A SPLENDID SCHOOL STORY. NEVER BEFORE PUBLISHED.

By E. HARCOURT BURRAGE,

Author of "Ching Ching," "Monkey Mat and Roving Dick," "The Brave Boy of the Basilisk," &c.

THE LAMBS OF LITTLECOTE

Don Prabin.   Jack Ford   Tom Drummond

Professor Lingo's Introduction to the "Lambs."

Formosus Snicker proceeds to Extremities.

Penny Bunn and Awful Rooker in search of Snicker.

A Handsome Coloured Plate Presented with Every Number.

PRICE ONE PENNY.

No. 2 GIVEN AWAY WITH No. 1.

THE LAMBS OF LITTLECOTE
A THRILLING SCHOOL STORY.

CHAPTER I.

DONOVAN PEEBLES LEAVES HOME—ARRIVAL AT LITTLECOTE.

IT was an advertisement which decided Mr. Peebles to give his only son Donovan the finishing touches to his education away from home. Nothing could be more inviting. It was an alluring advertisement, couched in terms that were of the nature to move the parental heart, especially when the parental pocket was not particularly well lined, as was the case with Peebles, senior.

He was an ironmonger in the not very thriving town of Smallwell, and business, owing to competition, where there were very few customers to compete for, had been going the wrong way for years. As a father he wished to give his son a good education, but he wanted, for reasons stated, to get it given to his off-spring on the most reasonable terms.

Therefore, when he read the advertisement in the morning paper as he sat at breakfast, he looked up at his wife and son, saying: "Here is the very thing."

"What are you referring to, my dear?" asked Mrs. Peebles.

"It is an advertisement of a boarding school, which will just suit our darling."

Their "darling," a genuine specimen of the only son, a spoilt child, stopped short in the hasty consumption of a boiled egg, and stared at his father.

"A boarding-school for me!" he exclaimed; "what is the good of that?"

"You must be educated if your are to make your way in the world!" answered his father, gently, "for I regret to say that, owing to the way trade is cut into nowadays, it is as much as I can do to pay my way. An education may be all I shall ever have to give you."

"It isn't much," grumbled Donovan. "Let's hear the advertisement, and if I like it, I'll go."

"It will be hard to part with him," sighed Mrs. Peebles, a wan, melancholy-looking woman. "But if he goes to a school where he is kindly treated, and his tastes considered, and he isn't taught any wickedness, I don't know that I should mind. Anyhow, I'll endeavour to bear up."

Mr. Peebles carefully turned down the paper so as to get conveniently at the advertisement, and slowly, and with emphasis in the salient places, read as follows:

EDUCATION—Good, and on the most moderate terms, at Littlecote Abbey, near Mumping Malford, Wiltshire. The situation of this popular school is on elevated ground, commanding a splendid view of a rich country. The soil is sandy, and the ground of the school spacious. The pupils have the privilege of roaming over a considerable tract of land. A limited number only of the sons of highly respectable persons taken. References exchanged. Terms from thirty pounds, all found. Principal, Mr. Fontenoy Snicker; assistant master, Mr. P. Y. Bunn; second master, Mr. Rooker. All branches of education taught by experienced teachers. Foreign languages a speciality. Pupils prepared for college examination. Matron, and general supervisor of cleanliness and morals, Mrs. Fontenoy Snicker. Prospectuses post free.

"There," exclaimed Mr. Peebles, as he laid down the paper. "What do you think of that?"

"It sounds very nice," answered Mrs. Peebles.

"I could go there and try it," said Donovan, cautiously. "And if I don't like it, I can come home again."

"Of course you can, my dear," replied his mother.

His father said nothing on that score. Wiltshire was a long way off, and if Donovan was sent there, he would have to give Littlecote a fair trial before he would be allowed to come home again.

As things were so far satisfactory, Mr. Peebles wrote at once to Fontenoy Snicker, Esq., and in due time received a prospectus. It was even more satisfactory than the advertisement, and as there was no special application for a reference, nor such a thing offered, Mr. Peebles, who had an Englishman's horror of being bothered that way, let the matter slide.

Arrangements were made for Donovan to start for the salubrious air of Littlecote at the end of the week, "so that he might have Sunday to rest from the fatigue of travelling," as his mother put it, and on the Saturday, at seven in the morning, he left his home.

Being market day, his father could not accompany him any of the distance, but his mother would not let him go alone, for fear that he should lose his head or his hat out of the railway window, or tumble out through the action of those doors that, in the minds of anxious parents, are always opening as soon as a child leans against them.

They went to Swindon, where they changed and took train for Chippenham, a dreary little place, very much behind the age.

It was arranged that one of the masters should meet Donovan there, and take him on to school in one of the flys to be hired in the town at a public house run to seed, which was dignified by the name of hotel.

Mrs. Peebles had not more than half-an-hour to wait, and she was considerably perturbed on hearing that Mr. Fontenoy Snicker had been there, but had been called away on important business, but he would be back in an hour.

She had therefore to leave her precious one to look after himself for awhile, and she took leave of him with many tears.

"Now, mind, my darling," she said, "that if there should be any wicked boys in the school, you are not to make friends with them. Choose nice, steady boys, who keep their collars clean and wash their necks every morning."

Donovan promised to do as she wished, and having received a little pocket-money to comfort him, sat down in the coffee room of the inn to await the coming of the master.

Donovan had no fears. He had always had his own way at home, and he was pretty sure he would go on the same way at school. If he did not, he should leave at once, and that was all about it.

But he did not know that his father had, on the application of the schoolmaster, paid a year's money in advance as a guarantee of good faith, it being one of the Littlecote rules to settle things in that way at the outset.

His father was not in a position to forfeit so much

as thirty pounds, and Donovan, whether he liked the school or not, was practically booked for twelve long months.

In complete ignorance of this dismal arrangement, he awaited the coming of the principal of the school, who, to his astonishment, was not more than five minutes after the departure of the train that bore the weeping mother away, ere he appeared.

Mr. Fontenoy Snicker had, as a matter of fact, only been just round the corner, it being an item in his policy not to show himself to parents or guardians more than he could help, he not being among the most favoured of men.

He was very short, thick-set, and had a face which Nature must have originally intended for a racecourse welsher, and his legs were of the extended class, being of the bow order of structure.

To cover his natural defects he dressed in what he considered to be the highest order of gentility. His garments consisted of a black dress coat, a white waistcoat, enormous stand-up collar, a big satin tie and check trousers. On his head was a broad-brimmed and remarkably shiny hat.

"Master Peebles, I believe," he said.

"That's my name," replied Donovan, hardly knowing what to make of the strange figure before him.

"My name is Snicker," said the schoolmaster, "and I'm your principal. Are you a good walker?"

"I think I am," answered Donovan.

"If that is the case," said Mr. Snicker, cheerfully, "seven miles won't hurt you. I've arranged for Milky Whey to bring on your luggage. He comes up our way on Monday with fish, and will make room for your boxes on his barrow."

"Father paid for a fly," said Donovan, feebly.

"That," answered the schoolmaster, sternly, "is a matter he will have to settle with the flyman. There's two funerals on here, and every blessed fly is engaged."

"He said the money was sent on to you," persisted Donovan.

Mr. Fontenoy suddenly became very stiff and solemn. "I'm not given to argufying—I mean harguing—usually with my pupils, especially about a fly. You've got to walk. D'ye hear?"

Donovan heard, and hardly knew whether to be openly rebellious or to cry, either way being in turns his method of settling any dispute about what he was to do. Eventually he decided on the latter, and began to dig his knuckles into his eyes. The next moment a strong hand was laid upon his collar, and his head was bumped against the wainscotted wall.

"No bellowing in my company," hissed the schoolmaster, ferociously, "especially away from home. My boys when they are with me have to look cheerful as if they loved me, and all their ways at Littlecote are ways of pleasantness, and all their paths are peace. Stand up."

Donovan stood up, cowed by the bullying air of his senior. But he ventured to say something more.

"I'm so hungry, sir," he said.

"Are you?" returned Mr. Fontenoy Snicker, drily. "You can have what you like if you are able to pay for it. Any money about you, eh?"

"A little, sir."

"Hand it over."

Donovan produced the money his mother had given him, and the schoolmaster counted it as it lay in his hand.

"Humph!" he muttered, "not more than enough get you a small lemon and a captain's biscuit. This is an awfully dear place, I can tell you."

He rang the bell, and when the waiter appeared he ordered the refreshment he had named for Donovan, also a glass of cold Scotch and a sandwich for himself.

"When I was a boy," he said, as the waiter disappeared, "I never ate more meat that I could help. That is why I am so strong."

A wicked and rebellious spirit was in the breast of Donovan, but he dare not let it loose, and as he really was hungry, he ate his captain's biscuit and drank his "small lemon" with exceeding relish. Mr. Fontenoy Snicker likewise enjoyed his more palatable fare.

That done, they started for the school.

Seven miles on a dusty road on a hot early summer day is a pretty good tax upon the energies of a boy, and long before half of the distance was traversed Donovan had had enough of it. But the schoolmaster ignored his grunts and gasps of fatigue, keeping on at a stiff pace, as if he were thoroughly inured to the exercise, which he probably was.

It was not a bad road in its way, but it was sadly lacking the livelier elements of life. Trees, fields, a cottage here and there, and a church now and then, erected in the most inconvenient place for the natives, was all Donovan saw as he shuffled along a pace in the rear of the schoolmaster.

The only vehicle they met on the way was a four-horsed waggon, with the driver fast asleep on the shaft, nodding forward, and swaying to and fro at the imminent risk of falling off and becoming a sacrifice to the agricultural Juggernaut car.

At length they turned down a lane and entered a wood, which Mr. Fontenoy Snicker said was a part of Mumping Malford.

"This village," he added, "covers ten square miles of ground, and there are one hundred and twenty inhabitants, including the parson, with his seven sons and five daughters."

Donovan, on the verge of a collapse with fatigue, was not interested, but he contrived to gasp out:

"I shouldn't have thought it."

"Thought what?" curtly demanded the schoolmaster, turning upon him.

"That there had been so many people hereabouts," answered Donovan, in a hesitating manner.

"I don't suppose you think much at all," grunted Mr. Fontenoy Snicker. "Now we come to the hill. A steady pull up it, and we are there."

It was all very well for him to talk about a steady pull up, but with the feeling of his legs having swollen to the size of gate-posts, and each foot weighing a good half-hundred weight, Donovan was anything but regular in his paces. He wobbled from side to side, grunting and groaning to the closed ears of his schoolmaster, and just as he had made up his mind to lie down and die right away, the summit of that parlous hill was attained.

"There's the school," said Mr. Fontenoy Snicker, in a jerky way, he having been pretty well pumped out at last; "what do you think of it?"

Donovan could not say anything against its outside appearance even if he had dared to do so, for the building was a goodly pile, having once upon a time really been an abbey. It was an extended pile of stone buildings on the verge of a steep descent, surrounded by a high wall, with massive iron gates, and two or three smaller ones on the right and left.

From the elevation there was a good view of a flattish and rather dismal-looking country, mainly pasture land, over which cattle were thickly scattered. There was also a small river winding about, and a distant view of a water-mill.

"Up here," said the schoolmaster, "you may holler your heart out and nobody will hear you. It's right out of the world, and although I don't own the property, I'm monarch of all I surveys—I mean *survey*, and lord of the boys and the brutes. Them—I mean *those* who go against me get wrong, but if I'm obeyed and not worried, there's easy times. You've come to a good school, young Peebles, and don't you forget that I'm master of it. Come along."

He led the way round to one of the side gates, which he opened with a key he took from his pocket, and they passed into a well-kept garden. The house itself looked very fine from there, but the windows had a meagre appearance. The blinds were shabby where any were on view, which was not in more than one out of three of the windows.

They crossed the garden, and entered the school by a door over which the honeysuckle in bloom hung in careless profusion.

"This is my door, you must know," said the schoolmaster. "A boy comes in this way at the start, and he goes out when I have done with him. If he tries to use it on his own account, I flay him."

———

CHAPTER II.

THE LAMBS OF LITTLECOTE.

IN the hall into which the schoolmaster conducted his charge was an old grandfather's clock, solemnly ticking off the moments as they passed. There was also a small rickety table, an umbrella stand, and three Windsor chairs.

The clock pointed to half-past three, and Mr. Fontenoy remarked that they had got over the ground pretty well.

"I always walk from Chippenham," he said, "because it's 'ealthy—healthy, ahem! I can time myself when alone to the minute. It's when I gets boys trailing after me I lose ground. Come upstairs and I will show you where you are to sleep."

He took Donovan up to a long room on the first floor, which had the appearance of a hospital, with from fifteen to twenty beds.

"New-comers," explained Mr. Fontenoy Snicker, "always sleep next the door, on account of the draught. He moves up as others arrive. That's your bedstead."

Donovan looked at it, and did not like it.

It was a narrow, cheap iron one, with a thin mattress, and a paucity of bed linen which did not promise much comfort. After that he was taken downstairs and shown the dining-room, an ill-favoured apartment with a stone floor. There were two long dining-tables, with forms on either side, and the air was laden with the odour of boiled beef, which had been kept out of the pot a day or two too long. At one end was a long latticed window, and at the other a huge old-fashioned open fireplace.

Over all there was a ghostly shadow which made Donovan palpably shiver.

"There's a quiet elegance about this place you don't find in every school," said Mr. Snicker; "we go in more for solidity than show. Here you can remain until the afternoon studies are over. I will just look in to give the boys a few final touches."

He walked out, leaving the door open, and Donovan saw him take from a cupboard in the hall a stout pliable cane, which he swished to and fro to test its qualities. The nature of the final "touches" he had referred to was thus made apparent.

He walked away down towards the back of the house, and soon, between the opening and shutting of a door, there floated the sound of many murmuring voices towards the listening boy.

Shortly after a yell, muffled, but anything but stifled, reached the ears of Donovan.

"He's laying into somebody," he muttered, "but he must not touch me. I'll write home to-night, to say that I can't stay here."

He passed a wretched hour alone, meditating on there being school on Saturday afternoon, and upon what he had seen and heard, and then the school was over.

Donovan heard the door open, and an authoritative voice, which he recognized as the physical property of the schoolmaster, calling on the boys to behave themselves. In response they came tearing down the passage and burst into the dining-room like water from a broken mill-dam, to see the new boy.

They were about thirty in number, respectably clad, but decidedly noisy, and some of them a bit rough in their manners.

Before Donovan could guess their purpose, they had picked him up and plumped him down upon the dining-table.

"Stand on your feet and let us have a look at you," said a tall boy of fifteen or so. "What's your name?"

"Donovan Peebles," haughtily answered the new arrival. Whatever he had to put up with from the schoolmaster, he was determined he would not stand any cheek from the boys.

"You seem to be a bit of a don," was the cool reply. "Hurry up. Get on the table so that all can see you."

"Sha'n't," replied Don, much in the way he would have answered his mother at home.

Immediately on a signal being given from the boy who had spoken to him, half-a-dozen of the others sprang upon the table. Don was collared, hoisted up, and held so that he could be inspected.

He writhed, he kicked, he even bit at them, but they had got him fast, and held him tight until it was their sweet will to let him go.

This they suddenly did when he made an extra effort to free himself, with the result that he went headlong down, and would have got an ugly tumble on the floor, but for the intervention of the youngster who had questioned him.

As Don came down, he caught him in his arms, and dexterously tilted him upon his feet.

"Steady, whoop, my war-horse!" he cried; "what do you mean by going on the rampage?"

"You are a lot of beasts," hissed Don. "I'll write to my mother to-night, and go home to-morrow."

A roar of laughter followed this declaration, in the midst of which the boys were seen to break away into two sections, and Mr. Fontenoy Snicker was observed by Don standing with the cane in his hand ready to cut at the nearest. But the boys got out of his reach and kept there.

"What's all this about?" demanded the schoolmaster; "didn't I hear somebody talking about writing home to his mother?"

Not a boy answered him, and after a glare around, he turned upon Don.

"Was it you?" he snarled.

"Yes," replied Don, with the boldness of despair, "I did say it, and I mean it. This is a hateful place."

"Impudence," said the schoolmaster, "cannot be tolerated here. My plan is to make myself understood from the first so that there may be no error afterwards."

He pounced on Don as a hawk goes for a sparrow, and he gave the boy, on whom scarce a finger had ever been laid, a bitter thrashing.

At first Don cried out, but when he had experienced half a score cuts with the cane, he suddenly froze up, and not a sound escaped him until it was all over and he lay on the form gasping for breath.

"Now," said Mr. Fontenoy Snicker, "are you going to write home to-night?"

The boy looked at him with a strange light in his eyes, but made no reply. The schoolmaster, apparently satisfied with his work, turned upon his heel and stalked from the room.

The boys gathered round Donovan and two of them raised him into a sitting position.

"What's the matter with him, Jack?" said one of the pair.

"He's dazed or stunned or something," was the reply. "Wake up, old chap. It's all right. You will get used to this sort of fun by-and-bye."

But Donovan made no answer and the boys became alarmed. A suggestion was made to carry him to the lavatory and place him under the tap. It came from a youngster with a face as brown as a berry.

"Not a bad idea of yours," cried the youth, named Jack. His other name, by the way, was Ford.

There was no lack of help in carrying Donovan to the lavatory, which was at the far end of the passage. It was a long, narrow place, with a trough lined with lead running down one side of it. There was also a tap at each end.

Hanging on the wall on the opposite side were half-a-dozen jack towels. It was here the boys went through their ablutions in the morning. The dormitories had no washstands. There was no room for them.

They put Don's head under the tap nearest the door and turned it on. The first rush of water brought him round, as well it might do, for fully a pint of it went down his back.

"Let me alone," he said, freeing himself from their grasp. "I'm all right now."

"You will have to take a licking here in better style," said Jack Ford, "or your life will be a misery."

"It wasn't the pain of it," answered Donovan, as he began to dry his head and face upon one of the towels; "it was the shock. At home I never was thrashed. I didn't know what to make of it."

"It completely flabbergasted you," said Tom Drummond, a broad-shouldered youngster, with a plain but kindly face.

"Poor mammy's darling," sneered a big fellow, who was seated on the edge of the trough swinging his legs to and fro.

"Now, isn't that like Roger Hone," exclaimed Tom Drummond, "always ready to depreciate a new fellow?"

"Which he oughtn't to do," remarked a youngster named Bedstone, "as he isn't much himself."

"Be quiet, you little beggar," growled Hone.

"Who funked his share of peppering old Snicker with peas?" demanded Bedstone.

"Stow your chaff, Tombstone," said Jack Ford. "We've got a new fellow here, a bit soft, but of the right sort of material to harden. If he's a bit pappy, it is the fault of his people at home. Here, old man, permit me now to introduce you to the kiddies of this place, known to the scattered world outside as 'The Lambs of Littlecote,' an agricultural sarcasm of our don't-stand-any-nonsense qualities."

Tombstone, by the way, was a cheerful schoolboy corruption of the name of Bedstone, at first resented by the recipient of the cognomen, but afterwards endured as a thing which could not be cured.

It will not be necessary here to give all the names of the boys to whom Donovan was introduced, but a few are essential for the present purpose of our story.

There was Soppem Smith (why Soppem was not explained; it could not be his rightful Christian name), Herbert May, the school-poet, Gyp Tanner, Bob Stockton (Prince of Politeness, Jack said he was, but a good fellow for all that), Roger Hone, "given to roaring, but nothing to be afraid of," and so on.

Bedstone was nicknamed as we know, and Tanner was called Gyp in recognition of the hue of his countenance, and Donovan himself straightway became simply "The Don."

By the time the introductions were got through with tea was ready. It was announced by a cadaverous youth, attired in black, and wearing a dirty white tie, who put his head into the lavatory, and announced it in a sepulchral tone, in simple fashion.

"Tea!" he said, and vanished.

"It's Awful Rooker, our pupil teacher," said Jack Ford, "the most miserable beggar on the face of the earth. He takes in fretting for other people, I fancy. Contracts to relieve them of their grief at so much an hour, you know."

Donovan laughed. He was getting a little more reconciled to his new abode, and finding in the novelty of a number of companions something he had vaguely been in want of all his life.

Away they went, every boy apparently making as

much noise as he could with his feet, to the dining-room, where Donovan found another stranger at the head of the table. The pupil-teacher was seated at the foot of it.

"That's P. Y. Bunn, our second master," whispered Jack Ford; "did you ever see such a guy?"

Mr. P. Y. Bunn, who was honoured with the nick-name of Penny Bunn, Penny for short, was indeed a peculiar-looking man. It was difficult to tell his age, as he might have been anything between five-and-twenty and forty. He was tall, thin, dark, and sallow. A straggling goatee garnished his chin, and his nose was of the colour of a faded cabbage rose. On his face he had a fixed vacant smile, and, in contrast to the pupil-teacher, he assumed a cheerfulness, if he did not feel it. His attire was an enlarged edition of that of his junior.

"Ha!" he exclaimed, as he espied Donovan. "New boy, eh, Ford? Introduce him."

Jack did so, and Penny Bunn shook hands with Donovan with fervency.

"Welcome to Littlecote," he said. "I hope we shall be friends. You will take your seat between Ford and Tanner, vacated by the departure of Stormer, who was of a wicked and defiant nature. He has gone to sea, I hear, boys, and will probably be wrecked on an island. He will make a good Robinson Crusoe, for he was ingenious and self-reliant. Boys, sit down and be orderly, if you please."

Jack explained to Donovan, in a quiet way, that Stormer had a few days before terminated rather a stormy year at the school by hurling an inkstand at the principal with so good an aim that it hit him between the eyes and "made a speckled nigger of him." For this daring act he was thrashed, "taking his gruel like a thoroughbred lamb," and expelled.

"Snicker was getting afraid of him, or he wouldn't have sent him away" explained Jack, in conclusion; "and now, Don, bless you and save you from such a fate. Anyway, it won't happen for a year. Your guv has, of course, paid the usual."

"I don't know," replied Donovan.

"But I do," said Jack. "Snicker always lands the first year's money, and if you don't like it, then you can leave it; but he doesn't return any of the lucre to the suffering parents. Try the bread, old man, and when you strike a spot of butter on it make the most of the treasure. Don't waste the greasy bits, but roll them in your mouth and keep the flavour going. It's your only chance of escaping the feeling that you are eating dry bread."

Matters were not quite so bad as that, but Donovan discovered that the bread was very thick, and the butter remarkably thin.

Gyp Tanner further explained to Donovan that Mrs. Snicker beat a pound of it out with a gold-beater's hammer until it was thin enough to cover two acres of ground. Then she cut it up into suitable sizes and laid them on the slices of bread.

It had been computed by Bedstone, who was good at figures, that a pound lasted the house six weeks and two days.

"You needn't believe it unless you like," said Bedstone, carelessly; "but after you have been here awhile, work it out for yourself."

Donovan laughed, and said he did not think he would give his time to it, and then, being really hungry, proceeded to make the best of the humble fare upon the board.

CHAPTER III.

THE ROPE TRICK.

BEFORE tea was over the patter of rain upon the window panes was heard, and Penny Bunn, rising, went and opened the latticed sash to get a look at the prospect.

"Boys," he said, "it is going to be a wet evening. Outdoor exercise must be given up for the more quiet recreations of the schoolroom. Lessons for Monday to be taken up and conned at *half-past seven.* It will give me great pleasure to assist you in passing the first part of the time away."

"You will see some fun, now," whispered Jack Ford in Donovan's ear. "When Penny Bunn joins in our recreations we generally get a rise out of him. You can lead him on to do anything."

"What is he?" asked Donovan. "A born fool?"

"Blessed if I know," answered Jack. "Sometimes I think he is, at other times I fancy he is playing the double game, running with the hare, and hunting with the hounds."

"Hunting," said Donovan, with a puzzled look.

"Keeping in with us, so as to get at our little games, to betray us to Snicker," explained Jack Ford.

"Oh, I see," said Don, as we shall in future call him, "that's mighty mean, isn't it?"

"Of course it is," assented Jack, "but it is precious little he gets out of us. All he gets for his pains is being made a fool of, and put upon all sorts of wrong scents."

The boys growled a bit about the weather, but they soon gave it up, and by the time they were all in the schoolroom, had reconciled themselves to being confined indoors for the evening. Don, drawing aside, sat down upon a form and looked at the future field in which he was to graze and consume the food of learning.

It was big and square in shape, and barren in appearance, as schoolrooms always are. On the right were two latticed windows, and near them the head-master's desk. Another for the use of Penny Bunn, which was lower down.

There was no desk for the pupil-teacher, as he sat among the boys when not engaged in instructing some of the juniors.

There were maps on the walls, and the usual desks and forms for the boys. On the other side of the room was a door, which had the appearance of being nailed up.

Tom Drummond, after a whispered conference with Jack Ford and two or three more, came over to Don, and in response to his questioning about the opposite door, told him that it was fastened up with screws, which had become rusty with years.

"There are two rooms beyond, as far as we can discover from the outside," he added, as they walked across the room together. "One of them with a window heavily barred with iron rods. The other has a skylight. It sticks out from the rest of the building."

"But why were they closed up?" asked Don, whose curiosity was naturally aroused.

"Ah! there you puzzle me," replied Tom. "I know for certain that they have not been opened in Snicker's time. It was in the lease, I believe, that he was not to make any alterations or changes in the arrangements of the old abbey. Snicker did not object. He got the place cheap. There is enough room for his requirements as things are, and he is not at all curious to find out what lies on the other side."

"Skeletons, perhaps," suggested Don.

Tom Drummond shook his head and smiled.

"I don't think so," he answered; "my opinion is that they are empty rooms, and nothing more. The merry monks of old were not in the habit of leaving skeletons about to give them a bad name in after days. I only hope the rooms are empty."

"Why?"

"That's tellings, for the present. Jack and I are working up a little game which you may know more of by-and-bye."

"You may trust me," said Don, a little haughtily.

"Well," coolly responded Tom, "I am inclined to think we can. But the game we have conceived is rather a serious one, and it is much too good to be spoiled. It will be such a flare-up as hasn't been seen or heard of in any school for many years. Be content to wait a bit.'

"Very well," said Don. "Of course I know I am a bit of a softy, having been brought up at home. I find things very different to what I expected, and I've got a strange feeling on me of having suddenly become years older."

"You are waking up," said Tom, encouragingly; "it's companionship of boys with grit that is waking you up. Have you had a look from the windows?"

"No."

"Come and have a peep, then. It's a pretty view, and especially pretty to us, as it will be of great assistance to us when the time comes."

Don's curiosity was keen, but he had to restrain it, as Tom Drummond evidently did not mean to confide in him for the present.

They walked to the windows, and Don looked out.

The schoolroom was on the ground floor, as we have already intimated, but, as far as those windows were concerned, it might have been on the fifth, for outside there was a steep descent for a hundred feet or more.

This part of the building stood on the verge of a part of the hill, which had been cut away, for the purpose of using the sand, perhaps, many years before.

Since then bushes and briars had taken root there, the birds having brought the seeds and dropped them on the face of what may very reasonably be called the cliff.

"It would take a sure-footed and cool-headed man to climb up there, wouldn't it?" said Tom.

"It would," assented Don.

"And that is why we like it," said Tom. "Before long that cliff may become historical in school life. Hallo! here's Penny, as fresh and as frank and as boyish as ever, bless his simple heart."

The under-master was in the middle of the room, looking around him with his perpetual smile.

"Well," he said, "here I am, boys. Now what shall we do to kill time for the next hour or so?"

He rubbed his hands and waggled his goatee in what was to Don an exasperating manner, but it was not for him to show his opinion of it by word or look.

"Remember," continued Penny Bunn, waggishly, "this is freedom's hour. Consider me one of yourselves. Do just as you please, avoiding of course any unnecessary noise, as our respected senior is at dinner."

"Respected grandmother," muttered Gyp Tanner, as he climbed on one of the school desks and squatted down monkey fashion.

There was evident expectation on the part of some of the boys, who gathered round the under-master. Jack Ford was one of the foremost.

"Did you ever hear of the rope trick, sir?" he asked.

"Hum," mused Penny Bunn, "the—ah, rope trick?"

"It's easily done," put in Bob Stockton, suavely. "You, sir, will see through it easily. It is no use trying to deceive you."

"I must confess," said Bunn, "that I am not often imposed upon. Of course I have heard of and seen the rope trick, but my memory is faulty, and for the moment it has escaped me."

"We thought it would amuse you, sir," pursued

Stockton, " and as it is not washing-day, we have ventured to take the clothes-line from its accustomed hook outside the scullery to show you how it is done. With your permission we will now proceed."

"Certainly," replied the under-master.

"Ford," said Bob Stockton, wheeling round to face his chum, "will you illustrate the rope trick to Mr. Bunn? I know it will be nothing more than refreshing his memory, but doing anything for one who takes so much interest in us is a real pleasure."

"Bob's got his oil-works well in order to-night," whispered Tom Drummond for Don's benefit.

Jack Ford stood up in the middle of the room with his arms close to his side. Bob Stockton, with the air of a tailor measuring an aristocratic customer, proceeded to wind the rope about him.

He put it round his neck and chest and arms and legs, knotting it at intervals, until Jack looked like a thoroughly corded-up Egyptian mummy.

"The trick, sir," said Bob, taking up the attitude and air of a showman, "is to get out of that rope with the least possible delay."

"Yes, I remember now," said Penny Bunn, tapping his forehead; " of course. I have done the trick many times. How could I have forgotten it?"

"Your mind, sir," answered Bob, "is generally occupied with higher things."

"Oh, stash it," muttered Tom Drummond.

"Ford," said the suave Bob, "you will now proceed to release yourself. I give you two minutes to get out of the rope."

Jack, who had been tied up in the good old spirit-rapping, swindling style, was out of the rope in seven seconds. The boys clapped their hands, and shouted their approval. Penny Bunn alone remained unmoved.

Holding up his hand as a signal for silence, he soon obtained it, and said:

"Boys, you must not demonstrate so loudly. Do not forget that our respected senior is partaking of the meal of the day he most appreciates. Ford, you did that well, but I have seen it done quicker. Indeed, my record time for the trick is, I believe, five seconds."

"I have not had your experience, sir," said Jack, apologetically; "of course, it is a trick anyone can do. You're tied up, and when it is done you give your wrists a turn like this, and the rope tumbles off."

"Just so," said Penny Bunn, approvingly; "for a boy you did it smartly. You turned your wrist to the right, I perceived. I always turned mine to the left."

"It doesn't matter which."

"Certainly not."

"I should like to see it done both ways," said Bob

Stockton, dreamily; "but it would be troubling Mr. Pen—ahem!—Mr. *Bunn* too much."

"Not at all," replied the under-master, briskly. He was as certain as he could be that it was, as Jack explained it, quite a childish trick, and why should he not show the boys how a man could do it?

"Stockton," he said, "as during the hours of recreation I am one of yourselves, I shall be glad to show you my style of doing the rope trick. Will you please bind me, avoiding, if you can, my right hip, where a carbuncle is, I regret to say, putting in an appearance."

"They are painful things, sir," said Bob Stockton, sympathetically, "but, I believe, are useful in relieving the system of poisonous matter. I have heard our family doctor at home say so."

Then, with a respectful air, he proceeded to bind up the form of the intended victim.

<hr>

CHAPTER IV.

PENNY BUNN IN A FIX.

A S it is inconvenient to have to describe a man in different ways, we will, for a time at least, adopt, when referring to the under-master, the name which had in private been bestowed upon him by the boys.

Bob Stockton proceeded to bind him, and anyone at all acquainted with the art of knotting a rope would have seen that he was a past-master of it.

Without making it inconveniently tight, and avoiding the carbuncle with the skill of a hospital nurse, he put the rope around Penny Bunn, knotting it here and there, until he was as securely bound as if he had been fettered with riveted manacles.

And he did it all with such delightful politeness, oiling the job, as it were, that the hapless man had no suspicion of a trick.

As a pet lamb lies down unsuspecting to the shearer, so he stood up to be made a victim of.

When it was done, Bob drew aside, and with respectful interest asked him if his bonds hurt him anywhere.

"No, indeed," replied Penny Bunn; "I fear you have, in your courtesy to a senior, made the trick too easy."

"Not intentionally, sir," rejoined Bob, with pellucid truthfulness. "How long are we to give you, sir?"

"I think," replied Penny Bunn, who had made a secret effort to loosen his bonds, and not found them quite so yielding as he expected, "that I will take the full seven seconds."

"Have ten, sir."

"No; seven will suffice."

"Very well, sir. Ready. Clear yourself from the rope."

And then ensued a scene that was a joy and a priceless boon to the youthful beholder.

Mr. Penny Bunn turned his wrists to the right, and then to the left; he made corkscrews of them, and all that came out of it was that the rope tightened itself about the rest of his body.

Then he writhed like a contortionist, perspiring as a harvestman does on a very sunny autumn day.

All the boys laughed. First in a quiet, stealthy way, then, in spite of their efforts to control themselves, in an uproarious fashion. And the more they laughed, the more the agonized Penny Bunn contorted.

He could not understand how it was that he was defeated. Being one of those self-satisfied men who think they can do anything and everything without going through the preliminary practice, and also burdened with a natural density which prevented his grasping the truth, he kept on fighting against the captivity he was enduring, and in a sense putting up fresh prison bars with every additional movement of his body.

The light of the evening faded before his eyes. A dark haze, speckled with sparks of fire, took its place; his limbs ached, his throat burned, and his tongue became parched, but he still struggled on.

Bedstone dived under the desk of the head-master, and brought out the dunce's cap. Springing upon a form, he was about to put it on the head of Penny Bunn, when the door was thrust open, and Mr. Fontenoy Snicker stood on the threshold.

The riot of laughter was now at its height, and although his lips were seen to move, nobody could hear what he said.

Whatever may have been the terror inspired by his presence, it did not stop the merriment, in a degree owing to the fact that Penny Bunn, unconscious of the arrival of his principal, was still making the most strenuous and ludicrous efforts to get free.

Mr. Fontenoy was not by nature a patient man. When disturbed at a very unseasonable time, as he had been that evening, he was apt to lose his head entirely.

He lost it that evening.

When he put in an appearance he had his eyeglass in his eye. He had great faith in it as an awe inspirer, but he could not keep it there.

Dropping it, and with both his eyes glittering like those of a hungry snake, he first of all charged at the under-master and sent him to the ground, where he lay like a log, wondering in his confused state of mind what had happened.

The next movement of Fontenoy Snicker was to get possession of his favourite weapon, the cane. Having unearthed it from behind his desk, he made a general raid among the boys, hitting out right and left, and making the recipients of his unwelcome attentions skip like young frogs chivied by schoolboys.

Having exhausted himself at this work, he knelt down by the side of the still prostrate under-master, and with a penknife lashed through the rope in a dozen places.

"Get up, you ass," he hissed in his ear; "will you never learn common sense?"

Penny Bunn got up with a mind partly cleared, but still far from having recovered from the shock it had received. Fontenoy Snicker turned to the boys, and favoured them with a shake of his ponderous fist.

"Let me hear so much as a whisper from any one of you to-night," he said, huskily, "and I will—will—I—I—"

He could get no further, but he had made himself sufficiently clear, and in a white heat he hustled his assistant from the room.

The door closed, and the boys were comparatively silent for awhile. Those who got a taste of the cane, mainly the younger and less nimble of their number, rubbed the afflicted spots and softly groaned. The unhurt restrained their mirth.

"That rope's done for," said Gyp Tanner, bending over the severed mass of cordage.

"It's his own, and he did it himself," replied Bob Stockton. "I don't see that we are in any way to blame."

"This is the final bit of fun we shall have with Penny," said Tom Drummond.

"Don't you run away with that idea," answered Jack Ford; "the more people of his breed are taken in, the more they like it. I give Penny Bunn three days to get over it and then we can go at him again."

"All I can say is," remarked Don as he wiped his eyes, from down which the tears of laughter had been flowing, "that if he is taken in by you again, he is a fool."

"He is that and nothing more," softly sang Jack Ford.

They could talk no more about the affair just then, for Rooker, the pupil teacher, now put in an appearance.

"Mr. Snicker has sent me to keep order," he said "and to see that you do your lessons. I am to take down all the names of those who are disobedient."

"Give him a ream of foolscap," said Jack Ford, scornfully; "he will want it."

"Oh, let him alone," grumped Bedstone; "he isn't worth howling about."

Awful Rooker produced a pocket-book, of the class to be obtained with a pencil for twopence, and made a feint of making a memorandum therein. Somebody's hands were placed over his eyes from the rear and the pocket-book snatched out of his hands. He was then projected forward, and when he had fallen and got up again, the boys were all in their seats.

"You are a nice lot, you are," he said.

There seemed to be so much truth in his remark, that none of them took the trouble to deny it. In silence they went on with the task of getting up their lessons for Monday.

CHAPTER V.

IN THE HEAD-MASTER'S ROOM.

"SIT down, Bunn," said Fontenoy Snicker, with a snarl, "I want to have a word with you."

"Certainly, sir, assuredly," answered the under-master. "I am very sorry it has happened, but it was quite an accident. The rope got round a carbuncle, I—"

"That will do," interposed Fontenoy Snicker, curtly. "Now tell me exactly what has been done."

It was not in the nature of things that the victimised Penny Bunn should tell more than a part of the truth. He left his boasting out of it, and declared that he had tried the rope trick, by way of experimenting on the elasticity of the human body.

"They make a pantaloon of you," growled the irate head-master, "and I will test the elasticity of your body in another way, if you don't act more like a man of common sense. Anything new?"

"No, sir," answered Penny Bunn, "beyond that I think there is *something* afloat."

"There's always something afloat," said Fontenoy Snicker, pacing the room, "and it's in my lease that I am to keep an orderly, well-conducted school. If I don't do that much, they will turn me out. There's a man after it."

"For another school, sir?"

"No stupid, he's a geological, or some sort of ogical, fellow, who wants it because its old and musty."

"Couldn't you let him have it at a price?" hinted Penny Bunn, with the slyest of sly glances at his superior's face.

"No!" thundered the head-master. "Where should I find another place like it to suit me? It's out of the way, ain't it?"

"It certainly is, sir."

"And isn't it an out-of-the-way place I want? Are you the sort of figure for a town? What would anyone think of the school if you were shown to him as a specimen of its masters?"

"There isn't much beauty about the house," said Penny Bunn, with child-like simplicity.

Fontenoy Snicker glanced at him, to see if that was meant as a reflection upon himself. But the face of his assistant had nothing on it to guide him but the old vacant smile.

"It's a dead sure thing," continued Snicker, as he waddled about on his bow legs, "that we must keep a quiet school, or if there is anything unusual going on, that we must keep it quiet at any cost. Perched up here, I am free from the interfering visits of friends and relatives. They have to take my word on trust, and when I've nabbed a boy for a year, whether he goes or stays, it pays me. Is the new boy a good feeder?"

"He put away seven slices of bread and butter," answered Penny Bunn. "I kept a steady eye on him."

"If he goes on like that he must be regulated," said Snicker, "but I don't think he will. He arrived peckish, and wanted to have something to eat at the hotel. I put him off with a captain's biscuit and a small lemon. So of course he was hungry. What is it that makes you think there is something in the air?"

"Ford, Stockton, and Drummond are always whispering together, and there is a look of their having a secret between them."

"Humph!" muttered the schoolmaster, "it's likely enough they are hatching mischief. After that Stormer affair, one doesn't know what to expect. Can't you get at it somehow?"

"They don't half trust me, although I play up to being one of themselves."

"You ain't clever enough for 'em," said Fontenoy Snicker; "they see through you. But it won't do to have a disturbance that will be talked about."

He seemed to be in a very uneasy state of mind. Littlecote was a paying concern, and he hoped, after a few years' arduous labour, to retire and live at ease. But he knew that he had no chance of succeeding as a schoolmaster in a more public place.

If he had been of a poetic turn of mind, which he certainly was not, he would have probably paraphrased the poet thus:

> Boys may come, and boys may go,
> But I go on for ever.

That is, until he had made money enough to retire.

"Bunn," he said, after a silence, "how would it do for you and me to be at war?"

"I don't understand you, sir," answered Bunn.

"By being at war, I mean always quarrelling in public."

"That is, sir, you are to pitch into me a little stronger than usual."

"Just so. It is to blind the boys and get them to look upon you as an object for their pity. If they do that, you will get into their confidence."

Penny Bunn sat thinking a moment, and then looked up with a sigh.

"You lay it upon me rather heavy now," he said. "To excite much sympathy in the boys you will have to make it very thick."

"I might strike you," suggested Snicker, "or put you on a shorter allowance of food."

"I don't think you need do that," hastily interposed Bunn. "I'll find out what is going on before many days are over. I know they grumble about the meat. They say it isn't fresh, and Tanner vows its horse, for he can smell the saddle."

"That was a joke" said Snicker, "but I'll take the fun out of them."

"Hone wants to write home, sir. He spoke to me about it this morning, but I forgot it."

"Let him write, and let 'em all write," answered Fontenoy Snicker, savagely, "all letters to be put into the post-bag and taken to my room. I must see what is in 'em afore—I mean *before*—they go."

"Won't the parents see the letters have been opened?"

"No, stupid. I will take care of that. Now go back to the boys and sham being angry with me. Say you won't stand any more of it, and will leave if you are not better treated. That will touch their young tender 'arts—I mean *hearts*. Dash it! I've often wondered what fool shoved the letter H into the alphabet. It isn't any use, except to aggravate people by not always coming up to time, that I can see."

"That reminds me," said Penny Bunn. "Yesterday I heard young Short say that you could make a Mosaic pavement with the aitches you've dropped since you came here. He's a chum of Tanner's, and they are a pretty pair."

"I will make it my business," answered Fontenoy Snicker," to water the schoolroom floor with the tears of Short to-morrow morning. Anything else?"

"Whymper drew your legs on his slate, and wrote under the sketch, 'Model for a railway-tunnel.'"

"A what?" cried Snicker.

"Model for a tunnel," repeated Penny Bunn, edging nearer the door, "in allusion, I fancy, to their not being straight as the legs of—of—of *common* people."

He was close to the door now, and waited to see the effect of this communication.

The schoolmaster looked at his legs, held one up for inspection, put it down again, and then said:

"I suppose you saw the drawing?"

"He left it on his slate as he was finishing off just at the dismissal. That is how he forgot to wipe it out."

"Good," said Fontenoy Snicker. "As true as my name is Jerry—as—as—I mean *Fontenoy*—what are you grinning at, you starved porpoise?"

"I did not intend to grin, sir," Penny Bunn hastened to say.

"Then don't do it again. Remember this. I'll make Whymper into a model for a humpback. The young fiend. What's the matter with my legs? Do you see anything objectionable in them?

"I've never seen any like them," answered the alarmed Penny Bunn, hardly knowing what to say in reply. "I—I wish I had such legs?"

"So do I,"growled Snicker,and Bunn,seeing a chance to get away, vanished from the room.

He went back to the schoolroom, and found the boys busy with their lessons. As a preliminary to the new game to be played, he walked up to his desk, and sat there with his face between his hands.

"What's up with Penny," whispered Tom Drummond.

"Nothing," replied Jack Ford; "he's looking at us to see what we're doing. Look here."

Jack stood up, and staring straight at the undermaster laid a finger upon his nose.

In a moment the head of the under-master was erect.

"Ford," he said, "I am surprised at you."

"Beg pardon, sir," answered Ford, "but my nose itched," and down he sat again.

"You see," he said a moment or two later, "he was watching us. He is not to be trusted, for I'll vow that he is a sneak as well as a fool."

CHAPTER VI.

IN THE DORMITORY.

IT was a strange sensation to Don going to bed in a room with a number of boys. At home he had of course slept alone, and was always glad to tumble in and go quietly to sleep. But in the dormitory it was a very different matter.

By the arrangements of the house the boys were supposed to be in bed by nine o'clock. At that hour they went upstairs, but not to sleep.

The parsimony of Fontenoy Snicker allowed only one short end of candle to each dormitory, two in number. Half an inch was the length of the bit apportioned that night to those who were thenceforth to be Don's bedroom companions.

"Every night," said Gyp Tanner, "Mother Snicker makes this thing shorter and shorter. What licks me is where she gets all the ends from."

"Chuck it, candlestick and all, out of the window," growled Tom Drummond; "here, give it to me."

He took the offending light from Gyp's hand, opened the window, and tossed it away.

"The girl will find it in the morning," he said; "she won't say anything. A very good girl is Black-Eyed Susan."

"What's her name," exclaimed Don.

"Her full name is Jane," answered Tom, "but we call her Black-Eyed Susan for short."

"Oh!" said Don, and the way the word came from his lips set all the rest laughing.

"You have a lot to learn about our playful little ways," continued Tom. "Now, boys, there is a bright moon to night, and that is a better lamp than any Snicker is likely to find for us. I say, Don, where are your traps?"

"They're coming on to-morrow," replied Don. "A man named Milky Whey is going to bring them on his barrow."

"Milky coming," exclaimed Bedstone, who was leaning on the window-sill looking out upon the moonlit landscape. "I owe him one for shying a cod's head at me when he was last here."

"Did it hit you?" asked Jack Ford.

"No, but the old thief's intention was good," answered Bedstone, "and that is enough for me. We shall have fish for dinner. Oh, lor!"

"I like fish," said Don.

"So do most people," assented Bob Stockton, "but not when it has been knocking about the world for a month or so. Milky buys his at a fish-shop at Chippenham, when it is just on the verge of dissolution. He pumps on it to make it fresh, then he takes it home and puts it under his bed while he has a day and night on the drink. That's his average. Afterwards he brings it to this benighted place, and what he can't sell to the yokels Snickey buys as a job lot. We have to eat it holding our noses with a grip of iron."

"The worst of it is that we get all sorts," grumbled Short, who was squatting on the floor clasping his knees with his hands, "and it is served to us mixed. You never can tell whether you are eating mackerel, soles, whiting, cod, or herring. Generally there is a strong flavour of whelks running through the lot. Who comes round to-night to take away the candle?"

"Penny," replied Whimper, who was sitting on Don's bed whittling a stick with his knife.

"Shall we shy the pillows at him?"

"Do what you like," said Jack, carelessly, "only mind you don't kill him. I wonder what the beastly things are stuffed with?"

"Wooden chips," said Gyp Tanner. "Here he is."

The door opened, and Penny Bunn came sidling in. The boys made a feint of undressing.

"Hallo," exclaimed the under-master, "not in bed again. How slow you are. Where's the candle?"

"It's out, sir," replied Drummond, with evasive truthfulness.

Penny Bunn sat down on Don's bed, which was near the door.

"Boys," he said, "I think I shall be going away from you shortly. I cannot stand the treatment I receive here."

"You certainly are put upon," said Bob Stockton, as he shied his bolster at the dolorous Bunn.

He was sitting with his head bowed, and it just missed him.

"Dear me," he cried, as the bolster whizzed over him, "what was that?"

"There's bats about this old place," answered Stockton, serenely, "of the vampire breed, I think. So you are going, sir. We shall all miss you sorely."

"I must either do that or something," said Penny Bunn. "Boys, Mr. Snicker is a cruel, remorseless man. I often wonder you put up with his treatment."

"We are only boys," said Jack Ford. "What can we do?"

There was a silence of a moment or so, broken by a sigh from Penny Bunn.

"I think," he said, "that something might be done, if we put our heads together."

There was another pause. No suggestion of what ought to or might be done came from the boys. Penny Bunn sighed again and rose to his feet.

"I suppose we must go on enduring," he moaned, "for the present, anyway. Get into bed as soon as you can. Good-night, boys."

"Whoop!" shouted Stockton; "another bat, a whopper."

He had got possession of Tanner's bolster or pillow, or whatever it may be considered, a miserable thing about eighteen inches long by twelve deep, and taking better aim as Penny Bunn turned away, hit him fairly on the back of the head. With a crash the under-master fell against the door, closing it with a bang that shook the house.

"Good gracious, sir!" exclaimed Bob Stockton, rushing forward, "has it bitten you?"

He whipped up the pillow, tossed it back into its place, and with a show of great anxiety seized Penny Bunn by the arm.

"I don't think I am much hurt," was the faint reply. "What a monster it was. Is it gone?"

"It whizzed out of the window," answered Gyp Tanner; "there it goes, right away over the garden. It's almost as big as a wild goose."

"Good-night, boys," said Penny Bunn, as he fumbled at the lock and opened the door, "close your window. It isn't safe to sleep with it open with such things about."

He shuffled out, shutting the door behind him.

"The worm!" said Jack, "he is trying to get over us. He not stand any more of Snicker's nonsense! He will stand anything because he's got to. Now listen, all of you. No fish to-morrow for us."

"Of course there won't be," said Drummond; "it's Sunday."

This fact appeared to have been overlooked by most of the boys, but it brought them no comfort.

"All the worse for us," groaned Short. "Monday's fish is always worse than any other."

"Sunday or Monday," said Jack, "we are not going to eat it. You leave it to me. I'll choke Milky Whey off coming up here with his rubbish. What a cheese we had for supper to-night. It was made out of brown paper, I should say. But there, for the present we must endure, but not for long, dear boys, not for long. Now for an evening song, and then to sleep. Herbert, old man, lead off."

Herbert May, the young poet and writer of the school songs, of which we shall hear more anon, started off with a sweet voice, softly singing as follows:

> There's a good time coming, boys.
> Wait a little longer,
> When Snicker will be up a tree,
> And we little kids be stronger.
>
> No more we'll mop his washy tea,
> Or dine on bread and leather,
> The butter it will thicker be,
> Or there'll be stormy weather.
>
> The days of cruel treatment must
> Very soon be over,
> Or Snicker will be turned to dust,
> And his cane laid up in clover.
>
> Ah! There's a good time coming, boys,
> Wait a little longer,
> When Snicker will be up a tree,
> And we little kids be stronger.

The last part of this song, simple enough and thoroughly boyish, was of course the chorus, which was chanted by the whole room—except by Donovan, who was strangely stirred as he listened to it—so softly that the sound of their voices floated out of the open window like the humming of bees.

Softly as they sang, the words were very clear, and there was a peculiar earnestness exhibited which set Don thinking that there was more than the simple singing in it.

He had seen enough of his new friends already to understand that behind the natural cheerfulness of boyhood there was a strong feeling of discontent.

Then he recalled the hint Drummond had given him in the schoolroom, and while he was thinking of it, he fell asleep.

CHAPTER VII.

GREASING THE SCREWS.

A SOUND of movement in the room aroused Don, and sitting up, he saw the boys out of bed, hurrying on their clothes, just anyhow and nohow.

"Get up, Don," cried Drummond, "we must be ahead of the other dormitory in the lavatory, or the towels will be so beastly wet that wiping ourselves dry will be impossible. It's Sunday morning, and the towels being fresh, it's a real treat to get at them."

Don slipped on his trousers and socks so quickly that he was ready to form part of the tail of his companions as they poured out of the room. Downstairs they raced, to find that the getting ahead of the others had been successfully accomplished.

The taps were turned on, and the sluicing commenced, all getting through it as quickly as possible. Splashing, rubbing, scrubbing, chattering and laughing, one would not have thought that they were the boys of a school which was a swindle upon parents, and practically a place of torture to the pupils.

"Halloa, boys!" said Gyp Tanner, "we've got through, and here comes Soppem Smith and his lot."

Soppem Smith was the head of the second dormitory, and he now came rushing into the lavatory with Roger Hone and a dozen others close behind him.

"Up before time," he cried. "If Snicker hears of it he will warm some of you."

"Dry up," said Tom Drummond. "Why don't you get out of bed sooner?"

"Towels, gentlemen," said Bob Stockton, politely.

He held one away from its roller, and, like the rest, it *was* a towel. If it had been drawn through a tub of water it could hardly have been wetter.

A howl of rage burst from the late arrivals.

"Look here," shouted Roger Hone, "no water. Whose turn is it at the force pump?"

"Why, yours, of course," answered Jack Ford.

"It isn't."

"Anyway, gentlemen," said Bob Stockton, with exasperating suavity, "the exigencies of the situation will compel you to pump your own water, or to abandon the idea of a wash. Mrs. Snicker overhauls your necks this morning, don't forget."

The water supply, as it does in most country places, came from a well, and a force-pump of the ancient order was used to fill certain tanks fixed about the lower part of the house. Working one of these pumps is taxing to persons of ordinary strength, and half-a-dozen boys had to unite their energies to work the ancient thing which filled the lavatory tank.

"I'll be even with you for this," snarled Soppem Smith. "You have wasted the water on purpose. Get along, some of you, and set that pump going."

The triumphant early-washers went away laughing, and Jack Ford, taking Don's arm, invited him to come and see their playground.

It was on the cliff side of the old abbey, where the wall was broken and in ruins. Jack took his seat in one of the openings made by time, with the assistance of the lambs of Littlecote, as he remarked, and coolly looked down into the depths, the cliff at this spot being within a degree of the uprightness of a wall.

"Mind you don't fall over," said Don, to whom the position of Jack appeared to be perilous.

"You are all right if you keep your head," answered Jack. "See here!"

He stood up, and bending over, gazed down at the wooded ground below. If he had overbalanced, he would have dashed his life out on the ground, or perhaps impaled himself on the top of one of the fir trees.

"Don't do that," said Don, drawing back and shuddering.

"Come here," replied Jack, jumping down and resuming his seat! "sit beside me. You will soon get used to it. I've been down there many a time."

Don stared at him incredulously, and Jack bit his lip.

"Perhaps I am saying too much to you," he said, "but I rarely make a mistake in taking to or disliking a fellow. I saw at the outset that you were rather raw, but all right. In a day or two I hope to make you one of us."

"But am I not one of you already?" inquired Don.

"Of the school, certainly; but not one of the inner circle," rejoined Jack. "You see what sort of a crib it is. A fraud. Of course, I could write home and split upon this rascal Snicker, but what would be the result? I should simply be taken away and the thing would go on. What a lot of us are aiming at is to play old boots with him. Now, then, do you twig?"

"Can't say I do," answered Don.

"We are going to make history," said Jack, "but it will not be just yet. There are plans to be arranged and worked out. It's a brute of a place, as you will find out. Have you seen Mrs. Snicker yet?"

"No," said Don, "that is a pleasure I have not had."

"It is a joy in store," returned Jack, laughing, "but you will be sure to see her this morning. At half-past eight we parade for inspection, and that is real fun. If you want to be flayed, just turn up with dirty hands. It doesn't matter in the week-day, because nobody outside sees us, but on Sunday that old hypocrite Snicker parades us to church, and then we must be models of cleanliness. Come into the schoolroom. I've a little job to do there."

The other boys, including the second washing party, were now in the playground, behaving with as much decorum as could be expected from boys under any circumstances whatever.

Jack and Don passed through them, and entering the house, made their way to the schoolroom.

The boys had no lockers. It was a school luxury Fontenoy Snicker did not think it necessary to indulge them with. The class books were kept upon a shelf near the door.

Stooping down and groping under the desk of the head-master, Jack unearthed a small bottle of oil and two screws.

"I am going to oil these," he said. "It isn't much of a job, but it can't be done when everybody is about."

It was not much of a job, as he said, but he was so cautious over it that he asked Don to stand by the door and give him a word if he heard anyone coming.

Don, of course complied with his request, and standing by the door he listened, and at the same time watched Jack do his oiling.

The screws appeared to be very old and rusty. Jack rubbed the oil into them with a small piece of rag, finally giving them a thorough soaking and replacing them under the desk, wrapped in the rag.

"You do not understand it," he said, as he joined Don at the door.

"I do not," replied Don.

"It is one of the items of the programme for the coming *Cust*," answered Jack. "Now what's the row?"

The latter remark was inspired by the sounds of a woman's voice, followed by a squall from one who was evidently a boy.

"That's Little Jiggers," said Jack, "and he has been prigging the tommy, as usual. We are all kept close, and know what hunger is, but Jiggers, though small, is a natural cormorant. Let's go and see the fun."

The fun, as he termed it, was going on in the hall, where a small boy, of dogged appearance, was being heartily cuffed by an old lady, attired in the fashion of our grandmothers, bombazine petticoat, big bustle, faded silk skirt, corkscrew curls, and cap garnished with a liberal display of artificial flowers.

"Don't deny it," she was saying, "I saw you coming out of the kitchen. Look at the grease on your waistcoat, and you have a rasher now in your mouth."

She pounced upon Little Jiggers, chucked him violently under the chin, and out popped a half-masticated rasher of bacon upon the floor.

This was undeniable evidence that Little Jiggers had been foraging in forbidden lands. He made no further denial of his guilt, but proceeded to plead extenuating circumstances.

"What if I did bone a bit of bacon?" he said, ferociously. "Wouldn't you do the same if you were kept as short as I am? And wasn't there enough bacon for ten people, and only you and Mr. Snicker to eat it?"

It was an unfortunate thing for Little Jiggers that Fontenoy Snicker should at that moment put in an appearance. He had evidently heard the disturbance, and he come provided with the means of quelling it—the dear, too dear, familiar cane.

Jack and Don kept back in the shadow of the staircase, being powerless to save or soften the punishment of the culprit.

"Now," said the schoolmaster, "let me see what is the matter!"

Mrs. Snicker, for it was no less a personage whom Don was beholding for the first time, proceeded to explain.

She had been preparing breakfast, and left the kitchen for a few brief moments, to give some instructions to the servant who was in the private dining-room. Returning, she met Little Jiggers, greasy with spoil, hurrying out of the domestic sanctum, and had pursued the young marauder as far as the hall, where the closed door stopped further progress.

"And not a single rasher has the young villain left upon the plate," she finished with, gasping for breath.

Mr. Fontenoy could forgive little, and certainly not an invasion on his domain of luxury. He rolled up the cuffs of his coat, and laying one hand on Little Jiggers, he utilised the other in giving him a most unmerciful thrashing.

The boy writhed and howled, but he might have made ten times the row and not been heard, save by those who were used to such vocal demonstrations.

At length he fell upon the floor, and with one final parting cut, the schoolmaster finished his vengeful punishment.

"How does that taste," he panted, "after a plateful of bacon?"

No reply was given him, and slowly turning down his cuffs, he swung round to depart, when he espied Don and Jack.

"What are you doing here?" he roared. "I'll have no spy upon my actions."

"We're waiting for breakfast, sir," answered Jack.

"I'll give you both a breakfast that will taste in your mouths for the rest of the day," said Snicker, with a hiss. "Get out of my sight."

It was the only thing they could do, and as he aimed a blow at them, they dodged it, and skedaddled to the playground.

"What do you think of that?" asked Jack, as they reached the open air.

"Brutal," replied Don. "I felt as if I could have killed him."

"You are already as good as one of us," said Jack.

This was a pretty beginning to the day of rest, but more remained behind.

Shortly after, it began to rain, and there was in the gathering clouds a full promise of a wet day. The boys, instead of being paraded in the grounds after breakfast, were told to assemble in the schoolroom, which they did under the care of Penny Bunn and Awful Rooker.

In due time Mrs. Snicker arrived, and overhauled them one by one. Those who were clean were put on one side of the room, and those who had made a failure of their ablutions were pushed to the other side. It was a case of dividing the sheep from the goats.

Out of the thirty odd boys nine were in the black list, and they were all members of the second dormitory. Their excuse was that the towels were wet, and they could not get the pump to work, so as to give them a sufficient supply of water.

But it availed them not.

Fontenoy Snicker was summoned, and, strong from the breakfast table, fell upon them like a giant refreshed.

Don in the whole course of his life had never seen so many tearful boys assembled together as the schoolmaster finally left behind him.

The rain beat against the windows, accompanying their wails with its mournful sound.

Owing to the state of the weather, they all remained at home, umbrellas being wonderfully scarce in Littlecote Abbey, and were requested to keep in the schoolroom.

It rained right away until the evening was far advanced, and in some respects it was the most mournful day Don had ever spent.

Somebody or something was going wrong all the time.

It was impossible to keep the boys quiet, and all amusement being denied them, they were up to all sorts of tricks with each other. The alternate presence of Penny Bunn and Awful Rooker acted as a poor deterrent.

Fontenoy Snicker was in and out, and he never came in without his cane or went away without using it. It was a pastime and recreation to him, and, like some other evil habits, it grew upon what it fed on.

Altogether it was a time to be remembered by one like Don, who had been spoilt at home, and knew nothing of the cruelty of school life under such men as Fontenoy Snicker.

CHAPTER VIII.

MILKY WHEY.

"HERE yer are, mackerel, fresh mackerel, three a shilling!"

It was a voice that might have been heard half-way across the desert of Sahara which fell upon the ears of the boys as they trooped out of the breakfast room on the following morning.

"Milky Whey, by jingo!" exclaimed Tom Drummond, "a full two hours earlier than usual."

"He is afraid his fish will tumble to pieces before he can sell it," explained Gy Tanner.

"Tom, Bob, Gyp, Tombstone, Don, a dozen of you," said Jack, "come with me. I've sworn that there shall be no fish eaten here to-day, and I will keep my oath."

Away they went pell-mell, out by the side door and across to the iron gates. There they found a flush-faced man of the coster class with some fish and a couple of boxes upon his barrow.

"What!" cried Jack, "you will come here in spite of all the warnings you have had?"

"I beant had no warning," replied Milky Whey, with a strong Wiltshire accent, "and you let I alone. I've brought the young gentleman's boxes."

"Shove 'em inside the grounds," said Jack to the boys; "Black-Eyed Susan will see to them. Snicker isn't out of bed yet. He always somehow bowls himself over on Sundays. That's it. Now, Milky, off you go, and don't you come within five miles of us for the rest of your days."

"I beant a-goin' to be ordered off by you," cried Milky Whey. "Muster Snicker is bound to buy a bit o' fish o' me. Fine fresh mac— Pah! Poof! Murder!"

Jack had taken up one of the fine, fresh fish, and hurled it at him with so good an aim that it struck him in the mouth, and set him spluttering.

"Boys," said Jack, "we've got an hour for the funeral. Let's run this fish down to the churchyard, and bury it."

"Ye let my barrer alone!" roared Milky Whey.

But Jack had already seized the shafts, and the rest, Don included, lending a willing hand, away they went, with Milky Whey in hot pursuit.

"Scissors!" exclaimed Tom Drummond, "how it smells!"

"Bear it for the good of the cause," said Jack. "No more fish until Milky clears out of the country."

The path taken by them was across a corner of the field in which the Abbey stood, and down a path that was new to Don. It was rather precipitous, but not dangerously so, and at a smart pace the barrow was trundled down.

Maddened by the prospect of a ruinous loss, Milky Whey tore down after the boys, favouring them with some choice specimens of Wiltshire dialect, usually reserved by the natives to express their anger.

The descent was effected without an accident, and level ground was reached. A lane, rather rough with ruts, lay ahead, and beyond that there was a glimpse of the high road, which, as usual in the wilds of that county, came from some unknown place, and led to nowhere in particular.

Bumping the barrow along, the boys kept on, blind or indifferent to the fact that they ran a great risk in being away from school without leave.

Here and there they left a record of their progress in the form of a fish of some sort, in a state bordering on decomposition.

Milky Whey stopped to pick up one or two at first, but finding that he was thereby losing ground, he reserved the rest of the picking up until he had recovered his main stock-in-trade.

On reaching the high road he began to gain ground, for the pushing of the heavy barrow began to tell upon the boys.

Raising his voice as he drew nearer, he promised them all sorts of things when he got hold of them. But, undaunted, they kept on.

"He is getting precious close to us," said Tom Drummond, who was running by Jack's side.

"All right," replied Jack, "you do as I tell you. When he is quite close to us, I'll give the word to swing the barrow round. Then you will see something."

A hundred yards or so ahead of them they could see the gate of the churchyard, where, in jest or earnest, Jack had declared his intention of interring the fish. The question was, would they be able to reach it?

"I'm on you," bellowed Milky Whey, from the rear.

"Turn!" cried Jack.

All assisting with the barrow knew by that time what was expected of them, and, with a simultaneous movement, the humble vehicle was swung round so that the unsuspecting Milky Whey came into violent collision with the upper end of it?

Breathless he fell sprawling upon his stock-in-trade, scattering the odorous fish to the right and left.

"Now we've got him!" shouted Jack. "Let us bury the lot!"

With a lightning-like movement, the barrow was again headed for the churchyard, with Milky Whey, who had rolled over on his back, still upon it.

The manœuvre, of which he had been the victim, was so thoroughly successful that it cowed his vengeful spirit, and reduced him to complete submission.

"Young gents," he pleaded, "have a bit of mercy on a covey as is trying his mortiul best to get a livin'."

Here the barrow came to a rough bit of road, and he was subject to the usual jolting. "I—I have p-a-aa-aid a 'igh p-p-ri-i-ce for this-s-s barrererer-load at the mon-n-nger in Chipp-py-py-py-am, and who-o-o says fi-i-ish is chea-a-ap to-day is a li-i-i-ia-a-r-r-r!"

"The gate's locked!" sang out Tom Drummond.

"Never mind," replied Jack, "here's a ditch. In with the lot!"

And in the lot went, Milky Whey first, and his fish afterwards. The barrow was tossed over all, and, hot and panting, Jack, pulling off his cap, shouted: "Hurrah, boys! No stale fish to-day."

They echoed his cry, and then turned their gaze

A SPLENDID SCHOOL STORY.

NEVER BEFORE PUBLISHED.

By E. HARCOURT BURRAGE,

Author of "Ching Ching," "Monkey Mat and Roving Dick," "The Brave Boy of the Basilisk," &c.

A Handsome Coloured Plate Presented with Every Number.

No. 2.

THE LAMBS OF LITTLECOTE.

A THRILLING School Story.

AN UNEXPECTED, BUT VERY LIVELY, PIG HUNT.

 PRICE ONE PENNY.

ALDINE PUBLISHING CO., 9, Red Lion Court, Fleet St., and 1, 2, & 3, Crown Court, Chancery Lane, London.

upon the fallen coster, whose dismayed face was just visible, as he peered out of the ruins of his stock-in-trade.

"Will you swear never to bring us any more stinking fish?" demanded Jack.

"I sells as I buys," answered Milky Whey, humbly, "and I'm not responsible for the hodour.."

"Do you mean to say," asked Gyp Tanner, "that they give it to you for nothing?"

"You are a nice lot," said Milky Whey, evading a direct answer to this very plain question; "lambs of Littlecote, indeed. I calls you raging sarpints."

"Your life is spared for once," said Jack, with lofty magnanimity. "Remember that the next time you turn up with fish more than six hours old, you die. You hear, you *die!*"

"I hears," answered Milky Whey, "and from what I sees of you, I don't think you'd mind doin' of it. You don't make no 'lowance for us bein' so fur away from the sea. Fish ain't shot out of a gun to Chippenham."

"Mind you are not shot out of one, you poisoner of boys," said Jack. "Keep there until we are out of sight, or we will bury you in earnest."

"It ain't likely I'm goin' to move if you don't wish it," returned Milky Whey, humbly. "I ain't onreasonble, and I hopes as you will see your way to have a whip round for this. All that stands atwix me and the workus," he added, pathetically, "is the barrer and what I sells from it."

They were out of hearing by the time he had finished this pathetic intimation of his financial state.

He lay still for awhile and then sat up.

"No offence if I gets up, gentlemen, I hopes?" he said.

There was no reply, for they were half-way down the lane, hurrying back to school so as to get there before they were missed.

Not receiving any reply, Milky Whey ventured to rise. He had so many scales of his fish about him that he looked like a mermaid in a worn-out, under-the-sea suit.

But that was not of much consequence to him. For many years he had lived with the persistent odour of over-day fish about him. It was the general upsetting which had exasperated him.

"They're a lively lot, werry," he muttered, "and I'm lively, too, when I'm put about. I'm a-coming up to the Abbey again, one day, young gentlemen, but it is not to sell fish. No; it's for summat else as will be worse than a few mackereel a bit gone. You must have got a lot o' dainty stomachs among you. Pah! sich stuck up mucks o' boys makes me sick."

Having righted his barrow, he picked up as many of his fish as could be picked up at all. Some were

made passable with a little rubbing on the grass, and others required a cautious scraping with his knife.

But he was a past-master in the art of "faking" up that class of food, and in about an hour he had cleaned and arranged his fish upon the barrow to his satisfaction.

But he did not return to Littlecote. Being on the level ground, he prudently remained there, making for some of the scattered houses forming the village of Mumping Malford.

High on the morning air rose his stentorian voice, crying:

"Fresh macker-re-e-el! All in this morning, three-e a shilling! All alive o!—macker-re-e-el!"

CHAPTER IX.

THE ART OF WALKING BLINDFOLDED.

THE boys raced back up the hill, and reached the gate of the playground just in time to see Awful Rooker emerge from the house with a book in his hand. One of his pleasant duties was occasionally to call the roll of the boys, to make sure that none of them were absent.

In the performance of this duty he had to put up with much irritating matter, as the youngsters were in the habit of treating it as a joke.

Rooker saw the gate swing open and shut again, but owing to there being a number of the boys intervening, his view was obstructed, and he could not tell whether somebody had gone out or just come in.

"The assemble for the roll-call!" he cried, in a squeaky voice.

At first there was a general shamming of not hearing, and he had to call out three times ere he got them in a body in front of him.

Then the fun of giving aggravating replies began.

"Walker," he cried.

"In bed with the measles," replied somebody who was not Walker.

"It's a lie!" shouted the real Walker; "don't believe him, sir."

"Ridge," said Rooker, as he ticked off Walker as being present. He knew that if he went into any argument about the original reply, he would have a good ten minutes' wrangling to get through with.

"Run away," was the answer.

"Who said that?" demanded Rooker, losing his caution in his anger.

"I—I—I!" shouted a score of voices.

The moment silence was restored, Gyp Tanner squeaked like Punch, and imitating the voice of that popular character, cried out: "Put 'em all down in your book, sir! Report 'em, sir! Report 'em!"

"Noakes!" shouted Rooker, wildly.

"Playing a Jew's harp in the cellar," was the answer this time.

"You are worse than ever this morning," said Rooker, savagely. "I've a good mind not to call the roll at all."

"I really wouldn't, sir," said Bob Stockton, sympathetically; "they're not worth the trouble."

"I will report you, anyway," said Rooker, as he put a black mark against Bob's name.

"May I ask what I have done?" inquired Bob, in his politest fashion.

"You have been insolent," answered Rooker, flushing.

"That's a deliberate lie!" said Bob, coolly; "and I will call the whole school to bear witness to my having merely spoken sympathetically to you when performing a trying duty. Report away."

"Ford!" cried Rooker.

"Here," said Jack.

"Don't believe him!" howled Short. "How can he stand there saying such a thing, when he knows he's out?"

This was too much. Rooker lowered his book, and glared at the laughing faces in front of him.

"You think it great fun," he said, "to worry me, but you dare not try it on with Mr. Snicker. You are all afraid of him."

"You have said that many times before," said Bedstone. "Why don't you sing it for a change? Chorus, boys."

Immediately they all burst out with a fragment of one of their school songs, written by Herbert May, poet laureate to Mumping Malford:

"Yes, we are all afraid of Snicker,
For he is a champion licker.
He makes you dance, and madly prance,
Quicker, and quicker, and quicker,
Until you cannot dance any more,
And finish by wriggling on the floor.

"You are a lot of little beasts," said Awful Rooker. "But you shall all smart for this."

"Calling names is a punishable offence," said Bob Stockton; "see rule 249 of the school."

Then Rooker did what he had often in despair done before. He counted the boys as well as he could, and, as ever, found it a parlous task, for they would not keep still, but shifted about like little pigs in a sty.

He feigned in the end to have done it to his satisfaction, and ordered them, in as peremptory a tone as he could assume, to go in to breakfast.

This was an order that they were willing enough to obey, and trooped in grinning over the discomfiture of the white-faced Rooker.

Mr. Fontenoy Snicker, who might very justly have been suspected of having been christened Jerry, having heard from his spouse that Don's boxes had

arrived, wondered how it was that Milky Whey had not asked for payment for his services, or offered any of his fish for sale. The mystery of this double omission was explained by the receipt in the course of the afternoon of a note from the itinerant fishmonger.

It was written on a dirty piece of paper, smelling very strongly of tobacco and beer. A boy, whose duty was to scare crows in the adjacent fields, delivered it, owing to the cautious spirit in the breast of Milky, which led him to avoid, for that day at least, the dangerous region of the school.

It ran as follows:

DARE SUR,—Mi barrer was runned orf with this mornin' by your boyes, and habout three stun of good sound fish spiled bi bein' put atop of me in a ditsh. I only want the vally of 'em, wich is fore ans sicks, the same bein' my doo. Pleas forrard a chek for saim to the Pig's Hed, Chippinhem. yures truley, MILKY WHEY."

The brow of the schoolmaster grew very dark as he read this precious communication, but he made no reference to it then. After school hours he set out for Chippenham, to interview the sufferer, so as to get at the names of the culprits.

He was, by the way, always glad of an excuse for going into the town, where he had a snug little inn in which to spend a social hour with some of the tradesmen. It was his habit to come back from these expeditions in a state known to the boys as "coxey-woxey."

As he usually returned at a late hour, the fear of being seen in that condition by any of the inhabitants of Mumping Malford was reduced to a minimum, as the lively people of that severely agricultural district were in the habit of retiring at a very early hour.

It was soon known among the boys that the terrible head of the establishment had betaken himself to the town, and, as they were wont to do, they proceeded to make the most of the opportunity afforded them.

One of the things suggested to be done was to "get at" Penny Bunn again.

It was early days, of course, so soon after the rope trick, but, as Tom Drummond said, they could only try their level best to lead him on to something, and, at the worst, fail.

Once more the rain was falling, and the evening had to be spent within doors, and, of course, ought to have been passed in the schoolroom.

A scheme was soon set afloat, and the talk turned upon the capability of some persons to walk blindfolded.

"It is impossible to keep straight," said Jack Ford, "for the natural tendency is to bear to the left. Travellers in a forest, when walking in the dark, invariably walk in a circle. Is it not so, Mr. Bunn?"

Penny Bunn, playing up that night as usual to being a companion to the boys, was of opinion that a man who could not walk straight must have some physical defect or be a fool.

"I am sure," he said, "that I could keep on in a direct line for hours." Jack shook his head.

"I think, sir," he answered, "that I can go further than that. You would not be able to walk straight, with your head simply covered, say, the length of the corridor on the first floor.

"Pooh! Nonsense!" returned Penny Bunn, rising like a fish to the bait.

"Will you try it, sir?" suggested Bob Stockton. "It would be interesting for us to know whether the theory is a false or true one."

"We must get something open to cover Mr. Bunn's head with," said Don, admitted for the first time as one of the joking fraternity.

"A foot-bath placed over the head of Mr. Bunn would suffice," hinted Walker, a boy with a face naturally stolid, a mask to conceal a very lively disposition.

Mr. Penny Bunn smiled. The idea that he could not walk straight with such a thing over his head was too absurd. However, he had no objection to trying the experiment.

Having got thus far, the rest was easy.

There were two staircases leading to the corridor, one at each end. One was used by the boys and servant, and the other was reserved for Mr. and Mrs. Snicker. The start was to be made from what was be called the inferior end, and the under-master may to walk down the corridor and back again.

Tom Drummond stole away first to get the foot-bath from a cupboard where several were kept, and in a few minutes Penny Bunn, with the boys at his heels, ascended the staircase.

All were so quiet and orderly that nothing more in that direction could be desired. Tom was by the door opening on the corridor with the bath.

"Now, sir," he said, "you are not to touch it when on your head, as it would be a guide, and that is what the traveller in the forest doesn't get. Shall I place it on your shoulders?"

"If you please," replied the smiling victim; "you may tilt it a little forward if you like."

"No, sir," said Tom, generously, "we will have the thing that is fair."

Meanwhile, an emissary, in the person of Gyp Tanner, had been dispatched to the kitchen, in search of Black-Eyed Susan, who was seated at the table darning her stockings.

"Lor', Master Tanner," she exclaimed, "what do you want?"

"There's a smell of fire upstairs," replied Gyp, feigning the greatest alarm, "and I believe it is in Mrs. Snicker's room. Where is she?"

Black-Eyed Susan sprang up, saying she would find her mistress, who was in the linen room, looking out the washing.

Gyp hastened back, so as to be present at the *denouement*, which all the conspirators fondly hoped would be brought about.

Penny Bunn, with the foot-bath upon his head, was about to start.

"Go slowly at first, sir," advised Gyp, as he winked at his companions to imply that his part of the work was done. His object in advising a slow movement was to gain time.

"All keep quiet there," said Jack; "talking might confuse Mr. Bunn."

"Or," said Tom Drummond, "it might act as a guide to him."

"I want no guide," interposed the under-master, his voice from within the foot-bath having a hollow, muffled sound.

Here the distant voices of Mrs. Snicker and Black-Eyed Susan were heard.

"Off," said Tom Drummond, in a whisper.

Penny Bunn started with the utmost confidence, and, as one may guess, experienced no difficulty in getting along. Half-way down the chosen track he paused for an instant, and at the same moment Mrs. Snicker came hurrying into the corridor.

The boys waited just long enough to get a look at the utter amazement depicted on her face, and then, closing the door, slipped away as if they were ghosts, and returned to the schoolroom, where they gave way to a full enjoyment of their mirth.

Meanwhile, Mrs. Snicker, recognizing the form of the undermaster, although she could not see his face, asked him, in her shrill fashion, what he was doing. He did not recognize her voice, as it came to him within the hollow of the foot-bath, and answered waggishly:

"Oh, you don't deceive me by slipping in front. I know the way I am going. Get out of the road, or I'll run over you."

This was meant to be a jocular threat, but Mrs. Snicker, not being in the secret of the performance, took it offensively.

She was a vinegar and pepper old woman, apt to lose her temper with those she considered to be her inferiors, and instead of merely enlightening Penny Bunn as to her identity, she seized hold of the foot-bath, and dragged it violently off his head.

"Oh, stash that!" he cried, keeping up his character as a playmate of boys; "it isn't fair."

Then he saw the eagle-eyed old woman before him, and his heart stood still.

"Mr. Bunn," she said, viciously, "you have been drinking. I've noticed lately that the beer barrel runs out very quickly. You've got a false key of it."

Penny Bunn turned his eyes towards where the

boys ought to have been, and saw nothing but a closed door.

"The little fiends!" he gasped.

"Mr. Bunn," said Mrs. Snicker, "will you explain yourself?"

"Madam," was his feeble response, "I was experimenting on the possibility of walking blindfolded."

"Then don't play your foolish tricks with my foot-bath," said Mrs. Snicker, viciously; "as for walking blindfolded, I think you do it always. Your eyes are never open. Why are you not looking after the boys?"

"It is the hour of recreation," he replied.

"Yes," Mrs. Snicker said, tartly; "and I believe they have, as usual, been recreating at your expense. You will hear what your principal thinks of this. Go away, you idiot."

"Madam," said Penny Bunn, getting on his dignity stilts, "if I were an idiot, I should not be in my present position. Don't forget that it is I who educate the boys. Mr. Snicker is an ignoramus, and cannot work out a sum in practice."

"You dare to tell me that!" screamed Mrs. Snicker; "you miserable workhouse worm, who came here without so much as a character to your back! Why, you—you—"

She was going for him, but he prudently turned tail and fled.

Mrs. Snicker hurled the foot-bath, after him, but, being a woman, could not throw straight, and so missed her mark.

As he vanished she turned to Black-Eyed Susan, who had arrived upon the scene, and was standing behind her mistress as demure as a kitten.

"Open the door of my room," she hissed.

Black-Eyed Susan complied with her request, and the angry woman just glanced in.

"As I expected," she said; "no fire, or a bit of smoke. Who was the boy that brought that fool's message to you?"

"He only just looked into the kitchen, ma'am," replied the girl, "and I didn't take any particular notice of him."

"That's lucky for the boy, whoever he is," muttered Mrs. Snicker; "if he could be marked down, he would have to repent of his fooling when Mr. Snicker returns."

Waggling the flowers of her cap with wrath, she hastened down the stairs.

"As if they were not beaten enough without my saying things to get 'em into trouble," said Black-Eyed Susan, as she closed the bedroom door. "No, ma'am, you don't get anything out of me to make their young lives harder than they are."

Jane, called Black-Eyed Susan, for short, was not a bad sort of girl.

CHAPTER X.

MR. SNICKER HAS A LITTLE MISHAP.

THE fact of Mr. Fontenoy Snicker not having returned at the time the boys went to bed, did not create any surprise. The schoolmaster, when he got into Chippenham town, generally remained there until the public-houses closed, and afterwards he would get home with the best of his ability.

There is little doubt that he was in the habit of taking his time, even to the extent of having short naps by the roadside, for he rarely turned up at Littlecote Abbey before two o'clock in the morning, and he had, at times, been as late as three, or half-past.

Mrs. Snicker took upon herself the task of sitting up for him, because it was better that her eye alone should behold him on his return, and if Black-Eyed Susan, or one of the masters—Rooker was a master in the prospectus, you know—sat up, they would not be fit for their duties in the morning.

At ten o'clock Mrs. Snicker had her supper, and then got out the usual sewing to while away the time.

She did the mending for the boys, and, although there were no extras in the school bill, there was always a little account for "tailoring" appended thereto. These bills were her perquisites.

For two hours she sat putting on buttons and mending the rents in the clothes of the boys, some of them of the nature of ghastly wounds; then she took a rest, and mixed for herself a little gin and water.

It was raining hard outside, and it was with a grim smile upon her face she sat listening to the swishing of the heavy drops against the window panes.

"Jerry," she said, "will be getting a-soaking outside, as well as in, to-night, and serve him right. I hope he will have an attack of rheumatism, as it will keep him quiet for a time."

It was her habit, thinking or communing about her husband when alone, to refer to him by his rightful name. She had married him as Jerry, and Jerry he would be to her to her dying day.

The Fontenoy was only a professional prefix to Snicker, and it had no reality to her.

She sipped her gin and water slowly for a time, listening to the rainfall, and then resumed her labours.

One o'clock was at last boomed out in a muffled way by the grandfather's clock in the hall.

"He ought to be back soon," she muttered, and as if in derision of the idea, there was an extra swoop down of the rain, and a gust of wind that whistled through the keyholes of the old place with dolorous effect.

Mrs. Snicker was not usually anxious about her husband, nor was she superstitious, but an uncanny feeling crept over her as she listened to the increase of the storm.

"What a fool he is," she muttered, "to be out on a lonely road on such a night, and all for a bit of low company and a lot of drink."

She rose up and walked from the room into the hall. A small lamp was burning on the table. In the house there was no sound but the aggressive ticking of the old grandfather's clock.

> And from its station in the hall,
> The ancient timepiece says to all,
> For ever—never!
> Never—for ever!

Mrs. Snicker recalled these words, part of a poem she had learnt in her girlhood, and shuddered.

"Something's happened to Jerry, I'm sure of it," she murmured. "I've got the creeps."

After a moment's hesitation, she opened the front door, and a sheet of rain swooped in. It cost her an effort to close it again.

With a sickening feeling in her heart, she sat down and waited.

Grandfather's clocks are always very deliberate in their movements, but surely there never was so slow a clock as that in the hall. It seemed the better part of a day ere it tolled off the hour of two.

Fully now impressed with the conviction that something had happened to her Jerry, she took up the lamp and ascended to the room occupied by Penny Bunn.

Taking on herself the privileges of matronship, she opened the door and went in. The under-master was sound asleep, and snoring.

She aroused him with all speed, and bade him arise and go forth to seek his employer.

"And you had better take an umbrella and a lantern," she added, "for it is rather wet and very dark."

Breathing internally compliments of a varied nature on his superior, Penny Bunn got out of bed and struggled into his clothes. Being averse to lonely midnight expeditions, he next sought out the pupil-teacher Rooker, and aroused him from dreams of a happy life, which he had never in reality enjoyed.

"Mr. Snicker has lost his way," Penny Bunn said, "and we have to go out in search of him."

Awful Rooker breathed hard, but he could only obey, and having attired himself in a slipshod fashion, he went down to the hall, where Mrs. Snicker was impatiently awaiting them.

To hasten their movements she had lighted a lantern, which she handed to Penny Bunn. He had brought his umbrella from his room. It was an ancient thing, faded, and with leaks in it, but still presumably of some service.

The door having been opened, he asked the shaking Rooker to hold the lantern, while he put up his umbrella to shield himself from the storm. Mrs. Snicker closed the door.

At the same moment a fierce gust of wind caught the half-opened umbrella, turned it inside out, and whisking it clean off the stick, bore it away over the precipice into some far away spot in the lower ground, where it was lost to its owner for ever.

"Hang Snicker," said the under-master, fiercely; "poison him! blow him!"

"I don't think it's any use trying to find him," moaned Awful Rooker.

"Anyway," muttered Penny Bunn, "we must go a little way. Hold the lantern low, so that we keep the path. If we fall over the side of the slope, it will be all over with us."

The path ran dangerously near the edge of this slope, which varied in places from a steep descent to an absolute precipice. There was indeed need of the exercise of much caution.

At a snail's pace the miserable pair crawled along, the wind threatening to blow them over, and the rain viciously beating upon them.

Presently there was a momentary lull in the storm, and close by they heard a voice crying for help.

"That's Snicker," said Penny Bunn. "I could swear to his howl anywhere."

"I thought it sounded somewhere below us," gasped Rooker, shaking from head to foot.

"Help! murder! help!" rose up the voice again, nearer than before.

"Stop!" cried Penny Bunn, "he's close here."

"Some tramps are murdering him."

"No, Rooker. He has fallen over the side of the hill. Hold the lantern higher."

Rooker did so, and as if to oblige them, the wind suddenly lulled.

"Mr. Snicker," cried Penny Bunn, peering over the side of the slope, "where are you?"

"Here," replied a faint voice below. "I've fallen a hundred feet, and broken every limb in my body."

"Not so bad as that, I hope, sir," said Penny Bunn, cheerfully. The idea of his principal being injured was rather a thing to rejoice over than otherwise.

"I think I can see him," said Rooker, holding the lantern high and peering down, "there, where the ground sticks out a bit."

Just there the slope was not so precipitous as it was in other places, but it was a very uncomfortable spot to fall down on a dark night.

"Wait a moment, sir," said Penny Bunn, who knew the ground well, "I'll try and come to you."

Bidding Rooker hold the lantern steadily, he cautiously began the descent. There was not much peril in it to a sober man, and in a few minutes he was near his principal, who was lying on a projecting portion of the broken soil upon his back.

He had not broken any bones, as it happened, but he had given himself a severe shaking, and he was plastered with sticky mud from head to foot.

His face, from the same cause, was totally unrecognizable.

"You must be nice sort of fellows," he snarled, "to let me lie here for hours. Do you mean to say you did not hear me hollering—I mean *hallooing?*"

"We did not, sir," answered Penny Bunn, firmly but respectfully; "people, when they get to bed, have something else to do than to lie awake listening for the bawling of others who go tumbling about."

They got him on his feet, and having found on examination that he was not seriously injured, they proceeded to assist him to get to the higher ground.

This was not an easy job, for the schoolmaster, in addition to having had a full cargo of drink, had fairly knocked himself out of time by his fall.

But, with many groans and explosive utterances from the sufferer, it was accomplished, and a man more heavily caked with mud, neither of them had ever seen.

"It appears, sir," said Penny Bunn, "that you must have mistaken your way and fallen over."

"You don't imagine, you fool," growled Fontenoy Snicker, "that I went down there as a matter of choice. What's the time?"

"Going on for three, sir."

"And I was earlier than usual to-night. I must have been down there since twelve o'clock."

"It's sobered him, anyway," thought Penny Bunn.

The rain and wind, as if to make amends for the recent lull, now renewed their fury, and it was as much as they could do to keep their feet.

The broad-brimmed hat of Fontenoy Snicker was naturally gone, and the others had to hold theirs tightly on their heads. At last they got to the side entrance, and all peril from the elements was past.

But Mr. Snicker had to run the gauntlet of another danger.

Mrs. Snicker, on seeing that he was alive, but in a muddy condition, experienced a revulsion of feeling. Her grief and anxiety vanished, and wrath took their place.

"This," she said, "is the result of low company and drink. Come into the kitchen and let me scrape you down."

Fontenoy Snicker murmured something about a warm bath, to keep off rheumatism, but he was cut short with the intimation that there was no hot water to be had that night.

Mrs. Snicker unceremoniously hustled him along, and so he vanished from the gaze of his assistants.

"He is sure to be laid up after this," said Penny Bunn. "Rooker, we shall have to brace ourselves up to keep the boys in order without him."

"I wish we may be able to do it," replied Rooker, gloomily, "but—"

He said no more, but, filled with all sorts of forebodings, wended his way to bed.

CHAPTER XI.

JUSTICE ABED.

THE morning brought with it a fulfilment of the under-master's fears. Mr. Fontenoy Snicker was overcome by his experience of the previous evening, and could not rise from his bed.

His legs ached, his arms ached, and he had a head which seemed to be swollen to twice its usual size. As for his tongue, if it had been smoke-dried for a year, it could not have been harder.

It was hard to bear of itself, but when it is supplemented with grudging attentions from a shrew of a wife, it is exquisite torture. She kept him waiting for a cup of tea he was dying for, and when she brought it, she nagged at him, and it scalded his parched throat.

When he told her that he thought he was going to die, she simply asked him what he expected to do after his goings-on.

"Men who get intoxicated, and go about falling down precipices," she said, "haven't any right to live. What's the matter with you now?"

"This piller—I mean pillow—doesn't seem comfortable," he replied.

"It's more comfortable than you have a right to look for," she answered; "it's more than you have a right to, to get a pillow at all."

Her next move was to insist upon washing his face and hands, performing that office with venom.

He got some soap in his eye, his nose was rubbed as if it were a door-knob in need of polishing, and when he said he wasn't dry behind the ears, he was told to dry himself by rubbing his head upon the pillow.

"If I was to die doing for you," said Mrs. Snicker, "you wouldn't be thankful."

"I think I should," he said, with a gleam of cunning in his eye.

"Oh! you brute," she cried, as she bounced out of the room, "you wish me dead, do you?"

In an hour or so he felt a little better. Mrs. Snicker, returning, asked him if he were going to get up and attend to school.

"I can't, and you know it," he replied.

"Then send the boys out for a holiday," said Mrs. Snicker, "for the two fools you have to assist you won't be able to keep them in order, and I'm not going to have the house in a state of riot."

"A little quiet would do me good," he said, pathetically. "The boys can have a holiday, and let 'em take their dinners with them. They will be satisfied with bread and cheese. Before they go, I should like to see Drummond and Ford and the new boy— what's his name?"

"Peebles," snorted Mrs. Snicker, "and he'll give you a twisting one day, if I can read the face of a boy. He's a willain."

"Say *villain*, my dear," pleaded the schoolmaster; "it's better."

"Pooh," was all Mrs. Snicker said, as she pranced out of the room.

In a few minutes the trio summoned to the bedside of the schoolmaster were ushered into the room.

Fontenoy Snicker turned in his bed and groaned.

"I'm down with a complaint I inherited from my father," he said; "its called brow ague, because it starts over the left eye, and runs all about the body. Its a thing that must run its course, for the doctors can't touch it. Drummond, you are laughing."

"I beg your pardon, sir," answered Drummond, "its the toothache distorting my face."

"If I wasn't down with—with my father's complaint," said Mr. Snicker, "I'd distort you. Now just you listen to me, you three. I went yesterday to Chippenham to interview the fishmonger, whose stock-in-trade was ruined in the morning. If any of you feel inclined to confess, now's the time."

It was one of the schoolmaster's pleasant ways to get a boy to confess, if he were weak enough to do so, and then thrash him. But he had two old and wary birds to deal with, and Don, the third, was getting his school feathers on him. They were all dumb.

"Then you have nothing to say to me?" said Fontenoy Snicker.

"No, sir," they answered in chorus.

"All right," he said, "but you won't escape, if you were in it, as Milky Whey is coming to identify the parties. I'm not the man to be took—taken in —ahem! —by boys. You've got a holiday to-day, so as to give me a chance of getting over the brow ager—I mean *hague*. Mind you don't get into trouble with anyone. D'ye hear?"

They said they heard, as they could not very well be off doing, and he dismissed them.

Just as they were going out of the door, he called Don back.

"T'other two—I mean the *other* two," he said, "can go, and they are not to listen at the door."

Jack and Tom departed, and Don demurely advanced to the bedside again.

Fontenoy Snicker fixed his bloodshot eyes upon him.

"You are new here," he said, after a pause, "but you are already getting old in sinful ways. I just give you the tip—dash it, I mean a hint—that I won't stand it. I'm going to break in the whole school to better manners, and I'll start with you. Dy'e hear?"

"Yes, sir," replied Don, "but will you kindly tell me what I have done?"

"I tell you," hissed the schoolmaster, "I am the sitting justice of this 'ere 'ouse—*house*—and am I to tell a boy of your age why I lick you? Not me. If you don't like it, go home!"

"My father," said Don, quietly, "has, I believe, paid for a year. Of course, if you wish to return the money—"

A sort of shriek burst from the lips of the schoolmaster. If he had been asked to lay his head upon the block, to save the life of another, he could not have been more astounded.

"Return the money!" he cried, in a choking voice; "do you think I am mad? It's enough, hearing you talk, to put a man into a b'iling—I mean *boiling*—rage. I'll return your money back. Git out—dash it—*get* out of the room."

Don was rapidly being hardened, and he was not much afraid of Fontenoy Snicker now. There was a smile on his face as he turned and walked away.

He went to the dining-room, where Mrs. Snicker was doling out parcels of bread and cheese to the boys, and, at the same time, instructing them as to their behaviour during the day.

"If you go doing any mischief," she said to Tom Drummond, "and get into prison, you will have to stop there."

"Yes, ma'am," replied Tom, demurely.

He winked at Don as he moved away, whispering as he did so: "Meet me outside. Want you particularly to-day."

Don had to wait a few moments ere his turn came to be served. When he had his dole of bread and cheese, wrapped in a piece of newspaper, he hurried outside, where he found Tom awaiting him.

There were other boys on ahead, singly and in twos and threes, some scattering over the fields, but the greater part taking the path that led to Mumping Malford wood.

"Don," said Tom, as they moved off side by side, "you have only just come among us, but you are going to be taken into the band, established for the confusion of Snicker, and to secure the rights and freedom of boyhood."

"What on earth is that?" asked the wondering Don.

"You will soon see," rejoined Tom. "About half the boys are in it. We take them on as we feel they can be trusted. I won't say any more just now, as we must hurry on. The meeting is held in the haunt of Robin Hood."

"Robin Hood!" ejaculated Don. "I never heard of his having been in this county."

"Well," said Tom, "it would have been his haunt, if he had happened to live here."

At this moment he turned from the path, and after a cautious look round, began to descend the steep hill-side, signalling to Don to follow him.

CHAPTER XII.

THE HAUNT THAT MIGHT HAVE BEEN ROBIN HOOD'S.

THE wood of Mumping Malford was a fairly extensive one. There were portions of it in which solitude might be said to reign supreme.

The reasons for this arose from the paucity of the population, and the fact that there was but a feeble attempt made to preserve game. The owner of the property was a minor, and his guardians were not in favour of sport. The parson, an old man, was left to do what he liked with the wild portions of the land.

The labourers having nothing to poach in the wood, and not being romantic, held aloof from it, and the women, who went gathering dead wood, to eke out their miserable purchases in coal, could get what they wanted nearer home.

Hence arose the peculiar isolation of the spot.

There was no direct path. The way Tom Drummond took was first down the bush-covered slope, and then through the tangled undergrowth, from which rose up the tall and stately trees.

But he seemed to know his way perfectly.

Without any hesitation he kept on until he came to a spot where the ground rose up suddenly in the form of a huge mound. There the undergrowth and the trees were so thick that the greater part of the daylight was excluded, and one might have thought that the evening had come.

"Widdy, widdy, whoo," Tom shouted.

Immediately, close to their feet, a dead bush shot out of the ground, giving Don a shock of surprise, disclosing a hole about three feet in circumference, and the head of Walker popped up.

"The word," he said.

"True as steel," answered Tom.

"Enter true as steel and all's well," said Walker, as he drew back.

"Follow me," said Tom, in a low and solemn tone.

Don, with his keen eyes on the stretch, followed Tom into the hole, and was bidden to keep still while the bush was being replaced.

Tom, having done this, told Don to crawl on a few feet and then stand up.

Don did so, and saw, to his astonishment, that he was in a chamber, roofed with stone, and of considerable extent.

Its proportions were revealed by the light of three ordinary tin oil-lamps fixed against the sides.

From the lamps his gaze wandered on to a circle of boys seated on the ground. They were sitting as silent and as still as statues, and on their faces there was the appearance of their being very much in earnest.

"Our new brother," said Tom Drummond, bowing to the circle.

They all rose to their feet, and bowed in response. Don saw that Ford, Stockton, May, Tanner, Short, Whymper, Little Jiggers, Walker and Noakes, boys whom he had taken the most notice of, were of the number there assembled.

"As the president of this band," said Jack Ford, "I declare that it is requisite our new brother take the oath."

Bedstone arose, and from a box behind him, which Don had not hitherto observed, produced a long bright dagger, apparently of ancient make.

"Don," said Jack, "what we are doing may at the first appear to you to be merely fun; but let me assure you that we are serious enough, although fun may come out of what we propose to do. You need not join us unless you like. All we ask is, if you funk being made a brother, say so right away, and give your word that what you have seen to-day will never be mentioned by you, so long as you are in Littlecote School."

"I will join you," said Don, firmly, "and I don't care a hang what you may be up to. Whatever it is, I am in it."

"Well said," returned Jack Ford. "You will now take this dagger in your right hand, and repeat after me:

"I, Donovan Peebles, do, on my solemn oath, swear never to reveal any of the doings of the band, nor will I act in any way contrary to their interests, or directly or indirectly do anything to thwart any purpose they may have in view. If I should do so, may I become an outcast among all as a mean and most contemptible cur, unfit to associate with boys who hold honour dear."

Jack spoke deliberately, as if he wished Don to weigh well the import of the words he uttered; and Don repeated them slowly, but unfalteringly.

The oath was taken, the new brother made.

Then a change came o'er the spirit of the scene.

The boys broke up, and talked among themselves for a time. Jack and Tom shook hands with Don.

"We're glad to have you with us," said the former; "every day we are getting stronger."

"But what is it all about?" asked Don.

"I am going to address the band," replied Jack, "and if you listen to me, you will hear all that is necessary to enlighten you. Brethren, we will now to business."

Immediately the boys resumed their seats, and Don, by Tom Drummond's direction, seated himself by his side.

"Brethren," said Jack, "in accordance with our custom, when a new brother is sworn in, I will now explain the object and aim of our band."

"Hear, hear," chorused the boys.

"It cannot be denied," continued Jack, "that our life at Littlecote is very hard, and that the whole show is as big a fraud as you would find from John o' Groat's to Land's End."

"It's all that," said Gyp Tanner, "and a yard or two over."

"It would be useless to apply to Snicker to ameliorate our lot," Jack went on, "and as for writing home, upsetting our mothers, and riling our governors, we are not going to do that, save as a last resource. The question then comes in, what are we to do to bring Snicker to his senses? In accordance with our custom, as aforesaid, we ask our new brother to propose a remedy."

Don, thus suddenly appealed to, looked up with a startled face.

"A remedy from me," he said. "I do not think there is any way of curing Snicker, except by killing him, which, of course, cannot be thought of for a moment."

"Well said," cried the others.

"Our new brother," said Jack, "has admitted the nature of the evil under which we suffer, by stating that the only remedy is to put an end to Snicker. It is strange, but true, that the same thought has been in the minds of many, but in the heart of none to carry it out. We are not bloodthirsty villains; but simply wronged and ofttime cruelly treated boys, who have made up their minds to put an end to the tyrannical conduct of the fraudulent Snicker, or, if I may use such an expression, burst up the school!"

There was an outburst of cheering, checked by the upraised hand of Tom Drummond.

"Don't forget," he said, "that if by any chance anyone is outside prowling around, that cheering might betray the secret of our retreat. Please express your approval in a more quiet fashion.

"For many months," Jack resumed, "a few of us were putting our heads together to find a remedy for the state of the school. Many plans were suggested, but put aside as impracticable, until our brother, Bob Stockton, the Prince of Politeness, came forward and suggested a *barring* out!"

There was another threatened outburst of enthusiasm, promptly suppressed by Tom, who, for the time, seemed to be acting as general director."

"You must be quiet," he said. "Blow it, can't you keep your heads a bit?

"A barring out," said Jack, "was, as you know, the extreme measure taken by boys to remedy school evils in our grandfathers' time. It fell into disuse as schools improved, and masters, under pressure, became

kinder. With a return of the evil which led to barrings out in the old days, I see no reason why it should not be again adopted."

There was a chorus of softly-spoken assents, as Jack sat down and Bob Stockton got upon his feet.

"Brethren and chums all," he said, "our president, as good and daring a fellow as ever lived, has spoken well, and, like the truly brave, he is ready to adopt a dangerous course. I, too, am willing to go that way, but if we tackle a barring out, it must be well done. There must be no weak, half-hearted nonsense about it. 'In for a penny, in for a pound.' We must work upon a system. Them's my sentiments."

"The system you have, of course, got in your head," said Gyp Tanner.

"I have," answered Bob.

"Then turn it out, and let us see what it is," said Whymper.

"A barring out for a day," said Bob, "is no good, nor for two days, or even a week, unless Snicker gives in."

"The question is," said Belstone, "whether, after he has given in, he can be held to his promise."

"What are we going for?" asked Don.

"Better food, and more of it," answered Jack, "and the total abolition of the cane."

"You won't get that," said Tom Drummond, emphatically; "but there is a great deal too much of it, without a doubt."

"We can ask for its total abandonment," said Jack. "If we don't get it, the only thing which will move Snicker is the fear of being turned out of the Abbey. That I know, for I heard him tell his wife one day, not long ago, that it would be his ruin. A barring out, if generally known, would lead to an inquiry, at, least might lead to one, on the part of the owner of the Abbey. Now, a barring out, to be successful, must be arranged, not only broadly, but in every detail. We must have food and water, some means of sleeping, however rough, and barricaded doors, which cannot be broken down by ordinary means."

"Snicker will have a fight for it," remarked Noakes.

"Just so," assented Jack, "therefore, we must be prepared to stand up strong against him."

"How long do you think it will take us to prepare?" asked Herbert May.

He was lying on the ground, behind the president, scribbling on a sheet of paper.

"A month, at least, from this time," replied Jack. "As you have done me the honour of electing me as manager of this business, I have given much thought to it, and I hope to have the details arranged in a few days' time."

"Will all the school be in it?" asked Whymper.

"Yes," answered Jack, "whether they like it or

not. Some, of course, will not know what is going on until the right moment comes. For instance, none of us would think for a moment of trusting Soppem Smith. If ever he tried to keep a secret, he would make a mess of it."

"There is one thing we must not forget," said Tom Drummond; "it will cost money."

"I forgot to mention that," said Jack, "although I intended to do so. It will be the duty of the brethren to get hold of all the tin they can, and hand it to Tom Drummond, who will fill the position of caterer. Write home, beg and borrow, sell things you don't want; in short, do your level best to get as much money as you can, and give it to the cause of boyhood's freedom. I do not think I will keep you any longer here to-day, as the sun is shining, and we all like to make as much of an outing, especially with Snicker safe in bed, as possible. We will conclude our meeting with the song of freedom, written by our esteemed poet, Herbert May, who will, as usual, sing alone the first few lines. Chorus to be chanted in the dormitory tone."

Herbert May stood up, and this was the signal for the rest to rise. With hand joined in hand, they sang the following

SONG OF FREEDOM.

Arise, wronged boys of Littlecote,
　Ere long a glorious day shall dawn,
When to regions far remote,
　Followed by the voice of scorn,
The cruel time of the past shall fly,
And terror in the graveyard lie.
So cheer, boys, cheer, no more of schoolboy's sorrow,
It may be very dark to-day, but surely will be very
　bright to-morrow

The song, sung with a quiet intensity, stirred the heart of Don, as the chant had done in the bedroom on the first night of his arrival at Littlecote. And it was none the less impressive for being sung in a place that gave to every sound an echo.

To his inexperienced heart, it was all very weird.

As soon as the song ended, there was a movement for the outside. Walker, who played the part of janitor, pushed out the bush that stopped up the entrance, and others extinguished the lamps, leaving them as they were upon the walls.

Don, on emerging from the retreat, dignified by the name of Robin Hood, was, for a spell of time, blinded by the glare, imperfect though it was, of the daylight.

Jack gave the word to separate, and meet again on Screwgray Bridge.

"Tom will take you there," he said to Don.; "by the way, boys, it's club day. Would this not be a good time to square up with old Charley Blotch?"

A general expression of approval followed, and Jack, promising to "think something out," hurried off with Bob Stockton.

Tom Drummond and Don remained to the last, the former carefully closing up the mouth of their meeting place.

"I don't believe," he said, as he stamped the earth round the roots of the bush, "that anybody but ourselves, now living, knows of this crib. Jack discovered it about two months ago when we were prowling about the wood."

"What was it made for?" asked Don.

"Ah!" exclaimed Tom, "there you ask me a conundrum I can't answer. But at a guess I should say it was made either as a sort of prison for some offending monk in the olden times, or as a retreat for one of those hermits we read of. Whatever it was intended for, it was never made for schoolboys to conspire in."

"What is club day?" was Don's next question as they began their journey towards the appointed spot.

"It's a day set apart for the meeting of everybody in the neighbourhood," answered Tom, "nominally for the members of a benefit club, but in reality for a general bu'st. The gentry make a big show of taking a pleasure in it, and they join in the sports of the humbler people. They eat and drink, and laugh and dance, with them, and the sons of the big nobs have all sorts of larks with the daughters of the farmers. It's done to keep up the good feeling of all classes towards each other. The game, of course, is to make those who have to work hard to keep the swells in clover contented with their lot."

"It's bunkum, then," said Don.

"Rather," returned Tom, "but it goes down with everybody here. The farms are practically deserted, and that is why old Charley Blotch's place can be dropped on with impunity."

"But why on his more than any other?"

"Because he is a selfish, cantankerous beast. His farm is in Smudgem Bender, a village about a mile beyond Screwgray Bridge. We were over there a month ago, having a run at hare and hounds across his farm. The hares took a course through his farmyard, and the hounds had to follow. The old beggar had a garden-engine filled with manure water ready for us, and you never saw such a state as some of us were in. Polecats couldn't hold a candle to us."

"It must have been very disagreeable," said Don, with a grin.

"Disagreeable isn't the word," growled Tom. "We had to strip, wash our clothes in the river, and dry them as well as we could, but we are going to get even with Charley Blotch for that to-day, or my name is Jack Ass."

Smarting under a sense of injury, Tom was so energetic that Don was obliged to stop to laugh. After a moment or two had elapsed, Tom laughed, too.

"I'll give you a peep of the club people a little higher up," he said; "but you musn't show yourself. It won't do to let them know we are out to-day. Of course, they have a list of our regular holidays in their capacious minds, but they little dream we are abroad now."

"Suppose they did know it?" suggested Don.

"Then some of them, notably old Charley Blotch, would be waddling homeward to stop any little games we might be up to. Bless you! we have been at war with some of the mutton-heads hereabouts ever since it has been a school. That is why we are called the Lambs of Littlecote."

He had worked his way to one of the sides of the wood by this time, commanding a view of an adjacent field, in which were a number of people and several tents.

A band of local celebrity was discoursing sufficiently sweet music for the yokels to kick up their heels to, and there they were, capering about with the gentry of the neighbourhood feigning to be as much entertained as they were.

"I should say that there are not a dozen natives of the place absent from this show," said Tom. "What a glorious opportunity for the exercise of our just vengeance. Come along, old man. Away, away to the bridge, to the trysting spot for the avenging brethren!"

Tom, at a pinch, could be wonderfully dramatic, and he now struck one of those penny plain and twopence coloured attitudes so much in favour with youngsters who get up an amateur play.

Skimming along the side of the wood, he presently came to the high road, and a trot of two hundred yards brought them to Screwgray Bridge.

A nice little band of the avengers had there assembled, including those who have figured in the most favourable light in our story.

Jack was there of course, and he had not as yet hit upon any plan of action.

"We had better go on to Blotch's farm," he said, "and see who is about and who isn't. If we go down by the fourteen-acre meadow, we shall be able to get up close to the farmyard without being seen."

The fourteen-acre meadow was not far from the bridge. It was part of the farm occupied by the offending Blotch, and having gained it, the boys, walking in Indian file, and keeping close under the hedge to escape observation, moved down on their road to vengeance.

The farm house occupied by Charles Blotch was not far from the highway, as it stood in the heart of the village called Smudgem Bender—a collection of about thirty houses of various sizes, on one of the roads leading from Mumping Malford to Chippenham.

The inhabitants were a dreary lot of yokels and petty tradesman, who, living apart from the world, had an immense idea of their importance to the nation.

It was generally supposed by them that the eye of London, whatever it might be, was on their movements, and that the voice of Smudgem Bender was virtually the chief guide to the government of the nation.

They were also a lot of petty scandal-mongers, lying against their absent friends and neighbours, and scandalising everybody around without stint or mercy. Blotch was the great man of the place. He could not read or write, but he had made a bit of money somehow, and he was also a churchwarden. When he opened his mouth no other Smudgem Bender dog was allowed to bark.

It may therefore be seen at a glance that to take any liberty with so great a man was a very serious thing.

Strange to say, the Lambs of Littlecote did not think so, unless they should do it at the wrong time.

Everybody but one old man was away from the farm that day; and the solitary guardian of the place was putting down the beds for the horses, all of whom were in the stable, when the boys crept up to the farmyard and looked over the gate.

It was very early for the putting down of the bedding, but the old man was bent on getting a taste of the glories and the joys of the club meeting. Jack looked carefully round, and came to the right conclusion that the coast was clear, save for the one old man.

"The key is in the stable door," he said. "Bob, you go and lock him in."

Bob Stockton skipped over the gate, and ran across the rotten straw of the yard with a swift, silent foot.

In a moment the door was closed and the key turned.

The next instant the head of an old man, covered with a shabby soft hat, with a hole in the crown, through which a few spiky white hairs protruded themselves, appeared at the side-window, and two eyes, dim with years, stared at the boys who were tumbling over the gate into the yard.

"Dang all things," he was heard to mutter. "If 'ere beant them werry Lambs. Here you," he bellowed, "let Oi out, Oi be a-goin' to the club, Oi be."

"Next year, I suppose," said Bob Stockton, with painful politeness.

"Next year be danged," cried the old man. "Oi be a-goin' this ere year."

"Get out of it," said Tom Drummond, as he banged to the wooden shutter of the window and fastened it with the usual wooden button; "we are going to put the place to rights for you."

"Let Oi out," roared the old man, "or I'll drive a fark through you."

"Keep your wool on," advised Bob.

Having got the guardian of the place fairly boxed up, the next thing was to see what could be done to avenge the foul water wrong inflicted on them a month earlier.

The first thing done on the inspiration of the moment was to open the doors of about a score of pigsties, and out came more little pigs than Don had ever seen at one time in his life before.

One of Blotch's specialities was pigs. He called them pegs, as do all the wise men of Wiltshire.

They were of various sizes, and with their ponderous, grave mammas formed a goodly throng.

Then there were a score of calves bleating in their stalls, which having been let loose, capered and skipped among the little pigs, adding thereby to the liveliness of their movements.

In an inner-yard was a pen of sheep, and their numbers were also added to the collection in the yard.

It was a sight to see such a variety of domestic animals gathered together. The place was as full as a well-crammed theatre.

"Now," said Jack, "the next thing is to find where the garden engine is, and spoil its working for a day or two."

The farmer's garden was on the other side of the house, and Tom and Don volunteered to go there in search of the engine. There was a way round the side of the building, and as they trotted through the gate they caught sight of a stout, red-faced man, with a half-a-score others at his heels, coming hurriedly up the garden path.

"Blotch and his men, by Jingo!" said Tom, seizing Don by the arm, and dragging him back. "They must have got a tip that we were here. Off with you, old man. Don't make a row. The quiet hint to the rest is what is wanted."

But it was too late for that.

The pair were espied, and with a terrific simultaneous yell, the farmer, and those with him, came tearing on.

The row they made was heard in the farmyard where Gyp Tanner was delighting all beholders by riding, in a masterly way, on the back of a rebellious sow.

Jack knew at once the full portent of that sound.

"'Ware hawks," he cried; "scatter. Everyone for himself. Meeting place the White Oak."

Away went the boys, and Don, on hastening into the yard again, saw them breaking off in various directions. Some were making for the high road, others for the fields, and all displaying the activity exhibited by lively youth when clearing out of danger.

Tom Drummond went on the trail of those who were hurrying for the road, and he seemed for the

moment to have forgotten Don, for he sprang over the gate, and, without looking back, bolted away.

Don had turned in the opposite direction, but he now harked back, which was a fatal thing to do.

To get clear off he had to pass the garden gate, and as he did so Blotch, with a thick, short stick in his hand, emerged therefrom.

Don had to keep close to the house, to avoid the central filth of the yard, and so came near enough for the stick to reach him. Blotch struck him heavily on the head, and he fell as if a cannon ball had struck him, losing all consciousness.

CHAPTER XIII.

DON IN DURANCE VILE.

"MEASTER be kind o' skeered, and he be gone for Lamplick to see what can be done for he."

Don heard the voice, but at first was unable to realize that the words in any way referred to himself.

He could make very little of anything indeed, for he had a strange singing in his head, and he felt as if the crown of it had been flayed.

But in a few moments he began to recall recent events, and then all came back to him in a flood, and he looked around him.

He was lying in a small cell-shaped chamber, with one small window high up, and a double door. His bed was a lot of short-cut hay and straw; in short, he was in the chaff-house of Blotch's stables.

A man was outside the door, the upper half of which was open, and he was leaning against it, with his back to Don.

"Measter will hit someun too hard by-an'-bye," was the reply to the above recorded remark. "Wun o' there yere days he'll be hauled up 'fore 'e bench and fined."

"But them there Lambs be warmints," said the man by the door.

"Human warmints can't be treated like stoats," was the sententious rejoinder.

Don now fully realized his position, and the question arose in his mind, what was to be done?

He was getting along in acquiring the arts practised by schoolboys, and he was also developing a spirit which would have amazed himself a month ago. It was a great support to him, for the blow he had received was a very heavy one, and in the time when he was at home would have completely cowed him; but now he was, in spite of it, as dogged as a mule.

"I'll sham being done for," he muttered, "and look out for a chance to get away."

Then he began to groan, as a preliminary part of his plan, and the man at the door, wheeling hastily round, revealed the wide-mouthed semi-vacant face of a Wiltshire yokel.

"Be 'ee took bad?" he asked, as if he had just made a great discovery.

"Somebody's been trying to murder me," moaned Don. "Do you know anything about it?"

"Noa," cautiously answered the yokel, "'cept that I seed a party give 'ee a whack over the head wi' a bit of a stick."

"Go for the police," gasped Don. "I want that man to be taken up and punished. Oh! oh! It will all be over in a few moments with me."

The other man now showed his head at the door, and proved to be a duplicate of the first, as far as appearance went. His face was almost intelligent with excitement.

"He ort to hev his dippersitions took," he said; "there be several magistraiks at the club. Run for one, Jacob."

Jacob hesitated a moment, for he had been placed as a guard over the boy. But the exigencies of the case prompted him to act on the suggestion of his companion.

"Stand 'ee here," he cried; "I'll fetch somebody along."

Away he went, and the second man took his place. For the better and easier keeping watch over the Don, he rested his chin upon the top of the half-door, and stared at him, goggle-eyed and wondering.

"Oh—oh!" groaned Don again; "why doesn't somebody come to help me?"

"The doctor 'll soon be here," said the yokel.

"See if he's coming down the road," wailed Don; "he must be very quick. Oh—oh!"

With a visible effort the yokel lifted his chin from the door, and, with heavy-footed haste, tore across the farmyard, to see if the doctor was coming.

The moment he disappeared Don got upon his feet.

He felt giddy and rather sick, but he resolutely ignored the feeling, and softly opening the door, stole out. He found himself in an adjoining stable, where the horses were serenely enjoying their feed.

Don looked through the outer stable door, and saw the man he had dispatched in search of a doctor standing on a gate, peering up the road.

There was an opposite gate, leading to the fields, which was the only way open to Don, and he was about to take it, when the yokel uttered a shout and descended from his elevated position.

Now there was no way of retreat, and Don, after a look round, rushed to a ladder fixed against the wall, by means of which the loft could be reached.

He scrambled up, and found above a considerable stock of loose hay upon the floor. He threw himself on the top of it and covered himself up.

But, although out of sight, he could still hear, and presently the voices of two men were heard in the yard.

One was that of Blotch, who spoke hurriedly, as one in trouble.

"What are you hollering for?" he demanded.

"The boy's dead," was the answer of the yokel.

"Impossible!" exclaimed a strange and more refined voice than that of Blotch.

"Come and see, sur," cried the yokel, excitedly; "he wor at his last gasps a minnet ago."

There was the sound of hurrying feet, and more exclamations, an oath or two, and then the voice of Blotch.

"You thief and liar, you hev let 'un go."

"I ain't," roared the yokel. "I seed him when he told me to look up the doctor, or he said he'd be gone."

"You chucklehead," hissed Blotch. "He's tuk you in. There ain't no trick as them boys ain't up to."

The doctor laughed in a quiet way.

"Boys will be boys," he said.

"I wish there warn't none," growled Blotch. "Shut up the stables and git out of it, you mutton-head. Doctor, we may as well go back. They won't come this way any more to-day."

The doctor assented, and the sound of their moving away was heard by Don. The bang of the closing gate followed.

"Dang that 'ere boy," the yokel muttered, as he begun to climb up the ladder, with the object of shutting the loft window; "he tuk Oi in, sure. Oi reckon he warn't get over Oi again."

He came into the loft, and was moving towards the opening through which the hay was delivered, a sort of window and door in one, when Don, urged by the demon of mischief, popped his head out of the hay, and uttered a yell worthy of a wild Indian.

The startled yokel ran for the opening, and before he was aware of having reached it, was out and upon his back on the soft and highly-odourized material in the farmyard.

Don was in turn alarmed, and, jumping up, ran to see the full extent of the injury the man had received.

Beyond having thoroughly steeped himself in the moister part of the farmyard material, he had not suffered much. Don saw him scramble up, and go splashing straight through the manure to the gate, which, after two or three nervous failures, he succeeded in opening, and fled, howling, up the quiet village street.

The way was now clear, and Don lost not a moment in getting to the fields, observing, as he passed through the yard, that the pigs and sheep had been restored to their pens.

He had a good mind to let them out again, but time might be precious, as it was possible for the yokel to fall in with somebody who would return with him to the loft to see what sort of ghost had scared him. So he made tracks, and doubling under the hedges, in imitation of the way he came, soon put a wide expanse of ground between him and the scene of recent troubles.

***

CHAPTER XIV.

THE STRANGER BY THE WHITE OAK.

WHEN fairly out of breath, Don stopped, and sitting down under the shadow of a hedge, thought over matters, recalling the cry uttered by Jack Ford, for his scattering forces to meet him by the White Oak.

Now where was the tree thus named?

Of course, the rest were aware of the locality, but Don was a stranger to the country, and knew no more than a child unborn where to look for it.

After he had got his breath again, he washed the fair-sized wound inflicted by Blotch on the crown of his head, in a pond hard by. Then he climbed up the lower branches of an adjacent elm-tree, and had a look around.

Far away he saw a big white tree. It was an oak, stripped at some time or other by the fierce lightning. Under it were a number of small specks shifting about, which he joyfully judged were the boys.

Taking the bearings of the spot, he descended, and wended his way towards it.

Ignorant of the risk he ran as a trespasser, he took a bee line, forcing his way through gaps in the fences, and in a general way making himself free of the country.

It was further than he expected; but at length he got upon a piece of common land, on which stood the tree, stripped of its bark, and there, sure enough, under it were the boys, partaking of their humble dinner.

Close by them was a travelling-van, such as showmen use, and near it an old horse was steadily making a meal of the scanty herbage.

Don forgot his injuries, and breaking into a trot, was soon espied by the delighted boys, who, springing up, came running towards him, uttering cries of welcome.

"Don, old man," said Jack, as he grasped him by the hand, "we were afraid you were nicked, and were just planning a rescue."

"I have been nicked," replied Don, "but I got away. As soon as I have had a bit of peck I'll tell you all about it."

They escorted him back to the tree in triumph, telling him he was the last to assemble at the appointed spot. Seated on the gnarled roots was one of the most extraordinary-looking men Don had ever seen.

He had a very big head, with close-cropped hair, red nose, and long moustache, curled at the ends. His eyes were small, dark, and inconceivably cunning in expression. His attire consisted of a gaudy-patterned sleeve-waistcoat, corduroy breeches, gaiters, and heavy boots. By his side on the grass was a very broad-brimmed, conical-crowned felt hat.

"The last lamb of the flock," he said, with a friendly nod; "welcome."

"Professor Lingo," said Tom Drummond, by way of introduction.

"It was feared," said the professor, "that you had fallen into the hands of the Philistines. But now the anxiety of your friends is assuaged. Sit down and be merry."

"Who is he?" whispered Don.

Soft as the utterance was, it reached the ears of the person referred to, and he proceeded to answer for himself.

"I," he said, "am the world-renowned Lingo, purveyor of every human requisite, which I offer to the public at ruinous prices, and live by the loss. By turns I am a public entertainer, and teacher of the arts and sciences, illustrator of the mysteries of legerdemain, and a foe to tyrants at all times."

The boys laughed, and resumed their seats. Don brought out his dinner from his pocket, and fell to.

"Why, Don," exclaimed Gyp Tanner, "you have had a whack on the head."

"Blotch gave it me," answered Don, "as I was trying to get out of the farmyard. It knocked me silly, and that is how I came to be nabbed."

He told them all what had transpired since, and they enjoyed it amazingly, commending him, with unstinted praise, for the pluck he had exhibited.

"Truly one of us," said Jack, as he patted Don on the back. It was, in Don's opinion, a full reward for his recent sufferings.

Professor Lingo was eating also, and having shortly after finished his meal, he filled his pipe, and, lounging on his elbow, smoked placidly as he listened to the chatter of the boys.

He watched them closely, and, from a few words dropped here and there, seemed to get possession of more facts than they intended to reveal.

He was, as Don heard later on, up to that day, a complete stranger to the boys.

A quiet smile settled on his face, and his small eyes twinkled with pleasure.

"My lads," he said, suddenly, "why don't you trust me? I can see that you are in one of those confounded schools, where the treatment would shame a slave plantation. It is right for you to combine to put an end to it. Say, how can I help you?"

They gazed at him in dismay, and the smile on his face developed into a hearty laugh.

"Of course, dear boys," he went on, "you did not mean to tell me anything. But I have keen ears, a quick intuition, and I read faces better than most men read books. You may print a lie, and the ink be as dark and clear as when recording solemn truth; but the face will not show the false without giving an inkling of the true."

"What we are doing is of a nature we cannot reveal," said Jack: "it concerns only those who have sworn never to betray it."

"Then make me one of you," said the Professor, readily. "I'm a man in build, but a boy in heart. I tell you that I've heard of this Snicker, and I don't like him. Look at my hand; it's rugged, but honest as ever the hand of man was. I'm smart in business, but I don't play the low-down game on youngsters. Say, now, will you make me one of you or not?"

"Let us have a talk over it," suggested Jack.

"Certainly," answered Lingo, jumping up; "but don't you take me on because you see that I've guessed at something. If I was mean enough to split on you now, it wouldn't be wise to trust me any further."

He walked away a short distance, leaving the boys to confer among themselves. The consultation was a hasty one, but the conclusion they came to was that the stranger had better be made one of themselves.

"We shall want somebody to do a lot of things outside for us," said Tom Drummond. "I've been thinking that over, and it will be absolutely necessary if we are to hold out for any length of time."

"Trust him, then," said Bob Stockton, and so said they all.

Professor Lingo, on being called back, received their decision with much satisfaction.

"You will never repent it, boys," he said. "I shall be around this neighbourhood, going to and fro, for some weeks, and all you have to do is to let me know what you want. Tell me the game you are up to."

"A barring-out," answered Jack.

The professor whistled, in a drawling kind of way.

"My eye!" he exclaimed. "You do mean going it! A risky job."

"We mean to risk it."

"And it must be well done."

"Just so."

"Now we come to the way you are to communicate with me."

"Easy enough," said Jack. "By telephone."

A general exclamation of surprise and incredulity followed, but there was a confident look on the face of Jack.

"Give me your address," he said, "and in a few days I will write you all the particulars. It can be done as easy as saying your A B C."

"A letter addressed to the 'Blue Boar,' Calne, any time within a week, will reach me," said Lingo.

"Within a week you will hear from me," said Jack.

Then they shook hands with him as a newly-made brother, and he proceeded to hitch in his horse, preparatory to starting for the club ground, which it appeared was his destination.

"About seven to-night," he said, with a wink of intense meaning, "all the good people of Mumping Malford and Smudgem Bender will be in a mellow state. It will be then that I will offer them some of the unrivalled bargains I have in that van. I shall send them home, happy with such handsaws, pocket-knives, hair-brushes, combs, etc., as they never before dreamt of. Good-bye, my lads, and good luck attend you."

They answered him by taking off their caps and waving them. Then, at a signal from Jack Ford, they fell into a line, and marched away, singing:

> There's a good time coming, boys—
>   Wait a little longer—
> When Snicker will be up a tree,
>   And we little kids be stronger.

Presently the words and air were changed, the professor standing still and listening, with a smile of pleasure on his face.

> We had a dream, a happy dream,
>   A thought that we were free,
> And Snicker was laid up in gaol
>   For brutal cruelty.
> His food was skilly, his work oakum picking,
> And when he shirked it he got a stiffish licking.

> In these good times coming, boys,
>   For which we wait but little longer,
> For Snicker each day weaker be,
>   And we boys are getting stronger.

Herbert May, as usual, led off, and in the open air proved that he had a very strong, sweet voice. It rang out across the common as clear as a bell, and when the others struck up in chorus the effect was very good.

To the professor it was something touching, for his face softened as he listened, and when the voices had died away to a low rising and swelling sound in the distance, he put up his hand and brushed away a tear from his eye.

"Bless the lads," he murmured. "Help them! Ay, that I will, right honestly, as I am a man, and as good a Cheap Jack as ever rattled the yokels. Help 'em! Yes, and for more reasons than one. Snicker, old man, get your muscle up. You'll want it."

———

CHAPTER XV.

A FINISHING TOUCH TO THE DAY.

ONE of the advantages of the club was that strangers were welcome, and they came in pretty fair numbers from all parts. They were mainly of the humbler classes, and among those who came from Chippenham was Milky Whey.

One of the rules of the meeting was that no man should have more than a sufficiency of tickets to purchase two pints of beer, but there was nothing set down to prevent the sober from selling their share to the beery inclined.

Thus it happened that Milky Whey had got on the kind side of no less than five teetotalers, and secured their tickets at a reasonable price.

Armed with the means of getting twelve pints of beer, and knowing from bitter experience that anything over seven rendered him speechless and incapable, he looked round for a friend with whom to share his liquid joys.

His eye lighted on no less a person than Penny Bunn, who, as usual, was in a state of impecuniosity which qualified him for a night in any of the casual wards of the kingdom. He had come thither to get a little cheap enjoyment out of the spectacle.

Milky Whey was not proud, and addressing the under-master as an old friend, he bade him come and refresh himself.

Penny Bunn was at the outset disposed to resent the offer as an insult, but the day was hot, and his throat a bit parched, so he graciously accepted the invitation, and they had a pint of beer together.

They had another, and, in short, shared the twelve together ere the shades of evening had begun to fall. Then, as ill-luck would have it, they fell into the company of a cheerful old gentleman, who, fearing the beer would not suffice to make him properly drunk, had brought with him a bottle of strong gin.

A casual word was passed, friendship struck up, and the bottle produced and emptied.

It was getting dark by that time, and the fun being all over, the trio prepared to depart.

The hospitable gentleman knew his way right enough, and with a corkscrew gait departed.

Milky Whey and Penny Bunn had only the haziest notion of the path to take, but they succeeded in getting upon the high road, and there sat down in the middle of it, to consider the situation.

"Way's ri-right," said Penny Bunn.

"Lef'," insisted Milky Whey.

"Bet you sov—hic—ren it 's right!" said Penny Bunn.

"Done," responded Milky Whey. "Sha' han's on it."

They shook hands on it, and after several conspicuous failures, succeeded in getting upon their feet again.

"The yabby's there," said Penny Bunn, with a sweep of the arm, covering three-fourths of a circle.

"Show me," said Milky Whey, "that yere abbey-babby, or you're a li-i-i-iar."

They set off once more, performing miracles of eccentric walking, and yet keeping their feet, and, guided by that sweet little cherub who looks after the inebriate, arrived at last at the school-house gate.

It took time, but they were there, and Penny Bunn gasped out:

"Now, isn't that yabby?"

"No," answered Milky Whey, obstinately, "not bit like it. No more yabbeybab—hic—by than I am."

"It's gate, ain't it?" said Penny Bunn. "You give me that shuverin."

"Man an' monish ready," said Milky Whey, "when I shee abberrabby."

"Come up to house and look at it," sputtered Penny Bunn, angrily.

He wrenched the handle of the gate round and threw it open, without perceiving that Milky was leaning against it. The consequence was that the travelling fishmonger fell upon his back with a whack.

"Here!" he yelled, "who yer knocking down?"

"Didn't knock anyborry down," answered Penny Bunn; "but I'll pick you up."

He stooped to do so, but not being in a condition to preserve his balance, he fell heavily upon the prostrate form of his companion.

A struggle ensued, but neither were in a state to do much injury to each other, and they soon got up again.

Then Penny Bunn conducted Milky Whey up to the house, tacking across the playground, but the obstinate loser of the bet would not believe his eyes.

"It's not the abberabby," he said, thickly; "I believe it's the *church.*"

"Have a looksh at the in—hic—side," said Penny Bunn, bent on having the sovereign he had won somehow.

He opened the door showing the hall, but the unbeliever was not yet convinced. He was certain now that it was the parsonage, and Penny Bunn, losing his head in his wrath, ushered him in.

"Come and see schoolroom," he said.

It was the rashest thing he had ever done in his life, for the boys were in that schoolroom, and the appearance of two wobbling men therein could not but be productive of some fun at their expense.

Moreover, the warm, close air of the house finished what the day's potations had too well begun.

By the time the pair had got into the schoolroom their minds were in a state of complete disorder, and

A SPLENDID SCHOOL STORY.

NEVER BEFORE PUBLISHED.

By E. HARCOURT BURRAGE,

Author of "Ching Ching," "Monkey Mat and Roving Dick," "The Brave Boy of the Basilisk," &c.

A Handsome Coloured Plate Presented with Every Number.

No. 1.

THE LAMBS OF LITTLECOTE

MILKY WHEY IS TREATED TO AN AWFULLY JOLLY RIDE ON HIS OWN BARROW

 PRICE ONE PENNY.

ALDINE PUBLISHING CO., 9, Red Lion Court, Fleet St., and 1, 2, & 3, Crown Court, Chancery Lane, London

A SPLENDID SCHOOL STORY. NEVER BEFORE PUBLISHED.

By E. HARCOURT BURRAGE,

Author of "Ching Ching," "Monkey Mat and Roving Dick," "The Brave Boy of the Basilisk," &c.

No. 3. *A Handsome Coloured Plate Presented with Every Number.*

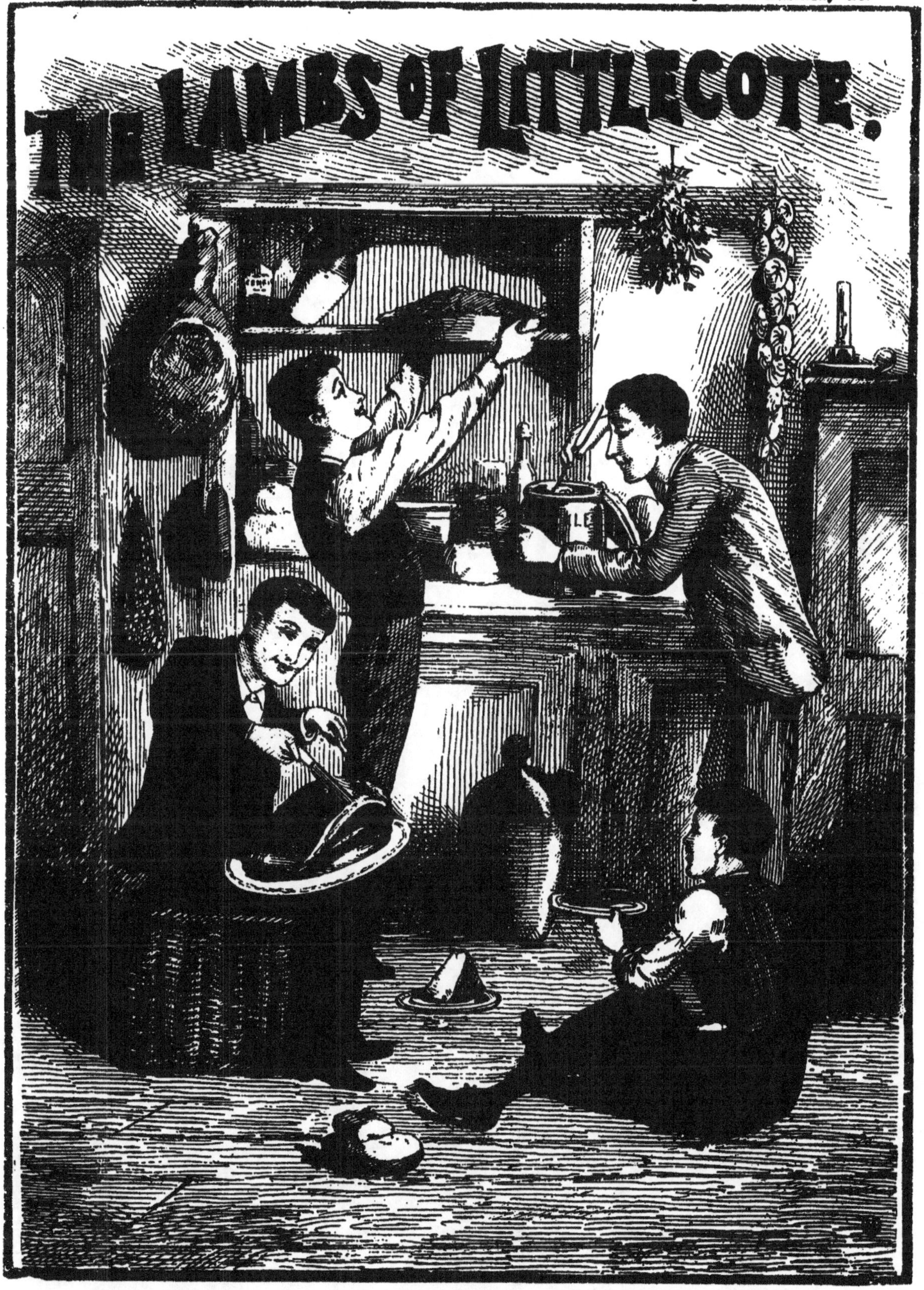

THE LAMBS OF LITTLECOTE.

THE MIDNIGHT FEAST IN THE SNICKER LARDER. A REAL TREAT.

PRICE ONE PENNY.

the speechlessness of the drunkard had come upon them.

They stood just within the door, holding on to each other, swaying to and fro, and staring at the boys, whom they saw as shadows in a mist, with wide-opened, meaningless gaze.

At first the youngsters were too astounded to do more than return their stare. Then, in a moment, the position was realized, and the fun began.

Finding that the two men were quite incapable of offering more than the feeblest resistance, they hustled them into a corner, where they subsided, like a sinking billow, in a heap, and in a moment, as it seemed, both were asleep.

The next thing done was to disguise them as far as possible.

Ink was first brought into use, and the face of Milky Whey was made as black as that of a thorough-bred African nigger. His coat was taken off, turned inside out, and replaced with the tails over his head. Then his necktie was removed from his bulldog throat and tied about his eyes. Finally the old poker from the fireplace was put into his hand as a sceptre.

Penny Bunn was next attended to, and around his eyes two broad black rims were daubed. A moustache in imitation of that of Professor Lingo was painted by Tom Drummond under his nose, and his boots taken off and hidden in his desk.

The revelation that the under-master wore odd socks excited some merriment, but little surprise, for it was known that he was put to sore straits to keep up appearances. A suggestion from Hone that they should be removed and stuffed up the chimney, was negatived on the score that it was possible that he had but another pair, and that in the weekly wash.

"We don't love him," said Bob Stockton, "but we do not wish to see him go about barefooted."

An old newspaper was fashioned into a rough resemblance of a King James the First collar, and put about his neck, which was considered a sufficient embellishment, and the work was done.

To avoid any sneaking, all had to take a share in this joyous labour, and, as it was then supper-time, the boys decided to go at once to the dining-room, without waiting for the usual summons from Awful Rooker, who had not dared to trust himself in the schoolroom with the boys.

"Now, no more fun to-night," said Jack Ford. "All be on your best behaviour, and go to bed as quiet as mice."

Meanwhile, the continued absence of Penny Bunn had caused a feeling of anxiety to arise in the breast of Rooker, and it was with fear and trembling that he took his seat at the supper-table unsupported by his superior.

But, to his gratified amazement, the behaviour of the boys was perfect.

They ate their stale bread and leathery cheese in comparative silence, and when the time came for retiring, adjourned to the dormitories in admirable order.

The only way Rooker could account for it was that they were hatching mischief in some direction, of which he would learn presently. He was sagacious enough to guess at half the truth.

"I wonder what they will do when they wake up?" said Gyp Tanner, as he was undressing.

"Don't talk about them," advised Jack, "for fear that somebody may be listening. Of course nobody here knows anything about the business. Get into bed and go to sleep. Wait for developments."

This advice was taken in a proper spirit, and in a little time the house, as far as the boys were concerned, was in a state of profound repose.

CHAPTER XVI.

FONTENOY SNICKER REPENTS OF HIS SINS.

IT was the custom of Mrs. Snicker, when anything upset her in the house, to retire to a certain room to sleep, which was especially her own. It was at the top of the house, well out of the way of the other occupants.

Fontenoy Snicker had, by his recent jaunt to Chippenham, angered his spouse a little more than usual, and at an early hour she left her husband to the full enjoyment of the solitude of his chamber.

He was better in many respects, but still in a very jumpy condition. A man at his time of life does not get over a debauch, followed by a fall down a cliff, and supplemented by hours of exposure to inclement weather, without giving himself a tolerably stiff shaking. The schoolmaster was, therefore, still far from being well.

He lay in bed, very wide awake, listening to the sounds of the inmates retiring for the night. He could tell by the variety of sound who was moving, and positively the last to ascend the stairs was Mrs. Snicker.

He heard her soft, shuffling footsteps as she was passing the door of his room, and putting on a plaintive tone, he called on her to come in and see him.

"I'm still in a bad way," he added, mournfully.

"Go to sleep, you idiot!" she tartly replied.

He groaned with the hope of softening her heart, but she passed on, and the dolorous sound ended in something like an oath.

"If ever she goes a-blundering down a cliff," he muttered, "I'll let her lie there. Blow her for a cast-iron old hag!"

The house was now still, and he was left to his reflections. They were not so agreeable as they might have been, and he was steeped in bitterness. As a mental pastime he arranged a series of castigations for the boys as soon as he was able to administer the same.

An hour passed away, and it was one of the longest hours he had ever known. He would have thought that half the night was gone if he had not his watch hung up near him by the side of the bed to tell him otherwise.

Suddenly the stillness was broken by a blundering sound upon the stairs. It was as if somebody had tripped and fallen. A muttering of a gruff voice followed, and then, whoever it was, came on again.

"Who on airth—earth—is it?" he asked himself, with a creeping sensation all over him. "Is it bur-r-r-rglars?"

Instinctively he grasped his watch, and put it under the small of his back in the bed. A profuse perspiration burst out upon him from his head to his feet.

The blundering footsteps came on, and he could hear that whoever it was, experienced the difficulty of moving about in the dark, and was groping his way along the wall.

Presently the visitor got hold of the handle of the door, turned it and came in.

It was Milky Whey, just as the boys had ornamented him, and, therefore, unrecognisable by the terrified schoolmaster.

As the light in the bedroom was a dim one, he could only imperfectly see the hideous figure, and the overturned tails of the old black coat, which Milky had put on as a holiday attire, stood out, bearing, to the distempered imagination of Fontenoy Snicker, the appearance of sombre wings.

Milky still retained the poker which the boys had put into his hand, carrying it upon his shoulder so that it had the look of a sceptre. His black face was horrible to look upon.

Fontenoy Snicker had not the shadow of a doubt that his last hour had come, and that some fiend had called for him.

"Is thish rabbybabby?" asked Milky, thickly.

The simple interpretation of the words was: "Is this the abbey?" Milky still retained some dim consciousness of his being in quest of the schoolhouse. To the terrified Snicker it was the language of another world.

"Oh, don't, please don't," he groaned; "spare me this time, and I'll be a better man."

Milky Whey looked hard at him, then about the room, but did not seem to be able to make much of either. He staggered a step or two nearer, and put the question in another form.

"Warry wanter know," he said; "am this shrabby or babby?"

"If you would speak the language I've been used to, sir," said Snicker, humbly, "I would be able to understand you. I think you must have called on the *wrong party.*"

Milky Whey made no reply. The interval of dim consciousness was passing away, owing perhaps to the stuffiness of the bedroom, for Snicker was one of those people who religiously deny themselves as much fresh air as possible. With half-closed eyes the itinerant fishmonger moved up to the bedside and sank heavily into a chair.

Putting his elbows on the bed and breathing heavily, he stared at the fear-stricken man, whose sight was going fast, and once more sought information from him about the abbey.

"Bunn shay rabby," he said; "I shay not rabby, for shoverin. You bigger fool shan he is. Pay up."

The intense ferocity with which this demand was made caused Snicker to jump up a foot in the bed, and then come down heavily upon his watch. He heard the glass go crack, and felt some of the small pieces of it penetrate through his night-shirt to his back. But that was nothing compared to the presence of this dreadful and unintelligible visitor.

"I've been a wicked man," he moaned, "and as a schoolmaster I'm a blooming fraud, I admit it freely; but do, sir, please, your majesty, gimme another chance. I'll go easy with the boys and improve their wittles—*victuals,* sir. The next farmer who brings me a sheep, killed in a hurry, so that it don't die, I'll hand over to the police."

"Snork!" was the only reply he received.

It was a terror-inspiring sound, although it was only Milky gone off into a sound sleep. To add to the awfulness of the situation, the candle began to flicker as a preliminary to expiring.

The effect of a luminary thus troubled is to make all things within its influence caper about in a hideous fashion. To the distempered sight of the appalled Fontenoy Snicker, everything in the room was dancing about as if in joy over his predicament.

Twenty moments later the candle expired.

"Mercy!" gasped Snicker.

"Snork, snork!" was the answer from the nasal organ of the soundly-sleeping Milky Whey, and Snicker, overcome by the terror he felt, became unconscious.

And in that condition he lay for hours.

From dreams of a most hideous nature, he was aroused by a terrific scream, and opening his eyes, he discovered that daylight had returned. He recognized that he was in his room, of course, and that he was alone, but for a while could grasp no more. Then came a rush of feet, and Black-Eyed Susan burst into his room, wildly waving a house-broom.

"Oh, sir! oh, mum," she gasped, "there is a himp

downstairs in the schoolroom, making all sorts of hantics, and goin' on frightful."

Having got so far, she stopped short and uttered another piercing scream, for from the floor to which he had subsided in the night there arose the awful figure of Milky Whey, the better in some respects for his sleep, but not at all improved in personal appearance.

He stared hard at the petrified girl, then at the frozen Fontenoy Snicker, and hoarsely asked:

"Where the bloomin' Moses hev I got to?"

It flashed on the schoolmaster that he knew the voice, and the daylight removing some of the terrors of Milky's get-up, he feebly gasped out:

"Whomsoever you may be, you ain't got any right to be here. Who are you?"

"As if you didn't know old Milky," was the reply. "Come, that's a good 'un."

Black-Eyed Susan had sunk to the floor, and was working her eyes and jaws like an automaton. She was, however, beginning to perceive that it was no spirit from another world she was gazing on, but some novel specimen of the genus man.

"You, Milky," said Fontenoy Snicker. "You scoundrel, what do you mean by getting yourself up like that?"

"Me get myself up!"

"Look at yourself in the glass."

Milky did so, and staggered back.

"Well, I'm blowed, if this 'ere ain't a game," he exclaimed. "I must hev been got at by somebody."

At this moment another footstep was heard in the corridor outside, and a feeble voice addressed those within the room.

"Don't be alarmed. It's only me, P. Y. Bunn, the under-master."

"Come in, you fool," growled Fontenoy Snicker.

Then the "fool" came in, exhibiting himself in all the glory of his facial adornment and stockinged feet.

"Oh!" cried Black-Eyed Susan, covering her face with her apron, "that's the himp!"

"Himp, indeed!" ejaculated Fontenoy Snicker. "Now then, you two, explain yourselves."

Neither had anything to explain, for their minds were now a perfect blank as to all that had occurred since they started from the field in which the club revels had been held. Penny Bunn remembered fraternising with the gentleman with the gin bottle, and it was his opinion that his out-door entertainer with his spirituous liquor was responsible for the whole thing.

"I fear, sir," he said, "that we were both hocussed at the club. I met Milky there, and a person of low origin induced me to take *one* glass of beer. It overcame me, sir. I can say no more."

"Yes, we was injuiced to take a drop," murmured Milky, "and it must have had a pinch of snuff or summat in it."

"Not another word from either of you!" hissed Fontenoy Snicker. "Is your missus—I mean *mistress* —up, girl?"

"No, sir," answered Black-Eyed Susan, uncovering her face.

"Then it is possible to conceal this outrage from her. Milky, take yourself orf—*off*. Bunn, go and wash your ugly mug—countenance. Dash it! Jane, I rely upon your good feeling for a kind master not to say a word about this awful business."

"I've lost a day by bein' brought here," said Milky Whey, "and I want my expenses paid. I consider I'm five bob out."

Fontenoy Snicker grabbed at his trousers on the other side of the bed, fished out his purse and produced the money.

"There it is," he said. "Bunn, see him off the premises, and be sharp about it. Jane, there is a shilling for you. Bunn, if you say a word to Mrs. Snicker, I'll punch that turnip head of yours. Git—*get*—along."

Penny Bunn, who was all to pieces in a nervous sense, and totally unable to show a bold front to his angry employer, took Milky Whey by the arm and led him from the room. Jane, having deposited the shilling in a pocket about the size of a hand-bag, attached to her petticoat, also departed, and Fontenoy Snicker was left alone.

The first thing he did was to furiously kick up the bedclothes, the next to howl with pain arising from his having aroused his rheumatism, and lastly to anathematize his pupils.

"They got hold of them idiots," he growled, "and did 'em up in that style. All right, my lads. As soon as I've got this cussed—*cursed*—rummu—roomy —hang it!—tism out of my bones, I'll level up matters with you. I owe you a bit all round for the scare I got last night. I'm bothered if I didn't think it was the—the—but there ain't no such person. Bless my bones! They are bein' twisted round like corkscrews."

CHAPTER XVII.

SNICKER IS BETTER, WHICH MAKES IT WORSE FOR THE BOYS.

THANKS to Jane, who, although bribed to say nothing to her mistress, felt herself at liberty to talk to other people, the boys before noon were acquainted with the salient points of the recent night of terror. It is needless to say that they were much comforted thereby, save by the reflection that Fontenoy Snicker would guess at the truth and exact a full measure of revenge.

"Not that it matters," said Gyp Tanner; "we are sure to be licked, anyway."

Fontenoy Snicker got up about ten o'clock, and, with the aid of a stick, went down to the schoolroom. He found it as he expected, much in need of his strong, governing hand. Penny Bunn's authority was of the weakest, and Awful Rooker absolutely useless as a keeper of order.

Taking his seat at his desk, the schoolmaster slowly surveyed the boys, all as quiet as mice and on study bent. He said not a word, but his eyes were eloquent, and those who furtively glanced at him mentally prophesied wriggling times in store.

He was not in condition to use the cane that morning, but he laid up a store of joy for himself in the future by setting the boys impossible tasks, and when they went wrong making records in a note-book of punishments to be inflicted later on.

Before the day was done he had them all down for something, and he assured them, in sarcastic tones, at the end of the afternoon studies, that none would be forgotten.

Jack passed the word round for a meeting of the "band" to be held in the schoolroom half-an-hour before the main body of the boys were expected to be there to attend to their evening studies. Accordingly, in a quiet way, they slipped early from the playground and foregathered there.

Warner was put on guard at the door, and Jack, mounting upon a desk, addressed his followers.

"My lads," he said, "Snicker is on the warpath, and you may expect rough times from the brute. I ask you to bear it manfully. It won't—it can't—last for ever. We must push matters on, and I want to know who among you is ready to give up part of your sleep to-night. I only want two or three."

It was a startling question, and all sorts of things flashed through the minds of the boys. Was it Jack's intention to do something to Snicker? If so, what was it?

But none held back. Every hand went up, and with a smile he thanked them for their ready support.

"Since all are prepared," he said, "you must draw lots. Tear up pieces of paper, one for each of us. Put crosses on three of them, and leave the rest blank. The crosses have to be with me to-night."

It was soon done, and the crosses fell to Don, Bob Stockton, and Tom Drummond, to their great joy. The rest bore their disappointment philosophically.

"What we will attempt to do," said Jack, "need not be talked about here. What we succeed in doing, you will all, as brethren of the band, know to-morrow."

Warner at the door here began to cough in a peculiar manner, and the meeting was instantly dissolved. A rush was made for books, and in something under half a minute they were in their places in earnest search for knowledge.

But ere they could acquire any, Fontenoy Snicker entered the room.

He stopped near the door, snarling at them for a time ere he spoke.

"Why are you in here so early?" he demanded. "What imps' mischief are you hatching now?"

There was no reply for a moment, and then Bob Stockton rose in his seat, and with gentle politeness addressed the schoolmaster:

"To-day, sir," he said, "we were all wrong in our lessons, therefore we thought it better to get them well up for to-morrow."

"Indeed!" sneered the schoolmaster, "your studious conduct will not be forgotten. Mind you *are* well up to-morrow. There will be no supper to-night for any of you. Your conduct has been infamous to-day. Fasting is good for people at times. It's so in Scripter—*Scripture*—Peebles, you are laughing."

"Yes, sir," replied Don, demurely.

Fontenoy Snicker hobbled up to the desk and stood over him.

"Your answer was an impudent one!" he hissed.

"You said I was laughing, sir," answered Don, quietly. "And it was true, I was."

"At me, in course," said Fontenoy Snicker, furiously, as he struck the boy on the side of the head with his clenched fist. "Do you deny it?"

"No," answered Don, boldly. "I did not mean to be impertinent, but I couldn't help it."

"You couldn't help it!" exclaimed the schoolmaster, striking him again. "No more can I help doing this—and this. Now, then, laugh again, will you?"

Don was very white, for the blows hurt him, but he sat quite still and made no reply. A buzz of indignation passed round the room.

"Hey, what now?" ejaculated Fontenoy Snicker. "You don't like it, hey? You will like it less as we go on. I'll clear the lot of you out of here, and get a fresh stock of boys. I'll be master in my own house."

He turned away and moved slowly to the door, white with the evil passions raging in his breast. Naturally a violent man, the poison of rheumatism made him worse than usual. He was seething with malevolence.

But he felt he was in peril of doing something of which he might afterwards repent, and he wisely decided to retire. As he went out and closed the door, a general yell of execration burst from the boys in the room.

It was an involuntary testimony of the feeling with which they viewed his conduct. The cane, to an extent, they had learnt to look upon as a legitimate instrument of punishment, but for a man to strike a boy with his fist exasperated them almost beyond endurance.

"Quiet there," said Jack Ford, and immediately the room was still.

The schoolmaster stood by the door, wrestling with a desire to return a visit of his wrath upon him, but prudence, assisted by the warning pangs of rheumatism, led him to abandon the idea, and growling to himself, he went away. Ten minutes afterwards, the rest of the boys poured into the class-room, but not a word was said to them about the conduct of the schoolmaster. That, as Tom Drummond said, was a matter for the band to adjudicate upon at some future time.

CHAPTER XVIII.

OPENING THE DOOR THAT WAS BLOCKED.

TRUE to his word, the schoolmaster sent the boys supperless to bed. They were all hungry, and many a bitter word was uttered against the man who could be so mean and cruel.

"All the better for our cause," said Jack in the dormitory; "he is playing into our hands. The others are ripening for the great day. Herbert, old man, we will have a song to-night."

"Which shall it be?" asked the school-poet, as he got into bed.

"Let us have 'The Voice,'" replied Jack.

A murmur of approval was heard among the rest. Don asked Tom if there was anything special in the song.

"It is rather a sad one," was the reply, "but very sweet, and Herbert sings it A 1. The chorus is done in a low whisper, and it always makes me think of the rustling of wings. Why, I don't know, but it does."

The boys having got into bed, and put out the light, settled down, awaiting the coming of Rooker, whose duty it was to go round that night. He came sneaking up, opened the door softly, and seeing all was dark, vanished swiftly, fearing a possible missile of some sort.

But he was let go free that night. The boys were waiting for the song from Herbert May.

There was complete stillness for a time, and then he began to sing:

THE VOICE.

I heard a voice some years ago,
A voice that sounded sweet and low.
It sang of joys of schoolboy life,
And never whispered of the strife,
Nor piped a solitary note
Of the pangs and wrongs of Littlecote.
    It lied to me,
    As all can see,
The voice that sang so long ago.

But of late another voice has sung,
And that with no uncertain tongue.
Pain and wrong has had its day,
And speedily will pass away,
    It sings to me
    With truth, you'll see,
The voice that has so lately sung.

The last three lines of each verse were sung in whispering chorus by the boys, and Don got an inkling of the feeling which had moved Tom Drummond. It certainly had upon the ear the effect of rustling wings.

It was like the other compositions of Herbert May, very simple, but it was a boy's song inspired by a miserable life, and it went home to the hearts of his companions. It inspired them, and it was with resolute hearts to fight against the oppressor that the majority of them went to sleep.

The trio who were to accompany Jack on his night expedition remained awake, occasionally exchanging a whisper with him or with each other.

In due time there was complete stillness in the house, and the minutes crawled away until midnight.

In the quietude of a still night they heard the church clock of Mumping Malford record the hour, and then Jack whispered the word to get out of bed.

They responded with alacrity, and dressed speedily.

Jack, having attired himself as the rest had done, in a perfunctory manner, left the room to "scout."

He was soon back with a lantern in his hand, one of the ordinary stable things of fifty years ago, which had been found by him in an odd corner of the Abbey, and declared the coast to be clear.

They had slippers, but as an additional precaution, they carried them in their hands until they reached the schoolroom, which was their first halting place.

Jack put the lantern down, and having closed the door, placed one of the master's stools under the handle so that it would be difficult to force a way in.

"Now," he said, "we are ready to go to work. Every screw but one is loose, and can be removed without any trouble. The question is, with the screws out, can we open the door? That I am here to find out to-night."

Don had guessed what was the object of their being there. The long, closed-up door was, if possible, to be opened, and the nature of the rooms beyond ascertained.

One by one, as was afterwards explained to him, one of the band had loosened and taken out the old rusty screws, which had been oiled and replaced awaiting the time when it might be necessary to remove the whole expeditiously.

That time had now come.

It seemed that the under part of the head-master's desk had been used as a store-house for several things.

The desk stood on four short legs of three inches

high, so that the space under it was limited, and as Jack informed Don, it was too confined to attract the attention of Black-Eyed Susan, whose morning broom never did more than travel over the open spaces of the schoolroom.

A better hiding-place for the screw-driver, a bottle of oil, and the twelve-inch crowbar which the "band" had brought into use, could not have been found.

Jack fetched them out, and set Tom to work on the last screw, which it was necessary to remove ere they could open the door.

Bob Stockton held up the lantern to assist him, and Tom went to work.

It was some time before he could get the screw to stir, the others standing by, watching the result of his efforts with absorbing interest.

At length it stirred, and they drew a deep breath of relief.

"I thought the beggar was fixed for good," said Bob Stockton, "and you can't draw a screw like a nail."

Tom turned the screw carefully, and the slit in the head of it, sound as it had been a hundred years before, held the driver close.

At length it was out, and exclamations of satisfaction escaped those who had watched the operations.

The other screws—there were a score in all—having been previously removed and lubricated, gave no trouble worth speaking of, and Jack, as they were drawn out, one by one, took charge of them.

"Now," he said, "we have to see if it will open. The lock of the door is free, not having been turned by the people who closed it up. Perhaps they had lost the key."

He carefully inserted the small crowbar, so as not to make a dent in the wood, and with the skill of an embryo burglar proceeded to open it.

At the outset the door refused to stir, but at length it was seen to shift a bit, and a lot of dust tumbled out upon the floor.

"Brush that away with your handkerchief," said Jack; "we must leave no trace if our night's work behind us."

Don and Bob Stockton performed this office, and Jack, renewing his efforts, was rewarded by seeing the door slowly open on creaking hinges.

As soon as it was wide enough to admit of his entering, he passed through.

"Hold up the light," he said, "and give me the oil bottle."

There was a feather in the bottle, with which he carefully oiled the inside of the hinges, moving the door slowly to and fro, until the creaking ceased.

Then the door was pushed wide open, and he invited the others to follow him.

"The air is foul here," he said. "Move slowly, in case it should overcome you."

They did so, and the door having been pushed wide open, they waited awhile to let in the purer air. By the light of the lantern they could see that they were in a big bare room with an inlaid oaken floor. The ceiling was covered with cobwebs, so thick as to appear like a draping of crape.

"It puzzles me," said Bob, "what spiders find in these out-of-the-way places to live upon, but there must be something, or they would not go to the trouble of making webs."

"It is no use worrying about how spiders live," returned Tom Drummond, sententiously. "Let them look to their own affairs."

"We shall have to take that lot down," remarked Jack, "before we can live here at all."

"It is only a question of a broom," said Tom.

When the air was in a measure purified they went on to the inner apartment, and this also was found to be without furniture of any description, but there was something there which astounded them. It was a well.

There it was, just as we see them in outside places, with the windlass and all complete, to the iron handles and rope.

Jack walked up to the well and put the lantern down near it.

"This," he said, "beats cock-fighting."

There was a low border to the well, and a double lid so as to prevent any unwary person from tumbling into it. On Bob Stockton's testing the working of the handle, it stirred but with the slow, creaking way of rusty things. Once more the oil bottle was brought into use, and then the whole worked freely.

The four youngsters all went to work on the double handle, and they turned and turned until they began to think they were labouring at an endless rope, but suddenly the two portions of the lid parted, and a bucket filled with water appeared.

"At last!" said Tom Drummond. "What is the depth of that blessed well?"

"Quite two hundred feet," answered Don. "I reckon by the quantity of rope round the windlass. We used to have big rolls of rope at home, and I know something about the way of estimating a quantity in them."

"The water is as sweet as a nut," said Jack, who had been tasting and smelling it. "Dear boys, what will this be worth to us in the barring out? Why, with solid food we can hold out for a month—a year."

"Longer," exclaimed Bob Stockton, enthusiastically. "Say that we get our linen and everything here, why could not we live all together? We could even do our own washing."

"We shall have some fun, anyway," said Don. "What is the height of the cliff?"

"Oh, not so deep as the well," replied Jack, "or there would not be any water. The merry old monks of old knew how to take care of themselves. They were always ready for a siege."

"Here is something else," cried out Tom Drummond, who had been prowling round the room, which, like the other, was of considerable size. "A trap-door, my boys."

It was in one of the corners of the room, and there was an iron ring in the centre of it, but they could not raise it up.

In vain they tugged at it in turn, until Jack laughingly called on them to stop.

"It is screwed down," he said, "and the holes covered in with some sort of cement. Look here."

He pulled out his pocket-knife, and with one of the blades picked some mortar-like substance out of a hole, disclosing the head of a rusty screw.

Working his way round the trap-door, he finally revealed at least a score of these protective things.

"It is too long a job to-night," he said, "or we might see what is under the trap-door. That is a task we can leave for another time. For the present we have discovered all that is to be seen. But what a gem of a place for us. No windows to this room, and those in the other crib are so heavily barred that no man, without smashing up the whole show, could get in from the outside. Make the schoolroom secure, and we can defy Fontenoy Snicker and all his works."

There was a lot of dust in the old place, of course, but a broom and a dust-pan would remedy that.

For the present the young adventurers confined themselves to seeing how the retreat they had opened could be utilised in the barring out.

Jack, as the originator and leader of the movement, explained his ideas, which met with hearty approval.

"The well-chamber, as I shall call it," he said, "must be the store-room. This one with the windows we must sleep in, and when the time comes we must divide ourselves into two watches, keeping time as they do on board ship. The schoolroom, with the door well barricaded, is absolutely impregnable. The windows open on the cliff side, and no man can scale the steep descent without the aid of a rope fastened to the house, and he's got to put it there. Boys, we shall be in a fortress which will fog Snicker to carry by assault."

"You have said that he will not get help," said Don.

"My dear boy," answered Jack, "he dare not ask for it. Unless this school is quietly conducted he has to go, and where is a rotten old impostor of his breed to move to and prosper as he does here? I assure you

that if we once get well boxed up we shall have him on toast."

The face of the boy was bright with enthusiasm, and he inspired the others with a kindred feeling. They were as slaves who see emancipation marching toward them with rapid strides.

The time passed rapidly, mooning about the strange old rooms and discussing the situation, until the old Mumping Malford church clock was heard proclaiming the hour of two.

Then Jack announced it was time to seek rest.

"Why not visit the larder?" suggested Tom Drummond.

"We ought not to do anything to give an inkling of our night movements," said Jack, doubtfully.

"Let us get up a sort of burglary," said Bob Stockton. "We can force the scullery window from the hinges, the sash is as rotten as tinder, and then break open the larder."

"Won't that show we have been at work?" said Don.

"Not if we do the thing right," replied Bob. "There is not much to steal; but why not bone all the knives and forks and spoons?"

"And what are we to do with them?" asked Tom.

"Why, bring them *here*," answered Bob. "Won't they come in handy to us by-and-by? So will a tablecloth or two, and the table in the kitchen. We've two hours before us. Let us make a clean sweep of the domestic portion of the establishment."

It was a daring suggestion, but it seemed to be a good one. Jack, after a short reflection, agreed with it. The only thing to be done was to work without making the least noise. The utmost caution was necessary.

"Say we are successful," he said, "nobody would dream of looking here for the lost things. Bob, you are a genius disguised as a model of politeness."

All were hungry, and in their socks they wended their way to the kitchen, and from thence to the scullery. Jack broke open the window, making no more noise than he would have done if the sash had been made of gingerbread. Then they went for the larder door, which the prudent Mrs. Snicker invariably kept fastened. The lock was a poor one, and they were soon revelling in roast beef and a bottled fruit pie, which were intended for a cold dinner on the morrow, to be enjoyed by the schoolmaster and his wife. Then they proceeded to carry out the rest of the programme.

All the knives and forks in the kitchen drawers, and the spoons from the plate basket, were carefully collected together, and conveyed to the chosen hiding-place.

Kettles, saucepans, a cooking oil stove, several lamps, and a huge carboy, containing ten gallons of paraffin, shared the same fate. In short, having begun the work, they carried it out thoroughly, and fairly denuded the kitchen.

No mauraders of the olden time ever made a more satisfactory haul in a single night.

The delighted boys could hardly contain themselves, but the steadying hand and voice of Jack were near, or they might have betrayed themselves with their tongues.

He ordered them to keep silent, closed the door of the two rooms, rubbed some dirt over the heads of the oiled screws, and, having assured himself that they left no trace of their labours behind them, led the way to bed.

CHAPTER XIX.

GREAT EXCITEMENT IN LITTLECOTE.

WHEN the four young adventurers were in the dormitory, Jack, who had been thinking on his way upstairs, beckoned to the others to come near him.

"What we have done to night," he said, "is too big a thing for all to know of it. Suppose we simply say to the brethren that we found two empty useful rooms, and leave the rest for a surprise by-and-by?"

"It won't do," said Don. "They will, on hearing of the kitchen business, guess the rest."

"We ought to sham having overslept ourselves," suggested Tom Drummond. "We need not say too much, and I don't like deceiving the fellows, but it is only prudent."

"Some of them might lose their heads," said Jack. "We are a secret society, and we must act up to the lines of it. Only the heads ought to know exactly what is done, and when the time comes to order the move."

"I vote for having gone to sleep and made a night of it in bed," said Bob Stockton. "After what we have done we must take upon ourselves to become the inner circle of the band."

It was agreed it should be so, and Jack was left to "work the blind" in the morning. He said he could do it with a few words.

Having settled matters thus, they got into bed, and notwithstanding their excited condition of mind, soon fell asleep.

The boys in the dormitory were awake early, anxious to know how the quartette had got on in the night. Jack awoke, too, and sitting up in the bed, exclaimed:

"Hang it, if it isn't morning!"

"Do you mean to say that you've been asleep like the rest of us?" said Gyp Tanner, with a disgusted air.

"I haven't a patent for waking up just at the moment I want to; have you?" retorted Jack.

"Surely there are more nights than one to carry out what we have to do?"

He said no more, and after a few expressions of disappointment, they became reconciled to the situation. Of course there were many more nights for the task Jack had undertaken. Tanner and Bedstone offered their services on the following night to keep awake, and see that there were no more mistakes.

"Thanks," said Jack, "it will be just the thing. Here comes Rooker to rouse us up."

Awful Rooker opened the door, but instead of simply calling the boys, he came into the room. His face was yellow with fright, and he was shaking all over.

"It's a good thing," he said, "that we have not all been murdered in our beds. The house was broken into last night. The burglars have taken everything out of the kitchen. They meant to have emptied the place, but must have been interrupted. There is such a scene below. Mr. Bunn has gone for the police."

"Don't you come playing old jokes upon us," said Jack.

"It is all true," rejoined Rooker, rubbing his damp forehead with his coat sleeve; "the house has been robbed. You never saw such a clean sweep as the fellows made in your life. They've emptied the very larder."

And away he went to carry the startling tidings to the next dormitory.

The astonishment of the boys he left behind him was overwhelming, and none were more astounded than the four who could have told exactly how the robbery was effected.

"It is lucky you beggars did not wake up," said Warner; "if you had tumbled across those burglars, it might have been bad for you."

"They might have murdered us," said Bob Stockton, gravely.

It took but a very few minutes to put on their clothes, and then down they hastened, mingling with another stream of excited boys from the other dormitory.

In the passage below they encountered Fontenoy Snicker, with a poker in his hand, boldly searching for any of the burglars who by some off chance might be still hiding on the premises.

"Oh, sir!" exclaimed Bob Stockton, "what a horrible thing it is. Can the Abbey have been robbed in the night?"

"I am as nigh—*near*—ruined as a man can be," replied Fontenoy Snicker, waving the poker threateningly. "The cost of the job will have to be spread over your bills, and so I tell you. There ain't no knives or forks to eat with, and you will have to put up with your fingers till I've runned—*run*, blow it! over to Chippenham."

He finished with a short war-dance, which sufficiently expressed his feelings, and as he seemed to be inclined to relieve himself by hitting somebody with the poker, the boys retreated to the lavatory.

There was the usual scramble for the first wash, and a lot of skylarking in the general joy arising from the loss the schoolmaster had experienced. By the time they had finished, and were hastening to the playground, a policeman had arrived.

He was the Mumping Malford official, and having been up all night going his rounds, was not in the best of humours, or so clear about the head as he ought to have been.

Penny Bunn, acting on his suggestion, had gone on to Chippenham to get further police assistance.

The Mumping Malford man looked at the kitchen and surveyed the forced scullery window. Then he went outside, where he discovered some footmarks on a muddy spot left by the recent rains. They were made by Black-Eyed Susan the day before, while hanging out some small household things she had washed to dry, but nobody thought of that, and the officer measured them carefully with a tape yard measure Mrs. Snicker lent him, and he made a record of the length and breadth thereof in his pocketbook.

Mr. Snicker was present, and he asked him if he had an idea whose footmarks they were.

"I can lay my hand on the man with that fut!" replied the sagacious officer.

"Then go and do it," said the schoolmaster. "Don't let him get out of the country with my property."

"Things has, in these cases," answered the officer, "to be done regular and accordin' to law. You keep quiet and leave them to work the job as knows how to do it."

The burglars had left one old knife in the kitchen drawer, and with this Mrs. Snicker cut a lot of thick bread and butter for the boys, telling them they must eat it as they could and drink water that morning, as no regular breakfast table could be laid.

The boys enjoyed the perfunctory meal, without sighing for the wash that was ordinarily given them under the name of tea, and made a morning picnic of the meal in the open air.

In the midst of it a gig drove up with an inspector and another policeman in it. Mr. Snicker came out to meet them, and asked where his assistant-master was.

"He's spreading the news in Chippenham," replied the inspector, "and all sorts of people are treating him to rum and milk. He's having a high old time of it with them."

"The blatant ass!" muttered Fontenoy Snicker; "what sort of state will he come home in?"

The inspector was a calm man, and he took the robbery easy, inspecting much but saying little. There was no particular reason why he should put himself out, as the vanished knives and forks and other kitchen requisites were not his.

"It's a clean done job, the work of an old hand," he said, when he got at all the facts. "In my opinion you will never hear any more of the things."

On being pressed to give a more definite opinion of the robbery, he said it was impossible to do so. A good many affairs of the sort had been carried out all over the country, and there was no trace of the workers. There might be only one man in it, and there might be ten. He couldn't say.

In short he was only able to surmise, and when he went away the mystery was as deep as ever. Fontenoy Snicker was left in a fog.

But one thing was certain, he would have to provide a fresh supply of kitchen requisites with the least possible delay. It was a piece of business he could trust to nobody but himself, and until Penny Bunn returned from Chippenham he was unable to leave the Abbey.

"I'll murder him when he comes back," growled the irritated schoolmaster, "going a rum-and-milking at other people's expense, and letting out goodness knows what about the school."

However, he could only await the return of his subordinate with such patience as he had at his command, which could have been put into a thimble, and in due time the boys were summoned to their morning duties.

CHAPTER XX.

PREPARATIONS GOING ON—MORE BURGLARIOUS WORK.

THE morning was about half over when Penny Bunn suddenly put in an appearance in the schoolroom. He opened the door with a jerk, shut it with a bang, and like a torpedo shooting through the water, gained his usual seat.

There was a reason for this rapid movement. Had he walked in the ordinary leisurely manner, he would have wobbled a bit, but by expeditious movement he preserved his balance.

He seemed to be in a cheerful mood, and was smiling and rosy of countenance. The fact of his having gone to Chippenham in his slippers did not appear to have embarrassed him in the least.

The fact was he had not as yet found the pair of boots the boys removed from his feet on the night of his adventures with Milky Whey, and his only other pair were away at the cobbler's for repair.

He had, therefore, been about the house in his slippers, not an unusual thing, nor calling for especial observation.

Fontenoy Snicker looked at him from under his heavy eyebrows, and decided that while the boys were near he would not question him about his morning jaunt to Chippenham. It might lead to something undignified.

Of course the boys, as far as they dared, took stock of the undermaster, and they were gratified with the spectacle of his hilarious, yet business-like expression of countenance. Opening a book with his head thrown back, he scanned it with the air of some ancient alchemist struggling with a chemical problem.

He stared intently for a moment, then frowned, pursed his lips and shook his head. Finally, with a sigh, he shut the book and took up a pencil.

Casting his eyes about the desk in search of the ruler, and failing to find it, he smiled sadly. Then he raised the lid of his desk, turned over the various things therein, until at the very bottom he laid his hand upon his boots.

He drew them out, and, holding them at arm's length, regarded the well-worn leather structures with the affectionate eye of one who has fallen on long-lost friends.

"Blessmer," he exclaimed aloud, "how did you two beauties get in there?"

It was too much for the gravity of the boys, and explosions of irrepressible laughter were heard, like the popping of big corks out of bottles, in various parts of the room.

"Mr. Bunn," thundered the schoolmaster.

Penny Bunn started violently, dropped the boots, and gazed around him as if just awakened from a dream. There was a dreadful silence.

"Did you speak, sir?" faintly inquired the undermaster.

"Leave the room," cried Fontenoy Snicker.

"Leave-r room," repeated Penny Bunn; "whar for?"

"Do as I bid you," said Snicker, with an intensity which showed the white heat he was in. "I trust you do not want me to *assist you*?"

"No sir," answered Penny Bunn, with ineffable dignity, "I do not. Your word is law here. S'pose I can pick up my boots first?"

His superior made no reply, but he looked a great deal more than words could have conveyed. Penny Bunn stooped down, and having, after twice falling on his hands, succeeded in picking up his boots, prepared to retire.

He was sufficiently conscious of his condition to know that he must, as he had done on entering, make a rush of it. It was on that account necessary for him first to take the bearings of the door.

This he proceeded to do with all the gravity of a ship captain taking the latitude at high noon.

Holding up a forefinger, he got it in a line with the door, and started. In the matter of straightness he left nothing to be desired, but he made a mistake in getting too much way on, so that he was unable to pull up ere he had collided violently with the woodwork.

Fontenoy Snicker, now almost beside himself, jumped down from his desk and rushed towards him, but Penny Bunn, having by good luck found the handle of the lock, opened the door and vanished, just in time to escape a serious blow aimed at him.

There was no laughter among the boys, but the effort to restrain it swelled some of them nigh to bursting. They dare not show their mirth with the principal of the school in that boiling rage.

He returned to his desk, called up the classes, and finished the morning by harassing their young lives to the verge of distraction.

"You're a nice lot," he said, as he dismissed them; "not one of you have took—*taken*—the least trouble to get anything by heart. Now, mind this, I've got to go out this afternoon—*afternoon*—on business. You will stop in here and study a double dose, so as to be ready to-morrer—*morrow*—and if you aint improved matters, I'll put the lot of you on bread and water for a week."

They got outside as as well they could, and breaking up into groups, proceeded to discuss the events of the morning. There had been a certain amount of comedy to edify them, but there was tragedy looming up from the horizon for the days to come.

"Bread and water," snorted Short; "why that's the food and drink they give murderers. If he comes to that it will be time to do something."

"What can you do?" asked Soppem Smith.

"There's a lot of bluster and brag about some people here," sneered Roger Hone, "but they do precious little."

"What would you do," asked Jack, "if you were put to it?"

"I should *strike* against it," returned Hone.

"Strike, how?"

"Oh, somehow!"

"That's a fool's answer," remarked Don, in an aside to Tom Drummond.

But Roger Hone overheard him, and turning sharply, said:

"You call me a fool again, and I'll make you eat your words."

"Indeed," said Don, quietly. "I did not say you *were* a fool, but that your words were those *of* a fool, and I can't give you much credit for wisdom."

"That," hissed Hone, "is the same thing as saying *I am* a fool."

"Very well," rejoined Don, "let it stand at that."

Hone advanced with a threatening air; but on seeing Don did not flinch, he drew back again.

"I'll settle with you, one of these days," he said.

"Any time you please," said Don; "give me five minutes' notice when you want me."

Hone walked away, followed by the laughter of some who had witnessed the scene. Tom Drummond took Don's arm and drew him aside.

"I say," he said, "are you anything of a fighter?"

"Never had a real fight in my life," Don replied.

"Then, if I were you, I would have a lesson how to use your fists. It's no good being plucky alone if you want to win in a fight. Pluck gives you the strength to take punishment, but alone it doesn't help you to give it to the other fellow. Hone handles his fists scientifically, and if he had the courage with the art, none of us could stand up against him. I must give you a few boxing lessons, as he is sure to have a go at you one day."

"Why not to-day, then?"

"Well, Don, it's this way with Hone. He hasn't tried it on to-day, because he's got a fit of funk, but he will be chaffed about it, and that will work him up to tackle you, and he will *lick* you heavily, unless you know how to get at him. I'll be your trainer."

Don thanked him, and the subject dropped for the time.

As with breakfast, so with dinner. Mrs. Snicker could not, or would not, have a regular meal laid out.

Sandwiches were cut with the solitary knife left for use, and sent out to the boys.

The undue preponderance of bread over the meat excited some adverse comment, but, as Gyp Tanner said, it was no great loss, seeing that the beef provided was a portion of some old cow as tough as leather.

"Cow," exclaimed Short. "I wouldn't mind if he stopped at cow. This is a cut of a rhinoceros. I heard of one dying in the London Zoological Gardens last week."

"Stow it," said Bob Stockton; "remember some of us have tasted decent food in our time."

"That reminds me," said Tom, drawing Jack aside from the rest. "In the good time coming we must have tinned meat, and we shall want a lot of it. Have you written to Lingo yet?"

"Yes, and I've appointed for him to be at the bottom of the cliff to-morrow night. One of us will have to go down to meet him. Do you think the clothes-line is strong enough?"

"It hasn't much to spare," said Tom, dubiously; "the lighter the fellow the better. Don is a good stone less than I am."

"And the same in comparison to me," said Jack, musing; "how about his nerve? You see, it only wants one to go down, taking with him a cord I've got ready, so that the things Lingo will bring can be hauled up. There's the getting back, of course. It would hardly be fair to ask him to do it."

"Let us hear what he says. By the way, Tom, we shall want all the funds we can get."

"The band has come out well. And, in addition to nearly a pound in coin, I've got the promise of no end of things to sell. Some of our togs will have to go."

"That's a necessity," assented Jack; "I can spare a coat and a pair of sit-upons. We must make up a parcel and get Lingo to sell the things to the best advantage, as some people would say."

"By the way," said Tom Drummond, "jam is not a very bad thing, is it?"

"Who the deuce said it was?" asked Jack, opening his eyes.

"There is a cupboard full of it on the second floor," continued Tom; "of course it is not intended for us, but—*why* should we not have it?"

"It's under lock and key, I imagine," said Jack, thoughtfully.

"Yes; but what a lock—one turn of the jemmy and there it is—the door open as wide as the gates to let the king pass through."

"Tom," said Jack, "this is a thing we must do alone. We must have an inner circle to the band. Let us be bold. Will to-night suit you?"

"Like a bird."

"Then to-night, at the hour of twelve, we will get up another petrifier for Snicker. This time the front door had better be found open."

"Anything you like."

They parted, and went about the ordinary business of schoolboys, which is getting as much pleasure as possible out of the most meagre materials, and in due time, assembled with the rest in the classroom for an afternoon of study.

Fontenoy Snicker had gone to Chippenham. That was known as a fact, but it was expected that, owing to his recent experience, he would not be late. Meanwhile, Penny Bunn and Awful Rooker had charge of the school.

Whether the headmaster had interviewed the under one or not was not known, but it is certain that Penny Bunn was in a most depressed condition of mind. In mercy to him the boys were on their best behaviour, and only indulged in a little mild skylarking among themselves.

Snicker was not so early as he might have been that night, for he was, as other men, full of good resolutions when sick, and weak when in a state of convalescence. It was eleven o'clock when he returned, carrying a huge parcel of kitchen necessaries.

Nothing serious had happened to him, save that on the way he had lost about a dozen cheap forks out of the parcel, and he was almost, but not quite, sober.

Having had his supper, flavoured with tart comments on his general conduct by his spouse, he went to bed and slept soundly.

The morning brought with it another period of alarm and surprise.

He was dreaming of being knighted by the Queen for the masterly way in which he conducted his school, when he was aroused by Mrs. Snicker.

"Get up, Jerry," she said, "here's another break-in. They mean to clean out the house!"

"In the name of Jehosophat," he cried, as he sat up in the bed, "what's the matter now?"

"The jam and blanket cupboard have been broken open and cleared of everything," replied Mrs. Snicker. "Jane found the front door ajar. The burglars must have hidden themselves somewhere in the house during the day."

Snicker arose in a tremor of mystification and fear, and having got his clothes on somehow, went upstairs to look at the burglared jam and blanket cupboard. It was a sad and solemn truth that it was denuded of its valuable and toothsome contents.

"What do you make on it?" he exclaimed.

"I make nothing *of* it," replied Mrs. Snicker, correcting his English. "All I can think is that they've made a dead set on the Abbey and mean to ruin us."

"It's a licker," said the schoolmaster, scratching his head.

"What has liquor to do with it?" demanded Mrs. Snicker.

He did not answer her, his mind being at work with the problem presented to his notice by that empty jam cupboard.

"I've got it!" he exclaimed. "The boys!"

"You idiot!" returned his wife, "as if they *dare* do such a thing!"

"They dare anything, Mrs. Snicker, and I say the boys. Are they out of the dormitories yet?"

"No, but they are getting up."

"Anyways they ain't had time to wash. Come on! You stop 'em from coming hout, and I'll examine them in the rooms."

_____

CHAPTER XXI.

TRULY A MYSTERY—LINGO COMES TO LITTLECOTE.

THE unexpected appearance of the schoolmaster in the dormitories astounded the boys, and in some cases alarmed them not a little. In as few words as possible he told them what he had come for, and proceeded to look around the room.

There was not the least trace of jam, nor of the empty pots, not the fragment of a clue to the robbery.

The outside of the house was examined with a like result, and Fontenoy Snicker was obliged to confess that he had been mistaken.

"I don't know what to think of it," he muttered, as he walked into his dining-room scratching his head; "it whacks bull-baiting."

"Now you have proved yourself to be in the wrong, as I said you were," replied Mrs. Snicker, "shall I tell you what I think of it?"

"I shall be glad of your wallyble—*valuable*—blow it!—opinion," he answered.

"Then I think it is the police," asserted Mrs. Snicker, with a confident air. "Didn't you see how they hummed and ha'd over it yesterday, looking as guilty as possible? They did it."

"If that is the case," said Snicker, aghast, "we 'ave nuthin' to do but to sit down, or go to bed, and let 'em go on till there's no more to take."

"That is one of your bright ideas," said Mrs. Snicker, sarcastically. "What a dunderhead you are!"

"Ham—*am*—I?" he retorted; "and what are you, Mrs. Cocksure? If it's the police, how are you goin' to ketch 'em?"

"Say *catch*, my dear."

"I'll say a plate at your 'ead," he replied, "if you go on worriting—"

"*Worrying*, Jerry."

"Here, you've got something in your 'ead," said the harassed Snicker. "What is it?"

"Get a London detective down here," she replied, "as quiet as you can. Don't let anyone know what he is. If he is seen, say you've taken on a gardener. There's lots of 'em always advertising in the papers. Write to one of them."

"I will," said Snicker, "and if it is the perlice—*police*—I'll sue the county for damages. Gimme a rasher and a egg. Blessed if ever there was sich—*such*—goings on as this."

After breakfast he looked up a daily paper a week old, and ran his eye down the list of private enquiry advertisements. Finally he settled on one in which a certain Mr. Copps advocated an immediate application to him in case of need, as he was about to depart, unless prevented by home engagements, for Russia, there to investigate the last half-dozen attempts on the life of the Czar.

"I should not have that man," said Mrs. Snicker; "he brags too much."

"But what a name he's got," urged Snicker; "it sounds like a man-trap. Oh! he's a worrier, I'll bet!"

"You are, if he is not," said Mrs. Snicker, as she left the room.

Snicker wrote the letter, and put it into the bag for the postman to take away with him when he called. Owing to the position of the Abbey, he did not, as a rule, deliver the morning letters before eleven o'clock.

Meanwhile Jack and Tom had communicated with Don about the affair that was to come off in the evening. Somebody would have to go down the cliff to confer with Professor Lingo, and help to convey certain things he had brought with him to the school-room above.

Neither Tom nor Jack would have hesitated a moment about venturing the descent, but for the fact that they had not a very strong rope at their command, and it was better that whoever went should be as light as possible.

Furthermore, it was advisable to have the stronger hands above to assist him who descended in return-ing. Don willingly undertook the task.

"All you have to do," said Jack, "is to hold on and go slowly. A rush will make the rope burn in your hands, and then you will have to let go."

Don said he was not afraid, for it would be dark, and he could not see down.

"I am getting more nerve every day," he said.

The appointed hour was midnight, about an hour after all the inmates in the Abbey were expected to be asleep.

As the old clock of the church was recording the time the trio of boys were on their way down the stairs to the schoolroom.

Jack led the way, and having reached the passage below, he glided away to get the rope from the nail on which it usually hung by the scullery door. They could have taken it earlier, but feared it might be missed, and suspicion aroused.

Tom went on with Don, and softly opened the schoolroom door. All was dark therein, and to make sure that nobody was hiding around, Tom lit a match and peeped into all likely places, finding nothing.

By that time Jack had arrived with the rope, which he handed to Tom to examine, and crossing over to one of the windows, he opened it and leaned out.

Beneath him was a sheer descent of more than sixty feet, and he had a faint glimpse of the tops of trees growing in the lower ground. After waiting for a moment, he saw the flash of a light below.

"All serene," he said, backing into the room. "Lingo is there. Now, Don, if you feel the least nervous, say so. An accident to you, or indeed to any of us, would put an end to all our schemes and hopes."

"I am a bit excited," replied Don, "but not the least afraid."

"He'll do," said Tom Drummond; "his voice hasn't the tenth of a shake in it. I'll lower the rope, and if we give it one turn round the leg of this fixed desk, we shall be able to keep it fast."

One end was thrown out of the window and lowered to the ground. The other was partially secured in the way Tom suggested. Don grasped the frail clothes-line and slipped over the sill.

Then for a moment he felt terrified, but remember-ing what was expected of him, and what he had to do, he screwed up his courage and began the descent.

The others could not watch him, as they were en-gaged in the schoolroom steadying the rope. Though put round the leg of a desk, it still demanded some effort to keep it from slipping down.

Don went on inch by inch at first, and, as he gained confidence, increasing the distance from grasp to grasp. And as he went down, getting nearer to the ground, his spirits rose higher.

"Steady, youngster," said a soft voice, "by the Pope. I wouldn't have risked that journey on that rope for a pound or two."

"It had to be done, you know," said Don, panting with excitement.

"This rope ain't half strong enough for the work," replied Lingo, handling it with the air of a con-noisseur. "It ought to be twice as thick. I'll bring you one along next time."

He had a big carpet bag with him, which he opened, and took out a parcel.

"This is a telephone," he said; "only a toy, but it works wonderful. Here's a cord from your pals above."

"And something at the end of it," returned Don, who was now seated on the ground in the thick of the undergrowth at the foot of the cliff.

The parcel affixed to some twine lowered by Jack or Tom contained money. Professor Lingo opened it, and examined it by the aid of a dark lantern he had with him.

"Bless you, boys!" he said. "I don't want this yet. I was going to run the job on tick, but as I never send back ready money, I'll keep it. You may have a regular debtor and creditor account rendered by-and-bye."

He put the money in his pocket, and opened the package he had taken from his bag. It contained a coil of wire with a cup-like article at each end. Attaching one to the twine, he gave a soft whistle, and up it went.

Don watched him by the feeble light, paying out the wire until two-thirds of it was gone. Then it stopped.

"Too much of it?" he said; "a good fault."

With a small file he took from his pocket he cut off the wire to the required length, and refixed it, like a man accustomed to the work, to the cup again.

"Now," he said, "we are ready."

Placing the cup to his mouth, he whispered a few words into it, and immediately shifted the cup to his ear.

"Right as rain," he said; "you can hear as plainly as if you were in the room with them. Try it."

Don took the cup and whispered into it: "Are you there, Jack?"

"There, and all there," was the reply.

"Now it's my turn again," said Lingo, "and we must get on with business. Up there."

"Below," was the response.

"Lower the cord for packages. I've brought some handy tools, not out of my stock, and a couple of tins of meat for a start. I've likewise brought two packets of salt. I'll bet you would never have thought of that?"

"No," replied Jack, from above.

"I knew it," chuckled Lingo; "and yet you would have been ill without it. Haul away."

The cord had come down, and was duly hoisted again with a packet attached to it. This was done three times, and the bag was empty.

"So far, good," he said; "and now I've got something here which you will have to take back carefully with you. I had better tie it to your back, as it won't stand knocking about."

"What is it?" asked Don.

"Pills that may be of use, perhaps," said Lingo, "but not to be used unless in a case of extremity. They won't kill or maim anyone, but a couple of them would clear a thoroughfare in twenty seconds."

"Does Jack know of these?" asked Don.

"Yes; I leave my clients to explain things to their friends," answered Lingo. "I assure you there is no real harm in them, but they may be very useful."

He had a piece of cord in his pocket, and with it he securely lashed the box to Don's shoulders. Then he communicated with Jack, above, and after that Don was told he might return.

But the difference between going up and coming down, to a novice, had been overlooked, and Don, on essaying to return by the way he came, found himself beaten.

He climbed up a few feet, and had to come down again.

"I can't do it," he said, with a gasp.

"This is a pretty how'd'y do," remarked the professor, as he removed the package from his shoulders; "Why on earth did you come down?"

"Because I'm the lightest of us, and the rope's weak," replied Don.

"Let us hear what your chums say," suggested the Professor.

Lingo communicated with Jack through the telephone, with the evident result that he was staggered on realising the state of things. After a short consultation with Tom Drummond, he informed the professor that there was nothing to be done but for Don to make the journey round, and he would let him in at the side door.

"It's as dark as pitch," replied the professor, "and the way up through the wood would be too much for him. He had better remain with me till the morning, and then you must smuggle him in."

Before Jack could send back any reply to this suggestion, the window immediately above the school-room was heard to open. It belonged to the chamber of Fontenoy Snicker, and it was the voice of that worthy humbug which fell upon their ears.

"Hallo, there," he cried, "I can see you! A nice thing for the county perlice to turn burglars, ain't it? I'll send a report to headquarters that will make you sit up. Now, then, are you going, or shall I fire my blunderbuss?"

"Has he a blunderbuss?" whispered the professor

"I never heard of it," answered Don, in the same tone.

"Then he ain't got one," returned Lingo. "If he had, you boys would have known of it. He's on the bounce. Just keep still."

"I can see you sneaking orf—*hoff*, hang it—and just you keep clear of this crib in futer. I'm not the man to be trifled with."

Down went the window, and for a moment or two his muffled voice was heard talking to his wife, but what he said could not be distinguished. Then all was still.

Lingo put his ear to the telephone, expecting to hear a communication from Jack. He was not disappointed.

"I think your idea is a good one. Only do not keep Don too late in the morning, I will unfasten the back door and outside gate. He had better be home by five o'clock."

A "good-night" was exchanged, and the rope having been drawn up, Don was left to the care of the professor for the rest of the time intervening between then and morning.

CHAPTER XXII.

DON AND THE PROFESSOR—THE RETURN TO THE SCHOOL.

"I'VE got my van about a mile from here," said the Professor, as they moved away; "you can have a doss there for an hour. Give me your hand. 1 can see you are not accustomed to travel in the night, in a wood, anyway. Mind the briars. Put your arm up in a line with your face, or you will scratch your eyes out."

Don found this piece of advice useful, for during the next ten minutes he was continually brushing against thorns and bramble bushes. But at length they got into the open, and then the way was comparatively easy.

A walk across a plot of common land brought them to the high road, and a short way down it the professor turned into a lane where he had posted his van. The old mare could be heard close by cropping the grass and slowly moving about.

"Here we are," said Lingo, pulling up in front of a dark mass, which Don at first failed to recognise as the van. "Looks bulky, doesn't it?"

"I thought it was a haystack," replied Don.

"I've got hold of a job lot of baskets of all sizes, and wicker chairs, and so on. They can't be got inside, so I put 'em out, with a tarpaulin over 'em."

He ascended the three short steps and unlocked the door. Then he struck a match and lighted a candle on a bracket fixed in the wall.

"Come in," he said; "my home is small, but it is uncommonly snug."

So it was. Don had never seen anything like it before. There seemed to be every requisite for home comfort, and yet no appearance of crowding. There was, in short, a place for everything; and everything was in its place.

"I've a ham in cut," said the professor, opening a metal-lined box, "and a nice crusty loaf. A bit of grub won't hurt us. Nor will a cup of tea."

He lit a small spirit lamp, with a frame of stout wire over it, on which he placed a kettle of water. Then he turned up a flap fixed in the side of the van, which made a good table. Upon it he spread what he called the festive board, consisting of bread and ham, cheese and condiments.

"There we are," he said, "help yourself and fire away."

Don needed no second bidding, and they fell to. In a few minutes the kettle was boiling, and the professor made the tea.

"You don't mind a mug," said Lingo, as he filled one for Don; "boys ain't squeamish. How would you like my life?"

"Very much, I think," answered Don.

"It's as good as any going," said Lingo, thoughtfully, "but sometimes it's a bit lonely. A man now and then feels the want of a wife and child. But I shall never marry now."

"Why not?" asked Don; "you are not too old."

"Old?—no," said the professor; "it isn't that. Do I look as if I had been disappointed in love?"

"No," replied Don.

"But I have, though," rejoined Lingo; "the woman I was to have married took up with a low menagerie man. She was a pearl of a woman. No man on the road could do the patter like her. She would have made such a female Cheap-Jack as never was, but she has lost her chance. How a woman of her gifts could sink to the level of taking money at the door of a menagerie licks me; but I'll bet that she feels sorry by this time. Heigho!"

He was very quiet for a time after having thus opened his heart to Don, but he soon brightened up again.

"Here's luck to her, anyway," he said, holding up his teacup. "Never bear malice, my lad. It doesn't help you in anyway."

Don was not disposed to sleep, nor Lingo either, so the latter whiled away the time by showing the boy a lot of conjuring apparatus, which he used on occasion at the fairs or in the schoolrooms of villages.

He made no secret of the way they were worked, but asked Don not to talk about what he showed him.

Afterwards he exhibited a variety of things, including a case of small bottles containing what he called his world-famous Elixir of Prolonged Existence.

"It's for old men who want to go back to their youth," he explained.

"And will it take them there?" asked Don, innocently.

Lingo looked at him for a moment, twirling his long moustache, his eyes twinkling.

"If," he said, "liquorice water, with a suspicion of spirits of wine and a dash of gentian root in it, will send the old fools back again, my elixir will do it. My lad, there is no going back for anybody, and a good job, too. 'Hark forward,' is the motto of humanity."

The time passed rapidly away, and Don, was rather sorry when the professor said that it was time for them to be moving.

"We have a long round to do," he remarked, "and I had better go a part of the way with you."

"But you must be tired," hinted Don.

"My boy," was the answer, "I am never tired."

He opened the door, and showed that there was already a faint light in the eastern sky. It was past three o'clock.

Having closed and carefully locked the door, he set out with Don, as brisk and cheerful as if he had just been aroused from a long, refreshing sleep.

He led the boy round by the wood, so as to keep out of sight, in case anyone should be prowling about, until they came to the path by which Don had travelled with Fontenoy Snicker on the first day of his coming to Littlecote.

"Here, my lad," said Lingo, "we part. Good-bye. Get back as soon as you can, and if you are bowled out by old Snicker, of course you have nothing to say about me."

"Certainly not," replied Don.

They shook hands and parted, Don, with the aid of the growing light, finding his way easily enough. He encountered nothing worse than a scared rabbit until he had reached the Abbey.

Jack had undone the fastenings of the side gate, and the door also. Thus far Don was all right.

But as he was creeping along the passage leading

to the stairs, he was suddenly confronted by Fontenoy Snicker, fully dressed and ready to go out.

The schoolmaster was standing on the mat at the foot of the stairs, very quiet, or Don would not have fallen on him unawares. He felt that now he was indeed in a fix.

He expected to be collared and asked to account for his being out at that unearthly hour, but instead of doing that, the schoolmaster wheeled about and bolted upstairs yelling for help.

Don paused a moment, staggered by this unexpected action of Fontenoy Snicker. Then it flashed upon him that the schoolmaster had not only failed to recognise him, but had mistaken him for a burglar, and fled in terror.

The best move, therefore, was to get to bed as quickly as he could.

He accordingly bounded upstairs and whisked into the dormitory, undressing as he went. He had just time to tumble into bed, when he heard Fontenoy Snicker again calling for help.

Then came a response from above, and footsteps hurrying downstairs. The noise that was made woke up Jack Ford and two or three more.

Jack glanced at Don's bed, and, seeing him there, uttered an exclamation of satisfaction.

"Been back long, old man?" he asked.

"Just this minute returned," replied Don. "That row is all about me. I met Snicker in the hall. He seemed to be scared, and ran away."

"Then he did not recognise you," said Jack, "and that's all right. What a row!"

There was indeed a great commotion going on below, in the form of loud voices, and an opening and shutting of doors. Presently somebody was heard coming upstairs.

"All asleep," said Jack, hurriedly, and the wakeful ones promptly feigned the soundest repose.

A few moments later the door of the dormitory was cautiously opened, and the head of Fontenoy Snicker was thrust in. Behind him were Penny Bunn and Awful Rooker, one looking over his shoulder and the other peering under his arm.

"The fellow would never have the audacity to come here," said the schoolmaster, in a low tone.

"Perhaps he is under one of the beds," suggested Penny Bunn, his voice sounding like the upper notes of a cheap American organ, with the tremolo-stop out.

"A man of six feet could not get under one of them there—*those*—beds," said Fontenoy Snicker. "I am not sure he wasn't six feet three. I don't remember having seen so tall a man before."

The door closed, and they were heard moving up the corridor. Jack opened his eyes and said:

"You are all right, Don. He hasn't the least idea who it was. Try to get an hour's sleep. You must want it."

"I wonder what got Snicker up so early," said Tom Drummond, who was one of the wakeful ones.

"He may have crept down for a drop of something," replied Jack. "Black-Eyed Susan told me the other day that he often comes down early for a nerver. But don't talk. Don wants forty winks."

Don did indeed, and, what is more, he obtained them, as he almost immediately fell asleep.

CHAPTER XXIII.

COPPS, THE LONDON DETECTIVE.

IT is astonishing what the shortest sleep will sometimes do towards refreshing the weary. Don got barely an hour of it before the usual morning summons, and when he awoke he felt as well as he had ever done in his life.

He had little to tell that was of importance to the great scheme in hand, but his description of the box, which Lingo had bound and taken later on from his shoulders, aroused the curiosity of all except Jack. He seemed to know all about it.

"It contains pills for Snicker," he said, "but they will not be wanted yet. Mind, all of you, not a whisper about them, even to each other, if you think there is a chance of being overheard."

They all promised to be cautious, and Jack advised a complete silence about the affairs of the band until they got a chance for a secret meeting. Holidays were not fixed in Littlecote as they are in other schools. Nominally the boys had Wednesday and Saturday afternoons, but the schoolmaster very often, without any visible reason, changed the order of things, stopping a usual holiday, or giving it on another day. He was never governed by anything but his own sweet will.

This was one of the minor grievances of the boys. Often, when they had made their arrangements for one of the usual half-holidays, they would, at the last moment, be told that there was to be no holiday at all. Sometimes it was done to punish the youngsters for a real or imaginary offence, and on other occasions it was designed to worry the undermasters, as it invariably fell to their lot on these occasions to have the entire charge of the school.

Fontenoy Snicker, having once got it into his head that he had seen a man in the house, speedily improved upon the original assumption, and put a uniform upon him. In short, he worked him up into a policeman, and congratulated Mrs. Snicker on her having hit upon the correct authorship of the burglaries at Littlecote.

A SPLENDID SCHOOL STORY.

NEVER BEFORE PUBLISHED.

By E. HARCOURT BURRAGE,

Author of "Ching Ching," "Monkey Mat and Roving Dick," "The Brave Boy of the Basilisk," &c.

A Handsome Coloured Plate Presented with Every Number.

No. 4.

THE BARRING OUT.—GENERAL HIGH JINKS.

PRICE ONE PENNY.

ALDINE PUBLISHING CO., 2, Red Lion Court, Fleet St. and 1, 2 & 3, Crown Court, Thames

"But," he said, "we can do nothing until Copps comes, and he'll get at 'em. There is nothing like having a London man on these jobs."

Copps was expected some time that day, and Snicker had arranged for him to play the part of a gardener. The garden wanted weeding—it always did—and he could amuse himself by attending to it.

"Some fellow who wrote a book," asserted Snicker, "said that the occupation of gardening gives opportunities for reflection. Copps will be able to work, and think out the moves he intends to make."

The baker who brought the bread was told of the coming of a gardener, by the express wish of Fontenoy Snicker, on the ground that he would be sure to talk about it as he went his rounds. He would thus do his part in blinding the police of the neighbourhood.

But the best designs of man will sometimes go astray, and the detective from London entirely upset the plans of the schoolmaster.

As one might expect from a man of his calling, he came down disguised, but not as a menial.

At Chippenham he said he was the Reverend Jopson Copps, and he had come on a visit for a month to Littlecote.

Having hired a fly, he was taken to the old Abbey, where he arrived early in the evening. The boys were in the playground when the vehicle, which had to go three miles round to get there, thus adding very materially to the fare, stopped at the gate.

Copps got out, and seeing a number of young faces at the entrance, addressed them as became a gentle of the parsonic persuasion.

"Ha, my little ones," he said, blandly. "How do you do?"

"Who is he?" asked the wondering boys, staring at the pseudo cleric.

"Mr. Snicker in?" asked Copps.

"Yes," chorussed a dozen voices.

"Will you kindly tell him that his old friend Copps has come from over the ocean to see him."

Now Fontenoy had announced to the boys not only that he was going to keep a gardener, but his name also. It was too short—sweet and novel to be mistaken, and expressive looks were exchanged by certain members of the band. They began to smell a rat.

"I'll go and tell Mr. Snicker you are here," said Jack Ford.

"And at the same time," said Copps, blandly, "inform him that I have unfortunately nothing but cheques about me, and I shall be glad if he will send out the money for the fare. How much is it, my man?"

"Nine bob without the driver," was the gruff reply.

"Isn't that rather heavy?" inquired Copps.

"Well, the hills are heavy," answered the driver, "and that's how we levels up things down here."

Jack hurried into the house, and asked Jane where the schoolmaster was. She told him he was in the parlour with "missis." To the parlour Jack went, and knocked at the door.

"Come in," cried the schoolmaster.

Jack entered the room, and saw that there had been some warm talking going on between husband and wife, for both were flushed, and Fontenoy Snicker had the tail end of a snarl upon his lips.

"A gentleman named Copps is at the gate," said Jack, "and, as he has no change, he wishes you to pay the fare. It is nine shillings without the driver."

"How much?" exclaimed Snicker, aghast.

"Nine shillings, sir."

"Jigger—I mean *bless* his cheek."

"He looks like a clergyman, sir," added Jack. slyly, "and he talks like one. He spoke to us as his little children."

"Did he?" said the staggered Snicker; "what a fo——, what a mistake. Go along and say I'll come directly."

Jack vanished, and having executed a short derisive dance outside the door, hurried back to the playground.

"Jerry," said Mrs. Snicker, "as usual, you have made a mess of this business."

"How could I tell he would start on this idiotic racket," growled Snicker. "I meant to have written to him to say that he was to be a gardener, and I believe I did so."

"You know you did nothing of the sort," returned Mrs. Snicker, coolly. "Go along and make the best you can of your own muddle."

Snicker left the room, feeling uncommonly small, and in a boiling rage. But he, like the villain in the play, had to dissemble. It would never do to have a quarrel with the private inquiry man at the outset.

He had of necessity to pass through the boys, and, although they feigned to be occupied in various games, many a pair of keen eyes were upon him.

Copps meanwhile had kept by the gate, regarding the boys with a well-feigned benevolent interest in them. He was tall and lank, with a thin, hatchet face, and his assumed garb became him uncommonly well.

On seeing Fontenoy Snicker, who had screwed his eyeglass into his eye, and put on his best pedagogue style, he rushed forward and fervently embraced him.

"After so many years, old friend," he gasped, "what joy it is to meet again."

As they had never set eyes on each other before, this was about as cool as a thing could be. It was a fair knock-out blow for the schoolmaster, and all he could say was uttered in feeble voice.

No. 4.

"You have come in a fly, I see. I usually walk. It's more healthy."

"You haven't any busses here," replied Copps, rather abruptly, "so I took a cab. My time is vallyble."

"Certainly," said Snicker, feebly, fumbling for his purse. "Nine shillings, I believe?"

"And at least three bob for the driver," said the man, unceremoniously. "*My* time is vallyble as well as other people's."

The man had to be paid, and Fontenoy Snicker groaned as he counted the money into his hand. The rejection of a shilling with a hole in it did not improve his temper, and he was almost speechless with rage by the time the transaction was concluded.

Copps had a carpet bag with him, which he calmly handed to Snicker to carry into the house, and smilingly passed through the boys, with the schoolmaster by his side anathematising him.

When they arrived at the seclusion of the hall Fontenoy Snicker ventured to remonstrate with him.

"Copps," he said, "you ought not to have turned up in this style. I've given out that you were to be my gardener."

"Then all I have to say is," replied Copps, who had already measured his man, "that it was like your confounded cheek to do such a thing. A gardener, indeed! Why did you not at once make me your footman or boy in buttons? No, sir; I don't play quite so low as that."

"I thought you detectives," said the schoolmaster, "did not mind any sort of disguise."

"Some play one thing," said Copps, "'tothers another. I go in for the hairystocratic line. I'm to be your guest, a friend, or nothing. It's for me to say what I am, not for you to arrange it. If you don't like that, you can pay me a month's money and let me go. Ten pounds a week and railway exes is my charge.

Fontenoy Snicker turned white, and felt for a moment as if he would liked to have settled the detective with an axe or some kindred weapon. But that, of course, could not be.

"You had better stay," he said. "I suppose you don't mind where you sleep. We have arranged a room for you at the top of the house, being crowded like."

"Then let somebody else enjoy the crowding," answered Copps. "I want a room on the ground floor. What good should I be in the attic, do you think?"

"This is about the bloomingest mess I ever was in," helplessly muttered Fontenoy Snicker; aloud, he said, "We will see what can be done for you. Come and pay your respects to my wife. She has a better head than mine for arrangements."

"So I should suppose," candidly returned Copps.

CHAPTER XXIV.

COPPS BEGINS TO WORK.

"I CAN'T quite make that parson out," said Tom Drummond, as the door closed upon Copps and the schoolmaster.

"He's not a parson at all," said Soppem Smith, who was standing close by.

"How do you know?" demanded Tom.

"I guess so," was the answer.

"Oh! he's a soapy one," remarked Roger Hone. "I should say he's been a missionary. Didn't you hear him talking of having come from abroad? What do you say, Ford?"

"I am no judge of parsons," answered Jack, "and whoever he is, I don't see what he has to do with us."

Notwithstanding this opinion, Jack had already serious doubts about the new arrival. Having been previously announced as a gardener, and not appearing in that character, what was he?

"He's a spy, brought here to find out something," was his decision, after some thought.

Then came the fear that Snicker had got an inkling of what was going on in preparation for the barring out. If that were the case, there was danger in the air.

He took what opportunities were afforded him to confer with some of the band, single, or in twos and threes, as he was able, and they were all of his opinion. The coming of the mysterious Copps boded them no good.

"We must lie quiet for a few days and do nothing—absolutely nothing," was the advice he gave to his followers. "Meanwhile, we ought to do something to make it hot for the spy."

He felt depressed, but did not show it to anyone save Don, for whom he already felt a strong, growing friendship.

As they sauntered to and fro in the playground, he put before them his views of the probable result of the coming of Copps.

"It will, unless we are careful, spoil the whole thing I reckon this man is a sharp fellow. His eyes have the cunning of a fox in them."

"He won't be long here," suggested Don, hopefully.

"Not if we can help it," said Jack, "but he may be here just long enough to find us out. We shall not be able to blind him as we have done Snicker."

"What's the confab?" inquired somebody in the rear.

They turned quickly, and saw Soppem Smith and Hone close behind them.

"Were you listening?" asked Jack, curtly.

"No," replied Hone. "Is it likely you would be talking anything worth listening to?"

"I wouldn't say that," said Soppem Smith, with a short laugh. "Jack and his set have got some game in hand. I don't see why they should be so precious close about it."

"Oh! don't bother," said Jack; "it is nothing that concerns you."

He walked away, and Don followed. When they were out of earshot, Jack said: "There are clouds in the atmosphere, old man. But I am sure that Smith and Hone only suspect at present."

"Suppose they knew?" hinted Don.

"They would, in sheer malice, blow upon us," replied Jack.

"But when the time comes, and we are successful in the first part of the you know what, how are we to get them to come in with us?"

"They will have to come," answered Jack. "In every revolution there are a lot who object, but they have to run with the crowd. At least half of Smith's dormitory are ripe for the thing, and would be enrolled in the band but for the fear they might let something leak out. Oh, if we can make all our preparations without hindrance, we shall work it."

To add to the growing fears of Jack, that evening, as they were in the schoolroom, Copps came in and had a chat with Penny Bunn, who was there, keeping guard, as usual. After that, he sauntered round the room in a prying sort of manner, and, to the terror of the band, stopped by the closed door and stared at it for a time.

"Where does this lead to?" he asked, turning to Penny Bunn.

"To some empty rooms, I believe," answered Penny Bunn.

"You believe? Don't you know?"

"No. The door has not been opened in our time. It is in the lease that it is to be kept closed."

"Oh!" was all Copps said, as he came back to his seat by the undermaster's desk. Jack would rather he had said more.

"Shall I try to get a rise out of him?" whispered Bob Stockton.

"If you like," replied Jack, whom he addressed; "but mind how you go about it. He's a keen one."

"All right," said Bob, "I'll be careful."

Rising, he turned, and having caught the eye of Copps, proceeded, in schoolboy parlance, to "work" him.

"Will you do us a favour, sir?" he asked.

"With pleasure, my son," answered Copps, unctuously.

"We shall soon have got up our lessons," pursued Bob, "and when they are done will you kindly tell us a story about the savages you have visited?"

"I do not remember having spoken to you about savages," said Copps, with a cunning light in his small eyes.

"No, sir," said Bob, "but we understood you to say when you arrived that you had been abroad."

"And from that you jumped to the conclusion that I have been a missionary?"

"Yes, sir."

"If you usually jump in that style at your lessons," said Copps, "you will make very clever men. I'll tell you a short story when you are ready."

"Thank you, sir," replied Bob, gently, and sat down.

"He has tumbled," he whispered to Jack.

"I don't know," was the doubting reply; "wait until he has told the story."

As the whole of the school had heard what passed, there was a general hurrying up with the lessons, and the books were closed much earlier than usual. Meanwhile, Copps had been talking with Penny Bunn in an undertone, and seemed to be on very good terms with him.

The boys faced round, and quietly waited for him to see that they were ready, and presently he observed them in their varied attentive attitudes.

"Ah!" he said, "you want a story from me. It will be a very short one. Listen!"

"Once upon a time—a good old style of beginning, isn't it?—there was a king who ruled over a country. He was very tall and strong, but his people were quite small—lilliputians, indeed, they were—and the king was mighty cruel to them. He walked about with a thick stick and beat them at all times, whether they deserved it or not. As a rule, they were a cheeky lot of little beggars, but they did not do much that was criminal, and the king was unjust.

"Now, this king had a certain portion of his kingdom, shut off from the rest. It was believed to be uninhabited; anyway, the inhabitants of other places were not allowed to get so much as a peep at it. But some of them made up their minds to see what that part was like, and they burrowed under the wall which had been shut off from them, and they entered the forbidden land."

Here Copps paused, with a curious, dry smile on his lips, and looked at the boys in turn with a searching expression in his small cunning eyes. He seemed to linger for the fraction of a second longer on the faces of a few, and among them were Jack Ford, Don Peebles, and Bob Stockton.

There was a solemn stillness in the room. The boys wanted to know what was behind the wall the tyrant had put up.

But after the pause, Copps said, quietly:

"I told you my story would not be a long one, and, short as it is, I am not going to finish it to-night. It is like the serials in a journal, to be continued in our next."

"Oh, that isn't a story at all," cried a dozen voices.

"Oh, yes, it is," he answered, "a part of a real one. It isn't fiction. The next time I get a chance to talk to you, you will know what was behind that wall. Perhaps some of you have already guessed."

Many said "No," but others were dumb, among them those who knew what was beyond that closed door.

Meagre as the so-called story had been, it terrified the band with the conviction that Copps had already detected the opening up of the long closed rooms.

How much more did he know or guess?

It was an appalling and disheartening thought.

But those "not in the know" were irritated in another way, and when Copps coolly marched out of the room they called him a variety of hard names, in which "fraud" and "duffer" were conspicuous.

As for Penny Bunn, he could make nothing of the affair at all, beyond that he could see in a dim way that there was something in it he did not understand.

Those most concerned said nothing then, but when they went to bed that night Jack passed the word for all to keep awake, for a consultation.

It was not until all the household were in bed that Jack, as leader of the band, opened the meeting by desiring Gyp Tanner to take his stand outside the door to watch and give warning of the approach of anyone playing the spy. Having taken this precaution, he proceeded to express his views.

"This man Copps is a police officer," he said, "and he has been brought here to ferret out something. Snicker has somehow got an inkling that there is trouble in the air. Copps could see that the door in the schoolroom has been opened."

"What a blessed sell," groaned Warner.

"We are not done yet," said Jack. "Of course, if he persuades Snicker to have the door opened, certain things will be discovered, and then it will be all u-p with the barring out. Our one chance is that Snicker won't consent to it, as his lease expressly forbids him to make any alteration in the present condition of the Abbey."

"A poor one, I should say," remarked Don, "for the detective, if he is one, will try the thing on himself. They are a prying lot."

"You are right," said Bob Stockton. "What is to be done?"

"When a great general sees the enemy advancing on a weak position," said Herbert May, "he goes in for a diversion. I've read about their making flank movements, whatever they may be."

"I shouldn't be surprised," growled Jack, "if he is not already at work. Hush! here's Gyp."

Softly as the door had been opened, his quick ears had heard it. Gyp came into the room to make a report.

"Somebody with a light moving about below," he said.

"I'll see who it is," said Jack; "now, all quiet, please."

He stole out of the room, leaving many palpitating hearts behind him. After an absence so long that it seemed Jack must have fallen into the hands of the enemy, he returned.

"It's that fellow Copps," he said, with a moan. "He has gone into the schoolroom, and we are done. To-morrow there will be trouble for somebody, but remember your oath, brethren, and, if you are tortured with red-hot pincers, be dumb."

"There is one comfort," said Tom Drummond, "they can't fix it on one more than the other. It is a case where the innocent will have to suffer as well as the guilty."

It was poor comfort at the best, and with the feeling of culprits, for whom the scaffold would be prepared on the morrow, they sought oblivion from their troubles in sleep.

CHAPTER XXV.

IN NUMBER TWO DORMITORY—ANOTHER PLOT.

THERE was an equal amount of restlessness in the other dormitory that night, in a measure arising from the idea which Soppem Smith and Roger had got into their heads, that Jack Ford and his set had something afloat in the way of skylarking or trickery in which they did not share.

But, at the same time, they had not the least inkling of the nature of it.

Added to this there was a smouldering fire in the breasts of the followers of Smith, created by the treatment they had to endure.

"It's licking all the day, and bad grub at the table," said a youngster, named Dorey, who was of a lively erratic disposition, and ever getting into trouble. "Why haven't we a few more Stormers in the school?"

"Because the game doesn't pay," replied Roger Hone. "Who here would care to go home expelled? We live apart, and when it came to the pinch, our friends would think that we have not done as we ought to, especially when they get a hypocritical letter from that beast Snicker."

"With the grammar corrected by Penny Bunn," said Dorey, "and copied out by Awful Rooker."

"If Ford is getting up anything," said another youngster, George Philter, "why can't he take us in?"

"Because we cannot be trusted, I suppose," said Soppem Smith, savagely.

"There are fifteen of us here," said Roger Hone; "why not get up something between ourselves? If the number one lot can be secret, so can we."

"It wouldn't be a very great sin to shoot Snicker," muttered Roger Hone. "Did you notice the butter to-night?"

"The what?" asked Dorey. "You must be thinking of the cart-grease just imported for us."

"I know what would give Snicker a shaking," said Soppem Smith, "but then you fellows wouldn't do it."

"Let us know what it is," returned Philter, "and then we can make up our minds."

"You won't go jawing about it, I suppose?" said Soppem Smith.

"We can all take an oath of secrecy," suggested Hone. "Now, then, all of you come out of bed and stand together. No shirking. Who is that in that corner?"

"I would rather not have anything to do with it," replied a weak voice.

"But you've got to have to do with it," answered Hone; "so none of your crawling out of it."

Barnes was the weakest and most nervous boy in the school. When he received a thrashing it was painful to see him writhe and hear his cries. Snicker took especial delight in administering chastisement to him. The manifest torture he endured seemed to be such a good return for the outlay of castigatory labour.

"I won't peach," said Barnes, miserably, "indeed, I won't. But you know how I get laid into with that everlasting cane, and if anything comes out, I shall get it worse than the rest."

"Come and make one of us," insisted Hone; "we are past taking the word of anyone here. You must take the oath. Jack Ford has sworn in his lot, or we should have heard something before now. Stand there. Now all of you join hands."

They did so, and Hone, by the direction of his leader, Soppem Smith, administered an oath he had acquired by heart from a brigand story.

It was a little too strong, perhaps, but the boys of number two dormitory were getting screwed up to the sticking-point, and they meant business, now that the subject of resisting the tyrant had been fairly mooted.

The most frightful penalties were to be exacted from those who betrayed the rest, and when all had assented to the conditions that were imposed, Soppem Smith proceeded to unfold his scheme.

It lacked the boldness of the idea developing in the other dormitory, being of the light guerrilla order of attack, a series of harassing movements, in short, which were to make the life of Snicker unendurable.

The first thing to be done was to provide the material for sundry plans Soppem Smith had in his head.

He named gunpowder, string, putty, and liquid glue among other things, and advised, or rather instructed, his followers to invest their pocket-money in obtaining a supply.

They undertook to do so on the first occasion they could find, which would be, of course, the next half-holiday—when they got it.

Having settled matters thus far, they retired to bed, feeling more contented with their lot, from the bare fact that they had arranged something to ameliorate it.

It is a curious fact that it is in the nature of us all to derive a certain amount of satisfaction from *intending* to do this or that. We all feel as if the work were done in part.

But intentions are not deeds, as we shall soon see, for a series of obstacles was about to arise in the path of the second band of malcontents.

CHAPTER XXVI.

DETECTIVE COPPS SEES HIS WAY CLEAR.

IT was three o'clock in the morning, and Copps had not yet retired to bed. As a matter of fact he had only just come into his room, which, in accordance with his wishes, had been arranged for him upon the ground floor.

Copps had been very busy for hours.

He had, as Jack suspected, detected the fact that the old door, supposed to have been closed for years, had been recently opened, and he strongly suspected that the boys had been beyond it.

Accordingly, as we know, he only waited until everybody was in bed, or presumed to be, to make his first move to ascertain what was behind that door.

He never travelled without a certain handy pocket-knife with all sorts of things attached to it, from a tooth-pick to a small screw-driver.

Armed with this, he felt certain he could open the door, and he succeeded in doing so.

One by one he removed the screws, carefully laying them on one of the boy's desks in due order, so that they could be exactly replaced, and then he turned the door back upon its hinges.

It was twelve o'clock by that time, as he had proceeded slowly and carefully with his labour, so as not to make any noise.

He expected to make some sort of discovery, but not of the startling nature which was disclosed to him.

Here, on the night of his arrival, he had solved the mystery of the school robbery, and, with professional care, he proceeded to make a list of the things the boys had accumulated in his pocket-book.

He examined the place thoroughly, noting the well with amazement, and discovered the fastened down trap-door.

As the boys had done, he reserved the task of opening that for a future time, for he saw that it had not yet been disturbed.

"I don't think I ever came nigh such a game as this," he muttered, as he held the light aloft and surveyed the property accumulated together. "What the deuce will boys be up to next?"

He was quite charmed with it. It was something so fresh and new to him as a professional man. He lingered there, as people do at a free show which pleases them. Thus it happened it was nearly three o'clock ere he returned to his room.

Nor could he go to bed when he arrived there, but sat down upon his couch, and dwelt upon his discovery with amazement and unalloyed joy.

"The question is," he thought, "shall I enlighten Snicker? On the whole, I think not at present. The little imps won't stop there, but will go on. I'll let 'em go right up to the top of the ladder, and then bring them down with a run."

At last he undressed and got into bed, but he could not sleep for an hour or more. He had never been so utterly taken aback as by his "big find," as he called it. The whole thing was so adverse to what he expected.

He had put down the robbery to some yokels in the neighbourhood, for, having had a look at the forced scullery window, he could see at once that it was not the work of a professional hand. It was the rough and ready doing of a complete novice.

He slept at last, and did not awake in the morning until Snicker came to his room and roused him.

"Nearly nine o'clock," he said; "you are a good sleeper."

"I have been about all night while you were snoring," returned Copps, as he sat up in the bed, "and if I had not been, it would be no business of yours. I must have a free hand, and do exactly what I please."

"No offence," murmured the schoolmaster. "Of course you can do as you like at all times. I won't ask you if you have discovered anything. It is too early yet."

"I have discovered enough," replied Copps, with the calm pride of genius, "to say that I can lay my hand on the parties almost any moment I choose."

"Then why don't you?" exclaimed the amazed Snicker.

"Because laying on the grip with a moral certainty of their being the people isn't always enough to convict," said Copps; "they must be taken red-handed."

"You can't do that so long after the robbery."

"They haven't finished yet, but will be at it again. That I'm sure of. Now don't you bother me too much. You will know all in time, and if you don't have about the biggest flabbergaster you have ever known, may I lose my business. It will be a record. How about breakfast?"

"There's some left for you," replied Snicker.

"Left for me! What do you mean by that?"

"Well, me and Mrs. Snicker have had some rashers and heggs—eggs—and we didn't eat the lot. There is —are some left."

"Then give what is left to the pigs," said Copps, as he got out of bed and proceeded to dress. "You seem to be a rough lot down here, living anyhow and nohow. Ask the cook to prepare me some fresh bacon and eggs, and I like a devilled bone or two to top up with. I hope the coffee is good, as I can't drink it poisoned with chicory."

"We allus—always—drink tea," murmured the schoolmaster.

"Do you mean to tell me that you haven't any coffee in the house?"

"No."

"Then get some at once. How far have you to send for it?"

"Three miles."

"Then I will put up with tea this morning," said Copps, graciously.

Snicker left the room, muttering to himself:

"This ere fellow will cost me a fortin—fortune—blow the words, I can't even think 'em right. I'd better have let the burglars clean me out. It would have come cheaper."

Acting up to his character of a clerical friendly visitor, Copps, after a breakfast of vast proportions—insomuch that when Mrs. Snicker reckoned up the consumption of good things he had eaten she saw famine and ruin advancing with giant strides—adjourned to the schoolroom to assist with the classes.

"I can harry some of the younger boys," he whispered to Snicker.

"Very well," answered the schoolmaster, who wished him at Jericho.

So Copps took a class, and as he was about as well up as the most ignorant of them, with all his professional knowledge, some novel scholastic things were said and done.

Among others he took charge of was little Jiggers, who had some history of the time of the early Saxons to get through with. Jiggers, having, as usual, a poorly filled stomach, had been thinking more of unsupplied food than the Saxons, and was not well up with his subject.

He mixed up the Gunpowder Plot with the Heptarchy, and was sent back to his seat to read up his lesson.

" Hey !" cried Snicker, " what's the matter there ?"

" My little friend," answered Copps, " doesn't quite know his lesson."

" Then your little friend," rejoined Snicker, " will get a taste of the cane. Come here, Jiggers."

" One moment," said Copps, " before you proceed Snicker. Allow me to ask you a question. Did you ever try the power of moral force ?"

" Moral force," said the irritated schoolmaster— he was getting tired of the presence of the detective— " be blo—be bothered. Jiggers, down on your knees."

Jiggers knew what was coming, and shivered. Going down on his knees was a preliminary to his crawling between the bow-legs of the schoolmaster, and his journey was accompanied by several severe and telling applications of the cane to that portion of his anatomy provided by Nature for him to sit upon.

He was such a mite of a boy that only a brute or a fool could have looked upon the chastisement inflicted upon him unmoved and Copps, whatever else he might be, was neither.

He did not say anything, but his brow darkened a little, and the rest of his class made all sorts of blunders without being reproved, much less sent down.

Little Jiggers, smarting and tearful, returned to his seat and had another go at the Saxons. Presently Copps came over to him and took the book in his hand.

" My boy," he said, in a low tone, " I am a man of peace, or I would recommend you to chuck something at his blooming head the next time he comes that game.' Aloud, he said : " We will now resume our studies, my little friend."

Jiggers got through his lesson all right this time, although he was wrong in many portions of it. Copps was not going to place him under a second ordeal of the cane.

But there was no lack of use for it that morning. Snicker was in a cantankerous mood, and he was very busy. Not half-a-dozen boys in the school escaped punishment, more or less severe.

" I understand the meaning of the game, now," thought Copps, as he retired from the schoolroom shortly before the close, " but I have my duty to my employer to perform, as my professional reputation is at stake in the result, but I'm blessed if I don't afterwards make a second job out of this. I'll get a cruelty society to fall foul of that brute Snicker. If he would only *kill* a boy, what a job I could make of it !"

As with him, so it is with the world generally. Business is the guiding force of our movements. Copps was sorry for the boys, but he could not champion them, at present, anyway, without incurring loss of reputation, and money, too. And that he was not going to do.

It was a melancholy lot of boys that adjourned to the outer air, but there was a hope rising in the breasts of some of the members of the band.

" I think you must be mistaken, Jack," said Tom Drummond. " Copps is not a detective, or, if he is, he hasn't discovered anything. I watched him a good deal this morning, and never once found him looking in the direction of the door."

In addition to Jack, he had as companions Don, Short, and Whymper, and they were seated on the wall by the edge of the cliff. It was a custom of the band not to gather in force in the playground, lest they should excite suspicion. It therefore transpired that although many of the others were anxious to have a chat on the situation, they held aloof.

" His not looking at the door is no proof he has not been behind it," replied Jack. " I am sure he has tried to open it. I haven't had a chance to examine the screws, but I could see from my seat that one of them was not covered up with dust in the way I did it."

" Then he has been at work," said Don, dismally.

" For a cert," answered Jack. " Now the question is, ought we not to risk the job at once ?"

" Surely," exclaimed Short, " not *the*—"

" Yes *the*—" answered Jack. " I have written a letter to Lingo to bring along to-night the boarding to fasten the door. He is staying in Smudgem Bender, and I only want a messenger. As soon as I get the material we start. I hope it will be to-morrow morning."

This declaration fairly took away the breath of his companions, and for a few moments they were silent. Now that the important moment appeared to be at hand they began to realize the magnitude of the task, and to measure the probable results of the success or non-success of it.

" It's rather sudden," said Tom, breaking the silence.

" The greatest things have been done with a rush," replied Jack. " I am certain it is now or never. Copps is our rock-ahead, and he will smash up the show unless we get ahead of him. If you funk it—"

" Hang it," said Don, " don't talk in that way. Funk it ! Not me, and I'm a baby among you. The rest, I think, are staunch."

" I hear a yokel whistling outside," said Jack, rising, " If he is going Smudgem Bender way, he will give my letter to Lingo."

Jack sauntered off, and as soon as he was out of hearing, Short had something to say. " It would be madness to attempt it," he asserted ; " we have nothing ready. Where's the grub ?"

Short knew nothing of the doings of the inner circle. Tom smiled.

"You have to trust Jack. I dare say he knows what he is doing."

"Of course we must trust him," said Whymper; "but to-morrow. It is precious near."

At this moment Soppem Smith came sauntering up and sat down beside them.

"Jawing together as usual, you number one fellows," he said. "Now don't rile up, Drummond. I am not going to ask you to tell us your secrets, but to let you into ours. *We* of the number two have had enough of the doings of Littlecote, and we are going to *kick !*"

"Kick whom?" asked Tom.

"Snicker."

"And he will hit back again—precious hard."

"Then we will kick once more," said Soppem Smith. "We intend to worry him into fiddle-strings."

Jack at this moment was seen returning. He had found a messenger to carry his letter in the person of a plough-boy, who was going to Smudgem Bendor.

"Take the letter to the Professor, and he will give you a nice four-bladed pocket-knife," said Jack. "See, I have written on the outside for him to do it." Jack scribbled the request with a pencil as he spoke. "Hurry up with it."

The boy promised to do so, and Jack, as we have stated, returned to his friends.

CHAPTER XXVII.

PLOT AND COUNTERPLOT.

"SMITH says he won't have any more of Snicker's nonsense," said Tom.

"Indeed," replied Jack. "What is he going to do? Shoot an inkstand at his head, as Stormer did, or run away?"

"Neither," said Soppem Smith. "We are bent on harassing him in every possible way."

"Not a bad idea," rejoined Jack, approvingly, "but it occurs to me that we might first try the *suaviter in modo.*"

"Soap won't touch the brute," grumbled Smith.

Jack sat quiet for a moment, as if reflecting on something which had just flashed into his mind.

"Suppose we try what a petition will do?" he suggested.

His friends stared at him in wonderment. Such a proposal, coming from Jack, was equivalent to a caving in and throwing up of the sponge. They were amazed, and Don felt a bit disgusted.

"After all," he thought, "it has been nothing but idle bounce."

"Who is to get it up, and present it?" asked Smith.

"I will write it out, and present it," replied Jack, "on condition that the whole of us sign. My name shall head the list."

"He will give us all a thundering licking," said Soppem Smith.

"Well, it won't be for the first time," answered Jack, coolly; "at all events, if he refuses our reasonable requests, he will only have himself to blame for what follows. Pass that idea round. It can be done in five minutes, and let me know the general opinion on the suggestion. If the fellows like it, I will have the petition written out before we grub, and you can sign it immediately afterwards. About three o'clock I will lay it before Snicker, and ask him to read it."

"He will half murder you," said Soppem Smith.

"That will be my affair," returned Jack. "Now hurry up, and let me know what the fellows think o. it."

Smith hastened away, and was seen moving around pretty briskly. Judging by the demeanour of the boys, the idea, in the expressive language of modern times, seemed to "catch on."

"Isn't a petition harking back a little?" said Tom Drummond.

"It looks so," replied Jack; "but there is one thing it will certainly do."

"What is that?" asked Don."

"Make the whole school a party to the—the—you know?"

"I see the move," said Tom, enthusiastically. "As heretofore, and ever will be, you are right, old man."

"There will be a blazing scene over the petition," said Jack, "and the floor of the schoolroom watered with the tears of the sufferers."

"Some of them, Jack."

"Some of them, then. I don't suppose we shall all howl, but there must be allowance made for the younger kiddies. Snicker will go right off his head. So much the worse for him, so much the better for us."

"To an extent, I suppose," said Don.

"Right up to the hilt," continued Jack. "What could be more in correct sequence to a scene of hitherto unrivalled—unrivalled—"

"Whoppings," suggested Tom.

"Yes, whoppings," said Jack, "to be followed by the event. We shall scoop the lot into the boat with us. And, once in, they can't go back."

"Suppose they won't join?" hinted Short.

"Didn't I say they were to be scooped in?" returned Jack. "Leave all to me. Here comes Smith, and if a face is anything to read, the petition is agreed to."

It was so. With one exception—Barnes—all were in favour of it."

"But Barnes doesn't count, anyway," said Soppem Smith, "and he *has* to come in. Some of the fellows say that, if it doesn't do anything else, it will upset Snicker's liver, and make him bilious for a week."

"That is one way to look at it," said Jack. "I am of opinion it will upset him longer than that. He won't get over it for a month."

Jack left the playground, and spent the next half-hour in preparing and writing out a petition that was to play an important part in consolidating the whole school for the impending rebellion.

He was a good hand at the work, and towards the latter portion of the time he gave to it he had the assistance of that master " of the soap trade," as he had been called more than once—Bob Stockton.

It is worthy of being set down here verbatim.

To Fontenoy Snicker, Esq,
Head Master of Littlecote College.

We, the undersigned pupils of the above-named college, respectfully appeal to you, as the founder and ruler of this establishment, to read the following list of our grievances, and consider the necessity of removing the same, so that the harmony and good feeling which should exist in a college of the high standing of Littlecote may prevail :—

1. The quality and quantity of the food provided for our consumption.

2. The amount of corporal punishment inflicted upon us on every possible occasion, too often of great severity ; and we respectfully ask that it may be reduced to infinitesimal proportions, or abandoned altogether.

3. The irregular way in which we receive our holidays, the usual plan at other colleges being to give half-a-day on Wednesday and Saturday, or a whole day on Saturday, whereas, we sometimes get a half-holiday at these times, and sometimes do *not*. We never know exactly whether we are to remain in, or go out to seek the change which is so beneficial to us all, and our health is thereby endangered.

4. The hour for retiring to bed is too early. We ought to have another half-hour to sit up and spend the same in reasonable recreation.

5. Games that are popular among boys are not sufficiently encouraged in the college. We have no cricket or football club, and there is no gymnasium to assist in developing our muscles.

Lastly. The washing arrangements are very poor. We want at least three times the number of towels, and something better than a horse-trough to wash in. A few cheap washstands placed in the dormitory, or in the corridor outside, would supply the deficiency. It would also be more convenient for the pupils. Having to go downstairs to wash is trying to them, especially in the cold of winter.

Trusting you will receive our petition in a kindly spirit, and soon make the changes we venture to suggest,
We remain,
Your Anxiously Awaiting Pupils.

The signatures were to follow in due course, and Jack Ford and Bob Stockton set theirs down at the head.

It will be seen at a glance that, though apparently a most polite and humble petition, it was of a nature to excite a man of Fontenoy Snicker's disposition to a pitch of frenzy bordering on madness.

This, we may as well admit, was the deliberate design of the two composers of it. They wanted a scene that would justify, apart from all else that had gone before, the desperate step they were about to take.

"It will make him *boil*," said Bob, gleefully. "Jack, we shall be like a flock of the sons of Lazarus, covered all over with sores."

CHAPTER XXVIII.

PRESENTATION OF THE PETITION.

AS Jack Ford, and Bob Stockton had signed the petition, there was no holding back for the rest. They had to follow suit, and they did so, although more than a third of their numbers were in fear and trepidation.

"We shall be all-alive-o'" said Gyp Tanner. "What an afternoon it will be. I wish I had a yard or two of cotton-wool to tuck in somewhere as padding."

But as there was no cotton-wool obtainable, he found the best substitute he could in the form of two or three old dusters lying in the drawer of the hall table, and concealed them under his clothing in places where the cane was most likely to be applied.

Armed thus, he was prepared for the coming lively time, and felt more at ease than many of his companions.

Jack folded the petition neatly, and endorsed it : " Petition from the pupils of Littlecote to their head master, Fontenoy Snicker, Esq.," so that it had quite an official appearance.

With it in the inside pocket of his coat, he took his seat in the schoolroom, and calmly watched for an opportunity to present it at headquarters.

Nothing had been seen of Copps since the morning. He was, in fact, away from the school, as we shall explain anon. Snicker, when the time came, would have a clear field, and no one to interrupt the course of Littlecote justice.

There was a hush upon the room.

The boys endeavoured to fix their attention on their lessons, with but indifferent results. Not a whisper was heard and the usual hum of the studious, permissible at times, was markedly absent.

So still was the room that Fontenoy Snicker observed it, and his mind was soon busy endeavouring to get at the reason for this unwonted state of things.

He, like the undermasters, always associated ultra good behaviour with the hatching of something forbidden.

When he desired to see anything with extra clearness he dropped his eyeglass, as that aristocratic article was to him more ornamental than useful. Releasing it from his eye, he took a long and steady look round the room.

The anxiety on the face of the majority of the boys could not escape him, and, with a frown upon his beetling brows, he muttered :

" The little fiends have done something, or are going

to do it. They had better not let me find them out this afternoon."

Taking the cane from the corner behind him, he smote the desk with it, and called "First class, jogra—*ge-o*-graphy."

Accustomed as they were to his verbal corrections of himself, there was, nevertheless, a slight titter which he failed to locate. At the same time he understood what it meant.

"Silence!" he roared.

The first class left their seats, and ranged themselves before him.

Jack pondered a moment, and then his mind was made up.

The iron was hot—uncommonly hot—and now was the time to strike.

"Pardon me, sir," he said, advancing a step, "but before we are examined will you kindly read this paper?"

As he spoke, without the scintilla of a tremor in his voice, he laid the petition upon the master's desk, and resumed his place in the class.

The excitement among the boys was now intense.

Those who were standing up felt a slight sinking sensation about the knees, and those still seated held on to the forms and desks to ease the palpitation of their hearts. Fontenoy Snicker was taken aback for the moment, but after a curiously wild stare at the petition, he opened it and began to read.

He got through it the first time like a man who has been hit on the head with a brick. Then, without removing his eyes from it, he started afresh and went over it again.

His mind cleared as he went along, and the height, and breadth, and depth of that document became apparent to him.

He did not say anything for a full minute afterwards, but spent the time in smoothing the paper out upon his desk, snarling with his upper lip, as angry collie dogs often do before they bite.

Then he took up the cane and descended from his perch.

The first class stood firm, prepared for the worst.

Penny Bunn, with his elbow resting on his desk, and his hands clasped before him, sat white and still. He had seen Snicker in his wrath, many times, and trembled, but never before like this. Awful Rooker shook as the aspen-leaves quiver in the evening breeze.

"So," said the schoolmaster, in a voice husky with passion, "your wittles—*rittels*—isn't good enough for you. I'll answer that ere part of the per—*pe*—tition first."

He raised the cane and went to work. One cut, and a most unmerciful one, for every boy in the school.

In his blind rage he favoured Awful Rooker with

one as he passed him, and made that notable assistant master twist like an eel.

The school, filled with wriggling boys, had the appearance of a cauldron seething with boiling humanity.

"Answer number one," said Snicker as, having paused a moment for breath, he resumed his congenial labours.

"The amount of punishment is too much, is it?" he said. "In my opinion, I've been too heasy—*easy*—jigger it—with you. Had I used the cane as I ought to have done, that petition wouldn't have been written. You darsn't have done it. Accordingly I now make up for lost time."

He made another round of the school, giving to each of the sufferers *two* cuts. Rooker got under the desk, and on being asked by the savage Snicker what he was doing there, explained that he was looking for a piece of pencil he had dropped.

"Come out," said Snicker, aiming a futile blow at him. Rooker came out as soon as it was safe to do so, and, shivering, awaited further proceedings.

Penny Bunn was getting into a petrified condition. He was wondering how many clauses there were in that petition, and whether Snicker would have to give in from exhaustion, or end in flaying half-a-dozen boys.

"You don't get your holidays regular, don't you?" continued Snicker. "Well, the regular ones in future will *be none at all.* D'ye hear, you infer—you impudent young beggars? *None at all!* And to impress that fact on your minds, I'll make another notch on every one of you."

This he did by giving them *four* cuts apiece. He was multiplying them like the nails in the horse-shoe of the famous sum, once so well known in schools.

Having done that, he walked out of the room and left them for awhile, but not for good, as the wiser among them knew.

"He's gone for a liquor up," said Bob Stockton, bitterly; "the worst is to come."

So apparent was this that a sort of numbness came over some of the sufferers. They were getting into the state of the martyrs of old, who, after a course of torture, without a doubt became insensible to further pain.

There was scarcely a movement in the room until Penny Bunn was heard to speak.

"Boys," he said, "you have done a wrong thing. How could you do it?"

"Wasn't there sufficient cause for the petition?" demanded Jack Ford. "Isn't this the most beggarly swindling school under the sun? Are you a man to put up with his nonsense as you do? We do not want your interference, Mr Bunn, thank you. We perfectly understand the game you have played."

Before Penny Bunn could make any retort to this

very plain speaking Fontenoy Snicker returned, refreshed by one of his favourite potations.

"We will now resume our examination of this charming petition," he said. "Fourthly, it appears you go to bed too early. As in the case of the holiday, you have got hold of the wrong end of the stick. You sit up too late. That is what I've allowed you in the kindness of my art—*heart* to do. From to-night you will go to bed directly after evening studies *without your suppers*. It will be a saving of health to you, and a saving of my pocket also. And you want to develop your muscles, I see. I'll develop 'em, hang the lot of you! I'll harden 'em!"

Which he proceeded to do with another doubling of the blows.

Some of the younger boys, notably Barnes, implored him to have mercy upon them, but they might as well have appealed to an Indian on the warpath. He spared none.

He read the last clause in the petition huskily, for, in spite of the "stimulator" he had indulged in, he was getting played out. But for all that he could still strike hard, and he went here and there hitting the boys anywhere and everywhere as they skipped about the room until the place was like a small Pandemonium.

But it came to an end at last, and, with a livid face, Fontenoy Snicker stopped near the door. He was in need of another refresher.

"I am going out for a few moments," he said. "*Be dumb* while I am gone, will you?"

He went out and the boys of the first class having resumed their seats, Tom Drummond, in a whisper, asked what was to be done.

"Nothing!" muttered Jack. "Sham being cowed. Snivel if you like. *Deceive* him until to-morrow. He will get a shock then that will wake him up."

"Jack's right," said Don, who was smarting horribly, but refused to show that he felt it. "I should say that *all* are ripe now for anything."

"*Anything*," assented Jack.

So the word was passed round for the band to play the part of cowed boys, and when Snicker returned he found them all either in tears, or rubbing the spots so lately afflicted with the cane.

"I've settled 'em," he muttered, exultingly. "There won't be any more nonsense for a day or two."

He said as much to Penny Bunn later on when the afternoon studies were over, and the boys had gone into the playground, but the undermaster was not quite so sanguine.

"In my opinion, sir," he said, "they will forget it to-morrow, and go on as bad as ever."

"Not they," answered Snicker. "I've broken 'em. You see if I haven't. Come into this room and have a look at 'em in the ground."

He opened the door of a room in the hall, and they entered it. There was a window commanding a view of the playground and the boys therein.

No play was going on. They were sauntering about in twos and threes, or standing disconsolately about, some—and they were of the number one dormitory for the most part—exhibiting their weals and bruises to a sympathetic audience. The whole of them looked like lambs indeed.

"Now then," said Fontenoy Snicker, "what d'ye think of 'em?"

"They're quiet enough now," replied Penny Bunn, "but—well, sir, you ought to know best. We shall see how they behave to-morrow."

"I'll be at 'em again if need be," said Snicker. "Where's that Copps?"

"He has been out since just before dinner, sir."

"That's a dinner saved," answered the schoolmaster, "but, for all that, I'm not going to pay a man——"

He stopped short on seeing a look of surprise on the face of his assistant.

"I forgot," he said; "you don't know who Copps is. Can I trust you not to blow on me?"

"You can, sir," replied Penny Bunn, fervently. "In your interest I can be dumb."

"In your own interest, you mean," snarled Snicker. "Well, then, Copps is a private detective."

"Bless me, sir! You don't say so?"

"But I do say so, don't I, you fool! He is a detective brought here to find out who has been robbing me, and he says he has as good as done it."

"I hope he has, sir," said Penny Bunn, "but I—I —pardon me, sir—do not think that he looks much like a policeman."

"If he did," said Snicker, "would he be fit for a detective?"

"I suppose not, sir," answered Penny Bunn.

CHAPTER XXIX.

THE NIGHT BEFORE THE STORM.

AT half-past seven o'clock the boys were sent supperless to bed, and they retired without any signs of rebellion.

In number one dormitory there was some whispering, but nothing more till midnight, when Jack and all the members of the inner circle got up and dressed.

The moon was shining brightly, giving sufficient light for what they had to do.

"The first thing to be done," said Jack, "is to fasten up the door of Copps's room. I have a bit of rope here that will do the trick."

He suggested that he should go down first and perform this task alone.

"There is a nail handy in the wall outside," he said. "I spotted it this evening, and that, with the handle of the door, will serve as the other thing to tie it to."

He was absent from the room only a few minutes. On his return he had a startling piece of news for them.

"The man is not in his room," he said: "his bed hasn't been disturbed."

"Perhaps he is in the schoolroom," suggested Donald.

"No," rejoined Jack; "I have been there. The fact is he hasn't come back since he went out in the morning. It is all right for us."

They spoke of necessity in a low tone, and walking in their stockinged feet, they crept down the stairs. Jack slipped away to get the clothes-line, for he was expecting Professor Lingo to bring a parcel of good things to the foot of the cliff, and they would have to haul it in by way of the window.

Owing to the night being remarkably clear, and the moon shining straight into the schoolroom windows, it was, as the saying goes, almost as bright as day.

As soon as Jack arrived with the rope it was lowered, and in a few moments there was a jerk from the other end.

"Hurrah," said Jack, in a whisper, "the Professor hasn't failed us. Don, can you see to take the screws out of the door?"

"See them?" said Don; "rather."

"Then go to work, old man."

Don knew where to find the screw-driver, and he was soon busy. Meanwhile, the rest, after waiting a little time, received a signal from below, and hauled in the rope.

Attached to the end of it was a box, which they succeeded in pulling in, but it was still work.

Removing the cord around it, they discovered that the lid was not nailed, and on opening it a number of small packets were disclosed.

"We won't stop to examine them now," said Tom Drummond. "How are you getting on with that door, Don?"

"All the screws out but two."

"There is something more to come, I suppose, Jack?" said Tom.

"I should think so," replied Jack. "I wrote for Lingo to bring us all he could in the way of eatables. I left the choice to him. He knows what we are likely to want. Stop a minute. I will communicate with him by telephone."

The toy apparatus was hidden under Fontenoy Snicker's desk—oh! if he had only known it, what a lot of bother he would have escaped—and Jack, fishing it out, prepared to communicate with Lingo below.

He threw out the lower speaking cup, as it may be termed, and gradually lowered it. The watchful Professor below soon espied it, and got it in his grasp.

"What do you want?" he asked.

"Anything more to come up?" inquired Jack.

"What do you think? How long do you imagine you could live on that handful?"

"Send down the box," said Jack to his friends, "and don't let it bumble against the cliff more than you can help."

The box was lowered, and while it was being filled, the things already arrived were stored in the inner rooms, Don having got the door open by that time.

About five minutes elapsed, Jack keeping his ear at the telephone, and then came the signal:

"All ready. Haul away."

The box was hauled up for the second time, and returned again. In this way it performed four journeys, and then everything, including some stout pieces of planking and a box of tools, had been safely landed.

"Screw up the door," said Jack, "while I have a word with Lingo. Below there!"

"Here, my lad," was the response.

"Awfully kind of you to do so much for us."

"If you say another word about that, I'll punch your head by telephone."

"All right. Won't offend again. You are a good fellow, and we can never repay you. Can you be here to-morrow night?"

"Certainly. Are you going to make a move?"

"We bar out in the morning."

"What time?"

"Immediately after breakfast."

"I suppose you know you have had a 'tec in the house?" whispered Lingo.

"Copps, you mean?" returned Jack.

"Yes," answered the Professor; "you need not worry about him. I have him all safe. What time can he safely come back to-morrow?"

"Any time after nine," replied the wondering Jack; "but what have you done with him?"

"He followed the boy you sent with the letter, and thought he had got hold of something, I suppose. I saw he was on the pry, especially when he come the parson with *me*. It wouldn't do—I know the real breed too well. He wasn't half stuck up enough."

"What did he want to know?" asked Jack.

"Nothing," replied Lingo, "not openly, anyway. But he has got hold of something. Whatever it is I am sure he is on the wrong tack."

"Where is he now?" asked Jack.

"Excuse me if I don't tell you," answered the Professor; "to-morrow night at twelve."

"Yes. But it is a shame to trouble you."

"It's a pleasure, my dear boy. I am on this job, I can tell you. It is the best bit of fun I have been mixed up with for many a day. Are you all staunch?"

"I think all are ripe for anything," said Jack, "but

it is too long a story to whisper through the telephone. Bring us a strong, knotted rope if you can."

"Right you are. I meant to have done it before. I'll send Copps home to-morrow about ten. Bye-bye, dear boy."

"Good night," responded Jack.

The clothes-line was hauled in and wound up in the usual fashion. Meanwhile the door had been screwed up again, and Don and the others wanted to know what the Professor had been telling Jack.

They could hear what their chum said, but without the intervening matter it was all Dutch to them. Jack imparted the necessary information.

"He's been too much for Copps," said Bob Stockton, "that's certain."

"And by keeping him away until ten o'clock the thing can be done," remarked Jack Ford, serenely. "Now for a few final instructions to you fellows."

They gathered closer to him, sitting in the moonlight, that shone through the window, a somewhat weird but interesting group.

"In the outset," said Jack, "*every* boy of the school must be in here at a quarter to nine o'clock."

"Before school time," said Tom Drummond; "but how are we to get the number two fellows here?"

"If it is wet," suggested Don, "they are sure to be here."

"I want a fine morning," continued Jack, "or they will be all crowding in here directly after breakfast, and that won't do. Now, my plan is this. The band to assemble here as secretly as possible soon after we have partaken of the luxurious morning meal that beastly Snicker provides for us. Then we make our preparations for a smart closing up and securing of the schoolroom door."

"We must be smart," said Don.

"If Snicker gets the alarm, we cannot do it," said Jack. "Now as to the way we shall have to deal with the fellows of number two. We must send them a sham message that they are wanted in the schoolroom, presumably by Snicker."

"And suppose they won't bite?" suggested Tom.

"They will rise to a call from Snicker like minnows at a red-worm," replied Jack. "Gyp Tanner will do for that. They won't suspect him of a joke, because he is of a size Soppem Smith and Hone can lick. Don and Tom, I leave the fastening of the door to you. I shall be busy in quelling the excitement of the outsiders. I see that the Professor, who is, I fancy, up to every move, has had the planks cut on the slant for us, which makes the nailing down easy and the holding firm. We must have three fixed. One just over the lock, a second by the hinges, and the third in the centre. Nothing less than a battering ram or some explosive will then break down the door. As for

getting in anywhere else, I consider it impossible Look at the cliff. Who is going to scale that? Not Snicker, or Penny, or Rooker. As for outsiders, unless Copps comes in, I do not fear their being employed."

"But there is one thing you have forgotten, Jack," said Tom Drummond.

"Well, what is it?" calmly asked the leader of the rebellious movement.

"How are we to communicate with Snicker as to terms of capitulation?"

"There the petition comes in," remarked Don—"at least, I think so."

"You are right, dear boy," said Jack, "it *does* come in. I shall simply write a line or two to this effect: 'Snicker, when you feel you can assent to our petition, let us know, and we will open the door, *but* not before, if we starve to death.'"

"And the answer—how are we to get that?" asked Don.

"Oh, we will do the thing regular. Wait a bit, as I, of course, do not pretend to have got every detail ready. Don't forget that we have been rushed at the last."

"I say," said Bob Stockton, "what about a rebellion inside the barring out? Suppose Hone and that lot won't remain with us?"

"Wait until to-morrow," was Jack's reply.

They sat talking a little while longer over the various details, and then, finding it getting rather chilly, returned to the dormitory.

"How do you feel?" asked Bob Stockton, as he got into bed—"I mean in the general way. I've got a sensation that I'm going to be in the rush of a forlorn hope in the morning."

"We must all feel a bit that way," said Jack. "It is all darned rot for a man or boy to say that they never feel fear. The secret of brave men is *that they don't show it*, but just make up their minds to go in and win. That's how I feel to-night. I know we are about to risk a pile, but I would rather die a dozen times than go back."

"And so say all of us," hummed Don. "I wonder what my pacific governor and my anxious mother would think if they knew all?"

"None the less of you for standing up against a tyrant," remarked Jack. "Go to sleep, boys.

> " 'There's a good time coming, now,
>   For which we wait no longer,
> To-morrow Snicker's up a tree,
>   And we little kids the stronger.'

Good night, my brethren."

"Good night," they responded, and in five minutes had forgotten everything in sleep.

CHAPTER XXX.

THE MONSOON BURSTS.

"MRS. SNICKER," said Fontenoy to his wife, as he scraped his chin with a razor, "I have got them there boys under complete control at last."

"It is time you did," replied Mrs. Snicker, as she opened the door to go downstairs, "but I will believe it when I see it."

"Women always were skepters," said Fontenoy Snicker, with a growl.

"You mean sceptics, of course," coolly suggested Mrs. Snicker, "but skepters is near enough for a schoolmaster. Oh, Jerry, why didn't you take to the greengrocery line, as I wanted you to do? We might then have been prosperous and happy, and not as we are now, both walking shams."

"I've a soul above weighing out pounds of taters," said the schoolmaster.

"*Taters!*" repeated Mrs. Snicker, with infinite scorn. "Will you never remember the *per*?"

Snicker, in a fury, worked the razor a bit too vigorously, and made an incision in his chin.

"Look, now, what you have done with your nasty insinivations," he howled. "Look at it, I say."

"I am looking at it," she answered, "and the only thing I see to object to is that it is not in the right place, and as a cut, not deep enough."

Then she vanished, and left him to work out the meaning of her retort.

The boys were at breakfast when this little connubial scene was being enacted. Penny Bunn and Awful Rooker were in their accustomed places. The silence in the room was very marked.

Penny Bunn no longer played up to his *rôle* of being one of the boys. On the previous day he had, to a great extent, been disillusioned as to the success of his performance. He sat quietly watching the boys, whom he could not at all understand.

"They seem as if they were waiting for an explosion," he thought; "it would not surprise me if they blew up the whole place with dynamite."

He was also troubled about the absence of Copps, who had not been seen at the Abbey since the previous morning.

Penny Bunn strongly suspected that the detective, having to an extent exhibited sympathy with the boys, had gone to lay information against the establishment.

The under-master was not concerned for Snicker's sake. As an especially agreeable morning entertainment, he would have joyously gone to see his principal hanged. The thing that worried him was, "How far would he be implicated in case of a row?"

After breakfast the boys dispersed quietly, and for the most part hastened to the playground.

There were exceptions to the rule, however, in the persons of Jack and Tom Drummond.

These two, as the leaders of the great movement, lingered behind for a moment or two, and then hastened to the schoolroom.

"Out with the screw-driver," said Jack, with his face aglow; "the hour has come. We strike for freedom, and we win or die."

"Or get a jolly good licking," said Tom, coolly, as he dived under the nearest desk as a short cut to where the screw-driver was hidden.

He soon got it out, and went to work on the old door. Jack, meanwhile, kept watch, with Fontenoy's own ruler in his hand, ready to strike down a pertinacious intruder.

Presently a footstep was heard, but Jack recognized it, and made no sign. Bob Stockton appeared, and hailed his leader.

"How goes it?" he asked.

"Why, well, comrade," was the answer.

He motioned for Bob to go to the assistance of Tom Drummond, and immediately after another footstep was heard.

It was Don, who, aglow with excitement, came hurrying along the passage.

"Have I been in too much of a hurry?" he asked.

"No," answered Jack, "the sooner you are all in, the better."

"Have you given your message to Gyp?"

"What do you think? Everything is arranged up to the time of closing the door. Tom, don't you bring out anything but the planks at present; and the nails and hammers, of course."

"Will you want the mallet?" asked Tom.

"Certainly, to drive the barricades home."

And now the members of the band came hurrying into the schoolroom until they were all there but Gyp Tanner.

"Be quiet for a few moments now," said Jack to his excited followers, some of whom were rather white about the cheeks. "I won't be long."

Jack hurried out and soon came to the door of the private room of Mr. Snicker. Listening a moment, he could hear the schoolmaster wrangling with his wife, and, with a smile of satisfaction, he hastened to the hall.

He had the letter for the unsuspecting Snicker ready for him, and he laid it in a conspicuous part of the table there, and then ran to the door used by the boys to go in and out of the house.

Gyp Tanner was waiting for him there.

"Now run the others in," said Jack. "Remember, Snicker wants them very particular, and they are to come at once."

"All right," said Gyp, and Jack returned to the schoolroom.

"Put those bits of timber and tools behind the door," he said to Tom, who, with Don, stood ready to go to work, "and some of you stand so as to hide them as Soppem's lot comes in."

This was done with feverish haste, and as soon as the planks, stout and strong, had been hidden, there was a rush of feet, and the rest of the boys came hurrying into the room.

Soppem Smith looked about him, and, not seeing the schoolmaster, shouted out: "A sell of the number ones."

"Nothing of the sort," cried Jack; "are you all here?"

He had been counting them, and was hardly in need of the responding "yes."

"Close the door," he fairly yelled.

Tom and Don dashed it to; Bob Stockton whipped up one of the stout planks which had so judiciously been cut on the slant.

Immediately the rest of the band, acting on instructions they had received from their leader, formed across the room and pressed the boys of the other dormitory back.

"What's the game here?" cried Roger Hone, trying to break through.

"Stand still if you don't want your head punched," answered Jack. "I'll explain everything in a moment."

Soppem Smith jumped upon one of the desks, and stared at what was going on at the door, where Don and Tom were engaged in nailing down the first part of the barricade.

"Number twos," he screamed, "it's a *barring out* they've planned."

"Never mind what it is," shouted Jack, his voice rising above the turmoil these words created, "don't any of you interfere. You are all in it whether you like it or not. Stop that row and hear what I have to say."

"Three cheers for Jack Ford," roared Warner.

They were given by the whole of the members of the band, a considerable portion of the suddenly enlightened number twos joining in.

Soppem Smith and Roger Hone stared at each other aghast.

Of all they had ever conceived, nothing one-tenth so daring as this had entered their heads.

A *barring out*!

It was like renewing the warfare of the mediæval age. It was equivalent, in their eyes, to a general civil war in the land.

The band stood firm, ready to resent any interference with their proceedings, and Don and Tom, with a few lusty blows, drove home a nail and secured the door.

The first holding plank was in its place over the lock, and no mortal man, without the aid of some more powerful means than natural muscle, could force a way in.

"That will do for the time," said Jack, who was keeping one eye on the work; "now all of you be silent there and listen to me."

They could hear his ringing voice above the din, and in a short space of time silence was obtained.

Jack walked over to the desk that was the rostrum of Fontenoy Snicker, and mounting into it, stood there a moment, with the light of triumphant success upon his face.

"Chums all," he began, "there are many here whom I need not tell that this move has been long conceived to bring the most ignorant and brutal schoolmaster in the British Islands to his senses. To others it is a startling revelation. To the latter I am now going to especially speak. First, is there one here who has a good word to say for Snicker?"

There was no reply for a moment, and then the voice of Barnes was heard.

"Oh, please let me out," he said; "we shall all be murdered for this."

"Better be that than go on with things as they were," answered Jack, "but don't you be afraid, old man. We have got Snicker on the hop. He will get such a turning over to-day as he never had before. Here we are, and here we remain until he undertakes to treat us as if we were flesh and blood, and not wooden images to be beaten and bawled at just as he chooses. Soppem Smith, you and I have not been very close friends, but we ought to work with each other now. Say out right away what will you do. Will you stand the racket of this business, or do you funk it?"

"I hardly know what to say," replied Smith, "it has come so suddenly on us. Why did you not give us the tip?"

"There were enough in it as things were," replied Jack. "Hone, which way are you going?"

"I'm with you," answered Hone, "but it is a desperate thing to do. How are we to keep out Snicker? When he gets in he will beat us to a jelly."

"It will take all his time to force that door, even as it is," said Jack, "and we are going to make it stronger yet. He can't get in."

"But he can get help," said Soppem Smith, dubiously.

"I tell you, as I have told my chums, the brave lads who have worked with me throughout, that he *dare not* He has to draw us alone, and if we are united, he has a whole family of badgers to get at. He is a poor dog, anyway."

"He will starve us out," said Smith.

The old door, so long closed, was now, by Jack's command, thrown open. Don did this, disclosing the heaped up things which had been accumulated there. The sight of them was as much a surprise to the greater part of his followers as to the complete novices.

"In those rooms," continued Jack, "we have food and drink and bedding. I have to apologise to some of my band for keeping a portion of my movements a secret. But I know they will forgive me, as they are aware that I never do a thing without there is a reason for it. When what is in there in the way of grub is exhausted, we can have a further supply, as you will soon learn, without so much as going out of the rooms. In my opinion, we shall not be here more than a day or two. But should it be necessary, I will undertake that those who desire it shall have an *occasional* outing. Now have a look in yonder, all of you, and make as little noise as possible, for school-time is at hand, and we shall soon have somebody knocking at the door."

There was a veritable stampede to the inner rooms, to see that which had so long been hidden from their eyes, and the amazement of all but those who had previously visited them was complete.

The name of Jack Ford, coupled with those who had worked with him to attain their object, was enthusiastically on the lips of the number twos to a boy, and the barring out was an accomplished fact.

"We'll stand to it," said Soppem Smith, addressing his followers, "and obey Jack Ford as soldiers obey their general. This is about the jolliest thing going."

And none dissented, unless Barnes is to be taken into account.

The poor nerveless lad, none the better for the ill-usage he had been subjected to at the hands of Snicker, had not a word to say.

All he did was to sit down by the edge of the well and shed a few silent tears. He almost, but not quite wished he were at the bottom of it.

CHAPTER XXXI.

TURMOIL IN THE HOUSE OF SNICKER.

THE rioting in the schoolroom was heard about the house, and it penetrated to the room where the schoolmaster was finishing his breakfast; but he did not consider it to be anything out of the common.

"That there idiot, Bunn," he said, "isn't looking after my precious lambs, as usual. I'll give him a bit of my mind, by-and-bye. Isn't he aweer—*aware* that a man disturbed while eating his meals is likely to get indigestion?"

"I have no doubt about it," replied Mrs. Snicker, "but he doesn't bother. The man knows that whatever happens he is safe in his situation."

"How safe?"

"You dare not discharge him."

"Dare not, Mrs. Snicker?"

"No, Jerry, you dare not. How are you to get another at the price, and what man of education would be made a tool of by an ignoramus like you?"

"You seem to have got into a way of speaking to your husband, Mrs. Snicker, in a most unbecoming style."

"I'm speaking the truth and nothing else, Jerry."

"I wish," said the schoolmaster, "that you wouldn't 'Jerry' me. Not even in private. You will be doing of it in public one of these days. Jerry is dead, but Fontenoy is alive and kicking."

"Ring the bell," said Mrs. Snicker, curtly, "and ask that Bunn fellow to look to the boys, they're hammering the walls down, I should think."

The schoolmaster rang the bell with a jerk, and Black-Eyed Susan promptly appeared. The girl seemed to be in a rather excited frame of mind.

"Find Mr. Bunn," said Snicker, "and tell him I want him."

"He's a-trying to get into the school-room, and can't do it, sir," answered Black-Eyed Susan.

Mr. Fontenoy Snicker opened his eyes until they had reached their utmost dimensions, which was not anything to brag about. Mrs. Snicker calmly poured herself out another cup of tea. She was not at any time surprised by the doings of the boys.

"Can't get in!" exclaimed Snicker; "why not?"

"The young gentlemen won't open the door," replied the girl.

"I'll open it for them!" snarled the schoolmaster.

He made for the door, and as he was going out, after Black-Eyed Susan had hastily retreated, Mrs. Snicker shrilly called after him:

"Do consider your digestion, Jerry."

He muttered an uncommonly naughty word, which made his ungracious spouse chuckle, and, half-mad with wrath, dashed on for the schoolroom.

It was dark by the door, and before he well knew he was there, he had collided with Penny Bunn, who was making an effort to get a view of the room through the key-hole.

In this he was foiled by somebody inside, who was now engaged in stuffing it up with paper.

The boys were all as quiet as sheep in the early morning just before sunrise. As far as they were concerned, that room might as well have been empty.

"Bunn, you ass," said the schoolmaster, "what are you doing there?"

"I am trying to make out what the boys are up to," replied Penny Bunn, "and, with all respect and politeness, I beg to say I am no more an ass than you are. Possibly not so much of a one."

A SPLENDID SCHOOL STORY. NEVER BEFORE PUBLISHED.

By E. HARCOURT BURRAGE,

Author of "Ching Ching," "Monkey Nat and Roving Dick," "The Brave Boy of the Basilisk," &c.

THE LAMBS OF LITTLECOTE.

A Handsome Coloured Plate Presented with Every Number.

No. 5.

DISCOVERY OF THE TREASURE IN THE VAULTS OF THE OLD ABBEY.

PRICE ONE PENNY

"They are quiet enough now," said Snicker. "Go in."

"Try the door yourself, sir," replied Bunn; "it is as fast as a rock."

Mr. Fontenoy Snicker tried it in various ways without succeeding in opening it.

He turned the handle this way and that, pushed and pulled, but it did not budge the tenth of an inch.

"It's very odd," he said.

"Try higher up, old man," said somebody in the room: "roity-toity."

It was a derisive squeak of the Punch pattern that followed this piece of advice, and it would have exasperated a better-tempered man than Snicker.

"Open the door!" he roared; "I'll flay you for this."

"You have not so completely subdued them as you thought you had, sir," mildly hinted Penny Bunn.

"Get out of the way, you fool!" said Snicker, roughly pushing the under-master.

"Get out of the way yourself," retorted Penny Burn, elbowing him back again. "This is a land of liberty — for men, anyway. Go and knock Mrs. Snicker about, and see what comes of it."

"Bunn," said the schoolmaster, adopting a milder tone, "can you give me an idea what they are up to?"

"I cannot, sir," stiffly replied Penny Bunn. "The door is fast, and that is all I know."

"Mr. Snicker," cried a voice from the room. It was not the one that had been derisively exercised in an imitation of Punch.

"Who is that?" demanded Mr. Snicker.

"Ford, sir."

"Well, Ford, perhaps you will be good enough to open the door."

"Not yet, sir. It will be done only on conditions."

"On—on—your grandmother's tabby Tom-cat!" cried the schoolmaster, suddenly losing his head, "Open, I say, at once, or I will murder you!"

"You will find the conditions written in a letter left for you upon the hall table," cried Jack. He had to raise his voice to make himself heard, but he was apparently quite calm. "The door will not be opened until you have read them and acceded to our wishes."

"Quite subdued—thoroughly broken in," murmured Penny Bunn.

"Look here," said Snicker, cutting an uncouth caper in his rage, "if you give me one ounce more of your cheek, I'll knock you down and jump upon you, and take the consequences."

He strode off to the hall, Penny Bunn shuffling at his heels in a state of unqualified but hidden delight.

Much as he had suffered at the hands of the boys, he had always temporarily forgiven them when they played something extra good on Snicker.

The letter was in the hall, and the schoolmaster tore it open and read it. We give it as Jack wrote it:

"DEAR SIR.—As our petition was not acceded to, but met in a most abominably rough manner, we have been driven to adopt the expedient of a barring-out. If you do not know what it is, Mr. Bunn will probably be able to explain. Until you assent to all our demands *in writing*, the door of the schoolroom will remain *closed*.

"Yours very obediently,
"J. FORD."

"Read that, Bunn," said Fontenoy Snicker, in a helpless way, "and tell me what you think of it. It's a licker to me."

Penny Bunn's mind was now in the condition of a man who has recently figured in a prize-fight, and received an unusual number of fistic compliments about the head. He took the letter, stared very hard at it, and apparently read it, but all he did was to hand it back again, and gaze at his employer in a dumbfounded fashion.

"Well," said Fontenoy Snicker, "what's your opinion on it?"

"It's Ford's writing," vacantly answered Penny Bunn.

The schoolmaster cut a gouty kind of caper, and shook his fist at his assistant.

"Of course it is!" he roared; "but what do you think of it?"

"I think," answered Bunn, with a sudden lighting up of his face, "that they've closed up that door uncommonly tight, and it will take you all your time to get in."

"I shall be a-lossing—*losing*—of my temper in a minute," hissed Snicker, yellow with rage. "Can't you answer a straightforrard—"

"Forward," corrected Penny Bunn, with a simper.

"I shall be the death of you," muttered Fontenoy Snicker, looking about him for a weapon of some sort.

Happily there was nothing lighter than the hall table and the old grandfather's clock available for chastisement of the tutor, so he did nothing.

"What I want to know is—what's your hidear—idea—of the chances of them young beggars holding out? They can't live on hair—*air*—and they must have something to drink."

"I think," said Penny Bunn, feebly, "that they probably have food, for I detected Short yesterday in the act of pocketing a crust, and although Whymper left a piece of fat on his plate on Sunday, I have reason to believe that he surreptitiously afterwards acquired possession of it. There are indications of their having, in a measure, provisioned themselves."

Fontenoy Snicker stood for a full minute looking at the vacuous countenance of his under-master, evidently reduced to temporary helplessness by the exasperating nature of his conclusions. At length he found speech, and his words came forth from his lips like a fusillade of ginger-beer corks.

"A crust—" he said, "and—a—bit—of—fat—won't —keep thirty odd boys going, you—you— Here— don't stop anigh me, or there will be an inquest over you afore the week is out."

"Mind there is not one on yourself," returned Penny Bunn, with alarming ferocity—"mind there isn't one on your old woman—"

"My *what?*" gasped Snicker.

"Your old woman," repeated Bunn, "the wife of *Jerry* Snicker, Esquire. Ha, ha! And you be careful that there isn't also an inquest on *the whole of the boys*, for it is my opinion that they mean to *starve*, rather than put up with your little games any longer."

Fontenoy Snicker reeled under the blow of this suggestion.

An inquest on a lot of starved boys was an appalling picture to mentally contemplate.

He sank into a sitting position on the low hall table, and was still in a speechless condition, when the door opened, and Copps, the London detective, appeared.

CHAPTER XXXII.

COPPS TELLS A PITIFUL STORY OF MAN'S CUNNING AND DECEIT.

IT was evident at a glance that Copps had been having a rough time of it. He still wore his clerical garb, but it was in the condition which apparel gets into when a man has made a night of it, and slept anywhere but in his lawful bed.

There was a wildness in his eyes, and a pallor on his face, which had not been observed before. He stared hard at the tutor and schoolmaster for a moment, and then huskily asked:

"Has anything happened since I went away?"

"The boys have fastened theirselves up in the schoolroom," replied Fontenoy Snicker, in the tone of a man who announces that he has lost all that is worth living for, and is about to die, "and we can't get in."

"Did you ever hear of a barring-out?" asked Penny Bunn.

"Oh, lor!" gasped Copps. "What a fool I've been! I thought they were up to quite another game."

"How come you to think of anything at all?" demanded Snicker. "I didn't get you here to look after the boys."

"You duffer," said Copps, "they were the *burglars!* Somehow they got that door in the schoolroom open, and they've stored away food and cooking utensils, and bedding, and the Lord knows what besides.

They can live there for a couple of months. There is *jam* enough for a week."

"Jam, *my* jam!" screamed a feminine voice; "the little willains—"

"*Villains!*" groaned Fontenoy Snicker, from mere force of habit.

"Go and get it out at once!" cried Mrs. Snicker, appearing on the scene with the air of an avenging spirit from the shades below. "Don't stand there, you three, but have it out at once. Break the door down."

"Stop!" cried Fontenoy Snicker. "The outside panels of that ere door are covered with carving, which is valleyed—*ralued*—at two hundred pounds. We can't get in by violence that way. There's no hurry for an hour or two. Let us put our heads together."

"I should like to knock 'em together," muttered Mrs. Snicker; "you are a lot of softys to let a parcel of boys strip the house. Get my jam out at once. I *will* have it."

"Blow your jam!" snarled Snicker. "If there wasn't more than jam in it, I shouldn't care. But look here, Mr. Copps, how do you know they've collared these things?"

"Because I suspected they had opened the door, and the night before last I took out the screws myself, and saw what they had been doing."

"And you niver—dash it, *never*—said a word about it to *me?*"

"I thought the youngsters had stolen the things to sell," groaned Copps; "it was a natural thought for an officer of the force, and for a man in my line."

"Even then," grunted Snicker, "you needn't have been quite so close about it."

"I thought, as they were thieves," said Copps, with a savage jerk of his head, "that there was also a receiver. I wanted to find out who it was before I said a word, and have the whole thing in one penny number complete, as it were, ready for you."

"Unkimmon — *uncommon* — clever of you," said Snicker, with bitter emphasis; "but you've come a buster over it."

"Who wouldn't?" angrily demanded Copps. "Did you, with all your learning, guess at the game they were up to? I thought the boys had been tempted to rob you, and that there was a receiver, and so I watched 'em."

"And what come of that?"

"This, Mr. Snicker. Yesterday, while I was prowling round outside, I saw that young Ford come out of the playground and look about him as if he wanted to find somebody. A plough-boy comes along, and Ford gives him a letter."

"A dummy, to deceive you?"

"No, it wasn't, Knowall," said Copps. "It was

addressed to a cheap Jack in the village of Smudgem Bender, and his name is Lingo. I thought that I'd got my man, after I'd given the plough-boy a penny to let me look at the address, and I dropped into the village shortly before noon. My game was to make friends with the Professor."

"Which you didn't," said Penny Bunn.

"You can keep quiet, if nobody else does," said Copps, fiercely. "The moment I saw the man I knew that my cleric get-up wouldn't take him in, so I got into his company at a public-house, and pretended to confide in him, saying I was roaming on the cross."

"You needn't have gone outside to be cross," said Mrs. Snicker. "A little more or less of ill-temper here wouldn't have hurt us."

"Travelling on the cross, madam," said Copps, with forced politeness, "is a professional term meaning that the party is on the look out for plunder, and not particular where he gets it. Apparently the Professor tumbled."

"Did you hit him?" asked Mrs. Snicker.

"Madam," said Copps, with the hair of his head bristling, "if I am to tell my story clearly, I cannot be pulled up every moment to explain my language to you. Ask your husband afterwards to enlighten you. He appears to me to be a man well acquainted with many things besides schoolkeeping."

"Never mind what I've been," said Snicker. "Let us hear how you got on with the Professor."

"Apparently, as I said, he tumbled," said Copps, with a startling wail. "I confided in him, and he confided in me. I asked him if he thought there was a chance of our getting anything out of the neighbourhood, and hinted that the Abbey would be a good place to work in, and he asked me how it was to be done. I suggested that the schoolboys might be asked to do something, and he as good as admitted that something was already done."

Copps stopped to wipe his brow. He had evidently a lot on his mind that was conducive to copious perspiration.

"Somehow I got all, as I thought, clear at last. I fancied I was working *him*, and all the time he was working *me*. He must have regularly scooped out what was in my head, for at last he tells me he is going that night to receive a consignment of goods from the Abbey, and he asks me to stay and help him ship it to the van. Like a fool I did it."

There was something quite plaintive in the agony of the overmatched private inquiry man. If he had not been reduced to a state of mental weakness, bordering on madness, he would never have made his revelation, as he did, so full and complete.

"I stayed in his company," continued Copps, "all the day and through the evening. At ten o'clock we started to receive that blooming blessed consignment of goods

from the Abbey. I had, of course, to be guided by him, and he led me out into the fields, saying that we had to get to the other side of this old place. On the way—we were in a meadow at the time—he stops and asks me to have a drink out of his flask. I did so in a friendly way, and the moment I had finished a stiffish pull I saw all the stars and creation generally waltzing around, and then of a sudden I went right off. There isn't a particle of doubt the beggar hocussed me, although he swears now that I was as tight as a fiddler before I started and the last drop finished me."

"As it did, and serve you right," said Mrs. Snicker. "Men can never walk a dozen yards without having a drink together."

Ignoring this interpolation of a highly feminine flavour, Copps went on with his story.

"I remember no more until I awoke early in the morning, and found myself in a dirty cowshed, out in yonder fields, handcuffed and chained by the leg to an ox-stall. I was in a perfectly helpless position, especially as there was no house near, and I might have hollered myself hoarse—which I did, and nearly blind, too—without making anybody hear. In that place I stopped until an hour ago, when that beggarly Professor came to set me free."

"And did he do it?" asked Snicker.

"He did."

"And what did you do when he had released you? Didn't you give him something for himself?"

"The Professor," said Copps, emphatically, "is a man to be approached with caution. If possible, he ought to be assailed in the rear—if at all—and then you must be mighty quick to catch him fairly on the hop."

"Then you did nothing?"

"I told him that I should take proceedings against him, and what do you think his answer was?"

"Goodness only knows. Something cheeky, I should imagine."

"He said I was so violently drunk that he was afraid I was going to commit suicide, and that he chained me up to prevent my doing an injury to myself. He then gave me a short lecture on the evils of drink, and insisted on my taking a tract, which he said an estimable old lady in the village had given him, and which, he was sure, would help to lead me back into the paths of honesty and virtue. It was all cheek, of course, and I nearly boiled over; but he is a stiff 'un to deal with, and, on the whole, it was just as well I came away quietly."

"And what do you make out of him?" asked Fontenoy Snicker. "Fooling about with the Professor couldn't help anyone?"

"Can't you see that he is in league with the boys?" groaned Copps, "and that he was mugging me all the time for their sakes? All round we've been taken in, and there's an end of it."

"There will be no end to it," said Mrs. Snicker, "until I get my jam."

"You may say good-bye to that," said Copps, turning himself, for the moment, into a Job's comforter. "I should think that by this time they've licked the very jam-pots clean."

"It's no use worrying over it," said Snicker; "let us have a quiet talk, we men, and see what is to be done. When I've explained to you, Copps, how I'm fettered by my lease, you will see that we have to rely on tragedy rather than force."

"You mean strategy," suggested Penny Bunn.

"I'll mean you a dazzling punch of the head," said Snicker, half beside himself, "if you cut in with your corrections. You keep that sort of thing for the school, and look after your work there."

"I will, sir," said Penny Bunn, briskly, "as soon as the ordinary duties are resumed."

This reply, intentionally of an irritating nature, caused Fontenoy Snicker to assume the appearance of a boiled-beef model of a man. He was like the rosy morn done up in a human parcel, and he felt that he would gladly have given ten years of his valuable life if he could have crumpled up Penny Bunn into the shape of a ball, and kicked him up to the moon.

But the joy of doing it, for more than one reason, was denied him, and, at a pace in harmony with his heated condition, he led the way to his room to hold a consultation on the parlous state of affairs.

CHAPTER XXXIII.

NO GOING BACK—IN FOR EVERYTHING NOW.

WHILE the discussion was going on outside the schoolroom door, there was no lack of movement within.

Having started the great barring out, the promoters of it were not going back, or even to think a bit.

As Napoleon, in the hour of his great victory over many nations, received some of his leading foes into his councils, so did Jack Ford invite Soppem Smith and Roger Hone to co-operate with him.

"We are all in it now," he said, after the colloquy with Fontenoy Snicker through the door, "and we have to stick to each other to gain the victory. Giving in won't help you any more than it will me. Fontenoy Snicker, with the upper hand over us now, would be a raging demon."

They were fair to admit as much, and both avowed that they would stick to the barring out through thick and thin.

Meanwhile Tom Drummond and Don Peebles had not been idle. Their appointed business was to strengthen the barricade of the schoolroom door. It was the only vulnerable point in their little fortress.

Right well was this work done. The three pieces of timber, technically termed, we believe, "braces," were fixed against the door and fastened to the floor with long nails.

That done, they put in a few screws at the top so as to hold the whole arrangement to the door, and the barricade was complete.

To force a way through two things only could be done. Either the barricade must be pulled down or the door literally burst in.

The latter Fontenoy Snicker dare not do, for the panels on the outside were specimens of the rarest carving of three hundred years ago.

Two hundred pounds was merely a nominal value to put upon them. Given a seeker after that class of work with a well-filled purse, there is no knowing what he might be disposed to pay for them.

Fontenoy Snicker, with the terrors of his lease and an action for damages before him, dare not force that door in its present condition.

It is not easy to describe the state of the minds of the boys as a body.

Some, as we know, had been prepared for the daring attempt to humiliate Snicker and bring him to his senses, but the rest had been suddenly brought into it, and for a while could not realize the magnitude of the venture.

The feeding of thirty odd boys alone was a task to the "officials," but, thanks to what had already been done, they were all right for a day or two.

The council of war was held in the main room, at which Jack had spoken as recorded.

One of the necessary steps was to swear in all who had not yet joined them, and this was done with all solemnity.

Barnes tried to shirk it, but Dorey, an excitable youngster, kindly repeated the oath for him, and the nervous youth was thus enrolled by proxy.

Sentinels were posted at the windows and the doors, so as to give notice of any movement on the outside, but for several hours there was no sign of the enemy.

This period of time was utilised to arrange the best beds their material would allow them to make up, and to divide the whole school into watches.

They were three in number. Jack took charge of one, Tom Drummond of the second, and Don of the third.

Bob Stockton was offered the last-named post, but he politely yielded to Don with the remark: "Rising genius has to be encouraged. When Jack retires it's odds on your being our leader."

As a matter of course, Don was flattered, and he resolved, if possible, to make himself worthy of the post which might be in store for him. At the same time he marvelled at himself.

Was he really and truly the spoiled child of Peebles, the quiet country tradesman? It seemed incredible, but it was a fact. Thus do time and circumstances mould us into shape, if we are made of the right stuff.

It was about noon when Tom, who was on guard at the schoolroom door, reported a voice outside. He had some difficulty in making himself heard, as the youngsters, having got over their first surprise, and in some cases alarm, were indulging in various sports and pastimes their position afforded.

Bob Stockton had undertaken, during the suspension of ordinary school duties, to enlighten the minds of the rest, and was giving a lesson in geography which would have been a staggerer to Copps, who, as we know, had a great deal to acquire in that direction.

Short, to add tone to his lecture on the origin of the Cannibal Islands, was giving illustrations of the variety of the savage countenance by lying on the desk on which Bob stood, and producing a variety of grimaces between his legs.

Jack was by the window scanning the landscape without by the aid of a field-glass, which the thoughtful Professor Lingo had put up with the other things in his parcels.

Don sat at the desk behind him in a thoughtful mood.

Others were engaged in unpacking parcels hitherto untouched, and in other congenial pursuits.

"Silence there, will you?" roared Tom.

By degrees the bubbling and seething among the boys subsided, and then Tom was able to report to his leader.

"One of the old fools outside," he said.

"Who is it?" asked Jack.

"I think," rejoined Tom, "that it is that putty-headed Penny Bunn."

"Ask him what he wants," said Jack.

Tom accordingly stooped down, took out the paper plug from the keyhole, and conferred with Penny Bunn as follows:

"What do you want?"

"Mr. Snicker would like to have a talk with some of you."

"Then why isn't he at the keyhole?"

"He would rather see you in his private room."

"Would he? It is very kind and gracious of him; but there is plenty of time for that. Has the bold Copps come back?"

"He is with Mr. Snicker."

"Is he quite well?"

"He appears to be in his ordinary health."

"That's a comfort. Give him our love, will you, and ask him how he likes his new pal, the Professor?"

"Do not yield to levity, but act like sensible boys, and open the door."

"We can't; the screws are in too tight. We must remain here until some of you clever gentlemen come in and let us out."

Here ensued a moment's pause, and murmuring voices were heard outside. Tom, by planting his ear close to the keyhole, could distinguish the tones of Snicker, as he said:

"Tell 'em that all they ask is agreed to, and you will be a guarantee that I keep my word."

Penny Bunn stooped down at the keyhole, and bawled through it:

"Let me in, and it will be all right. Mr. Snicker never was more kindly disposed in his life. He sees that he's been wrong throughout, and will in future be easier all round with you."

"Ask him to come to the keyhole," said Tom, "unless he is at dinner. We do not wish to do anything to upset his digestion. How is dear Mrs. Snicker? As a maker of jam she deserves a pretty medal. Will you tell her that the red currant would have been better if she had boiled it half-an-hour longer?"

On receipt of this message the voice of Snicker was heard asking: "If there ever was such blessed cheek!"

Then Penny Bunn was jerked away from the keyhole, and Fontenoy Snicker took his place.

"Who is that on the other side of the door?" he asked.

"Drummond," was the reply.

"Ah! Drummond," said Snicker, in the oiliest of tones, "one of the best boys of the school, who wouldn't do nothing wrong."

"Thank you, sir," answered Tom, "for your kind opinion. But why not be more grammatical? I would not do *anything* wrong, sir, unless it was for a good object."

"You will open the door, won't you?" pleaded Snicker.

"Yes, sir," replied Tom, "when the time comes. Sign the paper left in the hall to-day, roll it up very small, and push it through the keyhole. Then we will talk it over."

"Do you mean to drive me to break this ere door down?" demanded Snicker, with a sudden loss of temper.

"It would take a lot of work to do it," said Tom. "Let me beg of you, sir, to keep your temper. Think of your digestion and your liver."

Here Snicker exploded, and a sound that might

have emanated from a suffering tom-cat burst through the keyhole.

There was some more whispering outside, a shuffling of retreating footsteps, and all was still.

"Party outside gone," reported Tom.

"Close the keyhole," commanded Jack, "and hold no more conferences until to-morrow."

"Gone away in a wax," said Whymper.

"Oh dear, oh dear," groaned Barnes, who was sitting in a corner with his head between his hands. "What will he do when we open the door?"

"Not half so much as we will do," replied Little Jiggers, "if you keep snivelling there. Here, I vote we kill Barnes and eat him."

"Order, there," cried Jack; "no suggestion of cannibalism at present, if you please. By-and-bye, when reduced to the last extremity, we may think of it."

"We can't eat Barnes, anyway," said Gyp Tanner.

"Why not?" asked Hone.

"Because he is already nothing but skin and bone," answered Tanner. "After a few days fretting, *what will there be but the poorest picking?*"

"I wish you would not talk in that way," moaned Barnes. "I think it very wicked."

"So it is," said Bob Stockton, soothingly, "and we shall all suffer for our sins."

"Don," said Jack, handing him the field-glass 'there is something moving along the road yonder. I can't make out what it is. Have you good eyesight?"

"I think so," answered Don, as he took the glass. A minute later he reported:

"It is a van and very much like the Professor's."

"Surely he is not going to desert us," muttered Jack.

Don remained by the window, watching the van until it disappeared in the distance. He was certain by that time it *was* the van of the Professor.

"He is gone right away," he said; "got a scare, I suppose."

"We may see when night comes," returned Jack. "We can hold out without him for a week. After that, if Snicker hasn't softened, we are beaten, up *to a certain point.*"

"Shall we have to give in?" asked Don, dolorously.

"Can't say," replied Jack; "personally, I mean to hold out, if I starve.'

During the afternoon there was no sign of the enemy without, and Jack and two or three of his special chums employed the time in loosing the screws of the trap-door in the inner room.

They found them tighter in their places than those previously loosened in the door; but they were persevering, and got them out one by one.

It was growing dusk when the last was extracted

"That will do for the present," said Jack; "now w will have an early supper and all but the watch, and few more I shall appoint for a special purpose, mus go to bed."

It was astonishing how soon discipline had bee established. Throwing off some of their upper gar ments, the boys not on duty rolled themselves up i their blankets and lay down to sleep.

A hard floor was counterbalanced by the novelty o the situation.

The lamps already fixed in their places and bein lighted, some of the gloom was dispelled, but th effect of the whole scene was rather ghostly.

"I feel," said Don, "just as I used to do years ago when reading about robbers in their haunts."

"To me," said Bob Stockton, "the sensation i that of being shut up in a castle, besieged by a power ful enemy."

It was, in short, to them, that mixture of the agree able and the perilous, which is so enjoyable to th young.

Jack, like a great general, was not yet disposed t sleep. He had a plan in his head, which would entai more work yet, ere he could hope to get any rest.

"The inner circle of the band will explore the vaults, or whatever is beneath that trap-door," he said to Don.

"Will it be safe to leave the others on guard?" asked Don.

"I think so," answered Jack. "We are all in it, and there is no escaping the consequences. Give Bob and Tom the tip. I think we had better leave it till midnight. The enemy will be at rest then."

"Copps may not be," hinted Don.

"I am not afraid of Copps now," said Jack.

He left Don, and moving round among the boys, who were still awake, exhorted them to be as quiet as possible, which was in a sense superfluous, for after the excitement of the day, they were all pretty well worn out.

Some had stretched themselves upon the desks of the schoolroom, as little children in ordinary life, when sitting up late, lie down upon the sofa or floor —not to sleep, of course, but just to keep still for a moment or two.

Jack, seeing the condition of things, resolved to let them sleep if they chose.

"It is practically impossible for Snicker to break in, and he can't come up by the cliff."

He gave a hint to the other three of the inner circle, and when they saw one of the boys going off, they let him go. By ten o'clock all but those bent upon exploring the vault were asleep, and the variety of attitude taken up by those who had no bed was very entertaining.

Some lay at full length upon the desks and forms, others were curled up hedgehog fashion; two had their faces resting on their knees, and three were on the floor.

Up to half-past ten sounds of movement about the house were occasionally heard, but there was no further challenge at the door.

"The enemy is laying a mine," said Bob, with a quiet grin.

"He has one chance of getting at us, which we have not thought about before," said Don.

"What is that?" asked Bob.

Don pointed to the ceiling, and the face of Jack darkened.

"Bother it," he said, "I certainly overlooked that. And Snicker can do what he pleases with it, for, unlike the rest of the room, it is comparatively modern."

They all looked at the ceiling, and the more they looked, the less they liked it. If Snicker did not think of getting at them that way, the sapient Copps would be sure, sooner or later, to grasp the idea of it.

"Well," said Jack, after a long silence, "it is no use meeting trouble half-way. The kiddies all but ourselves seem to be asleep. Let us have a go at the vaults. It's odds on our finding nothing but frogs, toads, and spiders."

Stepping lightly, they passed through the sleeping-room, Jack carrying a lamp, and Bob with a screw-driver, went to work prizing up the trap-door. It stuck a bit, as might be expected after being closed so long, but he eventually succeeded in opening it.

CHAPTER XXXIV.

THE TREASURE IN THE VAULTS.

"BE careful," said Jack. "Here, let me go first. I have a splendid nose for foul air."

"It smells fresh enough for me," replied Don, as he gave way to his leader.

Jack thought it inclined to be muggy, but much better than he hoped to find it.

Under the door was a flight of spiral stone steps, worn away by much use in the days so long ago. Even here there were spiders, who, as Bob said, must periodically go through the bankruptcy court for want of business, or they would never be able to exist.

Down, down they went, not finding, as they thought they would, a cellar almost immediately beneath. Fully thirty stone steps were left behind them ere Jack saw the end of the journey in view.

"I see an opening," he said, "as dark as pitch. Go easy there behind me. It may be a well beneath. In the old times, you know, they often constructed places like this, with a deep pit at the bottom for their victims."

"Deep holes tell no tales," suggested Tom.

Jack went cautiously on until the light of the lamp enabled him to see what was ahead of him. It was no well or trap, but a vault, apparently of considerable size, and he stepped lightly upon the floor.

The moment he did so an exclamation of surprise burst from his lips.

"Boys," he gasped, "look here!"

They pressed on behind him, and beheld what it was that had given rise to his astonishment. The same feeling was amply responded to in their breasts.

Piled up in a heap on one side of the vault was a vast collection of the gold and silver plate, such as they had read of as being possessed by the abbeys of olden times.

There were chests, too, brass and iron bound, and secured with strong locks, but the whole had not been methodically placed there. On the contrary, there was ample evidence of the treasure having been hurriedly cast in a heap by men who had little time to spare.

Jack put the lamp down upon a chest, and sat himself on the bottom step.

He had not the power to express himself, and the rest had to sit down also, being in a like condition of surprised helplessness.

The inner circle ought to have been accustomed to surprises by this time, but here was something considerably above high-water mark, and they were, to use a popular term, floored.

They looked at each other and at the heaped up record of ancient wealth of the Church, and after a gasp or two, Jack found his tongue.

"I suppose it is real," he said.

"I shall be glad to introduce a pin into some tender part of your frame as a convincer," murmured Bob.

"Thanks," rejoined Jack, "but I think I can do without that. *It is real.* Now comes the question—what are we to do with it?"

"Isn't there a law that this sort of thing belongs to some fellow who calls himself the lord of the manor?" asked Tom.

"There is," said Jack; "I have heard my dad speak of him. But he always taught me that the lord of the manor had no real right to it, and I am one of those good boys who accept the teaching of their parents. This is *our* find, and we must do our best to keep it."

"What about those fellows up stairs?" inquired Bob.

"They are in the way, no doubt," said Jack, "but we can act squarely with them up to a certain point. They shall have some enjoyment out of the proceeds."

"How are we to dispose of these things?" asked Don.

"The Professor will help us," answered Jack. "We can only do one thing, unless we make up our minds to lose everything, and that is to keep the secret of it to the inner circle. I will hint to the fellows above that they had better not venture down here, and they won't dream of coming. Don, slip upstairs, and see if all is quiet there. You can find your way in the dark, and bring another lamp back with you. While you are gone, we can start on the job of overhauling the find."

Don nodded, and left them to their labours.

All thoughts of sleep were now driven away, and they began the task of overhauling.

First of all, the lighter things—the chalices, cups, and other things appertaining to the Roman ritual—were carefully taken up and laid aside. All were massive, some of silver, some of gold, and richly chased.

Each fresh article gave them cause for additional admiration and surprise.

Then they came to a mass of plate for the table, and some vestments embroidered with silver and gold. The silken material on which the embroidery was laid had rotted, and fell away to powder as they touched it; but the filigree work was held together like the outline fibre of skeleton leaves.

"All worth money," said Jack. "By jingo! it *is* a find."

When it came to moving the chests, they had to exert themselves, and some, as they dragged them aside, gave out an inspiring though muffled sound of the chink of metal.

"Money!" the boys gasped in concert, as this agreeable sound reached their ears.

So engaged were they with their labour, that they failed to notice the lengthened absence of Don, which extended to half-an-hour.

At length he came down with a lamp in his hand, and joined them just as they made a fresh discovery.

"Boys," he said, "you seem to be busy. So have I been."

"Look here!" exclaimed Jack.

Don turned his eyes in the direction indicated by a sweep of Jack's hand, and beheld a heap of weapons, which hitherto he had only read of or seen in the British Museum on a visit he paid with his father a year ago.

There were swords, and daggers, and pikes, and maces, bows and arrows in sheaves, steel breast-plates, and pieces of chain-armour mingled with monkish vestments, which seemed to have been packed among them hurriedly, to save them from the rust.

The collection lay partly in the vault itself, and partly in a recess about ten feet deep.

Tom picked up a jewelled-hilted dagger, and drew it from its sheath. It did not come from its covering very readily, owing to the rust outside, but so admirably was the fit that the blade had suffered very little from the action of time.

There were a few spots on the steel, but not sufficient to seriously injure it, and the edge and point were both as keen as they had been when the weapon was worn for use.

"There is too much for us to look over to-night," said Jack; "we must leave it till to-morrow."

"How about keeping our discovery dark?" asked Bob.

"Two of us must come down," replied Jack, "and the others remain above. We shall simply have come to explore, of course. As we have two lamps here now, we can leave one to use to-morrow. Now, Don is there anything wrong aloft?"

"No, all right there."

"Then let us get back," said Jack, "and in the schoolroom you can tell us what you have been doing."

They were loth to leave the scene of so great a discovery, but the suggestion was a good one, and, having extinguished a lamp, and placed it where it could easily be found, they ascended to the upper regions.

The trap-door was lowered quietly, and some of the screws replaced. Then they passed again through the room where the boys were sleeping to the other, and, the night being warm, they sat down by the open window.

"Now for your report, Don," said Jack; "after that, if you don't mind, I will take an hour's snooze. I really want it. I should like all of you to watch till four, and then wake me. To-night the regular watch will have to be given up. Let the rest sleep as they are."

CHAPTER XXXV.

THE THOUGHTFULNESS OF THE PROFESSOR—SNICKER BEGINS TO CONCEIVE PLANS ON HIS OWN ACCOUNT.

"ON coming upstairs," began Don, "it occurred to me that I might just as well have a look out down the cliff to see if anything of the Professor could be found. I was agreeably surprised by seeing a light below. It only lasted a moment, and was, in fact, no more than the striking of a match."

"His usual signal," said Jack.

"I whipped out the telephone, and lowered his end and then we had a palaver.

"'Hallo,' said he, 'what are you all doing? Fallen asleep?'

"'No,' I replied, and then I told him that we were exploring the vaults, and did not expect him that evening, as we had seen him going away.

"'That was a blind,' he said, with a chuckle. 'I have had such a game with Copps, and, as he may be hand in glove with the police, I thought I would get out of the district and lie close awhile.'"

Don then related what the Professor told him, which was substantially the same story Copps had related to Snicker on his return to the school.

"The only thing that seems to worry Lingo," said Don, "is the notion that he did not carry things far enough. But he said he meant to make up for it in the future."

The Professor had not come for the purpose of telling what he had done to Copps, but had made his visit memorable by his thoughtfulness.

He had brought with him forty pounds of bacon, a dozen big loaves of bread, and a small sack of ship-biscuits, to add to their store of provisions.

There was, likewise, a box which was marked, "handle with care," and this was to be given to Jack.

It was filled with small pellets, not quite so large as an ordinary pea, and with them there was a paper with written directions on it.

"What are they?" asked Tom Drummond.

"Practically the same thing he meant to have sent up with Don that night," replied Jack. "We must make a small paper tube so as to run a few of them through the keyhole. The enemy will not be able then to approach without giving us a good chance of knowing the very moment they arrive."

"But what will these things do?" asked Bob Stockton.

"They are simply detonators of the Professor's own make," answered Jack. "He says they will make more row than anything else in the wide world of double the size."

"What is in them?"

"Goodness and the Professor knows. All we have to do is to make use of them."

They made a small tube of paper, pushed it through the keyhole, and sent several of the pellets on their mission. That done, Jack climbed up on one of the desks, made a pillow of his right arm, and went to sleep immediately.

"Good old Jack," murmured Tom Drummond. "What a splendid fellow he is."

His opinion was echoed by the rest, and to keep themselves awake they squatted on the window—inside ledge—which was very deep, and let the cool breeze of night fan their foreheads to cool them.

Meanwhile, the enemy outside had been debating the position, and nothing had been come to that could be called a decision.

The fact was, Copps, after his recent adventures, was hardly in a frame of mind and body to attend to business, and as he and Snicker discussed it during the afternoon they had passed in private, calling in the aid of a bottle of spirits to assist them, he was early in the evening reduced to a state of semi-idiocy.

Diverging from practical matters, he became abusive, and told Fontenoy Snicker exactly what he thought of him, finally declaring that, if the boys would let him in, he would make himself their ally.

Having got thus far, he lay down upon the sofa, and snored in a villainous manner for an hour, while Snicker, also a bit overcome, slept in an arm-chair.

From slumbers that were heavily peaceful, the schoolmaster was aroused by the word "Jam" being rung in his ears. He opened his eyes, and saw his wife with an axe in her hand.

"Scissors!" he gasped, "what are you going to do?"

"I am going to get my jam," she answered, "since you are not man enough to do it."

"Will you listen to me?" implored Snicker. "You cannot get into that there room without doing more damage than we can pay for. Let the jam go."

"I'll bet it's gone," said Copps, from the sofa, where he had just woke up. "There's nothing left but the pots. Bet you two smokes on it, Snicker"

"Look here, I don't want your smokes," replied the goaded Snicker. "And I can do without you."

"Oh, indeed," sneered Copps.

"Yes," said Snicker; "it's through your messing they've got the jam at all. I'll work the job alone, and you can take yourself off as soon as you please."

"I am going to stay here," answered Copps, obstinately, "and see this job out. It is the most interesting case I ever was mixed up in. A lot of boys against an old rascal. I bet on the boys."

"So do I," said Mrs. Snicker. "That husband of mine always was a muddler. Jerry, I shall go in for a divorce."

"Do," said Copps, gallantly, "and marry me; I'm single, and with no encumbrance worth speaking of. We should make a good thing of it together. Lord love you, how could you marry a man with them legs?"

"Stop a moment," said Snicker, livid with wrath; "You forget that this is my 'ouse—*house*."

"Madam," said Copps, addressing Mrs. Snicker. "I am sorry for you. I consider you a lady thrown away on a—a—a bear. It is a pitiful case of self-sacrifice."

"It was the opinion of some of my friends," replied the pleased Mrs. Snicker, "that in marrying Jerry I was a-throwing myself away."

"You not only threw yourself away," said Copps, warming with his subject, "but you deprived a superior class man"—he smiled and bowed meaningly—"of the joys and advantages of having you for a wife."

And then Copps leant back and sighed deeply.

Mrs. Snicker looked at him with open commiseration.

"I fear," she said, "that you are not very well."

"I have a headache," replied Copps, softly, "arising from thoughts that have troubled me since I have been here. It always pains me to see a first-class lady married beneath her."

"A cup of tea might relieve your headache," murmured Mrs. Snicker; "shall I get you one?"

"Madame," said Copps, lightly kissing the tips of his fingers, "you do me honour, and you make me happy and proud."

While this tender colloquoy was going on, Snicker surveyed the speakers in turn from under his heavy eyebrows, and when Mrs. Snicker, with a sudden restoration of a long-laid-aside juvenility, skipped from the room, he, with forced calmness, addressed himself to Copps.

"I suppose," he said, between his teeth, "that you think I am going to stand this sort of thing?"

"I fear you will have to do so," was the cool reply, "and a lot more before we have all done with you."

"I've come to something at last," hissed Snicker. "Fust—*first*—the boys getting up barrings houts, and then you are a flowering fraud, and now my old woman in her dottage—"

"*Dotage*," corrected Copps.

"None of your cheek," roared Snicker; "whatever it is, she is gone wrong, and you are a-laughing at her, and she's too chuckle-headed to see it. Blessed if I don't think the 'ole—*whole*—of creation is going awry."

"Snicker," said Copps, with the air of a solicitous friend, "do *not* excite yourself. At your time of life, it must be injurious to a painful degree."

The door opened, and Mrs. Snicker appeared with a cup of tea upon a small tray.

"I do hope," she said, with a smile, "that I have made it to your liking—*Oh-oh-h!*"

To his liking or not, Copps would never taste that cup of tea, for Fontenoy Snicker, carried away beyond the regions of prudence, kicked up the tray and sent it flying over the head of his astounded wife.

Luckily for her, she did not receive any of the scalding contents of the cup; but a small jug, containing milk, struck her on the chin, and bespattered her with the lacteal fluid.

"Go and get him another," bellowed Snicker, "and I'll choke the pair of you! Now then, try it!"

Being naturally of a repulsive cast of countenance, he was especially so when roused in anger. So demoniacal was the expression of his face, that both Copps and Mrs. Snicker were alarmed.

"Jerry," said Mrs. Snicker, quaking, "I'm surprised you should give way like this for nothing."

"Hout!" he answered, pointing to the door, "and don't you come a-nigh—*near*—that broken-down fraud of a second-hand bobby until I give you leave. As for you," turning to Copps, "come that game again, and I'll—I'll—try it, will you?"

His wife had already gone, and he, following her, sought out Penny Bunn, who, with Awful Rooker, was engaged in playing a game of draughts in the lumber-room.

As a preliminary to entering into conversation with his assistants, Fontenoy Snicker seized the draught-board, and threw it into a corner of the room.

"Now," he said, "I want to talk to the pair of you!"

They both stared at him aghast, thinking that too much irritation had driven him mad. Penny Bunn thought of flight, but his superior was between him and the door, and he had to remain.

"Bunn," said Snicker, "this ere job of the barring-out have got to be settled by us. That Copps is a perambulating fraud."

"It has struck me," murmured Penny Bunn, "that he was not quite up to his work."

"He's up to nothing," growled the schoolmaster. "He's a bigger fool than Rooker!"

Having enlivened his junior assistant with this almost direct estimate of his intellectual capacity, Fontenoy Snicker sat down upon an empty box, and proceeded thus:

"We three have got to get at them 'ere boys, and if you think we can't do it alone, I fancy Milky Whey might be made useful. What is the first thing we have to do?"

"Get into the schoolroom," Bunn replied.

"But how?"

"There are two ways of getting in," continued Bunn, speaking like one inspired.

"Two of 'em!"

"Yes, sir: the door and the windows."

"It would be ruin to bust—*burst*—the door, and how are you going to get up to the winders?"

"There are difficulties, no doubt, sir," answered Penny Bunn; "but they may possibly be overcome."

"There is a third way," said Snicker, reflectively, "the chimbley."

"Yes," murmured Bunn, "the *chimney!*"

"I was a-thinking," continued Snicker, ignoring the correction of his assistant, "that as the flue may be in places rather small, that *you*——"

"Pardon me, sir," interposed Penny Bunn, firmly, "but I really could not think of it. The man who goes down that chimney will have to do so with full powers to *act*. He must have both moral and physical influence to support him. Unless he has, the boys, in their present frame of mind, might possibly murder him."

" You think so ?" said Snicker, frowning.

" Yes, sir," said Bunn. " Now, if you—"

He was stopped by the overwhelming savage expression of the schoolmaster's face. Murder was there, if it was not in the hearts of the boys.

" Me go down my own chimbley !" said the suffering Snicker. " I wonder what next I shall have to *enjure.* Here, come along. I will give them boys a last chance of giving in without their being flayed alive. If that doesn't come orf—*off*—I'll dynamite the whole Abbey, and put you and Rooker on the roof to make sure you got your full share of the blow-up."

He strode off with a determined air, and they followed him. Both were grinning. It was so funny to see and hear Snicker in his futile wrath.

Down the passage to the schoolroom door strode Snicker, and there he began his parley, destined to be very brief.

" Boys !" he yelled, with a stamp of his foot, and then—*bang !*

Something went off with a terrible violence, losing none of its effect in that confined space.

Snicker staggered back, and was seen to fall. Bunn and Rooker, wheeling about, fled for their lives.

Unconscious of whither they were going, they plunged in the direction of the kitchen, arriving at the door just as Mrs. Snicker and Black-Eyed Susan emerged therefrom.

Bunn only avoided a collision by pulling up smartly, and thereby making a buffer of himself for Rooker, who collided heavily with him and fell back against the wall.

" What is it ?" cried Mrs. Snicker.

" They've blown him up," gasped Penny Bunn. " The boys have got some infernal machines. Your respected husband is no more."

" Don't you tell no lies," bawled the supposed dead man, as he came limping along the passage ; " it isn't so bad as that, but it is bad enough, in all conscience. They've got powder and all sorts of explosives, and I was as nigh blowed up in the passage as I could be.'

" In the passage ?" said Mrs. Snicker. " How foolishly you talk. If it is in the passage, how could they place it there ? They must have a confederate outside."

" Copps !" yelled Snicker.

" You've got that poor man on the brain—if you have any brain," said Mrs. Snicker ; " he hasn't been near the schoolroom door this morning."

" Bunn !" hissed Snicker, " it is you, then. Confess it."

He was in such an excited frame of mind that he made a dash at the throat of the startled usher, and shook him as a dog would a rat.

There was a possibility of his murdering the innocent man outright, and Mrs. Snicker, seeing it,

grasped her husband by the collar of his coat and dragged him back.

" It seems to me," she said, " that you have gone quite cemented."

" *De-*mented, you old idiot !" roared Snicker. " Is it to be wondered at if I went *anything* with one and t'other of you ? Here, I am going to work out this job alone, and don't any of you come a-nigh me till it's *done.* Bunn, take yourself off to Chippenham, and send on Milky Whey here. He and I will—"

" Do you call that doing it by yourself ?" demanded Mrs. Snicker. " If you can't get along without a low fishmonger, you had better give in to the boys."

" I give in—I, Fontenoy Snicker, Esquire, of Little-cote Habby—*Abbey ?* It seems to me that you don't quite know the man you've married, ma'am. Bunn, do as you are told."

" May I trouble you for a shilling on account of my salary ?" asked Penny Bunn. " So long a walk will make a little refreshment imperative."

The schoolmaster had nothing less than a two-shilling piece, which he handed to his assistant, desiring him not to squander it, but to faithfully bring back the change.

" And take that ninny with you," said Snicker, pointing to Rooker ; " he isn't any good here. And mind this, if either of you chatter about the barring-out, I swear I'll murder you."

Bunn and Rooker, glad of the opportunity to get out of the disturbed Abbey, hastened away, and Snicker, after a snarl at his wife, retired to think out and mature some plan to circumvent his youthful enemies.

But it requires a cool head to conceive plans, and the schoolmaster was just then mentally red-hot.

He was a human volcano, boiling and bubbling over with lava. He puffed with rage—there were big black spots dancing before his eyes. Internally he was in a state of chaos.

" I'll go outside and think," he said. " Was there iver—*ever*—such a job as this ? I feel as if I could make an example of a boy by *b'iling* him."

CHAPTER XXXVI.

MILKY WHEY ARRIVES.—SCALING THE CLIFF.

" RASHERS for breakfast ! "

The boys, when they assembled in the schoolroom after a night's rest, heard the announcement made by Bob Drummond that this unwonted luxury was in store for them with amazement.

During all their experiences of Littlecote not one of them had lawfully tasted such a thing.

Little Jiggers, as previously recorded, had levied blackmail on a dish prepared for Snicker, but the others had almost forgotten what the flavour of bacon was like. The oil stove, which had been obtained during the great foray into the kitchen, was brought out and placed upon the window seat. Bob Stockton was appointed to cook; Tom, as chief caterer, cut the rashers, and Soppem Smith and others arranged the breakfast tables on the desks.

Considering all things, admirable order prevailed.

The bacon was splendidly cooked and served. The aroma of it tickled the nostrils of the boys, and, creeping under the door, found its way all over the house.

Fontenoy Snicker smelt it, and came forth from the retreat of his private study to make sure that he had not made a mistake. The odour was too pronounced to admit of doubt.

"_Rashers for boys!_" he exclaimed, breathlessly. "We shall have farm labourers tasting mutton and beef next. The whole world is turned upside down. But where did the little beggars get it from?"

He thought he would ask his wife if she missed any of her store, but on second thoughts he decided not to do so. "Let her suffer," he growled; "she will will have to pay for it out of her allowance."

He did not venture near the schoolroom, although he would have liked to do so, but, for the second time that morning, went out of the house to see what he could make of it. He walked across the playground to the cliff side and sat down upon the wall. The window of the schoolroom was open, and there was quite a rush of breakfast aroma, the wind bearing it towards him.

He could hear the murmur of voices, and laughter such as had never been heard at a table of his providing. He passed his hand over his brow, and wondered for a moment if, after all, he might not be the victim of a dreadful nightmare.

"It's a hallelujahcination, that's what it is," he groaned, "or perhaps I've gone quite off my head, and this ain't Littlecote at all, but a 'sylum."

This dreadful thought turned him cold and made him shiver. It was fearful to have such a thing in his head, so he fought against it, and brought on a profuse perspiration.

This was helpful to him, and he felt better.

"It's all true," he said, "as true as I am sitting on a stone wall. Hallo, they are singing."

So they were. After a moment or two of silence, broken only by the voice of Jack calling on Herbert May to take the lead, the whole of the Number One boys burst into song, the others falling in as well as they were able.

And this is what they sang:

We will fight to the end, and never yield
    To Snicker and his crew,
But die upon the battlefield,
    To our cause all true.

We've barred the door, we've shut him out,
    And there he'll have to stay
Until he turns himself about,
    And works another way.
For the good time has come, dear boys,
    And we shall wait no longer,
For Snicker's is now up a tree,
    And we little kids the stronger.

At the conclusion of the song there was a wild burst of cheering, Snicker listening to it, standing stiffly on his feet in a semi-petrified condition.

When the noise had subsided to the buzz of ordinary conversation, he moved slowly away, and walked out of the gate ere he could find speech.

"I do _not_ think," he groaned, "that I can stand anything more. 'For Snicker is now hup—up—a tree, and we little kids the stronger.' That is what they sang, and they seem to have got it pat enough, and it ain't the fust time they've sung a thing of that sort. One on 'em must have wrote—_written_—it. Fancy me being troubled with a poet in _my_ school."

It was such an overwhelming thought that he was obliged to find relief in walking hard down the slope through the wood.

Having got so far, he thought he would go on a little way and meet the itinerant fishmonger whom he had called in to assist him.

He reckoned that ere then Penny Bunn had got to Chippenham, and Milky Whey was on the road.

It would not hurt him to stroll as far as Smudgem Bender, where he could see if any inkling of the doings at Littlecote had got abroad.

As the best place to obtain information was undoubtedly the inn (there was but one in the village), thither he betook himself, and, walking into the parlour, called for a pint of mild ale.

Charles Botch, the farmer, was the only other person there, and he was indulging in cold gin and water.

"Good morning," said Snicker.

Botch made no reply, but stared at the schoolmaster as if he had taken an unpardonable liberty.

"I said good morning to you," said Snicker, angrily.

"What if you did?" asked Botch. "I don't object. Say it again, if you like. Go on saying it for a arf-hour, if you think it will do you good."

"You are mighty perlite," growled Snicker.

"I'm a man as knows my place," retorted Botch. "There are some men as don't."

"It's a nice thing for a clodhopper," said Snicker, "to talk to a schoolmaster in this fashion."

"A schulemaster!" sneered Botch. "'Ighly hedicated—werry."

And then he laughed in a most unmistakably offensive way.

It was not prudent to quarrel with the man at that time, and Snicker bottled his wrath. Botch drank up his gin and water with great relish, and walked out of the room.

Snicker sat there, fuming, for a good half-hour, during which period of time he had his beer mug three times replenished. Fortunately, it was the beer of a local brewer's make, and not endowed with intoxicating properties to get into the head of an old toper of Snicker's stamp, so he remained sober.

Having paid his score, he sauntered to the door just in time to see Milky Whey coming up the road at a smart pace.

"Hallo, Snicker," he cried.

This was a most unwarrantable and offensive way of addressing a man of the schoolmaster's social position, but he was getting used to anything now, and only feebly smiled.

Milky Whey, on drawing near, held out his hand, and Snicker had to take it.

"My old friend, Bunn," said Milky, "have been explaining to me wot's up, and all I can say is that I'm dead on the job. And I'll do it cheap, for I owe them boys something."

"Don't talk here," whispered Snicker; "I want the thing kept close."

Milky Whey laid a finger on his nose, and winked.

"All right," he said, "Bunn knows I'm the man to be trusted, and he out with the lot. Afore we start on smoking 'em out, I vote we have one drink."

It was impossible to refuse him so modest a request, and they returned to the inn, where they had not only one, but two drinks, for which the schoolmaster paid.

Then they set out for the Abbey.

As soon as they were beyond the village, and well on the road, Fontenoy Snicker proceeded to discuss the method of procedure he thought best under the circumstance.

"Are you good at getting down a chimney?" he asked.

"No chimney for *me*," replied Milky.

"Can you climb a cliff, then?" demanded Snicker.

"Ah! There I'm ready for you," was the cheerful response.

"Then come round to the foot of it, and let me see what you can do."

To get at the necessary spot they had to make a considerable detour, and work their way through some rough ground, covered with trees and brushwood. At length they stood immediately beneath the schoolroom window, and Snicker bade Milky Whey take his bearings, and select his upward route.

Their coming had not been unheeded, and there were half-a-dozen heads out of the window above, peeping down at them.

Snicker was able to distinguish the faces of Don, Jack, Tom, and Soppem Smith.

"Hallo there!" he roared.

"Good morning, sir," replied Jack, politely.

"For the last time, are you going to open that door?"

"Will you sign the agreement?"

"Go on, Milky," said Snicker, angrily.

"It seems to be a stiffer bit of climbing than I thought," mused Milky Whey.

"If you strike along that bit," said Snicker, "and take the hangle—*angle*, jigger it!—by that bush you will be able to get along to the bit of a shelf, and there you are."

"I'll try it," said Milky, as he pulled off his coat; "anyways I can't do more than venter."

He started on the upward journey, and succeeded in getting about fifteen feet up the cliff.

There he found a resting-place, a knob or excrescence on the side of the cliff, and sat down upon it.

"My eye!" he said, as he drew out what some people would have thought was a long-used dish-cloth, and wiped his brow, "this *is* work."

"If you don't hurry up," growled Fontenoy Snicker, "you won't get to the top this side of Christmas."

"It would take you ten years to do it," retorted Milky Whey.

His movements had been watched from above, and the boys now for a moment disappeared. Tom Drummond speedily reappeared at the window with a bucket in his hand. Snicker recognized it as a domestic utensil he had often seen about the schoolhouse when scrubbing operations were going on.

"Look out!" he shouted, warningly.

Instead of looking out, Milky Whey looked up, and immediately was blinded by a rush of greasy, dirty water. It had been used for washing up the breakfast things.

"Murder!" he roared, and swaying forward, down he came with a run, landing on the flat of his back at the feet of Snicker, who, according to his habit when exceedingly excited, cut an uncouth caper.

"Why didn't you duck your head?" he asked.

"Why couldn't you tell me what was a comin'," gasped Milky, as he wiped his face with his coat sleeve. "Poof! wot on earth is the muck?"

"It's the breakfast washings," said Snicker, watching the remnant of the "shoot" trickling down the cliff; "I see bacon rinds in it."

"Anyways," muttered Milky Whey, "I didn't come here to be soaked with sich stuff as that, and you had better go up yourself and get the next lot."

"Don't be faint-hearted," urged the schoolmaster; "you made a good start of it. Try again."

"Not me," replied Milky Whey, "I can stand any amount of fish, but not house-slops. You'll have to get a ladder."

"A ladder!" gasped Snicker. "You talk like a fool!"

"Hi, there!" shouted Tom from above.

"What do you want?" roared Snicker, adding in an undertone, "You little warmints—*vermin.*"

"Would Milky like a towel?" asked Tom; "a wash must be a refreshing change to him."

Milky said something in response, but it was not of a nature to be put into print, and the schoolmaster cut another caper.

"What are you going to do, Milky?" demanded Snicker, "hup or not?"

"Not," answered Milky Whey; "it isn't good enough. Them boys have got too much in hand that way. You pay me for my day's work and I'll get back again."

"I'll pay you when you've done your work," snorted Snicker.

"And I don't leave yer until I *am* paid," answered Milky. "Now then, old bandy-legs, shell out like a man."

Fontenoy Snicker, white with rage, stalked away snorting and puffing, and Milky Whey, using his dishcloth handkerchief to remove the greasy moisture from his countenance, strode after him.

CHAPTER XXXVII.

THE WORKING OF JEALOUSY—RETURN OF PENNY BUNN AND AWFUL ROOKER.

ON the way homeward Fontenoy Snicker said little more to Milky Whey, who doggedly stuck to him. During the walk the schoolmaster reflected on the position he was in with regard to the itinerant fishmonger, and the conclusion he arrived at was that, for the present, he had better keep him in tow.

If he allowed him to return to Chippenham, he would naturally talk of what he had seen, and this was a thing the schoolmaster especially desired to be avoided.

"I had better do it," he muttered; "he must stay at the Abbey, but if things go on in this way, with detectives and so on, I sha'l have the place chockfull of 'em."

At the gate of the Abbey Milky asked him if he meant to pay up or not, and getting no reply followed him into the house.

The moment they entered their noses were saluted with an odour of mutton chops.

"Somebody is a-going of it again," growled Shicker. "It can't be the boys this time."

Following up the scent with dilated nostrils he traced it to his own dining room and indulged himself with a peep through the key-hole.

The spectacle he looked upon was enough to drive him mad.

Seated at the table were two persons, Copps and Mrs. Snicker, and they were having a friendly chop and bottle of stout together. Copps was engaged in telling some humorous story, judging by the action and expression of his face, and Mrs. Snicker was smiling as Snicker had never seen her smile since he led her to the altar.

Jerking his eye away he put his ear in its place, and succeeded in getting hold of some of the light and airy talk the detective was indulging in.

"He is certainly the most ridiculous fellow I ever met," he said, "a blundering booby, who fancies he knows everything and knows nothing."

"Me in—*of*—course," muttered Snicker.

"And the fun is not all over," continued Copps; "indeed I may say it has only just begun, and if you, my dear Mrs. Snicker——"

The outraged listener did not wait to hear anything more, but straightening his back in his wrath he turned the handle of the door and stood upon the threshold of the room, wild-eyed and ferocious.

Mrs. Snicker raised her eyebrows in a slightly surprised manner.

"I didn't expect you back so soon, Jerry," she said.

This was cool, anyway. The volcanic energies of jealousy at once began to play with extra power in the breast of the schoolmaster.

"Come out of it," he hissed, glaring at Copps. "Let that chop alone, you brassheaded Copps. I am not going to be eaten out of house and home by a—a—a—a—a scoundrel of the shoddy detective pattern!"

Copps opened his eyes, and calmly addressing Mrs. Snicker, asked:

"What is the matter with the man?"

The next moment he was on the floor, with Snicker above him, grasping the chop, which he had snatched from the plate, in his right hand. He used it as cleanly mothers do a flannel upon the countenances of their little ones.

He rubbed it over the eyes, nose, and mouth of the offending Copps. He greased every feature with it, he scrubbed him with that seven ounces of mutton and bone until he did not know whether he was lying on the ground or standing upon his head.

Mrs. Snicker looked on with dismay; Milky Whey surveyed the scene with approval.

For a cheap entertainment for the poor there is nothing so popular as a fight, with themselves for spectators.

Milky, in common with his class, did not think of

inquiring into the justice of the assault. It was enough for him that it was provided for his edification.

At length, when he had rubbed all the meat off the bone, Fontenoy Snicker gave in. Rising to his feet, he thus addressed the dismayed Mrs. Snicker:

"I give you ten minutes to get out of this house. If I find you in it after that time, I'll murder you."

And he looked as if he would do it. Quaking all over, Mrs. Snicker left the room and sought the protection of Black-eyed Susan in the kitchen.

To the girl she imparted the startling information that her master had suddenly gone mad, and their lives were in peril. Thereupon, Black-eyed Susan suggested they should barricade the door, which was done with a recently-purchased kitchen table and the fender.

Meanwhile, Copps, relieved from further assault, had risen to his feet, with a countenance so greasy that it shone like the setting sun.

He surveyed the panting Snicker, and the satisfied Milky Whey in turns.

"This is the first time in my life," he said, "that I ever went to a place and paid for a loin of mutton and treated the woman of the house, and had the primest of the chops put aside for the master, and then been oiled all over with the bit I reserved for myself."

"You paid for them there chops?" exclaimed Fontenoy Snicker.

"I did," answered Copps, "wishing to act friendly with you. But I'll have a yard or two of law over this job. Look here, my man, I don't know who you are,"—he was now addressing Milky—"but I can see that you are honest and truthful, and if you are paid your expenses, will give your evidence in the box. So I reckon you will be ready to stand up for me."

"Certainly," said Milky Whey, charmed with the word "expenses"; "I'm ready when you want me."

"Copps," said Snicker, "I'm afraid I've been rather hasty, but when I see you and my wife so lovingly together, I——"

Copps burst into a roar of laughter.

"Well," he exclaimed, "if this doesn't beat all; he's jealous of her! Ha, ha! hold me up somebody, or I shall split my sides. Ha, ha, ha! if it doesn't lay over anything I ever met with."

The schoolmaster looked foolish to the edge of idiocy, and as Copps rolled about in the agonies of uncontrollable laughter, he felt that he would be thankful if the floor would sink down to the bowels of the earth, and take him with it.

It is impossible to say what he would have done, but at that moment footsteps were heard in the passage, and immediately the sound of voices singing followed.

The weather being hot, and teaching slow,
To Chippenham we resolved to go,
　　On the grand, on the grand, on the grand;
And there we had some rums and milk,
And other drinks of that 'ere ilk.
　　Understand, understand, understand.
I'm glad we're not with Snicker,
Or he'd have swallowed all the liquor,
　　Out of hand, out of hand, out of hand!

"Whoop-la! Hooray! three cheers for the barring out."

The above words were uttered with a shout after the singing, and Snicker listened to the uproar like a man in a dream.

"It's Bunn and it's Rooker!" he gasped; "but can I believe my ears?"

If he could not, he had good reason to believe his eyes a moment later, when the two undermasters appeared at the door of the room.

They were arm in arm, as much to ensure a necessary amount of the perpendicular to keep them on their feet, as from affection they had for each other.

Both were in a state of hilarity, and Penny Bunn kissed his hand to his superior as he hiccoughed and addressed him as follows:

"We have got back safe and sound. Returned to the buzzum of Snicker, as I may say, if I am allowed to bust into poetry. We've had a good time in Chippenham, and public opinion is divided on the matter of burning you in person or simply doing it in effigy."

"What are you saying?" snarled Snicker.

"Some want to hang you," explained Rooker, breaking into the conversation with a hiccough. "The betting is two to one the boys will win."

"If I find you have been talking about my affairs," said Snicker, with blue lips and white face, "I'll kick you both out of the Abbey."

"Do it at once," urged Penny Bunn, politely, "and take the sconch-conk-conser-quenchers. Got it at last, Rooker. Try it, Snicker. We are ready."

Here Snicker suddenly collapsed and broke down. Tears came into his eyes as he sank into a chair, a pitiable object.

"I am done up, now," he moaned, "every man, woman and boy have perspired—*conspired*, jigger it— to bring me to ruin. I shall be glad if you will all get out of the room and give me a chance of pulling round."

"Come to my room, dear boys," said Penny Bunn, addressing Copps and Milky Whey, with a wink, "I've got a drop of something in my pocket that will help you to bear up. I've got a pack of cards, too—borrowed them at the Blue Boar—and we'll have a game of nap. Snicker, old man, don't be surprised if the Chippenham undertaker comes to measure you for your coffin. I've laid three separate sixpences that you commit shew-soo-*snew*-a-cide before five o'clock to-night."

And then he went away, followed by the others,

one and all willing to partake of the liquid he had brought back with him, and not averse, in Copps's case, to a friendly game of cards as a relief to the excitement pervading the Abbey.

CHAPTER XXXVIII.

SECOND NIGHT OF THE BARRING OUT—A PROPOSAL FROM SNICKER.

"IT seems to me," said Bob Stockton, on the evening of the second day of the barring out, "that we shall have to make some arrangements for fresh air."

"There is draught enough here," said Roger Hone.

"I was not alluding to that," replied Bob, "but to the necessity of exercise. We may be here a week or more, and it will never do to have any invalids. There's heaps of rope about, and why cannot we make a ladder to go down the cliff with?"

"I don't think it will be wanted," remarked somebody close behind him.

He turned quickly, and saw Jack, who, with Don, had been in the vaults for the last two hours.

The boys, who had been lounging and strolling about the schoolroom, hearing what he said, crowded around him.

"But ere giving them any further particulars," continued Jack, "I must ask you to wait until to-morrow. It will be necessary for the inner circle to fully investigate the discovery, made this afternoon by Don and myself, ere going further into the matter."

There was a buzz of voices as this announcement was made. Soppem Smith put a question to Jack.

"If we can get out, will not Snicker be able to get in?"

"Perhaps," answered Jack, "but at present I can only speak to the fact that there is an opening. We have not been outside, nor tried to. Nor have we actually seen it."

"Then how do you know there is an outlet?" asked Bedstone.

"We heard the cows lowing in the meadows," answered Don, "and the whistle of a distant train. You would not hear such things through the solid earth."

"Hear, hear," chorussed a dozen voices.

"I think that we had better leave the whole matter to the inner circle," said Whymper. "Meanwhile, as it must be nearly six o'clock, we had better have tea."

Another "hear, hear," saluted this observation, and Tom Drummond proceeded to set the assistant caterers of the day to work.

The oil-stove had been lighted some time before, and the water to damp the tea was boiling.

Tom put the requisite quantity of the grateful herb into an old urn of huge proportions, part of the spoils of the kitchen, and having done that, and put more water over the stove, busied himself with buttering the bread they had—two slices for each boy, with as much biscuit as they could eat, and jam upon them to follow.

Jack took a seat upon the window of the classroom through which all their communications below the cliff were made, and with a feeling of pride, surveyed the busy scene.

So far, the triumph was on his side, and he already saw that, come what might, he had not fomented a rebellion against the tyranny of Fontenoy Snicker in vain.

And then his mind turned to the great discovery he and his closer friends had made in the vaults.

What was to be the outcome of that?

He had no qualms of conscience about the rightful ownership of the plate, money, and arms. The original possessors had been dust for centuries, and there was no trace of their heirs. And as for the lord of the manor, whoever he might be, Jack had been reared in a school that denied the right of the high-born to take possession of treasure discovered by others. It was, morally, the property of himself and his friends.

But how were they to retain it?

If the affair got wind, as it would most certainly do if the whole school were in it, then the powers that were would step in and rob them of their prize.

In the perplexity of thought that arose in his mind he saw that there was only one living person who could settle what ought to be done, and that was Professor Lingo.

But did he know enough of the man to trust him with such a vast secret?

It was a natural doubt that arose in his mind, but, with a boy's disposition to trust one he had already found to be so true, he decided that as soon as possible Lingo should be made acquainted with the facts.

His meditations were interrupted by a hand laid upon his knee. Looking down, he saw Barnes, the timid, standing near him.

"Ford," he said, in a low tone, "I want you to do something for me as soon as you can."

"What is it?" asked Jack.

"The moment you are sure there is a way out will you let me go?" pleaded Barnes. "I'll go right away and find my road home, somehow. I shall die of fright if I remain here."

"Die of fright!" repeated Jack. "Nonsense. People don't die that way."

"I can't stand it," said Barnes. "When you were

A SPLENDID SCHOOL STORY.

NEVER BEFORE PUBLISHED.

By E. HARCOURT BURRAGE,

Author of "Ching Ching," "Monkey Mat and Roving Dick," "The Brave Boy of the Basilisk," &c.

THE LAMBS OF LITTLECOTE

A THRILLING SCHOOL STORY.

No. 6.

A Handsome Coloured Plate Presented with Every Number.

PROFESSOR LINGO ARRIVES IN THE VAULTS WITH STARTLING EFFECT

 PRICE ONE PENNY.

down in the vaults last night I was wide awake, although I pretended to be asleep. And it was while you were down that I saw *something*."

"Well," answered Jack, unmoved, "what did you see?"

"It was a *ghost*," said Barnes, shivering.

"Bosh!"

"It was—it must have been—for it could have been nothing else. It came up from below while you were there."

"Oh! indeed. We scared the ghost, did we?"

"It was a figure in a gown and hood," continued Barnes, "like the pictures we see of monks. I did not see any face, except two sparks that looked like eyes. It came up quickly, and seemed to melt away. Then I fainted right off, and heard and saw nothing until the morning."

Jack was troubled, but he was not going to let Barnes see it. His matter-of-fact father had always taught him to disbelieve in ghosts, and he felt it would be unworthy of him if he allowed Barnes to make him think different.

"Why have you not spoken of this before?" he asked.

"Because I was afraid the boys would laugh at me," replied Barnes.

"And they will do so, although I shall not," said Jack. "The fact is you scare yourself into fiddle-strings about nothing. If it was a ghost it must have been a poor specimen, for when we went down it bolted out of the vaults. It was afraid of us, don't you see."

"That may be," replied Barnes, in all faith, "but it terrified me, and I want to go away from here."

"I will see what can be done for you to-morrow," answered Jack.

Barnes thanked him, and crept back to a corner of the schoolroom where he had spent most of his time since the barring-out began.

"I'll ask Lingo to take him into the van," thought Jack; "he will feel safer there."

Tea was now ready, and the orderly way in which the meal was carried out showed that discipline was in no way relaxed, but had rather been strengthened.

The youngsters were, in a subdued way, as merry as heretofore, and the talk turned on the fact that since the morning nobody had been near the school-room from the outside.

Some were of opinion that the schoolmaster was getting ready to take the place by assault, but others fancied that he had given up the task as hopeless, and simply meant to starve them out.

"Not he," said Bob Stockton; "he won't be able to do it in a year. His great chance will be faint hearts growing up in our midst."

There was a chorus of declaration that this was

impossible. All meant to stand firm except poor Barnes, and he said nothing.

After tea they gathered in groups to play quiet games, or tell yarns in the twilight. Outside the night was fine and clear, and some lay upon the window seats watching the cattle wend their way homeward to the farms, with the herdsman and his dog behind them.

It was a pretty scene, and Herbert May, more than all the rest, dreamily enjoyed it.

In front of him he had a pencil and paper, on which he at intervals jotted down a line or two. He was writing a vesper song for the Littlecote rebels.

Gradually there settled down with the darkness a stillness on them all. The usual tones of the speakers sunk into whispers. The influence of the hour was upon them.

Suddenly all were startled by a heavy blow upon the door. Ejaculations of alarm sprang from a score of lips, but Jack, with a word, quieted them down.

"It is only a herald from the great Mogul," he said, "or it might be the great Mogul in person."

He crossed over to the door, removed the plug from the keyhole, and asked who was there.

"Me," replied a voice, apparently some distance down the passage.

"Can't you come nearer?" asked Jack.

"Not if there are any more of them bombshells about," was the reply.

"It's Snicker," thought Jack. "How did you knock at the door?" he asked.

"I threw a brick at it," answered the schoolmaster. "I want to tell you that if you don't open the door you will have the life of a man on your hands."

"What is his name, sir?"

"Snicker, and he has had enough of it. What with you and the fiends I've got in the house, I'm done."

"Very sorry for you, sir," answered Jack, politely, "but you can do as you like, of course."

"If you let me in I'll sign the paper."

"No, sir; not to-night, anyway. Besides, I've altered my mind about it. A friend of mine may probably call on you to-morrow."

There was a moment's silence, and then Snicker was heard to gasp out:

"A friend of yours, did you say?"

"Yes," replied Jack. "He knows all about the barring out, and he will see us through it."

"May I ask the name of that there—dash it!—that 'ere—*that* friend?"

"You, may, certainly," returned Jack, "but I shall not tell you what it is. I may say, however, old boy, that he is known throughout the county."

"It isn't the owner of the abbey?"

"No, only a particular friend of his. I can't go on

talking through a keyhole. Give our love to Mrs. Snicker, and remember me kindly to dear old Copps. The next time you employ a detective, do not not get one *quite* so clever."

Then, as an explosive sound was heard from the schoolmaster, Jack corked up the keyhole and reported to the boys the substance of the conversation.

" Perhaps he means to give in," said Roger Hone.

" If he does," answered Jack, coolly, " he will have to sign to that effect in due legal form. It is now dark, and all not on duty had better get to bed. Smith, you are on sentry. The inner circle are about to resume their inspection of the vaults, and they hope to report something that will fetch the lot of you to-morrow."

Tom Drummond was already busy lighting the lamp, and Bob Stockton, having raised the trap door, Jack gave a glance around.

It was strange how tired some of the boys were, considering the little exercise they had, and those at liberty to go to bed were actively preparing for rest. The bedding, rolled up when not in use, was being spread out, and clothing taken off with commendable rapidity.

Herbert May came in from the outer room with the paper he had been writing on in his hand.

" Chums all," he said, " I've put together a few lines, and, if you are willing, I shall be glad to sing them to you."

A chorus of assent responded to his offer, and, standing in the middle of the bedroom, he asked for silence.

" It is to be sung very softly," he said, " and the first verse is the chorus. I will sing the words slowly so that you will remember them."

He was a good-looking boy, with a wonderful light in his eyes when under a poetic inspiration. It was in a crude form at present, but the spirit of it was growing within his breast.

He always sang sweetly, but, as his hearers afterwards said, never so sweetly as that night.

EVENING SONG.

The stars are out, the night is here,
    And the light of hope is shining ;
The earth may all be dark and drear,
    But with us there's no repining.
      Good night ! Good night ! And sweet repose,
      Rest on us when our eyelids close.

Our friends at home may be thinking of us now,
    And picturing us on peaceful study bent ;
Little dreaming of the barring out I vow,
    Or, how our days and nights are being spent.
           CHORUS.

They little dream that we have here unfurled
    Above the Abbey the banner of the free ;
And in the tyrant's teeth defiance we have hurled,
    And will not yield, though death our portion be.
           CHORUS.

Within these aged walls, like prisoners we're confined,
    But the captive's sorrow lies not on our breast ;
Self-chosen prisoners we, with one thought in our mind,
    To stay here until victory crowns our crest,
           CHORUS.

Perchance the day will come when other boys will sing,
    Also our friends at home, with no discordant note,
The praises of the barring out, a very daring thing,
    That brought better times to the Lambs of Littlecote.
           CHORUS.

The song was received with the utmost enthusiasm. The dressed and half-dressed alike joined in a general cheer that greeted its conclusion.

Even poor, hesitating, miserable Barnes, felt for a moment inspired with a spark of resolution.

Through all ages up to the present time it is the songs of the people that have most influence with a nation ; and thus it was at Littlecote. Herbert May provided the fuel, and Jack worked the machinery.

After they got to bed, some of the boys still kept on softly chanting " Perchance the day will come when other boys will sing," and the rest of the chorus. There was a stimulant in the thought alone. They would be enrolled in the scroll of fame, as great liberators are. They all felt it would be so, and if Snicker could have dived into the feelings of his pupils that night, he would have seen how hopeless it was for him to expect that yielding would come from their side.

" Herbert, old man," said Don, as he took the arm of the young poet, who was one of the guard of the first watch, " how do you feel when you are writing your verses ? "

" As if I were sitting in front of a big fire—all aglow," replied Herbert.

" And that is how it makes me feel when you sing," said Don ; and being hailed by Jack for the further inspection of the vaults, he left the young poet to his reflections.

CHAPTER XXXIX.

INTO THE OPEN AIR—A SURPRISE FOR PROFESSOR LINGO.

IT was while inspecting the arms discovered on their first visit to the vaults, that Jack and Don had met with the further surprise of the discovery that there was somewhere handy a communication with the outer air.

How they came to that conclusion we know. And this, their third visit to the vaults, was to determine the exact nature of that communication.

The inner circle of four descended to the vaults, Tom Drummond carrying a lighted lamp in one hand, and a trimmed one in the other. Provision was thus made for many hours' illumination below.

Bob Stockton closed the trap door, securing it with a wooden peg he had cut for the purpose, so as to stop any attempt to intrude upon them. Although there was a wonderful unanimity among the boys, the inner circle did not as yet entirely trust Roger Hone or Soppem Smith.

How far this doubt was justified time will tell.

Meanwhile, we must spend a little time with the young and daring explorers in the vaults.

Jack said nothing to his chums about the vision Barnes had seen, but it stuck to him nevertheless. As he followed Tom into the vault he fancied for a moment that he saw in the shadow beyond a dim outline of the figure of a monk shaking his fist at them with a threatening air.

But as it vanished instantly he put it down to fancy engendered by the story of a nervous boy.

He and Don had during the afternoon taken out most of the arms and laid them aside. The chief thing now to be removed appeared to be a pile of bows and arrows that completely blocked up the end of the inner vault.

"Be careful how you handle those arrows," said Bob Stockton, "some of them may be poisoned."

"I never heard of Englishmen poisoning arrows," said Don.

"No," answered Bob, "but I have read that the monks of old were first-rate makers of the choicest poisons, and when they hit a foe with an arrow, that man surely died."

"I don't think they used poison," said Tom, "but anyway it is as well to be careful."

As the bows and arrows were shifted it became apparent that they had been stacked in a third opening branching at right angles from that in which they were.

It was very narrow and dark, but a strong draught of air showed that there was an opening somewhere from the outside.

Tom went forward with the light and the rest followed. The passage was artificially made, for the roof of it was perfectly formed in the approved shape of an arch. The sides, though roughly hewn, still showed the marks of the excavator's tool.

For a few feet it was straight and then it turned to the left, suddenly terminating with a mass of roots of trees and bushes.

It was through the tangled mass that the draught came, and by their feet lay some earth which had recently fallen down.

Here was the mystery of the fresh air solved.

"The roots have grown and pushed away the earth," said Bob Stockton, "and the air comes through some of those places that look like black spots."

He pointed to some inky places among the roots of a bush, and stooping down so as to get a clearer view

of them, Don saw a solitary star twinkle through one of the orifices.

He laid hold of the roots of the bush, tugged, and rolled over on his back with the bush on the top of him.

The whole thing was so sudden and unexpected that he lost all power of speech and his companions were dumbfounded. Luckily Tom held on to the lamp and the light of it remained to assist them.

But a greater surprise, not to say alarm, was in store for them.

As they stood—and in Don's case lay—a voice was heard outside, exclaiming:

"Here's a go. I didn't know you youngsters had taken to mining."

Jack was completely staggered, and, like the rest, did not recognize the voice. All felt that their little game was up and they had fallen into the hands of the Philistines. The treasure was, of course, lost, and a groan burst from Jack's lips.

And then there appeared in the opening made by the drawing out of the bush—which, by the way, was like that in the haunt of Robin Hood, dead and rotting—a *face*.

"The professor!" gasped Don.

"Yes," replied the new arrival, "it is your own Lingo. But what *is* the game on now?"

"Do you think there is a chance of our being seen from the outside?" asked Tom, quickly.

"I should say so," answered Lingo, "seeing that I was drawn to the spot by seeing the light streaming through a hole in the side of the cliff. Douse the glim for a minute and tell me how you came here."

Tom blew out the lamp, not downward, as some foolish people do at the risk of exploding it, but across the top, which extinguishes a lamp in perfect safety.

Then the boys crept out of the hole and found themselves on level ground at the base of the cliff.

There were thick bushes and trees around, and it was not possible to quite make out where they were.

"Are we far from the schoolroom?" asked Jack.

"Not more than a dozen feet," answered Lingo, "and that is why I was made aware of your vicinity. I was just about to give the signal when I saw a pencil of light flash out of the side of the cliff, and I can tell you that it gave me a startler. If I had not been an old night traveller I might have got it into my head that some of the old monks were rising out of their graves, and bolted off. But being accustomed to all sorts of strange phenomena after dark I waited to see what it was, and found *you*. Now, boys, tell me how you got down here."

They told him all, in a whisper, lest there should, by any chance, be spies around, and he listened in silence, more amazed than he, as a man of vast experience, cared to own.

When the last word had been said he sat for a moment thinking. It was certain he had a very large nut to crack.

"Now, boys," he said, "I can guess that you have got an idea into your heads that these things you have found are as much yours as anybody's. In that opinion I entirely concur, but the law is dead against your keeping them."

"What!" cried Tom, dismayed, "do you advise us to give them up—money, jewels, arms, and goodness knows what?"

"What are you to do with them?" asked the professor.

"Sell them, and keep the money."

"My dear boys, the moment you put anything you have found upon the market, all the relics-of-the-past hunters would want to know where you had got them from. That is, unless you have somebody in the market with samples before you. Now, my advice is, *split the deal.*"

"Split the deal!" exclaimed Don.

"Yes," said the professor; "clear out half your prize, and then announce the finding of the rest to the authorities, who will reward you for your honesty. But do it before Snicker can put his claws on any of it."

"I know where we could hide a lot of stuff," said Jack, "if we could only get it there."

"You are thinking of the haunt of Robin Hood," remarked Don.

"I am."

"It was in my mind, too."

"And mine, and mine," said Bob and Tom together.

Jack explained to the professor the nature and position of the hiding-place they had thought of, and he said it would do.

"Nothing can be done to-night," he said, "but to-morrow I will go and reconnoitre the ground. As soon as it is dark I will bring my van close in here and load up. My advice to you all is to leave everything to me. Go back to the school and keep there until you hear from me, which may not be for a day or two. I've brought some bread and fresh meat for you which can be taken in by the vaults. It will save the bother of hauling up, and you can explain as you like how you got it into the place. I've already brought the sacks close in handy, so as to save trouble. I don't think there is anybody about, and one of you can go back to the inner vault, and light up there."

Don took this office on himself, and the rest remained to assist the professor with his stores.

Groping his way back, with a box of matches in his hand, Don was about to light one, when he fancied he heard a movement near.

"Who is it?" he inquired, quickly.

There was no answer, and having listened for a moment or two without hearing anything further, he struck the match and lighted the lamp.

He glanced somewhat apprehensively around, and discovered, to his great relief, that he was undoubtedly alone. Sitting down, he waited for his comrades, who ere long came staggering in, each with a sack containing provisions upon his shoulders.

The professor came last, bearing a box, which, as he set it down, he informed them contained the better part of a sheep ready cut up and prepared for cooking.

"Eat it all right away," he said; "good fresh meat won't be thrown away upon you. The bacon you you have will keep, and this won't. Now let me look at the find."

He went over it, examining everything but what was inside the heavy chests. Their contents, by reason of the strength of the fastenings, could not be got at.

"They will have to be opened elsewhere," he explained, "and the best of burglars' tools will be wanted for the job. Two of them will have to be left behind for the lord of the manor, just to show how honest we are. The rest, I reckon, are yours."

In this way, he cursorily divided the spoil, giving one third to the authorities, and the remainder he reserved for the boys.

How the prize was to be eventually shared he left for after consideration.

"Now, my lads," he said, finally, "you go up aloft, and lie close. Fasten down the trap-door so that it looks as if it had never been opened, and tell the boys it is not a place for them to venture into just yet. I'll wait here while you get the tommy upstairs, and then take my departure. You may rely upon me to shut up the hole in the cliff so that nobody, if they should happen to prowl around, which isn't very likely, will suspect it is there."

As the sacks were heavy, the contents had to be divided, and the food taken up in smaller quantities. The work occupied the better part of an hour, Lingo watching outside to guard against interruption.

The door of the schoolroom was shut so that the sleepers only could have seen what was going on, and as the quartette of the youngsters did the task very quietly, storing the bread and meat by the well, nobody had any suspicion awakened.

At a late, or rather, very early hour of the morning the work was done, and they took leave of the professor, who made no promises about being honest and true to them; but they knew that he might be wholly trusted, and their minds were at ease on that score.

Having returned to the upper part of their domain, as Bob Stockton called it, the trap-door was lowered and the screws replaced. Dirt was rubbed into the crevices, and wearied out, they adjourned to the schoolroom.

There they found every member of the watch fast asleep, but it was of no consequence. There was not the slightest prospect of anyone breaking in without disturbing them, and Jack and Tom, having elected to lie upon the floor by the door that was barricaded, the other two stretched themselves upon one of the desks, and in something under a minute all were fast asleep.

CHAPTER XL.

THE LONELY SCHOOLMASTER—HE CONCEIVETH AN IDEA, AND GETS TO WORK UPON IT.

THE evening song, sung by so many voices, could not, of course, fail to be heard by the inmates of the house. There was a lively party in Penny Bunn's room who heard it, and, strange to say, approved of the melody.

"They are the cheekiest lot I ever met with," said Copps, who was lying at full length on Bunn's bed, smoking a short pipe, "and I must say I like them none the less for it. The chief thing that amazes me is, however, the way they circumvented *me.* I am perfectly certain that they guessed I had found out something and pushed on matters."

"They had a man behind 'em," growled Milky Whey, who was seated in an old easy chair he had coolly appropriated from Snicker's own room. "They was put up to lots of things by somebody that's cute."

"It's the cheap Jack," said Penny Bunn.

"Bosh!" exclaimed Milky, "he's a stranger to 'em. It is somebody in the house as did it."

Here Rooker put in a word.

"I could name the man," he said, with a leer, born of unusual consumption of strong liquor. "Now, Bunn, why don't you own it?"

"Own what?" asked Penny Bunn, with a smirk.

"That you are at the bottom of the whole business," answered Rooker, "and that you done it out of the spite you have against Snicker. Nobody here loves him, and you can speak out."

"What I've done," said Bunn, carelessly, "I *have* done, and there is an end of it. I may, however, say that I am not a man to be trifled with. I warned Snicker a score times that he would go too far, and he turned a deaf ear to me. Let him take the consequences, and if the boys choose to betray me—why, they must. That's all."

"You're a cute un," said Copps, eyeing him keenly.

"I am prepared to admit," replied Penny Bunn, "that I am not quite a fool."

It was his weakness—he could not help it. The desire to pose as a clever man was insatiable within him.

"You have some cards, do you play?" asked Copps, after a short silence.

"I used to," answered Bunn, "but here I have never touched one."

"What is your favourite game?"

"Whist," replied Penny Bunn.

"I never travel without a pack," said Copps, "on the off chance of getting a game of nap in the train."

But it turned out that the only game Milky could play was all-fours, and Rooker had never touched a card in his life. So the idea of whist had to be abandoned. Cards were a failure.

A proposition from the detective to cut all round for sixpences was also negatived, and then he asked what they were to do to pass the time?

"Suppose we spend the evening at Chippenham," suggested Penny Bunn, "it will be nine o'clock before we get there, but we shall have two hours."

"I've took an oath," said Milky Whey, "that I'm not going outside this den till I've been paid for my day's work."

"And I am also a resident here," added Copps, "until Snicker shells out."

"We can get out by a side door and back again," said Bunn, "and Snicker none the wiser."

"If I thought that," said Copps, hesitating, "I'd go with you."

"It's awful dull here," said Milky Whey.

Eventually Penny Bunn went out to reconnoitre, and if the coast was clear, they would steal out and have a few hours at Chippenham, and return by-and-bye to sleep.

He returned after a short absence with the information that Mrs. Snicker and the girl were barricaded in the kitchen, and Snicker in his bedroom.

"I found that he had the door locked," said Penny Bunn, "and asked if I could speak to him for a moment. He swore at me in the most unbecoming manner, and looking through the keyhole, I saw him lying on his bed, smoking a long clay pipe. There was a whisky bottle and glass by his bed side."

"He's good for some time," said Copps. "Is he often on the whisky lay?"

"Mrs. Snicker does her best to regulate him," was the cautious reply of Bunn.

The feverish spirit of adventure and defiance was in the tutor's breast. In his veins the remnant of certain potations he had partaken of in the morning still lingered. He was ripe for anything.

So the party set out for Chippenham without anyone in the house noticing their departure. But shortly after they were gone, Fontenoy Snicker arose from his couch in a pot-valiant condition, resolved to act as chucker-out of the Abbey, and forcibly remove Copps and the obtrusive Milky Whey.

He sought them all over the Abbey, and found them not. Then it flashed upon the schoolmaster that they had left the place, and a brilliant thought flashed into his gifted mind.

"The boys," he growled, "have got their barring out, and I'll have *mine*. Blowed if I don't keep the lot out in the cold and risk it."

He foraged up a padlock and chain, which he took outside and put upon the main gates of the playground. Then he barred and locked the other entrances, and *his* barring out was done.

Returning to the house, he met Mrs. Snicker, and Black-eyed Susan, who, not being disturbed, had ventured out of the kitchen into the hall, where the latter was engaged in lighting the lamp. He told them what he had done, and tersely informed his wife that if she let anyone into the house without consulting him, he " would murder her."

"I'm going to get at them there boys alone *to-night*, d'ye hear?" he hissed.

"Lord help you for a fool," was all Mrs. Snicker said, as she hurried to the kitchen, followed by the girl.

"What will be the end of all this?" she moaned, wringing her hands; "the boys are shut up, your master has been drinking, and there's not a man in the house if he should be took bad. More than likely he will set fire to the Abbey."

"I'll fill the buckets," said Black-eyed Susan, simply, " and we can keep an eye on him."

But this precaution was knocked on the head by the sudden appearance of Snicker in the kitchen, with a crowbar in his hand.

"Come on, you two," he said, " before I start on the job of getting at them little fiends, I must have you boxed up."

"Jerry," said Mrs. Snicker, shaking all over, " what are you going to do?"

"Take up the floor of my bedroom," he replied, " and get at them through the ceiling," he answered, with grim ferocity; " and when I *do* get among 'em, this is the cane I intend to use about their backs."

He had, as was feared by the leaders of the barring out, hit upon the apparently only vulnerable part of their retreat. Mrs. Snicker saw that it would be dangerous to permit him to carry out his purpose. But how was he to be prevented?

There he was, as unseemly a ruffian as one would care to look upon. The events of the last three days had engendered a state of excitement, which, in a man of his temperament, was dangerous, and it had been fostered and fed with an extra indulgence in his favourite liquor. Of what avail would reasoning be with such a man?

Mrs. Snicker hit upon an expedient.

"Jerry," she said, " can't we help you?"

His answer was a snarl, and the raising of the crowbar as if to strike her. After that she argued no more with him, but hurried out of the kitchen with Black-eyed Susan by her side, and two minutes later he had them safely locked up in a bedroom, at the back of the Abbey.

Fontenoy Snicker now had the place practically to himself.

With a lighted lamp in his hand, he sought his bedroom, which was immediately over the schoolroom, as we have described, and having first rolled back the carpet, surveyed the floor.

To his surprise it was not the ordinary boards, but inlaid woodwork.

It was a fine piece of work, and it bade him pause ere he did anything to destroy it.

"Was there iver—*ever*—such dashed luck as mine?" he muttered. "All things play into the hands of them boys. I wonder, if I took it up if I could put it down again. It's a regular big puzzle."

The more he looked at it, the less he liked it. The wood was laid so closely that there were no real intersections available for the use of a crowbar, without doing mischief. He tried a dozen places with the same result. To get a crowbar inserted, a portion of the inlaid wood must be broken.

But he was in a desperate state of mind, and acting on a sudden impulse, he violently thrust in the tip of the weapon and wrenched out a triangular piece of walnut, splitting it into fragments in the act.

The first act of vandalism was done, and the rest was easy.

Immediately under the flooring was a course of cement, which he judged was the ceiling of the schoolroom, and before beginning on that, he was bent on having a sufficiently broad opening to admit of the passage of his body.

As he was a stout, thick-set man he allowed plenty of room, and prized up portions of the inlaid work, until there was an opening in the floor, fully three feet each way.

This was not done without irreparable mischief to the various woods, of which the floor was composed. Time had made the material dry, and rather rotten, so that it split in every direction. And what was more to be considered, all the king's horses and all the king's men could not replace that flooring again. It was irreparably ruined.

He knew it; but, perspiring and puffing, he laboured on, so silently that the boys below had no inkling of what he was doing.

It is true that they occasionally heard sounds of movement above, but attributed them to the necessary going to and fro of the schoolmaster, preparing for bed. Not the least suspicion of the peril they were in, dawned upon the boys.

Before tackling the cement beneath the floor, Snicker took a long and steady drink. He wanted it, for he was pretty well pumped out.

It spurred him on to increased exertions, and he went for the cement with a light heart, that is, a comparatively light one.

He dug the crowbar into the crust, pierced it, and struck—*metal.*

It was a short, sharp ring that fell upon his ear, but it sufficed to tell him that his labour had been in vain.

Between the ceiling of the schoolroom and the floor of the bedroom there was *a sheet of steel.* It was an exasperating discovery, and for a moment he was blind with wrath.

As heretofore, everything worked against him. Even the flooring of the Abbey was in favour of the boys.

"I'm bothered," he muttered, as soon as he could speak, "if I don't think the blooming old monks did this a-purpose. They got hold of what I was a-going to do somehow, and shoved this ere sheet iron into the ceiling, to put me to all sorts of trouble and expense for nothing. Here's a mess I've made of the woodwork! What *will* it cost to put it right?"

He finished with a groan, and as a temporary means of relief, had one more go at the whisky bottle.

Having done that, he threw himself upon the bed, and tried to find a refuge from his still increasing troubles in sleep.

And strange to say, that drowsy god, that oft refuses to come to good men when wooed, came to him, and in a little while he was snoring, as he always did, like a choking pig and a grampus rolled into one.

CHAPTER XLI.

THE RETURN OF THE REVELLERS.—COPPS ONCE MORE ON THE TRAIL.

THE adventures of the night were not yet over. At eleven o'clock the four revellers who had gone to Chippenham were desired by a local publican to vacate his place of business, and they turned into the street with a few natives, who hastened home to their more or less loving wives.

Chippenham by day is the home of dreariness, late at night it is the Catacombs out for an airing. The popular belief is that there is a policeman, or perhaps two, on guard throughout the night, but no living man has ever seen these guardians of the peace, after the public-houses close. What they do and where

they go is one of the mysteries of modern social existence.

The revellers were, to put it mildly, hardly in the condition to walk back to Littlecote.

Something was the matter with the legs of Penny Bunn and Awful Rooker. The latter's were as limp as those of a doll from which the sawdust has been extracted.

Ere he had walked a dozen yards he sank into a doorway, and lay there, not wholly unable to go on, but incapable of giving a reasonable explanation of his weakness.

Penny Bunn, swaying to and fro, remonstrated with him.

"Thish." he said, "won' do. You got to come back 'r Abbey. Pull yourshelf 'gether."

The only answer was a dismal moan. Copps became impatient.

"We must leave him there," he said. "A nap will pull him round. He knows his way home."

Penny Bunn burst into most unaccountable tears.

"What!" he exclaimed, "leave the companion of my daily labourers? No. Go back by 'shelfsh, you two, and leave us to die 'gether."

Thereupon, Penny Bunn likewise collapsed on the same doorstep, with his hat on the back of his head, and his arm upon the prostrate form of Rooker.

"I'll never leave you, ole man," he said, "for you are a fatherless orphan. Go 'way, ever'borry else."

"What is to be done with them?" asked Copps.

He and Milky Whey were a bit thick about the head, but they were all right about the legs. Milky scratched his head at first, and said he was blessed if he knew.

But light came to his aid.

"There's my barrer," he added, after a moment's reflection. "Between us we might get 'em home on it. It runs easy."

"Is it handy?" growled Copps.

"I keeps it up a yard just above the Hangel Hinn," answered Milky.

"Then get it, man, and let us make a start," rejoined Copps.

Milky was not long in fetching his barrow, and Penny Bunn being by this time as unconscious as Rooker, the pair were lifted up and put upon the crazy vehicle without offering any remonstrance.

"We must shove 'em forrard," said Milky, "so that the barrer can run light."

This was done, and, lying side by side, with their legs dangling over the front, the senseless pair were propelled through the town.

Outside it there is a long and stiffish hill, which taxed the strength of Copps and Milky to the utmost. But they got the barrow to the top without doing anything more serious than upset it once.

The human luggage was replaced, still in a comatose state, but very gritty, owing to the dusty state of the road.

The two propellers took a rest, and spent several minutes in regaining their breath and cursing the pair who were giving so much trouble.

But with the way comparatively easy, they proceeded onward along the silent road. It was horribly lonely, and soon became oppressive to the active mind of Copps.

"I can't do seven miles of this," he said, when the first had been covered, "and, besides, I ain't used to barrow work."

"Aperiently not," replied Milky, sarcastically, "for like some horses as runs double, you have 'lowed me to do all the work."

"Suppose I go on and see how things look at the Abbey?" suggested Copps. "I don't mind giving you a shilling or two for you to run the barrow along."

"All right," answered Milky, with alacrity, "shell out."

Copps gave him two shillings, and set off alone for Littlecote with a lighter step. If he succeeded in getting back without any further trouble he was not particularly concerned about what became of the rest.

Inside of the Abbey he was master of the position. Outside he was at a distinct disadvantage.

The brisk walk helped to clear his head, and by the time he arrived at the village of Smudgem Bender he was as cool as ever. It was then, he reckoned, about half-past one o'clock, and the place was as deserted in appearance as if all within it were dead.

"What a horrible little hole to live in," he muttered. "How do they stand it year after year?"

It was certainly a problem to a town man, and it lay heavy on his breast until he came to a point where the road divided, V-shape.

He bore to the left instead of to the right.

The way he took led to the country lying at the bottom of the cliff.

It must be remembered that he was a stranger to the district, and, furthermore, it was night. Therein lay ample justification for his going on and on even after he had begun to suspect that he was not on the right road.

He scanned the dark horizon in search of the outline of Mumping Malford wood. As soon as he could see that he would be certain of the way to take. But there was no glimpse of it, and with gathering doubt in his heart he went forward until he arrived at a broad expanse of common, and then he knew for certain that he had mistaken the road.

"Hang it!" he muttered. "Here's a fix. Where the deuce am I? Not a house in sight, nobody moving, and a country not quite so lively as the desert of Sahara."

As he communed thus to himself, the oppressive stillness of the night was broken by the sound of wheels upon the hard road.

The vehicle, whatever might be its nature, was, as yet, afar off, but, as he judged it was approaching in his direction, he was able to derive some comfort from the rumbling break upon the silence of the hour.

He had a quick ear, and could distinguish sounds, so that on listening, he decided that it was neither a light cart of the ordinary pattern, nor a waggon that was advancing towards him. His curiosity was roused, for in addition to the noise of wheels, he was able to distinguish the voice of a man singing.

As the vehicle drew near to him, he strained his eyes to make out what it was like, and the outline of a van gradually grew out of the gloom.

"It's that fellow Lingo," muttered the detective. "It is his voice. What is he doing out at this hour?"

Nothing in the world would have given him greater pleasure than to get the upper hand of Lingo somehow. If he could only land him in a criminal prosecution it would be joy indeed.

The indignities which the professor had put upon him rankled in his mind, and were likely to do so for many a day to come. He was burning to avenge them.

Lingo was singing as he walked beside his horse, and his song was one that the boys of Littlecote had often sung,

"There's a good time coming, boys,
　　We need not wait no longer,
　For Snicker he is up a tree
　　And the little kids are stronger."

Lingo made a slight alteration in the original words of the song to suit it to himself. He was not one of the boys, and had of necessity to leave himself out of it, but he sang it with evident gusto, insomuch that Copps was struck by it.

"What makes him so sweet on the youngsters, I wonder," he muttered.

He crouched down among the bushes to let the van go by. His intention was to shadow the professor so that he might know something of the object of his travelling at night.

But he was much disconcerted by the van pulling up short directly opposite him, and Lingo calling out:

"Hallo, my friend. Anything wrong with you?"

There was no help for it. Copps had to disclose himself, which he did, walking very feebly.

"I've lost my way," he said, "and am completely done up. If you, kind sir,"—he shammed ignorance of the personality of Lingo—"would kindly give me a lift to the cross ways I shall be grateful."

"Copps," said the professor, calmly, "I wonder at you, I do."

"Wonder at me!" exclaimed the detective.

"Yes," rejoined Lingo, "pretending you don't know me, when you were skulking there with the idea of following me."

"Good Lord!" cried Copps, "can you read what's inside a man?"

"Of some men," answered Lingo. "Now, you are not a fool, but you are not quite clever. When you try getting over me, you are bound to go wrong. Why? Because I am the stronger man. You are sure to rebound from me, and fall a buster. Get on the shaft, and have your ride. I'll walk beside you, and talk."

Copps got upon the shaft on the near side, feeling as if he had been considerably reduced in size. The professor had in a moral sense punctured him, and he was like a collapsed balloon.

"You are at the school still?" said Lingo.

"Ye—es, in a way," was the hesitating reply.

"And what do you think you are doing there?"

"Well, I was hired to find out who was robbing the place, and——"

"And you found out all you are likely to know. All round you are a poor lot. Snicker, his tutors, yourself and the old woman. I don't know that I ever came near such a scrubby lot in my life."

"Mighty complimentary, I must say," muttered Copps.

"I am one of the few men with truth in them," serenely answered Lingo, "and what is more, it is bound to come out of me. Here's a bit for you to digest. You won't do any good by trying to spy on me. But I am not spiteful, and would like to do you a good turn. In the main, you ain't a bad sort of of fellow. Your fault is that you are a little weak and foolish."

"I shall soon begin to think I am," said Copps.

"Now," said Lingo, "I am, as you guess, not here on regular business, but for all that it is *straight*. You understand that?"

"I suppose I must believe you," said Copps, with a sigh.

"Straight," repeated Lingo; "but there is money in it. Now, I can't make it all myself, and I am willing to put a bit in your way. It's only just come into my head to do it, but you may reckon on me. I want you to meet me three nights hence, say at twelve o'clock, at the spot where I picked you up. Will you come?"

"No gammon in it, I hope?"

"No; all fair and square. On my word, as a man. Meanwhile, you are to lie close in the Abbey and talk

to nobody. You can help Snicker to unearth the youngsters if you like. It is a bit of work you can take your time over, as *it can't be done*."

"Snicker can do his own dirty work," said Copps. "I've had enough of him. All I want is my money."

"Certainly," said Lingo; "and I wish you may get it. Here is the place for you to drop down, and you know your way home. Remember, three nights hence at twelve o'clock, by the spot where I found you playing on the artful. Don't fail, and don't try to play me double, for if you do, you will go wrong."

"I'll drop the crooked," replied Copps; "it won't do with you. I suppose you can't give me any idea of what you want me for?"

"I can," answered Lingo; "but I am not going to do it. You be easy till the time comes. Good night —or rather, good morning."

Copps responded, and being now on the right track, set out for the Abbey.

"What on earth is it he wants me for?" he muttered. "I'm inclined to think it is some game he has in his head, and yet he did not speak as if it were so. I had better keep the appointment. But it is very odd, uncommonly so."

So it was. The ready professor had got an odd idea in his head, but he was the man to work it out and bring it to a successful issue.

———

CHAPTER XLII.

THE FAILURE OF ONE BARRING OUT.

IT was with considerable astonishment, mingled with dismay, that Copps, on returning to the Abbey, found that he was unable to get in.

He tried the door by which he and his companions had left, and found it well secured. Then he wandered round the three open sides of the Abbey, and discovered that every means of entrance was closed against him.

"Done—and by Snicker," he gasped.

He confounded himself most heartily for having been induced to go to Chippenham, but he did not despair.

It flashed upon him that on the morrow some of the tradesmen might call for orders, and give him an opportunity of getting in. It would, however, be requisite for him to be very wary in his action, and if possible keep out of sight.

The morning was advancing, and already there was a faint light in the eastern sky. Moody and distraught, weighed down with fatigue, and utterly miserable, he wandered round to the gates of the playground and peered through the iron bars.

He looked at the lock and chain which Snicker had fixed upon the gates, and while turning over the former a light suddenly sprang into his eyes.

"Good Lord!" he exclaimed, "what a fool I am. But it is so long since I did a bit of lock-picking that it is no wonder it did not come into my head right off."

The only thing he needed was something wherewith to pick the lock. He had none of the regular tools about him, and on trying his pocket-knife he found the blade of it was too wide.

"A bent nail is all I want," he muttered, looking about him as most people would have done in the same case.

It is strange but true that rusty nails and pins can be found almost anywhere, if people will but take the trouble to search for them. Copps discovered what he wanted not far from the gates, fixed in the wall, for some purpose, long ago. He wrenched it out, bent the point to the requisite angle, and went to work.

The ordinary padlock is, as a rule, a weak production of the mechanical arts, and Copps soon had it undone. Having got into the grounds the rest was comparatively easy. He replaced the lock, turned it back with the same simple tool with which he had opened it, and sauntered towards the house. His mind reverted to the scullery window on which the boys had operated on that night when they made a clean sweep of the kitchen, and thither he wended his steps.

It had been repaired and strengthened, but that did not matter, as Black-eyed Susan had left it open for ventilating purposes.

He crept through it and made his way to his room without disturbing anybody, and, wearied out, got into bed.

Fontenoy Snicker was about early in the morning. Having dressed himself he first of all released his wife and servant from confinement, and told them to go to work getting breakfast ready. They were told not to open any of the doors or leave the Abbey on peril of their lives.

"Oh, Jerry!" cried Mrs. Snicker, "why don't you end it all?"

"I'm going to do it," he growled, "would you have me give in to the boys?"

"Yes," she answered, boldly, "because I feel you will have to do it. I dreamt last night that I saw you, like that picture in Gulliver's Travels, lying full length on the ground, and all the boys dancing about, and upon you."

"Bother your dreams," he muttered, as he strode away.

He sauntered into the playground where he took up a position by the wall, and listened. Inside the schoolroom there was apparently the stillness of a deserted mansion. He could not hear the slightest sound.

"They are dogged as mules," he muttered. "Their backs are as stiff as pokers, but I'll bend them, or what will be the good of my keeping on with the school?"

"Mr. Snicker," said a faint voice, in the direction of the gates.

He turned round and saw two dismal faces against the bars. They belonged to Penny Bunn and Awful Rooker, and never had the countenance of the latter been more in harmony with his name.

Both were covered with mud and had a generally bedraggled appearance which is associated with sleeping in the open air in showery weather.

"What do you want?" demanded Snicker.

"To return to the shelter of your hospitable roof," answered Bunn, in quavering, respectful tones.

"Is that villain Copps with you?" asked Snicker.

"No, sir," replied Penny Bunn, "we are alone. Milky Whey *was* with us, but we left him in Smudgem Bender knocking at the public house door with, as we believe, the futile hope of getting the landlord up to supply him with rum and milk on credit."

"You are a nice pair, ain't you?" demanded Snicker, grinning viciously at them through the bars. "If I let you in will you help me to keep Copps out?"

"I assure you, sir," said Penny Bunn, "that the chief aim and object of my life henceforth will be to avoid the company of that man."

"He's a beast, sir," said Rooker, with a groan.

Snicker looked at the pair with a lowering glance. He had no great faith in either, but his life was horribly lonely just then, and any sort of companionship but that of Copps, the betrayer, would have been acceptable.

"Come in," he said, as he brought out the key and unlocked the gate; "but you mind this, run against me again, and I'll—I'll——"

He did not finish the threat, and perhaps it was unnecessary. Throwing back the gates, he let in his woebegone assistants, who were in the last stage of misery.

"Where did you leave Copps?" asked Snicker; "no lies, you know."

"At such a time as this," replied Penny Bunn, "the utterance of the truth is imperative. After your generously yielding to my request for admission, it would be utterly mean and base of me to deceive you."

"Well," snarled Snicker, "where was he?"

"He was lying upon his back," answered Penny Bunn, with the air of an apostle of the truth, "senseless with drink. It was a terrible spectacle, and in the opinion of the parish doctor, who had been called to his aid, he could not recover."

"I hope he won't," said Snicker, rubbing his hands with satisfaction. "By the way, Bunn, are you anything of a carpenter?"

"I have an especial gift in that direction," said Bunn, "as an amateur, of course. But in some of the industrial exhibitions of my native place I have carried off prizes when competing against regular workmen."

"Good," said Snicker, "I ask the question because I have a job for you. I've been taking up a portion of the flooring of my room, and want it put down again. You can tackle the job by-and-bye."

"With pleasure, sir," answered Penny Bunn, "meanwhile, if you did not object, I should like to indulge myself with a few hours' much-needed repose."

"Wash yourselves before you get into bed," growled Snicker.

Penny Bunn, who, with Rooker, had passed a dreadful night, was only too glad to get to bed on any terms, and he murmured something to the effect that it was his intention to wash himself all over before he ventured to get between the sheets. Then he and Rooker staggered into the house, and went to bed just as they were. Penny Bunn was so overdone and dog-beaten all round, that he went to rest in his very boots.

Meanwhile, Snicker, not very sorry to get his garrulous tutor again beneath his roof, returned to his bedroom, and surveyed the damage that he had done the night before. It certainly would require a man who knew his work to put it right again.

"But if Bunn really can do it," he thought, "it will be all serene. And he will work cheap, because I sha'n't pay him anything extra."

As it was time for him to partake of a morning refresher, he indulged in one from the bottle, and sat thinking for awhile. Referring to his watch later on, he found it was seven o'clock, and as breakfast was probably ready by that time he went downstairs.

The savoury odour of ham and eggs saluted his nostrils as he reached the hall, and he was so far gratified; but on entering his dining-room a tremendous shock awaited him.

Seated in an easy-chair—his own easy-chair—was Copps reading the day before's paper.

If some monster, fresh from the vasty deep, had been there, it could not have been a greater blow to him. He could not speak, but Copps looked up, and gave him a friendly good morning.

"That case in the divorce court," he said, "is a rum 'un."

"May I ax—ask—who let you in?" Snicker inquired, with an effort.

"Who what?" asked Copps.

"Who let you in?"

"Nobody. Who said I was out?"

"Do you mean to say," said Snicker, with rising wrath, "that you didn't go out last night?"

"I can't talk to a man of your stamp," returned Copps, with a curled lip; "you do put such fool's questions. If I went out last night, how is it I am here now? I slept in my bed as usual."

Snicker said no more. It was a puzzler, but he had his suspicions. Copps might deride the idea of his being jealous of Mrs. Snicker, but after all there was something in it. In his private opinion she had secretly let him in, and they had better beware, or they would find the avenger on their trail.

As for Penny Bunn, he had of course drawn a fancy picture of the detective dying of drink. Even the parish doctor attending upon him was a fiction.

"I'm surrounded by a gang of liars and impostors," thought the schoolmaster. "It's no use standing up against fate. I give in."

CHAPTER XLIII.

CONSPIRATORS IN THE FOLD.—NIPPING A REBELLION IN THE BUD.

"STOPPEM," said Roger Hone, "what do you think they have been doing in the vaults?"

He and Smith were engaged in one of the duties of the morning. It was their turn to fill the buckets from the well, and they were alone in the inner room.

"Blest if I know," replied Smith.

"They seem to be mighty secret about it," continued Hone, "and just look how carefully they have fastened the trap-door down."

"What is the good of bothering about it?" said Smith, impatiently.

"Because it may be a matter that concerns us," said Roger Hone. "In a job of this sort there ought to be no secrets among us. I vote we ask Ford to give us an explanation."

"Do as you like about that," assented Smith, carelessly.

"Will you back me up?"

"Yes, if you want me to."

It was the old story over again. Antagonistic natures never really mix. They may, to an extent, assimilate for a little while, but, in due course, the old state of things is resumed.

In the first excitement of the barring-out, Smith and Hone had joined the rebels, and the bonds of friendship, of the nature of allies in a war, held them together for a time, but now they were weakening.

The truth was not suspected by Hone; he had no idea of the real value of the finding in the vaults. All he felt was a sense of being left out of something in which he had a right to share.

He had already spoken to some of the other boys of No. 2 Dormitory, and if they had not been dissatisfied before, he had made them so.

"Why can't we have a look at the vaults?" was the main question put to them.

While Smith and Hone were at the well, Barnes came into the room. He was, as usual, in a shivering, nervous condition, and he at once began to talk about getting out of the place.

"It isn't fair to keep me here," he said, "if I don't want to stop."

"Jump out of the window, and end it," said Hone, impatiently.

"But Ford said he would see if he could arrange for me to go," rejoined Barnes, miserably, "and now he says I must stay here for three or four days longer. The vaults won't be open again during that time. There is a way out from there, I am sure, and why can't he let me go?"

"When did he tell you that the vaults are to be kept closed?" inquired Hone.

"Just this minute," answered Barnes. "He said he forgot all about me, or he might have arranged for my leaving last night."

"Closed for three days," said Hone, looking at Smith. "What for?"

"You had better ask him," advised Smith, yawning, "and I don't think you will get much for your pains. The Number One fellows mean to keep on with the bossing business."

"I'll have a hand in it!" said Hone, resolutely. "Now, then; one bucket more, and we have done."

Breakfast was laid as usual in the class-room. The spread was a good one, for there was fresh meat for all. The odour of chump and loin chops made the very air heavy.

Bedstone and Gyp Tanner were the cooks, and the way they prepared the meat provided by the professor was worthy of a club *chef*.

No questions were asked about the meat at the outset. It was generally supposed, when any of the boys took the trouble to suppose at all, that it had arrived by the accepted road, through the school-window.

The meal was nearly over, when Hone, from the upper part of the table, addressed Jack Ford, who was seated at the lower end with the other members of the inner circle.

"I say, Ford," he said, "would you mind my having a peep at the vaults to-day?"

"I should, very much," answered Ford, calmly

"But why?"

"Because I can't allow it. The vaults won't be open for inspection for three days."

"By that time the barring-out may be at an end."

"Possibly; but don't make sure. Any way, you can't go down to the vaults till I say you are to do so."

"I say, isn't that bossing us a bit too much?" said Hone, looking round the table, or, to be more correct, around the desk.

"I thought," said Jack, "that it was an understood thing that I was to be boss here."

"It was decided so at the start," interposed Don, "and what is the good of trying to make a fuss about the vaults? In good time all you boys will be allowed to get a peep at them."

"Allowed!" exclaimed Roger Hone; "that is a good word to use among chums."

"Wait until breakfast is over," said Jack, "and then I will hear what you have to say."

Hone muttered something under his breath, but as he was not supported in any way—even Soppem Smith held back from a possible disturbance—he said no more just then.

And in all likelihood he would not have renewed the subject, feeling that he was really alone in his dissatisfaction, but Jack was determined to nip all objections to his rule in the bud.

As soon as the boys had eaten all they required and the washing up was done, he called an assembly of the whole school.

The boys ranged themselves before him without any attempt at order, and he took his stand on the desk of Fontenoy Snicker, and, glancing over them, said:

"A question, or rather, an insinuation, was levelled at me this morning. It came from Hone, and I want to know what it means. Are any of you funking or getting dissatisfied with the way the barring out is managed?"

A murmuring followed his question. It was all in support of him. Hone, who stood well in the background, looked uneasy.

"That we have discovered something in the vaults," pursued Jack, "is a fact. But whether you will ever know what it is, remains to be seen. All I can say is that if any of you make an attempt to go down without the leave of the inner circle it will be very bad for you."

"I only thought that you might confide in us," said Hone.

"You can think what you please," answered Jack, coolly, "but we are not bound to be governed by that.'

"Is there really a way out?" asked Soppem Smith.

"There is," replied Jack. "I may tell you that much. But it cannot be used just yet. There are reasons, of course, but the why and the wherefore will not be told at present. I am sorry to speak in this way, but unless my authority is for the time to be absolute we had better shut up the show. I'll put it to the vote. Who is with me? Hands up."

Up went a small forest of hands. All but Hone and Soppem Smith were for him.

"Now, against me," said Jack, as the hands sunk down again.

Not one was held up in opposition. The two dissentients did not desire to make themselves ridiculous.

"I hope this will be the last time I shall have to put the question to you," said Jack. "All I can say is that if you are patient for a short time you will meet with your reward, as the good people say. I think we will have drill exercise this morning. Put the desk up against the wall. I know a little of them and will take you in hand. It will kill the time anyway."

This was a part of recognized modern education which Snicker had not introduced to his pupils. It came as a refreshing novelty to the boys, and they spent the morning in acquiring a knowledge of the goose step and other elementary features of military drill.

There was no interruption, save a muffled knocking overhead at intervals. It was Penny Bunn engaged in the hopeless task of restoring the broken inlaid floor to its original condition.

Fontenoy Snicker was there part of the time, and the pair laboured together, but five hundred fragments of wood, split in every possible way, offered them a puzzle they were unable to put together.

"What is to be done with the beggarly thing?" asked Snicker, in despair, after they had been on the job for three hours, and were no nearer the end than when they started.

"I can only suggest one thing to be done," said Penny Bunn.

"What is it?"

"Remove the *whole* of the flooring and lay down another. When they find it out, swear you know nothing about it."

"But who is to do it?" demanded Snicker.

"On a straightforward job like that," replied Penny Bunn. "I may conscientiously declare that I have few equals. I recognize the fact that secrecy is necessary and you may rely upon me, sir."

"I suppose the planking could be obtained," said Snicker, doubtfully.

"Easily," answered the confident Penny Bunn. "Now, the first thing to be done is to clear the room, the next to take up the remainder of the flooring, and then Rooker and myself will fetch the planking on a truck and complete the thing."

"How long will it take to do it?" inquired Snicker.

Penny Bunn made a mental calculation, and thought that he would have the place in order at the end of two days.

"Go ahead, then," said Snicker. "Anyhow, things can't be worse than they are."

This was apparent, and Penny Bunn started forthwith on the job, pressing Rooker into his service.

The furniture of the bedroom was moved into an adjoining apartment, rarely occupied, and to work they went, ripping up the ancient valuable flooring until not a square inch of it was left in its place, and the whole of the plastering above the sheet-iron laid bare.

It was peculiar of the room that there were none of the ordinary joists visible in the floor. The whole thing, when the woodwork was removed, was an open square.

As the plaster had suffered during the removal, Penny Bunn decided that it would be as well to take it entirely away, and he and Rooker proceeded with that additional labour. The inevitable noise they made during the operation, attracted the attention of the boys below, and set them wondering.

CHAPTER XLIV.

DOUBTS AND FEARS.—IN A NIGHT OF ANXIETY.

IT was evening again when the continual thumping above became a matter of talk in the schoolroom.

"What the deuce are they up to there?" said Dorey, the excitable boy of number two dormitory.

"It sounds as if somebody's head was being thumped upon the floor. I hope it is Mrs. Snicker giving it to the *beast*."

It was Short who made this suggestion, but it was voted as hardly probable, the sound being continuous, and no head could have stood so much thumping, not even "the wooden structure," as Tanner called it, owned by the principal of the school.

Jack and his closer intimates had their opinion of what was going on, and it made them uneasy, but they did not say anything to spread the feeling around.

Obeying a whispered command from Jack, the quartette stole away into the well-room, and shut themselves in.

"I say, boys," he said, "things look queer. Snicker has hit upon the notion that troubled me. He is coming through the ceiling."

"If he does," remarked Don, "what is to be done?"

"I hardly know," said Jack, "it will spoil our fun

with the discovery we have made. The prize that was ours by every right, will go."

"To Snicker," interposed Tom Drummond, with a groan.

"Not if I know it," said Jack. "It goes right away to the lord of the manor, whoever that noble bloke may be. I think we ought to be prepared for anything that may happen. How long would it take you, Bob, to remove the screws of the trap-door?"

"I could do it in a quarter of an hour," answered Stockton.

"Then they can remain as they are for the present," said Jack. "We can let things go on as usual, unless there is an attempt made to get through in the night. Then we must tell the kiddies exactly how things are, and not allow them to undress."

"It is a bit of a sell," remarked Don, with a grimace.

They returned to the schoolroom, where their absence, if noted, was not commented on.

It was then getting dusk, and the window sills were filled with the youngsters, looking out upon the darkening landscape.

The thumping above had ceased.

So far they were comforted, and had they known of the sheet iron covering overhead they would have been quite at their ease.

But had they known of it, their feeling of security would have been a false one, for Penny Bunn was on the verge of a great discovery.

The end of the barring out was drawing nigh.

When darkness had fallen the lamps were lighted, and the main body of the boys set to work amusing themselves and each other in various ways.

They had improvised draughtboards with sheets of paper, ruled and divided into squares, and made cardboard men. These afforded occupation for a few. Others read such books as they had; some told stories they had acquired by previous reading, and a small percentage sat quiet, thinking of home and friends.

The four members of the inner circle were busy with their thoughts, and it was Don who was the first to conceive that it was necessary to communicate with the Professor without delay.

They all knew that he would be in the cave by-and-bye, but for obvious reasons would not arrive until a late hour. Don put the idea before Jack, who approved of it.

"If there is nothing more going on above," he said, "we are safe till the morning, but ere another day is gone we shall have him through. I think the best plan for seeing Lingo will be to go down the cliff with the rope. I'll undertake the little job after the main lot are asleep."

"Why not open the trap-door?" asked Don.

"Well, Hone and Smith appear to be curious, and unless we are obliged to let them know all, I would rather keep them in the dark for the present. Lingo will be sure to find us a way out of the trouble, if there is such a thing in store for us."

As there was no further movement above, the rest of the evening passed quietly. At ten o'clock the word was given for bed, and Jack announced that all who desired to sleep could do so, as he intended personally to watch until dawn, when he would be relieved by Drummond and Stockton.

"You are knocking yourself up with continual night-work," said Little Jiggers. "Most of us have gone to bed as usual. Why not let me sit up for once?"

"You shall have your turn, little man," said Jack, with a smile, "if we are kept here long enough."

Hone, as he was preparing for bed, gave Soppem Smith a nudge on the arm, and whispered in his ear:

"They are going down the vaults again to-night. If so, I mean to have a peep at the place, and chance it."

"You will get your head punched," was all Smith said in reply.

He went to bed, and soon fell asleep. Not so Hone. He lay awake, and watched for the inner circle to come through the room. But they did not.

The door between the bedroom and the other remained closed, and after he had heard the clock of the old church strike the hour of midnight, he became impatient.

He could hear them roving about, in a quiet way, and, getting up, he tried to get a glimpse of what they were doing, through the keyhole. The light was out, and he could see nothing.

His next move was to try to open the door, but something had been placed against it, and it refused to budge. He was in a state of perspiration, arising from unsatisfied curiosity.

"Hang the lot!" he muttered, "what are they doing?"

Then it flashed upon him that they might simply be preparing to go to sleep, and another idea entered his head.

Why should he not, on his own account, endeavour to find out what there was in those mysterious vaults below?

All he wanted was a screwdriver, or what would answer the purpose of one, and he could soon get the trap-door open. He reflected a moment, and then determined to make the attempt.

Don had taken the precaution to hide his tools away, so Hone was reduced to the necessity of trying what he could do with his pocket-knife.

It was a strong one, with a blunt-topped big blade, which promised to be all that he required. As usual, one of the lamps was left burning, and cautiously taking it from the hook on which it hung, he entered the well-room, and prepared for work.

He found that he had an easier task than he expected. Having removed the dirt which Don had rubbed across the screws, he discovered that his knife fitted the slits in the tops, and speedily brought out the first.

The only thing he did was to make a slight stratching sound upon the metal until, when he had drawn all but one, he dropped his improvised tool upon the wooden door.

The sound it made in falling was nothing great, but it brought his heart into his mouth. Trembling, he remained kneeling, expecting every moment to hear the schoolroom door open, and the voice of Jack asking what he was doing there.

But, to his vast relief, the sound apparently had not been heard.

He waited a full ten minutes, and then proceeded to remove the last screw.

All was ready now, and, with a palpitating heart, he raised the trap-door

Below all was inky-blackness, for the lamp, by the aid of which he had worked, was too far away on the floor to throw any light through the opening.

He thrust his leg through until it rested on the first stone step.

Then immediately a most appalling thing took place.

A cold, icy hand closed round his ankle, and held him tight.

He tried to cry out, but his tongue clave to his mouth.

The hand gave him a tug downward, and unable to bear anything more, he fainted away.

CHAPTER XLV.

THE PROFESSOR AND THE INNER CIRCLE GO TO WORK. —PENNY BUNN'S DISCOVERY.

MEANWHILE, Jack and his friends had been on the lookout for the professor. Quiet as mice, they lay by the open window listening for some sign of his moving below.

Midnight came and passed, and they heard nothing. One o'clock struck, and all was silent below. Where was he?

"Something has happened to detain him," suggested Bob Stockton.

"I had better go down and wait for him," said Jack, "he is sure to come."

They had previously lowered the rope, and Jack, having assured himself that it was securely fastened,

swung himself out, and hung there for a moment to listen again.

"Mind how you go," said Tom.

"I'm all right," was the cheerful reply.

He slipped away out of sight, and with his feet against the cliff to steady him, went down hand under hand. He made very little noise on the way, scarcely more than a cat would have done, performing the journey in a minute or so, but there was somebody below who had heard him coming.

It was the professor, who first coughed to prevent his being scared, and then spoke in a low tone.

"Very well done. What's up to bring you down here?"

"We have been watching for you," replied Jack, as soon as he had recovered from a shock of surprise, "and we thought you had not come."

"Did you expect me to announce my coming by blowing a brass trumpet?"

"No, but we expected you would make some sort of a noise."

"My lad," said Lingo, "on a job of this sort noise won't do. I was here at eleven o'clock and I've already got one fairish load safely stowed away. I came back a moment ago for another lot, and hearing you come down the cliff, I waited to see who it was. I reckoned that it was you."

"I thought I came down like a ghost."

"Ah!" said Lingo, "that was your innocence. You made a lot of noise, quite enough for me to hear. I suppose you never went out poaching? but, of course, not. I've done a bit in my time, if hard up for a dinner, and when a man knows there are sure to be keepers around he learns to listen as he lays his snares. They nick the deaf ones, but they never landed *me*. But this isn't business. Once more, what's up?"

Jack told him of the fears that had taken possession of himself and friends, and the cause of them. The professor listened, and when all was told softly whistled.

"That's an element in the affair we haven't reckoned on," he said." Do you think Snicker will get through the ceiling to-morrow?"

"I should say so," answered Jack.

"Then what we have to do has to be done to-night. We must get out all that we intend to keep of that treasure trove. I'll get it away somehow. By the way, I had an adventure to-night, but that will keep. It was more of a joke than anything else. Get your friends down to help us. Two more will do, for it is astonishing what a lot can be done with a few people when they open their shoulders to it."

"I think Don had better remain above," said Jack, "he is not used to climbing. But he will be A 1 at it when he has had a little practice."

Jack shook the rope, which was an arranged signal for the telephone to be lowered. In a moment it came gliding down.

Jack whispered his instructions through it, and was speedily joined by his two assistants.

"The lamp is just inside the cave," said Lingo; "while you are lighting it I will have a word with Don above."

They did not stay to listen to what he had to say to Don, although they wondered what it was, for time was precious.

The lamp was found, lighted, and placed in position near the piles of treasure ere Lingo joined them.

It was seen that he had already removed a quantity of the lighter material, notably the smaller weapons and two of the heavy chests had also vanished.

"I've picked out the best as far as I've gone," he said, "as we must leave something it won't be the choicest."

He seemed to know a great deal about the value of the armour and so on, for as he proceeded to sort the things out he explained what they were and what he believed to be their market value.

In an incredibly short space of time he had divided the entire stock into two lots, one for removal, and the other, as he remarked, "for the next party who came along that way."

"Which will be Snicker," said Tom.

"It may be," said Lingo, "but I'll bet against it. I could put my hand on the man, but never mind that just now."

One of the chests was to be left behind, in company with the heaviest armour and the coarsest weapons, with just a few of the bows and arrows. The rest they carried at once to the open air.

It was a heavy task, but they worked as niggers never worked, and never will, the proverb concerning the ebony race notwithstanding.

Having got what was recognised as their share outside, they helped the Professor to load up his van.

He had backed it into the wood, so that it could not be seen by any passer-by, though it were day.

After it had been half filled with the heavy material, which, considering its weight, was a fair load for a single horse, he decided to leave the rest.

"I must chance moving it by daylight," he said, "but I shall not attempt to store it in the other cave until night comes again. Meanwhile, I must lie quiet where no prying jackasses are likely to come across me. Now, my brave boys, back you go. We shall win all round yet."

"Suppose Snicker breaks through the ceiling, what are we to do?" asked Bob Stockton.

Lingo lowered his voice, and whispered a few instructions to them. They were received with delighted approval.

"Good night, dear boys," he said, finally. "Time is precious. We must not waste it in talking."

He moved away with his van, and the boys hastened back to the cliff. They were all expert climbers, and in ten minutes were with Don once more.

"Snicker is at work again," he said, "listen!"

They all stood still. The thumping overhead, early as the hour was, had been resumed.

But it was not Snicker. Penny Bunn was the man at work, and he was on the eve of a great discovery.

CHAPTER XLVI.

THE IRON TRAP.—SNICKER FEELS THERE IS A GOOD TIME COMING.

IT was all through a dream that the tutor was up and at work so early.

He went to bed fairly pumped out with his day's labour, and for a few hours was unconscious of everything. Then he had a vision.

His mind reverted to the scene of his recent operations, and he dreamt that under the iron flooring there were bags of gold. He saw them—in his sleep—in rows too numerous to count, and when he set his foot upon them the pleasant jingling of the king of metals fell upon his ear.

The sound of it increased until it was a perfect peal of bells, and then he awoke to find himself in a state of perspiration and half out of bed.

It was still dark, but so thoroughly was he awakened that he had not the slightest hope of getting another wink.

After ruminating awhile on the vision of his sleep, he decided upon rising and resuming operations on the off chance of the dream coming true.

Suppose, indeed, he should discover a lot of money, he was resolved to appropriate it to his own use, and as he attired himself by the light of a cotton dip candle, he pictured to himself the pleasures he would indulge in.

He had all the necessary longings to make a dissipated man. Where he had hitherto run short was in the means to gratify his wishes.

Anything more desolate than the uprooted room by candlelight, he had never seen.

It made him shudder, and if he had not clung to the hope of finding the gold he would have put off the task until daylight came again.

"I could do with a drop of rum and milk to start on," he muttered, as he placed the candle on the sheet iron and took up a crowbar with which he had been breaking up the plaster covering.

He had still about four square yards to clear away,

A SPLENDID SCHOOL STORY.

NEVER BEFORE PUBLISHED.

By E. HARCOURT BURRAGE,

Author of "Ching Ching," "Monkey Mat and Roving Dick," "The Brave Boy of the Basilisk," &c.

THE LAMBS OF LITTLECOTE.

A THRILLINC SCHOOL STORY.

LINGO MEETS AN OLD ACQUAINTANCE. A TOUCHING GREETING IN MEMORY OF EARLIER DAYS.

PRICE ONE PENNY.

ALDINE PUBLISHING CO., 9, Red Lion Court, Fleet St., and 1, 2, & 3, Crown Court, Chancery Lane, London.

nd it was under this he hoped to find a response to is dream.

So he began to work, watching with eager eyes the esult of every dig of his crowbar.

Suddenly, instead of striking metal, it went deep own into something that crunched in response to the low. He stopped short, and breathing hard, stared bout him.

"I've struck something," he gasped, in a broken oice. "What is it?"

Not gold, certainly, for it did not jingle in the least. Ie stepped across to the candle, which he had left in ie middle of the room, and brought it nearer.

There was not much to be seen, beyond the last ole the crowbar had made, so he laid hold of the laster with his hand and pulled off a cake of it.

Then he saw something, and the sight of it sent him aggering back.

It was a human skull!

It lay upon its base, with the vacant eye-orifices and he grinning teeth towards him. The iron bar had roken a portion of the cheek bone, giving it a more han usually sinister appearance, even for a skull. The hock numbed every fibre of his body.

To add to his terror, the candle he had placed near im suddenly toppled over and expired, and he was eft in complete darkness.

It only wanted this to make the awful horror of the ime complete.

He got out of the room somehow—he never exactly new how—and with a vague idea of getting somebody o help him to do—he knew not what — he vandered down the dark corridor until he came to he staircase.

Not being in a state of mind to know where he was, ie fell headlong down, with a clatter and a crash, ningled with screams of pain and terror, sufficient to aise an entire parish.

He awoke Snicker, also his wife, likewise Black-eyed Susan, and even Copps was aroused from a dreamless tate of repose.

As speedily as shaking limbs would allow, they vere all out upon the landing attired in the loose and iry fashion of those who arise in a fright.

"What is it?" asked Snicker, "cats, or an airth— orth—quack—quake?"

Notwithstanding the violence of his fall, Penny Bunn was in a conscious state, and he recognized the voice and style of his superior.

"It is your assistant, sir," he moaned.

"What's happened to you?" asked Snicker.

"There has been a murder committed in this house," answered Bunn, as he arose and rubbed his aching body.

An exclamation of horror burst from the lips of three of his hearers. The fourth, Copps, merely

pricked up his ears. A murder was of professional interest to him, but nothing more.

Penny Bunn crept upstairs as if he had rheumatism all over him, and stood before the limited audience he had summoned from bed. Mrs. Snicker was fearful and wonderful to the eye in her *dishabille*, and Black-eyed Susan looked like the maiden all forlorn, connected with the house that Jack built; but neither thought of their appearance in the excitement of the moment.

As for Fontenoy Snicker, although he was prepared for anything almost, a murder was more than he had calculated on, and the expression of his face was ghastly.

"Who's been killed?" he asked in a quavering voice.

"I don't know," replied Penny Bunn, "the—e—e remains are in that room."

He pointed to the chamber he had recently so abruptly vacated, and Copps moved towards the door with a professional air.

"Don't tell me it's one of the boys," groaned Snicker.

"I don't know who it is," said Penny Bunn.

They entered the room, Copps leading, with a candle held over his head.

"You've been at work here," he said.

He looked around, but not seeing anything approaching the appearance of a corpse, turned savagely upon the startled Penny Bunn.

"You've been drinking," he said, "and got 'um again."

"Got what?" demanded the tutor.

"Why *them*, the usual *anythings* that come before the eyes of a man who doesn't know when he has had enough."

"Look there, then," said Bunn, bitterly. "Can't you see *that*?"

Copps saw it now it was pointed out to him, and without any display of fear, he picked up the skull and held it at arm's length in disgust.

"Is this your murder?" he growled.

"Yes," replied Bunn, "isn't he dead enough for you?"

Mrs. Snicker and the girl, who stood by the door covered their eyes with their hands. The grinning skull was quite enough for them, as it was for Snicker.

He was green with horror, but Copps was not the man to be alarmed or troubled in any way with the contemplation of dry bones.

"You are about the biggest———" he began, and then, unable to control his rage, he hurled the skull at the offending Bunn, who ducked his head, and Snicker received it on the chest.

In mortal terror, for, in common with all bullies, he

was a most arrant coward, he screamed more like a frightened child than a man, and darted from the room. Mrs. Snicker and Black-eyed Susan also fled.

"You people don't make any fuss certainly about nothing," said Copps, addressing Penny Bunn: "why I've seen dozens of these dug up out of old buildings. This thing is hundreds of years old."

He picked it up again and turned it over as if it had been an ordinary fossil. Penny Bunn retreated to the wall, and stood there shivering.

The detective returned to the spot where the discovery had been made, and proceeded to pull up more of the plaster with his hands.

"There is a full bushel of bones here," he said, and another skull. The second one is a woman's, I reckon, by the size of it. What a fine lot of teeth she had."

He busied himself in calmly laying out the bones, Penny Bunn watching him with shivering interest. Presently he made another discovery.

"There's a sliding trap in this iron flooring," he said. "I wonder what that was made for?"

"What did you say?" asked a quavering voice at the door.

It was Snicker, who had crept back, because he was afraid to be alone in the room he occupied by himself.

"Here's a trap-door," answered Copps. "It used to open so as to get at the room below."

"Put those bones away," said Snicker. "I can't abear the sight of such things."

"No, I won't," impatiently replied Copps; "what was this floor taken up for?"

"I wanted to get at the boys."

"Then you can get at them now as soon as you've cleared some of this rubbish away. All that is wanted is a bit of grease to set the trap going. I can see how it works. What games them old monks must have been up to!"

Daylight was now creeping into the room, and it gave sufficient heart to Penny Bunn to allow of his advancing to the spot of his great discovery, with shaky knees. Copps pointed out the way the sliding trap had been made to work.

It stood up about two inches higher than the rest of the iron flooring, and moved to and fro on two small iron rails, not unlike those of the modern railway. One end of it was secured with a hasp, so that it could not be opened from below, and the whole was rusty enough to prevent its being moved until it was well lubricated.

"This is a lucky find," said Copps; "if there is nothing but the ceiling of the schoolroom under this, the barring out is over."

"And won't I warm 'em all round when I get among the young fiends," said the schoolmaster, exultingly. "Copps, I can forgive you a lot for having discovered this. Let us shake hands."

"You will pay me for my services like a man?"

"I will."

They shook hands fervently, and then Penny Bunn put in a word.

"I rather think," he said, "that I had something to do with this discovery."

"You found the bones," replied Copps, "and you are welcome to them. Get a sack, and take them away."

Penny Bunn glared at him as he exchanged a grin with Snicker. Being good friends again, it was only natural they should share a joke at the expense of the tutor.

"What we shall want," continued Copps, "is a small ladder, just long enough to reach the floor below. As soon as we get through that ceiling we can drop it down, and then you, Mr. Snicker, can drop yourself, and let 'em have it."

"I've got the ladder in the tool-house in the garden," said Snicker, "and while you are oiling that trap, I'll get a cane ready that will tickle their young hides for 'em. I've got a treat in store for me to-day. How long will it take you to get that trap ready for action?"

"It may take an hour or more," answered Copps. "We had better have an early breakfast, and then get to work."

"We won't make too much noise over it," suggested the schoolmaster; "I should like to give them a bit of a surprise. They gave me one a few days ago."

"They staggered me a little," admitted Copps, "and that is why I want to get even with them. Otherwise, I rather admire the pluck of the boys. It goes against the grain of all professional men to be done."

"I'll pluck 'em," said Snicker. "What do you say to just one thimblefull, to give us an appetite for breakfast, eh?"

"I don't mind," said Copps.

"Mr. Snicker," said Penny Bunn, as the pair were moving out of the room, "allow me to remind you that I have during the last hour or so suffered from a state of excitement, which, in the ordinary course of nature, has been followed by painful reaction. A thimbleful would not hurt me."

"Ask Rooker to pump upon your head for a quarter-of-an-hour," snarled Snicker; "that will do you more good."

"And when you feel better," added Copps, "you might clear away those bones."

Then they left him, and Penny Bunn realized how fickle is the gratitude and friendship of man.

"It is enough," he muttered; "but, Snicker—dog —pig—brute, I am independent of you. I have the least drop in the world, of the usual, in a bottle in my room. I will partake of it, and drink confusion to a rascal. I think I know of a way to be even with you. Ha! ha!"

And with the air of an avenger of the olden time he swaggered from the room, casting one quaking glance back at the pile of bones as he passed through the doorway.

CHAPTER XLVII.

THE DESCENT INTO THE SCHOOLROOM.—END OF THE BARRING OUT.

THE days, and the very hours, of the barring out were numbered. We need not make any secret of this fact. The trap-door really opened upon the ceiling of the schoolroom, which was nothing but lath and plaster, and all that had to be done when the said trap was opened, was to break through it, drop the ladder down, and descend upon the rebels.

Fontenoy Snicker had no doubt of the issue. Bad as he considered the boys to be, he could not conceive their attacking his sacred person, especially when he would be supported by Copps.

Wicked boys that loaf about the streets occasionally "small-gang" grown-up people; but his pupils surely would never dare to attempt such a thing. He might have rightly conceived also that they would not be cowardly enough to act in that dastardly way.

After partaking of a liberal breakfast, Copps and the schoolmaster prepared to carry the boys' retreat by storm.

The former provided himself with a bottle of oil and a feather, the latter fetched the ladder that was required, and armed himself with a stout cane from his little store of castigating weapons he kept in the hall.

"A drop of ile," he said, "won't hurt it. It fills up the pores, and adds to the sting of it."

"You seem to know all about it," returned Copps, a little drily; "quite a past master in the art of licking youngsters, I should say."

"I've laid into 'em pretty freely in my time," answered Snicker, with a grin, "but it is poor work to what I shall do to-day."

Copps began his labours, oiling the run of the trap, and, having raised the hasp, soon succeeded in getting it to stir a little. But it was of necessity a long job, and two hours or more had elapsed ere he got it fully open.

It was not a very wide trap, but it would admit of a ladder being thrust through it, and still leave room enough for a man to pass.

Nothing now remained between Snicker and the room below but a few laths, and a peck or so of plaster.

"Everything is quiet below," said Copps. "I suspect they know you are coming, and are preparing to give you a warm reception."

"You will follow me down and back me up, won't you?" said Snicker.

"I've promised to do so," answered the detective, "and I'll keep my word."

"Then jam the ladder through, and let us get at 'em."

Copps sent the lower end of the ladder through the plaster with a crash, and forced it down to the flooring below. A cloud of dust shut out everything below, and enveloped the two men in a sort of fog.

"Down you go," whispered Copps.

Snicker, now that the moment of his triumph had arrived, shook from head to heel with excitement. He would have shrunk in his cowardice from the task he had set himself, if his fears had not been counteracted by his malice.

He had, moreover, stimulated himself for the work, and was ready to do all that he had threatened.

Stepping upon the ladder, he descended rapidly, and stood in the midst of the cloud of dust which was being rapidly dispersed by the draught coming in from the open windows.

He soon had a clear view of the schoolroom, and he stared around him, utterly dazed and confounded.

Not a single boy was to be seen.

The whole place was in confusion. The breakfast things were lying upon the desks, unwashed, with remnants of food, and through the open door that led to the inner rooms, he could see the blankets and other articles of bedding carelessly piled in a heap.

But that was all.

The boys had vanished as if they had been so many ghosts, dispersed by the daylight.

"You're taking things quietly there," remarked Copps, from aloft.

"Come down," said Snicker, in a hushed voice; "the last of the lickers is to be seen here."

Copps came down the ladder, and, the room being now nearly free from the dust, he had a clear view of the state of things.

"They can't be gone," he said; "the door is still barricaded. They must be skulking in that inner room. Come out, you imps!"

"The room, as far as I can see—isn't there a well in it? You were telling me something about it."

"There is," said Copps, with a gasp.

Snicker sat down upon a form, and, unconscious that he had also seated himself upon a greasy plate, left there by a careless boy, covered his face with his hands, and shivered.

"I know what they've done," he moaned. "They've been and gone and chucked theirselves down that rather than face me."

"Look here," exclaimed Copps, suddenly, realizing the terrors of the situation, "I'm out of this job. I don't want any payment for what I've done—you are welcome to that; but I've got a particular appointment in London this afternoon, and I'm off."

"Copps," cried Snicker, clinging to him, "don't leave me now. You are a witness that I didn't mean to be unkind to the boys, and that I come down here in the most friendly sperrit. If you stand by me, all will be well."

"No," returned Copps, firmly, "it is not my affair. You sent for me to find out who had been burglaring about your place, and I've nothing to do with anything else. If I make a move at all, it must be to arrest you for driving them to wholesale suicide."

He had got thus far in his repudiation of the schoolmaster and his works, when a slight shuffling sound was heard in the well-room.

Snicker looked up, and both turned their eyes in that direction.

"What is it?" asked the schoolmaster, in a hollow voice.

"It's somebody moving about."

"Save me!" shrieked Snicker; "who is it?"

It was only poor Barnes, white and trembling, who came creeping out of the well-room, holding his hands before him in an appealing fashion; but the schoolmaster's nerves were in such a state that the sight of the wan lad appalled him.

Copps was a little—not much—cooler, but he had a clearer head at all times. Seeing it was only a boy, he took heart, and asked him what he was doing there.

Barnes stared at him, unable to utter a word.

"Where are the rest of the boys?" enquired Copps.

Barnes made a sign, but the purport of it neither of the troubled men could understand.

"Oh, sir," suddenly burst out Barnes, falling on his knees. "Don't beat me. It will kill me, I am sure!"

"Beat you, my dear boy? No, indeed. I feel like a father towards you. I now know what a bereaved parent's sufferings must be, although I never knowed —know it before. You are Barnes, ain't you?"

"Yes, sir," replied the boy.

"Then you are a witness as I meant kindly by the rest when I come down here," pursued Snicker. "They hadn't any reason to do it."

"Do what, sir?" asked the wondering Barnes.

"Why, what they did," said Snicker.

"I was afraid to go that way," said Barnes, "for fear I should fall, and so they left me behind."

"What are you talking about?" demanded Snicker, changing his manner of address.

"I was afraid to go down the rope by the cliff, sir——"

It was a yell, an oath, and shriek mingled together that leaped from the lips of the schoolmaster. Copps burst into a roar of laughter.

"My stars!" he cried, "if they don't whip all I ever came upon! Give in, Snicker. Don't be a bereaved father any more, but call 'em back and embrace the lot. What a lucky parent you will be to have thirty odd prodigals to kill the fatted calf for. You will have to buy a bullock. It's the best thing I ever came near."

"Down the cliff?" muttered Snicker, glaring alternately at the detective and Barnes.

"Yes, sir," answered the boy, "and Ford said that I was to unfasten the rope and throw it down to him, as it was his private property. Stockton said he was afraid you might rashly hang yourself with it, and they haven't taken anything of yours away, but all the jam and the pickles are eaten, and they took their stores with them——"

Barnes had found his tongue, and was running on at a great rate, until Snicker cut him short with an angry movement of his arm.

"I don't want to hear no more," he said. "Down on your hands and knees. I'll warm one of you for a start."

"No, you don't," interposed Copps.

"What has it to do with you?" muttered Snicker.

"To do with me or not, don't touch that kiddy," said Copps, determinedly. "He isn't in the state for your brutality to be exercised upon him. If you lay a finger on him you will have to take off your coat to me."

The schoolmaster threw his cane into the corner of the room nearest to him.

"I give in," he said, "but mind this, you won't get any money from me."

"We will see about that by-and-bye," said Copps. "I say, young 'un, do you know where the rest have gone to?"

Barnes shook his head.

"Ford said," he replied, "that as I wasn't coming with them it was no use my knowing."

"Well, Snicker," said Copps, "it is no good our hanging round here. If you give me a hand we can soon take away the barricade and open the door. The barring out is ended."

It took them but a few moments to break up the planks that had held the door so fast, and, it having been opened, they passed into the passage with the solitary boy they had found in the room.

The barring out was, as Copps said, at an end, but the fun attendant on it was far from over. The clouds which had gathered round the head of Fontenoy Snicker, Esquire, had thinned a bit, but were not by any means entirely dispersed.

CHAPTER XLVIII.

THE thing that worried Fontenoy Snicker now was, "What had become of the boys?" To have them wandering about the country, and up to all sorts of mischief, of course, meant absolute and irretrievable ruin. Something would have to be done to get them back again with all speed.

But first Mrs. Snicker must be enlightened concerning the, end of the barring out, and that estimable woman having been informed of the facts, hastened with Black-eyed Susan to inspect the schoolroom and the adjoining chambers.

The result of this proceeding was that she realized that there was an appalling amount of washing to do, and a great deal more than could be put out, on account of the expense.

"Start the copper, Jane," she said, "we shall have to keep at it day and night until it's done. Bless the boys, they must have done nothing but wallow about the floor with these blankets round them."

No doubt the youngsters had made them in a terrible state of dust and dirt, and her wrath was in a measure justified. Jane, otherwise Black-eyed Susan, started on her heavy task, and for the next half-hour was preparing for the biggest wash that had ever been undertaken since the school began.

It was to be expected that Mrs. Snicker would have another wail over her lost jam and pickles.

"I feel," she said, with the intensity of a very angry woman, "as if I *could* skin 'em."

There is little doubt that flaying a boy would just then have been a very congenial task to her. But there was only Barnes in the house on whom to perform that operation, and he was hardly to be numbered among the guilty.

He could, however, be punished for what he had not done by being made useful. Mrs. Snicker determined to make him assistant laundryman.

He was set to work to light the copper fire, and fill the boiler with water. Having done that, he was commanded to take off his coat, roll up his sleeves, and be ready to assist Black-eyed Susan at the washtub.

Barnes did not relish the prospect before him, and he hoped and prayed that the knowledge of his having done such humiliating work would never be known to the boys; but it was not so bad as being licked by Snicker, so he assumed a cheerfully responding air as he obeyed the injunction of the schoolmistress.

Meanwhile, Fontenoy Snicker had once more thrown himself into the arms of Copps, and asked him for his help and advice.

They were on the roof of the Abbey at the time, whither they had gone to see if they could discover any signs of the boys roaming about the country.

Nothing was to be seen but the old dreary prospect of flat meadow, scattered houses, browsing cattle, and here and there a rustic, plodding heavily along in the pursuit of his daily duty.

"The first thing to be done," replied Copps, "is to find out where they have gone to."

"What do you think about it?" asked the schoolmaster.

"It's no use thinking, Snicker. We have thought before, and all our thoughts have come out wrong. For instance, you thought this morning that you had them all safe, like little pigs in a sty, and that you were going to have a whacking treat—but it didn't come off right."

"They are enough to drive a man wild," said Snicker, with a sigh. "It's my luck, I suppose, to have got hold of nothing but bad boys."

"Boys," rejoined Copps, sententiously, "are pretty much what their elders make 'em. Now, my advice is to get at what has become of them without delay. We can soon find out if they are about the country. If they are not, it is my opinion that the whole lot have gone home."

Fontenoy Snicker smiled.

"That won't hurt me much," he said. "They all pay in advance."

"What of that?" asked Copps. "You are the blindest fool I ever met."

"Thanks," interposed Snicker.

"But you are," continued Copps. "Now, what sort of tale do you think the boys have gone away with? I tell you, as a man of the world, with his head screwed on the right way, that you stand a good chance of having actions brought against you, and damages to pay that will take your last rag from you. I'll also lay you an even fiver, and post the money, that you will be criminally prosecuted for obtaining money under false pretences. What sort of figure do you think you would cut in the dock? Fancy your posing as a schoolmaster! You are an unmitigated fraud."

"Plain speaking is one of your gifts, Copps," said Fontenoy Snicker, with a ghastly smile, "if I'm not edicated—*ed-jew-ca-ted*—quite so well as some people, I have a good master for the boys."

"A penny bun, slack-baked," said Copps, sarcastically. "Now, then, we're wasting time jawing here. You get away to the station at Chippenham, and if your boys have gone away by train, you will be sure to hear something about it. I'll start Bunn and

Rooker perambulating the country, and roam about in a casual sort of way myself. I'll have a chop at Smudgem Bender about two o'clock. Perhaps you can get back by that time."

Snicker was certain of it, and the plan of action proposed by the sapient Copps was at once acted upon. All that remained of the inhabitants of the Abbey in a quarter of an hour, were the trio engaged in washing pursuits.

Fontenoy Snicker, a man of independent spirit when dealing with those who could not help themselves, did not take the trouble to inform his wife of the arrangement made, and left her in ignorance of the place being so nearly evacuated. Unsuspecting, and intent upon her labours, she spent the next hour or so, and then was startled by a ring at the great bell of the principal gates.

As a matter of fact, this bell was rarely rung at all. The tradesmen came to a side door, and respectfully knocked, and if by chance a visitor arrived, it was at a time when the gates were open and they could approach the front door.

It was a noisy, aggressive bell, which seemed when it was rung to be trying to make amends for a long enforced silence by clanging its loudest.

"Mercy on us," exclaimed Mrs. Snicker. "who can that be? Jane, you are not fit to be seen, and I'm all of a muck-wet. Boy, go and see who is there."

Barnes, with his sleeves rolled up and a green baize apron pinned to the front of him, was hardly the figure to be presented to persons of such importance as had arrived.

On opening the door and peering out, Barnes saw a carriage at the gate and a gorgeous flunkey peeping through the bars.

He, instead of asking what was wanted, dashed back breathlessly to Mrs. Snicker, who at once fell into a flurry.

"Find Mr. Snicker," she said, "quick!"

Barnes ran off upon a fruitless expedition, and he had barely started when the bell clanged again, louder than before. The people outside. whoever they might be, were getting impatient.

Barnes soon discovered that the schoolmaster was absent, and imparted the tidings to the dismayed Mrs. Snicker. The bell rang a third time with a noise that was almost appalling.

"I had better go and see who it is." said Mrs. Snicker, as she whipped off her apron, "It is so like Jerry, to get out of the way when he is most wanted. It is his viciousness."

Smoothing her hair with her hands, and muttering all sorts of topsy-turvy blessings on the head of her absent husband, she hurried out, just as a portly gentleman was descending from the carriage to assist the flunkey with a fourth tug at the bell.

On seeing Mrs. Snicker he desisted in the attempt, and glared at her with an eye like Mars, to threaten and command.

"We have been ringing here for the last half-hour," said the old gentleman; "is the place deserted?"

"No, sir," replied Mrs. Snicker, as she threw back the gates; "but I am almost alone. Mr. Snicker is out with the boys, at—at—at morning exercise. It is washing-day, and myself and the servants were at the back of the house when you first rang."

"Washing-day!" exclaimed the lady in the carriage. "Oh, I cannot bear the smell of it. We must come again another day."

She was rather a pretty woman, much younger than the gentleman. He turned with a deferential air towards her.

"As you please, dearest," he said, "we can come to-morrow. There will be no washing about then, I presume?" addressing Mrs. Snicker.

She, scenting the coming of a pupil, and possibly a good paying one, promptly replied, "Certainly not, sir."

"Then we will say to-morrow," said the old gentlemen, "we are in the neighbourhood for a few days only. You do not appear to recognise me."

"I do not, sir," answered Mrs. Snicker.

"I am Sir Charles Barstow," he said.

"The owner of the Abbey!" exclaimed Mrs. Snicker, aghast.

"Yes," was the complacent reply, "this is Lady Barstow. We have been recently married, in fact, and are on our honeymoon trip. I wish to show her the antique beauties of the place. There is an inlaid floor, in an upper room, unapproachable in the beauty of its workmanship I am given to understand, which I especially desire her to see. Perhaps Mr. Snicker will be at home to-morrow?"

"Yes, Sir Charles," said the terrified Mrs. Snicker, faintly.

"The school is in a flourishing condition, I hope?"

"It is, Sir Charles."

"It is a noble pursuit," continued Sir Charles. "training the youthful mind in the way it should go. I hope we have not inconvenienced you by calling. Good day."

He stepped into the carriage, and Mrs. Snicker, in a mechanical way, bobbed a charity school curtsey by way of parting salute.

The carriage disappeared down the road which the boys once took, when they ran Milky Whey and his barrow out of the district of the school.

"Training their minds the way they should go." moaned Mrs. Snicker, "and they are all gone. Wants to see the inlaid flooring, unreproachable for its beauty, too. Oh! Jerry, Jerry, you have got yourself into a precious mess. It's ruin, stark staring, ragged ruin, as you've brought yourself to now. But you always were a fool."

Having paid this tribute to the ability of her husband, she returned to the wash-tub, weighed down with a feeling of coming woe, insomuch that she had not much harassing power left in her, and her assistants had a comparatively easy time of it.

Snicker, unconscious of further misfortunes hanging over his head, walked into Chippenham, hung about the station, visited the chief Inns, and heard not a word about his boys.

This was a great relief to him, and in a better and happier frame of mind than he had been for some days, he wended his way back to Smudgem Bender.

Copps was just about attacking his chop when the schoolmaster appeared. He had nothing to report.

"Not a sign of them anywhere," he said.

"It's skew—*cu*-rious," mused Snicker.

"They are not far away," said Copps, confidently. "It's early times to find them out. They are in one of the woods, according to my belief. After a night in the open, they will be glad to come back again."

"Seen anything of Bunn and Rooker?"

"I noticed them down by the river, and it seemed to me as if they had got hold of some tackle and were fishing."

"I'll bet they are not putting themselves out of the way," muttered the schoolmaster.

He ordered a chop for himself, and by the time he had partaken of it, and smoked a cigar with Copps, it was four o'clock, and time to be going homeward. Accordingly, feeling in a more and more easy condition of mind, Snicker paid the score, and they returned to the Abbey.

Mrs. Snicker, hearing them enter the hall, appeared and told her husband the short but staggering story of the visit of Sir Charles Barstow. He could have better borne a thrashing with the butt-end of a hunting whip.

"As I told you," said Mrs. Snicker, "you had the chance of giving in to the boys at the outset, and you ought to have done it."

"Say another word to me," yelled the schoolmaster, "and I'll murder you."

He dashed away upstairs, and was heard to enter a room and shut the door with a bang. It was the apartment on which he had operated with such a ruinous effect.

Copps went upstairs also, followed by Mrs. Snicker, and they stood listening at the door for awhile. Snicker was very busy inside, moaning, and moving the broken bits of flooring about.

"He will go mad on that," said Copps.

"Can't it be put right?" asked Mrs. Snicker.

"Not in forty years," was the consoling answer.

It was past six o'clock when Penny Bunn and Awful Rooker came back. It was quite true that they had been fishing, and they brought back with them a string of perch, and roach, and dace, in number about thirty, and their united weight something under a pound and a quarter.

Having got on the kind side of Black-eyed Susan, they asked her to cook their fishy game for supper. She promised to do so, and to bring it up to the room occupied by Penny Bunn.

"Missus is gone out for a walk," she said; "it's no use working here any more, she says, and the washing is to be left until the end of the week. You shall have a nice supper for once in a way, Mr. Bunn."

"On my word," said Penny Bunn, as he and Rooker walked upstairs, "that girl seems to be quite devoted to me."

"You don't mean to tell me that she is spoony on you?" said Rooker.

"I do," asserted Penny Bunn; "and it's not the first time I've had a woman in love with me, and been unable to reciprocate their affection. I once had a lady of title dead gone on me."

"Gammon!" exclaimed Rooker.

"Fact," insisted Penny Bunn; "she was young, wealthy, and beautiful, but there was something about her I did not quite like, and nothing came of it."

He pulled his collar up and wriggled his neck, in the way of some youths of gallant proclivities. Rooker hardly knew whether to believe him or not, but he decided not to cast any further doubt on his assertions until after supper.

It was about nine o'clock that night when, with the fish on a dish before them, the pair were about to partake of a relishing supper, when the great bell at the outer gates again clanged loudly.

They looked up, and stared at each other with pallid faces.

"What's that!" exclaimed Penny Bunn.

"The—e—e bell!" gasped Rooker.

"I know that," said Bunn, "and it is the big bell at the gate. But who is it ringing it at this time of night?"

"Shall we go and see?"

"I think so. Something must be wrong."

In the hall below they encountered the entire household with the exception of Barnes, who had been sent to bed half-an-hour before, without his supper, because he had been extravagant with the soap during the washing operations of the day.

All were wondering why the bell should be rung at that late hour.

They went out in a body to respond to it, and crossing the playground, had additional cause for dismay on discovering that there was nobody at the gate.

Copps and Snicker, as the two boldest of the party, went outside and made a feint of examining the ground around, but they discovered nobody.

"It is a rum district for a runaway ring," said Copps, as they returned towards the house.

"Save us," exclaimed Mrs. Snicker, "there is something sticking in the door!"

There was, indeed, and of all things in the world, it was an arrow, not a mere toy, but a genuine weapon of the olden time.

Appended, or rather wrapped round the shaft, was a piece of paper secured with a cord.

Copps tried to draw the arrow out, but the feat was not to be accomplished, and he had to snap it off short, leaving the head in the door.

"It wasn't a baby who sent that home," he said, "now let us see what this precious missive means."

He loosened the cord, and unrolled the paper. As he expected, there was writing upon it.

"Just listen," he said ; "of all the games—but there, it is no use talking about that."

Raising his voice, he read with due emphasis the following message to the schoolmaster :

"To FONTENOY SNICKER, Esq. (?) OF LITTLECOTE ABBEY.

"If you desire to end the state of war at present existing between you and your pupils, come to-morrow morning at the hour of ten, to the old elm tree, at the corner of Smudgem Bender Lane. Furthermore, let it be understood that your coming will not reduce the said pupils to submission. Therefore, in consideration of your own welfare and peace of mind, see that ye fail not.

"THE FOUR OF THE INNER CIRCLE."

"It is like reading of something in the olden time," murmured Penny Bunn.

"Stay a moment," said Copps; "that is not all There is a postscript where the paper is folded. down."

Reassuming the air of a public reader, he read as follows :

"Come alone. If you venture to bring an associate with you, or induce anyone to play the spy at a distance, you will both surely repent it. Obey the call made upon you, and no harm will ensue."

"This wants talking over," said Copps. "Snicker, we can't do it until we have had supper and settled down to a cigar."

This remark led Penny Bunn's thoughts back to his supper, and as the schoolmaster and the detective, with Mrs. Snicker and Black-eyed Susan departed, he and Rooker hurried upstairs.

The room was there, the table was there, also the plates and the knives and forks, but the fish was gone.

A top of a nice crusty loaf had also gone to keep the lighter food company.

"Rooker," said Penny Bunn, "what is the meaning of this?"

Now, as it happened, neither of them had been informed of the presence of Barnes in the house. Fontenoy Snicker had made them acquainted with the fact that the boys had got away, leaving out the part of the story referring to the lad they left behind them.

The disappearance of the toothsome fish was therefore for the time a complete mystery.

"Everybody in the place," said Penny Bunn, after a dismal silence, "was with us just now, and we do not keep a cat or a dog. Rooker, what do you make of it?"

"Skeletons don't eat, I suppose?" said Rooker.

"I don't know," answered Bunn, wearily; "but where is the fish?"

It was a problem that was worrying them until they, later on, went to bed and to sleep.

And yet how easily it could have been solved.

The meanest creature on earth, when it is hungry, will go a-prigging, and Barnes, prowling around, had come upon the open door of the tutor's bedroom. Inside was the savoury fish awaiting consumption, and in two minutes he had wolfed the lot and hurried back to bed.

CHAPTER XLIX.

THE MEETING BY THE OLD ELM TREE.—"SHALL AULD ACQUAINTANCE BE FORGOT?"

IT was the opinion of Copps that the appointment ought to be kept, and his advice, summed up in two words was "Give in."

"Even if you have to wait a bit," he said, in conclusion, "a month, a year, or suppose you are not able to ease off your bile on this lot at all, you will have plenty more boys in the future you will be able to warm to your heart's content. Give in."

"I will," assented Snicker.

On the following morning, at nine o'clock, he started for the trysting tree. The lane referred to was about a furlong from the village, and it was one of those minor thoroughfares that lead to nowhere but to fields. The experienced know them by the extra quantity of grass growing in them, but the novice, wandering for pleasure, sometimes thinks he will try one for a short cut, and when he has walked a half-mile or so, he discovers that he has to come back again.

At a quarter to ten Professor Lingo and the four boys, composing the inner circle, arrived at the old elm tree, and the boys climbed into its branches. The object of their being on the spot was to play the part of witnesses, in case it should ever be necessary for them to do so.

"And I have a surprise in store for you," said Professor Lingo, as they settled in their chosen places. "A little more to the left, Drummond. I can see one of your legs."

Shortly after they had got into place, Fontenoy Snicker arrived. He expected to see the boys, in full force, or a portion of them, at least, and it was his intention to settle the matter right away, as it would be necessary for him to be back at the school as soon as possible to receive Sir Charles Barstow.

The lurid light of his previous troubles faded into nothingness compared to what he anticipated would ensue when his landlord found out the mischief which had been wrought by him, in his eagerness to get at his refractory pupils.

On seeing Lingo he stopped, and stared with an expression of dismay upon his mobile features. It was clear to Jack Ford, who was on one of the lower branches, that they were not strangers by any means.

"Lingo!" exclaimed the schoolmaster.

"Yes, Lingo," was the calm reply, as the Professor advanced towards him, "your old pal with whom you ran a curiosity show, and one night when there was a full house and you took the money at the doors, you bolted with the mopusses. That is the last I saw of you until this day."

And then, with a sharp movement, he laid hold of Fontenoy Snicker by the nose and gave it a wrench that threatened to uproot it.

"Oh!—mercy!" gasped the schoolmaster.

"I swore I would do that and more," calmly returned the Professor, "but that will do for the present. Don't try to run away, or I will lash you with my whip up to the very door of that den of yours. I am here to arrange matters between you and the boys."

"What have you to do with them?" asked Snicker, and he rubbed his aching nasal organ, "I didn't know you were in the neighbourhood."

"Well, I am here," said Lingo; "and now to business. Here is a paper, practically a copy of that which the boys have already submitted to you. Will you sign it or not?"

"I came here to do so," answered Snicker, humbly, "but I have one thing that I think is reasonable to ask, before I do it."

"Out with it."

"It is, that so long as I keep to my part of the agreement, they won't write home or talk about what has been going on."

"I will undertake," replied the Professor, "that they will do as you wish. But if you come any more of your games, I'm hanged if I don't see that all the country knows of it. More, I vow that you shall be prosecuted as a fraud and a swindler."

As he uttered this threat and warning combined, he drew out a paper from his pocket and a traveller's bottle of ink with a suitable pen. Selecting a smooth spot upon the ground, he spread the paper out, and told Snicker to kneel.

"It is an attitude suitable for the occasion," he said, "and necessary, because I forgot to bring my library table with me. Go ahead and get it over."

Fontenoy Snicker did as he was desired, signing with a somewhat tremulous hand, but appending his usual signature. Professor Lingo, with a flourish, attached his name as witness, and the thing was done.

"You can go home now," he said, "and be smart in clearing away from here, for my fingers are itching to have another tug at that protuberance on your face which passes with some people for a nose. Morris—cut it—*bolt!*"

He raised his whip as he uttered the last word, and Snicker backed into the road.

"Tell me where the boys were last night," he cried.

"They were in a place they will shunt to again if ever you give them cause," replied Lingo. "And I'll bet that neither you nor all your private detectives will ever track them down. One word more, you are not to talk to Copps about my having played the part of peacemaker. If you do I am sure to hear of it, and then look out for squalls."

"I won't breathe a word consar—*cer*—ning you," answered the schoolmaster.

"Right," said Lingo, "I know you will keep your word, because you dare not break it. Off you go!"

Fontenoy Snicker was glad to get away, and hurried off, consoling himself with the reflection that he could in private tell what version he pleased of the settlement.

"The boys will be back to-night," bawled Lingo after him.

Snicker signified by a motion of his hand that he heard, and vanished round a bend in the road.

"You may come down now, dear boys," said Lingo.

They came tumbling down the tree in rather a reckless manner, but all alighted without injury to life or limb.

The first few moments were devoted to cutting sundry capers, and then they took off their caps and tossed them into the air.

"Victory!" cried Don. "Hurrah!"

"Not so much noise, dear boys," said the Professor, complacently, "let us be moderate and reserved in the hour of triumph. A quiet shake of the hand all round will suffice for successful generals of our kidney."

"We owe our success entirely to you," said Jack Ford, enthusiastically.

"Some of it, without a doubt," answered the Professor, "but it is a fact that the best of architects and builders cannot put up anything worth looking at unless they have good materials to work with. Now we will return to our anxious friends, and put their minds at rest."

They started off down the lane, the four boys softly chanting the burden of their old song:

> There was a good time coming, boys,
> We wait for it no longer,
> For Snicker is now up a tree,
> And we little kids the stronger.

The subject thus sung about was by that time well on his way back to the Abbey. Now that he had in a sense, got the burden of the boys off his mind, he had leisure to think of the prospective visit of Sir Charles.

What was he to say to him? How was he to evade the consequences of his rash goings-on?

The man could not be murdered and hidden away, because he would be accompanied by a young wife and two liveried servants. It was impossible to dispose of the lot, although the schoolmaster would not, on moral grounds alone, have hesitated to go to that length.

He was in the thick of the wood when a bright idea flashed upon him. It was so good that he stopped short, blinded by its brilliancy.

It was to put the whole thing on burglars.

He could vow that the room had been unoccupied for a considerable time, and the villains having got into the house went thither in search of treasure, a report having got abroad that there was something of great value hidden in the Abbey.

There was Copps in the place, a genuine detective, and if he could be persuaded to assert that he had been sent for to track out the offenders the thing was as good as done.

Of course he would want to be paid, but a pound or two would not matter now. It was really a splendid notion.

He fairly broke into a run, in his eagerness to get home and lay out the details of the idea, and did not pull up until he reached the hill, which he scaled in a panting, breathless condition.

But do what he might, conceive what he would, everything seemed to go against him. On reaching the summit of the hill, he was once more bowled over like a skittle on seeing the carriage of the baronet standing at the gate.

Its occupants had left it, and the footman, in an attitude of careless grace, rarely found, save among those accustomed to wear livery, was leaning against the footboard of the box, chatting with the coachman.

Snicker hobbled along as if his feet had been suddenly transformed into stumps, and on coming up to the carriage, paused to have a word with the two servants.

"Your people have just come," he said, feebly.

"They've been here a full arf hour," answered the footman, haughtily.

Snicker gasped out something, and staggered along into the house. In the hall he encountered Barnes, engaged in impotent efforts to catch bluebottle flies.

"My boy," he said, tenderly, "where are them—*those*—people?"

"Upstairs with Mrs. Snicker, sir."

The schoolmaster braced himself up, made an effort to hang his hat upon the peg, missed it, and leaving his chapeau upon the floor, hastened upstairs.

The door of the fatal room was shut, and all was silent within, but there were voices further on, in the chamber usually occupied by Penny Bunn.

Snicker went forward, and the door being open, he peeped in. Everybody he had left at home, barring Barnes, was there.

The furniture, including the bed occupied by Bunn, had been piled up on the far side, and the carpet wisped into a heap. Beneath it was another inlaid floor, in an uncommonly dirty condition, and Mrs. Snicker was explaining to the baronet that she would not allow it to be washed too often, for fear it should "warp."

"I must commend you for your thoughtful care of it," said the baronet. "Dearest," addressing his young wife, "observe the complete harmony of the thing. The various woods selected are laid so as to match or contrast with a force that makes it a perfect poem of the art of flooring."

"Yes, I see," responded her ladyship, "it is very pretty, but I do not think the person of the house is particularly clean."

She was evidently bored, probably because she had little taste for the antique, and looked out of the window at a number of crows flying past.

Snicker went forward, and bowed deferentially.

"Ha!" exclaimed the baronet, "Mr. Snicker. How do you do?" He shook hands with him graciously. "I am thinking that this room of all in the Abbey, ought not to be occupied. Your young man," he looked at the blushing Penny Bunn, as if he were uncertain whether he was odd man or scullery wench, "tells me that he sleeps here."

"I placed him in this especial room," said the veracious Snicker, "because he is careful and cleanly in his habits, and is, moreover, a lover of this sort of antic—*antique*—jigger it!—work."

Lady Barstow raised her golden eyeglasses, and looked at the schoolmaster as if he had been something to distinctly object to. The baronet, wrapped in admiration of the flooring, did not, apparently, observe his *lapsus linguæ.*

"Whatever he may be," said Sir Charles. "I do not think he ought to make use of the room."

"His occupation ceases this very hour," answered the obliging Snicker.

"Thank you," said Sir Charles; "and now, my dear, I should like to show you an adjoining chamber——"

"If you will spare me to-day," murmured Lady Barstow. "I am not very strong, and the—the—excitement of looking at so much ancient beauty is trying."

"But it may be months ere we come into this neighbourhood again."

"Yes, my love, but the floorings and the other things will not run away. I beg of you to excuse me."

The baronet looked disappointed, but he was too much in love with his wife to press the matter.

"As you please, dearest," he said.

It may be imagined with what close interest Fontenoy Snicker listened to this colloquy. His life, as it were, hung upon the turning of it.

It was a reprieve, new existence, to him when Sir Charles, with a courtly air, offered an arm to his wife, and carefully escorted her downstairs.

Snicker followed them, with a bearing that put ordinary flunkeyism into the shade, and never left them until they were seated in the carriage.

Then he backed, and bowed like a Chinese figure in a tea shop, until the vehicle had disappeared.

"The closest shave I've ever known," he gasped. "Now, with all respects to you, Sir Charles, I don't want to see you again. If you can get run over, or drowned in a yacht, or go a-mountaineering and fall over a precipice, or get rid of yourself somehow, I'll bless your blessed name foriver—hang the word—evermore."

CHAPTER L.

THE RETURN OF THE BOYS.—FIRST NIGHT UNDER THE NEW REGIME.

THE relief experienced by the long-troubled schoolmaster must have been very great. It is not easy to describe the full force of it in words. He was, in a metaphorical sense, down in a coal-pit when he came back to the Abbey that day, and now he was high above the clouds, free and soaring in the realms of peace.

The majority of men, under similar circumstances, would have felt an additional kindly feeling towards his fellow creatures. Not so Fontenoy Snicker, of Littlecote Abbey.

His thoughts, now that he was himself relieved, turned to revenge.

The boys had got the upper hand of him for the time, but anon he would level matters. It would hardly be prudent to attempt to do it at present. He would be wise to wait a bit.

Perhaps the Professor would go right away out of the county, or get into trouble of some sort, or die. Then again, the rebels would, ere long, be thinning in the school. Some would go away in due course, and there would be new boys on whom he could exercise his peculiar arts as a pedagogue of the old, cruel type.

Meanwhile, he wanted somebody on whom he could vent the spite that was in him.

He dare not try it on Copps, and Mrs. Snicker, although of late subdued, was hardly a safe subject. He had got her for life, and one day he might be ill again, and then it would be her turn. Only two persons were left for him to have a go at—Penny Bunn and Awful Rooker.

He hated the former more than the latter, because, with all his weaknesses and follies, he was in some things a better man than his master. He was in a degree fitted for his work, and Snicker was, as a teacher, worse than nothing in a school.

"I'll have a few minutes with Bunn," he muttered, as he strode into the house.

He found him in the schoolroom contemplating its disordered condition, only in part removed by the labours of Mrs. Snicker and Black-eyed Susan.

Barnes was in the well-chamber, sweeping up the floor under feeble protest.

"Bunn," said Snicker, sharply.

"Sir," replied the tutor, wheeling round, with tightened lips, and a nose raised in the air.

"You have made a nice mess of taking up that flooring. What did you do it for?"

"I was under the impression, and am still imbued with the belief, that I acted entirely under your orders, sir."

"My orders be jiggered! Hadn't you the sense to see that in taking up that there floor you would ruin it?"

"Sense," said Penny Bunn, with marked emphasis, "is of little service where your orders are concerned. As you appear to desire that your commands should in future be jiggered, I shall only be too happy to act as you wish. But, first, I will ask you to explain the verb ' to jigger.' It appears to me to be slang of a very low description."

"Now, don't you put my back up," said Snicker, with a face of saffron hue. "You will be sorry for it if you do."

"Up with your back," said Penny Bunn, " or up with your fists, too, if you like. What do you mean by worrying me about the floor? Didn't you begin the job yourself?"

"Bunn——" began the schoolmaster, but the tutor saw that he was quailing, and promptly interrupted him.

"Snicker," he said, calmly and steadfastly engaged in rolling up the cuffs of his coat, "there are some positions in a controversy—you know what a controversy is, I suppose?"

"In course I do," answered Snicker. "Do you think I've been livin' in a Abbey all this time without finding that out?"

"What is it, then?" demanded Bunn.

"A controversy," said Snicker, with the air of an authority on the subject, "is a place where the monks used to eat their wittles—*victuals* in."

"That," said Bunn, with a dry laugh, "is a refectory. But your answer is near enough for you." Snicker breathed hard, and looked all sorts of things, but said nothing. "A controversy is an argument, a debate, a disputation between parties. Make a note of it, will you? There comes a time in a controversy, as I was saying, when words are futile and useless. That time has arrived with us, and the ordeal by combat is all that is left. Before beginning the fray, I will just, in passing, mention that in my youth I took lessons in the noble art from a practised pugilist, who had killed his man in a sixteen-foot ring. Now, sir, if you are ready I am prepared."

Fontenoy Snicker was not prepared, for he was an arrant coward, as we have previously pointed out. To the immeasurable relief of Penny Bunn, who was on a level with his principal as far as real pluck was concerned, the schoolmaster held out his hand.

"Bunn," he said, "I was only joking. The school can't go on unless we pull together. I am pleased to see you show such a noble sperrit—*spirit*—and let us shake hands."

"Certainly," replied Penny Bunn, in an exasperatingly patronising manner, "if it will make you feel any better, sir, I'm agreeable."

So they shook hands, and Fontenoy Snicker retired to a secluded part of the Abbey, where he for a time wasted some of the sweetness of his disposition in verbal explosives on the air.

Then he sought his wife to hurry her up with the preparations to receive the boys.

This done, he had an interview with Copps, on whom he pressed the advisability of his evacuating the Abbey as speedily as possible.

Copps promised to go as soon he had transacted a little private business of his own in the neighbourhood.

The business was of course his appointment with Professor Lingo.

"And so the boys are coming back," he said, "that's a good job for you. What are the terms?"

"My terms," answered the schoolmaster with hauteur. "Is it likely that I would yield to a parcel of little whelps?"

"It certainly appeared to me that you would have to do so," said Copps, with a smile. "However, whatever the terms, it is a good thing all round. Take my advice. Conduct your crib on a better and more manly principle, and you will get on, if you don't, the word *bust* but feebly expresses what will happen to you."

"Much obliged, I'm sure," said Snicker, "nuthin'—*nothing* helps a man on like a bit of advice, free, gracious, and no charge made."

"Gracious or gratis," said Copps, "you are welcome to it."

As the evening approached all who were residing within the Abbey showed an increasing interest in the prospective coming of the boys.

The question agitating the mind of Fontenoy Snicker was, "How would they come home?"

Would they return in a quiet or a bounceable fashion? Would they return in twos and threes, or come in a body to support each other in a continued defiance of authority?

Again, "How was he to deport himself?"

It would never do for him to metaphorically rush into their arms, and again the difficulty of bearing himself in a dignified manner was apparent.

He eventually decided on deputing the office of receiver to Penny Bunn, and from some hidden spot take note of the way the boys behaved.

If there was anything the tutor dearly loved it was to be placed in a position of absolute authority. He readily undertook the task of receiving the returning rebels, and laid out a programme in his mind for the occasion.

His attitude was to be that of a forgiving father welcoming a host of prodigal sons.

The twilight was approaching when Penny Bunn, Awful Rooker, and Copps, with Barnes hanging in their rear, went down to the gates of the playground to see if there were any signs of the boys.

After a wait of five minutes' duration, the sound of voices chanting a song was heard. The returning host were coming up through the wood.

"In that way the old pilgrims of Canterbury used to sing as they wended their way along the high road," explained Bunn to Copps, anxious of course to show off his learning.

"There isn't much of the pilgrim about your youngsters," said Copps, drily.

As the boys advanced the words of the song they were singing could be distinguished. They sang in admirable time almost as one voice. It was very sweet to the ear. Copps remarked that it "was worth sixpence to listen to 'em," and Penny Bunn scooped an imaginary tear out of his eye.

"They are a little wild and wilful," he said, "but their hearts are sound as—as—as——"

"Young pertaties," suggested Copps.

"Your simile," rejoined Bunn, "is not the one I was endeavouring to think of, but it will serve. As sound as young potatoes, certainly."

"Listen to 'em," said Copps.

By the hill of old Malford when evening is nigh,
 We return to the Abbey with the wreath on our brow;
The banner of victory flutters on high,
 And peace should reign in the old Abbey now.

"Good," said Copps, "decidedly good. Take them all round, I never met with such a lot of lickers. I wonder who it is that writes their poetry for them?"

Penny Bunn smiled meaningly.

"That," he said, "is not for me to explain."

"You don't write it," exclaimed a weak voice in the rear.

It was Barnes who had thus dared to put a spoke in the wheel of the tutor. Penny Bunn turned, and stared at him haughtily.

"Silence, boy," he said.

"It is Herbert May who writes it," insisted Barnes; "he writes all our songs."

The appearance of the leading boys emerging from the wood, cut short any further controversy on the subject. They marched four abreast, and foremost were the members of the inner circle.

They saw Penny Bunn, of course, but no notice was taken of him at first. Bearing a little to the right, the boys filed from the wood, and when all were clear, the voice of Jack was heard.

"Halt!"

Instantly all were still.

"Left-half-turn. Eyes front."

It was done.

Jack then advanced a pace, and saluted, military fashion.

"Mr. Bunn," he said, "we have, in accordance with our agreement, returned to Littlecote Abbey, trusting that in the future there will be peace between us and those who have us in their charge, and that Mr. Snicker will be as true to his part of the compact as we will, most assuredly, be to ours."

"Yes, certainly," replied Penny Bunn, totally oblivious, in his amazement, of the part of the forgiving father he intended to play.

"We also hope that there will be no reference whatever to the past," continued Jack; "and with your permission we will now enter the playground, and amuse ourselves until the supper bell rings. When the meal is ready, we shall be ready, too. Stand at ease. Break away."

With a cheer, the column broke up, and the boys rushed past the staggered tutor and his companions into the playground. Barnes was immediately sur-rounded by some of the younger boys, and plied with questions concerning the treatment he had received during the last day or so.

He had nothing to report, or rather declined to report anything beyond the fact that Fontenoy Snicker had not whacked him, and Mrs. Snicker was in a fearful wax about the consumption of her jam and pickles. Not a word about the humiliating washing did he breathe.

Penny Bunn and Copps, after a short survey of the boys, who resumed their habits in the playground as if nothing had happened, went into the house, where they found Snicker awaiting them in the dining-room.

"They take it coolly," he said.

"Cool isn't the word," replied Copps.

"They set a good example to their elders in deportment," added Bunn. "Mr. Snicker, congratulate yourself. Your boys are *gentlemen*."

The schoolmaster did not make any immediate reply. He, as well as his assistant, had evidently received a facer. The bearing of the boys confounded him.

"If I may give another word of advice," began Copps—but Snicker interrupted him.

"Which you may *not*," he said. "What is the good of advice when it bears on what we don't know is going to happen. What did they say?"

The words of Jack Ford were reported to him. Snicker smiled a kind of snarl, but did not make any further direct remark on the subject. He fell back on his accustomed panacea.

"I feel," he said, "as if just one little drop would do me good, and I'm sure you two won't say no. We will have it. Bunn, you must preside at supper to-night. There is a fairish cheese in the store-room. Ask Mrs. Snicker to put it on the table."

They had their little drop together, and Penny Bunn afterwards had an interview with Mrs. Snicker. She was disposed to resent putting the "fairish cheese" upon the table, as it was one reserved for her own table; but she yielded to his arguments, and the boys had a better supper than they had ever before partaken of in Littlecote.

Their conduct all round was subdued, but it was the quietude of those who had fought and won, and were disposed to wear the laurels of victory with modesty.

When the time came for retiring, they went quietly to their dormitories, and comparative peace was on the Abbey.

The beds had been made in haste, and were rather bumpy, a fact that was speedily discovered.

"Chums," said Jack, "no fuss to-night. Remember that a lot of extra work has been put on Black-eyed Susan. You may take your affidavit that Mrs.

Snicker hasn't put herself out of the way, and it is no use worrying about trifles. We will give Snicker a fair chance of reforming, and if he doesn't come up to the scratch like a man, we can have another rumpus. I promise you that the next will be a *settler*."

So they went to bed like good boys, and for a brief spell of time there was peace upon the house.

CHAPTER LI.

THE NEXT DAY.—THE REMNANTS OF THE TREASURE.

THERE could be little doubt that the boys had been well coached by somebody in the line of conduct they were to take on their return.

At the usual hour on the following morning the call bell rang, and they arose, dressed, rushed for the first wash at the taps, and in all things comported themselves just as if there had been no barring out or levanting from the school.

Likewise did they adjourn to the playground to disport themselves according to established ideas, and in due time assembled in the schoolroom with Penny Bunn at his seat at his desk, and Awful Rooker in his at the head of the boys, both feeling very much like persons in a dream.

The door between the class-room and the inner chambers was closed, and, furthermore, nailed up.

Snicker had himself done it late on the night before, without taking stock of the peculiarities of the inner apartments.

He was induced to do this to insure himself from any further trouble arising from a breach of agreement. Little did he dream of how this course of action played into the hands, and furthered the schemes, of his pupils and Professor Lingo.

But that will be apparent anon, and we need not dwell upon it now.

Fontenoy Snicker was late. Modesty or nervousness was the cause, and when he at length appeared, he cast a quick glance around to note the behaviour of his flock of recovered lambs.

Beyond a slight flushing on the faces of two or three, there was nothing to lead a stranger to suppose that anything out of the usual course had happened.

But Fontenoy Snicker was not going to let the matter rest without *one* word.

Mounting his desk, he once more surveyed the lambs, all feigning to be doing something of a scholastic nature, with more or less success.

"Boys," he said, in a harsh, croaking voice, "after a short severance we meet again. Things isn't exactly as they was—*were*, and may never be so again. Any-

way, this is *my* school, and *I* am master here. I hope that will be recognized."

Not a sound, but the faces of the boldest were turned towards him. He had evidently primed himself for the occasion, and was disposed to be aggressive.

"I," he resumed, "am *master*. Is there any of you disposed to deny it?"

No answer.

"Is there any of you here," he went on, raising his voice, "who is disposed to deny it? Ford, what have you to say?"

"You are the principal of this school, sir," answered Jack, quietly, "and as such we *ought* to respect you. I fear, sir, that recent events are already fading from your mind."

"They will never fade," returned Fontenoy Snicker, "but I'm not going to say anything more now. Mind this, however—*don't go too far*."

It was a lame and impotent conclusion to an address, and he was sensible of it. He was, in short, beaten by the bearing of the boys as a body.

They neither quailed before him nor showed a rebellious spirit. He hardly knew what to make of them.

It was a loose kind of morning all round, for, of course, no lessons had been prepared. Desultory examinations were the order of the time, and quite a blank was created by the non-appearance of the cane.

The fingers of the schoolmaster itched to use it, but it lay in its corner untouched. It was early days for him to risk another outburst from his pupils, but it was very trying to have to wait and watch for revenge.

Then again the dinner was better that day than it had ever been. The meat was fresh and good. As Bedstone said, it hadn't the least flavour of the saddle about it. There was an abundance of potatoes, and unlimited bread. Thus far the compact was being kept.

But the claws of the tiger were only sheathed and not drawn.

The whip of public exposure for the time subdued him. The condition of things was a truce rather than a cessation of the war.

Mrs. Snicker kept away from the boys. With the jam and pickles still fresh in her memory, she dare not trust herself in their company.

"I feel, Jerry," she said, as they sat at dinner, "that if I go near them, I must scratch their faces."

"Then you keep away from them," growled her husband; "we don't want any of your high-falutin's here."

If the elders felt strange, so did the boys. There

was a sense of strangeness even in the most familiar places, and some of them could hardly believe in the reality of the immediate past.

"I don't believe that we shall get peace now," said Don, as the boys gathered together in the playground after tea.

There were about a dozen of the youngsters near him, among them Roger Hone and Soppem Smith, Jack Ford, Drummond, Little Jiggers, and Whymper Will were also there. Some were seated on the wall, others squatted on the ground.

"Peace," said Roger Hone, "I should think not. How would you feel if you were in Snicker's place?"

"I should make the best of things," answered Don. "The man has been wrong throughout. It's all bosh thinking you can have your own way in everything in this world."

"We shall not have ours," said Soppem Smith, significantly. "Did you twig how he kept glancing round the room to-day? Did you ever see such an expression on a man's face?"

"He will be quiet enough for the time," said Jack Ford, "and we needn't bother. Time enough to worry when he begins the old games again. I don't think we shall see it in our time."

"To-morrow is the usual half-holiday," said Bob Stockton; "suppose it is not given us?"

"Then we take it," said Jack.

Soppem Smith and Roger Hone severed themselves, and walked away across the ground. They were attracted by a group of boys examining the front door, and they walked over to them. Dorey, Philter, Short, and a few others were examining the broken arrow sticking in the panelling.

"What is it?" asked Short.

"Snicker has gone into archery while we were away, perhaps," suggested Philter.

There was a widish crack in the panel, and Dorey put his eye to it.

"It isn't the sort of arrow they use in these days," he said, "I can see that it has a big barbed top to it."

Penny Bunn, who had emerged from the side entrance, approached the group, waggishly shaking his head.

"Now, which of you boys played that joke on our respected principal?" he asked.

"None of us," they replied.

"But you must have done it," said the tutor. "Attached to that arrow was the request for Mr. Snicker to meet you and settle the terms of peace."

"I assure you, sir," said Dorey, "that we had not such a thing as a bow and arrow among us."

"That is strange," murmured Penny Bunn. "I have the message here. Mr. Snicker dropped it in the hall, and I picked it up."

He brought out a folded piece of paper, which he handed to Roger Hone, being the nearest to him, to read. He looked at it and passed it back again with a meaning look at Soppem Smith.

"I have never seen it before," he said to Penny Bunn, "and that is all I can say."

He left the group, and Smith following him, they moved down to the gate, where they leant against the bars with their faces to the boys.

"It is Lingo's writing," said Hone, "disguised a bit, but he has a way of making an 'S' that no one can mistake. The meeting was at the corner of the lane. Why were we not told of it? Soppem, old man, there are some fellows in this drum who are a mighty deal too close."

"And you can't draw them," returned Soppem Smith. "I wonder where the arrow was got from?"

"Does it matter?"

"Somehow, I think it does. There has been a lot going on we knew nothing about. I, for one, am sick of it."

"We must wait a bit. Something will crop up by-and-bye to let daylight in upon us."

"What are you two conspiring about?" asked somebody on the other side of the gate.

They turned quickly, and saw Copps, the detective. He had been out for a stroll down to Smudgem Bender, where he had, in a casual way, inquired after Professor Lingo. No tidings of him could be obtained there, and the detective was inclined to think that the appointment had been made to make a fool of him.

"We are not conspiring," answered Hone, gruffly; "we were merely talking about the arrow-head which is sticking in the door."

"By the way," said Copps, "have you any more like it?"

"No," answered Smith, "and we never had that."

Copps opened the gate and came in. He stayed awhile talking with them, and ascertained beyond a doubt that they had nothing to do with the arrow or the message attached to it. More than that they could not say.

He had a good look at as much of the remnant of the old weapon as could be seen, and it set him thinking. He could see what he had not observed before, that it was many years, probably centuries, old.

"Where did the youngsters get it from?" he asked himself, and found no answer.

Like all men of his class, he hated a mystery unless he was on the way to solve it. By-and-bye he was to find it out, and then it would be too late.

That night Professor Lingo came on foot to the secret entrance to the vaults in the cliff, and he brought with him a miner's drill and two small dynamite cartridges, such as are used for blasting rock.

He had also in his possession a lantern, which he lighted after he had got into the vaults.

With the aid of it he drilled two holes in the intersections of the stonework on either side of the entrance to the inner vault. Then he transferred the remaining portion of the treasure to the passage leading to the open air.

That done, he put out the lantern, and returning to the outside, sat down by the roots of a tree and filled his pipe.

It was about half-past ten o'clock, and he smoked on quietly until the old church clock proclaimed the hour of eleven.

Then he arose and backed into a position commanding a view of the rooms of the Abbey.

There was but one light burning and that was in a room Mr. Snicker had taken to after he left the one where the flooring had been taken up.

Lingo did not stir until he saw that light out, and then he returned to the vaults, relighted the lantern and carefully placed the dynamite cartridges in the intersections he had made.

After a deliberate examination of the fuses, he leisurely lighted them and sauntered once more into the open, and resumed his seat.

In a minute or two, a short, sharp, crackling sound was heard, followed by the crashing fall of masonry.

He kept his post with his eyes upon the Abbey. The sounds had not been heard, and there was no alarm.

Having given ample time for any indication of movement above, he returned for the third time to the vaults to inspect the work he had done.

The cartridges had faithfully performed the task he had set them to do. The passage to the stone stairs leading to the well room was completely blocked.

"Good," he said, approvingly; "the rest is for Copps the wise."

The lantern was again extinguished, and in his easy way he walked away through the wood, and crossed the open ground to a distant lane where his van, with the old mare in the shafts, was waiting for him.

Taking hold of the reins, he led the animal away, and did not halt until he came to a secluded spot seven miles from Mumping Malford.

———

CHAPTER LII.

COPPS KEEPS HIS APPOINTMENT.

AS the eventful hour drew nigh for the appointment with Professor Lingo to be kept, Copps betrayed a certain amount of nervousness.

He had to keep it from his host, who that night was in a convivial mood, and showed a tendency to make a high time of it and to have his guest for company.

Copps had announced his intention of going away on the morrow, and money matters had been satisfactorily settled.

By pleading indisposition, the detective succeeded in getting free of the schoolmaster's companionship in time, and with all speed he wended his way to the appointed place. It was a long walk, and he was pretty well pumped out when he arrived. Lingo was there, quietly smoking his favourite pipe.

"Punctual almost to the moment," he said. "I do like a business man to deal with. Now, before we go on, allow me to explain why I have brought you here."

"I hope it is something for our good," said Copps, facetiously.

"It is for the good of both, I hope," answered Lingo, gravely. "The fact is, I have made a great discovery, and I don't know how to make use of it without your assistance. You know I have been helping the boys in their little game?"

Copps nodded and smiled.

"Well," continued Lingo, "one of the things I did was to come now and then to the base of the cliff and send up provisions to them. On one of these expeditions I chanced to find out a cave."

"Yes," said Copps, suddenly keenly interested.

"In that cave there is a lot of things," continued the Professor, "arms and armour, and a chest, I am sure, that is filled with money, probably hundreds of years old. Of course, it is all the property of the lord of the manor, but there is a reward attached to it, and you are to get it and share it with me."

"But why don't you get it alone?" asked Copps, suspiciously.

"In the first place," said Lingo, "I don't want it to be known that I had anything to do with the recent barring out. A man of my stamp is always subject to all sorts of suspicions, and in a rumpus is likely to get into trouble. I have been had up two or three times for poaching, and the police would come in with their speechifying. You ought to know the line they would take. Perhaps they might get hold of my share of the find, and how could I ever get it out of them? As half a loaf is better than no bread, and as I know you to be a man they could not play tricks upon, I picked on you to take the honour and half the profits of the business."

"What is the find worth?" asked Copps.

"I don't know," answered the Professor; "how should I? Hundreds, anyway. Sir Charles Barstow's cousin is lord of the manor, and he is owner of the property—I have found out that much—and therefore would be disposed to be liberal. He is also one of those old gentlemen who thinks more of things of

A SPLENDID SCHOOL STORY. NEVER BEFORE PUBLISHED.

By E. HARCOURT BURRAGE,

Author of "Ching Ching," "Monkey Mat and Roving Dick," "The Brave Boy of the Basilisk," &c.

THE LAMBS OF LITTLECOTE.

A THRILLING SCHOOL STORY.

TOBOGGANING EXTRAORDINARY. PENNY BUNN EXPERIENCES THE JOYS OF TRAVELLING WITH AN AVALANCHE.

PRICE ONE PENNY.

ALDINE PUBLISHING CO., 9, Red Lion Court, Fleet St., and 1, 2, & 3, Crown Court, Chancery Lane, London.

the past than he does of the present. Say, are you in the job or out of it?"

"In it," said Copps, earnestly; "but how am I to say that I found it?"

"That I leave to you," replied Lingo, modestly, "I'm not a very good hand at faking up yarns. You may say that you were prowling around and tumbled on the cave, or something of that sort. Go right away to Sir Charles—he is staying at Reading—and it won't take you a month to get there. See him before you breathe a word about it, and tell him that you came straight, as you were sure that Snicker was not to be trusted. There are lots of people in the world who would bone a bit before they talked of what they had found. Naturally I dursn't do it, for where could I dispose of the things? They are not in the cheap Jack line."

"Lingo," said Copps, "you are really more honest than I thought you were. Will you shake hands with me?"

"Am proud to do it," returned the Professor.

They shook hands like the two good honest men th y were, Copps chuckling over the fact that he had found a flat, and trudged off to the cave.

There its mysterious position and contents were shown to Copps, who saw at once that he had tumbled upon a good thing.

They conferred as to the method of conveying the information of the discovery to Sir Charles, and before parting, an appointment was made at Chippenham on the following night, when Copps would report the result of seeking an interview with the great man.

Finally they took an inventory of the contents of the vault and left it, carefully closing the entrance as heretofore.

"Now we will have an hour together," said Lingo. "My van isn't far away, and I can give you a bit of supper, and perhaps something after it."

"Lingo," replied Copps, quite overcome, "you are my friend for life. If ever you get into trouble, send for me, and I will get fifty witnesses to prove an *alibi*. Not the common ruck, but men that not a judge or a warder knows, and whose looks would win the hearts of any jury."

"If ever I do want help," said Lingo, "you are the man I shall come to."

The van was on the common, where it had been since dusk, and Lingo, as good as his word, entertained the detective most royally.

The promised hour of enjoyment was extended to a longer period. In short, Copps passed the night in the van, and did not get so much as a wink of sleep.

CHAPTER LIII.

THE HALF HOLIDAY—TOBOGGANING EXTRAORDINARY.

IT was a great surprise to Fontenoy Snicker to find on the following morning that Copps had not been in the Abbey during the night, and when he turned up shortly before school time looking rather yellow about the chin, he asked him where he had been.

"On business that may one day surprise you," replied Copps, emphatically. "Meanwhile, if you will just settle my account, I will go away."

"Anything wrong again?" inquired the schoolmaster, anxiously.

"Wait and see," said Copps, with a mysterious wink.

More he would not say, but, having received his money, amounting to eleven pounds—he let Snicker off very light he declared—he shook hands with that worthy and went his way.

He was in such an uncommon hurry to go, that it made the schoolmaster uncomfortable, and he worried himself with all sorts of fears that had not the least foundation.

It was during the morning lessons that he had another surprise. Jack Ford, when his class was called up, reminded Mr. Snicker that it was the usual half-holiday, and he asked if it would be necessary to get up their lessons before going out or after they returned.

There was no asking if they might have the holiday? It was, as a matter of fact, a quiet way of testing the schoolmaster on the line he intended to take—whether he meant to keep faith with the boys or not.

There was a moment's hesitation on his part, but he yielded. He thought the evening would do, as they would be back by seven o'clock, and in a feeble way he warned them not to go too far afield, or to do anything to get themselves into trouble.

It was a cementing of the late victory, and the boys exulted. Jack was the hero of the school. Even Soppem Smith and Roger Hone admitted that nobody could have introduced the subject and carried it through so well as he had done.

On what may be called the upper side of the Abbey, the part beyond Mumping Malford wood, the cliff lost something of its precipitous nature. A quarter of a mile away it was a huge slope, down which the native boys had of late been accustomed to slide on rude imitations of the Canadian toboggan.

As a rule, the Lambs of Littlecote went the other way, but on this occasion they took that direction, keeping, with few exceptions, together, and with Penny Bunn accompanying them.

He had again put on the garment of friendship for the boys, being actuated thereto by a burning desire to get from them some of the details of the recent barring out. He had, indeed, in his chameleon disposition, volunteered to his principal to pump them on the subject.

Above all he was commissioned to ascertain where they had passed the time after they left the school.

As the youngsters straggled along in a broken line, playing little jokes upon each other, bursting out into short games of leap-frog, and singing snatches of songs, he tried his fortune with Little Jiggers and Don, who were walking side by side.

"It seems like old times, doesn't it?" he said.

"Old times," repeated Don, with a semi-vacant stare.

"Yes; our being all so happy together," said Penny Bunn. "I have had quite a desolate life since the feud began. When you left the school I was ill with apprehensions concerning you."

"We were all right," replied Don, disdainfully.

"I feared you would—would catch cold sleeping in the open air," continued the tutor.

"Well, you see we are all right," said Don. "Jiggers, I'll give you ten yards start and race you to that old oak tree."

"Right," shouted Jiggers.

He took a liberal ten yards, and away they went, leaving Penny Bunn to make the best he could of a failure.

"Not to be drawn," he murmured, "truly they are a most extraordinary lot of boys."

"Ya—hip! Who-o-o-oa there! Clear the way!"

It was not any of the Lambs from whom these sounds emanated, but the yelling of half-a-dozen country lads getting ready to slide down the cliff.

A clump of bushes hid them from sight, and the Littlecote youngsters ran forward to get a view of what was going on.

The sport was quite new in the neighbourhood, having been introduced there by a young soldier, a native, who had been in Canada and come home on furlough.

He went away again, but the sport remained behind, and became popular.

There were three sledges, each of which, with a little crowding, would carry five, or even six, passengers. One of them had a pole to steer the toboggan if it showed a tendency to swerve from the direct course.

There were about a dozen yokels engaged in the pastime, and having taken their seats away they went, whooping and yelling. The Lambs of Littlecote gathered on the verge of the cliff watching the descent with rather envious eyes.

"Great fun that, I should say," said Gyp Tanner.

"A 1, copper-bottomed," added Short. "I wonder if those fellows would let us have a ride."

There was a generally expressed desire to try the joys of tobogganing, and Jack Ford said he would try to make an arrangement with the yokels for the loan of their crude vehicles for an hour.

Pending their return, Penny Bunn, whose presence was getting rather aggravating, went on with his pumping business, and found it very dry work.

His motive was as clearly seen as if he had been made of glass, and his thoughts printed inside him.

"It looks as if he meant to stick to us all day," said Bob Stockton. "I wish he would hook it."

"I'll get rid of him," said Jack, savagely.

"Very good fun, tobogganing, sir," he said, addressing the tutor.

"Yes, most excellent," was the reply; "but it seems to me that those rustic boys are mere novices at it."

"They would be grateful for a lesson, sir, from you," said Bob Stockton, politely.

"I shall be pleased to give them one another day," answered Penny Bunn. "The secret of the whole thing lies in the management of the pole."

"They rather muddle the handling of it," said Bob. "Tom, you can do a bit of tobogganing?"

"Rather!" was the reply.

It seemed that there were at least half-a-score of boys there who had in the winter time indulged in the pastime at home. So, when the yokels had, by a circuitous, and less precipitous route, brought back their crude vehicles, Jack drew them aside, and made a bargain for the loan of the toboggans during the rest of the afternoon.

Money being scarce with the yokels, and Jack liberal, the business was soon transacted, and the vehicles got ready for a descent.

"I can steer one," cried Jack, "who will take the others?"

Don and Tom Drummond volunteered for the posts, and then came the question of passengers. Some of the more timid and inexperienced held back, and Penny Bunn remonstrated with them.

"Really," he said, "there is nothing to be afraid of. The rush down must be most exhilarating."

"Come with me, sir," said Tom Drummond.

A sickly smile spread itself over the face of the tutor.

"I do not think it would be kind," he replied, "to deprive the boys of a pleasure."

"You will deprive them of nothing, sir," said Bob Stockton, "and by your calm bearing you will inspire us with courage."

Boys are very ready in seeing when there is a "bit of barney" on, and now they all began to protest that they would not think of going unless Penny Bunn showed them how to do it.

"You can sit in front, sir," said Tom. "And I'll steer."

"In front?" said Bunn. "Isn't that the most—a—a—insecure place?"

"You would be in a position, sir," said Bob Stockton, in a velvety voice, "to perceive any sign of danger, and give a note of warning. With your experience of tobogganing, sir, I venture to say that no harm could befall us."

"Well," said Don, gruffly, "if these yokels can manage it, I can't see how we are going to fail. Mr. Bunn is not a coward."

"A coward, indeed," said the tutor, rearing his head proudly. "No, I come of a valiant stock. I have a remembrance of the sword my father wore in the—the yeomanry. Boys, it is my duty to show you that I do not fear. I *will* go down the declivity before us."

They encouraged him with a loud cheer, and he flushed with the pride of a great performer who receives an ovation on his entering upon the stage.

"Get ready," he said, firmly.

The first toboggan was pushed over the head of the cliff, and volunteers were asked to steady it until the voyagers were seated. There were plenty for the office, and Penny Bunn, his heart bursting with a deadly misgiving, slowly slipped over the side, and got upon the crude vehicle.

"Hold it tight, boys," he said; "if you let go before the others are seated you—you—you will deprive them of the pleasure of a journey."

"Tom," whispered Jack, "what are you going to do?"

"Follow me, and let Don come third," replied Tom, in the same low tone. "If I don't give him a treat he never had before, and won't want again, write me down an idiot."

Mr. Bunn had by this time slowly settled himself in front of the toboggan, where he tucked his legs under him in an attitude strongly suggestive of a jobbing tailor at work. He feigned to be looking ahead, but his eyes were closed, and he was breathing a prayer for his safe descent.

CHAPTER LIV.

TOM, with the guiding pole in his hand, slid down behind the tutor, and soon ascertained that he was surveying the scene with tightly closed eyes.

"Fine view from here, sir," he said.

"Remarkably so," answered Penny Bunn, in a cracked voice. "I never really appreciated its beauties so well until now. Don't you think this—a—a structure has a tendency to-o-o-o wriggle?"

"It is the pliancy of the wood, sir," returned Tom. "Now, are you fellows ready there? Remember that we must have three seconds clear start, or we shall run into each other, and then there will be broken bones."

"One mome-e-ent," said Penny Bunn. "I thi-i-i-i-nk I left my handkerchief behind. Dro-o-o-opt it. It is a familililly heir-lo-o-o-om."

"Get it in a minute, sir," said Tom; "when we come back. Let go there."

Two or three more had settled behind Tom, and the boys above holding the toboggan rope having let go, away they went.

A cry, that was a scream, a yelp, a wild howl in equal proportions, burst from the lips of Penny Bunn; but all the world could not save him now. He had started, and he had just *got* to go.

When a man of weak mind shuts his eyes, he invariably opens his mouth. Thus did Penny Bunn the moment he got under way. And by opening his mouth he offered a very wide cavity for the reception of the rushing air.

It dashed into his throat with such force that he would have choked on the spot, if there was a spot in the question, considering the speed he was travelling. But it was to Tom Drummond he owed an immunity from that unpleasant result.

As soon as the toboggan was fairly started, Tom proceeded to carry out an idea that was in his mind. Instead of utilizing the pole he carried in his hand for steering purposes, he quickly thrust it under the legs of Penny Bunn, and used it as a lever to propel that unhappy man from the conveyance.

The tutor, feeling something under him, leant forward, and fell off in front. The toboggan passed over him and went down like a shooting star to the ground below.

He knew what had happened as he lay for the fraction of a moment upon the sloping cliff. Then he sought to rise, and succeeded in getting upon his hands and toes.

"Hi, there! Out of the way."

It was Jack Ford, coming along with a party on toboggan number two, who yelled out this warning. But there was no time to profit by it. The second toboggan dashed upon the tutor with a force that sent him flying onward, rolling over and over, and he, in a whirligig mental fashion, recognizing the apparent certainty that he was doomed to destruction.

"Sorry, sir," screamed Jack, as he went by with a

fearful rush; and Penny Bunn was in a dim way congratulating himself upon his second escape, when the third toboggan descended with irresistible force.

This time he completed his journey. Don, with his party, carried him down to the level, rode over him, and shot ahead for fifty yards or so until stopped by the gradual rising ground.

The boys rolled off their conveyances, and lay upon the soft sandy soil, gasping for breath. No doubt the rush down had something to do with their condition, but it did not account for the distortion of their countenances as they fought to restrain their laughter. From the summit of the cliff descended the sounds of hilarious mirth.

As soon as they were able they rose up and went to the assistance of Penny Bunn, who lay upon his back coated all over with gritty particles as if he had been a piece of dough shaken in a bag of sand. He had not the least idea of where he was or what had happened to him, and when he was asked by Tom Drummond if he were hurt, he only stared at him and smiled as men do when they hit their thumb-nail with a tack-hammer.

"No bones broken, sir, I hope?" said Bob Stockton.

As he still was dumb, they raised him into a sitting position, and propped him against the side of the cliff. Then after a while he began to recover, and presently was able to respond to further questions put to him.

"How was it, sir," asked Tom Drummond, "that you fell over?"

"I was heaved up," replied Penny Bunn, "just as if there had been an earthquake."

"Well," said Tom, looking solemnly around, "I felt a queer sensation as we came down; but I must say, sir, that you exhibited wonderful coolness under the circumstances."

"I am not accustomed," replied the tutor, with a ghastly smile, "to a loss of nerve, no matter how suddenly a startling phenomenon is presented to me."

"Better luck next time, sir," said Gyp Tanner, cheerfully.

He had been one of Tom's party, and, therefore, in a position to enjoy the whole calamity.

"Well," said Jack, "let us get these things up again. I'll take Mr. Bunn with me this time."

"Excuse me," said Penny Bunn, as he rose up and started off with a rheumatic walk, "but I cannot conscientiously usurp the place of the boys who have not enjoyed this—this exhilarating sport. There are a few poor people in the neighbourhood on whom I am accustomed to call at intervals to read to, and in a general way amuse and elevate. At another time, my dear boys."

He would not wait any longer lest he should be tempted to indulge in another dose of the exhilarating exercise which had given him such a shaking up as he had never known before.

He walked just far enough to get out of sight of the boys, and then he sat down upon the roots of a big oak tree, and carefully felt himself all over.

"The little devils," he muttered; "they did it purposely. I never felt anything like it in my life. It was just like being shot out of a gun and a steamroller immediately going over me. It is my belief that Snicker is being punished for his sins by having all the imps of creation sent to him as schoolboys. But that is no reason why I should suffer, and if I don't get even with them before they are much older, may I be burnt at the stake."

He took off his coat and turned up his shirt-sleeves, so as to get a view of his elbows. Then he rolled up his trousers and surveyed his knees.

"There is not a nubbly part of my body that hasn't suffered," he moaned. "It will take a pint of arnica and Friar's Balsam to restore me to a sound condition. Snicker, I suffer vicariously for you. Hang you for an unmitigated old villain!"

He took a long rest, occupying the time in carefully soothing the afflicted parts of his anatomy, and then he arose, and keeping along the base of the cliff, went on his way. He had Smudgem Bender and an inn therein before him in his mind's eye.

He kept on, pausing at intervals to screw up his face and softly touch some aching limb, until he came into view of the spot where the cavern under the school was. To his surprise, he saw Copps and two men there, one an elderly gentleman, in whom he recognised the august personage of Sir Charles Barstow.

The detective had a spade in his hand, with which he was digging a hole in the side of the cliff. The other two were merely looking on.

In the distance, with the driver on the box, stood one of the flys to be had on hire at Chippenham.

"What on earth are they doing?" thought Penny Bunn, as he hastened forward, forgetting his recent injuries in the surprise of the moment.

He came up to them, and raised his hat to the baronet, who, after a brief stare at him, responded with a cool nod. Apparently he failed to recognise the tutor.

The other man was about fifty. He was very grey, and upon his face there was the absorbed look generally to be found in the countenances of men of scientific pursuits.

"Excavating, Sir Charles?" queried Penny Bunn.

Hearing his voice, and recognising it, Copps left off digging, and looked round.

"You here?" he said.

"It is a half-holiday," answered Penny Bunn, "and

I have been strolling around, pursuing my favourite amusement—botany."

"Oh, indeed," said Copps, drily. "Well, you won't find anything in that line here."

"There is no occasion for secrecy," said Sir Charles, in his dignified manner; "let him remain and assist with the digging."

Copps grunted in a dissatisfied manner, but he handed the tutor the spade, and told him to dig away the earth from the roots of the dead bush which blocked up the mouth of the cave.

"A great discovery has been made here," said Sir Charles, "and you shall be rewarded for your trouble."

Penny Bunn thereupon took the spade, and, although he was in no condition for manual labour of that description, his curiosity acted as a stimulus, and he proceeded with the work until Copps was able to pull out the bush, thereby disclosing the orifice. Copps then widened the opening, until there was sufficient space for them to enter. Finally, he drew a dark lantern from his pocket and lighted it.

"Now, Sir Charles," he said, "we can go in, and I believe that you will say I have not in any way exaggerated the find."

They all entered the cave, and there they found the remnant of the treasure which had so long been hidden from the light of day. Apparently the full extent of the underground vaults was revealed, and there was nothing to show, thanks to the ingenuity of Lingo, that there was any communication with the Abbey above.

The baronet was delighted, and the scientific man, who was a well-known professor of archæological tastes, looked like a hungry man before whom a splendid feast was laid. They both complimented Copps upon his keenness, which had brought this great store of good things of the past to their knowledge, and, above all, they warmly eulogised his honesty.

"Some men," remarked the baronet, "I may say the majority of men, would have kept this discovery a secret and sought to profit solely from it. Trust me, my worthy man, you shall be suitably rewarded."

He stepped aside with the learned man, and they held a short whispered conference together. Then Sir Charles told Copps that they considered he was entitled to the sum of two hundred and fifty pounds at the least. Would he be satisfied if he received that sum?

Copps said he would be more than satisfied, and thanked Sir Charles for his generosity. Penny Bunn watched the whole proceeding — a dumbfounded man.

"Everything here," said Sir Charles, "ought to be at once removed to a place of safety. Possibly a farmer in the district would lend me a waggon for the purpose. A room could be hired at Chippenham to store these valuable articles, until I can arrange for their removal to my residence."

He was in a generous mood, and turning to Penny Bunn, he asked him to take the carriage that was in waiting, drive into Smudgen Bender, and ask Mr. Botch if he would oblige his landlord with the agricultural conveyance he needed, at the same time tendering the tutor a ten-pound note as a reward for his late trivial exertions.

Penny Bunn took the note, murmured something that was intended to be thanks, but which only sounded like the babbling of a distant brook, and staggered out of the cave like a man in a dream.

He got to the fly somehow, grasping the note in his hand, and told the driver in a broken voice what he had to do. The man stared a little, but he was used to all sorts of customers, drunk and sober, and he started off without saying a word.

All the way to Smudgem Bender, Penny Bunn did nothing but gaze at the ten-pound note, and wonder if such things could be? He had never possessed so much money, at a time, in the whole course of his life.

Arriving at the farmhouse of Botch, he found that worthy in the farmyard, contemplating a promising family of little pigs, and gave him the message. The farmer was only too glad to oblige his landlord, and one of the men was desired to harness a team forthwith, and proceed to the spot, which, being immediately under the Abbey, could easily be found.

Then Penny Bunn, with two thoughts in his head, sent the fly back and remained behind. His first idea was to regale himself, and his second was to avoid the possibility that Sir Charles might, as other men occasionally do, have repented of his impulsive generosity, and would ask for his money, or a portion of it, to be returned to him.

Inflated and strengthened by the possession of ten pounds, the tutor placed his hat over his left eye to express that he at the time considered himself to be as good as any man, and a trifle better, and swaggered off to the parlour of the nearest inn.

It was the one Fontenoy Snicker visited occasionally and, as it happened, he was there that very afternoon.

He was surprised, and not over pleased, to see his assistant enter with a lordly air, and he was disposed to resent the friendly nod he was favoured with, but he thought better of it.

"Your glass is nearly empty," said Penny Bunn, "have one with me?"

This was a facer. Penny Bunn standing treat was a social phenomenon of a bewildering order. But Snicker was used to moral floorers by that time, and he said he would take a little Scotch cold.

The tutor rang the bell and ordered the drinks, one for his employer and another for himself. In payment he offered the waitress the ten-pound note.

"All gold please," he said; "I do not want a fiver in paper."

The girl left the room, and Penny Bunn took a sip of whisky, affecting an air or unconsciousness of the wide-eyed expression of the Snicker countenance.

The change was brought, and Penny Bunn having counted it, and given the girl threepence for herself, she disappeared.

"Have you been a-robbing anybody?" asked Fontenoy Snicker, with an effort.

"No," replied the tutor, airily; "I have simply been assisting Sir Charles Barstow to unearth a treasure valued at many thousand pounds, which being immediately under the Abbey ought to have been discovered long ago."

"Under the Abbey!"

"Just under it, in a cave which I should judge is immediately beneath your classroom."

"What's it wuth—*worth?*" demanded Snicker.

"Many thousands, as I told you," answered Penny Bunn; "but its exact value has yet to be ascertained."

"How did the old barrenight diskiver—*discover* it?" asked the astounded Snicker.

"He did not discover it," said Penny Bunn, with a dry smile upon his face.

"Who did, then?"

"Mr. Snicker," said Penny Bunn, firmly, "in all things appertaining to your academy I am your servant. Untold gold would not tempt me to diverge one hair's-breadth from the path of duty. Outside that I am a free agent. But even there I am guided by those principles on which the security of society is based."

"Bunn," said Snicker, after a pause, during which he wiped his brow with a big red handkerchief, "you might have let me known of this. Sir Charles have got no end of money. He's busting—*bursting*—with it. Now you and me are poor men, and we could have shared it, and nobody the wiser or the wuss—*worse*—blow the words—for it."

"Mr. Snicker," said Penny Bunn, "I am pained to hear you talk in this fashion. Hitherto I have been inclined to look upon you as a man of honour, although I must confess that I have now and then detected a slight warp in your moral character, which has led me to think otherwise. I am surprised and grieved."

He finished his whisky, and rang the bell.

"I am so moved to sorrow," he said, "that I feel I must have one drop more."

Fontenoy Snicker glared at him like an ogre in a trap, but said nothing until Penny Bunn was supplied with further refreshment.

"Hout with the pertiklers," he then said, curtly.

"I am not in a position to give them," answered Bunn, calmly, "nor is Copps, although——"

"Copps!" yelled the schoolmaster; "what has he to do with it?"

"He will receive his share of the reward generously given by Sir Charles," replied Bunn. "It is, I believe, two hundred and fifty pounds. I have received a small sum on account, as you with your eyes can see. Have another drink?"

"Copps is gone to London," said Snicker, ignoring the offer of further hospitality.

"He has *not*," rejoined the tutor, "for he is at this moment with Sir Charles in the cave where the treasure was found."

Fontenoy Snicker could bear no more. His wrath and mortification fairly overwhelmed him. Rising, he jerked the crusher out of his glass, threw it at the head of Bunn, hitting his hat so hard that it sounded like a small drum and fled from the inn.

CHAPTER LV.

LINGO'S NIGHT VISIT TO THE SCHOOL—SOME IMPORTANT EXPLANATIONS.

AFTER a glorious half-holiday, tobogganing, and enjoying the outing in other ways, the boys came back to the Abbey, being fairly punctual to the hour of seven, when they were expected to return.

Soppem Smith and Roger Hone were the exceptions, however, for they had shared in none of the sports, having been away alone in secret conference over their dissatisfaction at the reserve exhibited by Jack Ford and those who were more intimate with him.

But immediately on entering the Abbey, all the private troubles and joys of the boys were forgotten in the astounding news imparted to them by Black-eyed Susan, who had learnt it from her mistress, who in her turn was indebted to her husband for the information, of the discovery of the treasure in the cave.

It caused a terrific hubbub, and none were louder in their exclamations of astonishment than those who had known all about it before.

The mind of Roger Hone immediately became busy with speculations bearing on the vault which he had essayed to enter with a painful, wringing result, the full extent of which will immediately be made clear.

He lost no time in getting his chum Soppem Smith away from the rest to impart to him the ideas that had entered his head.

"That cave," he said, "was right under us, close to

the vaults. Now I wonder if Ford and his lot found anything?"

"If they did," replied Smith, "they never brought it up from the vaults."

"No; but they might have left it there to take away another time."

"If they did they have lost it, for Snicker has nailed up the door in the schoolroom again in a way that will puzzle any of us to open it. You have got hold of a mare's nest, Hone. Do they look or talk like fellows who have tumbled across anything worth having, and by fooling about, lost it again?"

"I can't say they do," said Hone, thoughtfully, rubbing his head. "Did Sue say that the cave communicated with the Abbey?"

"She doesn't know any more than that a lot of armour and weapons and a chest of money have been found and taken away in a waggon. Also that Snicker has done nothing but rave and talk swears about it since he came home. Penny Bunn discovered it."

"Never!"

"Sue says so. She heard Snicker tell his wife that Bunn was in Smudgen Bender this afternoon, throwing ten-pound notes about as if they were wastepaper."

"Where is Bunn?"

"He hasn't been home since he started with us this afternoon."

"Well," said Hone, "It *is* an eye-opener."

The inner circle, possessors of the secret of the truth of the whole business, studiously held aloof from each other. It would never do for them to give the least clue to the boys in general to the knowledge they possessed.

As the Professor had warned them, that would be fatal. They would lose everything, and the others gain nothing.

Not any of the youngsters outside Hone and Soppem Smith suspected that the inner circle had concealed anything. It was impossible for them to associate the cave with the vaults unless they had some information given them. On the morning when the boys left the schoolroom and so ended the barring out, Jack, as leader, had simply announced that the way to leave was by the cliff, and without telling a lie upon the subject he had led them to infer that there was no other road to take.

The reader will clearly see that, if the schoolboys as a body had [been allowed to depart that way, a complete exposure would have been inevitable.

They would have had to pass out by the passage where the remnant of the treasure was lying, and the result would have been all sorts of suspicions and inquiries which would have let the whole cat out of the bag.

But Lingo had blocked the way, the vaults by the explosion of dynamite had been severed from the cave, and if the inner circle could keep their own counsel, the richer store hidden in the Mumping Malford wood was safely concealed for their future pleasure and profit.

Awful Rooker was obliged, owing to the absence of Penny Bunn, to preside at eight o'clock at the table, on which was laid a meal serving for both tea and supper.

The continued improvement of the viands provided was the marked feature of it. Fontenoy Snicker was tortured in so many ways that he was afraid of raising another rebellion, and much against his will he told his wife to give the boys an ample spread of bread, cheese, and butter, and not to stint the mild decoction which passed as beer in the precincts of the Abbey.

At half-past eight they left the table, and as the evenings were long they were requested to get up their lessons before going to bed.

On entering the schoolroom they got out their books, but there was precious little work in the boys. They were tired with their day's outing, and lounged about yawning and mildly skylarking. Jack and Don climbed up to the window seat, and sat there looking out upon the stretch of meadow, lighted up with the deep-coloured rays, thrown down by the clouds illuminated by the sun which had just sunk below the horizon.

"It is a splendid evening," remarked Don, dreamily, "not a soul about, however, in the meadows to enjoy it."

"The yokels have no eye for beauty," said Jack; "what do they care for the landscape, or the sun, or, anything save as things that have something to do with their getting produce ready for the market? Hark! what is that?"

They both leant out of the window, stretching their ears. Jack had heard a peculiar cry which he believed was of portent to them. After the lapse of a few moments it was repeated.

"Too-whit-too-who-o-o!"

"Lingo," said Jack; "he is down by the gate. He wants one of us. Will you go?"

"If you like," answered Don. "I suppose there is no chance of tumbling across Snicker?"

"He will give Lingo a widish berth," returned Jack, significantly.

Don laughed, and slipped quietly out of the room, his going scarcely noticed by anyone. Hone observed it, and being, as usual, suspicious, was about to follow him when he was confronted by Jack, who said:

"You need not play the spy, Hone. Don has gone to have a chat with Lingo, and you shall know all about it when he returns."

Hone, with a growl, went back to his seat, afraid to refuse to take the broad hint given him, but more than ever convinced that there was something that he ought to know, hidden from him.

Don found the way clear to the gates of the playground, and outside nobody was to be seen. He opened one of them and went out, and there was Lingo leaning against the wall, calmly smoking his pipe.

"Oh, it is you, is it?" he said. "I thought I should make one of you hear me."

They shook hands, and the professor drew out a bag from his pocket.

"You will find five pounds there, in shillings, sixpences, and coppers," he said. "I thought it better to let you have it all in small money."

"Who is it for?" asked Don.

"The boys in general," answered Lingo; "but you of the inner circle must act the part of treasurers. Did you ever hear of conscience money?"

Don said he had not, that he knew of.

"Conscience money," explained Lingo, "is the mopusses sent to the Chancellor of the Exchequer now and then, say once a year, by people who have been dodging the Income Tax all their lives, and in their old age get the repentant knock. Considering that ninety-nine per cent. of tax-payers do their level best to make a false return to the assessors, the number of repentant sinners appear to me to be remarkably small."

"But this," said Don, holding up the bag, "is not *your* conscience-money, surely?"

"I have precious little money," said Lingo, with a grin, "and no conscience worth naming. No, it is the conscience-money of the inner circle. You are obliged, against your will, to conceal from the other lads the fact that you have, practically, in your possession, a fortune. All you can do is to let them have as much of it as will be *safe* to give them. What you have to do is to divide this among your four, or one can dispense it, and be liberal with it in the way of youngsters. When it is gone you can have a little more."

"I suppose," said Don, thoughtfully, "that it is all we can do?"

"It is all we *dare* do," returned the Professor, warmly. "Now don't worry any more about the matter. You discovered the things, you four, and they are yours. But for your pluck there would have been no barring out. We had one narrow escape of the whole thing being blown up, however. I forgot, in the rush of events, as the poet says, to tell you of it. Do you remember that night when I was removing the things from the vault?"

"Of course I do."

"It was arranged, you know, that none of the inner circle were to open the trap-door that night. Well, I had barely got into the vault, and was moving quietly about, in the way I have when there is need of it, when I heard a noise above, just over the trap."

"Who was it?"

"Wait a bit, and you will hear. I put out the light, popped the lantern down where I could lay my hands on it, and crept up the stone stairs. Somebody was working, in a sneaky way, at the screws. I'm a good judge of sounds, and I could tell when one was drawn."

"You must have keen ears."

"I'm all ears when there's a necessity," said Lingo, with half-closed eyes, "and it is a good job I am. To resume. Naturally, I wondered who it was, and all sorts of ideas came into my head. I knew it was none of the inner circle, and I was certain that it was one of the boys. Then I settled in my mind that it was somebody who wanted to know more than was good for him or you. So I lay still, waiting for him, with no real plan in my head, but bent on spoiling his little game, somehow."

Lingo paused to indulge in a quiet laugh, and Don smiled, too, in sympathy. But the feeling of curiosity was the stronger emotion within him.

"A youngster—it was Hone—got the trap up," resumed the Professor, "and stood a bit, listening. Then, in a fearsome way, he put a leg down through the opening. In a moment the idea I wanted comes to me, and I lays hold of his leg just above the ankle. I expected he would squeal, and bring you down upon him, but he didn't. He just faints right away. I knew he had been horribly scared, and wouldn't dream when he came round, of trying the game again. So I let him lay, and gently pulling the trap-door down, went on with my work. Did you ever hear anything about it?"

"Jack found Hone the next morning doing something to the screws. He had taken one out," said Don.

"That is where you were mistaken," chuckled Lingo; "*he was putting the last one in*. I can see it all now. He must have laid there until the morning, and then come round. Fearful of being found out, or perhaps he fancied that ghost that laid hold of him wanted appeasing, he put the screws back again, and Ford came upon him as he was finishing the job."

They both had a laugh over the affair, and then Don said:

"Hone is very close. I don't suppose he has mentioned the matter to anyone."

"He will now be more convinced than ever that it was a spectre which objected to his coming into the vaults. It was, and is, an uncanny place, you know."

"I think so," assented Don, with a shiver.

"Whether it's vapours, or what, I don't know,"

pursued the Professor; "but I saw a misty kind of figure rise from the ground, and float across the place. I had almost finished my job then, and I got away as soon as I could."

"But you are not afraid of a ghost?"

"All men are afraid of things they can't tackle or understand," said Lingo, sententiously. "Well, I mustn't keep you here. Good night, and remember this, *hold your secret close*, you four, for in days to come great things may be done with the property stored away yonder."

"You may trust us," replied Don, as they parted.

―――――

CHAPTER LVI.

PENNY BUNN'S PURCHASE.—MELODY FOR THE ABBEY.

IT was close upon ten o'clock, half-an-hour after the boys were in bed, when Penny Bunn returned to his quarters at the Abbey. He had been partaking of refreshment, and was in a lively condition, but no magistrate would have fined him for being intoxicated.

He had an oblong square parcel under his arm, something wrapped in brown paper and tied with a piece of cord in a perfunctory manner, and he was very careful with it.

When hanging his hat up in the hall, which was not accomplished until he had dropped it twice, he laid that parcel tenderly upon the rickety hall table. Having finally placed his hat on the peg, he took his parcel up and went aloft to his room.

Rooker was there awaiting his return, and the junior master was in a very bad temper.

"You are always out," he grumbled, "leaving me to preside at the table. One of these nights you will do it once too often. What good am I alone with that gang of imps?"

"Rooker," said Bunn, extending his hand, "forgive me. I know I have of late trespassed upon your kindness, but trust me you will not in the end repent of it. I have brought with me a bottle of fluid of invigorating qualities. There is a footless wine-glass and a tin mug in the washstand drawer. Bring them forth and we will imbibe. I have not entirely neglected myself in the matter of stimulants, but I feel that one drop more will not be absolute destruction to me."

Rooker, in a mollified frame of mind, opened the drawer and brought out the drinking vessels as desired. Bunn produced a big flat bottle and poured out some of its amber coloured contents.

"Drink," he said, "and forget your sorrows."

"Is it true about your having discovered a lot of valuable armour and handed it over to Sir Charles Barstow?" inquired Rooker.

"At present," replied Penny Bunn, "my lips are sealed upon the subject. Anon, dear boy, you shall know all."

"What is in that parcel?" inquired Rooker.

"Oh! of course, the parcel," said Penny Bunn, who had seemingly temporarily forgotten it; "certainly. In this package I have an instrument lately the property of one of the greatest musicians of the day. Quite an impresario he is. His name is Signor Bonelucci. Did you never hear of him?"

"Never," answered Rooker.

"Strange," murmured Penny Bunn; "but then you have never mixed in society as I have done. Bonelucci has for years charmed the nobility and gentry of this country with his performances on this instrument. To secure him for their garden parties and re-unions, they have been obliged to engage him three months in advance, and pay him a retaining fee."

"What is it?" asked Rooker, staring at the parcel.

Penny Bunn whipped off the string, and opening the paper, disclosed an enormous accordion. It was quite an outsize thing, and must have been made to order. It had the appearance of having been freely played upon, and subject recently to rough handling, for there was mud upon the keys.

"Where did you get it from?" asked Rooker, suspiciously.

"Have I not told you," demanded Bunn, haughtily, "that it was presented to me by my old friend, Bonelucci? After a long series of successful performances in our land, he has compiled a fortune, and to-morrow he returns to his native land to enjoy the fruits of his peerless genius, under his own vine and fig tree."

But Rooker, although he said nothing, looked dubious, which Penny Bunn observed, and with additional impressiveness, continued his story.

"Long years ago," he said, affectionately patting the accordion, "the original owner of this instrument was an unknown man. But he had a friend, who could introduce him into the highest society, and it was done. I will not name that man, for I am modest as well as proud, but the thing was done, I say, and the fortune of Bonelucci was made. In gratitude, he gives this to his friend" (here Penny Bunn was affected to tears), "as a combined memento of happy days, and a testimonial of the esteem he had in his heart for that friend, a *benefactor*. Rooker, one question, *do* you think I am a liar?"

"Can you play upon it?" asked Rooker, fencing the query.

"In my youth I was a Bonelucci in the bud," said Bunn, "but the art is in a measure lost to me. But is my intention to restore it, and one of these nights I will charm you with a tune. Have one drop more, and then away to bed."

They had it, and retired, Penny Bunn taking with him to bed the precious instrument he had received as a parting gift from the gifted Bonelucci.

CHAPTER LVII.

A QUIET MORNING.—FONTENOY SNICKER ON A NEW TACK.—BONELUCCI THE TALENTED.

THERE was nothing to show on the following morning that anything had transpired of an unusual nature on the previous day. The boys arose in the morning, and in due time appeared in the class-room to go through the accustomed curriculum of study. The only thing noticeable was the palpable absentmindedness of Fontenoy Snicker.

Most of the morning he was in a brown study, and the subject on his mind was the recent discovery in the cave presumably made by the detective, Copps.

It occurred to the schoolmaster that if there were one treasure in the neighbourhood, there might be more. And, if that were the case, where would the hidden wealth be concealed?

In or near the Abbey, of course.

The merry old monks of old invariably laid hold of the good things of this world, and, what is more, adhered to them. They were good receivers, but bad at parting.

Therefore, it flashed upon the brilliant mind of Fontenoy Snicker that by diligent search around the premises in which he lived, something worth his attention might be unearthed.

Penny Bunn was not in a condition to be hypercritical with the pupils. He put the usual questions to the boys, and he took their answers. Whether they were correct or not he had not the least idea.

He, too, was in a brown study, and it was on the way he would, ere long, perform on the wonderful accordion he had brought home with him on the previous night.

There was a stirring within him to excel as a musician, and he verily believed that in the sweet, musical by-and-bye he would be able to astonish a few people. His first victim in the astonishment direction was to be Awful Rooker.

Between the dreams and hopes of Fontenoy Snicker, and the aspirations of the under-master, the boys had a good time of it.

At noon, as usual, they were turned into the playground. There was a slight, drizzling rain, but not enough of moisture to ensure their being kept within doors.

One of Fontenoy Snicker's theories was, that no boy ought to catch cold, or, if he was sufficiently foolish to do so, it was his bounden duty to make the best of it, and not worry his elders for remedies to relieve him.

To the surprise of the boys, there was a foreigner outside the gate.

That he was a foreigner there could be no doubt, for his dress and air were that of an Italian who had devoted a considerable portion of his earthly career to entertaining or exasperating the public with the grind of an organ, or playing upon some kindred instrument.

He was aged, but still of a vigorous build. He also was uncommonly dirty—without dirt few foreigners are completely attired and ready for their daily avocations—and his dark eyes gleamed with venom.

Instinctively, the boys looked about the stranger for the usual organ and monkey; but he had neither, and there was a strange appearance of being imperfectly fitted out about the man.

"Hi!" he exclaimed; "you leetle boys. What now? Say, have you a gentleman here of ze name of Penare Bung?"

He had got hold of the name of the tutor near enough for the crowd of youngsters who gathered at the gate to admit that such a person was to be found there.

"I vant to zee him," said the stranger. "Say, now, is it diffeecult for so to do?"

"I dare say that, if you particularly want to see him," replied Whymper, "he will come out."

"He is a very obliging man," added Bob Stockton. "Shall I fetch him here?"

Before the Italian could give an answer one way or the other, Penny Bunn and Awful Rooker emerged from the house, and being spied by the applicant, he hailed him with a screech:

"So then I see you," he cried. "Come here, you."

Penny Bunn saw him, and changed colour from the saffron shade he had exhibited all the morning to that of sage green. He would doubtless have beaten a retreat but for the boys, who surrounded him, saying in chorus:

"Here's a foreign gentleman asking for you, sir."

"I see him," replied the tutor, with a smile of anguish; "what does he want?"

"Hi, then!" bawled the Italian; "you give me back my museek!"

Rooker looked at his companion wonderingly; meanwhile, the boys were pressing towards the gate.

"You gif him back to me," continued the Italian, violently. "What for you make me drunks and gif me two sheeling for him? It is not enoughs. They tell me you are here, and I behold you. Gif me back my museeks!"

"Is this Bonelucci, your friend?" asked Rooker.

"One moment," said Penny Bunn; then assuming a virtuously indignant air, he addressed the Italian.

"My good man, what is it you want?"

"My museek," was the answer, "two shilling is not enoughs. I was so drunks I know not what I do. So then, let me haf him!"

"This is not Bonelucci," said Penny Bunn to his companion Rooker, "but an impostor. But rather than enter upon a discussion with a low class foreigner, he shall have the accordion on payment of two shillings. There are times when it becomes every denizen of this sea-girt isle to stand upon his dignity. My good man, if you will hand me two shillings, the instrument shall be returned to you."

"I haf dem not," said the Italian, "for behold, as I am drunks in ze road ven ze landlord roll me out, some of ze vile mans peek my pocket. I haf zem not."

"In that case," said Penny Bunn, "I cannot yield to your request."

"Vhat!" screeched the Italian, "you not gif me my museek?"

"Certainly not."

"I get ze money," urged the Italian, "if you gif me my museek. For see, I take him, and I go play sweet tune, and I get ze money. Zen I bring him to you. I *svear* it."

It is impossible to convey in writing the intensity he put into the oath which he registered with his hand in the air. But Penny Bunn was not moved to compassion.

"I must have the money first," he said, "before I give up the music, as you call it. Go away!"

Then the Italian became a monument of passion, and his withered face quivered with wrath. He put his hand into his pocket, drew out a knife, and opened it, exhibiting a blade about eight inches long.

"You not gif him!" he hissed. "You see dat?"

Bunn saw it, but stood his ground, blue in the face but very firm.

"You threaten in vain," he said, with the tremolo stop inside him in full play; "without the two shillings I do not part."

"Zen," returned the Italian, with a world of spite in his tone of voice, "I gif you zis—so mooch."

And to illustrate how much of the weapon it was his intention to bestow upon the anatomy of the tutor, he laid his finger across the blade about half way down.

But Penny Bunn, with so many inquiring eyes upon him, was still firm.

"I am, as a native of our island home," he said,

"not to be cajoled, or threatened, or intimidated into yielding up my possessions without a due equivalent. If you do not go away, the police will be sent for."

"Send for him," sputtered the Italian; "what zen? He is avay. I see him long off doing noting, but sit on ze gate and smoke. He not to be found, and he no come."

"Anyway," said Penny Bunn, turning upon his heel, "you will not bully me into giving up that which by the law of my country is my own."

He walked back with inconceivable dignity to the schoolhouse, followed by Awful Rooker.

"Rooker," he said, as soon as they were under shelter: "did you ever see the like of that?"

"But is he that Bonelucci you were telling me about?" urged Rooker.

"*He* Bonelucci?" said Penny Bunn; "let me ask you as one who have known me well, is that the sort of man *I* should traffic with? *No*, a thousand times, no. But, Rooker, as I said, rather than have any vile dispute about such a thing as an accordion, I would yield it up to him again and again, provided, of course, that he comes supplied with the necessary equivalent in current coin of the realm."

"But you said it was given to you as a testimonial," said Rooker, persistently.

"Look here, Rooker," rejoined Penny Bunn, "there is a limit to the endurance of even such friendship as exists between me and you. Drop the subject, or I may forget all else but my wrongs, and give you one on the optics which will incapacitate you for your afternoon duties."

"It is no business of mine," said Rooker, "but if I were you I should give up the thing, especially as you cannot play it."

"Never—*never*," answered Penny Bunn, as he stalked away.

CHAPTER LVIII.

BONELUCCI'S STORY.

THE Italian was too good, as a bit of fun, to be allowed to go away at once, so the boys gathered close up to the gate, and questioned him as to the reason for his coming thither.

From what they could gather from his replies, given in broken English, and interspersed with violent adjectives, native and foreign, original and acquired, he had met Penny Bunn on the previous afternoon, and been engaged by the tutor to play "all he knew" upon the accordion for the especial edification of the tutor.

And lest they should be interrupted by the vulgar

herd, Penny Bunn had lured the performer into a good dry skittle ground attached to the Smudgem Bender Inn, and there being no players of the game in the afternoon, they had a good hour to themselves.

The flight of time was oiled with libations which were of a varied form, and in the end the Italian was a bit overcome. Under the influence of generous liquor he parted with his instrument for the sum of two shillings, of which he had, as he stated, been afterwards robbed.

But robbed of it or not, two shillings was not a tenth of the value of the instrument, and the Italian wanted it back again.

By making inquiries, when he got sober, he learnt where the purchaser was to be found, and he had walked to the Abbey to endeavour to soften the heart of the tutor to give him a chance of recovering his lost means of living.

He failed, as we have seen, and after a time he went away—murderous.

It was an amusing episode, quite a ray of bright light in the daily life of the school, and the thought of Penny Bunn as the possessor of an accordion was in itself a sufficient thing to excite their hilarious mirth.

He referred to the meeting with the Italian, and the late interview at the dinner-table over which he presided with his usual grace.

"It is my duty," he said, "to clear the air of any possible imputations against my honour, which may have been conveyed by the manner and words of the unprincipled foreign ruffian who was at the gate to-day. That he is a fraud and an impostor must be apparent to the meanest intellect at the table. It is a case of attempted extortion, aided by intimidation, without a parallel in my experience. It has been a great trial to me."

This statement was rather vague, but he was not denied the support of the boys. When he stopped for breath, a murmur of sympathy buzzed round the table.

"I could see, sir," said Bob Stockton, in his peerless impudent style, "that you were supported entirely by conscious innocence. Would it be asking too much, sir, to ask you how you met the man who has dared to accuse you of bamboozling him out of his accordion?"

"I never met the man in my life before," said Penny Bunn, who had been sticking to the original tale told to Rooker when discussing the affair with his junior. "The man must by some means have become aware of my having been presented with the instrument by a professional friend of mine, who is now on the way to his native land, sunny Italy. Should there be legal proceedings instituted in this matter I shall certainly ask him to return here as

witness on my behalf. Bonelucci is a true friend, and will not desert the man who made him. We were boys and budding musicians together. He studied the art and became famous. I neglected it and it is gone. What an illustration of the necessity of being studious through life. How it enforces the teachings of that unrivalled book for boys 'Sandford and Merton.'"

He sighed, and shook his head, as one who grieves over a degenerated people, but soon brightened up again.

"He is, however, gone," he said, "I trust, to return no more. Jiggers, if you eat so hurriedly you will choke. Boys, to-night in the hour devoted to study I will show you *my* accordion. At another time, when I have procured an instruction-book, I propose to give you lessons on it."

"We should be delighted to learn how to play it," said Don, and many others said the same, and Penny Bunn, strengthened by their support, felt that he could defy the machinations of the man who will henceforth, whether he was the rightful owner of the name or not, be referred to as Bonelucci.

"If I were you," said Rooker again, after the boys had been dismissed from the table, "I should give it up if ever that man called again. I never in all my life saw anybody look so murderous."

"Conscious of being in the right," replied Penny Bunn, as he brushed the crumbs from his lap and arose to depart, "I shall not yield to cajolery or threats. What you want is *nerve*, my dear Rooker, and the resolution that defies the machinations of the impostor. I have already recalled how to play the scales on that instrument, and shall go on with it."

Rooker said no more until his brother tutor had disappeared, and then he slowly followed him from the room, softly murmuring:

"The idiot ! he will be assassinated as I live. The Italian fellow will stick him, as sure as eggs are eggs."

CHAPTER LIX.

SNICKER MORE UNHAPPY THAN EVER.

THE desire to become possessed of wealth is a general one. Even the more industrious are haunted with it at times, and to a man like Fontenoy Snicker it had always been a passion.

All through his life, which, as we may judge from the facts already revealed, was a varied one, with many ups and down, he had longed for the time to come when he would have the means of gratifying his desire for unlimited drink and ease. Hitherto he had not got far on the road towards the goal he aimed at, for although he had of recent years made a very good thing out of the rascally way he conducted his school, something was always turning up to rob him, as he expressed it, of "his hard-earned money."

The agony he endured on learning that he had all the time been living over property worth thousands, which was "as much his as anybody's," was almost unendurable. He could scarcely bear the thinking of it, much less talk about it.

That Copps had become the recipient of a nice little sum of money as a reward for his honestly revealing his discovery was a fact, for the detective in a humorous mood took the trouble to write and inform him of the fact.

"It will please you to learn," (he wrote in a sarcastic way) "to learn that not only did I make a tidy job out of you by acting as a private discoverer of burglars in your school, but, thanks to the discovery I made, which you could have done yourself if you had a pair of eyes in your head, I am *some hundreds* the better for my stay in this salubrious county. I rather fancy that that eyeglass of yours is more ornamental than useful to you."

This was a decidedly offensive style of writing, and Snicker fumed over it. But he could do nothing except relieve himself by anathematising his tormentor Copps, like a good many other people, could not tell the exact truth. His share of the reward was a hundred and twenty-five pounds, not a bad thing, but it was a decided exaggeration to call it "some hundreds." This, however, is the way of the world.

"I am sure," said Mrs. Snicker one evening as the pair of that name sat alone, she engaged in mending clothes and Snicker brooding, "that if we only looked about we should find a lot of things."

"Look where?" growled the schoolmaster.

"Well," said his wife, "when me and Jane were cleaning up the mess those boys made in the back rooms, we noticed there was a trap door in the floor. It was screwed down, but I have no doubt that it would be worth our while to open it."

"Why didn't you mention this matter before?" he snarled.

"Because I supposed such a wonderful sharp man as you are would have noticed it."

"You are mighty perlite," he said. "I may have noticed it—I don't remember. I was in a sort of turmoil just then. It can't be of any importance."

"Jerry, there are no rooms under there, and the trap must lead into vaults and cellars. It is in sich places where things are hidden."

"I've nailed up the blessed door so that no mortiul —*mortal*—person could open it without breaking the woodwork to pieces."

"Then break it, if you must. If your imps could open it before, I should think you are man enough to open it now."

"I'll try it," said the schoolmaster, after a pause, "and if I come on anything worth having, I shall not be such a fool as Copps to say much about it. I wonder how much that ass Bunn got out of the barrownight—*baronet*."

"He's been spending pretty freely," replied Mrs. Snicker, "he has some sort of musical instrument in his bedroom. It sounds like a small organ with something wrong with the bellows."

"Oh! that is what's [o'clock, is it?" said Snicker, "I was passing his room last night on the way to bed, and heard what I thought was groaning. I fancied he was taken ill, but as I'm not a doctor, it was no business of mine."

"And he has some whisker producer in a bottle on the drawers, also a bottle of Macassar oil for his hair. Then his box is locked."

"Perhaps he keeps his money there," suggested the schoolmaster, with an ugly light in his eyes.

"He may," said Mrs. Snicker, "but surely you wouldn't rob him of it?"

"I don't know that," was the ready reply of her husband, "but before I go on that lay, I'll try my luck at finding a fortune. To-morrow is Saturday, and the boys will be out in the arternoon. I'll give the time to getting open the door."

It was not long to wait, but when a man sees a prospective El Dorado before him, and cannot touch it for a time, he is harassed with impatience. It ended in his not being able to wait until to-morrow, and after supper he took a candle and sundry tools with him to proceed with the work of opening the door.

But he found to his cost that he had most effectually closed it, and midnight came without his having done more than draw half-a-dozen of the half-hundred nails he had driven into the woodwork.

Worn out, he gave up and went to bed.

Daylight revealed to the most casual observer the signs of his overnight labour. There was not a boy, when the school assembled there at the usual hour, who did not promptly observe the holes and splintered woodwork resulting from the schoolmaster's nightwork.

Now the majority of them, as we know, had never been down to the vaults, but they all knew that they were in existence, and that the leaders of the barring out had visited them, apparently without profitable result. Some comment had been made on the fact of the schoolmaster having never sought to explore the underground part of the Abbey, mainly by the quartet who were acquainted with the place.

On seeing what the schoolmaster had been doing, it flashed upon the mind of Jack Ford that Fontenoy Snicker was going down on an exploring expedition.

He did not think of the real object of the schoolmaster, but inferred that he had obtained a clue to recent events, and was desirous of investigating everything. It was possible in that case he might be the means of revealing that the outer vaults had been cut off from the inner ones by artificial means. The result, if he did arrive at that conclusion, might lead to all sorts of disagreeable things.

Sooth to tell, it made Jack very uneasy, and he lost no time after the work of the morning was over in confiding his fears to them.

Dinner was served earlier than usual, " to enable the boys to make the most of the afternoon," the schoolmaster said, as he dismissed them, but the true reason was to give himself more time to renew his assault upon the door.

Saturday was always an off day in the food direction, and the boys declared for bread and cheese as sufficient for the day. They did this more readily, as a rumour was abroad that Tom Drummond had been the recipient of a very liberal remittance from " a distant relative," and meant to act towards them in a generous spirit.

This rumour proved to be correct, for immediately after dinner the word was passed for the whole of them to dodge the tutors and make their way to Chippenham, as the nearest town, where a sufficiency of good things could be obtained.

The dodging was very easily effected, for Awful Rooker had no taste for the company of the boys, and Penny Bunn had arranged with himself to hie away alone, and in the solitude of Mumping Malford Wood have a few hours' practice on the accordion.

He bought a second-hand instruction book, and a glance over it promised that he would speedily acquire the art of playing on the instrument, which we may, once for all admit, he had purchased from the hapless Bonelucci, under circumstances that stamped the deal as being rather one-sided.

Jack's friends, Don especially, saw nothing to fear from any investigations the schoolmaster might make.

" What does it matter?" he asked, as the four closer intimates of the Abbey hastened down the path leading through the wood. " What is there for him to find out?"

" Suppose he ascertains that the blocking up has been recently done?" urged Jack.

" Something in that," remarked Don.

" There is a lot in it," said Bob Stockton; but nothing to show that we did it. And who is to suspect the Professor?"

" He has taken good care to make the whole thing as dark as pitch," said Tom Drummond; "nothing could have been better done. Copps *dare not* admit that he has told a lie. Of course he may suspect something if Snicker should find out that the place was recently blocked, and the two get their heads together, but that is hardly likely to come to pass. Don't worry, and above all don't show that you do.

Here come Hone and Smith, whispering as usual. I fear them more than I do a dozen Snickers."

" I say, Drummond," said Roger Hone, as he came up, " it is awfully good of you to offer to treat us all. What kind relatives you must have. I wish I had a few of them. Your uncle has sent you a fiver, I believe."

" I did not say it was uncle," answered Tom, drily, " nor that it was a fiver. The fact is I got the money from my aunt's—on my mother's side—second cousin's grandfather. The relationship is a bit off the track, but that doesn't matter so long as it results in lucre."

" Perhaps Hone thinks you stole it," suggested Don.

" I don't think anything of the sort," replied Hone, violently, " and you need not put in your spoke."

" I shall put it into the wheel of anyone who acts as you do," said Don. " Why are you two always whispering together? Is there anything you want to know, or have you any grievance? Out with it if you have."

" We are not the only people who go about whispering," said Hone, savagely.

" Look here, old man," said Tom Drummond; "it just comes to this: I have announced that some money has been given, and the donor wished that it should be spent with the freedom of a genuine schoolboy. I am going to do as he wishes, but there is no compulsion. Don't come in with us unless you like."

Tom increased his pace, and his friends doing likewise they soon left the lagging Hone and Soppem Smith behind.

" I'll swear they've landed something," said Roger Hone, excitedly; " I could see it in their faces. There's no relative in the business. I'll watch and find it out. Are you going on to Chippenham?"

" I was thinking of doing so," replied Soppem; " what is the good of allowing your ideas, which may be all darned stuff, to keep us out of a treat? Tom Drummond has got a trouser pocket-full of money. I saw it bulging out of it and it jingled as he walked. Don't be a fool, Roger."

But Hone was in an obstinate mood. He was originally going with the rest, but his back had been put up by Don and Tom, too. Towards the former he had always entertained the strongest feeling of dislike. It would end in blows " some day."

" You can go sneaking around them," Hone said, with a sneer, " do as you please. I'm off somewhere else."

" Where?"

" Anywhere," answered Hone, curtly; " don't wait for me. Cut it."

His manner irritated Soppem Smith, who hurried

on in the direction taken by the others. Hone, after thinking awhile, turned back to the Abbey.

CHAPTER LX.

A ROYAL FEAST.—PENNY BUNN MEETS HIS EVIL GENIUS.

BOYS seldom, when they are in a generous mood, do things by halves, and the members of the inner circle were the last of their fraternity to do the mean thing.

Professor Lingo had handed over the sum of five pounds in coin of the realm, and they meant to spend it.

The amount gave to each boy about two shillings— a little under—and it was a royal sum to be spent in one day.

The limited displays of the confectioners' shops of the town of Chippenham, were swept away, as if the tarts had been straws caught by the whirlwind. There was also an unparalleled run upon ginger beer, and if there had not been a manufacturer in the town, the consequences might have been serious.

We may here content ourselves with stating that the youngsters had a splendid time of it, and if they did take to skylarking when replete with tarts and ginger beer, it was only what might be expected of them.

Chippenham has a mayor, generally selected from the most prominent, if not the most intelligent, of its tradesmen. At the time of our story, a local brewer was in office, and it may be said of him that he filled it as well as his predecessors, and those who have come after him.

To be a mayor of an important centre like Chippenham, all the qualities which make up a commanding man are essential.

The mayor must be equal, when called upon, to read the Riot Act, and the local brewer was very near doing it, when the Lambs of Littlecote were exercising their exuberant spirits upon the too utterly too-too pacific inhabitants of the town.

But as no serious result ensued, we may pass on, and wend our way to Mumping Malford Wood, where Penny Bunn was engaged in the laborious task of teaching himself to play the accordion. It was a much harder thing than he had anticipated.

He had selected a small dell in the heart of the wood, right away, as he fondly hoped, from his fellow man. It was a place where one would expect in the hours of darkness to find fairies tripping their uncommonly light fantastic toes, and to see the elfins of legendary lore indulging in their impish sport.

It was about twenty feet in diameter, and, therefore, sixty in circumference, and entirely surrounded by ash and willow trees. Quite a sylvan retreat of A1 quality it was.

And there Penny Bunn sat him down, placed the instruction-book against the trunk of a willow tree, and started exercise number one.

How much more difficult it seemed than he had anticipated from reading the preliminary instructions!

There were the notes to find upon the instrument, and to read them on the book at the same time. The wind had also to be kept in the accordion, and dispensed on economical and judicious principles.

The tutor drew the most extraordinary sounds from the instrument, the like of which he had never heard before. He had not previously conceived that anything of its size could have produced such a variety of unhallowed noises.

They chiefly resembled groans and screeches, and were strongly suggestive of dogs with tin kettles tied to their tails, and cats caught in a gin-trap.

Penny Bunn, haply for his own comfort, had no more ear for music than a wooden image. He could tell the sounds he created were of a varied character, and endowed with considerable novelty, but that was all. So he sawed away, and filled the air with the most uncanny melody ever produced by one man from so comparatively small an amount of wood, bone, and leather.

But, although he fondly hoped he was in complete seclusion, there was one who heard the strains and recognized them. It was Bonelucci, who was again on his way to the Abbey to claim his own. The unhappy Italian had been making a series of futile efforts to get together the small, but all-important sum, to him, of two shillings. But, alas! the cold, hard world turned a deaf ear to him, and he was as poor as ever as he wended his way through the wood.

He heard the accordion, and recognized its notes, drawn out by a novice hand, as a father recognizes the voice of his offspring suffering from maltreating hands. The original tone is there, though it be smothered in wails of anguish.

With eyes that blazed with anger, and his hand upon the knife he had in his sash, he crept towards the spot where Penny Bunn, having got tired of the instruction book, was indulging in some extempory work, such as only the stone-deaf could have been near without shuddering.

Cautiously picking his way through the wood, the defrauded Bonelucci at length reached a spot where nothing but a low stunted bush intervened between him and the man who had first made him "drunks," and then took advantage of his condition to effect a most unfair deal.

Bunn was in the seventh heaven of delight, squatted on the ground with his legs tucked under him, and sawing away as if he had taken the job on by piece-work.

Suddenly he saw two eyes glaring at him, and the melody came to an end with an abruptness that was illustrative of its being cut in two with an axe. He felt an icy drop of water, or what appeared to be one, travel down his back, in a line with his spine.

Then out from his sheltering-place came the embittered Italian.

"I say, you," he cried, "how you play him—my museek—you see-saw zee ting—you make him ill! Now give him to me!"

Bonelucci was not so very violent in his words or bearing, and Penny Bunn quickly recovered his nerve.

"I trust," he said, "that you have brought the two shillings with the *interest*. I consider that the money was simply invested as a favour to you."

"Vat you vant?" screeched the Italian, throwing off his quiet bearing.

"Two shillings with interest, at the rate of five per cent.," replied Penny Bunn, with the dignity of a conscientious money-lender; "you can reckon it up for yourself."

"I gif you dis!" hissed the Italian, whipping out his knife.

In a moment—Penny Bunn never exactly knew how he did it—the accordion was raised in the air, and descended with a crash upon the head of Bonelucci, who fell in a heap, and lay still. There was no motion or sign of life to be observed in his curled-up, withered body.

Penny Bunn stood aghast, with the accordion fully distended, dangling in his hand.

What had he done?

He backed a pace or two away, and stood for a minute looking down at the prostrate man.

"Boney, old man," he asked, "have I hurt you?"

There was no reply, and no sound beyond the chirp of a robin, the sole witness of the scene.

"You gave yourself a stiffish knock against your accordion," pursued the tutor. "It was no fault of mine. Get up, and we will go to Smudgem Bender, and have just one together. As for the two shillings, you can pay them back to me in instalments. Three-pence a week will satisfy me. Come—get up."

But the fallen Bonelucci never moved, nor was there the remotest indication of his breathing. Penny Bunn shivered, and he became painfully knock-kneed. His eyes stood out of his head.

"I've *killed* him!" he gasped.

He glanced hurriedly around. Beyond the chirping robin, which seemed to be enjoying the spectacle, no living thing had witnessed the crime. The wood was rarely penetrated so far into by any of the inhabitants. Who would be able to charge him with the crime?

Unless he confessed his guilt, who was to bring it home to him? And was there not time for him to flee away and get to some spot, where in the society of man or woman he could lay the foundation for an *alibi*? Yes. He could do that, so he turned and fled.

Away through the wood he sped, got clear of it, and on reaching the high road felt a little better. But there was still the awful thought that he had the life of a fellow creature upon his soul.

Of course he was only a foreigner, but he would count for something—as everything in the eye of the law—and it was with trembling steps that the tutor hastened to Smudgem Bender, and entered his favourite inn by a side door.

There were voices in the bar, the voices of rustics speaking a language that is a compound of Dutch and Chinese to a stranger. The men who owned them were indulging in jokes of a hazy order, and laughing loudly. Oh! how Penny Bunn envied them their freedom from crime.

The coffee room was empty, and he sat there for a time to recover his equanimity. It was not an easy thing to bring himself back to his normal condition, and when he was half-way there, he happened to cast his eye upon the accordion, which he had placed upon the table, and on the corner of the bottom of it was a *dark red stain*.

It was the life-blood of Bonelucci!

That must of necessity be removed at once, and he was about to remove it with his handkerchief, when he reflected that that would be evidence against him. So he looked about him for something that would serve his purpose. There was nothing but a mug without a handle, filled with pipe-lights.

He used them all, and then it seemed this awful indication of his deed was removed.

Then came the question—what should he do with the pipe-lights?

It was summer time, and there was no fire in the grate, which was filled with curly strips of newspaper. To burn them would create an amount of ash, which would raise suspicion, so he put them up the chimney and rang the bell with a desperate hand.

The usual waitress was busy, and the landlord responded. He was surprised to see his guest, and to mark that he lay back in the corner of the seat as if he were ill.

"Took bad, sir?" he asked, anxiously.

"I have been eating early apples," replied Penny Bunn. "Will you please bring me some brandy—a shilling's worth—neat."

The landlord hastened to obey the order, and when he returned with it, Bunn drank off the fiery potation at a draught. Mine host, meanwhile, missed his pipe-lights, and looked about the room and under the table for them.

A SPLENDID SCHOOL STORY.

NEVER BEFORE PUBLISHED.

By E. HARCOURT BURRAGE,

Author of "Ching Ching," "Monkey Mat and Roving Dick," "The Brave Boy of the Basilisk," &c.

THE LAMBS OF LITTLECOTE

A THRILLING SCHOOL STORY

THE FACE ON THE CLOCK—A COUNTERFEIT OF HER HUSBAND TOO MUCH FOR MRS. SNICKER.

☞ PRICE ONE PENNY. ☜

69, 2 Red Lion Court, Fleet St., and 1, 2, & 3 Crown Court, Chancery Lane, London.

"I'll swear," he muttered, "that I filled that 'ere mug 'arf-an-hour ago."

He scratched his head, and Penny Bunn trembled.

To divert the thought of the man, he ordered more brandy, and the landlord left him again. Barely had he departed, when a most awful thing flashed into the brain of the terrified tutor.

In his haste to get away from the scene of his crime he left his instruction book behind him!

And only that morning he had proudly shown it to Awful Rooker, and inscribed his own name therein to stay the hand of a possible purloiner.

CHAPTER LXI.

HONE AND THE SCHOOLMASTER.—IN THE VAULTS.— A PRISONER.

THERE was a heavy burden of dissatisfaction lying on the breast of Roger Hone. He was one of those boys who, when alone, are always weighing the *pros* and *cons* of his daily life, and it was his nature to prejudice his judgment by looking at things through a glass coloured with the smoke of discontent.

He was shrewd also, and he was certain that there was a great deal being hidden from him by the members of the inner circle. So far, we know he was right. But, of course, it did not dawn upon him why they should hold anything in reserve.

He could not grasp the fact that in his own untrustworthiness lay the necessity for hiding something from him, and from others also.

Some of our readers may also be of opinion that it was not right to have anything that took the form of concealment, but we have no doubt that in the course of our story, the action of the inner circle will be amply justified.

Hone walked very slowly back to the school. Ounce by ounce, if we may use such a simile, he weighed the various matters and divergence of disposition which severed him from his schoolfellows. He could not find the balance anywhere in the favour of friendship.

His only companion, in a strict sense, was Soppem Smith, but the tie between them was a mere thread, and Hone felt he could not, after what had transpired in the wood, trust him any more.

A sense of utter loneliness came over the brooding boy, and with it a revengeful feeling gathered in his breast. What he could not share in, he would do his best to spoil. He was acting on the lines of the boy who, being refused a portion of apple pie, maliciously threw a handful of grit into it, and thereby prevented others from enjoying it.

"I will go over to Snicker," was his mental resolve as he entered the house.

His shrewdness had all through enabled him to read the schoolmaster like a book. The humiliation, the struggles, the cowardice of the man were all clear to his eye, and he believed, not without good grounds, that he would be welcomed as an ally. In other words, Hone, in his revengeful mood, was bent on turning sneak.

He both hated and feared Jack Ford, and he knew the penalty of his being discovered as a spy or agent of Fontenoy Snicker, but he was determined to work mischief, because he felt he had been unfairly dealt with.

Instinct, rather than design, turned his steps toward the schoolroom. He gravitated as naturally in that direction as the toper on emerging from his home, goes to the public-house. He had no idea of finding anyone there, nor had he any scheme of action in his mind. He went there because it was the part of the house he was most familiar with, that was all.

It was therefore a shock of surprise to him, when, on opening the door, he saw Fontenoy Snicker hard at work with his task of removing the nails and screws he had used in closing up the two inner rooms.

The schoolmaster had, as some people say, "got his work cut out," and he was labouring at it like a bow-legged Titan, gasping and groaning, and occasionally putting in a word more forcible than polite.

Hone stood still watching him for a time, hardly knowing whether to remain or retreat. As usual with him, he proceeded to mentally weigh the matter, and before the scale of reason could be turned, Fontenoy Snicker paused suddenly in his labours, and facing about, saw him.

"Hallo, there!" he cried, "what the de—— What do you want?"

"I do not want anything, sir," answered Hone. "I came in here by chance."

"This is a arf—*half*-holiday, ain't it?" growled Snicker.

"Yes, sir."

"And haven't all the boys gone out?"

"Yes, sir, and I went with them, but I thought that I would——"

"Come back here and play the spy on me?"

"No, sir. I had not the least idea that you were here."

"Then you know it now. I'm big enough to be seen, ain't I?"

"I only wanted to——"

"You want nothing," interposed Snicker, violently. "You came back to play some trick on me, and I happened to bowl you out. What have you got your hands in your pocket for? Anything in the way of gunpowder there?"

"No, sir," answered Hone, "I——"

"Turn out your pockets and let me see 'em. Not a word. Inside out, sharp!"

The air of the schoolmaster was very threatening. He presented all the dangerous qualities of a wild beast that is cornered, and means to have a go at its foes. So Hone promptly emptied his pockets, which contained nothing but the usual delightful collection of odds and ends, without which no boy's outfit is complete.

"It's well for you there is nothing what I spected—expected!" snarled the schoolmaster. "Be off with you!"

"I should like to say one word to you, sir," began Hone.

Fontenoy Snicker, with a suppressed howl, picked up a chisel from the floor, and looked so ferocious that Hone promptly vanished, not only from the room, but from the house.

The schoolmaster did not follow him, and was, therefore, not cognisant of his having left the Abbey. It was enough for him that the boy departed from the schoolroom, and left him to pursue his labours.

He was in a terrible state of irritation, and led away by his ungovernable passion, pounded at the door, and split it up, finally tearing it down and utterly ruining it. After that he cooled a bit, and went away for some refreshment.

Now it so happened that day, Jack, prior to leaving the school, had been overhauling his box, in the way boys have, just for the pleasure of contemplating their possessions. He, having his attention called away as he was putting it right again, gave no further thought to it, but, hurrying off, left the key in the lock.

He thought no more of it until he and his companions were returning from Chippenham, and then calling it to mind, and coupling it with the fact that Hone had gone back towards the school, and had not been seen since, it made him uneasy.

There was nothing of any great importance in the box, but his letters from home were in it; and he knew that Hone, if he got a chance, would not object to read them, but would rather take a delight in doing so.

He, therefore, after having explained the state of the case, set out at a run for the Abbey, and arrived there fully an hour before the time appointed for the return. He saw no one on entering the house, and bounding upstairs to the dormitory, was pleased to find the key still in the lock, and the contents of the box apparently untouched.

In hastily turning it over, he came across the remainder of the packet of explosives which Professor Lingo had sent him. Some of them had, as we know, during the barring-out, been used with considerable success. Jack had forgotten them, and he put them into his pocket, thinking they might be useful in some way.

As he was going downstairs, he saw the schoolmaster entering the class-room. The fact was that Fonteney Snicker, when he went in search of refreshment, sat down in an easy-chair to rest; also, being a little worn-out with his exertions, fell asleep. He had only just woke up again when Jack was examining his box upstairs.

Not seeing the boy, he entered the room, and then Jack, listening at the door, heard him go into the inner chambers.

"What was he doing there?" Jack asked himself.

Cautiously opening the door, he peered through the opening, but could see nothing, so he boldly entered, and on tip-toe walked across the room.

He smiled as he observed the smashed door, guessing why it had been operated on in that violent fashion. Through the opening he could see the schoolmaster busy removing the screws of the trap-door.

A smile of pleasure spread itself over the face of Jack, as he watched Fontenoy Snicker carefully lay each screw in turn upon the floor. By his side was a lantern, ready lighted.

"Going down prying," thought Jack. "All right, old man; I'll give you a treat!"

It was not a long task taking out the screws; and having raised the trapdoor, the schoolmaster had a look at the dark staircase that led below. He was a terrible coward, and it was plain to Jack that he half feared to venture down.

The schoolmaster would certainly have sought a companion to accompany him, if he had not been in search of a possible hidden treasure, and cupidity finally mastered his fears.

Cautiously he descended the stone steps, and disappeared. The next moment Jack was standing by the trap-door, carefully lifting it to turn it down.

An idea flashed upon him.

Out come the little packet of explosive pellets he had in his pocket, and, with reckless prodigality, he threw them down the stone steps.

Being made of some light soft substance they made no noise in falling. Then over came the trapdoor into its place without the slightest sound, and two minutes sufficed to replace the screws sufficiently tight in their places to hold it fast.

Exulting in the complete success of his undertaking, Jack fled away, leaving Fontenoy Snicker a prisoner in the dismal vault.

———

CHAPTER LXII

A TERRIBLE TIME FOR MORE PERSONS THAN ONE.— HUSH MONEY.

THERE was nothing in the vault to reward the schoolmaster for his trouble. Damp and gloomy to a degree, it was not the place for a man of his cowardly disposition, and he shivered as he held the light aloft and looked about him.

On one side, where the professor had used the dynamite cartridges, there was a chaos of shattered stonework. Elsewhere there were damp walls ; and pendent from the ceiling a number of crape-like cobwebs.

"I'll get Phœbe to come down with me," he muttered. "I can't stay here alone."

"Phœbe" was the name of his spouse, and he rarely used it unless he in a troublous state of mind. In his softer moods he occasionally addressed her by her christian name. In his harder state he was given to employing the first epithet that came into his gifted mind.

So after a look round he began to re-ascend the stairs, and he had got about half-way up, when what appeared to be a most tremendous explosion took place under his feet. Down he fell, unnerved completely by the alarming noise, and banging his lantern upon the stone stairs, he not only put it out, but smashed it of shape and utterly ruined it.

For fully three minutes he lay there, enduring all the agonies of a mortal terror. Then he made an effort, and getting upon his feet, crawled up slowly until he reached the trapdoor against which, not expecting it was closed, he violently bumped his head.

The blow temporarily illumined the darkness around him with the usual shooting stars, but he gave little thought to them. His agonized mind was concentrated on the closed door.

Who had put it down and fastened it ? Everybody he believed was out the Abbey, but himself and Hone. The boys and the tutors were away, and even Mrs. Snicker and Black-eyed Susan had gone for a walk. Only Hone could have done this thing.

"I'll half-kill him when I get out," hissed the imprisoned schoolmaster.

But he was not yet out, and as he thumped upon the trapdoor, shouting at the same time, he gave a passionate stamp with his foot.

Bang !

He dropped in a heap upon the stairs, and lay there groaning with terror. What was the meaning of it all ?

So soft and insignificant in size were the pellets that he did not feel them beneath his feet, and could not associate any movement of his with the appalling noise. All sorts of wild speculations as to their origin flashed through his mind.

Were they gas explosions such as he had read of in mines ?

Were they of a supernatural nature ?

Was he being fired at by some hidden foe ?

His thoughts took the wildest forms, and all in a moment as it were, the ideas being jumbled together. Acting upon an uncontrollable impulse he began to yell as if he were in open ground, pursued by a wild-eyed Zulu with an assegai.

Suddenly his vocal performance was checked by a knocking on the trapdoor above. He ceased to yell, and then he heard a voice crying out :

"Who is it down there ?"

He recognized the dulcet tones of his own Phœbe, and felt more kindly towards her than he had done for many a day.

"It's me," he answered, feebly.

"Who's me ?"

"Your Fonty."

"My idiot !" he heard her mutter, and then aloud she asked him, "what do you mean by screwing yourself up in that cellar ?"

This was a peculiar question which could have only come from a woman, and the exasperation of it made him see red and blue lights darting to and fro. A pause of ten seconds or so ensued ere he could find an answer.

"I didn't do it," he said at last, "there's a screwdriver handy. It won't take you long to loosen 'em."

"I can twist them out with my fingers," she replied.

This she proceeded to do, and in three minutes he emerged from his prison whiter and more ghastly in appearance then any ghost ever yet seen by man.

His wife, who had her mantle and bonnet on, just as she had worn them when out for a walk, stepped back and uttered an exclamation of surprise.

"Jerry," she exclaimed, "what's come to me ? You look like a piece of b'iled veal."

"Why don't you say that I am a calf at once ?" he growled, all his tenderness gone now that the peril was over, "and not, woman-like, chuck an insult at a man in bits."

"But what have you been doing down there ?" asked Mrs. Snicker.

"I was a-thinking," he replied, feebly, "that the cellar below might be made useful for coals."

"That's a lie, Jerry," she rejoined, "and you know it. Coals, indeed ! And who do you think would take the trouble to fetch 'em up from there ? I should say you were digging a grave for me.".

But this, of course, he disclaimed as an impossibility. Mrs. Snicker smiled dryly.

"You'd do it if you durst, Jerry," she said, "but you are too much of a coward to commit murder. Go and wash your face, and brush them cobwebs off your back. Then come to tea, and have it in peace afore the boys come home. That Bunn has been at it again."

"What, drinking?" ejaculated the schoolmaster.

"He looked like it as he came into the house a minute or two ago, walking with his eyes straight fixed ahead, and when I spoke to him all he said was, ''struction book, blood on 'cordion, pipelights.'"

She mimicked the manner and speech of the hapless tutor to perfection, and a curt laugh of approval burst from the lips of her husband.

"He's been lavishing some of his ill-gotten gains on liquor," he said. "Have you seen anything of young Hone?"

"He is outside, mooning about," answered Mrs. Snicker.

"You go and get the tea ready," said Snicker; "I'll jine—*join*—you directly."

"But afore I go, Jerry," said his wife, "tell me what you have been firing off powder for. If you have been trying to blow out your brains, give it up. You must get some first."

"I dare say you think that is witty," he sneered, "you bag of bones in a bombazine dress and thirty-shilling mantle. It so happens that I haven't been firing off anything."

"Who was it, then?"

"I don't know," he roared. "Will you go and get the tea ready? I want to have a word with Hone."

Mrs. Snicker, muttering something about a pig of a bear with a sore head, stalked away, and the schoolmaster walked into the schoolroom, from whence he presently emerged with a stoutish cane in his hand.

"I haven't had a fair smite at one of them since the barring out," he hissed, "but I'm going to have one now, if I die for it."

Roger Hone was, as Mrs. Snicker said, mooning about outside the school grounds. He had been for a walk, and tiring of his own company, had come back to await the return of the boys.

A short time before he had caught a glimpse of Jack Ford hastening back to meet his friends, and he was wondering in his speculative way what had brought him back to the school, when Fontenoy Snicker, white hot through, and with the hand that held the cane behind his back, emerged from the grounds.

He came towards Hone in a quiet, stealthy manner, fearing he would run away, until he was close up to him, and then with a tiger-like spring he was upon the boy.

Hone yelled out with surprise, and immediately after began to exercise his voice in anguish, for the schoolmaster, seething with fury, beat him with the ferocity of a savage.

Now that he had resumed his old amusement, of which he had been for some time deprived, Fontenoy Snicker partook of it ravenously, as a starving man might of food when placed at his disposal.

Hone cried out in vain for mercy. The only ears that heard his cries at the outset were those of the schoolmaster, and they were deaf to the call.

The frantic appeals of the boy added fuel to the fire of his savage nature, raising the flames higher and higher, until there was a prospect of his beating Hone into a state of insensibility, or even killing him outright.

But this was happily prevented by the main body of the pupils, who were in the wood. Hearing the yells, and not knowing from whom they might emanate, they came tearing up the slope to the rescue, and arrived in time to stop the brutal exhibition.

The moment Fontenoy Snicker saw them, all his ferocity evaporated. His hand dropped to his side, and, but for the utterly cowardly nature of the proceeding, he would have turned and fled into the house.

But he had just sufficient courage to stand his ground and address himself to Hone in a miserable, sneaky way.

"You do it again and I won't let you off so easy as I have done this time."

Then looking at the boys who, out of breath with running, stood panting and gazing at the pair, thrasher and victim, wondering what was up, he told them tea wouldn't be ready for awhile, and they could stop out another half-hour.

He walked in, leaving them to hear what Hone had to say. It was not much, for he had not the least idea why he had been thrashed, as he had done absolutely nothing to deserve it.

"I haven't been inside the beastly den of an Abbey these two hours," he said, as he rubbed his aching arms and legs, "nor had a word with him or anyone."

"How did the row begin?" asked Whymper.

"There wasn't any row," replied Hone, "he came out in a quiet way with his hand behind his back, and dropped on me suddenly. He did not say a single word."

"It looks as though he had gone mad," said Bob Stockton.

"So it does," chorussed a dozen others and many an anxious glance was exchanged. A mad Snicker would be a very serious sort of man to deal with.

"When you left us where did you go to?" asked Don.

"I came back here," was the sulky reply.

"What for?"

"That is my business."

"Well let it be your business," said Don, "it is entirely a question between you and Snicker. Of course, if he is right in his head, you must have done something, and it is no use your pitching a yarn to the contrary into us."

"I am not going to pitch any yarn," retorted Hone, "I know you were all jolly glad to see me being flayed, but there is one comfort. As he has begun again he will go on, and it will be the turn of some of you directly."

As this was more than likely there was a decidedly uncomfortable look upon the faces of a few of the more timid, but on the countenances of those who were determined not to endure any more of the "Snicker physic," the expression was of a harder character.

"If the game really has begun again," said Jack Ford, "we shall be obliged to think over what is to be done. Come into the wood, all of you, for a moment. Hone, won't you come too?"

"Not me," was the answer; "I'll have nothing more to do with your plots."

"Going to turn sneak, eh?"

"I'll turn to what I like."

Hone lounged off, pausing every few steps to rub his aching anatomy, and all the others accompanied Jack down into the wood again.

"Now, boys," said the bold young leader, "a few words will settle this matter. Are you going to put up with Snicker's blackguardism again?"

"Never, never!" was the cry.

"And suppose he tries it on, will you be guided by me?"

"We will—we will."

"That will do, then. No more of it, is our motto," said Jack. "If any of you think otherwise, now is your time to back out. There is no compulsion in the matter."

They all reiterated their determination to stand by Ford, and accept his counsel and his advice in all things.

"Remember this," he said, as a final word upon the subject; "if we stick together we are strong, but if we are divided some of us will have a rough time of it. Don't forget the fable about the bundle of sticks."

"And bear in mind," said Bob Stockton, "that Snicker is only *one* stick, and a precious one into the bargain."

They laughed at his little joke, and the party breaking up, they returned in scattered form to the playground. But there were a few sinking hearts among them, and some whispered talk about writing home and getting out of the place.

Awful Rooker shortly after passed through the playground and entered the house. He went upstairs to his room, but on passing peeped into the apartment occupied by Penny Bunn, and saw the hapless man sitting in a heap in his chair with his face in his hands.

"I say," he exclaimed, "what is up?"

Penny Bunn raised a woebegone face and stared at him in a ghost-seeing fashion.

"What do you want?" he asked.

"Bunn," said Rooker, "you look as if you had done something—*something awful.*"

The vast majority of men would have kept their own counsel upon such a serious subject as that which lay like lead upon the breast of Penny Bunn, but his natural tendency to brag led him away as it had often done before. Rising, he walked to the door and closed it.

"Rooker," he said in a sepulchral tone, "can I confide in you?"

"I should think so," was the answer.

"And trust you?"

"You know you may."

"Then—bear up I beg of you—but perhaps you had better sit down. The shock won't be so great."

"I can keep my feet," returned Rooker, "and stand it."

"Rooker," groaned Penny Bunn, "in me you behold a *murderer!*"

Awful Rooker was startled, but he did not stagger or cry out or do anything but stare at the man who had confessed that his life was forfeited to the gallows.

"The impostor," continued Penny Bunn, "the sham Bonelucci, assailed me in the wood, and I slew him."

"Never!" said Rooker, in a stifled tone.

"He demanded the instrument, the testimonial accordion, of me," pursued Penny Bunn, "and threatened to injure me if I did not give it up. I naturally declared that I would not part with such a valuable gift while I had life. Then he drew a knife, the same with which he once threatened me in your presence, and we closed.

"It was a terrible struggle," continued Penny Bunn, after a dismal silence of a few moments' duration, "and but for my skill as a wrestler, he must have prevailed. 'Your life or mine,' he said. 'Be it so,' I answered, and it is his life that has been sacrificed."

"How did you kill him?" asked Rooker, slipping into a chair, probably because the awful revelation had shaken him up a bit.

"I wrenched the knife from his hand," replied Bunn, "and, maddened by my wrongs, plunged it into his heart. He gave a gasp and fell. 'It is but right that I should die,' he groaned, 'and no just law will punish you for it.' His absolutely last words were ' My wife, my children, my country, farewell!' Then he smiled and lay back still in death."

"I say," said Rooker, "this is rather a warm business. You will be hung for it, certain."

"Not unless I am betrayed," cried Bunn, wildly, "Rooker, you are the sole possessor of this terrible secret. My life is in your hands."

"That is all very well," answered Rooker, "but I don't see any fun in being accessory to a murder. You know, if ever it comes out, they will hang me as well as you. I dare not be in it."

"Rooker," groaned Penny Bunn, sinking upon his knees, "I beg of you to keep my story locked in your breast."

"I must be paid for the risk," replied Rooker, firmly; "you have a lot of money, and beyond a drink of very poor whisky, I am none the better for it. How much of the change of that note have you left?"

"Between seven and eight pounds."

"Then hand it over to me."

"Eh?"

"Hand it over to me, I say."

"What, *all* of it?"

"Every penny, or I go at once to the police."

"But, Rooker, *all* of it? It will leave me stranded on the shore of poverty again."

"Better that," said Rooker, sententiously, "than hang. Fork out the tin."

"This is a merciless proceeding," gasped the suffering Penny Bunn; "take half."

"All or none," insisted Rooker. "Now, be sharp, or I am off for the police."

He half rose from his chair as he spoke, and Penny Bunn uttered a stifled cry for mercy, pushing Rooker back into his seat.

"You shall have it," he said, "but I think I made a slight mistake about the amount. It is four pounds ten."

"You shell out the lot," said Rooker, ferociously, "all of it. Do you think I am going to risk my life for four pounds ten? Turn out all your pockets."

There was no help for it, and the tortured Bunn handed over all that remained of the generous gift of Sir Charles Barstow. Rooker counted the money, and finding that it amounted to seven pounds five shillings and fourpence halfpenny, was satisfied.

"Now I am dumb," he said; "but look here. It will never do to have the body found. Did you bury it?"

"Bury it?—no," answered Bunn, with a shiver. "I had no tools."

"Tell me where it is to be found, and I will go and complete the job. He's only a beggarly Italian, and nobody will miss or make inquiries after him."

Penny Bunn was both amazed and pleased to find so much latent coolness in his junior, who, hitherto, had not exhibited anything remarkable in the way of pluck, at home or abroad.

"And you will do this?" he exclaimed.

"Certainly," replied Awful Rooker, " for the safety of us both. You take the tea-table, and I will slip away with the spade from the tool-house, and put the body out of sight. Tell me exactly where I can drop upon it."

Penny Bunn, with a growing reverence for the developing qualities in Rooker, gave him a minute description of the spot where the unfortunate Bonelucci fell and died. Rooker said he could find it, and departed.

In due time the tea was ready, and Penny Bunn took the head of the table, shaking from head to foot with apprehension. He wanted Rooker back to make sure that he had performed his work without detection, and every moment increased a fear that he had been seen in his task of burial and arrested.

But during the meal he did not put in an appearance, nor was it until nearly nine o'clock that he returned to the Abbey.

Penny Bunn, unable to remain in the society of the boys with his awful fear within his breast, took refuge in his room.

At last the door opened, and Rooker walked, or rather staggered in.

His face was horribly pale, and he had the appearance of one who has been very ill.

"Bunn," he said, in a hollow voice, "I have buried him, and then——"

He stopped short and shivered, and with a wave of his hand, the meaning of which was not clear, he vanished from the room.

He left behind him the odour of somebody's full-flavoured, unrivalled twopenny cigars. Bunn, even in that hour of mingled anguish and relief, recognized the especial aroma, for he had on occasion indulged in that class of the narcotic weed.

CHAPTER LXIII.

THOSE BONES.—A NEW FACE TO THE CLOCK.

"HALLO, Don, what have you there?"

It was Tom Drummond who put the question as the two chums met in the passage outside the lavatory.

Don had a small box in his hand, which he opened, and exhibited the contents to Don.

"Goodness, bones!" ejaculated Drummond.

"Yes, bones," said Don, " human bones. I found

them in the bottom of the boot cupboard. I fancy they must be the lot Penny Bunn routed out of the floor of the room Snicker used to sleep in. Sue told us all about it, you remember."

"Of course I do. I wonder who put them in the cupboard? One would have thought that they would have been taken right away."

"Here comes Sue. Let us ask her if she knows anything about them."

Black-eyed Susan, with a bucket in one hand and a sweeping brush in the other, came hurrying along, and, with a smile, would have passed the boys, if Tom had not stopped her.

"Sue," he said, "we have got a box of bones which were in the boot cupboard. Do you know who placed them there?"

"Lard sakes!" exclaimed Black-eyed Susan, "they went right out of my head. Missus told me to bury them in the garden."

"And she supposes you have done so?"

"She does, and master, too; also Mr. Bunn."

"Then let 'em think so," said Don; "you are not afraid of bones, I hope?"

"Bones," said Black-eyed Susan, "is bones to me, and nothing else."

"And if you should hear of them being about the house, you won't take any notice of it, will you?"

"Certainly not," answered the girl, with a twinkle in her eyes; "it isn't my business, and I don't love any of 'em so much as to put myself out of the way for them. Oh! Master Drummond, do you know what is the matter with Mr. Bunn?"

"No," said Tom, "but he looks awfully pale the last day or two. Been worrying himself about something, I suppose."

"Then there is Mr. Rooker," said Susan. "He's sort of wild like. Last night, as I went by his room, he was screeching like, and talking to himself in the funniest way you ever heard."

"What was he saying?"

"I couldn't catch all he said, but I did hear him cry out, 'Buried in the wood,' and then he says, 'Ha, ha!' also 'Ho, ho!' likewise 'He, he!' and finishes off by kind of bawling out 'The scaffold waits for the murderer!'"

"It is very odd," said Don, thoughtfully.

"Perhaps he was reading from a book," suggested Tom.

"It isn't books, but," here Susan lowered her voice and put her lips near to Tom's ear, "*Licker.*"

"Do you mean drink?" asked Tom.

Black-eyed Susan pursed her lips, and nodded her head.

"It is that, and nothing else," she said. "He has a flat bottle under his linen in the drawer, and there is whisky in it."

"Fancy Rooker going that way," murmured Don.

"It is the bad example set him," said Black-eyed Susan; "master does it, and look at him. Did you ever see such a face as his? and he is always prowling about, and looking into all sorts of cupboards and places, and I heard him tell missus that he believed there was fiends in the house, for when he was down the vaults—he got shut in there, you know—he see 'em, and they opened their mouths and spit at him, and when they did it the noise was like the firing of guns."

"And does your mistress believe that yarn?"

"She do, Master Peebles, for she heard the bang, and that was what took her into the well-room, and then she let master out of what he calls durance bile."

"Durance *vile*," corrected Don.

"*He* said bile," rejoined Susan, "and missus said he was wrong. Then he called her a fool, and asked her who taught her edication, and they went at it hammer and tongs, and missus told master that the next time he was shut up in the vault, the fiends might bile and frizzle him alive before she would come and let him out. The state of the Abbey is dreadful."

Shaking her head in a solemn, portentous way, Black-eyed Susan departed on her way, and Tom and Don had a quiet laugh together.

Of course they knew what Jack had done, and the real cause of those explosions now attributed to fiends.

The bell for morning studies interrupted their mirth, and, the boys appearing from the playground, they hastened to their seats. It was three days since Fontenoy Snicker had thrashed Hone, and he, up to the present, had made no sign of his intention to favour others with a similar castigation. Roger Hone had no sympathisers in the school, and the rupture between him and Soppem Smith was complete. Smith had gone over to the enemy.

The tutors followed the boys almost immediately, and guided by the revelations of Black-eyed Susan, Tom and Don took notes of the appearance of both their faces.

Penny Bunn had the appearance of a hunted man. His face was absolutely colourless, and his eyes were ever roaming to the door. The least noise out of the usual course made him jump with fright, and anything in the way of door-knocking and bell-ringing out of the daily routine set him trembling from head to foot.

Rooker also was clearly nervous, but it seemed to be a different class of that form of weakness. He was not troubled by knocking or ringing, but had an all-round shakiness that would arise in anyone afflicted with unstrung nerves from whatever cause.

The schoolmaster was later than usual that morning, and when he came scowling into the room, it was plain that he had been upset, and was in one of his worst humours.

"Thunder in the air," whispered Bob Stockton to Don, who nodded his head. Once upon a time he might have been troubled by the announcement, but he had been strengthened and developed by events, and was as cool in a difficult and dangerous position as Jack Ford himself.

"Boys," said Fontenoy Snicker, as he mounted into his seat, with the screwed up face of one who has rheumatism or gout, "I hope you are well up in your lessons this morning. If not it will be the worse for you. Mr. Bunn!"

"Sir-r-r-r," stuttered the startled tutor, who was in a day-dream when addressed.

"You will not allow any shirking, if you please."

"Certainly not, sir-r-r."

Rooker also received an admonition on this subject, and the schoolmaster called for silence.

Then he glared round the room with his eyeglass, a strange picture of the burlesque and the brutal—a full-blown specimen of educational incompetence and the cruel pedagogue combined.

The door he had broken open to get at the vault having been too much shattered to be replaced, he had boarded up the opening with some planking that had been lying for years about the grounds. It gave the room a dismal, chilling appearance.

Now Jack Ford could see that another of the momentous struggles was about to begin, and unless something could be done to divert the attention, the breaking out of a second war appeared imminent, and the time for it was not yet ripe. He was debating in his mind what to do, when a piece of paper was passed up to him from Don. He opened it and read:

"Snicker thinks that it was fiends in the cellar, popping fire at him. He swears to his thinner half that he saw them spit fire at him, and she believes it."

Jack tore up the paper into minute fragments, and slipped them into his pocket. He had got an idea out of the communication which Don simply meant should be amusing to him.

Jack sat at the top of the desk near the schoolmaster. Behind him, and a little to the left, was the boarded up doorway. Turning in his seat he stared hard at it, and continued to do so until Fontenoy Snicker observed him.

"Ford," he cried, "attend to your work."

"Yes, sir," answered Jack, with a start.

He turned to his books, but was soon looking round again. The watchful schoolmaster pounced upon him verbally in a moment.

"Ford," he snarled, "am I to tell you a dozen times to confine your attention to your books?"

"I beg pardon, sir," replied Jack, "but it is the noise behind there that interrupts me."

He pointed to the planking, and Snicker turned pale. Jack hit him again while he was hot with fear.

"I fancied I saw an eye, too, at one of the cracks between the boards," he said.

The entire school was now dumb and observant. Those who knew Jack most intimately guessed that he was playing some game; others hardly knew what to think of it.

"Ford," almost yelled Fontenoy Snicker, "how can anyone be there?"

"I don't know, sir," answered Jack, quietly, "perhaps I am mistaken."

Here Bob Stockton thought it was time for him to come forward as a confirmatory witness.

"Look, sir," he cried, sharply, "isn't that an eye? There by the hole that was a knot in the wood."

It is a well recognised fact that, if a persistent person publicly declares that so-and-so is to be seen if you will but look hard enough, others will fancy they see it, and bear witness accordingly. It was so now with Barnes who, in his usual nervous way, was ready to see or hear anything. Jumping up in his seat he cried out hysterically:

"I can see it, too, sir."

Before the startled schoolmaster could express any opinion upon his evidence, two more witnesses came to the fore, in the persons of Awful Rooker and Penny Bunn.

Both declared that they could see an eye, and what was more, believed it.

The ball thus set rolling, something like a panic ensued, which was increased as Jack got up from his seat, and walked with apparent firmness to the barricaded doorway.

"Don't go there!" cried a dozen voices, his chums being leaders in the cry of warning.

But Jack, with an assumption of despising those who were afraid, put his hand up and his ear to a crack in the boards. The double action was expressive. He was listening to somebody, and immediately silence returned to the room.

"Will you kindly speak again," said Jack, addressing the imaginary person in the inner chamber.

Again did the imagination of the more nervous of the watchers aid him in his trickery. Not only did Barnes, the two tutors, and some half-dozen boys imagine they heard a speaker replying to Jack in a hollow whisper, but Fontenoy Snicker likewise yielded to the weakness of his nerves. But the sounds he fancied he heard were groans.

"I don't know what to make of it," said Jack, drawing back, "it is such an odd voice, and not at all plain, but I can make out a few words. He wants to know what has been done with his bones?"

"Mercy on me!" gasped Penny Bunn, as he subsided first into his seat and then to the floor, where he remained meanwhile in a state of terror and bewilderment.

"Will you make yourself a little clearer?" Jack asked the imaginary person.

He listened a moment and shook his head. This implied that there was no answer, and none of the victims of previous imaginings heard anything, of course.

"Shall I pull the boards down, sir?" inquired Jack.

Not getting an immediate answer either way, he thrust his hand into a widish opening at the end of the boarding, and tore one of the planks down. It opened a space just wide enough to permit him to slip through, and he boldly passed in. The silence was again intense in the schoolroom. The ghost of a pin might have been heard if such a thing had dropped upon the floor.

Jack, in the inner rooms, moved about with a light step, but it sounded very clear to the listening throng. After a minute or two he reappeared with a white, wondering face.

"There is nobody in there, sir," he said, with plaintive dismay, as he looked into the pea-green countenance of the schoolmaster. "I must have been mistaken about anybody being there."

"It was the wind, perhaps," answered Fontenoy Snicker, hoarsely; "replace the board. I will see that it is nailed up by-and-bye."

He was completely cowed, for the time at least, and the determination with which he had entered the schoolroom that morning, to make one more grand effort to resume his old-time authority, vanished like the spirit of a dream.

The quietude with which the rest of the morning passed away was very remarkable. At the termination of the course of studies, carried out, it must be confessed, in a very perfunctory manner, Fontenoy Snicker announced that he had business which would take him away for the rest of the day, and the boys could have a half-holiday.

Having made this unexpected announcement, he hurried from the room.

There was no cheering, or even thanks uttered in acknowledgment of this boon, for one and all knew well that Fontenoy Snicker did not bestow it upon them as a kindness, but as a personal necessity. The mysterious eye and voice from behind the boarding had, as Whymper remarked, "shaken all the fight out of him, "and he was simply going to shirk his work because he was no longer fit for it.

Whymper was right. The schoolmaster was shaken to pieces, and the superstitious part of his disposition was in a ferment.

Had Jack been the sole authority for the phenomenon, he might have suspected the reality of it; but, supported as he was by outside evidence, and adding to it his own experience in the vault, what other conclusion could a vulgar, ignorant-minded man come to?

Nor did he get much comfort from his wife, when he told her of the strange occurrence of the morning.

"Jerry," she said, "you was allus a bad 'un, and I've orfen thought that in your early days you must have murdered or pisened somebody."

"If you are going to accuse me of that," muttered Snicker, "say P-O-I-soned."

"The luck has always been dead against you," pursued Mrs. Snicker, ignoring his correction; "nothing goes right, and I am not surprised to find that as a last punishment, you are to be haunted."

"Women are a pack of fools," was all the troubled schoolmaster could say by way of retort.

Thus it was that the boys got an unexpected holiday, which put them in a light and cheerful mood.

They set off in a body, after dinner, and hastened away towards Smudgem Bender, marching in column, and singing one of their songs, written for them by Herbert May.

> Hurrah for the Littlecote Lambs,
>   Hurrah for the brave and the free;
> Down with all pedagogue shams,
>   And fight for your liberty.
> That boy shall be branded a fool
>   Who bends his neck to the yoke,
> Once worn in the old Abbey school,
>   As if each boy was a moke.
> But the yoke has been shattered, and Snicker may frown,
> Now his ears have been clipped, and the dog's tail is down.
> Then hurrah for the Littlecote Lambs, etc.

Their voices went before them to the village, and several of the more prudent folk who sat by the doors sunning themselves, went into their cottages, and remained there until they had passed by. As they drew near Botch's farm, a proposition was made by Bob Stockton that they should call and just ask how the old man was.

"It is only common politeness," he said, "and we need not make a very long stay."

The suggestion was made with a charming gravity that tickled his hearers, and the proposal, in a modified form, was accepted. It was decided not to call in the usual way, "which is vulgar and commonplace," remarked Don Peebles, but to foregather by the farmyard gate, which the reader will remember opened on the high road, and call for Botch until he came out. A few words of greeting "more or less polite," as Dorey hinted, "could then be exchanged, which, being done, they could go on their way, and Botch return to his home to "blow off the steam."

One of the farm men was engaged in feeding the pigs as the boys swarmed up to the gate. They had ceased to sing a hundred yards from it, and by the direction of their leader, advanced in silence.

The man had heard the singing in the distance, and knew who was coming; but when it suddenly stopped, he concluded that the boys had turned into a side lane, and departed in another direction.

He was congratulating himself upon being relieved of a possible encounter with the Lambs, when a most terrific yell, from a score of lusty young throats, fell upon his ears.

This was a terse and true account of the affair up to the time when Botch, who was having an after-dinner snooze, heard it too. Before he was half-awake, or had made any attempt to rise to his feet, he roared out: "The Lambs, fur a ten-pun note."

He jumped up, laid hold of a riding-whip, and dashed out of the house. His man was engaged in a violent struggle with a calf that had got loose, which he held by the fore-leg and one ear.

The boys were quiet now, their mirth having settled down to grins, but there was little doubt about their thoroughly enjoying themselves. Botch never could see why he should provide an entertainment gratis for the boys, and he went for them.

"Stand your ground," cried out Jack Ford, "we have done nothing, and this is the high road. Let him touch us if he dares."

Botch was a man of wisdom, or rather prudence, and he knew that Jack was right.

There was no breach of the law in their stopping to enjoy the spectacle of a farm labourer struggling with a calf. But he wasn't obliged to have a mob of boys about his premises, and he therefore ordered them off.

"Get away here," he cried, "here comes the constable. Danged if I don't lock you up."

The Smudgem Bender constable was indeed approaching. He was a mild specimen of his class, and, outside his uniform, there was nothing to be afraid of.

He had heard an unusual rioting going on and had come to see what was the matter.

Botch peremptorily ordered him to move the boys on.

The youngsters, taking their cue from Jack, were all now very quiet. They were doing nothing whatever to bring them within the iron grasp of the law. The constable smiled in a deprecating manner, but did nothing more.

"D'ye hear?" roared Botch, "move 'em on."

"I think," said the constable, addressing the boys, "that if Mr. Botch wants you to go, why then, you had better be goin'."

"Is this a public road?" said Jack.

"It be," was the reply.

"Are we doing anything wrong?"

"Not as I sees, but Mr. Botch——"

"Mr. Botch," said Jack, quietly but firmly, "be jiggered."

"I should like to know," here interposed Bob Stockton, "on what grounds Botch disturbs a whole neighbourhood with his pigs? My father is a solicitor, and he practises in the courts of London. His speciality is pig cases and public nuisances. I have often heard him say that, by law, you cannot keep pigs within a hundred feet of any public highway, nor wherever they may be, allow them to accumulate filth so as to be odorously offensive. Now I am certain that those sties are too near the road, and as for the odour arising from the accumulation of dirt it can be nosed five miles away."

"I've kep' pigs," said Botch, he called them "pegs" "going on for forty year——"

"Then I should like to know," interrupted Bob "what the authorities here have been doing? They ought to have summoned you long ago, fined you heavily, and compelled you to remove your pigs to the far end of yonder field. However, as they seem somewhat lax in the affair, I shall, as a public matter, communicate with my father, who will write to the Treasury, giving the particulars of the case, and I have not the least doubt about your being publicly prosecuted, Botch, as a keeper of a nuisance; and you," to the constable, "will certainly be removed from your post for having so long neglected your duty."

Bob finished with a flourish of his hand, and Jack, seeing that a good point had been made, gave the signal for departure.

"Fall in," he cried, "form fours, left half turn. *March!*"

Away they went, with a quick, regular step, the outcome of the training they had had at the time of the barring out, leaving Botch and the constable to dwell upon the warnings they had respectively received.

"Darn their cheek," exclaimed Botch, after taking ten bars rest to recover himself.

"It was a hevil day the old Abbey was turned into a school," said the constable. "This used to be a quiet, peaceful place, but now there's a regular stirring up going on. Mr. Botch, if it is the law for you to put your pigs further back, and that young gentleman's father is a lawyer——"

But Botch cut him short with a powerful explosion of a vernacular form, and in the strongest dialect of the district.

It is bad to swear in any language, but when it comes to doing it in the Wiltshire style, then it is time for all decent or timid people to sheer off, and accordingly the policeman, who was both timid and decent, departed as quickly as his official dignity and his heavy boots permitted.

———

CHAPTER LXIV.

STILL HAUNTED.—A RELIEF AND A REVELATION.

IT must be horrible to be haunted with the memory of a crime—to walk abroad with the knowledge of having the life of a fellow creature on one's hands. To enjoy the scenery and the beauty of the varied life around us, thus burdened, is an apparent impossibility to those who are free from crime. And so, indeed, it was with the incomparably wretched Penny Bunn.

It is true that he had not meditated a murder, or, indeed, intended to do any form of bodily injury to the unfortunate Bonelucci, but the fact remained before his eyes that he had hit the Italian, in a moment of haste, over the head with the most ponderous accordion of modern times, and slain him. There was no getting over that, nor of the fact that the law would consider it murder in the first degree, and hang him for it if he were found out.

It was a mad thing to trust Awful Rooker with his secret. Might he not, when he had spent the remnant of that ten-pound note, think it desirable for his own sake, to give the murderer up to justice ?

It was odds on—as betting men would say—his doing it, and it was in a state of apprehension bordering on stupidity that the tutor left the Abbey to make the best of the unexpected half-holiday.

But of what benefit was it to him ?

"Holidays in halves or wholes," he groaned, " will never be enjoyed by me any more, even if I escape justice. I wonder how a man feels on the morning of his execution."

He stopped short, shivering, and then he thought of the way he was going. How could he travel alone through the wood which held the remains of his victim ?

Rooker had taken himself off as soon as he could, to avoid, as Penny Bunn very well knew, the society of a murderer, who, in addition to his being immersed in sinfulness, was also penniless, and would have to be treated. The boys were gone, and Snicker was having a glass of something in solitary state. Penny Bunn had no companion, and he must go through that wood alone, unless he went on the other side of the Abbey, which, however, led nowhere but into the most cheerless and uninviting bit of country in the world.

Nerving himself, he started on again, and entered the wood. The day was fairly bright, but there was very little sun, and within the shadow of the trees a gloom prevailed.

Penny Bunn hastened down the sloping path, which as old country ways invariably do, wound here and there, just as if short cuts were shortest when of a curly nature. He hurried on with shaky knees, glancing apprehensively about him on either side, but, seeing nothing of the shade of his victim, was beginning to congratulate himself on being free from all horrors for the time, when, on swinging round a bend he came in sight of the *dreaded form !*

Yes, there was the figure of the dead and buried Bonelucci, clothes, and even his original dirt, included, seated upon a mossy bank, resting its elbows on its knees.

The head of the grim form was lifted up, and their eyes met. Penny Bunn staggered back and would have fallen but for the trunk of an adjacent tree, against which he stopped short and found the support he needed.

Then up rose the form of the outraged Italian, and with glaring eyes came stealthily towards him.

"Mercy !" gasped Penny Bunn, " keep off. I never meant to kill you."

"You gif me my mu-sick. How I live if you gif him not ? Now then, say it. How ?"

The form was solid, the voice had its original tone. Could it be that Bonelucci was still alive ?

Penny Bunn, shaking like a jelly in a confectioner's shop window when a waggon rumbles by, hardly dared to believe it. But there was the hope newly springing in his breast, and it gave him back a little of the strength of mind and body he had lost.

"Bonelucci," he murmured, " I thought you were dead !"

"How ?" demanded the Italian.

"Why, I hit you an awful whack over the head with that accordion, and you went down like a soldier shot on the battlefield. I certainly thought you were a goner."

"You hit me ! Poof ! I larf at so much. I go down to ze ground to een-joy him. A blow on ze head. How care I ? Not mooch. If it be your head zat hit with him music, it go crash—bang ! and you die. But not me. I haf better head. Mooch *thicker.*"

Penny Bunn was so overcome with the feeling of relief upon him that he was obliged to slide to a sitting position on the ground.

"Bonelucci, old man," he said, " we won't talk any more about that. As you say, that blow on your head was a thing to laugh at. We both enjoyed the joke."

"It is for me to larf, not you," screeched Bonelucci.

"All right," assented Penny Bunn, with alacrity ; " don't let us have any more quarrelling over what after all ought to be a friendly affair. You shall have your music back free of all charges and interest. Now, tell me, do you know Rooker ?"

"Am zat ze young mans of you school, weak eye, poor head?"

"Yes, that is the party," said Bunn, recognising the brief description of his associate as correct enough for the purpose of identity; "you know him?"

"I see him one time."

"Very well. Tell me when it was you saw him and where?"

"It zee day you tink you gif my strong head ze knock. He come to me at ze village where I look for food and drinks and not get zem. He take me to ze inn, he gif me drinks, also ze cegar, he smoke himself, and he very ill. He go out of ze room and fall on him back in ze road, and he mooch seeck, he bad indeed."

"'Tis well," murmured Penny Bunn, complacently, "the full-flavoured peerless twopenny smoke was too much for him. Proceed, my friend, proceed."

"He haf a drink and he bettare, zen he say to me, 'Go right vay and I gif you five shillings.' I take ze money, and I say to him 'I go.' But I say to myself, 'you come back again, you Bonelucci, and get you museek,' and I am here. Now zen, how? Will you gif him to me? I see zis Rooker leetle time ago, and he say to me, 'Go in ze town and I bring him to you your mu-seek. I wait here, and I see you.'"

"The double-dyed traitor," muttered Penny Bunn, "but he shall suffer for his treachery. Bonelucci, wait here while I fetch your accordion. I suppose you have not any of that five shillings left?"

"No, I spend him all."

"Well, it can't be helped. I was thinking that if you had any of it left, we might have adjourned to the hostelry at Smudgem Bender, and celebrated the renewal of our old friendship in just one of the usual. But, no matter, another time. Remain here while I fetch your priceless instrument."

He shook hands with Bonelucci, and, with a tremendous burden lifted from him, hastened back to the school. There he sought for the accordion out of which so much trouble had arisen, but he could not find it. It was not in the drawer where he usually kept it, nor in his room, nor could Black-eyed Susan give him any information concerning it, beyond that she had seen Mr. Rooker go out with a biggish parcel under his arm when he left the Abbey immediately after dinner.

"It isn't of any consequence," said Penny Bunn, "I was merely going to practise a bit in the seclusion of the sylvan woods."

It was impossible to avoid the old style of thing even then, when it was literally thrown away upon Black-eyed Susan, who smiled scoffingly as she walked away.

Bunn went to the room occupied by Rooker to see if by any chance he could find the accordion there. It was not to be found, but in a corner of one of the drawers he discovered an old sock in which was a quantity of money.

It was the remnant of the sum of which Penny Bunn had been blackmailed. With a heart that throbbed with ecstasy, he counted it, and found that Rooker had spent about two pounds, and five pounds odd remained. It was still a sum not to be despised, and he dropped it into his pocket with a sigh of relief.

Then he hastened back to Bonelucci, and told him that he was unable to get at the accordion that night as one of the domestics was engaged in cleaning his room, but he should certainly have it on the following morning.

"Meanwhile," said Penny Bunn, "I will see you are well taken care of and lack nothing. We will away to the hostelry and drown all our animosities in the flowing bowl."

CHAPTER LXV.

ROOKER AND THE BOYS.—PENNY BUNN'S REVENGE.

ONLY about half the boys went as far as Chippenham that day. There was no treat on, and some of them preferred a run in the woods of Cowley Park, which, in point of beauty, beat anything in the country round.

It was about five in the afternoon when, as Whymper and Little Jiggers were crossing the bridge over the Avon in the town, they saw Awful Rooker, with a big parcel under his arm, wandering about in rather an aimless manner. He was, as a matter of fact, looking for Bonelucci, whom he had appointed to meet in the town, but the Italian, in his impatience to get hold of his "music" again, had walked up to the wood to meet him, and they had somehow missed each other.

In searching for Bonelucci, Rooker had of necessity gone into two or three of the inns, where he had partaken of some of the local beer. It had got into his head, and, although he was not intoxicated in the legal sense, and could still walk straight, his ideas were getting hazy, and he was, when the boys met him, not exactly certain whither he was going, or what was the object of his wanderings.

He stopped and greeted the boys with a smile.

"How long you been out?" he asked, thickly.

"Since dinner," answered Jiggers.

"Blessmer," said Rooker, feebly, "You do not shay sho."

Then he appeared to forget what he had under his

arm, and, in the act of rubbing his chin, dropped the parcel.

But it did not fall to the ground, for Whymper smartly caught it, and was about to hand it back when he saw that the tutor had, without saying anything more, walked on.

"Here's a go," exclaimed Whymper.

"Buffy," said Jiggers, disgusted, "I wonder what is in that parcel?"

"It's an accordion," replied Whymper, feeling about the paper covering; "it must be the one Penny Bunn is sometimes blowing. Do you think Rooker knows we've got it?"

"No, he is as stupid as an owl. I'll bet he won't even remember that he met us."

"Then I vote we keep this accordion, for a time, anyway."

"Certainly—why not? Perhaps Bunn will offer a reward for it."

With the parcel under his arm, Whymper set out for the Abbey. All the others who had been into the town had gone back, and they had lingered behind watching a monkey on a barrel-organ.

On the way home they resolved to keep their "find" to themselves, or only let a few of their closest friends into the secret of their being possessed of it.

Meanwhile, Rooker had wandered up and down the town trying to get his thoughts into trim, until suddenly he remembered the accordion, missed it, and was instantly sobered.

It was not so much the value of it that frightened him, but the fact that he had so faithfully promised to restore it to Bonelucci, who valued it highly as an instrument that had no equal. It could not be replaced.

As Bonelucci had said to him, prior to that meeting in the wood, of course, "Ze oder one, he of ze name of Bunn, lie to me. It is enough, I have no more of him. You lie to me and I kill you. I make no misteek zis time."

It was the thought of being under the ban of Bonelucci that terrified him into sobriety.

He had a dim idea of having met two of the boys, but could not recall who they were, or what he had said to them. Nor did he think that the meeting had anything to do with the loss of the priceless accordion.

His belief was that he had left it in one of the houses devoted to the sale of intoxicating liquors, and he went to all he had been into before, and into some he had not patronized, without avail.

He even, in his anxiety, visited some of them twice on his errand of search, and was very rudely rebuffed.

Nobody had seen anything of it.

"What on earth have I done with it?" he groaned, as, after nearly an hour's inquiry in the little town, including the police station, he was obliged to give up the accordion as lost.

"I must keep out of his way," he thought, "or shuffle the responsibility back upon Bunn. I wonder where that beastly Italian has been all day?"

The parish church clock of Smudgem Bender was striking the hour of seven when the weary and dispirited Rooker entered the village.

He was late, and ought to have been back at the Abbey by that time, but he trusted in Penny Bunn being there to look after the boys. Of course, having, as he supposed, the whip hand of him over the Bonelucci affair, he could laugh at any reproaches he might receive. It was therefore something of a facer for him, when, as he was passing the Cowley Arms, the voice of Bunn was heard sternly calling upon him to halt.

He stopped short, of course, and Penny Bunn emerging from the inn with the gait of a stage baron, took him by the arm.

"Rooker," he said, "a word with thee. Let us adjourn to the skittle-ground. It is somewhat remote from the house, and in an unoccupied condition at the present moment."

"What do you want?" asked Rooker, sulkily. "There is nobody at the Abbey to look after the boys."

"The boys are quite able to look after themselves," said Bunn, as he led his companion through the yard gate, and down to the skittle ground. "Here we are. Permit me to close the door. There is light enough from the glassless orifice which serves this humble pleasure ground for a window. Take off your coat. As man to man we are *going to have it out.*"

"Bunn, you are drunk!"

"With coats on, then," said Bunn. "I'm at you; guard yourself. One in the eye," he illustrated the remark with a blow on the spot named. "Another on the nasal organ;" he delivered it straight from the shoulder. "A third in the receptacle for food;" it was duly given. "And a final one in the breathing region."

Rooker was down among the skittles, knocked out of time, and Penny Bunn was avenged. Satisfied, he opened the door and stalked back to the parlour of the inn.

A few minutes elapsed, and Rooker recovered sufficiently to take stock of his injuries. One of his eyes was closing fast, and his nose was the size of an Orleans plum. He still felt the pain of the blows in the less markable regions of the breast and stomach, and boiled with thoughts of revenge.

But what could he do?

It flashed on him that he could go to the village constable and declare that Penny Bunn had confessed to having committed a murder.

He need not say whose murder, or when it was committed.

Perhaps he might induce the official to lock up his brother tutor.

So he went out quietly, inquired where the constable lived, and found him at home.

Rooker told his story, adding, by way of embellishment, that it was because he had announced his intention to communicate with the authorities that ▶ ● had been assaulted.

"It is a curious thing, sir," said the constable, "but I have often thought that Mr. Bunn had something on his mind. He seemed so unsettled like. One day, not long ago, he went into the Cowley Arms, and the landlord fancied he looked odd. He asked for brandy, and while it was being fetched, all the pipelights on the table vanished. He was asked about 'em, but said he'd seen nothing of 'em, but arter he was gone a reg'lar search was made for them, and where do you think they was found?"

"I couldn't say."

"Up the chimbley, sir, and they was *stained with blood*, which could not be accounted for; but I had my suspicions. I'll go round and have a talk with him. Perhaps he will commit himself, and then I'll run him in!"

CHAPTER LXVI.

DEFYING THE LAW.—ROUGH TIMES FOR ROOKER.

IT was not without considerable trepidation in his breast that the police officer wended his way to the Cowley Arms to arrest that nefarious murderer, as he believed him to be, Penny Bunn, the Littlecote tutor.

Ever since that pipelight affair he had been thinking it over, and the fact of anything stained with blood being concealed up the chimney was an assurance of something criminal having been done. The one great obstacle in the way of the constable was the non-discovery of the body of the victim.

Still he trusted in his acumen, which, in common with all country policemen, he believed himself to be possessed of in a remarkable degree, insomuch that it had often been a matter of wondering speculation with himself at the non-recognition of his talents from Scotland Yard, the headquarters of the London Police.

The Smudgem Bender officer had brought more than one malefactor to justice.

For instance, when Mrs. Strubber, who kept the toffy-shop, lost her old gander, it was this officer who traced its remains to the back yard of a local cobbler.

The man was arrested, and fined one pound five for unlawful possession. The next day a tinker in his cups confessed to have stolen the goose, and exhibited the feathers in proof of the truth of his confession. The cobbler got his fine back again, and the tinker went to prison for a month, quite cheerful and happy, because, as he told the magistrates, "Business was slack, and he may as well lay up there as anywhere else."

This record case of Smudgem Bender crime naturally elevated its one policeman in the eyes of the populace, and he was, for a time, proud of it, to the borders of arrogance. Now he had a chance of still further distinguishing himself by bringing a murderer to justice, if the culprit would only assist matters by declaring whom he had killed, how he had done it, and where he had placed the body.

With these few facts to guide him, the Smudgem Bender officer was satisfied that he would carry the rest of the case through in a style that would compel the head of the Metropolitan Police to recognize his merits and make an inspector of him.

Penny Bunn, satiated with vengeance, and a bit gone in liquor, was in the coffee-room of the Cowley Arms with Bonelucci and two or three labourers, all of whom were indulging at the expense of the tutor.

To them entered the police officer with the stealthy footstep of a detective on the trail.

He gave Bunn good evening, and took a seat near him.

"What will you have, officer?" asked Penny Bunn, with the air of a monarch giving a feast.

The officer thought he would take two of rum, and Penny Bunn ordered sixpennyworth.

"I," he said, "could never sit in a room with a man who drinks twopennyworths. In my home—I may mention, by the way, that it was palatial—we drank only the choicest wines. My father never could be induced to indulge in port wine out of a sherry glass. Everything had to be *ony regal* under our roof. We kept two butlers."

"It must be a come-down to you, sir," murmured the officer.

"A come-down!" exclaimed Bunn; "it's a fall from a mountain-top to the gutter. Snicker is only an educational scavenger."

"It allus struck me," remarked one of the labourers, "that he wasn't up to much."

"A man who has bow legs," said Penny Bunn, gravely, "is the image of incompetence. With a crooked foundation no house can stand. Snicker's days at the Abbey are numbered. I am at this moment negotiating for the possession of the school. Here's your rum, officer."

Sixpennyworth was a very strong dose for the official, but he was too much of a man to shirk it.

Moreover, he was induced to take another, and yet another, until he dare not have any more.

Bonelucci and the labourers were all by this time fast asleep, in various attitudes that made them look like big dolls just thrown down anyhow, and Penny Bunn, having taken note of the fact that everything in the room had a tendency to double, or even treble itself, thought it was time to go.

"Officer," he said, "I will see you home."

There was just sufficient light in the brain of the policeman to recall the fact that he had come there to arrest a murderer, and that the culprit was unconsciously playing into his hands. The amount of cunning expressed in his eyes would have filled an ordinary-sized bucket. His very head seemed to swell with it.

"Rightyrare," he answered, in the run-into-each-other speech of the bibulous.

He and Bunn left the inn arm-in-arm, and, like twin corkscrews, wended their way up the winding street of the village. The policeman's residence was a strongly-built cottage in a lane near the church, and it possessed one windowless room, which on emergency was used as a cell.

Into that cell the officer was resolved Penny Bunn should go.

It was a marvel the pair reached the house at all, for Bunn was in a state of semi-unconsciousness, and the policeman's brain in a ferment. But he retained one stationary idea, which may be compared to a straw in the centre of a whirlpool, and that was he had to lock up his companion.

On arriving at the cottage, Penny Bunn suddenly became quite brisk.

"Here we are, officer," he said. "Goo' night."

"You mus' come inner minute," was the answer.

"*Must* to *me!*" exclaimed Bunn, haughtily. "Varlet! wretch! who are you talking to?"

"I've got a warrant for yer 'res'," said the policeman; "leaseway, I get one to-morrer for murder."

Penny Bunn laughed hoarsely, derisively, defiantly.

"It is true," he said, "that in the course of my wild career I have often shed the blood of those who have thwarted and defied me. I shed some this day, three ounces, if a drachm of it. But if you think that you can stop me from pursuing the course of vengeance, take *that!*"

"That" was a blow fairly upon the nose of the officer, which first dashed him against his own front door, and then dropped him in a heap upon the step thereof.

"Arrest me!" said Penny Bunn, scornfully; "I, who have defied——"

Here the door suddenly opened, and a vixenish-looking woman, with a candle in her hand, peered forth.

"Is that you, Joseph?" she inquired.

"No," answered Bunn; "your Joseph lies there. Take him in, and comfort him. I will call to-morrow and leave a card of inquiry about his condition. Perhaps it will be as well to have medical bulletins pasted on the door to allay the popular excitement. How have the mighty fallen! Fancy one blow on the proboscis laying such a noble form as this in the dust!"

By this time the wife of the officer had arrived at a tolerably clear view of things. Her husband was in a heap upon the doorstep, with a nose that had indubitably been assaulted, and the man of haughty bearing had probably hit him.

Having grasped these facts, she sprang over the form of her spouse, and went for Penny Bunn. He fled.

The martial spirit yielded to the attack of lovely woman, so he ran, and what is more, ran well, pursued for a while by the enraged woman, and afterwards by her screams for assistance.

But she might as well have cried for help in the heart of Salisbury Plain. Penny Bunn got clear off, and as the clock was striking eleven passed into the precincts of the Abbey.

Fontenoy Snicker was sitting up for him in a towering rage, and came into the hall with a candle in his hand.

"Are you aweer—*aware*—of the time?" he asked.

"I am," replied Penny Bunn; "the clock in the old church tower boomed the hour of eleven as I passed the portal."

"You are intossicated—*intoxicated*—sir."

"So are you, or if you are not, it is something unusual."

There was a moment's silence, both breathing hard. Fontenoy Snicker was the more sober of the two, but he had not omitted taking something. He was just sober enough to be prudent.

"Go to bed, sir," he said. "I will talk to you in the morning," he added, between his teeth.

"On the morrow," answered Bunn, "I may have something to say to you. Meanwhile, take heed of this. I have this day pounded one man in a skittle-ground to a jelly, absolutely to a jelly, and I have, moreover, evaded capture by overcoming a policeman in his uniform. The country will be alive with my prowess to-morrow."

Then Penny Bunn stalked upstairs, and got to the top with only two stumbles, the schoolmaster standing below, glaring angrily up at his retreating form.

"What has the fool been up to now?" he muttered. "I must get rid of him, or he will bring disgrace upon me. I'll get another tutor, I'm bothered if I don't, and risk it."

Growling to himself, Fontenoy Snicker retreated to

his private room, and sat there an hour thinking. The upshot of his meditations was that he resolved Penny Bunn should go.

He had really good grounds for complaint, as neither of the tutors had put in an appearance at the table, and the boys had been having high jinks all to themselves.

Snicker was out, but his wife on his return informed him that there had "been paddlemonium" in the dining-room, and a fight between two of the boys, Little Jiggers and Short, which ended in a broken cup and two plates. The dormitories she believed to be in a state of wreck and ruin, but had not been up to see.

As the boys were quiet when the schoolmaster came home, he had not visited them, but his wrath was very great. Rooker had no pay to speak of, and it was not worth while saying much about dismissing him, but Bunn was different. His days were, in the imagination of Snicker, numbered in the Abbey.

Rooker, on his return, had barricaded himself in and gone to rest. He slept fairly well, but on awakening in the morning discovered that he had a nose still of abnormal proportions, and a black eye that was quite a picture.

In a state of mind bordering on despair, he crept downstairs and walked into the playground. He was certain that his garnished face would attract attention, and subject him to many pertinent inquiries; but as they must come some time or other, he thought he had better get them over.

But, to his surprise, none of the boys took any notice of him. They did not give him good morning, or even look at him.

The majority were sauntering up and down in twos and threes, and in the course of their peregrinations, they had to pass him as he stood a few yards from the front door.

It was his duty to call the roll about this time to see that all the boys were in the grounds, and he had the book and pencil in his pocket, but he had not the heart to begin. The silent contempt of the boys, expressed in their carriage, was too much for him. It was more than he could bear.

Presently Hone, with a book in his hand, conning a lesson neglected the previous night, drew near, and Awful Rooker stopped him.

"Hone," he said, nervously, "I want a word with you."

Hone closed the book, and looked up without making any reply.

"How odd the boys all are this morning," continued Rooker. "I have had an accident," he touched his eye as he spoke. "I was afraid they would notice it, and think that I—I—I have been fighting."

"That would not have bothered them," answered Hone; "we all fight at times, don't we?"

"Ye-es, I suppose so."

"You know it, and what is a black eye to them? Somebody seems to have been giving you beans."

"Hone, it is horrible to be so friendless as I am, and you don't appear to have many chums in the school."

"I have not one," curtly interposed Hone.

"Then why should not we be friendly? I am a sort of half-and-half creature here. Part of the school-boy, and part of the tutor. Too old to be one, and too young to be considered the other."

"It's rough, I daresay," said Hone, unmoved, "if you really want me to be friends with you, I don't mind. I have not, as you said, a chum among the lot, but they speak to me when I speak to them, which is more than they will do to you for a time. *They* have sent you to Coventry."

"Why, in the name of goodness?"

"Because you were *drunk* yesterday, and, although we may laugh at a grown man like Penny Bunn kicking up a shine, we don't care to see one little more than our own age making a beast of himself."

Rooker hung his head.

"Is that your view of the matter?" he asked.

"Oh! I have no opinion of it at all," said Hone, "you may go and do as you please for all I care. I am simply quoting the words of Jack Ford, and his lot. And what they say here is law among the rest."

"And they despise me?"

"They have always done so, and that you know, so you need not fret over it."

"But they despise me more than ever, I mean?"

"They do—a heap. And to look at you one would think you cared for their opinion."

"Well, don't you?"

"Not a straw. Nor the opinion of anybody else. You are out with Bunn, are you not?"

"Yes, we have had a quarrel."

"Did he give you that whacker on the eye and smeller?"

"He did."

"And you did not hit him back again?"

"I can't fight a man."

"Call Bunn a *man*, indeed!" ejaculated Hone. "Bah! I would rather tackle him than a dozen of the boys I could name here. If you had hit back, he would have caved in."

"Do you really think so?"

"I am dead sure of it. But I won't stop here talking to you any longer. We had better have our confabs in private."

"Yes, in my room," said Rooker, eagerly. "Come up in the evening between study hour and supper-time."

"All sereno," assented Hone, as he took out his book and walked on.

A SPLENDID SCHOOL STORY. NEVER BEFORE PUBLISHED.

By E. HARCOURT BURRAGE,

Author of "Ching Ching," "Monkey Mat and Roving Dick," "The Brave Boy of the Basilisk," &c.

THE LAMBS OF LITTLECOTE.

A THRILLING SCHOOL STORY.

No. 10. A Handsome Coloured Plate Presented with every Number.

BLOTCH COMES A CROPPER BY THE BROOK. THE LAMBS SING A SONG OF JOY AND GLADNESS.

PRICE ONE PENNY.

ALDINE PUBLISHING CO., 9, Red Lion Court, Fleet St., and 1, 2, & 3, Crown Court, Chancery Lane, London.

Hone, as he said, was in want of a companion. Every hour saw the breach between him and his schoolfellows widen and widen. It was not the result of any machinations on the part of anyone, but the natural severance of elements that would never mix.

Hone had seen two letters, which Black-eyed Susan had fetched from the Smudgem Bender post-office the previous evening. There was no second delivery at the Abbey, and one of these letters was for Jack, and another for Don, and both were addressed in the handwriting of Professor Lingo.

Why should he write to them and both be so close about the nature of the communications? Was not that a clear indication that they had a secret between them, in which he and the rest of the boys, outside the inner circle, did not share?

By making friends with Hone, he would not only have somebody to talk to, but also one who might be able to help him with certain schemes he had in his mind.

CHAPTER LXVII.

THE LETTERS OF THE PROFESSOR.—THAT FACE!

HONE was not wrong in his belief that the letters addressed to Don and Jack were from the Professor. But one thing he had omitted to notice, and it was that they were addressed to the Smudgem Bender post-office, "till called for."

Black-eyed Susan could be trusted, Jack knew, and she was, therefore, commissioned, whenever she was out in the evening, to call for the letters, and had done so. The boys were home by seven, and the mail was not in at the office until half-past, which shut them out from obtaining them in person.

We will give both letters as written, and here is the one addressed to Jack:

"MY DEAR BOY,—I saw your uncle to-day, and he is not at all averse to letting you have the bits of rag to make a tail for a kite with. So I shall send them on to-morrow with a few other things for your friends. I am glad you are so comfortable at the Abbey. Mr. Snicker must be a nice sort of gentleman. Always respond to his treatment in a proper and becoming way, *whatever that treatment* may be.
            "Your loving cousin,
                    "O. GNIL."

And this was the one addressed to Don:

"DEAR DON,—As I am sending on a parcel to my relative Jack I enclose one for you. Together they make up a biggish bundle, and as the carriers of the railway are always so rough I intend to send it on by special messenger, and he will arrive some time this evening. I had a letter from a pal of mine, who is working your native place on Saturday nights with some of the cheapest and most useless cutlery that ever was. I am thinking of running over by rail to see him. If any message for the old folks send on to Calne by return. I shall certainly give your father a look up and tell him how happy you are. Shall call in my clerical rig.
            ' Your affectionate friend,
                    "O. GNIL."

These letters might be a bit enigmatical to some people, but the boys understood them, all but that part about the clerical rig. It was, no doubt, one of the disguises which Lingo assumed in his varied callings.

However, Don would hear more about it that evening, as the special messenger would, as he knew, be the professor in person, who might be looked for about seven or eight o'clock.

It was about half-past the earlier hour named when the boys, being in the schoolroom getting up their lessons for the morrow, were startled by hearing the cry of an owl. Perhaps the better term will be to call it the hoot, for it is a melancholy, hollow sound.

It floated in by the open window, and rapid glances were exchanged by Jack and Don. One of them ought to go to the professor, who was outside the playground by the wood.

Don signalled "I'll go," and, rising from his seat, asked if he might go upstairs for a handkerchief.

Penny Bunn, who had been wrapped in reflection on the dismal consequences likely to arise from his having assaulted a full-blown policeman, started as he was spoken to, and said: "I respectfully appeal to the bench for leniency to be shown me—I—I—beg pardon, Peebles, what is it?"

Don repeated his request, and Bunn graciously gave him the required permission.

"And should you see Mr. Rooker on your way upstairs, please remind him that it his duty to be here to-night."

Don said he would, and was lucky enough to be spared hunting up the under tutor by meeting him in the hall.

He was very white, and Don could see that he was trembling. He gave his message and expressed a hope that Rooker was not unwell.

"No," replied Rooker, "nothing is the matter with me. I have lost some money, that's all."

Don did not stay to inquire where he had lost it, or how much it was, but hastened out across the playground and opening the gate saw Lingo with a parcel in his hand waiting for him.

"Glad to see you, Don," he said, "take this parcel. It contains something that will help to foster the playful instincts of you boys. You twigged my signature, of course?"

"Lingo spelt backwards is O. Gnil," answered Don, with a smile.

"Just so. Now about money. I need not ask how much of that which I gave you remains in hand. Naturally it is all gone."

"Every penny."

"Coin, in the hands of the young," said Lingo, reflectively, "immediately acquires the properties of red hot iron. It cannot be held. In the possession of the aged it takes on a coating of glue. I have brought Jack two pounds more, all in the form that admits of easy spending. As I told you in my letter, I am off at once, and it may be weeks ere you see me again. While I am gone it must be distinctly understood that it will be dangerous to seek the fictitious haunt of Robin Hood. How are things looking generally?"

Don told him that there was not much stirring, but he thought that the schoolmaster was in a very uneasy frame of mind.

"Sooner or later that man will have to be driven out of the Abbey. The questions bearing thereon are two in number. I reckon that you boys do not want to part just yet."

"No."

"Which you would have to do if the school was broken up. The questions then are: How is Snicker to be got rid of, and who is to take his place?'"

"I am afraid," said Don, shaking his head, "that it will take a lot to make him budge."

"We shall see," rejoined the professor in a musing tone, "patience and water gruel work wonders when used with discretion. Don't let the old tyranny raise its head for a moment. You know what you have to do if it does?"

"Certainly, and all the boys are with us but one.'"

"And who is that one?"

"Hone."

"Oh, that big lad with a face that has always a discontented look upon it. He will come to a bad end. He is cut out for it. I met Snicker on the way here."

"Did he speak to you?"

"No. I did not give him the chance. I shammed lighting my pipe and he thought he was not seen. You should have twigged him shin past me. It was a treat."

Lingo did not stay long. After a short chat with Don on general matters he shook hands with him, sent his love to the boys, and went away singing.

Don, with the parcel in his hand, returned to the house. "Hang it!" he said, "I forgot to ask about the clerical attire."

As he had no time to examine the gift of Lingo, he ran upstairs and slipped it under the bed, pending the arrival of a more fitting time to examine it.

Shortly after the studies coming to an end, the youngsters went out for recreation before supper, and Don having imparted to his chums the particulars of the interview with Lingo, went up to the dormitory with Tom Drummond to inspect his parcel.

It contained nothing but a hideous mask, of the pantomime property order. Attached to it was a label on which was written, "Snicker, Esq."

"Well," said Don, "what are we to do with this thing?"

"It would about cover the face of the hall clock," answered Tom, "and if we hung it up there it would give Mrs. Snicker a scare. About this time she is everlastingly popping out to see what is the time, in case we should get five minutes extra fresh air."

"That's the place for it," said Don.

So they hung it up over the face of the grand-father's clock, when they got below, and hastened off to the playground.

Meanwhile, Penny Bunn and Rooker had been left behind in the schoolroom. On the face of the elder there was a look of sneering triumph, on the countenance of Rooker a determination to have back the money he had lost, or risk another fight with his redoubtable senior.

Bunn feigned to be engaged in arranging some books upon his desk. Rooker walked up and stood there staring at him with a basilisk expression in his weak eyes.

"Mr. Bunn," he said at last, with an effort.

Bunn shammed waking up from deep meditation, and turned a pair of rather shifty eyes upon Rooker.

"Oh, it is you, is it?" he said.

"You knew it was. I want my money!"

"Your money?"

"Yes, *my* money you stole from the drawer in my room."

"How did that money come into your possession?"

"That is my affair. Are you going to hand it over to me?"

"Rooker," said Penny Bunn, "I am *not*."

He descended from his perch as he spoke and laid himself out for a walk from the room in a state of dignified contempt. But the best laid plans and efforts of mankind sometimes go astray, and in this case the walk was speedily changed to a run, for the exasperated Rooker, snatching a ruler from the desk, dealt his senior a whack over the crown of the head that sounded like a single knock at the front door.

An ordinary display of fireworks was as an illuminating failure compared to the coruscations that danced before the eyes of Penny Bunn as he bounded forward, from the schoolroom into the hall.

Rooker pursued him with the fury of a Matabele on the trail of a flying Mashona, and as the first lights were fading away gave him another whack.

Then Penny Bunn, goaded to madness, turned upon his assailant and they closed.

Neither could wrestle worth a cent, and the result was that they immediately fell together. Once upon the ground they held on tight and, gasping, lay still.

"Do you give in?" hissed Bunn.

"I'll die first," roared Rooker.

"Mercy on me, you two," exclaimed a female voice, "what are you doing of?"

It was Black-eyed Susan on her way to the evening duty of turning down of beds in the dormitories. She stood over them with her eyes pretty well out of her head with wonderment.

"Are you both taken ill?" she asked.

"Let him give in," replied Penny Bunn, "and I will forgive him."

"I will *not* give in," returned Rooker, with unswerving resolution.

"Give in and get up both of you," said Black-eyed Susan, "or I'll call missus, and she will, in her present temper, throw a bucket of water over you."

"With me," said Penny Bunn, "the voice of gentle woman prevaileth always. I will arise. Rooker, the struggle between us is held in abeyance. Susan or Jane, as you are indifferently called, you look positively pretty to-night."

"And what business is that of yours?" demanded Black-eyed Susan, bridling up.

"It is much to me," replied Bunn, with a sentimental languor stealing over him, "notwithstanding the impassable social gulf between us, I will take just one."

"There it is," said Black-eyed Susan, smartly, and then he got the one—an open-handed smack on the cheek, and it was as far removed from the sweetness of the salute he intended to bestow upon her, as a brickbat is from a lollipop.

Susan marched off, leaving Penny Bunn standing against the wall in a state of bewilderment. Rooker, exulting over the discomfiture of his colleague, skipped away upstairs.

From a dream of miserable meditation, Penny Bunn was aroused by a piercing scream in the hall. Instinctively he reeled off in the direction, and discovered Mrs. Snicker seated in a fainting condition upon one of the hall chairs.

Facing her was the clock with the hideous face upon it, and it really was enough to give an unsuspecting woman a "turn."

Penny Bunn stared at it vacantly, and slowly read the words upon the label out:

"'Snick-er, E-squire.' How like him!"

CHAPTER LXVIII.

SNICKER JEALOUS AGAIN.—ARTICULATING SOME BONES.

MRS. SNICKER gave vent to a gasp and a groan, kicked up her legs, and then became still again. Penny Bunn was still mentally far from clear about his surroundings.

"Is this an untimely death or drink?" he murmured. "Mrs. Snicker, you—you have received a shock. In the absence of your husband, I suppose it is my duty to restore you."

To that end he fanned her with the tails of his coat, still with the vacant look upon his face. Then, as she remained unconscious, he gently raised her in his arms, and looked plaintively into her face.

"Fair maid," he began; "I mean, Snissers Micker —Mrs. Snicker—jigger it, as that man you have thrown yourself away upon, would say: I beg of you to compose yourself. If we were found thus together, we might both be seriously compromised, and——"

"Here, what's the matter, now?" roared the familiar voice of Snicker, as he plunged into the hall. "Hang it!—Blow it!—Bunn, what do you mean by that? Drop her!"

Bunn obediently let go of the lady, and she fell upon the floor in a heap, only to recover her entire senses immediately, and rise like a Venus from the ocean, with the additional charm of being in a boiling rage.

"Jerry," she said, "you are a brute. You always were since you left the coal and tatur line. I've been in a fainting fit, and Mr. Bunn was only acting the part of a man."

"I am a modern Bray Hard—I mean, Bayard," murmured Bunn, in a confused way. "I found the maiden, that is, Mrs. Snicker, insensible on that chair, and I tendered her assistance. Behold the cause of her emotion."

He pointed to the mask which seemed to be grinningly enjoying the whole thing, and Snicker started violently.

"Who put that there thing there?" he demanded.

"I know not," replied Bunn. "Mr. Snicker, if you think that I have wronged you——"

"Get out of the way, you idiot!" snarled Mr. Snicker, thrusting him aside. He stalked up to the clock, and laid hold of the mask, giving it a violent jerk, so that the clock came over with a run, fell upon him, and the pair, man and time-giver, went to the floor together.

"Now, isn't that like you, Jerry?" exclaimed Mrs. Snicker; "so unkimmonly hasty."

"Say un*commonly* hasty, you hag," hissed the schoolmaster.

He lay at right angles with the clock, and that valuable piece of furniture was upon his manly breast, impeding his utterance, but he managed to put an astounding amount of vigour into his correction.

"I'll say what I like," she answered, tartly, "and how I like. Get up, and don't lie there like a Hirish Banshee ghost."

"Bunn," said Snicker, feebly, "be good enough to lift this clock off me. I'm stifling."

"First of all," said Bunn, haughtily, "I will ask for conditions."

"Oh, blow your conditions. Can't you see I'm being stifled? This 'ere blessed old wheezing brute of a clock weighs half-a-ton."

"Do you withdraw your imputations cast on my honour as a man?" insisted Bunn.

"I'll withdraw any blooming thing," answered Snicker.

"And also retract your unjust insinuations against your wife?"

"Anything—everything I tell you. Oh my ribs!"

"And you will furthermore——"

But Snicker could stand no more. With an effort that cost him two brace buttons, and the back buckle of his waistcoat, he rolled the clock from his chest, got up gasping, and would have committed murder if the pair, wife and tutor, had not fled.

For the lack of some other object on which to vent his wrath, he picked up the clock and banged it against the wall. This violent movement was followed by the rattle of falling wheels and weights inside the old grandfather's timepiece.

"Now I've done for it," hissed Snicker, "and all through them boys as put this 'ere figurehead on the clock. But was it them there boys? Pussonally—personally I do not think so. It was that hag and idiot that did it. They put it up there to get a laugh out of me, I did think that when Copps went away I should have no more of them games, but, as I'm a sinner, I'll do for both of 'em."

He had suddenly developed his old jealous fury, and was for the time as mad as a hatter. His thoughts turned to an axe as the more suitable implement for his purpose, and hissing like a small steam engine, he walked in his bowlegged style down the passage. In his hand he had the mask which had been so unwarrantably labelled with his name. The nose of it had been flattened by the clock falling upon it, but otherwise it had escaped injury.

On his way he had to pass the store-room, the door of which stood open. Inside was Mrs. Snicker composing her nerves with something from a bottle, labelled "Lemon Juice." She started on seeing him, thrust the bottle into her pocket upside down, with the cork out, and faced him boldly.

"Now, Jerry," she said, "I can see that you are decomposed——"

"*Dis*-composed, hang you," he roared.

"My mother," retorted Mrs. Snicker, in her most dignified manner, "always told my father when *he* was put out that he was decomposed, and she wasn't a woman to make a mistake. But it don't matter. Try and keep cool, Jerry, or one of these days you will lift the top of your 'ed right off."

"Cool!" he exclaimed, with his face the colour of the brightest vermilion, "look 'ere. What do you mean, you two, by a libelling me with this ere thing?"

He held up the mask as he spoke, his hand shaking with passion. With its flattened nose the hideousness of the thing was multiplied ten-fold.

Mrs. Snicker regarded it with the utmost composure.

"Who did you say put it on the clock?" she inquired, suavely.

"You and that there thief of a Bunn."

"We didn't do nothing of the sort, Jerry, and you know it. I ain't given to lowering myself by mixing up with a tutor who came here with one shirt, and not a button on it. But, as I said afore, it doesn't matter. So you call that a libel on you, Jerry, do you?"

"I do," he answered, with an emphasis that showed he had no doubt about it.

"Dear me," sniffed Mrs. Snicker, "I had no idea, Jerry, that you were so conceited."

"Conceited?"

"Yes, Jerry——"

"I wish you wouldn't Jerry me so much."

"I shall Jerry you as much as I like, for a Jerry you was born, a Jerry you was christened, and a Jerry you'll die. A libel! What!—it's a *compliment*. If you was arf so good-looking as that article, I'd feel prouder of you than I do."

Snicker could bear no more. He had to flee away or kill his wife, and he bounded out of the store-room like an Indian on the war trail. He even whooped as a relief to his overtaxed feelings.

There was a scampering of feet ahead, followed by the banging of a door, and he knew that it was some of the boys who had witnessed and overheard at least part of his humiliation. Utterly helpless, however, he rushed to his private room, where he shut himself in, locked the door, and worked off some of the steam by dancing thrice round the table.

Then he opened a cupboard, and taking out a bottle, put the mouth of it to his lips and drank a long draught of the fiery liquor.

"Something will happen," he muttered. "Every hand is ag'in' me. I'm a Hiss Male; is that right? Hiss—Ish—mael, now I've got it! I'd give a trifle if Bunn would run away with my old woman. But he won't do it; nor any other man with eyes in his 'ed—*head*. If I was half as good-looking as that there thing! It won't bear thinking of. I'll have another drink."

The boys who had accidentally overheard the little domestic discussion in the store-room were Herbert May, Little Jiggers, and Short. They had come into the house from the playground to get some water to drink, and it was as they emerged from the lavatory that they heard the voice of Snicker lifted up in anger.

Guided by it, they cautiously approached the scene

of domestic commotion, and arrived by the door just in time to see him raise the mask and ask the question which we have recorded.

The attitude of the man, boiling over as he was, and the calm bearing of Mrs. Snicker, made up a picture that delighted the youngsters as they lingered in the gloom of the passage until they were startled by the sudden bounding out of the frantic schoolmaster.

Then they fled, and, having by the exercise of youthful agility, avoided detection, reached the playground, and told the story of what they had seen and heard.

While they were talking and laughing over it, Mrs. Snicker appeared at the door with the mask in her hand.

"There, boys," she said, "amuse yourself with that."

As only a few of the boys had previously known of its existence, the mask became an object of delight to them, and Short, holding it before his face, executed a wild dance, but was checked by a roar that was like unto the bellowing of a bull.

It was Snicker at a window. He was shaking his fist at the school collectively.

"Take that thing away," he yelled, "and put it in the dust-bin."

Then he banged the window and disappeared.

"Give it to me, Short," said Don. "I'll put it away. It seems to disturb the Snicker nerves."

"What are you going to do with it?" asked Bob Stockton.

"Put it into Bunn's bed, I think."

"All right; make the best use of it you can."

As Don departed on his mission, Bob crossed over to the wall by the cliff, on which Jack Ford and Tom Drummond were seated in close confab together.

"Jack," he said, "what did you do with those bones?"

"I have them all right," answered Jack. "Why do you ask?"

"I have been thinking that we might do something with them. Is there a complete skeleton?"

"Pretty near. I should say."

"Then what do you say to trying our hands at putting them together?"

"I stored them in one of the cupboards in the attics," said Jack, "we might do the work there. Sue says that Mrs. Snicker never goes into that particular room as she believes it is haunted."

"I don't see why we shouldn't have a ghost here," said Bob, in a meditative manner, "for such an old place as this I think we are very short of them."

"Ghosts," said Tom, "are not a very big success in the summer time."

"Well, we can work up one or two in readiness for the winter," suggested Bob. "I have a reel of fine wire that will do for articulating the bones with. If the skeleton isn't quite complete it can still be made to work wonders."

"A skeleton with a rib short is just as good as the complete article," said Tom. "Now we must mind how we go into the house. Snicker is on the rampage, and it would not do to tumble over him. Put on your most casual air, dear boys."

They tacked about the ground a bit, and then in a listless way bore towards the house. At what they deemed to be a favourable moment they slipped through the doorway, and met Don as he was coming out.

"Put the thing in Penny's bed?" carelessly inquired Bob.

"No," replied Don, with a grin of delight. "I found the door of Snicker's open, and the bed ready turned down for the night. There was a night-cap of dear old Phœbe's hanging on the back of a chair, so I popped it on that figurehead, and put the composite article into bed. With the clothes drawn up to the chin you have no idea of the effect of it. I don't think I ever saw anything before half so beastly hideous. It's enough to give a man a month's staggers."

Hearing the object on which his friends were bent he joined them, and with due caution they scaled the two flights of stairs that led to the upper landing. From thence the way to the attics was by a short ladder which could be taken away if desired.

There were several of these upper chambers in the roof of the Abbey, not half of which were in use. Black-eyed Susan occupied one, and Mrs. Snicker used another for lumber, but the rest were given over to dust, spiders, rats, and mice.

In every room in the Abbey there were one or more cupboards, good roomy places such as the housekeepers of old revelled in. The attics were no exception to the rule.

In one of those receptacles Jack had stored away the bones which Penny Bunn discovered under the floor of the chamber originally occupied at night by Fontenoy Snicker.

As the four chums surveyed the ghastly relics of the past, which Jack spread out upon the floor, they could not repress a tendency to shiver.

"I say," said Tom Drummond, with unwonted gravity, "suppose that fellow who owned these bones ever so long ago should cut up rough over our getting fun out of them."

"That would be no joke," said Jack Ford.

"If he is a reasonable sort of chap," drawled Bob Stockton, "he will take the matter easily. It seems to me a sort of a dog-in-the-manger business for a ghost to kick up a row about his bones. They can't be the least use to him."

"Something in that, Bob," said Jack.

"And it would be unreasonable on other grounds, too," pursued Bob. "Here are these bones lying idle under the flooring of Snicker's snoozing room, just as if they were so many little parcels waiting to be called for. Nobody calls. The original party who trotted about in them did not come near the place, and to come forward now and claim them would be, in a legal sense, ridiculous. I rather think that the Statute of Limitations would come in here."

They laughed at Bob's view of the subject, but there was not the usual full hearty ring in their voices. Jack arranged the bones upon the floor, the others looking silently on. It took a little time to get at which was which, and when all had been placed, the left leg was short.

"It would be a hopping ghost if it came at all," said Bob, thoughtfully. "I have an idea, boys. When we have got it together, we must fit up the poor thing with a wooden leg."

"Hang it, Bob, what next?"

"I am sure that the ghost, when it turns up, will take it as a kindly act on our part. Or, it may be"—here he became brighter of face and more rapid of speech—"the wooden leg would be a disguise, so that the ghost, if it came trotting round here, would not know its own bones."

"Let us get to work," said Jack, laughing. "Who's afraid? Hand out the wire, Bob. Tom, you cut it up into lengths of about eight or nine inches."

They went to work. The first natural feeling of delicacy or nervousness, whichever you will, passed away, and if they addressed each other in a low tone, it was more because they were on forbidden ground than from any feeling of superstitious fear.

Their labours would not have pleased a professional man in the line, but they succeeded in building up a very fair skeleton, barring the one leg short. To make the thing complete, Bob routed out of the cupboard an old broom-handle, which he cut partly through with his pocket-knife, and broke in two.

One moiety of it was utilized for the requisite wooden leg, and there was the thing complete.

"Stand him up against the wall," said Bob, "and let us feast our eyes upon his handsome proportions."

"It is a horrible-looking thing," said Don. "Are you sure, Bob, that it is the skeleton of a man?"

"No," said Bob, "I only guess at it."

"If it is a woman's skeleton," remarked Tom, "she won't rest. Do you think that Phœbe Snicker would put up with boys skylarking with her bones? Why, I——"

"Who is it up there?" shrilly inquired the lady from the bottom of the ladder leading to the attics. "I am sure it is you boys, or, some of you, I mean. Come down this instant, or I'll come up and flay you."

CHAPTER LXIX.

THE WORK OF THE SKELETON.—A CASE OF DOUBLE SUFFERING.

"SCISSORS and pantiles," exclaimed Bob, "here's a go. It is the lovely Phœbe herself."

"Now then," screamed Mrs. Snicker again, "are you coming down or not?"

Of course nobody answered her. The youngsters stared at each other in search of some suggestion to help them out of their difficulty.

"Why not leave the skeleton there," said Don, "get into the cupboard and take our chance?"

"If Phœbe ventures up," whispered Tom, "she will get a turn."

"It will be a somersault," murmured Bob.

"I can hear you," cried Mrs. Snicker. "You don't get over me by your whispering. Come down this moment, or I'll half-kill some of you. What business have you up there?"

Don opened the cupboard door, and the others, one by one, filed into it as if they had been spectres. Mrs. Snicker continued to command and threaten from below.

"If I do come up," she said, "you shall know it. Come down, all of you!"

Getting no reply, she began the ascent of the ladder, and the boys, through the crack-like opening of the not quite closed door, could hear her muttering as she ascended:

"Jerry may be afraid of 'em, but I ain't—a nice thing—in the hattics—goodness only knows what they are up to. Are you little imps coming down, or——"

She had reached the door of the attic by this time, and opening it with a savage wrench, stood there as one petrified.

Inside there was nothing for her to look at but the bare dusty room, and a grinning skeleton leaning against the wall in an attitude that might have been associated with an undue consumption of strong liquors.

Through all the changing scenes of her varied life she had never received such a shock.

"A skellington!" she gasped, and then staggered back, feeling in a feeble way, as one in a dream, with her feet for the opening that led to the ladder.

She found it, but in her haste to get away from the grim spectacle in the attic, unfortunately missed the top step, and went sliding down the ladder, with her face towards it, alighting in a heap upon the floor below.

But she only remained a moment. Fear gave her strength, and springing to her feet, she bounded away, like a gazelle troubled with rheumatism, down the two flights of stairs to the hall below.

"Jerry!" she screamed, in a voice as loud and shrill as a factory steam whistle.

Jerry heard her, and recognizing from the tone that something was wrong, came hurriedly forth from his room.

"What is the matter now, you cattlemount?" he asked.

"Skellingtons in the hattics!" she gasped.

"You and your skeletons," he growled, contemptuously; "go along with you!"

"Go up and see," she said, "if you are a man. I tell you I saw 'em a-leaning against the wall in the hattic next to the gal's room. They were grinning at me as impudently as ever was."

"I don't believe it," said Snicker.

"Go and see," urged Mrs. Snicker. "Take the gal with you if you are afraid. Jane!" she screamed.

"Yes'm," was the response from the distant kitchen.

"Come along here. Your master wants you."

"I don't want her," growled Snicker, "but she can come along with me, just to see what a fool you have made of yourself. Here, Jane, Mrs. Snicker says she have seen skellingtons upstairs, and she wishes us to go and scare 'em away."

"Very well, sir," said Black-eyed Susan, quietly.

"They are in the attic," said Snicker; "but don't be afraid, girl. I'm with you."

There was a very dry smile on the face of the girl as she led the way upstairs. Snicker came next, and at a cautious distance his trembling Phœbe.

"In the attic, Jane," she said, "the next one to yours."

"Yes'm."

On they went up the ladder to the attic in question. The door was wide open, and inside there was nothing but dust. Neither skeleton nor boys nor anything could be seen.

Black-eyed Susan, with her practised domestic eye, observed footmarks and other signs of the recent presence of somebody on the dust-laden floor, but she said nothing. Her thoughts were her own and she kept them to herself.

She went in, and Snicker remained in the doorway. Throwing open the cupboard, she showed that it was empty.

"There's no skeletons, sir," she said.

"Of course not," growled the schoolmaster. "Here, you old image, what do you mean by coming along with that cock-and-bull story? What's the matter with you? Why don't you leave the bottle alone? I was dead sure you would soon have 'em on."

Mrs. Snicker had come half-way up the ladder, and was only visible from her waist upwards.

"Nothing there?" she gasped.

"Nothing!" said Snicker, emphatically. "Perhaps if you come up you will see 'em agen."

Mrs. Snicker came up and stared into the room.

"I'll swear," she said, "that I heard 'em talking first, and when I came up I see 'em real livin'—I mean bony skellingtons, leaning agin that very wall, laughing."

"No wonder," snarled Snicker. "You would make a tom-cat, with his tail cut off, grin all over his face." Here he sniffed. "Hang it! if you ain't smelling strong with whisky."

"I upset the lemon-juice bottle in my pocket," replied Mrs. Snicker. "Jerry, you are a brute, an unmanly brute, and if you say I didn't see skellingtons, I'll scratch you on the nose."

"All right," said Snicker, coming toward her, "you see 'em. Regiments of skellingtons. It's all right. Lemon-juice, was it, you spilt? Well, I gives a guinea a gallon for it. Get out of the way!"

She descended, and he followed her.

Mrs. Snicker, troubled and angry, hastened below, and Snicker went into his bedroom. Black-eyed Susan, girl-like, popped into her room above just to tidy her hair.

As she took up the brush she heard the voice of Snicker below bellowing with rage.

She dropped the brush, and hastened below. Snicker had already gone down to the hall. He had left the door of his bedroom open, and the girl, peering in, saw what appeared to be a monstrous creature sleeping in his bed.

But Susan was not afraid, and, running in, saw at once what it was.

It was the arrangement of mask and nightcap which Don had made.

"Bless them boys," exclaimed Black-eyed Susan; "they are always up to something."

In a moment she had the mask out of bed, and the nightcap back in its proper place on the back of a chair.

Then, with one movement of the hand, she put the bedclothes straight, and slipped away to her attic again.

Meanwhile Snicker had been raging and tearing about before his wife, calling her names that cannot be printed, and capering about like a Zulu chief on his we'ding morn.

"I knowed there was some game 'on," he hissed. "You got me upstairs to skeer—scare—me. What d'yer mean by it?"

"I see them skellingtons," insisted Mrs. Snicker.

"I'm not talking about skellingtons," he roared, "but about something you've shoved in my bed. Don't say you didn't do it."

"Jerry," gasped his wife, "if I've been near your room, may I——"

"I tell you I won't have no lies about it," he bellowed. "Come up and look at it; it's got your nightcap on."

"My nightcap?" exclaimed Mrs. Snicker. "What imperence!"

"Come and see it," snarled Snicker, seizing her by the arm.

He half-dragged, half-led her upstairs to his room.

"There, look at it!" he cried. "Cast your leary old optics on it, and then say——"

It was his turn to stop short and stare. The bed was smooth; everything was in its place.

"Well, I'll be somethinged!" he muttered.

"Jerry, Jerry," said Mrs. Snicker, mournfully, "you had better see a doctor, and sign the pledge."

He made no answer, but stood there staring and muttering to himself, until Black-eyed Susan appeared on the scene.

"Jane," said Mrs. Snicker, "your master has licker visions again. Get him to go to bed."

"It seems to me, ma'am," replied Susan, "that neither of you is quite well, and I don't wonder at it."

They both stared at the girl, and then at each other, silent and troubled.

"Phœbe," at length said the schoolmaster, feebly, "do I look queer?"

"You are hollow under the eyes," she answered, "and I feel pale."

"You are white as a muffin," he said. "I think we had better go downstairs. Jane, you ain't to talk about things, you know."

"Oh, no, sir!"

"There is sixpence for you to buy a bit of ribbon with. Phœbe, we are two unfortunates, and it's our duty to support each other through the trials of life."

"I always said so, Jerry," she sighed, "but you wouldn't believe me. Shall I make some strong tea?"

"Jane will make it," moaned Snicker. "Be as quick as you can, girl."

"Yes, sir."

Black-eyed Susan disappeared, and the afflicted husband and wife, for the time linked together in a common misfortune, walked into the room of the former.

For a time, at least, the jarring sounds of domestic war were dumb. A feeling of peace, tempered with the fear that both were on the road to an attack of that terrible affliction of the lover of intoxicants, the dreaded delirium tremens, was hovering around them like a cloud.

While all these things were disturbing a portion of the household, two individuals, also connected with it, were in close conference in the class-room. They were Awful Rooker and Roger Hone.

It was the first time they had secured an oppor-

tunity to confer together, and they were going through a preliminary discussion on their relative positions in the school.

"For my part," said Rooker, "I am neither one thing nor another, and get sat upon by both sides. Bunn used to be tolerably friendly, but he has rounded on me."

"In what way?" asked Hone.

"In every way, and he has set a beastly Italian on me worrying about an accordion."

"I fancy I heard one after I got into bed last night," said Hone. "Only a note or two, but I won't make sure."

"It wasn't possible," said Rooker, "for I lost—— But let it go. The boys are down on you, I believe?"

"Yes, and why?" said Hone. "They have a secret from me. That find under the cliff isn't the only one which has been made hereabouts."

"You don't say so?"

"I am certain of it. When the barring-out was on, some of the fellows, Ford, Peebles, Drummond, and Stockton, went down into the vaults, and I am sure they dropped on something, and it must have been money, as they had no chance of getting anything bulky away."

"Have they been flush of late?"

"They spent a lot at Chippenham a short time ago. The whole of the fellows, except myself, had a blow out of tarts and ginger beer, and all sorts of things. It was a perfect feast. I believe they have something hidden away, and if I could only find it, they would have to whistle for it."

"Hone," said Rooker, "we must get at that money."

"We must."

"We will watch and follow them about until we find out where it is."

"We will."

They shook hands upon it, and Rooker, warm with a new friendship, invited Hone to come up to his room on the morrow after supper, to compare notes of such discoveries as they might make in the meantime.

Then they shook hands again, and were preparing to part, when Hone thought he heard a slight noise outside the door.

He was considerably troubled on rushing up to it to find that it was ajar, but there was nobody but the Snicker cat outside, a black cat of exceeding vicious disposition.

"It must have been this brute," said Hone.

"Sure to have been," replied Rooker, confidently. "Who could be listening? All the boys are outside. There goes the bell for supper. Quick, to the door, and count them as they come in."

They raced across the hall, and were just in time to

see tne first boy, in the person of Bedstone, tear into the house.

He was followed by a stream of laughing, chattering boys, none of whom appeared to take the slightest notice of the pair, as they stood covertly counting them.

Not one was missing ; they were all there, and the two allies were satisfied. They let the boys go on to the dining-room, and then slowly followed.

"It *was* the cat," said Hone. "I haven"t the least doubt about it now."

"I was certain of it right through," said Rooker.

CHAPTER LXX.

BONELUCCI TURNS UP AGAIN WITH A COMPATRIOT—A TIME OF TERROR.

TIME does not, as some people think, fly swiftly with the young. It rather lags, as a rule, especially when the days are spent at school. But for all that, it does pass, and the welcome holidays of various length come round in due course.

Once more it was half-holiday at the Abbey, and Fontenoy Snicker, who had been in a subdued frame of mind since that evening of adventure with the mask and skeleton, made no effort to curtail their enjoyment.

He made no reference to the trick played upon him, and Black-eyed Susan keeping her own counsel, the perpetrator and his friends were puzzled.

"It isn't like Snicker to allow anything of that sort to pass without comment," said Don.

"No, it isn't," said Bob Stockton, "but I believe he has changed his tactics. He is lying in wait, perhaps, for a clue, as they say in the newspapers, to the guilty parties."

"He will have to lie in wait for a long time," remarked Tom.

They were preparing to go out for the afternoon, their destination, the White Oak. In any other school cricket would have been encouraged, but Snicker had always set his face against boyish amusements, and there was not a bat or ball in the school.

One of the questions recently agitating the minds of the leaders of the Lambs was whether this state of things ought to be allowed to continue.

A meeting had been called by the White Oak, sacred through its being the place where they first met Professor Lingo, and some of the boys had already started off, others were following in twos and threes.

The members of the inner circle were the last to go. Neither of the tutors had as yet left the Abbey.

As the four friends sauntered across the playground they were surprised to see two men come up and peer through the gate. Still greater was their surprise when they recognized the unfortunate Bonelucci. His companion had a barrel-organ slung across his back.

"What is the move now ?" exclaimed Jack.

"Hi you! all of you !" cried Bonelucci. "Say, is he of ze name Rookare home ?"

"You had better inquire at the front door," replied Bob, with his usual politeness. "Knock once, ring twice, open the door, and walk in."

"I see ze choke," replied Bonelucci. "You boys laf to see me kick out wif ze pails of watare on ze tops of me."

"Well," said Bob, "if you are averse to adopting the usages of polite society, wait here until he comes out."

"He no out," said Bonelucci.

"He is at this moment oiling his hair."

"I oils him back when he comes," said Bonelucci.

He turned to his companion and said something in Italian. Both glared fiercely, and the boys all thought they had never seen such a pair of forbidding-looking ruffians.

"What can they want with Rooker ?" asked Don.

"I think we had better wait and see," replied Jack.

They were not kept long. In a few moments Rooker emerged from the Abbey, and Bonelucci and his companion drew on one side, so that they were not seen until he was clear of the gate.

Then they confronted him.

"Come now," said Bonelucci, flourishing his arms, "my mu-seek. Where is he ?"

"Look here," said Rooker, feeling strong in the company of the boys, "I can't be troubled in this way."

"You gif him, or see he here, my friend, of ze name Tappilooni, he help me to put you in preeson."

"Bosh !" exclaimed Rooker.

Tappilooni divested himself of his barrel-organ and placed it on the ground.

"I haf you to ze poleece," he said.

Rooker backed into the school-ground white and scared, followed by the two Italians, crouching as if preparing to pounce upon him like tigers.

Bob looked at the defenceless barrel-organ, and a bright idea flashed upon him.

"A little music would help us along this afternoon," he said, softly. "I think we could carry it."

No more was said. Bob and Tom Drummond laid hold of it, and away they went, unperceived by the owner, down into the wood.

Knowing they would assuredly be pursued, they soon turned aside from the beaten track and lay up under some bushes.

"If the worst comes to the worst, we can clear off," said Bob, "for the Italian will, when he re-collars his barrel-organ, be glad to stick to it."

"And weighted with it," said Don, "if he pursues us still, we could give him seven furlongs in a mile."

Meanwhile Rooker, seeing matters were getting serious, suddenly turned tail and fled back to the Abbey. The Italians pursued him, but only succeeded in getting the door banged in their faces.

"Hey, then!" bawled Bonelucci, "you tink you laf at us; but you laf on ze inside cheeks to-morrow!"

"It is enuf," remarked his companion, "I can do no more. You wait for him—he ze tief—I come back by-ze-bye."

He left Bonelucci growling by the door, and walked outside the grounds. A glance round showed him that his barrel-organ had disappeared, and he set up a howl that would have scared a mad dog.

Bonelucci came hurrying out to him, with a gait that was a compound of the hop and the wobble.

"Tappilooni—friend—brother, speak! How is it?" he cried.

"You bring me here!" yelled the other, capering about. "You say—come help me to get my mu-seek, and zen see—I lose mine also. Curses on you thick head of flour colour!"

"Gone!" said Bonelucci, wildly. "Who shall take him?"

"Ze boys of four. Was he not here?"

"It shall be so—friend—brother."

"And haf zey not take him?"

"I see it is so. You know ze boys if you shall see zem?"

"No. I look a leetle—not mooch. I haf eye for se Rookare, no more. But you, Bonelucci, you see zem, sure?"

Bonelucci bent his head upon his breast, and groaned aloud.

"All ze English boys am ze same to me," he said, with a sob. "I know zem not."

"You bring me here—for your mu-seek," hissed Tappilooni, "and now is not so. Mine gone—and not mine. I haf him for ze hire of ze Padrone. It is too much."

"Ze boy cannot fly wif ze organ," said Bonelucci. "Say, if we go to find him, shall it not be so?"

"I keel zem all," hissed Tappilooni, and to show that he meant real business, he took out his knife and brandished it in the air.

Bonelucci, probably to keep him company, and to cheer him up, did the same. Then down into the wood they plunged in hot pursuit.

The boys, in their hiding-place, heard them as they went by jabbering and gasping, and as soon as they dared give vent to their feelings, laughed until their sides ached.

"The next thing to be done is to get this article to one White Oak," said Don.

"There is only one way to do it," said Jack, "we must lower it down over the cliff, work our way round, and pick it up. The Oak lies direct west from here. Bob, you nick back to Littlecote, and borrow the Snicker clothes-line."

"All right," replied Bob, as if about to carry out an ordinary commission.

Don volunteered to go down the path as scout, so that notice might be given of the Italians returning, and away he went. In ten minutes Bob was back with the rope.

"Rooker was in the hall," he said, "and when I went in suddenly, he tried to get into a cupboard in his fright. He is thoroughly scared. I asked him if he were coming out, but he shook his head, and said, 'Not to-day, thank you.'"

"What a lark it is," grinned Drummond.

"But suppose one of these Italians stab him one day?"

"Well, *we* can't help it."

"Rooker wants to know if we will speak to the police."

"Certainly, why not?" replied Jack; "he shall have the whole force of Chippenham at his back—if they will come."

The rope was put securely round the barrel organ, as they thought, and it was carried to the edge of the cliff, and lowered. When near the bottom, it suddenly slipped out, and went down to the bottom with an audible bang.

"My eye!" exclaimed Don, who came up and joined them at that moment, "that has put it out of tune."

"We shall see all about it," answered Bob, "when we take to grinding it at the White Oak."

As the rope was free, they hauled it up, and hid it where they would be able to find it on their return. Then they set out at a trot for the base of the cliff.

On reaching the end of the wood they stopped for breath, and to look about them. Far away on the high road they could see two figures, which were unmistakably Bonelucci and Tappilooni. The coast was, so far, clear, and, turning into the fields, they worked their way round until they came to the spot where they rightly judged the barrel organ had fallen.

"It doesn't look as if it was much hurt," said Don; "shall I try it?"

"No," replied Jack; "these beastly things can be heard miles away in the country. Wait till we get to the other fellows."

The White Oak was fully a mile-and-a-half away, across rough common ground, and by the time the boys had got there with it, they had had enough of the labour entailed in its transit.

The rest of the boys had arrived before them, and when they saw them struggling along with it, all sorts of speculations were set afloat about the nature of the burden.

Little Jiggers was sure it was something to eat, a box full of buns and tarts being his conception of the contents of the box, as the barrel organ was supposed to be.

Gyp Tanner was inclined to think it was fireworks, and recommended Barnes, who dare not let off a squib, to go and help them along with it.

"If anything explodes," he said, "it can't blow you very far."

Barnes declined to assist, so Tanner and Whymper ran forward and lent a hand with it.

"A barrel organ!" shouted Whymper; "where did you get it from?"

"We found it outside the Abbey gate," replied Bob Stockton; "some good fairy must have left it for us to play with."

They carried it up to the tree, and set it down.

"What does it play?" asked Bedstone; "hymns, or frivolous music?"

"We will see in a minute," replied Jack. "Take off the cover, Bob."

The green baize cover was whipped off, and cast aside. It was immediately appropriated by Dorey, who put it over himself.

As it covered his head and arms, some of his lively friends promptly laid hold of the strings, and drew them tight. Then, having knotted them, they set him free.

"Blind man's touch!" screamed Philter, giving him a push. "Now, Dorey, who is it?"

"And who is this?"

"And who am I?"

There were a dozen at him in no time, and he was pushed this way and that as he furiously struggled to get free. But he was fairly caught, and as helpless as a bird in a snare.

During the uproar attendant on this impromptu bit of fun, Jack and his friends had tested the organ, and discovered, to their disgust, that it only played the most solemn and the slowest of tunes.

There was the inevitable "Old Hundredth," and "When I lay me down to sleep," and others of a most dolorous order.

"What's to be done with the beastly thing?" said Don, eyeing the offending instrument with strong disfavour.

"I intended to have had a witches' dance to it under the Oak," said Tom Drummond.

"So we can now," said Bob Stockton; "you leave this thing to me. Now, boys, all for the witches'

dance. Everybody kick up his legs just as he pleases, independent of each other; but you must keep moving, and the more novelty you can throw into the thing, the better."

"What on earth is this?" cried Jack Ford, as Dorey, in the green baize covering, came tumbling up, and fell upon the barrel organ with a bang.

"Let me out," answered Dorey, with a muffled, roaring sound.

"Don't!" yelled a dozen voices; "make him dance the British hornpipe inside it."

"I won't!" screamed Dorey, wriggling frantically.

"Won't he be in a wax when he comes out?" said Bedstone to Gyp Tanner.

"A tiger will be a shivering lamb to him," was the reply.

Dorey was a very excitable lad; all right so long as he was not irritated, but when roused, not easily appeased.

He was subject to what is known as fits of blind rage, that is, in his anger he was reckless, and apt to do mischief to somebody.

"Now, Dorey," said Tom Drummond, lifting him up and putting him on his feet, "you have got to do the hornpipe, and the sooner you get it over the better."

"I'll die first!" replied Dorey, his voice sounding like the distant bellowing of a bull.

It was excruciatingly funny to see the agitation of his legs, and the partly-defined movements of his arms within the bag-like covering.

Don began to grind furiously at "When I lay me down to sleep," but nothing could make it a lively air. The organ was also handicapped by some injury it had received in its fall, which had broken a few of the teeth of the barrel, and therefore deprived it of a few notes necessary to complete the air.

As Dorey would not dance alone, Tom and Don took him in charge, and lent him what assistance they could. To dance the hornpipe to such music was practically impossible, but they cut strange capers, and the boys roared with delight.

The only one who did not enjoy it was Dorey, and his state for the time may be described as absolutely murderous.

CHAPTER LXXI.

A MUSICAL BREAKDOWN.—TAPPILOONI ON THE WAR-PATH.

CRACK!

"Stop a minute!" cried Bob Stockton, as he ceased to grind, "there has been an explosion in the works."

He gave the handle a few more turns, but it went

round much too easily, and there was not the slightest sound in response.

"It's lying down to sleep," suggested Don.

"I'll set it for another tune," said Bob.

He shifted the stop, and turned again, with the same result.

"Hushed is the harp, the minstrel's gone," sang Herbert May.

"I'll try again," said Bob.

But all the stops were tried in vain; the organ had, in a sense, breathed its last.

"Come out, old man," said Tom Drummond, as he unfastened the strings of the cover, and dragged it over Dorey's head; "awfully sorry to ask you to stop when you were beginning to foot it like an opera *danseuse*."

"I'll kill somebody for this!" yelled Dorey. "Who was it tied me in? I think it was you, Bedstone."

"No fighting, Dorey," said Don, throwing his arms around him. "Why can't you take a joke in good part?"

"Joke!" screamed Dorey; "a joke! You have it put over your head, with your arms pinned to your sides, and then be hustled about. Will you let me go?"

"Not until you say it is all right. What is the good of your trying to fight forty fellows. Dry up!"

"Dorey," sang out Bob, "you are a bit of a mechanic, are you not?"

Dorey was, and he was rather proud of it. He turned an inquiring and slightly-softened eye upon Bob, who had just taken off the top of the barrel-organ.

"Well," he growled, "what if I am?"

"Come and see what is the matter here."

"Now, Dorey," urged Don, "do your work, and fight afterwards."

Dorey nodded assent, and being released, went over to the organ. Kneeling down, he examined it carefully, and finally expressed his opinion that it was "done for."

"Done for!" ejaculated Bob; "what have I done? I only turned the handle *a little faster* than ordinary."

"The cogs are smashed," said Dorey, "the guiding pin is bent, and the spring is snapped."

"In that case," said Bob, with an air of resignation, "we must give up the idea of any further melody."

"Who wants a light job?" cried Don.

"I do," sang out Barnes.

"Good. Then just run up to the Abbey with this organ. Ask Snicker to take care of it for us."

"Look out there!" yelled Whymper.

Every eye was turned upon him for a moment, and then in the direction he was pointing.

Coming across the waste land at a smart run on the part of one, and a wild hobble on the part of the other, were the two Italians.

From afar they had heard the wild music extracted by Bob from the organ, and Tappilooni had recognized its voice.

"Clear away!" shouted Jack Ford; "scatter and make for Meagray Churchyard."

Away the boys went like so many rabbits and hares, with a start of a good two hundred yards, thus putting the Italians for the time out of the running.

As they melted away in the distance the frantic pair came on. Tappilooni, by reason of his superior speed, was a long way ahead.

He was gasping with rage, but knew not the full extent of his loss until he was under the White Oak, and could see the inside of his instrument.

"Ach!" was all he said, and then for ten seconds or so he was blind.

Rage overwhelmed him.

Bonelucci came up, and laid a hand upon his shoulder. He was as sorry as one friend can be for another, which, as the world goes, isn't anything very great, but he could not speak for want of breath.

Presently Tappilooni recovered his speech and breath together.

"You see?" he said.

"Alas! it is so," answered Bonelucci.

"What will ze Padrone say? How much swear? Is it for me to go to him to be kicked, to be cuffed, to be down-knockered? Say, then?"

"It is for us to go to ze schoolmaster, he of ze bent legs, and say: 'Behold him, my museek organ. Say, then, was it not you boys who do him? Pay, zen. Take him. Give him new stomach—inside.'"

"And if he does not do him, he must die!" said Tappilooni, fiercely. "You knife-cross him."

They drew out their knives and crossed them in the air.

"By our country."

"In ze name of true liberty."

"Ze accursed boys, and he of ze bent leags, shall mend ze organ, or all die!"

"So it shall be."

They put on the lid of the instrument, fastened the catch, and looked around for the cover. It was on the ground, with the strings broken, a tear or two in it made by the frantic Dorey, and terribly trampled on by the boys in their flight.

"More swear!" hissed Tappilooni. "Ze Padrone see him, and gif me more knocker-down. He, too, gif his wife and children hard digs with him foot. Ze Padrone go mad."

They put on the cover as well as its condition permitted, and carrying the ruined organ between them, started for the Abbey.

It was a long way to go, but they were used to travelling on foot, and in two hours they would be there.

Meanwhile, the boys had gone on to Meagray Churchyard, which had been, on the spur of the moment, selected by Jack as a trysting-place. It was suitable, on the double ground of being in an out-of-the-way spot, and easily recognized as one of the features of the country.

The church was old, and the yard attached to it extensive. Among the scattered population it was quite a pet spot for the final residence of their bodies.

The boys, moreover, had visited it before, and the distance from the White Oak was considerable. It was hardly probable that the Italians would attempt to follow them so far.

By the churchyard, Jack naturally meant outside it. He had no lack of reverence for the dead, and would have been one of the first to object to an unseemly capering about among the tombstones.

The church stood away off from the road, and was accessible through a lane with a perfect avenue of trees. It was also surrounded with high elms.

In this secluded spot the boys assembled to review the position, and to decide what was to be done.

"What is the cost of a barrel organ?" asked Whymper.

Various answers were given. Some said they could be had "almost for nothing," and others declared that they cost from fifty to a hundred pounds. It was patent to all that it was not in their power to pay for it.

"Let the macaroni fellows fight it out with Snicker," said Bob Stockton. "But I can tell you one thing we must be careful about, and that is how we go home."

"There is but one way," said May. "What do you mean?"

"We must go in a body, and be prepared to resist any attack made upon us. These Italians are a murderous lot, and I should not be surprised if they tried to kill some of us."

"We ought to return to the Abbey," said Don, "just as if we were invading an enemy's country. Scouts must be thrown out in advance to prevent an ambuscade."

"Barnes is the boy for that work," suggested Little Jiggers.

"I won't be anything of the sort!" howled Barnes. "Oh dear, oh dear! why don't you fellows leave these murderous people alone!"

"I'll be a scout!" cried Dorey. He had already forgotten the green baize cover business. "I've read how it ought to be done."

"The first thing," said Jack, "is to arm ourselves with sticks. Go to work. There are plenty of trees. Cut off the small branches with the bark close, as they are tougher. Where the bark is very open the branches are as soft as pap."

Fortunately for the boys, it was a very secluded spot, or the row they made, as they broke or cut off the branches from which to fashion sticks, would have brought some authoritative person to the churchyard to stop the performance.

But they were not interrupted, and eventually all were ready to meet the foe.

That some of their number should be a little nervous was to be expected. It was rather a serious matter to have to run the gauntlet of two grown men, who would not hesitate to use the knife. Of course, they might not show up, but the chances were very strong that they would do so.

Barnes cried bitterly, and was chaffed by two or three, but Tom Drummond told them to let him alone.

"He can no more help being nervous than you can the size of your nose," he said. "Barnes, keep close to me; I will take care of you."

The timid lad thanked him, and dried his eyes.

As they had spent a considerable time in arming themselves, and there was a long way to go, Jack said they ought to be making for the school. Falling in, in military order, they started for the Abbey.

CHAPTER LXXII.

THE AMBUSH.—MR. SNICKER TRIUMPHANT.

THERE was need for the precautions the boys had taken to defend themselves, for Bonelucci and his friend, Tappilooni, were on the war-path.

After the most strenuous labour, they had succeeded in getting to the Abbey with the injured organ, and presented themselves at the door. Black-eyed Susan answered their somewhat peremptory ring, and that they should have the audacity to pull the bell of the principal entrance excited her unbounded indignation.

"Why do you come here?" she demanded, "especially before you have played."

"See here," cried Tappilooni, "ze organ."

"I can see it," replied the girl. "I am not blind. Be off with it. Master and missus is out, and I've got no coppers. If I had I would not give 'em to you."

"We ask to have him—ze organ of museek—repair," said Tappilooni.

"Carry it to the blacksmith," replied Black-eyed Susan. "We don't take in jobs here. If you are not off, I will set the dog on you."

The dog was a fiction, often brought out for the benefit of tramps. But there was no uncertainty about the emphatic way in which the door was shut in their faces.

"How now?" asked Bonelucci. "How you do with him?"

"Ze Snickare—ze misses—who zey?" growled Tappilooni.

"Zem of ze place—teacher, schoolmaster."

"Shall it be we wait for zem?"

Bonelucci had had enough of carrying the organ about for the time, and he readily acquiesced in the idea of waiting.

So they went to the outer gate, and there sat down with the ruined instrument, with the idea of waylaying Snicker on his return.

It seemed as if every hour, and day, and week, brought fresh trouble for that much persecuted man.

He and his wife had been to Chippenham, shopping, and they came back in a fly as far as the base of the wood. Laden with parcels, they walked, with staggering footsteps, the rest of the way, Mrs. Snicker, who had suggested the stopping of the fly below, to save expense, reviling her husband because it had been done.

"So like you, Jerry," she said, "never thinking of my poor legs, but of a penny saved."

"Bother your legs," grunted Snicker. "Didn't you yourself say that the fly was to stop there?"

"What if I did? Couldn't you, like a man, have ordered it to go on? I call it mean; but you allus—"

"Say always," wrathfully interposed the schoolmaster.

"Allus," repeated Mrs. Snicker, perversely. "You stick to your language, which is mostly ignorant rubbish, and I'll stick to mine. It's mean of you, Jerry, and you can't deny it."

He was too much blown by exertion to retort with fitting power, and therefore said no more. But it will be readily conceived by the reader that he was hardly in the frame of mind to listen to an appeal from the organ-grinder or his friend.

He saw them sitting by the gate, and they rose as he approached. His beetling brows were bent, and the scowl he favoured them with was as dark as a thunder-cloud.

Mrs. Snicker stalked by them, and her heated husband would have followed her, but Tappilooni intervened his odorous person.

"I say, sare," he cried, "behold, I have a museek organ."

"Hang your organ," growled Snicker; "get out of my way."

"He haf to be ze repair, to haf new insides," cried Tappilooni, quivering with wrath.

"Get it new insides, outsides, bottoms, and tops," hissed Snicker. "Get another organ. Two, three, a dozen—what you like! But don't bother me."

"Ze boys, zey of your school, take him avay from ze gate, right off to ovare zare, and grind him double quick and break him."

"Then break the boys—if you can do it," roared Snicker, "but don't bother me. Out of the way."

He thrust himself against Tappilooni, forgetting his parcels for the moment. There was a cracking of glass as the Italian fell upon his barrel-organ in a sitting position.

"Blow it," growled Snicker, "there goes a lamp glass. Was there ever a man so bothered as I am by all the natural vermin in creation? Look here, you two, be off, and if you come here again, I'll lock you up and give you a month apiece for mendashity—mendish—dicity."

With his very coat-tails alive with wrathful excitement, he hurried across the playground and bounced into the house.

"How now are you, Tappilooni?" said Bonelucci; "shall he pay?"

"It must be ze boys," hissed Tappilooni. "Monies or lifes, as ze roadway men use to say. See here, ze knife to scare zem—pay up all of you. Zey come back soon. We meet zem at ze bottom of ze wood."

He motioned to Bonelucci to lay hold of the barrel organ, and together they departed wearily.

It was about an hour afterwards, a little more, in fact, when a shouting outside the Abbey was heard by Snicker, who had shut himself up in his room. Rushing to the window, he looked out and saw some of the boys in the playground and others formed in a line across the gate.

Among the latter he observed Jack Ford, Tom Drummond, and Don Peebles. The air was alive with sticks whirling over the heads of the youngsters.

"What is the riot now?" he muttered.

Popping on a smoking-cap and seizing a stout cane he dashed out of the room to the playground, arriving in time to see the boys at the gate rush forward with a shout of victory.

Then it was he obtained a glimpse of the two Italians backing towards the wood, wildly gesticulating and bleeding about the head. Neither of them had a hat upon his crown.

"It isn't the boys' fault this time," said Snicker; "leastways, I told them savages to be off, and they haven't offed—*gone* I mean, so here's at 'em."

The fact was, the Italians were, in his way of thinking, the safer game. He broke through the astonished boys, many of them prudently getting out of the reach of the cane, and there was a shout as he came to the front.

Bonelucci saw him and turned tail. Tappilooni, blind to all but the boys, continued to threaten and gesticulate, until he was seized by the schoolmaster, and felt the first sting of the cane.

Then they closed, and one of the most exciting struggles that the boys had ever witnessed began.

"My goodness!" exclaimed Little Jiggers, "this is a treat."

On the rest a great silence had fallen. The shouting ceased, and every eye was on the two men, and at the outset those who understood anything of the art of wrestling could see that Snicker had some knowledge of it.

The Italian had also an inkling of it as practised in his own country, and he was perhaps the stronger of the two. Altogether they were evenly matched.

To and fro, bending this way and that, the struggle went on. Suddenly the heels of the Italian flew up, and he went to the ground with a whack.

A shout of approval went up from the boys. They could be generous enough to recognize a feat of arms, or rather legs, on the part of their natural enemy.

Tappilooni had had enough of it.

"I gifs in," he gasped, and Snicker, flushed with victory, rose to his feet.

The boys cheered him again, more for the fun of the thing than anything else, and he walked proudly into the house.

When he got into his room again, he threw himself into his chair, with the light of exultation in his eyes.

"Got the better of somebody at last," he said. "I think I will celebrate my victory with just one little drop."

And he did so.

Among the boys there was also the spirit of exultation.

The two Italians, hiding near the wood, had allowed them to pass on their way home, and then attacked them in the rear.

They had been so far successful at the outset as to seize Don, and were dragging him off a prisoner, but his friends speedily rushed to his aid.

The Italians drew their knives, but flourished them in vain. They could not resist the rush, and letting Don go, they stabbed about them in a wild, futile manner.

As the boys slowly retreated up the wood with their bolder members defending, Bonelucci and Tappilooni followed, occasionally making sham rushes and uttering the most fearful threats, but it was not until the playground was reached by the foremost youngsters that they really attempted to carry out their presumed intention—to kill one of the boys.

It was then that they were maddened to real mischief, and but for the gallant stand made by the party at the gate, without a doubt some of the weaker boys would have been seriously injured, if they had not been killed outright.

But none suffered harm, and when the schoolmaster, after his "glorious" victory over Tappilooni had retired, Jack and his friends of the inner circle retreated to the conference place on the wall by the edge of the cliff.

"I have one of their knives," said Jack. "I knocked it out of the hand of the old man—hit him over the knuckles. Who has the other?"

"I have," replied Don, "in my pocket."

"Keep it there. We needn't show them. They are the spoils of war. But look here, boys, we have got the upper hand to-day, but we have not quite got rid of the foe."

"The worst of such fellows," said Bob Stockton, "is that they are cunning, as well as cruel. I shouldn't wonder if they did mischief to some of us for this."

"Can't be helped," said Don. "We must not, for a time, at least, go about except in strong parties. If we do, some of us stand a very good chance of being murdered."

"It is all the fault of that barrel-organ," remarked Bob, pathetically. "Like poor old Barnes, it was weak in the inside. Got no real heart, and caved in the moment it was put to serious work. Well, the thing is done—

"'And all the Lambs' horses and all the Lambs' men,
Can't set the thing up a-grinding again.'"

CHAPTER LXXIII.

DON GETS A LETTER.—MORE FUN WITH THE FAILING OF THE SNICKERS.

ON the following morning Don got a letter from his mother. A post-office order was inclosed for two pounds, which made him stare, but the origin of this unlooked-for bounteous gift, and, as he knew, beyond his mother's means, was explained in the epistle.

"MY DEAR DON,—We received your last letter, and were glad to find, more from its tone than words, that you were reconciled and quite happy. I miss you very much, but as I believe your being away is for your good, I try to reconcile myself to it.

"Last night a clergyman from your district called upon us, and a nicer man I never met. He did not begin to talk as if he were better than we are, but sat down and had a cup of tea with us quite friendly. It was he who gave me two pounds to send on to you to be distributed among the boys. He said that it is the gift of a charitable body known as the Lambs of Littlecote, which I suppose are a sort of Quaker body in your neighbourhood.

"He gave us glowing accounts of the progress you are making, and hinted that for good conduct you are nearly at the top of the school. I was very glad to find it so, as at times you used to be very troublesome at home.

"Before leaving, our visitor did a very strange thing for a clergyman to do. He bought all the overdate and odd stock of the shop. Of course he got it cheap, but it paid your father to sell, as we could not get anything at all for it here.

"Your clerical friend said that the goods were for distribution among the 'flats,' meaning, I suppose, those new sort of poor buildings in London where there are a number of families under one roof. He must be a charitable man.

"A cart called for the things after dark. A strange man came with it. Your father says he thinks he has something to do with the shows we have had in our town, but I fancy he is mistaken. Your father sends his love, and hopes you will not lie about the grass at any time. It is sure to lay in a stock of rheumatism. With both our love,
"I am, your affectionate
"MOTHER.

"P. S.—What a strange thing! Your clerical friend never said who he was. More than that—he did not mention his name, or the church where he officiates.

"P. P. S.—Mr. Snicker has written to your father, marking his letter 'private.' But, of course, it was shown to me. He asks if we would rather have you remain there during the coming holidays, as it is such a long way to travel. If so, he will keep you for a moderate extra charge. As you are so happy with him, we were thinking that it was the better thing to do; but we would like to hear what you have to say on the matter."

Don showed the letter to his friends, and they had a hearty laugh over the part that referred to Professor Lingo, but there was the reference to Snicker, which gave rise to serious reflection.

"He can't have written to other of our parents," said Jack Ford, "or we should have heard of it. What is his game?"

"It is a feeler, in my opinion," said Tom Drummond; "we may hear more about it by-and-bye."

"I shall write home, and say that I would rather not stay unless the rest of you do. If that should be arranged, I would not mind, to save expense."

But the mystery of it was not long in abeyance. That very afternoon, when the school was dismissed, the schoolmaster sent for the four members of the inner circle, whom he must have singled out as the leaders of the school, to meet him in his private room.

They went, wondering, and expecting a squall of some sort, but were surprised to find Fontenoy Snicker in a most gracious mood.

"Sit down, boys," he said. "I want to have a little private talk with you. But, first of all, what do you say to a piece of plum cake? It's good. I gave tenpence a pound for it at Bib's in Chippenham."

The amazed quartette said they would have some of this double-extra cake, and Snicker brought it out from a sideboard. He gave them a good-sized piece each with a visible wrench, as if it wrung his heartstrings to be so unwontedly generous.

"Now," he said, "I'll come to the pint—point—with you all, and explain why I have sent for you. Of course, you have heard of the treasure that that low fellow, Copps, found under the cliff?"

"We have, sir," they chorussed, with immovable faces.

"Well," continued the schoolmaster, "to come right to the head of the matter, I will tell you that it is my belief that there are other treasures stowed away."

It required all their efforts to keep composed faces. Snicker, with an air of friendly confidence, went on:

"Now, if there is more to be found, why shouldn't we find it? I don't mind telling you, boys, that I think you are unkimmon—common—ly sharp, the brightest in the school, and that is why I want you to help me."

They tried to look grateful for this burst of confidence, and succeeded passing well.

Snicker, rubbing his hands, resumed:

"While the ordinary school is going on, it would not be possible to search the place, as, naturally, all the boys will be in it if anything is found. So I want you four only to jine—join—me in this 'ere business, and if anything comes to light, 'arf will be divided between you, and the t'other—other—'arf for me."

"Will it not interfere with our ordinary duties?" inquired Don, innocently.

"Not if we work in harmony and peace, as good old Doctor Watts used to say," replied Snicker. "It must be left until the holidays, when I should like you to spend the time with me. I've written to Mr. Peebles, and he is agreeable for his son to stay if he chooses. Then comes the idea that if you boys would like to stop with him, I'll write to your friends also. What do you say?"

"The holidays begin in about a month," said Jack, musingly.

"About then," replied Snicker.

"May we take a little time to talk this over?" asked Bob Stockton, "say, a few hours, sir?"

"You can give me your answer in the morning," answered the schoolmaster, briskly, "and don't forget that if we should find something, what a fine thing it would be for you. You can go now. Would you mind asking Mr. Bunn to step here to see me?"

They promised to deliver the message, and did so to the tutor, catching him as he was going out for a walk.

He was dressed in a light check suit, and had a flower in his button-hole. Never before had they seen him half so spruce.

"Won't by-and-bye do?" he asked.

"Can't say, sir," replied Jack. "Mr. Snicker certainly led us to think that he wanted you for something very particular."

"I will see him," said Penny Bunn.

Accordingly, he assumed a fashionable lounging air, which was highly edifying to the spectators, and lounged in the direction of the master's room.

"Come on," said Jack, "let us go to our consulting crib, the old wall by the cliff. We must try and get at Snicker's little game."

———

A SPLENDID SCHOOL STORY. NEVER BEFORE PUBLISHED.

By E. HARCOURT BURRAGE,

Author of "Ching Ching," "Monkey Mat and Roving Dick," "The Brave Boy of the Basilisk," &c.

No. 11. A Handsome Coloured Plate Presented with Every Number.

THE LAMBS OF LITTLECOTE

A WEIRD, MYSTERIOUS VISITOR GIVES FONTENOY SNICKER A SHOCK.

 PRICE ONE PENNY.

CHAPTER LXXIV.

BUNN IS MYSTERIOUS.—AN EXCHANGE OF AFFLICTION.

IN saying that Fontenoy Snicker, Esq., was astounded by the gorgeous appearance of his tutor, is but to mildly describe his feelings. If Penny Bunn had waltzed into his room attired as a ballet girl, he could hardly have been more astounded.

"Here," he exclaimed, when he could find his breath, "are you going to a fancy ball?"

"This is one of my evenings out," replied Bunn, with the chilling hauteur of an outraged aristocrat, "and whither I wend my steps is my own affair. Fancy balls are not usually held at this time of year, which, of course, a man of your birth and breeding would not be expected to know."

"Look here," said Snicker, wrathfully, "do you think that I am going to enjure—*endure*—these 'ere insults?"

"Permit me to observe," replied Penny Bunn, "that you began it by referring to my apparel. If you wish to know why I am attired thus, I do not mind telling you that it is to bring myself up to the standard of the society I mix with in my hours of leisure."

"What society?" sneered the schoolmaster.

"Mainly of the fair sex," answered Bunn.

Snicker burst into a roar of laughter. Penny Bunn stiffened his back, and regarded him with icy hauteur.

"Please to state what you want with me," he said, "as I 'ave an appointment of some importance to keep."

"It is only this," said Snicker. "As a rool—*rule*—you have spent your holidays here, owing, I suppose, to your having nowhere to go to."

"Thanks to your trumpery pay," said Bunn, sharply.

"I pay you all I can," said the schoolmaster, "and as much as you are worth. Now, can you make it convenient to spend the vacation away from here?"

"I will let you know later on," said Bunn.

"I was thinking, too," continued Snicker, "that while you were away you might look about you for another berth."

"Indeed," said Bunn, craning and wriggling his neck. "That is equivalent to my getting the sack, I presume?"

"You may make it equivalent to what you like," said Snicker. "I have arranged for another tutor to take your place. He will be here in a few days to get an idea of his duties."

"I shall be prepared for him," replied Penny Bunn. "Anything more?"

"Nothing more at present," was the answer.

Bunn opened the door, and, to show his independence of the schoolmaster and all his works, put his hat upon his head before he was out of the room.

Snicker, suddenly enraged, hurled a dictionary at it, but missed his mark, and knocked a plaster cast of Lord Byron's bust off a bracket in the passage outside. Bunn deliberately trod upon the pieces to increase the mess that was made, and went his way.

Meanwhile the boys of the inner circle had held a consultation, and had come to the conclusion that the schoolmaster had got an inkling that they knew of something hidden from the general eye, and was bent on getting at their secret.

It did not make them uneasy, for they knew that they could trust each other. The one point wherein there was any cause for uneasiness lay in the possibility of their treasure, hidden in the wood, being discovered by accident by somebody.

"But we must take our chance of that," said Don, cheerily. "And now, boys, I want you to consider a little scheme I have in my noddle. Of course you all love Snicker as much as ever?"

"Just as much, and no more."

"And you forgive him for having squandered cake away upon us?"

"We do, most heartily."

"Very well, then. My scheme is for the comfort of himself and that peerless old image, Mrs. Snicker. Pop your heads together for a few moments."

They put their heads together, and in the whispered conversation that ensued, there were frequent expressions of delight.

The words "skeleton," "mask," and "Sue," could also have been heard by an attentive listener, but the other youngsters, engaged in various sports, did not come near them.

Don's scheme, whatever it was, having been approved of, they shortly after slipped quietly into the house to carry it out.

Of late, as the reader knows, there had been a renewal of affection on the part of Snicker and his wife, based on suffering of the delirium tremens order.

Both were firmly convinced that the skeleton on the one hand, and the hideous figure in the bed on the other, had been nothing more than phantasies of the brain.

Linked by the terror of the situation, they now spent much time together without any wrangling worth speaking of.

On this evening they were in their room about the hour of nine, when Black-eyed Susan came in and asked if she could lay out the supper.

"Suttinly—*certainly*—" replied Snicker, "and I'll draw the beer, Phœbe."

"Do, dear," answered Mrs. Snicker.

No. 11.

"And please, ma'am," said Black-eyed Susan, demurely, "will you give out master's things to air?"

"I'll fetch 'em down, Jane," said Mrs. Snicker, rising.

Accordingly, she took one candle and went upstairs, and Snicker with another wended his way to the cellar.

Just ten seconds later a fearful scream was heard above, and a yell, accompanied with the crash of a broken jug, from the direction of the cellar.

Then Mrs. Snicker came tumbling downstairs, and the schoolmaster rolling in from the direction of the cellar. Both made for their room, from which Black-eyed Susan had vanished.

"Phœbe!"

"Jerry!"

Their voices were hollow, and their faces white. Both their eyes stood well out of their heads, showing a lot of the white.

"What did you scream for, Phœbe?"

"And why did you holler, Jerry, and drop the jug?"

"I see something standing agin the cellar-door—a skellington, Phœbe."

"And when I went into the bedroom I saw a hideous figger in the bed. It was like what you saw, Jerry."

"And I've seen *your* skellington, Phœbe!" groaned the schoolmaster. "*We've exchanged driddledrum trimmings.*"

He sank into one chair, and Mrs. Snicker collapsed into another. There they sat gasping for awhile, but at length the schoolmaster again found his tongue.

"Phœbe," he said, in a piping tone, "it's a bad job for us, but we must bear it. Will you mind pouring me out just a little drop? I'm shook all to pieces."

"Jerry, I'm that limp," replied his trembling wife, "that my legs are no more use than the limbs of marynettes without the strings. If you are a man, get up and give me a drop—the least as ever was."

Snicker, feeling that it was his duty, as a man, to obey, rose up, and with the gait of one whose feet were all corns, hobbled and staggered across the room to a cupboard, from which he took his favourite bottle.

"Just one drop as a nerver, Phœbe," he squeaked. "It won't hurt us, and then we will give it up for good. We must keep to light wines and beer."

"We must, Jerr-r-e, dear," she answered, with chattering teeth.

Then they had their little drop, which gave them back some portion of their lost nerve, and hearing the footsteps of Black-eyed Susan, who was bringing in the joint of cold meat, Snicker whispered:

"Pull yourself together, Phœbe. It will never do

to let the gal know there was anything the matter with us."

So they pulled themselves together as well as they could, with the result that when Susan appeared, she saw two artificially stiffened figures with faces like wooden dolls, with all the paint washed off, sitting in their respective chairs.

She placed the meat upon the table, and vanished as quickly to the kitchen as she possibly could, where she went into a fit of semi-stifled laughter that nearly choked her.

———

CHAPTER LXXV.

HOW IT WAS WORKED.—IN THE SPRINGTIME OF LOVE.

"OH! if you young gentlemen had but seen their faces, you would have split your sides with laughter."

"I have no doubt we should," said Jack.

The quartette of conspirators had come into the kitchen before going to bed, to know how the thing had worked.

"I did just as you told me," continued Black-eyed Susan. "I stood the skellington up against the cellar door, and I put the other hideous thing into the bed, and asked missis for master's clothes. Then away they both went, and before you could say Bobbinson, I hears missus scream and master bellowing like a bull, and He breaks the jug, and them two goes staggering as if—if—if they was in their frequent condition, and then I takes in the meat, and if there was ever two people scared right out of their precious wits, it was Mr. and Mrs. Snicker as I seen 'em. I listened, too, before I went in, and master said as they had exchanged deriddlelum trimmings. Oh! how I was fit to laugh, but I dursn't, not until I finds my way to the kitchen."

"Well," said Don, "we are very much obliged to you, and if it was quite proper, we would kiss you all round."

"Thanky," said Susan, simply, "but I has a young man, although I don't often see him."

Then they all laughed, and Jack having promised to get the girl some ribbon or something for her trouble, they hurried out of the kitchen.

It was time for them to be in the dormitory, and all the rest of the boys were already there, undressing, and chattering about the events of the day.

But ere they could reach their place of rest they were for a short time detained by Penny Bunn, who, as they reached the hall, came in by the front door.

He showed a wonderful elasticity of step, and his eyes were very bright, but he was perfectly sober. It was not alcohol, but good spirits that affected him.

"Good evening, boys," he said, as he sank into a chair and stretched his legs.

"Good evening, sir," they responded, and waited to see what was coming. From long experience, they knew that the undermaster was bursting to speak of something.

"Boys," he said, "in me you behold the happiest of men."

"Indeed, sir," they softly chorussed.

"Yes," rejoined Bunn, "and down in yonder vale I have this night left behind me the happiest of women. The springtime of love is upon us. I have, after strenuous endeavours, won her heart, and there only remains for my peerless one to name the day."

"We wish you every happiness," said Bob Stockton, but the rest were too dumbfounded to say anything.

"Life without love," pursued Penny Bunn, musingly, "would be a double blank, which is only elsewhere to be found in a box of dominoes. It would be a desert without an oasis in it. Woman is the mainstay of man, especially when she has a trifle in the funds, and a natural desire to work hard enough to make her own living. The problem of the sexes is solved when a loving pair come together linked with the tenderest feelings, yet able by their gifts and possession of private property to be independent of each other."

This was getting too deeply into social problems for the boys, and they were silent.

"In the steady marching of time many changes are to be seen," continued Penny Bunn. "I left here tonight with a geranium in my button-hole. It has been exchanged for a bit of mignonette and a pansy, bound together with scarlet thread. The significance of this change will not be lost upon you. Good night."

He smiled upon them, hung up his hat, and bounded up the stairs two at a time, until he came near the top. There he missed a step, and fell upon his nose. He likewise barked his shins, but concealing his agony, he sprang up, and, humming the first bars of "She wore a wreath of roses," disappeared.

"I wonder what Bunn has been up to," said Jack.

"Courting," growled Tom.

"I should like to see the woman who is sweet on *him.*"

"We may all see her one day."

They hurried upstairs, and as they entered the dormitory there was a chorus of voices asking them what they had been doing.

"You shall know ere long," replied Jack.

It was an understood thing between him and his closer friends that there might be a still greater future before the skeleton and mask, and, therefore, they kept their secret for the present.

"You might tell us," grumbled Whymper.

"Patience," said Bob Stockton, "is one of the greater virtues, and it never fails to be duly rewarded."

There was some slight dissent from this, but it was soon forgotten when Herbert May, on being called upon, softly chanted one of his newest songs—

A SCHOOLBOY'S LIFE.

They may sing of the joys of a warrior bold—
    The delights of a life at sea;
Or of tales that are by travellers told,
    But a schoolboy's life for me.
Many a trouble will come to his lot,
    As he treads on his blithesome way.
He may suffer, but for that not a jot
    Does he care, but cries "Hurray!"
There's lessons to learn, and whackings to take,
    But his eye will never grow dim;
And he fights at times with his sturdy foes.
    And it's all the same to him.
He's as bright as the sunshine, as free as the air,
    And the days by swiftly skim;
He laughs at trouble, and casts away care,
    He is filled with joy to the brim.

    So hurrah for a schoolboy's life,
      Hurrah for the young and the free;
    Down with all sorrow and strife,
      And stand up for our liberty.

As the last line was chanted in chorus, the door opened, and Fontenoy Snicker put his head in.

"What's the row there?" he growled.

For a moment there was nothing said in reply, and then some undistinguished voice squeaked out:

"Please sir, I think it is the rats."

"Who said rats?" demanded Snicker; and instantly realizing that he had put an absurd question, he banged the door, and was heard no more.

"He will dream of rats to-night," said Jack Ford, when the subdued laughter had subsided. "Good night, dear boys."

"Good night," was the general response, and in a little while there was stillness in the room.

———

CHAPTER LXXVI.

THE OLD CLOCK UNDERGOING REPAIR.—NATURAL INDIGNATION OF FONTENOY SNICKER.

ONE morning, Mr. Botch, farmer, rose at his usual hour, after having been to market on the previous day, at eleven o'clock, and ordered his horse for a constitutional ride.

He was regular in his goings out and comings in at all times. When he had not been to market, he was up at five in the morning, and as fresh as paint. When he had been to the market he could never rise until the hour named. The reason was that he invariably laid in a stock of liquor that held him captive for many hours.

Sometimes he returned from dealing with his fellow-men sitting, but rolling like a ship in a storm in his seat. At other times he was brought back to his domicile by his intelligent horse, lying on his back in the cart, with his heels in the air. Hence the need of a nerver on horseback on the following morning.

On the particular occasion referred to he was more shaky than usual, having indulged extensively in fiery potations "enough to float a man-of-war," as some people say.

He could just sit in the saddle, and that was all.

To make matters worse, his horse was very fresh, and showed a tendency to shy at every little thing.

It was particularly troubled with milestones and posts by the wayside, so he eventually turned aside into the meadows, and about one o'clock came across a party of Lambs out for a run.

A man in liquor is occasionally good-tempered, but one just recovering from a bout is rarely, if ever, so.

Botch was in a very irritable mood, and in a thoughtless moment, he shook his fist at the boys, who had no intention of molesting him.

They responded with a defiant yell, which startled his horse, and away it went straight towards a brook, a little too wide for a horse to take with a sixteen-stone man upon its back.

But the noble animal, defying the hard-pulled rein, went in for it, to do or die.

It rose gallantly at it, and Botch, with a loose seat, was shot far away over its head, so that he landed on his ribs near the opposite bank, but well in the water. He still held the reins as he climbed out, which had been drawn over the head of the horse, now tumbling about in the water.

Botch, who was constitutionally as hard as nails, climbed up to the land, and began tugging at the head of his steed, while the delighted boys performed a wild dance of exultation on the opposite shore.

In a few moments the horse got the better of the man by breaking the rein, and swimming down a short distance, crossed over on the side of the boys, and with a contemptuous kick up behind for the benefit of its master, galloped away.

To get home Botch would have to walk at least five miles, there being no bridge within half that distance. He stamped and raved, and the boys on the opposite shore capered about, deriding him until he was half-mad. He threw his whip at them, which they promptly picked up and decamped with.

"That's enough!" roared Botch. "It's theft! and I'll have you up for it!"

And he meant exactly what he said, for he had thought he had taken sufficient notice of the boys to swear to some of them.

That afternoon he made his preparations to bring everlasting confusion and disgrace upon the Lambs by calling upon one of the locally-residing magis-

trates, and securing from him a promise that on his ascertaining the names of the offenders, they should be at once summoned to answer for their offence.

It was five o'clock when he got home, and having been about in his wet clothes, which were, however, now nearly dry, for many hours, he felt it incumbent upon himself to forthwith undress and go to bed, where he laid the first stone towards convalescence, after his chilling experience, by swallowing a big tumbler of hot brandy-and-water.

In case it should not be sufficient for the purpose, he took another, and fell asleep until the following morning.

Passing on from this event, we must, ere relating the issue of it, describe a scene in the Abbey, which arose out of an attempt to repair the grandfather's clock in the hall.

The reader will remember that on a memorable occasion, when a mask had been fixed thereto, Fontenoy Snicker, Esq., had pulled it over, to the great detriment of its works and his own personal injury.

After a lapse of time, it was thought necessary to repair it, and on this day a little watchmaker, named Bibbins, from Smudgem Bender, was the person selected for the job.

He was a very worthy little man, and as honest a teetotaler as exists in the wide world. He conscientiously acted up to his creed.

But, unfortunately, he suffered from some complaint that gave him a red nose, which was apt to set the idle and thoughtless thinking that he was a temperance fraud.

He was nothing of the sort, but if he had been a heavy drinker he could not have been more nervous.

It was the nature of the man.

Somehow it became known among certain of the boys that Bibbins was expected about five o'clock to attend to the clock, and shortly after that hour he arrived, with his little black leather bag filled with the needed tools.

Not one of the Lambs was at home, it being Saturday, and Fontenoy Snicker in person pointed out the clock to Bibbins.

"You'll find it fairly well shaken up," he said, "and if you think it will cost too much, we can let it be."

Then he left him and sauntered back towards his own room, but ere he could open the door, he heard a rushing of feet behind him, and turning, saw the little man approaching at the pace of a champion runner, with his hair erect and his eyes fixed and staring.

"Here, what's the matter?" cried Snicker, in alarm.

"The clo-o-o-o-ck," stuttered the watchmaker. "You-u-u-u oughtn't to play tri-i-i-icks on a 'specta-a-ble man."

"I play tricks!" said Snicker, haughtily. "What do yer—*you*—mean?"

"Yo-o-o-ou have put a skel-el-el-teon in it!" cried Bibbins.

Snicker had got the door of his room open, having mechanically turned the handle, and hearing this awful announcement, he reeled into the apartment.

Bibbins, now getting over his fright a little, changed to a wrathful mood.

"Yo-ou know I am a nervo-o-ous man," he said, "and that is why you di-i-i-d it."

"A skellington—*the* skellington in the clock," said Snicker, as he sank into a chair. "What new 'orror—*horror*—is there afore—*before*—jigger it!—me?"

"It's shameful—it isn't manly," continued Bibbins; "it's a nasty, stupid trick."

"Wait a moment," said the schoolmaster, pulling himself together; "you say there is a skellington in the clock?"

"No," returned Bibbins, scornfully; "I said a *skeleton*, not a skellington."

"We'll leave that for a moment."

"Leave it for a month if you like. There isn't such a thing as a skellington. And you a schoolmaster! Bah!"

"You say there is a *skeleton*," continued Snicker. "I say there *isn't*. Now then."

"Come and look at it," urged Bibbins.

"I don't think I'll do that," replied the schoolmaster, with a visible shudder. "We'll have an impartial witness."

He rang the bell, and Black-eyed Susan appeared.

"Anyone at home?" asked Snicker.

"No, sir. The young gentlemen isn't due till six and missus is at Chippenham."

"Very well, my gal—*girl*," continued Snicker. "Now Mr. Bibbins says there's something more than works in the clock in the hall. Just see what it is."

"Yes, sir."

"That girl ain't afraid of nothing," said Snicker, as she disappeared. "If there *is* a skeleton there, she'll have it up by the roots, in a manner of speaking."

"It *is* a manner of speaking," sneered Bibbins.

Black-eyed Susan came back with a serene expression of face.

"There's only the broken works in the clock, sir," she said.

"What did I tell you?" said Snicker.

"I saw a skeleton," insisted Bibbins.

"Here," said Snicker, "let us go and see if it has come back again."

He assumed a jocularity he did not exactly feel, but it was necessary that he should put a bold face on the matter.

"And, Jane," he added, "you come with us."

"Yes, sir."

So they all went, and the schoolmaster, strong in the support of his general servant, boldly opened the door of the clock.

Only the works were to be seen.

"Now, you see," said Snicker, immeasurably relieved on his own account, "there's nothing in the clock."

"I saw a skeleton," said Bibbins.

"If you did," said the schoolmaster, suddenly becoming virtuously indignant, "is it not because of your 'abits—rabbits—blow it!—*habits*."

"My what?" cried Bibbins.

"Your habits," returned Snicker; "your drinking habits."

"*I drink!*"

"Of course, you do; only such a confirmed drunkard could have such a nose as I see on your face."

Bibbins brought out a memorandum-book, and with trembling hand wrote down the libellous words.

Then he slowly read them out.

"That is what your master said, I believe?" he asked Susan.

"Yes, sir; the exact words," she answered.

"And I stand to 'em," said Snicker, recklessly.

Bibbins made a further entry of this mad assertion, and then began to put his tools into the bag.

"I'll put this into the hands of a lawyer to-morrow," he said. "The law of libel comes in here, *I'm* thinking."

"I don't want any law," said Snicker.

But the little watchmaker had packed his tools, and without deigning to exchange another word with him, vanished from the house.

"He seems out of temper, Jane," said Snicker.

"Yes, sir," was the demure reply.

"I don't think he heard 'zactly what I said."

"Oh! yes, sir, he did, the very words."

"Would you go against your master, Jane?" asked Snicker.

"I must tell the truth, sir," she replied, "for if I committed perjury they would send me to prison."

"All right," said Snicker, as he beat a hasty retreat, "even you ag'in me. The life of a man like me ain't of the vally—*value*—of tuppence."

Then he banged the door of his room, and Black-eyed Susan retreated, laughing, to the kitchen.

———

CHAPTER LXXVII.

AN INSPECTION AND A SUMMONS—TRIAL OF THE OFFENDERS—STARTLING DENOUEMENT.

BLACK-EYED SUSAN was on the watch for the return of the boys. Among the foremost were our four particular friends, who were just as eager to see her.

By appointment, they made their way at once to the lavatory, where, it will be remembered, the youngsters performed their ablutions in the morning. The girl was awaiting them there, nominally engaged in arranging the towels and putting the place to rights generally.

"Well," said Jack, "how went it?"

"Oh! lovely," replied Black-eyed Susan. "It took that little watchmaker so sudden, that he was fairly off his head, as you young gentlemen say. Then master rung the bell for me, and as I had got the skellington away, I answered it. We all had a talk, and went into the hall. Of course, there was no skellington then, and Mr. Bibbins, who had stood out there was, looked worse than ever. Master told him he had been drinking, and he is gone away to put a lawyer on him."

They all had a hearty laugh over it, and then Don asked Susan what she had done with the skeleton.

"I ran upstairs and popped it under my bed."

"Where will you put it next?" asked Bob.

"It had better stop there a bit," said the girl, serenely, "as missus don't come into my room."

"Are you not afraid of sleeping with it there?" ejaculated Tom.

The girl opened her big black eyes in surprise.

"No," she said; "why should I be?"

"Well," said Tom, "some people would be."

"Some people," said Black-eyed Susan, "are afraid of anything. Bones are nothing but bones, wheresoever they may come from."

They did not argue with her. It was convenient, anyway, that she should entertain such a view of the uncanny thing.

Of course, the moment the schoolmaster really knew that there was a skeleton about, all the terrors he at present laboured under would vanish. And that would not be in accordance with the wishes of those who had perpetrated the series of jokes upon him.

They went to bed perfectly happy, unconscious that the sword of justice had been lifted up by Botch, and might ere long inflict a fatal wound upon them.

It was on the Monday morning that the blow fell.

The boys had just breakfasted, and were in the playground, when Botch appeared, accompanied by the village constable.

He walked straight up to the Abbey door and rang the bell.

Black-eyed Susan having responded, he asked for Fontenoy Snicker, who in due time appeared.

"Mornin'," he said, eyeing the visitors curiously.

He had been in so much hot water of late, that he would hardly have been astonished if they had, there and then, arrested him for murdering the Lord Mayor of London.

"Mr. Botch," began the village constable, "was riding the other day, and in jumping his horse over a brook, dropped his whip. Some of your boys picked it up and ran away with it. He hollered after 'em, and they wouldn't pay no heed."

"Well?" said Snicker, inquiringly.

"Mr. Botch is here to identify the culprits, and to take action agin 'em."

"I wish you joy of the job, Mr. Botch," said the schoolmaster. "You are bound to go wrong on it. But do as you like with the lot."

He came out with them; and Botch, on whom every eye was fixed, singled out Jack Ford, Little Jiggers, and Don, as a trio of culprits he could swear to.

"And will you give them in charge?" asked Snicker.

"I does," was the firm answer.

"Then take 'em," said Mr. Snicker.

The constable thereupon signified to the boys that they had to accompany him before the local magistrates, who were holding court that morning at Chippenham, in the Town Hall.

"But what have we done?" asked Jack.

"The charge will be entered against you at the police station," was the answer.

Little Jiggers was a bit scared, but seeing that neither Jack nor Don was much worried, put a bold face on the matter.

"I haven't done anything," he said, "and I don't care."

There was considerable commotion among the boys, for not one there seemed to have the least idea what was the matter.

Bob Stockton fell in by the side of Jack as he walked to the gate, and asked him, in an undertone, "what the row was about?"

"Blessed if *I* know," answered Jack; "do you, Don?"

"Not the least idea," said Don.

"If it should be a case of fizzle," whispered Bob, "you will have a fine case of false imprisonment against Botch."

"We'll let you know more about it when we come back," said Jack, cheerfully; "don't worry."

Mr. Snicker hurried back to the Abbey for his hat

and coat. Of all in the school, he most feared and hated Don and Jack. It would be a luxury to him to have to write home to their friends that they had been guilty of robbery, and had been sent to prison, if only for a week.

Hastily summoning Penny Bunn, he told him to look after the school until he returned, and then hastened after the prisoners, who, with the constable and Botch, were now descending the path in the wood·

The boys were perfectly cool, being, as they had declared, totally unconscious of having done anything criminal. Jack was sure that some egregious mistake had been committed, out of which a considerable amount of fun and, as Bob had stated, some profit, would be derived.

They did not walk to Chippenham, for Botch, to save his own legs, had provided a waggonette, which was waiting for them below.

They got into it, and arrived in the dismal little town shortly after ten o'clock, and were dropped at the police-station, and there the charge was entered against the boys.

The inspector, a sensible man, took Botch aside, and asked him if it was not a very trumpery affair, which could be easily settled out of court.

But the farmer told him he was determined to proceed, as he had been "a great sufferer" from the depredations of the "Lambs," and was determined to make an example of some of them.

After that, nothing was left but to proceed with the case.

The hour for the sitting of the magistrates was eleven, but, in the leisurely, indolent style of the great county unpaid, the bench was not occupied until a quarter to twelve.

Then a retired colonel, with a moustache like a hair brush, and a nose as big as a prize tomato, and the mayor of the town, an ironmonger, took their seats.

There were two drunken cases to be disposed of, which they were—sharp—by hearing the story of the police, and listening to a feeble defence, with fines in one instance, and a caution, with dismissal, in the other.

A tramp was next charged, and sent to prison for a month, for despoiling a gate to make a fire to camp by—truly a righteous sentence, for men of that class are a pest anywhere—and then the boys were about to be put into the dock, when the magistrate, having read the charge, suggested that their standing in the front of it would meet the requirements of justice.

Accordingly, they took up a position there, a trio of bright-faced boys, sufficiently impressed with the gravity of their case to preserve an appearance of respectful decorum towards the court.

Snicker took his seat in the place set aside for witnesses, and prepared to enjoy himself.

Botch got into the witness-box and told his story. It was practically the same he had given at the Abbey.

The colonel frowned, and the mayor smiled pityingly.

"It is a very small affair," he said.

Then Botch came out strong with the general depredation theory.

He had not had an hour's peace for "ever so long" from the boys, who, whenever they had a day's holiday, invariably favoured him with a visit.

He dwelt strongly on the letting out of his pigs and sheep from the sties and pens which has been recorded in this narrative, and of their general tendency to work ruin to his crops in the fields.

He was quite eloquent, and the perspiration upon his brow made him look as if he had been freely washing his head, and was looking around for a towel.

"Now, you lads," said the mayor, "you have heard the story of the prosecutor. What have you to say to it?"

"What can they say?" put in the colonel; "this sort of thing must be put a stop to."

"We admit letting out the pigs, partly by accident," said Jack, acting as spokesman. "But we know nothing about the whip. We were not in the meadows that day."

"Where were you?" asked the mayor.

Jack hesitated. He and his friends were in the wood, as it happened, having a look at the closed-in cave of Robin Hood, just to see that it had not been disturbed. How was he to explain that?

"Guilty, of course," muttered the colonel, and Fontenoy Snicker looked exultant. Now, indeed, some of his sufferings would be avenged.

The mayor hesitated. He was a kindly-disposed man, and had boys of his own, who had now and then given him and other people trouble. What was he to do?

If they desired it, the boys could be sent for trial; but if they elected for him to settle it, he must act fairly, in a legal sense, as to poorer offenders, and send them to prison.

He was about to ask them what course they would prefer, when a stout man pushed his way through the public from the back of the court, and cried out:

"Stop a moment. I know something about this case."

"For the prosecutor or the prisoners?" asked the mayor.

"For the lads," was the reply.

"Swear that man," said his worship.

He was hustled into the witness-box, and sworn accordingly.

"Your name?"

"Daniel Figg."

"Occupation?"

"Dealer in fowls."

"What do you know about this case?"

"On Saturday last," began the witness, "please your wusship, I was drivin' along the road not fur from Smudgem Bender, when some boys come out of a meadow. They was a-laughing like winking."

"Like what?" tartly asked the colonel, who did not approve of witnesses for the defence in any case.

"Well, anyhow, just as boys laugh when they have been having a bit of fun," said Daniel Figg. "I stops to look at 'em, as I takes kindly to boys, having nine of my own, and one of em 'listed—Lord help him for a fool! He will find more hard work and no pay than glory in that sort of fun."

"You are not called upon to run the service down here," said the colonel. "Keep to the facts."

"One of them boys [comes up to me," pursued the witness, "and asks me to leave a riding-whip at the house of Mr. Botch, with their compliments, and hopin' that his turning a summysalt in the brook 'adn't addled the little brains he's got. Them was the werry words."

"And you took the whip?" said the mayor, interposing to stop some offensive remark from his brother magistrate.

"Yes," said Daniel Figg; "but I told 'em that I was going t'other way, and shouldn't be back in Smudgem Bender afore Monday morning. They said as it would do."

"Are these the boys?" asked the mayor.

"Not one of 'em was there," said Figg, emphatically.

"And what have you done with the whip?"

"I left it at Mr. Botch's house an hour ago."

Snicker shrank back into the collar of his coat. Botch looked as if he had been knocked down and jumped on.

"I had to come on to Chippenham," continued this valuable witness, "and having an hour or so to wait for a party with a lot of houdans he has to sell, dropped inter the court permiscous."

"The evidence of this witness settles the case," said the mayor, "unless the prosecutor wishes for the prisoners to be put back until his statement is verified."

"Let 'em go," said Botch, huskily.

"I have one comment to make on this case," said the mayor, ignoring a pluck of his gown by the colonel, "and that is, it is a most unwarrantable and, I believe, malicious prosecution, which, I hope, will be taken notice of by the parents of these young *gentlemen*. They are pupils at Littlecote Abbey, I believe?"

"We are, sir," said Jack.

"Then where is your schoolmaster?"

Snicker was preparing to vanish, but Jack promptly pointed him out, and he was ordered to stand forward.

"May I ask," said the mayor, "how it is that you have taken no steps to defend these lads?"

Fontenoy Snicker never looked more like a plain Jerry than he did when he stammeringly tried to explain that he was just going to say something about their general good conduct, when he was cut short by the mayor.

"From what I have heard," he said, "you are, in more ways than one, most unsuitable for a schoolmaster. Your conduct in this matter is very reprehensible."

"But I ain't charged 'em with doing anything," pleaded Snicker.

"Remove that man from the court," said his worship. "My boys, you may go. I advise you to write to your parents, so that they may take steps to get you damages for false imprisonment."

A police officer promptly led Snicker to the door of the court, and, with a short, sharp, offibial jerk, propelled him into the passage outside. Then his hat, which he had left behind, was thrown after him, and, as he was putting it upon his head, Botch came out, looking very yellow about the cheeks and chin.

"I told you that you would go wrong with them," said Snicker. "If they had been ten times guilty, they would have got the upper hand of you."

Botch stared at him in a heavy-eyed manner, breathing hard; but, without making any reply, wobbled out of the building, and wended his way to the nearest inn.

Thither in a few moments the schoolmaster followed him. Both stood keenly in need of a reviver.

CHAPTER LXXVIII.

THE MAID THAT WAS WON BY PENNY BUNN—THE COMING DISCOMFITURE OF SNICKER.

A GREAT change was pending at the Abbey, and would be brought about by a lady who hitherto has not figured in our story.

Her name was Miriam Jaggers, and she was a dressmaker in the village of Smudgem Bender.

She lived alone, which was nothing to her detriment. Her age was something in the forties, and in figure she was inclined to the scaffold-pole order of architecture.

It was this fair maid whose heart had been won by the enterprising Penny Bunn.

They met first one day when the tutor was wending his way home from a walk. It was about the time when he recovered his money from Rooker, and he was in a very smiling mood.

It was a lonely spot, near a stile, and the lady was about to step over. Penny Bunn gallantly offered his assistance, and as they were going the same way, they got into conversation.

To be communicative was part of the nature of the undermaster, as he preferred to be called, and as the new associates had a long way to walk, he had time to put the gentle Miriam into full possesssion of all the important facts connected with the life at the Abbey, and a few things that were entirely the produce of his vivid imagination.

"Snicker," he said, by way of a peroration, "is the presumed master of the school; I am the real one. I have him under my thumb."

"How is that?" was the soft query of the fair one, with a sidelong glance at her companion.

Then Bunn, after just one moment's hesitation, told her of the nature of the lease, and how if anyone communicated with Sir Charles Barstow about the shattered flooring in the room lately occupied by Snicker, that he would be a "gone coon."

"The baronet," he said, with a flourish, "would have him out like a shot, and sue him for wanton damage."

"But you took up the flooring, Mr. Bunn," hinted Miriam Jaggers.

"By his orders, and in ignorance of the clauses in the lease," said Bunn. "I am in no way to blame."

"And suppose the Snickers were turned out," suggested Miriam, "then the school would be broken up?"

"Not if the right man—myself, for instance," returned Bunn, "could get the right side of the baronet. But there's one thing that is the stumbling-block, the lack of filthy lucre. At the present moment my entire capital, save a few pounds, is tied up in some land in India. Negotiations are going on for the sale of it, but things move slowly out there, and it may be a year or two ere the thing is settled. You cannot run a school without capital."

"Or a lady at the head of it—the lawful mistress," murmured Miriam.

"Yes; she is also essential," assented the undermaster, with a tender glance at her.

She blushed, and Penny Bunn, with a resolute movement, offered her his arm.

"You are fatigued," he said; "lean on me."

She leant on him rather heavily, and from that moment they were fast friends.

Before parting, they thoroughly understood each other.

Miriam Jaggers had two hundred pounds in the bank, left her by her father, who was a "china dealer," that is, he was a niggardly old sinner, who,

when alive, travelled about the country with crockery on a cart, and made money by it.

She did not say outright that she was willing to invest this sum in a husband and home, such as the Abbey would be for her, but it was implied, and Penny Bunn returned to the school with his brain teeming with all sorts of wild dreams.

They met as often as they could afterwards, and always in quiet places. Miriam had a cool head, and a knowledge of business habits. She saw light ahead, but bade her lover, which Penny Bunn now was, go ahead steadily, and under her guidance.

She could see that he was a born blunderer, and wanted a steadying hand.

In the course of their love-making, he enlarged upon his imaginary property in India. Having once started "on the job," he was unable to stop.

He even went so far as to declare that he was born there, and used to ride to school when a boy upon an elephant.

On one occasion he asked her how she would like a black servant to fan her in the heat of summer with a "punkah of peacock's feathers," and on her declaring it would be delightful, he made a memorandum of it on an old envelope, so that he might, by the next mail, send out a request "to his agent" to "pick out a few rajahs," and send them over for Miriam to choose from.

"By the time they arrive," he said, with emotion, "I trust that you will be my wifey."

Then he embraced her, and so went forward—to his doom.

Matters were in this condition when Fontenoy Snicker announced to Penny Bunn that his days were numbered at the Abbey.

This declaration being carried to Miriam, she said that a forward movement must be made, and advised her lover to communicate at once with Sir Charles Barstow.

Between them they concocted the following letter:

"To Sir CHARLES BARSTOW :—

"RESPECTED SIR,—It is with considerable hesitation that I write this letter to you, as it may seem to be a betrayal of the interests of my present employer, but a desire to do what is just, and a natural disinclination to be made a party to anything but what is honest, leads me to communicate the following facts to you.

Here followed a statement of the damage done to the bedroom and schoolroom door.

"I should like to add, sir," the letter went on, "that at the time I assisted in the acts of vandalism I was unaware that there was anything in the lease to prohibit such things being done. Moreover, I was led to believe by Mr. Snicker that he was about to purchase the Abbey from you. Now I know it to be false. He is, I am sure, in pecuniary difficulties.

"Finally, sir, I should like to take the Abbey off your hands, if it should be vacated, and give my time to restoring the flooring to its original condition. I have taken care that not a single piece of it has been mislaid, and as I have devoted a considerable portion of my time to the study of ancient inlaid woodwork, the labour entailed would be a pleasure, and the result all you could desire. No charge would be made by me for this work. As stated before, it would be a labour of love.

"Awaiting a communication from you on this important matter, I am, respected sir, your obedient servant,

"Py. Bunn.

"P.S.—If it would not be asking too much, I shall be glad if an appointment could be made for a meeting. I could then more fully explain matters.—PY. B."

Miriam posted this letter with her own hand, and Bunn, feeling that the train of the mine that was to blow Snicker sky-high was laid and fired, returned to the Abbey, and in his elated condition told the boys, in part, the story of his love.

CHAPTER LXXIX.

BOTCH COMPROMISES AN ACTION.—HE IS ASTONISHED, AND COMES OUT STRONG IN THE RIGHT DIRECTION.

THE defeat of Botch in the police-court sent the boys home in an exulting mood, but the chief charm of the matter was that Fontenoy Snicker had "got a towelling," as Bob Stockton put it, as well.

"What did he mean by coming there?" Little Jiggers scornfully. "The mean skunk. I saw him grinning when things looked bad. What could they have done to us if we had been found guilty?"

Don shook his head, and put on his best legal-adviser air.

"Imprisonment, of course," he said; "but I could not tell you for how long within a year or two."

"What!" exclaimed Jiggers, "could they have transported us?"

Then seeing that Bob was laughing, he grinned, and called himself a duffer for having been taken in for a moment.

"The mayor was all right," said Jack, "and I dare say he would have given us a day, which means that we should have been discharged at the rising of the court. But the taint of the prison would have been on us, and that would have suited Snicker. He could have sent us home hopelessly disgraced."

Botch had, as stated, driven into Chippenham, and having had his refreshment, he started for home.

Half-way there he overtook the boys, and reined up beside them, to their great astonishment.

"I want a word with you, boys," he said, and then paused, looking rather foolish.

"The fact is," he went on, with a catching in his breath, "I made a mistake in that there police case, and as I shall have to pay damages sooner or later, I should like to know what will satisfy you?"

Jack and Don exchanged glances. A similar idea was in the mind of each of them.

They exchanged a few whispered words, and then said something to Little Jiggers. He nodded as if in approval.

"Mr. Botch," said Jack, as spokesman for the other two, "you ask what will satisfy us, and we say—*nothing*. We do not want any damages out of you. The fun we have had with you will be set off in our minds as squaring accounts. All we hope is that there will be no malice on either side."

Botch stared, first at one, and then at the others, with an expression of bewilderment upon his face. But it slowly cleared away.

"Do—you—mean—to—say," he said, slowly, "that you are not going to have a shot at me in the law courts?"

"Certainly not," replied Jack, with a smile.

"Well—" began Botch, and then he stopped short, as if quite overcome.

He kept his eyes upon the old roan mare in the shafts, and after a long silence, came abruptly out of his day-dream.

"Will you boys mind getting into my trap?" he said.

"Are you going to give us a lift?" inquired Jack.

"I am, and I want to have a word with you, but I can't say it here. I'm kind of flummaxed, like."

There was room for two more in front, and one got in behind. As soon as they had settled down, Botch gave his steed a whack with a whip, and on they went for home.

Not a word did he utter until he reined up at his gate. Then he bade them get out and come into his house. They obeyed him wonderingly.

He ushered them into the parlour, furnished well, but in a stiff, old-fashioned way, with horse-hair chairs and sofa. There he rang the bell, and in response a prim old dame appeared.

"The girls are busy," she said, looking at the boys with her eyes wide open. "What is it you want?"

"Wine and cake for these lads," replied Botch. "They are good fellows, every one, and as long as I'm on this 'ere farm they will be welcome to drop in whenever they please. I'm a childless man myself," he added, with a curious touch of pathos in his voice. "If I had young 'uns of my own, I might not have been so cantankerous with them of other people."

"A change has come over you," said his wife, as she left the room.

Personally, she had always been fond of children, and taken no part in the occasional warfare with the boys. Now that her husband had changed about, she was entirely satisfied, and quite indifferent as to the reason why.

She brought cake and wine for the boys, and

Botch, "to keep them company," took a little drop of gin-and-water. As an assistant to the clearing of his thoughts, he also lighted a long clay pipe and smoked with the solemnity of a sage.

After they had partaken of a sufficiency of refreshment, and began to talk of leaving, he would not let them go.

"You must come and look at the stock," he said. " I've some shorthorns and Southdowns that will take the wind out of a lot of 'em at the next Royal show."

The spectacle of Botch walking about his farmyard with some of the hitherto much-hated Lambs in tow was almost as much as the men could stand.

To one—it was he who had had that little adventure with Don when he was a prisoner—he seemed to be utterly dazed.

"Master must have been took with the deriddlerum trimmers," he said, in an aside, to a brother yokel. "It don't seem nateral to Oi."

"You lat master be," said the person he addressed, contemptuously; "he ain't got brains 'nuff for him to go wrong on."

Having seen and duly admired the stock—and they were creatures worthy of the fullest admiration—the boys again talked of going.

But, as before, Botch would not hear of it.

"You have got to stay and have a bit of dinner with us," he said.

And stay they did to as good a dinner as ever they would care to sit down to. Botch did the honours, and without referring to any of the disagreeables of the past, which, to say the least, was courteous of him.

At the hour of two, after he had had one pipe after dinner, he at length consented for them to go home.

"But I drives you," he said.

They were nothing loth. It would be a fitting crowning to the events of the morning, and behold, a little later on, they were on their way to the Abbey.

It chanced that they drove up just as Snicker arrived a few yards ahead of them, worn out with the day.

"Hallo there!" roared Botch, "here we are."

Fontenoy Snicker faced about, and on seeing the boys in a dogcart belonging to Botch, with that notable owner driving, he was almost petrified.

"Brought 'em back, you see," said Botch, cheerily. "Now, if you treat them well in the future, they will be good boys to you."

"I always treated them well," said Snicker, with a snarl: "and a nice fellow you must be, with your paltry prosecution, and then cavin' into 'em. How do you think I am going to manage them arter—*after*—this ?"

"Do your best," said Botch. "Now, boys, here you

are. A shake of the hands and we part the best of friends, don't we ?"

"We certainly do," answered Jack, "and if we had known each other before, we need not have ever been enemies."

They shook hands, and the boys hurried into the Abbey, whither Fontenoy Snicker had hurriedly preceded them.

"Everybody is making friends but me," he muttered. "and everybody is against me. Fancy old Botch and the boys cottoning to each other !"

He mentioned it to Mrs. Snicker, whom he found in the dining-room assisting Black-eyed Susan to lay the table for tea.

"What do you think of it ?" he cried.

"I haven't time to think of anything in that way," replied Mrs. Snicker, "I'm so worried with other things."

"What's the matter now ?"

"Oh, the boys have been going on just anyhow," she replied. "Stockton and Hone have been fighting, and the eyes of Hone are quite stopped up. Why don't you stop at home and attend to your business ?"

"Wasn't it my business to go and hear that police case ?" snarled the schoolmaster. "It was my duty to see that the boys were properly defended."

"Now don't lie to me, Jerry," said Mrs. Snicker. Jane pricked up her ears. "You know that you said as you started that you wanted 'em to be sent to prison. You was a talking to yourself in the hall, but I was on the stairs and heard you."

"Well, you needn't talk afore—*before* the gal."

"She heard you, too. We was together, and she's been saying it is shameful of you."

"So it is," said Black-eyed Susan, with spirit. "I should like to know what anyone would think of it ?"

"So them boys have been fighting," said Fontenoy Snicker, abruptly returning to the other subject. "Where did it come off ?"

"In the playground, right under your winder."

"Say *window*, for goodness' sake !" howled Snicker. "And what was Bunn doing ?"

"He was upstairs. I sent for him, and he said as I was to send for a policeman, or take a broomstick to 'em."

"Insolent !" muttered Snicker, between his teeth, "but his time here shall be cut short. The new fellow is coming to-morrow. Get me a cup of tea. I have had a hard day, and not a bit to eat, or a drop to drink have I had, since I left this morning."

"Then you have picked up the hojour of whisky on the way home," returned Mrs. Snicker. "Jerry, the truth isn't in you. Lying comes as nateral to you as blinking them eyes of yours. Jane, put a kettle of water on the fire." The girl left the room, and the loving wife and husband were left together.

"Phœbe," he said, "you are rough on me. I didn't expect it, after what we have suffered together."

She made him no answer, but after glancing up and down the table to see if everything was there, she walked, indifferently, from the room.

"If I could throw off a wife as easily as I shall that fool Bunn, away you would go, my lady, like an old shoe."

CHAPTER LXXX.

HOW THE FIGHT CAME ABOUT.—THE NEW TUTOR IS SEEN AT THE GATE.

IT was quite true that Bob and Hone had been fighting. It was shortly after the school had been dismissed in the morning that it was unexpectedly brought about by their meeting in the hall. Hone was with Rooker, and Bob, coming unexpectedly upon them, heard the former say to the latter:

"I'm with you against the fellows in all things. Don't forget that."

Bob, took no notice of it at the moment, and as he walked straight into the playground the two confederates, who had been startled by his sudden approach, thought that he had not heard a word.

Rooker went upstairs, and Hone adjourned to the playground.

Bob, meanwhile, had called all the youngsters together, and having told them what he heard, asked them what they thought of it?

Only one answer could be expected from them, and it was in condemnation of one of them who could meanly associate himself with a tutor against the whole school.

There was a suggestion that he should be made to run the gauntlet and other punishments to be inflicted upon him, but Bob asked to be allowed to deal with him alone.

"Hone and myself have had many little nigglings," he said, "and it is time affairs came to a head with us. I will talk to him when he comes out."

And when he did come out, Bob walked up to him, and told him he was a sneak and a cur. Hone began to bluster and threaten, and then Bob knocked him down.

Hone had now to fight, or to ever after be at the disadvantage of being called a coward.

Maddened, he whipped off his coat, and Bob having done the same, they went to work.

The boys formed a ring, and kept as quiet as they could to prevent interruption, but it was such a desperate encounter that they could not help cheering at times.

We have heard from Mrs. Snicker that they were not interrupted, and the reason why. The fight went on to the finish, when Hone, cowed, beaten, and blinded for the time, lay upon the ground suffering, with other pangs, the agony of defeat.

Tom Drummond and Whymper helped him to rise, and assisted him to the lavatory, where they washed his face, and bathed his eyes, but they could not open them.

He was a lad inclined to puffiness, and the swelling continued to increase until there was not a vestige of his eyes to be seen.

"You will have to go to bed, old man," said Tom, "and sleep the swellings down."

He went to bed accordingly, and they promised to do what they could to get food and drink for him, and went below to see how it was with Bob.

He had not come off scot-free by any means, for Hone was muscular, and when he got a blow home it told with effect.

Bob had a lovely black eye, as Dorey called it, "quite a picture," and his nose was swollen, but he was in high spirits, and made light of his punishment.

"It was bound to come to it one day," he said, "and it couldn't have happened better. There will be a row with Snicker, of course, but I cannot help that."

But the schoolmaster made no reference to it downstairs. All he did, when he heard that Hone was in bed, was to go up to him.

He thought he saw a chance of making one friend in the school.

"So you have been fighting, Hone?" he said, as he took a seat by the bedside.

He spoke in what he meant to be a kind tone. But Hone answered him, surlily:

"Yes, and suppose I have?"

"Hone," said the schoolmaster, severely, "I did not expect this from you."

"And what did you expect?" asked Hone. "You gave me a thrashing for fastening you in the cellar when Ford was the culprit. What did you care? All you wanted was to thrash *somebody*."

"If Ford did it," said Fontenoy Snicker, "I am sorry."

"Very well. That will do. I have had enough of this place, and as soon as I can get up, I am going to write to my father to take me home. And if you don't refund some of the year's money, he will bring an action against you."

The schoolmaster, whom a sympathising person might very well call "poor old Snicker" in the accepted style of condolence, was now beginning to think that he had arrived at his last plank, and there was nothing left for him but to go under the sea of misery, and end the whole thing.

But he had a considerable amount of tenacity, and he still held on.

"Hone," he said, "it is true I whacked—*thrashed*—you on that day, but why didn't you tell me you had not done it?"

"Because you did not say what it was you punished me for," replied Hone.

"Well, that had something to do with it," said Snicker, thoughtfully, rubbing his chin. "But you don't see things in the right light."

"I can't see at all just now," grunted Hone. "All I know is that I've had enough of this school. It's a regular swindle."

"Hone," said the schoolmaster, "there is such a thing as an **action for libel**." Then he thought of Bibbins, and turned cold. "Not that I would bring such a thing. I couldn't be so mean."

Hone turned round so that his back was to the schoolmaster, and made no reply.

"I am sorry to find you have such a sperrit as this in you," said Snicker, rising. "You can write to your father as soon as you like, and so will I."

He stopped a moment, hoping that the boy would say something, but he continued sulky and silent, so he left him.

It was while the schoolmaster was with him that a letter was brought to the Abbey by one of the tradesmen's men. It came in by the second post, and in the ordinary course would have lain at Smudgem Bender until the next morning, there being no late delivery at the Abbey. But Mrs. Snicker had lately asked for any letters to be sent on when possible. Hence its arrival.

The man, on arriving at the door, met Penny Bunn, who was just going out, and gave it to him, thinking, of course, that he would hand it over to his principal.

The undermaster glanced at the writing, and saw that it was neat and scholarly, evidently the hand of a teacher.

It flashed upon him that it might be from the new tutor, and he thrust it into his pocket.

"I'll see what is in it before Snicker does," he muttered.

For a moment he hesitated, for he knew that he was about to do a very serious thing—bordering on a crime, in fact. It was running a risk, and might get him into serious trouble. But if the new tutor once got into the house, and Bunn dismissed therefrom, his chance of becoming the head thereof would be reduced to a minimum.

Desperate positions induce desperate efforts to escape therefrom, and Penny Bunn, on getting outside the playground, took out the letter, and recklessly tore it open. With feelings we had better not attempt to describe, he read as follows :

"FONTENOY SNICKER, ESQ.

"DEAR SIR,—I am pleased to learn from you that my testimonials are satisfactory, and that I may enter upon my duties at once. Though a native of India, I only passed my boyhood there, and, having spent many years in the schools and colleges of England, I am fully qualified for the post. Your request that my capabilities must be tested before we arrange the terms of payment is, I think, a reasonable one. I have no fear of the result. I purpose arriving at the Abbey on Monday evening next. The train reaches Chippenham about four o'clock, and, as my needs are few, my luggage is light, and I shall walk over with it. Pray do not put yourself out to meet me, unless you think I may lose my way. I am, sir, your obliged and obedient servant,

"CHUNDER LOO."

Penny Bunn, having perused this epistle, thrust it into his pocket, and stared ahead of him. He really could hardly credit the evidence of his senses.

"A nigger," he gasped, "a wily, oily Indian, to take *my* place. And the way the beggar's letter is worded, too! He is up to snuff. What will Miriam think of it?"

He entered the wood, and sat down upon a knoll by the side of the path to think. Something must be done, and promptly, too, for he was certain that if this Chunder Loo once got foothold in the school, he could not be got rid of without a deadly struggle.

Every word of his letter breathed of wiliness, and a sort of serenity that is attached to craft. It was a bit of a crusher, and just at the time when he was preparing to spring a mine upon Snicker. Unconsciously, a countermine had been prepared for him.

Penny Bunn could not make up his mind to any plan of action. He would have given anything, almost, to have had Miriam by his side. Was there time to consult her?

"This nigger must come by way of Smudgem Bender," thought Bunn. "I must keep my eyes open for him."

He hurried down through the wood, meeting nobody.

On the way to the village he only encountered two persons, neither of whom could possibly be the Indian.

One was a gipsy woman, and the other an agricultural labourer, sixty years of age.

He reached the abode of the fair Miriam, and although he had, for propriety's sake, been forbidden to come there, he thought he might venture to call at the door. So he knocked.

There was no answer, and, after a second knock, he rightly came to the conclusion that she was not at home.

As he was turning away, disheartened, he saw a stranger approaching, who was unmistakably Chunder Loo.

He was a taller man than Bunn, and looked taller than he was, owing to the plain, long garment he wore.

It was of a reddish hue, and simplicity itself in cut. It might, in a tailoring sense, be declared to have no cut at all.

So closely did it fit his spare body that, hanging, as it did, down to his ankles, it gave him a very snake-like appearance.

His face was of the hatchet description, long and thin, with dark eyes set close together. In his hand he carried a small, square parcel, about the size of a cash-box.

The latter was no doubt his luggage, of which his needs, as he had stated, were small.

Penny Bunn " sized him up," and thought that he could tackle him verbally or otherwise. But what was he to do with the man?

Suddenly he was inspired with a brilliant thought, and his mind was made up. Advancing, he met the stranger, and raising his hat, said:

"Chunder Loo, I believe?"

"That is my name," was the quiet response, which very composed—most composed. Chunder Loo was evidently a person not to be taken aback by trifles.

"My name is Snicker," said Penny Bunn, recklessly.

There was a slight raising of the Indian's eyebrows, but that was all the acknowledgment of the information he made.

"I came to meet you—not to show you the way to the Abbey," continued the undermaster; "but to make a statement, which I regret must be very painful to you."

Penny Bunn paused to see the effect of his words. Apparently it was nil. Chunder Loo's composure was not at all disturbed. The undermaster being in for a penny, now went forward to the pound.

"I presume," he said, "that while acquiring your knowledge of the English language that you have not neglected our customs and habits?"

"I am English in all things," was the answer, "save in my skin, and, possibly, features."

"Then," said Penny Bunn, briskly, "what do you say to adjourning to the Cowley Arms with me, to partake of some refreshment? It will be better talking there than here."

"I shall be delighted," responded Chunder Loo.

Bunn felt in need of something to strengthen himself, that he might continue to play the part he had begun.

He had also a deeper purpose, and that was to reduce this wily Indian to a state of helpless intoxication, and render him unfit to keep his appointment.

On the morrow Sir Charles Barstow might appear, and then the blow might be struck at Snicker. After that, Chunder Loo was of no consequence whatever.

It was too early for the usual frequenters of the coffee room, and Penny Bunn and Chunder Loo had it all to themselves.

On being asked what he would take, Chunder Loo left it to the undermaster.

"I have acquired a knowledge of all your drinks," he said, in a smooth, musical way, "and have no choice."

"Whisky hot, then," said Penny Bunn.

He ordered sixpennyworths, and they sat down. The offer of a cigar was likewise accepted.

"Now," said Penny Bunn, "let us come to the point of business right away. You cannot come to the Abbey."

"But I have been engaged to come," said Chunder Loo, serenely.

"That is so," assented Penny Bunn, "but, owing to the strong objection of the boys to be taught by a foreigner, I am compelled to rescind the agreement, if it can, indeed, in the present stage of affairs, be so termed."

"Your letters," said Chunder Loo, as he emptied his glass, "are, I am sure, sufficiently binding to make you pay me a month's salary, or, it may be, more, and my expenses down here. That, I presume, you will do?"

"If it is your legal claim," said Bunn, "it will of course be recognised. But I must consult my solicitor first."

"That," said Chunder Loo, "is perfectly fair. You will do so to-morrow, of course?"

"Assuredly," replied Penny Bunn. Then seeing the empty glass, he added: "You will have another with me?"

"I shall be delighted," answered Chunder Loo. "Shall we have a change to brandy this time?"

Penny Bunn sat a moment aghast. But he speedily recovered himself. The mixture might be trying to himself, but he was certain it would be a settler for Chunder Loo.

They had brandy, and continued to converse on the topic of the broken engagement. Chunder Loo was perfectly pliable, to all appearances, and only wanted "what was legal and fair."

He drank his brandy, and the undermaster recklessly did the same. He also suggested something more, and the placid Indian assented, suggesting gin.

"I have tried all your drinks," he said, cool as ever, "and like them every one."

Penny Bunn was now in the state when a man either leaves off or makes a fool of himself. He decided on the latter course without a moment's reflection.

So gin they had, and before the undermaster had got through his potion, he saw two Indians seated opposite him, serenely smoking big cigars.

He was smoking himself, and his weed was apparently a very full-flavoured one.

He had just sense enough to think that he ought to get outside, and he accordingly rose. Holding on to the table, and assuming the attitude of a nigger stump orator, he said :

"Sho' all's shettled. I 'shult shlisheter in the morning. You go backsh town to-nightsh."

"Pardon me," said Chunder Loo, "it will he impossible for me to do so. I am fatigued with my long walk, and intend—if I can be accommodated—to stay at this inn for the night. You had better call on me in the morning, and we can go to your solicitor together."

Penny Bunn was getting into a deep fog, but he saw light in this suggestion. He held out his hand.

"Shunder Loosh," he said, "you are man affer my own heart. Shake hands."

The Indian put forward a long, lean paw, and it closed with the effect of a leather band round the palm of the undermaster. They stood thus for fully a minute, linked together. Emblematical of the future that lay before them was the attitude, Bunn trying to think of something more he had to say, and utterly failing to fish up two consecutive words to the point. Suddenly tearing himself away, he reeled out of the room and from the inn.

He left a half-filled tumbler behind him, which Chunder Loo quietly emptied, and lit his third cigar.

CHAPTER LXXXI.

THE COURSE OF TRUE LOVE IS RUFFLED.—COMMOTION IN THE ABBEY.

ON getting clear of the inn, Penny Bunn shot straight across the road, because he could not help himself, and was pulled up short and sharp against the railings outside a cottage garden.

It was now dark, and there was, fortunately, no witness to this involuntary performance. The shock sobered him a little, but not much. It enabled him, however, to think a bit, and he called to mind the recent interview with Chunder Loo with a feeling of exultation.

"I've nobbled him," he thought—"done him. What will Miriam think of me now?"

Had he given utterance to those thoughts, the words would have been thicker, but no man lisps or stutters mentally, and had he not been the unutterably conceited donkey he was, and more sober, he would have hesitated ere he visited his loved one that night.

But, bursting with pride over the great success of his manœuvre with the Indian, he felt it was his bounden duty to convey an account of it to his Miriam.

Having straightened himself, and taken the bearings of the village, as well as his condition permitted, he started afresh, and, with only three tumbles, and one collision with a post, arrived at her abode.

There was a light in her window, the room in which she worked, and his heart throbbed with joy.

"My loved one, I come," he murmured, as he kissed his finger-tips.

He bore towards the door, but halted on the step, and laid a finger on his nose.

"Shstay," he said, half-aloud, "am I fit for shiety of peerless beauty? Berrer have resht. Shoon be all right."

And where could he rest better than upon the threshold of her home? Accordingly, he gently subsided upon the doorstep, and, laying his head against the lintel of the door, fell asleep.

Now, Miriam Jaggers had a little dog, a yapping little mongrel she had named Dolphus, being, presumably, an abbreviation of Adolphus.

It was her custom, about this hour of the night, to open the door and let him out for a short run before retiring for the night. He slept on a mat at the foot of her bed, at once a companion and a protector.

The manner of letting out was as follows :

Miriam would rise at the usual time, and say : "Come, Dolphy, and look for cats."

Then Dolphy would immediately become the victim of a mad excitement, and, the moment the door was opened, shoot out like a cannon-ball, and tear down the road, barking and yelping, to the everlasting wrath of all who heard him.

Miriam, little suspecting the presence of her lover, opened the door, and Dolphus, who was a canine idiot, without any nose to speak of, or he would have smelt a stranger around, shot out, and was brought up short by colliding with Penny Bunn, striking him in the small of the back with tremendous force.

Dolphus rolled over, stunned, and Penny Bunn woke up. Miriam, on seeing the figure of a man, apparently rising from the ground, in the gloom, began to scream for the police.

Bunn rubbed his back, and then his eyes, hazily wondering what had happened, and where he was.

By the exercise of considerable mental exertion, he got at a dim knowledge of things, and rising, with a sickly smile upon his lips, he lurched towards his betrothed, who was leaning against the passage wall like a frozen figure.

"All's clear, Mirum," he said, thickly; "we ash good as in Rabbey."

"Monster," she gasped, "away !"

"'Way?" he said, dismally; "wharfore?"

"On, this is cruel," said Miriam, beginning to sob; "look at poor Dolphus. You have slain him."

Following her outstretched finger, Penny Bunn's eyes beheld the form of that hapless dog, lying quite still and apparently dead.

"Bless me," he said, "who did it?"

Miriam reeled towards the prostrate pet, and picking him up in her arms, carried him into her little parlour.

Penny Bunn staggered after her, and dropped upon a chair.

"Mirum," he said, "life's nothing without you."

"Go away," she said, wearily, "you are intoxicated."

"I am heart-broken," he replied, as he brushed away a tear. "I am not tossicated. Never was in my lifsh. Tossicated! _Me!_ Mish Jaggersh, you forget the man you 'dressing."

"If you don't go away," said Miriam, "I'll scream again, and have you locked up."

"Mish Jaggersh," said Penny Bunn, rising and holding on by the table, "I am not the man to remain where not wanted. Seemsh to me that you think you only woman in the world. It not so, by long chalksh. There are two, three lovely—girls—in the 'jacent town of Chippenham ready for me to speaksh. It a great mishtake on your part to throw 'way man like me. Good nightsh."

He made for the door, intending to depart in his most dignified manner. His exit was, however, a partial failure, owing to his colliding with the door of the parlour, and falling over the mat in the passage. But he got out at last, and to show how little he cared for the woman who had sent him forth, he, on reaching the open air, burst into song.

"Of all the gu-u-u-urls that are so-o-o smart,
There's no-o one like pretty Sa-a-ally.
She is my own ja-a-am tart.
And lives in Chippenha-a-am Walley."

"Walloy," said Bunn, gravely. "That won't do. _Valley_, as our friend Snicker would say. Mirum! You've made a false move to-night, my gu-u-url. Already I was tiring of thee, and thou has left me free to choose a wife from the ranks of refinement. I'll do it. Now P. Y. Bunn, Esquire, steady yourself, and don't give way to motion—Emotion—hang it! I hope I am not going to take on Snicker's lingo, as well as his school. Now for Rabbey."

Earlier in the evening Fontenoy Snicker had been terribly upset by the reception of a telegram.

In the first place, owing to the position of the Abbey, he had to pay two shillings porterage, it being over three miles from the nearest telegraph station. In the second place, the message was full of portent of coming trouble.

It was from Sir Charles Barstow.

"Coming to visit Abbey in a day or so. Hope to find everything in order."

"Everything in order!" gasped Snicker. "What _will_ he say when he goes into that room upstairs. I can't hope for him to pass it over this time. Phœbe!" he roared out.

"What do you want now?" asked his wife, from an inner room, where she was busy with some household matter.

"Come and see what I want," he rejoined, tartly. "I don't want to holler—_halloa_—for all the world to hear."

Mrs. Snicker came to the doorway, and standing there, said, curtly:

"Now, then, tell me what it is."

"Sir Charles Barstow is coming again."

"Oh, is he?"

"And he 'opes—ho'es—_hopes_—to find everything in order."

Mrs. Snicker smiled grimly.

"You had better be packing your portmantle, Jerry," she said. "You will have to go this time. Not content with sp'iling your bedroom, you must go and bust up——"

"_Burst_, woman!"

"Bust," calmly insisted Mrs. Snicker. "It was bust with you when you were in the 'tater line, also when you was a cheap showman, and bust it will be with me until I die. You've bust up the schoolroom door. Sir Charles will have you out in a chinkling."

"Twinkling," said Snicker. "Now, Phœbe, we've been on good terms latterly, and I don't see why we should again go in for the old wrangling. Sir Charles won't be here for days perhaps. He's a slow old party, and takes his time always. Couldn't you and I do something with that floor?"

"We might."

"A woman is handier than a man in these 'ere small jobs."

"Small jobs!" echoed Mrs. Snicker. "I think it will be a big one. Where is the flooring to come from?"

"Why, there's the material left, isn't there?—a little broken up, but it can be fitted together."

"Not in this world," said Mrs. Snicker, shaking her head; "it's all burnt."

"It's all—all—_bur-rnt!_" gasped Snicker. "Who burnt it?"

"We was short of kindling for the kitchen fire, and I told Jane she could use the stuff. It was nothing but chips."

Fontenoy Snicker leant back in his chair, tightly grasping the arms of it, and staring straight at his cool, unmoved spouse with the wild gaze of an Indian idol.

"Used for kindling!" he said, in a slow, methodical

A SPLENDID SCHOOL STORY.

NEVER BEFORE PUBLISHED.

By E. HARCOURT BURRAGE,

Author of "Ching Ching," "Monkey Mat and Roving Dick," "The Brave Boy of the Basilisk," &c.

THE LAMBS OF LITTLECOTE.

A THRILLING SCHOOL STORY.

HAULING IN THE PROVISIONS FOR THE FEAST OF CELEBRATION.

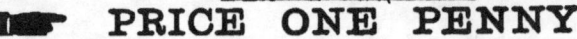 **PRICE ONE PENNY.**

way, as if he was trying to get at the meaning of the words. "A floor worth *hundreds* used for the kitchen fire. You idjot!"

"Idiot, Jerry, dear," said Mrs. Snicker, "since you must use the word. The wood only littered up the room, and you didn't say it was vallyble. You and that miserable wretch, Bunn, had both tried your hand at putting together the floor, and couldn't do it. How was I to know that you would care to try it again?"

Fontenoy Snicker jumped up with a howl, and, tearing off one of his slippers, hurled it at the head of his offending wife. It was a poor, feeble act, almost childish in one way, but it was a spark to very inflammable matter. Mrs. Snicker promptly fired up.

"Two can play at that game, Jerry," she said.

Snicker was rather great in plaster busts. He was imbued with the belief that they gave an air of learning to a room, and there were many upon brackets about the house.

One of Archimedes was handy for Mrs. Snicker, and seizing it, she hurled it at her husband, striking him between the eyes, smashing the cast, and covering him with plaster of Paris.

Then, as he stood there using language not fit for refined society, she went for him.

Although she was, in ordinary times, rather afraid of her Jerry, she was, when roused, a dangerous woman.

We need not go into the details of the punishment she inflicted upon him. He fled from the room, and she followed him. Outside there was a long broom, which she laid hold of, and, like a Malay inspired to run amuck by the possession of a knife, she scampered after him, swinging the weapon over her head.

He was a coward, as we knew, and terror took possession of him. It was the feeling of one pursued by a murderous savage. He wanted a place of refuge, and was not particular where it was. In his flight, he ran in the direction of the schoolroom, and, opening the door, he rushed in.

The boys were there, getting up their lessons for the morrow, and, in surprise and alarm, they jumped up from their seats.

If Fontenoy Snicker hoped to escape from his wife by taking refuge there, he made a great mistake. She cared for nothing and nobody, not she, and dashing in at his heels she, in the presence of the boys, gave him three hard blows with the broom handle, and laid him prostrate upon the floor.

"There," she said, "you keep your slippers to yourself in the future. Throw one at me again, and I'll kill you outright."

Taking no notice whatever of the boys, she marched out with the broom upon her shoulder, a striking and impressive specimen of the latter-day Amazon.

Surely now the humiliation of Fontenoy Snicker was complete.

Thrashed by a woman, and before the boys!

Was there any deeper depth for him to be plunged into?

He got upon his feet with aching bones, and endeavoured to explain matters, instead of leaving them for the youngsters to make the best or worst of them as they pleased. Fool that he was! It was making another rod for his wretched back.

"Mrs. Snicker," he said, "is a bit excited to-night. I don't hold *her accountable for all she does.* I must get a doctor to see her."

The inference to be drawn from this was plain. He imputed insanity to his wife, but, as far as the boys were concerned, it fell flat.

When he had shuffled out of the room and gone his way, the general joy was very complete. Even Hone, with his two "all highly-coloured" eyes, joined in the demonstration.

Some gave vent to their feelings in laughter, others cut capers, and Whymper called for three cheers for Mrs. Snicker, which were heartily given.

And Snicker outside, with his ear to the keyhole, heard it all, and groaned in spirit.

"I thought, weeks ago, that I had as much as I could bear," he muttered, "but what I had then was in *ounces*: now I have to bear it in *pounds*. I don't think that I can bear anything more without going——"

He stopped short and shuddered. Might not that which he had falsely imputed to his wife recoil upon himself? How long would he be able to endure the strain upon him without going *mad?*

CHAPTER LXXXII.

LETTERS AND OTHER THINGS.—A NOBLE MIND O'ER-THROWN.

ON the following morning several important missives were delivered at the Abbey. By post there were letters for some of the boys, which Black-eyed Susan saw were delivered to them without being pried into by the schoolmaster or his wife.

It is possible that neither would have cared to interfere with the correspondence on that particular occasion, for both were in a sorely troubled state of mind, and, in the case of Snicker, of the body also.

He did not rise at his usual hour, being stiff and sore from the chastisement he had received from his wife, who, woman-like, was sorry, now that her passion had evaporated, that she had given way to her wrath.

It had opened up quite a new era of her married life, and it was not a pleasant one to contemplate.

In contrast to her violence on the previous evening, she was now all kindness to her husband.

She took up to his bedroom a breakfast of tempting toast and eggs, and, although she was very brusque in her manner, there was no sting in her words.

"You shouldn't aggravate me, Jerry," she said, "but you never had any sense, and don't know how to treat a woman."

"How can you expect me to have any sense," pathetically asked Snicker. "if you knock it all out of me with a broomstick?"

Mrs. Snicker went away without favouring him with an answer to this very direct question.

There was a letter for Don that morning from his mother, and another from Lingo. The former was of the usual class, loving, kind, with a few words of well-meant advice and a post-office order for five shillings.

Lingo's letter was a brief statement that he was going very well, and hoped one day to see his young friends again. Meanwhile he was preparing to dispose "of a lot of old iron and stuff," which he believed would sell amazingly well, as "there was a great demand for it."

"Genuine old iron and other metals [one paragraph stated] fetch almost any money just now. Hoping to see you one day, your affectionate friend.—OGNIL."

"I suppose," said Don, "that it is just as well he should be absent from here for a time."

"You may leave Lingo to do the right thing," replied Jack Ford. "He is as cute as a fox, and as honest as the sunlight."

It promised to be rather a lively morning in the schoolroom, for it was early known that Fontenoy Snicker would not take his usual seat, and Penny Bunn, who had not, as a matter of fact, been able to get into the Abbey on the previous night without rousing everybody, which he was not willing to do, having slept in the wood shed on a pile of empty sacks, was not in a condition to do justice to the work. Rooker, as heretofore, hardly counted as an assistant.

Most people who had been spending a night as Penny Bunn had done would look very queer, but few would have presented a more miserable appearance than the undermaster did as he took his seat at the desk allotted to him.

He was white, and yellow, and green about the face and cheeks; no chameleon ever presented on a single occasion such a variety of colour. Externally he was a horrible picture, internally he was a boiling cauldron of remorse.

He had quarrelled with the only woman who had ever inclined towards him, and in addition had shut himself out from the prospect of being the master of the Abbey.

He could not take the post without means and a wife. Miriam had the money, and she would have, as he believed, made him a suitable partner in life.

And now he had quarrelled with and insulted her. It was all the work, in an indirect way, of Chunder Loo. He cursed the lithesome Indian with all his heart, as he prepared for the duties of the morning.

"Boys," he said, wearily, "owing to the absence of our respected principal, the main labours of the morning fall upon me. You can see that I am not well, and I trust you will give me as little trouble as possible. I am a great sufferer from *suppressed gout*, which I inherit from my ancestors, who were heavy drinkers of port wine. It was the habit of the period so to do. But the times have changed, and we drink no more. At least, only what is sufficient for the requirements of health. We will now proceed."

And proceed they did, in a fashion that would have driven a conscientious schoolmaster to the verge of distraction.

Boys are but mortal, and when they get a chance of "taking a rise" out of their teachers and superiors, they are sure to do it. The morning was a record one.

They scamped their tasks, larked among themselves, made all sorts of jokes at the expense of Bunn, drew caricatures of him upon their slates, and enjoyed themselves thoroughly.

Penny Bunn was too weak and shaky to even remonstrate with them. He sat quietly, bearing it all, and longing for twelve o'clock to arrive.

It was close upon that hour when a man, wearing a seedy suit of black, and carrying "lawyer's clerk" upon his face, appeared at the door of the Abbey. He rang the bell, and when Black-eyed Susan responded, he asked to see Mr. Snicker.

"He isn't well," replied Susan, "and can't get up."

"But he will see *me*," said the stranger, insinuatingly, "when you tell him that I have brought the present for him. I was to be sure to deliver it into his own hands."

"I'll tell him, sir," said the girl, "but I don't think he will see you. Won't missus do?"

"No," answered the man, "the present is for Mr. Snicker, and his wife isn't to know anything about it. Will you tell him so?"

Black-eyed Susan faithfully delivered the message, and Snicker asked her to show the man up. He wondered who could possibly have sent him a present his wife wasn't to know anything about. Perhaps it came from some lady in the neighbourhood who had taken a liking to him. Such things happened to other men, and why not to him?

So the man was shown up, and Susan shut him in by closing the door.

"Mr. Snicker, I believe?" the man said.

"That is my name," replied the schoolmaster

"I have something for you," continued the stranger, producing a piece of blue paper about six inches long, by four broad, and a strip of parchment—"a writ, at the suit of Signor Tappilooni, for one hundred pounds for the loss of a barrel organ and deprivation of means of living. This is the original, if you would care to see it."

He laid the slip of blue paper upon the bed, and Snicker, who was propped up with pillows, looked vacantly at it.

Not getting any reply to his remarks, the man who had so successfully served the writ slipped out of the room, and departed from the Abbey chuckling.

Fontenoy Snicker did not move for awhile, but kept his eyes upon the blue paper, fascinated thereby as if he had been a poor sparrow under the gaze of a hawk.

At length he slowly bent forward, and looked closer at it. Then he picked it up, and held the legal missive at arm's length.

"A present," he groaned; "wife not to know. I wish she had been here to get hold of that chap. *He'd 'a'* gone away hopping, I reckon. But what does it mean? Have I *stole* a barrel organ? Stop! I remember two thievish grinders at the gate. But *where* is the organ? I haven't it. I'm piled up now. Go it, all of you; Fontenoy Snicker is on the p'int—*point*—of being bust up. Don't spare him—tread on him—*crush* him. Ha, ha!"

"Good gracious, Jerry!" exclaimed Mrs. Snicker, thrusting her head into the room, "if you can't laugh at a joke better than that, don't do it at all."

"Phœbe," he answered, wildly, "the time has come for me to be done for, right orf—*off*. I'm an all-round ruined man. Never mind, we will have just the least possible drop together, and be merry while we can."

Mrs. Snicker closed the door, and, on the landing outside, stood for a moment wringing her hands.

"I've been afeard of it," she groaned; "there's been too much put upon his poor brain. He's gone clean demented. I must get the doctor to see him, in case he should be violent with it. I should be sorry to see him in a strait waistcoat, but it will be better for him to have one on, rather than have him work ruin and mischief. His eyes is as wild as a mad March hare's."

Ten minutes later, Black-eyed Susan was hurrying off to fetch the doctor to see her master, who was raving and tearing, and Mrs. Snicker, instead of supplying her husband with the "least drop possible," in spite of his continuous roaring for it, was keeping guard over his bedroom door with the original broom.

CHAPTER LXXXIII.

CHUNDER LOO COMES TO THE ABBEY.—BUNN'S DESPAIR.

EITHER Black-eyed Susan could not find a doctor —there was really only one within reach of the Abbey, and he resided in Smudgen Bender—or she did not attempt to carry out her mission, for at noon the required medical man had not appeared, and she had not returned.

The boys were dismissed, and hurried into the playground, unconscious of the serious state of the schoolmaster's domestic affairs. Mrs. Snicker, meanwhile, tired of keeping on guard, had secured the door of the bedroom with a string, and come downstairs.

She met the boys as they were trooping out, and asked them not to make so much noise.

"You have done for Mr. Snicker," she said, "and you must now have a little mercy on me."

"*We* done for Snicker?" exclaimed Short, in disgust; "was it us who handled the broom?"

"I wonder what is the matter with him?" said Gyp Tanner. "He must be bad, as he hasn't been down all the morning."

"Got connubial affection on the brain, I should think," suggested Short.

It was not to be expected that the boys would be overwhelmed with grief on account of their tyrant's condition, but they were possessed of sufficient good feeling to restrain their youthful spirits for fully three minutes after they were in the playground. Then the usual noises began to rise in the air, and Jack Ford called some of the most vehement to order.

"If you want to kick up all that row," he said, "pop outside the gate, and let fly there. Snicker has been a brute to us, but if he is really bad, we need not kill him outright."

The suggestion was acted upon by the majority of the youngsters, and there was quite a lively party by the wood, later on, when a sinuous Oriental emerged therefrom. It was Chunder Loo.

He was soon marked, and as he stopped, bowing and smiling, he was speedily surrounded by the boys, who wondered what had brought him there.

"Pupils of Mr. Snicker, I presume," he said, in a voice that was like the high notes of a flute.

"We are the Littlecote Lambs," they roared in concert.

"And we don't want any rhubarb to-day," squeaked some boy from behind.

"Pardon me," said Chunder Loo; "but I am not a native of Turkey, but a son of India, who has been reared in England, and acquired English habits and tastes. I wish to see the principal of the college."

"You can't," said Bedstone; "he is in bed with the broomstick fever."

"Again pardon me," said the unmoved Chunder Loo. "What fever did you say?"

"The broomstick fever," replied the unabashed Bedstone; "he caught it from Mrs. Snicker."

"It is a complaint I have never heard of," said the Oriental, placidly. "Is it infectious? I am not afraid of it, but it is as well to know."

A perfect riot of opinions was poured in upon him by the boys. One said that the fever was infectious when you caught it. Another said that it was more fatal than the original plague, and twice as nasty. Bob Stockton said that it was nothing when you were used to it. And Chunder Loo listened with the gravity of a judge who hears counsel wrangling over some point in the law.

In the midst of all sorts of confusing remarks upon the subject of Snicker's ailment, Penny Bunn emerged from the house, and came across the playground. He did not see Chunder Loo, who was in a stooping, listening attitude, as one who is endeavouring to get at the meaning of a multitude of utterances, and was well upon him ere he saw his *bête noir* in the thick of the crowd of boys.

At the same moment, Chunder Loo saw him, too, and straightened himself up as a preliminary to a most elaborate bow. The boys became silent.

"I presume," said Chunder Loo, "that I am addressing one of the officials of the establishment?"

Penny Bunn gave vent to a gasp of surprise. Was it possible that the Oriental had failed to recognize him? If so, it was, in a sense, a great relief.

The undermaster rose to the occasion.

"I am," he said, "the second master of Littlecote Abbey College."

He spoke in a deep, sepulchral tone, to add to the hiding of his identity.

Chunder Loo bowed again.

"That being the case," said Chunder Loo, "I may appeal to you to conduct me to the presence of the master."

This was about the last thing Penny Bunn would have willingly have done on his own account, and he made an effort to fence with the matter.

"Mr. Snicker," he said, "being indisposed, I can give you any information you may require."

"My business," replied Chunder Loo, "is with the headmaster alone, and I must see him."

"He is in bed."

"He may be up presently."

"Not for hours."

"I can wait."

Nothing could be more polite, and at the same time more firm, than the bearing of Chunder Loo. Penny Bunn felt that he was being cornered.

"I cannot take any message for you," he said, "nor can I permit you to intrude upon my superior, in the present stage of his indisposition."

Chunder Loo slightly raised his eyebrows, and stroked his hatchet face.

"At least," he said, "I may be permitted to see the lady of the house?"

"Tell me what you want," said Penny Bunn, desperately.

Chunder Loo shook his head.

"It is a most serious matter," he said, "but all I want with him is a few words ere I sail for India. I have this morning taken my passage for Calcutta and I must see him ere I depart."

"If you are really going away," said Penny Bunn, with sudden briskness, "that is another matter. Please to step into the Abbey, and I will see what can be done for you."

Chunder Loo bowed his thanks, and followed him into the Abbey. Behind the pair came all the boys in an irregular train.

The Oriental had his parcel of clothes, or whatever he considered his luggage, with him, and as he glided into the house, he gently swung it to and fro.

Bunn dared not look back upon him, for he was in mortal fear of his being recognised. Chunder Loo made no sign of having met him before.

Into the hall they went, and Penny Bunn asked the visitor to take a seat. Instead of doing so, the Oriental opened the door of the sitting-room and walked in.

Mrs. Snicker was there engaged in mending socks. She rose up in some trepidation, hardly knowing what to make of the visitor. She half-feared that he was another of those phantasies of the brain which she believed she had of late been troubled with. Bunn stood upon the threshold, ready to put in a suitable word.

"Mrs. Snicker?" said Chunder Loo.

"That is my name," she replied.

"Permit me to kiss your hand as your most humble slave."

Royalty could not have done it better. Mrs. Snicker, having got over her first fright, was charmed.

"I am the new undermaster," said Chunder Loo: "at your leisure I shall be glad if you will instruct one of your dependents to show me my room."

"Mr. Snicker said something about your coming," said Mrs. Snicker, "but I wasn't aweer that it was settled."

"It is quite settled," said Chunder Loo: "last night we ratified the agreement."

Mrs. Snicker was puzzled. She had heard of the coming of a new master, and understood from her husband that he was of foreign extraction, but she was not prepared for anything quite so pronounced in that direction as Chunder Loo.

"My husband is asleep," she said. "He is poorly, having got an attack of depressed gout, which allus flies to his 'ead. You had better wait until he wakes up."

"May I be permitted to spend the time in your charming society?" inquired Chunder Loo.

"Certainly," answered Mrs. Snicker.

"Then I need not trouble you any more," said Chunder Loo, turning suddenly upon the staggered Penny Bunn. "Thanks, many."

"May I be allowed to say one word?" asked Bunn, with a flushed face. "This intrusion is to me the most unwarrantable proceeding. I———"

"Pardon me," interposed Chunder Loo, "a lady is present. If you have anything to say about the conduct of Mr. Snicker, please to reserve it for a more fitting occasion."

Then in a moment Penny Bunn, hardly conscious of being pushed, so gentle was the movement, found himself outside the room, and the door quietly shut in his face.

He reeled to the nearest chair, and sat down. Here was a situation that was for the time too much for him.

"The black beast!" he muttered, his eyes out of his head with despair. "I'll bet anything he knows me. It is his cheek. Ruin, stark, staring ruin, is before me. Oh, Miriam, if I had not been a fool and offended *thee*, now would have been the time to prove the stuff you are made of."

He jumped up, dashed his hat to the ground, then picked it up again, and kicked it half-way up the stairs. After a few wild gestures, expressive of hatred and bloodshed, he bounded up after it, and took refuge in his room.

———

CHAPTER LXXXIV.

MORE STRANGERS FOR BUNN.—CHUNDER LOO IN FULL POSSESSION OF THE FIELD.

AFTER a short rest in the sanctitude of his room, Penny Bunn once more roused himself to action, and, with a determined expression of face, sought the chamber of his principal.

Without any ceremony—he was past all that—he opened the door and walked in. Snicker, just aroused from sleep, struggled up to a sitting position, and savagely asked him what he wanted.

"Sir," said Penny Bunn, "a nigger has just put in an appearance in this abode, and is exercising his impudence by virtually ousting *me* without ceremony.

He says that he has been engaged by you to supplant me—a cruel thing, after such a long and faithful service."

"I don't know nothing about faithful service," replied Snicker, curtly, "not having seen it in you or anybody else, but it is certain that in the present state of affairs I don't want any niggers trotting round my place. I asked him to write to say when he was coming. Why didn't he do it?"

Penny Bunn flushed. Too well he knew how it was that his principal had not been informed of the coming of Chunder Loo.

"I may inform you, sir," he continued, "that this man is a most impudent and unduly familiar fellow I left him practically *cuddling* Mrs. Snicker in the parlour."

"Well, if she don't mind being cuddled by a nigger," said Snicker, indifferently, "I see no need to interfere. Anything else?"

"I want to know what is to be done with him?" said Penny Bunn.

"Go and fight him for the place," replied Snicker, lying back again. "Chuck him out, if you are man enough. Do what you like with him. I don't want him, but if he suits Mrs. Snicker, I have no objection to his remaining. I'm tired of the whole show. D'ye hear?"

"I know nothing about shows," answered Bunn, meaningly, "not even penny shows"—Snicker winced—"but, in defence of my rights, I will act upon your instructions. I will eject this blackamoor. There goes the dinner-bell. After the meal I will proceed to action."

"Proceed to Jericho if you like!" growled Snicker.

"It will be a memorable struggle," muttered Penny Bunn, "unless this swarthy menial thinks proper to depart."

He left the schoolmaster, who seemed to be quite resigned to his fate, and strode down the stairs to the dining-room. The boys were all in, and the door stood open. Seated in his accustomed chair, the enraged under-master beheld Chunder Loo calmly carving the joint, a round of cold boiled beef.

For a moment he was positively blind with rage, and then he felt that now or never the day must be won. Assuming a calmness that was not by any means felt by him, he walked into the room and up to his usual seat.

"Thanks," he said, "obliged to you for beginning for me. I am prepared to go on."

"There is a seat reserved for you," replied Chunder Loo, smoothly, "down at the other end of the table. Permit me to assist you to some beef. Do you care for fat?"

The fall of a pin would have had a startling effect upon the listeners, so still were they. Penny Bunn was in a statuesque condition for several seconds, and then he made a last effort to stand up for his rights.

"Until my time here has expired," he said, "my place is at the head of the table."

"I should be happy to evacuate the post," replied Chunder Loo, with quiet but overwhelming courtesy, "but for the fact that it is by the request of the lady of the house I assumed it. It would be a bad beginning here for me if I disobeyed her slightest wishes."

"I take it," said Penny Bunn, with dilated nostrils, "that you mean to stick to that seat?"

"I do," was the reply, given in a sweet, dulcet tone of voice.

Penny Bunn began to roll up the cuffs of his coat in a very demonstrative manner. Expectation lighted up the eyes of the boys. A struggle between the old and new usher for supremacy would have been delightful. But it was not destined to come off just then.

Chunder Loo continued to do the honours of the table with an immovable serenity.

He cut himself a plate of beef, looked round the table, suggested to some of the boys that they might require more, and asked Tom Drummond to pass the potatoes. He was no more impressed by the threatening demonstrations of Penny Bunn than a blind and deaf man would have been.

"For the moment you triumph," hissed the deposed tutor, "for on reflection I forbear to exercise violence on one so worthless as you. I have a legal remedy, and I shall avail myself of it at once. My solicitor at Chippenham will take action at law."

"You had better dine before you go," suggested Chunder Loo, sweetly; "it is a long way to walk."

Penny Bunn, scorning to hold further conference with such a man, stalked from the room, and ascended again to the chamber of his principal, at whom he intended to fire a parting shot.

"Snicker," he said, as he thrust his head into the door, "I am going."

"Very well," was the answer.

"And I am about to enter an action against you for unlawful dismissal. I shall also expose the school management to the world."

"Do exactly what you like, I say," snorted Snicker: "do you think that it matters to me *now* what you do? Blaze away, the lot of you. I'm an old sea hulk, riddled through and through, and agoing down fast to the bottom of the deep blue sea."

"You are an old fool," said Bunn. "I am sorry for you. Keep an eye on Mrs. Snicker and the nigger. Good day!"

He closed the door as the enraged schoolmaster hurled a pillow at him, and hastened to his room.

There he packed up his few effects in a wooden box with only one hinge and a small portmanteau without straps.

He corded both, and labelled them thus:

P. Y. BUNN, Esq.,
CARE OF LADY TOLLEMARCH,
BELGRAVE SQUARE. LONDON.

It is almost needless to state that he knew nothing of Lady Tollemarch. It was the name of an aristocratic family that cropped up in his mind at that moment, nor had he so much as set his eyes on Belgrave Square since he was born, but he loved to make effect on the slightest provocation, and felt that, when Mrs. Snicker read those labels, she would feel that a bright light had gone out of her home.

It consoled him a little, but not much.

As he departed from the Abbey, he felt intensely miserable. It was so different to what he expected.

Then there was the additional misery of having shattered the heart of his Miriam, who, of course, must despise him. Could he have flown to her and laid his sorrows and troubles before her, she might have pitied him but for his having so hopelessly disgraced himself.

"But now," he cried, with a wail, "I must go forth into the world alone, and what I am to do for a living I can't tell. In a month I shall be down to the match trade—retail—with the streets for my place of business, or perhaps I shall be going in for 'Cards of the races, gents,' or dying in casual wards—supplanted by Chunder Loo, a Blackamoor, a skinny Othello, a human eel. I wish I had poisoned him last night."

Bewailing his lot, breathing threats, and uttering vain regrets, he strode on through the wood, intending to call at the carrier's and request him to bring on his box to Chippenham Station. Then he asked himself if he should venture to call, for the last time, on Miriam Jaggers, and was still debating the matter with himself, when Smudgem Bender hove in sight.

Meanwhile Chunder Loo presided at the table until dinner was over.

He was such an amazing problem to the boys that they did not venture on any breach of discipline during the meal, but conducted themselves with unexampled propriety.

He, on his part, did not appear to be conscious of anything unusual in his sudden elevation to the post of tutor, or to be disturbed in any way by the novelty of his surroundings. If he had been tutor there for several years, he could not be more at home.

There was a hubbub of voices in the playground during the short time allowed for recreation, and the cause of it was Chunder Loo.

"Who is he?" was the general question. "Are we really to have him in the place of Penny Bunn?"

Herbert May declared that he looked like the

magician in the play of "Aladdin," only "more wicked and sly." But opinion was divided about the character of the stranger.

Some thought him a demon, others were inclined to think that he was not a bad sort of a fellow, but all agreed that he had been too much for Penny Bunn.

"Poor old chap," said Don. "I never saw a man so flummaxed. I wonder where he is."

"He is not in the Abbey," replied Bedstone, "and his boxes are labelled, as I suppose, for the carrier to take away. I peeped into his room and saw them."

"He will turn up again," said Bob Stockton, confidently: "he will not let that Oriental chap have it all his own way."

When the boys were summoned by the bell into the schoolroom, they found Chunder Loo there before them. He had taken possession of Fontenoy Snicker's desk, and was calmly looking over the books.

The youngsters slipped quietly into their seats, and sat still until, as they expected he would, he addressed them.

"Boys," he said, "I see that the line taken by your principal is, in an educational sense, rather crude. I must presume that Mr. Snicker is not an educated man."

"He is a duffer," blurted out Little Jiggers, and a general titter followed.

"The term used by my young friend," said Chunder Loo, singling out the speaker with his eye, "is not a portion of the accepted language of Great Britain and Ireland, but as it has got into common use in schools, I must allow it to pass. I shall, however, endeavour to introduce here a more refined tone than appears to exist at present. Though a native of another land, I have been through a course here that makes me English in everything but my skin."

He paused, turned over the leaves of a book, and frowned.

"I fear," he resumed, amidst a breathless silence, "that ere I can enter on the new code of instruction, which I consider is essential to you all, much has to be done. My conscience will not allow me to proceed with the methods I here find have been in use. Therefore, I feel it incumbent on myself, owing to the unavoidable absence of Mr. Snicker, to give you all a half-holiday."

The boys did not cheer, nor utter a sound, or for a moment or two make a movement, they were so utterly taken aback by this unexpected termination of the address.

"It is due to Mr. Snicker," pursued Chunder Loo, "that I should consult the principal of the college before making fresh arrangements. He is not in a state of health to be troubled to-day. Boys, you may go."

They went out in comparative silence, too much astonished to express their pleasure at the boon of an additional outing. In the hall they took down their caps and went out. In the playground the general feeling was embodied in a few words, uttered by Whymper:

"I never saw anyone like him. I'm flabbergasted."

Then they went forth, still wondering what manner of man had come to guide them through the intricate paths of learning, and slowly wended their way through the wood.

CHAPTER LXXXV.

LOVE TRIUMPHS OVER ALL.—SIR CHARLES BARSTOW ARRIVES.

LEAVING the boys to make the best of their unexpected holiday for a time, we must follow Penny Bunn.

It was well for him that, in his desperation, he resolved to pay a last visit to his lady-love. Having been, in a way, cast off by her, he could not suffer much loss by having another dose of rejection. The question was, what line of action was he to take?

He could call upon her, of course, but as he had always been forbidden to do so, he thought it would be risky. The better plan would be to hover around her residence and see if she would come out to greet him with sweet words of forgiveness, or order him away on peril of being moved on by the police.

That she would do one or the other he was pretty well assured, and, assuming an agonising expression of repentance, he pulled up opposite her abode.

He did not look towards the house, but he could see her out of the corner of his eyes working near the window. He feigned to be so abstracted in his misery, that he was unconscious of being so near her.

Leaning against a garden wall on the other side of the road, he put a hand against his side and groaned. If he had been in mortal pain, he could not, by his face, have expressed deeper anguish.

Miriam "spotted" him instantly, and laid down her work. He saw the movement, and shook in his shoes.

"She's coming at me," he muttered; "but how?"

After a short delay the door opened, and Miriam Jaggers, with her bonnet and light cloak on, came forth. She came over to Penny Bunn, and, in a peremptory tone, said:

"Now, come along with you."

"Eh?" he exclaimed, in feigned amazement, "who is it? *Miriam!*"

"No theatricals, or any of your Christmas actings for me," she said, shortly. "Come along, I say."

"Where to?" asked Bunn, as she grasped him by the arm and led him up the street.

"You will see," she answered, between her set teeth. "I will have no more of it."

Penny Bunn was startled—alarmed. Whither was she bearing him? Was it her intention to marry him right away, or to hand him over to the police? The latter, when he thought of the episode of her pet dog, appeared to be the most probable.

Resolved to know the worst, he gasped out, as he was hurried along:

"How's Dolphus?"

"Dolphus," said Miriam, curtly, "has, I am happy to say, survived your brutal assault upon him. His head is still slightly affected, just as if he had short spells of *intoxication*, but I hope he will grow out of them."

"I am glad the dear dog isn't dead," said Bunn, feebly.

"Small thanks to you," she said. "In all the course of my life I never heard of so mean a trick as a man's sitting down on a doorstep to be an obstruction, and stun a poor little dumb creature. P. Y., of all men, I should not have expected it of you. Here we are."

She ushered him into a cottage, such as is in the ordinary occupation of the labourer. The door opened into a room without any preliminary passage, and seated at work was one Hiram Stiff, the Smudgem Bender cobbler. He looked up, and greeting Miriam with a hard smile, laid down his awl.

"Mr. Stiff," said Miriam, "I've brought a gentleman to you who wishes to *sign the pledge*."

Penny Bunn did not wish to do anything of the sort. It had never entered into his head as a possible contingency, but he did not dare to say anything to the contrary. He saw his chance of being restored to favour, and yielded like a lamb.

"Why, certainly," said the cobbler. "I'm glad of another brand plucked from the burning. Drink is the cuss of the nation and of the indervidewal."

He was the leading light of the temperance party in the district, a hard, ill-favoured man in some respects, but a well-meaning one. He had a stock of pledge cards constantly on hand, and in a few minutes Penny Bunn was pledged, thenceforth and for ever, to abstain from the use of all intoxicating liquors.

"Now I will have a walk and talk with you, P. Y. If ever you drink again, I will cast you off for ever."

"Miriam," said Penny Bunn, almost overwhelmed with emotion, "it will be my pride and glory to abstain. I will shun intoxicating liquors as I would the serpent in its lair, and avoid alcohol as a wolf in the fold."

"Mind you do," said Miriam. "Good day, Mr. Stiff."

"Good day, ma'am," said the cobbler, as he resumed his seat. "Keep an eye on your young man. He looks as if backsliding is in him."

"I shall live a shining light among the sober people of this drink-sodden land," said Bunn, warmly. "Miriam, dear, we will walk in the fields and commune; but prior to going thither, I should like, with your permission, to partake of a captain's biscuit and a bottle of lemonade."

"Come home with me, and you shall have both," she answered. "I will not trust you in a public-house."

"You might trust me in the cellar at the hour of midnight," solemnly averred Bunn, "and I would abstain."

She took him home, and gave him some bread and cheese and a bottle of lemonade. While partaking of them, he told her of the events of the morning.

She was not by any means so disturbed as he expected she would be.

"Sir Charles Barstow is the only man we have to look to," she said. "As for this Bundle——"

"Chundle," corrected Bunn.

"Much the same thing," said the gentle Miriam. "When we get the power, I will soon arrange matters with him. I am not afraid of any living white man, and I don't think that a black one will scare me."

"You are a priceless woman," murmured Penny Bunn.

As they sat talking, Penny Bunn saw Black-eyed Susan sauntering through the village in the direction of Chippenham. The girl seemed to be troubled with something, for her cheeks were white, and she had, to all appearance, been crying.

"Miriam," said Bunn, "I wonder what is the matter. That girl is our domestic at the Abbey. She has been upset by something."

"I will ask her in, and perhaps she will tell us what it is."

Hastening to the door, Miriam called to the girl, who crossed over and inquired what she wanted.

"Mr. Bunn is inside," replied Miriam; "he would like to see you for a moment."

"I am waiting for the doctor," replied Susan; "he has been out for ever so long, and Mr. Snicker is so bad."

"What is the matter with him?"

"Raging lunacy."

"I should not have given him credit for sufficient brains to suffer that way," said Miriam, composedly. "I would not be upset if I were you."

"It isn't that, miss," said Susan. "Mr. Snicker isn't the sort of man I respect. What I'm afraid of is that while I am waiting for the doctor he may get up and murder some of the dear boys."

"Well, here come some of them," said Miriam, as a

shouting was heard up the road, and a number of the boys hove in sight. "He has spared a few of the precious lambs."

They watched the youngsters as they came along at a trot. Foremost was Whymper, with an accordion in his hands.

Every few steps he drew a discordant note from it, that was about as sweet as the braying of an ass.

"Goodness me !" exclaimed Black-eyed Susan; "what game are they playing now ?"

She might well ask, for the faces of the half-score boys behind Whymper were on the grin, and every few steps one of them would look back, as if expecting some one on their trail.

Seeing Susan standing by the door of Miriam's cottage, they gave her a friendly nod, and Whymper, opening the accordion to its full length, closed it sharply, extracting from it a combination of hideous sounds by way of salute.

On they went, and disappeared in the distance.

A minute later, as Black-eyed Susan was about to enter the cottage on the invitation of Miriam, Bonelucci appeared up the village street, coming on the trail of the boys with such speed as his years and bones could make.

CHAPTER LXXXVI.

PEACE FOR BONELUCCI.—ARRIVAL OF SIR CHARLES.

THE Italian halted by the two women, and saluting them by taking off his cap and bowing, he asked them if they had seen the boys go by.

"What do you want with them ?" asked Black-eyed Susan.

"I vant noting of zem but my museek," answered Bonelucci. "I hear zem, I see zem, and I cry out for it. So zey vork him—my museek, so zat I run. Zey keep so far away, and laugh. 'Come for him—your museek,' zey say, and I come, but zey run, run, and I not catch zem. Vhen I do——"

He stopped short, and the expression of his face was sufficient to indicate the nature of the punishment he would inflict upon them. It was murderous.

"You can go and find them," said Black-eyed Susan.

Bonelucci glared at her, malevolently, and passed on. Susan and Miriam entered the cottage, where Penny Bunn received the former graciously.

They had a long talk together, and the upshot of it was that Susan was, for the time, persuaded there was no necessity for a doctor, and she had better defer looking for one, for a few hours at least.

"Snicker is vicious," said Penny Bunn, "but he is not mad."

Black-eyed Susan allowed herself to abandon seeking the doctor, and remained where she was for a time. Bunn and Miriam conversed in an undertone for a quarter of an hour, and then rose.

They were going for their long-deferred walk, and they asked Susan to accompany them.

"We will walk as far as the doctor's with you," said Bunn. "After all, he had better see Snicker, and if he is at home, you can go to the Abbey with him."

The doctor's house was at the end of the village, and he had not yet returned. As the patient he was visiting resided in a cottage on the Chippenham road, they decided to walk in that direction.

A short distance from Smudgem Bender, they came upon Bonelucci, sitting by the roadside. He had his accordion upon his knees, and was fondling it as a mother would a long-lost child.

"Hey, now, you see," he cried, holding it aloft, "I haf him, my museek."

"I congratulate you," replied Bunn, with a gracious air. "You are fortunate in getting anything back from the clutches of the Lambs."

"Ask him to give us a tune," whispered Miriam; "I am fond of music."

Her wish was law to Penny Bunn, and, with a patronising air, that would have become a burlesque monarch on the stage conferring a favour on one of his subjects, he made the request.

"Alas !" sighed Bonelucci, "I cannot, for, behold, as I come round ze corner, my museek fly ovare ze hedge like a bird, and smite me here "—he touched his breast—"and ze bellows zat make ze wind go 'bang.' But no mattare. I haf him, my museek, and I mend him. It is enough. I go 'vay, nevere to come back here."

He rose up, saluted the ladies, and walked away, hugging his recovered treasure close to his breast.

And that was the last ever seen of him in that district.

Yet another meeting, and one of more portent to the fortunes of Penny Bunn, was destined to take place that day.

They arrived at the cottage just as Doctor Lamplick came out. He was considerably astonished on hearing from Penny Bunn that he was required at the Abbey. And Black-eyed Susan was even more astonished when she heard Penny Bunn state it to be his conviction that his late employer was mad.

"You said a short time ago that he was nothing of the sort," she said.

"That," replied Bunn, with his usual readiness, "was but a preliminary opinion. I diagnosed the case too hastily."

The word "diagnosed" settled Susan, and ended all further discussion upon the subject. Doctor

Lamplick said that he could not go alone, as the law demanded the evidence and certificates of two members of the profession. He advised their going on to Chippenham, where he could obtain the help of a brother practitioner. As he was on foot, they all went on together, and arriving at the drowsy town, the doctor suggested some refreshment before visiting his brother practitioner.

Miriam admitting a feeling of fatigue being upon her, they all adjourned to the Black Bear hostelry.

In the coffee-room Black-eyed Susan sat modestly apart, but, as she had had no dinner, expressed herself as thankfully willing to partake of bread and cheese and beer; Miriam, "feeling so low," declared for gin and water warm and a biscuit; and the doctor took whisky and water. Bunn's lady-love said he had better have a bottle of ginger-beer, and, with affected joy, he said it was his favourite drink. He did not require anything to eat.

He drank the inflating ginger-beer with the stoicism of a martyr, and noted how Miriam disposed of her gin and water like one to the manner born. He drew his own deductions therefrom, but wisely kept them to himself.

While they sat there a train came in, and one of the stablemen was observed from the window running up to the inn, and calling out for a carriage to go at once to the station.

"And hurry up," he roared, "for it is Sir Charles Barstow who wants it."

"P. Y.," said Miriam, "there is something Providential in this."

"I feel as if I were about to be rewarded for my turning over a new leaf and signing the pledge," murmured Penny Bunn. "Shall we go and meet him?"

"I will," said Miriam. "You stop here awhile. Doctor Lamplick, you would not mind waiting for Sir Charles, I hope. It is possible he may accompany us to the Abbey."

To ride through the country with the owner of the estate the doctor would have waited a week, for he was, in common with most of the rural practitioners, simply a poor man's doctor, and was never sent for by the big swells. He assented gladly.

So Miriam went forth, and they sat by the window and watched. There was a short cut to the station through a narrow way, used only by foot passengers. By taking that route, she would be there some minutes before the fly ordered for the baronet could arrive at the railway.

"A smart woman, that," said Penny Bunn, admiringly.

"Very," replied the doctor, drily, as he looked at him covertly and smiled; "she is a match for most men, I should say."

Black-eyed Susan sat still, thinking in her quiet way, and wondering what would be the end of the day's adventures.

Presently Penny Bunn, who kept close watch upon the street outside, saw the fly coming back from the station. It was an open one, and Miriam was by the side of Sir Charles Barstow, who, above all things, was a gentleman, and courteous to all women.

"Sitting beside Sir Charles," said Bunn, exultingly. "I am proud to be loved by such a woman."

Black-eyed Susan stifled a giggle, and the doctor openly grinned. But Penny Bunn was oblivious of both. All his senses were concentrated on Miriam, sitting composedly riding by the side of the baronet.

The fly drew up at the inn door, and Sir Charles, stepping out, gave her a hand to assist her to descend. She accepted it with the grace of the high-born, and Bunn was overcome with admiration.

"There is a woman who will raise me to the highest society," he murmured.

The new arrivals did not come into the coffee-room, for the baronet, as became a man of his position, ordered a private apartment. Shortly after, the doctor was requested to walk upstairs by a waiter who entered the room.

"There was a message for me, too, I presume?" said Bunn, sternly.

"No, sir, you wasn't mentioned," replied the waiter. "The lady said the doctor was wanted."

"There has been a mistake somewhere," said Penny Bunn, haughtily, "and if it lies with you, I shall make a complaint. No matter. You will mention, doctor, that I am here, waiting."

"Certainly," answered the doctor.

He looked at himself in the glass over the mantelpiece, straightened his necktie, ran his fingers through his hair, and was bowed out of the room by the waiter, who was about to follow him, when Bunn peremptorily called out:

"Stop!"

The man stopped, in no way alarmed.

"Did you speak, sir?" he inquired.

"I did," returned Bunn. "Now, think again, you are sure I was not mentioned?"

"Yes, you was," replied the waiter, after a moment's hesitation.

"I thought so," said Bunn, triumphantly. "Then how dare you say that the lady only named the doctor?"

"Well, sir," answered the waiter, "I didn't like to say it before him, for I respect the feelings of the humblest. The lady said I wasn't to let you come upstairs on any account, and if you ordered any drink you wasn't to be supplied with it."

"Indeed!" ejaculated Penny Bunn, with a gasp.

"Feller, you may go."

And the "feller" went, holding back a grin until he was outside, and had closed the door.

CHAPTER LXXXVII.

PREPARATIONS FOR THE DISLODGMENT OF SNICKER.—
PENNY BUNN AS LEADING CHUCKER-OUT.

MIRIAM had told all she knew of the goings on of Snicker, with such embellishments and additions as a woman endowed with the gifts of a novelist could think of, and the doctor and the baronet were discussing the matter.

"What is your opinion?" asked Sir Charles. "I really think the man must be mad."

"I have no personal doubt of it," said the doctor, "and it will only be necessary to proceed in due form. He ought to be removed from the Abbey at once, and the school placed in the care of a man more fit for the post."

"It is not for me to place the man under proper care," said Sir Charles, thoughtfully; "that, of course, rests with his wife."

"Certainly."

"I understood you to say, Miss Daggers——"

"Jaggers, Sir Charles," simpered Miriam.

"Well, Jaggers," said the baronet, as if it were all the same to him or anybody else. "I understood you to say that this man, Snicker, would not suffer any pecuniary loss by his immediate removal."

"None at all, Sir Charles. He receives all the school fees in advance."

"And that you, on behalf of Bunn, guarantee that the boys will receive their education up to the expiration of their respective terms without additional fees?"

"Yes, Sir Charles. The majority of them expire shortly. The loss will not be very great, and it will be accepted cheerfully."

"And you are about to be married, as you inform me?"

"We are to be married in three weeks. The banns will be read in church on Sunday next for the first time."

"Meanwhile, there will be a woman in the house?"

"Yes, Sir Charles, I have a maiden aunt who will take charge of it."

"All is well so far," said Sir Charles. "Now the hold I have upon this madman is a strong one. He has broken his agreement, and done a vast amount of damage. Your future husband will repair it, as promised, free of charge, which will be embodied in the agreement between him and me. So far, good.

Now what had we better do, doctor, to ensure the speedy removal of this man, Snicker?"

"First of all, he must be seen by Doctor Bloomer and myself; then the requisite certificates must be made out, and after that his wife must decide what is to be done with him. All that you need to do, Sir Charles, is to enforce his departure by the power you have over him."

"He has a certain amount of furniture," mused the baronet.

"Which you, Sir Charles," promptly remarked Miriam, "ought to seize in part payment of the damage done."

"I could hardly do that," said Sir Charles, "but I would not mind making him a small allowance for it, and you, when you are married, Miss Maggers"— Miriam did not correct him this time—"could repay me by instalments, or in bulk, at an appointed time."

"I will undertake to do so, Sir Charles."

"Good. Now as to the method of his removal. What about that, doctor?"

"I should have some men ready to enforce it if necessary. As a lunatic, he could not bring an action against you. Mrs. Snicker might, but, under the circumstances, I think that she would prefer to let the matter rest."

"Where are the requisite men?"

"How many will you want, Doctor Lamplick?" asked Miriam.

"Three would suffice."

"Mr. Bunn and two others?"

"Yes."

"Then I will see to it at once," said Miriam, rising.

"Let them go forward in a fly," said the doctor, "and await our coming outside the Abbey."

Miriam hesitated a moment before going.

"May I ask, Sir Charles, if you will honour Doctor Bloomer and myself with your company?" inquired Doctor Lamplick.

"Assuredly I shall go with you," replied the baronet. "Nothing can be completed without me, and Miss Baggers will accompany us."

Miriam bowed graciously, and swept towards the door.

"If Doctor Bloomer is at home, we shall be there in an hour and a half," said Lamplick. "Ask your husband to secure two strong men without delay; the rougher the better."

"It shall be done," said Miriam, and she departed with a heart as light as one made of cork.

She found her coming husband, as yet ignorant of the happy day being named, sitting gloomily by the window with a twopenny cheroot in his hand. As it did not come under the head of drink, he had been supplied with it. She took it from his hand, and threw it into the grate.

"P.Y.," she said, "this is no time for indulgence in any form of vice. We have the reins in our own hands, and win. Listen to me, and drop that scowl, or I will box your ears."

"Am I scowling?" he asked, dropping his frown like a very warm potato.

She did not say anything more on that head, but imparted to him as much of the interview as was necessary, in her way of thinking, and asked him if he knew where to get two suitable men. Naturally, he said that he could lay hands upon a hundred.

"Then off with you," she said; "and here is a little money to give them something to drink and pay for the fly; but touch a drop of strong liquor, and I have done with you for ever. I know a man who will jump into your place in five minutes."

She knew of nothing of the sort, but, like her lover, she could draw a stiff long-bow when it was required.

"Miriam," murmured Penny Bunn, "hast thou already forgotten my *pledge?*"

"No," she said, curtly, "and don't you forget it, either. Off with you, and secure the men. Go on with them in a fly, and take the girl with you."

"Thanky, marm," said Black-eyed Susan, promptly, "but I would rather walk. I can get home in time."

So Susan went her way at a brisk pace, and Penny Bunn started forth to get two juniors for the work of chucking out.

Now Penny Bunn, notwithstanding his bold declaration, knew of only one man whom he could call upon as an assistant, and that was Milky Whey, but he was pretty certain that, having got hold of him, he would be able to find him the third person required. The question was, would he be able to secure the itinerant fishmonger.

Fortunately, it was an off-day for that worthy man, and Bunn landed his fish without any delay in one of the dirtiest beer-shops in the town. It was not difficult to find Milky Whey when he was at home, for he was invariably in one of the public-houses, and where he was there was sure to be wrangling also.

A single inquiry of a small boy sufficed for Bunn to be directed to his whereabouts, and, on entering the beer-house, the coming husband of Miriam discovered him, with a quart pot in his hand, talking loudly and offensively to a broken-nosed man, who was apparently making fun of him.

"Milky," said Bunn, patronisingly, "can you give me a moment?"

Milky Whey turned, and seeing him, lost all his rancour, and became exceedingly chummy.

"What, you, old pal?" he cried. "Have a drink."

Penny Bunn would have resented this familiarity, but he knew it was not politic. Furthermore, there was the quart pot, and it shone like the eye of the Evil One tempting him.

"I am pledged," he thought, "but, for Miriam's sake, the sacrifice must be made."

Then he drank, long and quickly, down to the very bottom of the tempting pewter.

"Thirsty, guv'nor, I should say," remarked the man with a broken nose.

"Not so," said Bunn, coldly. "But what is worth doing at all is worth doing well. I drink to one of my humble friends—a most worthy man. The goblet shall be renewed. Host, fill again."

The landlord did so, and Bunn, drawing Milky Whey aside, told him of the mission he was on, and it was received with joy.

"As it is a job for Sir Charles, I know I shall be paid handsome," said Milky Whey. "As for the second party, there stands the werry man, once the champion bruiser of the West of Hengland. You have heard of the Bath Brick, in course?"

Penny Bunn had never heard of the man in his life, but he hastened to say that he had followed his remarkable career with unflagging interest, and gloried in his many victories in the ring.

"If he hadn't been knocked out by the Walham Tickler," said Milky Whey, "he would have been champion of Hengland. Brick!"

"Wot now?" demanded the Bath Brick, rather sulkily. He did not approve of whispered conferences in his company.

"This gentleman have got a good job for you—a chucking out of a party. The pay's sure to be good."

Thereupon the Bath Brick became brisk and business-like, and in a few minutes everything was settled.

Penny Bunn having taken another pull at the replenished pot—again for Miriam's sake—departed to get a fly. When he returned, the pair of junior chuckers-out suggested that they should take a bottle of gin with them as a gentle stimulant, which Bunn paid for, and they were ready.

The day being warm, the carriage was an open one, and the two ruffians, each with a short pipe in his mouth, took the two back seats therein. Bunn, warmed into recklessness by his recent potations, lit another cheroot, which he had purchased on his way for the fly, and they started, an amazing spectacle to the people in Chippenham.

Many of the tradesmen stood by the doors of their shops, which was apparently one of their chief pursuits, and the spectacle of Milky Whey and the Bath Brick in a fly could not be otherwise than astounding. Penny Bunn being in their society, adding to the charm and novelty of the sight.

There were a few boys abroad, and they, acting on their youthful instincts, ran behind, cheering. All the mongrel dogs—and everybody in the town kept one—joined in, barking their loudest, and thus, with much commotion, the chuckers-out left the town behind them.

"This is better than shoving a barrer," said Milky Whey. "Brick, uncork that 'ere bottle."

Not having any corkscrew with him, the Bath Brick rose to the occasion, and with the blade of a big clasp knife dexterously removed the top of the neck of the bottle. Penny Bunn, feeling in the best of humours, was overcome with admiration.

"I never saw anything so cleverly done," he said.

"I'd like to have a pound in my pocket for ivery bottle I served the same way," growled the Bath Brick. "Drink, guvnor."

"Well, really," murmured Penny Bunn. "I take very little in this way. I suppose you did not think of bringing a glass?"

"Glasses be blowed!" said the Bath Brick. A man as can't take it out of a bottle ought not to drink at all."

Penny Bunn smiled, murmured something about its being a matter of education and habit, and drank. He nearly choked himself in so doing, but he managed to imbibe about a gill of the coarse, fiery liquor. By the time this precious trio reached Smudgem Bender, the bottle was empty, and they were all merry.

The suggestion of the Bath Brick, that a second bottle should be obtained at the Cowley Arms was not dissented to for a moment, and it was obtained. The driver was also treated, and the cork having been drawn and Bunn being favoured with a loan of a wine-glass with the foot off, the journey was renewed.

The Bath Brick forthwith began to sing in a voice that was like the growl of a bear with a cold, and Milky Whey extemporised a chorus. Penny Bunn, not to be behind as an entertainer of his friends, also started a song of his own. In this style they went up through the wood of Mumping Malford, and dismounted from the carriage at the summit.

Penny Bunn, on stepping out, missed the usual means provided for alighting, and fell in a heap upon the ground. Rising, he stared long and steadily at the steps as if it had played a joke upon him he was disposed to resent.

"Skewrus," he murmured. "I don't undershand it. Coshman, whatsh your fare?"

The man told him, and Penny Bunn, after some difficulty in getting the coins right and in order, handed over the amount. Then the man drove away, with a story to tell that night as he smoked his pipe with his brother drivers in the tap-room.

Milky Whey and the Bath Brick, being hardened to ordinary potations, were not very much the worse for the drink, but Penny Bunn was conscious of a growing weakness in his legs, and of a tendency in his eyesight to double, and even treble, objects before him.

So he sat down to think, and thinking, fell asleep.

His companions exchanged a few words, and then, proceeding to turn out his pockets, relieved him of the remnant of the cash therein. That done, they turned them in again, lighted their pipes, and left him to repose.

Penny Bunn was not the only festively inclined party that day at the school, for the boys of Number One dormitory had made up their minds to celebrate the indisposition of Snicker with a feast in the seclusion of their sleeping place.

A box of provisions had been obtained from Smudgem Bender. Blotch kindly sent it on in one of his carts to the foot of the cliff, and the boys hauled it in by the schoolroom window.

"It reminds us of the glorious barring out times," they said.

Having conveyed the box to their dormitory, and hidden it under one of the beds, they cleared out of the Abbey again, and were seen no more until some very portentous events had transpired.

CHAPTER LXXXVIII.

MR. AND MRS. SNICKER PLAY INTO THE HANDS OF THEIR COMING FOES.—A SERIES OF STARTLING EVENTS.

IT was late in the afternoon, and only three persons were left in the Abbey, Mr. and Mrs. Snicker and Chunder Loo.

Fontenoy Snicker was still in bed, and he had called aloud many times in vain for "a drop of the usual." His wife refused to either hearken or obey.

Once he got out of bed, and, on trying the door, found it was looked on the outside, so he got back again, and lay there brooding, and gradually working himself up to a dangerous pitch of frenzy.

Chunder Loo did not make himself intrusive, but wandered stealthily about the place, peeping into the various rooms, and seeing in some of them matter to set him wandering. The chamber without the flooring, which Snicker had torn up, especially set him thinking, and it appeared to trouble him deeply.

He was either shy of intruding too much upon Mrs. Snicker, or really found no joy in her society, for more than once, when he heard her soft, shuffling step about the house, as she went here and there in the performance of her domestic duties, he took especial pains to avoid her. Once he hid in a cupboard and remained close, scarcely breathing until she had passed by.

It was about half-past four when he heard a sound of beating open a door above. He was in the schoolroom at the time inspecting the master's desks, in and out, above and below. He seemed to be very thorough in all he undertook.

Impelled by curiosity, he went into the passage, and there encountered Mrs. Snicker with a small tray, on which was a cup of tea, in her left hand. In her right hand she held the house broom.

"Somebody is knocking upstairs," he said.

"It is my husband raving for drink," replied Mrs. Snicker, "and this is all he will get, if he bangs the house down. Will you come upstairs with me? I am afraid of him in a violent condition."

"Sweet madam," said Chunder Loo, with a quiet bow, "I am Indian by birth, but I have been reared in your country, and cultivated the ways of your people, among them the art of boxing. I will protect you."

"Oh, thank you so much," exclaimed Mrs. Snicker, completely overcome by the gracious manners of Bunn's successor.

So they went upstairs, where Snicker, a prisoner in his room, was hammering at the door with a bedroom poker. Mrs. Snicker being also armed with her favourite long broom, she smote the door with it. The banging inside ceased.

"Who's there?" roared Snicker.

"Me, Jerry," answered his spouse.

"Oh, it's you, is it, you hag?" growled the schoolmaster.

"Yes, Jerry. Do you want anything?"

This inquiry, uttered in a soft voice, to a man who had been groaning for his "special Scotch" for hours was more than exasperating—it was maddening.

"Do I want anything?" he repeated. "Ain't I famishing for it? You know what I want."

"You can't have it, Jerry. I have brought you a cup of tea. Will you behave yourself if I open the door?"

There was a short silence, and then, with an apparent effort, the answer came:

"Of course I will. Ain't I always as peaceful as a lamb when I'm not worried?"

Mrs. Snicker handed the cup of tea to Chunder Loo, and softly whispered:

"You hand it in to him when I open the door. If he rushes out, I'll stop him with the broom. For all his speaking so soft he can't be trusted."

It was too true. Snicker was meditating a dashing out with a force that would upset his wife and the tea at the same time. Tea for a man in his condition! It was a miserable way of insulting him, and whatever he might put up with in ordinary times, he was not going to endure it now.

Chunder Loo took up a position about the middle of the door, and quite close to it. Mrs. Snicker, standing a little on one side, thrust the key into the lock.

"You are sure, Jerry," she said, "that you are not going to be violent?"

Again he took time ere he answered, and now it came huskily from his throat.

"I'm all right, Phœbe."

Then she turned the key, and opened the door.

With a war-whoop he sprang out, as he thought, against his wife, but in her place encountered the elbow of Chunder Loo, thrust forward so as to catch him just under the breast-bone.

Snicker went down as if he had been bowled over with a skittle-ball, but Chunder Loo did not budge an inch.

"Cup of tea, sir," he said, in a flute-like tone.

Snicker lay there gasping and staring at him, not having for the moment the least conception of who he was. He really thought for a moment that he had got another form of his old trouble upon him, and that his mental faculties were distorting his Phœbe into something horrible and unnatural.

"Now, Jerry," said Mrs. Snicker, thrusting her head round the side of the doorway, "you said you would not be violent, and now you've nearly upset the tea and Mr. Chunder Loo, who is here to take Bunn's place."

"Oh!" said the schoolmaster, as he slowly got upon his feet, "this is the nigger who's been cuddling you, is it?"

"Jerry!" screamed Mrs. Snicker. "How dare you?"

"How dare I?" he yelled. "I'll show you how I dare. You are a nice sort of wife. Where's my poker? I'll smash the pair of you!"

He had dropped that domestic article of common use, and as he scrambled up and looked madly about for it, Mrs. Snicker pulled the door to and locked it.

"Oh! Mr. Chunder Loo," she gasped, "you see how he is. What is to be done?"

"He must have somebody with him," replied Chunder Loo. "Gentle madam, as he will not drink this tea, may I partake of it?"

She signified her assent with a motion of her hands, and he drank it, as it seemed to her, with one gulp.

"That gal ought to have been back with the doctor long ago," said Mrs. Snicker. "Oh, what a fearful thing it is! Will you go upstairs, and look out of one of the top winders to see if they are coming? I'll stand here, and if he breaks down the door, I'll knock him down with the broom. He's my lawful husband, but I'll do it."

"Are you going to get me anything to drink?" yelled Snicker from the inside of the chamber, as Chunder Loo glided up the attic staircase.

"You'll get no more of that sort of drink which has made you what you are," replied his wife. "I won't deceive you on that, Jerry. Do try and be patient."

"Patient, you hag! I'll get at you somehow."

Once more he renewed his attack upon the door with the poker, and Mrs. Snicker took up the attitude familiar to military circles, as preparing with the bayonet to receive cavalry.

The part of the broom that is used for sweeping she held nearest to herself, and the top of the handle pointed so that when Snicker rushed out, he stood an even chance of impaling himself thereon.

The din he made was frightful, and the crash of the door, which he was splintering by degrees, sounded ominously in the ears of his wife. She trembled, but did not budge. If Snicker did succeed in getting out, she felt that even alone she could with her weapon be a match for him. And furthermore, had she not Chunder Loo to assist her in an emergency?

She called to him by name in a loud, screeching voice, thereby adding to the riot. Snicker heard her and grew madder, pounding at the door with a vigour that threatened to destroy it very speedily.

Suddenly, Mrs. Snicker felt herself grasped by the arm, and, turning her face round, saw Doctor Lamplick by her side, and close behind him was a white-haired, grave-looking gentleman, whom she remembered to have seen in Chippenham, and believed to be a resident physician there.

Three other persons were also present, Milky Whey, the Bath Brick, and Sir Charles Barstow, who, in his most dignified manner, had taken up a safe position in the rear.

"Mrs. Snicker," cried Doctor Lamplick, "what is the meaning of this horrible disturbance?"

His voice must have been heard by Snicker, who suddenly ceased to perform upon the door, and her reply was plainly heard by all.

"It's my Jerry," she said, quaveringly. "He's gone quite dementled."

"Don't believe her," roared Snicker. "It is she who is off her chump—I mean head—and she's been playing all sorts of tricks, cuddling niggers, and keeping me here all day without anything to drink. Is that you, Bunn?"

"Really," murmured Doctor Bloomer, "this is a very sad case."

"And to say that I cuddled niggers! Oh, it is too bad," sobbed Mrs. Snicker.

"You must not give way," said Doctor Lamplick, soothingly; "it may be only a temporary derangement. What can have led him to refer to niggers?"

At this moment the face of Chunder Loo appeared on the attic staircase. His dark eyes flashed over the group, and then he quietly vanished upstairs again.

"He says all sorts of things," replied Mrs. Snicker, evasively, "and there isn't any truth in 'em."

"No doubt, no doubt," said Doctor Bloomer. "Has the unfortunate man locked himself in his room?"

"No, sir, I have the key."

"Then please admit us. I think our two assistants had better go first. Stand forward, men."

"Here," replied the Bath Brick, as he took the foremost place, "give me the key, missus, and you stand off a bit. Milky, you grab him by the legs when he pops out. I'll look to his head."

By looking to that portion of Mr. Snicker's body the Bath Brick meant that it was his intention, on the least sign of violence, to administer to it a blow that would effectually knock the patient out of time, that being, in his opinion, the shortest road to a general peace.

Snicker, hearing so many voices, was dumbfounded thereby, and not being able to make head or tail of their presence, thought he had better slip back into bed, and did so.

When the door was opened, and the two agents employed to protect more peaceful people got ready for action, it was seen that for the time there was no immediate need of their services.

Only the upper half of the face of the suffering Snicker was visible, and the expression of his eyes was dove-like.

The entire party glided into the room, except Sir Charles, who remained in the doorway.

The two doctors stood by the bedside, looking down critically at the patient. Behind them Milky Whey and his chum, the Bath Brick, stood ready for anything that might turn up.

"Well, how are we now?" inquired Doctor Bloomer, as if he were making the inquiry of a sick child. "Better, eh?"

"I'm all right," growled Snicker. "I suppose there are no more of you to come in? Who is that by the door?"

"Jerry," pleaded Mrs. Snicker, "do behave yourself. It is Sir Charles Barstow."

"Murder!" muttered Snicker, "it is all up now, I suppose. Look here, gentlemen, I want to tell you something about that woman there, my wife——"

"Another time, my friend," interposed Doctor Bloomer. "You were saying something about niggers——"

"Yes, I was, and there is one in the house."

"You referred to your wife having an undue liking for him."

"If people don't like each other, I suppose they don't cuddle!" growled Snicker.

Mrs. Snicker began to sob again, but Doctor Lamplick laid a hand upon her arm, soothingly.

"Don't give way," he whispered. "It is only temporary."

"You saw them, as you term it, cuddling?" continued Doctor Bloomer, in pursuit of his professional examination of the unfortunate man.

"No, I didn't," replied Snicker, "and I don't want to talk about it any more."

"Quite right," assented the doctor. "Put out your tongue, please."

"Look here," said Snicker, suddenly becoming violent, "I didn't send for you, as I do not want any doctoring, and I won't have it. All I want is a toothful of whisky, and then I will get up."

Doctor Bloomer turned to his brother practitioner, and they exchanged a few whispered words. Then the chief physician addressed Snicker again.

"If you do not want us," he said, "of course we shall not remain. Mrs. Snicker, will you come downstairs with us? We must have a few words with you before we go."

CHAPTER LXXXIX.

A CHOICE OF EVILS.—MRS. SNICKER UNDERTAKES ALL THE RESPONSIBILITY.

THEY went outside for a few minutes, the doctors last, and one of them closed the door.

"Now you two men," said Doctor Bloomer, "you have a duty to perform, and I trust you will do it creditably."

"Whatsoever I goes in for I'm here," replied the Bath Brick. "I mean winning every time."

"Amen," growled Milky Whey, thinking it was appropriate to say on such a solemn occasion.

"Go back to that room, and remain there," continued the doctor, "and remember this, you are not to talk about things that do not concern you to the patient. If he asks why you are there, you will say that you will be going away directly, or something evasive. Watch him closely, and do not let him get out of bed."

"If he gits out," said the Bath Brick, "he'll be put in again sharp. What say you, Milky?"

"He'll go in like a thunderbolt," answered Milky Whey.

"Go then, and do your duty," said the doctor.

They returned to the room, and found the schoolmaster in the act of getting out of bed.

"Steady there," said the Bath Brick; "in you goes again. It's the doctor's orders."

Snicker was about to say something abrupt when he was hoisted with little ceremony into bed again, and the clothes drawn over him up to his chin.

"You move agen," growled the Bath Brick, "and I'll choke you with a blanket. And don't you talk neither. Our orders is to keep you quiet and happy."

"Suttinly," said Milky Whey, "that is wot we was brought here for."

"This is some game of the boys, I suppose," said Snicker, feebly.

"Niver you mind who's game it is," said the Bath Brick, "but lay low. No jawing allowed. That's the matter, and keep them legs of yours still, or we'll tie 'em together."

Snicker, dumbfounded, amazed, and terrified, fought no more against fate, but lay still, employing his mind in endeavouring to make out what it all meant.

It is needless to say that he utterly failed to get the least idea of the true state of things.

Meanwhile, Mrs. Snicker, the two doctors, and Sir Charles Barstow held conference below, and there could only be one outcome of it. She and her husband would have to promptly leave the Abbey that very day, within an hour if possible.

"If you desire your husband to be taken care of," said Doctor Bloomer, "that matter can be arranged for you. I have not the least doubt that he is suffering from alcoholic dementia."

Doctor Lamplick confirmed this opinion, and they gave Mrs. Snicker a few moments to reflect.

"Jerry is very odd at times," she said, "and unkimmon violent, but I'm not afraid of him, for he is a fearful coward. There's no call to put him away. If he will only let the drink alone, as I do, he won't get into trouble. It's been his ruin—in the tater line—in the show puffession—here and everywhere."

"He can never pay for the damage he has done," said Sir Charles, "but if he will go quietly, I will let him have twenty pounds as a gift to start him fresh, and take no action against him."

"Very generous," murmured Doctor Bloomer.

"Kindness unparalleled," said Lamplick.

"I am sure I thank you, Sir Charles," said Mrs. Snicker, "and it is the best thing we can do. The place for a long time has been a worrit to us, and nothing less. I don't pretend to be troubled about the boys, because I ain't. Somebody will see to them, I suppose."

"We have arranged for that," said Sir Charles. "You need not take another thought about the matter. My advice to you is go at once. Your furniture, such as you are in a position to claim, can either be paid for, or sent after you with your clothes. Go out of the Abbey without delay."

"I will see Jerry at once," replied Mrs. Snicker, "and I have no doubt he will be glad to go."

She left them talking together, Sir Charles remarking that it was almost time Penny Bunn appeared on the scene to take possession.

"We have not seen him since he left Chippenham," said Doctor Lamplick, "but I am inclined to think that it is prudent of him to keep out of sight at present."

"Just so," said Sir Charles.

A SPLENDID SCHOOL STORY. NEVER BEFORE PUBLISHED.

By E. HARCOURT BURRAGE,

Author of "Ching Ching," "Monkey Mat and Roving Dick," "The Brave Boy of the Basilisk," &c.

THE LAMBS OF LITTLECOTE

A THRILLING SCHOOL STORY.

JACK RECOGNISES A FRIEND BY HIS BOOTS AND BREECHES.

PRICE ONE PENNY.

ALDINE PUBLISHING CO., 9, Red Lion Court, Fleet St., and 1, 2, & 3, Crown Court, Chancery Lane, London.

In a few minutes Mrs. Snicker returned with the information that her husband had assented to the conditions of departure, and would now be dressing but for the two men, who refused to permit him to get out of bed.

"The moment he moves," she added, "one of them pounces on him. That man with the broken nose is sitting on his legs, and Milky Whey is turning things topsy-turvy looking for a bit of rope."

"It will be as well to relieve them of their duty," said Doctor Bloomer, hastily, and Lamplick hurried upstairs to do so.

Sir Charles Barstow made a rough draft of the terms of giving up the Abbey for the departing schoolmaster to sign before he left it. The two doctors would be the witnesses of the deed. The pith of it was as follows :

1. To leave the Abbey undisturbed from that day thenceforward.

2. To only take away clothing, until it could be seen if the new tenant deemed it advisable to purchase the rest. The price to be settled by a valuer, selected by Sir Charles Barstow.

3. All claims upon the pupils to be forfeited.

4. Snicker not to attempt to open another school within twenty miles of Mumping Malford.

5. On breaking one or more clauses of this agreement, Fontenoy Snicker was to be held responsible for all the damage done in the Abbey.

It was just six o'clock when Fontenoy Snicker, Esq., leaning on the arm of his wife, came creeping down the stairs to perform the last act of humiliation in the stirring drama of his life as a schoolmaster

He was very pale, and his legs were in a very shaky condition. Moreover, every ounce of nerve had left him, and he was a temporary wreck, for he had suffered sorely.

Phœbe ushered him into the room where the three gentlemen awaited him.

"Good evening, gentlemen," he said, as if they had not met before.

"Mr. Snicker," said Sir Charles, "you will please to put your name here. If you like, I will first read the document to you."

"No occasion for that, Sir Charles," replied Snicker. "all our other dealings have been straightforrard—forward—how sickness upsets the langwidge of a man, to be sure. You would not do anything but what is right and kind, I'm sure."

Sir Charles assented stiffly, and handed him a pen to sign his name. Snicker appended it to the document with a stifled groan.

"Is 'ard—hard—to part with the old place," he said, "for I've spent a werry—very—'appy—happy, low it !—time here. I hope there is no ill-feeling on

either side. And you was a-mentioning twenty pounds, Sir Charles, as Phœbe tells me."

Sir Charles, without a word, brought out his pocket-book, selected four five-pound notes therefrom, and handed them to him, still silent.

"Thanky, I'm sure," murmured Snicker. "Now, Phœbe, I think we will tear ourselves away from the hold—old, jigger it !—spot. Good evening, gentlemen, and thanky once more for all your kindness."

They responded with a grave inclination of the head, but said not a word.

As the door closed upon the pair, Sir Charles turned to Doctor Bloomer, and inquired :

"What is your real opinion of that man ?"

"He is better out of the Abbey than in it, Sir Charles," was the reply.

"Quite so ; just my opinion. Now we have only to await the coming of his successor, arrange preliminaries, and depart."

As the baronet said this, the door opened, and Miriam entered the room.

CHAPTER XC.

SETTLING FOR BUNN.—AN EXCITING TIME.—WILL CHUNDER LOO GO AWAY?

MIRIAM said she was so sorry, but the excitement of the day had upset Mr. P. Y. Bunn, who had gone to his room, and lying down there, had fallen asleep.

"He is a very sensitive man," she further explained, "and keenly feels the fall and degradation of the unfortunate man with whom he had been so long connected. If you wish, Sir Charles, for me to arouse him, I will do so, but any engagement I may enter into will be confirmed by him, as my future husband."

Sir Charles did not think it at all necessary to disturb the new possessor of the Abbey. Perhaps it would be better to defer the signing of papers until the deeds had been prepared by a qualified practitioner. The baronet assured Miss Jaggers — he called her Waggers on this occasion—that his word was his bond. She, on the part of herself and Bunn, expressed herself as well content.

So the doctors and their aristocratic companion departed in the fly, and Miriam went in search of Penny Bunn, who, so far from being in a state of repose, was in the schoolroom, suffering agonies of remorse and fear.

He sat at his familiar desk, with his head bowed down upon his hands.

"Now," said Miriam, sharply, "having found you in the wood sleeping off intoxication, and smuggled you in here, and having, moreover, made your path smooth for you, I want to know what you have to say for yourself?"

Penny Bunn raised the most woebegone of faces, and stared at her like a bit of waxwork representing Mournfulness. In a few moments he huskily replied:

"Miriam, your censure is just, but, although I have fallen, it is in a good cause. Neither of those men would budge a step until I had drank with them. Have they departed?"

"I don't know, but I believe so," answered Miriam, shortly.

"Well, if they are here, they will confirm what I have said," returned Penny Bunn. "I made every appeal to them, but they were as deaf as the adder that crawls among the withered leaves of the forest."

"Don't be unnecessarily poetic."

"I won't, Miriam, dear. I put the case to them from every point of view, and they were not to be moved. So I said I would sip a drop from the bottle, and I verily believe that they played some prank upon me. Anyway, I was immediately overcome, and remembered no more until I heard your welcome voice in the wood."

"I am afraid I cannot quite believe you," said Miriam, doubtfully, "but if ever you do it again——"

"I won't. I swear it!"

"Very well. Then let us have a look round the place. I have telegraphed for my aunt, and she will be here to-night. Her name is Miss Astracan Jaggers."

"Astracan!" exclaimed Penny Bunn, staggered.

"Yes. She is, I believe, of foreign extraction on her mother's side. I do not know exactly how it is, but she was named in honour of the country where one of her ancestors distinguished himself."

"It is a most extraordinary name, Miriam."

"It is, P. Y., and you will find her an extraordinary woman."

They walked out of the schoolroom, and as they sauntered into the hall, the voices of some of the boys were heard in the playground.

"The lambs are returning," said Penny Bunn, relapsing into pathos, "little dreaming that they have lost their shepherd."

"Lost their grandmother!" said Miriam, tartly. "I wonder where that girl is? She helped me to *carry* you indoors, and I haven't seen her since."

"Miriam, I think I walked. Be just to one who loves you dearly."

"P. Y., your legs were about as useful to you as two long sandbags, which people put along the windows to keep the draught out. What is the girl's name?"

"Black-eyed Susan. That is the name the boys have given her."

"Susan is enough," said Miriam; "now show me the way to the kitchen."

Penny Bunn did so, and there they found Susan, from henceforth engaged in getting the tea ready for the boys.

They told her what had been done, and informed her of the coming of a new mistress—a temporary one—that night. Susan seemed to be rather sorry for Mrs. Snicker, but she bore up pretty well.

They left her busy, and proceeded upstairs. On the landing Bunn received a staggerer by suddenly encountering Chunder Loo, who stood bowing and wagging his head for the benefit of Miriam, who was dumbfounded.

"Hallo!" exclaimed Penny Bunn, "you not gone?"

"I ventured to stay," replied Chunder Loo, "thinking, sir, that I might be of some slight service to you, for a while at least. I require no salary during the first month, which I shall be glad to look upon as a time of probation."

Penny Bunn stared at Miriam, and she kept her eyes fixed on Chunder Loo.

"Though a native of India," he went on to explain, "I have been educated in England, and have acquired some knowledge of your ways, especially those relating to the education of youth."

He bowed again low and gracefully, directing the obeisance with surpassing cunning to Miriam more than to her future lord and master.

"Really," said Penny Bunn, who was not by any means in fighting trim, "I hardly know what to say to you."

"If I am not suitable for the post of your servant," said Chunder Loo, in his sweetest tone, "it will be easy to say to me when the month is up that I am to go."

"He has a most agreeable address," murmured Miriam.

"Yes, that is the worst of him," said Penny Bunn, in an undertone, "and there is no getting at him."

"But you must have some sort of help."

"Yes; but fancy a nigger!"

"He is hardly that. He reminds me of those rajahs on your estate in India that you have told me of."

This was a facer for Bunn, who had forgotten all about that little yarn he had so thoughtlessly spun. It now occurred to him that if he kept Chunder Loo for a time, he might, by his evil ways, disgust Miriam with all things Indian, and the rajah business be allowed to drop.

"I don't mind his staying for a time, if you wish it," he said. "The holidays will soon be here, and he can't do much harm."

"We'll talk it over, and, as you will be better away

from the table with the boys, suppose he takes your seat to-night?"

"Miriam, your judgment is always good. It shall be so."

Chunder Loo was informed of this decision, and he expressed his gratitude in a few well-chosen words, and then retired gracefully.

"Now, you and I, P. Y., will have a cup of tea in the private room of the Snickers, and stay until my aunt arrives. She has been a matron in an orphan asylum, and will know how to look after the boys."

"If she has had a free hand with the fatherless," said Bunn, with feeling," I have no doubt but she will be a priceless acquisition to Littlecote Abbey."

They adjourned to the room lately occupied by Fontenoy Snicker and his wife, and, when Susan eventually served up a tea, they sat down to enjoy themselves.

Miriam was in a good humour, and all the little peccadilloes of her future husband were forgotten.

"P.Y.," she asked, "do you feel at home?"

"I feel," he answered, "as if I was the reigning monarch of this kingdom, blessed with a queen whose light is as the sun in the firmament."

"You take milk and sugar, I believe," she said, sweetly.

"I do," answered Bunn. "Oh! Miriam, light of my eyes, we have a brilliant career before us."

He spake in the joy of the hour. Could he have obtained a peep into the future, he would certainly have modified his statement. But then nobody knows what lies in the future. There are rocks ahead for us all.

CHAPTER XCI.

COMMOTION IN THE SCHOOL.—ARRIVAL OF MISS ASTRACAN JAGGERS.

"SOMETHING'S happened, but what is it?"

It was Tom Drummond who addressed this remark to Don at the tea-table, presided over by Chunder Loo. Rooker sat at the foot of the table, as much mystified as the boys.

The above remark originated in the coming of Penny Bunn into the room for a moment, and smiling benignantly upon them all. They expected to see him make another rush at Chunder Loo, but he merely asked that inscrutable individual if the boys had all they required, and, on receiving a respectful reply in the affirmative, walked lightly from the room.

"Bunn doesn't look as if he were going," remarked Jack Ford.

The amazement of the boys was shown in every face, but no solution of the mystery was to be obtained at the table. Rooker was unable to give it, and nobody thought for a moment of asking Chunder Loo.

Bob Stockton suggested that one of them should, after tea, look up Susan, and ask her what had been done in their absence. This was voted by all within hearing to be a good idea.

There was no trouble in finding Susan, as she was looking out for them, bursting with the news she had to impart for their comfort.

They found her in the passage, and the moment the first of them appeared in the dining-room she cried out: "The Snickers have gone for good!"

"Gammon, Sue!" cried Tom Drummond.

"It is true," she said, "but I can't tell you about it here. May I go into the schoolroom? Nobody will come there."

Of course she might, and away they trooped with Susan at their head, and the boys having all assembled, the door was shut. Rooker was not there, he having gone upstairs to his room.

Susan was a little roundabout in her way of telling a story, but she soon put the boys in possession of the facts, and when she stopped for breath, they cheered lustily, not so much on account of their own emancipation as over the downfall of their tyrant.

"Mr. Snicker is gone," said Susan, when silence was restored, "but I don't think we have heard the last of him. What sort of a master Mr. Bunn will make, I won't pretend to say, but I think we shall have a missus who will look after you. And now I must go, for I have to see to the room for the new matron, who is coming to-night."

After she was gone, the schoolroom was for a time in an uproar. Whatever the boys had looked forward to, it was not this.

Then there was the question of staying under the new arrangements, and the verdict was, generally, in favour of it. None of them were afraid of Penny Bunn, and after all, in the teaching, he had been the real master. It was a question that would be mainly settled by their friends.

No master or tutor came near them that night again. They had a room all to themselves, and as for getting up lessons, it was a mere farce. Who on earth, in their state of minds, could study, or require anything outside information on the absorbing topic? Jack Ford, like Susan, was certain that, although Fontenoy Snicker had left the Abbey, they had not heard the last of him.

"He will never allow Penny Bunn to rule in peace."

Tea having been served, they went to bed at the usual time, but it was long before they were all asleep. There had been, practically, a revolution in the Abbey, and the elements of a general turmoil were abroad.

It was ten o'clock, and Penny Bunn and Miriam were still in the Snicker room, the former engaged in framing a circular to the parents of the boys. Miriam had some crochet work, and was very busy stitching and thinking.

"Your aunt is late," said Bunn, looking up suddenly from his work.

"She will be here as soon as possible," replied Miriam. "How are you getting on with the prospectus?"

"It is finished, my love," answered Bunn; "shall I read it to you?"

"Do dear."

How dove-like they were. All was told by that time, and Bunn was aware that the banns would be read for the first time on the following Sunday.

Leaning back in his chair, and holding a sheet of foolscap at a convenient distance from his eyes, he read as follows:

DEAR SIR (OR MADAM):—I have the pleasure of informing you that I have recently acquired from Mr. Fontenoy Snicker (who has retired from the avocation of schoolmaster owing to ill-health) the goodwill of the College of Littlecote Abbey, wherein I have for a period served in the capacity of second master. That I have practically been the head of the school for some time is a fact your son will convey to you when he comes home for the vacation, but I have still further claims on your good will as master, being duly qualified, and one of a long line of teachers of the young. My father was one of the resident proctors at Cambridge, and I have at this moment two uncles headmasters of colleges abroad. My certificates are numerous and valuable, and copies of them will be forwarded as soon as they are received from the printer.

Should you elect to entrust me with the care of your son —or sons—it will be my earnest endeavour, not only to fill their minds with useful educational matter, but to feed and sleep them in a way worthy of their position in life—in short, Littlecote will be a home and school in one.

Awaiting your reply,

I am, Sir (or Madam),

Your obedient servant,

P. Y. BUNN.

"What do you think of that, Miriam?" asked the author of this precious piece of academical literature.

"It will do," she replied, coolly. "It is, I must say, very Bunny."

"Very *what*, Miriam?"

"Bunny, like yourself. There is a good deal of the drum in it. Noise, you know."

Penny Bunn leant on one side, and put a hand upon his heart, as if in pain.

"I expected a kinder criticism from you, Miriam," he said.

"No doubt you did," answered Miriam, "but it is as well not to expect too much at any time. Listen! I hear wheels. Dear Aunt Astracan has arrived."

She tossed her crochet work upon the table, and hurried out. Penny Bunn got upon his feet, gave himself a shake, and muttered, "Blow your aunt. I

hate having cold water thrown on my work. There is not another man in the country who, in my place, would have compiled such a prospectus as that."

"I am sorry I am late, dear," said a deep bass voice, "but it was the driver's fault. He said I was a woman who ought to ride in a fly and a half, and his horse wasn't used to hauling more than a ton. The man was excessively rude."

"He shall be reported to his employer," Miriam was heard by Bunn to declare.

"That would not do any good," answered that deep voice, which made Bunn turn cold and shiver, "for the master was fetched to look at me before we started. The man was doubtful if the springs of the fly would bear my weight. The master said if I broke them down I should be held responsible."

"Merciful Heavens!" exclaimed Penny Bunn, "what is coming here?"

He listened intently, and heard a snorting in the passage, drawing nearer and nearer. It was accompanied by a shuffling footstep.

Bunn resumed his seat, and feigned to be absorbed in his reading, until he heard Miriam's voice again.

"P. Y., dear, my aunt."

Penny Bunn got up with sham briskness. He was screwed up for the worst, but did not expect anything so overpowering as Miss Astracan Jaggers.

She was six-feet-two, if an inch, and turned the scale at something over twenty stone, if she weighed an ounce. Her features were masculine, of the Duke of Wellington order of build, and her eyes were dark and staring.

They were not intelligent eyes, but had that fixed look we see in inferior waxwork. To add to her charms, she breathed hard, and in a jerky way, as if she was a steam pipe connected with a stationary engine.

"We-e-e-elcome to Littlecote," gasped Bunn.

"Of all the out-of-the-way places," said Miss Astracan Jaggers, "this is the worst. What do you mean by sticking your house on the top of a hill? Why didn't you have it down in the valley?"

"Really," murmured Bunn, "considering that it was built hundreds of years ago."

"I have nothing to do with that," interposed Miss Astracan Jaggers, "you ought not to have had it put up here. I don't see any tea ready for me."

"We were not quite sure, aunt, when you would arrive," murmured Miriam; "I will get you a cup directly. The girl has gone to bed, as she has to be up very early in the morning."

Miriam flew out of the room, and Penny Bunn was left alone with the Gorgon-like woman. They sat facing each other, and he tried, with but a poor result, to appear at his ease.

One of the chief causes of the embarrassment he felt

was the peculiar expression of Miss Astracan's eyes. Though apparently staring him out of countenance, there was, as stated, no expression in them, and it was impossible to be certain whether she was looking at him intently or absorbed in thought.

After Miriam's departure there was a short silence, which was broken by the new-comer. In a voice that seemed to come from a cellar below, she inquired, "Where's the boys?"

"They have retired for the night," replied Bunn.

"All in bed?"

"Yes, Miss Jaggers."

"Say Miss Astracan. I prefer it. It is one of the few joys of my life to know that I am an Astracan."

"Certainly," murmured Bunn, as a profuse perspiration burst out all over him, "it must be a great comfort to you. It would be so to me."

"You," said Miss Astracan, with marked emphasis, "couldn't ever have been one of the forlorn but noble race. Boys in bed, you say?"

"Ye-e-es."

"Tucked up and comfortable?"

Bunn began to think that there was something unearthly about this woman, with her meaningless eyes, deep voice, and curious catchings of the breath. It was only by struggling with his feelings that he was able to reply: "I believe so. I don't know."

"When I have had a cup of tea," said Miss Jaggers, "I will go and see them. If you help me a little, I can get upstairs."

If he helped her a little, she could get upstairs. Bunn sat staring at her, aghast, his eyes unconsciously being in a sense, a duplicate of hers.

"Boys," continued Miss Astracan Jaggers, "if they ain't tucked up, kick off the clothes as they sleep and get cold in their legs. I had no end of trouble with the Orphans at the Asylum, but I didn't mind it while my breath was right."

Penny Bunn felt that it would be utterly impossible to go on talking with this woman and retain his reasoning faculties. So he got upon his feet and begged her to excuse him, while he looked to the doors and windows before retiring for the night.

He reeled out of the room and hastened to the kitchen, where he found Miriam engaged in blowing up the fire with the bellows to make the kettle boil.

"Miriam," he gasped, as he sank into a chair, "that aunt of yours—oh!"

"What is the matter with her?" asked Miriam, composedly.

"Look at her size!"

"She is stouter than when I saw her last, but *that* is no crime."

"And she wants to go upstairs to tuck up the boys in bed. Fancy the Lambs of Littlecote being tucked in at night!"

"Where's the harm of that?" asked Miriam, calmly working the bellows. "If it pleases aunt to see that the boys are comfortable, let her do it."

"You don't understand," said Bunn, despairingly.

"Surely," said Miriam, "you don't think there is any impropriety in it?"

"No, no," returned Bunn, "but think of the fun the boys will make of it and her."

"They won't make fun of her *twice*," said Miriam, as she turned from the fire to look for the teapot. "She used to manage her orphans all right. I hope her bedroom is comfortable. Will you go up and look at it? She will occupy Mr. Snicker's room, and as it is so late, I will stay the night and sleep with her."

"That is kind of you, Miriam," said Bunn, gratefully. He had no objection to go up to the bedroom. Anything rather than return alone to that Gorgon of a woman.

"She has come like a shadow on my prospects," he muttered as he lit a candle and left the kitchen; "can her arrival be an omen of future trouble?"

It was so. Could he but have foreseen the dread time to come, he would have fled from the Abbey that night and returned no more. But the life forward is hidden from all men by a veil which no eye can penetrate.

CHAPTER XCII.

A BREAK-DOWN IN THE NIGHT.—BUNN FEELS THAT HE IS IN FOR A GOOD THING.

IT would be dwelling too long on one subject to go into details of the next hour; it was a day of misery to the wild-eyed Bunn.

Miss Astracan, as she preferred to be called, carried out her programme of going round to see if the boys were comfortable, and she tucked the unconscious sleepers in one by one. Bunn was in mortal terror all the time that some of them would be aroused, but luckily they slept on.

At length the ponderous lady got to her room with her niece, and Bunn, worn out, retired to his, which was two doors off. He was so utterly fagged out that he had no strength left, and it was only by degrees that he was able to undress himself and get into bed.

It was some time before sleep came stealing over him, owing to the excited state of his mind. But at last he was sinking down into the valley of unconsciousness, only to be aroused by a hoarse yell.

"Heavens!" he exclaimed, sitting up in the bed. "What is that?"

There was a murmuring and a groaning not far away, which by strenuous efforts he located in the chamber to which Miss Astracan had retired.

"Something has happened to the old girl," he muttered; "if it should be fatal I shall start housekeeping by paying her funeral expenses."

A minute later there was a tapping at the door.

"Who's there?" he asked, quaveringly.

"Me, Miriam," was the reply; "Get up at once. You have put aunt into one of them lace-up sacking beds; the poor thing has gone right through it. The ropes are broken in a dozen places."

"But what can I do?" asked Bunn, wildly.

"You must help me to make up a strong bed for her somewhere. Surely you do not expect her to sleep on the floor?"

"I'll come in a minute," said Bunn, resignedly, adding to himself, "if you have got any more aunts running loose anywhere, I hope they are thinner."

He was stiff all over, but he lit the candle and managed to make himself presentable in the matter of attire. Then he went outside and found Miriam wrapped in a counterpane waiting for him.

"It has given her such a shock," she said, "and the trouble I had to get her out of the frame of that bed you wouldn't believe."

"I am in that state," said Bunn, "I can believe anything."

Miss Astracan was seated in an old arm chair, swathed in blankets for decency's sake. She was still gasping, and her eyes looked more fixed than ever.

"You ought to have had a wooden upright bedstead for me," she said, viciously. "Haven't you any sense, young man?"

"I am afraid I haven't much left," said Bunn, dolorously.

As there were no other rooms ready for occupation, it was imperative that something should be done with the bedstead, and Bunn, after surveying the wreck, suggested that he should get some planks to put across it for the night. He thought he could find some below.

Miriam sent him away in search of suitable material, and, after rummaging in the kitchen, scullery, and cellar, he succeeded in getting together a lot of stout planks, which he and Miriam utilized as a foundation for Miss Astracan to sleep upon. Finally the bed was made up.

"Now mind this, young man," said Miss Astracan, as Bunn prepared to depart, "you must get a good strong iron bedstead for me to-morrow."

"But your stay is so short," murmured Bunn.

"I don't know about that, young man, for I feel as if, having got up to this place, I shall never have the heart to try to go down again."

He gave her a hurried good night and vanished. In his own room, after an hour's groaning and tossing about, he found refuge from his troubles in sleep.

On the following morning Miss Astracan was unable to get out of bed, and the boys, who had heard of her arrival from their usual informant, Susan, were denied the pleasure of seeing her. Chunder Loo presided at their table, and Miriam and Penny Bunn breakfasted together. He was in low spirits, but Miriam was very bright and spry.

"Now that aunty is here," she said, "you will be able to get on without me, but I shall come to and fro until we are married. I must dispose of my business, and there is a lot to do, you know."

"Yes," he said, in a hollow voice, "a lot to do. Things haven't begun very well."

"You must not give way," said Miriam, sweetly, "we must look to the future. When you have realised your Indian estate"—Bunn shivered—"and two or three black rajahs have arrived to help us, the house will go along swimmingly. Indians make such splendid servants, I have read."

"Yes," said Bunn, "but I heard the other day that there has been a run upon rajahs, and they are getting rather scarce."

"With your family influence," said Miriam, brightly, "you can get what we want. Have another egg, dear?"

"I think I will," said Bunn; "not that I am hungry, but I feel I must be kept up."

He made a very good breakfast, considering, and the hour for his attendance in the schoolroom having arrived, he went forth to labour.

The boys were all in their places, so was Chunder Loo, and he was in the principal desk.

Penny Bunn went up to him, and reminded him of having made a mistake. The other desk was his.

"If you would not mind it, sir," said Chunder Loo, "I would rather remain here, as a strong light affects my eyes. Of course, I am willing to do as you wish, but——"

"It doesn't matter," said Penny Bunn, "you can remain where you are during the time of your probation."

He was resolved that when Chunder Loo had spent a month at the Abbey, he should go. That would end the whole business, and it was not worth while to have any disputing about where they were to sit.

So he took his old place, and the work of the morning went on.

But not in the old style.

Chunder Loo had already laid out new plans, and proceeded to work upon them. He reversed the method of teaching in many instances, and it seemed to the boys that he improved matters. Their way on the road of learning was assuredly much smoother. Chunder Loo helped them along in a quiet, unobtrusive way, that was very comforting.

Penny Bunn naturally resented this new order of

things, but he put up with it, saying nothing. The man was only there for a month, and what did it matter?

More than once there was urgent need for the application of the cane to boys who were unruly, especially in the case of Little Jiggers, who was caught in the act of playing marbles under the desk among the legs of his companions. Chunder Loo reproved him quietly, as Bunn got out the cane, and that somehow was deemed sufficient. The old weapon was put back into its place unused, nor was it brought out again that morning.

The swarthy teacher found favour in the eyes of the Lambs, but for all that, he was not liked by the keenest of them. Jack Ford was of opinion that, as yet, none of them had seen the real man. He had, in Jack's opinion, the look of a man who *was playing a part*, appealing to the gallery for applause, as people say when a person works to gain the good will of the greater number.

The whole thing seemed to be unreal.

Before the school broke up that morning, Penny Bunn addressed the boys on the sudden change in the management of the school, and, in the pride of authorship, read to them the draft of the prospectus he intended to forward to their friends. He trusted that they would stand by him, remembering " the happy days they had spent together in the past."

The response was nothing to speak of. Rooker tried to raise a cheer, but it was early days for the boys to give their alliance to the new *régime*, and for the most part they were silent.

In the playground there was no general discussion, but a number of Jack Ford's more immediate followers gathered on the old stone wall, and held a long conference on the turn of events.

None of them cared to leave the Abbey School, as they had so many friends there, and in the minds of those who once formed the inner circle of the great rebellion against Snicker, there was the knowledge of the treasure hidden in the wood to influence them. If they went away, might not that be lost to them for ever?

"I, for one," said Don, "shall come back, for there are six months due to me. Of course, now that things have so changed, none of us will think of remaining here for the holidays."

"Why not?" asked Tom Drummond, " we ought, I think, to keep an eye on—say Bunn."

He was really going to refer to the things hidden in the cave of Robin Hood, but checked himself in time. It did not appear to the majority that there was any need to keep an eye upon their new master, and the majority declared for home. Finally, only the four members of the Inner Circle decided to remain.

" It has been practically settled so by our friends," said Jack Ford, " and it would look stupid to try and alter it. Naturally I want to see the old folks at home, but they will get enough of me after next term, when I must leave you for good."

From this subject they diverged to that of Mr. and Mrs. Snicker, wondering what had become of them.

" We haven't seen the last of that cheerful couple," said Bob Stockton. " Snicker, when he went away, did not know Penny was going to take his place. As soon as he hears of it there will be ructions."

Then Miriam and Chunder Loo came in for a share of their attention, and Miss Astracan, likewise, was talked of. So the time was whiled away until the hour of recreation was passed and the bell summoned them to dinner.

CHAPTER XCIII.

FAIRLY SETTLED.—THE SHADOW OF COMING MYSTERIES.

SIR CHARLES BARSTOW, like other big men with property, had an agent who settled all his business affairs. This important personage in two days had the agreement ready for Penny Bunn, who was requested to meet him in Chippenham, there to sign and have the same duly attested.

Miriam could not play any part with the pen and ink, but she was there, and she saw that her affianced had nothing stronger than lemonade and tea. Penny Bunn under a temperance *régime* was improved in every respect.

To attend the meeting they hired a pony and cart of a Mumping Malford general dealer, and, barring a bit of jibbing and a tendency to fall down on the slightest provocation, the horse was all that could be desired.

Bunn was not entrusted with the reins, and every time the animal came down, which it did on seven different occasions, Miriam asked the hapless Penny what *he* was doing? His invariable reply that he had nothing to do with it did not save him from a scorching lecture on his general ability for blundering.

But they got home at last, and the erewhile tutor was master of Littlecote School, as firmly established as pen, ink, and paper could make him.

Fontenoy Snicker, named in the deed as *alias* Jerry Snicker, was to give up all claim to the payment of bills due, and future proceeds of the school, on condition of receiving the sum of eighty pounds, which Miriam found, and so far the new possessors of the place started independent of Sir Charles Barstow.

As all the parties concerned had to meet on the day of settlement, there had been present all the elements of a disturbance, but nothing serious happened. Bunn maintained a calm dignity that well became him, and Snicker bottled his wrath.

He was not going out of the neighbourhood, having taken a cottage in the village of Smudgem Bender, next door to the abode of Bibbins, the watch and clock maker by courtesy, mender in practice.

The downfall of Snicker had suspended proceedings for libel on the part of Bibbins, he being wise in his generation, and knowing that blood could not be extracted from a stone. But it was a most unfortunate thing for both that Snicker should have chosen an adjoining house to dwell in. It was impossible for two such neighbours to live in harmony.

Snicker had no definite future beyond a determination to be the ruin of his late tutor. The deed signed and sealed, he was free of all responsibility in connection with the Abbey, and it chanced that the house he had taken was one of the few in the district that did not belong to Sir Charles Barstow.

He was therefore able to act as he pleased, and he forthwith set his mind on carrying out some scheme of vengeance to be hereafter revealed.

Tappilooni's action against him also fell through, as it was brought by a speculative lawyer who hoped to fasten upon him the responsibility of the act of the boys.

This man of law, who lived at Swindon, came to see Snicker the day after all was settled, and, strange to say, ere they parted a perfectly amicable understanding was established between the pair.

It was decided that Penny Bunn might be worth worrying, and worried he was accordingly.

On the very morning after he came into possession of the Abbey, in a legal sense, a fresh writ was issued against him at the suit of the organ-grinder, but that a mistake had been made was soon demonstrated.

Penny Bunn, in a tremor, took the writ down to Miriam, who, having ascertained the facts, promptly trotted off to Bath, saw a first-class lawyer, and a legal letter was sent back to Tappilooni through his legal adviser informing him that he would be prosecuted for endeavouring to obtain money under false pretences, if he dared to proceed further in the matter.

This, for the time, put an end to that affair.

Thus did Miriam, at the very outset of her rule, show that she was not to be trifled with, and Penny Bunn congratulated himself on having secured a priceless pearl of a woman.

Meanwhile the school jogged along without any incident of import to the welfare of the boys.

Miss Astracan, on the third morning after her arrival, declared that she was well enough to get up and take upon herself the duties for which she had been summoned to the Abbey.

Bunn, Rooker, and Chunder Loo were all pressed into service to get her down without an accident, and once below she declared it to be her intention to sleep in the future on the ground floor. The room that had been occupied by Copps was available, and it was put in order by the active Susan for her use.

Miriam Jaggers worked only half days at her business now, and every afternoon she came to the Abbey to have tea with her aunt, spent a few happy hours with the devoted Bunn, and returned home in the twilight.

Her lover had, of course, to accompany her, but she would not permit him to come further than the entrance to the village, with the double object of saving him from a collision with Snicker, and keeping him from the temptations of the Cowley Arms.

Though an enforced teetotaller himself, he could not shut out Miss Astracan from one of the established comforts of her laboured life. It was in the form of gin, prescribed by a London physician, as an anti-fat and a preventive of a threatening dyspepsia.

For her use she had a gallon stone jar of the liquid imported to the Abbey, and it was put into a cupboard in her bedroom, and locked therein.

The lock was an old one, but it was deemed sufficient for the purpose, especially as only herself, Miriam, and Susan were supposed ever to set foot in the chamber. One night, Penny Bunn, having seen his lady-love home, was returning by way of the wood in a pensive mood. He was what the poets would call "sadly happy." All things appeared to be going right with him. The boys were behaving fairly well, and in a fortnight they would, with the exception of four of their number, be going home. Who these four were we know.

Penny Bunn, though in part ignorant of the reason for their staying, did not object to it. The arrangement, he believed, had been made by Snicker, and as he had taken the Abbey with all the responsibilities he was not disposed to alter it.

Miriam assented too, for Chunder Loo would be there, and her aunt, and Susan also.

Two days after the breaking up, the happy pair were to be married. Miriam had never seen the sea, and Penny Bunn was going to take her to the briny shore of some convenient place, and show her the glories thereof. The length of their honeymoon was undetermined.

Penny Bunn was dwelling upon his coming joy with a slight suspicion that there would be a little vinegar with the sweets, when a curious howling sound echoed through the wood.

He stopped short, and thought of that horror to so many nervous people—a mad dog.

He had nothing but a dandified little cane, affected in recognition of the new order of things, with which to protect himself. It was about as much use as a straw to a man in defence against a dog afflicted with rabies.

His blood seemed to turn to ice water, and he felt as if his heart stood still. What was he to do?

Climbing trees had never been an exercise in which he excelled. Ascending any height worth mentioning from the ground also affected his head. It was a horrible position to be in.

But, as he dwelt upon it, vainly trying to settle upon some line of action, the howling was heard again, and in a moment was followed by the voice of a man singing.

The two sounds so opposite came from the same direction, and evidently emanated from the same source.

It was a great relief to him, and curiosity took the place of fear. Believing it was some person who had given way to an undue indulgence in strong waters, he stole in the direction of the sounds, and presently heard another variation of them.

This time the person, whoever it was, had started off with an address of some sort. The words were at the first unintelligible, but, drawing nearer Penny, he heard the following short but powerful address delivered in the accepted style of public oratory.

"Though born in India, I have been reared and educated in your country, and have acquired the taste and habits, as I may say, the aspirations of your people. If you want a man of independent principles, to represent you in parliament, here I stand offering myself to you as a candidate for your suffrages. The people's cause is mine. I am for (here he burst into song)

"'Eight hours work, eight hours play;
Eight hours sleep, and eight bob a day.'

Those, gentlemen, are my principles, and if you think they fit in with your views, then give me your vote and support."

"Chunder Loo," gasped Bunn, "as I am a sinner!"

He moved on stealthily, and presently he saw the Oriental, not as he expected, in the attitude of an orator addressing an audience, but waltzing round and round in an opening in the wood.

Chunder Loo's footsteps were always soft, but now he positively made not the slightest sound as he gyrated about. His face, as he turned it towards the amazed Penny Bunn, exhibited a fierce excitement, held in a measure under control.

"He's a wild man," thought Bunn, and fearing to be caught in the act of playing the spy, he drew back and hastened to the Abbey, which he reached without further adventure,

"I've got something at the Abbey now," he thought, as he paused by the gates of the playground. "What a difference in the brute! No savage ever looked fiercer, and what am I to do with him? Shall I tell

Miriam? But why should I rouse a tremor in her gentle breast? At the end of the month he goes. I wouldn't keep a wild man, especially when he can be so oily, if I were paid a hundred a year to do it."

He was appalled by what he had seen, not that there was anything very terrible in the exhibition, but it seemed to put all sorts of possibilities before him.

A man who could exhibit such an entire change of demeanour might develop into anything.

The scene lay like a waking nightmare on his breast, and when he encountered Miss Astracan blowing off steam in the passage of the Abbey, she was an angel in his eyes compared to Chunder Loo.

He went into the private room, once Snicker's, and now his own, and threw himself into a chair. It was almost dark now, and there was a lamp upon the table ready to be lighted when required. From the schoolroom came the faint murmur of the boys at play.

"I would like to change places with anyone of them," he muttered.

A knock at the door, a very quiet one, brought his heart into his throat.

"Come in," he cried, "and don't stand there thumping."

It was Roger Hone who shuffled into the room and apologised for disturbing the master.

"I wouldn't have troubled you, sir," he said, "but it is a very serious matter. There is a thief in the school."

"Hone," said Penny Bunn, "you will please be careful what you say."

"I wish to be so, sir," said Hone, "but the truth is the truth, and I don't mind who says it; I am not telling a lie."

"I don't assume that you are guilty of such a thing," replied Penny Bunn; "let me know what has given rise to that belief in your mind."

"I had three shillings in my box," said Hone, "and it is gone."

"Where do you keep your box?"

"In the dormitory, as we all have to do."

"Why don't you keep it locked?"

"It was locked, sir."

"You think so, but of course you found it open?"

"No, sir, it was locked, but the things were tumbled about anyhow. Somebody has been to my box and taken the money."

"Will you make this statement before the rest of of the school?"

"Yes, sir, for it is the truth."

"Come with me to the schoolroom."

Penny Bunn rose up and motioned for Hone to go before him. It was a very disagreeable thing he had just heard, but it was nevertheless overshadowed by the affair of Chunder Loo's altered face and voice as seen in the wood. It was even a relief to have something to turn the direction of his thoughts into less disagreeable channels.

The appearance of Hone and Bunn in the school-room cut short a series of antics and skylarkings going on there. The more prominent culprits expected to hear that Hone had been playing sneak to get them into trouble, and they were glaring at him threateningly, when Penny Bunn opened a statement upon the more serious question.

"Boys," he said, "Hone tells me that the lock of his box has been picked and three shillings taken therefrom. I ask you, one and all, to say if you have done this in jest."

There was a dead silence. Amazement was written on every face.

"Speak one at a time," added Bunn, "a simple no will do."

A running fire of negatives followed, and in tones of great variety of scorn and disdain. Not one held back.

"I must believe you," said Bunn; "you hear them, Hone?"

"Yes, sir," was the sulky reply. "I can't say that I have the least idea who did it, but I have lost the money. It came from home only two days ago."

"Did you mention to any of your schoolfellows that you had this money," inquired Bunn.

"No, sir."

"That is strange."

"Hardly so, sir," said Bob Stockton. "Hone has never mentioned a tip from home. He spends all he gets upon himself. And I for one believe he has spoken the truth. We all know how he looks when he is lying."

This was a left-handed testimonial to the veracity of Hone, but it was, in a sense, a confirmation of his story. He was pleased so far, and looking into the face of Bunn, said:

"You see, sir, *they* believe me."

It was a fact. The general conviction was that Hone had lost the money. The way he spoke and his air were both convincing.

But who was the thief? In turn and in concert, the boys denied all knowledge of the affair, until they heard of it from the lips of Penny Bunn. Their manner in giving the denial was also convincing.

"Well, boys," said Penny Bunn, "I must leave things where they are for the present, but I hope, for the good of all, that the culprit will be soon discovered."

He left them, and Hone remaining behind, entered more fully into the details of his loss. The lock had not been forced, he was certain, and it was not a feeble one that could be easily picked. No ordinary thief of the age of the boys could have got at the money.

But who was the culprit was not solved, and it was destined to remain a mystery for a time. When the day came to reveal it, other matters of dark import would be made clear.

CHAPTER XCIV.

THE APPROACH OF BREAKING-UP DAY.—ANOTHER MYSTERY IN THE ABBEY.

MISS ASTRACAN, as housekeeper, was what the boys called a "real treat."

It was quite clear from the outset, that she had notions that they were a little out of harmony with their position in life. She treated them as if, like the orphans, over which she had ruled in earlier times, they were objects of public charity, who had no right to dissent from anything that was said or done for them.

She was not unkind, but she was too fussy to be pleasant. From morning to night she was constantly overhauling them in some way, save, of course, in the hours they spent in the class-room.

She was very methodical too, and looked to them in sections, a dozen at a time.

For instance, when the morning studies were over, Susan would be found outside the door of the class-room, waiting with a list of names of those who had to go to Miss Astracan to be inspected. She had a book, in which she set down a list of the pupils, and she never made a mistake. All had to suffer in turn.

The inspection was at first received in a humorous spirit. The boys had to turn down their jackets, take off their collars and exhibit necks free from dirt. They were questioned as to the number of shirt buttons they had in use, and where one was short a note was made of it. Then they had to take off their boots to see if there were holes in their socks. Finally she made a minute examination of their teeth and hair, reproving or commending them according to the condition of cleanliness revealed.

"I could stand it well enough," said Soppem Smith, after he had gone through the ordeal, "if she wasn't blowing off steam all the time."

"I was awfully polite to her," growled Bob Stockton, who was engaged in cutting his initials on the gate-posts of the playground, "but I don't mean to be so any more."

"Why not?" inquired little Jiggers, who was watching him at work and thereby taking a lesson in amateur carving.

"Because she told me I was a little gentleman," replied Bob, "*and kissed me.*"

A roar of laughter burst from the lips of those around him, but Bob maintained his gravity and went on with his work.

"It is all very well for you fellows to grin," he said, "but it was a trial which I hope you will never have to undergo."

"Did you say anything?" asked Tom Drummond.

Bob did not immediately reply, but indulged in a soft whistle. Then, in a deliberate way, he answered the query:

"All I said was that I was pleased to find favour in her eyes, and that *if she kissed the rest of you, all the lot would be as good as I am.*"

A howl of indignation responded to this confession. In the midst of it they became aware of the presence of Penny Bunn.

Elevation to the post of principal of the college did not seem to have made quite a happy man of him. During the past few days he had been in a very low, nervous condition, and had lost what little colour in his face he previously possessed.

Jack Ford said that it was the prospect of his coming happiness as the husband of Miriam that worried him. He had heard his father say that women always entered into married life as if it were Paradise, and men trembled as if they were going to execution. He considered his paternal parent was an authority on the subject.

"You are merry, boys," Bunn said, in a hollow voice; "it is at the expense of somebody, I presume."

Bob Stockton faced about on hearing him, and suddenly conceived that now or never was his time to speak. With his accustomed coolness he entered upon the subject.

"We were discussing, sir," he said, "the extraordinary things we have to endure under the generic term of inspection. Miss Astracan hauls us over as if we were so much linen going to the wash. The dirty articles are put aside and the cleanly ones hailed with approval. I myself was, on account of my meritorious appearance, kissed."

"Boys," said Penny Bunn, "I will not disguise from you that I think that Miss Astracan's method of procedure is not wholly approved of by me. It smacks of Institutions which are as wide apart from Littlecote Abbey as the poles. But she is not tyrannical or cruel, and you will do well to bear with her during the short term she will reside with us."

"It isn't worth while, sir," replied Bob, "making any fuss about, under those circumstances, but I trust you will agree with us that it is rather unusual for schoolboys to be cuddled by the housekeeper."

"I do," said Bunn, "but as it is kindly meant by one whose stay here is drawing to a close, let it pass."

He went his way, after reminding them needlessly that it was a holiday, and he trusted they would be good boys abroad, and return home punctually.

He was going to meet Miriam, who was coming to the Abbey to spend the afternoon with her aunt to assist her in overhauling things generally.

She came in due time, dined with them, and after dinner Bunn announced his intention to walk abroad, "just to see that the boys were not getting into mischief." As he was of no use at home, but rather in the way, Miriam permitted him to depart, with one of the now too familiar warnings about the need of abstaining from all things intoxicating.

As he was going out he encountered Chunder Loo, who, since that day when he had witnessed his performance in the wood, Bunn had studiously avoided as much as possible.

"I may remind you, Mr. Loo," said Bunn, with a quiet dignity he had worn like a garment since his accession to the throne, "that there is some work to do in the school. The copying books have not been ruled of late."

"I will depute Rooker to see to them, sir," replied Chunder Loo, and glided from the house.

Penny Bunn confounded his impudence in an undertone, and slowly followed him, sadly thinking. Joy lay upon his shoulders like a heavy burden.

The ladies left together, had a cup of tea before going to work, and while partaking of it, Miss Astracan made a startling statement to her niece.

"You remember, dear," she said, "that to meet my wants a gallon jar of gin was ordered for me?"

"Yes, aunt," replied Miriam, "I ordered so much, as it is the cheaper way to buy it."

"Now, dear," continued Miss Astracan, "I am not a humbug in the matter. I require a little gin, and I take it openly. Never do I touch it in secret, and at the outside I do not drink more than an eighth of a pint in the day. Some days I do not touch it at all. According to that measurement, there ought now to be six and a half pints left in the jar, but judge of my astonishment this morning when on inspecting it I found it nearly empty."

Miriam stared at her aunt in astonishment, mingled with wonder and alarm.

"Nearly empty?" she repeated.

"Yes, dear, I do not suppose there is half-a-pint left. It is the first time I have handled the jar, as I always before gave Susan the key of the cupboard, and asked her to get what I required. She takes with her a wine-glass to measure the quantity."

"Are you sure that the cupboard has been kept locked?"

"Quite sure. I try the door every night before going to bed. The question is, was the jar full when it arrived?"

"Full and sealed," said Miriam, emphatically. "I put it into the cupboard myself."

"That the girl is sober, I am convinced," asserted Miss Astracan. "We must, therefore, come to the conclusion that somebody has a false key, or picks the lock so as to steal it."

"It must be P. Y.," said Miriam, with a frown. "In spite of all I have said to him, he will not give up that which will be his ruin and mine."

"If I had drunk it," said Miss Astracan, "I would not deny it for a moment. As I said before, I am not a humbug about what I take."

Miriam sat for a time in deep thought, evidently worried. Having drunk her tea, she went on with the subject.

"P. Y.," she said, "looks very queer, and as we were coming through the wood to-day he kept on looking about as if he expected to see a ghost. I am sure he is ill, and he need not be if he keeps sober. I will speak to him about it when he returns."

Poor Penny Bunn! He was in for it again, and as luck would have it, he came back early for a cup of tea with the ladies.

Then he was put through his facings by Miriam, in the presence of Miss Astracan, and he denied all knowledge of the loss with the utmost fervour that could be put into a denial.

"I have not touched a drop," he said, "since the day I took possession of the Abbey, and I find myself awfully low in consequence. As for having another key, I haven't the least idea of the size and make of the original one. Nor could I pick a lock, if I would, to save my life."

Notwithstanding his earnest denial he was not believed, and after a rather stormy scene with Miriam—Miss Astracan held aloof from it—he left them in a very heated condition of mind and body.

Miriam, a woman of many resources, suggested a plan whereby the culprit could be detected. The remnant of the gin was to be put into a bottle, and a colourless liquid, which she could compound, put in its place in the jar. Whoever took so much as a sip of it, would be immediately taken ill.

"And whoever it is, won't get over it for an hour or two," said Miriam, viciously.

This arrangement was carried out that evening, and she left early without seeing anything more of Penny Bunn.

<hr>

CHAPTER XCV.

THE MYSTERY ASSUMES A MORE POIGNANT FORM.—THE BREAKING UP.

IT was on the following day that Miss Astracan was taken with one of her usual attacks. She was in the kitchen at the time, and she at once dispatched Susan to get her the usual quantity of the prescribed remedy.

She, when taken bad, rolled her eyes and exhibited other symptoms of agony, appalling to a girl li Susan, who dropped the broom she was sweeping u with, and made for the door.

"It is in an ordinary bottle!" gasped Miss Astraca "under the bed!"

Susan, with the glass, sped away, and speedil returned with it half-full. The sufferer tossed off th liquid with a gasp, and immediately uttered shriek.

"Where did you get it from?" she cried.

"From the bottle under the bed," answered Susa

"Is it possible?" moaned Miss Astracan; "run fo Mr. Bunn. I am dying!"

Away sped Susan, charging into the schoolroom where she screamed out the message. Penny Bun nearly fell off his stool, and would have done so if h had not grasped the side of the desk with both hand The boys leaped in their seats. Chunder Loo alon remained undisturbed.

"What is the matter?" cried Penny Bunn.

"Miss Astracan has taken poison!" answere Susan.

Bunn jumped down and rushed from the room wit the girl, leaving a wild, excited mass of boys behin him.

In the kitchen he found the ponderous woman gasping and rolling her eyes about, still in her chai but leaning upon the table.

"Villain!" she moaned; "look upon your work."

"What have I to do with it?" roared Bunn.

"Get me to bed," was all she said.

Penny Bunn and Susan got her out of the chai somehow, and the trio, reeling and staggering, worke their way to the bedroom. How fortunate it wa that it was on the ground floor. Had it been upstair nothing less than a lift would have taken he thither.

"Go for Miriam," murmured Miss Astracan, as sh sank upon the side of the bed, "I want her to hea my last words."

She really looked as if the time had come for her t leave this vale of tears, and Penny Bunn felt that h must needs obey.

Rushing out, he got his hat, and without waiting t explain matters in the schoolroom, ran out of th house, and down through the wood.

He had to stop for breath several times on the way and when he arrived at Miriam's cottage he was fairl done. She was at home, and the arrival of her love in such a state naturally excited in her breast th liveliest alarm. But having got at the facts, sh whipped up her bonnet and mantle and put them on just anyhow, in preparation to depart.

"P. Y.," she said, "this ought to lie heavy on you breast."

He did not answer her, because he had no idea ho

she could put it justly upon him. They went out of the cottage, and Miriam locked the door.

She was on the whole wonderfully calm, but her face was pale and her lips set. There was more anger than terror in the expression of her face. She was in the position of an engineer who had been hoist with his own petard.

Without exchanging a word with Penny Bunn, she walked rapidly back to the school, arriving there about noon. At the door they were met by Susan, who gave them the welcome tidings that Miss Astracan was better, and had fallen asleep.

"She will not waken to-day," said Miriam. "Does anybody but ourselves know exactly what has happened?"

Susan had not said a word to anyone, and so far all was well. Miriam enjoined silence, and bade her go about as if nothing had happened.

"Nor are you to speak of it," said Miriam to Bunn; "it is our affair unless aunt dies, but I have no fear of that."

"You seem to know more about it than I do," said Bunn.

It was a chance shot, but it hit home. Miriam glared at him for a moment, as if she were about to say something bitter, but she abstained and went on to see the patient.

Penny Bunn was deeply mystified as well as harassed, and it was with a weary heart that he went about his ordinary duties.

While he was engaged in the afternoon, Miriam inspected his room, turning over the drawers and searching every hole and corner of it. Whatever she sought, she did not find, and she came downstairs as deeply mystified as Bunn himself.

He came into the room where she was engaged in sewing, and sat down in a chair.

"Miriam," he said, "I am suspected of having poisoned your aunt. On what grounds, may I ask?"

"It was all a mistake," replied Miriam. "Aunt has not been poisoned at all. She has partaken of something out of the wrong bottle. You need not worry any more about it."

Her manner had entirely changed towards him, and he was content. So many mistakes had been made by himself at various times, that he was not astonished errors were made by others.

From a subject that was disagreeable to both, he turned to school matters and general things connected with their future. The circulars he had sent to the parents of the boys, which had been issued a few days before, had been answered in many cases favourably. But it seemed that some of the youngsters had been writing disagreeable letters home, and he would lose some pupils.

"Then we must get others to fill their places," said Miriam. "A few strangers will be an advantage. The present lot want leavening."

He assented, as he always did, although he was inclined to think that in the process of leavening, he might get hold of worse material than he had to handle at present. Future events were destined to prove that he was right.

It is sometimes better to bear the ills we have, rather than fly to others that we know not of.

Of Chunder Loo, Penny Bunn never spoke. He was inspired with a combined fear and hatred of that wily Oriental, but he sank his feelings in the prospect of getting rid of him, when his term of probation had expired.

Miriam referred to him occasionally in an approving way, as a very able teacher and man of unsurpassed manners. Penny Bunn would assent with a nod or a low exclamation that might mean anything, and let the matter drop.

Among the boys there was much mystification about the affair with Miss Astracan, especially when Susan told Tom Drummond that she was under orders not to speak about it. But they soon forgot it in the preparations the majority were making to go home for the holidays.

And had Miriam quite abandoned the suspicion that Penny Bunn had been surreptitiously getting at the gin jar? Not she. He was still, in her eyes, the culprit, and she was determined to catch him in the act, if possible. But that was not to be yet.

CHAPTER XCVI.

BOTCH IN IMMINENT DANGER.—HIS DEBT OF GRATITUDE INCREASES.

MOONING about became the habit of the boys, for a feeling of restlessness was on them. All things at the Abbey were in an unsettled condition.

Discipline naturally relaxed, and Penny Bunn was himself the victim of excitement that rendered him unfit for his duties. He was glad when the next half-holiday came round, and he resolved, in a gracious spirit, to extend the time of absence to an hour later than usual.

The boys went off in bodies, save in one instance—that of Jack Ford. He thought he would like to spend an hour with Botch, the farmer, and he was pretty well assured of a warm welcome.

So he went away to the farm alone, and there learnt that the farmer was away somewhere in the fields, riding a new mare he had purchased, testing it, in fact, on the grass prior to trusting himself upon the animal on the hard, high road.

"And I do wish," said Mrs. Botch to Jack, "that a man of his weight would not try new horses, especially when they are sperrited, like this one he's got. I don't like the look of her. She has too much white of the eye showing."

Jack was fond of horses, and he thought that the spectacle of Botch testing a spirited mare might be interesting.

The farmer was no coward in the saddle. Notwithstanding his weight, which was too much to risk a fall, he would get across almost anything, as he had a good seat and a firm hand.

But the best of riders gang astray at times, as Jack found out that day.

He left the farmhouse, after receiving directions as to the route taken by Botch, and started across a portion of the farm, known as the Witch's Meadow, through which ran a narrow brook, fringed with some swampy land.

The place gained its uncanny name from its having the reputation of being the scene of the death of an old woman, many years before, by drowning, in the broadest part of the brook.

She was what they called in those days being tested. If she floated, she was a witch. If she sank, she was an honest woman.

So they threw her in, and she, like a good, honest woman, went straight to the bottom, and was drowned. Her innocence being established, she was buried at the cost of the parish, and everybody was happy.

Jack got down to the brook, selected a narrow part of it, and took it at a bound. The opposite side was fringed with willows.

As he lighted on the bank the thud of a horse's hoofs fell upon his ears. From the right a saddled steed was galloping towards him, head up, ears pricked, and nobody mounted thereon.

It was Botch's new mare. Jack had no doubt that Botch had come to grief somewhere, perhaps ended his career by breaking his neck.

In the direction from which the mare came there was a hedge, over which the mare had most likely leaped. Jack ran towards it, fought his way through a thin portion of it, and on the other side beheld a spectacle that literally staggered him.

Sticking out of one of the pools of the marshy ground, a mixture of water and mud, were a pair of top-boots and leathern breeches. That they were the property of Botch Jack did not for a moment doubt, and he went to work rescuing the unfortunate man.

He succeeded, after strenuous efforts. Botch was not dead, but he was very near it.

Covered down to waist with slime and weedy matter, he gasped and sputtered until he was able to speak. His first words were: "Never been thrown before in my life—never!"

Don Peebles, taking a short cut to the village, was a witness of this scene from an adjacent stile. He had a quiet laugh over it, but did not stay.

Jack helped Botch home, when, having been duly rated by his wife, he went away to dress.

On coming down again he brought with him small parcel, which he slipped into Jack's hand.

"I ain't a man of words," he said, "but actions. ten-pun note, and if you don't take it, I'll shove into the fire. If you hadn't come along, I was a gor 'un, and it would have cost double that money bury me."

Jack did not argue with him, but put the mone into his pocket, and considered himself well paid.

On his return to the school he mentioned th matter in a casual way. Jack hated fussing over sma matters, as he called them, and showed Don the te pound note.

"It will help us along through the holidays," said.

There the matter ended with him, but not wit Botch, who long remembered his rescue wit gratitude.

But it taught him no useful lesson, for his mar having been caught and brought home, he rode he again the next day, and, what is more, he soon mad her as tractable as a lamb.

Meanwhile time was moving on, and the days fle by until it was the eve of the breaking up, and th boys had gathered together in the schoolroom There were no lessons to learn, for the meeting t gether there in the morning only entailed a listenin to the master's dissertations on the past term.

Their curiosity was excited as to what Penny Bun would say in reference to the stirring events of th time. They looked forward to something edifying.

"Whatever he says," said Tom Drummond, "it wi not be in condemnation of us. He will, of course, la it thickly upon Snicker. By the way, has anybod seen him since he left?"

Nobody had, but it was certain that he was still i the neighbourhood, "lying low" for the chance giving a return blow to Penny Bunn.

"I wish you would all listen to me for a moment cried Jack Ford, as he mounted into the desk no during school hours occupied by Chunder Loo.

There was a call for silence, and the hubbub voices subsided. Jack glanced over the eager fac lifted up to his.

"To-morrow," he began, "we shall all be too bus to say much to each other about the prospect of mee ing again under the shadow of the old Abbey. B it is pretty certain that some of us will go away nev to return."

Here Barnes began to weep, for he was one of tho that would be seen no more there, and Whymp hustled him into a corner.

"You need not snivel," he said; "the place has been all lollipops to you."

"I can't help it," said Barnes. "I cry at most things."

"A situation at the waterworks would suit you," muttered Whymper, as he turned his attention again to Jack.

"During the past term," he was saying, "we have fought and won a great battle. Of all the tyrannical frauds that ever attempted to keep a school, Jerry Snicker is the worst."

A yell of execration responded to his name. Jack held up his hand.

"No more noise than you can help, if you please," he said, "as I do not want to be interrupted by outsiders. We fought and won, I say. In the hands of a good man there should have been nothing to complain of, for of all the places that would be delightful to boys, I think the Abbey is at the top of the tree."

"It takes the cake," said Dorey.

"It does," assented Jack, "although I fear that your way of expressing your admiration must jar upon the sensitive, poetic mind of our respected friend, Herbert May."

"Not at all," said Herbert. "I like to hear people express themselves in a way natural to them."

"There spoke the considerate spirit," said Jack. "Well, then, the question we now have to consider is, what are our prospects in the future? Looking at Bunn, I cannot say that I am overcome with admiration, but, as a master, he is better than Snicker."

"Oceans ahead of him," cried Soppem Smith; "but nothing to brag about."

"Bragging," said Jack, "is not becoming. Now, I, for one, am going to give the new arrangement a trial. With three of my chums, I shall spend the holidays here, and I dare say some of you are very sorry for us; but you need not be, as we are, for more than one reason, well content to remain."

"May I ask what those reasons are?" inquired Hone.

"You may," replied Jack, suavely, "but we do not intend to give them to you."

A roar of approving laughter followed this retort, and Jack resumed his address.

"I hope that as heretofore we are united in the resolve not to put up with tyranny from anyone. If things go on all right and reasonably, well and good; if not, I for one shall kick. Now, the purpose of my speaking to you is to find out from yourselves if you are of one mind with me. All who are will please hold up their hands."

All but Barnes, who was employed in drying his eyes, held up their hands, and Jack smiled his approval.

"Next term," he went on, "I hope to see things glide along pleasantly. Of course, nobody can tell what may turn up. Personally I think we shall witness something stirring, for if there are not exactly clouds in the air, there are portents of coming events.

My firm belief is that next term will either see the place firmly established as a school, or the Abbey cease to be one for ever. It is only a fancy, of course, but it is a very strong one. For myself, I have to thank you all for the allegiance you have shown me in the past and if in the future you retain me in my position as leader I will most assuredly devote myself to your interests. If, on the contrary, you should find one more worthy to fill the post, I shall accept my chucking out with a philosophic resignation that ought to excite your lasting admiration."

He stepped down from his rostrum amid cries of "Good Old Jack! We'll stand by you for ever!" and so on. He had not lost one iota of his influence among them. It is doubtful if any among them dissented from the virtual re-election of their leader, except Hone.

He had not got over the old envious bitterness. It was not in his nature to entirely forget or forgive.

But there was no jarring that night. The morrow would soon be there, and then for six long weeks books would be laid aside, and the majority of them taste the joys of home, sweet home.

"I forgot to say," Jack said, a little later on, "that I do not think it will be advisable for any of you to make any statement at home about the barring-out. It might prejudice the chances of our new master, and I should like him to have a show. He is a bit of a fool, but—— Well, you understand me, I dare say, and there's an end of it for the present."

They laughingly assented, and returned to the various pursuits Jack's address had interrupted.

CHAPTER XCVII.

AU REVOIR.

ON the breaking-up morning Penny Bunn appeared in all the glory of a new suit of black. It had been made by a tailor in Smudgem Bender, and in the matter of collar and fit in the back was open to improvement, but it made him wonderfully respectable.

"He looks as if he had been turned into an angelic pedagogue," said Bob Stockton, in an undertone to Don. Don smiled his approval of the simile.

Penny Bunn had very little to do on this, the last morning of the term.

There were no prizes to distribute—there never had been such things at Littlecote—and he had only to deliver his address and dismiss the boys with a few cakes for their luncheon, and his blessing. But the latter was to be accompanied with a few comments on school matters in general.

Chunder Loo upon his perch was the image of Oriental meekness and resignation to his lot.

"Boys," began Penny Bunn, "during the past term

many events have taken place " (here he referred to a string of notes he held in his hand) " all more or less of an improving nature. It would ill become me to make any comments on the gentleman who has vacated, under heavy pressure, the post I now hold. His conduct, in common with all mortal movements, speaks for itself. He was a narrow-minded man, impudent, arrogant, overbearing, and when out of temper, bitter and cruel. His knowledge of the English language was limited, but tempered with a gift of correcting himself when he blundered, rarely equalled and never surpassed. Of foreign tongues he had no knowledge whatever, and looked upon them as entirely superfluous for man and entirely unworthy of being cultivated." Penny Bunn paused for breath, and Bob Stockton, ever ready to help the weary traveller onward, put in a " Hear, hear."

" Fontenoy Snicker is gone," pursued Penny Bunn, again referring to his notes, " and by good fortune I reign in his stead. Thus does the tide of life shift those who gloat—I mean float—upon it. Of Mrs. Snicker it would also ill become me as a man to speak in just terms. She was a woman of a thousand, on which creation generally may congratulate itself. She was a worthy spouse of a most unworthy man."

He considered this ought to be one of the greatest hits in his address, but it only secured a " Just so," from Don.

With a slightly dispirited face he went on.

" Of myself the least said the soonest mended, perhaps."

A perfect storm of approving applause broke in here, and the invidious nature of it plainly staggered him. But he rallied and pursued the thread of his address.

" We have been friends together——"

" Chorus, boys," said Bob, in a low, clear tone, and there was a burst of laughter.

" Friends together," repeated Bunn, with emphasis, " and I have always, in my heart, been able to recognise the great truth, as immovable as the mountains, that boys will be boys. You must all be aware of that."

He waited for a response in the affirmative, but it did not come, and, with assumed cheerfulness, he resumed his address.

" Although we have never been of one view on all matters, I believe that in the main issue we have been agreed, the school should be conducted on liberal principles " (here burst in a roar of applause), " and it will be my earnest endeavour to do so. I am, as some of you may be aware, about to espouse a lady of high principles and undeniable virtue. She has been an ornament to the sphere in which she has previously moved, and I am sure that her previous career will not be falsified by her bearing here."

He stopped again, but nothing beyond a few dubious murmurs could be heard. Then he concluded as follows:

" Time tries all things, and it will try me. That I

may be weighed in the balance, and not found wanting, is my earnest desire. Boys, Heaven bless you, and a happy time to you all, until we meet again."

They cheered then, their loudest, and he was comforted. It would have been churlish had they done otherwise. Chunder Loo moved no portion of his anatomy during the address, save his eyes, which wandered restlessly to and fro.

The boys, knowing the end had come, broke up in inevitable confusion, and hurried off to get their few things yet unpacked together.

Three carts had been hired to convey their luggage to the station. The boys, partly for economy's sake and partly from choice, intended to walk. And they were going in military procession, in fours, to make their departure more impressive to the people of the village and cottages they would pass by the way.

Perhaps the quartette who were going to remain behind felt a twinge of pain at being left, but they hid it successfully, and when giving a hand to their chums in packing were very merry.

At least, it was not a case of being very solitary and they bore up bravely.

" Write to us all you can," said Jack Ford, " and we will let you know how things are going on here. No doubt I shall have some very interesting tidings to impart."

There was always a cheery ring in Jack's voice, and it was never more cheery than at that moment, but somehow the listeners, in a dim way, felt there was a tinge of sadness in it.

They thought of it afterwards, although they had no time to dwell upon it then. There was another thing which the more thoughtful among them observed, and that was the remarkable change in the physique and general appearance which of late had come over the quartette whom they recognized as the inner circle of their community.

It was not to be all accounted for in the more elder style of apparel they had of late adopted, but it was in their walk, their manner, voice, and in their very features.

So strongly was this change observable, that on Herbert May's sensitive mind there flashed a double picture—the four friends as they had been six months before, and as they were then.

It was the outcome of the earnest work that had resulted in the humiliation of Snicker.

But the time for absolute peace at Littlecote had not come. That was a certainty, and Herbert, as he gave Jack a final grasp of the hand, said, in a low tone: " Jack, old boy, you have carried us through a lot of trouble, and if more should arise, we shall have a sturdy champion in you."

" I know and feel," replied Jack, in the same tone, " that other storms are gathering about us, but school

A SPLENDID SCHOOL STORY.

NEVER BEFORE PUBLISHED.

By E. HARCOURT BURRAGE,

Author of "Ching Ching," "Monkey Mat and Roving Dick," "The Brave Boy of the Basilisk," &c.

The LAMBS of LITTLECOTE

PENNY BUNN SAYS GOOD-BYE TO THE BOYS.

PRICE ONE PENNY.

ALDINE PUBLISHING CO., 9, Red Lion Court, Fleet St., and 1, 2, & 3, Crown Court, Chancery Lane, London.

life has a lot of April in it. It has its alternate storms and sunshine. We must take the life as it comes. I had a strange dream last night of coming strangers, but I won't bother you with it now. You are such a fellow to think, and it might worry you when you should be enjoying yourself at home."

"And you believe in dreams, Jack?"

"Yes, when they come true," was the answer, given with a smile.

"I should like to know what you dreamt," said Herbert, hesitatingly.

"Well," said Jack, "it was all vivid when I first awoke, but during the last hour or so it has been getting hazy. I suppose it is the bustle and confusion of breaking up that is the cause of it. But the vision will come back to me, I am sure. It was a mixture of a curiously mean face—a woman—Chunder my Loo, and a body lying in the wood. I remember, in recall dreams, I knew who it was lying there, but I can't it now. Anyway, Herbert, dear boy, it wasn't you."

"That is something to congratulate myself upon," returned Herbert. "I know you, Jack, so well that I am sure you are shamming having forgotten. But you may be right. It is as well I should not know too much, because I am foolishly sensitive."

"I wish there were more fools of your pattern," said Jack; "then the world would have an increased number of good fellows in it."

Then they shook hands again, and Herbert went away to give a final touch or two to his packing.

Penny Bunn was at the gate when the time came to go, and the boys trooped out of the Abbey in a body. Miriam watched the scene from a window, she having come up to help Susan to put away the bedding and other things, and to witness the breaking-up. Chunder Loo was not in evidence, and Miss Astracan, having another attack of her complaint, was in the kitchen in agonies.

There was a sound of many voices, a score of good-byes to those left behind, and then Herbert May assumed the position of leader, and called on the boys to fall in. The carts had already started with the luggage, and were rumbling through the wood. The sound of the wheels could be plainly heard.

Away they went with a steady marching tramp, and ere they had got far their voices burst into song:

> "There's a good time coming, boys,
>   We are waiting now no longer,
> Snicker is lying in the dust,
>   And we little kids are stronger!"

"They are gone," said Jack Ford, as their voices died away in the wood; "gone from a life that was at one time the most miserable ever known to boys in a school of this class. They are happy in the belief of a better future. I hope they may not be disappointed."

"I'll say amen to that," said Don; "but, as my father said when the bull from the market ran into the shop, and upset the whole of his stock, and broke the window, you never can tell what is going to occur."

CHAPTER XCVIII.

PENNY BUNN'S COMING WEDDING.—A DROP OF GALL IN THE CUP OF BITTERNESS.

IT was noon when the main body of the school departed, and shortly after Susan laid dinner for four in the long room, once the refectory of the Abbey, and under whose rafters many a merry party of the monks of old had sang, and laughed, and quaffed.

There was no master or usher to sit at the head of the table that day. It was tacitly understood that the four boys were to live with the freedom of a home in all things. Jack Ford took the top of the table, and proceeded to carve the joint of cold boiled beef thereon.

"Well, here we are," he said, "and the old den looks dull enough without the rest. But I dare say we shall get accustomed to it. Has anybody seen Chunder Loo?"

"Not since the breaking-up," replied Don, "nor Rooker, either."

"Rooker," said Bob Stockton, "goes away to a maiden aunt of his to spend the vacations. If he hasn't gone already, he will steal away quietly by-and-by."

"I would rather Chunder Loo had gone in his place," said Jack, thoughtfully; "can't make that fellow out, nohow."

"Though born in India," said Tom Drummond, "he seems to have acquired some of our tastes and habits."

They all laughed quietly at the repetition of the favourite stock phrase of the Indian teacher, but Jack Ford looked upon him as a very serious subject for discussion.

"Boys," he said, "I would rather have fifty Snickers and four hundred Penny Bunns to deal with than one Chunder Loo."

"What have you got into your head now?" asked Don Peebles.

"Nothing very clear," answered Jack, "but there is a misty something that worries me a bit. However, we will not talk about it now. What shall we do this afternoon?"

"What do you say to running down to Botch's?" suggested Bob Stockton, "He will be glad to see us."

"Yes, that will do," said Jack. "Now, last term a great discovery was made under the Abbey"—here he lowered his voice and looked around. "Of our share in in it I will not speak at this moment. It will be better for us to be mum within the walls of the Abbey, as we have been heretofore, as far as possible. But I can say, without fearing anything wrong will come out of it, that I believe other, and possibly greater, discoveries may be made. We have several weeks before us, and we need not hurry to begin a second course of searching."

"Penny Bunn will be married on Monday," remarked Tom Drummond; "after that we shall have a free hand."

"Not exactly," returned Jack; "there will still be Chunder Loo. But for him we should have had an entire week to ourselves. Sue and Miss Astracan would not have interfered with us in any way."

"Give me a little more beef," said Don. "Don't forget that fat, Jack. Of all the fats, commend me to that of boiled silverside. Talking of Chunder Loo, don't you think that we might, in some way, get rid of him?"

"How?"

"That we must talk over. I wonder what the beggar does with himself in his leisure time. I never see him about."

"Well, drop him now," said Tom Drummond. "Is there a pudding to-day?"

"Not likely. Sue and the future Mrs. Bunn are busy putting away the rags in the dormitory. Now, there's a woman we shall be obliged to keep an eye on."

"Sharp as a needle," said Bob Stockton. "She is very different to the departed Mrs. Snicker. By the way, wouldn't it be fun to give the old people a look in as we pass by?"

"Anything for a change," said Bob Stockton.

"Any of you want more beef?" asked Jack.

An answer in the negative having been given, Jack rose with the rest and they slowly sauntered from the room. In the hall they met Susan, who asked them if they had seen Chunder Loo.

"No," replied Don; "do you want him particularly?"

"Mr. Bunn wishes to know where he is."

"Haven't seen him," said Bob, "since the morning."

The boys went off to spend the afternoon, and Susan hastened to the newly-appointed master of the school with the information that she was unable to find the Hindoo tutor.

Penny Bunn, in all the glory of his new black clothes, was sitting before two mutton chops, which his loving Miriam had cooked. One was for Chunder Loo, with whom the head of the establishment desired to have a little talk.

"Not to be found?" said Bunn. "Where the—where is he?"

As he impatiently put the question to the girl, Chunder Loo, with his tightly-clothed, snake-like form, dark, close-set eyes, and hooked nose, glided into the room.

"I understand, sir," he said, "from the boys, that you wish to see me."

This was not exactly true, for Chunder Loo, while the boys were at dinner, had been hidden in a big cupboard in a corner of the room, and had heard all they had said to each other. Why he should take the trouble to hide himself will be apparent by-and-by. Gliding out immediately after their departure, he overheard Susan inquiring for him, and that was how he followed so readily on her heels.

"Sit down," said Bunn, curtly, "and have a chop. Susan, you can go."

Susan vanished, and Chunder Loo, with a wriggling action, took a seat at the table.

"You eat chops, of course?" said Bunn.

"Though born in India," began Chunder Loo, "I——"

"Certainly," interrupted Penny Bunn, "one is a chump, and the other from the loin. Which will you have?"

Chunder Loo preferred the chump, and it was handed to him.

"Now, Loo," said Bunn, as he peppered his chop freely, "let us come to business at once. I don't think you will suit. As you are here on a month's probation, and the boys won't be back for six weeks, of course there will be no chance of your being tested any further. What I propose to do is to pay you board wages for the rest of the time and let you go."

Chunder Loo cut off four square inches of his chop, gave the piece one bite, and swallowed it.

"It is not convenient for me to go," he said, with all the coolness imaginable. "Though born——"

"Bother where you were born!" interrupted Bunn, "and also your convenience. You've got to go."

Chunder Loo shook his head, cut off a bigger chunk of chop, put it into his mouth, and swallowed it without a bite at all.

"I was going to say that, though born in India"—Bunn wriggled in his chair—"but in deference to your wishes I will, for the time, omit to make a statement that I have found to be imperative on occasions, to make myself understood, and come to the point of law on the subject. I am here for a month, and a month I must, in duty to myself, stay."

Then he took up the rest of his chop, and it vanished down his throat as if he was doing a conjuring trick.

"Do you always eat in that way?" demanded Bunn, at a loss what to say.

"According to the days in the week I eat," answered Chunder Loo, as calmly as ever. "In that one thing I remain true to my caste. It was the religion of my progenitors to eat according to the time and the position of the moon."

"You belong to the Bolting Fakirs, I suppose?" said Bunn, grimly venturing on a joke, although he felt anything but jocular in his heart.

Chunder Loo bowed.

"That may be the true translation of the title of our caste," he said. "Is there any other subject you desire to speak upon?"

"I don't know that there is. You say you won't go?"

"I do."

"All right; then there is an end of the matter *for the present.*"

"Then I will depart, as my faith calls me away to other duties of the day."

He arose, bowed, and in a moment he was gone.

Penny Bunn looked at the ceiling, at his half-empty plate, and, after a struggle with his feelings, went on with his meal.

"So I have got a Bolting Fakir in this show, have I?" he muttered; "a nice look out. Here is a drop of bitterness to start on. A Bolting Fakir! Hang it! he's a human snake. I wonder whether he could be got to eat something tough enough to choke him?"

CHAPTER XCIX.

A VISIT TO SNICKER.—THE WEDDING MORN.

FONTENOY SNICKER, Esquire, sat by the door of the humble cottage to which his change of circumstances had reduced him. He had a newspaper in his hand, but he was not reading it. His whole attention was occupied in listening to a wordy warfare going on between Mrs. Snicker and Mrs. Bibbins, who were exchanging volcanic compliments across the wooden fence that divided the little front gardens, and the ex-schoolmaster was thoroughly enjoying himself.

The subject-matter under discussion was a broken window in the Snicker cottage, shattered by a stone from a penny catapult, known to be the property of one of the Bibbin boys, and supposed to have been deliberately used by him to destroy a portion of the Snicker residence.

Mrs. Snicker we know, but Mrs. Bibbins has not hitherto appeared in the Littlecote records.

She was a small woman, not more than four feet ten high, and exceedingly spare in form, but what she lacked in substance she made up in spirit.

"Whatever my husband may be," she was saying, "he isn't a libelling lump of refuse throwed out of a school. As for my boy, if you lay a hand on him, I'll take your bonnet off for you!"

"I wouldn't bemean myself to fight," retorted Mrs. Snicker.

"Say *de*-mean yourself, Phœbe," said Snicker, softly.

She heard him, and turned sharply.

"You mind your own business, Jerry," she said, with her nose in the air. "If you was a man, you would go and throw that pottering little watchmaker down his own well. But you allus took the part of any *worm* that insulted me."

Jerry, *alias* Fontenoy, Snicker suddenly became absorbed in his newspaper, and Mrs. Snicker returned to the charge.

"*You* take *my* bonnet orf," she cried, "you wisp of a woman! Come and do it!"

As she spoke she leant over the fence to give emphasis to her challenge, and so put herself within reach of the foe. Perched on her head was a well-worn bonnet which had seen better days, but was still a faded thing of beauty, being garnished with about half-a-peck of artificial flowers.

Mrs. Bibbins gave a cat-like leap towards it, and in a moment it was gone, with a false front of hair to keep it company.

Having gained possession of this valuable trophy of war, the watchmaker's wife proceeded to throw it scornfully upon the ground and execute a festive dance thereon.

Mrs. Snicker, after one frantic, futile effort to get over the fence, made a dash for the gate, intending to invade the enemy's country, and there let slip the dogs of war. Snicker, seeing matters were getting serious, and might lead to legal consequences, threw down his paper, and, springing up, rushed in pursuit.

"Stop, Phœbe!" he yelled; "don't do anything on *her* ground, or you will get the worst of it!"

But Mrs. Snicker was not in the frame of mind to hearken. She had been despoiled of a bonnet and a front, and revenge she would have at any cost. Whisking round to the other gate, she dashed into the Bibbins's garden, followed by her husband, and the watchmaker, who had, up to that time, lain *perdu*, rushed out of his house.

Mrs. Bibbins stood her ground, and in a flash all four were locked in a deadly embrace in the thick of a promising bed of autumn cauliflowers.

In three seconds Mrs. Snicker was *hors de combat*—lying on the ground and, furthermore, deprived of a chignon which had adorned her head at the back, and a wisp of lace round her neck. Snicker also became conscious of his being the recipient of two remarkably stinging blows in the region of his left eye, and of all his own energies being wasted on the empty air.

A loud hurrah burst from some lusty young throats in the road, and, wheeling round, his one available optic showed him that the four boys to whom he owed his fall from the Littlecote high estate had arrived upon the scene.

Bibbins, being either ignorant of or deliberately ignoring the chivalry of fistic warfare, hit him on the side of the head, and sent him staggering to the garden wall.

"At him, Snicker!" cried Bob Stockton. "Don't be whopped by a man half your size."

It was a horrible yell that burst from the lips of the schoolmaster. One of his old fits of blind rage came over him. He forgot the present, and recalling the past, sprang into the road and went for the boys.

It was Mrs. Snicker's turn now to sound a note of warning. She had just risen to her feet, defeated and humiliated, but her mind was fairly clear, and she saw the red light up in the wild action of her husband.

"Jerry, you fool!" she screamed, "let the boys alone."

"Don't funk him!" cried out Jack Ford; "we are four to one."

As Snicker charged at them, hissing like a boiler on the point of bursting, the boys opened out, and having let him pass, charged from the rear.

They did not hit him, but simply threw themselves against his back, and their weight toppled him over upon the dusty road.

He fell rather heavily, and rolling over upon his side, saw Botch, the farmer, reining up his horse hard by.

"Well done, lads," sang out the yeoman; "what is the old bully up to now?"

A number of the people residing in the village, hearing the commotion, came out of their houses, and there was quite a throng around as the defeated Snicker rose from the dust.

"Schoolmaster," said Botch, "there's a horse pond not far from here that would be glad of your company."

"Why do they come here worriting—*worrying* me?" hissed Snicker. "Isn't it enough that they've lied agin me and ruined me, and put a nincompoop in my place? Why ain't they gone 'ome—*home*, blow it!—with the rest of the little wipers—*vipers?*"

"We did not interfere with you," said Jack; "all we did was to cheer when the watchmaker gave you a whacking."

"This man," said Bibbins, coming forward, "is a low-bred scoundrel. He is howling half the night, and spends his days in threatening my children. I'll take him afore the Chippenham Bench."

Snicker loweringly glanced at him, then at the laughing boys.

"Look here," he said, between his teeth, "listen to me, you four! All that I've enjured—*dured*, hang it!—comes from you. And before long I'll be even with you, if it costs me my life. Phœbe, where are you?"

Phœbe, having been reduced to a state that made her unpresentable in public, had quietly retreated to the seclusion of the cottage in which she dwelt. Mrs. Bibbins, the victorious, stood smiling by her gate.

"Go indoors, schoolmaster," advised Botch, "and don't give out murderous threats that one day may be brought up against you."

"I mean what I say," cried Snicker, quivering with wrath, as he moved across the road; "let them look to it."

Many who saw the late schoolmaster of Littlecote slouch into the cottage remembered, in after days, the words he uttered at that memorable time, and, above all, the expression of his face. It was fiendish.

The lookers-on broke up, and the boys walked away with Botch, who asked them if Snicker ever looked like that when he kept school. They laughingly replied that at any time, when he was in a venomous mood, he was not a pretty picture.

"He's a bad 'un," said Botch, sententiously.

He wanted to know how it was that the boys had not gone away with the rest, and they told him it was by their own wish that they had stayed behind. It was a vague reply, but it seemed to satisfy him.

They went on to the farm with him, and he asked them in. There they spent a pleasant hour or two, and returned to the Abbey early in the evening, without anything transpiring worthy of note.

Time sped on, and things at the school remained much as they were. Chunder Loo did not beat a retreat, and Penny Bunn, who had tried an experiment upon him and failed, took no further action.

The preparations for the wedding kept Miriam and her aunt busy.

At length the auspicious morn arrived, and Bunn arose from his couch with the feelings of a man who was going to execution, and had not the slightest hope of reprieve.

There was nothing novel in his sufferings, for they are the common lot of man, and arise more from a nervous temperament than from any justifiable fears that the coming life will be more miserable than that which has preceded it.

Penny Bunn had never passed his days or nights upon a bed of roses, and, whatever was in store for him, he could hardly be worse off than he was before.

As Miriam did not encourage extravagant outlay, he was going to be married in the black coat and waistcoat he had worn on the breaking-up day, with a new pair of light trousers.

Unfortunately he selected the pattern by candle light, when the material appeared to be a rich grey. When made up and exposed to the glare of the brighter day, the grey colour proved to be rather a pronounced blue.

He dressed himself, and on leaving the room he had slept in, his nostrils were saluted by an odour of burnt meat. Tracking it along the corridor to its source, he discovered that it emanated from the chamber occupied by Chunder Loo.

Having tried the door and found it locked, he knocked thereat, and after a short delay Chunder Loo opened it.

The rush of the odour from the room nearly overpowered Bunn.

"What are you doing in there?" he demanded.

"I, sir," replied the Hindoo, bowing low, "have been roasting a small pig in the grate."

"In the name of everything," exclaimed Penny Bunn, startled by the answer, "what for?"

"It one of the customs of my caste, to bring good fortune to a friend on his wedding day," replied Chunder Loo.

"Where did you get the pig from?" asked Bunn.

Chunder Loo, without the least hesitation, answered: "Found him."

"Found him? Whose pig is it?"

Chunder Loo shook his head. He had not the least idea. He discovered the little pig trotting about outside the Abbey gates on the previous evening, and he had conveyed him to his room forthwith for the necessary sacrificial purposes.

"Then you have had the little brute in your room all night?"

Chunder Loo bowed as if he had done a meritorious action.

"I can't have this sort of thing going on," cried Penny Bunn, hotly.

"It will happen no more," said Chunder Loo, with an overwhelming simplicity, "until you marry again."

Penny Bunn put his hand to his brow. He hardly knew what to say or do. This dark-eyed, imperturbable son of the East was altogether too much for him.

"What are you going to do with the pig?" he feebly asked.

"Bury him, *deep*," answered Chunder Loo.

"But what is the game? Where is the good? *Cui bono?*" asked Penny Bunn.

"Only Hindoo knows," was the reply.

Bunn walked away with uncertain steps, and by sheer instinct found his way to his private room, where breakfast awaited him. Miriam was, of course, at home, and would meet him, in due time, at the altar.

"He roasts a pig on my wedding morn," said Bunn, staring out of the window, "for luck. But what sort of luck? Hanged if I don't think I've got a fiend, a juggler, an alchemist, a worker of evil

spells, in the house. What is going to be the end of it?"

"Are you ready for breakfast, sir?" asked Susan, appearing at the door.

"I am ready for anything," hissed Penny Bunn. "By the way, have you any arsenic in the house?"

"No, sir," replied Susan, calmly, "but there is a packet of mice poison."

"Put it into an omelette for Chunder Loo," said Bunn, "and bring me a rasher and an egg."

Susan whisked away, muttering to herself:

"I never see a man so much upset by his wedding day. But there! All men seem to be afraid of it. He will be better after breakfast."

CHAPTER C.

THE HAPPY PAIR.—THE DESERTED ABBEY.

A WEDDING in a country village is a great event, and all but the bedridden think it is their bounden duty to be present inside the church, or in the ground attached to it.

Before the church clock struck the hour of ten, the graveyard was alive with old women and children, who had taken up points of vantage to see the chief actors in the joyous drama pass by.

Hard by Miriam's cottage, which she was to leave that day for ever, the young maidens congregated, and at intervals sought to get a glimpse of her through the window. As she was past the time of life when women are wooed, her having gained a lover was deemed a latter-day miracle, and created excitement in proportion to its strangeness.

There was peace in the village, outside the natural excitement. Even the warfare of Mrs. Snicker and Mrs. Bibbins was suspended, and they stood by their respective gates awaiting the passing of the bride without firing a single shot at each other.

Fontenoy Snicker was going to the church. It was something to do, anyway, and he wanted to see how his successor bore himself under the trial.

If he got a chance, he amiably meant to put a spoke in the wheel of the proceedings.

One of the early arrivals was Chunder Loo, whose general appearance terrified a lot of little ones, from six years old downwards, into a spell of silence. He carried a small parcel in his hand, and he bowed very politely to all the old women he passed as he made his way to the church.

He was the very first of the public to enter therein, and he modestly took a seat that belonged to the squire of the parish, and, naturally, was in a very prominent position. It was, as a matter of fact, in the chancel, close to where the bridegroom would have to stand.

Presently the clock struck eleven, and then the outside feminine public began to flock in and secure the better seats. A quarter of an hour later the four youngsters who had remained behind in the Abbey appeared, and close upon their heels came Penny Bunn.

He walked with feigned composure to the altar, and at first did not see Chunder Loo. The pew-opener, an old woman of eighty years, but upright still, came up and touched him on the arm.

"Who is the best man, sir?" she asked.

"Bless me," exclaimed Bunn, "I have forgotten him. Is he necessary?"

"Yes, sir," replied the old woman; "it is Miss Jaggers that told me to remind you. She says that she never thought of it until this morning."

"I haven't one," said Bunn, dismayed.

"My husband would have stood for you," said the pew-opener, "but he is in bed with the rheumatics, and he is as deaf as a post. Oh, here is a gentleman."

It was Chunder Loo, who had glided out of the squire's pew, and stood there bowing.

"Though born in——"

"Oh!" gasped Bunn.

"*Another* land," continued Chunder Loo, "I have frequently attended your wedding festivals, and know how to comport myself. I will be your best man."

Before Penny Bunn could refuse this offer, as he intended to do, Miriam appeared, leaning upon the arm of a local publican, who had volunteered to play "pa" for the occasion. Two of his daughters, giggling and blushing, acted as bridesmaids.

The parson, at the same moment, glided out of a side door and took his place inside the altar rails.

There was no time to repudiate Chunder Loo and get another in his place. Penny Bunn bowed his head to the decrees of Fate, and allowed things to slide.

Miriam, coolly triumphant, walked up the church without a falter, until her eyes fell upon Chunder Loo, meekly occupying the place of best man.

Her eyes flashed fire, and for a moment it seemed as if she were about to turn and leave the sacred edifice, but cooler reasoning instantly prevailed.

Gliding up to Penny Bunn, she favoured him with a cool, cutting whisper.

"And this is *your* idea of a best man?" she said.

Penny Bunn would gladly have offered an explanation, but there was no time for anything of the sort. The parson was in a hurry, as he expected some friends to luncheon, and not being particularly interested in the bride or bridegroom, he rattled through the marriage service at express speed.

Some of the responses of the bridegroom were a little wide of the mark, and for the most part unintelligible, but that did not trouble anyone, and in a few minutes he and Miriam were bound in wedlock.

Chunder Loo, as best man, occupied the attention of the greater part of the audience. Standing just behind Penny Bunn, he went through a series of contortions, presumably the outcome of his emotions, that terrified and appalled all the little boys and girls, and set the old people wondering. Fontenoy Snicker, seated at the back of the church, watched him with increasing interest, and felt inclined to congratulate himself on having escaped such a weird creature for an undermaster.

The ceremony was over, and the usual signatures having been appended to the register and the fees paid, the happy pair walked to the Cowley Arms, where a breakfast had been prepared for the principal actors in the matrimonial drama.

It was laid in the parlour for six, bride and bridegroom, the host who gave Miriam away, his two daughters, and best man. There was no shutting out Chunder Loo, as he managed to get into the room just two seconds before the newly-married couple, and to the eye of Bunn he was the skeleton of the feast.

Everybody but the bridegroom had a glass of champagne, but he was, by virtue of his pledge, called upon to drink the necessary toasts in soda water.

It was as dismal an affair as ever took place in connection with a wedding, and everybody but Chunder Loo was glad when it was over.

Miriam had been married in a travelling dress, to save expense and the bother of changing, and the cab being at the door, there was nothing to cause delay.

"P. Y., dear," said Miriam, as she drained the last of her champagne from the glass, "will you go and see if all the luggage is on the carriage? There are three boxes of mine, your portmanteau, and a hand-bag."

Penny Bunn, inflated and depressed by an undue indulgence in soda water, rose up and went forth. He had a vague idea that now or never was his time to flee away from all his troubles and be at rest, but he had not the courage to act upon it.

Outside he found all the little children of the village awaiting the departure of the happy pair, and seated on one of the forms by the door of the inn were the four pupils who were still resident at the Abbey.

Bunn cast an eye over the luggage, and then turned to the boys, who rose up and came towards him to say good-bye.

Jack had a letter in his hand.

"This came in by the second post this morning,

to the post-office here, sir," he said. "I called in to know if there was anything for me. As it has the crest of Sir Charles Barstow upon the envelope, I thought it might be important."

"It may be," said Bunn, regarding it as he would have looked at a lighted bombshell. "Thank you. Boys, one word before I go. Beware of *Chunder Loo.* There is evil in the man. Enough—no more—she comes."

And she came, accompanied by her bridesmaids, to kiss at the door of the hired fly, which stood there, with a saturnine driver on the box.

Chunder Loo waited behind a moment to drain all the bottles and glasses. But he did it expertly, and was there to say adieu before Bunn had taken his seat.

"Gracious lady," said Chunder Loo to the bride, "farewell. Vishnu watch over you. The shadows of the blessed rest on you. Farewell."

Miriam, quite overcome by this presumably Oriental form of blessing, gave him her hand, which he raised respectfully to his lips.

The next moment he was jerked away by Penny Bunn.

"That will do," said the bridegroom, haughtily; "we don't want anything of that sort from your breed."

Just for one brief half-second—all the four watching boys saw it—there was a quivering turn of the upper lip of Chunder Loo. It was like that often shown by an irritated Collie dog, and then that dark face was as inscrutable as before.

"The breed of a man," said Chunder Loo, "is not of his own choosing. Though born in India——"

"Here, get away!" cried Bunn, as he sprang in. "Hurry up, driver, or we shall miss the train. Born in India—I wish to goodness the beggar had died there."

"My dear," said Miriam, "you are too hasty with the poor creature. I always pity the unfortunate people who are born with black faces."

"Don't talk about him," groaned Bunn, "he won't bear thinking of. Here is a letter from Sir Charles Barstow, our knightly landlord. I wonder what it is about?"

"Open it and see, dear."

Penny Bunn tore open the envelope, and read as follows :—

"DEAR SIR,—In your proposal to take over the Abbey, you offered to reinstate the flooring in the chamber occupied at one time as a bedroom by Mr. Snicker. I shall be glad if you will get on with it as quickly as possible, as several friends of mine are anxious to see it. I have found an old drawing of it, which I will forward by hand, as it is a very rare work, in the course of a few days.
"Yours very truly,
"CHARLES BARSTOWE, BT."

"Blow it !" ejaculated Bunn. "I had forgotten all about that blessed floor, but I think I shall be able to manage it with the help of the drawing."

"I fear not, Penny dear," said Miriam, softly, "for I have learnt from Susan that the pieces of wood have been used for firewood."

Bunn leant back in the corner of the carriage and put his hand over his eyes. Thus he sat for awhile without moving. Presently he dropped his hand and groaned.

"This is a good beginning to a honeymoon. Miriam, we are as good as already chucked—chucked I say—from the Abbey."

"Don't be vulgar, and don't talk nonsense," said Miriam. "You leave things to me."

But he only groaned again. There was no light around, and not so much as a single star in the dark prospect ahead of him.

———

CHAPTER CI.

KEEPING AN EYE ON CHUNDER LOO.—LETTERS FROM CHUMS AND LINGO.

"WE are to keep an eye on Chunder Loo," said Jack. "Certainly."

The boys drew back and, unseen by him, resumed their seats by the door of the inn. The carriage drove away, followed by a yelling crowd of youngsters for a distance, and Chunder Loo remained where he had said adieu.

He stood quite still, presenting his profile to the boys, and his dark eyes were fixed in the direction of the departing carriage. The expression of his face was something to set one thinking.

For fully two minutes he did not move, and then he slowly turned away, and, with his peculiar gliding step, went away down the village. Apparently he walked very slowly, but he was so soon gone that his pace must have been very brisk.

"What do you think of him?" asked Don, as he vanished round the bend of the road.

"Crafty," said Jack, "but what else I am not sure of."

"And cruel, I should say," remarked Tom Drummond; "but on the whole he is a puzzle. I wish we had Lingo to help us to fathom him."

"I have a letter from Lingo in my pocket," said Jack," and others from some of the fellows, Whymper, Dorey, Tanner, and two or three more. I did not make a show of them before, as there may be something of importance, in Lingo's, at least."

"Would it be safe to read them here?" asked Don.

"Yes, but we need not do so. I told Sue that we might not be back to dinner, and as I have some lucre, what do you say to a chop inside here?"

A ready assent was given to the proposition, and

they entered the inn. Jack ordered chops for four, and they adjourned to the scene of the recent festivities. A servant girl was engaged in removing the remnants of the feast and appropriating certain fragments thereof, which would not be missed.

Jack sat down in a corner away from the table and the others stood by the window awaiting the departure of the domestic. They could not, of course, talk of their private affairs before her.

As Jack looked carelessly about him he espied, lying under the table, what seemed to be a big, black worm.

Startled, he stared at it, expecting it would move, but it remained quite still. Then he next observed that around its neck, as it may be called, close to the head, was a thin golden band. Whatever it was, it showed no sign of life, and was probably an ornament or a toy.

He was about to call the attention of the girl to it, when it flashed upon him that it might be something peculiar, with which the people of the inn had nothing to do. So he waited until the girl had gone out with a pile of empty plates and dishes on a tray, and then quietly picked it up.

It was not a worm, but a small, stiff, and still snake, the smallest, as a matter of fact, he had ever seen. The eyes were closed, and he judged it had been expertly stuffed.

There was a peculiar colouring in the scales, and the ring about its neck was undoubtedly gold. It was engraved all over with minute hieroglyphics.

"Something of Chunder Loo's," thought Jack, and he thrust it into his pocket. For the present he resolved not to say anything to his companions about his find.

In a little while the table was prepared for the boys, the chops were served, some mild ale ordered, and they sat down.

Jack brought out the letters, and opened that which came from Lingo first.

"Hope to be with you shortly," was practically the sum and substance of it.

"It will be jolly to have him here," said Bob Stockton. "Pass the pepper, Don, if you please. Thanks. Lingo will be invaluable to us."

"I think I had better write to him at Calne, his old address," said Jack. "He will sure to go there first, and I am certain he ought to know something about Chunder Loo."

"But we can tell him everything about him when he comes," suggested Tom.

"Lingo may think it necessary not to show himself to Chunder."

"Something in that, Jack. And, after all, we may be worrying unnecessarily about the darkie."

"If we are, there will be no harm done. But one

false step may ruin all. Suppose, for instance, he were to get a clue to——"

Jack stopped short. He sat facing the door which the girl had left ajar, and fancied he saw it move.

"Tom," he said, softly, "there is somebody listening. See who it is."

Tom got up quietly, and glided to the door. Throwing it open, he saw that nobody was there.

"You are mistaken, Jack," he said.

"The door moved," replied Jack, "and there is not a breath of air about. Drop all private matters for the present."

This they did, and went into "schoolboy talk," of lessons and games, and what they would do when the school began again.

Ten minutes later Chunder Loo was seen to pass the window, and he came right on into the room.

"Ha! young gentlemen," he said, rubbing his hands together, "you are enjoying yourselves. You drink to the bride and bridegroom."

"Not as yet," replied Don, "but we don't mind doing it. We do not wish either any harm."

"Why should you?" exclaimed Chunder Loo, with apparent warmth; "they are most excellent people."

"Though not born in India," put in Jack, drily.

"No," said Chunder Loo, gravely, "not born there, and well for them, and for you, too. It is the land of the weird and the accursed—a country of magic and mystery--the land of what your Scotchman would call 'the uncanny.'"

"Fakirs live there, for instance," said Don, humorously.

"You do not believe in the fakirs," said Chunder Loo.

"I can't swallow all I read about them," answered Don. "For instance, there is that yarn about the fellow who was buried alive for six months, his grave covered with earth, wheat grown over it, cut when it was ripe, and then when they dug him up again he was alive. A yarn of that strength wants a little salt."

Chunder Loo, who had been gliding about the room, his eyes wandering restlessly here and there, sat down in the seat Jack had occupied when he first came into the room, and glanced keenly under the table.

He was certainly ill at ease. The boys had never seen him so restless before. The next moment he was on his feet again.

"The fakir who was buried was not alive when they dug him up," he said.

"Then the story is a lie?"

"No, they brought him *back to life.*"

"I can't believe it," said Don.

"I saw it done when I was a boy," said Chunder Loo, his eyes still wandering about. Jack was certain by this time what he was seeking. "I knew the fakir, no man better, and he was buried, and the wheat grown upon his grave. It took all the day, when they dug him up, to bring him back to life. They were just in time, for the sun was going down. Had night fallen upon him unrestored he would have been truly dead."

There was a fierceness approaching wildness in his manner, as if he were earnestly supporting truth against falsehood, but it immediately disappeared.

"I don't expect to be believed," he said, with a curious little laugh, "and it is just as well you don't. What has this country to do with buried fakirs? It is a land of solid fact, and not of magic and mystery. Will you mind my staying with you to have an English drink to the happy pair?"

They could only answer in one way, in courtesy, although they wished he would go. It seemed to them that in his changed bearing he had, for a time, presented to them another, a more powerful and dangerous, Chunder Loo.

So he ordered some brandy and water, and when the girl brought it in, he made a remark to her that the room was very untidy about the floor, and she had not swept it that day.

"Yes, I have," said the girl; "it is always done the first thing in the morning."

"But you have not swept it since."

"I can't be allus sweeping, sir."

She answered him with a flushed face, annoyed by his remarks. He gave her the change out of a shilling, and mollified the wench.

The boys had now finished their dinner, and rose to leave. Jack had to be cautious in surveying their visitor, but he managed, in a careless way, to note that Chunder Loo was scrutinizing their faces to see if there was anything, as Jack judged, to give him a clue to the lost snake.

It is almost superfluous to state that Jack presented an inscrutable countenance. He had quite a gift in that direction.

They bade Chunder Loo good-bye, and went out to the bar to pay. Jack laid down half a sovereign, and while the landlord was getting the change, he stole to the door of the public room, and peeped through the keyhole.

He could just see a portion of Chunder Loo's lithe figure, as he knelt by the table and groped about the sanded floor.

"Looking for what I have got," thought Jack as he returned to his companions. "There must be something special in it of which he does not care other people to know, or he would have asked for it. There is something decidedly mysterious about Chunder Loo."

"Why the keyhole trick, Jack?" softly inquired Don.

"Come right away from here," said Jack, as he took up the change, "and I will tell you. If we haven't got the unmentionable one to deal with in Chunder, we have a near relative, or I am very much mistaken."

He gave the landlord sixpence for the girl, and walked out, followed by his companions.

As they passed the window of the public room he glanced in, and saw nothing of Chunder Loo, save a pair of slippered feet protruding from under the table. The Oriental was still engaged in looking for his lost snake with the gold ring around its neck.

"We will go right away to the wood," he said. "Let us have a trot. I want to get away from that fellow."

As boys of their stamina are not troubled with thoughts of indigestion and other ills arising from hurrying after meals, they broke into a trot, and, led by Jack, eventually into a run, gaining the wood in double quick time.

"Right into the heart of it," he said.

"To the Cave of Robin Hood?" queried Tom.

"No. Anywhere but there. Let us get to Fern Dell, on the other side."

CHAPTER CII.

THE MYSTERIOUS SNAKE.—MISS ASTRACAN IN DISTRESS.

THE Fern Dell was a secluded spot in the wood that wanted finding out, even by those who were tolerably familiar with its locality. There was no regular path to it, and it was almost completely surrounded by dense and long-neglected undergrowth. But Jack was a sure guide to it, he, among his other mental endowments, being blessed with the gift of locality.

To the Fern Dell they therefore hied, and there he softly told his story, and produced his treasure trove, laying it on the ground.

"That is what he was looking for," he said, "and what he came back for. Now, doesn't it strike you that it is one of those beastly charms fakir fellows carry about with them?"

They stooped down, and looked at it with something akin to awe. It was none the less uncanny because it had no visible eyes. The usual glass substitutes used by taxidermists were absent.

"It is a nasty thing," said Don. "What are you going to do with it?"

"Keep it, I think," answered Jack.

Tom Drummond cautiously touched it with his finger, and immediately drew back with a sharp scream.

"Tom," said Jack, "don't make that row."

"Look at it!" said Tom, breathlessly; "it is alive!"

They all stared at it with a terror they could not control. The eyes were open, and shifting restlessly about. Though small, they looked remarkably like those in the head of Chunder Loo.

Not one of them would have touched it now for a trifle. They drew back with their eyes fixed upon it, dumbly watching. Presently the tip of the tail turned up, as that of an angry centipede. Then a slight undulating movement was observable through its short, sinuous body.

"It is going away," hissed Don, breaking an awful silence.

"Let it go," cried Tom.

"No, kill it!" said Jack, between his teeth.

He sprang forward to put his foot upon it, but instantly it was endowed with the vigour of full life, and shot into the undergrowth.

They seized upon sticks, portions of broken branches, that were lying on the ground, and darted in pursuit.

In a sort of frenzy, they beat the bushes, cut them away with their pocket-knives, and searched around, but the snake was gone.

It was no wonder, perhaps, that so small a thing should have eluded their vigilance, but they could not but consider there was something unnatural in its disappearance.

"Fancy my having carried it in my pocket!" said Jack, with a shiver.

"It is such a queer little beast," said Don. "Small snakes are not uncommon, but this one appeared to be fully grown."

"And about a hundred years old," said Tom Drummond. "I never saw such a leery look as there was in the eyes of that wormy little beggar as it opened them and looked at me. 'Not so dead as you seem to think,' it seemed to say to me."

"Come back to the Abbey," said Jack, "and don't let us worry any more about it. It has the whole wood to live in, and the chances are much against any of us seeing it again."

And there did not seem to be much probability of it, but, then, you can never tell, as the sage says, what is going to happen in this wondrous world of ours.

Half-an-hour later, they were at the Abbey gates, where they were saluted by a tapping at the window. Glancing in the direction of the sound, they saw that it was Miss Astracan, who, owing to her ponderosity, had not been able to attend the wedding. She was in the old private room once occupied by Fontenoy, *alias* Jerry Snicker, Esquire.

Inferring, from the sound, that she wanted to see them, and hear something about the wedding, they went there in a body "to share the sorrows of the story with her," as Bob Stockton remarked. But,

strange to say, it was not the wedding she wished to talk about.

Without making any reference to it, she plunged right away into another subject.

"I want to ask you how long you have been at school here?" she said, as she slowly subsided, like an enormous billow, into a chair.

They named the respective times of their stay at the school. Jack Ford had been there the longest.

"Then I will appeal to you," said Miss Astracan. "Have you, during your stay here, heard anything about ghosts?"

"Lots of times," replied Jack.

"From people who have seen them?"

"Oh, no. In a place like this fellows have to talk of ghosts, whether they believe in them or not."

"But have you ever seen one?" asked Miss Astracan.

"I have seen things that might be made into ghosts," answered Jack, "but I should be sorry to swear to them."

"I am a great judge of human nature," said Miss Astracan, "and I make a study of it, especially in boys, for, as you may have heard, I once was matron in an orphan asylum, where I met with every variety of the male juvenile. Now, I have studied the boys here, and I have come to the conclusion that in you four I see the leading spirits of this establishment."

"The leading ghosts?" exclaimed Bob Stockton, feigning amazement and horror.

"You know very well what I mean," said Miss Astracan, nodding her head, "and perfectly understand the difference between a leading spirit and a ghost. Now, I am also aware that talking to you about such things won't put you into fits, as it does some lads, and I am going to tell you something which has happened to me."

They were all ears now, and Bob Stockton, abandoning the facetious inclinations upon him, was as grave as a judge.

"Last night," said Miss Astracan, "I went to bed as usual, pretty well worn out with the fatigue of helping my niece in matters relating to the event of to-day. By-and-by you shall tell me how it went off, but at present I will stick to the subject uppermost in my mind."

"Quite right, ma'am," murmured Bob, and immediately raised his eye to the ceiling to avoid meeting the gimlet-like gaze she fixed upon him.

"It is my custom," she went on, "not only to lock and bar my door, but also to barricade it. Previous to that, I have the girl in to look into the cupboards and under the bed, also to the fastenings of the windows. For a barricade I use two chairs and the washstand, having great faith in a crash of crockery as a means of scaring a would-be burglar."

"That," said Bob, gazing at her approvingly, "is a distinctly good idea. I have a maiden aunt, ma'am, who will be glad of a hint upon the subject, if you would not mind my mentioning it."

"I shall be very pleased," said Miss Astracan, gratified. "Well, last night, I had made myself secure and got into bed. It takes me time to do that, as I have—have——"

"To go easy," suggested Bob.

"To be careful with my breath," said Miss Astracan, severely; "and having put out the light, I tried to sleep, but I could not."

"Did you count sheep going through a gate, ma'am?" asked Don. "My mother always does it when she is restless."

"I did everything I could think of without getting up. Walking the room is a good thing for thin persons, but I, who—who——"

"Am inclined to be stout," said Bob, once more giving her assistance.

"I am *very* stout——"

"But not so stout as some people," insisted Bob, with his mind on a fat woman he had once seen at a fair.

"I dare say there are stouter people than I am," said Miss Astracan, "and I am sorry for them. But that is not to the point. There I lay thinking and thinking for a good two hours, and then a most extraordinary thing happened. All in a moment there was a light in the room."

She paused for breath, and even Bob maintained silence. He was getting powerfully interested.

"A light," repeated Miss Astracan, "that was all round the head and partly down the person of the tallest woman I have ever seen. She was not stout, as I am, but otherwise the most monstrous creature in petticoats I ever beheld."

"She wore petticoats?" said Bob, apparently relieved.

"A dress, at all events," said Miss Astracan, "of some soft, diaphanous material. She was moving slowly about the room, and did not seem to be aware of my being awake until our eyes met, and then she suddenly vanished."

There was a short silence, and then Don was heard to murmur, "Vanished?"

"Yes, vanished," repeated Miss Astracan, "instantly. I need not tell you that I was terribly scared, and the way I shook fairly rocked the bed. I hadn't a bit of voice for screaming, and in that case only one thing could happen, and that was, I fainted away.

"Now, there is the whole story, boys," she added, after a short rest for breath; "there is nothing more to tell. I did not come to myself again until the morning, and then things were exactly as when I lay down the previous night."

"There was nothing disturbed in the room, I suppose?" asked Jack.

"Not even the washstand?" said Bob, in an undertone.

"Nothing," she replied. "Nor was a single thing taken away. Have you ever heard of such a midnight visitor before?"

None of them had, and they could offer no solution of the mystery.

"Well, then, I must suppose," said Miss Astracan, with a sigh, "that it was a ghost which has favoured me alone with its company. Do not run away with the idea that I am afraid, because I am not. If I had expected the ghost, or whatever it was, I should not have fainted away. The next time it comes I shall be prepared for it. I hope I have not alarmed you?"

"Not at all," said Jack, replying for them all; "but if I may venture to give you a piece of advice, ma'am, I should warn you against mentioning it to Susan. She is a plucky girl, but as she sleeps alone in the attics, it might upset her."

"I have not spoken of it, nor shall I," returned Miss Astracan. "You have had your dinner out, I believe?"

"Yes, ma'am, but we should like our tea at home," said Tom.

"Come in and have it here with me at five o'clock," said Miss Astracan, "and then we will try to arrange some way of solving this affair. I don't mean to be haunted by ghosts if I can help it!"

She nodded as an intimation that the interview was at an end, and they departed, hastening to the class-room, now shorn of all signs of daily study, save the desks and seats. There they closed the door and sat down to talk matters over.

CHAPTER CIII.

IS THERE A REAL GHOST?—A HORRIBLE SPECTACLE.

"WE have something to work out now," said Don. "The old girl has told a very circumstantial story."

"She *must* have been dreaming," suggested Tom Drummond.

"I do not think so," was Jack's view of the matter; "whatever it was, she saw it. I should like to have a good look about her room."

"What good would that do?"

"Well, Bob, it would enable me to try and find out if there are any secret passages in it. The old abbeys all had them, and there are some here, I'll wager all I'm worth."

"Which, after paying for the chops to-day," said Bob Stockton, "isn't much to brag about."

"All I am likely to be worth then," said Jack,

"since you are so critical. The room is panelled, I believe ?"

"It is," said Don. "Copps slept there, if you remember."

"And he saw no ghosts," said Tom.

"It would be rather a delicate thing," grinned Tom, "to ask permission to inspect the chamber."

"Leave it to me," said Bob. "Miss Astracan once favoured me with a chaste salute, which you probably remember——"

"We shall never forget it until our dying day," said Don.

"No more shall I," said Bob. "Well, say she gives us leave and we find out a secret passage, what then ?"

"All depends where it leads to," replied Jack.

"But the ghost was a lanky woman——"

"It is no use speculating," said Jack. "Our first duty is to get leave. That done, we will go to work, and if the mystery can be solved, we are the boys to do it."

"Certainly," assented Bob, and then he burst into song :—

"We are a solving family, we are, we are, we are."

They talked no more on the subject, but strolled into the playground to moon the intervening hour or so between then and tea-time.

How solitary the old place appeared in their eyes. So still in comparison with what it ordinarily was. It was quite depressing, and in no humour for play of any sort, they sat on the wall by the cliff and looked down into the depths below.

"Hush !" said Bob, suddenly, "somebody is moving down there. Look there among the bushes. By the living Emperor of Germany, it is Chunder Loo !"

They all leant over and peered down, and there, sure enough, was the Hindoo, winding his way among the bushes with that snake-like mode of progression with which they had grown familiar.

He was walking slowly, with his head bent forward and his hands spread out, the attitude being very suggestive of a feeble, blind man groping his way in a place full of pitfalls for the unwary.

But for the uncanny influence this strange man had already gained over them, they might have been disposed to laugh, but as matters were they remained quite still, with a chilly feeling in their breasts, wondering what had brought him there, and why he should carry himself in that mysterious way.

As he crept along, he was every moment weaker, or shammed being so. Suddenly he sank upon his knees, and, with a despairing gesture, fell upon his face, with his arms extended, so that his body was in the form of a cross.

The boys remained quite still. They were scarcely breathing, so absorbing was the spectacle.

They waited and waited—how long they never knew ; it might have been two minutes or twenty, for they lost all count of time—and he never stirred.

Presently Jack softly slipped from his seat, and glided back into the centre of the playground.

Obeying his beckoning call, the others joined him there.

"Don't speak above a whisper," said Jack. "What do you think of it ?"

"Unearthly !" replied Tom Drummond.

"Do you think he knew we were looking down upon him ?" suggested Don.

"No," answered Jack ; "we went up quietly. He was already groping his way along, and while watching him, we certainly made no sound."

"It occurred to me," said Don, "that he is playing a sort of game—endeavouring to impress us with a sense of being something more than mortal."

"He certainly isn't an ordinary man," said Jack, "but that is no reason why we should be afraid of him. Keep still a moment. I'll just see if he has shifted his ground."

To make sure of getting back to the wall without making the least noise, Jack removed his boots, and, in his stockinged feet, glided up to it. He took his cap from his head on the way, and peered over the wall with the utmost caution.

With a shudder of repulsion he drew back, and speedily rejoined his companions.

"Come in," he said, with a shiver.

They followed him as he hastened into the house. Instinctively he hastened to the classroom.

There he sat down and put on his boots.

"Boys," he said, "that beggar was still there. You know how thin he is ?"

"Yes," they replied.

"Well," said Jack, "thin as he was an hour ago, nay, ten minutes ago, he seems, as he lies there, to have shrunk to *half his usual size !*"

"Save us !" exclaimed Tom Drummond, with a gasp.

"It may have been my fancy," continued Jack Ford ; "but if he is really, for some mysterious reason, shrinking away to nothingness, and is about to vanish for good and all, I for one will put up with the horror of the mystery so long as we are rid of him."

"But," urged Bob Stockton, "if the fellow has the power of shrinking up that way, may he not also have the gift of coming to life again ? May he not be a hitherto unknown species of Fakir ?"

"I don't know," answered Jack. "Suppose he is, who cares ? All the Fakirs of India could not keep the Britisher out when he went to conquer the country. Don't let us bother any more about him."

It had always been Jack's policy to show a bold front to his followers, even though he had reason to think there was a very serious state of things, and possibly disaster, impending. In one sense, he felt no fear. But he was not blind to peril or to the peculiar developments of an unnatural nature now going on with Chunder Loo.

"The Fakir," he resumed, after a short silence, "does wonderful things with his own body, but I don't remember having read that he did much with those of other people. I hear a footstep without. I fancy it is the gentle Susan with the coal-black eyes, come in search of us to announce that tea in the private apartment of Miss Astracan is ready."

It was Susan, and the announcement she had to make was of that import. Miss Astracan awaited their coming at the festive board.

"And she's got the thinnest of bread and butter," said Susan, smiling all over her face, "some jam, potted meat, and a cake. I really think that when Mrs. Bunn comes back and hears of such goings on, she will go stark, staring wild."

Having thus led the boys to perceive that she already understood the economical gifts of Miriam, Susan vanished, and the boys, after a hasty wash and brush up in the lavatory, adjourned to the room where Miss Astracan awaited them.

CHAPTER CIV.

A PLEASANT TEA-PARTY.—EXAMINING THE ROOM.

"I SUPPOSE you all take milk and sugar?" said Miss Astracan. "Yes, of course. I needn't have asked. Help yourselves to the bread and butter."

Bob Stockton politely handed the plate to her first, and she smiled graciously.

"I do like good breeding wherever found," she said. "I never could *quite* get it from my orphans. But there, take them all round, they were not a bad lot—poor little mites."

She sighed, and having handed them their tea asked if they would ever have taken her for an orphan. The question was to all of them, including Bob Stockton, a bit of a floorer.

He managed to say that it had never occurred to him to look upon her as being bereaved of her parents.

"And yet I have been an orphan all my life—as long as I remember," she said. "Ah, me! Pass the cake, if you please, Ford."

"We have been thinking over what you told us, Miss Astracan," said Jack, as he held the plate of cake to her, "and we think it is a matter that ought to be investigated."

"How?" inquired Miss Astracan.

"Well—ahem!" coughed Jack, "it is—— Bob, as the plan is of your arranging, you had better explain it."

Having thus shifted the explanation to Bob, Jack went on with his tea. The "politest boy in the school" took the task upon himself with his accustomed *sangfroid*.

"In the first place, ma'am," he said, "we were thinking that there are certain little articles—toilet necessaries and so on—which you might wish to be packed away in your box. There are harmless secrets in the lives of ladies which the sterner sex have nothing to do with. I allude to hair-washes, complexion-revivers, and the like."

A feeling of dismay came over his companions. They felt that for once Bob had entered on a delicate task in a clumsy fashion, and they expected he would promptly get a wigging from Miss Astracan.

But she simply looked at him in a puzzled manner, and said:

"I do not quite understand you, Stockton."

"It would facilitate the examination of the room," suggested Bob.

"I have not many fal-lals about," said Miss Astracan, "and they would not incommode me when examining the apartment. Nor would they trouble Susan."

"But it was not you or Susan," said Bob; "we were thinking of who ought to look into the matter."

"Good gracious, Stockton! You do not think it an affair for the police?"

"Oh, no," said Bob, serenely, "we were thinking of doing it ourselves."

"And who is *we?*" asked Miss Astracan, with a stony eye.

Bob, with a wave of his hands, indicated himself and friends as the proper persons for the job. Miss Astracan drank her tea, set down the cup, and deliberately surveyed each in turn.

"It is a cool proposition," she said, "because it implies that you are sharper than I am. Now, that is the sort of thing elders are always disposed to resent. I know I have a keen eye——"

"Gleaming with intelligence," murmured Bob, and Jack gave him a kick under the table to admonish him not to go too far.

"Thank you," said Miss Astracan, accepting the compliment in all faith; "the eye *is* the indicator of the mind."

"I wish to say here," interposed Bob, "that it is not the eye or the mind that is in question. Had it been so, we should never ventured to put ourselves forward. It is a physical question. To thoroughly examine your room will entail a deal of stooping, and we, being *slimmer* than you are, Miss Astracan, we venture to offer our services."

"I see it as you do," said Miss Astracan; "you are right. It is a physical matter entirely. As soon as the room can be arranged for you after tea, you may investigate its structure. Not that I think you will discover anything."

Thus Bob had gained his point, and the rest of the tea-time was taken up with ordinary conversation. When the boys were dismissed to await a summons to the room, they sauntered out to the Abbey gate, and squatted on the ground near it.

"On my word, Bob," said Jack, "I think you went perilously near making a hash of it."

"Success must not be questioned," replied Bob. "All the old girl has to hide away is, in my opinion, a bottle with something stimulating in it. We shall not be kept waiting long."

Nor were they. Susan soon summoned them to their task, and they joined the girl by the door. It struck Jack that she looked rather pale.

"Has Miss Astracan been talking to you about anything?" he asked.

"No, Master Ford," replied Susan, "except that she feels a draught in her room, and wants you to find out where it comes from. As if she couldn't do it herself!"

"But you have been upset by something, Susan?"

"Yes, I hates 'em."

And the girl shivered from head to foot.

"Hate what?" asked Jack, with his eyes intently fixed upon her.

"Snakes!" said Susan. "I was in the scullery, when a nasty little thing came creeping in at the open door. It wasn't more than seven inches long, if it was as much. Ugh! It gave me such a turn."

"What colour was it?" Jack inquired.

The faces of all the boys had a white, still expression, seen only in those who are in a state of suppressed excitement.

"A kind of reddish yellow," said Susan.

The boys breathed more freely.

The hideous little snake that had vanished in the wood was nearly black.

"I suppose," said Jack, hesitating—he dreaded the possibility of its being the little reptile after all—"that it had nothing round its neck."

"Good gracious!" exclaimed Susan. "What could a thing like that have about its neck?"

They were still more relieved. Bob, recovering his ordinary demeanour, informed Black-Eyed Susan that the latest fashion among snakes was to wear frilled fronts. This made them all laugh. But Susan was still perturbed.

"I never saw such a peculiar snake," she said. "It came in as bold as brass, as if it rented the place, and went across the scullery in a slow, quiet way that put me all agog. It had an eye that you couldn't help noticing, although it was so small, and never as long as I live shall I forget the look of it. It was so awfully cunning."

"What became of it?" asked Don.

"It went into the kitchen," replied Susan, "and then I rushed in with the broom to sweep it out, and although the door was closed, and it couldn't get any further to save its life, *it wasn't there.*"

They understood the perturbed condition of the countenance of Susan now. She could not understand what on earth had become of her strange visitor.

Of course, there were a hundred places where so small a creature could hide away, and they told her so, but Susan was too upset to be easily comforted.

"It was a horrible little thing!" she said. "And it has given me the creeps."

As they could not explain the nature of the snake, or help her to a solution of its disappearance, they let the matter go. The task they had in hand was the examination of Miss Astracan's room.

And they examined it thoroughly, as they thought. The chamber was panelled, and they tapped every inch of the woodwork. In no way did it give out a sound indicative of hidden passages, on which so many old romances have been founded.

In one of the cupboards Bob raked out from a lot of odds and ends, an empty jar.

Bob Stockton removed the cork, smelt it, and said:

"There is the ghost of Old Tom in this thing. The spirit of departed gin rests in it."

"Could that have been the ghost?"

"Might have been," said Don.

"No," asserted Jack, confidently, "I feel assured there is something in her story which will be explained by-and-bye. We must report 'Nothing found,' and let it rest for the present."

They did so, and Miss Astracan said she was sure of it. But, for all that, she was of the opinion that Jack Ford entertained.

"It was the sort of ghost," she said, "that a stick would knock the nonsense out of." Then a sudden thought came to her. "I hope you are not playing a trick upon me yourselves. If any of you are the ghost, I could not expect you to find yourselves."

They assured her they knew nothing whatever about it, and she believed them. So the matter of the strange visitant to the room of the ponderous lady was left for the time.

The evening was spent in wandering about. None cared to look over the wall until twilight had come, and then the curiosity that was consuming them all asserted itself.

"I must have another peep over the wall, if I die for it," said Jack.

"I was thinking of it myself," said Don.

In short, they all were of the same mind, and in a

body they strolled out to the wall and peered over.

The form of Chunder Loo was no longer there.

"Vanished—melted away," gasped Bob.

Jack said nothing. He was very pale, but quiet.

As the others moved away, with the intention of going into the house to supper—not even the mystery of Chunder Loo's vanishing could take away their appetites—he resumed his seat by the wall, and gazed into the darkening depths below.

There was nothing to solve the strange affair —nothing but the gloom of night gathering over the wooded ground.

The others called to him as they reached the door of the Abbey, and he signalled with his upraised hand that he would follow them presently.

They vanished, and he lingered for awhile, and, meditating, walked to and fro.

When he entered the house, he could hear the voices of his companions in the dining-room. They had left the door open, and were talking in a somewhat boisterous manner, something like the people who speak at the top of their voices or whistle as they pass a churchyard at midnight, their object being to let ghosts know they are not afraid of them.

Jack was about to join them, when he heard a strange sound from somewhere upstairs.

It was a cry that might have emanated from one suddenly and joyfully surprised.

He stopped short, crept to the foot of the stairs, and listened intently.

There was no further cry, but in its place a low, droning sound, that reminded him of psalm-singing in a cathedral, heard afar off.

He braced himself up—there was need of it, all things considered, and, with a light step, he bounded up the stairs.

On the landing, by the long corridor, he could hear the sound more plainly. In a few moments more, he traced it to the chamber of Chunder Loo.

What did it mean?

He had heard nothing—seen nothing of the mysterious man since he had watched him lying in the wood at the base of the cliff.

And yet here he was, in the Abbey—or was it his ghost?

Jack was not afraid of the supernatural, whatever he may have thought. He did not believe that a spirit could harm him. If he "felt a little pale" as he walked up to the door of the room, who will blame him?

Without a doubt, Chunder Loo was there. And he was chanting some sort of song.

It had a religious tone and twang, but Jack did not give the Hindoo much credit for piety. He sacrificed his distaste to playing the spy, and placing his ear at the keyhole, heard him chanting thus:

"Lost for awhile, oh, my beloved—lost! But you will return to me as the breath of the morning.

"Life is as naught without my loved one—my light, my guide, my friend, my counsellor and comforter.

"Shall I be evermore without thee? I ask of the sun, and the moon, and the stars, if it shall be so, and they answer: 'Nay; wait awhile, and he will return to thee. Be comforted. Rejoice.'"

Then the voice of Chunder Loo burst into a screech that was almost unearthly in its frenzied joy, and Jack perforce retreated, for he could bear no more.

"He has come as a curse to the Abbey," he muttered; "but is it worth my while to tell all I believe to the others? I think not. For the present, therefore, I will be dumb."

So he went back to his comrades, and not a word of the chant he had heard passed his lips that night.

It had been a weird day enough, in all conscience, for them all without his making any addition to it.

CHAPTER CV.

THE RETURN OF PENNY BUNN.—EXTRAORDINARY EFFECT OF TOTAL ABSTINENCE.

IN the morning the boys were up earlier, but Chunder Loo was before them. He was in the woods at dawn, and before the sun was well up was standing at the Abbey gates, with his face to the east, singing in a low, monotonous way, which presently ceased as the boys came out for a morning stroll before breakfast.

He greeted them as if nothing out of the common had transpired, and spoke of the beauty of the morning as if the weather was, of all things, the most interesting to him.

They answered in suitable terms, and got away from him as soon as they could without being rude. The man was repulsive to them.

From that time to the day when Penny Bunn returned from his brief honeymoon, they only saw Chunder Loo occasionally. Without exhibiting any desire to avoid them, he was far from being obtrusive.

He partook of his meals alone, was in and out the Abbey, and went about and comported himself as an ordinary tutor might have done under the circumstances.

Penny Bunn and his bride came back a day before the appointed time.

Something had gone wrong with the finances or

something. A telegram preceded them by an hour, and when a cab brought them to the gate, the way Miriam flounced out of it showed she was like beer after a thunderstorm, a "little off."

Nobody had told Chunder Loo that the happy pair were expected, but he was at the gate to receive them. The boys were there by accident.

Chunder Loo received Mrs. Penny Bunn with a salaam that would have done credit to an Eastern potentate.

"Welcome," he said, "back to the shelter of your future home."

"Will you kindly see to the luggage, Mr. Chunder Loo?" said Miriam. "Mr. Bunn has lost one of the trunks on the way. I cannot trust him more than a child."

"Who, after a long course of ginger beer and lemonade, can be trusted?" asked Bunn, as he descended from the carriage.

Nobody offering a reply to so deep a question, Penny Bunn brought out the fag-end of a cigar, and lighted it. Leaning against the gate-post, he sarcastically watched Chunder Loo as he checked off the luggage from the roof of the cab.

His looks of contempt were thrown away upon the Hindoo, who, in the coolest manner possible, performed the duty imposed upon him, and vanished into the house.

The cabman waited for a moment, and then asked Penny Bunn if he intended to pay.

"My good fellow," replied Bunn, "I intend nothing. I am nobody but a piece of bread—a mere crust—cast upon the matrimonial waters. Perhaps you may find me, with the wherewithal to pay you, after many days. Meanwhile, I will give you sixpence for yourself, and ask you to put the cab down to my account."

"Master said you hadn't any account," feebly returned the cabman.

"True, quite true," answered Bunn, briskly. "The element of truth is in your employer. It is time I had one, and I open it with this job from Chippenham."

The man was not proof against this suggestion. All respectable people had accounts with his master, who was the chief proprietor of cabs in Chippenham, a business he combined with keeping a public-house. He saw that it was time Bunn had an account, and drove away with the set object of spending the tip given him in conviviality in Smudgem Bender at the Cowley Arms.

"Boys," said Penny Bunn, "I have returned to you, more or less—principally less—in a joyful frame of mind. I won't ask you how Miss Astracan is, but merely inquire—has she increased in weight?"

"We are not in a position, sir," replied Bob Stockton, in his most unctuous manner, "to give you any information on that point, beyond the assurance that she has not visibly decreased."

"'Tis well," said Penny Bunn, gloomily. "One more question: Have you ever heard of the injurious results of non-alcoholic liquors—of the utterly depressing effects of aerated waters—of the murderous thoughts engendered by seltzers and sodas at all times and seasons?"

None of them were able to give him any information on that head, and having shaken hands with them all round, and thanked them "for their kindness and forbearance," he left them.

"What is Bunn suffering from?" asked Don.

"Ginger beer, and too much of it," answered Bob.

They saw little more of Bunn that day. Miriam, for some reason, got him to bed early, and he had a refreshing sleep ere she came to rest.

She had a lot to tell her aunt, and at eleven o'clock or thereabouts she sought her room. Penny Bunn was awake.

"Miriam, dear," he said, humbly, "what has Chunder Loo been doing to-night?"

"He retired at nine o'clock," she answered.

"That accounts for it."

"Accounts for what?"

"A sort of humming I have heard in his room."

"Bosh!"

"Listen. He is at it again."

They were quiet for a moment, but Miriam declared she could hear nothing.

"It is perfectly plain," said Bunn.

"You have been full of fancies of late," said Miriam, severely.

Bunn sighed, and laid his head upon the pillow.

"The deleterious effects of teetotal compounds," he murmured, "are ruining me body and mind."

"Are you sure you kept to them?" demanded Miriam, tartly.

"My dear," he said, "I am pledged."

"I have known temperance reformers to be found in the public streets insensible, and taken home in wheel-barrows," said Miriam. "Go to sleep."

"I suppose the humming is an illusion," groaned Penny Bunn.

Whether the humming was heard by Miriam or not, the fact remained that Chunder Loo was softly chanting in his chamber until after midnight, and then the sound suddenly ceased.

Shortly afterwards, a figure very much like his was prowling about Mumping Malford Wood.

The night passed, and the morning came. When Jack came down, rather late, there was a letter waiting for him.

It was lying upon the hall table, and prior to opening it he carefully examined it.

A SPLENDID SCHOOL STORY.

NEVER BEFORE PUBLISHED.

By E. HARCOURT BURRAGE,

Author of "Ching Ching," "Monkey Mat and Roving Dick," "The Brave Boy of the Basilisk," &c.

No. 15.

A Handsome Coloured Plate Presented with Every Number.

IT WAS PROFESSOR LINGO DISGUISED AS THE OLD GYPSY.

PRICE ONE PENNY.

He knew not why he did so, but of late he had learnt to be suspicious.

There was a dinginess about the part where it was gummed that led him to think it had been opened and read. But on inquiring of Susan he learnt that, late as he was, he was the first person down.

Chunder Loo had rung his bell, and when Susan went up to his door he asked for a cup of tea to be brought up and left outside, "for he had a headache."

Chunder Loo with a headache! Prodigious!

The letter was, as Jack knew, from Lingo. It was written in vague terms, but it conveyed the intimation that he might be expected any hour after dark, and would communicate through the channel of the telephone.

Jack therefore resolved that evening to keep watch for him, and having conveyed the intelligence to his companions, they decided to be in the classroom as soon as it was dark and keep watch there.

The day passed uneventfully. Nothing occurred to ruffle the even tenor of the lives of any at the Abbey. Penny Bunn was busy with sundry books relating to the school accounts, and Miriam was making domestic arrangements for the proper future management of the place.

The boys mooned the time away, and when the evening came assembled in the classroom. The view from the windows we have described before.

It was an extensive one, and if not beautiful, it was at its best at twilight.

The boys lay upon the desk by one of the windows, lounging at their ease, and talking in an undertone of the coming of Lingo.

"He must have something important to tell us," said Jack.

"Seems so," assented Don. "I hope nothing is wrong."

Before any further comment could be made, the door opened and admitted Penny Bunn.

He was as much surprised to see the boys as they were to see him.

"I came here," he said, "for temporary quietude, to commune with my thoughts. Probably you have done the same."

"We came here for a quiet chat, sir," Jack admitted.

They wished him at Jericho, but could not tell him to go away.

He sat down on the form close to their feet. Each moment the darkness of night drew nearer.

"Life," said Bunn, "is a strange problem. I often wonder why I was born."

"It is a bit of a puzzle, sir," softly assented Bob.

"Stockton——"

"I beg your pardon, sir. I spoke generally."

"In that case," said Bunn, "the remark is pardonable."

He was about to pursue the theme, when a hooting was heard in the depths below the cliff.

"Dear me!" exclaimed Penny Bunn, "how strange. An owl abroad so early."

The boys had heard it, and knew that it was the professor below, but they kept their countenances wonderfully.

"An owl, sir!" said Tom; "where is it?"

"Did you not hear it?" asked Penny Bunn. "There it is again."

"Too-whit-too-whoo——"

They looked at him in feigned surprise, taking their lead from Bob Stockton.

"I heard no *owl*, sir."

Bob spoke a Jesuitical form of truth. He had not heard an owl. It was Lingo.

"Do you mean to say that you did not hear it?" gasped Bunn. "There—there, listen!"

"Too-whit-too-who-o-o-o-o."

"There is certainly no owl near here," said Bob. "You do not look well, sir. Had you not better go and lie down."

"I suppose I had," muttered Bunn. "Miriam said that she could hear no humming last night. Am I suffering from a long course of enforced abstinence and going to be ill?"

He opened the door and left the room, omitting to close it behind him. Tom got up and did this for him, and Jack in a moment had the window opened and the telephone lowered.

It was almost instantly jerked from below, and he put his ear to the cup.

"Is it Ford?" was the question asked.

"Yes."

"Do you think you can keep anyone locked up to-night? It is only to make sure of him. Try what you can do. I won't stay now. If you succeed, put a light in the dormitory window by half-past eleven o'clock."

"All right. For the present, good-bye."

"Farewell." There was another jerk of the telephone, and Jack drew it in. The little that was necessary to impart to his friends he told, and then they entered into a discussion of the way to ensure the keeping of Chunder Loo in his bedroom.

That he was the person referred to was undoubted; but why should Lingo be so anxious about him? He had not shown any desire to be abroad at night.

"Anyway," said Jack, "we will fasten him in somehow. A rope from the handle of his door tightly stretched across to the opposite one will do it."

This was settled on as the right thing to do, and Jack went away in search of the requisite material.

Chunder Loo did not go out that day, as far as they knew, but he was seen in the house, but had talked to the boys in the afternoon about ordinary matters.

The rain fell as it poured all day, and the playground was covered with little pools of water, presenting a most dreary spectacle.

At the usual hour the friends went away to bed. There was no change in the weather, and the rain dashed against the window of the dormitory with the force of a storm heralding another deluge.

"If I did not know Lingo as I do," said Jack Ford, "I should be inclined to think that he would shirk the work to-night. But he will be there."

"Without a doubt," said Don.

All was prepared for the work to be done later on. By eleven o'clock the seniors of the house would, unless something unforeseen occurred, be in bed.

At that hour Jack was to steal softly to the room occupied by the Hindoo, and with a rope, already prepared with a slip-knot, fasten his door to the opposite one.

This task Jack resolved to carry out alone, and then he would display the signal agreed upon to guide Lingo to a knowledge that Chunder Loo was safely shut in.

"Four of us about in the dark might lead to a blunder; one is enough," he said.

There was wisdom in the idea, and they let him have his way without any demur. Accordingly, at the hour selected for operations, he slipped out of bed, and with his trousers belted round him, he, with the rope in his hand, stole forth from the dormitory.

He had nothing, not even his socks upon his feet. In walking he made not the slightest sound. Outside the storm was howling, and the rattle of the rain upon the roof was as the pattering of a thousand footsteps from afar.

The corridor was dark, but he, knowing every inch of the way, made no mistake. He reached the door of Chunder Loo's room, and placing his ear to the key-hole, listened.

The Hindoo was there, softly singing, not in the impressive chanting style Jack had heard on a previous occasion, but as one who is at peace and engaged with pleasant thoughts.

Wasting no time, Jack slipped the rope over the handle of the knob, carried it the door opposite, and then stretched and tied it fast.

Upstairs he sped, and in a few moments a light was burning in the dormitory window. He left it there to burn for half-an-hour, lying down and thinking until he felt certain that it had been seen. Then he arose and extinguished it.

"The next thing," he said, as he composed himself for sleep, "will be to wake early and remove the rope before anyone is up. If discovered there, we might say it was a joke. That might do for Bunn, but not, I fear, for Chunder Loo."

CHAPTER CVI.

A HARD NUT TO CRACK.—SNICKER IS TEMPTED.

THE majority of people, if they go to bed with a strict determination to wake early in the morning, will nine times out of ten succeed. Jack Ford was awake at four o'clock, or shortly after, and immediately he sprang out of bed, put on some of his clothes, and hastened out of the dormitory to remove the tell-tale rope.

It was daylight, of course, but the full glare of the later hours was not there. The soft glow of early morning crept through the windows with a soothing effect that is given by no other time of the day.

It had been raining all night, but the storm was now fleeing before the sun. The horizon in the south was still dark with clouds and overhead there were big patches sailing away with their watery burdens before a brisk breeze. Everything promised a fine, pleasant day.

The rope was still in its place, untouched and apparently not strained. Jack, delighted with the success attending the manœuvre, swiftly removed it and hied back to bed.

But having once fully awakened, he had a dislike, common to healthy natures, to sleeping again. So he awoke the rest, and asked them what they thought of getting up and having a run before breakfast.

"Nothing could be better," replied Tom Drummond, and the other two, after a yawn, said that as they had been roused, they might as well get up, but it was "a beastly shame."

"I want to see Lingo, if possible," said Jack. "There is a chance of our doing so if we run as far as Smudgem Bender."

"We can get some milk if we pop in upon Botch," said Bob. "They have the cows into the yard at five, and as there are six of them, it takes an hour and a half to get through the job."

They dressed, and, after a hurried wash below, went softly out of the house by the back-door. As Susan was not up, they left a short note on the kitchen table, explaining how it was the door was unbarred. Then away they sped, down through the woods to Smudgem Bender.

Milking operations at Botch's farm were nearly over, but they were in time to have a draught of milk, really fresh and warm from the cow. Having drunk it, they went into the extensive dairy, and saw what was done with the rest preparatory to turning it into butter and cheese.

Botch came into the dairy while they were there, and asked them to stay to breakfast; but they were compelled to decline, as they had not left word at home whither they had gone.

A second invitation to dinner was cordially accepted, as they could make arrangements for that, and then they went on their homeward road.

As they drew near the wood, the smoke of a small fire was soon rising in the air from the left.

"Gipsies!" exclaimed Bob. "Let us give them a look. I wish I had been born one of the Romany people. It would have spared me such a beastly lot of book study, washing, and other things. Heigho! but I suppose it is too late to turn back, and strike out a new line in life."

Tracing the fire to a clump of bushes on the left of the wood, they discovered a tent, with a bent old woman in the act of hanging a pot on three sticks, tied together in a triangular form, and placed over the fire.

As they went up, she just glanced at them with a pair of dark eyes, but took no further notice of them.

The lower part of her face was muffled up, and she coughed in a hollow fashion that made Bob Stockton shiver.

"Rather damp weather for you, old lady," he said. "And where on earth did you get dry sticks, after all the rain we have had? Did you sleep on them?"

"The Romany woman," she answered, fiercely, "sleeps where she wills, and as for dry sticks, they can be found by any but the fool who never think of looking below the surface."

"Don't be angry, old lady," said Bob. "I meant no offence."

"But you are offensive," she replied, quivering all over her body, but still keeping her back to him, "and I, as the queen of my race, curse you for it! Away, dog, to your kennel, and die!"

"I say, old lady," exclaimed Bob, aghast, "draw it mild. I don't, as a rule, place so much faith in curses, as I do in blessings, but you people have a reputation for leaving a mark upon those who offend you. There is no reason for your being so dreadfully riled."

Then the old woman began to chant something in a low tone, spreading her hands weirdly over the fire. The boys stood watching her, in a sense, spellbound. Bob had never felt more uncomfortable in his life.

"Look here, old lady, queen of the thingummy people," he said, "let us try and square this business. I have a piece of silver, which I shall be glad to cross your hand with——"

A wild shriek of laughter burst from the old woman, and wheeling round, she threw back her hood, revealing the face of—Lingo!

It was a bigger staggerer to the boys than the old man who had injured his back in his youth, and was reduced to selling pencils. They fairly reeled under it.

"Sold again," said Lingo, delighted; "and nearly got the money. Here, Stockton, my boy, don't faint."

"You really ought not to do it—you oughtn't, indeed," murmured Bob, glaring at his laughing companions. "It was such a beastly sell."

"Well, if I cover my face again," returned Lingo, "as a necessary precaution, will you be satisfied that I am not really somebody else. Chaffing an old woman of nfy years! Fie! Bob Stockton. And you the Lord Chesterfield of the school, too! I blush for you."

"Drop it," growled Bob, "or I shall faint away in earnest."

"All right; away it goes," said Lingo. "I suppose you have got some excuse for placing that light in the window last night, and nearly bottling up the show."

"I placed it there," replied Jack, "because everything was right. I secured the door, and I unfastened it myself in the early part of the morning."

"But you did not shut up the man," asserted Lingo.

"I did, I vow," returned Jack. He was singing in his room when I put the rope up."

"And you made it fast?"

"It was stretched like a telegraph wire. No man could have opened the door without breaking it."

"Then here is another nut to crack that will try all our wisdom teeth," said Lingo. "Chunder Loo was in the wood last night, and it was more by luck than wit I did not run against him."

"Tell us all about it," said Jack.

"I must be brief, then," replied Lingo; "and I must do it while I am cooking, for as soon as I have satisfied the inner man, I must be off and away."

He turned to the fire, putting the sticks together, and the boys gathered near, assuming the attitude and general bearing of casual listeners to nothing in particular.

"I brought the van up to the bottom of the wood, congratulating myself on having such splendid weather for the job. There was no fear of even the casual coming of the night policeman, for, naturally, he would not prowl about the wood in a howling storm of rain. I tied the head of the old mare to a tree, and told her that, if she coughed, I'd let her have it warm when I came back, and then I took a bull's-eye lantern, and started for you know where. Before I had got half-way there, I heard the cracking of a stick, not the ordinary crackling of the falling twigs which you can hear at any hour of the day or night in any wood of more than two acres, but the sharp breaking of a stick that is stepped on. I immediately put my lantern behind me, for although it is supposed to be a dark-lantern turned off or on, it shows some light to keen eyes. Getting behind a tree, I waited a bit, and then there came stealing down a tall, lithe figure, and stopped within three yards of me, looking about him. It was too dark to see his face, but having once seen the man, no mistake was possible. It was Chunder Loo."

"Could you see his dress?" asked Don.

"The form of it, and there is nothing like it in these parts. He stood there listening for fully ten minutes, I should say, and what I suffered, fearing that old mare of mine would cough, I cannot tell. Luckily, she didn't."

"How was it he did not see you?" asked Tom.

"He would have seen me," answered Lingo, "if I had stood upright, but I knew a game worth two of that, and I knelt down so that my face was not more than a foot from the ground. He would not expect one to be looking up from there. Anyway, he didn't. After standing for awhile, he went slowly back, soaked, I should say, to his very skin, as I was. The drip from the trees was like a heavy shower-bath."

"Did you see anything more of him?" asked Jack.

"No, for I was too wide to follow him. There was no knowing what I might have done in the way of blundering over the roots of a tree, or anything else, in the dark. But I went early this morning, and had a look at the 'spot,' and it was all right. As for attempting to move anything last night, I dare not do it. It would have been madness."

"Do you think," inquired Don, "that he has an idea of what is hidden there?"

"No," answered Lingo, "because I don't see how he could have the least idea of it. But he is here for something. Don't forget that all the country, or a great part of it, has heard, or read, of the great find of ancient armour in the vault under the Abbey. It was in nearly all the papers. This fellow, whom I will swear I have seen somewhere before, comes here, in my belief, on a finding game. He's cute, and he is not going to throw away a chance from any quarter. Of course, it is only my opinion, but he was in the wood last night, and he wasn't out for the fun of the thing."

They all admitted that. It was a great disappointment to find that the work of removal had not been done, and how Chunder Loo had got out of his room and back again was a harassing mystery.

His window opened upon the cliff, and to attempt to get out that way could only end in his neck being broken. And even if by a miracle he escaped a mortal injury, he, when once down, would not be able to get back again.

Then there was the rope, found untouched, to prove that he had not passed in and out by the door.

Only the secret passage theory remained to offer a solution to the affair.

But how was it that this stranger, a foreigner, had gained a knowledge of such places, provided, of course, they were in existence?

"It's a licker," said Bob Stockton.

"Well, go away, boys," said Lingo; "you must leave me to reflect and act as I please for a time. Don't worry. We shall come out all right, I hope. Bob, if you should feel at all 'incommodated' by the old gipsy's curse, any qualms or quiverings coming on, I can let you have a few pills——"

"Oh, stash it!" growled Bob. "Be satisfied with having sold me out and out. Good-bye."

They parted with him, and went home in a somewhat harassed state of mind. On arriving at the Abbey, they hastened to the refectory, where Susan was laying the cloth.

In response to a query, "If everybody was up?" from Jack, she said, "All but Chunder Loo," were, and he was going to have his breakfast in bed.

"I am to leave it at his door," said Susan, "and he will take it in."

"What is the matter with him?" asked Tom.

"I don't know," answered Susan, "and I don't care. He's a horrid creature."

There was no doubt now that Chunder Loo had really been seen by Lingo in the wood during the night, and, in Jack's opinion, he was staying in bed more because he had no dry clothing, and this opinion received verification by the discovery, after breakfast, that the lengthy outer garment of the Hindoo could be seen, by bending over the wall in the playground, blowing from his bedroom window.

"We can make up our minds," said Jack, "that he was there."

"And he must have known that we were making a move through Lingo," said Don.

"I am afraid so. But cunning as he is, we ought, with Lingo, to be more than a match for him."

Jack, like Lingo, wanted to think over the matter, and when the others proposed strolling out for the morning, he elected to remain at home.

"You needn't worry about me," he said, "as I want to be by myself for an hour or two. I shall take a book and lie down in some quiet place, read a bit, and then think. That is my way of solving puzzles."

So they left him, and, with a copy of one of Scott's works under his arm, he sauntered into the wood.

But he did not go very far. On coming across a tree that offered a snug resting-place among its lower branches, he climbed into it and stretched himself out to read and think.

He was not more than five feet from the ground, and his back was turned from the Abbey. Anyone coming from the direction of Smudgem Bender could have seen him lying upon the gnarled branch of the tree, about on a level with the head of a man of medium height.

The growing heat of the day, the stillness of the wood, and the soporific influence of steady thinking and reading, soon told upon Jack, and he sank into a sleep that was firm and peaceful.

Shortly after, Fontenoy Snicker came prowling up by the path, on his way to get a peep at his old home. He was out for a walk, and he had no particular design outside seeing the Abbey, but he was in a brooding mood.

Things were not going well with him. The money he had received as compensation from Sir Charles was running out, and the time was advancing when he would have to do something to make a living. He could not quite see his way clear to what it ought to be.

As he strode along he thought of those who had been instrumental in removing him from the Abbey, and he cursed them, viciously striking the air with a heavy knotted stick he carried in his right hand.

"I hate 'em all," he hissed, "from the bottom of my 'art—*heart*. I could cut their——"

And then he paused, for within three feet of him was Jack Ford, peacefully sleeping.

He crept up until he could see the face of the boy, and on making sure that it was indeed the leader of the rebellion against his power, all the venom of his nature surged into his bosom.

How easy it would be to kill him as he slept!

But not with the knife. There was no need to shed blood.

One blow with that heavy stick would do it.

Or say that it would require two or three, the first dealt him would surely stun the boy.

There would be no struggle and no disturbance. As Snicker came towards the wood he had met no living being, and the chances were against his meeting anyone on his way back. All the people were busy in the distant hayfields.

"Why shouldn't I do it?" muttered Snicker; "he's been my ruin. Curse him—*I will!*"

His face became distorted with passion, and with a sweeping movement he raised the stick to strike.

CHAPTER CVII.

TWO EVIL SPIRITS.—BUNN HAS HIS NERVES TRIED.

WHAT trivial things sometimes intervene to stop the commission of a great crime! In another moment the blow would have been struck that would have cut short a promising life, and qualified Fontenoy, *alias* Jerry, Snicker for the gallows.

But the something intervened.

It was only the slightest cough in the world.

It was no more in sound than the first peck of the woodpecker on the hollow beech tree, but it sufficed. Fontenoy Snicker staggered back, and his arm fell by his side as he turned his head in the direction of the sound.

Leaning against the trunk of a tree, with a cigarette between his lips, was Chunder Loo.

"How do you do?" he said, politely.

Snicker could not answer him. All he could do was to stare and gasp.

"You do not like the boy there," continued Chunder Loo, adding, after a moment's pause, "no more do I."

"I wasn't going to hurt him," muttered Snicker; "it was all fun."

"Ah!" said Chunder Loo, "that was clearly written upon your amiable countenance. Go on with your fun; it will not disturb me. Though born in India, and inheriting the extra gravity of a wise race, I have learnt to enjoy an English joke. Knock his brains out. It will amuse me."

"That is, of course—your fun," remarked Fontenoy Snicker.

"Come with me," said Chunder Loo, "and I will tell you the sort of joke I enjoy."

He walked up to Snicker, took his arm, and led him down the path. Not a word was said until they were well without the reach of the hearing of Jack, should he awake. Then Chunder Loo paused, and coolly planted Snicker against a tree.

"You are a rascal!" he said.

"Here," began Snicker, "what do——"

"One moment," said Chunder Loo; "so am I. There are two of us, and we should make a pair if we matched better; but we don't. You are a coarse, sorry ruffian, and I am a refined scoundrel. That being understood, let us proceed to business."

"To business!" repeated Snicker, vaguely.

"Yes, to business," rejoined Chunder Loo. "Now, we all have people whom we dislike, and we always call them our enemies, whether they have injured us or not. That is human nature. Now, if we have enemies, we desire to get rid of them. Say that you have a wife whom you wish to get rid of?"

"I have one," said Snicker, with considerable emphasis, "whom I will sell—a bargain."

"Good," assented Chunder Loo; "but you must get a buyer, if you sell at all. Now you are very fond of Bunn, I believe."

Snicker ground his teeth.

"You adore the boys."

Snicker clenched his hands and rolled his eyes.

"Good," said Chunder Loo. "I see you are ripe for action. Hating Bunn and the boys, what would you say to me—how reward me, if I rid the world of the lot of them?"

"Of—the—lot—of—them?"

"Yes, of the boiling—you see, that, though born in India, I have your slang at the tip of my tongue ready for use. Come, what will you give me?"

"But how will you do it?"

Chunder Loo thrust his dark face close to that of

the ex-schoolmaster, and, like a serpent's hiss, the reply came from his tongue:

"*By poison!*"

Snicker's eyes bulged out of his head, and every fibre of his body quivered.

"P—*poison!*" he groaned.

Chunder Loo nodded, and taking a cigarette-case out of his pocket, lit another of the small but insidious smokes.

"Poison," he said, "is the product of the East. It has a hundred forms, and those in the true secrets of the manufacture can kill and leave no sign. The victim pines away, the doctors talk of pulmonary complaints, and by-and-bye give a certificate for consumption. See here." He brought out a small packet from his pocket. "Try this on your wife. You need not kill her unless you wish it, but give her some, and mark the effect in a few days' time."

He thrust the packet into the hand of Snicker, and with a smile and a bow vanished.

"Well," gasped the recipient of this peculiar form of bounty, "of all the——"

He looked at the gift, and for a moment was tempted to throw it away, but he changed his mind and put it into his pocket.

"Phoebe," he murmured, "is now a-continually grumbling about the hardness of her lot, and says it would be a mercy for her to be took—*taken*, blow it!— and borne aloft. It can't be much of a crime to try on her how it works. I'll have a shot at it."

There is a weird delight felt by those who hold the life of another in their hands, and Snicker experienced it. With this unholy feeling in his breast, he wended his way homeward.

When Chunder Loo returned to where Jack had been sleeping, he found that he had awakened, and was on his feet, yawning and stretching his arms. There was a smile on the crafty face of the Hindoo as he said:

"You enjoy a little sleep in the open air, and it is good."

"I suppose so," answered Jack, carelessly, "although I did not mean to indulge in it."

He waited a moment to see which way Chunder Loo was going, intending to direct his steps the other way, but the Hindoo did not stir, so Jack went on to the Abbey with the swarthy one by his side.

At the door of the house Jack mustered courage to say: "You will excuse me, Mr. Chunder Loo, but may I ask if you are better?"

"Better!" repeated the Hindoo.

"Yes, sir. I heard you were not well this morning."

Chunder Loo looked at him with half-closed eyes and laughed.

"Oh! clever boy," he said, laying his hands on Jack's shoulders. "You think I am as strange a man as ever you met. You want to know why I should be cold on a summer day, eh? When you can see as clearly through an oak door *as I can*, you will know all about it."

Nodding his head and laughing—or was it snarling? —he vanished into the house, leaving Jack rather sorry he had asked after the health of Chunder Loo.

Presently he sauntered into the house, and found Penny Bunn in the hall, staring at the old grandfather's clock, which had never been repaired since that memorable time when Snicker, in a rage, pulled it down upon himself.

"Ha, Ford!" he said, "you are back early. Where are your companions?"

"Out for a stroll, sir," answered Jack. "I cannot say for certain where they are gone."

"I wish that one of you would call on Bibbins at Smudgem Bender, and ask him to come and repair this clock."

"He came some time ago, sir."

"Yes, I know. I have heard the story. He fancied there was something inside the case, and Snicker was very rude to him. But, of course, it was all fudge. Who ever really saw a skeleton in a clock? And if they did," added Bunn, with a smile of scorn, "what then? A skeleton is nothing more than a bag of bones."

"Most people are scared by skeletons," said Jack.

"It is exceedingly foolish of them," remarked Penny Bunn.

"I will run down to the village this afternoon, sir," said Jack, "and tell Bibbins you would like him to call to-morrow."

"Do, Ford."

Jack thought over the recent affair, and, in his opinion, Bibbins would decline to come to the Abbey. Perhaps if he did, some fun might be got out of it.

For some time past Jack had forgotten all about the skeleton, and calling to mind the fact that it had been entrusted to the care of Susan, he looked up the girl and asked her where it was. She said it was still under her bed. She had kept it there for the want of a more secure place.

"Do you think you could smuggle it into the old clock in the hall?"

"What, again, Master Ford?"

"Yes. You might do it while we are at dinner."

Susan promised on condition that she was not to be troubled with it again. Though not in the least afraid of all the skeletons in the wide world, she was not disposed to have it in her room again.

"Missus is such a one to go routing about," she said, "that she will be sure to drop upon it one day. Then I shall get into trouble."

Jack told her that she would never be asked to take charge of it more, and the matter was settled.

As the whole house, with the exception of Susan, dined at the same hour, she would be able to place the imperfectly articulated lot of bones within the clock without much fear of detection.

And it was done.

The three chums of Jack came back in time for dinner, and in the afternoon they all went on to the village of Smudgem Bender. Meanwhile Jack had laid the whole thing before them, and it was the general hope that things might work round so as to test the nerves of Penny Bunn in the presence of a skeleton.

Jack went to Bibbins, and told him what he was wanted for. Bibbins was dubious of the job.

"I am not fond of the Abbey at all, and I don't like that clock."

"None of us are," replied Jack. "Since you were there last, nobody has so much as ventured to open the case."

"Tell Mr. Bunn," said Bibbins, after a moment's reflection; "that although I don't like to throw away work, I would rather a Chippenham man undertook the job."

This was what Jack wanted, and the four friends went off for a bathe in the river that ran through the adjoining meadows. Word had been left that they would not be home to tea, and they timed their return so that they arrived at the Abbey when twilight was on the earth.

Jack went off to the sitting-room of Bunn and knocked at the door. Being requested to come in, he entered. They were all there—Bunn, his wife, Miss Astracan, and Chunder Loo. Mrs. Bunn was winding wool, and the obliging Hindoo held it outstretched on his dingy hands.

"Well, Ford," said Penny Bunn, who was reading a paper, "what do you want?"

"I have been down to Bibbins, sir," answered Jack, "and he says that he won't come."

"Eh? Now, what does he mean by that piece of insolence?"

"I don't think he meant to be rude. I judge from what he said that he is afraid of the clock."

"Why should he be afraid of it?"

"He says there is a skeleton in it."

Miriam stopped winding her wool, and Miss Astracan grunted contemptuously. Chunder Loo softly smiled.

"Pooh! A skeleton," said Bunn. "The man is a fool."

"Bibbins says that the last time he was here he saw one in it," said Jack.

"I heard a whisper of it," returned Bunn; "and I laughed at it, naturally. A skeleton every man has in

his house, but he does not keep them in grandfathers' clocks. Go and see for yourself, Ford, if such a thing is there."

"I think, P.Y." said Miriam with a curled lip, "that it would be more proper for you to see to it."

"Don't ask him to do it, dear," said Miss Astracan. "You know what a poor, nervous creature he is. I'll go."

"You sha'n't, indeed, aunty," said Miriam, pushing her gently back into her chair; "why should you be worried? You must have a life of ease or you will be seriously ill."

"I should like to say," said Penny Bunn, rising from his chair, and looking haughtily about him, "that there is no particular necessity for *any* one of us to look into the clock. I thought it would put Ford's mind at ease to see that nothing was there."

"You need not worry about him," said Miss Astracan, "he has forty times your nerve."

"As there seems to be some doubt about my courage, which will be poorly exercised in this matter, I will, for the satisfaction of all here, go at once and look into the clock."

Jack could have capered with joy. All things played up to his little scheme, and his friends had been posted in places of vantage to see the effect of that skeleton on the valiant Bunn.

Snorting with rage and contempt, the schoolmaster hastened out of the room. Jack hesitated a few moments, and was about to follow him, when a most fearful yell was heard.

"There *is* something in the clock," said Miss Astracan. "Miriam, dear, help me to get up. I must see what it is."

CHAPTER CVIII.

A JOKE WITH THE WRONG MAN.—POOR BUNN.

AS Miss Astracan required time to rise, there was sufficient lapse of it between her request for assistance and the moment she got upon her feet to enable Bunn to stagger down the passage and roll into the room.

A more abject specimen of scared manhood would have been difficult to find. His hair bristled, his eyes bulged out, and his legs were as limp as two sticks of boiled celery. In a heap he tumbled into his chair.

"P.Y.," said Miriam, sharply, "what is the matter with you?"

"The clock!" he gasped. "There is a skeleton in it!"

"I don't believe it," said Miriam; "you fancy it is there."

"I saw it," said Bunn, "plainly. I think it spoke. It was laughing at me."

"And well it might," said Miss Astracan. "I'll see what it is. Don't bother, Miriam, dear. No thank you, Mr. Chunder Loo. I don't want your arm." He had risen and offered it. "Ford will help me along."

She waddled to Jack's side, and laid a hand upon his shoulder, and for the first time he had a fair idea of her weight. But he was stronger than Bob Stockton, and did not give way under it.

The pair went slowly away, and Miriam spent the time intervening between their departure and return by calling her husband all the poltroons she could think of.

When they came back Miss Astracan had a housebroom in her hand, one of those articles with a very long handle.

"This is all I can find in the clock," she said.

Miriam gave vent to a shriek of laughter and Chunder Loo, apparently inspired by some uncontrolable emotion, cut a wild caper, tossing his feet alternately into the air. Only Jack was a witness to this movement, and it let a little more daylight into his mind about the hidden nature of the Hindoo.

"A broom!" said Miriam. "You donkey! So this is your skeleton?"

"I will swear," said Penny Bunn, violently, "that I saw a skeleton inside the clock."

"You want some physic, Bunn," said Miss Astracan, "and you must have a strong mustard poultice on the back of your neck when you go to bed. And Miriam, dear, if you have any cayenne pepper in the house, a sprinkling of it will help the poultice along."

"I won't be poulticed," howled Penny Bunn.

"But you must, and will," coolly replied Miriam; "aunty, you will get him one ready? Now, P.Y., come to bed instantly."

Bunn looked for a moment as if he would resist, but a glance round showed the hopelessness of his position.

"Put me into my coffin, if you like," he said, drearily. "It is all one to me. Ha, ha! If there was no skeleton in the clock, there are a hundred in the house—thousands—millions!"

"Take him upstairs," said Miss Astracan, "and I'll have the poultice ready in two minutes. I used to make them for the orphans, and they did a power of good. None of 'em, having had a poultice on, was ill for a month afterwards."

Bunn and his wife departed, and Jack, shirking the duty of escorting Miss Astracan to the kitchen, hastened away in search of his friends, who had taken refuge in the classroom.

"Whose thought was it putting the broom in the clock?" asked Jack.

"Don's," replied Tom.

"It completed the thing. What have you done with the skeleton?"

"Put it into Chunder Loo's bed for a change," replied Bob Stockton.

For a moment Jack looked grave, but he soon brightened up.

"He won't mind it, and if he does, it will show him that we are not so scared by his uncanny goings-on as he seems to think. That lot of bones has done us yeoman service, and now they may go."

"I wonder what he will say?" said Tom, musingly.

"Wait and see," advised Jack.

It was assumed by the boys that Penny Bunn had his poultice duly put on, and derived great benefit therefrom, but they heard nothing about it. Nor did Chunder Loo in any way refer to the little practical joke played upon him. Not the slightest further reference was made to the skeleton, and he met the boys, and talked to them, when they could not avoid his company, as if there had not been such a thing in existence.

"I don't like that," said Jack one night, as the chums wandered in the meadows. "It is your silent men who work evil. I have heard my father say—and he knows. Chunder Loo will even up matters with us somehow."

"But how?" asked Don.

"Wait and see," said Jack, falling back upon his favourite piece of advice in a difficulty.

So they waited, and nothing came of it.

The life they spent was enjoyable in many ways. They had perfect freedom, and lived practically in the open air. Botch still acted up to his hospitable instincts, and welcomed them heartily at his farmhouse whenever they chose to go, and they enjoyed the sunshine, and the bathing, and the semi-gipsy existence of the time, but there was a shadowy mass of cloud over it all.

They felt that they had reason to fear Chunder Loo, and not a word or sign came from Professor Lingo.

So the time passed, and the day for the return of the boys was drawing nigh, when a dreadful event happened in Smudgem Bender, to which we must devote a very short chapter.

It happened on the eve of the day previous to the time when the pupils of Littlecote Abbey were expected back from their homes.

The holidays were over, and the time of study and worry, fun and adventure, was about to be renewed.

Whatever in the past worried the boys had now vanished, but new sources of fear had arisen, and problems of import would have to be solved. The inner circle looked forward to the coming time with anxiety, but not dread.

CHAPTER CIX.

THE POISONER AT WORK. — SNICKER'S DYING REQUEST.

WHEN a man of the temperament of Fontenoy Snicker, Esquire, finds himself getting into difficulties, and all the world against him, he invariably begins to brood in a revengeful spirit.

Thus it was with the ex-schoolmaster of Littlecote Abbey, who may be fairly considered to have put himself outside the court of public complimentary criticism.

No man in Smudgem Bender would associate with him.

He tried what may be called the upper classes of the place first, the village doctor and the parson, and they threw him heavily, openly declaring that he was a disgrace to the neighbourhood.

Then he went for the tradesmen, who were few, but potent in their sphere, and they sat upon him.

They showed their love for him as a neighbour and a friend by utterly refusing to supply him with so much as a rushlight, unless the money was first planked down on the counter.

In despair, he fell back upon the agricultural labourers, and they offered "to keep him company" if he paid for all the drink they wanted, and did not come into the room they affected at the Cowley Arms more than once a week.

The terms, in the eyes of Snicker, were a little too one-sided, and he declined to close with them.

So he fell back upon his home, with no other company than his wife, who, in accordance with her nagging nature, would not give him a moment's rest.

Day after day she put the following questions to him, much as if they had been a series of conundrums, especially got up for the pleasing exercise of his gifted mind :

Why didn't he hang on to Littlecote Abbey?

And having left it, why did he not rise up like an industrious man, and go back to the coal and 'tater line? There was a living for an active man in it, anyway.

Why did he not go out like a husband, and thrash Bibbins, the watch and clock maker?

Why did he not summons Mrs. Bibbins, and make her pay for Mrs. Snicker's bonnet and front, both of which had been damaged, in the encounter recorded, beyond repair?

To all of these queries Snicker had but one form of reply, and that was of the brimstone order.

At last he began to think that he ought to try the effect of the medicine given him by Chunder Loo on Mrs. Snicker. He had it in a packet, in the form of a small powder, and it was in his desk, which he would have carefully kept locked, if the lock had not been long out of repair.

Meanwhile, the worry of things had made a great change in his personal appearance. He lost what little colour he had, and took upon himself a general sickly appearance, which caused much anxiety to Mrs. Snicker.

In common with her sex, generally, she was always anxious to administer physic of some sort to her husband, and she suggested to him one morning that he would be better for a "little cooling mixture." His answer was of a nature that is unprintable. It appalled Mrs. Snicker, who ought, by that time, to have become hardened to the verbal explosives of her spouse.

To an extent she was daunted, but not utterly defeated. Her Jerry wanted medicine, and medicine he should have.

One morning when he was out, she was overhauling his desk, and came across the powder, hidden in in one of those old-fashioned secret drawers which are immediately found out.

A powder was a powder—that and nothing more, to Mrs. Snicker, and, in her opinion, it was the very thing for Jerry. He must have it, and she thought it would go down undetected in a cup of tea.

So that afternoon she put it in a cup, and placed it on the table. It was a small, colourless powder, and without close examination would not have been seen at the bottom of the cup. Snicker, who came home in time for tea, did not look for it at all. Phœbe handed him his portion of ceylon, and he drank it, unsuspecting what lay hidden in it.

About an hour afterwards he was seated in the porch, when a sudden spasmodic feeling laid hold of him. He jumped from his chair and called out :

" Phœbe!"

" What do you want?" she asked from the region of the back kitchen.

" I'm took bad. Bring me a drop of something!"

" How do you feel, Jerry?" she asked, as she emerged from the doorway.

" I've a pain all over here."

" Oh, that is nothing. It is only the powder beginning to work."

" What powder?"

" You haven't looked so well as you ought to do of late, Jerry," said Mrs. Snicker, as she wiped her hands upon her apron, " and, as you wouldn't be agreeable, I thought that you ought to be dosed without your knowing it. So this afternoon I gave you a powder in your tea. I found it in your desk——"

A cry, the most horrible that had ever sprung from his lips, burst from the agonized Snicker, and aiming a blow, which she expertly dodged, at his wife, he fell upon the ground.

"I'm a dead man!" he groaned. "You've given me poison!"

She was a thin woman, and none too young, but she was strong and wiry, and, grasping him by the collar, she dragged him into the house.

"What was the poison, Jerry?" she asked, in an agony, "was it for mice or rats?"

"Get the doctor here," was all he said.

She laid him on an old sofa that formed a part of the furniture of the room, and throwing a shawl over her head, rushed out for Doctor Lamplick. Fortunately, he was at home, and they were back in three or four minutes.

Snicker lay groaning and writhing upon the sofa, endeavouring, in a wild, incoherent fashion, to utter words of repentance for his past sins.

"Gimme a chance of living on," he groaned, "and I'll be a better man."

"Come," said the doctor, "don't make all this fuss. Let me see what is the matter with you? Mrs. Snicker said she gave you poison by mistake. It was a powder you had in your desk. Where did you get it from?"

"It was given to me by a friend. Oh! the hagony—agony—I enjure—dure. It is offal—awful!"

"Who gave you poison, and for what purpose?" demanded the doctor, angrily.

"It was Chunder Loo, at the Abbey," groaned Snicker, as he rolled about, "and I don't know what he gave it to me for."

"Strange," muttered the doctor. "Keep still, man! How am I to know what is the matter with you if you wriggle about like an eel on a toasting fork?"

The doctor pushed him back, and held him down while he looked steadily into the face of the ex-school-master.

"You are very bad," he said. "Mrs. Snicker, find somebody who will run up to the Abbey and ask this Chunder Loo to come here at once. I must know the nature of the poison before I attempt to find an antidote to it."

"Wouldn't the stomick—ach—pump do no good?" inquired Snicker, tearfully.

"No," was the curt reply. "Keep still until this man comes."

Mrs. Snicker was gone, and the two were left alone. The doctor sat down by the sofa and brought out a briarroot pipe.

"A little smoke will do you good," he said; "anyway, it won't make you worse."

"Doctor," said Snicker, "do you think I'm really dying?"

"If I can't get at the nature of the poison," replied the doctor, "how am I to help you? All depends on the speedy coming of this man who gave you the stuff."

"And suppose he don't know the name of it, doctor?"

"Oh, then I can do nothing."

"Oh, dear!" groaned Snicker. "Perhaps I ought to make a last dying speech and confession."

"Just as you like. Fire away."

"Oh, doctor, you don't seem to feel the awful position I'm in."

"I don't. How should I, not being poisoned? Now out with what you have to say."

"I've been a great rascal, doctor——"

"We all know that."

"When I married Phoebe I was a salesman in a 'ole—whole—sale 'tatur shop—and I used to send out sacks of 'taturs to a little shop I'd started unknown to my employer—and they wasn't never put down in the book."

"Just what might be expected of you," said the doctor.

"We didn't thrive in the 'tatur line," pursued Snicker, "for I was found out by master, who thrashed me with a cart-whip, and sent me about my business. He was a vilent—vi-o-lent man, and couldn't, as he said, wait for the slow course of justice, and so laid it on me thick. I was sore for days."

"Glad to hear it," remarked the doctor. "Well, what did you go into next?"

"We had coals with the 'taturs, and they wasn't helpful to an honest man," said Snicker, in a snivelling fashion. "Bu'sted in both, we took to shows, and exhibited the fattest woman on earth for a penny. She was fat, and it took a lot to keep her, but she drew. We made a bit of money, and got up so that we went into partnership with a man as would have robbed me if I hadn't robbed him."

"That will do," said the doctor. "I don't want to hear any more. In my private opinion, you ought to be poisoned."

The doctor puffed at his pipe, and Snicker wriggled and groaned for another ten minutes, and then Mrs. Snicker and Chunder Loo unexpectedly appeared.

"Sich a fortunate thing, Jerry," she said, "I met Mister Bungalow out a-walking, and I told him what he was wanted for, and he's come."

"I understand," said Chunder Loo, with hauteur, "that I am charged with having poisoned this man?"

"No," replied the doctor, "he says he has been poisoned by a powder you gave him. It was accidental, and I want to know the exact nature of that powder."

"He complained of the toothache," said Chunder Loo, "and I gave him a camomile powder."

"As I thought," said the doctor, rising and taking up his hat, "the fool is not poisoned at all! The next time you are taken that way, my man, send for another doctor."

He stalked out of the house, snorting in anger, and Chunder Loo, turning to Mrs. Snicker, asked her to leave the room for a minute.

"I have something to say to your husband," he said.

Mrs. Snicker smirked by way of assent, and left the room. Chunder Loo drew in chair and sat down by the bed of the sufferer, who had now recovered with almost magical rapidity from his indisposition.

"You are the man to trust, surely!" hissed Chunder Loo. "Don't you know, you worm, that the true confederate dies a hundred deaths rather than betray his brother knave? You have been weighed in the balance and found wanting. Hear me. *You have taken poison!* Had you not sent for me as you have, it would have been easy for me, any time within three weeks, to have given you the antidote. I alone know it."

"But you will give it to me now, in course?" pleaded Snicker, feebly.

"I give it to you?" hissed Chunder Loo. "Not to save my own life. Hear me, you miserable dog and cur! *The poison is in you,* and it will remain there until the moment comes for it to act. I cannot tell when that will be. There is no knowing, save that it will not be for a week, anyway, or not for a month, or even a year; but it *will* act when the moment comes."

"I'll tell of this," groaned Snicker.

"Do so," answered Chunder Loo, with a horrible laugh, "and they will tell you that you *lie.* How is it to be proven, unless you die, and the poison is found in you? *But it cannot be done.* Ten minutes after you are gone it *will vanish.* I doom you, as a traitor and a worm, to a short life of terror and a speedy death."

And then in a moment more he was gone.

When Mrs. Snicker, after waiting a long time, ventured to peep into the room, she saw her husband lying senseless on the floor.

CHAPTER CX.

THE COMING OF A NEW BOY.—BUNN PULLS HIMSELF TOGETHER.

THERE was much scrubbing and cleaning going on in the Abbey, for which three old women had been engaged as assistants to the active Susan.

Miriam and her aunt were arranging the sleeping accommodation, and to ascertain the number of beds required, were in conference with Penny Bunn.

Movement produces harmony in a household, and there was peace among the trio.

"Now, P. Y.," said Miriam, "tell us how many beds will be wanted. You have, I presume, received all the replies to your circular that you expected?"

"As a matter of fact," replied Bunn, referring to a list he held in his hand "*all* have written, and I find that I lose seven pupils. The rest are coming back, as I fear, just to work out the various terms which have been paid for."

"Any new pupils?"

"Not one."

"That is not promising, but we must be hopeful, and advertise. Who are among the missing?"

"Smith—the boys, for some reason, nicknamed him Soppem—is one; Bedstone another, and Whymper. These are three boys I should like to have kept. There are a four more boys not coming back to school. Their time was up, and their parents did not think it desirable they should come again. In the letters they send there are some very unpleasant remarks. Shall I read you some of them?"

"I can guess what they are," said Miriam; "denunciations of Snicker, I presume."

"They certainly lay on thick there," said Bunn; "but for some reason they have not spared *me.* One mother writes to ask if it is likely that, having been imposed upon by a rogue, she is likely to trust her son to a fool? I," added Bunn, impressively, "am the fool referred to."

"'Woe unto you if all men speak well of you,'" said Miss Astracan.

"As far as my life has gone," returned Bunn, "I have escaped that peril. Nor have I run the gauntlet of all-round praise from the other sex. If shying stones was pecuniarily beneficial to the man they are directed at, *I* should at this moment be a Crœsus."

"You are too sensitive, P. Y.," said Miriam.

"Too soft," asserted Miss Astracan. "Will you want thirty beds?"

"No; twenty-seven or eight will do. Oh! by the way, I have received from Sir Charles Barstow another reminder that the flooring of that accursed room ought to be nearly completed."

"Sit down, and write to him as I dictate," said Miriam. "Now, are you ready?"

"Quite," replied Penny Bunn.

"DEAR SIR CHARLES,—I am in receipt of your letter, and, in reply, hasten to inform you that the flooring is progressing as fast as is commensurable with good work. If you desire it I can hurry on, but the result would be disastrous. The whole thing would be ruined. I have been looking over some old records of the laying of a similar floor, and I find that it took two ancient skilled men close upon *two years* to carry it to a successful completion. Do not forget that I work single-handed. I am at your command always. If I am to hasten the work, let me know by return. "I am, Sir Charles.
"Your obedient servant,
"P. Y. BUNN."

"Miriam," said Bunn, as he finished this Jesuitical letter, "you are a marvel of a woman."

"Then live as if you were thankful for her, and don't be always worrying the poor creature," said Miss

Astracan, warmly. "I am sure that there is never a night that I don't shed a lot of tears in my room when I think of her."

"Grief," said Bunn, with a dry smile, "seems to have the same effect upon you as it did upon Falstaff."

"And how did it operate on him?" asked Miss Astracan, innocently.

"According to the statement of that peerless old man," answered Bunn, "it blew him up like a bladder."

For a moment both the women stood aghast at this unparalleled piece of audacious wit from Bunn. He was himself staggered by the tremendous weight of the bolt he had hurled at the head of Miss Astracan.

She, on her part, having fought for breath and come out victorious, turned to Miriam, and said, huskily:

"Darling, will you give me the poker? I dursn't stoop. No orphan I ever had to deal with—and they come it strong sometimes—ever had the audacity to say a thing like that to me."

"Don't bother about the poker," said Bunn, as he retreated to the door. "I am sorry you cannot take a jest in the proper spirit. I am going out for a walk."

He departed accordingly, leaving Miss Astracan to fight out an attack of the old spasms, assisted towards her convalescence by her niece, and a drop of the rare old liquor, which she, as heretofore, kept ready for such emergencies.

It was not until he was well within the shelter of the wood that he allowed himself to thoroughly enjoy his joke at Miss Astracan's expense.

"It was almost as good as hitting her with a brick," he cried, and then off he went into a fit of laughter, in part restrained, but sufficiently free to put him through some of the most extraordinary contortions ever seen in connection with the human form.

He was so occupied with the reflections on his success as a wit, that he did not hear the footsteps of two persons who were coming up the path.

Close behind them was a fly, with some luggage on the roof.

The strangers, for such they were, consisted of a woman of thirty-five or so and a boy of fourteen.

The former was stout, in a moderate sense, and had been good-looking once upon a time, but was now rather coarse in features.

The boy was stout, thick-set, and of rough general aspect. But his clothes were good, and in both there were indications that there was no want of money in connection with them.

"I say, mum," cried the boy, "look at that covey; he's got the twisters."

Penny Bunn heard his voice, and casting off his

mirth, became straight and dignified in a moment. On seeing two persons unknown with the fly and luggage, he promptly scented a new pupil. That he should have been discovered going through such a performance was a little embarrassing, but he rose to the occasion.

"Pardon me," he said, "but whatever the twisters may be, I am not suffering from them. I was practising the first steps of the Pyrrhic dance of the Greeks, which has now become a portion of the gymnastic exercises of all well-conducted schools."

"It was a blooming fine way of amusing yourself," said the boy, with a grin.

"Mulberry," said the woman, "be quiet; you can't know anything of it. Brought up as you was, how should you? Do I see the head of Littlecote School, sir?"

"I have the honour to be the principal of that college," said Bunn. "May I ask if you desire to place your son under my care?"

"Sich was my intentions," replied the woman. "My name is Cork, and his Chrisen name, which you perhaps ketched as I spoke, is Mulberry. I want to place him at a school where he can be made a gentleman of."

"Then allow me to say, ma'am," said Bunn, solemnly, "that some guiding angel must have led your steps hither. It has been a recognised fact that Littlecote Abbey School has turned out more *real* gentlemen, from the roughest material, than any ten other establishments in the kingdom, including the Universities."

"You hear that, Mulberry?" said Mrs. Cork.

"Yes," replied Mulberry, with a tinge of scorn in his voice, "I hear the bloke, but he don't take me in."

"Excuse me, madame," said Bunn, "but I think the matter uppermost in your mind can be better discussed by ourselves in the seclusion of my study. Permit me to offer you an arm to escort you to the Abbey."

Mrs. Cork smiled and simpered, and having taken the arm of Penny Bunn, the pair walked on. Mulberry dropped back to the side of the fly, and looking up at the driver, said:

"It's a game of my mother's to put a bit of polish on me. She's got a idea that I'm short of manners—*manners*," he repeated, bitterly; "what is the good of 'em? I hate 'em."

"You'll get a lot of manners up there—of a sort," replied the driver. "The boys, if nobody else does, will knock 'em into you."

"A fly lot, I 'spect," said Mulberry.

"They are rushers," said the driver.

Meanwhile Penny Bunn had escorted Mrs. Cork to the study, and despatched Susan to watch for the fly and assist with the luggage.

"Before we enter into business," said Bunn, "may I offer you some refreshment?"

"I could do with a toothful of something," answered Mrs. Cork—"anything, so long as it isn't water."

"Excuse me one moment," said Bunn. "I will bring Mrs. Bunn here."

He had no difficulty in finding her, and cutting short a threatened storm, told her about the new arrivals.

"There's money," he said, "and ignorance at the back of it. Will you come and see her?"

"I think I had better," said Miriam.

She whipped off the overall she was wearing, smoothed her hair with her hands, and sent Bunn back to do the honours to the guest while she fetched her aunt's special bottle from her room.

When she appeared, she had it, with a glass, a decanter of water, and some biscuits on a tray.

"Mrs. Bunn," said Bunn.

"Hope you are well?" said Mrs. Cork.

Miriam bowed, graciously, and placed the tray upon the table.

"Will you help yourself," she said.

Mrs. Cork did so, liberally.

"Here's luck to all," she said, raising her glass. Having drunk freely, she put it down, and went on:

"If there is one thing I'm fond of, it's good manners. *You've* both got 'em, but I ain't."

"I was only just remarking to myself how exceedingly pleasant you were," murmured Penny Bunn.

"Pleasant I 'opes to live and die, but manners ain't in my line. Nor in Mulberry's, either."

"Mulberry," explained Bunn to Miriam, "is this lady's son. A very promising youth."

"He ain't a bad sort if you scratch him right," said Mrs. Cork, "but if you rub him the wrong way, he's okkard. Just like his father."

"Dead, I fear," murmured Bunn.

"No," replied Mrs. Cork, with some embarrassment, "he isn't 'zackly dead, or—well, it don't matter where he is so long as he isn't here. That's my motter."

Miriam now interposed. She saw that it was time to take matters in hand. Bunn, having once got off the track, might run goodness knows whither.

In five minutes that peerless woman had secured a pupil for the school at the rate of one hundred pounds per annum—terms, payment in advance.

"I admit," said Miriam, with her most lady-like air, "that you are paying a little in excess of our ordinary terms, but the case is exceptional. Most of our pupils come *as* gentlemen. They have the requisite polish, and much time and labour is saved. But your son is a rough diamond, and it will take time to polish him."

"We *have* gone as high as two hundred," here interposed Bunn, but a look from his wife cut him short.

"I don't mind the money a bit," said Mrs. Cork, taking a cheque-book from a reticule she had brought with her, "and I reckoned it would be references or money down, and if the blunt is planked on the table, it stops a lot of jaw."

"It does," said Miriam, "P.Y., dear, will you see Mulberry is not being worried in any way? He may be anxious about his mother having left him."

"Not he," exclaimed Mrs. Cork, laughing; "it would take more than that to worry Mulberry. Whatever he may want in the way of clothing and linen I hope you will buy, ma'am, and send the bills on to me. I stops at the Langham Hotel, London, mostly. Send the bills on there. Money by return as soon as I has 'em."

She rose up, put her bonnet straight by the glass, and calmly helped herself to a little more gin and water, which she disposed of without a wink.

"Keeps you up, it does," she said, "until it knocks you down. But I never take more than I can carry."

They went out to the hall, where they found Penny Bunn and Mulberry, the latter with his hands in his pockets, softly whistling.

"All done, mother?" he said.

"Yes, my dear boy," she answered.

"They've got a pupil and the mopusses. Well, that's all right. If they treat me well, I'll not let fly more than once now and then, just to ease off the steam. I'm short of lucre. Hand us over a thick 'un."

His mother took a sovereign from her purse, which he on receiving spun into the air, and then transferred it to his pocket.

"Oh," said the fond mother, as she held him to her breast, "how proud I shall be of you when you are a gentleman!"

"I'll soak in some manners," replied Mulberry, "if only to please you, you bet. Good-bye."

Bunn, with all the gallantry at his command, escorted Mrs. Cork to the fly, and then hastened back to the house.

In the hall Miriam was awaiting him.

"Come into your room," she said. "I want to speak to you."

"Where's the boy?" asked Bunn.

"I don't know. He's gone off upstairs with *his hat on* in the house, the little wretch!"

They went up to the room, and as Bunn closed the door, Miriam sank into a chair.

"I don't often take it," she gasped, "but for goodness sake, P. Y., mix me a little drop. Two more minutes with that woman would have killed me."

"She certainly is a most remarkable creature. But there is much amiability under lying her eccentricities."

"Bosh!" said Miriam, curtly. "Thank you."

She emptied the glass, and handed it back to Bunn, who, meditatively, poured out a little for himself.

"I could not help feeling sorry for you, dear," he said.

Then looking round, and seeing she was sitting with a hand over her eyes, he emptied the glass, and put it down very softly. "It was such a contrast—vulgarity *versus* refinement."

"What do you think you will do with the boy?"

"Refine him."

"Send him home at the end of a month, or get him to run away. We have her cheque. I will take care of it--that is, I will get it cashed, and put the money away. We may want it one of these rainy days."

"It is the first streak of sunlight that has fallen on the school," said Bunn, joyously. "Ahead I see the coming of a glorious day."

Then as Miriam, forgetting the bottle, went out of the room, he helped himself to a second dose, and drank "long life to Mrs. Cork."

He had a third dose, and put some water into the bottle to make up for the deficiency. That done, he felt he was at peace with all the world, and went out for a stroll.

CHAPTER CXI.

MULBERRY CORK ASTONISHES SOME PEOPLE.

IT was with considerable astonishment that the four friends, on returning to the Abbey, where, as usual, they hastened to their private chamber for the nonce, the classroom, to hear, on approaching it, the sound of shuffling feet, accompanied by the whistling of a lively air.

"What's the matter now?" asked Don, as they pulled up short, and stared at each other.

"It isn't Bunn," replied Tom, "and it can't be Chunder Loo. A Hindoo never whistles."

"I would not swear to that," murmured Bob. "Hearken."

It was Mulberry Cork, of course, to whom they were listening, and now he burst into song, still pursuing his dancing.

> "I'm a gent, I'm a gent, a gent ready made,
> In Whitechapel born, and to kid 'em's my trade.
> 　　Houp la! on we go;
> 　　Walk up and see the show
> Of the gent, of the gent, the gent ready made."

"This whacks everything," said Jack; "let us see who it is."

He opened the door, and they walked in, just as Mulberry finished his Terpsichorean performance with a leap in the air.

On seeing the boys he stared hard at them, as if they were so many natural curiosities he had suddenly met with, but was not in any way troubled.

"How do you do?" asked Bob Stockton, politely. "New boy, I presume?"

"No, I am no newer than other boys of my age," was the reply, "and not so green as most on 'em. My mother brought me here to-day to have the corners chipped off me, and to be generally filed down and sand-papered into a gentleman."

"And who is going to do it?" asked Bob. The others could not find anything to say to this phenomenal boy.

"A longish chap, who is boss here, I fancy," answered Mulberry; "anyway, he has the old woman's brads, and he will have to work on the job."

"I wish him joy of it," said Bob; "it will be interesting to watch the progress of his labours."

Mulberry glanced sharply at him, and for a few moments was silent and thoughtful, as if he were engaged in getting at the full meaning of the words he had just heard.

"I reckon," he said, suddenly, "that you consider yourself a bit fly—up to snuff, and down to a thing or two?"

"Not at all," replied Bob; "it is for others to consider. Will you, in accordance with the rules and regulations of this school, duly made and provided, oblige us with your name?"

"If you think it will do you any good," rejoined Mulberry, "you can have it. Mulberry Cork."

"Novel and appropriate," murmured Bob.

"Look here," said Mulberry, with sudden anger, "if you, or all of you, with your fine manners and turn-up-nose airs, think you are going to get the rise out of me, you will find you have made no common error."

"There is no occasion to put yourself out," interposed Jack. "I presume that you have not been to a school of this description before."

"Neither before nor behind," curtly replied Mulberry. "What of that?"

"Well, you will have to learn to adapt yourself to its peculiarities."

"Oh!" was all Mulberry said, and then he walked out of the room whistling.

"I say," said Don, "that pattern won't do here."

"He is a regular rough," said Tom.

"Wait and see how he turns out," advised Jack. "He will give us some fun, if nothing else."

"But who will associate with him? Who can chum with such a fellow?"

"Nobody, while he is on that tack, but wait and see."

"Jack's stock bit of advice," said Bob, "and, like the landscape of the song, 'Ever charming, ever new, old as the hills, but always true.'"

There was no doubt that Mulberry Cork promised to keep the place alive. He was cool, impudent, and apparently cared for nothing and nobody. He was not even startled by Miss Astracan, and when they met in the hall later on, as she was waddling about, he calmly took stock of her from head to foot, and ejaculated:

" My eye !"

" What is the matter with your eye ?" asked Miss Astracan. "Come more into the light, and let me look at it."

Mulberry Cork walked to one of the windows, and opening the lid of his left eye with a thumb and finger, said:

" Have a good look at it, old lady, and, if you see any green in it, be sure you let me know."

" Green what ?" asked the puzzled old woman, who had heard of this youthful treasure, and was prepared for eccentricities of speech.

" Any sort of green," he answered ; " the green of the mug, the verdure of the chicken. See any, eh ?"

" I think you want a powder, and will give you one to-night. How old are you ?"

" Fourteen."

" Ah ! Then you are too old for teething powders. I never give 'em over ten. Gentian with a little ginger will do for you."

Mulberry dropped his hand from his eye as she waddled away, and appeared to be in his turn a bit flabbergasted.

" Now," he said, in a musing tone, "what is her line ? Is she on the barney lay ? Gentian and ginger for *me!* I'd like to catch myself taking the stuff. Blessed if I don't think I've tumbled on a rum lot here—a gawk for a schoolmaster; boys as swell in their lingo as West End toffs; an old gal that would be good for a pound a week and her beer in any show. Blessed if I don't think mother's done it this time."

He was plainly perturbed, and he fought shy of the people in the house the rest of the day, not even appearing at meal-time, but coming in late to tea, and eating from what was left as Susan was clearing away.

He thought he would ask her a few questions about the house in general, and proceeded to do so, in an affable manner.

" I say, old girl," he said, " is this a regular shop for cranking out gents, or only a dummy one ?"

" I don't understand you," replied Susan. " This isn't a shop; it is a school."

" Well, I am here to be made a gentleman of. Do you think they have the tools to do it ?"

Susan looked at him in a puzzled way, and did not answer him for a moment. He, meanwhile, was eating bread and butter in the unconventional manner of a young wolf.

" The only tool I have seen here," said Susan at last, breaking the silence, " is a cane, but it isn't so much used as it was."

" Let 'em try it on me," said Mulberry, with a ferocious glare in his eye. " I will slip into 'em if they do."

" I think you have done wrong to come here," said Susan; " it isn't your sort of school."

" Well, you must blame mother," said Mulberry: " I didn't want to come. I told her she might as well chuck her lucre into the river off London Bridge."

Susan took up a tray she had filled and hastened away. Mulberry Cork was something monstrous in her eyes. She could make nothing of a boy who could talk in that style. He was altogether out of the region of her previous experience.

In debating the question of where this novel addition to the Abbey was to sleep, Miriam and Miss Astracan were both of opinion that he ought to have a room to himself. For that night he might be put into number two dormitory.

" He will be horribly lonely," urged Bunn.

" Do as you are told," said Miss Astracan. " Stay with him until he is in bed, and see that he takes a powder I will get ready for him."

" I should think Chunder Loo might attend to him."

But the ladies demurred to that. Chunder Loo had been out all day, and had not yet returned. When he came back he would be too tired to be worried with this very strange boy.

" You are mighty considerate about him," sneered Bunn.

" All gentlemen," replied Miriam, " whether their skins be white or a rich mahogany brown, are entitled to the consideration of ladies. Don't talk nonsense, but do as you are told."

So at half-past eight Penny Bunn went in search of his promising pupil, and found him in the class-room alone. The schoolmaster had a mug in his hand, in which was the powder ready for the patient.

" It is time to retire, my boy," he said.

" Time to what ?" demanded Mulberry.

" To retire—to go to bed."

" Oh ! to bed. Well, I don't mind for once, although it is so precious early. What have you got there ?"

" A powder Miss Astracan has mixed for you."

Mulberry took the mug from his hand, looked into it, smelt the potion, and walking to the window, which was open, tossed the precious mixture out.

" What does the old gal take me for ?" he scornfully demanded. " I run alone, I do. I'm not a baby. Now, then, show me where to doss."

" Cork," said Bunn, with severity, " in this home, where refinement dwells, you will have to learn to speak of things in a becoming manner."

"Well, do you expect me to do it right away?" asked Mulberry. "Did you think you was going to earn a cool hundred right orf the reel? Blame me if I don't think you have got a cheek."

"Come to bed," said Bunn, with a growing wildness in his eye. "To-morrow the boys will be coming back, and then the usual routine of school will be resumed. You will take your place with the rest, and be duly instructed. I hope you will prove an apt pupil."

As it was not dark, in the true sense of the word, no candle was needed, and Bunn escorted his charge upstairs.

On being ushered into the dormitory, where fifteen beds were made ready, Mulberry sent forth a whistle of surprise.

"Why, it's better than a sixpenny doss," he said. "I suppose, being the first here, I can pick my bed?"

"No," replied Bunn, stiffly. "As a new-comer you will have to sleep next the door."

"Not if I know it," said Mulberry. "It isn't done anywheres. First comer takes his pick; if anybody wants his bed, they must fight for it. Whatever you do, governor, let the thing be fair."

"Do as you like to-night," said Bunn, "To-morrow the usual routine will begin, and you will have to conform to the rules."

He could not argue any further with this dreadful boy, but fairly fled from his presence.

Mulberry, left to himself, inspected each bed in its turn, turning down the counterpanes to see if the sheets were clean, and punching the mattresses to test the softness thereof.

"Pretty much of a muchness about the biling," he muttered. "Bar the position, there ain't much to choose. I'll sleep in the furthest from the door."

He was the general theme of conversation in the Abbey that night, and Chunder Loo, coming back in time for supper, heard all sorts of things about the phenomenon. He seemed to be more than usually interested in the subject.

"Will you take him in hand, Loo?" asked Penny Bunn, with a groan, "and make a—a—a—a *gentleman* of him."

"I will make something of him," quickly replied Chunder Loo.

CHAPTER CXII.

THE RETURN OF THE BOYS—OLD FRIENDS AND THE NEW FACE.

"I HEAR voices in the wood," said Bob, as he rose from the ground, on which he had been lying with Don. "It is some of the fellows returning to slavery."

It was near noon, and some who lived within comparatively easy distances from the Abbey were expected back in time for dinner. Jack Ford and Tom had gone down to meet them, and to prepare them for the new-comer's eccentricities.

The fact was Mulberry Cork had completely nonplussed the four chums, and they had not been able to settle on any definite line of treatment for him.

As he was, they felt that it would be impossible to make a chum of him. But would contact with a higher form of civilization than he had clearly mixed in before be of any service to him?

Was he an incurable specimen of low cunning? Or were his faults only on the tongue and on the surface of his nature?

They were anxious not to do him an injustice, but if he should prove to be no better than he was exteriorly, it would be impossible for them to associate with him.

"Bunn ought to be prosecuted for taking him" said Bob, and that was really the opinion of them all.

But Jack, as usual, advised them not to judge hastily, but to await the development of events.

There were about a dozen of the boys with Jack and Tom coming up by the wood. Among them were Dorey, Tanner, Short, Jiggers, and Hone. The latter appeared to be in a more amiable mood than he had been last term.

He was walking by the side of Jack, and talking with him as if he desired to be friends.

Jack was not the sort of youth to bear any grudge, or to foster ill-feeling of the past. As he was strong, so he could be generous. He met Hone halfway.

In accordance with an established custom, the youngsters had walked from Chippenham Station, leaving their luggage to be brought on by a carrier, who had been duly advised to meet them with his cart.

"Hallo, Don!"

"How are you, Bob?"

"Glad to see you back again!"

"Haven't you found it precious dull here?"

"Not at all—all sorts of fun going on."

"I say, it is odd Chunder Loo hasn't gone."

"What about the new fellow?"

And so the chatter went on, school matters being mingled with short yarns of the jolly times they had had at home from the returning ones.

All who had not seen Mulberry Cork were naturally anxious to get a glimpse of him, and they were soon gratified.

Dinner was served at one o'clock, and they had settled down a minute or so, and were waiting for Chunder Loo to take his seat at the head of the table with some impatience, all being hungry, when loud voices were heard in the hall.

A SPLENDID SCHOOL STORY. NEVER BEFORE PUBLISHED.

By E. HARCOURT BURRAGE,

Author of "Ching Ching," "Monkey Mat and Roving Dick," "The Brave Boy of the Basilisk," &c.

THE LAMBS OF LITTLECOTE

A SKELETON APPEARS TO THE TERROR-STRICKEN DON.

PRICE ONE PENNY.

"I tell yer I won't go in! I'd rather have my peck alone afterwards. I don't mind the cloth being a bit dirty; I'm used to it."

"You will precede me to the room, please," said a quiet voice.

"Mulberry Cork and Chunder Loo," whispered Bob Stockton. "Order, there, for the play!"

A marvellous stillness fell upon the room. Outside the voices had ceased, and there was a sound of hesitating footsteps. Presently Cork appeared at the door, with Chunder Loo behind him.

"Take that seat," said the Hindoo, "at the top of the table, on my left, and remember that it is yours until I change it."

"I ain't been used to dining with toffs——"

"Sit down."

Mulberry shuffled across the room, and sat down in the seat chosen for him, casting lowering glances round the table.

"Sit upright," said Chunder Loo, "and don't square your elbows that way. You incommode your neighbour. Will you have some cold mutton?"

"In course I will."

"That is not the way to answer. Say, 'If you please.'"

Mulberry Cork said it with an ill-grace, and was served with some cold mutton. Chunder Loo was a good and expeditious carver, and the requirements of the rest were soon attended to.

He helped himself, and turned to Mulberry again.

"You need not hold your knife half-way up the blade," he said. "The handle is all you need grasp. And—look, this is the way to use your fork."

"I can't eat my grub if I'm worrited," said Mulberry.

"Do as you are told, and there won't be much worry about it. Ha! Will you obey me, or not?"

The eyes of Chunder Loo flashed, and Mulberry Cork, who was looking at him, shrank back, terrified. He hastened, in a bungling way, to hold his knife and fork in the orthodox manner.

He gave no more trouble at the table that day.

As only a portion of the school had returned, the rest not being expected until the evening, there were no classes. It was to be considered a half-holiday, save that the boys were not to leave the precincts of the Abbey.

Mulberry Cork went out with the rest to the playground, and moved about among them in a high-shouldered manner that was rather offensive.

But they took no open notice of him until he burst out suddenly, addressing Little Jiggers, who was, in schoolboy phraseology "taking stock" of him.

"Who are you gaping at?" he demanded.

"I am looking at you just now," replied Jiggers; "a cat may look at a king."

"And a king can twist a cat's tail," growled Mulberry Cork. "Blessed if I ain't sick of this place already. You are a nice lot, you are."

"We have a reputation for being something special," said Bob Stockton; "more polite than peculiar."

"I don't mind you so much," said Mulberry, "toffs though you all are, but my gorge rises when I'm sat on by a nigger. Why, we had a blacky worth ten of *him* down our way, who got his living by worriting rats, and he warn't proud and uppish."

A sudden stillness came over the boys, for Chunder Loo had emerged from the house while Mulberry was speaking, and had drawn up close behind him.

They expected him to see him burst out in anger, but the Hindoo was quite cool.

"Cork!" he said.

The boy started, and his face flushed, but he did not look round.

"Cork!"

He slowly faced about this time, and was met with the smile that was so like a snarl.

"I am going for a walk," said Chunder Loo, "and you had better come with me."

"I don't want to walk. I'm tired," muttered Mulberry.

"I shall stroll quietly along," said Chunder Loo, "and we can sit down and have a nice little talk together."

He took the arm of the boy, who looked helplessly about him, and, for a moment, it seemed as if he meant to resist. But he was urged onward without any perceptible pressure from Chunder Loo, and the two disappeared into the wood.

They left behind them some who were exceedingly thankful they were not the objects of the Hindoo's special care.

"I am ashamed to own it," said Don to Bob Stockton, "but I am afraid of that man."

"So am I," candidly admitted Bob.

It was near upon the hour of five when Mulberry Cork came back, alone. He walked into the playground with a shuffling footstep, crossed it, and, without a word to anyone, entered the house.

"He is cowed," said Jack, "and will give no more of his cheek to Chunder Loo."

They could only guess at what had transpired in the wood, for although they saw Mulberry Cork at tea and afterwards, he had not a word to say to them. In the evening he brought out a book, and sat down by the wall to read.

As he did not peruse it in the ordinary way, but turned the leaves this way and that, as if referring to various places, some curiosity was felt as to the nature of the volume.

Little Jiggers, despite his having already got into trouble with the stranger, volunteered to saunter by, and bring back information on the subject.

He carried out his mission to perfection. As he passed Mulberry Cork, the boy did not heed him, but was, to all appearance, wrapped in the contents of the book.

"Well, what is it?" asked Hone.

"The title is on the back," said Jiggers, breathlessly, "but I don't know what it means."

"Let us have it," said Hone.

"The 'Racing Calendar,'" said Jiggers, "that is what it is."

"This is another facer," said Bob Stockton, after a short silence, created by this unlooked-for announcement. "A boy of his age studying that sort of thing!"

"Boys," said Jack, "he is out of place here. The sooner he is gone the better."

CHAPTER CXIII.

THE FIRST NIGHT AT THE SCHOOL.—A LIVING SKELETON.

BY night all the boys, except Herbert May, were back. The school poet was away in Scotland and not expected for a few days.

At the usual hour they retired to their dormitories, and then it was found that Mulberry Cork was not to sleep in number two, as he had done the night before. Where he had been sent to was not known at the time, but on the morrow it was discovered that he was to share the room of Chunder Loo. A small bed had been put up for him in the corner thereof.

Not one among the whole of the boys would have taken his place, let us say, for a pound a week pocket-money for a month.

But although he was a prominent subject of conversation, he did not absorb all the talk.

All had something to tell of home, and those who had remained at the Abbey during the vacation had also something to say about their goings-on.

The fact that Lingo had been there was, however, not mentioned. That was one of the secrets which the inner circle of four felt bound to keep.

It was a long time before the occupants of number one dormitory were asleep.

After Penny Bunn had been round to see if all lights were out, they lay in bed talking until nearly midnight.

Once during a pause in the chatter somebody said that he thought he heard a cry, as if a person was in pain, and he was certain it was in the house; but it was not repeated, and the general opinion was that he had made a mistake.

But Jack and his chums thought of Chunder Loo and the boy who shared his room with him, and shuddered.

The snake adventure was also held in reserve, for all those who had shared in that strange experience felt that silence was prudent. Above all things, they wished to keep it from Chunder Loo.

Don was positively the last to resist the insidious influence of sleep, and as the old church clock slowly and solemnly tolled the hour of twelve he was as wide awake as ever he was in his life. It is necessary to make this clearly understood to account for a strange experience he had shortly after the witching time of midnight.

It is true that the general opinion of it was, when he related his story on the following day, that he had been the victim of a dream. But he was ever after certain that he was at the time awake.

There was no moon, but the room, with the blinds drawn up, was fairly light, thanks to the time of the year and a sky filled with stars. One endowed with good eyesight could see any object moving about the room, provided it was bigger than a rat or mouse.

As Don lay there with his back turned to the window, he suddenly became aware of something moving about at the darker end of the room.

In a few moments it had defined itself, and he saw, to his horror, it was a skeleton!

Moreover, it was the very skeleton which he and his friends had roughly put together, as related in the earlier records of Littlecote Abbey.

There it was, with its loosely-fastened bones and the crude wooden leg, owing to the absence of the right one, which Bob Stockton in merry mockery had fixed upon it.

The identity of it was not to be denied for a moment.

It came up the room, dancing and covering the ground in a leisurely manner until it reached the bed of Jack Ford. There it stopped, and bending over, raised its bony arms as if threatening him. But it did nothing more.

From the leader of the school it passed to the next bed, where Tom Drummond lay in peaceful sleep. There it repeated its threatening action.

Don lay in bed stiff with horror.

Fain would he have dived under the clothes and found refuge there, but he could not do it. He had, whether he would or no, to lie still and watch the horrible thing as it capered and gesticulated.

From Tom it swung round with a loose movement, and crossing the space between the two rows of beds, approached the only conscious boy in the room. Don shivered, and he made an effort to cry out, but his tongue clave to his mouth, and, overcome by the terror he could not ward off, he fainted away.

*   *   *   *   *   *

When Don awoke in the morning the rest of the boys in the dormitory were still asleep. By the light streaming through the window he judged it was about six o'clock. In a few minutes the calling-up bell, which Susan tolled with religious punctuality, would soon be ringing.

His head felt heavy, and he experienced a slight sensation of sickness, the result of the emotion he had suffered from the previous night.

Since he had been at the Abbey Don had developed, under the influence of his surroundings, a stoical spirit, and he hated making a fuss about anything. Therefore, for some reasons, he would have preferred letting the matter of the dancing skeleton pass, but he felt that there was a portent of mischief in it, and he could not remain silent.

In all his anxieties and doubts he instinctively turned to Jack Ford, whose influence was indeed paramount in the school. Jack was endowed with a force and vigour of character that made him a born leader of his fellows.

Tom and Bob were, although of different natures, more on a level with Don. In ordinary affairs he might have looked to them for advice, but in things of serious moment Jack was the fountain head to which he turned for help.

By-and-by, when the boys were all up and in the open air, Don got the opportunity he wished for, and gave Jack an account of what he had seen. Jack in return told him of the face he had once seen flash out in the darkness of the room.

"We must set a trap for the ghost," he said, "for I do not think for a moment that there is anything supernatural about either. The fact that it was the skeleton that visited us this time is a conclusive proof of it. You must remember it was put under the bed of Susan, and we have not heard of or seen it since."

"But how did it get into our room?"

"That, Don, is what we have to find out. I will try to work up some plan to spoil his fun."

"There must be some secret way of getting into the room."

"I should say that the whole Abbey is honeycombed with them," said Jack, "and if we can find one it will, I hope, give us the key to the rest. One thing I am convinced of—Chunder Loo knew a lot about the Abbey before he came here. And he hasn't come for the sole purpose of acting as tutor."

"I think you are right, Jack. Well, as you would say, if we wait a bit we shall see what we shall see."

———

CHAPTER CXIV.

A MISSING CHEQUE.—SNICKER IN SACKCLOTH AND ASHES.

"I REALLY cannot understand it," said Miriam, as she walked up and down the room, looking about her with a distracted face.

"Understand what, my dear?" asked Miss Astracan.

"What has become of it," said Miriam.

Penny Bunn looked up from his book and asked what "it" was?

"The cheque Mrs. Cork gave us," said Miriam. "I laid it upon the mantelpiece an hour ago, and now it is gone."

"Laid it on the mantelpiece!" exclaimed Bunn, raising his eyes to the ceiling—"a cheque for a hundred pounds."

"It ought to have been safe there," returned Miriam, tartly; "who was to touch it?"

"Ah, indeed!" said Miss Astracan, "who was to touch it? I hope, Bunn, that you do not think I would steal it?"

"I don't think anything about it," said Bunn. "All I meant to convey was, that a cheque for a hundred pounds ought not to have been put upon the mantelpiece like a—a—pipelight."

"It was not put upon the place like a pipelight," insisted Miriam. "I am going into Chippenham this morning, and I laid it there so that I should not forget it. I meant to have paid it into the bank."

"It may have been blown down," suggested Penny Bunn.

"Then why don't you get up and help me to look for it?"

Bunn laid down his book, and they went to work rummaging about the room, but the missing cheque could not be found. Susan was sent for, but she had not been in the place since the early morning.

Nor did it appear that any one else could have been in there, as Miriam placed the cheque on the mantelpiece at eight o'clock, and five minutes past Miss Astracan entered therein.

"And if, Bunn," she said, with her eyes more fixed than usual, "you think that I have taken it, you had better have me searched."

"Oh, dear!" gasped Bunn.

"I haven't been out of the room since I came in, you know."

"I don't care if you have been in and out a dozen times," groaned Bunn in despair, "or if you have been up and down the chimney. I do not say that *anybody* has taken it. The window was open, and is open still. A gust of wind may have whisked the cheque out. It could easily have been done when the door opened."

There was some reason in this assumption, and Miss

Astracan immediately suggested that somebody should go out at once and look about the playground, and, if need be, into the wood and down at the base of the cliff, for the missing article.

"When once a bit of paper begins to blow about," she added, "there is no knowing where it may be taken to."

Bunn was, of course, the "somebody" who was expected to go on this mission. In vain he pleaded that he had not had his breakfast, and that duty would call him to the schoolroom in an hour's time. He was met by the telling retort that neither *his* breakfast nor the morning lessons of the boys weighed in the scales against a cheque for a hundred pounds.

"Of course," said Miriam, sarcastically, "if you are rolling in wealth, it doesn't matter, but as you haven't enough money *of your own* to buy starch for your collars, I think that you ought to go, and make no fuss about it."

And Penny Bunn went, reviling the folly of his wife, who could be so careless or stupid with such a valuable document in her possession.

"Women are such fools with money," he muttered. "They lay it about, put it into teapots and soup tureens, and hide it in places they can't remember, and then expect men to find it when lost."

The cheque could not be found.

Bunn hunted for hours, coming back to the Abbey once just as he was expiring for the want of food, or nearly so. Miriam and Miss Astracan were now getting serouisly alarmed, and they were so far disposed to be kind as to give him a chunk of bread and cheese and send him off again to eat it while he searched.

It was noon when he finally gave up that task in despair.

Wending his way back, he met Miriam by the door, her face inquiring and anxious.

"I can't find it, and only one thing can be done now. We must wire to Mrs. Cork and ask her to stop it at the bank and send us another."

"Can that be done?" asked Miriam, brightening.

"It can be, and is done every day," answered Bunn. "Cheques are constantly being lost in a hundred ways. We shall make it all right."

"Then I should like to know," said Miriam, "why you could not say so at first, and not waste your morning as you have done, besides putting the whole school on the shoulders of Mr. Chunder Loo?"

"It hasn't hurt him," muttered Bunn; "he is tough."

"And why isn't Rooker back at his post to assist?"

"I wrote to him to say that I thought such talents as he is blessed with were lost in our limited sphere, and recommended him to try a wider field. It was a polite way of giving him the sack."

"And you have not looked for another assistant?"

"No."

"Then do it at once. I think you ought to be more considerate of——"

"Chunder Loo, of course," said Bunn, sarcastically. "I suppose you will be going to Chippenham this afternoon?"

"Yes, and as my mind is easy about the cheque, I shall go with pleasure. Dinner is ready. We must have it early to-day."

"I'm ready for it."

The story of the lost cheque was all over the school, as a matter of course. Susan told of it, and in the comments made upon the affair Miriam came in for some dry remarks on her carelessness.

"I thought better of her," said Bob Stockton, "for generally I should think she is cute. I wonder who has nabbed it."

"Chunder Loo was out early, before eight o'clock," said Jack, "or upon my word I should have suspected him. It has been blown away, I suppose."

Miriam started early for Chippenham, taking Susan with her to bring home the purchases she intended to make. The girl also gave a tone as an attendant to the mistress of Littlecote Abbey, and it was with a proud step she wended her way towards Smudgem Bender. It was only right that the inhabitants of that thriving village shculd see that she had risen to the full dignity of her position.

On the road they met a man with a barrow laden with vegetables, and, to the amazement of both the women, it proved to be no less a person then Fontenoy Snicker.

Susan's mouth and eyes opened so wide that the chances of their being closed again appeared to be very remote.

Snicker touched his cap to Miriam. He was horribly pale, and had the look of a man utterly broken down.

"I was a jest—*just* going up to the Abbey," he said, "to see if you wanted anything in my line."

"I really don't know," answered Miriam, coldly. "Miss Astracan attends to the housekeeping. You can, of course, go and see."

"I can do 'taturs as reasonably as any man," continued Snicker, "and I must make a livin' somehow. Thanky, I think I'll run up and see the lady."

Miriam affirmed her permission with a gracious bend of the head, and sailed away like a yacht with every stitch of canvas set. Susan stopped for a moment to have a final look at her old master, who affected to be arranging his stock on his barrow.

"If I hadn't have seen you," said Susan, at last, "I couldn't have believed my very eyes."

Having thus expressed her astonishment in words, she started off and speedily overtook, and fell into the rear of, her dignified mistress.

Snicker was going to the Abbey, but not to sell potatoes so much as to see Chunder Loo, if possible.

Humbled, crushed, bowed down to the very dust, and haunted night and day with an unspeakable terror, he walked as one doomed by an inexorable judge to die. The only difference between him and an ordinary criminal lay in the freedom of movement he enjoyed in place of the convict's cell.

On arriving at the base of the wood, he made a. effort to get his barrow up the slope, but suffering and fear had weakened him, and he could not do it.

So he filled a small basket with sample potatoes, and having hidden the barrow among the bushes, went forward on foot.

It was just upon two o'clock when he arrived at the gates of the Abbey. The boys were in the playground. So was Chunder Loo, who was calmly smoking a cigarette.

It seemed to Snicker that everybody recognized him at once, and from the boys there arose an involuntary yell of execration.

It was a spontaneous outburst, expressive of their feelings towards him.

And there he stood at the gate, with his form bent and abjectness dimming his coward eyes, covered, in a sense, with sackcloth and ashes thicker than was ever mourner in the East.

Chunder Loo raised his hand and bade the boys be quiet.

"He is a dog," he said, "but he was master here once. You should deal gently with him. Go in. The bell is due, but it will not be rung to-day."

So they went in, with their eyes upon Snicker to the last, with one exception, and that was Mulberry Cork. He had his gaze on Chunder Loo, whom he had previously been following about at a short distance, like a dog.

When the Hindoo was present, he was the humblest of the humble, but he was still, at times, as much of an impudent young rascal as he was at first, as we shall see anon.

"Why do you come here?" asked Chunder Loo.

His eyes were half-closed as he languidly put the question, but there was fire flashing from them, nevertheless. Snicker put down his basket, and clasped his hands.

"I've come back to ask you to be merciful to me," he groaned.

"Get away from the gate," said Chunder Loo, curtly, "out of sight of the house, and I will talk to you."

Snicker drew aside, and the Hindoo followed him, bearing to the left of the Abbey wall until it hid them from the view of anyone within the building.

"You want me to be merciful to you?" said Chunder Loo.

"I can't bear it," moaned Snicker, as he wiped his forehead with his coat-sleeve, an action that seemed to be perfectly natural to him. "It's torter—*ture* —misery—a livin' death. Give me the anecdote to the pison."

"*Antidote,* you probably mean," said Chunder Loo, with a grim smile. "Suppose I did, how would you behave? Once out of peril, would you not be the most insolent of dogs?"

"No, I would be your slave," said Snicker.

"If you will obey me in all things," said Chunder Loo, after a pause, "I will make your life safe for three months, *certain.* After that, if you go on right, I will continue to help you, but *I will still hold you in the poison toils,* because only a mad fool would trust you out and out. You are an unmitigated, worthless scoundrel!"

"Yes," said Snicker, feebly. "That is a fact. But I am going to turn into a good man."

"Do that," hissed Chunder Loo," "and I will leave you to your fate. I *hate* good men. *They* are poison to me. What I want is men who will do *anything* at a pinch."

"Whatsomever you may want done," replied the ready Snicker, "I am prepared for to do it."

"Now you talk up to your character," said Chunder Loo, drily. "Hear me. I am going to send you on a journey to-night—a long one."

"I hope it won't be very expensive," pleaded Snicker, "for if iver—*ever*—there was a man stony broke, I'm one."

"You will not have to find a penny of the cost of it," said Chunder Loo. "All you have to do is to go and *obey me* in all things, and be *dumb.* Say but one word about the errand I shall send you on, and I will put you to such tortures that all you have gone through will be as pleasure in comparison. Now, get home, and keep there until I come. It will be some time this evening—possibly after dark. Not a word more. *Away!*"

He dismissed him with a sweeping motion of his hand, and, turning on his heel, disappeared through the Abbey gates.

Snicker, after another wipe of the forehead, on the same lines as before, took up his basket, and, bewildered, troubled, and shrinking with fear, hastened home.

It was well on towards dusk that evening when Miriam returned, with the long-suffering and much-enduring, but still buoyant, Susan at her heels. The girl was so laden with parcels that she presented an appearance comparable to a purveyor of toy-balloons.

She had so many about and above her that she threatened to stick fast in the doorway; and Bunn, who was on the look-out for his wife, assisted the girl by relieving her of a portion of her burden.

"You seem to have been busy, Miriam," said Bunn, smiling.

"Yes," she replied, " so many things were wanted, and the people in the shops will not show you exactly what you ask for."

"I hope they satisfied you in the end," said Bunn, rubbing his chin, and ruefully regarding the pile of purchases.

"Pretty well, although I think I ought to have gone to Bath."

"You wired about that cheque, of course ?"

"There, I declare!" cried Miriam, "if I didn't forget all about it. You made me easy in my mind, and it just slipped away."

"Never mind," said Bunn, making the best of a bad job, "I will send one of the boys down with a telegram to-morrow."

Ah! How often things are put off until to-morrow, and then the discovery is made that it is *too late.* But Bunn was satisfied all would be well.

CHAPTER CXV.

RUEFUL TIDINGS.—HERBERT MAY HAS A QUARREL WITH MULBERRY CORK.

WHEN the morrow came, Miriam thought it would be a pity to take any of the boys away from school to send on to Chippenham. She would spare Susan "by-and-by."

Bunn yielded, although his heart now misgave him that precious moments were being wasted. But Susan really did go—at twelve o'clock, when all her morning work was done. And, after all, she had to go no further than Smudgem Bender, there being a telegraph office there, a fact both the schoolmaster and his wife had for the moment overlooked.

Everything connected with that unfortunate cheque seemed to go wrong.

But Penny Bunn was at ease when he heard at last that the telegram had been sent, as Susan reported on her return.

All this time nothing had been said to Mulberry about the affair, and it occurred to Bunn that it would be just as well to name it to him.

So he sent for the boy, having first obtained the consent of the two ladies, to whom he was bound, by the oppressive laws of matrimony, to defer on all occasions.

Mulberry might be in a cowed frame of mind in the presence of Chunder Loo, but the wily Hindoo being absent, he did not care a straw for the trio into whose presence he was summoned.

Indeed, he felt inclined to vent his spleen upon them—"take it out of the lot" was his own expression.

"It seems to me," he said, as he entered the room,

"that there ain't no peace for a cove here. I ain't had five minutes to myself to-day."

"You have been sent for," said Bunn, mildly, "to acquaint you with the sad fact that your mother's cheque has been lost."

"Well," said Mulberry, in an injured tone, "I didn't se it, and you ain't got no call to worry me about it."

"You are not being worried," said Bunn, severely. "I do wish you would learn to comport yourself more becomingly in the presence of your superiors."

"Oh, you are my s'periors, are you ?" said Mulberry. "Well, I don't want to arger. What about the cheque ?"

"It has been lost," said Bunn, "and we wired to-day to your mother at the Langham to stop it and send us another."

"Well, what time did you wire ?"

"At one o'clock."

"Then it wasn't any blessed use."

"No use ?"

It was a triple and joint exclamation that burst from the lips of his superiors there assembled.

"Not a bit on it," continued Mulberry. "I got a letter from mother to-day, fust post, saying as she was a-going to leave the Langham at ten o'clock."

"But she will return ?" said Bunn, with his eyes coming out of his head in the old style.

"Yes," said Mulberry, "in three months' time. She's gone on a tower all over the blooming Continong, to see if *she* can't pick up manners. Furriners have got no end of 'em allus on hand, ready made, and they will turn 'em out to order."

"But they will send on the telegram to her," said Miriam.

"No," replied Mulberry. "Mother never has any letters or telegrams sent on to her. When moving about she isn't certain where she may be stopping. The people at the hotel will keep the message till the old girl comes back. She is sure *I* am all right," added Mulberry, fumbling in his pocket for the letter, "and she reckons that when she turns up she won't know me, I shall be so improved."

"When she comes back !" muttered Penny Bunn. "Don't wait, Cork. I must stop that cheque myself at the bank."

"If you go a-stopping my mother's cheques at her bank, she will have some of your wool off."

"My boy, you don't understand."

"But I *do* understand. What right has a party like you to stop *her* cheques. If you wrote 'em out, it would be different, but——"

"Cork," said Bunn, rising, "I request you to leave the room."

"Oh! I don't want to stop," said Mulberry, as he backed towards the door. "There ain't much to keep *me* here. You ain't pertieklerly lively company, any of you."

And then he vanished, and was heard growling about the cheque as he shuffled down the passage.

" He is the most dreadful boy I ever saw or heard of," said Penny Bunn, "and, as far as I can see, we have got him on our hands for three months, during which we shall have to wait for the second cheque."

" What about the first one ?" asked Miss Astracan.

" Lost," replied Bunn, "without a doubt. We need not bother about it. But I will write to the bank—by the way, *what* bank was it drawn on ?"

Miriam did not know, and Bunn, who had known once, could not remember.

Until the special bank could be got at, and the branch the cheque was drawn on, nothing could be done.

" I never met with such a case in my life," groaned Bunn.

" It is all your own fault, Bunn," said Miss Astracan. " You should have told the mother that the boy wasn't suitable."

Bunn rose up, and left the room. He could not trust himself to answer her.

So Mulberry Cork became a pupil in the Abbey, the very first for whom nothing had been duly paid in advance.

All round, he promised to be anything but a boon and a blessing to the unfortunate Penny Bunn.

All that day, and at intervals long afterwards, he was haunted with the dread thought that Mrs. Cork, having gone abroad, might get lost upon the mountains, or be waylaid and murdered by brigands, and never be heard of or seen again. In that case, it was possible he would have to keep Mulberry for an indefinite time, and perhaps for good.

He tried to extract from the youth some information as to his antecedents, and whether he had not some relative who would come forward and help in the matter.

" You see," said Bunn, "one of them might be induced to give me another cheque, and settle with your mother when she returns to England."

But Mulberry was not to be drawn either as to his original home, or about his relatives.

He hadn't lived anywhere in particular that he knew of. His mother was fond of moving about, and he just went with her. What else was he to do ? Did Penny Bunn think that he was an undutiful son ? If his mother wanted him to go up to the moon, he was ready to start.

" As for asking me about my relations," he went on, scornfully, " who do you think you are getting at ? Do you want to make me a foundling, or what ?"

But though indignant at the suggestion, it seemed to amuse him at the same time, for on leaving the presence of the depressed principal of the school he fairly doubled up with laughter in the seclusion of the outside passage.

" My relations !" he gasped. " One of 'em might give him a cheque ! Oh, my eye and Betty Martin ! what a covey he is, to be sure !"

It was two days later when Herbert May, the dreamy, thoughtful youngster who had been the school poet from the day he first appeared there, returned to his chums, and he was welcomed with delight by all.

Herbert was a boy who would be sure to make friends wherever he went, and rarely find an enemy. His office in life appeared to be to make those around him brighter and happier.

He was as brown as a berry with travelling about with his friends, and had a lot to tell of the places and things he had seen.

" But, first of all," he said to Jack, " you must tell me what has happened here."

Such news as could be discreetly imparted to him was told and, of course, Mulberry Cork figured therein.

Herbert saw him at a distance prior to having a word with him, and he at once took a strange dislike to the boy.

" I do not care for the look of that fellow."

" Wait till you hear him speak," said Don, with a light laugh. " It is not a question of tone of voice—that he cannot help—but the choice language that will charm you."

Herbert soon got a taste of the vernacular of Mulberry. They met by the door as the boys were going in to tea, and accidentally collided, but not violently.

" I beg your pardon," said Herbert, as a matter of course.

" Who are you a-shoving of ?" asked Mulberry. " I never see such manners as you toffs have got."

" We are not toffs, as you call us," returned Herbert quietly, " but we are not bears."

" Perhaps I'm one," said Mulberry, fiercely.

" Well, really," said Herbert, " if we should ever be inclined to think so, it will be your own fault."

Mulberry, being at a loss for a retort, shouldered him again.

Now, while Herbert May was as peaceful a youth as could be found here and there, he was not a coward, and when unduly pressed by a cantankerous adversary, he knew what was the right course to take. He adopted it on this occasion, and dealt Mulberry a stinging blow on the side of the head.

" Take that, you vulgar cad !" he said.

Herbert was slightly built, and looked more the smaller of the pair to the eye than he really was, and Mulberry was as much astounded as hurt by the blow. Tom Drummond, who, with two or three others, saw it given, felt that Herbert had possibly made a mistake.

But they did not interfere. Whatever happened to Herbert, he must fight his own battles. He had dealt the first blow and among the Lambs of Littlecote one motto was paramount. It was, "Justice to All."

Mulberry Cork had not endeared himself to any one there, but in a quarrel he was entitled to have fair play.

After the blow he stood a moment with his small eyes fixed on Herbert, then, with a sort of suppressed yell, he sprang at him.

But now Tom Drummond intervened.

"You can't fight in the house," he said; "it would only get you into trouble. Wait until by-and-by."

"I'll give him something he will remember," hissed Mulberry, "but if I do, I suppose I shall have the whole gang on me."

"What gang?" asked Tom.

"Why, the lot—the b'iling of you."

"There is no gang here. If it comes to a fight between you two, then whoever wins is safe. What do you think we are made of?"

"Blessed if I know," said Mulberry, with a sneering laugh. "When am I to have a go at him?"

"This evening, outside the Abbey gates," replied Herbert, quickly.

"All right," said Mulberry. The others, hearing the voice of Jack down the passage calling for them, hurried on.

Chunder Loo was at the head of the table, and he cast a quick glance at the boys as they came in. The countenances of the two antagonists were flushed and he seemed to interpret the addition of colour, for when Mulberry took his seat near him, he said:

"He is a smaller boy than you. But he is not a coward."

Mulberry Cork hung his head and went on with his tea, taking snappish bites out of his bread and butter as if he were eating an enemy in a cannibalistic fashion.

And Chunder Loo at intervals cast a sly glance at him and softly smiled.

CHAPTER CXVI.

THE FIGHT OUTSIDE THE GATES.

"I DON'T see how we can stop it," said Jack Ford, "but on my word it is not a fair thing. The fellow is wiry, and Herbert is such a delicate youngster."

They were all in the playground, and the boys had gathered in groups, discussing the probable outcome of the fight. Herbert May sat on the wall calmly reading a book, but his antagonist had not appeared since tea-time. An appointment had, however been made for seven, sharp.

"It can't be stopped for more than one reason, and the first that occurs to me is sufficient," said Bob Stockton. "Herbert would rather be torn piecemeal than called a coward."

"He would hardly be called coward if he refused to fight one so much bigger than himself," said Don.

"Somebody will have to second the other fellow," said Jack Ford.

"Who will care to do it?" asked Tom.

"Nobody will like it, but it must be done."

This was an undoubted fact. There was grim silence of a few moments, and then Jack spoke again.

"I think I had better do it," he said, "for Herbert understands me, and will know why I take on myself such a disagreeable task."

"I had thought of offering to take the job," said Bob Stockton, "but as you are boss here, I yield to you and make the sacrifice. With your permission, Jack, I will endeavour to console myself by looking after Herbert."

"Very well. It is close upon seven, and we had better have a few words with him."

So they crossed over to the wall and Herbert, hearing their footsteps, raised his eyes and quietly smiled.

"What a fine poem this is," he said. "I suppose you have all read 'Marmion?'"

"I had a look through it once," replied Tom Drummond, "and thought it fine."

"It is superb," Herbert went on to say, with the light of an enthusiast in his fine eyes. "With all his faults, Marmion died like a man."

"So he did," said Bob Stockton, "and you are going to fight like a boy?"

"Oh, of course," exclaimed Herbert. "I had for the moment forgotten. I have a row on with that fellow Cork."

There was no shamming or bravado in his way of referring to the coming fight. They could see that for the time he *had* forgotten it. As he closed his book, the clock of Mumping Malford church began to strike the hour.

As the last stroke was given, Mulberry Cork emerged from the house and walked across the grounds.

Herbert and his friends made a move also, and they were followed by the whole school. "May will be pounded to death by that fellow," said Hone to Gyp Tanner; "he hasn't a ghost of a chance with him."

"Both can't win, anyway," said Gyp, philosophically.

"You ought to be sorry for an old chum," remarked Hone, with a bit of a sneer.

"I may be sorry in one respect," said Gyp; "but

don't forget that we are all proud of Herbert, so don't sneer at him. Are you chumming up with Cork?"

"Not I," said Hone, surlily.

They found Mulberry Cork outside, in the act of taking off some of his upper clothing. His face was rather pale, but there were no signs that he desired to shirk the fight. Jack Ford went up to him and said:

"As somebody must second you, I offer myself for the post."

"I didn't expect that any of you toffs would do it," replied Mulberry, drily, "and so I didn't ask you. I see the other covey has *all* the school to help him along."

"You will have fair play," said Jack, "so pray don't talk a lot of bosh."

"I'll mark him," growled Mulberry; "but I feel that it is like fighting a girl in boy's clothes. He is as soft as pap."

Jack made no reply, but quietly assisted him to roll up his shirt-sleeves, observing at the same time that he was a very sinewy boy.

Herbert, meanwhile, with the aid of his second and others, had prepared himself for the fray. The only difference in his appearance to that of his normal condition was the light in his eyes, which was brighter than any there had ever seen before.

"Herbert means fighting," thought Don; "but how long can he stand up against that fellow?"

"This is a rough beginning of the term for you," said Bob, as he gave Herbert a few finishing touches. "A fight on the first day."

"A rough beginning," said Herbert, serenely, "often leads up to a smooth ending."

"*Time!*"

The two combatants entered a ring formed by the boys, and stood facing each other about four feet apart.

The contrast between them was very striking, not only in a sense physical, but throughout. They were types of two classes of boy. One so refined by nature, that if he had been the son of a travelling tinker, he would have been one of Nature's gentlemen, happily to be found among the poorest as well as the richest in the country; the other, hopelessly coarse and vulgar. All the purple and fine linen in the land would not have made him otherwise.

A feeling of pity for the gallant Herbert was felt by nearly all. Hone secretly exulted. It was his nature to take delight in the downfall of anyone whom he could not help in his heart admitting was his superior in so many ways.

The moment Mulberry Cork raised his hands, it was seen that he was not by any means a novice in fighting, but the style of the boy was recognised by Jack Ford and two or three more as that of the street lad. It was to an extent scientific, but the main feature of it was its *venom*.

Herbert, on the other hand, showed a better and easier style, but he was not very scientific. He had failed to avail himself of the benefit of the sparring bouts the boys used to have among themselves.

There was a steady drawing together of the combatants, a quick movement of the arms, an exchange of blows, and Herbert was down.

It was a blow on the chest that had floored him.

And it must have been a pretty stiff one, too, for as his agile second raised him up, he saw that he was gasping for breath, and there was a deadly paleness in his cheeks.

"Shall I throw up the sponge," he whispered. "That fellow is altogether too hot for you. Nobody will think the worse of you for not going on with a hopeless thing."

"Not yet," said Herbert, rallying himself. "I'm not half-beaten yet."

Mulberry Cork had gone swaggering to his corner, and then, declining Jack's assistance, he said, with a grin:

"Landed him one there, I think."

"No doubt," replied Jack. "I see no chance for him, but he is not beaten yet."

"I tried to give him the upper-cut," growled Mulberry, "and if I do it will stop his jaw for a day or two."

Jack could hardly repress a shudder. The blow referred to was a terrible one when it got home. It was the "knock-out" blow of the fighters of olden time. It would be terribly telling upon one so delicate in build as Herbert May.

But the fight must needs go on, if it led to the maiming of one of the combatants. The laws of the school, and the code of boyish honour, demanded that it should be so.

Herbert came forward again, weaker than at the outset, but with that resolute light in his eyes which speaks of the indomitable spirit.

He might be knocked out of time, or even killed, but while he had breath to speak, or a leg to stand upon, he would never yield.

Mulberry Cork took things coolly. He felt that he had a sure thing in hand, and he delayed the enjoyment of finishing his antagonist in the spirit of the epicure, who dallies over his plate prior to consuming a choice morsel.

His exultation and venomous confidence were alike perceivable by the lookers-on, and a feeling of intense hatred for him was roused in the breast of Herbert's more intimate friends.

Two at least, Don and Bob, made up their minds to try conclusions with the victor, as they deemed Mulberry Cork would assuredly be, as soon as opportunity presented itself.

The time soon came to finish the fight. Mulberry

Cork, unable to hold back long, went for Herbert with a rush that drove him back. The gallant youngster stood the onslaught with all the resisting power at his command, but weight and strength are sure to tell.

He received another blow on the chest, and was reeling with his guard thrown open, and Mulberry had sprung forward to administer the blow, the really terrible upper-cut, when an unexpected diversion took place.

A ponderous form broke through the ring of boys. It was Miss Astracan, with an old umbrella in her hand.

It was one of those structures known as gamps, and waddling at a pace the like of which no eye there had seen in her movements before, she came up behind Mulberry Cork, and in the nick of time dealt him a blow on the side of the head with the weapon. He fell—apparently, like Lucifer, never to rise again.

"I knew it," she gasped. "I was sure there was going to be a fight. And when I looked out of the window and saw the ground was empty, I says to my niece, 'They are at it.' I didn't have the charge of an orphan asylum for many years without learning about your ways. Get up, you horrible boy!"

Mulberry Cork lay upon his side, with one leg raised to ward off another possible blow from the umbrella. He was the very picture of snarling dismay.

"Why didn't you knock him down as well as me?" he demanded; "ain't we *both* fighting?"

"I can't hit two people at a time," replied Miss Astracan, "and one is enough to show that I won't put up with it. Besides, you are the biggest, and ought to set a better example. I always punish the bigger boys. Get up and go away to bed with you."

"Pardon me, gracious lady," broke in a quiet voice, "but, with your permission, I will take this unhappy youth away for a time, and endeavour to instil better principles into him."

It was Chunder Loo, standing a few feet away, who finished with a salaam. He was clad in a garment which the boys had not hitherto seen, as close-fitting as the old one, but it was of the richest material, being of satin, embossed with flowers.

His get-up was, with the addition of a new turban of snowy whiteness, quite dazzling.

Miss Astracan was as much impressed as the boys by his altered appearance. Now, indeed, did he look like a rajah from the East, one calculated to be a thing of beauty and joy as long as he stayed at the Abbey.

"Take the little wretch away," said Miss Astracan, "and never let me hear of his fighting a small boy again."

Chunder Loo simply fixed his eyes on Mulberry, and the boy, with a fascinated light in his small eyes, rose to his feet. Without a word he put on his clothes, never for a moment removing his gaze from the resplendent figure of the Hindoo, who did not by his face exhibit any consciousness of there being anything unusual in his attire.

He salaamed again, as Miss Astracan retired with her umbrella under her arm, and then made a few remarks to the boys about the beauty of the evening.

When Mulberry was dressed and ready to start, a fact he became aware of without looking towards the boy, Chunder Loo sauntered away, and Mulberry, with the air of a broken dog, followed at his heels until they were out of sight.

Herbert, meanwhile, had resumed his attire, and was congratulated upon the end of the fight.

"You were no match for him, old fellow," said Jack; "but after the way you stood up to him, who will dare say you are afraid?"

"I can't help it if they do," said Herbert, with a smile; "if he ever wants to finish the fight, I won't shirk it."

"I do not think he will attempt to renew it," returned Jack. "He has something else to think of."

The boys sauntered back to the grounds and resumed their sports, but some of them were much exercised and bothered by the garment exhibition of Chunder Loo.

"Where did he get it from?" was the general question.

"He came here," said Jack, "with a parcel no bigger than a cigar-box. Who has fitted him up with raiment that would make Solomon of old feel that he had something to live for?"

And none could tell. It was a mystery of mysteries.

CHAPTER CXVII.

THIS IS THE TRAP THAT JACK SET.

SINCE the night when Don had seen the skeleton dancing about the dormitory, nothing had occurred to disturb him or any of the other occupants.

The majority knew nothing of this strange visitation, or of the face that Jack Ford said he had seen at an earlier date. Happily for their peace of mind, they were kept in ignorance of both events.

An opportunity had been found by Jack to examine the walls, which were like most of those in the chambers of the Abbey, panelled. But, as it was in the case with Miss Astracan's room, he discovered nothing to help him.

But that there was some secret means of communication from room to room, he was thoroughly convinced.

As he strolled about in a favourite way of his

among the boys, yet communing with himself only, thinking over various things, he got it into his head that it was possible another visitation might be looked for that night, or, at all events, at an early date.

So he decided to carry out a plan which, he hoped, would prove once and for all the origin of these sources of terror.

If of a supernatural nature, he would throw away his time, but if the visitor was of material mould, the probabilities were that he would bring the author to confusion.

His plan was to stretch pieces of rope from the iron bedsteads across the room, about four inches from the ground. Any person coming upon them unexpectedly in the dark would fall. He or she would not have a ten to one chance of escaping it.

He had prepared ropes of the necessary length, and hidden them under the mattress of his bed. As soon as all but those who were acquainted with his object were asleep, he planned to steal out of bed, adjust the ropes quietly, and slipping between the sheets again, await the result.

That night it should be done.

As usual, he only confided in the members of the inner circle—Bob, Don, and Tom—all of whom promised to do their best to keep awake and see what came of it.

Neither Chunder Loo nor Mulberry Cork was seen any more that night. Penny Bunn presided at the supper-table, and he was as cheerful as a mute at a christening. It was said of him that never had he seemed to be so utterly cast down.

Part of his lowness of spirits arose from a letter he had received from Sir Charles Barstow, informing him that he expected the destroyed inlaid flooring to be put in its place by that day six months. Failing in this, Penny Bunn would have to give up the Abbey.

But, of course, the boys knew nothing of this. They put it down to a surfeit of matrimonial happiness.

"The joy of having a Miriam for a wife," said Bob Stockton, "could not be borne by a man of ordinary strength of mind."

At the accustomed hour the boys retired, and the major portion of the occupants of number one dormitory were soon asleep.

The members of the inner circle, true to their word, kept awake, and, acting on the advice of Jack, were as quiet as mice who know that pussy is within hail.

It must have been about half-an-hour after stillness prevailed—although it seemed to be much longer—when a slight creaking was heard at the far end of the dormitory. The listeners felt an increase in the action of their hearts, and a nervous feeling took possession of them.

Jack, it ought to be stated, had previously fixed his pieces of rope, five in number, according to his plans, and the question was, would the ghost fall over them?

It was in Jack's mind, when the whole four of the boys were startled by the crash of a fall upon the floor.

Not only did something like the body of a man come to grief, but there was also a rattle of something of a metallic nature and the sound of a suppressed curse of the most pronounced human tone.

Jack alone had the presence of mind to rise to the occasion. Feigning to be suddenly aroused, he sat up in his bed and called out:

"None of your larks there, boys. It is too late for fun."

The cue thus given was immediately taken up by his friends and two or three more, among them Herbert May, who had been awakened by the noise.

"What is the game?" asked Don.

"It is that little beggar, Tanner," cried Bob Stockton. "He can never let us sleep in peace."

"Keep quiet," said Jack, "while I got a light. I'll let him have what for, the little sinner."

He had the matches handy, but feigning to grope about for them, he allowed a minute or so to elapse ere he struck a light. As there was a candle in the room, he put the match to it, and jumping out of bed, walked down the dormitory.

At first he could see nothing but one of the ropes, loosened by some heavy body coming in contact with it. Stooping down to untie it, he saw something glistening under Tanner's bed.

It was a long, thin knife.

Without a word he secured it and slipped it up his shirt-sleeve. Then he proceeded to quietly remove the ropes, doing it so that only those who were sitting up—and they were confined to his more intimate chums—could see what he was doing.

"It is very odd," he said, "but I cannot find anything."

He would not have named the nature of his find for any money.

"Well," asked Tanner, sarcastically, "have you found me?"

"I only thought you were up to something," replied Jack. "Somebody was out of bed roaming about the room."

"Then he was a fool for his pains," said Gyp Tanner, as he curled himself up afresh. "I'm off again."

And true to his word, he was soon once more on his way to the land of dreams.

So far Jack's trap had met with success, but he had not been able to discover for *certain* who the intruder was. Could he have found Chunder Loo lying upon the floor, then indeed he would have had a clear case against him, which might have led to unpleasant explanations.

Bidding the others go to sleep, he got into bed again, and, truth to tell, not in the happiest frame of mind.

The fact of the intruder having brought a knife with him was a very unpleasant fact. It pointed to the probability of even murder being contemplated.

But what could be the motive for so deep a crime?

Jack could not see it at all, and he eventually conceived that it might have only been hidden in the dress of the stealthy visitor, and fallen out when he came so suddenly to grief.

Jack, in addition to his pluck and general acumen, was endowed with very clear reasoning powers, and he argued with himself that there was little prospect of their being favoured with a second visit to the dormitory that night.

Even Chunder Loo would not, audacious as he undoubtedly was, venture on such an experiment.

He would never attempt to come back for his knife in the dark, provided he missed it, and to bring a light would, of course, be fatal.

Satisfied that he had nothing to fear from that direction, Jack composed himself for rest, and as great warriors and statesmen, like Napoleon and Gladstone, were and are, reputed to be able to command sleep at will, he, too, obtained it almost as soon as sought, and sank away into unconsciousness.

Awaking, as was his wont, among the earliest to arouse themselves, he was hardly surprised shortly afterwards to see the door open and Chunder Loo come stealing into the room. He was now convinced beyond all possible doubt that here was the intruder.

Perceiving that Jack was awake, the Hindoo smiled and took a seat on the end of his bed.

" I am going for a walk," he said, " and I was wondering if any of you would care to rise and go with me. Though born in India, I know your proverbs, and the one about early risers getting the worm I think is one of the best."

"Thank you," replied Jack, yawning, "but I do not think I care for worms, unless I am going fishing."

" Your answer," said Chunder Loo, with his eyes wandering stealthily about, as they had done that day when the snake was found by Jack in the coffee-room of the Cowley Arms, "has the evasive humour of your people. You do not want to go?"

" I do not," said Jack.

"Very well," returned Chunder Loo; "then as the rest are asleep, I will not remain."

But for all that he did not go away. With one pretext and another, he contrived to keep there until the morning bell rang, and the boys, summoned by its clanging, roused themselves to meet the toils of another day.

He lingered on until they got up. With wondering eyes upon the Hindoo, and slipping on their clothes, they hurried down to wash.

Jack had slept with the knife up his shirt-sleeve, and he contrived to keep possession of it without revealing it in any way.

The Hindoo was left in the dormitory, and Jack, chuckling to himself, went down to the lavatory, leaving Chunder Loo to prosecute what he knew would be a fruitless search.

Later on he saw him mooning about the playground in troubled thought, his face betraying no common anxiety, until the boys went out for morning recreation.

Then he fell back into the original Chunder Loo, save in the matter of dress, for once more he had donned the gorgeous raiment of the previous evening, and he told them it was to be his dress of the future.

Penny Bunn announced at his own breakfast-table that he had secured a junior master, who would be with them during the day. There was a general expression of surprise on the faces of those who sat with him, manifested in a very pronounced way by his wife, and in lesser degree by Chunder Loo.

"You did not tell me, P. Y.," said Miriam, "that you were negotiating with one, although I spoke of it."

" It was so small a matter," replied Bunn, in some confusion, "that I did not think it necessary to trouble you with it."

" I am concerned with every change in the house," rejoined Miriam, tartly. "What is the name of the creature?"

" Anthony Gubbles," answered Bunn.

Miriam turned up her nose, Miss Astracan stared, and Chunder Loo showed his white teeth in his peculiar way of smiling.

"It is not a common name," said Bunn.

"It is worse than that," said Miriam; "it is low. Who ever heard of a Gubbles before?"

" I am not responsible for the man's name," said Penny Bunn, with a show of dignity. "He is a very good tutor, and will lend lustre to the school. I want nothing more."

"How do you know he is a good tutor?" asked Miss Astracan.

" I would prefer," said Bunn, "for him to prove it to you by his conduct here."

" If he is not up to the mark," said Miriam, "he will go out quicker than he comes in."

"Very well," said Bunn, "do what you like. Blow him into the valley with dynamite if you care to."

" He will want a desk. There are only two in the schoolroom," suggested Miss Astracan.

" For the present," replied Penny Bunn, "he can have mine. I will have a small table placed in the corner for my own use."

"Ah," said Chunder Loo, "is there not a poem in your tongue on one Jack Horner, who sat in a corner doing something with a pie?"

"Sir!" exclaimed Bunn, haughtily, but Miriam laughed, and Miss Astracan choked herself with her tea.

When Miss Astracan choked she did it thoroughly, going through all the popular contortions and emitting sounds promising a speedy termination to her career.

A scene of confusion followed. Miriam sprang up and went to the assistance of her aunt, smacking her back and imploring her to get it out of her throat, whatever it was, and uttering wails of alarm.

Chunder Loo also lent his aid by using some well-known methods employed to restore an inanimate person, which, of course, were exactly opposite to what was wanted.

Penny Bunn was alarmed, but was of no service, as he did nothing but stand up, grasp the hair of his head, and give vent to his fears in gasping ejaculations.

But Miss Astracan did not die. She came back to a quieter condition, with a face so inflamed that the setting sun, if it had been setting at the time, which it was not, would have had to take a rear seat in the matter of colour.

"I declare," she said, as soon as she could speak, "that it is a misery to sit at the table with that man."

"P. Y.," added Miriam, "you are too trying."

"I say nothing," said Penny Bunn, "save that if I am to be made a subject for a jest by a subordinate, the sooner that subordinate leaves this house the better."

"It is to be hoped," said Chunder Loo, gravely, "that the new-comer, Mister something, will not so far forget himself."

"Sir, I——"

"P. Y., let us have no more of it, for goodness sake!" cried Miriam.

So P. Y. collapsed, knowing it would be useless to say more, and Chunder Loo remained master of the situation.

CHAPTER CXVIII.

THE PROS AND CONS OF A DANGEROUS POSITION.

ACTING up to his resolve, Penny Bunn desired Susan after breakfast to place a certain table in the schoolroom, and, as a defiance to the jesting propensities of Chunder Loo, had it put into a corner, between the two desks. The purport of the change was early made known to the boys.

Before the usual lessons were gone on with, Penny Bunn announced that a new tutor was coming, a man of learning and high standing in the world.

"He comes here," he added, "to gratify a taste for a quiet life, and not from any sordid motive. He is well up in the arts and sciences, and has already made a name as a lecturer, that will be handed down to posterity on the roll upon which is inscribed the cognomens of such men as Huxley, Tyndall, and Darwin."

As he said this he glanced at Chunder Loo, who was apparently pleased to hear it, and grinningly bowed his delight.

The boys were indifferent to the announcement, not knowing how far the future bearing of the usher would come up towards the point of excellence Bunn declared he had attained.

"If he does nothing but blow Chunder Loo through the roof of this old shanty," said Bob Stockton, "he will have done something to deserve well of his country."

"And so say all of us," said Don, in an undertone.

The cane had been practically abolished, not from merciful motives, but because Penny Bunn feared to use it. He remembered the important part it played in bringing about the historical barring out, but it was not entirely abolished. He had announced as much on more than one occasion. If driven to it, he would have to again bring it forth.

That morning he was naturally in a very irritable mood. The scene at the breakfast-table lingered in his mind like poison. He had been subjected to a piece of impertinence from Chunder Loo he could not forgive or forget.

He would even up matters with that sapient son of the East ere long.

Gyp Tanner and Little Jiggers both got into trouble that morning. They were not well up with their lessons, which was nothing new, but on this occasion they were worse than usual.

"It appears to me," said Bunn, after examining the latter, "that you have not so much as looked at this book."

"Oh, yes, sir," answered Jiggers, with innocent alacrity, "I have seen it lots of times. It is my own book, sir."

There was a chuckling among the boys, and Chunder Loo laughed aloud. To do him justice, he remembered himself in a moment, and became as grave as a judge.

But he had laughed, and Bunn had heard the peculiar cackling of his voice. It was most offensive, and Little Jiggers was the origin of it.

Therefore Little Jiggers must be punished.

Penny Bunn rose from his seat, and with a stately walk left the room. He soon returned with the cane in his hand, which he switched ominously.

"Idleness and insolence," he said, "cannot be passed over."

"I am sorry, sir," said Jiggers, and he spoke the truth, "but the words popped out before I knew they were there."

"Hold out your hand," said Bunn, sternly.

At that moment he caught the eye of Chunder Loo, glittering with amusement.

Penny Bunn had come forward from his table, so that he was within the reach of his assistant. The look on the face of the Hindoo maddened him, and he forgot himself.

Instead of striking Little Jiggers, he gave the Hindoo a sweeping blow across the stomach.

It was, in a sense, a ludicrous thing to do, and a laugh rose to the lips of half the boys, but it instantly died away as they looked at Chunder Loo.

He had not stirred, nor did he speak. He simply looked at the rash man who had struck him.

The face of the Hindoo was composed. There was not an unusual line or crease in it, and yet it expressed the concentrated essence of malignity.

The silence that reigned in the room ere he spoke was short, but it seemed a little age to some of the youngsters.

"It is Jiggers you intended to strike, of course," he said; "go on with correcting him."

But Penny Bunn was not so inclined, and tossing the cane upon his table, he waved his hand for Jiggers to resume his seat. Nothing loth, the culprit, the innocent cause of much mischief in the future, glided back to his place, and the schoolmaster resumed his chair.

The routine of the morning work went on. Chunder Loo did not so much as look at Penny Bunn again, but performed his part of the teacher's labour in his accustomed quiet way. A stranger entering the room after the event would never have conceived that anything unusual had taken place.

Jack Ford, meanwhile, had kept to himself the fact that he had found a knife in the dormitory under the peculiar circumstances related, so as to weigh in his mind the *pros* and *cons* of the position, which he was bound to admit was a perilous one.

He thought the matter over as he sat in school, and decided eventually to impart the discovery to his three particular chums.

They had arranged a sign by which they would know from Jack when he desired a private conference with them. The place of meeting was always, in the first instance, to be on the wall in the playground, the old spot with the gap looking down upon the lower ground.

"The less appearance we have of secrecy the better," Jack had said. "Nothing could be more natural than that we should gather together for a chat, and it is easy to put on an air of talking of nothing in particular."

He passed the sign that morning, and as soon as was desirable after school, the quartette got together. They lay, or sat, in a careless fashion on the broken wall, and Jack, pointing down to the bushes below, as if they had found there a subject on which to talk, told them of the finding of the knife.

"It is a fine piece of work," he said, "two edged, and as pliable as a cane. The handle is of some hard wood, a deep brown colour, with a pretty grain, and it is inscribed all over with the same class of characters we saw on the gold collar of that beastly little snake."

"Surely," said Bob, "Chunder Loo did not come into the dormitory to murder any of us?"

"That might have been his object," rejoined Jack, with a shrug, "but I do not think myself it was. That he has a means of getting into the room, which we know nothing about, may be put down as a fact. He came last night and was not prepared for the mild form of trap I set for him. It was the sweet simplicity of it that took him in. What a crash he went down with."

Jack laughed softly, but the others were too much troubled with their thoughts to respond to his smile.

"If he had broken a limb now," said Don, thoughtfully, "none of us would have howled over it."

"Better his neck," said Tom Drummond. "Hanged if I don't think that we had better have gone on with Snicker than had this oily, creeping *worm* of a Hindoo here."

"It is a fine game that is going on," said Jack. "One of these days we shall know what brought him to Littlecote."

"Snicker engaged him, didn't he?" asked Bob.

"Snicker advertised for a tutor, and Chunder Loo answered the advertisement. And he did it in a style that ensured his being engaged. Why, even now he is not receiving any pay."

"You are sure of that?" said Don.

"As sure as I can be," returned Jack. "Susan says that Bunn and his wife were wrangling about it last night. Penny says he won't pay him a copper, and Mrs. Bunn isn't anxious to part with her own coin. Chunder Loo meanwhile rigs himself out in gorgeous style. What did that robe he is wearing now cost, do you think?"

"Twenty pounds, if a penny," said Tom.

"Very well," said Jack, "say that it is that sum, although I think it cost more. *Where did he get the money from?* And how did it get here? Susan says no parcel arrived for him in the ordinary way, and he has brought nothing home with him when he has gone out in the evening. Confound the fellow!—he is a very hard nut to crack."

"But you will crack him, Jack," said Don, confidently.

"I will do my best," answered Jack, modestly, "but I cannot promise you that I shall succeed."

"Have you the knife with you?" asked Bob. "I should like to see it."

"I have it in my pocket," said Jack, "swathed in cloth, for it is beastly sharp. I did a rash thing, sleeping with it up my night-shirt sleeve. Had I turned over and lain upon it, I might have seriously cut myself."

"Well, Jack," sighed Tom, "we look to you to take care of our lives. I can't say that I am so sanguine as you are that no crime was intended last night. Did you twig how he fixed his eyes on Bunn this morning?"

"We all saw it. He is a venomous beggar, no doubt, this Chunder Loo, but at the same time he is politic. He did not come here to murder us, but for something else. If we do not cross him—which we are, however, almost bound to do—he will not harm us."

"And if he finds we are crossing him?" queried Bob.

"Why, then we must look out for trouble. What we have to do is simply to lie close for a time, and do nothing."

"Oh, that Lingo were here!" murmured Don.

Jack's face slightly clouded.

"I must confess," he said, "that I am getting rather uneasy about Lingo. We ought to have heard from him in some form ere now."

"Do you think it possible he is murdered?"

"It is possible."

"And only one man would be able or willing to put him out of the way."

It was Don who made the suggestion, and from the expression of the faces of his companions, it was clear that a similar idea had been in their heads.

"The wood is thick," said Jack, "and there are a hundred hiding-places for a dead man's body. I should like to run over it to make sure that nothing has happened to our friend, but then you see his orders were that we must do nothing of the sort. Above all, we are not to go near the spot where lies you all know what. Boys, we can do nothing but keep our weather eye open, and, as I believe I have suggested before, *wait*."

CHAPTER CXIX.

MR. ANTHONY GUBBLES ARRIVES.

AS Susan knew everything, and told the boys all she knew, the arrival of Mr. Anthony Gubbles, who was to act as second tutor, or third master, according to the title conferred on him at different times, was not a startling surprise.

He came in the evening in a fly, and although he had but one portmanteau, he was well up in packing-cases and boxes.

The latter he allowed no one but himself to handle, taking them off the top of the vehicle, placing them on the ground, and finally transporting them to one of the attics, which he was to use as a laboratory, without any assistance whatever. Penny Bunn met him at the gate, and volunteered to give him a hand, but in a quiet way Gubbles said that it would be better if he carried the boxes himself.

"There are things inside that ought not to be shifted," he remarked, in a casual way.

In person Anthony Gubbles was short and stout. He wore spectacles slightly tinged with blue, his face was clean shaven, but the crown of his head was covered with short, stubbly hair of a straw colour. His features were as simple and placid in expression as those of a child.

Having got his things upstairs to the attic, he asked for a key of the door. Bunn told him that there had not been such a thing to any of the attic rooms as long as he could remember.

"I feared it would be so," said Gubbles, "and so I came provided with a padlock, staples, and chain."

From one of the boxes, which he opened with exceeding care, he brought forth the necessary tools for fixing on the padlock, and proceeded to do the work with the skill of an expert.

Bunn stood by watching him. In his heart he already warmed to Gubbles.

"Of course I am taking a great liberty," said the new-comer, "but this is a school, and schoolboys are up to mischief at all times. If they should get in here and break something, the damage would be very great—irremediable, I may say."

"Got a lot of delicate things in those boxes," suggested Bunn.

"Very delicate," was the quiet response.

The boys were busy with their lessons when he arrived, but as he was finishing his job their voices were heard below as they were hurrying out to play.

"Healthy lot there, I should say," remarked Gubbles; "vivacious, too."

"They are much too lively at times," said Bunn. "Now, if you are ready, I will show you your sleeping-room. It is on the next floor."

"I should, if you would not mind," returned Gubbles, "prefer sleeping here. I saw there was no bed in the room, and intended to suggest one being placed in this room."

"But if there are a lot of delicate thing in the room, the girl, when putting it to rights, might break some of them."

"The girl will not be required. I will look after the room myself."

"Bless me, what a strange man you are!"

"I am a student, Mr. Bunn, and sometimes sit up late. It is my whim to be let alone during my leisure hours. It was to have my own way in this respect that I offered my services to you for almost a nominal sum. In scholastic matters you will not find me remiss."

"I am sure we shall get along together," said Bunn, "By-and-by I may confide in you on certain troubles I have, with the hope that you will be able to assist me. Now, if you are ready, we will go down and you can have a peep at the boys."

"With pleasure," said Gubbles, as he locked up the room and put the key in his pocket.

They went down as far as the front door, and there Gubbles halted, and through his blue spectacles surveyed the boys at play.

He ran his eyes over them much as an expert in cattle would survey a lot of young heifers in the field. On the whole, he approved of them.

"Who is that stalwart youngster with his cap tilted on the back of his head, there, by the gate?" he asked.

"Jack Ford," answered Bunn.

"I like the look of him. Who is it he is talking with?"

"Peebles."

"I like him, too. And that fellow mooning about with his hands in his pockets?"

"Hone."

"I don't like Hone—too lowering in the face, and doesn't walk with sufficient elasticity in his step. He is a sloucher. Ha! Here comes a boy with a character. Who is he?"

"That," groaned Penny Bunn, "is a boy who came here under the most extraordinary circumstances. His name is Cork—Mulberry Cork."

Then Bunn told Gubbles, who listened attentively, the history of the arrival of Mulberry, and all that had transpired since, and naturally he embellished the story a bit.

"A hundred pounds," he said, "is a lot to pay for a boy at the school, and so I told his mother. But she would not pay a smaller sum. 'The reputation of your college, Mr. Bunn,' she said, 'is such that I should blush to pay you a penny less, knowing that my unhappy boy will give you a lot of trouble.'"

"It was very considerate of her," said Gubbles, in his even way.

"And now the cheque is lost," groaned Bunn, "and I don't know the bank—can't remember it for my life—ah! stop a moment. Let me think—I've *got it!*"

He shouted out the two last words at the top of his voice, and the astonished boys, having their attention drawn towards him, saw the head of the house cut a caper. Beside him stood the unmoved Gubbles.

"Pardon me," said Bunn, "but it was so suddenly that the name of the bank returned to my mind, it was quite a galvanic shock."

"I can perfectly understand your momentary excitement."

"The name of the bank is The London and Westminster, Oxford Street branch."

"I should communicate with them at once," said Gubbles, "giving all the particulars, and asking them to wire if the cheque has passed through their hands"

"I should say it is impossible."

"Nothing is impossible. You will do well to write to-night, and at once."

Penny Bunn admitted it was good advice, and went indoors to pen the necessary letter. Gubbles sauntered across the ground, and made his way straight to Jack Ford.

"You possibly guess who I am," he said, with a smile.

"Yes, sir," answered Jack. "Mr. Gubbles, I believe"

"That is my name. Yours, I understand, is Ford."

Jack bowed and smiled.

"As every kingdom has a ruler, and every house a head, I presume, Ford, that I may put you down as the leader of the school."

Jack was hardly prepared to hear this remark from one who was quite a stranger. It was a moment or two ere he made reply.

"I dare say Mr. Bunn has been good enough——"

"Mr. Bunn has nothing to do with it. Don't let your modesty stand in your light. You *are* the leader. Admit it."

"I am considered so," said Jack.

"So I thought," returned Gubbles, "and you are just the lad to lead them into a mess and out of it again. Kindly give me the names of the boys, pointing them out in turn. I shall remember them afterwards."

Jack did so readily. He was impressed by the new under-master, but in his cautious way was not ready to fall, metaphorically, into his arms. He even resisted a budding tendency to like him.

From Jack, Gubbles went to Mulberry Cork, who had no particular chum, not having attempted to gain the hearts of any of his schoolfellows. Hone spent a little time with him occasionally, but as yet they could not be considered intimate.

Mulberry Cork looked at him impudently as he advanced, and hailed him with "Hallo, gig-lamps!"

There was no response on the part of the tutor until he was close up to Mulberry, and then, with a lightning-like rapidity of movement, he gave him a stinging box on the ear.

"Drop that!" howled Cork.

A SPLENDID SCHOOL STORY.

NEVER BEFORE PUBLISHED.

By E. HARCOURT BURRAGE,

Author of "Ching Ching," "Monkey Mat and Roving Dick," "The Brave Boy of the Basilisk," &c.

The LAMBS of LITTLECOTE.

GIVING THE BOYS SOME IDEAS CONCERNING PHRENOLOGY.

PRICE ONE PENNY.

Gubbles seized him by the collar and shook him until the teeth rattled in his head.

"Let me have no more of your impertinence," he said.

Mulberry Cork would have backed away, but Gubbles held on to him.

"Where were you born?" he asked.

"I don't know," replied Mulberry, with a suppressed snivel.

"I can tell you where you will die unless you mend your ways," said Gubbles, sternly—"on the scaffold—do you hear?"

"I don't know why I should die there any more than——" *You*, Mulberry was going to say, but catching the eye of the tutor gleaming through the blue of his glasses, he merely said, "than other people."

"But I can tell you why it will be so. It is in the breed of you, my lad—*the breed*."

The eyes of Mulberry Cook bulged out of his head, and as he endeavoured to wriggle out of the grasp of his elder, he muttered:

"Let me alone, will you? I haven't done nothing to you."

"Take care you don't," said Gubbles. "Stand still and let me examine your head."

The boys by this time had gathered around the pair, not a little amused by the proceedings of the new tutor.

"There ain't nothing the matter with my head," roared Mulberry Cork.

"Not in the sense *you* mean," returned Gubbles. "I don't want to know what is outside it. I only deal with what lies under the skull. Stand still, will you?"

As he spoke he took off Mulberry's cap, and handed it to Gyp Tanner, who happened to be nearest to him. Then he fixed his hands on the head of the resentful Mulberry Cork with a claw-like action.

"I will take this early opportunity," he said, "to give you boys some ideas concerning phrenology, the science of the human mind, as connected with the organs of thought and passion, developed by the external undulations of the head or cranium. It is otherwise known as craniology."

Whether it was the language of Gubbles or the effect of his pointed fingers on the top of Mulberry's head, is uncertain, but the boy was reduced to a frozen state of passiveness by one or the other and awaited the revelations of the state of his internal head with the stillness of a figure of stone.

CHAPTER CXX.

HEADS OR TAILS?

"THE first duty of a phrenologist," began Gubbles, "is to be frank. He must also be truthful. I have here under my hands no common head"—Mulberry brightened a little—"in the strong development of the evil propensities"—Mulberry's light went out again—"which must, unless some mighty influence for good is brought to bear upon him, lead him to ruin."

"I ain't a-going to be preached at," said Mulberry, wriggling. "Why don't you take the head of another cove?"

"The bump of acquisitiveness is very strong," pursued Gubbles, "so bold indeed that it will be only by maintaining a resolute spirit that this youth will walk in the path of hon——"

Mulberry, with a howl and a jerk, got his head free, and, breaking through the group standing round, rushed off into the house.

There was a roar of laughter from the boys, who looked upon the whole thing as a joke, but Gubbles maintained his gravity.

"It is unpleasant to hear the truth at times, but it is good in the long run," he said. "Now, if there is another here who would like——"

But they all broke away laughingly, and got out of his reach.

"As you will," he said, with a sigh. "It would have been interesting to you all to have heard me explain *one* head thoroughly. But another time will do."

He left them, walking quietly across the ground and disappearing into the Abbey.

"I wonder," said Hone, "where Bunn picked him up?"

"We ought to get some fun out of him," remarked Gyp Tanner; "what do you say, Short?"

Tanner's particular chum thus addressed, thrust his hands into his pockets and looked doubtful.

"He knows such a precious lot. More than Chunder Loo, I'll bet."

"Nobody knows more than Chunder Loo," said Hone; "Mulberry says so."

"Indeed," said Jack Ford, quickly, "and what does Mulberry Cork say about him?"

"Nothing in particular," answered Hone. "He only says that Chunder Loo is awfully clever, and nobody can get over him if they tried until their heads fell off."

"Which, of course," returned Jack, with a curled lip, "he gets from Chunder Loo."

"Wherever he got it from," said Hone, "he believes it."

Penny Bunn shortly after came out of the house with a letter in his hand. The ordinary post had gone two hours before, but this letter, as the reader knows, was of the utmost importance, and he wanted it to be taken down to Smudgem Bender, where the post did not leave until nine o'clock.

He singled out Jack Ford to take it down, and bade him select one of his friends to accompany him.

"It will be better for you not to be alone, as it will be growing dark ere you return."

Jack picked out Don to accompany him and they set off down through the woods. The address on the envelope attracted Jack's attention. It gave him a clue to its contents.

"He is writing about that cheque, but in my opinion it will never be seen again."

"You think it was stolen ?" said Don.

"That I would not like to say, for certain. But I have an idea that I think will fill the bill."

"What is it ?"

"The cheque *was* stolen, and by one of us."

"Now, Jack, that is a very serious thing to say."

"By one of us, I mean one in the school. He is not, however, exactly one of us. I refer to Mulberry Cork."

"Jack, that is going far ahead."

"I look upon the whole thing as a fraud," said Jack. "Of course I may be mistaken; we are all liable to jump at wrong conclusions. You heard what Gubbles said as to the bump of acquisitiveness on Mulberry's head ?" asked Jack.

"I did."

"Well, that is what set me thinking. Mulberry comes of a queer lot, that I *will* stake my life on. Then comes the solution of the mystery. He steals the cheque, and his mother, mysteriously to my thinking, disappears. Result, no other cheque will be forthcoming. Row by-and-bye and Mulberry will be taken away without paying a cent for his food and teaching."

"I can't quite follow you there, Jack," said Don, shaking his head.

"Can you solve the loss of the cheque in any other way ?"

"No."

"Then you must confess that I have hit on a probable solution of the loss."

"I give in to you, Jack, in all things, as a rule, but in this affair I think you are wrong. Never mind ; it is not *our* business. Let us get rid of the letter, and on the way back I was thinking that we might have a bit of a look about for some signs of our old friend Lingo."

Jack did not immediately answer him. He had also an idea of doing something on the way back.

"Chunder Loo," he said, "hasn't gone out to-night. He is stopping in to do the work of the school. Now

Don, I should like to make sure nobody has been visiting you know where."

"Lingo said we were not to go near the place."

"But Lingo ought to have shown up or written before now. Don, I am mightily uneasy about our *property*, and whether it is right or wrong, I am going on *there* when this letter is posted."

"What you do, I do," was all Don said.

They broke into a trot so as to have as much time as possible to spend in the wood on their return, and without a halt arrived at the small post-office of the village. Having dropped the letter into the box, they were turning away, when Fontenoy Snicker came out of the post-office. He was licking a stamp preparatory to sticking it upon an envelope.

"You seem to have fine times now," he said. "Boys running about loose at this hour of the evening can't do no credit——"

"*Any* credit," said Jack, correcting him.

"No, or any, it is all the same," returned Snicker. "One of these times Bunn, when he sends you out late, will be a pupil short in the morning."

"This is not the first time you have threatened us," said Jack, "but we are not afraid of you. How's Phœbe ?"

"I resume—*presume*—you mean Mrs. Snicker," said Snicker. "Look here, you think that I don't mean what I say. Good. If I can't put a stop to some of it, I know who will. And if I so much as hold up a little finger——"

"Hold up the lot if you like," said Jack. "I know who you mean, and on my return I will let him know what you have said. He won't care about your bragging that he is ready to commit *murder* on your account."

"For 'Iven's sake !" gasped Snicker, his face suddenly assuming a leaden colour. "I only had a few words with Mister Chunder Loo——"

Jack burst into a roar of laughter.

"Thank you," he said, "for letting the cat out of the bag. I thought you were only lying as usual. But now I know that you have leagued yourself with a man *who would do anything* to serve his purpose. Messrs. Chunder Loo and Snicker, Dealers in Villainy. Sounds well, doesn't it, you bow-legged old ruffian ? Good night. Come along, Don."

Snicker, in an imploring tone, called on them to stop, but Jack would not in any case have humoured him, and especially just then.

He broke into a run, and with Don by his side did not halt until he had reached the wood. There they pulled up to get their breath into its normal condition.

It was the stilly hour of eve, " between the sun and moon," as the poet hath it, and the wood was as quiet as if it had never been ruffled with a breath of air.

No living creature, man or beast, was to be seen. High overhead the sky was clear as crystal and luminous, the sun, hidden from all mortal eye at Mumping Malford, having sunk below the horizon. A solitary rook, one of the more dissipated of its fraternity, was wending his way homeward in a sneaky kind of flight, as if he expected to hear of the crime of keeping late hours from the "missus."

Anyone much less impressionable than the two boys would have noted the almost supernatural stillness around.

"I feel," said Jack, "very much like one who has a primeval forest before him. There is the path ahead of us, it is true, but doesn't the wood look as if it had never been trodden by foot of man?"

"There is a peculiar loneliness about it," admitted Don, "but of course it is in our case all fancy."

"Which we have no time to indulge in," said Jack, "unless we give up the project of visiting the outside of the cave."

"Just as you like."

"Then I do like; we will go on. I stake our future on the hazard of the die."

Don laughed lightly.

"It is not so risky as that comes to," he said.

Jack was, without exception, the best guide about the wood in these parts. It is doubtful if one-tenth of the inhabitants knew a quarter as much as he did of its little hidden-away places, not excluding the keepers, who, when game had been preserved there, were, as a matter of duty, wandering about it in some part or other nearly every day.

But that was years before, and since the days when the pheasant and other game found shelter in the wood it had been entirely neglected. So the undergrowth had had its way, and obliterated many of the wood marks once familiar to the frequenters. Even rabbits were scarce, for the foxes who skulked in the depths of the wood played havoc with them, and lived a happy life secure in a country where they were rarely sought for the hunt.

But Jack had spent many a lonely hour and more with his friends in penetrating into the heart of the deserted wood, and that was how he knew better than anyone else where to find the long hidden cave, to which the name of Robin Hood had been given.

"The quicker we are there the better," he said. "In less than an hour we shall not be able to find our road home."

Leading the way swiftly, watchful as he went of sights and sounds, he worked his way through the undergrowth, stopping for a moment at intervals to mark some tree that was to guide them to the right road to take homeward.

At length he was near the spot he was in search of, and his heart beat quickly. The shades of night were falling fast, and there was a ghostly glamour on the wood.

"What," he said, in a low voice, "if we should find Chunder Loo there?"

"He will not be there," replied Don, confidently, "for had he not several hours work to do? I heard him say as much when we were leaving the class-room."

"What Chunder Loo says and what he does," said Jack, sententiously, "are things that often clash."

He parted two bushes ahead of him, and looked upon the spot he had been seeking. His first thoughts were for the Hindoo, but he was not here. A sigh of relief escaped him, only to be followed immediately by a groan of despair.

"What is the matter?" asked Don, who was standing behind him.

"The cave," said Jack; "*it is open!*"

He made way for Don, who advanced a pace, and looked upon the sight so fraught with the misery of a bitter loss.

On the sloping crown that concealed the cave there was a hole about three feet in circumference, gaping like the mouth of some huge beast.

Below it lay a heap of soft soil, which had been recently removed from above.

"Perhaps," he suggested, miserably, "the rain has washed the cave open."

"Come on," said Jack, desperately. "I have a box of matches with me. Let us know the worst."

They ran forward, and climbing up the three or four feet of slope, plunged into the hole.

"Stop," said Jack, "we must have a light."

Don could tell by the sound as he brought out the box from his pocket and struck a match, that his hand trembled. But he lit one at the first try, and as there was a lamp fixed in the soft wall they had used in the days gone by, when they held their secret meetings there, he took off the glass, and lighted it.

"We shall be able to see better with this," he said, and his voice sounded hollow and hopeless.

As the lamp flared up, it illuminated the small cave throughout, and then their worst fears were confirmed.

The cave was empty!

Empty in the bitterest sense to them, for the odd litter lying about did not count. All that had been concealed there by Lingo had vanished.

Jack leant against the earthen wall, and covered his eyes with his arm. Don shook from head to foot.

"Don't give way," he said. "Why not try to think as if *never had been?*"

"Let me be a moment," replied Jack. "I am not blubbering, but only trying to think the thing out. Lost—all lost, and there is only one man who could have robbed us. Don, the secret of Chunder Loo's new rig-out is now explained."

He dropped his arm, and Don saw that his face was white and fixed. His dark eyes scanned the cave through and through. On the floor, a few feet away from him, he espied a heap of old rags. Advancing, he picked it up, and with an exclamation of anger immediately threw it from him.

"It is the old dress of that beast," he said; "it was here he changed it for what he now wears. Don, we have now one thing to do."

"What is that?"

"Chunder Loo cannot have disposed of all he found here, or, say that he has, he must have the proceeds in the Abbey. He is not the man to trust it to a bank. Our business now is to conceal what we feel, find out where he has hidden the coin, and get it from him. Then I, for one, shall make immediate tracks from the school."

"Perhaps he has hidden the things elsewhere," suggested Don, miserably, rubbing his hands together.

"Then our duty is the same. We must find them again. I have never cursed living thing yet, but I feel as if I could do so now. Get out from here. We must hasten back to the Abbey, and there wear the mask of indifference over our pain. The cunning brute must never even guess what we have discovered here."

Don crept out, and Jack, turning the lamp down, followed him.

Though they had been there but a few minutes, it seemed as if night had come upon the scene with a rush. It was as much as they could do to see their way at all.

"I thought all along it was a toss-up if he did not get the better of us. It was a game of coin spinning—of heads or tails—and he has won. More to the right, Don, over that fallen tree, and then straight on."

CHAPTER CXXI.

ANOTHER BLOW FOR BUNN.

CONCEALING their loss from Bob and Tom was impossible, and when they heard of it, they both gave way to a momentary despair. It was then that the strength of Jack Ford's character came to their aid.

"Never give in," he said. "Let us live as if we never had anything hidden, and work as if we have good reason to believe there is something to be found. Mark every movement of Chunder Loo, and report all that you see to me. Don't, if possible, let a

look escape you. But, above all, show nothing for him to make a note of."

"We never wanted Lingo so much as now," said Tom Drummond.

"Lingo is done for," gloomily remarked Bob Stockton; "if it were not so, he would not have been away so long without a sign."

"It is useless to talk about it," said Jack. "Now let us go about as if we were in an ordinary school. Go in for fun, if you have the chance. Don't howl. Dissemble, like the villain in the play. If, as we believe, Chunder Loo has got hold of the things, then he has something to dispose of that will take time, although they may be removed from here. If he threatens to go away, there is one thing I shall do."

"What is that?" asked Bob.

"Blow the whole thing to Sir Charles Barstow, and let him wait on Chunder Loo. Anyway, I do not mean he should profit much by his cunning."

Acting on his advice, they tried to forget their loss, and went about their daily avocations in the spirit of schoolboys, just as if they had not a thought or care to worry them.

They were not the only distraught persons in the Abbey. Of all who suffered from the agony of an irreparable loss, none equalled the principal in that respect.

From the London and Westminster Bank there came a letter to him, conveying the terrible tidings that the cheque for one hundred pounds drawn by Sophia Cork, and endorsed with the name of P. Y. Bunn, of Littlecote Abbey, had been presented over the counter, and duly paid, not having been crossed, in the usual way.

It was a bombshell to him, and a terrible staggerer to his wife and Miss Astracan.

"You must go up to town," said Miriam, "and ask to look at the signature of the endorsement—unless you *have* written it."

"No," groaned Bunn, "I have not touched it. Indeed, for the moment, I had forgotten that an endorsement was required."

"You have two assistants," said Miss Astracan, "and the school can get on very well without you for a day."

So Penny Bunn went up to London, starting from the Abbey at six in the morning, so as to catch an early train. He returned at ten o'clock, weary and footsore, having walked both ways, to save the expense of a cab. It was Miriam who suggested he should do so.

"If you go on losing cheques for hundreds of pounds," she said, "you must be economical."

All the house but his wife and Miss Astracan had retired. There was supper on the table, and they were in a state of high expectancy.

The schoolmaster looked fagged to death.

"The signature," he said, "is a perfect imitation. If I did not *know* that I had not written to it, I could have sworn that it was my own writing."

"Bunn," said Miss Astracan, sepulchrally, "why not admit you wrote it?"

. "I warn you," said Bunn, taking up a knife, and viciously cutting off a chunk of cheese, "not to go too far with me. *I did not endorse that cheque.* Now, then, intimate again I did it, and——"

He flourished the knife, and went on with his supper. The two women were, for the time, cowed.

"I may," said Bunn, after a pause, "be a worm for a forty-stone woman to tread on, but the capacity of the worm is left to me. *I can turn.* Enough. Get to bed, and leave me to my reflections."

They thought it better to do so, and Bunn pursued his reflections, which bordered on the chaotic, with the aid of the contents of a small, flat bottle he had prudently kept in his pocket until the ladies had vanished.

He sat long over the meal, and afterwards smoked a cigar—a Capitan, of extra power—and then lighted the candle left for him.

As he left the room, the darkness and solitude of the Abbey, which a multitude of sleepers would not have dispelled, impressed him. He paused in the hall and looked about him. His eye fell upon the old grandfather's clock, and, to his amazement, it was going.

The solemn tick, tick, once so familiar to his ear, was resumed, and the hands pointed to the hour of midnight.

Was it a dream?

There was something terror-inspiring in this discovery, let him take it as he would. When he went away that morning, the clock was in a shattered, useless condition—now it was a thing of life.

Awe-stricken, he essayed to get upstairs out of the way of it.

Ere he had taken two steps, his nerveless hands dropped the candlestick, and the light went out.

Gasping and groaning, he groped his way up the stairs, and found the door of his bedroom—how he knew not.

There was a small paraffin lamp burning by the bedside, and he could see that Miriam was asleep, or had got up a very good imitation of it.

He blundered towards the bed, and laying a hand on her shoulder, awoke her.

"My love!" he groaned.

"Why do you wake me?" she asked, peevishly.

"The clock!" he gasped.

"What clock?"

"The grandfather of clocks. That unnatural thing in the hall. *It is going.*"

"I know it is," snapped Miriam. "Peebles and Tanner have been amusing themselves by trying to put it right. Peebles is a handy boy, and he discovered that there was nothing broken, but only a wheel off, or something. Really, if you think they have done wrong, you should have awakened them and said so. But you never throw away a chance of worrying *me*."

Bunn smiled a sickly smile, and was about to explain, but he checked the impulse and let the matter go. It was a relief to learn that there was nothing supernatural in the clock's resuming its labours as a recorder of time.

Miriam was soon asleep again, and Penny Bunn, with that mixture of joy and sorrow which is harder to bear than any distinct emotion, undressed and got into bed.

But he could not sleep for a time, and presently a distinct, but not very powerful, odour of sulphur pervaded the room.

Bunn sat up, and looked about him in search of indications of a conflagration. But the chamber was as dark as the catacombs.

"It's Chunder Loo," he muttered. "*Got a visitor,* I expect. Well, I don't care. If we are all stifled in our beds, it will be a merciful release."

Possibly he drew the soothing power from the contemplation of an early demise, or he might have been utterly worn out; anyhow, the sleep that had refused for a time to come now came to his aid, and the world of trouble for a few hours was a blank to his perturbed spirit.

CHAPTER CXXII.

ANTHONY GUBBLES LECTURES AND EXPERIMENTS.

WATCH as they might, and watch closely they did, the four friends could not discover anything in Chunder Loo to help them to regain that which they had lost.

The Hindoo went about his work as usual, occasionally going out for a stroll, sometimes alone, and now and then taking Mulberry Cork with him. The only thing observable about him, and it was noted by Jack, was that he made no effort to attach himself, in any way, to Anthony Gubbles, but rather held aloof from him, as he would have done from a small magazine filled with dangerous compounds.

Not that there was anything alarming about Gubbles, either in appearance or movement. He was, to the eye and ear, nothing more than a very good tutor in the school, and a nonentity out of it.

He took no part in the lighter life of the boys. After that brief lecture on the cranium of Mulberry Cork, he did nothing for a week to excite their attention.

As soon as school was over he would retire to his room in the attic, and there labour until meal-time. At the table he usually sat absorbed in thought, and, as soon as possible, disappeared again.

All this was bordering on the mysterious, but his appearance did not justify the assumption, entertained by Hone, that he was "a bad lot."

Susan spoke of strange sounds that came from the attic occupied by Gubbles, a "sort of sputtering," and a "kind of groaning," which was not, however, sufficiently definite to enable any one to form an idea of his doings in the secrecy of his chamber.

"He is a student of chemistry," said Bob Stockton, "one of those fellows who would not hurt a worm in their hearts, but are always finding out the most awful things for others to use."

One evening, when it was wet, Anthony Gubbles appeared unexpectedly in the schoolroom, where Chunder Loo was with the boys. The Hindoo was getting through some of the ordinary preparatory work, apparently heedless of the little pranks going on under his nose.

He looked up, and it appeared to the ever-watchful Jack that he was rather startled by the coming of the third master into the room.

The eyes behind the blue spectacles wandered pleasantly among the boys, who saw that something was coming, and were silently attentive.

"As it is a wet evening," he said, "I thought that a few experiments of a scientific nature might help to amuse you."

There was a chorus of joyous approval. Anything in the way of experiment, especially if it is likely to take an explosive form, is always interesting to boys.

"As you are willing I should show you something, I shall be glad if one of you will assist me to bring down a portion of my apparatus. Ford, will you come with me?"

Ford was only too pleased, and, jumping out of his seat, he accompanied Gubbles from the room.

But in a moment the under-master was back again.

"I shall require Mr. Bunn's table for my apparatus. Please to clear it. And you may also arrange the desks and forms, so as to make the room look as much like a lecture hall as possible."

The boys went to work, but Chunder Loo remained at his desk, going on with his labours as if he had no interest in the matter.

Presently Jack came down, carrying a mahogany box, which he carefully placed on the centre of the table.

"None of you are to touch it," he said. "Tom, keep an eye on it, will you?"

Tom crossed the room, and took up a position by the table. Chunder Loo descended from his desk, and looked at the box curiously.

"This," he said, "contains a small retort."

"For distilling?" queried Tom.

"I should say so," replied Chunder Loo, "but a retort can be used for a variety of purposes."

He returned to his seat, and remained there, abandoning his work and sitting quite still.

Jack soon reappeared with another box, and accompanied by Gubbles carrying a larger one.

"I shall require an assistant," said Gubbles; "a boy is hardly old enough."

He looked at Chunder Loo, who made no movement, but softly said:

"I am so ignorant of all science, that I should only be a hindrance to you."

"Very well," said Gubbles, "then I must get along with Ford."

As he made this announcement, Penny Bunn came into the room. The alteration in its arrangements, and the boxes on his table, excited in him the liveliest surprise, as was expressed by his mobile countenance.

"I am about to experiment for the benefit and amusement of the boys," explained Gubbles, "and I want an adult assistant. Mr. Chunder Loo professes to be ignorant of all science, so I am going to do the best I can with Ford, unless you——"

"Delighted, I am sure," murmured Penny Bunn. "Though not a practical exponent of chemistry, I have a theoretical knowledge of it."

"All I require," remarked Gubbles, as he proceeded to open his boxes, and take out from them a number of instruments and bottles, "is a strong, sure hand, such as we cannot hope to find among boys."

From the bottom of the biggest of the boxes he produced a number of pieces of white linen, about four or five inches square, neatly folded, and laid them on his left, and placed two of the bottles, filled with clear liquid, near them.

"Where shall I stand?" asked Bunn.

"On my right," was the answer, "and please hold this bottle firmly in your hand."

"Am I to remove the cork?"

"Not until I tell you."

The attitude of Penny Bunn was, alone, worth being there to see. If he had been the lecturer, and Gubbles the assistant, he could not have assumed a more imposing air. Holding the bottle aloft, he gazed at the boys with an expression which seemed to say:

"Keep your eye on me, and you will see something to astound you."

Chunder Loo sat with his face resting in his hand, and his eyes on the wearer of the blue spectacles, who did not exhibit any interest in him in return.

"My first experiment," said Gubbles, "will show you how, out of colourless liquids, permanent dyes of various colours can be produced. I take up this piece of linen, and from this bottle I pour out a few drops of what seems to be water. You see that it hasn't even a tint in it."

He held up the bottle and the piece of linen, on which he had poured a few drops of the liquid. Beyond a damp circle, there was nothing to show it was there.

"Now I will ask Mr. Bunn," pursued Gubbles, "whom, for the time, I will take the liberty of calling the Great Magician, to pour out something from this bottle, doing it with exceeding care."

Bunn took the piece of linen, and spread it on the flat of his hand. Gubbles handed him the second bottle, and peered into one of the boxes for something he required.

"About a teaspoonful will suffice," he said, without looking round.

Bunn tilted up the bottle, and about three times the necessary quantity ran out. But "it did not matter," he thought, as he felt it soak through and rest in the hollow of his hand.

The moistened spot on the handkerchief instantly became a brilliant blue.

Gubbles looked up, and uttered an exclamation of surprise and alarm.

"Take the rag from your hand!" he cried. "Quick!"

Bunn had the bottle in the other hand, and he had to first put it down ere he could obey. In his hurry, he spilt some more of its contents over a pair of shepherd's plaid trousers he was wearing.

Gubbles hastily snatched the linen from his hand.

"There!" he exclaimed. "As I feared, you have dyed your palm. Don't rub it, or it will be there for years. A surface drying will be better."

Penny Bunn looked ruefully at his palm, which was an ultramarine blue. His gravity, as he compared it to his whiter palm, sent the boys into fits of laughter.

Gubbles shook his head, and held up his hand.

"Boys," he said, "you must not laugh. It is a very serious thing for your principal."

"How long will this remain?" dismally asked Bunn.

"Impossible to say within a month or two," replied Gubbles. "I am experimenting on the subject, and hope, ere long, to find a compound that will remove these so-called permanent dyes. Speaking roughly, I should say that the colour will remain about a year."

"What?"

"A year, sir. I ought to have warned you, perhaps, but as you spoke of having a theoretical knowledge of chemistry, I opined that a reference to permanent dye would have sufficed for you to have avoided this catastrophe."

"For a moment I was at fault," said Bunn, with a ghastly smile. "It is some years since I took part in anything of this description."

Chunder Loo, of all in the room, was the one person except the lecturers, who did not smile. He seemed to be thoroughly interested in the preliminary part of the lecture.

"Perhaps," said Bunn, as Gubbles took up a piece of linen, hitherto not used—he had just found it in the box—"as I may, owing to want of practice, do more harm than good, I had better retire from the post of assistant."

"I will endeavour to manage without assistance," said Gubbles, quietly.

Penny Bunn took a seat among the boys, and, despite the warning he had received, he forthwith began to rub his hand upon his trousers, with the hope of getting rid of some of the permanent colouring. He was horrified, a minute later, on looking down at his trousers, to find that he had produced a broad patch of the most brilliant scarlet thereon. The liquid had acted upon some colouring matter in the wool. But rather than expose it to the public eye, he hastily covered it with his pocket-handkerchief.

"Blow the fellow's dyes," he muttered.

Gubbles, in serene unconsciousness, proceeded to show the delighted boys something else.

"In the making of dyes," he said, "the ancients excelled. All their colours had a permauency which is practically unknown to the ordinary manufacturer. Still, there are some who have got at the secret of permanent production. Brown is the easiest to produce—blue the most difficult of all."

Here he soaked a piece of linen by dipping it into the mouth of a bottle. Afterwards, he poured various liquids on it, changing its colour at every turn. The boys cheered and rattled their feet. Chunder Loo never stirred.

Bunn would have enjoyed himself immensely if he had not been set up with a blue palm and spoilt his trousers, but with the buoyancy of his nature he succeeded in rallying himself a bit, and smiled, "as they smile upon the rack."

"From dyes," said Gubbles, "I will pass to its kindred art—if I may so call it—the production of poisons. From the earliest age that dreadful instinctive desire in man to kill has led the more cruel of men to search for that which will take life and leave no sign."

A thrill went through the boys. Here was a subject, horrible, and yet interesting to a degree. They had all read of the Borgias and of other monster men and women of the earlier and middle ages, and wondered if he would refer to them.

"Now here," said Gubbles, holding up a small vial, "I have twenty drops of the most virulent poison in existence. It is not my intention to retain it, but I should, if possible, like to show you some of its effects, and for this purpose I have caught a mouse."

He coolly produced it from his pocket, and, amidst a breathless silence, uncorked the bottle with his teeth, and held the poison to the nose of the little creature so that it would inhale the odour of its contents. It was dead instantly.

"You see," he said, "the very aroma kills. And yet it is the product of an article we eat every day. I am not going to tell you what it is, but I have shown you that the old stories of ancient poisoners is no lie. And now I will dispose of this, as it is a dangerous possession."

He walked to the window, and hurled the vial out, having previously removed the cork.

"There are some others who boast of being able to produce such a poison," he said, as he came back to the table, "but they lie!"

"Wo-o-ould there be any trace o-of that poison?" tremulously asked Bunn.

"None at all in the human body," was the cool reply, and Bunn thought that he had got another perilous treasure in the Abbey in the person of Gubbles.

It will not do to give the rest of the lecture in detail, as it would take up too much of our time. To the boys it was interesting—absorbing.

He showed them how explosives could be made from the most simple materials, but declined to give them the proportions. And there was, moreover, always something he left unnamed which was vital to the production.

A grain of something which he dropped on the floor and rubbed with his foot went off like a pistol. It made the heart of Bunn leap in his mouth, and Mulbury Cork was heard to exclaim: "Criminy!"

The process of making that youth into a gentleman was up to that time exceedingly slow in action.

He had not moved one step on the road to refinement. The one thing, in the opinion of his mother, that was needful, he was never likely to possess.

Altogether the lecture by Gubbles was a great success, and it was growing dark when he finished with a specimen of "fire writing" on the wall of the schoolroom.

"Fire," he said, "without heat or flame. It is a discovery of the east. And this concludes my lecture, boys."

As he said this the supper bell rang.

They stopped one moment to give him a cheer by way of thanks, and then off sped the boys with Penny Bunn dolorously following behind.

He would have to account to Miriam for the condition of his paw, and come in for the usual rating. She would not blame Gubbles, of course, but ask Bunn why he interfered with matters he knew nothing

whatever about. He could almost repeat to himself the exact form of her address upon the subject, and Miss Astracan accompanying her with a running fire of ejaculatory comment.

Chunder Loo remained behind with Gubbles, who was engaged in packing up his boxes.

"Can I assist you?" he asked.

"No, thanks," quietly replied Gubbles, "there are some things which are dangerous for the inexperienced to handle. Every box here is a species of infernal machine. If handled carelessly or ignorantly an explosion might take place—perhaps I ought to say, *would*, do so, and blow the unfortunate person to atoms."

"Oh!" was all Chunder Loo said, as he drew back.

He hesitated a moment and then slipped away from the room.

Anthony Gubbles, whistling softly to himself, without any particular tune, finished his packing and then went to supper. It was his night to preside at the table, and he was in a cheerful mood, cracking little jokes as he had never done before.

All round he was looking up in the estimation of the youngsters.

After the meal he and Jack Ford carried the boxes upstairs again, and it was bed-time ere the latter reappeared.

"You have got in the good graces of Gubbles," said Hone, as Jack came down the stairs. Hone was just then going up.

"He is a very nice fellow," replied Jack, quietly, "and time slips away when people are talking upon some agreeable subject."

CHAPTER CXXIII.

SNICKER ON THE VERGE OF A PIT.

"THE person who changed the cheque," read Bunn, at the breakfast table on the following morning, "was a coarse man, with a head completely bald. He took off his hat to wipe his forehead as he was waiting for the money. He had a habit of correcting himself as he spoke, in the matter of pronunciation of words. For instance he said: It an un*kimmon* fine day, and immediately substituted *common* for *kimmon*."

Bunn, who had written for further information as an afterthought, stopped short and stared at his wife with the light of a great discovery in his eyes.

"There is only one man in the world to answer to that description, and that is the scoundrel, Snicker."

"How did he get hold of the cheque?" asked Miriam.

"Found it, of course."

"Is there not a saying in your country that 'findings is keepings,' or something to that effect?"

It was Chunder Loo who put the question in a general way. Bunn pressed his lips and looked troubled, but Miss Astracan knocked the bottom out of the remark by saying:

"Findings may be keepings if you are not found out. Then there is the fact that the name of Bunn has been forged on the cheque. That, I take it, is a criminal offence.

"He was a duffer with his pen," said Bunn, thoughtfully. "I don't think he could have done it."

"They had no knowledge of your signature," returned Miss Astracan, "just to write your name was enough."

"I'll go down to his place and make him disgorge the money," said Bunn, flourishing his knife and fork. "I'll have it, or lock him up."

"May I say one word?" interposed Chunder Loo.

"Oh, certainly," answered Bunn, sarcastically. "Go it. Advise us to let him spend the money and say nothing about it."

"P.Y.," said Miriam, severely, "I am ashamed of you."

"I merely wished to point out," said Chunder Loo, as he put down his teacup and wiped his lips with his napkin, "that what Mr. Bunn proposes to do would lay him open to the charge of condoning a felony. The law, I believe, gives as much as seven years for that offence. Now would it not be better to have the man arrested at once, and if the money is found upon him, or in his house, it will probably be recovered through the police."

"Excellent advice," exclaimed Miriam.

"It is just as a judge would speak," added Miss Astracan, in a voice that sounded like a muffled drum.

Bunn sat dumb. He could see that Chunder Loo was right, but on principle he was not going to admit it.

"If you will allow me to act in this matter," said the Hindoo, after a pause, "I will go on to the police-station at Chippenham, state the facts, and arrange for the arrest of Wicker."

"Snicker," corrected Bunn.

"I beg pardon, Snicker," said Chunder Loo. "Well, are you willing to leave it to me?"

"Oh, certainly," replied Miriam. Penny Bunn put three parts of a rasher into his mouth and masticated it viciously.

"Then the sooner I start the better," said Chunder Loo, rising.

He paused one moment more to finish his cup of tea, and then was gone. "I would rather have gone myself," grumbled Bunn, "it seems to me that I am only a sort of second fiddle here."

"Don't be a fool, Bunn," advised Miss Astracan, sharply, each word almost as resonant as the banging of a drum.

Bunn breathed an anathema on her head, and departed.

Chunder Loo was already on his way to Chippenham. Could any of those in the Abbey, who knew him only as a quiet, stealthy walker, have seen him as he *ran* like a deer through the wood, they might have wondered.

The pace at which he travelled was marvellously swift, and to facilitate his movements he had his tight-fitting garment drawn up to his knees.

Penny Bunn had one great failing, and that was he could not keep his tongue quiet. It was part of his nature to utilise every opportunity to speak on matters that, for the most part, had better be left unsaid.

He could not for the life of him keep the Snicker affair from the boys.

Just before school-time he sauntered into the playground, and told Jack Ford of it.

"You are at liberty to speak of it, of course," he said; "but at present I would not make too much of it. It is a deplorable thing that man should fall so low. It is not the money I care for—that might have gone, and very little said; but for the old master of this establishment to descend to robbery and forgery —it is *too* much."

Passing his hand over his eyes, as if he wept for the fallen Snicker, he glided into the house.

It was not likely that Jack would attempt to keep the matter a secret. He called the boys together, and out with it, right away.

"Now," he said, "don't forget yourselves to cheer. That is going too far. But if I said that I was sorry for Snicker, I should be telling a lie. He has been a knave, and he will meet with the end of a knave."

"He isn't the only thief about," said Hone; "don't forget that not long ago somebody boned my money. He couldn't have taken that, you know."

"When did you lose it?" asked Mulberry Cork. "I should like to know, because I don't want it put on me."

"It was taken last term," replied Hone, "and there was no occasion for you to ask about it. You were not here then, thank goodness."

"Well, you have got me now—blow the lot of you!" rejoined Mulberry, with a scowl, "and I am going to stop out that hundred pounds. Bunn had it, and lost it, like a booby. It isn't *my* fault. How much did you lose?"

"Find out," replied Hone, curtly.

"It wasn't much, I reckon," sneered Mulberry Cork; "threepence a week is about your allowance."

Hone's face flushed, and then turned deadly pale.

"You are a low-bred cur," he said, "and are about as ornamental to the school as a mangy dog!"

And then, with a swift back-handed movement, he struck him.

Mulberry was taken unawares, and was knocked down. He lay for a moment, and then slowly got up again.

"The last time I had to fight here," he said, "you took good care, the lot of you, I should get the knock from that old porpus in the house. This time, if I fight, I want to have it *got through with.* It must go on *to a finish.* There is a half-holiday to-day, I think."

He paused, and Jack nodded. It was the only answer he got. There was something fiendish and beyond his years, in the expression of the boy's face.

"Well, we have the whole afternoon," he said, "and there's piles of time to get right away where we can't be stopped. I won't have a mob howling at me either. We can have it out *alone.*"

"Just as you like," returned Hone.

"To a finish, mind you," repeated Mulberry Cork, "and we can go away together. Are you agreeable?"

"Yes."

"One moment," said Jack Ford, "I rather object to this sort of thing. There ought to be somebody to see fair play."

"I wouldn't mind it," said Mulberry, "if I didn't know that I was poison to the blooming lot of you. What is the good of your shamming friendship? Of course, if that hulky chap, Hone, is afraid of me——"

"That will do," interposed Hone. "I'll have it out with you. There's an end of the jawing. Ford, I'm obliged to you for what you said, and know the spirit you spoke in, but let the thing go. If I never licked a fellow before, I will give this cub a trouncing."

None there felt they could interfere further, and the two antagonists were left to make their own arrangements.

As Mulberry had said it was a half-holiday that day, and they had plenty of time to go miles away from the school if the combatants choose, Jack's general advice after Hone had spoken was, "Leave them to themselves to do as they please."

The morning passed away without any further event out of the common, and at noon Chunder Loo came back.

He reported to Miriam that he had made the necessary statement to the Chippenham police, who would at once proceed to arrest Snicker. She and her husband would be probably required, later in the day, to go down and enter the charge against the culprit.

"I suppose you have seen nothing of him?" asked Miriam.

"I saw him seated by his door smoking a pipe," replied Chunder Loo. "I did not, naturally, say a word to him. By the way, you had better remain at home this afternoon. As soon as the arrest is made, a messenger will be sent on Here for you to attend at the police-station as soon as possible."

"I hope he will be imprisoned for life," said Miriam, viciously.

Chunder Loo in response, simply smiled.

———

CHAPTER CXXIV.

THE CRICKET GROUND ON THE HIGH LAND.—TWO STARTLING THINGS.

IN the days when Fontenoy Snicker was master at the school, all the games dear to boys were tabooed. It was part of the policy of that utter scoundrel to make their lives as miserable as possible with the deliberate intention of breaking their hearts.

He succeeded in making many miserable, as we know, but it is also on record that he failed to break the spirit of the youngsters.

It remained unshaken, and was the rock on which he ran, and split himself to pieces.

Penny Bunn, more prudent, had gone on the other tack, and the boys had brought back with them sundry bats and balls, tennis rackets and so on, with which they hoped to make their leisure time more agreeable than it had been heretofore.

The ordinary playground did not, either in size or location, admit of games with the ball. The precipice being handy, the balls would, in the usual course, be sent over and lost in the brushwood below.

It was, therefore, requisite to select a suitable spot for cricket practice, and this Penny Bunn announced that day he had done.

It was a piece of common land away on the cliff, just beyond the wood, fairly well turfed, remote from the farmhouses and cottages scattered about the district, and only rarely frequented by the yokels.

Bunn wanted something to distract his mind from his troubles, and he proposed to accompany the boys to the cricket ground, as it was thenceforth to be called, and open it with due ceremony.

Luckily for him, Miriam omitted to name the request made by Chunder Loo that he was to remain at home, and the Hindoo being shut in his room when the boys gathered by the gates, Bunn was enabled to accompany them.

Jack Ford had spent a considerable sum of money from a boyish point of of view, having purchased two good bats, two balls of the best make, and a net for practising. A sprinkling of the others had bats, pads, and gloves, and there was everything needful to make the inauguration of the game a complete success.

"I hope you are all here," said Bunn, looking about him.

"All but Hone and Cork, sir," replied Bob Stockton, "and they are going for a walk together."

"They've gone!" cried out Gyp Tanner. "They went down through the wood ten minutes ago."

"Two strange boys," murmured Penny Bunn, "reserved and brooding. They will be congenial company for each other, I have no doubt."

There was more than one covert smile, as this remark was made. The congeniality promised to be rather rough in its course of action.

On the way to the chosen spot Penny Bunn spoke of cricket as "the noblest game ever conceived by man."

"It is some years since I handled the bat and ball, but in my youth I was selected to play for All England."

A sort of dumb astonishment came over the boys, who knew the requisites required for a representative player. Bunn, in happy ignorance of the peculiar thoughts in the minds of his listeners, went on:

"I shall never forget my great innings, when Hayward, the great bowler, bowled one hundred successive balls at me, and only knocked my stumps down twice. He afterwards hit one for the third time. Then, of course, I was out."

It is impossible to describe the feelings of those who had some knowledge of cricket, as they listened to his remarkable statement.

It was perfectly clear that Penny Bunn had only the most elementary knowledge of the game, probably acquired in some out-of-the-way town alley, where a couple of bricks served for stumps, a piece of the lid of a deal box for a bat, and a roll of paper bound with string for the ball.

The *third* time he was bowled by Hayward, he was out!

The vast majority of players, on being bowled *once*, retire from the field.

Thinking from the silence that followed his remarks that the boys were keenly interested, Penny Bunn went on with a few more staggering reminiscences.

"On another occasion," he said, with a smile, "it was my turn to bowl at both Hayward and Carpenter. I bowled them both six times, with six successive balls, but I would not declare them out because I knew they were professional cricketers, and leaving the yard —I mean ground—in which we were playing without making a score would have been their ruin. So I bowled again until they had made two runs together, and then ended the match."

"Were you ever umpire, sir?" asked Bob, suavely.

"On two occasions only," was Bunn's reply.

"And how many runs, sir, did you make?"

It was a most audacious question, and there was a visible perturbation among the boys, who expected to hear Penny Bunn administer a very strong rebuke to Bob, for his impudence.

But Bunn had no such thought in his mind.

After a moment's deep reflection, he said:

"On the first occasion, as far as my memory serves me, I only made forty runs, but on the second one I carried out the stumps."

This was took much. The boys had either to let out in some way or be taken ill. Led by Bob Stockton, they smothered their laughter in a cheer.

"Since that day," continued the veracious narrator, "I have rarely played. Possibly my memory may fail on some points of the game, but as far as lies in my power, you may rely upon me to assist you in acquiring some knowledge of it."

They thanked him as well as they could, and he complacently led them to the chosen ground.

As far as that position went it was remarkably pleasant, but what with the bushes dotted about, and the lack of level spaces, a great deal of work would have to be done, ere it was fit for real play.

But they pitched the stumps in the best available spot, and a bat was handed to Bunn, with the expressed hope he would take first innings.

"It is not a regular game," explained Jack Ford; "we shall merely bowl, and if you are caught or bowled you will have to give place to another player. We must be content with practice, to-day."

Bunn was very diffident about playing at all, but on being duly "plumbed" by Bob Stockton, he consented to do his best, although the want of practice would, of necessity, act against anything like a fitting display.

They had set up a double wicket, and Tom and Don undertook to bowl. As there was to be no running, the rest acted as a very liberal field. Poor Penny Bunn!

He was like the aspiring cricketer, who received an over from Jackson. The first ball hit him in the leg, the second in the eye, and the third put him out. Before he had so much as touched the ball with his bat, he felt compelled to retire from the field.

"The want of practice," he said, as he laid down the bat, and limped aside, "is dead against me. Cricket, also, seems to have materially changed its methods since the time when I was a proficient player. With your leave, I will look on."

Little Jiggers, took the bat, and showed that his size was not against his being a smart cricketer. One of his hits to square leg would have gone goodness knows where, but for Bunn, who happened to be in a line with it, and obligingly stopped it with his stomach.

As soon as he recovered his breath, Bunn declared that he had seen enough to know that the boys, for that day at least, could get on very well without him, and he would go for a walk. So he limped away, and when he was at a safe distance, they all lay down upon the ground, and laughed until they had hardly an ounce of strength left.

"He bangs everything," said Whymper.

"Well," said Jack, "let us waste no more time. I want to get you all in a condition to challenge some country team and give them a licking."

The game was then earnestly entered into, and for two hours the batting and bowling went on, Jack noting the different styles and estimating the capabilities of the various players. On the whole, he seemed to be satisfied, and even pleased with them.

"There is a lot of good material among you. We shall have a very fair team to represent Littlecote, in a month, if we can only get a decent amount of practice. We must try to get leave to run here in the evenings, if only for an hour."

Bob Stockton undertook to approach Penny Bunn, and it was considered as good as done.

At six o'clock the bats and so on were put together, and in small parcels doled out to boys to carry home. Jack arranged it all, dividing the labour among those who had done nothing towards bringing the things thither.

They wended their way back in high spirits, and when they came in sight of the Abbey gates they saw a boy seated on a big stone, holding his head between his hands.

It proved to be Mulberry Cork, who, hearing their footsteps, raised his head and exhibited a face, terribly bruised.

"You see," he said, speaking with difficulty, "that he was too much for me."

"Was this done in fair fight?" asked Jack, who had no very high opinion of Hone.

"*He* will tell you so," answered Mulberry, bitterly; "but it don't matter much how it was done. He's got the better of me to-day, but——"

He stopped short, and the most horribly malevolent look ever seen on the face of one so young, distorted his features.

They all turned away from him and passed on.

"I want to hear Hone's version of the fight," said Don.

Hone was in the playground sauntering about in that high shouldered way of his with his hands in his pockets. Apparently, he had not as much as a scratch about him.

"Hone," said Jack, with some sternness in his voice, "we have just seen Cork. He has had a fearful mauling. Where did you fight, and how long?"

"I didn't try to keep an account of the time," answered Hone. "I haven't a watch. We went down into the wood, pitched on a place, and I began

to undress. Before I had hardly got my coat off he came at me like a wild cat, and I treated him as one. I don't think any of you would have done otherwise."

"I can't say a word about that," said Jack, "it seems to have been rather a one-sided fight."

Then he turned away, and the others doing likewise, Hone was left to himself. He mooned about for a time, and then entered the house. As he passed through the doorway, he either was, or feigned to be, shaking from head to foot with laughter.

———

CHAPTER CXXV.

WANTED—FONTENOY SNICKER, ESQ.

"WHERE have you been, P.Y.?" asked Miriam, as her husband stood on the mat rubbing his shoes.

"I," he replied, lightly, "have been with the boys, teaching them the manly art of cricket."

"Then you ought to have let them teach themselves, which I dare say they could have done very well without your assistance, for you have been wanted here. The police called two hours ago. Snicker has disappeared, and is not to be found."

"I dare say he is merely out for a walk," said Bunn.

"The police hold a different view," replied Miriam, "they think that he has got scent of trouble, and has fled from the neighbourhood. A description of him is being wired in every direction. They want to know if you will offer a reward."

"I can offer one, certainly," answered Bunn, "but whether I can pay it is another matter."

"Bunn, you get a bigger fool every day."

"Thank you, my love. I was under the impression that I had stopped growing, and with my manifold troubles it is impossible for me to get fat."

She looked at him for a moment as if she entertained a private opinion that a little mauling about the countenance and rumpling of the hair would do him good, but she did not enter on that course of procedure.

"Do something," she said, "I feel certain that the police won't do much unless they have a stimulus. Go at once and see about it."

"My dear, I am tired. Cricket is a most exhausting game."

"Go at once, I say, and have a cab home from Chippenham. Every hour is of importance. Snicker may get on board an emigrant ship by the morning unless he is stopped."

Penny Bunn pleaded for a cup of tea before he started, and this being an absolute necessity under the circumstances, he was allowed to have it.

Then he went away, halting once at the Cowley Arms for a further refresher. Later he partook of another on his arrival at Chippenham, and then visited the police authorities.

The result of a conference with them was, that he authorised the printing and issuing of a bill offering a reward of fifty pounds on the apprehension and conviction of Fontenoy Snicker, erewhile schoolmaster of Littlecote Abbey, a late resident at Smudgen Bender.

Satisfied that he had now done all that was required of him, he had a third drink with the inspector, and in a cab set out for home.

There he learnt from Miss Astracan that she had discovered the condition of Mulberry Cork, also the name of the boy that had ornamented his countenance, and she "wanted to know what he was going to do in the matter?"

"Do?" he exclaimed. "Nothing. Boys will fight. When I was young I fought every day in my life."

"I have no doubt," said Miss Astracan, "that then, as now, you were anything but what you ought to be. All I have got to say is that you make the poultices for the boy yourself."

"He doesn't want any," grumbled Bunn, "but I will see him. Where is he?"

"In bed."

Bunn went upstairs and found Mulberry between the sheets, and Chunder Loo sitting beside him. The Hindoo rose up as his principal entered, and bowed. Bunn gave him a condescending nod of the head, that seemed to have an exasperating effect on Chunder Loo, for he grinned maliciously behind his back.

"Now, Cork," said Bunn, "what is the meaning of this?"

"Fight, and I got the worst of it," was the short reply.

"Miss Astracan says you are to have some poultices put on your bruises."

"Bother the old porpoise. Why can't she let me be?"

"Cork!"

"Well, ain't it aggravating that I can't have a licking without her coming around with poultices? I will make it right with him before I've done. I'd like to get that Hone down by the river one night—Wapping way—he wouldn't go about hammering many more covies."

"Cork, I am grieved and shocked to hear you talk in this way."

"Then don't stop any longer, and you won't hear it."

Penny Bunn turned to Chunder Loo, who was rubbing his hands together and grinning like the proverbial Cheshire cat.

"Leave him to me, Mr. Bunn," he said.

"I think it is the better thing to do," replied Bunn.

He saw neither pleasure nor profit in having anything more to do with Mulberry. Since the loss of the cheque, the task of turning him into a gentleman had become somewhat onerous. So he beat a retreat, and left the Hindoo alone with his charge.

Chunder Loo resumed his seat, and sat for a time with his eyes on the boy, who shifted about uneasily, without returning his gaze.

"So," said Chunder Loo, at last, "you don't know what you want to put your bruises right? But *I do*. What you groan for is revenge—*revenge!* If anyone, boy or man, had pounded me when I was your age, in the way you have been, *I would have killed him!*"

Mulberry Cork made no reply, but his breath came short and thick. He was labouring under intense excitement.

"Killed him," repeated Chunder Loo, "not as some mad fools do, openly, but *secretly—safely.*"

He paused, watching the boy, more uneasy than ever, but still he did not speak.

"*You*," continued his tormentor, sarcastically, "will do nothing of the sort. You have not the blood and breed to go beyond scratching and kicking. To-morrow, when you meet him, you will pass him sniggering and shamefaced. You *worm!*"

A fixed look came into the eyes of the boy, and Chunder Loo said no more. He could see that he had instilled the poison into his soul, and left him to his thoughts.

That night, as Penny Bunn sat up for half-an-hour after his wife and her aunt had retired, he sat reading a book, in the full belief that he was the only person in the Abbey who had not gone to bed.

Of late, it had been the custom of Miriam to accompany her aunt to her chamber, there to have a quiet chat, after the manner of women, who consider a bed-room bit of chatter the very cream of gossip. To Bunn, it was his brief spell of rest.

But that night he was worried with his stained hand. Frequent references to it on the part of the ladies had not served to dispel the sensation of discomfort it naturally created in his breast.

"It is just like the palm of a baboon," he muttered, as he held it out before him. "I'd give all I am worth, which isn't much, to get rid of it."

Hardly had the words been breathed, when he was startled by the opening of the door of the room.

Facing about, he saw the origin of the mischief, in the person of Anthony Gubbles. The usual quiet face of the undermaster was ablaze with excitement.

"Excuse my troubling you so late," he said, "but knowing you were sitting up, I came down to relieve you. *I have found it!*"

"Found what?" asked Bunn, with his mind instantly fixed on another haul of treasure.

"A compound, or rather a mixture, that will remove the stain from your hand," said Gubbles, in a low, thrilling tone.

His excitement, important though the discovery was in some respects, appeared extraordinary in the eyes of Bunn, who, however, experienced a throb of joy.

"It is a great relief to me," he said.

"I have it here," continued Gubbles. "Please hold out your hand."

"You are sure no further mischief will come of it, Gubbles?"

"It cannot harm you."

Penny Bunn held out his hand, and Gubbles poured out a few drops of a yellowish liquid into the palm.

Then, with a piece of rag, he gave it a gentle rubbing, and the stain was gone.

Bunn gazed at his whitened hand, and drew a long breath of relief.

"Gubbles," he said, "accept my assurance of eternal gratitude. The study of chemistry must be very pleasing?"

"It is fascinating beyond description," answered Gubbles, "especially when you hope by its aid to do something great."

"I have dabbled in it," said Bunn. "I think I told you so before, but I have lost what little I knew. If you would give me some instruction I should be further grateful."

"I shall be only too pleased," said Gubbles, "and to-morrow I will write out a short list of the things you will require. The outlay is merely nominal. I will now say good night."

Penny Bunn held out his hand, and they exchanged a fervent grasp. Gubbles then retired, and Bunn went off to bed once more for a brief spell—a happy man.

CHAPTER CXXVI.

JACK FORD PUZZLED.—ANOTHER LECTURE WITH DIREFUL RESULTS.

THREE days passed, and Snicker had not been found.

Stimulated by the offer of a reward, the police were even more active than usual, and every place they could think of, where he was likely to be in hiding, was searched without result.

Mrs. Snicker was allowed no rest. Two or three times a day, one or more of the emissaries of the law paid her a visit, on one pretext or another, and her answer to their inquiries was always the same.

"I don't know where he is, and I hope you will soon find him, and leave off worriting me."

As the item of news, concerning the failure of justice arrived at the Abbey the excitement among the boys increased. All sorts of rumours were afloat. Twice it was reported that the late schoolmaster had been found in the river, and once a man, returning home late, fancied he saw him hanging from a tree, on the verge of the wood.

But there was no truth in the first reports, and the man who saw him hanging from the tree failed to point out the exact spot, and was, moreover, declared by the Smudgem Bender officer, whom he knocked up for the purpose of getting him to cut Snicker down, in such an intoxicated state that it was utterly impossible for him to see anything clearly.

But in the matter of interest to the inner circle of boys at the school, even this affair sank into insignificance beside the fact that there was no sign from Lingo.

Nor could they, with the most careful watching, find out Chunder Loo doing anything unusual.

They learnt also that he had asked Mrs. Bunn to lend him half-a-sovereign until he had settled terms with the head of the house, and it had been given to him. This piece of intelligence was obtained from Susan, who was "dusting up the room" when the money was handed to him by the "missus."

"He has not been able to dispose of anything," said Bob Stockton, and the quartette of friends conferred together in the class-room, under the pretence of exchanging notes about their lessons.

"I am completely fogged," returned Jack Ford, "but it is only for a time. I'll get at the bottom of the whole business before I have done with him. The borrowing of the money may be only a blind. But still, I cannot see how he could have sold the stuff, or even exchanged any of the old coins for current money. He is never away from the Abbey more than a hour at a time, now."

"I wish you fellows would take me in with you," said Hone, as he came up and sat down beside them. "I am certain you have got something hidden, and it isn't fair."

"Whether we have or not it is our own business," replied Jack. "Take my advice, Hone, and don't poke your nose into things that don't concern you."

"But it does concern me," rejoined Hone, surlily. "I am not a fool, and I have often thought that you found something in the vaults and kept it to yourselves. You have spent a lot of money at different times, Ford. More, I should say, than your father allows you."

He glanced at the four immovable faces, and a dark frown settled on his own.

"Unless you trust me," he said, "I will, when I get at anything, split upon you, and so I tell you. Now then, how is it to be ? Trust or no trust ?"

"There is nothing we feel inclined to trust you with," said Jack, shaking his head. "Don't be an idiot, Hone."

Hone laughed curtly, and rising, left them.

They knew from his manner that the temporary league between him and Jack Ford was at an end.

"It is awkward," said Jack, " to have him bothering us again, but I do not think he will be able to do much mischief."

Anthony Gubbles was out that evening. It was understood that he had gone to Chippenham to purchase a few things he required. Chunder Loo had not put in an appearance and the boys were by themselves. But this state of things was put an end to by Penny Bunn, who came into the room with a pestle and mortar in his hands. Behind him was Susan, gingerly carrying an open box, in which were a number of paper packages.

"Boys," said Penny Bunn, " I thought it would amuse you to have another lecture on chemistry, and so I have arranged with Mr. Gubbles to give you alternate evenings, say, once a week."

He had done nothing of the sort. All that he had done was to take a few preliminary lessons from his undermaster on the art of compounding explosive materials, and he had been warned by his clever assistant not to attempt to do anything alone.

But want of confidence in himself was never a failing of Bunn's, and hearing that Gubbles was away from home, he thought it would be a delightful opportunity to exhibit his knowledge to the boys.

It was a fine evening, and the announcement of a lecture was not received with the enthusiasm he expected. One and all would rather, now that their lessons were disposed of, have gone off to practise cricket.

But when the king proposes to entertain his subjects the poor mortals have to be entertained whether they like it or not.

So the boys settled down and awaited developments.

"Bother him for a fool," muttered Short in Gyp Tanner's ear. " I wish he was at Jericho."

"If he went there," answered Tanner, miserably, "they would send him back again."

Susan, as soon as she had placed the box upon the table, hastily retired. Bunn emptied a packet of powder into the mortar and took up the pestle.

"Come nearer," he said, " draw up the forms and sit as close to the table as possible. The experiments I am about to show you are both simple and interesting."

There was a marked display of inactivity in response. The wiser among the boys kept to the back seats, and the front form, after they were shifted, was still left entirely empty. Bunn gazed at it and smiled.

"In your ignorance of the entire absence of danger, when these materials are manipulated by experienced hands," he said, " is excusable It is a very common thing for the world to shun a fancied danger. When you have gained a little more confidence I shall be pleased to see that vacant form occupied."

He proceeded to pound the powder in the mortar with the easy grace of an accomplished professor, flourishing the tool, and bringing it down with much force and precision.

This went on for a time, the lecturer pausing at intervals to test the fineness of the powder.

"It is necessary," he said, " to have it reduced to an almost impalpable state. I propose to mix three things. Two will be pounded together. Afterwards I will place a pinch of the double mixture on a piece of cardboard, and drop upon it a little of the third powder. The result is both unique and beautiful. I will now place the second chemical in the mortar."

He did so, and raising the pestle, brought it down *once.* He had no need to do more, for one of the most terrific explosions ever heard in a private house promptly followed.

Four-fifths of the boys were blown off the forms, and, although not seriously hurt, they were considerably alarmed, and some of the youngest howled for help.

The whole room was filled with a thick, creamy smoke, and breathing was difficult.

"Open the door, there !" Jack Ford was heard to cry.

Don was already groping his way to it, but he was spared the trouble by its being opened from the outside.

"May I ask what is going on here?" Miriam was heard to ask.

"Mr. Bunn was lecturing on chemistry," replied Don, coughing between the words, "and he has blown himself and all of us up."

"My love," a feeble voice exclaimed from the far end of the room, " I am safe."

"I am sorry to hear it!" was the angry reply. "Why don't you get up and help the poor boys?"

The only answer was a groan.

Happily one of the windows was open, and with the aid of the doorway, the smoke was rapidly driven out. As the room was getting tolerably clear, Miss Astracan came up, wheezing and groaning.

"Is it another barring out?" she asked.

"It's a blowing up," replied Miriam, bitterly, "P. Y. has killed half the boys

"Then he will be hanged for a fool!" said Miss

Astracan. "Really, he should have a keeper. Such a nincompoop ought not to be allowed about alone."

"I don't think any of us are hurt," said Jack Ford, coming forward, "but Mr. Bunn is lying in the corner with a lot of things on the top of him."

As it was possible to breathe now in the schoolroom, Miriam hastened to the aid of her husband, who was, as Jack said, lying in the corner with all his chemicals, the table, and Gubbles's desk, which had turned right over, on the top of him.

The explosion had caught him fairly on the head and in the face, for every hair he carried there was singed close, and there was quite an overpowering smell arising therefrom.

Miriam, aided by Jack and Don, proceeded to remove the desk. Bunn closed his eyes and groaned.

"Take it off gently," he said, "I am seriously, and I fear, mortally, hurt."

"And a good job, too," said Miss Astracan, from the rear. "Ugh! ugh! how can you be such a donkey after all the talkings-to I've given you?"

When the encumbrances were taken off Bunn, Miriam curtly bade him get up.

"I require considerable help," he moaned.

"You don't," said Miss Astracan, "you are only singed like a goose."

"Cruel—unnatural," murmured Penny Bunn, while the boys were choking with the effort needed to suppress their laughter.

Finding no assistance was offered, he got up slowly, a gruesome object to the eye, and endeavoured to screw his face into a smile.

"This comparatively minor accident," he said, "when viewed in the light of the magnitude of the subject, arose from my having forgotten that to expedite the experiment I, prior to my coming into the room, mixed two of the powders together. Having inadvertently added the third, the experiment was completed—completed earlier than I expected."

"Come along with you," said Miss Astracan, "and don't stand here as if you were the anthropoglossus machine to be seen for a penny. The next time you go a-mixing you will mix the roof off. Come out of the room and let me vaseline your head, or you will be an object for life."

She took him by the lapel of his coat and led him out, Miriam, frowningly, bringing up the rear.

Then, as soon as they dare, the boys went into fits of laughter, and hastened off to the cricket-field.

They had good reason to congratulate themselves on the recent experiments not being more injurious to them than they were. It afterwards transpired that Penny Bunn had narrowly escaped killing many, and blinding all of them.

CHAPTER CXXVII.

DOLPHUS COMES TO THE SCHOOL AND MAKES ENEMIES.

IT will be remembered that Miriam when single was possessed of a dog, to which she had given the name of Dolphus, presumably short for Adolphus.

Dogs, as a rule, are delightful creatures, truly the friend of man and woman, but this little yapping brute was a strong exception to the rule.

On the eve of her wedding Miriam confided her canine treasure to the care of the ostler at the Cowley Arms, he undertaking for the sum of one shilling per week to feed and take care of the animal.

The man was fairly faithful to his trust. He fed Dolphus when he could get any odd bits gratis from the kitchen of the inn, and he looked after the dog by keeping him tied up in one of the back places in the stable-yard, where having howled his heart out for three days and nights, Dolphus settled down to the firm conviction that he had been sentenced, for some unknown crime, to imprisonment for life, and became resigned to his fate.

On returning to the Abbey after her honeymoon, Miriam thought it would be advisable to get fully settled there before her pet was brought home. It was necessary that Dolphus should be made comfortable at the outset, and kept so.

Thus it happened that not until the events we have just recorded had transpired, did Miriam deem it advisable to ask the ostler to give up his charge. A letter was sent to the man, and the morning after Penny Bunn had given his disastrous lecture on explosives, Dolphus was led home with the aid of a string.

He was in a very excited state when he arrived at the Abbey.

In the first place, the bare idea of being once more in the open air had an intoxicating effect upon his active brain.

Then as he passed his old home he made a frantic effort to return thereto, and the ostler was obliged to raise him from the ground, and carry him out of the village like a dead rabbit on a string.

He finally conceived that he had been brought to the Abbey as a more secure place of confinement, a sort of transference from Pentonville to Dartmoor, and he made a last desperate effort to regain freedom.

The ostler, equal to the occasion, pinned him by the throat, and held him fast until Susan answered his ring at the door. She stared, as well she might, at sight of a man holding up a dog with his eyes well out of his head, and exhibiting about four inches of a quivering tongue.

A SPLENDID SCHOOL STORY.

NEVER BEFORE PUBLISHED.

By E. HARCOURT BURRAGE,

Author of "Ching Ching," "Monkey Mat and Roving Dick," "The Brave Boy of the Basilisk," &c.

BUNN, CHUNDER LOO, AND THE POLICEMAN DISCOVER A BODY ON THE GROUND.

PRICE ONE PENNY.

ALDINE PUBLISHING CO., 9, Red Lion Court, Fleet St., and 1, 2, & 3 Crown Court, Chancery Lane, London.

"I be a brought the dawg hoam," said the man.

Miriam, from the bottom of the passage, heard his voice, and came rushing forward.

"My darling!" she exclaimed.

The ostler dropped Dolphus, and with the canine power of recovery, the little brute instantly became himself again.

He recognized his mistress's voice, and having made one frantic leap at her, he, evading her longing arms, dropped to the ground, and ran round her again and again yelping and barking, so that his cries of joy penetrated to the schoolroom, and caused Penny Bunn, who was at his post, wearing a velvet skull-cap which Miss Astracan had made for him, to mutter something very far from a blessing on his canine head.

"Oh, look at him!" said Miriam, in an ecstasy. "Isn't he pleased?"

"He be, mum," replied the ostler, "and it a'most breaks me 'eart to part with him. He's been a j'y and comfit to me. We ha' been sich friends. Ain't we, old man?"

Dolphus declined to respond, and kept up his mad career until he ran against the umbrella-stand, and half-stunned his precious self. Then he subsided into a quieter mood, and Miriam took him in her arms.

Having paid for his keep, with an extra shilling as a solace for the grief of the ostler, expressed by his scooping an entirely imaginary tear out of his left eye, Miriam bore away the darling to her aunt, at whom Dolphus, with a recovered breath, barked and snapped viciously.

"It is only his play, auntie," said Miriam. "He is the most affectionate of precious creatures in the world."

"I hope he won't bite," replied Miss Astracan, dubiously. "I have a dread of hydrophobia."

Solitary confinement had not, in short, improved the temper of Dolphus, never of the best by a long way, but having been regaled with the remnants of two mutton chops and a saucer of milk, he settled down on the hearth-rug and took a much needed sleep.

From repose he was aroused by the voices of the boys, as they trooped out of the house to the playground. Waking up and seeing the door open he charged out upon them, it having been his custom, as a resident in Smudgem Bender, to harass, when an opportunity was given him, the children as they journeyed homeward from the village school.

To them he had been a terror, but he had boys of a different mould to deal with in the Lambs of Littlecote.

As Dolphus dashed into the thick of them in the hall, yelping and snapping, Jack Ford coolly gave him a kick that sent him like a football against the case of the grandfather's clock with a bang that threatened to once more stop that valuable timepiece.

Fortunately it did not do so, and Dolphus, humiliated and defeated, fell upon his back, lay there a moment to collect his thoughts, and then rising, bolted back to the place from whence it came.

"Where did that little beast come from?" asked Jack.

"It must be Mrs. Bunn's dog," replied Philter. "I think I have seen it in Smudgem Bender, near where she used to live."

"A nice sort of animal that," said Bob Stockton, laughing. "Don't forget, Jack, the old saying, 'Love me, love my dog.'"

Jack merely smiled, and the boys left the house.

Shortly after Chunder Loo wended his way to the dining-room, where Miriam had just settled down to look over an account-book before dinner.

The moment the swarthy tutor appeared, Dolphus, like one of the guards at Waterloo, was up and at him.

He rushed at Chunder Loo, and stopping just short of kicking distance, barked and growled and yapped while the Hindoo, with his dark eyes resting on him, stood still and smiled.

"Dolphus," said Miriam, sweetly, "I am quite ashamed of you. Be quiet, sir!"

But Dolphus refused to be quiet until she lifted him into her lap, and there he lay, with one eye on Chunder Loo, occasionally giving vent to his animosity with a low growl.

"We have no domestic dogs among the natives in India," said Chunder Loo, as he took a seat on the other side of the table, "but I am very fond of them. Your pet, Mrs. Bunn, will soon get used to me, and then we shall be most excellent friends."

"Dolphus," returned Miriam, complacently, "only wants to be approached in a conciliatory spirit to be the most charming companion."

Chunder Loo smiled in that half-snarling way of his, but otherwise he made no response.

Thus did Dolphus become an inmate of the Abbey, and within twenty-four hours he had made himself obnoxious to everybody, save his affectionate mistress.

But it was necessary for all to dissemble their feelings in the presence of Miriam, and she was imbued with the belief that the hated animal was well on the way to become a fixture in their affections.

But ere a second day had passed away, Dolphus had been again kicked, this time by Tom Drummond, whom he tried to bite, and broomed out of the kitchen by Susan.

Penny Bunn also secretly assaulted him with a

walking stick. Miss Astracan threw the tongs at him, and Chunder Loo was debating in his mind, on the possibility of getting the little brute to eat something of his providing, which would put a stop to his animosity towards men and boys for ever.

CHAPTER CXXVIII.

HONE AND MULBERRY CORK.—SOMEBODY MISSING.

TO the surprise of the school, nothing more in the way of a quarrel took place between Hone and Mulberry Cork. But on the contrary they were more like friends than enemies after a few days had elapsed.

Mulberry made the first advances, and he did it openly. Hone, who had fallen away from the rest as of yore, responded with a readiness that showed he had, as we all have, the need of companionship.

Unlike in everything but one point, and that was their antagonism to all around them, it struck Don that they much resembled a fox and wolf that had consorted together, and it was owing to him that they were so named during their brief term of friendship.

Hone, it may be said, had sorely disappointed Jack Ford, who was loth to think that he was so dead to his own interests to turn against the whole school as he had done before.

He trusted that a wiser thought would eventually prevail with him, but as matters turned out the estrangement was now to be final, irrevocable.

To the credit of the Lambs, and many were afterwards glad they acted in a commendable spirit, whatever might be their opinion of this strange friendship they did not make a single sarcastic reflection upon it, in the hearing of the oddly assorted pair.

Mulberry Cork seemed to be most anxious to keep in the good graces of Hone, and he openly fawned upon him, much to the disgust of those who noted it.

"I feel as if I could punch his head," said Philter to Gyp Tanner.

Gyp laughed, and asked what good that would do?

"If Cork likes to cringe," he said, "and Hone enjoys having the blacking taken off his boot with the other's tongue, it is their own affair. We needn't worry about it."

Thus things stood when a day arrived destined to be long memorable in the minds of all who shared in its doings and anxieties.

It was a Saturday, about a week after the curious alliance of the pair. As usual, it was a half-holiday, and all but Hone and Cork were going to the cricket ground. Penny Bunn and his wife were bound for Bath on marketing proceedings intent. Chunder Loo stole away early without saying a word about whither he was to wend his footsteps.

As the boys passed through the gates in a body, they saw Hone and Cork descend into the depths of the wood, and it was particularly noted that they appeared to be on the very best terms with each other. Hone was laughing at some remark made by his companion, who walked with one hand upon his shoulder.

"It seems too good a thing to last," said Jack Ford, as he shouldered his cricket bat.

"I wonder if, like some loving couples, they are on the eve of another quarrel?" said Don.

The afternoon passed pleasantly with the bat and ball, and as the eve drew nigh, the youngsters, tired out with play, were about to start for home, when they were considerably astonished to see Mulberry Cork approaching.

He was walking quickly, and on arriving within a short distance of them, hurriedly scanned them over.

"I thought I should find Hone here," he said. "What a rum beggar he is. He dodged me in the wood, saying that he was going to look for something, and would meet me here."

"How long ago was that?" asked Tom Drummond.

"About an hour—perhaps a little more."

"What was his idea, I wonder?"

"He said, he fancied he knew of something in the way of a cave that would please me, but before asking me to see it, would make sure that it was in the wood."

"A cave?" echoed half-a-dozen voices.

"That was what he said," replied Mulberry Cork, with a dogged look. "I thought it was all bosh, and that he wanted to be off to enjoy himself alone. Now I am certain of it. He is like the rest of you, a beastly swindle."

Mulberry swung round upon his heel, and slouched back to the Abbey alone. The others followed at their leisure, some laughingly commenting on the sudden termination of the "alliance of the wolf and the fox."

Tea-time arrived, and there was one absent from the table in the person of Hone. Chunder Loo had returned, and observing the vacant seat, asked where he was?

Mulberry Cork repeated his story of the way they had parted in the wood.

"Hone," said Chunder Loo, calmly, "is a boy who is inclined to bad company. The other day I saw him talking in quite a friendly manner with a low-looking poacher kind of a fellow. I reproved him, and he answered me, as I might have expected him to do, insolently. I will see that he is punished," he paused a moment, coughed, and then said, with a visible effort, "when he returns."

"Hone will get a tanning for this," whispered Bob Stockton.

There was more licence allowed to the boys, at table, on half-holidays than upon other occasions, and in the chatter of many voices, talking of cricket and other congenial topics, Hone was for a time forgotten.

But later his absence was again the theme of talk in the class room.

Mulberry Cork sat in a shaded corner of the room, with a book before him. His head rested on his hands, the palms pressed close to his ears, as if to shut out all sounds that would interfere with the due enjoyment of his book.

It was the first time he had been seen absolutely reading for pleasure, and Little Jiggers, stealing up behind him, observed it was a *Dictionary* that lay before, and it was *upside down.*

His discovery was circled round in whispers, and now, for the first time, Jack Ford began to think seriously of the absence of Hone.

Even then he did not entertain any great apprehensions on the subject. He was inclined to believe that Hone and his quondam-friend, Cork, had fought again, and the latter, by cunning, avenged the drubbing he had received on a prior occasion.

Shame, in that case, might be the cause of Hone's keeping away. Possibly he had stolen into the house and gone to bed.

Jack went off quietly to number two dormitory, to see if he could find anything of him, but he was not there. More perturbed than ever, he went down again and sought Chunder Loo, whom, as he expected, he found in the sitting-room of the schoolmaster. He was lying at ease upon a sofa by the window, reading the paper and smoking a cigarette.

"Ha! Ford," he said, pleasantly, "do you want me? Is there anything wrong?"

"Hone has not come back, sir," answered Jack; "he is two hours late."

"All the worse for Hone," rejoined Chunder Loo, "when he does return."

"I hope nothing has happened to him," said Jack, uneasily.

"What can have happened to him?"

"That I cannot even guess. But his continued absence is so very unusual that I thought——"

Jack paused, and Chunder Loo, carelessly folding back his paper, glanced over it.

"You thought—what?" he asked.

"That we ought to go and look for him."

"You are thirsting for a late outing."

"No, indeed, sir," answered Jack, earnestly, "I am not on the best of terms with Hone, and in an ordinary way would not have bothered about him. But I am troubled now."

"You need not worry, Ford. At least, that is my opinion. At all events, Mr. Bunn will be here by half-past eight. Then, if Hone has not turned up I will consult him as to what ought to be done."

His manner, as he yawned and turned the paper about, left Jack nothing to do but to retire and fall back upon his favourite method of procedure in time of trouble and doubt—to wait.

He made no reference to the interview with Chunder Loo, on mingling with his companions again, but watched for the return of Penny Bunn.

It was nearly nine when the schoolmaster and his wife came back. Penny Bunn was laden like a pack-mule in Mexico. Miriam carried one solitary paper bag, containing a new feather for her hat. This was her idea of a division of labour which, Bunn had been bitterly, but vainly, resenting on the road home.

"Never again," he said, as he delivered his parcel like a sack of coals upon the floor of the hall, "will you get me on such a bout as I have suffered this day."

"You seem to have forgotten," said Miriam, sarcastically, "that among those parcels there is a box of eggs."

"I had to drop the lot if there had been a ton of dynamite among them," growled Penny Bunn; "my senses were on the verge of leaving me."

"I am glad you have returned," said the voice of Chunder Loo, as the wily Hindoo stole into view, "one of the boys has not returned."

"Returned from where?" asked Miriam, sharply.

"From the usual afternoon outing," answered Chunder Loo. "He was last seen in the woods, by one of the boys. I think it was Cork."

"He must be sought and found," said Miriam. "P. Y. you ought——"

"From this Abbey," cried Bunn, clutching the hair of his head and snorting, "I do not budge one inch to-night. No, not if all the boys had vanished. I dare say Hone, who is troubled with a discontented spirit, has run away. Loo, is tea ready?"

"Miss Astracan is seeing to it."

"Good. Then I will refresh myself. Loo, suppose you go into the wood and look for Hone."

"I am a native of sunny India," answered Chunder Loo, stiffly, "and the night dews are not good for me. But if you command, I must, as your servant obey."

"You are mighty humble all of a sudden," sneered Bunn. "But don't worry yourself. If Hone comes back, well and good. If he doesn't, then that is his lookout."

With another snort he walked away, disregarding a curt inquiry from his wife about the parcels on the floor of the hall, as to who should pick them up and convey them to the sitting-room.

Chunder Loo volunteered his aid, and was sweetly thanked. Miriam sailed on, and the Hindoo, with a curious smile upon his swarthy face, proceeded to pick up and sort the parcels at his feet.

<hr />

CHAPTER CXXIX.

DOLPHUS MAKES A TERRIBLE DISCOVERY.

IT was eleven o'clock, and Hone had not returned. Penny Bunn, notwithstanding his rebellious mood, was getting into a state of deep anxiety.

The boys were in bed. Miriam and Miss Astracan had retired, and Bunn and Chunder Loo were alone.

The schoolmaster was horribly uneasy, and shifted about in his chair. Chunder Loo sat, in a composed and dignified frame of mind, steadily smoking a final cigarette.

"I suppose something ought to be done," murtered Bunn, after a silence.

"What *can* be done?" asked Chunder Loo.

"Somebody might go out and look for him."

"Where?"

Bunn did not know, and was obliged to admit as much.

"He was last seen in the wood, you said," he remarked.

"The wood is an extensive place. Difficult to travel about by night. A search there in the dark would have but one end—and that a failure. Now, if you had started immediately you came home——"

"Man, I am not made of iron. After being dragged into, and shoved out of, every shop in Bath, I had a right to consider that my day's work was done."

"I think that we ought to do something," said Chunder Loo. "The police could be communicated with. If you will sink your fatigue, I will risk an outing on a dewy night, and we can go down to Smudgem Bender together."

"Very well," said Bunn, in a tone of resignation, "I suppose it must be done."

They left the room and put on their head-gear in the hall. As Bunn opened the front door, Dolphus came bounding downstairs and rushed into the playground, barking furiously.

Dolphus had no love for Bunn, but like a dog, he was prepared to sacrifice his private feelings for the pleasure of a run.

Bunn, on his part, hated Dolphus with his whole heart, and he was about to anathematize the little beast, when Chunder Loo, with more tartness than he

generally displayed when speaking, called to the dog to come back.

That was enough for Bunn. If Chunder Loo objected to Dolphus being one of the party, the spirit of opposition prompted the schoolmaster to go upon the other tack.

"The dog wants a run," he said; "he had better go with us."

"I dislike dogs—at night."

"Then catch and bring him back."

But Dolphus, being in the open air, was not be cajoled or frightened into returning while one of his friends was abroad.

He treated the efforts of Chunder Loo to wheedle him back into the house, with contempt, and only barked derisively at his threats.

So they all went together, with Dolphus well to the fore, rushing here and there after imaginary cats and rabbits, and digging his head into rat-holes and old burrows, until he was half-blind with dirt and dust.

"After all," said Bunn, as he descended the path into the wood, "a dog is company on a dark night."

"Is he?" muttered Chunder Loo; "there he goes now, away among the bushes. Come back, you infernal beast!"

His excitement was so novel in comparison to his ordinary demeanour, that Bunn was astounded. He had a suspicion that his companion had been indulging during the evening in the strong waters of his adopted country, but he said nothing.

A row with a wily Hindoo in a dark wood, without a friend to see fair play, was anything but desirable.

Dolphus continued to rush about among the bushes for a time, barking his loudest, until suddenly he was dumb.

Bunn stopped short and listened.

"I wonder if the dog has gone back," he said.

"All the better if he has," grunted Chunder Loo.

"I would prefer having Dolphus with me," said Bunn. He called aloud : "Dolphus, Dolphus!"

There was a moment's silence, and then the dog answered him with a prolonged and most dismal howl.

"Bless me!" exclaimed Bunn, "he is caught in a trap."

"There are no traps in the wood," insisted Chunder Loo. "Come along."

"I must have the dog with me," said Bunn. "Dolphus, Dolphus!"

Again the answer was a howl as mournful as an Eastern wail for the dead.

"He hasn't stirred," exclaimed Bunn. "Something has happened to him."

"Come along," returned Chunder Loo, taking his arm, "the brute will follow us."

A third howl seemed to give him the lie, and Bunn,

now intensely excited, refused to go on. A profuse perspiration burst out all over him.

"He has found something," he said. "Let go of me, you black beast, will you?"

"I say you are a fool," replied Chunder Loo, between his teeth, "to make all this fuss about a barking dog."

"He is not barking, he is howling."

"What is the row there?" asked a rough voice, as the light of a bull's-eye lantern flashed upon them.

Bunn started back alarmed, but recovered himself when he saw that it was the Smudgon Bender policeman going his nightly rounds. As a rule he came as far as the Abbey every other night, if the weather permitted, and it was very fine just then.

"I want you to show us a light," replied Bunn; "you hear that dog howling? It is mine, and he is not the sort of dog to howl for nothing."

"He is after a rabbit," suggested Chunder Loo.

"Not he," asserted the officer. "He is either got into a trap, or found something more than a rabbit."

"Just what I said," cried Bunn.

With the lantern throwing its light before, the policeman plunged among the bushes, and stalked in the direction of the howling of Dolphus, which was now continuous.

The dog was fully two hundred yards from the path. As they drew nearer to him the sound increased in intensity until it was absolutely horrible to hear.

At last the officer, with Bunn close to his heels, and Chunder Loo, wild-eyed and furious, bringing up the rear, came in sight of the dog standing with its forelegs stretched out, and its head raised in the air, beside a long, dark object upon the ground.

There was a rush of the two foremost men, and the light of the lantern showed the form of Hone lying on his back.

He was quite still, and a glance at the half-closed eyes and fallen jaws sufficed to reveal the truth. The poor boy was dead.

───────

CHAPTER CXXX.

DARKER GROWS THE STORY.

DUMBLY the staggered schoolmaster stared about him. The time, the scene, and the sight of that still form all conspired to make him doubt the evidence of his senses.

Chunder Loo's eyes were ablaze with a lurid light, independent of the glare of the bull's-eye lantern, but he did not stir.

The officer, of more sluggish nature, was not deeply moved, but coolly raised the boy and put an ear to his lip.

"He is dead," he said, "as—as a door."

The simile was a feeble one, but it served.

"It can't be," groaned Penny Bunn.

"It's true enough, sir," repeated the man, "and look here, he's had an awful crack. Quite a smash on the head."

Penny Bunn groaned again. Chunder Loo now advanced, and stooping, looked into the face of the dead boy. There was more curiosity than sympathy in his gaze.

"He died instantly," he said, "and whoever hit him, must have been very strong."

"So I should say, sir," assented the policeman. "Will one of you gentlemen go for assistance? I want two men with a hurdle, or something to carry him down to the inn. And Doctor Lamplick ought to be fetched."

Chunder Loo did not volunteer his aid, so Bunn was obliged to go. His only companion was Dolphus, who walked quietly at his heels, now that his share of the work was done.

"I'll take a few notes of the spot while Mr. Bunn is gone," said the officer.

"I will assist you," volunteered Chunder Loo.

As they walked around noting the condition of the bushes, it was the Hindoo who espied a stout stick, about two feet long, lying on the ground. Unperceived by the officer, he picked it up, and coolly tucked it away under his long robe. Nothing else of importance was discovered.

The better part of an hour had elapsed ere assistance arrived in the person of two labourers, whom Bunn had aroused. Close upon their heels came the doctor.

He exchanged a cool bow with Chunder Loo, and proceeded to examine poor Hone's body. It was of a very perfunctory nature. Nothing more was necessary.

"He has been dead many hours," he said, "A blow of the description he received, would have stunned an ox."

It was three o'clock in the morning when the body was deposited at the Cowley Arms, there to await inquiry and an inquest.

All round it was considered the better thing to do, both for the sake of the inmates of the Abbey, and the convenience of the coroner of the district. Bunn wrote a letter there to Hone's father, which would, in due course, go out by the early morning post.

"A telegram would be a waste of money," said Bunn, "as the inquest cannot take place until the day after to-morrow."

All this time the Hindoo had the tell-tale weapon he had picked up, under his robe, and he carried it back with him to the Abbey. There he and Bunn discovered they had not been missed, and without a word they parted for their respective places of rest.

Chunder Loo, on entering his room, struck a match, and lighted a candle. In the corner of the room was Mulberry Cork's narrow bed, and with the light in his hand, Chunder Loo approached it.

The boy's eyes were closed, but he was not asleep. There was a slight quivering of the eyelids that betrayed him.

Chunder Loo turned the clothes over the boy's head, and then unlocked a drawer, in which he placed the stick. Having locked it up safely, he pulled back the clothes, and said, quietly:

"You may open your eyes now."

The small, mean eyes were revealed, with an inexpressible terror in their depths, and the boy shivered and shook in his bed.

"You went away with Hone, to-day," said Chunder Loo.

"In course I did," replied Mulberry Cork, with an effort to be bold.

"Where did you leave him?"

"In the wood."

"I have been out to-night with Mr. Bunn, and found him there."

"Then there ain't no more need to worry about him," said Mulberry Cork, turning over, and drawing the clothes up close to his face.

"Turn and look at me!" hissed Chunder Loo. "We found him dead!"

"I didn't do it," muttered the boy, with a thousand little drops of perspiration on his forehead.

"You liar!" said Chunder Loo.

Mulberry Cork threw back the clothes, and sat up in the bed. He was now more like a snarling reptile, or one of the lower brutes, than a human being.

"I swear I haven't touched him," he said, huskily. "I dursn't do it. Ain't he—wasn't he three times as strong as I am?"

"He was struck down from behind," said Chunder Loo.

"I can't help that," answered Mulberry Cork, as he lay down again; "I didn't do it. You can go and blow on me, if you like. I'd just as soon be dead as not."

He turned upon his side, and Chunder Loo, without speaking again, looked intently at the outline of the face upon the pillow, for a full minute or more, and walked away to his couch. He undressed rapidly, got into bed, and closing his eyes, lay there for a few moments thinking, ere he slept.

A deep horror, dark as a cavern in the bowels of a mountain, lay upon the school on the morrow.

It would have been sad enough to the boys if one of their number had died from illness—but to hear of one murdered! It was, for the time, overwhelming.

It mattered not a straw that Hone had made himself objectionable to them all. In the presence of death the ills that have been done are forgotten. Added to this there arises in the heart of us the inevitable feeling that we have been less kind than we might have been, to the one we have lost.

The latter emotion may be transient, but it is there for a time, and it is as lead upon the soul.

There was no attempt made to perform the usual school duties. Penny Bunn and Chunder Loo would, in all probability, be required by the authorities to assist the police in the investigation of the horrible affair.

Anthony Gubbles, having nothing to do with it, was deputed to remain at home with the boys, and see "that they got into no mischief."

He had a light task before him, for mischief is invariably the outcome of high spirits and thoughtlessness. The spirits of the Lambs of Littlecote were well below zero.

In the early part of the morning, up to ten o'clock, Penny Bunn and Chunder Loo remained in the Abbey. The latter was shut up in his room alone.

The boys were in the playground, talking in groups, and with hushed voices, about the crime, ever after to be associated with Mumping Malford Wood. The four members of the inner circle had been called together by Jack, and were seated on the wall, when a very simple matter took Don upstairs. He discovered that he had no handkerchief, and went off to the dormitory to get one.

He was absent longer than they expected—fully a quarter-of-an-hour—and when he finally appeared, his face showed that he had received another shock, or had been subjected to a painful surprise.

"What now?" asked Jack Ford, as Don sat down by his side.

"Chunder Loo!" replied Don.

"What has he done?"

"Nothing to me. You remember that little beast of a snake?"

"As if we could ever forget it," said Bob Stockton; "not while memory holds a seat in this distracted globe. What of it now?"

"It is in the Abbey," replied Don, with a shiver.

"Hang it!" ejaculated Tom Drummond, "the thing is impossible."

"I had been into the dormitory, and got my handkerchief," said Don, "and was on my way back, when I saw the little horror creeping along the corridor, in the direction of Chunder Loo's room. I stood still, as if I had been suddenly petrified. You can't imagine the turn it gave me."

"I think I can," said Jack.

"Well, I stood there staring at it, going slowly from me, luckily. Had it been coming towards me, I believe I must have gone right off. It slid up to the

the door of Chunder Loo's room, where it positively knocked."

"Now, Don," said Bob. "Draw it mild."

"It beat against the door with that metal ring round its neck, and although it was very faint tapping it must have been heard by Chunder Loo, who opened the door. I did not see him, only his skinny dark hand as it was thrust out to pick up that vermin snake. To my utter astonishment he began to talk to it as a mother would to a child that has been straying."

The eyes of his companions opened to their widest. Tom softly murmured :

"It isn't natural. But how did the thing get into the Abbey ?"

"I judged, from what he said—I cannot recall the exact words—that it has been there for some time, and had only strayed that morning, or during the night. One sentence that came from him with a peculiar intensity, I can give you word for word. 'Oh, Mehala, my life! how is it that thou wilt leave me, stealing away to mock and laugh at me, knowing that even as the earth grows dark when the sun is gone, so does my soul in thy absence sink to the depths of despair, even to the gate of death !'

"Those were the last words I heard," said Don to his amazed friends, "for as he uttered them, he closed the door."

"I don't understand it at all," remarked Tom, after a silence, "it isn't, as I said before, natural."

"It is devilish," muttered Bob.

"I will go so far as to say that it is incomprehensible," said Jack Ford; "and there we must leave it for the present. Chunder Loo is not the subject that has brought us together, but this awful thing— the death of Hone. Have any of you thought over the possibility of his having been killed by *one of us ?*"

They had no need to answer him. Already they had thought it over, and their minds pointed in one direction.

"I see you think as I do," continued Jack; "but our thoughts prove nothing. Have you seen Cork since breakfast ?"

None of them had, and he was not in the ground. At the outset, Jack had not suspected him. The idea of one boy killing another seemed too monstrous to be entertained for a moment. But it had been forced upon him by the demeanour of Mulberry Cork that morning as he sat at table.

He ate nothing, and never raised his eyes, save to cast a quick, furtive glance around. Every footstep heard in the hall brought the flush of alarm to his cheeks, to rapidly die away and leave him deathly pale.

The result of the first fight had never, in Jack's opinion, settled the feud between Cork and Hone. Judging by what he had seen of Cork, he was almost certain that he would not forget or forgive. But could his venom carry him to the extent of shamming friendship, and then committing a murder in cold blood ?

It was too horrible to think of, and foreign to the nature of boys in general as a thing could be ; and yet, now and then the most atrocious crimes have been committed by the young, and even by absolute children.

"I don't want you to try to fasten it on him," said Jack, without mentioning to whom he was referring —there was no need of that, as they had but one person in their minds—"but I wish you to help me to prove he did *not* do it. Much as I dislike him, I would give half of what I expect to have of the good things of this world if I could truly say : 'This crime was not done by one of us.' "

"Who could have done it ?" said Bob, musingly. "Is there no living person who would be likely to do such a deed ?"

"He must have had some object," suggested Don.

"True," said Jack, "and if it had not been one of us here, then those remaining might have looked in the direction of Snicker—provided, of course, he had not fled away."

"Milky Whey, in a fury, might kill a fellow."

"No, he is too much of a coward. We must look elsewhere."

"And, against our will, turn back to Mulberry Cork," said Bob ; "and see, here he is, coming in at the gate, as if he had been summoned to answer for his crime."

"Say for *the*, and not *his*, crime," said Jack, almost imploringly. "Put yourself in his place. Reared as he has been, with a hundred things to his prejudice, and yet possibly innocent."

"Generously spoken, Jack !" cried Don. "Cork is slouching our way. If he comes near enough to us, we ought to speak to him, I suppose ?"

"Certainly," assented Jack. "it is the time-honoured custom of our country to treat all people as innocent until they have been proven guilty."

CHAPTER CXXXI.

THE SEARCH IN THE WOOD.—ADJOURNED INQUEST.

MULBERRY CORK walked with his eyes upon the ground, oblivious of the many curious eyes upon him, until he was brought up short by Jack Ford hailing him.

"We have been wondering where you went to after breakfast," he said.

Cork stopped within a few feet of the four friends, glancing quickly from one to the other, and licking his dry, parched lips, ere he seemingly had the power to reply.

"I thought I would go down into the wood," he said. "There are a lot of people there, and half-a-dozen police. They won't let you go very near the spot where Hone was found."

"Did you particularly desire to see it?" asked Jack.

"I thought I'd like to," was the answer, given with a surly frown.

"What good would it have done you?"

"None perhaps—nor harm either. Most people I've known run off to see the places where murders have been committed."

"Well, what do the people say?"

"It is talked among them that it must have been a very strong man who hit him."

"A very strong *man*?"

"Yes. I heard a labouring chap say that he had seen the body at the inn, and *he* couldn't have give such a blow, unless he had a lot of beer in him."

"Did you hear if they have found the weapon?" asked Don.

"They ain't, I know," replied Mulberry Cork, "which is uncommon strange, for——" He stopped short, and bit his lip, flushing at the same time.

"Odd they have not found it?" said Jack, with his eyes closely scanning the embarrassed face of the boy.

"Yes," said Cork, with an effort, and a defiant nod of the head; "would you, if you had done it——"

"Which I could not."

"Say you had, then—by a miracle, if you like. Suppose, then, it was done with a stick, say; would you carry it about with you? No—the moment you killed a chap with it you would throw it away. Directly afterwards you *might* feel sorry you had done so, and tried to find it again so as to burn it, but in a wood like that you mightn't drop on it afore you heard somebody coming, and then what would you do? Why, run away, of course."

He was quite energetic—in a crude way, dramatic —as he laid before his attentive listeners the probabilities of the following of the crime. He spoke as one who had had experience of crimes of a similar nature, and was in a position to give the opinion of an expert. As he concluded, Jack abruptly rose to his feet.

"I think I shall stroll down. Will any of you come with me?" he said.

"I can show you the werry spot," offered Cork, eagerly. "Take you there as straight as a gun."

"Thanks," replied Jack, "but as you have already been there, we will not trouble you."

"You don't want my company. That's about it."

"Think so, if you like," answered Jack; "anyway, we wish to go by ourselves."

"Hang the lot of you!" hissed Mulberry Cork, violently. "Do you think I did it?"

How could they answer him? They could not tell him what was in their minds, nor deny that they involuntarily, and through the force of circumstances, associated him with the crime.

All that was left for them to do was to keep silent and walk away, and this expedient they promptly adopted.

They had got clear of the playground, and were just entering the wood when Mulberry Cork came tearing after them.

"You four!" he cried, derisively. "Leaders of the school, ain't you? Yah! A lot of mutton-heads. If you live for a thousand years, you won't prove who killed Hone!"

"Perhaps you know who is guilty?" said Jack, quickly.

"I think Hone committed *suicide*," answered Cork, with a strange leer, and then, positively laughing, ran back to the playground.

Jack strode into the wood, and his friends followed him. Ere he had gone far he pulled up sharp, and faced about.

"It seems too horrible to be true," he said, "but now I feel *certain* he did it."

Then he turned again, and hurried on, as one who flies from the presence of a hideous thing.

There was nothing much to be seen in the wood. The police were guarding the spot, and one of the chief officers had just arrived to inspect it. Stragglers, too, were coming in from Chippenham and the surrounding districts, but, as yet, there was nothing like a mob in the wood, as there would have been in a more populous district.

So the boys went on to Smudgem Bender, where they found a knot of people outside the Cowley Arms. The coroner, it seemed, was in the neighbourhood, and would expedite matters by opening the inquiry that afternoon.

While the boys were standing there listening to the remarks of the assembled people, a cab drove up, and a dark-faced man, of about fifty, got out.

"Is this the place where my murdered boy is lying?" he asked, "passing through Chippenham I heard of it."

Penny Bunn came rushing out of the inn, and grasped the stranger's hands.

"My *dear* sir," he exclaimed. "Mr. Hone, I believe?"

"Yes, that is my name," was the answer, curtly given. "Is what I have heard true?"

"My dear sir," returned Penny Bunn, "man is as

grass; he is cut down to-day, and gone to-morrow——"

"Will you be kind enough to come to the point without any cant or evasion? Is my son dead?"

"He is, sir, I fear."

"Then you are not quite certain?"

"Of course he is, sir. He was found last night—quite dead. He could not have been more so."

"And he is reported to have been murdered. Is that so?"

"I believe, myself, he has been slain," answered Bunn.

"Then," said Mr. Hone, "I shall be glad to know under what circumstances his life has been taken?"

"I will trouble you to come into the inn," said Bunn.

Chunder Loo now appeared. He first glanced at Mr. Hone, and then immediately discovered the presence of the four boys, which Penny Bunn had failed to do.

"Who gave you leave to absent yourselves from the Abbey?" he sharply demanded.

"Eh? What is the matter now?" demanded Bunn.

"Four of the boys are here without your leave," replied Chunder Loo.

Bunn glanced at the offenders, and sharply bade Chunder Loo not to interfere.

"They have my permission now to remain," he said, and disappeared into the inn with Mr. Hone.

There was that curious tigerish snarl of the upper lip to be seen on Chunder Loo's face, as he slowly wheeled round, and followed his principal into the Cowley Arms. Some of the bystanders stared, but they could make very little of the scene.

"Measter Bunn can be kind o' uppish when he loikes," remarked a labourer, and others solemnly nodded their assent to this criticism on the conduct of the schoolmaster.

"But I don't take much count of the black chap," said another man, by his dress probably a small dealer in cattle and pigs.

"Noa, he be too much loike a bad collie dawg."

Having ascertained that the inquest would be opened at three o'clock, Jack suggested that, as they had leave of absence, they should walk on to Chippenham, get a bit of luncheon there, and return in time to form part of the public in the court.

It would be better than hanging about, and Penny Bunn could have no chance of rescinding the leave he had given them.

At a quarter to three they were back again, and had just time to squeeze themselves into a crowded room, there never yet was a public place so full that it would not hold a few boys, when the coroner appeared, and the proceedings opened.

Twelve men of the labouring and small farmer classes had been got together. They were sworn in immediately, an inspector of police rose to ask that only one witness, beside himself, might be examined.

"There was no doubt," he said, "that a murder had been committed, but by whom it was impossible to say at present. All that would be necessary at present was evidence of identity, and a description of the injuries inflicted on the hapless boy. His father was present, and having seen his son would give the first portion of the requisite evidence."

He did not seem to be so deeply affected as he ought to have been under the painful circumstances.

The nature of the man was evidently hard, for in the midst of his evidence he spoke of the necessity of his getting back to town that night, as he had a very important business appointment early on the following morning.

"How like Hone," thought Jack.

It chanced that in the earlier stages of the inquiry, the coroner asked if any weapon had been found. The inspector of police replied that nothing of the sort had come to light, but the search for it would be renewed immediately after the court rose.

Chunder Loo, who had modestly, or cautiously, taken up a position against the wall near the door, immediately left the room, gliding out so quietly that his departure was not observed by anyone there.

Walking apparently at his leisure, he, nevertheless, travelled quickly, and was soon out of the village. On striking the wood he bounded up the narrow path with the swift silent step of a panther, and made his way to the Abbey gates.

There he stopped short a moment, and, drawing in a deep, long breath, became his ordinary self again. There were a few boys scattered about the ground, and he asked one of them "if Mr. Bunn had returned?"

The answer was "no," of course, and the question was but a preliminary to another. "Then, I suppose, Mr. Gubbles is still away, also?"

"Mr. Gubbles," replied the boy, "hasn't been out at all. He has been talking to us, and showing us all sorts of things, and has gone up to his room to study something."

Chunder Loo hastened into the house, and ascended to his room. Having taken the precaution to lock the door, he opened the drawer in which he had deposited the stick he found in the wood, and examined it carefully.

There was a deep, dark stain on the roughish knob at the top, and several reddish spots lower down.

It was a piece of holly, and there was a narrow band of silver round it, on which were engraved two letters—F. S.

"Let me think a moment," muttered Chunder Loo; "ought I to risk it? I think so. He will be better out of the way. Charged with the bigger crime who will listen to his talk about so small a matter as a lost cheque? Yes, it is a good thought— I will sacrifice him as a calf—equivalent for booby— on the altar of *my* safety."

He placed the weapon under his robe, and stole out again. Pausing in the corridor he heard a tapping sound in the attic above. It was, no doubt, Anthony Gubbles carrying on his studies.

From the Abbey to the wood was not a far cry, and the distance to the scene of the murder was but a few minutes swift travelling.

None of the idlers were there; they were all down at the Cowley Arms, where they could assuage their thirst, and get a little cheap excitement over the inquest at the same time.

Chunder Loo thrust the stick into the heart of a thorn-bush, and immediately was on the way to Smudgem Bender again.

In all, he had barely spent an hour in this performance, truly a creditable specimen of the activity of man.

The first stage of the inquiry was over, but the coroner had not long been gone, and all otherwise concerned had lingered for the inevitable "one drink," and a chat over the sad affair.

Chunder Loo was just in time to hear the inspector direct two of his men to return to the wood and renew the search for the weapon which might, according to the general opinion, be eventually found in its precincts.

Mr. Hone was gone, having given the requisite directions to an undertaker, who had appeared on the scene. The boys also had departed, but Penny Bunn was still there, washing down his sorrow with extra libations.

As Chunder Loo entered the coffee-room in which his principal was sitting with a number of the tradesmen and other inhabitants of the village, every eye was turned upon him. Penny Bunn frowned.

"I do not think," he said, huskily, "that this is a fitting time for you to thrust yourself upon me."

"Pardon me," said Chunder Loo, raising his eyebrows a little. "I do not understand."

"At this moment," replied Bunn, smiting the table with his clenched fist, "I am moved to the very depths of my soul by the memory of that dear boy who lies dead—here—in an inn, awaiting the last rites of mortal life!"

"Well?" said Chunder Loo, coolly.

"That being the case," pursued Bunn, amidst a breathless silence on the part of the rest, "I ask you again—why do you come here? You have crept like a small, venomous snake"—Chunder Loo started, and there was a sensible blanching of his skin under its swarthy hue—"like a snake, I say, worming your way into my domestic life, and marring it peace. Away, reptile, away!"

"Mr. Bunn," said Chunder Loo, "I am willing to excuse you, extraordinary as your language is, on the ground of your being intoxicated. It grieves me, as it will grieve your dear wife, to see you in this condition."

So cool, so insidious in his insults! It was maddening. Penny Bunn was on his feet, had thrust over a chair, and struck Chunder Loo full in the face, all in a moment.

The blood spurted from the nostrils of the wily Hindoo, as he drew back and thrust a hand beneath his robe.

But he withdrew it instantly, only to thrust it in again and bring out a handkerchief, which he applied to his face.

"You are a low dog," he said to Penny Bunn, who stood panting and glaring at him; "a *cur* to strike one born in India, and, therefore, not accustomed to your coarse fighting! *Go home*, and sleep off your drunkenness, and then I will talk to you."

His dress and dark countenance gave more dignity, perhaps, to his dramatic action than it was entitled to, and the whole scene made a strong impression on the rustic minds of his listeners.

They would have laughed at a bleeding nose in any other case, but it was a serious matter now.

Penny Bunn had half-sobered himself by his attack on the Hindoo, and the cool, cutting denunciation thrust at him did the rest.

"Chunder Loo," he said, in a low voice, "I was hasty, but you aggravated me. I have something to forgive in you. Let us cry quits."

"My answer is this," replied Chunder Loo, as he suddenly held up the forefinger of his right hand, stained with blood, and traced the figure of a moving snake in the air.

That was all he did, and he said no more, but wheeling round, vanished as if he had been a puff of vapour.

Not a word was said by the startled company until Penny Bunn, with a very white face, resumed his seat. Then the voice of the village barber was heard:

"I am glad I have not offended that chap."

"He is a strange fellow," answered Bunn, with a faint smile, "but he doesn't mean any harm. It is only his fun."

"Different people have different sort of jokes, I suppose," said the Smudgem Bender blacksmith. "When they lark in India, I should think they goes in for *murder!*"

Bunn smiled even more faintly than before, and rising, declared it was time for him to be going home.

A general break-up followed, and five minutes later

the inn was deserted by all the throng that had fore-gathered there after the inquest.

———

CHAPTER CXXXII.

THE WEAPON FOUND.—SNICKER IN HIDING.

THERE was a great cry in Smudgem Bender that night. The weapon had been found, and recognised as the property of Fontenoy Snicker. It was Bibbins, the watchmaker, who was prepared to swear to it.

"I've seen it in his hands a score of times since he came to live here. I noticed it particularly, because the band has been roughly put on, and the engraving ain't up to much. 'F. S.' stands for Fontenoy Snicker, too, I fancy."

The police went to his cottage, and asked the wife of the missing man if she recognised the stick. They told her, as in duty bound, that she need not say a word about it unless she chose.

All she did was to throw her apron over her head, and sob aloud:

"Oh, Jerry, Jerry, if you had stuck to the coal and 'tater line, it would never have come to this!"

Then there were communications made to the police about a certain day, which the reader will remember, when Snicker threatened some of the Lambs of Little-cote. The informants, among whom Mrs. Bibbins was prominent, could not say for certain who the boys were, but it was certain they belonged to the school.

"We've got him now," said one of the officers engaged in the case, as he walked away on the road to Chippenham.

"Yes," replied the other, sententiously; "when we've caught him."

The discovery of the stick left no doubt, in the minds of the police and the public, as to the identity of the murderer.

Fontenoy Snicker had a long, evil record to tell against him, even if he had not uttered that incautious threat in the hearing of the villagers.

Then the stick having been handed to the doctor employed by the officials, he tested it to see if it would tally in any way with the wound inflicted. It was seen the indentation indicating the cause of death, exactly corresponded in a cup form with the knob stained with the tell-tale blood.

One thing puzzled those engaged in getting up evidence, and that was—how came Snicker to be in the wood on that memorable afternoon?

Up to the discovery of the weapon in the thorn bush, it was believed that the ex-schoolmaster had fled the country. Was it possible he had been hiding in the wood throughout? And if so, where was his place of hiding?

Then, again, they had to think over the improbability of his remaining in the wood after the commission of his latest and more awful crime. Still, it was not impossible that he might be skulking there, and a party to beat the wood was organised for the following day. During the night a close watch was kept on all its recognised outlets.

There was a sensation in the Abbey among the elders, when the news of the finding of the weapon was brought there by Penny Bunn, who had lingered in the wood, in the evening of the day of the inquest, as it warded off a lecture he would have otherwise undoubtedly received from Miriam, for the lateness of the hour when he arrived home.

"It only wants the original schoolmaster of this place to be hanged for murder," said Miss Astracan, "and you, Bunn to be transported for a fool, to make the place live in the annals of the country."

This amiable remark was made the next morning at the breakfast table, where Chunder Loo sat as usual, with no signs of the affair of the day before, save a slight swelling of the tip of his aquiline nose.

"I should be well content to be transported, or even hanged, in your company," retorted Bunn, angrily.

"P.Y. !" exclaimed Miriam.

The door opened and Susan appeared.

"A policeman, sir," she said.

"A—a—a—a what?" stammered Penny Bunn, thinking that he might have done something to get *himself* into trouble.

"He wants to see you, sir."

"Very well. I'll come directly."

"If I could be of any service," said Chunder Loo, rising. "I——"

"Sit down," almost howled Penny Bunn. "I will not have your nose in all my affairs."

He flung himself out of the room, and Chunder Loo, resuming his seat, went on with his breakfast.

There was an officer in the hall, and he wished to explain to Bunn that at ten o'clock they would be beating the wood to endeavour to unearth the fugitive, Snicker, and they would be glad of any assistance he could render.

"All right," said Bunn, "I'll turn the boys out. They won't be sorry to have a hand in the job. I dare say they have done breakfast. I'll see."

"I think the smaller boys would only be in the way," suggested the officer.

"Then confine yourself to the bigger ones," said Bunn. "I have half-a-dozen here who will be as good as men to you."

He opened the door of the refectory, or dining-room, and peeping in, saw that the boys were about to rise from the table. Up to that time they knew nothing about the finding of the stick in the wood, not even having seen the usual purveyor of Abbey news, Susan.

Anthony Gubbles, in his capacity of third master, sat with them.

"Boys," said Penny Bunn, "your attention to me one moment, if you please. The man who murdered your unfortunate schoolfellow has been marked down, and is supposed to be now hiding in the wood."

There was a murmur of voices and an uprising from their seats. Mulberry Cork alone retained his, with a face that was scarlet for an instant, and then ashen.

"Last night," pursued Bunn, " or rather early in the evening, a stick was found in the wood with stains upon it. Little doubt exists that it was the weapon used by the murderer. Boys, I must say that, while I deplore the Abbey being in any way associated with such a deed, I am not surprised to find in the criminal your old master, *Fontenoy Snicker*."

The shouts of anger that burst from the boys' throats made the rafters of the old room ring again. It was some time before order could be restored. Mulberry Cork was, to all outward appearances, himself again.

"That monster," continued Penny Bunn, "is believed to be at this moment hiding in the wood. The police are about to have it beaten, and will be glad if some of you bigger boys will assist. Who volunteers?"

They all wanted to go, big and little, but the officer stepping forward, asked leave to pick out those who might be serviceable.

He selected about a dozen, among whom were Jack, Don, Bob, Tom, Walker, Philter, a stout-built, quiet lad named Noaker, and Gyp Tanner.

He advised them to arm themselves with thick sticks, and when in the wood not to stray away alone, but for two, and even three, always to be within sight of each other.

"The younger lads must be kept at home," he said to Bunn, " and the gates of the Abbey closed."

"It shall be done," replied Bunn. "Mr. Gubbles, I place the Abbey under your care. I will accompany my boys and protect them if occasion arises."

They would rather have gone without him, because he had such a happy knack of doing the wrong thing. But, as he had arranged matters, they could not offer any opposition.

As there was a good store of oaken faggots in the wood-house, the boys selected had no difficulty in getting their weapons wherewith to defend themselves, if attacked by the fugitive.

Jack advised them to have sticks of about the length and thickness of a policeman's cudgel.

"At close quarters," he said, " you will be able to use them better than anything longer."

They were marshalled at the top of the wood with a sprinkling of labouring men. Jack Ford succeeded in getting his closer friends, Don, Tom, and Bob, on either side of him.

There were two police officers to direct the rest, and at a given signal the whole party, in a line, marched into the wood.

Jack Ford had seen some beating for woodcock when he was in Ireland a year or two before, with his father. The cry of the beaters came back to his memory :

" Hi, cock-woodcock ! Hey, woodcock !" kept up so as to assure the keeping of the line as well as to rouse the game.

It flashed upon him that a similar cry might be of service now, so he started it.

" Hi, Snicker ! Ho, Snicker ! Catch Snicker !"

It was speedily taken up, and the wood resounded with the voices of men and boys, " Hi, Snicker ! Ho, Snicker ! Catch Snicker !" repeated over and over again, rising and falling in a strange, wild cadence, the like of which had never been heard among the beeches and elms and oaks within the memory of that parlous nuisance of village life, the oldest inhabitant.

CHAPTER CXXXIII.

UNEARTHED.—A SCENE OF TERROR AND DESPAIR.

THROUGH thorn bushes, briars and brambles, creeping under nut trees, and fighting their way through tangled grass and weeds went the boys.

Jack, the centre of the line, kept a close watch upon his younger friends, to see that they did not advance too far. Although he had no belief that they would unearth Snicker, he was one of those born leaders who have ever an eye to contingent possibilities.

" Hi, Snicker ! Ho, Snicker ! Catch Snicker !" resounded the mournful, and yet threatening cry in the wood.

" I wonder if he is really near enough to hear us?" said Don, who was on the left of his leader, Jack Ford.

" If he is, he guesses that he is wanted," was the grim reply of Jack.

" Close in a little, all ye Lambs," shouted Tom. " We are near the slope of—you know where."

They had come to the region of the cave, which, as we know, was in the heart of a mound. When Jack last visited it, in company with Don, he had left it open. Henceforth, the treasures being gone, it would be of service to a fox, perhaps, but not to the boys.

He was the first to catch sight of the mouth of the cave, and to his astonishment, the old plan of concealment had been adopted by somebody. It was closed up with a dead thorn bush.

Dead bushes, and trees for the matter of that, are no novelty in any wood, and this special one might have passed unheeded by a casual passer-by.

But those who knew what the blocking of the cave might mean, had good reason to marvel.

"All Lambs to the cave," shouted Jack.

The Lambs began to close in smartly, and there was a cry from the men mixed with them, to know what they were doing.

"It is Ford, our chief," they answered, "he has found something, and wants us."

So the men closed in with the boys, and among them was one of the police officers. On seeing nothing but a mound and a dead bush to gather them together, he waxed wroth.

"What's your game, calling us in?" he demanded.

"A few days ago," replied Jack, "that cave was open, now it is closed."

"What cave?"

"Pull out that bush and see."

The officer hesitated. The reputation of the Lambs had reached him, and he was afraid that even in a solemn search for a man charged with murder, they might still keep up their love of practical joking.

"That bush," said Jack, "blocks up the entrance to a small cave. I have been in it a score times, and more."

Then the officer, seeing Jack was in earnest, laid hold of the bush and pulled it out. The entrance to the cave was revealed.

"Is anybody in there?" demanded the officer.

"I won't be taken alive," answered a hollow voice, from within. "I'm inner—*inno*,—jigger it—cent of the crime!"

"Snicker," yelled the boys, in a chorus so fierce that it startled the men with them. What must it have been to the miserable wretch hidden in the cave?

"Let's have him out," cried Jack Ford; "he has been too cruel and mean to us in the old days for us to spare him now. Come out—*Murderer!*"

The men tried to stop the boys, but they were too nimble for them. Led by Jack Ford, they poured into the cave like a flood of water.

At the outset they could see nothing, and it might have gone hard with Jack if he had not kept his truncheon-like stick waving sharply to and fro, as a means of defence from assault.

When, as happened in a few moments, he could see with tolerable clearness, the ungainly figure of Fontenoy Snicker was seen crouching by the wall of the cave.

The men were creeping in now, but they had no real hand in the capture. It was to Jack Ford that the ex-schoolmaster yielded himself.

"If their wasn't a mob of you," he said, "I'd make some of you young war-*vermints* smart for this."

With Jack on one side and Don on the other, holding him by the collar of his coat, he was eventually led out of the cave, where the police-officer practically received him with open arms, and placed around his wrists, the unholy order of the criminal, in the shape of a pair of iron bracelets.

"There ain't no need for them things," he pleaded. "I'll go quietly. It ain't much of a job I'm charged with. I found the cheque——"

"Blow the cheque," answered the officer, "that's nothing. You are wanted for the murder of the boy!"

It must have been a most marvellous piece of acting, or the outcome of complete ignorance of the crime, that expression on the face of that long, but much deserving suffering Snicker.

"For—the—*murder*—of a boy," he said, with a pause between each word. "What boy?"

"One of your old pupils. Hone, by name."

"I commit murder?—*I*—it ain't reasonable nor possible. *I'm too big a coward.*"

"Anyway, you are charged with it," said the officer, unmoved. "And all you say now will be given in evidence against you. So talk easy. Say as little as possible, and if you can manage it, get legal advice—right away."

Snicker stared at him blankly.

From the man, he turned to the boys, and with his dull, despairing eye looking at each in turn.

No hunted wolf, wounded to death, ever showed more hopelessness in his gaze than he did at that moment.

Then suddenly, a wild light set his eyes ablaze, and speaking rapidly, he poured out an appeal to them.

"Boys," he said—"Ford, Peebles, Drummond—all of you *know* that I dursn't commit murder. Where was it done, and how?"

"The body was found not a hundred yards from here," replied Jack.

"Stop a moment," interposed the officer, "this isn't the place to go into particulars. The prisoner will have all the information he wants at the police station! Some of you boys break away and let the others know we've found him."

It was not a pleasant sight for the boys to look upon Snicker in his misery and degradation.

The terrible nature of the crime with which he was charged might have repelled them at another time; but just then—much as they had suffered at his hands —their generous hearts were touched, and they were sorry for him.

"Come along," said Jack, and they bounded off, leaving the prisoner to the charge of the men.

Before they were out of sight, Snicker called out to them to return and save him. What a moment of triumph it might have been considered! But, pained and troubled, they only hurried on.

As soon as they had vanished, Snicker threw himself down upon the ground, and cried out that he would not be taken to prison.

But he had rough, strong men to deal with, and they dragged him to his feet, roughly bidding him behave himself, "and just come on quietly."

He had to yield to combined moral and physical force. Rising, he allowed himself to be led away, but it was with tottering knees, and they had to walk slowly.

The tidings of his capture sped on before him. A messenger hastened on to Cowley Arms, to hire a horse and cart to convey the prisoner to the police station. When he appeared on the outskirts of the village, all who could leave their work or their homes were there to greet him with yells of execration.

One alone was not there, and that was his wife. She, too, had heard the news, and was lying senseless on the floor of their little front room, unthought of, uncared for, but happily unconscious of the scene, as her husband, with a howling mob around him, was led by.

They did not throw stones at him, or threaten to adopt the American principle of lynching, but all that tongue could do they did. And he answered them not a word. He was past all that, and walked like a man in a dream.

He was put into the cart waiting for him. They had to lift him in, and it was driven away. Then the execrators and the idlers turned to the inn, and for hours kept high holiday in celebration of the capture of the man of whom the more fervent among them was already speaking as "that notorious murderer, Snicker."

CHAPTER CXXXIV.

AFTER THE STORM.—MULBERRY CORK TRIUMPHS FOR AWHILE.

AFTER the storm comes the calm. That afternoon there was a stillness in the Abbey not often found there during term time.

Penny Bunn and Chunder Loo, as persons present when Hone's body was found, had been called away to give their evidence before a local magistrate, so that the prisoner might be committed to prison without delay.

Anthony Gubbles took upon himself the care of the class-room.

"You have been idle long enough, boys," he said, "and you can do nothing to further the ends of justice. It will be well for you to endeavour to forget it all for awhile."

He knew it was impossible, but it was sound advice. It is not good for the young to be haunted with sadness, or the memory of sin. The boys were in a subdued frame of mind, and endeavoured to learn something; but, in a school sense, the afternoon was almost a blank.

But Anthony Gubbles was kind. He did nothing more than gently reprove them for their lack of attention, and he was himself in a thoughtful mood.

So were many of our friends, especially those who had entertained the idea of Mulberry Cork being the author of Hone's untimely end.

It had seemed hideous, and almost impossible from the first. It was to them doubly hideous and quite impossible now.

The general feeling was that ample amends ought to be made to the unjustly suspected boy.

In addition, the obligation lay in the fact that he had been all through pretty well snubbed as an undesirable addition to the school.

A desultory conference, and passing of comment from one to the other led to the suggestion that Bob Stockton should take the matter in hand, and express the general feeling in the matter.

Accordingly when the school work, such as it was, came to an end, many of the boys remained behind, and Bob Stockton, privately intimating to Mulberry Cork that he was wanted with them for a few minutes, was one of those who stayed.

Anthony Gubbles, apparently unconscious of anything unusual being on the board, left them, closing the door partly. It was not by accident that he did this, but by design, for he deliberately stayed outside to listen.

"We have asked you to stay," said Bob, addressing Mulberry Cork, who was lolling against a desk with his hands in his pockets, "to frankly ask your forgiveness for having for a moment suspected that you had any hand in the death of Hone. We could never quite believe it, and now we are sure that you are as innocent as any here. We hope you will meet us in the right spirit and forgive, as we would fain forget."

"All I have to say to you," replied Mulberry Cork, as he straightened himself up, "is that you are a blooming lot of jays. If I hadn't better eyes and ears than yours are, I would do without 'em. Whether you are sorry or not, don't matter to *me*. The next time one of you gets knocked on the head, just let me alone, will you?"

With a curious twist of the mouth and a curt laugh, he slouched to the door, inserted his toe in the opening, and drew it back. Then he shuffled away, leaving them to follow or not as they pleased.

"Polite, anyway," said Bob Stockton; "perhaps he did not think I greased him sufficiently."

"I can make nothing of a fellow like that," remarked Philter.

"There is a lot of *something* in him," said Jack, as he walked to the door.

Mulberry Cork was in a very insolent mood that night—at his very worst.

He made no attempt to fraternise with his schoolfellows, but slouched, or stalked by way of a change, about the playground. At times he would stop short and double himself up with laughter that was too loud to be entirely genuine. Then he would whistle and dance in an uncouth fashion prior to laughing again. Altogether, his manner of betraying his triumph was highly objectionable.

"Confound the brute!" said Gyp Tanner. "I should like to punch that hideous head of his."

"A strange creature," remarked Herbert May. "Do you know who he puts me in mind of? Danny Mann in the "Colleen Bawn." He seems to have so little good in him."

And they all felt that Herbert May, as some people would say, "entirely filled the bill."

Nor did the peculiar bearing of Mulberry Cork end there. By-and-by he began to talk. Jack Ford was the first recipient of his verbal bounty.

"Fancy you," he said, as he drew up to him and looked him insolently in the face—"*you*, the boss of this show—the leading copper of the place—going on the wrong tack! It makes me laugh, it does."

"I believe I have been on the wrong tack, but even now I may be wrong."

"What d'yer mean by it?"

"Snicker isn't proved guilty yet. There may be a hundred things in his favour. For my part, I *don't* believe he killed Hone."

"Well, that belief makes you a bigger jay than ever."

"If you call me a jay again," said Jack, serenely, "I'll pull your ears till you howl an apology."

Mulberry Cork looked as if he were about to try his luck at another verbal shot, but altered his mind, and softly whistling, walked away.

After this he adopted what may be termed a general plan of annoyance, calling out to nobody in particular, a variety of names—"mugs" and "jays" being most prominent.

Even after they had retired for the night, and were in their beds, he had the audacity to come to the door and derisively shout:

"All the little mugs in bed, are they? Bless you, my children."

And off he went chuckling.

"I can't make him out," said Don.

"He is a fool, and doesn't know it," replied Jack. "Good night, dear boys."

CHAPTER CXXXV.

SNICKER COMMITTED FOR TRIAL.—ALARMING ILLNESS OF PENNY BUNN.

IT was almost certain that Fontenoy Snicker had been hidden in the cave from the time he first disappeared. If so, the question arose: who had supplied him with food?

Furthermore, how did he learn that he would be wanted for that cheque affair? And finally, how was it that he obtained possession of the cheque at all?

These things were problems to Jack and his friends, and in vain did they seek solution by talking over the subject.

But Jack had ideas in his head which he did not vent before his friends. Having made one mistake, as he thought, in suspecting Mulberry Cork, he felt it would be only right to be exceedingly wary ere he gave expression to another.

Now Jack had one good friend in the school who was an adult, and that was Anthony Gubbles.

Of late he had been, on more than one occasion, invited to the room occupied by that gentleman, and in the course of this present chapter, we will accompany him thither.

But first of all we will briefly state how Snicker was dealt with in the police-court.

He was brought up, and at the outset, fervently denied his guilt. He was cautioned by a kindly magistrate to say as little as possible, but to get legal advice. But he would talk.

Having insisted on making a statement, he plunged into the affair of the cheque, declaring that it had been given to him by a "party," whom he believed to be his friend, to get changed. All that he had received was his bare expenses, and in the list of his charges, some of the items had been disputed, and were still unpaid. He was, therefore, out of pocket by the transaction.

Furthermore, this same friend had warned him that he would be arrested, and had induced him to hide in the cave, while the whole affair would be explained and settled. Snicker was sure that in due time the explanation would be forthcoming.

As for the murder, he was not even aware it had been perpetrated until he was arrested.

The stick found in the woods was his, he admitted it like an honest, truthful man, but he had dropped it as he hurried to his hiding-place, where, as he pathetically stated, "he had passed a time that seemed to run into months of darkness and misery."

On being asked if he would name his mysterious friend, he hesitated, and said, that for the present he would not, but leave it to his honour to come forward and act honourably.

This statement was received with murmured derision —at once suppressed—by the spectators in the court, and he was committed to take his trial at the next county assizes. This was but anticipating the verdict of the adjourned inquest, when the jury recorded, "Wilful murder," against him.

He asked for his wife to be allowed to see him, under the usual restrictions, and permission was given him. Accordingly, Phœbe, in a tearful, hand-wringing condition, visited him in prison, and to her care, he entrusted the following pencil-written letter:

"To Chunder Loo, Esquire.
"Respected Friend,

"Knowin as you was true to your word in all things, I will ask you to come forrard and do as you would be done by in two matters, first giving me the aneckdote (he meant antidote) to what I has inside me, and next, to admit that you was the party as sent me to London with that ere check. I don't bear no spite aginst you, but look up to you as I have done ever since I had the plesure of making your ackquaintance. I respects you more than anny livin' man, so hoping as you will come forrard at once, I remains, your well-wisher,

"Fontenoy (allus Jerry) Snicker."

He impressed upon his wife the necessity of observing great secrecy in delivering this letter, but he did not entrust her with the nature of its contents.

Phœbe, with a fresh burst of tears, promised to do so, and left him, a mournful specimen of troubled womanhood.

As her ideas of secrecy were rather limited, she carried out her instructions by going straight to the Abbey in the evening, and asking to see Chunder Loo.

Susan, who answered the door, was in a flurried state, but she promised to deliver the letter as soon as possible.

"Mr. Chunder Loo," she said, "is out, and master is took bad with colic or something. I can't stop a moment."

Mrs. Snicker departed, and Susan, as a further assistant to secrecy, laid the letter on the table of the hall, and then rushed back to the dining-room, where Bunn was in a state bordering on collapse, no shamming this time, with Mrs. Bunn and her aunt ministering to him.

Lying limp in his accustomed easy-chair, his face white as the lily, and his eyes open and staring, he presented a woe-begone figure to the eye.

Miriam was really alarmed, and the better part of her womanhood was to the fore.

"P.Y., dear," she was saying, as Susan appeared, "make an effort to rally. It is only a passing indisposition."

"It is a passing away indisposition," he murmured; "leave me to die in peace."

"I think he ought to have another emetic," said Miss Astracan. "I am certain he has accidentally taken some form of vegetable poison. I remember one of my orphans eating fungi he found in the coal cellar, under the impression he was partaking of mushrooms. The symptoms are precisely the same."

"Another emetic," moaned Bunn, "would bring about a dissolution of my entire anatomy. Woman, try one on yourself."

"P.Y.," pleaded Miriam, "you must be patient with dear auntie. She means everything kindly. We all feel for you. Look at even poor Dolphus, curled up on the rug. I never saw a dog so completely heart-broken."

"Blow Dolphus," said Bunn, with feeble ferocity. "hang him up by one of his hind legs. I will not be—be emeticated any more."

"Well, then," said Miss Astracan, "would you prefer a little cold gin? I have some left in my bottle."

Penny Bunn softened at once.

"I think," he murmured, "if I tried hard, I could swallow about half a tumbler full—mix it half-and-half—not too weak."

So the bottle was fetched, and while Miss Astracan was preparing the required dose, Bunn looked into the face of his wife, and smiled.

"I am not breaking my pledge," he said; "the Rational Temperance teetotalers allow it to be imbibed medicinally."

"For this once, P.Y., you may have it," she answered.

And he had it, struggling so manfully to get the remedy down, that the entire contents of the glass slipped down his throat like an oyster.

The effect was at once apparent.

A little colour appeared in his cheeks, and he softly smiled. In addition he pressed the hand of his wife.

"The antidote has been found," he said; "repeat the dose, and I believe I shall be able to sit up."

Under the circumstances they could do nothing less, and Penny Bunn, having been favoured with a repetition of the half-and-half mixture, sat up in his chair, and joyously declared that the worst was over.

But on being questioned, he could not recall having partaken of anything that could have induced the sickness, and for the time, at least, the origin of it was a mystery

While the sufferer was thus being restored, the letter in the hall had been discovered by Jack and Anthony Gubbles, who had just entered the Abbey from the playground where they had met.

Anthony Gubbles had been for a quiet stroll, and on finding Jack there alone, invited him to spend an hour with him in his chamber.

Jack recognised the familiar handwriting the moment he looked at it.

"A letter from Snicker to Chunder Loo," he exclaimed; "what does that mean?"

Anthony Gubbles picked up the envelope and looked at the scrawling hand with a curious eye.

A SPLENDID SCHOOL STORY.

NEVER BEFORE PUBLISHED.

By E. HARCOURT BURRAGE,

Author of "Ching Ching," "Monkey Mat and Roving Dick," "The Brave Boy of the Basilisk," &c.

NO. 19. A Handsome Coloured Plate Presented with Every Number.

The LAMBS of Littlecote

A SPECTACLE MORE AMUSING THAN EDIFYING.

PRICE ONE PENNY.

ALDINE PUBLISHING CO., 9 Red Lion Court, Fleet St., and 4 & 5 Crown Court, Fleet Street, London

"Chunder Loo is out," he said; "I saw him going along the Chippenham Road, walking at a smart pace. It was half-an-hour ago. He won't be back for some time."

He stopped short and looked at Jack. A grave expression was on his face.

"It is an unpardonable offence," he said, softly, "to pry into a letter addressed to another, or to read one, even if it lies open before your eyes, unless you have permission to do so. But there are exceptional cases where it is pardonable. Ford, I am going to see what is inside this envelope, and I trust in you not to say a word until I give you leave to speak."

"I will do exactly as you wish, Mr. Gubbles," replied Jack.

Then Gubbles put the letter in his pocket, and ascended to his room.

———

CHAPTER CXXXVI

IN THE LABORATORY.—PLANNING A MINE FOR THE ENEMY.

THE attics of the Abbey varied in size, and that which Anthony Gubbles had selected for his scientific labours, was one of the largest.

One end of it was hidden from view by a curtain, attached to a wire cord, tightly stretched across the room. Behind that curtain was his bed, hidden from the view of a visitor.

By this arrangement the visible portion of the chamber was that of a laboratory. The fittings were those of a scientific nature, amateurish to an extent, but pleasing to the eye of a boy like Jack Ford, whose natural gifts embraced a love of the mysterious, and a desire to search into the hidden secrets of life, and of things inanimate also.

By the window were two small retorts and a number of curious-looking instruments, pretty to the eye, and doubtless of good service in the hands of an experienced man.

On the walls were a few pictures, mainly of the class we find in geography and similar books, and about a dozen volumes in a small hanging bookcase.

The furniture consisted of a second table, in the centre of the room, the other was by the window with the retorts upon it, and two very old lounging chairs.

"Sit down and shut your eyes," said Gubbles, "if you do not wish to be a party to my nefarious proceedings."

Jack smiled and sat down, but he did not shut his eyes. He was rather curious to see how his companion would go to work.

In a vessel of copper Gubbles placed a small quantity of water, and screwed upon the top a lid with a pointed spout. Then he lighted a spirit lamp, and placed it under the vessel.

In two minutes the water was boiling, and steam issuing from the spout. Holding the envelope over it, he speedily softened the gum that fastened up the envelope, and then opened it.

Having read the letter through, he took a memorandum book from a drawer in the table, and made a copy of it therein. Then he handed the letter to Jack.

"Read it while I slip downstairs to see if Chunder Loo has returned."

He was absent but a minute, and on coming again into the room, he said:

"Our friend has not put in an appearance at the Abbey yet. What do you think of that letter?"

"It clears up the mystery of the cheque," answered Jack. "Chunder Loo must have stolen it."

"Just so. But who is to prove it?"

"Snicker——"

"No, Ford. Snicker would not help us, anyway. Who would take the word of a man on his trial, or let us say, charged with murder? Would you?"

"I do not think Snicker's word generally was worth much. But I believe he writes the truth here."

"I think so, too, Ford, but proof must be found before we could act. Besides that point there is another. I fancy that something more serious than purloining a cheque will one day be laid to the charge of Chunder Loo."

"Snicker says here," said Jack, referring again to the letter, "that he lost his stick in the wood. He does not say how, but he *may* have put it down and forgotten it."

"He writes that he lost it in his haste," replied Gubbles, "and it is possible. But he will have great difficulty in getting a jury to believe that yarn. He has a bad character, and he has threatened you boys. Do not forget that these things incriminate him to a considerable extent. They are very helpful to the prosecution."

"But say that he *did* lose it," urged Jack, "and that Chunder Loo found it——"

"Why should Chunder Loo murder Hone?" interposed Gubbles. "He would not, in any case, commit a crime without having some strong inducement—hatred, or prospect of gain. He had neither in connection with Hone. Furthermore, I have ascertained beyond a doubt that Chunder Loo was not in the wood at the time the murder was committed."

"Then I am more puzzled than ever," said Jack. "I know what Snicker is capable of, but I do not believe he dare commit murder."

"That thought is a credit to your shrewdness. But you may be mistaken."

"I had no idea, Mr. Gubbles, that you were bothering much about anything outside your work here."

"I am fond of investigations," was the reply, "of course, I am only an amateur in the detective line, but I think, with your help, that the mystery of this murder will be cleared up."

"I don't see what use I can be," said Jack.

"There are two persons in the Abbey on whom we must keep a close watch—the boy Cork, and Chunder Loo. I suspect the boy knows something, if he did not actually commit the crime."

"It lies, then, between him and Snicker?"

"Perhaps."

There was a peculiar significance in the tone of this short but expressive reply. Jack looked up with a surprised face.

"If," he said, "it is neither Cork nor that Hindoo snake—I can't help hating him—then it must be Snicker."

"No."

"Who outside them could it possibly be?"

"Time will tell perhaps. I hope so."

Anthony Gubbles, who had been standing, hitherto, now took the unoccupied chair, and drew it up to Jack's side.

"Mr. Bunn was taken very ill to-day," he said.

"So I heard," answered Jack; "but——"

"He was poisoned."

"*Poisoned?*"

"Not to kill outright, but to worry and annoy. The man who administered the dose was Chunder Loo."

"You know that for certain?" said Jack, in a hushed way.

"As certain as one can be without seeing the thing done. I believe he intends to favour me with a similar attention, and with your aid I propose to lay a trap for him."

"He may poison us all one day."

"Not yet, at all events. Now, to-night I wish you to watch your opportunity to fill a water-bottle in the presence of Chunder Loo. You can say, in a casual way, that I have asked you to take it to my room. Then you must, with assumed carelessness, leave it—say in the hall—for a time, so that this swarthy scoundrel can, if he chooses, put something into it. When he has had time to do so, bring the bottle to me, and in two hours I will tell you what the poison is that he's using."

Jack readily undertook the task set him. It was simple, and on that account the more likely to succeed. Anthony Gubbles handed him the letter from Snicker.

"It is closed again, so that no eye can detect it has been opened, although it might be, with aid of the microscope. See that you are not observed when you place it on the table, and hold aloof from me till to-morrow. I will take good care to be absent from my room when you bring up the bottle."

Jack left him then, and finding the hall quite deserted, placed the letter on the table, and sauntered into the playground. Some of the boys were there. Others had taken advantage of the indisposition of the schoolmaster to wander into the wood.

Jack joined Herbert May, who was seated on the broken part of the wall reading a book.

"As usual," said Jack; "deep in the fanciful realms of poetry?"

"No," replied Herbert, "quite a different style of thing. I found this book in the schoolroom. I wonder whose it is?"

"'The Newgate Calendar!'" exclaimed Jack. "A little out of our style of thing, isn't it?"

"It is a horrible book," said Herbert, closing it. "I was fascinated for a few moments by it, as I might have been if I had come across poor Hone lying dead in the wood."

"Is there no name on the fly-leaf?" asked Jack, pretty well assured in his own mind, as to the identity of the owner.

"There is a name," said Herbert, "but I don't know it, and never heard it before."

He opened the cover, and read aloud as follows:

"Berry Mawston—his book. Whosomever takes wot isn't his'n, will be sure to be cotched and sent to prison."

"A time-honoured warning," said Jack, "and the writing is as cruel as it can be. I fancy the book belongs to Cork. And here he is, on the lookout for something."

Mulberry Cork emerged from the Abbey as he spoke, and cast a quick glance around. Espying Herbert with the book in his hand, he came on to the wall with a run, and when near enough, made a furious grab at his book, as it proved to be.

"Wot yer doing with that?" he demanded. "Is it yours?"

"No," replied Herbert, as he quietly yielded it up.

"Then wot yer mean by boning it?"

"I have not boned it, as you elegantly express yourself," answered Herbert. "I simply borrowed it for a few moments. *We* do not object to that sort of thing here."

"But I do," said Cork, as he tucked the book under his arm. "You let my things alone, will you?"

"You need not be so violent," remarked Jack; "nobody here wants to read such villainous stuff as that. We are not personally interested in criminal records, if you are."

The words were out before Jack had fairly thought of their portent. He would have hesitated in a cooler mood ere he gave utterance to such an unmistakable insinuation, especially to Mulberry Cork, but the thing was done.

He was not, even when he realized the force of his

utterance, in any way prepared to see the result take such a striking form.

Mulberry Cork stepped back a pace, and stood in a stooping attitude, with his eyes gleaming with the lurid light of a mass of glowing embers in a cavern. His nostrils spread out until his nose was like that of a negro, and his upper lip was twisted into an ugly snarl.

"You say too much, you Ford," he said. "What do you know about me? Out with it!"

"I know nothing about you," replied Jack, keeping cool, "but I should very much like to know who and what you are."

"Would you?" sneered Cork, "then you won't, Mr. Double Extra-clever. Keep your mouth shut, will you? If you don't, it may be closed for you!"

"Go away," said Jack, contemptuously. "Who cares for the threats of a miserable hound of your breed?"

Cork, with a frenzied gesture, hurled the book at Jack's head. It missed its mark, and flew over the wall, down to the depths below.

He plunged forward to stop it in its flight, and would have gone headlong over but for Jack, who seized him by the collar of his coat, and jerked him aside, so that he fell upon his back.

"You mad fool," he said. "If you can't control your temper, don't ventilate it at the risk of your life."

Cork got up, and peered over the wall in search of his book. It had passed out of sight, being hidden among the brushwood below.

"Let it lie there," advised Herbert May, kindly enough. "Reading horrible stories of depraved people won't help you, anyway."

"I'll read what I like," growled Cork.

"As you please, of course," said Herbert.

He and Jack walked away, leaving Mulberry by the wall, staring below as if he had lost a treasure in the depths of the sea. They saw him no more that night.

CHAPTER CXXXVII.

THE WATER-BOTTLE.—NEWS OF LINGO.

JACK managed so well with the task entrusted to him, that it was, in the preliminary stage, completely successful.

Chunder Loo did not return until nine o'clock, and as he passed into the hall, Jack appeared with a water-bottle, already filled, in his hand. Behind him was Tom Drummond, to whom he turned, and said:

"Mr. Gubbles asked me to take this to his room. I suppose he is not in a hurry for it. I will get that book for you."

He had promised Tom no book, but his astute friend, seeing some motive in the remark, merely replied:

"All serene. Where will you bring it to?"

"The class-room," answered Jack, as he put the bottle on the hall table, and sped upstairs.

Tom sauntered off to the class-room, and Chunder Loo was left alone. He waited until the boys were out of sight and hearing, and then, after a sharp look around, he brought out a small packet from a pocket in the inside of his robe. With a steady hand he opened it, and shook a small quantity of powder into the water-bottle.

It was colourless, and instantly dissolving, left no trace of its presence.

With his snarling smile upon his face, Chunder Loo glided to the sitting-room, where he found Miss Astracan.

"Alone?" he said.

"Bunn has been eating something that disagreed with him and has gone to bed," replied Miss Astracan. "Mrs. Bunn is with him."

"Temperance ought to be cultivated in eating as well as in drinking," said Chunder Loo.

"If all were like you, Mr. Chunder Loo," said Miss Astracan, "what a peaceable world it would be."

"I am a sinner with the rest," said the Hindoo, rolling his eyes, sanctimoniously; "but perhaps I might have been a better man if I had met you earlier in life. Oh! Miss Astracan, you are a charming woman!"

"Go along with you," said Miss Astracan, simpering.

"I mean what I say," continued Chunder Loo. "In the land which gave me birth—which you may have heard is India—men wisely love the woman who is—pray excuse me if I imperfectly express myself—in *full* condition. My people are no lovers of bones. Miss Astracan, I adore you!"

There was a wildness in his eye, not observable when he first entered the house. His face shone, and he had the appearance of a man who has imbibed freely and been suddenly overcome by a change of atmosphere.

As for Miss Astracan, she was staggered, but like a woman, rose to the occasion.

"Mr. Chunder Loo," she said, "it was my intention never to marry, but if—if—you *mean* it——"

He was by her side in a moment, and after a little manoeuvring, got his arm about a third round her ponderous waist.

"I must consult the head fakir before making a final proposal for your sweet hand," he murmured, "but I am sure he will put no obstacle in the way. Meanwhile, let us be happy in our love."

And then he kissed her.

Having got so far along the rose-strewn road of love, he withdrew to the opposite chair and sat down, waggling his head about in the strangest manner.

"I came home sober," he said, "but the intoxication of love is upon me. Excuse me a moment while I survey my happy lot."

He closed his eyes, and contemplated for about six seconds. Then a slowly-developed sound emanated from him, rising up to about G sharp, and then dying away.

Miss Astracan struggled out of her chair and waddled up to him.

"Chunder," she said.

He answered with a repetition of the sound.

"He's asleep and snoring," she said. "What a rum young man he is. But I don't care; rum or not, black or white, he's proposed to me, and if he doesn't come up to the scratch, I'll bring an action for breach of promise against him."

Nodding her head slowly, she waddled from the room and left her unlooked-for lover to sleep in peace.

It was fully three hours later when he awoke and found himself in the dark. The lamp had burnt itself out, and there was an unpleasant smell of smoky wick in the room.

Chunder Loo sat and thought out the situation until he had recalled, in a somewhat imperfect fashion, his recent exploit. Something between a curse and a growl broke from his lips.

"I," said he, with a savage wave of his arm, "though born in India, am as big a fool as any of them when I step over the border. It was the stuffiness of this accursed room that did for me."

He felt his way to the door, opened it, and went into the hall. There he paused and listened. With the exception of the scratching of rats behind the wainscoting, there was not a sound to be heard.

"A ghostly place—a dismal den," he muttered ; "but when the time comes it will *burn!*"

Creeping cautiously onward, he found the staircase and ascended it. The road to his room was easy.

He entered it, found the matches and obtained a light.

In the far corner of the room Mulberry Cork was sleeping, and he only just glanced at the boy.

"The fire-water of the white brave," he muttered, with a dry smile, "induces thirst."

There was a water bottle and the usual tumbler on the washstand. He poured out some of the liquid and tossed it off. Then throwing off his clothes, he crept into bed.

It could not have been more than half-an-hour afterwards, when there was a clamouring at the door occupied by the schoolmaster and his wife. They were both asleep, but after a struggle with the drowsy god the former succeeded in awakening.

"Mr. Bunn, Mr. Bunn!" cried a voice outside.

"Wha—a—a—at is it ?" asked Bunn, his teeth rattling together as if they were castanets in experienced hands.

"Mr. Chunder Loo is dying," was the reply, "and rolling on the floor, and a groaning as if to bust hisself."

"It's Cork, my dear," said Bunn.

"I hear," was the muffled answer from Miriam; "go and see what is the matter with that poor man."

"My dear—it was but a few hours ago——"

"If you don't go, P. Y., I must."

"I'll go," said Bunn, with a groan.

He struck a light, and having put on a dressing gown, the wedding gift of his wife, he opened the door. Mulberry Cork stood there, white and trembling.

"Hear him," he said, in a hollow voice. "He's got a pain that twists him about like a bloomin' snake. He's on the floor with all the clothes wound about him !"

As Bunn stalked along the corridor, an unwilling agent in a charitable business, he saw a light coming down from the attics. It was in the hand of Anthony Gubbles, who had no covering beyond his night-shirt.

"I have been awakened by a disturbance," he said. "I trust it is not fire ?"

"Chunder Loo is ill," briefly explained Bunn.

They entered the room together, where the Hindoo lay writhing on the floor, almost hidden from view by the bed-clothes which he had twisted about him.

Gubbles, with a strength one would not have given him credit for, picked him up and threw him upon the bed.

Then he removed the clothing, and Chunder Loo, in a tight-fitting garment of brilliant red, lay revealed.

He was now seemingly conscious of visitors for the first time, and made an effort to pull himself together. Gubbles asked him to locate the pain he was enduring.

"It is nothing," replied Chunder Loo, "and will soon pass away."

"You must have been eating or drinking something to upset you. Hey ! what is this ? The water-bottle is half empty. I have had my doubts of the purity of the well. The contents of this bottle ought to be analyzed. I am sufficient chemist to do it."

"I have not drunk any water," answered Chunder Loo, the perspiration induced by pain standing upon his brow.

"For all that," coolly answered Gubbles, "analyzing it won't do any harm. It will give me an hour's amusement to-morrow."

"I drank some water shortly before I was taken ill," said Penny Bunn, "from a bottle in the dining-room."

"It is in the water, depend upon it," remarked Gubbles.

"I am quite well now," said Chunder Loo, but his looks belied his speech. "And if the water is to be analyzed, I would rather have it done by a professor."

"As you please," returned Gubbles, as he replaced the bottle on the stand.

"It was kind of you to respond so readily to the call of my young friend," continued Chunder Loo. "It was a passing indisposition. I am better now."

"That being so, I will retire to my room," said Bunn.

He was not keenly sympathetic on Chunder Loo's account, and Gubbles also left the room without expressing any sentiment on the matter.

When the latter got back to his own chamber he sat on the side of the bed for awhile, laughing silently, until every vein on his forehead was swelled almost to bursting.

And after he was gone Chunder Loo bade Mulberry Cork close the door, and bring him the water-bottle from which he had drunk.

The boy obeyed him, and he held it up to the light, looking at it steadily for a few moments.

"Empty that thing out," he said, abruptly. "Gubbles is right. The water is not good."

When Mulberry had performed this office for him, he told the boy to go to bed and put out the light.

In the dark he lay thinking for awhile, puzzled and bothered. He knew now that the water-bottle he had designed for Anthony Gubbles's use had by some means found its way to his room, but how it came there he could not decide. Finally, he came to the conclusion that Susan must, in the performance of her ordinary duties, have brought it there, and with a good round curse on her head he curled himself up, as much like a snake as the body of a man permitted of, and fell asleep.

In the morning Gubbles told Jack of the affair, and from Jack it was conveyed to Don, Bob, and Tom, and they all enjoyed the joke, which had taken the form of a deserved punishment.

Gubbles had come to the conclusion that the shortest way to get at the nature of the poison—he had a firm conviction that Chunder Loo was using poison—would be to exchange the water-bottles of the two rooms.

This he had done when Chunder Loo was engaged in his impromptu love-making with Miss Astracan. The success of the idea was in every way complete.

By the morning post Don received a letter from his mother that was practically a bombshell to the four members of the inner circle.

After the usual long dissertation on home and local affairs, appeared the following startling statement:

"I saw your friend, the reverend gentleman, in our town a week or so ago. He was handsomely dressed as a bishop or dean, or one of the dignitaries of the Church. I am not certain which. He was riding in a carriage. I rather expected he would call, but we saw nothing of him. Give him our kind regards when he calls upon you."

It will be remembered by the reader that Lingo, when he first called upon Don's friends, was disguised as a clergyman, and now he was riding about in a carriage. And he had not called upon the Peebles', as he might reasonably be expected to do.

What did it mean?

And why had the boys heard nothing of him?

Was it possible that he had, after all, succeeded in getting away the treasure, and played the part of traitor by applying it to his own use?

It was only natural that the boys should entertain this idea, although both in conversation and in their hearts they strove against it.

After all he was but a man, and they really knew very little about him.

But what could they do if he had thus been false to them?

They could certainly, as Lingo would have put it, "blow upon the whole affair," by sending a full statement, which would be a confession, to Sir Charles Barstow, who would at once take steps to find out the whereabouts of Lingo, and deprive him of his ill-gotten gains, but it would practically be a revelation that would lead to trouble and confusion all round.

"I cannot see the wisdom of doing that," said Jack. "Lingo has been a good friend to us in the past—without his help the barring-out might have been a failure, and there may be sound reasons for his not communicating with us. We must fall back on our old line of action when in doubt and difficulty—just do nothing but *wait*."

And this was the opinion of them all.

CHAPTER CXXXVIII.

A CRICKET MATCH.—BUNN, AS USUAL, TO THE FORE.

FONTENOY SNICKER being committed for trial, the only other event connected with the tragedy, which for the time could be of public interest, was the burial of Hone.

He was laid in Smudgem Bender churchyard. His father came down to the funeral, arriving an hour before the interment, and departing immediately it was over. Penny Bunn also was there with a contingent of the boys, all, indeed, in the school who had a full suit of black clothes.

There was also a strong attendance of that class of

the public which never fail to get the most out of any public event, provided they can do so free of expense.

It was a glorious summer's day, and his old school acquaintances were deeply moved as they stood by the open grave, and thought of his untimely end, as compared with their brighter lot.

But emotions of this nature are happily transient. It would go ill with the world if our sorrowful thoughts were to be very lasting. In an astonishing short space of time, from the sentimentalist's point of view, the routine of school life was resumed.

Whatever might have been in the minds of many who play important parts in our story, there was no further outward expression of their sorrow.

Chunder Loo fell back into his old quiet stealthy ways, and apparently Miss Astracan had forgotten the love episode. Anthony Gubbles resumed his studies, and Penny Bunn returned to a buoyant, hopeful state.

In the evening the cricket practice was carried on with vigour, so that within a week Jack had got a very fair team together, and an advertisement was inserted in a local paper announcing that the boys of Littlecote Abbey School were open to a match on their own ground, or any other place within reasonable distance, with teams of their own *calibre.* Wednesday or Saturday afternoons they would be at liberty to play, the latter preferred.

Penny Bunn once more showed a strong interest in the peerless game, by being a constant attendant at practice, prudently confining himself to looking on, and occasionally making a comment of a nature that proved he was as ignorant of cricket as a man could be, and was never likely to rise above that dead level of dufferism.

In response to the advertisement, several acceptances were received.

Jack, as captain and secretary of the Littlecote Cricket Club, refused to close with some, on the ground of distance, and others on the score of age, as he did not feel they ought as yet to attempt to play adults, but he settled upon a team formed of the members of a school in Buffer Bassett, a small Wiltshire town, which time had reduced to the quietude of a village, about ten miles up the line. And after consulting Penny Bunn, he offered to play there.

Eventually it was arranged it should be so, and on the following Saturday afternoon, the 1.30 train was caught at Chippenham by all those at Littlecote who cared to go, and had the means to meet railway expenses.

In all, eighteen of the boys went, and Bunn and Gubbles accompanied them.

Very few people, seeing them for the first time, would have suspected, when viewing the joyous de-

meanour of the party, would have suspected that so many among them held deep secrets in their breasts, or had a thought or care to trouble them.

Much less would they have entertained the thought that tragedy had so lately visited them, and was still dogging their footsteps, to show itself again in startling scenes yet to be enacted in their midst.

Penny Bunn acted the part of schoolmaster and general boss to perfection.

He took the tickets, securing the usual reduction in the railway fares on taking a quantity, and away they went to Buffer Bassett.

Arriving there, a slight hitch occurred, in consequence of Bunn being unable to find the tickets.

He remembered distinctly putting them into one of his trousers pockets, loose and unhampered by any foreign substance in that receptacle.

But the tickets were not there, and after a close inspection of the lining, a gap in the stitches, creating a hole, was discovered.

The tickets must, therefore, have slipped through, but as he could not possibly have dropped them entirely, it occurred to Bunn that they must have slipped down his leg into one of the short Wellington boots he was wearing.

This proved to be the case, for the aforesaid boots were wide as a bell at the top, and the removal of the left one, and the subsequent revelation of the tickets therein, and also the sight of a hole in the sock as big as an orange, were matters of great interest to the Buffer Bassett station-master, the boys, and a few gaping idlers.

Bunn affected to regard the hole as something created since he left home. "Never in my life before has this misfortune befallen me," he said to Gubbles, as, with a cricket bat on his shoulder, just to let people see that he was heart and soul in the game, he left the station. "But it is the unexpected that always happens."

It was a commercial school team they were to meet, and the master of it was a Mr. Trully, a little, fat, fussy man, who met them a short distance from the station.

He cast a somewhat supercilious eye over the newcomers, and gave Gubbles good morning, addressing him as "Mr. Bunn."

The mistake was rectified, but already there were clouds in the air. Bunn did not take to Trully at all, but promptly in his mind put him down as an upstart, who would have to be treated with dignified coolness.

"Our cricket ground," said Trully, "is attached to my school. It is strictly private, but on occasions like this the public are admitted by card."

"Oh, indeed!" said Bunn. "Then a complete pack will admit fifty-two people."

"Sir !" said Trully.

" A jest, sir, nothing more," replied Bunn.

" I object to jests," returned Trully, "unless they are good, unobjectionable, and in season."

Anthony Gubbles said nothing. He did not even smile, but some of the boys were already on the grin.

" We shall have some fun to-day," whispered Bob to Don, who nodded and laughed.

They passed through the time-worn, worm-eaten old town, and came to a house that was as big as a small barracks, standing flush with the roadway.

" My academy," said Trully.

Bunn looked at it as he might have done at a work-house.

"There is a lot of it," he said.

This remark appeared to irritate Tully, for he rang the bell of the house with a jerk. The door was opened by a servant who had smudges all over her face.

" Mary," said Trully, " is this the way you answer the door ?"

" If you want me to be clean," replied the girl, " you must get missus to clean out the kitchen flues, instead of lying in bed, reading novels, while I'm made a born slave of."

Trully stalked through the house, followed by the Littlecote party. In the rear was a piece of grass ground, dotted all over with barren patches—playground and cricket-field in one.

There were two tents, one for spectators, and the other for the players and scorers. From the top of the first floated a flag. A number of boys, close upon forty, say, were grouped about, some in flannels, and the rest in ordinary attire.

Of the public, admitted by card, there was a conspicuous absence, not a single individual having wasted a strip of pasteboard to view the match.

Bunn was blind to his own shortcomings, but he had a quick eye for those of others. A good hand at bounce on his own account, he naturally objected to it in others.

"This match," he said, " does not seem to have excited the inhabitants around."

" I keep the place select," snorted Trully.

They were now within hail of the boys, a very priggish lot, judging by their demeanour. One of their number, a tall, lathy lad of fifteen, came forward, and speaking to the Littlecote boys generally, asked :

" Who's your captain ?"

Jack said he was, and the boy asked him to spin a coin for the innings.

Jack did so, and the Trullyite won. Then the boys went off to change their coats and jackets for flannels. One and all, to spare trouble, had come in their cricketing trousers, and Bunn, Gubbles, and Trully took their seats in the spectators' tent.

They were alone, as the boys on both sides preferred the open air, or the vicinity of the scoring tent. The wicket was already pitched, and no time was lost by the Littlecote boys in getting into the field.

The captain of the Trully team came out with one of his lot, walking with the air of a conqueror who was a stranger to defeat.

There was no doubt about it, the Buffer Bassett team were a stuck-up body of youngsters. The spirit of their master had permeated through them all.

This was evidenced by the way they held aloof from their opponents' friends. They all assumed a " standoff" air, common to small people who believe they are in inferior company.

Boys make fun of that sort of thing, or treat it with contempt. The Lambs of Littlecote adopted the latter *rôle*, and played it off to perfection.

Their two best bowlers were Tom Drummond and Don, the former a fast, with a high delivery, and the latter a slow, with a lot of break.

The Trully boys were showy in their batting, but their defence was really poor. Tom took a wicket his very first over.

" Your boys seem soon to tire," remarked Bunn, to the other schoolmaster.

" To do *what* ?" snorted Trully.

" To tire," repeated Bunn, calmly, " you would not find one of my boys so easily discouraged. Any one of them would have stayed at least another over."

Anthony Gubbles scraped his chin, with his forefinger, and smothered a smile. Trully stared at Bunn as if he beheld in him some monster intruding upon his sacred grounds.

" My good man," he said, tartly, " the boy *had* to go out."

Bunn smiled contemptuously.

" All my boys are taught to endure," he said, " but the high-class thing is one of my features in all that appertains to the education, and the cultivation, of the school."

" Really, sir," said Trully, " I must say that I was not prepared to hear such utter nonsense from you."

A shout in the region of the wickets, followed by a yell of delight from the Littlecote boys who had come to look on, stopped further argument between the two pedagogues for the time. Another of the Trully boys had come in, and been caught off Don's slow bowling. He left the wicket, and with a dejected air walked back in the direction of the scoring tent.

" See, there," said Bunn, to Gubbles, " one of our opponents is going out *before* he is even bowled."

" But he was *caught* out," exclaimed the exasperated Trully.

" It is the result of less stamina, and an imperfect

training," continued Bunn, ignoring the remark and still addressing Gubbles, who quietly said :

" I am no cricketer, and am no judge of the play."

" That," returned Bunn, "is a distinct loss to you. I am an enthusiast in the game, having been somewhat famous when I was young, both as a batter and bowler."

Trully shifted angrily in his seat. Gubbles rose up, and said he would join the boys by the other tent.

Thus the two schoolmasters were left together, and the game proceeded for a time without further friction in the tent. The third batsman made a fairly good stand, and put on ten runs before he, in trying a short run, ran himself out.

Bunn, on seeing Philter, who kept wicket, receive the ball smartly, and knock off the bails, indulged in a chuckle.

" Clever," he murmured, "very clever. It is the quickness of the hand that deceives the eye, as the conjurers say."

" Pardon me," said Trully, unable to contain himself any longer, "did you speak to me ?"

" I was merely uttering a thought on the expertness of my boys. Of course, if your representative thinks he is bowled and chooses to walk out——"

" One moment," said Trully, "let me explain. It is plain to me that you know nothing of the game——"

Bunn turned to him with his head on one side, and a sarcastic smile upon his lips.

" I fear," he said, "that you do not *quite* know the man you are talking to,"

" If I had," retorted Trully, "you would not have been here to-day. I can talk about cricket to a *player*, or a simple judge of the game, but when it comes to a man whose experience appears to me to be confined to skittles, I feel humiliated."

" I must ask you not to speak to me," said Bunn, "unless you recognize the fact that you are in the company of a *gentleman*."

Trully laughed, low and scornfully, and there was open war impending, when Gyp Tanner came up with a run from the field.

" Ford wants a handkerchief from his bag." he said, "and he has left the key at home, sir. He wishes to know if you will see if a key on your bunch will fit the lock."

" Where is the bag ?" asked Bunn.

" In the scoring tent, sir. There is another man in the field, I can't wait, but I will call to Jones to bring it to you."

Jones, on being hailed and told what was wanted, brought the bag to the tent, and Bunn took it upon his knees. He had no key that would fit the lock, and as he would not ask Trully to help him in the matter, and Trully stolidly refused to offer his own keys for the purpose, nothing was done.

Penny Bunn laid the bag on the ground, and renewed his attention to the game.

CHAPTER CXXXIX.

AN EXPLOSION IN THE CRICKET-FIELD.—A ROUSING UP FOR BUFFER BASSETT.

THE Trully boys were all out for forty-two, and as the last wicket fell, the whole of the Littlecote fielders came running towards the scoring tent.

It was the usual style of thing, but to Bunn it appeared to be something out of the common. For a long time he had not exchanged a word with his companion, but he now broke silence, saying :

" The match is over. Littlecote is victorious."

" This is only the first innings," replied Trully.

Bunn leant back, folded his arms, gazed up at the bright blue sky flecked with white patches of cloud, and smiled.

" I said, sir," repeated Trully, "that this is only the first innings."

" Surely," said Bunn, "after that humiliating exhibition of your boys you do not desire them to go on."

" They take the field now," grunted Trully, "and then we shall see what your boys will do with our bowling."

" Nothing," returned Bunn, "can retrieve this utter defeat. I say it, who ought not to, but it is entirely owing to my careful training that our team has been so easily, and completely, triumphant."

Trully took off his hat, and wiped his forehead with a big, red, silk handkerchief. Bunn, to show how much he was at his ease, produced a cigar and lit it.

It would have been well if one, or both, had now left the tent, but both doggedly kept their seats. Boys do not waste time between the innings, and in three minutes the Trully field was out, and Tom Drummond and Bob Stockton, at the wickets, prepared to do battle for their side.

Jack Ford, as became a modest captain, had put himself down to follow the third man out. He was in no hurry for the bag now, having only required the handkerchief to tie round his waist to assist him to run smartly, when fielding at long off.

He, therefore, did not look for it, but squatting on the ground with his own team, watched the two young batsmen with interest. He hoped to see them knock off at least half the runs before a wicket fell. Nor was he doomed to disappointment.

The Trully bowling was weak—it is a fact that cannot be overlooked—and there was nothing absolutely great in the speedy way in which the runs came.

Having "got their eye in," the young batsmen gave the fielders a lot of leather-hunting, and thirty-five runs were down to their credit, when Bob carelessly skied a ball, and was easily caught by the bowler.

"Bravo, bravo!" shouted Trully.

"Really," said Bunn, "a child could have caught it. No reasonable man would expect a batsman to go out for a miserable effort like that. Go back, Stockton."

"On my word," said Trully, rising in a heat. "You are too preposterous."

Bunn rose to his feet likewise, picking up the cricket-bag as he did so.

"I must ask you, sir," he said quietly, but firmly, "to explain yourself."

"I might give you the explanation," replied Trully, "but I fear I am not in a position to provide you with the intelligence to understand it."

This was going too far, and Penny Bunn, with a door-mat-beating movement, smote him with the long heavy bag. Moreover, he struck him in a region, which, if assaulted, leads to an entire absence of breathing power for awhile.

Trully was stout, and his physique could not but induce additional suffering.

He gasped and groaned as he staggered back, and every vestige of colour fled from his face, save at the tip of the nose, which suddenly assumed a vermilion hue.

"You—*you!*" hissed Bunn, "provide *me* with intelligence. *You*—a commercial pedagogue, as much beneath *me* as the stars are above—I mean as the earth is under the stars. I certainly must admire your cheek."

Then, just as Trully was getting back his breath, he smote him again, and in the same region.

Trully had no breath now. Only muscular action of the spasmodic order remained to him. He hit out in a round-arm fashion, and Bunn, who was in the act of replacing the bag upon the ground, received the blow on the most muscular part of his anatomy—the jaw.

Then ensued a scene, calculated to make the angels weep.

Hearing a commotion in the tent, the eyes of both lots of boys were drawn in that direction, and the spectacle of their two principals locked in a gladiator-like embrace, met their view.

A fight always meets with popular support, and even the little prigs of the Buffer Bassett School forgot all else for the time.

There was quite a stampede to the tent, accompanied by much shouting.

"Go it, Bunn."

"Let him have it, Trully!"

These were the cries of the respective youthful supporters, but instead of stimulating the fight, they brought the combatants to a sense of the position they were in.

They let go of each other, and, drawing apart, stood panting and glaring at each other, the boys, dumb spectators. Anthony Gubbles, in the far end of the field, was collecting specimens of Buffer Bassett grass.

"I think, sir," said Trully, who was the first to call back a semblance of composure, "that our best interests will be served by your retiring from the field."

"*Your* interest, sir," said Bunn, scornfully, "does not concern me. Boys, how goes the game?"

"Oh, we can lick 'em easy," replied Gyp Tanner.

"Lick 'em!" exclaimed Trully, with a curled lip; "the vulgarity of it!"

"Proceed with the game," said Bunn. "Give these upstarts a thrashing."

"I forbid the resumption of the game," cried Trully.

"It is really not worth playing such a lot of duffers," said Jack Ford. "Do not put yourself out, Mr. Bunn. Now then, all together, three cheers for Littlecote."

As the Lambs lifted their voices, the Trullyites groaned. It is astounding how soon the spirit of combativeness can be developed.

A nation may not like its monarch, but if any other monarch comes along and insults its king, they will fight for him, and fight well, too.

The more especially will they do so, if the insulting people have objectionable qualities.

All through the Trullyites had been offensive to the Littlecote Lambs. Not so much in word, as in air. They were, in short, an uppish, caddish lot, and if the meeting had been on neutral ground, there would have been "ructions" long before they actually took place.

The antagonism between the two masters led to the explosion. The cheering and groaning were the preliminary warning sounds.

It would have been better for Trully and his cubs, if he had thereupon curbed his rising wrath, and suggested an amicable parting. But he failed at the right moment to show a judicious spirit, and once lost, that moment came not again.

"Take your low-class boys off my ground," he cried.

"We will go in our own good time," replied Bunn. "Boys, after your noble exertions in the cricket-field, you must need a rest. Sit down awhile."

The Lambs promptly entered into the spirit of the thing. Though they had long odds against them, in case of a row, they were all eager to try conclusions with the Trullyites. There is nothing a sound-hearted boy detests so much as uppishness in those of their own age. When exhibited by their elders, they laugh at it.

They got their things together and squatted on the ground, with no more need of rest than an athlete as he rises from his bed in the morning. Trully drew aside, snorting, and his pupils gathered around him.

Anthony Gubbles came back, and stood for a moment regarding the two silent groups in surprise.

"Anything the matter?" he quietly asked.

"Sir," said Trully, with his nose standing up from his thrown-back head, like a model of the Eiffel Tower, "I have requested Mr. Gunn——"

"Bunn, if you please," interposed the owner of that euphemistic name.

"Gunn or Bunn," said Trully. "It is a matter of no consequence. Your insignificance——"

Bunn promptly cut short his offensive remarks by seizing Jack's cricket-bag and hurling it at Trully, with an aim so true, that he was bowled over like a skittle.

"Boys," he gasped, as he lay upon the ground in a semi-sitting position, head and feet up so that he resembled the letter V, "drive this scum from our ground."

Feeling bold in numbers, the Trullyites went for the scum, and the scum stood their ground so well, that in a few moments, half-a-score of the attacking party were lying prone upon Mother Earth, or holding their noses, or otherwise showing they had been smitten sorely.

Then Jack Ford called upon his followers to assume the offensive, and with a ringing cheer they dashed at their foes, and scattered them right and left.

Bunn, not to be behind-hand in deeds of bravery, hit Trully with the bag again as he was rising from the ground, and this time laid him out in a horizontal position, which he prudently retained, loudly calling upon his boys to fetch the police.

Away went half-a-dozen of the Trullyites, across the ground and through the house to bring the needed assistance, and those remaining, after being chivied by the delighted Lambs, made frantic efforts to get away.

Some broke through the thorn fence, and others, forgetting the tenter-hooks which Trully had fixed upon the gate leading to a lane, to keep out intrusive Buffer Bassett boys, climbed over it, tearing their nether garments in places vital to decency, and inflicting on their persons small but grievous wounds.

A few simply threw themselves down upon the ground and howled for mercy, the Lambs capering around them with the assumed ferocity of savages, but, of course, sensible to the code of honour that forbids a combatant to strike a foe when he is down.

Anthony Gubbles stood quietly surveying the scene, with an amused face, filled a briar-root pipe, which he lighted, and began to smoke with an air of enjoyment.

The victory was complete, and Bunn, panting with excitement, called the boys together.

"Gather up your cricket materials," he said, "and let us retire. This has been a glorious day."

It was soon done, and Jack, taking the command, desired the boys to fall in, as they had done before, on memorable occasions, in military order, two and two.

They did so with a smartness that was a revelation to Bunn.

Herbert May struck up the old song, with a slight variation.

"Cheer boys, cheer, no more of idle sorrow,
    We've whacked the Trullites to-day,
    And could whack them again to-morrow."

Chanting this simple, but effective and appropriate lay, they marched out of the ground, through the house, and into the street of Buffer Bassett, just in time to meet some of their defeated foes returning with a policeman.

The officer was astute enough to see that there was nothing for him to do. He could not arrest a score of schoolboys singing as they passed through the street. If they had recently been guilty of assault the usual remedy was to summon them, as he had not been present at the time. This much he told those who had called upon him to do his duty, and drawing aside, he let the procession go by, without a word.

Bunn walked behind the boys, with a air that would have done credit to an actor playing the part of Hannibal. Gubbles, with his pipe in full blast, sauntered along upon the cobbley pavement, enjoying the whole thing hugely.

Buffer Bassett was a dull, dismal town, where the sound of a barrel organ was ever the means of drawing people to their doorways, and a German band a source of popular excitement.

The song of the boys, sung with a sweet but powerful cadence as they marched, with a swinging step, came upon the stolid people as a revelation.

There was a noise of opening doors and windows in the houses they passed, the beershops were emptied of their frequenters, and quite a little crowd of boys, girls, men, and sprinkling of women accompanied the victorious band to the station.

Outside there was a stucco building devoted to the sale of liquor, and dignified by the name of "The Railway Hotel." Bunn called for a halt outside it.

"Boys," he said, "after our recent exertions, we all need something, and I am ready to pay for it. I will send you out some lemonade and ginger-beer. Mr. Gubbles, I shall be glad if you will accompany me to the interior of this hostelry to—to inquire when the next train for Chippenham arrives."

Bunn was nothing if not grandiloquent and dramatic in action. Before going into the hotel, he called for another cheer, which was heartily given.

A smattering of the crowd, experienced in the art of getting drink at the expense of others, followed him and Mr. Gubbles, with the object of sharing in the *finale* to that glorious day.

In due time a very liberal allowance of ginger-beer and lemonade appeared, and the boys, lounging on the outside seats, or reclining on a small grass-plot in front of the inn, imbibed the same, laughing and chatting over the outcome of their first cricket match.

It had not come exactly as they expected, but one and all voted that things could not have been better.

There was half-an-hour to wait, and during that time there was no further sign of the enemy. When the signal for the train went down, Bunn appeared with Gubbles and others, who had been drinking success to the Littlecote C. C. at his expense, and the departure from the station was worthy of the leave-taking of a victorious body of troops, who had fought for the honour of their country.

Penny Bunn was in a glowing state of pride, waving his hat out of the window until they were out of sight of the station. Subsiding into his seat, he said:

"Boys, I have always taken a strong interest in all you do, and this day you have shown the stuff you are made of. I rejoice in the knowledge that the example I set you, by laying that upstart. Trully, in the dust, was so promptly followed by your thrashing his insolent cubs. From the bottom of my heart I thank you."

Then he settled into his corner, with a somewhat vacant eye, and shortly after fell into a sweet sleep, which was unbroken until he was aroused by Gubbles at Chippenham Station.

CHAPTER CXL.

MYSTERIOUS MOVEMENTS OF MULBERRY CORK.—
GUBBLES CONFIDES AN IMPORTANT SECRET TO JACK.

"MIRIAM," said Bunn, a few days after the cricket match at Buffer Bassett. "I should like a little confidential talk with you."

"What about?" she asked.

"This incubus on the school, Mulberry Cork," was the reply.

It was evening, and they were alone. Miss Astracan was in the kitchen looking into domestic matters with Susan, and Chunder Loo was out.

Gubbles was known to be in his room experimenting as usual, and the boys were away at play.

"What possible good can come of discussing the boy?" murmured Miriam. "We must await the return of his mother."

"Do you think she will ever return?" asked Bunn, solemnly. "If you do, I am of a contrary opinion. I look upon the whole thing as a conspiracy between the boy, his mother, and Snicker to bring ruin and contumely on the school."

Miriam laughed, not lightly, but in a dissenting fashion.

"How could Snicker possibly know anything about the boy, or Mrs. Cork?" she inquired.

"That remains to be seen," said Bunn. "You remember Snicker's story about the cheque."

"Certainly."

"It was a lie, of course. Snicker was always a braggart and a liar. Now, I've been thinking the whole affair over, and have come to the conclusion that the boy stole the cheque, and handed it to Snicker."

"What need was there to get it changed?"

"Why, to cancel the debt to me. I had the cheque, and it is for me to prosecute the thief. The mother has nothing more to do with it."

"What makes you think that boy stole it?"

"Because I am sure he is a bad lot. He is not like other boys. Since Hone's death, he associates with nobody."

"They will not associate with him."

"They can't. He is a wrong 'un, as the boys say. He steals away whenever he has a chance, and who knows where he goes to?"

"Have you asked him what he does with his spare time?"

"No, for he would be rude, or tell a lie. I want to get rid of him. He must be sent away."

"You cannot do it without running the risk of getting yourself into trouble. Suppose the mother suddenly returns, and asks for her son, what could you say to her?"

Penny Bunn went through the action of tearing his hair, and groaned.

"It is the beastliest fix a man ever was in," he said.

"By the way, P.Y.," said Miriam, after a pause, "we have a thief in the house."

"It seems to me that we have everything that is villainous and objectionable here," grumbled Penny Bunn.

"The robberies are not serious," said Miriam, "but we cannot afford them. Food disappears daily from the larder."

"The boys may take it."

"Nonsense. They are well fed, and if they were

not, they would let us know by making complaints. They are bold enough to do it."

"Who, then, can be the thief?"

"P.Y., I don't know; but I thought that a man of your extraordinary ability would be able to find out."

It was a sarcastic shaft, but it glanced harmlessly from his seasoned hide.

"What has been stolen?" he asked.

"Bread, cheese, butter, and last night an entire loaf, and the remnant of a leg of mutton."

"The leg of mutton, though but a remnant," said Bunn, "is serious. An astonishing amount of hash can be made from almost bare bones. Who do you think——"

"I decline to think," interposed Miriam; "it is for you to find out the culprit."

"I fancy it is Cork," said Bunn, thoughtfully. "Of late he eats nothing at table. Gubbles told me so. I will keep an eye on him. He must carry on his nefarious proceedings in the night."

He arose and left the room, resolved to forthwith begin the investigation. He would, as a start, seek out Cork, and by insidious questioning, of which he deemed himself a past master, endeavour to get at something.

As he was leaving the house, he saw Anthony Gubbles descending the stairs with his hat on, to go out.

"Gubbles," he said, "which way are you going?"

"I was thinking of taking a stroll in the direction of the cricket-field."

"I'll go too. I want a word with you on a most important subject."

He was not prepared to find Gubbles interested, notwithstanding his statement that the matter was a most important one. But the undermaster, nevertheless, was so. He asked how long the thieving had been going on? Bunn thought, from his not hearing of it, that the depredations were recently begun.

Then he wanted to know the situation of the larder, and if it was locked at night.

"Of course it is," replied Bunn. "That is a phase of the subject I have not thought of before."

"Ascertain for certain if it is so," said Gubbles; "also if the lock is all right in the morning, and let me know as soon as you can. I am fond of investigating anything. It interests one, and takes one out of the common ruck of life."

"So it does," mused Bunn; "I have often thought that the detective element was very strong with me, but I have never had time to cultivate it. We will work together in this matter."

"With pleasure."

They went on to the common in company, and stayed with the boys until it was time to return.

Then they all came back in a body, the only absentee being Mulberry Cork. There was nothing unusual in that. He had never once joined in the boys' practice in the cricket field.

Bunn, on returning to the Abbey, made inquiries, and ascertained that the larder was always duly locked at night, and found in that condition in the morning. He reported this to Anthony Gubbles, who said he would think it over, and endeavour to get at something to work upon.

Later in the evening, as the boys were coming into supper, he intimated to Jack Ford that he would like to see him in his room ere it was time to retire.

"Come up quietly," he said; "and you need not mention it to anybody."

He managed to convey this request in an ordinary conversational tone, and in a semi-whisper, without any apparent secrecy about it. Jack said he would come as soon as he could do so unobserved.

There was nothing in the way of his keeping his appointment. After supper, the boys went for half-an-hour into the class-room, and Jack hied away upstairs. He had to wait but a few minutes when Anthony Gubbles appeared.

He sat down, lighted his pipe, and sat for a minute or so without saying a word. Jack saw he was thinking, and kept silent.

"Ford," said Gubbles, "I am now about to confess to you exactly who and what I am. First, let me tell you that I am here for the purpose of discovering the authors of a great and most unhallowed crime. Never before have I played the *rôle* of teacher in a school."

"You are a detective, then?" exclaimed Jack.

"Not in the sense you mean," returned Gubbles. "I have nothing to do with the police, and the police have nothing to do with me, professionally. I am simply a man of private means, who lost a most valued friend under the most painful circumstances.

"At present," he resumed, after a pause, "I will not tell you exactly who I am. It is a matter of no consequence. My relation to you will deal with the crime, and the difficulties I have met with in attempting to discover the authors of it."

"You know there are more than one," said Jack.

"I do," was the reply. "There were two. Men who, at the time, passed under the names of Aaron Brand and Berry Mawston."

Jack started violently, for it instantly flashed upon him that Berry Mawston was the name written in the "Newgate Calendar" which Mulberry Cork had claimed as his property. He was about to mention that important thing, when he decided to let Anthony Gubbles finish his narration ere he made any statement of his own.

"The name of my friend," said Gubbles, "I will give to you as Ruskin. He was a merchant in the City of London—a most liberal man, without any thought of evil of his fellow creatures. Shrewd in business, but outside his sphere—a child."

He stopped to press down the tobacco in his pipe, drew it into a glow, and resumed:

"He was, like myself, a bachelor. We were close friends, and spent much of our spare time, mostly in the evenings, together. I was interested in his philanthropy, and he was pleased to learn something of my scientific pursuits. He invariably told me all he did in way of helping his fellow man and woman, as the case might be, and one night he spoke of the two men I had named as persons who had applied to him for help under rather extraordinary circumstances. They professed not to want money, but to gain some knowledge of business, and they asked if he would, when alone, impart to them some information on the subject. He went so far as to offer to take them as assistants, but that they declined, giving as their excuse a statement to the effect that it was necessary, for family reasons, their desire for a time should be kept a secret.

"I ventured to point out to him that it would be undesirable for him to entertain the proposal, but he combated that view by declaring that the doing of good in that way would cost him nothing, especially, as he, unlike the majority of city men, lived upon the premises, in rooms tended by a solitary deaf domestic whom he had taken into his service. He did so, I verily believe, because her infirmity prevented her getting a place elsewhere."

"It speaks for the man," said Jack; "he must have had a noble heart."

"He had," replied Gubbles. "Well, the terrible upshot of it was that in spite of my warning, he received them one evening after office hours, and they there and then murdered him, broke open the safe in the office belonging to the clerks, emptied it of the petty cash, and with his keys got at his private safe and took away a very considerable sum in bonds."

Gubbles stopped short and with his hand veiled his eyes for a moment. The recollection of the crime was evidently very painful to him.

"At the outset there was nothing but what he had told me to guide the police to the authors of the crime. The old woman had not so much as seen them, nor had any of the clerks heard them referred to by their employer. But poor Ruskin was a very methodical man, and he made notes in his diary concerning the pair of scoundrels. He had gone so far as to describe their personal appearance. I have a copy of the entrance on the diary, which I will read to you."

He brought out his pocket book, from which he selected a paper and read as follows:

"'Two men, giving their names as Aaron Brand and Berry Mawston, called to-day to ask to be taught the methods of business, as an act of kindness to help them to start in the world. Brand is tall, thin and dark, with close set and rather shifty eyes. He has a quiet way, and seems to me to be a man who has travelled. He has a habit of rubbing his hands together when speaking. Mawston is stout and thick-set, with a face that is far from prepossessing. He speaks in the low-class dialect of the East End, and occasionally indulges in slang. I cannot like the man, but am not disposed to judge him as evilly inclined because he lacks education. He has a scar upon his left wrist.'

"With these slender clues to the identity of the men," said Gubbles, "the police went to work, and I must say that up to a certain point they did their work very well. They traced the murderers out as two notorious swindlers and scoundrels who had long been wanted for a long string of crimes, and they tracked them down into Wiltshire, to this very neighbourhood, and there they lost them."

"Into this very neighbourhood?" repeated Jack.

"Yes," said Gubbles, "and it is because they lost them here, and have put a cordon of watchfulness round the county, so close that they cannot escape, a fact the villains are doubtless aware of, that I eventually undertook the task of teacher in this school, being so near the very spot where Mawston was last seen. I am, moreover, guided by a conviction, that it is not far from here where the solution of the mystery of the murder will be obtained."

He ceased, and there was silence in the room for awhile. Jack could not see, without further information, how being shut up in the Abbey could help Gubbles in his search, and he expected additional matter to be placed before him. But Gubbles did not seem to have more at his disposal.

"There the matter rests for the time," he said, breaking the stillness. "I thought it right you should know who and what I am, because I feel assured that you will sooner or later be able to help me."

"You wish me to keep a look-out for these men?" said Jack.

"Just so."

"I can even now give you some slight clue, I believe, that may lead us to Mawston."

Jack then told him of the affair in connection with the "Newgate Calendar," which created in Gubbles a feeling of the profoundest astonishment. For once in a way his face was roused into an expression indicative of strong excitement.

"Ford," he exclaimed, "we must set to work and find that book. Are you fond of early rising?"

"I do not object to it," answered Jack.

"Well, then," said Gubbles, "be prepared to be

quietly roused by me a little before sunrise. We shall have time to get to the lower ground and give a hour to searching the spot before breakfast. It is time you went to bed. Good night."

They parted, and Jack went straight to the dormitory. The other boys had not yet come up, but he undressed and got into bed.

When the rest came trooping in they were considerably taken aback to find him there.

"In bed, Jack!" exclaimed Don.

"Got a bit of a headache," answered Jack, "don't talk to me. I want to get to sleep."

Jack with a headache was a thing hitherto unheard of. They were all very much surprised, but in deference to his statement, hastened to undress and quietly sought the realms of repose.

CHAPTER CXLI.

THE LOST BOOK.—A PEEP AT THE OLD TREASURE CAVE.

"THREE o'clock."

The words were whispered in Jack's ear, and he was awake in a moment. His faculties, as usual, were clear as soon as his eyes were open. Anthony Gubbles stood beside the bed, ready dressed to start on the searching expedition.

Jack lost no time in getting into his clothes. Time was precious, and he resolved to put off washing until he returned.

Without making the least noise they succeeded in going downstairs and leaving the Abbey behind them. In the wood they felt free to talk.

"I have thought over what you told me last night, Ford," said Gubbles, "and I am inclined to think it is most important. But I won't be sure, and until I am, I will say nothing more. I am reticent because I have had so many clues and hitherto been disappointed."

It was a long walk round to the base of the cliff, but they maintained a smart pace, and did the distance under the hour, Jack finding a short cut down the slope where it was less precipitous than it was near to the Abbey, when they were nearing the entrance to the wood.

The ground they had to search was liberally sprinkled with trees and covered with bush. Jack located the spot, where he judged the book had fallen, and they went to work.

As there had been no rain for a week and the sun shone brightly each day, the ground was hard. There were no indications of footsteps to show that another had been there before them. But after an hour's close searching they came to the conclusion that the book was no longer there. Not the least trace of it could be found.

"He has been for it," said Gubbles, "and must have it in his possession. We must get at his box, somehow. It would be an easy matter if he slept in one of the dormitories, but being in the chamber of Chunder Loo, it would be difficult to get a peep at his effects."

"We must give it up for the present," said Jack.

As they were about to leave the spot, Jack suggested that he should show the cave where the treasure had been found, to his companion. Gubbles assented.

It had been left open after its contents were removed, and was open still. Jack led the way in, but owing to their having no light they did not go very far.

"There seems to be a lot of fallen masonry here," said Gubbles.

"Yes," replied Jack, "and it appears to have been recently shifted. A month ago it extended only halfway across the cave, now it nearly covers the flooring."

"Where does it come from?"

"It is, I think, an intervening wall that has fallen down."

"Intervening between what?"

"This vault and others, I should say," said Jack; "that, at least, is my theory. No doubt the old Abbey has vaults under its entire length."

"Ford," said Gubbles, as they turned to seek the outer air again, "I have heard the story of the barring out. Why not tell me that whole secret of the vaults?"

"It is not mine alone, sir." answered Jack, "or I would gladly do so. I feel that I can trust you."

"You may with safety," was the response.

They left the cave, and Gubbles, on referring to his watch, discovered that they could proceed leisurely on the way home. The conversation soon reverted to Aaron Brand and Berry Mawston.

"They were both Englishmen, I suppose?" said Jack.

"What makes you ask that question," inquired Gubbles.

"It dawned upon me that one or both might possible be foreigners."

"I should say they were Englishmen," said Gubbles, "because Ruskin was such a methodical man, that, if either had been foreigners he would have referred to it in his diary. But it is possible that they had both travelled. Mawston, according to the police, is a low-bred fellow, but a consummate actor. He has extended his nefarious proceedings to the continent, and the independencies of our kingdom. His record covers a longer period than that of Brand, who suddenly appeared on the scene, as novelists say, about five years ago."

"In Mawston's company?"

"Yes. They came back together from the continent."

"If so much was known and seen of them, why were they not arrested?"

"The reports of their being in England were conveyed to the police by spies, who had no power to arrest either. When those who had that power went in search of them they had disappeared. The cunning of the fellows was, as one of the officers told me, a record in the history of criminals. But it is only lately that they added murder to their long list of crimes, and the prospect of being hanged has, no doubt, the effect of making them doubly cautious."

There was nothing more in their conversation that we need record. By six o'clock they were back at the Abbey, and had regained their rooms without meeting with any one.

Susan was up, and could be heard in the distance, banging about with the broom, but they did not set eyes on her, and she appeared to be the only person, beside themselves, who had arisen so early.

CHAPTER CXLII.

CONFIDENCE FOR CONFIDENCE — CHUNDER LOO'S DILEMMA.

JACK held a consultation with his three chums that day. First of all he confided to them who Gubbles was, for he considered they had a right to know, and were not likely, in schoolboy parlance, to "blab." Then he asked them if they were willing that their great secret should be confided to Gubbles in return.

After weighing the matter they decided to leave it to Jack.

"For you see," said Bob Stockton, "you are so much a better judge of people than we are. You are not the bird to be caught with chaff."

"I am certain that Gubbles is a brick," said Jack, "and I shall tell him everything."

In the evening he obtained an opportunity to do so, and Gubbles listened to the story with the face of a Sphinx. When it was concluded he suddenly burst into laughter.

"It is the best yarn it ever was my lot to hear," he said, presently, "and it has the merit of being true. There is a lot of material under the old roof for the making of great men, or if you go on the wrong tack, notorious criminals."

"I hope you do not fear we shall become the latter?" hinted Jack.

"It is impossible to say. Human nature is a complex machine, and when one of the wheels gets out of gear the whole thing sometimes goes utterly wrong. But I hope for the best, with the majority of you."

"What do you say about the treasure? Have we a right to keep it?"

"Not a legal one, as the law stands, but in my opinion a moral one. There is no living person who could justly call himself heir to it, and as to the lord of the manor, his claim is based on the law made when lords of the manors had everything their own way."

"And what do you think of Lingo?"

"Ah! There," said Gubbles, "you ask me a question I cannot answer. Looking at him in the light of his early conduct, I should say that he is sound."

"He could have taken everything at the outset, could he not?" asked Jack, wistfully.

"Just so," replied Gubbles, "so could have done in early life the confidential clerk who after years of faithful service becomes dishonest without rhyme or reason. A vehicle will travel for a long time and give no cause for anxiety, but suddenly some portion of it gives way, and then down it goes with a smash. You can help us by asking some of my detective friends to hunt him up. I need not say what you want him for."

"I think," said Jack, hesitating, "that I would rather—wait a little longer."

"And I think you will be right in doing so."

Thus matters were left for the present. Meanwhile, no less a person than Chunder Loo was getting into a position of discomfort, arising from his ridiculous impromptu love-making to Miss Astracan.

He had made no attempt to renew it, and the lady had apparently forgotten all about it, when on this very evening she, being left in his company, staggered him by suddenly referring to the subject.

"Chunder," she said, as she sat in her easy-chair, panting with heat, "I don't want to hurry you, but when is it to be?"

"I beg pardon," said Chunder Loo, looking up from the paper he was perusing.

With all the coolness the villain was naturally possessed of, he had plainly received a facer. There was a visible fading of colour under his swarthy skin.

"I am a reasonable woman," answered Miss Astracan, "and know that people of our years when love-making would only be making donkeys of themselves if they indulged in the foolery of younger people. We are old enough to take things easier. You have put your arm round my waist——"

"Not *quite* round," murmured Chunder Loo.

"Near enough round," said Miss Astracan, undisturbed by this interpolation bearing on her substantial build, "to answer the purpose, and you kissed me, too. Do you deny it?"

"No," replied Chunder Loo, "it was an act of reverence."

"An act of a lover," rejoined the undisturbed Miss Astracan, "or of a fool, or an impertinent scoundrel. Which will you have it considered to be ?"

"For the present," said Chunder Loo, "I prefer to leave it as a matter for future full discussion.

"I shall not leave it long," said Miss Astracan, "you may depend on that. I give you three days to come up to the scratch—like a man—or out of the Abbey you go !"

"Out of the Abbey ?"

"Yes. Hitherto I have not said a word about it to my niece or her husband, but if you refuse to fulfill your obligation, I shall certainly ask that you be promptly dismissed. If you demand any salary, I shall at once serve you with a notice of breach of promise, and, as I am a living creature, I will carry the action through. I may not be exactly the sort of woman most men would come wooing, nor are you the man many white women would care to marry. Englishwomen don't, as a rule, go in for niggers. They would make a lot of fun out of us in court."

"They would," said Chunder Loo, eagerly : "too much for one so delicate and sensitive as you are."

"Never mind how delicate and sensitive I am," said Miss Astracan. "I can stand the racket. Now, you have heard what I have to say. What will you do ?"

"With your gracious leave," replied Chunder Loo, resuming his ordinary manner, "I will take three days to reflect."

"Very well," said Miss Astracan, serenely, "do so : but I don't go an hour longer. If by three days hence you have not openly avowed our engagement, I shall speak to Bunn. You can go now."

He went out of the room with a curious grin upon his face. He had the look of a man who had been severely kicked, and was trying to extract a little joy out of it. When he got outside, and had closed the door, he suddenly seemed to bristle all over with wrath of the quiet sort that is always more dangerous than an open outburst.

"Three days !" he muttered. "Much may happen in that time, my lady. Stout people are suddenly called away to the Great Unknown. You are a bulky person, but you may not be allowed to bar my way. Curse you, and myself, too, for a pair of fools."

He was stealing on towards the front door, when Dolphus rushed out of a side room, and barked at him furiously, keeping, with canine prudence, well outside the reach of a possible kick.

It was not the first time Dolphus had shown his animosity to Chunder Loo, but he had hitherto been treated with contempt. The Hindoo was not now, however, in the frame of mind to bear the attack with equanimity.

He rushed at Dolphus, with the object of kicking the breath out of him, and settling him for good and all. But a small dog is not so easily got at, even in so comparatively limited an area as that of the Abbey hall.

He dodged the feet of the furious man with an agility that was maddening, keeping just clear of the slippered feet, and barking unceasingly.

In a few moments the appearance of Chunder Loo was more that of a black fiend than a human being, and Miriam, coming from above, stopped short halfway down the stairs, unperceived by Chunder Loo, stared at him in amazement and alarm.

It was the first time she had ever gained an inkling of the real nature hidden under his suave demeanour, and the discovery was far from being a pleasant one.

Recovering herself sufficiently to speak, she said, sharply :

"Mr. Chunder Loo, will you be kind enough to let my dog alone ?"

He heard her voice, but for a moment could not see her, so blind in his rage had he become. His eyes were bloodshot with fury. It was a sight to look upon him wrestling with his feelings, so as to assume his ordinary bearing, and still more surprising to mark how soon he was successful.

"Mrs. Bunn," he said, "we are only having a little fun together. I am on the best of terms with Dolphus."

"Indeed," replied Miriam, coldly, "I should not have thought it. One of those kicks you aimed at him would have deprived the poor little creature of his life. Dolphus, come here."

Dolphus had subsided into quietude, partly because he had nearly expended his valuable breath, and partly on account of the arrival of his mistress.

But he did not instantly respond, not being sure of her real object. More than once he had been treated to a specimen of the uncertain temper of women, and been slippered.

"Dolphus."

She spoke softly, and, stooping down, held out her hand to him. That was a sign of peace.

He allowed himself to be picked up and carried away by his mistress, who walked off with her nose in the air.

Chunder Loo had fallen in her estimation—never to rise again.

"What is coming to me ?" he muttered, on being left alone. "Am I losing my head ? Ruffled out of all reason by a cur ! Showing my hand to everyone like a fool ! But I am not beaten yet. Three days ! Much may happen in that time."

Muttering to himself, he shuffled up the stairs, and was seen no more that night.

A SPLENDID SCHOOL STORY.

NEVER BEFORE PUBLISHED.

By E. HARCOURT BURRAGE,

Author of "Ching Ching," "Monkey Nat and Roving Dick." "The Brave Boy of the Basilisk," &c.

"LAMBS of LITTLECOTE."

H.M.S. ~~~~SON
No~~~~

SNICKER BROUGHT IN UNDER THE CHARGE OF TWO WARDERS.

PRICE ONE PENNY.

NO. 20. A Handsome Coloured Plate Presented with Every Number.

CHAPTER CXLIII.

STRANGE PHENOMENA IN THE ABBEY.—A COUNCIL HELD
ON THE SITUATION.

THAT night there was confusion and terror among many occupants of the Abbey. Let us take the case of Miss Astracan first.

She was in a sound sleep, when she was startled into a wakeful condition by somebody shrieking in her ear. What was said she could not tell, beyond that there was the word "Hag!" in it.

It was to be expected that she should be alarmed, but Miss Astracan was made of more solid stuff than the majority of women, and did not entirely lose her wits.

Struggling into a sitting position in the bed, she called out to know who was there.

"Whoever you are," she said, "I am not afraid of you."

On a chair by the bedside, she invariably kept a candle and matches for any emergency that might arise, in the way of a night alarm. With a tolerably steady hand she obtained a light, and holding it aloft looked round the room.

Nobody was there, and getting out of bed, she took a survey of the region under her couch. No midnight intruder was to be seen.

Waddling to the door she tried it, and found it fast.

"I must have dreamt it," she said, "but it was horribly real."

She got into bed again, and, leaving the candle burning, lay there very wakeful. In the position she was in, she could not see much of the floor of the room, but that did not trouble her. She was convinced she had been dreaming, and there was an end of it.

Poof!

The candle was out, and she was sure she heard a short, sharp sound as of somebody blowing at it. This was a staggerer, indeed, and it was some minutes ere she could muster the courage to feel for the candle and matches again, so as to obtain another light.

But, eventually, she did it, and with a resolve not to be frightened, lay upon her side with her eyes fixed upon the meagre flame.

But, if the candle had been really blown out by anybody who had means of access to the room, the startling jest was not repeated.

Miss Astracan was aware that the Abbey, like all old buildings, had its full complement of draughts, that came from goodness knows where, and could not be kept out when there were winds abroad, by any device of man.

By degrees she came to the conclusion, that it was a sudden gust of air that had put out the light, and again found refuge in sleep.

She was disturbed no more that night.

But there were other sufferers, notably among the smaller boys, such as Little Jiggers, Short, and Herbert May in No. 1 dormitory, and Walker, Rudge, and Noakes in No. 2.

They were respectively aroused by having a hand passed over their faces, or their legs jerked, or an unaccountable heaving up of their beds.

On awakening, they thought they were being subjected to some form of practical joking, common among schoolboys, but on remonstrating, they were answered by a growl, like that of a wild beast, or a deep-voiced threat, which certainly emanated from a man. Some of the poor little fellows were literally stricken dumb with terror.

But the climax came when the voice of a woman was heard shrieking. It came from the room occupied by Bunn and his wife, and it was the voice of the latter creating the commotion.

So piercing were her shrieks, that all the boys, indeed all the house, except Miss Astracan, who had gone off into a sound sleep, were aroused.

Jack Ford, having the materials handy, got a light, and slipped on his trousers.

"You fellows keep quiet," he said, "I'll pop into the passage and see if I can make out what is the matter."

"Bunn must be murdering her," suggested Tom Drummond.

"He hasn't the pluck," said Don.

Jack, on emerging into the corridor from his dormitory, beheld Gubbles, attired in an antiquated dressing-gown, coming downstairs, and close behind him was Susan, with the counterpane of her bed wrapped round her like a Roman toga.

The shrieks were still going on, but were not so loud, and Penny Bunn was heard imploring his wife to compose herself. Gubbles, after a surprised glance at Jack, knocked at the door.

The sound of it had an apparent composing effect on Miriam, for her cries ceased, and, in a few moments, Bunn, with his hair resembling a confused mass of hog's bristles, opened the door sufficiently wide to thrust his head out.

"I feared something had happened," said Gubbles; "fire or burglars."

"Mrs. Bunn, has, I think, been dreaming," answered Bunn.

"Nothing of the sort," sobbed Miriam, from the region of her couch, "I was awake, and heard a footstep in the room. I asked who it was, and somebody said, 'If you don't want your throat cut, shut up.'"

"I have examined the room," pleaded Bunn, "and there is nobody here."

"Was your door locked?" inquired Gubbles.

"Yes; double locked and bolted."

"Then, I fear, we must consider Mrs. Bunn has had an attack of nightmare."

"It was nothing of the sort," angrily answered Miriam. "Bunn, is the window open?"

"Yes, my dear, as usual on these warm nights; I leave it so, but only a few inches."

"Look at it now."

"My dear, anyone going that way would break his neck."

"Draw the curtain aside and look at it, I say."

Bunn complied with her request, and found that the window was wide open. It was certainly not as he fixed it before going to bed.

"Well?" said Miriam.

"The window has been tampered with since we retired," replied Bunn.

"I should like to tamper with your ears," said Miriam, "for telling me I was not awake. The man got out that way."

"But how did he get in, my dear?"

"He was under the bed, I suppose. I forgot to look as usual, being extra tired."

"He has settled himself," said Bunn; "it is a sheer pitch down. I will make it my business at an early hour to seek his corpse. Gentlemen, I thank you for your ready response to the call of Mrs. Bunn, and will bid you good night, or morning, whichever it may be."

He closed the door. Susan skedaddled upstairs, and Gubbles motioned to Jack to lead the way back to his dormitory.

"I will have a word with you ere going back to my room," he said.

As they passed No. 2 dormitory, one of the boys cried out asking who was there? They went in and found the whole room awake.

Gubbles said nothing was the matter, beyond Mrs. Bunn having been awakened by a noise.

Then those who had been disturbed by the secret visitor told their story. Gubbles softened their fears by telling them that it was only some thoughtless boy indulging in fun, and he would investigate it on the morrow.

In No. 1 dormitory the same wakeful state was found, and there were similar stories to be told. But none of the four, comprising the inner circle, had been disturbed.

Gubbles sat down on the side of Jack's bed. He did not talk of a jesting boy there, but went into the details of the night's experiences.

Although nobody had been hurt the narratives were sufficiently startling.

"I do not think you will be disturbed any more," he said, after awhile, "but, as I am one of those un-fortunate people, who, when once aroused at night, cannot get to sleep again, I will bring down a light, a book, and a folding-chair, and stop with you until the morning."

"There is really no need for it," they chorused.

"It is a whim of mine" he answered; "allow me to do as I please."

He was not long gone, but by the time he returned, some were already off again to the land of dreams. Others soon followed, and at length, only Jack remained awake.

"Why don't you go to sleep, Ford?" asked Gubbles, seeing that he was lying with his eyes wide open.

"I want to," answered Jack, "but first I should like to tell you of something that happened here some time ago. You might think it over as you sit there kindly watching over us."

Gubbles came over to his bed and listened to the story, briefly put, of the strange visitant, who came to the room and had his coming stopped by the cord stretched across. Jack also mentioned that he had the knife he found on that occasion, hidden away.

"You can show it to me in the morning," said Gubbles, "as you say, I can think over what you have told me. It demands a lot of thought. We won't talk any more just now. Try and get some sleep."

Jack lost no time in obeying him, and in a short space of time, Gubbles was the only person awake in the room.

And he was very wide-awake and thinking.

CHAPTER CXLIV.

MORE STRANGE CONDUCT.—LIVELY DAYS AT THE ABBEY.

CHUNDER LOO had not, apparently, been disturbed by the events of the night, but in the opinion of those who were competent to judge, he was fully cognisant of them.

Nay more, he was looked upon as the chief offender, the author of them, in fact.

"I am as certain as I can be," said Jack, to Tom Drummond, "that this place is honeycombed with secret passages, and that Chunder Loo knows all about them."

"But how is it that he knows and everybody else is in ignorance?"

"That is the mystery, but Chunder Loo is an all-round mysterious fellow."

A complete change had come over the personage who so powerfully disturbed them all. Hitherto, as we have shown, he was a model of quiet deportment, but on appearing in the morning he exhibited the other side of his character.

He opened the ball, as we may term it, with Bunn, and the ladies, by giving himself airs at the breakfast table.

He complained of the viands, and the way they were cooked, and the tea, he vowed was nothing better than the advertised "family Congo at one-and-three."

"It is enough to poison a hog," he declared. "Bunn, will you tell me if it is you who is so preciously mean, or do you allow the women to govern everything here?"

"Sir," said Penny Bunn, "you are impertinent."

"I am *what?*" demanded Chunder Loo, with the cool ferocity of a duellist of the last century.

"I said you were impertinent," answered Bunn, in a milder tone.

"*You* said it, did you?" snarled Chunder Loo. "Indeed! I will ask you to repeat that observation, in a more convenient place."

Miriam, with a spirit that was worthy of her, went to the rescue of her husband.

"Mr. Chunder Loo," she said, "you are a low person, and a hypocrite. I will thank you to behave yourself at the table, or to take your meals with the boys."

"My dear," replied Chunder Loo, with an overwhelming insolence, "I should not be happy away from you. What have I done that you should turn and rend me?"

"How dare you address me as *your* dear?" cried Miriam.

Chunder Loo stared at her with affected surprise. His manner had the effect of reducing his small audience to a state of semi-petrifaction. It came upon them as such a sudden and overwhelming surprise.

"Miriam," he said, in a tremulous tone, evidently got up for the occasion. "I did not expect this from *you.*"

Miriam burst into tears, and Bunn felt that now or never he must assert himself.

Rising, he walked to the door and opened it. His face was very pale, and he shook a little, but he meant business.

"Leave the room, sir," he hissed. "I will talk to you anon. I can only attribute your conduct to drink."

"You are qualified to judge of the action of drink as well as any man I know," said Chunder Loo, rising also. "I will breakfast with the boys. Now, don't run away with the idea that I am afraid of you. If you say another word to me, I will pitch you into the fire-place."

With a grimace at the appalled Miss Astracan, and a mocking bow to Miriam, he glided from the room, and Bunn, having giving him time to get well away, banged the door to with great violence.

"What has come to the man?" sobbed Miriam. "The monster!"

"I knew what he was, all along," said Bunn, bitterly, "but you believed in him."

"And I allowed him to make love to *me*," murmured Miss Astracan, in a hollow voice.

"Hey! What is that?" exclaimed Bunn, and Miriam looked up at her aunt, in surprise.

"He has been making love to me," replied Miss Astracan, "and in two days it was to be settled, if we were to be married, or not. After what has happened I can't possibly think of him any more."

Bunn, with a vacuous expression of countenance, born of astonishment, stared at her for fully half-a minute, unable to say a word. It was Miriam who made the next remark on the matter, and it was very much to the point.

"Auntie," she said, "that man has been making a fool of you."

"I see no reason why I shouldn't marry as well as you," retorted Miss Astracan, "we are neither of us chickens."

There was a storm impending, and Bunn, to ward off a scene, threw himself into the breach.

"You have both spoilt the scoundrel," he said, "and now you suffer for it."

Then they both turned upon him, as a safe target to shoot at, and fairly overwhelmed him with reproaches. It had all been his fault throughout, of course. But for him, the man would have been sent away long ago, and so on. Bunn grinned feebly, as he went on with his breakfast, prudently declining to say a word more. By the time he had finished his morning meal they had pumped themselves out, and he left them to water their own, with tears of mortification.

"Well," he said, as he hastened out; "Time, the avenger, has done all I would have asked for. The fellow will have to go, now. I am satisfied."

But Chunder Loo was not done yet, and meant going in his own sweet time. He breakfasted with the boys, and at the bottom of the table, put on a jocular air that was almost as astounding to them as his previous conduct had been to the trio in the parlour.

He cracked jokes, asked conundrums, and told them short, humorous stories, at which they might have laughed if they had not been so completely taken aback.

The least disturbed at the table was Anthony Gubbles. He sat quietly at the head of it, exhibiting neither surprise nor interest. When Chunder Loo on one occasion addressed him, he made no reply, and the wily one took no further notice of him.

Penny Bunn was in the playground, where he hoped to see Chunder Loo, and bring things to a head.

The boys would be out for the usual half-hour before study, and he relied upon their presence as a moral support.

Not that Bunn was afraid of Chunder Loo—he scorned the very idea; but at the same time it would be as well, if they came to words or blows, to have witnesses.

Chunder Loo did not disappoint him.

He came out with the boys, and on seeing Bunn standing with his back towards him, affecting to be in deep thought, he glided up, and favoured him with a hearty smack between the shoulders.

"What cheer, old cock !" he cried ; "though born in India, I have acquired some of your more cheerful social habits. How goes it, old man ?"

Perhaps in all the absurd positions in which he had been placed at various times during his career at the Abbey, Bunn had never been in one so absurd as this.

The shock of the blow, and the surprise of it effectually cut off the tree of dignity at the roots. Nothing was left for him but to be violent, unless he consented to be laughed at.

On a previous occasion he had struck Chunder Loo, and the blow had not been returned. Why should he not, suffering, as he was, from a gross impertinence, repeat the performance ?

He was getting ready to strike, when, to his increased astonishment, Jack Ford glided between them.

"Don't do that, Mr. Bunn," he said, "the blackguard isn't worth it."

Penny Bunn could have embraced Jack on the spot. The brave lad had undoubtedly rescued him from an invidious position. But it flashed upon him that any demonstration of his feelings would only accentuate the affair. So he merely said, in a breathless way :

"You are right, Ford. He is not worth it."

Chunder Loo, on his part, was as much astonished at the boldness of the boy, as his principal. He stood erect, with his hands behind his back, his eyes on Jack's face, and rocking to and fro upon his heels.

"So," he said, in a slow, icy way, "I am a blackguard ?"

"Go indoors, Mr. Bunn," advised Jack, in an undertone. "A row with the fellow won't pay. Turn the rascal out, and if he won't go, send for the police."

"Ford," replied Bunn, "your advice is valuable. You show a wisdom in your words beyond your years."

He walked into the house, very stiff about the back, and scornful in look, and Jack, taking no further notice of Chunder Loo, sauntered away.

But the swarthy rascal he had called a blackguard, followed him.

"Young Ford," he said.

Jack wheeled about and looked him full in the face. There was a quick gathering of the clans, in the form of the boys around them.

"You called me a blackguard just now ?"

"Yes, and you are one. A low blackguard—a fraud —and a scoundrel."

As they exchanged these words, spoken quietly enough, deep and settled hatred developed in the eyes of the man, and scorn in the gaze of the boy.

"You run some risk in using hard words to me," said Chunder Loo.

"I care not a straw for that. You are like an evil spirit in the house. There has been a dark shadow in it from the moment you set foot in it. I hope Mr. Bunn will have the courage to send you away."

"He will be spared the trouble," answered Chunder Loo. "As I am going. Not to-day, nor to-morrow, but the next day. I choose my own time for that, as I do for other things. You are young and impulsive. You may get into trouble if you are not very careful. Cultivate reticence."

He left them then, returning to the house, and when the boys, after a fevered talk about the events of the morning, were summoned to the classroom, they found him in his usual place.

He was no more ruffled than he would have been if nothing unusual had happened. Jack Ford, for the first time, fully realized that this swarthy mystery could indeed be dangerous.

"He would kill the lot of us without hesitation," thought the boy, "if he could do it safely, but he will do nothing rash. Who, and what is this cold blooded schemer ?"

Well might he ask the question. It would have puzzled most men to answer it.

Anthony Gubbles came into the room, with Bunn at his heels. They had apparently been in conference together. The latter walked up to Chunder Loo.

"After what happened half-an-hour ago," he said, "you are out of place here. I must request you to leave the room, and the house."

"I can leave the room," replied Chunder Loo, "but not the house, because it is not convenient to do so. I can't find a crib in a moment. In two days' time, when I have made my arrangements, I will go."

"I must request you to go at once," insisted Bunn.

"I shall do nothing of the sort, you ass."

The intensity of the last word, in its utterance, showed the passion that was seething in the man. A sensation was created by the unexpected interposition of Anthony Gubbles.

"Why don't you behave yourself and leave the room ?" he said to Chunder Loo.

An insolent look flashed across the swarthy face, but it died away as the eyes of the two men met.

There was nothing overpowering in the physique of Gubbles, but there was something in his look that told on Chunder Loo.

He descended from his desk, and walked across the room. As he passed Mulberry Cork, who had a seat near the door, the boy raised his face and grinned. Chunder Loo gave him an open-handed blow on the side of the head.

" Stash it, will you?" howled Mulberry.

" Come out with me," hissed Chunder Loo; " I'll look after you."

The boy rose up, glanced at Bunn and Gubbles in turn, and hesitated. But neither made a sign for him to remain, so the pair left the room together.

" I don't understand that," murmured Bob Stockton to Don. " I wonder Bunn or Gubbles did not stop him."

" Mulberry is no ornament here," replied Don.

Penny Bunn took the head seat for the first time, and the routine of study went on. It was a quiet morning, with a suppressed feeling of excitement in the air.

Speculation was rife in many minds as to things that might possibly happen during the short term remaining for Chunder Loo.

It was impossible to say what would occur, so strange had been the sudden development of the character of this remarkable man.

CHAPTER CXLV.

CHUNDER LOO SECURES LODGINGS IN SMUDGEM BENDER.—HIS FAREWELL PRANKS.

NEITHER Mulberry Cork nor Chunder Loo was seen during the day, and it was getting late in the evening when they returned.

It so happened that the boys were just back from the cricket-field when the pair came out of the wood. Chunder Loo was in a swaggering mood. He had a big cigar in his mouth, from which he blew clouds of smoke as he passed the boys. Mulberry Cork walked with an unsteady step behind him.

Chunder Loo had not a word to say, but his companion was in a more communicative mood. He waited until his elder was out of sight, and then, with a preliminary vicious laugh, he began :

" The more I see of you"—he stopped and hiccoughed—" the more I *know* you are a blessed lot of jays. Jays!—do you hear?—all feathers and no sense !" He laughed again more vacantly than before, and, in an effort to draw himself upright, lurched a little to the left.

The silent boys, one and all, regarded him with unmitigated scorn.

" You may think you are clever," continued Cork, " but you are *not*. You are fools, every "—he stopped as before, impeded by that complaint known as a disturbance of the respiratory muscles—" hic—hic—one of you. I'm going away with good old Chunder."

He made this announcement as if he was imbued with the belief that his departure would be a very serious thing for the school.

But as before, they answered him not.

" Going 'way 'gether," cried Mulberry Cork, " him and me. We are going to stay with Mrs. Stick—Shick—Snicker. Chunder will make mincemeat of——"

He was cut short by a hand that closed upon the collar of his coat and fairly jerked him off his feet. It was Chunder Loo, who had come back for him. His eyes blazed ; his hair bristled with rage.

" You whelp ! you worm !" he snarled.

" Why don't you call him a snake ?" cried Jack Ford.

Chunder Loo started, and cast a fiercely inquiring look on the interlocutor. But Jack cared not for his looks, and returned his gaze unflinchingly.

" Another time," said Chunder Loo, " I will answer you."

Then, in a jerky fashion, he hauled Mulberry Cork into the house, and the door closed upon them.

" The little beast is *drunk!*" said Whymper, in disgust.

" He is," said Jack, sadly. " Whoever he may be, he is in bad hands. The boy hasn't a chance."

" Why doesn't Mr. Bunn keep him away from that nigger ?" asked Little Jiggers.

" He is not a philanthropist," returned Bob Stockton, shrugging his shoulders. He is a poor pupil. The cheque being lost, I am afraid he won't get another."

It appeared later on that the precious pair went straight to their room, and were quiet until everybody was in bed. Then they began to sing, and it was Mr. and Mrs. Bunn who got the full benefit of their vocal efforts.

At first the schoolmaster could not decide who it was that was thus disturbing the quietude of the place, but having located the sound, he got up and went to the door of Chunder Loo's room.

Not only were the pair singing, but dancing, too. Bunn, who had taken the precaution to bring the poker with him, smote the door with it.

The singing stopped, and the voice of Chunder Loo was heard.

" Who is there ?"

" Stop that row, will you ?" cried Bunn. " This isn't a pot-house !"

" More's the pity," was the jeering reply. Then again the speaker burst into song:

" Jim Crow's sister going to the ball,
    Tumbled down and broke her leg, and couldn't go at all.'

"I say, Bunn, what do you think of that? Come in and join us. You can howl a chorus."

Bunn had no time to answer, for a hand was laid upon his shoulder, and turning, he saw Gubbles with a lighted candle in one hand and something that looked like an ordinary squib in the other.

"Go on talking, but don't quarrel with him," he said. "I'll settle the noisy brute."

He lighted one end of the squib and thrust it into the keyhole. It was aglow, but did not give out any visible smoke.

"Talk to him," whispered Gubbles.

"Here, you, Chunder Loo," cried Bunn.

"What do you want, Socrates?" asked Chunder from within.

"Are you going to stop that singing?"

"Certainly not; and you have got to join in the chorus. Get the missis up, and we'll make a jolly night of it.

> "For to-night we'll merry be,
> For to-night we'll merry be,
> For to-night we'll merry, merry be,
> And to-morrow we'll get so—so—so—— Help!"

"Got him," said Gubbles, quietly. "He's down on the floor, and he will be there till the morning. The boy has gone, too. He went off quietly."

"What is it?" asked Bunn, shivering.

"An herb," replied Gubbles, as he withdrew the remnant of the squib-like thing and extinguished it with a wet forefinger. "The fumes of it, when burning, would stifle an ox, but it leaves no ill effects. I discovered it myself."

"In some foreign country, I suppose?"

"No; here, in this place, in the wood. It is not a common plant, but it is to be found by those who seek it. But, then, nobody but myself does so, as they don't know the use of it."

"I suppose," said Bunn, in a tremulous voice, "that if you had a mind to, you could just pop round one night and send us all off as good as dead."

"Yes," calmly replied Gubbles, "and murder you at ease. Good night."

"Go-o-o-od night," said Bunn, as he with chilly legs hastened back to his chamber.

"I will endeavour to keep friends with Gubbles," he murmured, as he laid his head down upon the pillow. "If thoroughly upset, he might do something that would be a good thing for the papers. Heigh! I don't think I should mind so much myself. I am tired of the whole thing. But some of the boys may want to live, so I will not ruffle the spirit of Gubbles."

After this episode Chunder Loo gave no trouble to anyone in the Abbey until the time came for him to depart.

He seemed to be conscious that he had something or somebody working against him with considerable success. He was subdued, and if not defeated, was bent on leaving his plans of vengeance, if he had any, for future carrying out.

Miss Astracan looked upon the love episode with the swarthy one as done with, but she did not even now thoroughly understand Chunder Loo.

The question of remuneration for services had been discussed between Bunn and his departing assistant, and it was arranged that two pounds ten shillings should be considered sufficient, that sum to be paid just prior to his departure, and in the presence of two witnesses—viz., Miss Astracan and Miriam.

The evening of the day came. Chunder Loo had been away almost all the intervening time, always taking Mulberry Cork with him, and the pair were going away together.

Bunn had demurred, as a matter of course, but the boy said he would not stay at the Abbey, and as they were going no further than Smudgem Bender, he would be handy for restoration to his mother, if ever she returned to claim him.

Chunder Loo hired a man to carry away their effects—his own were nothing to speak of—on a barrow, and having sent Mulberry Cork on ahead, sought the parlour, where the closing scene of his life in the Abbey, for the time anyway, was to be enacted.

They were all there—Bunn, Miriam, and Miss Astracan. The schoolmaster had written out a receipt, and two pounds ten shillings lay conveniently upon the table.

As the swarthy one entered the room, the trio maintained an all-round chilly, haughty demeanour. Chunder Loo, on the other hand, was very affable.

"It is a nice evening," he said; "and you all look jolly."

"Two pounds ten is the money, I believe," replied Bunn, stiffening his neck. "Please to sign here; our connection then terminates."

"As a schoolmaster and assistant," said Chunder Loo, as he wrote a scrawl supposed to be his name. "I always sign in Hindoo, a language you are probably familiar with."

"No, I have never studied it," said Bunn.

"Dear me! and you with Indian estates, too."

Chunder Loo coughed, and Miriam blushed. She had been confiding in the scoundrel, after all. Bunn waxed angry; but he kept outwardly calm. He had forgotten his having, prior to his marriage, boasted somewhat about his mythical estates in India.

"So far, all well," said Chunder Loo, regarding his signature with a loving eye. "The money is good, I suppose. You have no connection with a firm of smashers, I trust?"

Bunn did not reply. The women kept their eyes upon the ground.

"We now come to an affair of the heart," pursued

Chunder Loo. "I trust you will permit me to visit my *fiancée* now and then. It will be impossible for me to lead her to the altar before the end of September."

They all started, and fixed their eyes upon him. Miss Astracan opened and shut her mouth slowly, as if it were that of a dying fish.

"I see," said Chunder Loo, "I have given you all a pleasant surprise. You thought I was a scoundrel, who could win the heart of a maiden, ponderous but affectionate, and leave her to mourn my loss. Not me! I'm honourable, I am. Don't knock your heads against that wall, or you'll see stars. It's a hard fact that I mean to be faithful to the old girl I adore. Struggle up, my angel, and give me a kiss."

"Keep him off, Bunn!" shrieked Miss Astracan. "Turn him out! If he comes near me, I shall die!"

"My love!" murmured Chunder Loo, slowly approaching her.

She sank back in her chair, faintly gesticulating to her niece, who, without any hesitation, pounced upon Chunder Loo and boxed his ears.

It was a good, hearty, sounding smack, that was as much a startling experience to the recipient as to those who witnessed it. Before Chunder Loo could say a word in remonstrance or otherwise, he was favoured with another blow on the opposite side of the head.

Matters being balanced so far, Miriam opened the door.

"Will you go?" she said, in a close-set way, that showed she was very much in earnest.

"Ye-es," said Chunder Loo, "I am going."

"And if ever you dare to talk of love-making to my aunt again," continued Miriam, "I'll skin you!"

"I have only to say this," said Chunder Loo, standing in the doorway, "that if——"

Bang! went the door in his face, and Miriam, overcome with her exertions and excitement combined, fainted away in the arms of her husband.

Leaving him to the delicate task of restoring her, we will follow Chunder Loo, who, if a sneaky bearing goes for anything, was completely cowed.

"Hang the woman!" he muttered, as he rubbed his ears: "her hand is made of horn, or something in the tin line. And I can't—though born in India"—here he could not repress a vicious grin—"I am not the cur to fight a woman; not but what I would poison one," he added, thoughtfully, "if I had the chance."

There was no doubt about it—he would. There was not an atom of conscience in the man to stand in the way. It was the law and the method it had of dealing with murderers that hindered him.

He had to pass through the boys on his way out, and he plainly expected some sort of demonstration.

But they had been well coached by Jack Ford, and did not so much as look at him.

He felt this more than any words or action they might have indulged in. He paused two or three times on his way out, hoping they would say or do something; but they went on with their play, unheeding him.

At the gate he finally stopped, and, in a curious kind of frenzy, indulged in a very vulgar form of expressing what he felt. He put his thumb to his nose, and spread his fingers out.

It happened, unfortunately for his further peace of mind, that the greater portion of the boys at that moment looked in his direction.

They saw the action, and burst into a roar of laughter.

With a curse that rang out on the evening air like the shrill scream of a bird of prey, he swung himself round, and dashed into the wood.

"There goes a dangerous man," said Jack Ford. "May we never set eyes on him again!"

It was a vain hope. Chunder Loo was not done with yet by a long way.

CHAPTER CXLVI.

SNICKER SENDS A MESSAGE.—JACK FORD GETS A PEEP INTO A COUNTY GAOL.

IT was like the lifting of a dark cloud from the house, the departure of Chunder Loo. One of the first to feel the better for his going was Penny Bunn, who celebrated it with a private glass of grog from a jar he had smuggled into the house to take a drop now and then medicinally.

As he was kept rather short of money by his careful wife, he had put it up at the Cowley Arms for future payment, thereby laying in a store of future domestic trouble. It was a gallon jar, and was already half empty, which is a way jars have of diminishing when obtained for medicinal purposes.

Gubbles lost no time in overlooking the room Chunder Loo had left; but there was absolutely nothing to be found that could be of service to him as an investigator of mysteries.

If there was such a thing as a secret panel in the wainscoting, he failed to find it, and for the time he was nonplussed.

"There is one somewhere," he said to himself. "I am satisfied that Ford's theory is correct."

Next to the joy of losing Chunder Loo came the feeling of relief following the departure of Mulberry Cork. The boy was both hated and despised, and his going was voted a good riddance. For two days there was calm at the Abbey.

Then there came through a letter from Snicker, awaiting his trial, addressed to Jack Ford. It was, as might be expected, a scrawling epistle, filled with allusions to the "old happy days when he was master at the school"; but the pith of it was this: he desired to see Jack, to give him some "very valuable information."

Jack hardly knew what to do in the matter, but, after consulting his friends, he showed it to Anthony Gubbles, who offered to get him a visiting order, to arrange for a holiday, and accompany him to the county prison.

"He would not write to you on a trivial matter," said Gubbles, and Jack thought the same. He left the matter in the hands of the tutor.

Gubbles lost no time, and in forty-eight hours the order was forthcoming, and arrangements had been made for the requisite day off from school.

Their destination was Devizes, where Snicker was to be tried, and half the day was gone when they arrived there, and were driven to the prison.

The order admitted them without any demur. It was signed by one of the chief magistrates of the county, and they were shown into the room set apart for prisoners to see their friends.

After a short wait Snicker was brought in, under the charge of two warders, who withdrew to the other end of the room, to enable Snicker and his visitors to talk in secrecy and comfort.

But they kept their eyes open to see that nothing contraband exchanged hands.

Fontenoy Snicker had lost a lot of flesh. He was but the shadow of his former self in body, but he was precisely the same animal in spirit.

He was troubled on finding that Jack was not alone, as he hoped he would be, but the position of Gubbles having been explained to him, he, with assumed cheerfulness, declared that he was glad he had come.

"And now," said Jack, "will you as quickly as possible say why you have sent for me?"

"I want to tell you about a party," replied Snicker; "him, as I believe, has got me into this trouble. His name is Chunder Loo."

Gubbles turned so as to get a better view of the face of Snicker. Jack simply nodded his head, and said: "I guessed as much."

"I only want the truth to be known," continued Snicker. "I daresay I ought to be punished for passing that cheque, but as I am a living man I did not know it was stolen."

"But you knew there was something queer about it?" suggested Gubbles.

"Well, I did," said Snicker, "in a per-*pro*-miskus way. But, then, I was in the power of that man, as I am about to tell you."

Then he entered into his relations with Chunder Loo, giving the facts with tolerable truthfulness, and only diverging from the straight path when he came to himself as one who had struggled against the insidious tempter, and fallen.

That part of the story relating to the poisoned packet he intended for Mrs. Snicker he covered over with a statement that he wanted it for rats. Gubbles burst into laughter when he heard of that poison that was to remain so long in the veins of Snicker before acting. It tickled him immensely.

"He has played a splendid practical joke upon you," he said; "there is no such poison in existence."

"You are sure of that?" said Snicker, looking at him wistfully.

"Quite sure," was the reply.

"If I was certain of that——"

"There are poisons slow in their action," said Gubbles, "but they begin at once. That Chunder Loo knows the use of some poisons of an Eastern origin, I fully believe, but he is not a great man in dealing with them. He is an amateurish bungler. Rest easy. Your life so far is safe."

"I am glad of that," said Snicker. "Then all I want to prove is that I am not the murderer of that poor boy."

"Ah!" said Gubbles, dubiously, "that is another matter. There is a great deal against you."

"It was Chunder Loo who did it," said Snicker, clasping his hands together.

"Can you give us any proof?"

"He threatened to do for some of them, and he was in the habit of skulking about that cave. He'd got an idea that they would be coming along there one day. It was there I met him with a robe I bought him in London with some of that 'ere money, and he left his old one in the cave."

"I saw it there," said Jack. "Can you tell me in what condition he first found the cave?"

"No," replied Snicker, shaking his head, "except that it was open and empty when I saw it first. We knew that you boys had been there, on account of the lamp fixed on the wall."

"Snicker," said Gubbles, "I cannot accept your theory that Chunder Loo is the murderer. He was a long way from the wood all that afternoon, and until late in the evening. At the same time I do not think you were guilty of the crime."

"I thank you, sir," said Snicker, humbly, "it will be a comfort to me through all trials to know you was—*were*—of that opinion."

"I suppose you know," said Jack, "that Mrs. Snicker has a lodger?"

"Not heard a word on—*of*—it," replied Snicker; "who is it?"

"She has two. Chunder Loo, and a boy named Mulberry Cork."

"And how came that about?" asked Snicker.

Jack told him that Chunder Loo had been dismissed, and had taken up his quarters at the cottage. Why he had not gone clean away he could not tell.

"There's summat—*something*—uncommon queer about that chap Chunder Loo," said Snicker.

"Now let us come to another subject," said Gubbles. "What sort of counsel have you got?"

"None at all, respected sir. I really haven't the money to pay for legal assistance."

"I will see that you have it and of the best."

"I'm more than grateful to you, sir."

"You need not be," was the somewhat curt rejoinder, "because if you were alone concerned I should not in all probability take the least interest in you. You have been an arrant scoundrel, Snicker."

"I am too fully aweer—*ware*—of my shortcomings," was the humble response, "but I ain't a murderer. No, sir. I draws the line at bloodshed."

They shortly after left him, and as they drove away from the prison Gubbles expressed his disappointment at the result of the interview.

"I thought we should have got hold of something more to the point," he said. "All that he says would not go far towards convicting Chunder Loo—as Chunder Loo."

Jack was struck by the nature of the concluding remark, and especially its tone, and looked at him inquiringly.

"You seem surprised," said Gubbles. "Well, I have a private opinion of Chunder Loo, which I hope ere long to verify. But patience and watchfulness are necessary. I trust he will be fool enough to remain where he is."

"I don't see his object," said Jack.

"Smudgem Bender is a quiet, out-of-the-way place," returned Gubbles, with an enigmatical smile.

CHAPTER CXLVII.

GUBBLES AND THE INNER CIRCLE.—THE SEARCH FOR THE SECRET PASSAGES.

IT was late when they reached the Abbey, and after supper Jack was glad to get to bed. Penny Bunn was naturally anxious to learn the result of the interview, and was disgusted to hear that it ended practically in nothing.

Gubbles said not a word about his having volunteered to help Snicker with his defence.

"It was like his impudence to trouble you," said Bunn; "but cheek was always his special gift."

It was observed by those nearest concerned that after the departure of Chunder Loo and his chosen companion, Mulberry Cork, the depredations in the larder ceased. This led Miriam to definitely associate the thefts with the latter.

She mentioned it in the presence of Anthony Gubbles, who made a mental note of it. He saw more in it than met the eye of Mrs. Bunn, as we shall presently see.

Another Saturday came round, and a team from Chippenham came to the common to play the boys. They were mainly composed of the sons of tradesmen, with a retired sergeant of Artillery to assist them. Jack objected to the presence of a full-grown man in the team, but eventually yielded the point and played the match.

It ended in a draw. The Chippenham team went in first and made, with the assistance of the sergeant, a big score; and the Littlecote Lambs held out to the call of time with the loss of six wickets. It was a satisfactory and yet an unsatisfactory ending of the match. But it was better for the Lambs than losing.

"As we must have done," said Jack, when their opponents had gone, "if we had had another hour's play."

"It was like Chippenham," growled Tom Drummond, "to bring a hulking six-foot fellow with them. He bowled like a fifty-ton gun shooting at a target."

This was a fact, as many a bruise on the arms and legs of the boys witnessed. But they did not make an exhibition of their injuries before the powerful retired soldier.

On the return of the boys to the Abbey, Susan gave Jack a note. It was from Gubbles, asking him to come to his room at nine o'clock and bring his three chums with him. This was the first time Don, Tom, and Bob had been invited into the sanctum of the amateur detective, who posed so successfully as tutor.

There was not much to see, but they were interested in what there was. He explained to them the nature of his apparatus, and then, while he smoked a pipe, he went into the real business of the meeting.

"I think it is time," he said, "that we make an earnest attempt to get at the ways by which Chunder Loo went from one room to the other. There is not the least doubt he was able to do so."

"Not the least," assented Jack; "here is the knife that was dropped in the dormitory, the night I put the rope-trap up for him."

Gubbles took the knife from Jack and looked it carefully over.

"This is a very old piece of workmanship," he said, "and very rare. I have seen one like it in a museum in Vienna, but nowhere else."

"Perhaps it was stolen from there," suggested Don.

"Probably," said Gubbles. "It's as pliable as whale-bone, and as hard as steel can be made to be. It is worth money, Ford. Many a collector would give twenty pounds for it, or more."

His proposal with regard to the presumed existence of secret passages was that to-morrow afternoon should be devoted to the purpose.

"It's Sunday, I know," he said, "but is there not a saying about 'the better the day the better the deed?' Our principal and the ladies of his house will be indulging in a nap, and if the weather is fine the boys will be lounging about outside. Susan gets a half-holiday, and we shall to all intents and purposes have a free hand. I propose that at half-past two we quietly assemble in the room lately occupied by Chunder Loo."

They assented, and after a little general conversation the boys retired.

Sunday was always a quiet day at the Abbey. In the morning, weather permitting, there was the march to Mumping Malford church and back to dinner at half-past one. In the afternoon the boys were left to do as they pleased, provided they did not make a noise within easy distance of the Abbey, or go too far away.

Every other Sunday, Susan was allowed to go forth and receive the attentions of some love-lorn yokel who expressed the height and breadth and depth of his affection by staring at her and breathing hard.

All things favoured the search party on this eventful Sunday afternoon. Penny Bunn, it is true, did not indulge in a nap, but went for a drive and took the ladies with him. They were not expected back until the evening.

It was in reality an outing designed as a celebration of the departure and presumed confusion of Chunder Loo.

It was such a common thing for Jack and his three friends to steal away from the main body of boys to spend an hour together, that they were able to get to the appointed spot without exciting any attention. Gubbles was there before them, and as soon as all had assembled he closed the door and locked it.

The furniture of the room was in disorder, preparatory to a cleaning. The bedstead was bare of clothing and the drawers stood open, revealing their emptiness.

The carpet, rather a scrubby piece, was rolled up and put in a corner.

"I have already had a good look round this room," said Gubbles, "and am satisfied that the wainscoting is a fixture. There is not one movable panel."

Disappointment was written on the faces of the boys, and Jack gave it expression in words.

"Then we need not look any further," he said.

"Stop a minute," said Gubbles: "now let me ask you a question or two. Have you noticed the comparative lowness of the ceilings downstairs?"

"They are not so high as one might expect," replied Don.

"And have you not likewise observed the number of stairs leading to the first floor?" asked Gubbles. "Doesn't it strike you that the ceilings must be uncommonly thick?"

"It strikes me, now you name it," answered Jack, "but it never did before."

"My boys," exclaimed Gubbles, tapping the floor with his foot, "the secret of the passages lies *here!*"

The four listeners looked down at the flooring. It was like that of many other rooms in the respect of its being inlaid, but the work was far simpler than in other places, notably the room which Bunn, when a tutor, had been employed to pull to pieces.

"Here," repeated Gubbles, "between this flooring and the ceiling below—I believe it is the ceiling of Miss Astracan's room—there is almost room for a man to stand upright. Now let us go to work and find out the road to the hidden hollow."

The pattern of the floor was very irregular, but there was method in it, and the effect of the whole was pleasing. Squares, diamonds, stars, and a variety of shapes were deftly fitted into each other, forming a harmonious whole of woodwork of a dozen tints.

"It is, as I said, in this peculiar flooring that I hope to find out the secret of the hidden passages," said Gubbles; "you hitherto have only thought of the panelling."

"It never dawned upon me until you suggested it," replied Jack; "but I see that you may be right."

"I am certain of it, Ford. It is the only solution of the mystery."

"Which would never have occurred to us——"

"Very cunning men built this Abbey. Now to work my dear boys."

They began their labours, kneeling upon the floor and closely examining the inlaid woodwork. An exclamation from Don drew all eyes upon him.

"I have found it," he said, breathlessly.

With his pocket-knife he was engaged in prising up a piece of the flooring, shaped like the accepted form of a star. It came up readily, and proved to be thinner than the rest of the flooring, resting on a sort of ledge in the adjoining pieces.

It was just large enough to admit of the passage of a man's hand, and on its being removed they saw that the rest of the inlaid work could be lifted with ease. In short, it came to pieces like a puzzle, for the key of the whole had been removed.

————

CHAPTER CXLVIII.

FROM ROOM TO ROOM BY HIDDEN WAYS.—SOMETHING LEFT TO ASTONISH PENNY BUNN.

"WE shall want a light," said Gubbles, as he peered down into the dark hollow under the floor. "Run up to my room, Peebles, and get a dark lantern you will find upon the table by the window."

Don sped away, and was soon back with the lantern, which was already trimmed and ready for use. He found that the others, unable to restrain their curiosity, had descended to the bottom of the hollow, where there was just room for the tallest of the boys to stand upright.

"Lock the door on the inside, Peebles," sang out Gubbles, his voice sounding very strange, as if he was talking into some big empty vessel; "bring the key with you in case we should not return this way."

Don dropped down, and the lantern having been lighted, they cast its rays around; but its light failed to penetrate to the full extent of the gloomy hollow.

Overhead were the joists of the flooring, with supports like small columns, standing a few feet apart.

"I suppose the flooring could be replaced from here?" said Tom Drummond.

"With ease," replied Gubbles; "but for the present we had better leave it open. There is just a possibility that we might lose our way in the ramifications of these underground ways. As far as I can see there is nothing to guide us from one room to another."

"There are marks on the wooden supports," said Jack.

Gubbles held the light near one of them, and saw a deep notch cut in it. Others immediately around were distinguished in the same way. A short distance off the columns had two notches each.

"I see," said Gubbles, "by the number of the notches the room overhead is distinguishable."

They moved on, but had to proceed cautiously, as the false flooring on which they trod was covered with a fine dust, which, in a disturbed state, was very irritating to breathe. A few feet further on, Gubbles called a halt.

"There is another opening over our heads," he said.

Holding up the light, he showed them a square which had the appearance of having been recently disturbed. Below, the dust had been displaced by moving feet.

"Chunder Loo's slipper-marks," said Don: "there is no sign of heels, such as we have to our boots."

"You are right," said Gubbles.

He raised his arm and pushed up the square in the flooring above. It had four more pieces round it,

forming a sort of frame, and these having been removed, there was room for anyone to pass through.

"Up with one of you," said Gubbles.

Jack laid hold of the outside of the opening and pulled himself up so that his head was above the floor.

"Bunn's room," he said, "and the opening is under his bed."

"All right," replied Gubbles; "that accounts for the scare Mrs. Bunn had a few nights ago."

"May I go into the room?" asked Jack.

"What for?"

"Well, I was thinking another little scare would not hurt our valiant principal."

Gubbles laughed lightly.

"What can you do?" he asked. "Remember that it will be known you were left in the Abbey this afternoon."

"Mrs. Bunn, after Susan has done her room, always locks the door and puts the key in her pocket," said Bob Stockton. "She seems to have a most unreasonable fear of practical jokes."

"I suppose I must allow you to vent your natural desires up to a certain point," said Gubbles, "but do not go too far."

Jack pulled himself up and was followed by Don. Bob Stockton declared, with a simulated snuffle, that nothing would tempt him to do anything wrong on Sunday, and Tom had charge of the lantern, holding it so that Gubbles might examine the supports around.

Jack and Don soon returned, and as they volunteered no information about their proceedings, no questions were asked. Bob and Tom knew that in good time they would be let into the secret, and Gubbles felt that if he did not know, he could not be expected to tell or reprove.

From the bedroom, after the flooring had been carefully replaced, they went on to the dormitories, where they discovered similar arrangements. But with this difference: the flooring of the dormitories was not inlaid, and it was a short piece of planking that was removable.

So neat was the work, and the wood so thoroughly seasoned, that the possibility of its displacement would never have been suspected by any ordinary person.

At the end of number one dormitory they came to a narrow staircase, built in the wall, which was here of presumably immense thickness. It took them down to the hall, of which they had an imperfect survey through a crack in the panelling.

From thence they worked their way behind the woodwork until they arrived at a small cell or chamber, three sides of it apparently of solid stone.

But here again the ingenuity of the monks of old

was made manifest. One of the stones had an iron ring, to which was attached a chain, let into it.

"A prison for some poor wretch this has been," said Jack.

"Perhaps," replied Gubbles, dryly.

He laid hold of the chain, gave it a tug, and out came the stone. It was fully two feet square, and ought to have been of considerable weight. But Gubbles laid it aside as if it had been a wooden box.

"A sham," he said to the amazed boys, "hollow. Now let us see where we are."

Beyond the hole made, they saw a broad old-fashioned hearth. The opening was in the side of it.

"If I am not mistaken," said Jack, "we have arrived at Miss Astracan's chamber."

There was ample room to get through, and, in turn, they all made their way to the sacred chamber of the ponderous maiden lady.

Gubbles hinted that there, at least, no practical joking was to be indulged in.

"Certainly not," answered Bob, fervently; "the gods forbid. Besides, nothing scares her, and, in a way, she is horribly cute."

Gubbles sat down on a chair near the hearth, and after a thoughtful silence, said:

"Thus far we have been wonderfully successful in discovering the means by which certain things have been done, and the author of them we know. But how on earth did this man, as far as we can tell, a perfect stranger to the place, get at secrets which must assuredly have been hidden from residents here for at least a century? I have a guide to this part of the county, and the description of the Abbey is of the most copious nature, but there is no mention of what we have discovered to-day."

"Still, there may be an account of it somewhere," suggested Don, "and Chunder Loo, by some means, must have got hold of it."

"One day we may know all," said Gubbles, rising; "and now, boys, I think this must do for to-day. Any other time, given a good opportunity, we will explore further, taking the opposite direction from our starting-point. I purposely came this route to-day to put aside all doubt as to the means by which that unmitigated scoundrel Loo carried on his trickery."

"I am not at all tired of exploring," hinted Bob.

"No more am I," answered Gubbles, "but we must be prudent. The time has not come for any of us to reveal all we know. I propose that we return to the place from whence we came——"

"Like the fellow sentenced to be hanged," murmured Bob Stockton, in a tone scarcely audible.

"Just so," said Gubbles.

"I beg your pardon, sir," said Bob. "I thought I was only thinking."

"You were thinking half-aloud, and I have excellent ears. What I suggest we ought to do is to go for a walk, taking a direction that will enable us to meet our respected principal returning with the ladies."

"Respected principal," said Bob, heartily, "is *good*—distinctly good."

They all laughed as they crept back to the cell-like place. Gubbles carefully replaced the stone, and they returned to their starting-point.

The flooring in Chunder Loo's old room having been carefully put in its place, Don unlocked the door and sallied forth to remove the traces of their exploration, and go for a stroll, in accordance with the suggestion of their tutor.

They wandered about here and there, meeting with some of the boys and getting a brief glimpse of Susan and her lover as they sat on a distant stile, fixed in attitude with a foot or so of daylight between them, but no doubt inexpressibly happy.

"After all," said Gubbles, with a sigh, "the simplest nature is the happiest. To know nothing is to desire nothing. Without unfulfilled desires there is no carking care, or the thousand-and-one miseries of the gifted, inquiring mind."

"For all that," said Don, quickly, "I would rather have the mind and the misery than the dead level and the happiness of a nonentity."

"Well said," cried Gubbles, laying a hand tenderly upon his shoulder; "there is something in every boy who aspires."

"We are all going to make our mark in the world," said Bob Stockton, "or—I hope, sir, you will excuse my saying it—or *bust*."

"All who try to make their mark cannot hope to succeed," said Gubbles, with a smile. "Some must inevitably, as you forcibly put it—*bust*."

"A short life and a merry one," said Tom.

"Short and moving, anyway," said Jack.

They wandered about for an hour on the top of the cliff, and then, not seeing anything of their "respected principal" and the ladies, went home to tea. The other boys strolled in, two or three together, all wearing that repressed look one gets by habit from the keeping of an English Sabbath.

Nothing had happened to any of them worth recording, beyond a meeting between Mulberry Cork and little Jiggers, who was in the company of Short.

"He was sitting on a gate, with a young bird in his hand," said Jiggers, "and was pulling the feathers out of it."

"The cruel brute!" exclaimed a dozen voices.

"Just what we told him he was," continued Jiggers, "and then what do you think he did?"

"Threw a stone at you," suggested Philter.

"Swore at you," said Walker.

"Worse than that," replied Jiggers. "He whipped out a revolver, and said he would give us ten seconds to get away, and if we didn't start he would riddle us."

"And you went?" said Anthony Gubbles, who had been listening attentively to the chatter carried on in a softened tone of voice.

"Well, sir," said Jiggers, "he looked so vicious—and it being Sunday—and—and one thing and the other, we thought we had better go."

"You did quite right," returned Gubbles. "Only a fool braves a peril needlessly. The probabilities are that the young scamp was only threatening you, but he might have been mad enough to do you mischief."

After tea there was some quiet reading in the class-room, and a stroll in the open air prior to having supper. Mr. Bunn and his party had not returned, and the length of their drive was exciting comment.

"It isn't as if there were any tea-gardens within twenty miles to tempt him with their giddy joys," remarked Bob Stockton.

"Or as if he was still courting," said Herbert May, "and had forgotten the flight of time."

"Hallo!" exclaimed Don, "our special poet getting frivolous?"

"I often think jokes," said Herbert, quietly, "if I don't speak them on the slightest provocation as you fellows do."

"From the jocular mood to that of the grave censor," said Bob, sadly. "Herbert, old man, something is wrong with your digestion."

"I am getting rather anxious about Penny," continued Herbert; "you see, he is such—a—a—well, to put it plainly—fool, in some things. I noticed the driver of the fly. He was a very crabby-looking old man. Perhaps they have got to a fight over something."

"His crabbed face," said Bob, "may be but the mask that conceals the kindly mind. Possibly he may have allowed Bunn to take the ribbons, and our peerless principal would naturally go for the nearest post and take a wheel off."

Supper-time arrived, and Bunn had not returned. The anxiety deepened. It was almost a certainty now that something had gone wrong.

Even the serenity of Gubbles was disturbed, and he was in and out of the Abbey, listening for the sound of wheels, a dozen times between nine o'clock and half-past.

At length he gave orders for the boys to go to bed, and a like command to Susan.

But the girl would not go.

"Missus would be so angry," she said; "besides, I couldn't get a wink, thinking of poor Miss Astracan, who can't stand the night air. It brings on a garpsing with her."

"A garpsing?" exclaimed Gubbles. "What is that?"

"A ketching of the breath, sir," answered Susan.

"Oh, I see! a disturbance of a bronchial nature?"

"I suppose so, sir," said Susan, doubtfully; "anyways, she looks terrible when it comes over her."

Susan retired to the kitchen, and Gubbles once more walked to the door, intent on again listening for sounds of a returning vehicle.

CHAPTER CXLIX.

THE TERMINATION OF A HAPPY DAY.—STARTLING ADVENTURE.

A COOL, delicious twilight lay upon the earth. In the far west the faintest tinge of orange showed the road the sun had taken. Overhead the sky was a pearly grey. In the east a deep, dark blue, with the moon lying on it like a silver shield.

Gubbles walked across the playground to the gate, and stood there listening. There was no sound of wheels, but not far off there were angry voices, a male and a female engaged in warm discussion.

"Sounds like Bunn," thought Gubbles.

It was indeed the schoolmaster and his wife, returning on foot. When they came into view, both were walking slowly and painfully. Gubbles awaited their arrival home in the shadow of the gate.

"I cannot and will not be responsible for what has happened to-day," Bunn was saying as they came nearer.

"You will have to be responsible," said Miriam, "so don't talk nonsense, P. Y. dear. You hired the vehicle."

"Don't dear me!" snarled Bunn.

Gubbles thought it was time to show himself, and advanced from the shadow of the gate.

"You are very late," he said. "I fear something has happened."

"Something has happened," replied Bunn. "Miriam——"

"I cannot stop," she replied. "Susan must get me a cup of tea at once, or I shall die!"

She limped across the ground and disappeared. Bunn took off his hat and wiped his heated brow.

"I knew it," he said, "I was certain of it at starting. Gubbles, I must sit down somewhere in the cool for a bit."

"Come over to the boys' favourite seat on the wall," said Gubbles. "You are not afraid of looking down, I hope?"

"I am afraid of nothing," earnestly replied Bunn. "Not even of falling down. Life is a hollow thing!"

They crossed over to the playground and sat down upon the wall, never dreaming that their voices had floated into number one dormitory, by the open sash, and that all the occupants thereof had drawn up to the window in a little crowd, and were listening.

"I said so at the start," said Bunn. "No ordinary spring would bear the weight of that woman, especially if the wheel got jerked into a rut."

"You have had a break-down?" suggested Gubbles, amiably.

"We *have!*" answered Bunn, "far away on a moor, where I verily believe the foot of man never trod before. It happened about seven o'clock."

He paused and groaned. Gubbles kept quiet, and he soon went on with his story.

"For a while after we started," said Bunn, "all went as merry as a marriage bell. The road was smooth, and a slight incline leading to a valley below favoured the mass of flesh on four legs which was brought here to-day as a horse. May the knacker speedily claim his own! I pray that to-morrow may see the brute sacrificed!"

"I would not get excited," suggested Gubbles.

"We wanted a quiet drive," continued Bunn, "away from the habitation of man. It is easy to get from your fellow-creatures in this country, and the driver bore away to yonder moor, that even by day lies like the distant sea in the horizon. On reaching the level, the horse—I desire to be as complimentary as possible in speaking of the *thing*—dropped into a walk. Urged by my wife, I remonstrated, but the driver said the horse knew better than we did what he could draw and the pace he could go at, and if we objected to him, we had better get out and walk."

"An independent man, I should say."

"Gubbles, he was a nefarious, insolent hound. The horse crawled on over waste lands, with ne'er a house in sight, until it was, as I judged, about five o'clock. I then suggested that we should head for home. The horse was put about, and we, as I fondly hoped, steered for the Abbey. But the moor is a perfect maze of roads, sir, and the beast of a driver lost his way. At half-past six he pulled up and admitted that he knew no more where he was than the man in the moon. Not only was he a stranger to the district, but he was a new-comer to the county.

"It was bad enough to be lost, but worse remains behind," continued Bunn, after a painful pause. "For an hour or more I had been conscious of a gradual subsidence of the vehicle on the side which was graced by the substantial figure of the aunt I have acquired by marriage. I whispered as much to Mrs. Bunn and received a scornful sniff in reply. Ten minutes afterwards the driver drove into a rut—there was a pistol-like crack, a sudden heave over to the left where Miss Astracan reclined, and then we all rolled into the road. I might have been materially injured but for the feather-bed form of Miss Astracan, on which I fell head first."

"Was she hurt?"

"She was too much astonished to feel the momentary inconvenience she experienced. Mrs. Bunn, I have reason to believe, turned a complete somersault, but alighted with unequalled grace upon her feet. The driver maintained his seat, but rose to the occasion by using some of the most powerful and objectionable language it has ever been my lot to hear.

"Well, sir," said Bunn, with the tone of one concluding a narrative, "there we were, far from the madding or any other sort of crowd. What sound is that? I fancied I heard suppressed laughter?"

"I am not laughing, Mr. Bunn."

"No, I perceive you are not. I must have been mistaken. There we were, with a ruined vehicle, a lady of a substance that precluded her from walking a third of a mile, even for a wager, and a furious driver who showed so strong a desire to fight me, that I had great difficulty in declining to oblige him. Eventually, he and I went for help, and after a long ramble, came upon the cottage of a pig-dealer, who, on certain pecuniary conditions, offered to assist us with the loan of a cart. Its original use, I believe, was to convey turnips from the fields in the autumn, but it was just the thing wanted, and Miss Astracan is, I believe, coming hitherward in it. It required some inducement to prevail upon her to take a seat in so humble a vehicle, but, as it was that or nothing, she yielded.

"For ourselves," groaned Bunn, "we had to walk, after having received directions from the dealer concerning the road to take. As the horse in the cart had a heavy load, and could only travel slowly, we thought it better to come on and ease your minds of any possible anxiety you might have for our safety. We were hungry, too, not having partaken of refreshment in any form since our departure. Gubbles, I will now leave you, with the hope of finding that the board has been spread with viands for consumption. One more favour. Will you sit up and receive Miss Astracan on her return home? I confess I feel as if I had, like Captain Barclay, been walking a thousand miles in a thousand hours. Animation has deserted my legs. I am used up—done for."

He got up stiffly and walked into the Abbey with a stilty air. Gubbles, left alone, had a quiet laugh to himself. As he did so the sounds of merriment, long held in check in the dormitory, burst out, and there was a sound of many voices in No. 1, which could not be stifled by the window, which Tom Drummond prudently closed.

Penny Bunn had not been gone three minutes ere he came bounding out again.

"Gubbles," he gasped, "come indoors, for Heaven's sake! My wife is lying senseless on the top of the stairs."

Gubbles followed him as he dashed back into the house. There they found Miriam, not exactly senseless, but in a wild state, sitting upright on the top stair.

"My darling," murmured Bunn, "the fatigue of the day has been too much for you."

"It is not fatigue," she replied, with a shiver. "I had occasion to go upstairs to our room, and there I discovered two people *sleeping* in our bed."

Bunn reeled under this new horror, but Gubbles kept calm.

"Let us see who they are," he said.

Miriam had taken a light up to the room and, as it appeared, placed it on the dressing-table prior to making the startling discovery.

It was still burning, and by its aid the two men saw a sight that might well have scared a woman.

Two heads and four staring eyes, surmounted by a rough arrangement of towels in the place of nightcaps, were visible above the sheets. Bunn sank into a chair, but Gubbles proceeded to investigate the nature of the intruders.

"Two dressed-up milliner's dummies," he said.

With his original elasticity Penny Bunn became himself again.

"Dear me," he said, feebly. "Of course, they were in the cupboard. Mrs. Bunn used them in her business prior to our union."

"It is a boy's trick, I fear," remarked Gubbles, gravely, as he removed the dummies from the bed. "You should lock your door."

"It *was* locked," said Miriam from the doorway, "and I made sure that no other key would be used by placing a piece of cobweb over the keyhole. I mistrust boys all round."

"And that cobweb was there when you returned?"

"It was, Mr. Gubbles, and that self-same piece. Nobody has entered by the door."

"Yet another mystery," exclaimed Bunn, clasping his hands.

Miriam walked to the window and looked out. She found nothing there to help her to a solution of the affair. Then she had a peep under the bed, with the same result.

"I suppose it will be explained one day," she said, "and whoever is playing these tricks upon us had better keep clear of me. You need not remain, Bunn."

The two men went down and sauntered into the open air again. There Bunn went into the matter, making a variety of speculations on the mystery as wide of the truth as they could possibly be.

Gubbles, knowing it was the work of the boys, wisely said nothing.

The theories of the schoolmaster were eventually cut short by Susan appearing to ask him, as desired by her mistress, if he meant to come in to supper, or was he going to camp out for the night?

Penny Bunn thereupon vanished into the Abbey, leaving Gubbles to indulge in a quiet chuckle over the affair.

"It was a natural thing to do," he murmured. "I should have done the same thing if I had had the chance when I was a boy."

CHAPTER CL.

THE MOVING SHADOWS BELOW.—TIDINGS OF LINGO.

GUBBLES, left alone, returned to his seat on the wall, and sat there still as a statue, his eyes fixed on the dark region below.

He was thinking, and was not at the outset at all interested in the outlines of the trees, so still in the almost breathless air. Thus he remained for a time—how long he was never able to estimate—and then he was aroused from his dreamy state.

Somebody was moving below.

At first he could only hear them as they made their way through the bushes. The swish of the boughs as they pushed them aside and allowed them to swing back was very clear to the ear in the almost unearthly stillness of the night.

Presently he saw them, but very faintly. Looking down from that height, it was impossible to make out their age or sex. They were two figures, and nothing more.

They vanished at the base of the cliff, near, as he judged, the entrance to the old treasure cave.

"Visitors to that place at this hour," he thought. "I should like to know who they are."

But that pleasure was denied him. He had no time to get round to the spot, and his eyes were useless at that hour. He had not the least idea who they could be.

After a lapse of time they reappeared, and gliding away among the bushes, were lost to view.

He waited a long time to see if they returned, but there was no further movement below, and, as the dew was falling heavily, he went into the house, where he proposed to await the return of Miss Astracan.

All had gone to bed, but refreshment had been set out for the expected lady. Gubbles helped himself to a glass of gin and water, filled his pipe, and sat down to make the best he could of the interval.

It was exactly half-past one when the cart and its precious contents arrived at the Abbey. Miss Astracan was in a state bordering on a complete collapse. Fortunately the man with the cart was a strong fellow, and he, with Gubbles's help, got her into the house.

Seated in her easy-chair, she struggled through a glass of liquid refreshment. The man also had something, and then came the settlement for his services.

He was of opinion that the job was cheap at a pound. Miss Astracan thought he would be nobly paid with five shillings. Eventually half-a-sovereign settled the matter, and he departed.

Miss Astracan, after another stimulator, managed to waddle away to bed, and Gubbles sought the repose he stood very much in need of.

The morrow brought with it a startling letter, addressed to Don Peebles. It was from his mother.

The Monday morning post was always a light one, as only the cross-country letters arrived. There was no post from the town or from any place beyond the metropolis.

His mother being a pretty regular correspondent, and her letters not, as a rule, containing anything beyond domestic and other home matters, Don was in no hurry to open it. He popped it into his pocket, and there it remained until noon, when he recalled it to his mind as he sauntered in the playground with Jack.

"Hang it," he said, suddenly. "I had a letter from the mater this morning. What would she say if she knew that I did not read it at once?"

"And as the novelist says," added Jack, "devour it with avidity."

Don brought out the precious missive, opened it, and began to read. Ere he had gone far the expression of his face roused Jack's curiosity.

"Nothing wrong, I hope?" he said.

"Listen," replied Don, "here's a staggerer for you."

Dropping his voice a little, so that he might not be heard by any of the boys casually lounging about, he read the following extract from Mrs. Peebles's letter:

"You remember, my dear boy, my referring to your clerical friend, and to his not calling upon us. He passed me in a carriage, as you know. Well, the poor fellow must have shortly after met with an accident. I did hear at the time of a horse running away and smashing a carriage at Redstone Hill, but I never associated it with him. But him it certainly was, and he has been in our cottage hospital ever since. Delirious nearly all the time, too, poor man. I went to visit an old servant at the hospital—she is in there with a housemaid's knee—and saw him in one of the beds. He did not recognize me."

"Here comes a queer bit, which may lead to complications," said Don, and turning over the paper he read on:

"I told the nurse that I knew him, and that he was a clergyman from Wiltshire. The nurse laughed in my face and declared he was an actor, or something in that way. She told me he was always calling out: 'Walk up, walk up and see the wonderful show of the Lambs of Littlecote, and the secrets of the cave of treasure.' And when he got through with that he would go into a fit of fearful laughter. Isn't it sad? I saw the doctor before I came away and told him all I knew about your friend, and he promised to have enquiries made concerning him. I promised that you should write and tell him all about the dear man. Address, J. Morton, Esq., M.D., at our Cottage Hospital."

"There," said Don, in a tone of quiet despair. "I shall be glad if you can tell me exactly what I ought to do?"

"It is Lingo, of course," mused Jack.

"Is there any possibility of mistaking him for another, or another for him?" asked Don.

"I fancy not, it is a pity you are so far from home. If you were nearer you might pop in and see him. It is a sad affair, and puts everything out of gear. Poor old Lingo!"

"I really do not know what to do," said Don, with a groan. "I can't write and deny all knowledge of him; it would be making a fool of my mother, and that I am not going to do at any price."

"Don, old man," said Jack, "there is nothing you can do. Wait. Perhaps the doctor will forget what he has heard—they are awfully busy at these hospitals, and think more of the nature of the cases than of the personality of the sufferers. Lingo will pull through, and as soon as he is able, he will certainly send us a message of some sort. He is sure to relieve our anxiety."

Jack's advice was good, and Don accepted it. He could not do otherwise unless he wished to make additions to the complications that puzzled him and his friend to the verge of distraction.

CHAPTER CLI.

DON THINKS HE WILL ACT INDEPENDENTLY IN A CERTAIN MATTER.—HE HAS OCCASION TO FEEL SORRY.

THE adventure with the hired fly was not only expensive, but it had the serious effect of confining Miss Astracan to her bed for several days. Miriam was also worn out, and the stiffness of the limbs of Penny Bunn was evidenced by the careful way he walked about, and the deliberate way he sat down.

The days glided by until Thursday, and nothing was heard from the doctor of the cottage hospital. Don began to think that the opinion of Jack was the correct one. The practitioner had too much to do to think of the outside lives of his patients.

The quietude of these four days was only broken by the inevitable lively scenes common to all schoolboys. Whymper had a fight with a young yokel who come up to the cricket-ground and guffawed at his cricket. It was a perfectly fair fight, although the yokel was not accompanied by any friends, and the truth must be told—he was too much for Whymper.

He had no science, and Whymper had but little. He was the defeated, as Jiggers remarked when the battle was over, and the yokel had gone away to wash his bleeding nose in a brook. "What was the use

By E. HARCOURT BURRAGE,

Author of "Ching Ching," "Monkey Mat and Roving Dick," "The Brave Boy of the Basilisk," &c.

...S of LITTLECOTE.

NO. 21.   A Handsome Coloured Plate Presented with Every Number.

GUBBLES TRIES TO PREVENT A QUARREL BETWEEN PENNY BUNN AND CHUNDER LOO.

PRICE ONE PENNY.

ALDINE PUBLISHING CO., 9, Red Lion Court, Fleet St., and 1, 2, & 3, Crown Court, Chancery Lane, London.

secret, and to withhold anything from his dearest chums required a strong and resolute spirit.

This he was now in possession of.

As for getting at a solution of the thing by thinking, he soon found it was impossible, and gave up the task; not in despair, but quietly resolved not to bother with it.

When Saturday came he realized that it would be difficult to get away without exciting comment, unless he did so immediately after dinner, when Jack would be superintending the getting together of the cricketing materials. Of course on his return he could, if he chose, explain everything, which he was resolved to do.

If he made out anything of importance he would be all right, but provided the result was nil he felt that he might lay himself open to censure from his leader.

Jack was not jealous of his authority, but he had a theory, which is a perfectly correct one, that too many generals, like cooks engaged in the making of broth, are apt to spoil everything.

But that he must risk, because he had set his heart upon doing something, unaided and alone.

When the boys came out, and Jack ran his eye over them, he missed Don at once, and asked if he had gone on.

"Not alone, surely," suggested Bob Stockton. "Don isn't Mulberry Cork."

Philter went back to the Abbey for him, and returned with the information that he was not there. Mr. Gubbles, who was preparing for one of his botanising expeditions, knew nothing of him either.

"It's deuced odd," muttered Jack; "so unlike Don."

"Perhaps he has gone to Smudgem Bender for some lollipops," suggested Little Jiggers.

"All your theories, Jig," said Herbert May, "have the stomach for a foundation."

Jack marshalled his men and took them away to the cricket-field. Don's action puzzled him, and he was uneasy, but he was of opinion that he could take care of himself, and speedily ceased to think of his absence.

Meanwhile Don, having got well away without being observed, was hastening down through the wood to a spot where he could descend with ease and safety. He met no one by the way, and within the hour was in sight of the cave.

It was nothing to look at. There are thousands of such openings in the chalk and sand pits of the country. Only a boy would, without knowing the place, have been able to extract a grain of romantic thought from the sight of its meagre entrance, a mere spot in the cliff.

But to Don it was associated with events of a stir-

ring nature, and although he did not dream of danger, his heart beat quicker and quicker as he advanced towards it.

He stopped at the mouth and peered in, but could see nothing. Then after a slight hesitation, which made him smile, he entered.

He had advanced but a few steps when he was staggered by a heavy blow he received upon the head, and fell with a crash to the ground.

His mind was in semi-chaos, but he was still able to hear a growling curse, and to see a form standing over him ready to strike again.

With a feeling of astonishment, that made him forget the agony following the blow he received, and helped also to clear his brain, he saw that his assailant was *a woman!*

————

CHAPTER CLII.

GUBBLES DIRECTS HIS STEPS IN THE RIGHT DIRECTION.—HE HEARS AN ASTOUNDING STORY.

MR. ANTHONY GUBBLES was going botanising, as we have previously declared. All classes of science he loved, but the study of herbs was his passion. He was never so happy as when wooing Nature in her verdant garb, and luring her to tell with her still soft voice stories of her wondrous doings with the products of the wood and field.

Slung about his shoulders by a strap, was a bag for the larger specimens, in his pocket he had sundry boxes for the more delicate results of his searchings. In his hand he carried a strong, crooked Alpine stick, not to assist him in walking or climbing, but to enable him to get at the mosses and leaves out of ordinary human reach.

Unconsciously he followed in the track of Don, and contrary to his usual habit, he did not pause by the way. His destination was the wooded ground at the foot of the schoolhouse cliff.

Hitherto, he had not visited it as a scientific searcher, and he looked upon it as a veritable happy hunting-ground, wherein to spend a pleasant afternoon.

It was his intention to get a peep at the cave again, but that was quite a subordinate part of the outing.

Gubbles was, as usual, in a thoughtful mood. There was no ruffle on his placid face, but in the eyes there was an expression of deep longing to get at something at present beyond his ken.

He was not a man to enter wildly into the pursuit of anything, and if the first rush ended in a failure, to give it up, but rather one of those steady goers who start easy, and never abandon the task until the goal is attained.

If any man in the world could unearth the mystery of the murder of his friend Ruskin, he would do it. While life and intelligence lasted, he would never give in.

A glorious day it was—warm, with a soft wind that fanned the cheek, and gave new life to those who breathed its balmy odours. There were clouds in the sky, but so high up, that they were mere flecks of wool passing majestically and leisurely across the face of the sun, without perceptibly dimming its life-giving light.

It was the hour of stillness, when the cattle get under the shadow of trees in the fields, and stare with placid contentment at each other, replete with food, and too lazy to move about.

It was the hour when the tinker and the tramp stop to rest, and extract from a roadside *siesta* such fulness of joy as can be got from their wandering, friendless life; the hour when the village is as empty and silent as the city of the dead.

Gubbles felt the influence of the day and the time, and was in a contented mood, steadily trudging along until there suddenly burst upon his ears a cry for help.

He was within a furlong of the cave. On his right was the perpendicular cliff, speckled with bushes, planted there by seed-carrying birds and insects. On its head the old Abbey formed a crown of architectural glory.

From whence came that cry?

It sounded as if it arose from some place over his head, but he knew that it could not be so. It was the mocking echo that sought to deceive him.

Ahead he could not see very far, owing to the undergrowth and the trees, but from that way he was certain the cry came, and grasping his Alpine-stock firmly in his hand, he ploughed his way on; fighting through the bushes, as sea-bathers struggle through the waves for the shore.

Another cry was heard, and nearer.

He answered it with a shout, and increased his pace. The voice was shrill, yet sweet, that of a boy or a woman.

Gubbles had a resonant voice of his own, and it rang out like a trumpet blast, rousing a big echo and many minor ones from the nooks and crannies of the cliff.

It was that cry which saved Don's life.

Half-a-minute later he saw the boy reeling towards him, falling against the trees, stumbling over the roots of bushes and holding his head, from which blood was dropping, tightly between his hands.

He threw his arms around the boy as soon as they met, and supporting him, cried out in anguish:

"Peebles, who has done this?"

"After *her!*" gasped Don; "don't let her get away!"

"Her?" repeated Gubbles, as he applied his handkerchief to two fearful-looking wounds on the boy's head. "*Who?*"

"*Mulberry Cork's mother*," gasped Don, and fell back unconscious.

"Cork's mother," murmured Gubbles, bewildered; "the poor boy is *mad*."

It really seemed so. Unable to account for the injuries Don was suffering from, and not daring to leave him for what would have been a vain pursuit of the person who had injured him, Gubbles could only remain and do his best to restore him to consciousness.

There was no water handy, nothing that could be of real service, and practically it had to be left for Nature to bring him back. Nature, having her appointed time for everything, was very slow in reviving Don, and it was many minutes ere he opened his eyes and stared in dumb surprise at Gubbles.

"Something has happened to me," he said, faintly.

"Pull yourself together, Peebles," returned Gubbles, "and tell me exactly how it came about."

"I thought I would try to solve the mystery of those two men, or whoever they were, visiting the cave. I came to-day to do it."

"And you found somebody there?"

"Yes, I did. I think I can stand now, Mr. Gubbles. Anyhow, I can sit down by this tree. My head aches a bit, but otherwise, I am all right."

"You have two nasty wounds," answered Gubbles, "and they must be attended to as soon as possible. You were saying you found somebody in the cave."

"It was Mulberry Cork's mother."

"Peebles!"

"I am telling you the truth," said Don. "She knocked me down with a stick the moment I entered, but I did not lose my senses. In fact, seeing her, pulled me round a bit. I warded off the second blow, but the third she aimed at me, I got here. It was a stiff one, but still I kept my wits, and as she kicked at me, I laid hold of her foot and down she went, striking her head against the broken masonry on the ground, and that settled her for a time. I, however, was too much dazed to move, but after a time I managed to crawl out of the cave, slowly, and more like a snail than anything else.

"I can't say how long I was travelling fifty yards," continued Don, after a pause for breath, "but it must have been quite a journey. Then it seems she came round and left the cave to see what had become of me. I hid myself in some bushes and she was working round, just as a dog on the scent would, a good twenty minutes ere she found me out. I had pulled round a little, and managed to stand up and try to run for it. Swearing horribly, she pulled out a knife, and that was when I shouted—twice, wasn't it? Then—I suppose it was you—there came a shout back, and the vile woman fled."

"It is a most extraordinary story," said Gubbles, "and you are not, as I first supposed, suffering from delirium. But I can do nothing just now, except get you to some place where you can be attended to."

"We might get a lift to Smudgem Bender ont he high road," suggested Don. "Carts often pass along that way, and it is not far from here."

Gubbles picked up his Alpine-stock, and with his disengaged hand took Don's arm. Walking slowly, they got to the high road in a quarter of an hour, and soon had the pleasure of seeing a farmer's hay-cart approaching.

It proved to be one of Botch's, and the man was known to Don. A word sufficed for the required lift to be given, and at a slow pace they proceeded to the village.

The man was naturally curious to learn how Don came by his injuries, and Gubbles said he had been attacked by a tramp skulking in the Littlecote Cave, as it was now called.

The labourer declared that tramps were the pest of the neighbourhood, and ought to be put down "by hact of parlymenk."

Gubbles agreed with him, as a matter of course, and changed the subject by offering the labourer a pipe of tobacco from his pouch. The rest of the journey was given up to nicotine, and talk on agricultural topics in general.

In the village they encountered Botch in person. He was much concerned to find Don in a white and wounded condition. His house, he said, was at the service of the boy and the schoolmaster.

The story told to Botch was practically a true statement of the affair, but Gubbles asked him to keep it a secret.

"It was a woman who did it," he said (he had withheld the name of the offender), "and boys don't like the idea of being knocked about by women; they get such a lot of chaff from their chums."

"I can understand the feeling," said Botch. "When I was a boy I didn't mind a bit of cart-whip from my feyther, but a spank from mother used to drive me wild."

Don had a good wash and a glass of wine. Mrs. Botch found him some sticking-plaster—such a good housewife would be sure to keep it in stock—and he was almost himself again in an hour.

They stayed to tea, and afterwards Botch drove them home.

"I'll keep an eye open for that 'ere hag," he said, as they parted at the Abbey gates; "she be a bad lot."

"If you can lay hands on her," said Gubbles, "lock her up, and send for me."

Botch promised to do so, and Gubbles asked him to leave a telegram at the Smudgem Bender post-office as he passed on his way home. It was an after-thought.

That telegram was addressed to a well-known detective, whose headquarters were at Scotland Yard, London.

They were the first home, and they had the dining-room to themselves. The tea was already laid, but having refreshed liberally at Blotch's, they were in no hurry for it.

"Peebles," said Gubbles, "I must confess that I have received a floorer to-day. All sorts of possibilities, half formed in my mind, may come out of it. It certainly seems amazing that a woman who has stayed at the Langham Hotel, and banks at the London and Westminster, should have occasion to skulk away in that cave."

"She did not go abroad, as she professed to do?" remarked Don.

"That is certain."

"I have an idea concerning it," said Don, "but as it is rather misty, and my mind is still in a bit of a whirl, I won't worry about it now."

"Don't," advised Gubbles, "there is no hurry. I am convinced we can move easily now."

In three hours—it was about nine o'clock—a reply came back to Gubbles's telegram:

"With you in the morning. Have closed up every road. The lady is quite safe."

Gubbles went to Bunn with the telegram, and confided to him the facts of the day. It is needless to say that that grandiloquent gentleman was laid, morally speaking, on his back.

"I wish I had known the vulgar wretch was skulking so near me," he said.

"What would you have done?" asked Gubbles, meditatively.

"I should have arrested her as a fraud," replied Penny Bunn.

"Alone?"

"Surely, Mr. Gubbles, I am a match for a woman?"

"For some, perhaps, but this particular animal has a lot of the tigress in her, if I am not mistaken. You never know what any woman is made of until you tackle her."

"True," murmured Bunn, and then his own gentle Miriam rose up, like a sweet vision of the sex, before his eyes. He sighed deeply, shook Gubbles by the hand, told him he was a cute sort of fellow, and went away to supper.

He ate with his usual appetite, but scarcely heeded what he was eating. His gifted mind was dwelling on what he had heard, and he came to a conclusion thereon—a wrong one, of course.

CHAPTER CLIII.

LOBBS, THE LONDON DETECTIVE.—PREPARING TO UNEARTH MRS. CORK.

THE name of the expected detective was Lobbs, and he came down, as he promised, on the following day, and put up at the Cowley Arms. He was dressed as a dealer, and gave out that he was there to buy a consignment of the famous Wiltshire pigs.

Being Sunday, he could not, of course, go into business. As a mild, harmless way of spending the day, he said he would take a stroll, and sauntered in the evening up to the Abbey.

All he did there was to interview Bunn and Gubbles, in the latter's room, and receive all the information available from these sources.

Bunn gave him a minute description of the lady, and of the entire affair connected with the coming of Mulberry Cork under such peculiar circumstances.

Lobbs seemed to extract a great deal of quiet amusement out of the relation.

"It is a clever bit of work all round," he said. "I shall not stir until the morning. I will be here early, when I shall be glad to see the boy Peebles."

As he was going away in company with Bunn and Gubbles, who proposed to see him through the wood, he met Miriam on the stairs. She stared at him, and Lobbs, taking off his hat, said it was "a fine evening."

"A friend of mine, Mrs. Bunn," said Gubbles. "Mr. Lobbs."

"A wholesale dealer in porcine material, my dear," murmured Penny Bunn; "the only English rival to the mighty pork merchants of Chicago."

Miriam smiled sweetly. She was a great admirer of merchants. They all seemed to roll in money, which had been the hitherto unaccomplished aim of her life.

"Do you stay here long?" she asked.

"Possibly for a week, ma'am," he answered.

"If you can spare any time to visit us," said Miriam, "we shall be happy to see you."

Lobbs thanked her, and meant it, too. Nothing could have been more opportune, as he might possibly have occasion to pay several visits to the Abbey.

"Fine lady, that, of yours, sir," said Lobbs to Bunn, when they reached the open air. "Got quite an air, sir. If you wasn't the perfect gentleman, I should say she was high above her station."

"It is necessary to have a good tone in both the master and mistress of this establishment," returned Bunn, with lofty affability.

"That is clear to any human eye," assented Lobbs.

"Being of humble birth, I always feel a bit put out in aristocratic company. But I like it for one thing. You ain't made to feel your inferiority."

Bunn rose to the occasion, and his high-toned amiability was rather trying to Gubbles, master as he was of the art of keeping his countenance.

At parting, Lobbs deferentially took the hand generously offered by the schoolmaster.

"Now there is one thing I should like to say," said the detective, "and that is, you, sir, are not only a gentleman, but a man of common sense and prudence. You would rather die on the rack than go talking to people about my being here. You can hold your tongue, sir, you can."

"I believe so," said Bunn; "there are a few secrets here," smiting his breast, "of great people who have confided in me, that would astonish you."

"I should be astonished if there wasn't," returned the detective; "confiding in you comes as natural as saying, how do you do? I'll bet there isn't a boy in your school who *could* keep anything from you."

"They bring all their little troubles to me," said Bunn, with a fond smile.

"You are proud, too, in a right way," continued Lobbs, eyeing him closely; "you are not the man to sink your position by going to such places as the Cowley Arms. Not you; except when taken there on business."

Penny Bunn assured him that he had been obliged to visit that hostelry, under pressure of events on two or three occasions, but it had ever been a source of regret that he should be obliged to set his foot in a publichouse.

"Men like me," pursued Lobbs, "can't help ourselves. We are compelled to pop in now and then. I am staying there."

Having thus neatly shut off Bunn from a possible early visit to the Cowley Arms, he once more bade him good night, and went humbly on his way.

"A most discerning man, that," remarked Bunn, as he and Gubbles faced homewards; "reads characters at a glance."

"He is pretty shrewd in that direction," was the quiet reply.

School had begun in the morning when Lobbs arrived, and there was any amount of excitement when the two masters and Don were called out of the room in company.

Don's injuries could not be concealed, but only three of his friends knew the source from whence they were derived. Gubbles had agreed to his acquainting Tom, Jack and Bob with the facts, leaving them to make their own deductions. Don personally made none, and the others were practically at sea. The whole affair was beyond an ordinary mystery. It was incomprehensible.

Nor did it seem that Don would be able to help them. He was the first to return, and all he had to say was that a man, dressed like a dealer, who might be a detective, had asked him a number of questions about the morning in the cave, and he had gone away to examine the place.

This was about half-past ten o'clock. A few minutes before twelve the whole school was startled by a knocking at the planking which had been put in the place of the door that divided the class-room from the inner chambers.

Bunn, who by the position of his desk, was nearest to the spot, fairly tumbled out of his seat, and in the dread silence that followed, a voice was heard calling:

"Anyone on the other side?"

"It is Mr. Lobbs," said Gubbles. "Do not be alarmed, boys."

Don glanced at Jack and saw that he had lost some of his colour. Their eyes met, and Jack's seemed to say:

"This may lead to something awkward."

With the schoolroom poker Gubbles removed one of the planks, and Lobbs squeezed through.

"A most extraordinary thing has happened," he said. "I have been visiting the cave on the plain below, and find that it communicates with this house by a staircase and a trap-door. The latter was secured by a nail or two, but I managed to force it."

"I never heard that there was such a communication before," said Bunn, breathlessly.

"Well," returned Lobbs, "it *is* there, as you may come and see for yourself, if school is over."

"I am about to dismiss," said Bunn, and the boys were despatched about their "business."

Jack gave the meeting signal, and the inner circle promptly assembled on the wall in the playground.

"That Lobbs is a keen fellow," began Jack, "and all sorts of things will crop up in his speculative mind."

"Bunn will be sure to let out that we were down in the vaults during the time of the barring-out," said Bob, with a groan; "he can't keep that pendulum tongue of his still for a moment."

How well they understood the nature of their gifted principal! Bunn, having obtained a light in the form of an old stable-lantern, accompanied the officer to the vaults, and while the sombre place was being examined, he let loose his tongue and dilated fully on the barring-out.

Lobbs listened quietly, his eyes wandering here and there until they suddenly espied a lamp, one of those the boys had used in their visits to the vaults.

It had been left there and forgotten.

The officer took it up and examined it.

Bunn glanced at the lamp, and opening his eyes, exclaimed:

"Bless me. That is an old lamp I used to have in my room. It disappeared about the time of the barring-out."

"Then the boys were in the habit of coming down here?" inquired the officer.

"I don't know for certain. I forget."

"And how did the barring-out end?"

"The boys took themselves off, and were lost for a day or two."

"Where did they go?"

"Nobody knows to this day."

"Humph! They had no difficulty in getting away?"

"They risked their necks," said Bunn, with a shiver; "everyone of the young villains went down by the cliff, using a rope. No, one of them was afraid. He remained behind."

"Can I see that boy?" asked Lobbs.

"No, he has left the school."

Lobbs went on with the examination of the vaults. Presently he came upon a plate and a dish. In the latter there was a portion of meat pie. Hard by lay the bone of a leg of mutton.

"Mrs. Cork has not been starved while she was hiding here," said Lobbs.

Bunn looked at the mutton bone, then at the plate and dish.

There was the light of recognition in his eyes.

"These things," he said, "came from the larder attached to my establishment. I understand it all now. The vile woman must have been here some time, and her precious son robbed me to give her sustenance."

"So your larder was robbed?" remarked Lobbs, in a casual way.

"It was, and much anxiety it gave us; for we feed the boys in a way rarely equalled and never surpassed in the——"

"Just so," interposed Lobbs; "and feeding them in that way, you thought it more than cruel they should pilfer food from your larder. But stolen things are always sweeter than bread earned by honest labour."

"I can't understand why the woman came here at all," said Bunn, "or why she should want to be fed like a—a caged animal. She has a banking-account, and a good one, as I was assured when I went to town about that cheque of mine."

"Which, by the way," said Lobbs, "you have forfeited all right to by allowing the boy to go away."

"Can't I prosecute Snicker for it?"

"Well, seeing he is to be tried for murder, I should advise you to let him alone. Drop the cheque business; it may get you into all sorts of complications. As for Mrs. Cork and her banking-account, I daresay your curiosity will be satisfied on that head one day.

I have seen enough for the present, and will go out by the way I came. You will naturally take the short cut to your residence."

He handed the lantern to Bunn, and vanished through the opening that served as a mouth to the cave-like entrance to the vaults. The schoolmaster watched his form until it was lost in the woody surroundings without. Then he turned back, and slowly wended his way upstairs, thinking.

"I used to be good at conundrums," he muttered, as he stood by the trap-door above, and blew out the light in the lantern; "but I can't get at this business."

There was, indeed, a lot to fathom and explain. Keener and more experienced intellects than his were puzzling over some of the mysteries also, and none as yet saw a solution clearly before him.

The capture of Mrs. Cork would probably be of great service, and to that end the police were scouring the country. But the word had been passed to go to work quietly, and even in Smudgem Bender nothing was known of the discovery made by Don, nor of the arrival of Lobbs and the activity of the officials.

CHAPTER CLIV.

DON AND THE DETECTIVE.—CHUNDER LOO IN A FOG.

IT was not until the following morning that Don received a message from Lobbs to come down to the Cowley Arms, in a casual sort of way, and have a chat with him.

As the message came through Bunn, he had no difficulty in getting leave from school, and alone he wended his way through the wood shortly after nine o'clock.

He half-expected to meet with Mulberry Cork, or possibly Chunder Loo, and had taken the precaution to bring a stout stick with him, which, however, was not required.

He did not meet a living soul until he was approaching Smudgem Bender, and then it was but a labourer, or one of the old women of the district, he saw on the road.

As he passed the cottage inhabited by Mrs. Snicker he glanced at it, and saw Chunder Loo sitting by the window reading the paper. But as he had his back to the road, Don did not imagine for a moment that he had been perceived.

There was a lively scene at the Cowley Arms, for it had got abroad that a buyer, on an extensive scale, of the native pig had arrived.

The rustic mind, though slow at most matters, has the gift of romantic dreaming; and already it was considered an undoubted fact that the said buyer was from foreign parts, with a commission to give fabulous sums for porcine animals—provided, of course, they were of the Wiltshire breed, the like of which, in the estimation of the Wiltshire folk, no other spot in the world can produce.

Lobbs was a bit dismayed to find how fervent was the response to the announcement, but he was fully equal to the occasion. When Don arrived, he was outside the inn inspecting some of the pigs brought for him to look at, and exchanging a few words with the dealers generally.

"Of course," he said, "I can't settle on a deal *now*. My orders are to get nothing but the best, and to pay the best price. I must have time to judge, and if you will leave your addresses, I will look round or write to you. Meanwhile, order what you would like to drink."

He caught sight of Don, and nodded in a friendly manner, but seemed to be in no hurry to get away from the pig-owners.

Don prudently did not press forward, but remained quiet until the thirst of the men had been assuaged, and they had, after a struggle with their pigs as to the right road to take, gone their way.

Then Lobbs motioned for Don to enter the inn, and ascend to a room on the first floor, which he had taken for his private use.

"You have a cool head, youngster," he said, as they sat down. "I was afraid you would make a rush at me."

"I fancied you wished to be as cautious as possible," replied Don.

"I do. Caution is never thrown away. Now just tell me all about your struggle with Mrs. Cork, and if you have any impressions on your mind, I am prepared to hear of them with due respect. For, as I told you, you have a clear head, and are as likely a lad as there is up yonder, and the old Abbey has got some good specimens of the genus boy."

Don flushed a little; but he was inclined to think that the detective might be "taking a rise" out of him.

Having given the particulars of the meeting with Mrs. Cork, and a few ideas he had conceived thereon, Don found himself being led on to talking about the barring-out.

It was a subject he could always speak of with enthusiasm, and he was all aglow with it until Lobbs suddenly turned to the vaults.

"You boys have had a peep down there?" he said.

Don was immediately on the alert not to betray anything of importance.

"Yes," he said, thoughtfully, "we went down; but it was such a beastly place. Looked as if it was haunted."

"As if *you* would care for a ghost or two," remarked Lobbs, jocularly.

"I *do* care for them," returned Don, "and so does everyone who is not an absolute fool."

"I suppose you used to go in and out there?" continued Lobbs.

"We knew there *was* an outlet," replied Don; "but we did not make use of it when we went away. You see, only four of us had been into the vaults at all."

"Only four of you?" said Lobbs, quickly.

Don drew in a bit. He felt that he had said too much.

"The others were not eager to go down, because there was a talk about the ghosts I spoke of," he said.

"I can understand their feelings," said Lobbs, carelessly.

He asked Don if he would care to have any refreshment, and on receiving a reply in the negative, commended him for his abstinence.

"If you never touch strong liquors," he said, with the portentous gravity of a temperance lecturer, "you will never know an unhappy moment. Health will be your friend, and prosperity will keep at your heels like a dog. As you go downstairs, ask the landlord to send me up a glass of whisky."

Don smiled as he shook hands with Lobbs and went away, giving the requisite order as he passed through the bar.

Lobbs was standing by the window shortly after, staring at the quiet highway. His glass of whisky had arrived, but he had not touched it. Glancing up the street, he saw the sinewy figure of Chunder Loo approaching, with the air of a man who was coming to the inn to drink.

There is always something about a man as he approaches a house he frequents, a sort of overdone style of movement, implying, "I am not going into that public-house, although you may think so."

Lobbs understood it. In a moment he was on his way downstairs with his glass of whisky in his hand, and glided into the coffee-room with the stealthiness of a spectre.

He had barely settled down in the corner by the fireplace, and put on a feigned sleep, when Chunder Loo entered.

He stared at Lobbs, who opened his eyes and looked heavily about him.

"Having a nap, my friend?" said Chunder Loo.

"Dang the lot of 'em!" growled Lobbs; "nuthin' can be done with these dealer chaps without drink. I am a steady man as a rule, but the five or six glasses this morning ought not to have sent me off."

"But they did, it seems," remarked Chunder Loo, as he rang the bell. "I hear you have come down pig buying."

"I want pigs," answered Lobbs, giving himself a shake, "but I don't want them at the price these people are asking. They must think I'm buying for

royalty, whereas I am buying for my brother-in-law. You have heard of Howler's sausages in London, I suppose?"

"I have never been in London," replied Chunder Loo; then, as the girl at this moment entered the room, "Four of the usual, Mary."

"Not in London," repeated Lobbs; "then you landed in Liverpool?"

"Yes," said Chunder Loo, "years ago. Though born in India—by the way, what would you take me for?"

"Take you for?"

"Yes. I pursue some calling. What is it?"

"I should say," said Lobbs, after a long and heavy stare at him, "that you have tried the Turkey rhubarb line."

"Well, I have had a shot at it. Anything else?"

"There was a chap something like you at the revels here, I'm told. He ate fire. The landlord was speaking of him this morning."

"I am not a fire-eater," said Chunder Loo, meekly, "I am a teacher."

"Never!" exclaimed Lobbs, in breathless astonishment.

"It is true, and I was a teacher at the Abbey school."

"Where's that?" asked Lobbs.

"Up beyond the wood, Mumping Malford Wood." Lobbs shook his head.

"Don't know it," he said, and emptied his glass.

"Will you have another drink with me?" asked Chunder Loo.

"No, not now," was the reply; "my head won't stand it. I've had too much already, and shall be better for a walk."

"The Abbey is worth a visit," said Chunder Loo, "and I want a walk. Shall we go together? That is," he added, meekly, "unless you do not care to be seen with a foreigner with so dark a skin."

"Oh, blow your skin!" said Lobbs, "I'll be glad of your company. I've heard of a murder hereabouts. Perhaps you know the spot where 'twas done?"

"Everybody knows it," answered Chunder Loo. "I shall be happy to show it you, if you think it will interest you."

"Well," said Lobbs, with a laugh, "most people, if nigh a place of that sort, like to see it."

He said something about being ready in a minute, after he had had a wash, and left the room. Chunder Loo, alone, fell into a train of thought.

"I don't understand that chap," he muttered; "I am completely fogged. Dealer, is he? Maybe. Fool? No. But he is not wise in trusting himself with me in the wood."

He would not have doubted the wisdom of Lobbs if he could have seen him in his room just then.

He was engaged in preparing for the walk by putting a pair of revolvers inside the outer pockets of his loose coat, and in the right one a knuckle-duster, so that it could at a moment's notice be slipped over his fingers, ready for use.

————

CHAPTER CLV.

MORE AND MORE ASTONISHED.—DON AND JACK.

DON got back to the Abbey about half-past eleven. It was then, as he judged, too late for him to think of books, and he refrained from presenting himself before the masters prior to the dismissal of the boys. Then he thought it would be advisable for him to give in some sort of report to Penny Bunn.

Seeking that gentleman in the retirement of his private apartment, where he had the good fortune to find him alone, he told him of the interview he had had, and Penny Bunn listened to him with the air of a judge noting the observations of a leading witness in an important case.

"And did he express any opinion," he asked, "as to the probable early apprehension of that vile woman?"

"He did not," answered Don

"Humph!" muttered Bunn, "my faith in the ordinary detective is not great. In the end I may have to take this matter in hand myself."

Don could have smiled, but he did not. He merely remarked that it appeared to be necessary that somebody should do something.

"What the detective body in this country lack is—*go!*" said Bunn. "We have no Fouché on English soil."

"Fouché was a French detective, I suppose?" hazarded Don.

"He was, and the best," answered Bunn. "I am a descendant of his on my mother's side, and I believe the gift of unearthing the deepest mysteries has been in a measure transmitted to me. But I have never really cultivated it. I can recall the astuteness with which my mother—she was a very remarkable woman, Peebles—would, in a way, analyse my father on his return home, generally two hours later than he promised to be. 'You have been to the Rifleman,' she would say—the 'Rifleman,' I may remark, was an hostelry he occasionally frequented—'and you have been drinking and talking politics.' My father, a man of truth and honour, two virtues I inherit from him, always admitted politics, but denied the drink beyond one pint of mild ale. Now, I have an idea regarding this Mrs. Cork."

Don started, and looked at Penny Bunn, whose eyes were fixed upon the floor in a meditative way. But he said nothing, awaiting the further statement from the schoolmaster.

"Mrs. Cork," pursued Bunn, "is, in my humble opinion, not Mrs. Cork at all."

Don's face lost all its natural colour, and his breath was short as if he were taken aback by the prospect of some astounding revelation.

"Mulberry," pursued Bunn, "is not her son. He is one of those hapless children who have been adopted for a stated sum in response to an advertisement. He is, as I may put it, a full-blown specimen of the nefarious results of baby-farming."

Don felt so queer that he was obliged to sit down. Penny Bunn, speaking as one who unfolds a dark story, went on.

"Mrs. Cork at the outset doubtless intended to keep the child and bring him up according to the light within her. He disappointed her, and after many trials she resolved to foist him upon some person, and unfortunately selected me to take up the office she longed to abandon. Fearing that she might get into trouble, she resolved for a time to live a life synonymous with that of the hermits of old, and chose the cave beneath the cliff for that purpose. There Mulberry found her, and moved by a latent tenderness in his disposition, he resolved to give her some return for past favours by feeding her at my expense. It was a thought essentially human, for in all of us there is something that links us to common humanity."

Don could not help it. He burst into a roar of laughter and could not stop himself, even when Bunn fixed an indignant eye upon him.

"Peebles," he said, "explain your mirth, which at the moment appears to me to be slightly out of place."

"Pardon me, sir," said Don, "but I could not help it. The position Mrs. Cork found herself in must have been very comical, to anyone looking on."

"Just so," returned Bunn, with a gleam of suspicious doubt in his eye; "the whole thing is ridiculous, but the serious element in it is, that I have fed and given culture to that little villain without getting any adequate return. You may go."

Don went, and in the hall without had another laugh, but a quieter one. The revelation he had expected was very different from the one he received.

From the schoolmaster Don sought out Jack, to give him a more elaborate version of the interview of the morning. He found him, not in the playground, as he thought he would, but in the class-room, alone.

Jack received Don's statement with a listening face, and appeared to attach especial weight to the detective's questions concerning the vaults.

"I am afraid, old man," he said, "that Lobbs is not a Copps, but something far and away beyond him."

"He may be," answered Don, "but not so keen as you think he is."

"Well, we can leave him for the time," rejoined Jack.

"What do you think of Bunn's opinion of Mrs. Cork?"

"I would rather have yours, Don."

"Suppose I have none to give?"

Jack cast a quick look at him before saying anything further. He bit his lip, too, and seemed to have something on his mind.

"Are you acting quite straight with me?" he asked.

"I am straight in telling you all I know," answered Don, "but I would rather not indulge in speculations. They might only lead us astray."

"But you have some thought concerning her?"

"Yes."

"And you have named it to someone—Gubbles, let us say?"

"I have," replied Don, "and it is by his desire that I say nothing. He thinks my ideas are wild, but not impossible of being the truth. I don't like leaving you out, Jack, so if you will come with me we can hear what Gubbles has to say on the score of the notion I have in my head being revealed to you."

"I don't want to be confided in as a matter of justice to me."

"You'll have to come, Jack. If I held back, it was simply with the idea of showing you how clever I really am."

Don laughed, and the slight frown that had been on Jack's face disappeared.

"I see," he said, "you were ambitious to distinguish yourself without my aid. I respect the desires of an aspiring young man, and if you should be on the right track, you shall have all the honour and glory. Gubbles is upstairs. Let us go to him."

They went up to the room of their friend and were with him when the dinner-bell rang.

As Jack came downstairs with Don and the tutor in response to that melodious summons to eat and drink, his face was as bright as of yore. Indeed, it went further than that. It seemed to have the light of a fresh inspiration upon it.

Don's idea had been confided to him, whatever it was, and he was perfectly happy.

———

CHAPTER CLVI.

CHUNDER LOO SEEKS LIGHT AND FINDS ADDITIONAL DARKNESS.

ON that day Miriam was going to Smudgem Bender to partake of dinner with an old neighbour. At a quarter to one she sallied forth in all the glory of a new print dress, and a natty little hat to match it, with Dolphus at her heels.

That is, Dolphus kept at her heels until he was out of the Abbey gates, and then, with canine joyousness on finding that he was really bound for a long walk, dashed barking into the wood.

Presently he was silent, having discovered an old rabbit-burrow, into which he thrust his head, and sniffed the fading fragrance of a departed bunny.

No doubt it was otto of roses to him, for he sniffed until he felt the dust he had acquired thereby was leading up to a sneeze.

Withdrawing his head to the open air, so that it might have full play, he became aware of two men approaching. One was Lobbs, a stranger to him, and the other was Chunder Loo.

It was no doubt a severe shock to Dolphus to find that his old and hated enemy was still in the neighbourhood. Anyway, it warded off the sneeze, and produced another sound in the form a short, angry bark.

Chunder Loo stooped down and picked up a stick. Thereupon Dolphus began to bark in earnest, backing towards his approaching mistress in the wriggling fashion of a small dog which has to retreat with his eyes to a foe.

Miriam was almost as much astounded as her dog on seeing the two men, and Chunder Loo was, on beholding her, visibly discomposed.

Lobbs was the only calm member of the party.

"How do you do, Mrs. Bunn?" he said, raising his hat. "I was just about paying a visit to the Abbey."

"I am sorry to see you in such disreputable company," replied Miriam, "but you may not be aware of the character of the person you are with."

Chunder Loo grinned. Lobbs looked pained and astonished.

"I met this gentleman at the inn," he said, "and he offered to show me the country and the Abbey. He says he is a tutor there."

"He *was*," replied Miriam, "but he was dismissed for base conduct. If he sets a foot in the place, he does so at his peril."

She sailed on, with Dolphus keeping a wary eye on Chunder Loo until he was by, and then he barked until he was out of sight and hearing.

"I say," said Chunder Loo, frowning at Lobbs, "you seem to know Mrs. Bunn?"

"I guessed from what I have heard that it was the lady," was the cool reply. Lobbs was fully conscious of the fact that he had almost let the cat out of the bag. "She knows you certainly. I wonder at your cheek coming up here."

"I never meant to go as far as the Abbey," said Chunder Loo. "All I want to know is who are you?"

"Who I am?"

"Yes, and I mean to, or——"

He had got thus far when Lobbs slipped his right

hand into his pocket, and got the knuckle-duster fixed over his fingers. Then out it came, and Chunder Loo went down from a tremendous blow on the jaw.

It was so quickly done that it was almost like the visitation of a flash of lightning. Chunder Loo lay on the ground, conscious but helpless.

"I thought that you was a wrong 'un," said Lobbs, bending over him. "One of them chaps as get an ignorant man like me in a quiet place and then robs 'em. So I just put on this thing to protect myself. If you try to get up I'll scream murder and police."

"You've broken my jaw," muttered Chunder Loo, in a mumbling way.

"Oh, no, I ain't," replied Lobbs, "or you wouldn't be able to talk at all. You get up, and if I sets eyes on you again, I'll give you in charge. You are a three-card trick and a confidence man, that is what you are."

Shaking his fist indignantly at him, Lobbs wheeled about and disappeared upward in the direction of the Abbey.

It was some little time ere Chunder Loo got upon his feet, and it was slow work then. He leant against a tree, holding his jaw.

"Curse the fellow!" he growled; "he is nothing but a clown of a dealer after all. I have wasted my time, and made a fool of myself. Fancy his having a knuckle-duster about him!"

And then he cursed him again roundly, not as a more astute enemy who had circumvented him, but as a clodhopper of hard-hitting powers.

The light he had come to seek in regard to the personality of Lobbs had ended in his finding complete darkness.

"My friend," he snarled, shaking his fist in the direction Lobbs had taken—he had disappeared— "you are not worth the risk of murdering, or I would find out a way to settle you."

Then he grasped his jaw and cursed again. It was such an unexpected result of the outing.

CHAPTER CLVII.

IVAN'S TOWER.—VISITING FOR FUN AND FINDING SOMETHING ELSE.

LOBBS stayed and had luncheon with Bunn and Miss Astracan. To the latter he was a dealer in pigs, and with her he conversed about pork in its various stages, from the sty to the table.

Bunn, knowing him, of course, in another character, could hardly refrain from showing what he knew by some significant act or words.

But the watchful eye of Lobbs was upon him to check, as it did more than once, the tendency to commit himself.

After luncheon Miss Astracan announced that she had some household duty to perform, and waddled away, the household duty on that occasion being a nap in the silence and solitude of her chamber. Bunn brought out a box of cigars, obtained on credit from a tobacconist in Chippenham, thus laying in yet another store of future trouble, and invited Lobbs to smoke.

"I suppose nothing has been heard of Mrs. Cork?" he said.

"Nothing," was the reply. "She is a downy one."

"I have a theory concerning her," said Bunn, and then he repeated the brilliant idea he had previously laid before Don.

Lobbs did not laugh: he did not even smile, but listened with a grave, appreciative air. When Bunn finished he rose up and shook him by the hand.

"There ain't another man in the world who would have thought of that," he said.

"Then you think it a good idea?" murmured Bunn.

"A staggerer. You will excuse me now. I am expected in Chippenham at three."

"Oh! certainly. Will you have another cigar?"

"Not to-day. I am not accustomed to smokes up to this standard. Good-bye."

They shook hands, and Lobbs got out of the room. He hurried away through the playground to the seclusion of the wood, and there he halted.

"If I had stopped another minute," he muttered, as he mopped his head with his handkerchief, "I *must* have railed at him for a fool."

Shortly feeling better, he threw away his stump of cigar and filled a briar-root pipe.

With this between his teeth he sauntered on, musing as he went.

Nothing more was seen of him that day, for he went on to Chippenham, as he had declared he intended to, and remained there until late.

About four miles westward from the Abbey there stood an old ruined building known as St. Ivan's Tower. Around lay a mass of old stonework, which had been tumbled together long ago by the slow hand of Time, or the quicker action of war.

As to who St. Ivan had been, and to what special class of building the tower belonged, the rustic minds were in the dark. But superstition caused them to hold it in reverence, for it was reputed to be haunted, and the spot where it reared its hoary head being very lonely, it was shunned by day as well as by night.

A half-holiday having arrived, there arose the usual debatable matter among the boys. Where would they go? Was it to be cricket during the afternoon, or a ramble about the country?

Cricket has charms that never fail to please, and the majority of the boys elected to spend the half-holiday on their own ground. They were disappointed when they heard that neither Jack nor Don would be there.

Tom Drummond and Bob Stockton expressed their surprise in rather forcible torms.

"It isn't like you, Jack, to go off with just one chum," said the former, "and I call it a beastly shame."

"Gubbles asked me to show him St. Ivan's Tower, and I promised to do so," replied Jack. "The impression on my mind was that I was making a sacrifice by taking cn the office, and when Don offered to accompany us I was very grateful."

"You are a pair of martyrs, I have no doubt," said Bob, gravely. "I daresay you have some game on. But the king can do no wrong, and we have now to take the hump."

"Five would be too many, perhaps," said Jack, "but you can go with us if you like."

"No, thanks," answered Bob; "I respect St. Ivan's Tower for having on one occasion given us shelter. You remember?"

Jack nodded, and Tom having declared for cricket, too, he, with Don, sat down upon the old wall in the playground, by the side of which the foregoing conversation had taken place, to await the coming of Gubbles.

They saw their schoolfellows depart with the speed the demands of cricket imposed upon them, until they were left alone. Then Don spoke:

"I suppose you have some object in going to the Tower?" he said.

"Gubbles wants to see it."

"Then you have nothing on your mind. I thought you had."

"I have a good many things on my mind," replied Jack, "as you have. I was not in the humour for cricket, anyway, to-day."

"Nor I," said Don, rising. "Behold our Gubbles."

The gentleman named emerged from the Abbey and made for the gates. There the boys met him. He had his alpenstock and bag as usual when bent upon a botanising expedition.

There was the necessity of going through the wood until they came to a spot by which they could descend. It was getting a familiar way now, and Don remembered, with a shiver, the last occasion on which he traversed it alone. It was on the day he encountered Mrs. Cork in the cave.

Gubbles having declared he was fit for cross-country work, Jack, on reaching the lower ground, led the way across the fields, striking the highroad on their line of march.

Beyond the cattle, and a boy here and there keeping the crows off the scattered fields of wheat—the country was mainly grass land—they saw nobody on their way.

"The Tower has some interest to you?" remarked Gubbles, as the time-worn structure appeared in sight.

"It has," replied Jack, laughing, "for it was beneath it that the whole school took refuge at the time of the barring-out. I mean, of course, immediately after the barring-out was over, when we all disappeared. It was Lingo who told us of it as a hiding-place."

"That wonderful Lingo," said Gubbles. "By the way, I have some information for you concerning him. Bearing in mind what you have told me, I had inquiries made, in a quiet way, at the hospital where he was lying. My agent was just in time to learn that he had been discharged as cured. He gave the hospital a very liberal donation in recognition of the care bestowed upon him."

"When did he leave?" asked Jack, with close-set lips.

"Three days ago."

"And we have heard nothing of him!"

"I should not despair yet," advised Gubbles. "A man who has done what he has must turn a moral somersault ere he could betray the trust of a friend."

"Here is the Tower," said Don, changing the subject, as if he found that of Lingo painful to him; "isn't it a grim old ruin?"

It was as sombre a record of the builders of the past as one would desire to see.

The walls were wonderfully massive, and there was a tenacious look about the stones and mortar not observable in modern work.

The top of the Tower was worn away, but not to a great extent. On one side of it the ivy had grown to the very summit, but on the other side there was no parasite of that nature.

"They say that nothing will grow on this side," said Jack, "owing to that deep stain like the mark of dripping water. The legend goes that it was made by the blood of innocent men who were hung out from above alive, and the crows came and tore them to pieces."

"Like all legends," said Gubbles, "there may be some truth in it. I fancy this place was originally the centre of a castle, the outer walls of which were almost destroyed. There is just a faint outline of the original plan left. These piles of stones, brick, and mortar formed what was once the residential part of the castle."

The only visible entrance to the Tower was a narrow slit of a doorway, half-blocked by fallen masonry. Jack crept through, and Gubbles, following, found himself in a chamber with a stone roof, and the entrance to a winding stairway facing him.

"It was here," said Jack, "in various chambers on the different floors, that we lay concealed. Lingo provisioned it for us, and got in a stack of straw, on which we slept, and rather enjoyed it as a novelty."

"So I should imagine," remarked Gubbles; "boy-like, you would. Straw will do temporarily, but as a permanency it is open to objections."

Jack crossed over to the staircase, and having warned his companions to look out for the broken steps, began the ascent. A score of steps brought them to the first chamber.

It was not circular in form like the Tower, as the lower one was, for one side of it was flat, owing to an arrangement made for storing arms. It was a store-room, in fact, with a strong oaken door which, like the Tower itself, had made a good fight of it with Time.

"I'll show you the place when we come down," said Jack. "It was there that we kept our grub, and we left some tinned meat behind us."

"Which some tramp has probably appropriated for his personal comfort," suggested Gubbles.

"I do not think so," said Jack. "The Tower is out of the way, and it isn't inviting to a lone man even in the day-time."

They went up a second, then a third, a fourth, and finally a fifth flight of stone steps to the summit of the Tower.

In the uppermost chambers, the straw which the boys had slept on still remained, blown about by the wind, but otherwise, Jack imagined, not disturbed.

From the top of the old building there was as fine a view as the country afforded. That part of Wiltshire is not pretty, nor would anything ever make it so. It has a cold and repelling look, just as it had to Gubbles that day.

"There are some places," he said, "which two suns would not brighten, and this is one of them."

"We soon got sick of staying here," said Jack. "It fairly gave us the hump. That dark wood yonder hides a pretty part of the country Berkshire way, but the lookout towards the Abbey is not exhilarating."

"You cannot see the Abbey from here," remarked Gubbles.

"No," answered Jack. "The old castle was built on low ground, and the trees on that knoll there hide the Abbey. Now, Mr. Gubbles, *look there!*"

Jack seized the arm of the tutor that was pointing downwards towards the sombre wood beyond which lay a brighter portion of the country.

Tearing across the open ground in the direction of the wood was a woman.

"Mrs. Cork!" almost shrieked Gubbles.

There was no doubt of it, for the woman tallied with the description of that vanishing lady which had been circulated among the police.

"She was in the Tower," added Gubbles, with a groan of disappointment.

"In our old store-room," said Jack, breathlessly.

"What a fool I was to delay looking into it! But can't we——"

"No, pursuit would be useless," interposed Gubbles. "She has got too long a start of us. Our best course is to strike at once for Smudgem Bender and wire to the police."

"To think that she should be *here*," muttered Jack. "Who on earth would have dreamt of it?"

"It is that which we did not dream of which comes to pass," said Gubbles, sententiously, as he started down the broken stairway.

CHAPTER CLVIII.

TRUE AS STEEL.—BUNN MAKES SOME STRONG REMARKS.

IT was a stiffish walk to Smudgem Bender, but the pedestrians were indifferent to ordinary fatigue.

The hands of the old clock in the church were on the hour of four as they came out of the post-office after despatching their message, and on the suggestion of Gubbles, turned their faces towards the Cowley Arms with a view to refreshment.

"We can get some tea there," said the tutor, "and nothing pulls one up after fatigue better than a drink of the fragrant herb—the only thing worth having that China has given to less civilised countries."

"Less civilized countries?" echoed Jack.

"Precisely," said Gubbles. "China ages ago got as far as her ideas of civilization could carry her, and came to a dead stop. She hasn't advanced one step since the time when the Druids bossed Old England with their unholy, savage rites."

Jack and Don always enjoyed a talk with Gubbles when they got him out of the ordinary ruck of conversation, but there was a stopper put on it then by the appearance of Mulberry Cork coming sauntering up the village with a cigarette in his mouth.

He did not see them until they were almost upon him, for he seemed to be wrapt in thought, and not of the exhilarating order.

On raising his eyes and seeing them, he pulled up and half-faced about, showed a tendency to run away. But Gubbles, kindly enough, called on him to stay.

Mulberry faced about again and glared sulkily at them in turn.

"What yer want with me?" he asked. "I am surprised at you blooming swells stopping to talk to a low-down cove of my breed."

"I have wanted to see you," replied Gubbles, "and for your good."

Mulberry Cork laughed and grinned in a dismal way.

"There's a blessed lot of good any of you wish me, I dessay," he muttered.

"I wish you no harm, anyway," said Jack.

"You can afford to wish any cove good," said Mulberry, bitterly, "because you go along with everything to make a kid happy. *You* run a show that always pays, for people believe in you, and you may stuff them with anything; but as for *me*, who of the lot of you would take my word?"

"If you tell the truth," said Gubbles, quickly, "we must believe you."

Mulberry Cork lifted an eye to his face that was absolutely wonderful in its expression of deep cunning.

"Where is Chunder Loo?" asked the tutor, after a pause.

"He isn't at home, if you want to know," answered Mulberry, "and I tell you that because you could, if you liked, find out that much for yourself. But more'n that you won't get out of this child. Do you take *me* for a blooming jay? I'm a lock without a key to you, so you can save your breath."

"You are going the wrong way, Cork."

"Suppose I am, what then? I like the wrong way. I belong to wrong 'uns. Leastways," he added, hurriedly, "you think so, and what you think must, in course, be right."

"You are at an age," pursued Gubbles, taking hold of the collar of his coat with a swift yet quiet movement, "when, if you listen to the voice of those who would be your friends, you can be saved from utter ruin."

"You are piping the slum missionary tune," returned Mulberry, backing against the wall of a cottage garden; "but suppose I don't want to be saved from ruin, how then? If I like to be ruined, can't I be without your worriting me? Let me alone, will you?"

"You know who murdered Hone," said Gubbles, calmly, ignoring his request. "Tell the truth, and you will not suffer."

"Not from you perhaps," returned Mulberry Cork, disdainfully, "purwided I *do* know. No, you would take care of me and hand me over to some party to make a good boy of me, or shove me into a reformatory school, where I should be taught a lot I *don't* know, and not by the master or the parson either. Oh, yes! I am aweer that it would be a good thing for me. But then, you see, I don't know anything, and so you can let me go."

"I have made you a fair offer," said Gubbles, releasing the boy, "and now I warn you that when the truth comes out, as it will and must, you may find it a very serious thing for you."

"I know that," said Mulberry; "but look here, suppose you are right and I blabbed, what do you think could be done to me by them as I split on? Why, anything. I should have to go about guarded like a member of Parliament, threatened by a dynamiter. I don't want any more jaw on it, so let me go. And since you are so ready with *your* advice and warnings, let me give a tip to both of you. Jest you dry up prowling about and sticking your nose into other people's business, or one of these days you will be pulled up short. You hear me—*short!*"

"Go along with you," said Gubbles, giving him a quiet push, "you are incorrigible, I fear."

Mulberry backed away with a curt laugh, and to show his contempt for Gubbles and his companions, stopped to light another cigarette from the stump of the first, and then swaggered away.

"I had not much hope when I spoke to him," said Gubbles, with a sigh, "but now I have none."

"If he killed Hone," said Jack—"and it isn't at all certain that he did not—then you could hardly expect him to admit it."

"It is not quite certain that he did not, as you say," mused Gubbles, as they walked on, "but I cannot think he is responsible for the crime."

They reached the inn, and having stopped in the bar to order tea, sauntered into the coffee-room. A man was seated there, reading the paper, and he held it so that his face was hidden. They could see nothing of him but the lower part of his body and legs. His attire was that of a miller or corndealer.

Jack glanced at him and stopped short. There was something in the attitude of the man that struck him as familiar.

He motioned to Gubbles and Don to keep quiet, and walking across the room, addressed the stranger.

"Will you kindly let me have the paper after you have done with it?"

The paper was hastily dropped, and the man sprang to his feet.

"*Lingo!*"

"*Jack* and *Don!*"

They fairly fell into each other's arms, all three, and Gubbles, having nothing else to do, removed the spectacles he was wearing and wiped the glasses on his coat-sleeve.

There was no need to brighten them. It was the action of a man who was in a state of suppressed excitement, and felt bound to do something.

Yes, it was Lingo, but much changed. The old ruddy colour was gone from his face, and the traces of a long and severe illness were very clear upon it.

"My bold lads, it does my heart good to see your handsome faces again. I was just thinking how I could get at you on the quiet without attracting attention. Hallo! I beg your pardon, sir. I *didn't* see you."

"This is Mr. Gubbles," said Jack, adding, with emphasis, "one of *our* friends."

"Happy to see you, sir," said Lingo, as they shook hands; "down on a visit here?"

"I am one of the tutors at the Abbey," replied Gubbles.

"Indeed," said Lingo, raising his eyebrows, "I shouldn't have thought it."

"Why not?" asked Gubbles, smiling.

"Well, sir, you seem somehow—I don't quite know how—to be a cut above that sort of thing But then, you see, my experience of tutors is limited, as I never took kindly to the breed. What little love I had for them once on a time was choked out of me by Snicker."

"I think," said Gubbles, as he took a chair, "that we ought to know each other thoroughly right away. Our young friends here have fully confided in me."

For a moment Lingo looked grave, but a second glance at Gubbles reassured him.

"I am not surprised," he said; "you are a man an honest boy would confide in. He has told you everything, I suspect?"

"Everything."

Jack said they could not do anything by halves. All or none, was their motto.

"Well, I reckon he did the right thing. Especially as you did not hear from me for ever so long, and must have suspected——"

"Don't, Lingo," interposed Jack.

"My lad," said Lingo, earnestly, "I am a man of the world, and in my rugged way get at things in human nature pretty clearly. If you had not suspected me you would have been a blind fool—one of them softies who are taken in by every kind of blarney. Ready-made grub for sharpers and canting hypocrites, I calls 'em. Take it easy. I am not sensitive. I knew as soon as we met that the clouds would clear away."

The tea was now brought in, and Lingo having finished a glass of grog he had upon the table, joined them. As no other customers of the inn appeared, he told them the whole of the story of his mishap and how it was they had heard nothing from him.

"I got everything out of that cave," he said, "and without staying to close it, sped away. I had all the boxes ready for packing, and sent them, when the goods were in them, to London. I marked the lids 'Perishable,' leaving the railway people to put the contents down as bacon, or condensed milk, or watercresses, or what they liked, and got them safe to town, where I had arranged for the turning of them into ready money.

"I sold all the armour and so on, but I kept the boxes of coins, as they are money at any time, and in any country. As a safe place I left them at the Great Western cloak-room, till called for. I told the porters there to be careful of 'em, as they contained the machinery of a whole collection of waxworks, and the least jolting would put it out of order. So they were stowed in a safe corner. I tipped the men a bob each."

Then he went on to tell how he went down as a bishop to see Mrs. Peebles, intending her to write to Don to let him know that "his clerical friend" was coming to see him.

"I daresay I made a poor bishop," said Lingo, "for they are generally smart men, or they couldn't rise to the situation. But on getting into the town, I was spotted by Barney Griffin, an old pal of mine, who naturally wanted to know what lay I was on. I took him for a drive to explain it in a way I hoped would be satisfactory, if it wasn't the truth; but in the middle of it the smash took place. Barney was nearly killed, and I went as near to it as a man could do without kicking the bucket, and that was what I got for lying. Barney got well, I suppose, and went about his business. Anyway, I did not inquire after him, but as soon as I could I came away. The doctor asked me one day if I was not a Wiltshire parson; and I got out of him that Mrs. Peebles had been to the hospital, and nearly blowed everything. I told him that I had left the church, being disgusted with the way Wiltshire parsons go about playing croquet, or shooting at archery meetings, and then blowing about hard work, and that I intended to go upon the stage."

"And did he take that in?" asked Gubbles.

"No. I fancy he suspected I was an old stage bird, who had been playing the parson. But it wasn't his business, and he had a lot to do. So I got away, and here I am.

"The armour and stuff," he said, after a laugh all round, "being genuine, fetched five thousand three hundred pounds. The coins, I suspect, are worth more."

"Gemini!" exclaimed Jack.

"It is a tidy haul," said Lingo, gleefully, rubbing his hands, "and we must talk by-and-bye about what is to be done with it. I've a notion of spending some in a way that will be pleasant and profitable. But that can rest for a bit. I want to know what is being done in the murder of that poor boy."

They told him everything, including the affairs of Chunder Loo, as they understood them.

The professor listened with rapt attention, and confessed that he was considerably fogged by the narration.

"That Chunder Loo," he said, "has given me more mental twisters than any man I ever came across. I'll swear he is not quite a stranger to me, and yet I haven't the least idea where we have met. I've a good memory, too, and that is where the worrying comes in."

Shortly before seven o'clock they left him. It was considered advisable that they should not be seen together, and it was arranged that he should write to Gubbles and appoint a place of meeting, where they could talk over affairs. He was of opinion that Lobbs was a man to be wary of.

"Not that he isn't honest, as policemen go," he said, "but he will upset a lot by knowing a little of our private affairs."

They agreed with him, and left the inn, Jack and Don still in a repentant state over their having for a moment suspected the professor.

But they had glorious tidings to convey to their friends, and that comforted them.

The village was livelier in the evening, owing to the children being home from the school, and the men and women sitting at the cottage doors or pottering about their gardens after work. But on this especial evening one part of it was in an unusually lively state. This was in the region of the two houses occupied by Bibbins, the watchmaker, and Mrs. Snicker, with her two lodgers.

They were all outside, and a small mob of the villagers in the roadway. By the gate of the Snicker garden was Penny Bunn, violently gesticulating. Chunder Loo, with Mrs. Snicker by his side, was grinning with malicious delight.

CHAPTER CLIX.

CAPTURE OF MRS. CORK.—AN AMAZING DISCOVERY.

"NOW, I wonder what is the matter here?" said Don.

They pushed their way through the little crowd, and at that moment Penny Bunn, who had apparently been taking in a fresh supply of breath, burst forth again.

"You say I murdered the boy!" he cried. "You dark-skinned villain, I'll prosecute you."

"I said nothing of the sort," returned Chunder Loo, with a malicious grin. "I merely told you that it was just as likely to be you as Snicker."

"Snicker is a brute!" roared Bunn, "and undoubtedly murdered Hone, for which he will hang! He——"

"Here," said Gubbles, sharply, "this must be stopped."

He was beside Penny Bunn in a moment, and had hold of his arm. Drawing him back, he said, in a most decisive tone:

"You ought not to be quarrelling here with that fellow. It will lead to no good, and may possibly do you harm."

"Am I," cried Bunn, "the head-master of Littlecote Abbey, to be told that I killed Hone to save the cost of his keep for the remainder of the term?"

"You should not heed such rubbish," replied Gubbles, "and, in any case, ought to put a restraint upon your own tongue. Snicker is not convicted yet," he added, in a lower tone, "and you have no right to publicly declare him to be the murderer."

"Take him home," said Chunder Loo, derisively, "and ask that wife of his to put him to bed and keep him there. It is the only safe place for a fool."

"Put the jay in a cage!" sang out Mulberry Cork, who was standing a little to the rear of Chunder Loo. Mrs. Snicker at the same time made a plunge at Penny Bunn, with the obvious intention of making a record of the day with her nails upon his heated countenance.

But the watchful Gubbles swung the schoolmaster round out of her reach, and, with a steady hand, pushed him through the crowd. Beyond a buzz of excitement, there was no demonstration, for the Snicker party was not by any means popular, and Chunder Loo had become a terror to the more ignorant, a report having got abroad that he was possessed of the "evil eye," which, as everybody knows, is often fatal to those who gaze upon it.

Gubbles and the boys got Penny Bunn away, and bore him homeward in a vengeful mood, but pretty well exhausted. He was not handed over to Miriam, and Gubbles advised him to lie down somewhere for an hour and get cool.

Shortly after the main body of boys were back at the Abbey, and Tom and Bob were informed of the arrival of Lingo and the nature of the communication he had made.

There was great rejoicing among the four forming the inner circle. They were possessors of a thousand pounds apiece or more.

"What shall we do with it?" exclaimed Tom.

"Nothing, at present," replied Jack, "it would be too risky. As sure as fate, if we go gassing about with a lot of money some sharp fellow, like Lobbs for instance, will get at the facts, and then away will go the lot."

"Lingo will advise us what to do with it," said Don; "he said he had a plan in his mind for its disposal. I daresay if we want a pound or two we can have it now, and that ought to suffice."

"It will suffice," replied Bob Stockton. "Why, anyway, we are small Rothschilds."

Then there was the story of the discovery of Mrs. Cork, in the act of fleeing away from St. Ivan's Tower, to create additional excitement, but the amazing events of the day were to be followed by something more in the evening.

Shortly before nine o'clock, when the boys were at supper, a farm labourer came riding up on a carthorse of the lighter breed with a message from Botch, the farmer, to Jack Ford.

A SPLENDID SCHOOL STORY.

NEVER BEFORE PUBLISHED.

By E. HARCOURT BURRAGE,

Author of "Ching Ching," "Monkey Mat and Roving Dick," "The Brave Boy of the Basilisk," &c.

THE LAMBS OF

A Handsome Coloured Plate Presented with Every Number.

NO. 22.

"Come back, you fool!" said Jack, as soon as he could speak, "give yourself up." "Come down and take me!" hissed Mulberry.

PRICE ONE PENNY.

ALDINE PUBLISHING CO., 9, Red Lion Court, Fleet St., and 1, 2, & 3, Crown Court, Chancery Lane, London.

Jack was called out from the dining-room, and went to the door to the man.

"What is it?" he asked. "Nothing wrong with Mr. Botch, I hope."

"No, zur," was the answer, "he be as well and hearty as he has been all th' days o' his life. But he sent me to tell you that he ha' got that woman. She be a-lying in the old chaff-house, tied up wi' roapes, so that she du look more like a hay cloth ready to put away for th' winter than a mortiul bein'."

"Tell him that some of us will be there directly," said Jack, hurriedly. "Will that horse carry me as well as you?"

"I shouldn't think much o' he if he waddent," replied the rustic, with a grin.

"Then I will go with you," said Jack. "Stop while I have a word with Mr. Gubbles."

Jack had no right to make arrangements without leave to be away from the Abbey at that hour, but he felt that he might do pretty well as he pleased under the circumstances.

He slipped back to the door of the dining-room, and beckoned for Gubbles to come to him.

"Mrs. Cork is captured," he whispered, as the tutor joined him. "Botch has got her in his keeping, and I am going back on the horse the man has ridden here upon with the message. It will carry double."

"What can you do, Ford?" inquired Gubbles.

"See that the woman don't get away," answered Jack. "I hope you don't mind going. Perhaps you will follow."

"Certainly, with Mr. Bunn, and perhaps I may bring Don Peebles with us. The boy ought to be gratified with a sight of the wretch in custody."

"Shall I do anything before you come, sir?"

"In what way?"

"Communicating with the police. I do not suppose that Botch has taken any steps in that direction."

"No, wait for us. I fancy there is a surprise for a good many people in store."

"I think so, too, sir; but we won't be certain until," he added, with a bright laugh, "we are sure."

Jack sped back to the door of the Abbey, and springing lightly up behind the rustic, bade him make the best of his way back to Smudgem Bender.

"Be ye sure ye can hoald on, measter," asked the rustic.

"Try me," replied Jack. "If I fall off, don't you stop to pick me up."

"Hi, then, Smiler!" cried the rustic, addressing the horse. "Gang hoam wi' ye, and get to the corn in the mainger. Hi, lad!"

The horse seemed to understand him, and with a swift-trotting movement, wonderfully so considering his breed, started off. Down through the wood they went, with only the dimmest of light for them to see by.

It was a ride that would remain for many a year in the memory of Jack. He held on by the smock of the man, and gripped the body of the horse with his knees. That was all the hold he had.

It was not until they started that he realised the fact of the man having neither saddle nor bridle, only a halter, which he now practically abandoned, allowing it to hang loose.

He had a limp way of seating himself upon a horse, had this rustic. As the animal thundered through the wood, raising echoes on every side, he swayed this way and that, as if he was bound in the end to come the ground.

But he held on; it was his way of riding, that was all.

At intervals he would suddenly cry out, "Ware branch, measter," and then down went both their heads, and Jack would feel the sweep of leaves down his back for a moment, and then on again, down, down, the horse needing no guide, as his chief rider knew.

A man may make a mistake when riding in the gloom, or complete darkness, but the horse, if he has trodden the road before, never. The wise man trusts entirely to the noble animal, when he has a doubt of himself, at such a time.

Clear of the wood at last, and they were thundering along the hard highroad.

Not a soul about. The lights were out in the scattered cottages, if indeed there had been one that night. Your true countryman does not waste candles in the summer time. He goes to bed with, and rises with, the sun.

Smudgem Bender was reached. All still there. No alarm, not a sign that an adventuress, who had attempted to murder Don Peebles, had been captured.

Botch had evidently made no fuss over the matter.

The horse pounded up to the farm gate, and there stopped short. Jack rolled off, bucked over the five bars, and made his way to the stables, where a light was burning.

He entered, and saw Botch standing just within the open chaff-house door, with a gun in his hand. Down through the long intervening stretch of stabling the cart horses were quietly munching hay or chawing corn.

"Who's there?"

"Only me, Mr. Botch."

"You've come smartly, my lad."

"I rode back behind the man."

"Well done for you."

Jack entered the chaff-house, and there found the

form of Mrs. Cork, literally swathed in ropes. There was no movement of the face, but the eyes glanced venomously at him.

"I saw her making through the field for Chippenham," said Botch, "so I pops the saddle on the roan and goes after her, taking a cart rope with me. She runned for it, and took the fences in a way that flabbergasted me, but I can ride straight if I ride heavy, and I took her to Mallow Mesh" (Wiltshire for "marsh"), "and blessed if she didn't pull up and draw a pistol on I. But I goes straight for her, and she blazed away, puttin' a bullet through my hat. Then I gave her one on the head wi' my whip, the butt end, and down she goes, senseless. Off I gets, binds her, and lays her across saddle like a truss o' straw, and brings her on here. Haw, haw! it were a sight to see her lying that way, and when she cum round, cussin woful."

"That was well done," said Jack, enthusiastically. "Mr. Botch, you will be the hero of the county over this affair."

"I ain't got much leanin' for a hero," replied Botch; "now what be ye goin' to do wi' her?"

"We must wait until Mr. Gubbles and some others arrive. Have you seen anything of Lobbs, the de—— I mean the pig-dealer? He has been staying at the Cowley Arms."

"He wor here about seven o'clock," replied Botch, "goin' on friendly like with another strange party with a biggesh merstache. Blessed if this place ain't gettin' chock full o' visitors."

Jack was a bit startled to hear that Lobbs and Lingo had so soon come together, but he felt confident that the professor could take care of himself. He would have liked to send for his friend, but thought it would be more prudent not to do so.

Jack said nothing to the captive, who maintained a dogged silence. Botch talked of various matters until half an hour elapsed, and then Penny Bunn, Gubbles, and Don Peebles appeared on the scene.

Bunn came into the stables first, and, as might be expected, opened his mouth straightway.

"Where is the vile woman," he cried, "who could desert the child she had promised—for a consideration—to bring up in—in—in the way he should go?"

"There she is, sir," replied Botch.

"Yes," said Bunn, staring at the captive, how smiled in a dry, hard way, "that is the woman who gave me a cheque for a hundred pounds, and then instructed her adopted son to steal it."

"What the blazes do you mean by adopted son," demanded the prisoner, in a gruff, hoarse voice.

"You may have deceived others," said Bunn, shaking a finger at the prisoner, "but not me. You are one of those vile women who take up with baby-farming, and adopt children cast off by their unnatural parents."

It was a perfect shriek of laughter that burst from the captive, and the effect was so startling that Bunn skipped back out of the chaff-house into the stables proper.

Strange to say the rest, Botch excepted, laughed likewise.

"If this don't beat cock-fighting," gasped the prisoner—"the jay!"

"There spoke Mulberry," said Gubbles. "Don, run off to the Cowley Arms, and ask Lobbs to come here. Nobody else, mind."

Don understood, and was off like an arrow from a bow.

Nothing more was said while he was away, but occasionally Gubbles or one of the boys would indulge in a chuckle.

Bunn, standing in the doorway, regarded them with dignified surprise.

The dull sound of footsteps on straw was heard, and Lobbs, with Don close behind him, entered the stables.

He had been simply told that he was wanted, and was not prepared for the scene before him.

"Hallo!" he exclaimed, "so you've nabbed her. Who laid her by the heels?"

"It is not a woman at all," replied Gubbles, quietly.

"What is it, then?" asked the detective.

"A man," replied Gubbles, "and his name is Berry Mawston!"

CHAPTER CLX.

THE NET CLOSES IN.—DON AGAIN DISTINGUISHES HIMSELF.

SILENCE reigned for a moment on the whole party. The prisoner did not stir, but the light went out of his eyes for a moment, and when it returned it was lurid with a new-born terror and despair.

"Do not give me the credit for the discovery," said Gubbles, breaking the stillness; "it was Peebles who led up to it. When this supposed woman attacked him in the cave under the Abbey, he noted something in the action of this monster that led him to believe that it was a man in disguise. Together we came to the conclusion that he was the man I have been hunting down with another, who has yet to be found. The only other persons in the secret of our assumption were Ford, Drummond, and Stockton, all of whom are boys shrewd beyond their years. We have all worked to get hold of this supposed woman to prove that theory to be true ere we said a word."

"The she-fiend," gasped Bunn, with a dazed stare, "is a man!" Then he gave himself a shake, and brightened up. "I must say that I was not entirely deceived. There was something in the way he worked that cheque business which led me to suspect——"

Botch, who had been staring heavily at Bunn, here intervened.

"Mr. Bunn," he said, "if you say another word I'll lay you on the flat of your back!"

"Sir!" exclaimed Bunn.

"*On the flat of your back,*" repeated Botch, emphatically, "with a blow from this 'ere fist of mine. Not that I want to hurt you, but I feel it would be my duty to knock *some* of the *ass* out of you. Now then, go on, if you dorst."

Bunn did not go on. He merely smiled in a way that showed he was above wrangling with a man so utterly dense and unreasonable as Botch. He left the matter to the discriminating powers of the more intelligent people around him.

Lobbs went to work in a business way.

First he rummaged the pockets of the prisoner, and removed from the outer ones a number of articles, including an extra revolver, some papers, a purse, and a bottle labelled "poison."

There were several pockets in the dress.

Next he released his hands and put a pair of hand-cuffs on them, and after that untied the rest of the rope.

"Get up," he said, curtly.

The prisoner got up, slowly and painfully, glaring at the boy whom Gubbles had indicated with his hand as the originator of the great discovery.

"Do you deny your identity?" demanded the detective.

"I am a man," was the curt reply.

"Got any other clothes on?"

"Yes."

Then the dress was cut away, and he stood revealed in a tourist suit, with the trousers turned up. There was a wig upon his head, which was removed, and the picture of a low-bred cunning-looking villain was complete.

In the pocket of his coat there was a soft travelling-cap, which was put upon his head by the detective.

"All I want now is a trap to take him to Chippenham for the night," said Lobbs, "and if any of you care to come with me, well and good."

"We will all go," said Botch. "I'll have the horse put into the waggonette."

"The more the better," said Lobbs; "if not the merrier."

He held the prisoner by the arm, in an apparently careless way, but he had him securely enough. In a few minutes the trap was ready.

"You had better drive your own horse, sir," said the detective. "I'll have this fellow at the back, as he is a slippery customer. Will you, sir," to Bunn, "ride on the box with Mr. Botch."

"After his unseemly threat," replied Bunn, "I would prefer a seat in the rear of the vehicle."

"Then you must ride on the step," rejoined the detective, coolly, "for I reckon that the rest of us will take up all the room. There is no real need for you to go at all, unless you wish to."

"But my evidence as to the proceedings of this scoundrel——"

"Your evidence," said Lobbs, "won't be wanted in any case. And most certainly not to-night. He is wanted for something more serious than your blooming cheque."

"A faded cheque, I should say," murmured Don, and Lobbs laughed.

"Look here, youngster," he said, as they left the stable, "if you don't by-and-bye enter the force, you will miss your proper vocation."

Bunn was dumbfounded.

That his evidence should not be wanted, appeared to him to border on the impossible. Personally, he could not see how it could be dispensed with. As riding on the step would be a most undignified proceeding, he took a seat beside Botch on the box, and journeyed to Chippenham with the haughty air of an Eastern monarch compelled to associate for the time with one of his low-caste people.

They talked in the rear, of course, but not about the prisoner, who seemed to be utterly cast down. Once he was heard to mutter, "Brought up short by a boy. And I had a chance of cracking his skull, too," finishing with a curse.

They were otherwise a light-hearted party. Lobbs lit a cigar, and Gubbles smoked his briar-root pipe. To Jack and Don it was the very pick of adventures. They felt that they had not lived in vain. How sorry they felt for Tom and Bob who "were out of it."

The prisoner was received at Chippenham with all the honours due to a notorious criminal whose capture would give lustre to the dreariest town in the United Kingdom, and create for its inhabitants something to talk about until a travelling waxwork exhibition, or some other equally edifying exhibition, came down to rescue the limited population from their normal condition of stolid dreariness.

Chippenham, in the great scheme of Creation, may have been originally intended for a colony of dormice, but a class of people having been found suitable for it, they were allowed to settle down and vegetate according to their natures.

Once upon a time a short spell of ordinarily lively talk was heard from a visitor in this unique town, but it was too much for its people. Everybody went about as if he or she was drunk, for a week, and mental exercises beyond the comprehension of a limpet have not from that hour been encouraged by the corporation..

After Berry Mawston had been charged and secured for the night, Lobbs gave some interesting details of the career of the criminal, which had recently come to light.

There was no doubt that Mulberry was his son, but the mother had been dead for several years. Mulberry was therefore a party to the imposition played upon Penny Bunn.

"It is without doubt," said Lobbs, "one of the cleverest moves ever made by a man who was wanted. First, he sees the need of a disguise that will be a poser, and he gets himself up as a woman, and takes rooms at the Langham. Mawston is a man who would have made his mark upon the stage, for whenever he played a part, it was done to perfection."

"He did not quite deceive me," remarked Bunn.

"Oh, you," said Lobbs, "be jiggered! Don't interrupt, please."

Bunn was astounded. Could this be the man who had so deferentially treated him when on a visit to the Abbey? Was it possible that there were two Lobbs? Well, his conduct was strange anyway.

"Having done that," pursued Lobbs, "he knows that it is not a safe game to be there too long. What does he do? There is his son, who I don't doubt is up to many a move in the criminal game, he is to be disposed of. He must be put away in a quiet place. Why not a boarding-school for a year or so? It is done. Mawston comes down with him, makes arrangements, hands over a cheque——"

"Stolen afterwards," murmured Bunn.

"Can't you keep quiet for two minutes?" demanded Lobbs; "a champion parrot isn't in it with you. The cheque is handed in, and was met, although the right party did not get the money. Mawston gives out that he is going abroad, and is supposed to go, leaving a balance at his banker's, and this is the most artful move of all. But he doesn't go abroad; he comes down here, and there I come to a dead stop. Why did he return to this outlandish country?"

"Possibly," said Bunn, "he wished to take a final leave of his offspring."

"Take leave of his grandmother," said Lobbs. "Can't you keep quiet?"

"Really, you are very abrupt," murmured Bunn.

"Mawston came here to see some pal. I guess it is Aaron Brand, who is a yellow-skinned beggar with a face lightly tattooed. He could make himself up with paint and stuff so as to deceive anyone. In fact, the pair are consummate actors."

"This is the first I have heard of that," exclaimed Gubbles; "there is no intimation of it in the diary of my murdered friend."

"No," quietly replied Lobbs; "but I found a memorandum of his face having a peculiar appearance, among the odd pieces of paper in the office."

"Why was it kept from me?"

"Because I am a professional man, and don't care to be cut out by an amateur. I am not going into the whole thing, but I had a clue, and followed it up, and I got at this fact. Aaron Brand is a foreigner. He used to travel with a show as the wild man of Borneo, and even that was a cover to conceal that he was a burglar, and what not. The man is hereabouts somewhere, and when I've found him the work is done."

It was a strange story, and Jack and Don, especially the latter, listened to it with the closest interest. A vague possibility was developing in his mind into a conviction. But, whatever it was, he would not speak of it as yet. If Lobbs was desirous of excelling an amateur, in the person of Gubbles, why should not another amateur, in the person of Don, excel him?

Shortly after they parted with the detective and were driven home by Botch.

In the absence of Lobbs and his prisoner there was room behind for Bunn, and he took his seat there.

"Lobbs may be a very clever man," he said, as the trap went slowly up the hill, "but for all that I fear he does not look beyond the surface."

As nobody made any reply, the schoolmaster settled himself comfortably in a corner, and after sundry mysterious mutterings and suppressed ejaculations, expressive of contempt for Lobbs and all his works, he fell asleep.

CHAPTER CLXI.

CHUNDER LOO AND MULBERRY CORK.—A MEETING IN THE WOOD, AND ANOTHER DISCOVERY.

IN the morning all was known. It was impossible to keep the story of the capture from the public. Chippenham was roused to a pitch of excitement that reminded the oldest inhabitant of the day when the Queen was crowned and the Corporation expended twenty pounds in fireworks.

There were no fireworks on this occasion, it is true, but the running to and fro, the chattering, the comparing of notes, and the refreshment imbibed, made up for the lack of a pyrotechnic display.

The dull town was more disturbed than it was when the shop of Blobbs, the ironmonger, caught fire, and the place was expected to be blown up, and would have been, had not Blobbs remembered that he was quite out of gunpowder.

In Smudgem Bender it was known early. Botch had not been bound to secrecy, and he told his men of it in the morning as they sat milking the cows. From mouth to mouth the story spread.

Chunder Loo and Mulberry Cork, at eight o'clock, sat down to breakfast, with Mrs. Snicker presiding at the teapot. That estimable old woman faced the window, and as she poured out she saw a group across the road consisting of two old men, one on crutches, and three old women, two of whom were evidently partially deaf.

"What is the matter?" she exclaimed.

Well might she ask the question, for the aged crones were working their arms up and down as if they were moved by steam, and their heads turned this way and that with a waxwork expression of astonishment in their eyes.

Chunder Loo, who sat with his back to the window, faced about, and regarded the group for a few moments with close attention.

"Mulberry," he said, "go out and listen to their jaw. Something has happened, I reckon." Mulberry vanished from the table, and presently was seen hopping about the road, picking up stones, as boys often do with no other intention than to throw them down again, and listening with all his might.

Suddenly he gave up stone picking and stood erect; with the hair of his head bristling. Chunder Loo saw it and rose from his seat.

"Pour me out another cup of tea, Mrs. Snicker," he said; "I'll be back in a moment."

He went out, closing the door. Mulberry, with shaky knees, was just returning.

"Not a word here," hissed Chunder Loo, "come to the back."

They passed round to the rear of the cottage, where they were out of sight of the road.

"Now, what is it?"

"They've nabbed dad."

Chunder Loo stood for a moment transfixed. Then in a slow, forced way he asked:

"Who got hold of him?"

"Botch, the farmer," replied Mulberry, "saw him footing it to Chippenham last evening."

"The fool! the dolt!" hissed Chunder Loo, between his teeth, "I told him to wait until dark."

"He had no business to come here at all," said Mulberry; "it was all your fault. Why didn't you let him go abroad?"

"Because I couldn't trust him," snarled Chunder Loo; "he wouldn't give me a full share of the mopusses, and if he had got away I might have whistled for it."

"They'll come for me next," moaned Mulberry Cork, wringing his hands.

"What for, you little fool? They may give you a look to see what can be got out of you. All you have to do is to glue your tongue to the roof of your mouth and let it stick there. Utter a word, and away you go to limbo. We had better go back and finish our breakfast. I'll see then what can be done. But I must go to the wood to think."

"And to jaw to that little vermin snake of yours. It is the devil in disguise, I believe."

"What do you know of it, you whelp? I am a son of the torrid zone, born among a people soaked with arts that were rife in Egypt thousands of years ago. My snake never lies to me. Mehala is faithful. He can speak in a language that neither you nor any of your cursed dunderheaded race can understand. Had I parents, wife, children, the loss of all would be as nothing to compare to the loss of Mehala."

He poured out these words hotly, fiercely, and Mulberry Cork shrank from him. But in a moment Chunder Loo was his cool self again.

"Go in," he said.

When Mrs. Snicker asked what was the matter, Chunder Loo told her that somebody had been arrested for something. He could not exactly tell what.

"Poaching, of course," she said, and the subject dropped.

That morning Don had an early interview with Gubbles, before breakfast, in fact. Don wanted leave to go out for the morning as far as Smudgem Bender. Gubbles was in a position to give him permission to do so, as Penny Bunn, overcome by the excitement of the previous evening, was not up. He hoped to be in the class-room by ten o'clock. Meanwhile he left everything to his subordinate.

So Don got leave, and away he went on a journey of discovery. He took with him a stout stick, and the small bottle of liquid which Gubbles had given him for the removal of dyes. The latter, however, he had recently always carried in his pocket wrapped in a piece of rag. He had a fancy it might one day be of good service to him.

With a light, elastic step he entered the wood and glided down the dry well-trodden path. Ere he had traversed half its length he suddenly pulled up. His quick ear had caught a murmured sound on the left from among the bushes.

He stopped for a while, listening. The tone of the murmurer was familiar. It was Chunder Loo.

The heart of the boy beat fast, and he hesitated some moments ere he made up his mind to enter the deeper part from whence the sounds came.

But it was Chunder Loo he was in quest of, and now was the opportunity to see him at his best or worst.

Don crept through the bushes until he got a view of the man. He was standing with his back to the trunk of a beech-tree, holding Mehala in his hand.

"Oh, my own," he was saying, "wise friend, tell me

what to do? Shall I flee or stay? Look into my eyes, you who never deceived your worshipper. Tell me, tell me what to do."

He stooped and placed the snake upon the ground. Immediately it turned its lithesome body and glided in the direction of the boy's hiding-place.

Chunder Loo, with a wild cry of despair, followed it.

"Will you desert me, Mehala?" he screamed.

Don saw that he must be discovered, and for a moment he saw death. And then there came over him the courage of those who fight to the last.

Springing to his feet, he raised his stick, and as the snake was within two feet of him, he struck it a blow that literally smashed it.

There was nothing but a pulpy mass upon the ground to tell where the miserable little fetish had been.

Chunder Loo saw it done, and as his eyes beheld the completeness of the work of destruction, a horrible pallor that was like a film spread itself over his face.

He made an effort to draw something from beneath his dress, but his hand seemed to be palsied, and failed to do its work. He stared wildly at Don, around him, then his eyes closed, and he fell to the ground with a crash.

"Is he dead?" was Don's first thought.

He stepped forward and looked at the long, sinewy form upon the ground. There was no movement of the limbs, but his chest heaved. Therefore he was yet alive.

But was he playing the spider? If Don ventured to go near him, might he not fasten on him and avenge the death of his fetish? "But I *will* not fear him," said the boy.

He stepped out, drew near the still form, ready to strike if he was assailed. But there was no movement on the part of Chunder Loo.

"He has fainted away," said Don.

Then he knelt down, and whipped out the bottle he had in his pocket and poured some of its contents upon the rag around it.

Using it as a brush, he passed it over the forehead of Chunder Loo, and immediately the dark brown of the skin disappeared, leaving a lighter brown under it, and the skin covered all over with the most intricate fine tattooing.

"As I thought," cried Don, leaping to his feet; "*This is the other murderer known as Aaron Brand!*"

What should he do?

He could not carry the man away to the police-station, nor had he the means to bind him. He could only leave him there and return to the Abbey for help.

And back he sped at a pace that surprised him. School had just begun, and all in the room were startled by the sudden appearance of Don, panting

with excitement. He hastened to Gubbles and breathlessly spoke to him in a tone that reached the ears of most of the boys, although he endeavoured to speak in a whisper.

"Chunder Loo and Aaron Brand are one, and he is lying senseless in the wood. I killed his snake, and he fainted away!"

CHAPTER CLXII.

THE CHAIN COMPLETE.—NOT TO BE FOUND.

CHUNDER LOO and Aaron Brand one and the same person!

Of all in the room only two had suspected that they had even so much as heard of each other.

And yet the two were one!

Marvellous!

And it was Don who had first suspected it, for only that morning he had confided his suspicions to Gubbles. His object in going to Smudgem Bender was to endeavour to casually meet Chunder Loo, study his face as closely as he dared, and see if there were any indications of its being coloured so as to hide the tattooing.

Now that his suspicions had been aroused as they had never been before, Gubbles was prepared to fully investigate the matter, and he had given Don various hints as to the signs of a painted face he must look for.

The quest had suddenly come to an end in the most unexpected manner, confirming Don's ideas.

There was nothing more to be done, save to secure the second villain in that dark tragedy of the murder of the merchant, whom Gubbles spoke of as "Ruskin."

The amateur detective and tutor recalled to mind much that he had read of Eastern lore, and the worship of the serpent he knew was no modern fad. It had existed for ages, its origin being lost in the misty past.

Jack Ford called to mind that memorable scene when he sat upon the wall, and, looking into the valley below, had seen Chunder Loo wandering in search of his lost snake. Had he not seen him give way to weakness or despair, so that he lay upon the ground as one dead?

These, and many other incidents, were so many pieces of mosaic work in a remarkable story.

The school was now a secondary consideration in the mind of Gubbles. No time was to be lost. Chunder Loo must be secured.

The first thing he did was to hasten up to the room where his principal, Penny Bunn, lay in bed.

There was not much the matter with that highfalutin gentleman, but on hearing footsteps he immediately put on the proper expression for a hopeless invalid. It did not deceive Gubbles.

"You must get up, sir," he said, "or the boys will be left to themselves."

"What on earth do you mean by that?" cried Bunn, sitting up in bed, with a Jack-in-the-box action.

"What I say," tartly answered Gubbles. "I am off to assist in the arrest of Chunder Loo, and I am going to take with me four of the pluckiest boys in the school!"

Then he vanished from the room, leaving Bunn in a state of mind which may be termed mental hasty-pudding—it was such a terrible mixture.

The schoolmaster had no clear idea why his late tutor should be arrested at all, save as a rank and rotten impostor. But if Gubbles had gone to lay him by the heels, it was the duty of Penny Bunn to get up and look after the boys, unless he wished to have a riot in the house. And a riot among the boys meant a domestic disturbance with Miriam, who had but just now expressed her opinion on the feebleness of the indisposition of her husband.

"It is all a sham," she told him; "you are simply lazy, or are sleeping off the effects of one of your bursts of beastly dissipation."

So Penny Bunn tumbled out of bed and began to don his clothes.

"Life at Littlecote," he murmured, as he drew on his trousers the hind part before, "has to be experienced to be appreciated, and being experienced, it is a thing to give the chuck to. I've had enough of it, and the sooner there comes an end to it the better. Ho, there! ring down the curtain. Pick up the pieces of P. Y. Bunn, Esq., and bury them decently."

A source of further annoyance was awaiting him in the schoolroom, which he found had been deserted by Gubbles and the four members of the inner circle. As time was precious they had not waited for him, but, armed with sticks and a rope—it was the linen line that had been useful to Jack before—were on their way to the spot where Don left Chunder Loo lying.

But that wily scoundrel was gone, and the only record of the recent meeting was a dead snake, or rather its smashed remains, almost unrecognisable, so well had Don done his work.

The little gold collar that had been about its neck was, however, gone.

"If he had left that behind him," said Gubbles, "I might have been able to give you some clue to his worship of the reptile. But we must get on and give the alarm. Chunder Loo must not escape, for in my belief he excels even Berry Mawston in villainy."

They sped along to Smudgem Bender, where they first wired to the police at Chippenham the intelli-

gence of the discovery they had made. There, of course, it would fall into the hands of Lobbs, who would know how to act.

Then they hastened to the Cowley Arms, where they found a coffee-room full of people discussing the arrest of Mawston. Lingo was in the thick of them, listening, and occasionally putting in a word.

As soon as he caught sight of Jack's face by the door he came out and greeted the party. Two minutes sufficed to put him in possession of the story of Don and Chunder Loo.

"I fancied I knew him from the first," said Lingo, with unwonted excitement. "It was the skilful hiding of the tattooing that did me. He was with half a dozen shows that I knew of, here and there giving up his engagements on the pretext of not being well paid, or that his grub wasn't good. We used to call him the grumbling man of Borneo. But I see his game now. What he wanted was a shift from place to place."

"What pay did he get?" asked Gubbles.

"A pound a week, and all found," replied Lingo; "that would be about the average. Penny shows can't give the greatest curiosities a very high figure. Then you see this, how cunningly the whole thing was worked. A wild man on exhibition couldn't walk about in the daytime. He had to take his exercise in the air at night. This Chunder chap professed to be very fond of it, and sometimes would be away all night. What was he doing? Why, burglaring and robbing, or spotting places for his pal to work on. I remember its being spoken of at one time as a curious coincidence that housebreaking was common wherever the fair was. The show people generally got the credit of it. But they ain't, as a rule, thieves, although linen on a hedge is tempting to the poorest."

They stayed with him until Lobbs arrived. He had, as he stated, roused the entire force of the country to look for Chunder Loo, and communicated with the chief authorities in Scotland Yard.

"All that could be done, I've done," he said, "and now let me look at the place where he met this born detective."

It was Don he alluded to, who blushed a little as he demurred to the statement.

So they all set out together, and as they were going down the village street, Lingo said to Lobbs:

"There's Mawston's boy. Is he to go scot-free?"

"I forgot him," answered Lobbs, "it is a good idea. We will have him."

As they were near Mrs. Snicker's cottage, where Mulberry Cork probably was, Lobbs called a halt and ran over with the boys the probable avenues Mulberry would go for if he attempted to get away.

There were only two, the road in front and the fields in the rear.

"Well," said Lobbs, "you boys make your way to the back of the cottage and lie close until you hear my whistle. That will mean 'Look out,' if it is blown twice. If you hear it only once, you may reckon we've got him."

CHAPTER CLXIII.

AN EXCITING CHASE AND IMPORTANT CAPTURE.

"OUR best way," said Jack, "is through Botch's farmyard, over the gate, and along by the hedge that runs at the back of the houses."

"I hope we shall nail the young beggar," said Bob Stockton, "for he can, if anyone, clear up the mystery of the murderer of Hone."

"I don't now think that Snicker did the deed," said Tom Drummond.

"And I believe I could name the murderer," remarked Don, as he skipped nimbly over the farmyard gate.

"The born detective once more on the trail," said Bob, laughing, "go it. Knock the stuffing out of the pros. in Scotland Yard."

There was nobody about in the yard, and they passed through without attracting attention, save of an old sow who had had previous experience of the Lambs' visits, and grunting and squeaking, cleared off to a far corner, where she planted her tail against the stone wall, and eyed them viciously until they were over the other gate and out of sight.

At right angles with the yard was the hedge that backed the village gardens. It was of thorn and very thick, with here and there a gap made by some urchin or dog.

Mrs. Snicker's garden was about fifty yards down.

The boys, now silent, crept along until they reached the desired spot, and then lay down in the dry ditch that ran parallel with the hedge.

"Don't show so much as the tip of your nose," whispered Jack, "until you hear footsteps in the garden. Then up and be ready to nab him."

Three uncommonly long minutes elapsed, and then there was a rush of feet on the other side of the hedge. Instantly all four were on the alert. But the thorny mass was so thick that they could see nothing. They could only hear footsteps approaching.

Jack motioned for his followers to spread out, and as they were quietly shifting, the whistle of the detective was heard. It was blown twice.

Almost simultaneously, Mulberry Cork came literally flying over the hedge, dropped on his feet, half fell, recovered himself, and sped across the meadow like a fox with the hounds in full cry behind him.

"After him!" shouted Jack.

Mulberry had come into view so suddenly, the sound of his footsteps notwithstanding, that he had in a degree taken the four friends by surprise. Nor were they prepared for such an exhibition as he gave of his running powers.

Mulberry was fleet of foot, for he was one of those town boys who yearn to become professional runners. You may see lads of his class going through a crude form of training in the outlying districts of the East-end of London, generally on a Sunday morning. With a handkerchief tied round their waists, and accompanied by a number of sympathising friends, they go pounding along as if the future welfare of humanity depended on their getting over a certain amount of ground in a given time.

His fleetness of foot was a revelation to those in pursuit.

But then it must be remembered that he had never associated with the boys, nor joined in any of their sports, nor done anything to give them a clue to his ability as a runner.

Jack Ford was a good judge of athletics, and he saw at once that the stern chase which had started might be a long chase.

"Don't talk," he said; "save your breath and go steady. Give him time to lose his first wind, and then when I give the word, *spurt* for him."

Behind them there was a shouting of men, and Jack, glancing back, saw that Lobbs, Gubbles, and Lingo, and a number of rustics had got into the field. They were following up the boys, but had as much chance of overtaking them, while the chase was proceeding, as so may cart-horses would, if entered for the Derby, have a chance of winning that national race.

Straight across the field went Mulberry, ignoring a gate to the left, and taking the hedge at a bound. Five seconds later, the four pursuers jumped it side by side, and here Tom Drummond fell, putting himself out of the hunt. He came over with his head too much in advance, pitched forward, and spread-eagled himself upon the ground, with every puff of wind knocked out of his body.

He had not enough left to utter a single ejaculation in expression of his feelings.

The others knew that he had fallen, but could not stop to assist him to rise. It would have been a waste of time.

Now they were in a broad meadow, one of the largest in the neighbourhood. It contained fully forty acres, and at the foot of it ran the Avon river, narrow but deep in places, and away to the left was Screwgray Water Mill.

Over the bridge adjoining it Mulberry must go, unless he swam the river. Jack was wondering if natation was one of his accomplishments, when he suddenly shot away in the direction of the mill.

So swift was the pace that Bob Stockton was beginning to pant, and Don was mentally estimating how long he could hold out. Jack Ford, as he ran, brought out his handkerchief, whipped it round his waist, and tightly knotted it.

"Looks as if we were going to be licked," murmured Don.

In essaying to imitate the doing of his chief, Bob Stockton came to grief. While engaged in tying his handkerchief round his waist, he failed to observe a rabbit-burrow, into which he thrust his foot, and went down.

As he afterwards described his fall: "The earth rose up and knocked all the sawdust out of me."

Two pursuers only now were left. Mulberry twenty yards in advance of Jack, who headed Don by a quarter of that distance.

The party from the village had not reached the meadow, and nowhere else around was there a sign of human life.

Nor was the mill going. Across the bridge, and on the side nearest to them, was the ponderous wheel, with the water near it pouring over the waste fall. Across that fall was a narrow wooden bridge that also spanned the wheel, so as to reach a small side door of the mill. That door was shut.

Mulberry, after apparently being bent on going right over the main bridge, and away to the country beyond, turned to the narrow one we have described, rushed across it, and threw himself against the mill door.

It was fast.

Wheeling round, he whipped out a revolver and presented it at Jack Ford and Don, who were about to dash up to him.

"Stand off, or I shoot!" he gasped.

But neither heeded the threat. Their blood was up, and they were not to be daunted by anything.

As they still kept on, Mulberry Cork fired the weapon hastily. Twice it rang out, and the bullets sped harmlessly over the heads of his pursuers.

Then something went wrong with the weapon, and it ceased to act.

Jack was half-way across the narrow bridge, and Mulberry Cork, with a yell of despair, jumped over the railing on to the big wheel, where he lay gasping and eyeing his pursuers with the malevolence of a hunted wolf.

"Come back, you fool," said Jack, as soon as he could speak. "Give yourself up."

"Come down and take me," hissed Mulberry.

"I'll be at him," said Jack. "Don, there is a punt down there. Go to it, and be ready to give a hand to help us out of the water, for into it we are bound to go."

Don ran round to the side of the mill-pond, where there was a fishing-punt tied to a post. He loosened it and sprang in, picking up the pole to work it.

Then he looked up to see what Jack was doing.

He had dropped upon the wheel, and was cautiously advancing upon Mulberry Cork, who was shifting to a lower flange of the wheel.

Don was not an experienced punter, but he had common sense, and knew that to use the pole effectually he must keep in the shallow water.

So he began to push along under the bank with his face to the two boys on the wheel.

He had accomplished half the requisite distance to reach them, when suddenly he saw, to his terror, a great rush of water, and the wheel began to turn. Jack Ford at the same moment sprang upon Mulberry Cork, and the pair disappeared in the deep water below.

This was startling to Don, and for a moment he lost his head. Recovering himself, he pushed the punt out from the bank and was immediately caught in the swirl from the newly opened flush of water.

He was helpless now. The pond was too deep to use the pole, and could he have done so, what would have been his strength against the rushing, twirling, bubbling, eddying water? The punt was merely a big cork on the surface of it.

It was not long, of course—a time to be reckoned by seconds—ere Jack appeared again. He came up fully twenty yards from the mill, and he had Mulberry Cork by the collar of his coat, holding him out at arm's-length.

His captive was madly struggling, not to get free, but in the terror of those who are unable to swim and find themselves in deep water.

His efforts were directed simply towards the getting hold of something to cling to. It matters little to non-swimmers what it is—a plank, a stick, a straw, a fellow-being, anything.

But Jack knew that with Mulberry Cork clinging to him he must go down with the poorest of chances of ever coming to the surface again. He therefore put forth all his powers to keep off the maddened Mulberry, at the same time casting glances around to see if Don was near.

At the outset he had his back to the punt, but he soon espied it. It was being carried towards the further shore, as he, but being heavier than himself and the boy he had captured, it moved with less speed. Given a few minutes' time, he would overtake it.

He had calculated everything with great accuracy. Having succeeded in keeping Mulberry at arm's-length, he was soon near enough to the boat to give directions to Don.

"Stand by!" he said, "put down the pole. It isn't any use to you now—be ready when we are near enough to lay hold of Cork. Grab him by the hair of his head. It won't hurt him and he will keep quieter until I can pop into the punt, and help you with him."

It was neatly done. Don carried out the instructions given him to the letter.

As soon as he had hold of the hair of Mulberry's head Jack let go and climbed into the punt. Then the pair hauled in the exhausted boy, and laid him down, gasping like a fish, all his defiant spirit gone.

"Give me the pole," said Jack; "I can steer the punt clear of this eddy, and then we shall strike the bank."

As he took it in his hand a far-off cheer was heard, and the boys turned their eyes in the direction of the sound.

Standing in the gaps and upon the gate of the hedge on the upper side of the meadow were the men who had followed with such speed as they could command. Lingo, Gubbles, Lobbs, the villagers, Tom, and Bob, they were all there, witnesses of the scene ever afterwards to be spoken of by them as a record of boyish gallantry and daring.

CHAPTER CLXIV.

MULBERRY MAKES A CONFESSION.—SUFFERING INNOCENCE.

"WELL done, my lads!" sang out Lobbs, as the men approached Don and Jack, who were standing guard over Mulberry Cork.

There was not much fear of his running away, for terror and the drenching he had received combined to reduce him to a helpless condition.

"Looks like a drowned rat, doan't he?" remarked one of the villagers, staring at the sodden captive, as he lay limp upon the bank of the mill-pool.

"Can't you get up?" asked Lobbs.

Mulberry raised his woebegone eyes to him, as he feebly replied:

"I'll try to in a minute."

"We are not going to have any more of your nonsense, you know," continued Lobbs. "Now then, up you come!"

He assisted Mulberry to rise, and the boy stared about him with wild eyes. Presently he began to shiver.

"I wish I'd been drownded, I do," he muttered, "better that than be hanged. Where are you going take me to?"

"You needn't be told," answered Lobbs.

"To prison—I know," rejoined Mulberry, "and I shall die there. I say you, Jack Ford, and you, Don

Peebles, you think you've done a grand ing me down, don't you?"

"We want to know who killed Hone," replied Jack, "and you ought to tell."

"I could tell," muttered Mulberry, "and nobody would be the worse for it." Aloud he said: "If I tell, will you let me go?"

"You will be treated mercifully," replied Lobbs, "unless, of course, you did it yourself."

"I hadn't any notion of killing him," replied Mulberry. "We were going on with all sorts of games together. *It was my father who killed him!*"

There was a general exclamation of surprise save from two of the party, Gubbles and Don. They were quiet, but exchanged meaning glances, practically saying to each other, "Just what we thought."

"Take me away, gimme something to drink, and put on me some dry clothes," said Mulberry, "and I'll tell you all about it. It can't hurt my father now, seeing as you've nabbed him for another job. If you hadn't got him I wouldn't have split if you had rent me to shreds. It would have been good fun to have hanged old Snicker, too. What a howling row he would have made over it! *My father will die game!* You see if he don't."

It was strikingly hideous to see the flash of criminal pride that for a moment brightened up the boy. But it died away instantly, and with a shiver he said:

"Take me somewhere and let me have something to warm me. I've got the ager."

They took him back as soon as they could to the Cowley Arms, where he was put to bed, for he seemed to be in a bad way, and some brandy was given to him. This, seemingly, did him good, for he fell asleep.

Lobbs sat by his bedside until he awoke half an hour afterwards. The others remained below discussing the rapid clearing up of the great mystery of Hone's murder.

"I thought Mawston did it," said Don; "it came to me like an inspiration, but even now I don't see why."

"Wait," advised Jack, who was clad in a cricketing suit belonging to an absent son of the landlord, pending the drying of his own clothes.

It was now dinner-time, and a proposition from Lingo that they should all have a chop met with ready assent. In the midst of the humble repast Penny Bunn appeared, hot with a rapid walk and the seething of inward anger.

"On my word," he said, "you have an amount of coolness, Mr. Gubbles, which I did not give you credit for."

"Indeed," replied Gubbles, unmoved; "in what way?"

"You asked for permission——"

"Pardon me; I took it."

"Took permission, then, to visit the wood, and here I

find you at the 'Cowley Arms' with a mixed assemblage——"

"Am I the mixed assemblage?" interposed Lingo. "I am the only stranger here, you know."

"Mr. Gubbles," said Bunn, ignoring Lingo, "you will at once return to the Abbey and attend to your duties there."

"Return yourself," calmly replied Gubbles, "and go to Jericho."

Penny Bunn became as a frozen man for a moment, he was so white, straight, and stiff.

"You will understand," he said, slowly and painfully, "that your refusal to obey my commands——"

"Hang your commands!"

"Will lead to your dismissal."

"Bother your dismissal! I am going to send for my things, and there is an end of my life as your tutor."

"You will forfeit your salary."

"Keep it for yourself. You may want it on a rainy day, Mr. Bunn. I am a rich man. I came to the Abbey to work out plans of my own. The fulfilment of my hopes has come. Don't be a fool, Bunn. Sit down and have a chop with us. Afterwards we will have a cigar and a chat."

"But the boys," murmured Bunn, with a sudden change in demeanour.

"It is a half-holiday, sir," said Jack.

"Why, so it is!" exclaimed Bunn, beaming. "I forgot it, truly. Mr. Gubbles, I will join you with pleasure, and since I am to lose a most valuable fellow-instructor of the young, I shall be glad to part the best of friends. You are sure you do not want your salary?"

"I would not accept it," replied Gubbles, smiling.

"Will you mind giving me a receipt?" insinuated Bunn—"ahem!—just to keep my books clear."

"And to get a little bit extra for yourself, that the wife won't know of, you wicked dog," said Gubbles, giving him a playful dig in the ribs. "I'll give you two receipts if you like, and lend you a fiver to compensate you for the loss of my services. How's that for high?"

"Upon my word," murmured Bunn, glowing like a lighthouse lantern, "I did not think there was so much nobleness in man."

A chop was ordered for him, and while it was cooking a message came from Lobbs for all concerned to come up and listen to the full confession of Mulberry Cork.

It was already written out by Lobbs, who read it over to them. It is needless to give it in its entirety. The story, in short, was as follows: Mulberry Cork, on the day when Hone was murdered, went into the wood with him, where they mooned about for a time. Suddenly Mulberry heard a peculiar cry, which he knew emanated from his father, whom he believed at that time to be in London. He recognised it as the cry of warning given by men associated with his parent when there was danger in the air.

He managed to slip away from Hone and meet his father, still in woman's attire, of course, lower down in the wood. They drew aside, and got into conversation about their affairs, and, of course, Chunder Loo was mixed up with them.

Berry Mawston on entering the wood had picked up a stick, which was Snicker's property, as it eventually turned out to be. He was showing it to his son, and talking rather carelessly of himself, when Hone was espied hidden behind a bush watching the pair. Before Mulberry could intervene his father had sprung upon the unfortunate boy and struck him.

The blow, dealt by a strong, angry man, was fatal.

As soon as the deed was done Mulberry railed at his father, telling him that Roger Hone was a boy who could have been trusted, for he had openly avowed to him that he was ready to join in anything that would bring him money. He was, in short, a criminal in embryo.

Berry Mawston—to keep to his correct name—was aghast at the folly and needlessness of the deed, and he swore his son to secrecy. The weapon that was used to such complete and terrible effect was thrown aside, and recognising the desirability of his keeping out of the way for a time, he asked his son Mulberry —the real Christian name of his son, although Cork was fictitious—where he could hide in security.

Mulberry had heard of the discovery of the treasure from Chunder Loo, and he thought of the cave beneath the cliff. Thither his father hied, and there he was brought food by his son and the Hindoo, under circumstances that will be clear to the reader.

All that followed the taking refuge there we know.

This confession, duly read over and attested, was conveyed to Chippenham by Lobbs, who took Mulberry with him. And the pair were away before Penny Bunn had finished his dinner.

It was just as well he had partaken of it, for the relation rather upset his digestion.

"You were rash in speaking of Snicker's guilt as you did," said Gubbles, playing the part of Job's comforter to perfection, "and he will probably bring an action against you. My advice to you is, if he does so, *square* it."

Penny Bunn gazed at him fixedly for a moment, and then, in a slow, pained way, asked:

"Square it—with what?"

"Money!" answered Gubbles.

"At the present moment," said Bunn, putting a hand to his brow, "my entire worldly wealth consists of two threepenny-pieces and a penny with a hole in it. My wife has a small sum left of her own, and she has announced her determination to stick to it. She will keep her word. Debts are accumulating round me. Snicker can proceed with his action. I am a broken man. But for this afternoon I would fain forget my misery, and as you have proffered me hospitality, I will partake of a glass of gin, warm, and a mild smoke."

Gubbles laughed good-humouredly, and dismissing the boys with a nod, prepared to spend an hour, happy or otherwise, in the society of Lingo and his late employer.

CHAPTER CLXV.

A PLAN OF THE ABBEY.—THE HOME-COMING OF FONTENOY SNICKER, ESQUIRE.

THOUGH Lobbs had gone on to Chippenham with a most portentous confession in his possession, he had not forgotten other matters. Among them his original intention, before the capture of Mulberry Cork, to examine the spot where Chunder Loo had last been seen.

He deputed one of the county police—of whom there were three hanging about the village—to go thither and closely examine the place. Jack and his three friends, after leaving the "Cowley Arms," turned their faces towards the Abbey, and overtook the man.

He was an intelligent young officer, and recognising the boys, he got into conversation with them, and eventually told them of the errand he was upon. They naturally offered to assist him, and all went on to the wood.

There, after a short search, some pieces of paper, folded together, were discovered. On opening them, it was seen that they were portions of a very old book, part being a series of plans of a building, and the rest letterpress of a hundred and fifty years ago or more.

The plans were in a very dilapidated condition. Where the folds were they were almost broken through, and some of the details were hidden under blotches of ink and dirt.

At the bottom was some printing, obscured in the same way, but a portion of it sufficed to show what the plans were.

Through the holes and dirt the boys were able to make out the following:

"Ye plan o . . . . tlecote Abb . . . as desig . . . by . . . . most pious son of ye Holy Catho . . . Church . . . ther Anselmo . . . . secret ways theretoe, for ye . . . . ty of the Holy Fri . . ."

"Putting in the missing letters," said Jack, "I read it this way: 'The plans of Littlecote Abbey, as designed by that most pious son of the Holy Catholic Church, Brother Anselmo, with the secret ways for the safety of the Holy Friars.'"

"That's about it," said Bob.

"And Chunder Loo, who has, of course, dropped it," mused Jack, "having got hold of it he was able to play high jinks in the old place. I see now what brought him and Mawston down here. Somehow—from an old bookstall, probably—they got possession of this plan and the account of the Abbey. Chunder Loo may have had it in his possession for months, or longer. About the time when the two scoundrels were in need of a hiding-place, Snicker's advertisement for a tutor appeared in the papers. Then Chunder Loo and Mawston put their heads together, and laid out the whole thing."

"Jack is on the trail, as usual," murmured Tom.

"But of course they could not all come down together," pursued Jack, "so Chunder applies for the post of tutor, and Mawston gets himself up as a woman, takes the name of Cork, and in due time brings his precious cub here as pupil. Having done that, he intended to get abroad, but was kept hanging round here by Chunder, as Mulberry has confessed. I do not think we have anything else to learn."

Jack was right. He had picked up the lost threads, or all that was required of that strange story.

"I don't wonder at you boys being too much for old Snicker," remarked the officer, admiringly; "your heads are as clear as a bell."

They had another look round, but nothing more was discovered that could be of any service to the authorities, and the officer departed with the plans and letterpress, promising to take great care of both, for the boys hoped by-and-by to have the opportunity to examine the matter, and get full knowledge of the intricacies of the old Abbey.

Then they hurried away in search of their schoolfriends, to tell them of the startling results of their morning's work.

The tidings of Snicker's innocence were known that afternoon at Smudgem Bender, but the prevailing feeling was one of intense and unqualified disappointment. His popularity was of the doubtful character that everybody who knew him felt that justice had been led astray. Snicker, in the general opinion, deserved hanging, anyway.

There was one, however, who ought to have rejoiced, but did not, and that was his wife. She did not exactly desire him to end his days ignominiously, but she had had quite enough of him and all his works.

"Oh, dear! oh, dear!" she exclaimed, when she heard the news; "now he will be coming back, and worriting and snarling, and going on with all his aggrawating tricks. I am the most unfortunate woman alive!"

Desiring to be just to the innocent man, the police lost no time in placing the facts before the proper authorities. But there were certain things to be done ere the prisoner could be released, so he was doomed to spend one more night in the shadowy confines of a gaol.

But on the following morning, shortly after he had partaken of his breakfast of feeble cocoa and brown bread, a gaoler appeared and gruffly told him the governor wished to see him.

"Is there any other charges agin me?" asked Snicker, dismally.

"You will find out all about it," replied the warder. "Hurry up!"

The man was in a bad humour. He knew what Snicker was wanted for, but he was of opinion that never had a man less deserved to be found innocent, and it had put him out of temper.

Snicker was taken to the governor's room, where he was shown an order for his release, as no further charge would be made against him. For a moment the listener was dumb.

Then he drew a deep breath and pulled himself together.

"Oh! they've found out I'm not the party, eh?" he said.

"That is a fact, I believe," coldly replied the governor. "Some other man has been arrested for the crime."

"I told you all along," said Snicker, exultingly, "that I wasn't the man, but you were sich a set of thickhead——"

"Show this man outside!" said the governor.

Two warders performed this office, and Snicker was discharged at the gate of the prison with the scantiest of ceremony. Outside, he felt that he could hardly credit the evidence of his senses. While he was standing there the gate opened again, and one of the warders came out.

"Lay hold of this," he said, tossing half a crown towards Snicker. "It is from the governor to take you home. Get out of here smart! We don't want any of your kidney here."

Snicker picked up the money and looked at it.

"Is this enough?" he asked.

"It is all you will get," was the reply. "Your fare to Chippenham is about a bob. Hook it!"

It was the most unpleasant dismissal from prison ever experienced by an innocent man; but Snicker was getting fairly well used to hard knocks, and, with a snarl on his lips, wheeled about and wended his way to the station.

By eleven o'clock he was at Chippenham, where he rather expected to receive an ovation.

But there was no excitement, and to all appearance he was not recognised until he got outside, and there he encountered Milky Whey.

Milky had heard the news, and had just been ex-pressing his opinion on the matter by declaring, in an adjacent public-house, that if Snicker had not killed Hone he meant to do it, and ought to be hanged all the same.

But on seeing the released one, he suddenly went on the other tack.

"Welcome, old pal!" he said, holding out his hand. "I knowed you was innercent right through. My 'art have been a-bleeding for you."

It was the first expression of sympathy Snicker had received, and it moved him deeply. He accepted the outstretched hand and pressed it warmly. Tears stood in his eyes.

"Milky," he said, pathetically, "my suffer—suffer-in's have been excrutinating!"

"You ought to get heavy compensation for them," replied Milky, "and them as lives in Smudgem Bender should, if they acts manly, give you a grand deception. Them boys at the Abbey ought to be made to do something for you, too. Look here! We'll have a talk over it. I got up a rovation for the Bath Brick when he lost his fight with Walloping Jim on a foul, and I'll see you through your job. Have you got the price of a pint about you?"

Snicker admitted he had the price of several.

"Then come along to the 'Ship and Whistle,' and I'll derange the whole thing for you."

It would take up too much of our time and space for us to give the consultation between these worthies in full, but the upshot of it was that Snicker was to remain in Chippenham during the night, and write to his wife and the boys at Littlecote to do their best to give him a "warm reception" on the evening of the morrow.

"And we ain't going to crawl there on our feet," said Milky Whey, finally, "for I've got a moke on hire—leastways, his owner is doing a week for 'salting a constable, and I'm taking care of him. He about fits the shafts of my barrer. With a few hevergreens and bit or two of ribbon we can make a tidy show. We'll go home in style, as all innercent men do in story-books, and have a rousing night of it."

"We will," said Snicker; and finding he had still tenpence left, he ordered another drink.

CHAPTER CLXVI.

A VERY WARM WELCOME.

EARLY in the morning the postman wended his way to the Abbey, bearing with him, among other letters, one Snicker had written to Jack Ford as the leader of the school.

It came upon the boys as a flash of light comes on a dark, tragic scene.

We think it good enough to give it in its entirety.

"MY DEAR YOUNG FRIEND,

"In the sorrerful past there was bill feeling twixt us, risin' I have no doubt out of the matchinations of the idjiot who is now master of the school. I alwus felt that one day we should understand each other more puffectly, and as you are now aweer of my being innercent of the crime of murdering Hone, I feel sure that you will show the nateral good feeling by helping to give me a public reseption on my return to-morrow hevening punkually at the hour of seven. Milky Whey, a troo but humbel friend, have kindly lent me a webicel for the occasion, and will akkompany me.

"Your old and true friend,
"FONTENOY SNICKER.

"P.S.—Hone wasn't a bad sort of boy, but I niver could love and respeck him as I do you."

After the reading of this letter aloud in the play-ground there was a general opinion that the boys ought to do something to make Snicker's return to Smudgem Bender memorable.

"After this greasy letter," said Jack, "I feel that to throw away the opportunity to let him know exactly what we think of him would be a sin."

"Bags of flour," suggested Little Jiggers. "They make a lot of show."

"It is a pity there are no coloured ochres in this country," said Philter.

"He ought to have the word 'hypocrite' branded all down his back," said Herbert May, scornfully.

"I'll drop a line to Lingo," said Jack, "and give him a few suggestions. I daresay we shall be able to run down in the evening and see the fun. Don, you can go with the letter. Bunn won't miss you. He came home last night with a headache and something wrong with his legs, and Gubbles is gone. There ought to be some startling educational work done this morning."

Don expressed his readiness to go and risk what followed. He, too, had seen Penny Bunn on the previous evening when he came back to the Abbey, and a violent altercation between the schoolmaster and his wife had been overheard by all.

Things were indeed horribly mixed at the Abbey that morning.

No Gubbles—he had sent a man to pack and remove his effects—Penny Bunn in a state of trembles—Miss Astracan with the spasms, and Miriam furious. Susan had also lent her quota to the general disorder by giving notice to leave, and expressed her willingness to depart at once, as her young man was waiting to marry her.

The condition of things was almost as bad—quite as bad one way, perhaps—as during the time of the great barring out.

Bunn would not get up until he had had a cup of tea, and Miriam refused to let him have one. At nine o'clock he was in bed, moaning, and there was nobody to look after the boys in the class-room.

"This is the beginning of another breaking-up," said Tom Drummond.

"What could you expect," snorted Short, "with an *ass* for a scholmaster?"

The result of being left thus to themselves was inevitable.

Boys will be boys, and if they have nothing to do, they get help from Satan, who finds some work for idle hands on the shortest notice.

It was nobody's business to keep order, and none was kept.

Skylarking of the noisiest description soon became the order of the day. While some of the elders sat talking, as well as they were able, to each other in the din, the younger boys started a hare-and-hounds chase over the forms and desks.

The riot was at its highest, when the door opened and Penny Bunn was seen there framed in the dark doorway like the picture of a ghost.

Immediately there was a subsidence of the elements, and a gliding into seats with faces expressive of the most resolute determination to go on with their book-learning or die.

Jack and a few others remained where they were, looking at the forlorn figure in the doorway.

"Boys," said Penny Bunn, in a voice that seemed to be coming through a reed, "this conduct is unseemly, knowing as you do that I am this morning prostrated by an attack of—of—incipient brain fever."

"Impossible!" muttered Jiggers; "got no brains."

This remark sorely taxed the gravity of those nearest to him, and there were sounds of bubbling in the throats of the boys.

"Having a due regard to the necessities of health," said Bunn, "and feeling that repose is absolutely necessary, I request you all to go for a quiet walk. The duties of the school will be resumed in the afternoon—my health permitting."

The boys needed no second bidding. They were out of their seats in a moment, and as Bunn, with his hand to his brow, tottered off in the direction of his dining-room, they cleared out of the Abbey.

"Another step towards a break-up," said Tom to Jack; "the school is doomed. It can't go on."

This opinion would have been fully confirmed if the boys had witnessed the scene between Penny Bunn and his gentle Miriam, following his appearance in his private room.

There was no breakfast on the table, unless the remnants of her own—a teapot with some cold tea in it—could be considered in that light.

At first she took no notice of him, and he sat down. Having poured out some tea, and on tasting it found it was cold, he said, mildly:

"Miriam, this is *not* kind. Suffering as I——"

She was upon her feet with a springing action ere he could utter another word.

"Where are the boys?" she demanded.

"I have sent them for a walk," he replied; "my suffer——"

"You fool!" she cried, and then she struck him.

It was an open-handed blow, but it was a stinger, and it blinded him for a moment.

She had not gone to that length before, although she had pushed and hustled him occasionally.

Then she lost her head entirely and railed at him, using a torrent of invective that only a woman has at her command. Men use rough language at times, but on the score of cutting abuse they have no chance with the gentler sex.

Penny Bunn listened like a man who doubts the evidence of his senses. He said but little, but it was always at the right time.

When Miriam flagged, he uttered a conciliatory word, and on she went again.

At last the storm was over. It ended in a fit of hysterics, during which he left her and went out for a walk. He wanted a quiet hour to review his prospects, and a very bad hour it was.

He went no further than the entrance to the wood, where he sat down by the roots of a huge oak-tree, and reviewed the past and present, following it up by contemplating a possible future.

As with most men who practise deception on themselves or others, he could not take a personally impartial view of his share in events.

"I," he murmured, "have done my best to live at peace with man and woman—particularly woman. But the continuous condition of my existence is war, and, alas! never a victory."

He was affected to tears, shedding one from each eye; but his elastic nature rebounded from the rock of grief the next moment, and he got upon his feet.

"After all," he said, "it is not a hanging matter for me. A woman strikes me—good. She is my lawful spouse, and I am responsible for all her unlawful acts. I can do nothing but submit to the decrees of fate. Therefore I will submit."

Investigating his coat-pockets, he found the stump of a cheroot, and he lighted it, feeling that it was as well to enjoy the blessings of life while an opportunity was afforded him.

Two puffs and then a footstep.

He listened attentively for a moment, and then recognised it.

"My Miriam," he muttered, "going forth; but whither?"

He withdrew a few paces down the wood, and behind the trunk of a splendid beech-tree, waited for his loved one to go by.

CHAPTER CLXVII.

WOMAN'S LOVE FOR WOMAN.

THE cheroot Bunn was smoking had all the strength of the well-known, full-flavoured two-penny smoke. The faintest puff from it filled a considerable space with a very pronounced aroma, not entirely agreeable, even to a lover of tobacco.

Bunn, with ears distended, listened to the approaching footstep of the gentle Miriam as it drew nearer and nearer. After the experience of the morning he had no desire for more of her sweet company that day.

Suddenly the sounds ceased. There was a pause, and then a short, sharp sniff.

Right away from the nape of his neck down to his boots Bunn turned cold.

"Like a bloodhound," he muttered, "she scents me. Can she follow up the trail?"

The stump of the cigar was still burning.

Under more favourable conditions it would have given him the pleasure of a smoker for fully a quarter of an hour.

Now it must be sacrificed, and he groaned in spirit.

Dropping it to the ground, he put his heel upon the precious morsel of ill-favoured weed, and silently breathed a hope that he was safe from the further attentions of the gentle Miriam.

But much as he knew of her investigating powers, he did not know her full capability as a tracker of men who leave trails of tobacco behind them.

Moving on again, she came steadily and surely down to where he was hiding.

Feeling that detection was certain, he hastily drew an old letter—it was a peremptory request for the immediate payment of rates from his pocket, and holding it upside down, contemplated it thoughtfully, as if weighing the contents of an important document.

"P. Y.!"

The initials by which she once endearingly addressed him, but now used when in an acrid humour, fell sharply upon his ear. He started from his feigned reverie, and exclaimed:

"Miriam! Is it thou?"

"Don't be an idiot!" she returned. "You knew I was near you, and skulked, as usual, to avoid me. It is not manly or just, P. Y., to treat me as you do."

"If you will write me down a code of conduct for my daily guidance," he said, "I will endeavour to follow it."

She glared at him, thinking he was mocking her, and he was for a moment in danger of receiving a second dose of the chastisement he had previously received. But she saw that he was serious, and the half-raised hand was dropped again.

"Of all men I have met or known," she said, "you are the biggest fool!"

"Forcible," murmured Bunn, "but possibly not true, and, in any case, not polite."

"I am going to the village," said Miriam, abruptly: "you had better come with me."

"To the village, my dear?"

"I am about to pay a visit to Mrs. Snicker."

"Oh!"

What a world of expression there was in that interjection! Doubt, fear, dissent, deprecation, and what not, were all in it. But Miriam did not heed him. Marching on in front, she motioned for him to follow, which he did with the meekness of a poodle dog.

He did not ask her what she wanted with Mrs. Snicker, although he wondered consumedly. He could hardly think that there was going to be a wordy war, followed up by a fight; and the idea of Miriam paying the wife of the man recently charged with murder a visit of condolence was entirely out of the question.

"Why and wherefore?" Bunn asked himself, and Miriam, striding on in stern silence, gave him no satisfaction by answering.

She might have guessed what was in his mind, and probably did, but it was not in her line of action to relieve the man she had married and deemed herself so much above.

So they went on in silence until the village was reached, and the cottage occupied by Mrs. Snicker within a few yards of them.

"Need I come in?" inquired Bunn.

"What do you think?" asked Miriam. "Suppose we should have a quarrel, shall I not be in need of a witness?—and even a husband like you is better than nothing."

"As complimentary as heretofore," muttered Bunn. "Go on, woman."

"P. Y.!"

"I think 'woman' a term that you ought to be proud of. What shall I substitute for it?"

She could not fall upon him there, as some of the elder villagers were abroad with a number of children on whom the picture of matrimonial violence might have a startling effect.

Handicapped in this direction she stalked into the cottage where Mrs. Snicker dwelt, without the preliminary step of knocking at the door, and Bunn perforce followed her.

Mrs. Snicker was engaged in that oft-repeated duty in small households, sweeping up the hearth. When a thoroughly domesticated woman has nothing else to do she has a turn at that. An exclamation of surprise burst from Mrs. Snicker's lips.

"I am Mrs. Bunn," said Miriam.

"I am sorry for him," promptly answered Mrs. Snicker.

She saw war in the eyes of Miriam, and immediately put her armour on.

"Your husband has been charged with murder and is about to be released, I hear," continued Miriam; "probably by this time he *is* released. What do you intend to do when he returns?"

"That is my business," answered Mrs. Snicker.

Miriam had been met with unexpected opposition to some purpose she had in her mind. The position was a difficult one, if not actually humiliating.

"I came," she said, "to suggest that when your husband comes back you had better take him away as soon as possible."

"Thanks, ma'am, I'm sure," said Mrs. Snicker, very upright and perky about the head, "and suppose I don't do it, ma'am, perhaps you would like to take him away yourself. I am sure you are welcome to him."

Penny Bunn raised his eyes to the ceiling. This delightful scene compensated him for much previous suffering.

"*Me* take your husband away?" said Miriam breathlessly, "*me?*"

"Yes, ma'am," said Mrs. Snicker, calmly; "don't you run away with the conviction that I ain't heard of your artful ways, endeavouring to lure him from me. Not as I wants to keep him, for welcome you are to him, if you can see your way to getting rid of that poor creature behind you there."

"Woman!" cried Bunn.

"P. Y.," said Miriam, "be quiet. Mrs. Snicker—will you kindly tell me when I ever endeavoured to lure your husband away from you?"

"The last time as iver he was out with his barrer," said Mrs. Snicker, "when you was so sweet and pleasant to him that the idjot's head was turned, and he talked of nuthin' but your own luvin' ways all the evening."

"P. Y.," gasped Miriam, "help me out of this house! The bare sight of that woman suffocates me."

"Yes, take her home, and if she don't behave herself, *wollop* her," advised Mrs. Snicker, "that is what she wants. As for what I am going to do with my husband, that's my affair. Take her away, Mr. Bunn, and be a man in the future. *Don't stand her nonsense!*"

Miriam, who had come to vent some of her spite on Mrs. Snicker and insist upon her leaving the neighbourhood with her husband, being thus foiled, staggered out of the house.

Bunn paused a moment to wring the hand of Mrs. Snicker, and then hastened after her. But she was

A SPLENDID SCHOOL STORY.
NEVER BEFORE PUBLISHED.
By E. HARCOURT BURRAGE,
Author of "Ching Ching," "Monkey Mat and Roving Dick," "The Brave Boy of the Basilisk," &c.

The LAMBS of LITTLECOTE.

"Wo', I'm blowed!" exclaimed Snicker, as his eye fell upon the inscription. "Milky, it's a lot of the usual gammon they're up to. What shall we do?" "Go forrard," replied Milky Whey. "Wo''s gammon? It ain't poison. I don't see nothing wrong as yet."

PRICE ONE PENNY.

already far away up the road, gliding along like a puff of smoke before a brisk breeze, and Bunn, on reflection, decided not to follow her until her present condition of heat had somewhat cooled down.

Meanwhile, preparations were going on for the reception of Snicker. Lingo was conducting them alone, until the boys appeared unexpectedly and lent a hand. Then indeed things moved briskly.

As the nature of them will appear immediately in our account of Snicker's arrival home, we need not go into them now.

At half-past five precisely Milky Whey and Fontenoy Snicker started from Chippenham on the fish-barrow, decorated crudely with evergreens. At each of the four corners of the vehicle a tallish stick had been fixed with bits of coloured rag flying aloft.

Ample time had been allowed for the journey, as the donkey, entrusted to Milky's keeping, under circumstances already set down, was known to possess an uncertain temper, and given at times to lie down without any notice, and refuse to budge until it did so of its own sweet will

The journey to Smudgem Bender was one unbroken struggle between Milky and the beast. Being a man of forethought, he had provided himself with half a dozen sticks, the last of which was used up when they had still a third of a mile to travel.

Strange to say, no sooner was the last worn-out stump of the lot thrown aside than the donkey, which rejoiced in the name of Filberts, started off at a brisk pace, and there was much promise of a fitting entry into the village.

But the hopes of men are wont to "gang agley," and just as the houses appeared in the distance, a wheel came off the barrow and the occupants tumbled ignominiously into the road.

Filberts was thrown down, and gave vent to a hee-haw of double-extra donkey power.

The vehicle could be left, for it was not likely to be stolen by anyone unless they were hard up for fire-wood, but the donkey must be taken.

Filberts never objected to being led, and submitted like a lamb. On foot the two men with the animal set forward again.

"There's a lot of 'em waiting for us," said Snicker, shading his eyes with his hand and peering ahead. "I can see by the looks of 'em that there are a lot of the boys there, too."

"They was bound to meet you, and do justice to a man they've wronged. Come up, Filberts! What yer hanging back for?"

Yes, the boys were there, and the villagers abroad in force. At the entrance to the village two poles had been set up, and stretched across was a strip of calico on which was painted, in bold, black letters, the following appropriate words:

"SNICKER IS HINNER—*inno*—JIGGER IT!—CENT.
"*Hooray!*"

"Well, I'm blowed!" exclaimed Snicker, as his eye fell upon the inscription. "Milky, it's a lot of the usual gammon they are up to. What shall we do?"

"Go forrard," replied Milky Whey. "Wot's gammon? It ain't poison. I don't see nothing wrong as yet."

"But read that 'ere redress," pleaded Snicker.

"I would if I could, but I can't," answered Milky

"There's Jack Ford," said Snicker, "and, as I'm a livin' sinner, that chap Lingo! Milky, we must go back."

"Not if I knows it," said Milky. "I've got a thirst on me through wolloping Filberts, and I've got to swage it. Wot can they do to you? Ain't you got the law on your side?"

"I ain't had much on my side lately," moaned Snicker.

"But you are bound to go home, ain't yer?"

Snicker groaned again, and with a hesitating step approached the party of reception which had formed across the road. Jack Ford, with his particular henchmen, stood a little in advance.

There was a dead silence as the two men with the donkey between them drew up and halted, in obedience to a sign from Jack, a few feet away.

Herbert May put his hands to his mouth and gave out a very good imitation of the blast of a herald's trumpet.

"Oyez! Oyez!" he cried. "Silence all while Baron Ford speaks words of warning to the brazen Snicker. Silence!"

The boys, inspired to play their part, kept up a gravity that did credit to their powers of self-control. But the villagers, young and old, were on the broad grin.

Jack stepped forward another pace.

"Fontenoy, *alias* Jerry Snicker," he said, "in response to your request to give you a fitting welcome we are here this evening, marvelling at your cheek, but resolved to let you know, for good and all, what we think of you. You are the most unmitigated skunk and rascal known to any assembled here!"

"Ham I?" exclaimed Snicker; "anyways, when the governor parted with me at the gaol he wept coporously, and said I was a *hin—in—*blow it!—jured man."

"In the past," pursued Jack, with the air of a calm, practised orator, "you were a monster in your treatment of boys entrusted to your care and handsomely paid for. You were only restrained from ultra-fiendish cruelty by the fear of the law. We fought and defeated you. Righteously you were kicked out of the school, and you ought then, if you had had one iota of the man or a tinge of shame in you, have gone away and never shown your face here again. But, instead of that, what do you do ?"

" I had to go somewheres," snivelled Snicker.

" You were not obliged to remain here," said Jack, " and certainly not to associate with thieves and murderers. You were innocent of the murder of Hone, as you are innocent of the murder of any of us here, *because you are a coward !* You had murder in your heart all through. But to come to the point. We have had enough of you here, and we warn you that, if you will consult your comfort and safety, you had better turn back. We had enough of you long ago at the Abbey; they have had enough of you in the village. Begone! We give you ten seconds to start."

" They lay it on pretty thick," said Milky. " This is about as warm a reception as ever I heerd on."

Then Filberts hee-hawed again, louder than before.

" I'm going on home," said Snicker, with a livid face. " I've got the law on my side. Milky, foller up with the donkey."

The line of boys in front of him divided so as to make a lane for him to pass through. He thought that he had frightened them, and snarled triumphantly as he strode forward. Milky followed with the donkey.

When they were fairly between the lines the storm began.

It rained flour, chalk, yellow ochre, cabbage-stumps, rotten eggs, and all sorts of cheap and effective missiles.

In two moments the staggered Snicker and his companion were unrecognisable. Filberts also, owing to his position, got his share, and resented it.

Jerking himself free from the weakened hold of Milky Whey, he let out with his heels and favoured Snicker with a kick that doubled him up for a moment, and then with a final hee-haw tore away back in the direction of Chippenham.

Blinded and furious, Snicker staggered on with the shouting and laughing crowd behind him. People are prodigal of their ammunition at such times, and the storm was soon over. Milky Whey prudently dropped behind to rub the flour out of his eyes and indulge in the luxury of a private course of cursing. Snicker went on, half-blinded, for home.

There were women and children at the gates, who shouted and clapped their hands as he passed by. Some were ringing small hand-bells. Bibbins, the watch and clock-maker, with his wife, was beating gongs, and Botch fired off a double-barrelled gun into the air.

The uproar was prodigious.

Snicker staggered into his garden and tottered to the door of his house.

It opened, as if his loving wife was coming out to welcome him.

But only a feminine arm and a short brush appeared, and the latter descended upon his head— he had dropped his hat—with crushing force.

" Go away, you villain!" Phœbe was heard to scream; " I can keep myself charing, but not you in drunken idleness."

Then the door closed and the sound of bolts being drawn followed. Snicker dropped limp and exhausted upon the stone-flags outside.

" His reception is over," said Jack Ford.

" Complete," assented Lingo, who was standing near him. " I think we may leave him now."

" Home, boys!" cried Jack.

Away they went, falling instinctively into the old marching order. But they went quietly. The foe was done with now. They desired nothing more—a triumphant song would have been superfluous.

Lingo returned to the inn where Gubbles, who had taken no share in the demonstration, was awaiting him.

The villagers sought the shelter of their cottages, and Bibbins and his wife ceased their gong-sounding and disappeared.

Snicker was left alone, lying by the door of his cottage, pleading to be admitted.

" Phœbe—Phœbe, let me in ! I ain't been a good husband to you. But in the futer—*ture*—I'll act manly and fair to you. Do let me in !"

But the door remained closed. Phœbe was firm. She had thought the matter well over and henceforth, for good or ill, for weal or woe, she and her husband were to live apart.

———

CHAPTER CLXVIII.

THE FULL WEIGHT OF RETRIBUTION.

IT is hard for a man who has been in the wrong all his life to admit it. Insensibly he has learnt to think himself in the right, and to look upon all just punishments as undeserved.

So it was with Snicker.

It is true that he was innocent of the crime of murder laid to his charge, but it is at the same time an undoubted fact that he would have killed more than one person long ago, but for a lack of courage. He had all the necessary venom in his heart.

After endeavouring in vain to gain admittance into his house, he eventually turned away, and stared down the village street.

It was empty, and there came a feeling over him that he was in a deserted world.

Assuredly no man, however poor and vile, was ever more friendless. There was, in all probability, no living creature under the sun who cared a straw what became of him.

He had isolated every associate from him.

"What shall I do?" he muttered. "As far as I can see, there is nuthin' but the work-us—*house*—ahead of me."

While he stood by his gate, Bibbins, the watchmaker, emerged from his house and turned into the roadway. He glanced at Snicker, and, elevating his nose in the air, hastened down the street.

Snicker followed him.

"One moment, sir," he said.

Bibbins wheeled about, and stared at him coldly.

"What do you want?" he asked.

"I s'pose—*sup*-pose," said Snicker, hoarsely, "that you ain't got sich a thing as a tanner about you?"

"I believe I have—perhaps two," replied Bibbins.

"Well," continued Snicker, "I was a-wonderin' if you could lend me sich—*such*—a thing?"

"I could not," said Bibbins; "but I will give you a sixpence if you will undertake to leave the neighbourhood, and poison the atmosphere of Smudgem Bender no more."

"I wasn't aweer—*ware*—of the p'isoning," answered Snicker, humbly; "but if I really does it, then I feels as if I'm in duty bound to leave the s'lubr'us part of Smudgem Bender."

"You accept my condition, Snicker?"

"I does."

"Then there is your sixpence. Don't come any nearer, please."

Bibbins tossed him the coin, and Snicker having dexterously caught it, spat upon it, and transferred it to his pocket.

The act was so redolent of his mean past life, so clear a revelation of the low origin of the man, more in the way it was done than in the actual doing, that Bibbins first stared at him, and then burst out laughing.

"It isn't the first time you've played the cadger," he said, and hastened on.

Snicker slowly followed him, pondering as he went.

"Sure-*ly*," he reasoned, "if one party can get his art touched, another is open to it. I'll try Botch now."

The night was coming on now, and deep shadows were falling on the village. In a few minutes night would be fully there.

When Bibbins had disappeared Snicker was once more absolutely alone in the thoroughfare. Most of the inhabitants were partaking of the last meal of the day, and some were already in bed. He walked slowly on until he came to an empty shed attached to the premises of the wheelwright, and there he took shelter for a time.

When it was quite dark he emerged from his hiding-place. Save for the lights in some of the windows, and the glimmer of the lamps lighted in the inn,

there was nothing but gloom. Smudgem Bender was innocent at all times of anything approaching public illumination of any sort. It never indulged in it even at times of national rejoicing.

It was easy enough to single out the house of Botch, because there were two windows lighted up, and Snicker ventured as far as the gate and peered over.

The moment he did so a huge dog dashed up to the gate with a growl. Snicker turned and dashed up the street. Over came the animal, apparently bent on having his life.

He would have cried out if he could, but the power was denied him. But he could run, and run he did, at a speed he could scarcely give himself credit for.

The dog followed, keeping close up—within a few inches of his heels, in fact, growling in a low, menacing tone.

But it did not bite him, probably because it did not think he was worth it, or it might be suspicious of the quality of the man altogether. The sagacious brute contented itself with harrying him clean out of the village, and then turned back and joyously went home.

Snicker sank down exhausted by the roadside, and lay there, breathless and done for.

What would he have given for a good long draught of ale out of the pewter? But he knew they would not serve him at the "Cowley Arms." It was a thing he must long for in vain.

He knew of a roadside spring thereabouts, and having groped around until he found it, satisfied his thirst.

Then he resumed his seat, and set to thinking again.

"I can't get along without a bit of money," he muttered. "I'm bound for to get help from somewhere—but where?"

He thought of everybody he knew, and last of all the boys. Though he was fully aware of having been a brute and tyrant to them, he knew their kindly, generous dispositions, and it was to them he finally turned his mind.

"If I could see them," he reflected, "they would be good for something. But I must wait till the morning."

That was the worst part of the thing. He had no desire to linger any longer in Smudgem Bender. The place was metaphorically too hot for him, although his treatment may be, in one sense, considered chilly.

"Perhaps," he murmured, "if I hurries up, I may ketch them youngsters afore they go to bed. I could wentur to the back door and ask the gal if I could see young Ford. That's a pearly idea."

It was so good that he at once proceeded to act

upon it. Once more he wended his way through the village, keeping well on the opposite side of the way when passing Botch's place, and so on to Mumping Malford Wood.

Still wrapped in the contemplation of his own sagacity in fixing on the boys as likely prey, he hurried up until he was well in the wood, and then a ghastly thought took possession of him. It was there Hone had been murdered.

Would his *ghost* walk?

Snicker was too ignorant not to be superstitious, and the bare thought of seeing a ghost would have raised the hair off his head, if he had possessed any.

Would that the thought of such a contingency had entered his head before he had travelled so far into the sombre depths of the wood! But he was there, and the mortal terror that came over him rooted his bent legs to the spot.

"Heaven have mercy on me!" he groaned aloud.

Barely had the words escaped his lips when he was seized by the throat and thrown violently to the ground.

CHAPTER CLXIX.

THE VANISHING OF SNICKER.

SNICKER gave himself up for lost. It never dawned upon him that a ghost, being an insubstantial being, would not have the power to deliver a material blow. All he knew was that he had received an uncommon hard knock which laid him low with a brilliant display of fireworks dancing before his eyes.

A silence followed, the smiter apparently giving him time to recover. Then a voice was heard addressing him.

The very first words, more like the hiss of a snake than the utterances of a human being, acquainted him with the fact that his assailant was Chunder Loo.

"You worm! what do you mean by prowling about here at this time of night?"

"I come up here jest to be quiet," replied Snicker, "being a 'omeless man."

"Homeless, are you?" said Chunder Loo, whom he could now faintly distinguish leaning over him.

"Owin' to the workin's of my henemies," said Snicker, "even my wife, a armless—*harmless*—creetur as I've loved and chirruped—*cherished*—fondly, 'cordin' to the hoath took at the altar, have shut her door—which is mine, anyway, as the law goes—ag'in' me."

"What else did you expect?" demanded Chunder Loo.

Snicker had to think a bit before he furnished an answer to this query. The spirit of candour finally took possession of him.

"Really," he said, "I wasn't sure of anything. In this wale of tears things as you expect don't come off, and wicey wersay. But a man's 'ouse is his own"—he paused a moment, and then added, "'cept when the bailiffs is in."

"Get up!" said Chunder Loo, curtly.

Snicker rose with a peculiar alacrity, and backed, so as to have a few feet between him and Chunder Loo.

"You have not told me the whole truth," said the Hindoo; "why are you here?"

"I am that hard-up," answered Snicker, "that I'm glad of help from anybody, and I was a-thinking the boys might help me."

"So you thought that the youngsters whom you starved and beat in your time, and whose parents you robbed, would help you?"

"I had a 'ope—*hope*—of it."

"What a precious cheek you must have!"

"If you think it wrong, sir, I won't do it."

"I do think it wrong, and what is more, if you attempt such a thing, I will personally go out of my way and wring your neck!"

"Don't be hard on an old pal."

"*What?*"

"Servant, then, sir."

"I would wring it in any case," said Chunder Loo, "not because I want to take the part of those cubs—for I hate them with a deep and bitter hatred—but because the very thought of you excites the murderous propensities I was born with and inherited from my parents. But I will spare you——"

"Thanky, sir."

"Spare you, because I should not know how to dispose of your body in this place. I have no wish for anything in the way of additional excitement. You will therefore clear out straight away, and tramp to London. I will give you two pounds to keep you from starvation, but if ever we meet again, I will put an end to you."

"For the two pounds, sir," said the humbled Snicker, "you have my lasting gratitude. You was allus—*always*—kind."

"You liar!"

"I thought you meant to be kind, sir, even when you poisoned me in a jokeular sperrit. I will go to London or furder—*further*—if the two pounds will carry me, and niver trouble you no more."

"Lay hold!" said Chunder Loo, fiercely.

He held out a skinny brown hand that had a peculiar phosphorescent glow about it, as the quaking Snicker extended his, receiving two sovereigns, which he instinctively transferred to his pocket.

"Away with you!" said Chunder Loo; "but first a question: Do you believe I am a common man?"

" *I don't,*" answered Snicker, with the emphasis of one speaking the truth.

"I am not," rejoined Chunder Loo, "for I have occult powers that enable me to tell if you so much as whisper to anyone on your way that you have seen me here to-night. Personally, I am a free man. No authority in this country can reach me. I am here of my own free will now, and when I choose to go away I shall do so, and no man be able to trace me."

"I can well believe it," assented Snicker; "you are in many ways, sir, a complete staggerer."

"I am," said Chunder Loo; "now heed me. You must go away now, right out of this district. If you walk all night you will, in the morning, be far from here, in a place where nobody will know you. Should you be arrested—as you may probably be, if hang-dog looks have any influence with the police—you will be dumb concerning *me*. Say but one word, and your life won't be worth an hour's purchase!"

The luminous hand was raised, and the terrified Snicker saw a finger pointing down the path. It was a clear indication that he was expected to go at once, and murmuring a feeble "Good-night, sir," he went tremblingly away.

Down through the wood to the main road he stepped unevenly, and there he pulled himself together. And as he hastened on, he took the two sovereigns Chunder Loo had given him out of his pocket, and tested them by biting them with his fang-like teeth.

They were sound and good.

"It would have been like him," he muttered, "to have played a low-down trick on me with Hanoverian medals. But he's given me good 'uns. Perhaps he hadn't any bad 'uns about him."

It had been a fatiguing day, and he was pretty well done, but he kept on as far as Chippenham, spurred along by thoughts of the terrible man he had just parted from.

He hoped and prayed that he might not see him again.

This heartfelt wish was on his lips when he walked into Chippenham at a quarter-past two in the morning.

CHAPTER CLXX.

ON, AND ON, AND ON.

EVERY fresh trouble seemed to Snicker that it must positively be the last. After the meeting with Chunder Loo, he could not believe there was further evil in store for him.

But not being gifted with the true prophetic vision, there was still a small store of this awaiting him.

Chippenham, at that unearthly hour, was a still collection of inferior bricks and mortar. Ugly by day, it had no redeeming feature at night. There was no more life or beauty in it than one would hope to find in a Turkish cemetery.

As Snicker neared the bridge that spanned the Avon in the heart of the town, a most unearthly howling fell upon his ears. He immediately associated it with cats, and looked about him for feline disputants, or wooers, whichever they might be. Between the unseemly caterwauling of cats engaged in a row and the song of a tom-cat lover there is little to choose. To the ordinary ear the sounds are precisely the same.

But it was not the cats at all.

On the bridge sat a man in whom it was easy to recognise the form of Milky Whey.

Seated on the pavement, and under the influence of drink, he was engaged in what he was pleased to call singing.

In any other town, and at any other hour of the day or night, he would probably have had the police upon him in something under two minutes; but being where he was, he could indulge in his unearthly performance free from interruption for a good hour or more.

Snicker had to pass him as he squatted on the footway, with his eyes shut, and his mouth open to emit the dolorous sounds with which he was making the night hideous.

He thought—like that most aggravating of birds, the corncrake—that he was singing.

It was Snicker's intention to pass by him and get away unobserved, but it unfortunately happened that a certain little dog was abroad, and resenting the noise made by Milky Whey, it dashed up just as Snicker came down the street, and began to bark furiously.

Milky opened his eyes, and saw Snicker and the dog at the same time. The dog he did not care a straw for, but the sight of the other roused his anger, and hastily scrambling upon his feet, he called on Snicker to stop.

"Let me go," pleaded the miserable man; "I'm in a hurry!"

"You goes," said Milky Whey, with bitter gravity, "when you pays for that 'ere lost donkey, and not afore."

"Is the poor creetur lost?" asked Snicker, sympathetically.

"Is it lorst?" sneered Milky. "Don't you know as it is? I hates hypocrissy. That 'ere donkey is in the pound. They've put it in, and won't let it out until I pays five shillings. Hand the money over!"

"Milky, you know I'm poor."

"Hand it over, or I'll call the police, and swear it is *your* donkey, which you stole. Come, hand out the money!"

"I've only got a sovereign," said Snicker, faintly.

"Ho!" exclaimed Milky; "I thought you had no money. Sovereigns ain't generally lonely in people's pockets. They goes in companies, or not at all. Turn your pockets out!"

But this Snicker positively declined to do, being goaded to desperation, and Milky, in a drunken fury, dashed at him. Snicker ran up the street, and turning a corner at the top, sharply ran into the arms of a policeman, who, from the sweet seclusion of a doorway, had just awoke to the fact that he was wanted.

Closely following on his heels came Milky Whey, and both being recognised by the officer, he promptly collared them.

"Give in, and come to the lock-up," he said.

"To the lock-up!" groaned Snicker, and he thought of the warning conveyed to him by Chunder Loo.

He made no resistance, as Milky Whey, after a faint semblance of it, yielded himself up, and also went to the police-station like a lamb.

He would be able to get a sleep there, and, as far as his sentiments guided him, he would just as soon be there as at home in his wretched lodging.

At Chippenham, as elsewhere, the pockets of prisoners are overhauled before they are consigned to the cells, and the inspection of those of Milky Whey showed that, beyond a pocket-knife with one blade, and the point broken, he had absolutely nothing to get him into trouble. With Snicker it was different.

From his pockets, with various odds and ends, the two sovereigns were unearthed.

"Hum!" said the inspector, suspiciously. "Snicker, you went home to-day, I believe?"

"I did, sir," replied Snicker.

"What money had you in your possession on your return?"

"Nothing to speak of."

"Where did you get these two sovereigns from?"

"I'd rather not say. They was given to me by a friend."

"A man or a woman?"

"I can't say."

"Hum! How is it that you are here at this hour?"

Snicker looked wistfully about him, in a terrible fix. What was he to say?

He dared not tell the truth, and a lie would assuredly get him into trouble. A faintness, that exceeded his previous distress of body, came over him.

"They are my sovereigns," he said.

"They may be," said the inspector, coolly, "but you will have to prove it. You are leaving home, I believe?"

"I am on my way to London, sir—to—to look for work."

"On the tramp?"

"Yes, sir."

"You are not the man to tramp with so much money in your possession," said the inspector. "I really must have the matter explained."

"I can't do it, sir. My friend will not like it. I—I can go and ask him to speak up for me, if you will allow me."

"When will you go?"

"At once, sir."

"Very well; and you had better appear with him in the morning. There is no charge against you, beyond making a disturbance in the street in the middle of the night. That is, of course, a minor affair."

"I'll be back in the mornin'," said Snicker, in a perspiration.

The inspector would have detained him anyway, but for his recent incarceration and acquittal on a charge of murder. So he was allowed, out of pity, to take his departure.

"You may go," said the inspector, "but be here in the morning. The magistrates sit at eleven."

"Wot's to be done with me?" growled Milky.

"You will pass the night in the cells, being an old offender in this way."

"All right," said Milky, "I'm willin'; but it's a case of false imprisonment, and you may go wrong on it."

They hustled him into a cell, and Snicker was shown the door. He turned into the street as poor as when he went to Smudgem Bender many hours before, hoping to get a public reception that would atone for much recent suffering.

"Talk of luck," he moaned, as he hastened up the street. "Was there ever any like mine?"

As for going back in the morning, he knew it was impossible.

In the first place, he dared not ask Chunder Loo to come and clear him, or to mention that he had seen him. Miserable as he was, he was not willing to court what he believed would be certain death.

No, he must fly away from the spot, leaving the two sovereigns to swell the official coffers, and return no more.

It was hard—very hard, and it is not to be marvelled at that he pursued his lonely way with eyes blinded with tears.

But was he sorry for his past sins? Did he repent?

It is to be feared not, for he was not made of that malleable stuff out of which saints are made.

Given the opportunity, he would be the old Snicker over again, without being one atom the better for all his bitter experiences.

CHAPTER CLXXI.

IS IT RIGHT?—JACK FORD GOES TO SEE SIR JOHN BARSTOW.

THREE days elapsed, and nothing had been heard of Chunder Loo. How the cunning villain could have eluded the police, with so much about him to lead to detection, was a puzzle to everybody.

Meanwhile Berry Mawston had been brought before the magistrates and, as a matter of form, remanded. His ultimate committal for trial was a foregone conclusion.

Mulberry was being taken care of by the police, but where exactly he was the public did not know.

Penny Bunn, as sole master of the school, had enough to do, but with some of the elder boys looking after the younger ones, he got along fairly well.

After that scene with his wife he became a changed man when in her company.

That she may have been sorry for her outburst is probable, but, woman-like, she would not admit it. They rarely spoke to each other, and then only when compelled to on some matter connected with home affairs.

Miss Astracan, being a prudent woman, did not interfere. Susan was too much occupied with her prospective wedding to worry about the matrimonial troubles of other people.

But there were others who had thoughts that worried them on another matter. For some time past not only Jack Ford, but his three friends, had been privately exercising their minds on the *right* they had to the money obtained by the sale of the armour.

Lingo was a good fellow, and honest, according to the light within him, but it was not to be expected that he would entertain those finer notions of honour which are found in more delicate natures.

In addition, they thought of the fact that they could not trust their schoolfellows, or share with them.

This they had all secretly felt, for some time past, was not exactly right. There is a generous feeling among boys in the dealing with their possessions. They hate the miser and the mean giver. But, as we have pointed out, they could not follow their natural instincts without betraying the whole thing.

But recent events were destined to fully awake them to a sense of what was exactly *right*.

Don was really the first to broach the subject, when news came to the Abbey that the old lord of the manor was dead and Sir Charles Barstow appointed in his place.

Now Sir Charles had struck the boys as being a high-minded, noble specimen of the genus *gentleman*.

His bearing, when at the Abbey, and his general treatment of his two tenants, Snicker and Bunn, showed that he was a man who could not only be just, but exceedingly generous. He had a soul above the common ruck of grasping humanity.

It was a half-holiday and the four friends were together, lying upon the grass near Screwgray mill. They had come down to have another look at the spot made memorable by the capture of Mulberry Cork under striking circumstances.

"It is this way with me," said Don, shortly, after the subject of the treasure had cropped up. "I do not think it is quite honest to keep this money. If the laws of the country are unjust, we have still to obey them until they are altered. The money isn't ours. It belongs to the lord of the manor."

"Hitherto an indefinite quantity," remarked Bob Stockton: "but now Sir Charles Barstow."

"Well," said Jack, "I have thought of it too. We have no right to the tin *unless the lord of the manor approves*. I have a good mind to see Sir Charles and make a clean breast of the whole thing. What is the good of our having money if we are obliged to hide it like sneaks or *thieves?* Depend upon it, many a young fellow has begun with the idea of his being in the right, while he is doing the wrong thing, and it has ended in his becoming a Mawston."

"In one sense," said Don, "the money belongs to us more than to anyone in the school."

"That is right enough," replied Jack. "So far, I see no reason why we should not keep the secret of its existence. We discovered it, and all through we have been the leading spirits of all that has been done."

"Thanks to your good generalship," remarked Tom Drummond.

"The best of generals," rejoined Jack, "can do nothing without good officers and soldiers. Now we are all agreed that something must be done. Sir Charles Barstow is the newly-appointed lord of the manor, and he is owner of the Abbey. To him I had better write at the outset, asking for an interview. It would be difficult to make myself clear in a letter, and furthermore, it would not be so effective as speech. Are we all agreed on that?"

"We are," they answered, somewhat dolorously, for they felt afraid that after the interview they would have to bid good-bye to their dream of wealth. Still they all knew that it was the only thing to be done, if they were to live with clear consciences.

Striking while the iron is hot being one of Jack's gifts, he wrote the letter early in the evening, and that there might be no higgling or hesitating further about the matter, walked down to Smudgem Bender with Don to post it.

On the way there he read it to his chum, and we may as well give it verbatim as a manly specimen of a boy's confession of a possible danger of doing the wrong thing.

"To Sir Charles Barstow.

"My dear Sir,—I have for some time past been in possession of a secret concerning Littlecote Abbey, and that secret has been shared by three of my friends. As it concerns you as Lord of the Manor and owner of the Abbey, I shall be glad if you will see me privately, so that I may give you a fuller explanation. I ought to have told you before, and my mind has been troubled on the subject. But when you see the nature of the temptation to hold the secret, I am sure that you will, as a gentleman and a man of kind feelings towards others, make all allowances and forgive us. Nobody outside myself and three friends in the school have the least knowledge of the matter.

"I am, Sir Charles,
"Your obedient Servant,
"Jack Ford."

"A good letter," said Don; "the only thing I see in it to object to is a very small matter : it is the signing yourself Jack, instead of John, when writing to so important a person as Sir Charles Barstow."

"Dear boy," was the laughing reply, "I was christened Jack, and have no more right to John than you have."

"Never!"

"Fact, I assure you. I have a younger brother Tom, and we should have had a Bill if my dad could have had his way. But mother struck at Bill, and he was christened Joe. There is no nonsense about the Fords."

Sir Charles Barstow had a residence near Swindon, and it was there the letter was sent. Of course it was not certain he was there, for the amiable baronet was paying the penalty of having a young wife, by being trotted here and there whenever Lady Barstow felt desirous of a change. But fortune favoured the boys. Sir Charles was there at the time, and in two days Jack read a reply, appointing to meet him at the "Cowley Arms."

Sir Charles, it seemed, had some business with his agent there, and he could, as he put it in the familiar way, "kill two birds with one stone."

There was no difficulty in getting an afternoon off. Penny Bunn had fallen into a dejected state, that left him incapable of refusing the boys anything. The school had got into a go-as-you-please state that was not good for the youngsters, and they all saw that the end was not far off.

Nothing had been heard of Chunder Loo. He had evaded pursuit, and it was feared by the authorities he had left the country, or was hiding in that best hiding-place in the world—London.

Gubbles was of the latter opinion, and he had gone to the metropolis to give what help he could to ferret out the scoundrel.

Lingo was still at the "Cowley Arms," but Snicker was gone. As neither his neighbours nor his wife would have aught to do with him, he had departed, but whither was for some time afterwards a mystery.

We may, however, hear more of him.

Penny Bunn now took his meals with the boys, and it was after dinner when Jack, having waited till the rest had departed, made his request.

"You want an afternoon off, Ford?" said the schoolmaster, wearily.

"If you please, sir," answered Jack.

"Take it," said Bunn. "Where are you going to?"

"To Smudgem Bender, to meet a friend."

"Meet your friends while you have them, Ford. The time may come when you, like me, may have no friends to meet."

"I am sure you are not entirely without friends," said Jack, feeling rather sorry for Bunn, who looked at him as mournfully as the seal at the Aquarium gazes at the spectators watching it in its watery prison, which is about the most mournful expression of which any countenance is capable.

"Ford," said Penny Bunn, "I am a human feather, blown about by the winds of adversity. Occasionally I get into a quiet corner and have a spell of rest. But not for long. Soon the howling blast gets at me again, and I am whirled into the air to be carried hither and thither as it wills. You are a boy I can confide in. If I tell you something you will not betray me, I hope?"

"Assuredly not, sir."

"Then I *will* confide in you, Ford. The grim shadow of ruin rests upon this house. Owing to my having taken on the school with so many of your bills paid, and having no capital of my own worth mentioning, it has been impossible for me to meet the bills. The butcher is insolent and the baker offensive. There is a laundry bill also of sufficient magnitude to appal the stoutest heart."

"I am sorry to hear it, sir."

"Thank you, Ford. Sympathy is welcome, although it will not find blacking for our boots. The grocer also requests a cheque this morning by return. He can have the cheque, but there is no money to meet it. Lastly, there is the inlaying of that confounded chamber which I undertook for Sir Charles Barstow. I must say that the noble baronet is a gentleman, and if I had told him the truth at the outset, that our domestic used the priceless wood as kindling for the household fires, he might have forgiven me. But it is now too late. I lied to him—deceived him, and when he knows the facts I have not the slightest doubt that I shall be the recipient of a supply of moral shoe-leather—in other words, I shall get the kick-out."

"It is a very bad business, sir."

"It is a fearful business. No living man could

replace that flooring, even if I had the means to pay him for his labour. I see nothing but the life of a tramp ahead of me, and how I am to get along with a wife, and an aunt of the proportions of Miss Astracan, I fail to see. It would take us two months to get as far as Chippenham. But enough, Ford. Take your holiday, and be happy while you may."

Jack was glad to get away, for he really could not see how he could help Bunn, who certainly was in the queerest corners of Queer Street.

So he hastened off, and on arriving at the " Cowley Arms," ascertained that Sir Charles had put in an appearance, and was engaged with his agent in a private room upstairs. He had left word with the landlord that when " the young gentleman from the Abbey arrived, he was to be asked to wait."

CHAPTER CLXXII.

JUST AND GENEROUS.—ANOTHER MYSTERY.

IT was rarely that so important a man as Sir Charles put up at the Cowley Arms, and his coming being unexpected, it caused a flutter of excitement.

The news having flashed round the village, several of the tenants of the baronet dropped in, with the hope of having a word with their landlord about repairs which the agent had studiously ignored. Jack could hear the buzz of their voices, mingled with the clinking of glasses in the coffee-room.

It was no place for the boy, he being alone, so he walked to the door, and was hovering about, awaiting a summons to the presence of the great man, when he espied Lingo coming down the village-street.

Now, Lingo was one of those people whom Jack felt he could not at that moment have confided in about the nature of his errand to the inn.

He was doubtful if he would be able to get him to see the matter in the light in which the boys viewed it. There was also a sense of his being about to act in opposition to one who had been so true a friend.

It was, to a great extent, nullifying the labours of the professor.

But whether he confided in him or not, he could not avoid his wandering friend, because Lingo saw Jack as soon as Jack saw him.

He quickened his pace, and in a minute their hands met in a friendly clasp.

"What good luck brought you here to-day, Jack?" he asked.

"It is hardly good luck," was the reply.

"Nothing wrong at the Abbey, I hope?"

"Nothing that brought me here. I have come by arrangement, to meet Sir Charles Barstow."

" By arrangement?"

"Yes. It is no use my keeping it from you, Lingo. We have made up our minds to tell him everything."

He expected to see the professor flare up with righteous indignation, and to have a shower of remonstrances poured out upon his head. But nothing of the sort happened.

Lingo looked at him quietly and steadily for a few moments ere he said anything. When at length he spoke, he simply said :

"I knew you would do it, sooner or later."

"You knew it?"

"Why, yes, Jack. For I have studied you boys, and know you must be open and aboveboard, or nothing."

"It hardly seems fair to you, Lingo, after all the trouble you have taken."

Lingo laughed, as if he were immensely tickled.

"Don't you worry about me," he said ; "the whole thing has been a bit of fun to me, and nothing more. What I have done was done for the best right through. What will be the end of it depends, of course, on the way in which Sir Charles will take it. He appears to me to be rather a good sort; but you never can quite tell what a man is made of until you touch him on the raw."

"You are not angry with me, Lingo?" pleaded Jack.

"Angry, my boy!" replied Lingo, heartily; "not me. I am not going to quarrel with you over a few shekels. Why, you boys have been sunshine to me. The very thought of you is a comfort to me; being what I am, nothing more than a graceless wanderer on the face of the earth—a homeless dog. Angry with you? Not me!"

"If you knew what a relief it is to me to hear you say that!" said Jack—"but there, I can't express it."

"Then don't try to," advised Lingo, smiling. "When you can't express a thing, keep it inside you. Here is somebody who seems to want you."

It was the agent, a hard-faced man between fifty and sixty, who was standing at the door of the inn, critically examining Jack and his companion, as if surprised to find the boy in such company.

"Is your name Ford?" he asked.

"It is," replied Jack.

"Sir Charles wishes to see you. It is an appointment, I believe?"

"Yes."

"If you are the son of one of the tenants, and it is a matter of repairs that you wish to speak to him upon, I——"

"It has nothing to do with repairs," interposed Jack, "but quite a private matter."

He nodded to Lingo and glided past the agent, who frowned in a distrustful way upon him. Men of that class are very jealous of their authority, and do not approve of anyone approaching the fountain-head, except through them.

"Who is that boy?" he asked Lingo, as Jack disappeared.

"One of the pupils at Littlecote Abbey," answered Lingo.

"Oh, indeed! He brings a message from Mr. Bunn, I presume?"

"You can presume what you like, of course, and you are just the man who, in my opinion, would never lose an opportunity for presuming. As for pumping me, you might as well try to get the history of the people buried in yonder churchyard, from their tombstones."

The agent walked away down the village, snorting in anger, and Lingo, pleased with having had the opportunity to show the agent that he was "not yet everybody," as he expressed it, wandered into the coffee-room, where he was an established favourite.

To the farmers and small tradesmen. none of them mentally very brilliant, he was as a humourist, a dispenser of good stories, a shining light indeed.

Jack, meanwhile, had ascended the stairs with a fast-beating heart. As far as matters went with Lingo and his friends he had a mind at ease, but it was only natural that he should be a little perturbed on the point of the probable issue of the interview between himself and the baronet.

Sir Charles Barstow was in the best private room of the "Cowley Arms," seated at a table, with a quantity of papers before him. As Jack entered he rose and extended a hand to the boy.

"Ford, I presume?" he said.

"Yes, Sir Charles," was Jack's reply.

"Sit down," said the baronet; "I must confess that I am somewhat curious to hear what you have to tell me. I am a bit of an antiquary, as you have probably heard, and I have assumed that you have come upon something of interest to me."

"It should be of great interest to you. Sir Charles," answered Jack, gravely; he was beginning to feel more at his ease. "You remember the discovery of the arms and armour in a vault under the Abbey?"

"Assuredly. It was one of the greatest discoveries. in that direction, of the century."

"Sir Charles, you were greatly deceived as to the extent of that discovery."

The baronet fixed his gold-rimmed nippers on his nose, and stared at Jack as if he had announced a coming revolution. The dismay and surprise upon his face were almost ludicrous.

"Deceived!" he said. "Do you mean to tell me that I have been victimised into receiving a lot of bogus ancient armour?"

"No. Sir Charles," replied Jack. "What I wish to confess to you is that you have only received about one-third of the treasure."

"Who, then, has the rest?" demanded Sir Charles, flushing.

"It was kept back by myself and some of my friends," said Jack, "and it was not exactly discovered where it was found at all."

Sir Charles took off his glasses, put them on again, and sat down.

"Pray explain yourself," he said. "I feel bewildered."

Then Jack told him the whole story as fully laid out in the first part of the records of the Lambs of Littlecote; and to say that Sir Charles listened with the utmost amazement is but to feebly describe his feelings.

"You see, Sir Charles," said Jack in conclusion, "we argued with ourselves that the things belonged once to people long ago dead and forgotten. We assumed that nobody in these days had the least right to them. But we have come to the conclusion that in any case they do not belong to us."

"What have you done with them?" asked the baronet, thoughtfully, sitting with his head resting upon his hands.

"They were sold for five thousand pounds," replied Jack.

"To whom?"

"I do not know. But Professor Lingo could tell you.'

"Where can I find that man?"

"I hope, Sir Charles," said Jack, hesitating. "that you do not mean to harm him. He has been so honest and straight with us throughout that I am sure he did not intend anything dishonest."

"I can well believe that. He is safe from all prosecution from me."

"Then I may tell you he is in this house."

"Here? Then let me see him instantly!" cried the baronet, impetuously. "I cannot rest until I have seen the man."

Jack would have gone in search of Lingo, but Sir Charles bade him remain where he was, and rang the bell. When a servant appeared, he asked that Lingo. whom he called Bingo, might be sent up at once.

"It is the visitor here," explained Jack. "The gentleman with the moustache."

Lingo was not long in putting in an appearance. Whatever may have been his inward fears of the reception he would meet with, there was no trouble on his countenance. Outwardly he was as calm as a judge.

Bowing quietly, he stopped half-way between the door and the table, and waited to be addressed.

"You are the person who sold the armour to a dealer?" said Sir Charles.

"I sold it to a collector, on conditions," replied Lingo.

"On what conditions?"

"That it was not to be sold again for six months, and if claimed, to be returned on payment of the money with two-and-a-half per cent. interest."

Sir Charles sank back in his chair and gave vent to a sigh of relief.

"Then nothing has got into the hands of the regular dealers?" he said.

"Nothing, Sir Charles," answered Lingo.

"What a merciful escape!"

The face of the baronet was quite radiant. He looked, as Lingo afterwards remarked, as if he had come into a handsome property.

"Judging by what I have in my possession," he said, after a pause, "five thousand is a ridiculously small sum for this treasure. I shall only be too glad to pay it, so that I may secure the priceless things."

"We have the money untouched," Jack ventured to suggest.

Sir Charles paid no heed to the interpolated remark.

"But what security," he asked, addressing Lingo, "have you that the purchaser will hold to his bargain?"

Lingo, with unruffled composure, dived his hand into an inner pocket of his waistcoat and drew forth a small pocket-book, from which he extracted a paper.

"Read that, Sir Charles," he said.

The baronet glanced at the paper, and his face assumed the radiance of a harvest moon.

"Lord Hathwell!" he exclaimed—"my chief rival as a collector of antiquities. A man of honour. But it will break his heart to have to give them up. Nevertheless, he will have to do it, for your true collector shows no mercy to his collecting brother."

And then for a few brief moments he laid aside his portentous dignity and rubbed his hands, chuckling just like an ordinary mortal. Lingo and Jack prudently kept quiet.

"I am sure," said the baronet, when he had resumed his ordinary demeanour, "that I can never be sufficiently grateful to you boys for being the discoverers of this long-hidden treasure. But for that barring-out, when you showed a most commendable resistance to a tyrant, it might have lain there many years. At the very least, I might not have heard of it during the remaining years of my life."

"Then you forgive us," said Jack, anxiously, "for not having revealed it to you before?"

"I not only forgive you, but, as I have said, I am grateful. As for the money you have received, I must beg of you to accept it at my hands."

"Truly a noble gift!" murmured Lingo.

"I cannot see that," said Sir Charles. "I give you five thousand for property that will be worth twenty to me. Nay more, for it will give me an all-abounding pleasure to possess it. It will make me by far the richest collector of old armour and arms in England, if not in the world. Trust me, I shall not let my gratitude stop there. You have shown, both of you, that there is a wondrous honesty in your natures."

"Sir Charles," said Jack, sitting with bowed head, "I cannot feel that I deserve such praise."

"My young friend," replied the baronet, leaning forward and laying a hand upon the boy's arm, "I am only estimating you fairly. I can say that there is not one in ten thousand in the country who would not have hesitated ere they revealed any of the secret treasure until they had disposed of it and got away to some safe place with the money. The logic by which you at first arrived at the conclusion that you had no right to it had common-sense for a foundation. But while the law is as it is you could not rightfully hold it. So far good. But then comes in my conscience. I feel that you have enriched me by certain acts, and I cannot let you go without your reward."

"In addition, Sir Charles, to the armour," said Lingo, "there are the cases of coins, left at the station until called for. I have the ticket, which I have much pleasure in handing to you."

He laid it upon the table as he spoke, and drew back, rubbing his hands together as if he now washed his hands of the whole business. Sir Charles was silent for a moment, and then he said:

"As with the armour so with the coins. You shall all have a share in their value. I cannot allow you to refuse it. And now, if my young friend will excuse me I shall take steps at once with you, Professor Dingo."

"Lingo," murmured the owner of that name.

"Lingo—certainly—I beg pardon," said Sir Charles; "our young friend can return to school, and remain there until he hears from me. You and I, Professor Mingo"—Lingo was going to correct him again, but changed his mind—"must away at once, for I shall never rest until I have relieved Lord Hathwell of"—here he chuckled again—"of his ill-gotten property."

Jack, feeling happier than he had done for many a day, rose up and took leave of the baronet, who shook hands with him as if he had been a benefactor and a friend. Lingo accompanied him downstairs, promising Sir Charles that he would be ready to start in half an hour.

"Jack," said Lingo, as they halted at the foot of the stairs, "you have done the right thing, as you always will do if you can, and you have met with your reward. You can go back to the school and give the whole bi'ling of boys a blow out."

"They will not be forgotten," said Jack.

"I wish to contribute something towards it," pursued Lingo, "and here's a fiver. A line to your friends at home would not be amiss, either. Make everybody all round happy."

"I shall wait until I am sure there will be no hitch with Lord Hathwell," said Jack, with a sly look; "it is just as well to be safe, you know."

"Cool, brave, honest, and prudent, that's what you are," said Lingo. "Good-bye."

They parted, both in a high state of glee. In their most hopeful dreams they had never dreamt of the issue of the interview being so thoroughly satisfactory.

Jack lost no time in getting back to the school, arriving there about five o'clock, shortly before the boys were released from their afternoon labours. He was amazed to find Susan, Miriam, and Miss Astracan in excited consultation in the hall.

"Where have you been, Ford?" sharply inquired Mrs. Bunn.

"To Smudgem Bender," replied Jack, "I went to meet a friend. Mr. Bunn gave me leave."

"What time did you go?"

"Between one and two."

"Then he could have had nothing to do with it," said Miss Astracan.

"May I ask what is the matter?" inquired Jack.

"Certainly," replied Miss Astracan. "Mrs. Bunn and myself dined late, owing to household duties, and it was half-past three when we sat down to dinner. We had a leg of mutton, and ate only a small portion of it. As we were tired, we lingered at the table until half-past four, and then adjourned to my room for a few minutes. On returning to the dining-room we found *that the leg of mutton had disappeared*"

"Perhaps the dog took it?" suggested Jack.

"No," answered Miriam, sharply, "Dolphus has been too well broken for that. Besides, if he had taken it from the table he would have dragged it about the carpet. And he could not have eaten the bone."

"Then it is clean gone?" said Jack.

"Vanished," said Miss Astracan.

"Is it possible that a tramp has been here?" was Jack's next suggestion.

"No," said Miriam, "for Dolphus has been in the hall all the time, and he would have barked himself wild if a person had ventured to intrude, especially if he had been of low caste and origin."

"I hope that I am not suspected, ma'am" said Susan, "for I've been upstairs the last hour tidying myself."

"No, Susan," said Miriam, "nor can it be the boys, unless they have been allowed to leave the room."

"They are about being dismissed," said Jack, his ear catching the familiar humming, which showed that the work for the day was done. "Mr. Bunn will be able to enlighten you on that point."

But Mr. Bunn had no light to give, beyond making a positive statement that none of the boys had asked for permission, or been allowed to leave the room.

"Indeed," he said, "I have been entertaining them with a little light reading for a change."

"The school is coming to something now!" said Miriam, scornfully.

"It is coming to the final bu'st," said Bunn, as he walked away.

"All we can say is that the departure of the leg of mutton is a mystery," said Miss Astracan. "Miriam dear, we will not worry about it."

CHAPTER CLXXIII.

A SCHOOL FESTIVAL.—A CRY IN THE NIGHT.

JACK had something more important than the loss of the leg of mutton on his mind, and the subject for the moment passed away from him.

He was burning to tell his friends of the issue of his meeting with the baronet, and they were just as anxious to hear about it.

When he emerged from the house they were already at the favourite trysting-spot by the wall, having seen him in confab with the ladies as they left the class-room just prior to Penny Bunn being questioned as to the absence of the boys.

The tidings he brought with him could not be concealed by an assumed portentous gravity he worked up for the occasion.

"He has forgiven us!" exclaimed Don, joyfully.

"More than that," said Jack, and then he told them all.

"Well," said Bob Stockton, "if this isn't about as good as coming into a small estate, I'll go hang! What a brick the old fellow must be!"

"He was not to be outdone in honesty or generosity," remarked Tom Drummond. "Without wishing to detract in the least from his kindness, I think you will admit that some of us, if in his place, would have acted in the same way."

"Probably," answered Jack; "but before giving a decided opinion, I would rather wait until I am in his place."

They all laughed, for, when light-hearted, a small joke goes well with us. Then came the question of the feast for the boys.

"I vote that we simply give it, and make it a royal one; without saying how it came about," suggested Bob Stockton; "there is nothing like a bit of mystification: it is as good as sauce."

"It is now half-past five," said Jack, "or there-bouts. Now there is plenty of time for Tom and Don to run to Smudgem Bender, hire a trap, and drive to Chippenham. There they can get what they think will make a spread. If the confectioners run short, there are the station refreshment-rooms. Get a cab-load of something, and when you come back, drive up to the kitchen entrance. I will arrange with Susan for smuggling the stuff in."

"Bunn will miss us, of course," said Tom.

"Not he," replied Jack; "off with you, and have your tea in the town like two swells. If you are back by dusk, it will do."

Nothing could have suited the boys better. Risk-ing what might follow, they darted off, and in a few minutes the tea-bell rang. All fears of Bunn missing them were dispelled by his not being at the table to preside.

"Master wishes you to take his seat," said Susan to Jack; "he is looking for the bone of the leg of mutton. He says that Dolphus took it."

"Perhaps he did," replied Jack; and then it sud-denly flashed upon him that it was not, and could not be, the dog.

Where was so small a canine creature to stow away a leg of mutton? He could not have eaten it, and had he hidden it away, there would have been a trail of grease to betray him. But that was not the time to think out a solution of the mystery. The table called upon him to preside, and he hastened into the dining-room.

"I say," sang out Philter, "where's Bob?"

"And Tom Drummond?" added Short.

"Gone to the moon," replied Jack, suavely; "don't you worry about them. They will be back soon enough."

"I fancy Tom has enlisted," said Little Jiggers; "there was a recruiting sergeant round this way a week ago."

"He wasn't a recruiting sergeant at all," said Herbert May; "it was a private home on fur-lough."

"How do you know?"

"He told me so. I asked him if he had ever been in a battle, and he said he had, more than once; but there wasn't much for him to say about it, as all he could see was smoke and now and then a comrade dropping down dead beside him, or in front, or some-where close handy. 'When you saw that,' he said, 'it makes you feel as if you could make *mincemeat* of the enemy.'"

Jack went on serving the tea, while the talk shifted this way and that until the two absent boys were for-gotten. It was a noisy party, of course, but, barring a little skylarking, there was nothing to "put the stopper on."

After tea there was an adjournment outside, and

play until twilight set in. The usual hour devoted to the lessons for the morrow was not spent in the class-room.

Boys soon find out how far they may go with those in authority, and it was recognised that for the time they could do as they pleased. A complete demorali-sation of the school was not far off.

About the time appointed, Bob and Tom returned in a waggonette laden with packages containing good things, and then it was made known to the boys that there was a treat in store for them.

"Don't eat any supper in the dining-room to-night," was the word passed round by Jack; "we have something better for you. All are to assemble in No. 1 at bedtime."

They had no fear of being discovered if they kept fairly quiet, for, in addition to other duties neglected of late, that of going round to see if the boys were in bed had been ignored by Penny Bunn.

All they had to do was to keep as still as possible until their principal had retired, and after that make no more row than they could possibly help.

Susan was very much attached to the boys, and would have done anything to add to their pleasure. Now that she was shortly to leave them she was more kindly disposed towards them than ever.

On being told that her help would be required to get certain things upstairs with secrecy and despatch, she volunteered to do the whole work.

"You keep watch on master's door," she said, "and I'll have the things up in a jiffey."

No hitch occurred. The sundry packages, boxes, and bottles of home-made wine were duly conveyed to No. 1 dormitory, and stored under some of the beds.

Tom, as in some of the old days, acted the part of chief caterer.

Not only had there been a good supply of eatables and drinkables obtained, but also the means for quite an illumination. Instinctively it was felt that this would be the last feast they would ever partake of in the Abbey, and the disposition of those who had the arrangements in hand was that nothing should be done by halves.

The word having passed round for the usual supper to be ignored, Susan was told that she was not to lay it out. It was done to save her trouble and to ease her work, as a set-off for the labour en-tailed in carrying the things upstairs.

Nobody thought that Penny Bunn would think of appearing to preside at supper, but for some reason or other he did so.

Although Susan had not laid out the table, she had been advised to ring the bell in case the sound of it should be missed by the seniors, and inquired into.

Bunn heard it and responded, having been spending

a dreary evening in the society of his wife and her aunt.

The amazement expressed on the face of that gentleman when he found a barren table and not a boy present was something that would have been worth seeing by any student of the mobility of the human countenance.

Fancying that he must be the victim of a nightmare, he sat down and waited, expecting, as people do in dreams, to soon awake.

But the minutes passed by and nothing happened. Then Susan appeared to put out the lamp.

It was a shock to her to find Penny Bunn sitting there like a ghost, very white and still. For a moment neither spoke, and then Bunn pulled himself together, and said :

"Susan, I am under the impression that I am dreaming. Tell me if I am or not. Where is the supper, and where are the boys ?"

"The young gentlemen said as they hadn't any appetites," replied Susan, "so I didn't lay out no supper."

"But you rang the bell ?"

"I did that, sir, distinctively," said Susan, meaning, of course, "instinctively."

"No appetites !" exclaimed Bunn. "Boys unable to eat is a phenomenal thing, and must have its source in deep grief. They are sorrowing for me, their pastor and shepherd."

"I can't say why they didn't want no supper," answered Susan, evasively.

Penny Bunn sighed, and rising, left the room. His first intention was to steal away to bed, but on second thoughts he decided to pay a visit to the class-room, and beg of the boys not to give way for his sake.

He expected to find them sitting sadly and silently brooding over the shadow that lay upon him—the shadow of impending ruin. His calculations were considerably upset on finding that they were all in the highest spirits.

Opening the door quietly, he stood upon the threshold, watching them as they indulged in various little games to kill the time ere they retired for the night.

Some were having a friendly wrestle, others playing leap-frog, and the rest were sitting in groups, laughing and chatting.

Not one of them perceived him, and he softly closed the door again and wended his way to the staircase. Halfway up he sat down to think.

"I can't make it out," he mused. "It is not sorrow that overwhelms them. They have some game on. I wonder what it is."

As he sat there he heard his wife in the passage below, accompanying Miss Astracan to her room. They were talking of the coming ruin, and the old

lady was advising the younger one to pack up the most portable things and send them away to a place of security.

"I would never let Bunn's creditors have the linen and plate," she said.

"Not a bad idea," murmured Bunn, as the two ladies entered Miss Astracan's room and closed the door. "For myself I have nothing to pack and send away; I wish I had."

In a short time Miriam came out, and with a candle in her hand walked slowly up the stairs. Penny Bunn retreated quietly before her with his eyes upon her face, and it struck him that it looked very old and worn.

She was unconscious of being watched, and there was no forced composure of her features to conceal what she felt.

For an instant Bunn felt sorry for her, but the next moment he was espied, and then came the change.

"What are you crawling about there for ?" she sharply demanded.

"I am not crawling," answered Bunn. "I am simply enjoying myself in the dark, as there is no pleasure in the light of your company."

"You are a fool and a knave," she said, "luring me away from a good home and a thriving business to this dark hole of a place. I suppose you know that the baker has refused to supply us on the morrow ?"

"I was not aware of it," said Bunn, "although I have considered that sooner or later he would adopt a popular expedient, and strike."

"There will be no bread for the boys," said Miriam, bitterly, "and they must be sent home."

"I can't help it," answered Bunn. "Home is the better place for them, I should say."

"You," said Miriam, with a furious gesture, "will have to go out and work. I shall return to the dressmaking, and aunt will live with me. But I won't keep you."

"If keeping me is to be associated with the society of your aunt, of which I have had enough," said Bunn, "I would rather you did not do it. I hoped to find a more worthy spirit in you in the hour of adversity."

"Get away from me !" she said, angrily, "and keep away. I have done with you."

"Miriam," said Bunn, looking at her steadily, "I will not trouble you any more than I can help. But the day may come when you will bitterly repent of casting me off. The world is wide, and for a man who has energy, and certain gifts of which most sensible women would be proud, there is much to be done. If not at home, there are foreign fields to labour in."

"Go and labour, then !" she said, as she whirled into her room and banged the door.

Bunn stood there, with a curled lip and dilated

nostrils, a picture of the outraged husband bearing his sorrows and troubles with high-minded fortitude.

"It is spoken," he murmured. "The silver cord that bound us together is broken. Miriam, ere another sun sets I shall be far away from thee. Hallo! here come the boys."

He slipped into the room that was once occupied by Snicker, and where the flooring was still up, and lay there *perdu* until the boys passed by.

As he had left the door ajar, he could see them, and he noted, with amazement renewed, that they all went into No. 1 dormitory.

"As I thought," he muttered; "they have some game afloat. Would that I were a boy again, so that I could make one of them!"

But for the condition of things between himself and Miriam he would have gone to her for advice on the matter, but now the boys were at liberty to do just what they pleased.

All was over. The hour for the explosion was at hand. The morrow would see a sudden and last breaking-up of the Abbey School.

As he mused on the parlous prospect he was aroused by a sniffing at the door. It was Dolphus, which on his way to the door of his mistress's room had scented out his master.

Benny Bunn had always hated Dolphus, and never more than at that moment. He was not in a humour to be sniffed at by the cantankerous little creature, so he quietly opened the door another inch or two and grasped him by the neck.

Dolphus gave one fearful yelp, and then the hand of Bunn tightened on his throat.

"Cur!—mongrel!" he hissed, "this night you die!"

He closed the door, and holding Dolphus so tightly by the neck that he could only faintly expostulate with a gurgle, he cautiously felt his way over the joists of the flooring.

He heard the voice of his wife in the passage calling to her pet to come and comfort her, but his heart had been turned to stone, and he only sardonically grinned.

"In vain, woman," he muttered, "you call for this canine worm which has usurped all your affection. Never more shall he listen to your drivellings. *He dies!*"

The window of the room was open, and Penny Bunn on reaching it paused a moment to call up all the strength he was possessed of, and then, with a powerful swinging motion, he hurled Dolphus forth into the night.

The dog uttered no sound, being probably made dumb by astonishment. There was a short silence, and then a slight crashing sound from the depths of the valley below.

"It is done!" said Bunn, with a gasp. "Now call for a week, woman, and he will not come."

But Miriam was content to call but a minute or so, and getting no response, she retired again, and all was still.

CHAPTER CLXXIV.

A GUEST AT MIDNIGHT FEAST.

THE cry of Dolphus was heard in No. 1 dormitory, and the origin of it recognised, thanks to the stillness that prevailed in the room.

The youngsters were playing the fox until the whole of the house save themselves had retired.

"Something wrong with Miriam's darling," said Bob Stockton, softly.

"Miss Astracan may have trodden on his toe," suggested Little Jiggers.

"She has squashed it, then," said Short; "I never saw such a foot as she has, in my life. I wonder who her shoemaker is."

"No single bootmaker," said Philter, "would have enough leather in stock for her. Her boots must be made by a company."

"Don't talk quite so loud," advised Jack; "it is barely ten o'clock."

"Half-past," said Tom Drummond; "I heard the quarter of Mumping Malford clock go a minute back. I think I may begin to lay out the spread."

"Sit down, all of you," said Jack, "except Tom and his assistants. We must make a table of the floor. Will you have a light, Tom?"

"Yes; and bung up the keyhole, somebody, in case Bunn should come up and see it."

This was done, and Tom lit one candle, placing it on the floor so that it would give him the light he wanted. Don and two or three others gave him a helping-hand.

Then out from under the bed were hauled such a variety of good things as have rarely if ever been seen in any other school.

It seemed scarcely credible that so many toothsome articles could have been obtained in the district.

There were tarts, buns, sausage and beef rolls, patties, biscuits, sandwiches, bread, cheese, and slices of ham—enough, and more than enough, for nearly double the number of boys there assembled.

Those who had only been half-informed of the nature of the feast in store stared in bewilderment, calculating the cost of this regal entertainment, and wondering where the money could have come from.

It had, as we know, been decided by the inner circle that it was not necessary that everything should be known to the entire school. What they had come into they had now a perfect right to. It was a free gift from Sir Charles Barstow, and to mention it could only excite envy, and possibly ill-feeling, and do no good whatever. So it was arranged that Jack should simply say that he had come into some money, and had decided to spend some of it in giving an entertainment to his chums and the entire school.

Fully half an hour was spent in arranging the board upon the floor, for Tom was not disposed to have things done in a slipshod fashion. He was a lover of order, especially where the table was concerned.

The clock of the old church was heard to strike eleven, and then Jack gave the word for the general lighting up.

For this purpose three pounds of composite candles had been purchased, and by the simple expedient of melting the bottoms of the candles sufficiently to make them stick, and then fixing them on pieces of cardboard, candlesticks were dispensed with.

Set up in two rows, the effect was most brilliant. No scene in fairyland could have a greater charm in the eyes of those assembled.

"Squat down," said Tom, when all was ready, "and peg away. I'll be wine-steward, and see that you don't run dry. I have black and red currant and gooseberry wine. There is no lemonade or gingerbeer, as the popping of corks might be heard."

Then the boys fell to, and soon their tongues loosened so that there was a softened Babel of voices in the room.

Who among them that thought it was like the feast of Belshazzar, the last to be held by them in what Bob Stockton called that "lordly hall"?

He had risen to his feet, and it was seen that he was about to propose a toast. A word from Jack Ford brought about the necessary silence.

Having referred to the dormitory, as above stated, Bob went on: "Englishmen wherever they go carry their toasts with them. The fashion may have gone out to drink to each other in the highest circles, but that is because the upper ten are getting lazier and lazier every day, and even drinking to one another is too much of a bore to them."

"Of course you know that as a fact," interposed Don.

"I have it from the highest authority," calmly replied Bob; "but, of course, if you have later intelligence, that can be authenticated, from the upper circles, I should be very glad to receive it."

"Get along and don't wrangle," advised Drummond.

"There is no wrangling," said Bob. "Well, the toast I have to propose—Tanner, you are not attending to my address."

"I can't give full attention to a meat-pie and attend to you," retorted Tanner, "and, as a choice of subjects for edification, I prefer the pie."

"The intellectual loss is yours," said Bob. "As I was about to remark——Isn't there somebody outside?"

Short, who was near the door, got up and put his ear to it. The silence in the room was intense, and a dozen hands were ready to extinguish the lights.

"I hear *something*," he said, after a pause.

"Something!" sarcastically growled Don; "what is it like?"

"A cat purring," said Short.

Don got up and walked to the door, gently thrusting Short aside.

Swiftly opening it, he popped out, and as quickly closed it again.

The movement was so rapidly performed that he vanished like a ghost. In a very few moments he was back again, holding his hand up.

"There is no need to put out the lights," he said, as he returned to his seat, with a face of ultra gravity.

"Was there anyone outside?" asked Tanner, anxiously.

"There was *something*," replied Don, sadly shaking his head. "Short, how could you think it was a cat?"

Short snuffled and rubbed his nose with his forefinger.

"It sounded to me like one," he said.

"*Sounded* like one—on my word! But there, it's useless to talk to a boy of your natural density. It was *not* a cat."

"What was it, then?" demanded Short.

"*A kitten!*" replied Don.

"Oh, go to Bath, with your beastly sells!" said Short, exasperated by the chuckling around him. "You are not so clever as you think yourself. Every kitten is a cat, although all cats are not kittens. Now, then, stupid?"

"Short scores there!" said Jack Ford. "Get along, Bob!"

"I am doing so," said Bob; "but as long as I am subjected to interruptions, I cannot get on. The toast I have to propose is the health of one who is much respected among you. I may as well say that it isn't Jack Ford, because we all know that he doesn't want toasting among us. Nor is it Peebles or Drummond——"

"Don't tell us who it isn't, but who it is," growled Tanner, as he finished the meat-pie and took a tart.

"Your impatience," said Bob, "is embarrassing, for I am already in a quandary concerning the fitting words wherewith to express my admiration of the good qualities of the individual I am about to propose as a toast. He ought to be, if he isn't, foremost in your hearts or on a level with Jack Ford. His virtues ought to excite your daily admiration and emulation, and in drinking his health you will be doing more honour to yourselves than to him. Need I say, gentlemen, that this peerless individual is *myself?*"

A SPLENDID SCHOOL STORY. NEVER BEFORE PUBLISHED.

By E. HARCOURT BURRAGE,

Author of "Ching Ching," "Monkey Mat and Roving Dick," "The Brave Boy of the Basilisk," &c.

THE LAMBS OF LITTLECOTE

NO. 24.   A Handsome Coloured Plate Presented with Every Number.

"On my word, not bad !" said Penny Bunn.   "Thank you, Stockton, I WILL take a little more."   " Patties ?" said Don.

PRICE ONE PENNY.

There was a very pronounced howl of execration, which Jack stifled with a motion of the hand, as Bob, with ineffable grace, drank his own good health and bowed to the assembled company.

Good-humoured, quiet execration at his impudence came from every side. The refusal to drink with him was unanimous and complete.

"As you will," he said, composedly; "but as my health has been drunk by one, who is at least sincere, I will now proceed to return thanks."

But that was an infliction they positively refused to put up with. There was, in a manner of speaking, a rising of the clans against him, and he was threatened with being assailed with all the fragments of the feast as far as it had gone, among which was a bun in the hands of Drummond, as hard as a piece of pumice-stone—"worked in," as he declared, "by the confectioner upon innocent boys."

"On my word, Bob," he said, "I will hit you in a vital part with it, and then you won't go about toasting your wretched self again."

"I yield to undue pressure put upon me," said Bob, "but I have a private opinion of the lot of you that will not be uttered to-night."

"What is the matter with Herbert?" asked Don.

The sentimental boy of the school was sitting with his head resting thoughtfully upon his hand. He looked up, and replied:

"I am sad."

"About what?"

"Who were the prophets of old?" said Herbert. "Were they not the poets of old? Alas for them, to be the heralds of sadness! Boys, I feel that we shall not meet here again. This night is the breaking-up of us all."

"The dear boy is in one of his sad moods," said Bob Stockton. "Chums all, whate'er portends, let us be merry to-night. Short's cat is a creature of his imagination. The kitten is gone, and let us be merry."

All danger of being disturbed was considered to be at an end, but to the dismay of the feasters the door suddenly opened, and Penny Bunn appeared.

He slipped quickly into the room, and closing the door, gazed at the group, frozen into sudden silence.

"Boys," he said, "do not let me disturb you. I am not here to spoil your fun, but to join in it, if I may be permitted."

He paused for a reply, but nobody seemed to have one ready for him, and he continued:

"If the school were likely to go on, instead of coming to an untimely end, as it undoubtedly will, I would not permit this outrage on the rules for a moment. But as the days of Littlecote Abbey are numbered—as its *Mene, Mene, Tekel Upharsin* has been written on the wall, I see no reason why I should not relax and become one of you."

"Mr. Bunn," said Jack Ford, "I must confess that your coming here was unexpected, and in a measure not agreeable to us, for boys when engaged in this way prefer to be left to themselves; but as it appears that the school must break up, and all of us scattered far and wide, I personally see no reason why you should not join us, if you can derive any pleasure from doing so."

"Ford," said Penny Bunn, "you are a manly boy and a good fellow. I wish I could go back and improve upon my young days, so that I could be more like you. But it cannot be. It is not possible to turn back the hands on the face of time one single moment. But for this night only, probably for the last time in my life, I would be a boy again. Treat me as one of yourselves. Possibly in the future you may be able to look back with satisfaction to the time when you cast one ray of radiance on the darkened existence of the man who stands before you. Outside here all is gloom. May I sit down?"

"Certainly," said Jack. "Tom, hand Mr. Bunn the sandwiches. You must excuse the absence of plates. Pieces of cardboard are the nearest things we have to earthenware."

"I have nothing to excuse," said Bunn. "I will take two sandwiches. Really, they are delicious."

"Currant, gooseberry, or ginger wine, sir?" asked Bob Stockton.

"Gooseberry, for choice," said Bunn; "it is the nearest thing to champagne that graced the table of my boyhood. It was my father's weakness to have the best."

"At it again," muttered Don, with a wink at Jack.

"Let him go it as much as he likes," replied Jack. "It seems to amuse him, and it doesn't hurt anybody."

Bob filled a mug with gooseberry wine, and Bunn took a pretty long pull at it.

"On my word, not bad," he said. "It has often appeared strange to me that more attention has not been given to the production of native wines. Why should we not compete with the foreigner? Thank you, Stockton, I *will* take a little more!"

"Patties?" said Tom, offering them to Bunn.

"What charming pastry!" said Bunn, as he took one. "I understand now why you did not have any supper. It was a source of astonishment to me on entering the room to find nobody there."

Glances of comical dismay were exchanged. What a narrow escape they had had of having the whole thing ruined!

"Did you mention it to Mrs. Bunn, sir?" inquired Jack.

"No," replied Bunn. "In the state of domestic disruption which I at this time live with Mrs. Bunn, I did not think it necessary to confide in her."

No. 24.

"If you had, she might have guessed what we were thinking of doing, sir."

"If she had, Ford, she would have played old gooseberry with this glorious spread. Yes, I think I will take a little more gooseberry."

He eventually drank all the gooseberry, and then they plied him with the currant, and he ate so many tarts, buns, and sandwiches, that there were fears in the breasts of two or three of the boys that he would be taken ill. Little Jiggers, who had the reputation of being able to eat anything and any amount of it, felt that he had from that evening to take a seat to the rear.

The fact was, Penny Bunn was thoroughly enjoying himself. For a brief period he was a boy again, with a boy's appetite, and a youthful, keen sense of enjoyment.

He relished everything, the hour, the scene, the food, and the novelty of the banquet-table. The whole thing came to him as the refreshing dew to a traveller after a day in the scorching tropical sun.

Now it is an admitted fact that British wines, while they have the countenance of teetotallers, are not entirely devoid of the alcoholic spirit. They are produced by fermentation, even as foreign wines are, and if they have not the same body, they have undoubtedly intoxicating properties. A man who drinks sufficient of them can become hilarious, or *vice versa*, according to his nature when under the influence of strong drink.

Penny Bunn drank at least a bottle and a half of the wine, and it got into his head. He became jocularly happy, and for a time forgot his domestic troubles.

"Boys," he said, "to-night we will merry be, to-morrow we'll grow sober. Not that you are intoxicated," he added, gravely, "or that *I* am in the least overcome. No. To-morrow we'll grow sober—in bearing. To-night we will be jocular. Away with dull care! Blow it!"

He held out his mug, and Tom gave him some more wine. He was a guest, and could not be refused.

"We'll make an entire night of it," said Bunn, after another sip of black currant wine, "and I vote we have a song. Who is the best singer among you?"

"Herbert May," was the reply in chorus.

"I sing very little," said Herbert, in deprecation of himself. But they would have none of it.

"Tip us something, Herbert," said Don. "Sentimental, if you have one on hand."

"I should like to hear a song of the sea," said Bunn, "of the boundless deep. I had thoughts at one time of devoting myself to the briny ocean, but the tide of events turned me another way. Still it may not be too late. Sing us something about the sea."

CHAPTER CLXXV.

A SONG AND THE INTERRUPTION.

HERBERT MAY, though as modest a boy as ever existed, did not carry it to the extent some people do. He knew when to yield to an honest request for an exhibition of his abilities as a songster.

After clearing his throat, he began to softly sing the following song:

FAREWELL.

Farewell for ever, Littlecote,
Of all within its walls;
My forward path lies far away,
The voice of ocean calls,
And where I go I may not find
So many friends and true.
I still may hope to leave behind,
Naught but love for you;
We meet to-night, we part to-morrow,
May joy be ours, and banished sorrow.

'Tis here the monkish fathers rest,
Here living hearts there be
Who in the coming wandering days
May still remember me.
The birds at night may hither fly;
But we return no more,
Our rest in other places lie,
Upon some distant shore;
To-night we here will merry be;
To-morrow, wing our way to sea.

"It is an impromptu song," said Herbert, modestly as he concluded, "and you must take it with all its defects."

"Whatever you sing, Herbert," said Don, "no matter how simple, seems very sweet to me."

Penny Bunn was affected to tears, and he was now observed in the act of brushing them away.

"To-morrow we wing our way to sea," he said, dolorously; "certainly, why not? Wherefore should we linger here? May I trouble you, Stockton, for a little more of that currant wine?"

"I am afraid sir," answered Bob, holding up the bottle to the light, "that there is nothing but the dregs left."

"Nothing but dregs," exclaimed Bunn, looking heavily about him—"my life has been *all* dregs."

"Don't say that, Mr. Bunn," urged Bob, with affectionate interest.

"But I *do* say it," replied Bunn, smiting his two hands together; "I started into existence as human sediment, and in that condition I have been up to the present hour. But I am about to emancipate myself from that state. I shall rise and soar like a bird on the wing—

"'Bird of my breast, away,
And boundless heights explore.'

That's a beautiful song, but I don't sing it quite so well as when I was leading choir-boy at Westminster Abbey. How often have I melted the Dean to tears with my upper B flats and G naturals. Those were my choice notes, boys; I had no rival in them."

"I should think not," said Bob, mischievously; "will you have another jam tart, sir?"

"I might venture," said Bunn, staring heavily at the proffered dish of cardboard, "but I have slight doubts as to the wholesomeness of too much pastry, especially when it is made in a town like Chippenham, where all ideas of the manufacture of things eatable are in a crude and semi-savage condition. There is no more wine, you say?"

Bob opened his lips to reply, but ere he could utter a word a most appalling scream was heard.

It came from the corridor, and as far as the cooler among the startled boys could judge, it emanated from Miriam.

A dreadful silence and stillness lay upon them all for a moment, and then there was another cry.

"Help! help!"

Penny Bunn was sobered in an instant, and got upon his feet.

"It is Mrs. Bunn!" he said. "Boys, I will not ask you to see what is the matter—that is my especial duty; but will some of you open the door and ask what has disturbed her?"

"Help, help! *Fire!*"

There was no mistaking the force of the cry this time, or the nature of it.

Fire is the most awful cry to be heard in the dead of night, and there was a prompt rush for the door.

Without a thought of the viands still spread upon the floor, the boys trampled over them, and Don, who was the first to reach the door, opened it.

All doubts as to the serious nature of the disturbance were immediately set at rest. Miriam was in the corridor, in her night-attire, gazing wildly at the open door of her room, from which smoke was coming forth.

"Save me!" she cried—"save me!"

Bob Stockton, with a thoughtful gallantry beyond his years, pulled off a counterpane from the nearest bed and threw it over the distracted woman's shoulders.

As an effective garment for the occasion it rivalled the Roman toga.

"What have you done?" cried Bunn, reeling forward. "Have you set fire to the bed?"

"I have nothing to do with it!" she answered, wildly. "I put out the light and was asleep, when I felt a choking sensation, and awoke. The room was full of smoke."

"Take Mrs. Bunn downstairs, sir," said Jack Ford to Bunn, "and we will do what we can to put out the fire. Some of you run upstairs and wake Susan."

Susan, however, was already awake, and she now came tumbling downstairs in a variety of garments imperfectly put on, a figure to be impressed on the memory of the beholders for many a day.

"Oh, master!" she cried—"oh, ma'am, what is it?"

CHAPTER CLXXVI.

FAREWELL TO THE ABBEY.

"IT is all right, Susan," said Jack. "Mr. Bunn, you really must take your wife out of this. Boys, down you go and get all the buckets filled with water you can lay your hands on."

"I—I'll do what I can," replied Bunn, waltzing about distractedly. "Miriam, don't look so wild."

"I might have been burnt in my bed!" she cried. "The fire is under it."

Jack was already by the door of the bedroom, with some of the boys behind him. But they went no further, for the smoke was now very dense.

Still, the origin of it was clear to an extent. The fire was under the bed, and it seemed as if the floor was already burnt through.

"It comes from the secret passages below," said Jack to Don, "and it is the deliberate work of some villain!"

"The missing leg of mutton!" gasped Don, excitedly. "Chunder Loo is in hiding there!"

"He has been," rejoined Jack, hurriedly, "and this is his work. I don't doubt it. But we have no time to think of him; we must try to save the Abbey. Water, there, as smartly as you can!"

Penny Bunn being utterly unable to assist his wife, Susan gave her a hand and led the alarmed woman below. The boys for the most part were gone to seek out something to quench the fire.

Presently they came dashing upstairs with hose, buckets, and other utensils, filled with water, in their hands.

Jack seized each in turn and threw their contents in the direction of the fire.

But the result was only a sputtering and hissing. The fire each moment rose higher, and flames were bursting through the flooring.

"We can do nothing," said Jack, "save getting out our things as smartly as we can. The old place will burn like tinder. To work! Out with your boxes from the dormitories and run them into the hall. We have no time to spare."

He was the leader in that hour of trouble as he had been before. The coolest head and the strongest nerve were his, but he was backed up by many bold hearts, although many of the youngsters were, as they well might be, exceedingly terrified.

Penny Bunn was about as much use as a milliner's dummy would have been at the time. He could do nothing but stare, wring his hands, and mutter all sorts of irrelevant remarks, until Jack told him that if he did not go downstairs he would toss him over the balusters.

"You are only in the way," he said. "If you can do nothing else, run off for help."

"Certainly," replied Bunn.

And off he went half-way down the stairs, where he tripped and fell, going headlong to the mat. There he lay for a time endeavouring to arrange the stars which the hard knock he had received raised before his eyes.

That the fire had been well prepared was soon evident.

In three minutes the heat of it was felt under the floor of the corridor, and from there extended to No. 1 dormitory. Inflammatory materials had been placed under both places.

"Merciful Heaven!" thought Jack, "if we had all been asleep nothing could have saved us."

This was an evident and startling fact. The whole thing was the work of an incendiary, and had been carefully planned and carried out.

Jack bitterly reproached himself for not having thought of the possibility of Chunder Loo having taken refuge there. Still, the act was a bit of sublime audacity for which few people would have given the rascal credit.

The boys worked with a will, and their boxes were soon in the hall; but even there they were not safe for long. The cracks in the wainscoting revealed that there was yet another body of fire burning behind it.

With no water to speak of and no help worth mentioning, it was useless to attempt to save the Abbey.

The work of the incendiary had been too well done, and it *had* to go.

Whatever the boys may have suffered within those walls they loved the old Abbey, and if in the bitterness of the moment they called down vengeance on the head of the destroyer, it was a pardonable expression of their feelings.

"Outside, all of you!" said Jack. "Get up two or three carpets of the rooms. The women will want some sort of shelter. Don, will you hurry up Miss Astracan? We shall have the fire through the wainscoting in two minutes."

"And the back way is barred," sang out Tom Drummond. "From the lower part of the passage there is a fire going in the kitchen."

"The fiend planned well," said Jack, "but he has been foiled so far as the loss of life is concerned. Don, hurry up those women. Don't stand upon trifles. Go into the room and tell them that there is not a moment to spare."

Don sped away in the direction of Miss Astracan's room. Acting up to orders, he entered without ceremony.

Miss Astracan had just been got of bed by Susan and Miriam, and with their aid was making an effort to put on some of her clothing.

Espying Don, she set up a series of shrieks that would have appalled many a stout heart. But Don had a duty to perform, and he was not to be daunted by trifles.

"You must not stop to dress," he said; "in another minute the passage will be blocked by fire."

"Boy!" cried Miss Astracan, in a deep, tragic tone of voice, "leave my room!"

"Auntie," said Miriam, hurriedly, "you hear what he says. We are in danger of being burnt to death."

"I must leave the house in a presentable condition or not at all," said Miss Astracan.

Miriam signed to Don to leave the room, and, nothing loth, he hastened out. The smoke was now filling the hall and the time for escape was running short.

Miss Astracan must have taken alarm, for Don had just time to inform Jack Ford that he was afraid the ladies would lose their lives, when the ponderous form of the stout lady hove in sight.

She was covered in a crude way with the bed-clothes, and was an extraordinary spectacle; but it was no time to make fun of the appearance of anyone. All the boys but Jack and Don had gone outside, and Penny Bunn had also disappeared.

"Mrs. Bunn," said Jack, "you will find Drummond outside the grounds putting up a shelter for you and Miss Astracan, until we can get a conveyance for you."

"That is very thoughtful of you, Ford," replied Miriam.

"He is the dearest and sweetest boy in the school," gasped Miss Astracan, and she made for Jack as if to embrace him, but he dexterously evaded the honour by picking up a rug that was lying in the hall and leading the way out.

The shelter he had spoken of was being erected against the outside wall by Bob, Tom, and a few others. It was nothing more than a roughish kind of gipsy tent formed with a few poles, the clothes-prop among them and the carpets and rugs which Jack had ordered to be removed from the Abbey.

Poor as the shelter was, it was most welcome to the ladies. No immediate help was near, and it would have tried Miss Astracan, at all events, if she had been compelled to remain in the open air.

On the ground inside the boys had spread two hearthrugs and some blankets, so that, as Bob politely informed Miss Astracan as he helped her into the retreat, she could go to bed and get a few hours' rest if she desired it.

Susan being among the imperfectly attired of the fair sex, had to share in this hastily-erected shelter.

Whatever happened to the Abbey, it was at a sufficient distance to ensure that no harm would come to them.

Going for help was then brought under discussion, but Jack was averse to any of the boys being sent through the wood. He had a fear that Chunder Loo might be lurking there. The scoundrel who had been hiding in the secret passages of the Abbey and deliberately made arrangements to roast all the occupants, would not hesitate to crown his infamy by murdering one of his intended victims.

"It is a good thing," said Jack, "that we got up that feast to-night. Had we all gone to bed as usual I believe every one of us must have perished. By the time we awoke and realised our position, it would have been too late to get out of the place."

Penny Bunn had not been seen during the last few minutes. In response to an inquiry from Don, Herbert May said that he had observed him walking up and down on the borders of the wood, like a man distracted.

"Perhaps he has gone for help," suggested Philter.

"Not alone," said Jack. "I wish some of you would have a look round for him. Don't, however, go out of sight."

The entire school had now assembled by the gates, with their eyes on the Abbey door, which was open, and gave a view of the rapidly increasing fire within. The flames were already licking the lintels of the door.

Tom Drummond, Philter, Short, and Little Jiggers walked across the intervening space to the wood, and on the verge of it they discovered Penny Bunn lying on his back.

They picked him up, and saw by the flickering light of the fire that his face was covered with blood.

"Mr. Bunn," exclaimed Tom, " what has happened to you?"

"I saw him," moaned Bunn; "he came out of the darkness like a spirit of evil!"

"Saw who, sir?"

"I said to him, 'Stop, villain, and yield yourself up to me.' Then an arm that seemed to me to be telescopic flashed out from his body, and I fell."

"You have seen Chunder Loo, sir?" said Tom.

"I have," answered Penny Bunn, "and felt him too."

"Which way did he go?"

"My boy," said Bunn, as he proceeded to staunch the blood that was still flowing freely from his nose, "when you get a sledge-hammer blow between the eyes you realise that the power of observation of passing things is *gone*. Until you kindly came to my aid I had seen nothing but volcanic eruptions in the air."

Tom hastened back to Jack and told him what had happened.

"Chunder Loo cannot be more than half through the wood," he said; "if we arm ourselves——"

"We can do nothing," answered Jack, "until the police arrive. Surely one of the nightmen will soon see the fire and give the alarm. I am not afraid of Chunder Loo, Tom, but none of us are a match for him. His arrest is the work of men."

Penny Bunn now joined them. The bleeding at the nose had lessened, and he was gradually resuming his ordinary bearing. But his face for many days would bear record of the fistic powers of Chunder Loo. His nose was thrice its normal size, and both his eyes were swollen. On the morrow they would be black, and afterwards go through the various stages of coloured convalescence common to injuries of this nature.

"He was too quick for me," he said; "could I have got in the first blow he would now have been our prisoner."

"You are sure it was Chunder Loo, sir?" inquired Jack, who for the moment thought that it was possible the schoolmaster might have blundered against the trunk or a branch of a tree.

"It was either that unparalleled monster," answered Bunn, "or a personage I hesitate to name at this hour of the night. There was the hook nose, the wicked eye, the form so like the serpent. I could not have been mistaken."

All doubts on the point were at rest. It was without doubt Chunder Loo, who was making his escape, carrying away with him the knowledge that the chief part of his plan had failed.

His object for lingering so long had no doubt been to watch the progress of the fire, and possibly have an opportunity to gloat over the agony of his victims, conveyed to his ears by futile cries for help.

But that unholy joy was denied him, and he must have gone away cursing the ill luck that had attended his work.

But suppose it had been successful, what a dark mystery the burning of the Abbey would have remained to the world!

Who would have known the origin of it?

The whole thing would have been attributed to accident.

One man alone would have lived with the fiendish knowledge and joy in his heart of having in his malice destroyed nearly forty people, young and old.

It would have been a full and ample revenge for such wrongs as he perversely considered he had suffered.

These were the thoughts that ran through Jack's brain as he with his friends watched the rising of the fire.

It had got a good hold, and in a quarter of an hour after all had escaped to the open air there was a long tongue of flame protruding from the door and some upper windows.

The air was red, and as the volumes of smoke, tinged with the same colour, rolled away over the valley, the sight was one of the most impressive things any there had ever looked upon.

And no help came, although it would not have been of much service.

The farmers in their homesteads and the labourers in their cottages slept on. The police were some- where about, possibly, but they saw nothing of the burning until the ruin was practically complete. And then it was a far-off officer who saw the glow of it, and could only guess that some place, out of his beat, was burning.

The boys and the schoolmaster were the sole spectators of the scene, and as the fire gathered strength they looked dumbly on, awe-stricken by the power of the element that brought the old Abbey tumbling about like a house of cards.

There was a pair of owls living somewhere in the roof, and when the warmth reached them they were seen to rise in the air, and blindly, in the light of the flames, circle round and round until the smoke over- powered them, and then they came headlong down and perished.

As they plunged into the flames there was a general cry of horror. Though it was only a matter of the destruction of a pair of owls, the time, the scene, and the manner of their death acted power- fully on the highly-strung nerves of the spectators. They felt it for the moment almost as much as if two human beings had thus perished.

Higher and higher rose the fire, pouring out of the windows, leaping and roaring, until there was a mighty crash. The roof had fallen.

Then for a few brief moments there was almost darkness again.

But it was soon dispelled as the flames gathered strength again, and proceeded to destroy what little inflammable matter there was left.

The stars overhead and far away were hidden by the dense smoke. The wind, light at first, had entirely died away, and there was a solemn hush around broken only by the crackling of the flames, and the splitting of stonework in the heat of the fire.

It hardly seemed credible that the old Abbey was a thing of the past, but it was so.

It was gone for ever, with its record of man's faith, man's virtue, man's cruelty and crime.

Whatever there had recently been left to learn of its mysteries would now never be known.

All was over. Littlecote Abbey was no more.

CHAPTER CLXXVII.

AFTER THE FIRE.—HOUSING THE VICTIMS.

IT was not until the dawn that a stranger appeared upon the scene in the person of a labourer, who every morning had to walk four miles, by way of the Abbey and the wood, to work.

It seems incredible that any man should be called to live so far from his field of labour, but it was a common thing in the old time, and is not even now unknown.

Landlords of the old school had no more thought for labourers than they had for their cattle. Nay, not so much. Comfortable housing was provided for the beast, but the man had to live where he could, and work where he could get it to do.

This labourer, having been accustomed to glance at the Abbey as he passed, was considerably astonished to find it gone, and a few slight columns of smoke in its place.

He pulled up by the gates, and stared at the rough tent the boys had fixed against the wall. From the inside—it was completely closed up—there came sounds of a nasal character of great power.

Unable to comprehend what these things meant, he peered inside the gates, and beheld, ranging along by the wall fringing the cliff, the boys of the school, many of whom were fast asleep, and the others nodding and giving out signs of fatigue.

Not until then did the Wiltshire dullard realise what had happened.

"I'll be danged!" he exclaimed, "if t'old Abbey ain't been and got cotched afire and burnt down."

Then he went his way, as he had to be punctual at his milking work. In passing through Smudgem Bender, he only stayed to tell others of what he had seen.

Still it was only labourers who heard the news, and some were inclined to think that their informant, who, although not forty years of age, was called Old Turmer, had gone a little wrong in his head, or had his intellect stimulated up to the point of making a joke.

The old Abbey burnt down! The building, which seemed to be all stone, destroyed as a thatched cottage might have been! It did not seem possible.

But with the daylight came Jack Ford and others to make arrangements for the temporary accommoda- tion of those who had been burnt out.

They made their way to the "Cowley Arms," where they roused the whole house, and brought the host from his bed by loudly knocking at the door.

He thrust his head out of the window, and seeing the boys, asked what on earth had brought them there at that hour?

They told him of the fire, and that a vehicle was required to bring down the ladies, and breakfast prepared for the homeless ones. The inn was soon alive with preparations to receive the flood of guests.

Botch soon joined the boys, and heard all there was to tell. The story impressed him deeply.

"There will be no rest or safety for anyone," he said, " until that Chunder Loo is laid up in limbo. He be a cunning fiend, and as remorseless as a crocodile."

As the village became fully aroused, and the tidings spread, there was a flocking to the inn to hear of the event at first hand; but the boys were tired out, and Botch kept the curious ones at bay until after breakfast.

Those who had come down had it as soon as it could be served, and soon after others came flocking in, until the inn was alive with chattering youngsters, who were now disposed to regard the thing as a delightful adventure.

A cart had been despatched for their boxes, and a waggonette for the three women. Smudgem Bender had no fly to send.

Last of all came the village constable, who, according to his statement—received with a considerable amount of reserve—had been lying in some lonely spot on the lookout for poachers. On hearing the facts he started on foot for Chippenham.

In due time Penny Bunn arrived, heralding the coming of the ladies.

What with his swollen nose, black eyes, and the want of sleep, he presented a pitiable appearance, but he was fairly buoyant, and partook of rum-and-milk as a start towards the spending of a happy day.

"Misfortunes comes to all," he said to Botch, who paid for the drink, "and they are but blessings in disguise. It is our duty to meet them in a manly spirit."

"Just so," said Botch; "some of the tradesmen here just now were wondering if the burning of the Abbey would settle their accounts."

"It has settled them," said Bunn, "settled everything. I wash my hands of the Abbey and all relating to it, and begin the world anew."

Botch looked at him and laughed.

"I doubt much," he said, "if that 'ere sort of washing will not be objected to."

"Let them object," replied Bunn. "I care not a fig. Listen! the waggonette approaches. As none of the women have full apparel on, I would suggest that it goes round to the back to enable them to get upstairs without being observed."

This was done, and then came the question from the landlord as to who would settle for the accommodation of his guests. Botch said he would be responsible for the day.

After that somebody else would have to do it.

"Sufficient for the day" satisfied Bunn and his wife, and Miss Astracan, having been conveyed to an upper room, there to make arrangements for some needed clothing, the schoolmaster went about in a buoyant spirit which nothing could quell or even momentarily depress.

The butcher, the baker, and the grocer all tackled him in turn, with a view to ascertaining what prospect they had of getting their money. He assured them that it was his intention to immediately look into his affairs and see what could be done.

Meanwhile the agent of Sir Charles Barstow, having heard of the disaster, wired that gentleman, who simply sent a reply that the Abbey was fully insured, and expressing a hope that no lives were lost. A satisfactory rejoinder on this point was forwarded to him.

The boys, having had a bad night, mooned about and took short naps in convenient and inconvenient places. They were found on the straw in the stables, in the summer-house of the garden of the inn, and elsewhere, indulging in Nature's sweet restorer. Smudgem Bender had never seen so many sleepy youngsters before.

Ere long it became a question of what was to be done for the night. Bunn had no funds to send any of them home, and if he had, he would probably have kept the money for himself. All the boys could do was to write to their parents and tell them they wanted to come home, and please would they send their railway fare. Penny Bunn dictated a sentence for general use.

"Tell your parents," he said, "that all my worldly possessions have perished in the fire, and that I am a ruined man. Had it been otherwise, I would gladly refund the balance of the money paid for the term and send you all home first class."

About the middle of the afternoon he disappeared, and did not return to the inn until nine o'clock. He found then that the boys had been taken care of by the villagers, each of them accommodating one, two, or more according to the spare beds at their command. Bunn expressed approval of this generous conduct.

He was in a very cheerful mood, and partook of something warm, paying for the same with a sovereign, which he changed to show that he was not so poor as people might think.

As he went away in the afternoon practically penniless, this sudden accession of wealth puzzled Jack Ford, who happened to be in the inn waiting for Botch, in whose house he and Don were to pass the night.

Bunn went even further than this, for, in addition to changing a sovereign, he ostentatiously jingled other coins in his trousers-pocket.

The secret of this sudden acquisition of wealth did

not transpire until some time afterwards, but we may as well reveal it here.

Penny Bunn had been calling upon some of the big people in the neighbourhood, from whom he collected subscriptions to recoup the boys for the loss of their "little all" in the fire.

It was a happy thought, to his way of thinking, and it put him pecuniarily on his legs for a time.

With a plausible tongue he had done wonders, having collected over twenty pounds. But when his wife sent for him, and asked what had to be done about her needs, he calmly bade her fall back upon her own hoard.

"It is cruel," he said, "to taunt a man who is penniless with requests for money."

Miriam, having some of her own, had already made arrangements for the purchase of apparel, and her request was, as Bunn declared, equivalent to a taunt. It fell upon him harmlessly, however.

In a buoyant mood he left her, but was called back immediately.

"P.Y.," she said, "have you seen anything of Dolphus?"

The question came upon him like a thunderbolt. From the moment when he had hurled the dear dog out of the Abbey window, he had not bestowed a thought upon that priceless creature.

"Dolphus!" he stammered, "he—he—must have perished in the fire."

Miriam uttered a piercing cry, and was getting up a faint, when he hurriedly said he had an appointment with a friend, and left the room.

The word "Brute!" came after him like a missile, but it only made him smile.

"She will never know the manner of his death," he murmured, "and it is better so."

CHAPTER CLXXVIII.

RETURNING TO OLD HAUNTS.—FOOD FOR REFLECTION.

DON and the rest of the inner circle had written to their friends an account of the fire; but as it had been agreed between himself and his three friends that they would not go home until they had seen Lingo again, he did not speak of returning.

"It is impossible to say what may come out of the fire," Don wrote, "so you will have to wait until I write again before you know what we are going to do. You need not, dear mother, be at all anxious about me. I have lost nothing, and we have friends here who are taking care of us."

There was a letter in the morning from Lingo to Jack. It was of a very satisfactory nature.

"All is well," he wrote. "Sir Charles has as good as got the armour, and he is going to call for the boxes containing the coins as soon as possible. He is a tremendous toff, but that is what he was born and bred to, and he is under the starch one of the best fellows I ever met with. What is this about the fire at the Abbey? How did it come about? Drop me a line to Bing's private hotel, Pall Mall—fancy me at a private swell hotel, waited on by waiters who look like mashers got up for the evening—and I shall get it in the afternoon. Sir Charles merely said that the place was burnt down, and then went off again about that old iron and stuff we unearthed for him. He's quite gone on it."

By noon a number of the parents and friends of the boys had either sent money or had come in person for their sons.

Some of them were in an irate condition of mind, and Short's mother, a very voluble lady, told Penny Bunn some home truths that would have made him wince, if he had not had a lot of money in his pocket.

"I would never have allowed my son to come back this term if it had not been paid for. You are not fit to keep a school!" she said.

"There is the element of fact in your statement," replied Bunn. "I am of a sensitive, refined nature. Boys want a coarser man to govern them."

He was asked by some if he could not refund some of the money paid to Snicker, and he told them that he would be willing to entertain the matter as soon as his affairs were settled. Meanwhile, if they would estimate the amount due to them, he would give an I O U for the sum to be met out of the funds of "his estate."

Dorey, Jiggers, Short, Philter, and many more were gone in the evening. There were feelings within some of them as they parted which they strove to hide with but poor success, for they knew that the parting would, in most cases, be a long one, and perhaps they might never meet again.

So they drifted away, and on the morrow the rest went, save the four who had been so closely allied in the various adventures we have recorded.

They remained, Jack and Don at the house of Botch, Tom and Bob at the inn.

This arrangement was, of course, mainly for sleeping. The floodgates of the heart of Botch being opened, it was not in his nature to do anything by halves.

"I shall expect you," he said, solemnly, "to dine here—all of you—until further notice."

They accepted his hospitality readily, the more so because they knew their stay in Smudgem Bender would be short, and once they left it they might never set foot in it again.

There is something pathetic in the break-up of all

communities, especially communities of the young; and in the case of Littlecote Abbey there was something out of the common.

Not that the lives of the boys had been, for the most part, of the best or the brightest, for they had been far from that. No; the emotion was of a different nature.

Jack put it into words as he strolled with his chum through the wood that afternoon.

They started in company, simply for a walk, and drifted naturally towards the ruined Abbey.

"I am sorry for the old place," said Jack Ford, "as, with all its drawbacks, it has made me feel as if I were a man. I fancy it will take a lot of rough work in the world to knock me out."

"It has done something for us all," said Don Peebles. "Take my case—what sort of fellow was I when I first came down here?"

"Not much to look at," replied Tom Drummond.

"You were what the brick-makers call 'pug,'" said Bob Stockton; "a mixture of clay and cinders and goodness knows what. But there was neither make nor shape about you."

"I like you fellows," said Don, dryly, "you are so overpoweringly complimentary."

"Don, old man," said Jack, "we shaped you. But you were of the right sort of 'pug,' or you would never have made a brick of the class you are."

"Don't make him conceited," advised Bob; "he will bear a little more shaping yet."

"Snicker was an unconscious moulder of his kind," remarked Jack. "Bunn is too soft for a schoolmaster, although I would rather have had his pedagogue career cut short by something less sad than this."

They were on the summit of the slope now, with the ruins of the Abbey before them. It was indeed as sad a spectacle as the lover of ancient things would care to see.

Here and there a faint pencil of smoke was rising, but the fallen brickwork and masonry was rapidly cooling.

CHAPTER CLXXIX.

THE GIPSY'S PROPHECY.—A STORY OF THE PAST.

THEY entered by the old gate and walked to the wall, where they had so often sat in council. It had escaped the fire; but further on, where the old schoolroom once stood, the walls had shot down the cliff in avalanche form, taking with them a mass of earth. The whole had fallen so as to conceal the mouth of the cave.

"Nothing is left undone," said Jack, "to ensure that the Abbey and its story shall, in a few years, be forgotten."

"Some fellow will dig out the cave one day," said Don.

"Who that we know here would take the trouble?" said Jack. "The farmers, as a body, have no more sentiment than there is in a wooden figure, and one cannot wonder at it, seeing how they have to toil and scheme to live. The agricultural labourer won't give his spare time, if he has any, to it. No, my dear boys, they will let things remain as they are, and in a few years we shall be forgotten, or only dimly remembered as a tale that is told."

"But your names shall not pass away!" cried a croaking voice behind them.

Startled, they turned, and saw the form of an old gipsy, bent with more than four-score years, leaning on a stick, hard by.

Just for a moment it flashed on Don that it was Lingo playing another trick upon them; but one searching look at the withered face and the bleared eyes, still with some of their ancient fire slumbering in their depths, dispelled the notion.

"Don't stare at me," she said, turning her head and slowly scanning their faces in turn; "you know me not?"

"No," replied Jack, "I cannot remember having seen you before."

"But I have seen you in my dreams," she said. "I am Hecla, the gipsy queen, last of my family and my tribe."

Amazed, they could only stare at her and note the feebly passionate workings of her face.

"My people are all gone," she wailed. "In the old days we were free of the lanes and in some places of the woods. Now we have no resting-place. They drive us on and on. They take our children away to school; they fine us because we say we would rather be free to live the old life, and they imprison us because we cannot pay. Of our strong young men they have made burglars and thieves. My last grandson was taken from me two months ago, and for seven years he will be caged in walls of stone. He is lost to me for ever!"

It seemed to the boys that she was mentally overhauling her woes and repeating them aloud as much to relieve the sorrows of her heart as to let them hear of her loss. She stopped and mumbled for a time, shaking her head, and Jack quietly signalled for the others to steal softly away.

But the first movement they made roused her from her thoughts, and with a movement of incredible swiftness when her age is considered, she barred their retreat with her staff, holding it horizontally before them.

"I have seen you in my dreams," she repeated;

"and waking, I remembered you. I knew when I crept up here that I should find you."

Bob, standing partly behind Jack, made a wry face, as if dissenting from this statement. He was mentally calculating how long it would be ere she asked for a piece of silver to "cross her palm."

But, to his amazement and terror, she instantly took record of the movement, and fell upon him.

"Come forward, my dainty boy!" she said, imperiously.

Bob tried to escape the ordeal by shamming that he did not recognise any allusion to himself; but the imperious crook of her finger was too much for him, and he slowly came to the front.

"You think I want your money to tell you lies," said the old gipsy, shaking a forefinger at him, more in expostulation than anger; "but I'll have none of it. When the gipsy asks for money she has need of it. I need no more. Hold out your hand—the right one."

Bob had to do it. He could no more resist the request than he could have held back if chained to a moving horse.

"There is trouble and danger ahead of you," said the old gipsy, peering into the lines upon his hand; "but you will survive, for here by the thumb is the line of the long liver—bar accidents. Nature gives the line of life for good living; but it will not protect you from the dagger of the assassin! If you seek evil company, in their midst you will fall!"

She motioned to him to stand aside, and beckoned to Tom Drummond. Without being requested, he instinctively held out his hand, and the old woman peered at it for awhile ere she spoke.

"Strong and sturdy—plain and true," she said. "Not so tender-hearted as some, but kind in the main. You have the heart of the oak. As a young bison roaming over pastures, so will you go through the world—pacific while let alone, but let him who would attack you beware!"

She dismissed him, and then it became Don's turn to go through the ordeal. It must be confessed that he did so with some trepidation, for the manner of the old gipsy impressed him deeply.

"A son of a trader," she said, scanning his hand; "one of the class that is the backbone of the country. Yet shall you not be a trader, but in other lands find fame and fortune. True as steel, open as the day, honourable as one can be, you will carry a strong noble heart with you wherever you may be or what-e'er betide you."

Don stepped back, and Jack Ford, seeing the old woman made no movement, thought he was going to escape. But he was in error.

Instead of beckoning him to come to her, she suddenly advanced upon him.

"I want no hand from you," she said, peering into his face. "You carry with you as a heart upon your sleeve what you are—*a born leader of men*. He who will range himself under your banner in days to come will be led by one to whom falsehood and deceit are *impossible*. Fear you may know, but it will never be the fear of the weak, whom the world miscalls coward. As you are strong, so will you be tender to those who are not so blessed as yourself. To the evil-doer—he who lives by wronging others—you will be a scourge. The blessing of Hecla will follow you through the world."

She turned from him, and pointing towards the Abbey, said, in a tone of voice that rang out shrill and clear:

"Ye four sons of good men, in that Abbey I was born. You may not believe me," she added, turning to them, "but it is true. The old Abbey, at that time, had no house-dweller in its walls, and we wanderers on the earth, sometimes, when the weather was biting or sickness laid hold of us, used to shelter in its walls. It was there that I was brought into light, and for many years I came hither as one goes home—as you go home from school. Then came a time when they closed the gates against us and put a house-dweller there with dogs to keep us out, and I with my tribe wandered away. Through the long years of sorrow I have longed to return here, and I crept back at last but yesterday, only to find it in ruins. It was to be so, and it is in harmony with my sorrows. Tribe and people gone, why should not my birthplace follow? My children, you may leave me now."

She waved her hand to them by way of adieu, but she did not look at them again. Jack thought he saw a tear fall upon her ragged garment, and moved to compassion, he said:

"I should like to do something for you in your old age. We all would gladly do it. We have money——"

"I need none," she interposed; "go, I beg of you!"

She walked away from them with tottering steps, and feeling that their staying longer would be distasteful to her, they hurried out of the grounds and walked back to Smudgem Bender through the old wood.

"I want to look about the ruins a bit," said Jack. "We can come again to-morrow."

"What a strange old woman!" remarked Don. "Of course, there is nothing in her prophecies."

"I would not like to say for sure," replied Jack.

"They were very complimentary—or I ought to say, encouraging," said Don. "In her young days I should say she was a very handsome woman."

"Hardly that now," said Bob, lightly. "But there! it is no use my shamming. The old hag has deeply moved me. I am pleased we met her, and yet I am *not.* In short, I hardly know what I feel: it is a staggerer."

CHAPTER CLXXX.

PIGS IN TROUBLE.—THE SECOND VISIT TO THE RUINS, WITH A STARTLING RESULT.

ON returning to the farm they found Botch inspecting the pigs, with a view to picking out a few of the best, to be immediately turned into bacon.

He was leaning on the edge of a sty as the boys crossed the yard. Inside the sty, a dozen huge pigs moved restlessly about. It was a very large sty—a final fatting-place.

"Now," he said, "some people will have the rawdacity to tell you that pigs is fools. They are the most artful animals going. All these chaps knows what I am here for, and to get off being killed for a week or two, they've been a-hunching up their backs and getting theirselves up as mean as possible. Look at that chap with a black patch over his eye."

The pig thus referred to uttered an expostulatory squeak that made Botch laugh.

"He knows what I'm going to say," he said. "Well, look at him. Twenty-three stun, if a pound."

"So much as that?" exclaimed Tom Drummond.

"Eight pound to the stun," said Botch; "that's the weight we go by. Now that 'ere pig have been trying to make hisself look no more than sixteen stun. But he can't do it. He's picked out for one on 'em."

The unfortunate animal thus referred to, whether he understood Botch or not, now retreated into the house of shelter where he slept with his companions. The exhilaration of Botch was a sight. He fairly swelled with laughter.

"They are most amoosin'," he said.

But though they were amusing to him, it appeared that the pigs took *him* very seriously; for, on his calling one of his men to mark sundry occupants of the sty for slaughter, there was an amount of preliminary squeaking that was almost heartrending to hear.

At four o'clock Mrs. Botch announced tea, and they all went in to partake of it.

It was none of your fal-lal affairs, with a small pot of tea and two or three slices of thin bread-and-butter, but a very substantial spread which would have sufficed for some people's supper.

There was tongue, for a start, and a ham to go with it, or follow, according to the taste of the consumer; and brawn and potted meats, and goodness knows what; and Mrs. Botch was very uncomfortable when she found that her guests could not liberally partake of all.

"I am sure I never ate such splendid ham in my life," said Bob Stockton; and he meant it.

"Not even when Snicker was master at the Abbey," facetiously put in Botch.

This was such a good joke that Botch fairly choked over it, and the boys kept him company by laughing as heartily as they were able.

Snicker had, of course, his humorous side to them, but his hams were not a joke. He never had one unless it was in danger of being seized by an inspector as unfit for human food.

The wonder used to be that he did not poison his pupils.

After tea the pig-killing was arranged to begin, and the boys were invited to witness the "slaughter of the innocents."

As none of them had ever witnessed that thrilling ceremony before, they decided to sink their tender feelings and look on.

No public execution could have been more ceremoniously performed, or excited more public attention in Smudgem Bender.

It had gone forth that Botch was "killing" that evening, and all who had leisure time among the tradesmen and general inhabitants were on the spot.

The more intimate friends were admitted to the precincts of the slaughter-house, the labouring population stood about the doorway and the gate, and the farmyard was thronged with boys. The girls modestly stood in the road and peeped between the boys' legs.

As a first experience, killing a pig is an interesting performance.

The pig is so well aware of his impending fate that he resists the slaughterer and his myrmidons with all the muscular powers of his fleshy legs.

What he lacks in actual muscular strength he makes up in agility, and only the experienced can handle him with the ease and grace of a professional slaughterer.

Even he has sometimes as much as he can tackle, as he found in the present case when he went for the pig with the spot over his eye.

Though weighing fully twenty-four stone, afterwards proved by the steelyards, he was as corky and lithe as a ten-stoner, and he not only succeeded in embarrassing the slaughterer, but finally upset him and got free, as far as the farmyard was concerned.

Chasing and recapturing that pig was not a very long task, but it was an exciting one, for it landed several of the assistants in the mire in the centre of the farmyard, without which no similar area is considered complete.

But with an expedition that was creditable to the Smudgem Bender professional slaughterer, the whole of the selected pigs were finally put to rest, and having been duly scalded so that the bristles could be removed, they were hoisted up to a beam in the slaughter-house, there to hang until the morrow, when the same operator would cut them up into the recognised joint form, with spareribs and griskins, and bits for sausages, and so on.

The ceremony concluded with a liberal supply of beer to all who rendered assistance, and to some who had made no effort to bear a hand, but had made up for a lack of energy by giving abundant unasked-for advice.

The whole affair partook of the nature of a public festivity, "without considering the pigs," as Bob Stockton remarked.

But it must be confessed that nobody felt very much for the deceased animals, and the boys were amongst the merriest in the rugged festivities that finished the evening in the barn.

It was not until the following morning that Jack found an opportunity to speak to Botch about the meeting with Hecla, the gipsy. Rising early, he found the farmer already abroad and about to start to a distant meadow, where he had some heifers running.

A walk suited Jack, and they went together. On the way he told the story of meeting with Hecla, and it appeared that Botch knew her.

"Let me see," he said, "it must be many a year since I set eyes on her; a fine woman, well set up, with eyes as black as coals; and a way of looking at you that made a quiet man like me feel foolish. But to tell the truth, none of us people here took to gipsies."

"Why not?" asked Jack.

"Well," said Botch, "they are a rum lot! Kind of got dealings with a party I won't name. They ain't what we calls quite human."

"They are a romantic people," said Jack.

"So they may be," said Botch; "but when their romanticking led 'em on to come in the night and borrow your fowls with no intention of paying back, then we matter-of-fact people go agin 'em. Some of the young men among 'em alser took to taking horses, and that was a bit too thick."

"It was," assented Jack.

"But as for this 'ere Hecla," said Botch, musing, "I ain't nothing agin her. If I remembers rightly, she tried to keep her people honest, for the little they wants is earned, and they are a handy people at making brooms and rush nicknackers."

"Did she used to tell fortunes in those days?" inquired Jack.

"She did," answered Botch, "and some pretty true things she told some of us. I remember once when me and Bill Drodger—he is gone aloft these ten years through being throwed out of his market cart that night when he took the corner nigh the smithy too sharp, and ran against a post. I was with him,

and we was both throwed out, and we both come on our heads. He was killed and I wasn't, which is curious."

"It is," said Jack, slyly glancing at him. "Was it ever accounted for?"

"No, only in a jokerly way by them who've got heads as thick as mine and thicker. But she said that it would come orf the day when Bill horsewhipped one of the young gipsies till he was sore all over for stealin' eggs out of the fowl-house."

"How did she prophesy it?" inquired Jack.

"She come to us a-purpose, and told us that something would happen before long and one of us be killed. The jokerlar ones said there was nothing in that, and we both ought to have been killed before, seeing how we drove home on market days. But the woman was right, and there was a talk of having her up for witchcraft, or murder, or something that way; but the gipsies cleared out of the neighbourhood, and I don't think she's been here since."

So far, the experience of Botch did not add much to the romance of the life of Hecla, but, on going back to breakfast, the subject was mooted in the presence of Mrs Botch, and she had a score of thrilling stories to tell of the gipsy woman.

While in the neighbourhood she had been the terror of the good old-fashioned dames, who laid all their misfortunes with milk and poultry to her charge.

And, furthermore, even the sicknesses in the village were attributed to her, and, in the opinion of the good dame, Hecla simply went away because she was afraid of being burnt.

"Nonsense!" said Botch, "she wern't afraid of nothing. When quite a young woman, as she was when my mother was a girl, she was as venturesome a creetur as ever sat under a tent. Some chap, not a gipsy, made love to her—he was a commercial traveller, which the race is cheeky—and she beat him with a stick until he ran down the street, howling for his life."

"She was a hussy, for all that," said Mrs. Botch, with her nose in the air; "all the lot are."

Botch did not argue the point. In a way, his wife might be right, but not in the way she intended to be.

Jack purposed going up to the Abbey, and had appointed the early hour of nine for starting. Punctually his friends were there, and in company they started.

The journey thither was without incident, and on arriving at the gates Don remarked that the fire of the old Abbey was out at last.

There was no smoke visible anywhere.

They clambered up to the top of the ruins—no great height, for the whole place had collapsed, and it seemed almost impossible that a place could be so utterly wiped out, as far as its form was concerned.

But it was so, and they were unable to locate, save in a very vague way, the plan of the lower rooms.

In one spot, in the thick of some shattered stone-work, they came across a lot of half-calcined human bones, representing portions of at least half-a-dozen skeletons.

Beside them were a number of rusty iron chains, and there were circling bands for the waist, one of which still hung about the spine of a broken skeleton.

"Here is a story for you," said Bob, breathlessly. "You see what these bones mean?"

"Can't say I do," answered Tom Drummond.

"How dull you are! Here, once upon a time, when the Abbey was in its pride, the men who owned these bones offended the abbot or the monks that lived here, and they were bricked up in the walls. It was a favourite punishment of good men a few centuries ago."

"A cruel lot," said Don.

"All men were cruel in those days," said Jack, "and the time will come when they will revile us for taking a man's life on the scaffold, even though he has committed murder."

"But it is just," said Don.

"Oh, I daresay it is. But different ages look at things in a different light. That is all I wish to say. I am not moralising. You can't tell what the owners of these bones, as Bob calls them, did to earn their fate. We ought, however, to let the parson know they are here, and he will, no doubt, see that they are reverently interred."

The ruins were in a very uneven state, as one may guess, and they had to climb over masses, and to dive down into small valleys or hollows. In the latter there was still some slight warmth, and a remark had just been made that "many a tramp would be glad of such a sleeping-place," when an exclamation from Jack, who had climbed on a little ahead, startled them all.

He was standing on the summit of a mass of bricks and stones, peering into a hollow.

"She is here!" he said.

"Who?" asked Bob.

"Hecla, the gipsy, asleep, or——"

He slid down out of sight, and they climbed to a higher spot, from where they could again see him.

He was kneeling beside the form of Hecla, the gipsy. It required scarcely a second glance to tell that she was dead.

"I understand her last words now," said Jack, looking up. "This was her place of birth, and with naught left in the world to live for, she came here—to die!"

Death had smoothed out many of the wrinkles on the old woman's face, and she looked quite young in comparison to her aged aspect on the previous day. There was no doubt now that she had once been a very handsome woman.

Jack could do no more than cover the still face with his handkerchief, and with his desire to inspect the ruins now completely extinguished, he set off alone to acquaint the authorities with his discovery.

He left his friends behind him to keep a watch over the dead, lest some stray dog or bird of prey should mutilate it.

————

CHAPTER CLXXXI.

A MEETING OF CREDITORS. — ABSENCE OF THE DEBTOR A SLIGHT IMPEDIMENT IN THE WAY OF SETTLE-MENT.

ABOUT the same hour a most important meeting was being held at the "Cowley Arms." It had been called by the village baker, and been responded to by every tradesman who had had the honour of supplying Littlecote Abbey with goods.

Even Bibbins was present, although his claim was a small one; the cost of putting in a spring to Miss Astracan's watch, and cleaning the kitchen clock.

But the grocer and the butcher were heavy sufferers, and they were very much to the fore.

One would hardly have thought that so many creditors could be made to suffer in so short a time. But there were representatives from Chippenham to swell the host, and the throng in the coffee-room was a very imposing one.

The grocer was voted to the chair, and, supported on either hand by the butcher and the baker, he opened the proceedings.

"Gentlemen," he said, "afore we begins business I think we ought to have the debtor with us."

"Hear, hear!" chorussed the rest.

"I sent him a notice of the meeting," pursued the chairman, "and he showed his sentiments towards us by lighting a twopenny smoke with it. I see him do it with my own eyes."

"You wouldn't have seen it with other peoples' eyes," remarked Bibbins, with mild facetiousness.

"Mr. Bibbins," said the grocer chairman, severely, "this ain't the time or place for your irreverence. If you think it is a joking matter to supply a man with cartloads of grocery and then have to whistle for your money——"

"Pardon me," interposed Bibbins. "It was not my intention to make a joke of that."

"You was wrong to cut in with any sort of joke," was the cutting rejoinder, which met with approving reception from the whole room.

Bibbins again apologised, and the matter was

allowed to drop. Then a proposition was made that if the debtor would not honour them with his presence, probably his wife would be induced to do so.

It was admitted that she was the more business-like of the two, and she proved to be so, for, on a deputation waiting upon her to solicit the pleasure of her company below, she plainly told them she was not personally responsible for anything; and Miss Astracan, who seemed to be in a semi-wild state since the fire, informed the staggered deputation that if they did not depart forthwith she would rise up and " fall upon them."

The probability is that she did not mean to do so in a bodily sense, but verbally. They, however, took the matter in a literal light, and not being tired of their lives or longing to be crushed to death, the deputation precipitately vanished.

Left to their own devices, the creditors looked into Bunn's affairs, and the more they looked the less they liked them.

What they wanted was some proposition as to settlement.

" How much in the pound will there be ?" asked the baker ; adding, " We don't mind a little short weight, but we must have something."

" You needn't drag your business into it," said the village tailor, who had a considerable bill for clothing supplied and repairs.

" What do you mean by that ?" demanded the baker.

" You were speaking of short weight," said the tailor.

The baker fired up and made reference to " cabbage," and a fight was imminent, when the butcher, who was a convivial soul, suggested they should all have something at the expense of the baker and the tailor.

It was carried, and the two unfortunates had to shell out ; which was, however, but a preliminary to others doing the same, and the whole proceedings devolved into a convivial day.

Bunn, meanwhile, was out making appeals to those whom he called " the children of affluence," with less good results than the first day warranted him to anticipate. But, as he remarked on his way back— to himself, of course—" there is another day, and other cows to milk to-morrow."

On reaching the " Cowley Arms," he was pleased to hear the sounds of mirth in the form of a rousing chorus to a hunting-song. He was at no loss in locating the melody in the public parlour, and was on his way thither, when the landlord called him back.

" If I was you I wouldn't go in there," he said.

" Why not ?" inquired Bunn.

" Them's your creditors. They've been waiting for you all day, and been making the best of the time by singing. Keeping up their speerits, I s'pose."

" Oh !" said Bunn, " my creditors ? All I can say is that they are remarkably cheerful under rather trying circumstances. If you will cut me a sandwich or two, I will take them, with a bottle of bass, outside, and there partake of the refreshment I need. Please cut the sandwiches thick."

They were supplied him—for cash—and he adjourned to the stable at the back, where, in the company of the ostler, who had taken charge of Dolphus once upon a time, he spent a quiet hour.

Indeed, he so far manœuvred matters that he eventually slept on a heap of clean straw in one of the stalls.

" Here," he murmured, " I am at peace. No intruders will venture here. No shrill-tongued women will keep me from repose. Here I lie until chanticleer proclaims the morn. On my word, it is very comfortable. Perhaps a tramp's life would suit me. I might make the experiment. But, meanwhile, there is a shot in the locker, thanks to the benevolent. Bless them, and to the world good-night !"

CHAPTER CLXXXII

HORSE-TAMING.—A COMING OF AGE.—ROYALTY EXPECTED.

THE morning came fair enough to give promise of a fine day. There was a little haze about, but that was better than a too clear atmosphere with the rising sun.

Tom and Bob, who slept at the inn, were aroused in the morning by the sounds of hissing peculiar to ostlers when engaged in cleaning down a horse.

The why and wherefore of this sibillation has never yet been fully explained. Ask an ostler why he does it, and he will tell you he must do it or he cannot groom the horse. That is all he knows about it.

The window of the room occupied by the boys was over the stable-yard, and Bob opening it, looked out.

To his astonishment, Penny Bunn, with a few straws sticking in his hair, like the madman in the play, was watching the labouring ostler with a keen and critical eye.

That is, his eye was as keen and critical as it could be under its still visible discolouration. He had assumed the position of a judge of grooming by virtue of a pot of purl which he had paid for, and which he and the ostler alternately drank from.

The pewter stood upon the ground near the stable door, giving out the steam so fragrant to the nostrils of our humble forefathers.

" You will excuse me," said Bunn to the ostler— Tom had joined Bob by this time, and they were both quietly observing the scene from the window—" excuse me, but why do you make that peculiar sound as you toil?"

"Hosses won't stand the rubbing without it," shortly replied the ostler.

"Indeed!" said Bunn, drily. "I presume you never heard of Mr. Rarey?"

"No, not as I knows on," said the ostler, pausing in his work and meditating; "what was he—a circus man?"

"No," answered Bunn, "he was a horse-tamer; he could do anything with the most vicious creature that ever was harnessed. Indeed, he took them in hand before they were harnessed."

"What did he do wi' 'um?" asked the ostler.

"Anything and everything," said Bunn. "First of all he never hissed when he groomed them. If he beckoned, they followed him. He could sit on a bare-backed steed, and bang a drum, or fire a gun, or do what he pleased, and the beast would not wink an eye."

"Was the hoss deaf?"

"No, my friend; it was the power a *man* had over the creature. The secret of it he kept for years. But I happened to render him a signal service once upon a time, and in gratitude he imparted the secret to me, merely stipulating that I did not reveal it to others without due emolument."

"What's that?" gruffly asked the ostler.

"Pay, my friend."

"I'm not on," said the ostler.

"Excuse me," said Bunn, "it was not my intention to ask you for anything. The secret, after all, was nothing, merely a matter of the hand and eye."

"Bunn is going to make an ass of himself again," whispered Tom.

"A million to one on it," replied Bob, in a low tone; "but we won't spoil it by permitting him to see or hear us."

They drew back behind the muslin curtains, and remained quite still during the instructive scene that ensued.

"It is by the eye alone the trick is done," resumed Bunn. "I suspected it at the time, but would not be sure. Now here is a horse."

"Of a sart," said the ostler, in broad Wiltshire.

"As you say, of a sort," continued Bunn; "an humble, and, I may say, a depraved specimen of his species."

"He ain't no beauty, but he can do a lot of work," said the ostler, "and he wants driving. Afore his leg swelled he was in the Hearl's stable. A groom named Wosster used to ride him."

"Just so," said Bunn, lightly. "The animal has blood, I believe, and undoubtedly bone. Now see—first of all I stand in front of him and fix my eye on his."

Bunn fixing his eye on anything in its then condition was a comical sight; but the ostler had no sense of humour, and he looked on with stolid, grumpy gravity.

The horse, in response to the gaze of Bunn, rolled his eyes, showing a lot of the whites.

A grunt escaped the lips of the ostler, and he withdrew to a respectful distance from the brute.

"Having, as it were, fascinated him with my gaze," said Bunn, "I will now proceed to demonstrate that it is not necessary to hiss while at work. Oblige me with your wisp of straw."

The ostler tossed it to him, still keeping well out of the reach of the horse, which made no movement beyond rolling his eyes and slightly lifting one of his hind legs.

"Hissing," said Bunn, slowly gliding by the side of the creature, "is a waste of breath. It is a tax on the organs of speech, and, in truth, it has an irritating effect on all pacific animals like the horse. I will now——"

What he was going to do was never done.

The horse, tied to an iron ring fixed in the wall by an ordinary halter, suddenly spun round and lashed out.

Fortunately Bunn was close up, or there and then he would have paid in full for his temerity. It is the full-length kick that does the most mischief.

But even as it was Bunn was shot like a bolt from a catapult straight at the ostler, and both were thrown violently down.

The wisp of straw flew into the air and was carried away by the wind, in fragments.

Having performed this feat, the ill-conditioned brute clattered about the stones, tried to rear, and tugged violently at its halter, which fortunately held.

The ostler got upon his feet, and, true to his instincts, thought first of his horse.

"Whoa then, will 'ee!" he cried. "Gently, boy—whoa—whoa—whoa!"

Manœuvring round, he eventually succeeded in getting hold of the elated beast and subduing his antics. Then the ostler had time to look at Bunn.

He was reclining like Marius among the ruins of Carthage—overcome with mixed meditation. Apparently he had suffered no great bodily hurt. He was simply the victim of unqualified surprise.

"The next time you wants to go a-Rareyin'," said the ostler, viciously, "try it in another yard."

"I admit," said Bunn, as he clambered to his feet, "that my first experiment with that horse has not been marked with complete success. It is admitted by the best known authorities——"

"Who are they?" asked the ostler, as he detached the horse from the ring and proceeded to lead it to the stable. Bunn backed a bit, although he was well out of reach of those dangerous heels.

"The greatest authorities of the *present* day," said Bunn, " are Mr. Weatherby, the racing-calendar man, and *myself*. In the past we have Buffon, a mere closet student without personal experience such as I can boast of, and Cuvier, and a few others."

"I'll back myself to know a 'oss ag'in the lot," said the ostler.

He disappeared into the stable with the gallant steed, and Bunn, turning away with a supercilious smile upon his face, saw the boys laughing behind the curtain.

"Hail—all hail!" he cried, airily.

"Good-morning. Mr. Bunn," said Bob; "sorry to see you had an accident."

"A mere trifle—a mere trifle," replied Bunn; "one of the exigencies of experimenting with unknown quantities. By the way, boys, have you heard the news?"

"What is it?" asked Bob. "We have heard nothing out of the common. Is Chunder Loo captured?"

"I regret to say," said Bunn, "that that most nefarious of unmitigated ruffians is still at large. I was referring to a coming of age."

"Whose is it?" asked Tom.

"It is the son and heir of the Gimpson-Smiths, a family that has of recent years been the light of Malmesbury. Though not entitled to be considered blue blood, they go in for style, and hope one day to be among the *élite*. I heard of it yesterday on my rounds testing the charity of the world. It is my intention to walk there."

"To Malmesbury!" exclaimed Tom.

"Yes. I was a man of mark years ago as a walker."

"Is there to be much fun in the coming of age, sir?" asked Tom.

"Rather," said Bunn; "it is to be done in style. Free drink by the roadside. Luncheon for all comers. High festivities modelled on the olden time. The Gimpson-Smiths simply mean going it."

"This would suit us for a day's outing," said Tom, in a low tone.

"Do you think we could get Botch and Bunn out together?" suggested Bob. "Here, I'll run over to the farm and hear what Jack thinks of it."

Leaning out of the window, he told Bunn that they thought of going, too, and if they did they could drive and be glad of his coming.

Bunn did not immediately reply. He pulled out his handkerchief and blew his nose as one overcome with emotion.

"Boys," he said, "I am deeply affected. You stir me to my heart's core. I will gladly avail myself of your offer.

"I have only to add," said Bunn, as he pulled out some of the straws in his hair, "that Royalty is expected by the Gimpson-Smiths to grace their festival. No less a person than his Royal Highness the Prince is expected in the neighbourhood. He will be driving to a ducal seat where he proposes staying for a few days to recruit his health. He has promised on his way to stop at Bolsover Court, the home of the Gimpson-Smiths, and partake of a glass of wine and a biscuit."

"It must be a great day for the Gimpson-Smiths," said Bob, as he turned aside and proceeded with his toilet.

He was getting chilly about the legs, having witnessed the horse-taming scene in his nightshirt.

CHAPTER CLXXXIII.

BOTCH ARRANGES FOR A BIG DAY.—THE COMING OF AGE IS NOT SO SUCCESSFUL AS THE GIMPSON-SMITHS COULD WISH.

WHEN Bob got to the farm,—it was but two minutes' walk—he found Botch with Don and Jack engaged in looking on at the milking.

Seventy cows were ranged along a shed of abnormal size, and half a dozen milkers, all men, were getting through their work with the expedition of experts.

Bob soon made his wishes known with regard to the coming of age, and Botch fell in with him before Don or Jack could speak.

"I want a day off," he said, " or a day on, whichever you considers it—and I'll take the lot of you in the waggonette. We can carry a few meat-pies to eat on the road, and a drop of something light, so that we are not too dry. What do you say, boys?"

Of course they were delighted, for it was certain, as they had not heard from Lingo, that they would be there yet another day. Anything that killed the time was acceptable.

Mrs. Botch never objected to her husband going out. She had given up that sort of thing long ago. Furthermore, she had a liking for "bossing the men," which she could only do in his absence, and the men preferred the master.

He was not half so strict, and had not so keen an eye to petty omissions.

So she raked out from the larder a big hamper of provisions, which proved to be acceptable not only as a relish on the way, but as something needed, notwithstanding the hospitality of the Gimpson-Smiths.

As there was a long way to go, Botch proposed to start at ten o'clock, although the festivities did not begin until two; his object being to give the roan mare a rest on the way.

A SPLENDID SCHOOL STORY.
NEVER BEFORE PUBLISHED.
By E. HARCOURT BURRAGE,
Author of "Ching Ching," "Monkey Mat and Roving Dick," "The Brave Boy of the Basilisk," &c.

THE LAMBS OF LITTLECOTE

NO. 26.   A KINDLE COLOURED PLATE PRESENTED WITH EVERY NUMBER.

Suddenly Penny Bunn was roused from rather dismal reflections by something cold touching his hand. He glanced downward and saw a small dog—"DOLPHUS." But was the dog alive?

 PRICE ONE PENNY.

Bunn, on receiving the intelligence, was once more overcome, and bemoaned the state of his eyes, which he declared, were not fit for society.

But Bob rose to the occasion.

He borrowed a box of water-colours from the landlord, which had been left by a travelling artist as a surety for a debt, and painted Bunn with the flakewhite round the eyes, until he was almost presentable.

It is true that the effect was somewhat ghastly, but, as Bunn said, "One had better look indisposed than present the appearance of a defeated prize-fighter."

Avoiding his wife meanwhile, he breakfasted in the coffee-room, and a little before ten o'clock started for the farm. Botch and his young guests were ready, and so was the roan mare. In the body of the waggonette was a huge hamper laden with provisions, sufficient for a troop of soldiers for the day. There were also certain strong waters and lemonade, and, in short, all the necessary things to make a happy day.

Botch and Bunn shook hands, the former regarding the eyes of the other with curiosity.

"You must have had a stiffish knock, sir," he said.

"Well, yes," said Bunn, assuming an indifferent air, "a tap of some magnitude it was, without a doubt; but to one who has so many hard knocks as I have received in the course of my life, nothing to howl about."

The two men sat in front, and the boys got in behind. There was just room for them with the hamper.

As they drove towards Malmesbury, they overtook many others on the way thither. They were mainly farmers and their families going to share in the merrymaking of the coming of age.

Occasionally they came upon a man on horseback, and some were making their way along on foot.

Botch knew them all and exchanged a word of greeting with each as he passed.

Penny Bunn, with arms folded, sat in dignified state, thereby conveying to the general public, or intending to do so, that he was in humble society, but not ashamed of it.

As they neared Malmesbury the road presented a thronged appearance, but the people, instead of going into the town, turned aside a short distance from it into a short by-way that led to the mansion of the Gimpson-Smiths.

Now indeed they came upon a scene of revelry, illustrative of the merriment of the olden time, and it was not altogether pretty.

Barrels of beer by the roadside look very well in a picture, so do the hearty old Englishmen in the picturesque attire of two hundred years ago jovially drinking therefrom, but in these modern days things are different.

Around the Gimpson-Smiths' barrels were as fine a collection of rustic ruffianism as ever got together; scrambling, wrangling, and even fighting for the beer.

And the man who got to the tap with a mug, though fortunate in some respects, was not allowed to hold his position in peace. He was pushed this way and that, and the beer spilled all over his clothes, insomuch that many there were not only soaked inside but outside also.

The air reeked with beer, and was cloudy with ruffianism.

"Well," said Jack Ford, as the waggonette slowly made its way through the noisy throng, "if this is the good old days, I, for one, am not sorry they are gone."

"Them chaps," said Botch, sententiously, "will be quiet enough afore dinner-time." Meaning thereby that they would render themselves speechless with the Gimpson-Smiths' beer.

At the top of the short road were the gates of the new park—good specimens of cheap modern ironwork. There was a lodge with a grinning rustic at its door, and inside the drive quite a jam of vehicles, and men and women on horseback.

"Really," said Bunn, "this is a lively spectacle. Right royally has the day begun."

"I s'pect the finish will be a job for the perlice," replied the matter-of-fact Botch.

It was indeed already a scene of confusion, for the originators of the festivity, while providing amply for the public in eating and drinking, had omitted to obtain a proper supply of men to preserve law and order.

One thing was certain, there was no stabling for the horses to speak of, and Botch, not caring to keep the roan about in such a crowd, decided to turn back and drive on to Malmesbury. There was, however, the encumbrance of the hamper.

"I think," said Bunn, "that the boys and myself can look after it. We had better convey it to a quiet corner of the park."

"If you can find one," said Jack Ford.

He stood up on the seat of the vehicle and looked around. Some distance away was a lake of fair magnitude, and on its shore a brand-new Swiss cottage, intended to serve as a boat-house. There did not seem to be many people in that region.

"We can take the hamper there," said Jack, "and perhaps, Mr. Botch, you will join us—or would you like some place nearer?"

"Anything is better than the stuffiness of this crowd. But, as I may be gone for a bit o' time looking for a crib for the mare, you had better not wait for me, but peg away at the luncheon."

They got out, and the hamper was removed from the vehicle. Nobody around thought anything of it, the general assumption being that it was something just arrived for the Gimpson-Smiths.

Nor was the conveying of it across the lower part of the grounds in front of the house observed. Everybody was occupied in looking after him or herself; for, judging by the crowd that was gathering fast, the Gimpson-Smiths must have provided sufficient for a besieged town, or somebody would go short.

On a terrace in front of the house there was a gay company of the select. Parsons, and small gentry, and country doctors, and provincial lawyers, and land-agents, all were there to do honour to the occasion, and give a hearty welcome to the expected Royalty.

Mr. Gimpson-Smith, a stout man with a pompous bearing, was moving here and there, supported by his son, a languid youth of the modern masher type. In front of the terrace a huge marquee was erected, with the Royal banner floating from the top.

It was within that tent a most gorgeous luncheon had been spread for certain guests, and it was hoped that his Royal Highness would condescend to enter therein and partake of something.

Every seat had been apportioned, and the names of the fortunate ones written on a card, so that there might be no mistake.

Never were preparations for a good old-fashioned day more complete, but over it all there was the glamour of vulgar ostentation.

The boys with Bunn conveyed the hamper to the Swiss cottage, and finding the door unlocked, boldly entered.

"In times of such abounding hospitality," said Bob Stockton, "one may take the slight liberty of intruding on a combined bath and boat-house."

CHAPTER CLXXXIV.

THE GLORIOUS DAY AND A GLORIOUS ROW.

THAT was exactly what it was—a combination of the two houses.

For bathing and other purposes there were three chambers, and at the end of the third a door opened on a flight of steps leading to the boats below.

For the sake of privacy the boys carried the hamper to the third room—they opened one upon another—and then had a peep at the boats below.

The water-shed was of considerable size, big enough to hold several rowing-boats, canoes, and a punt, perhaps.

There were, as a matter of fact, two rowing-boats and a canoe there, and Bob pointed out that a punt was probably out on the lake, for there were poles used for punting in a rack overhead.

This was not particularly interesting information,

but as it has a bearing on after-events of the day we give it here.

There were lounging-chairs and a table in the room, and many arrangements for the comfort of those using the place. Bunn volunteered to open the hamper and spread the festive board.

It was a task congenial to him, and he spent a pleasant quarter of an hour in artistically arranging the eatables and drinkables. The boys meanwhile had a look round the lake from one of the windows, and Don remarked that the punt Bob referred to was not in sight.

"It may be lying among the rushes along the bank," replied Bob, "but a punt there is, I'll take my davy. They use it for fishing, perhaps."

As Botch had desired them not to wait for him, they began luncheon and soon did ample justice to it. Just as they were finishing, Botch came in with face all aglow with the haste he had made.

"Boys," he said, "it will never do for us to mix up with that lot outside. Why, there will be a riot afore the day is out."

"How is that?" asked Bunn, as he cleared a place at the table for the farmer to sit at.

"Well," said Botch, helping himself liberally to meat-pie, "the lane is choked with parties the worse for beer, and the trains have brought in some hundreds of men from the Swindon works. There are roughs from London, too, I hear, and the park is a seething mass of humanity."

"There's a room upstairs," suggested Jack, "suppose we go up there and look at the fun?"

To get at the staircase they had to go to the outer room, and there they observed that Botch had taken the precaution to bar and lock the door.

From the outside there was a roaring of voices strongly suggestive of an angry sea.

"Something is moving," exclaimed Bob, as he bounded up the stairs.

The room above was without furniture. It contained nothing but a chest for keeping towels. Facing the park was a window wide enough for all the boys to see out of comfortably.

Bunn had not followed the youngsters. With an appetite stimulated to renewed exertions by the sight of Botch's vigorous attack on the pie, he had begun again, as he facetiously remarked, "To keep his host in countenance."

What a scene it was outside!

During the time the boys had been in the cottage the arrivals must have come in their hundreds.

The lawn was crowded with a host of men from town and country. The women and children were working their way out of the throng, finding the heat and crushing too much for them.

But the most observable thing was the apparent

animosity between the swells on the terrace and the mob on the lawn.

The latter were howling and calling out all sorts of offensive things, which the former pretended to hear with composure and proud disdain. Above all there was a cry for something to eat and drink.

Mr. Gimpson-Smith presently came forward and held up his hands for silence. He was dreadfully pale, and had to lean against the terrace rail for support.

There was a call for silence, and with the object of hearing something to their advantage, the crowd subsided into quietude.

"Friends!" roared out Mr. Gimpson-Smith, "I cannot lay tables for all comers. In the lane I had thirty barrels of beer——"

"It's all drunk or spilt!" yelled the crowd.

"And two cartloads of bread and cheese and sandwiches——"

"All eaten or throwed about!"

"That being the case," said Mr. Gimpson-Smith, loftily, "I can do no more for you!"

"Then we must do summat for ourselves!" yelled a stentorian voice. "At the tent, my lads!"

And they went for it—the royal refreshment tent with the royal banner floating over it—at the table laid out with all the elegance imaginable, and they scattered its contents in every direction.

The spirit of mischief was abroad. The mob had their appetites—an instinctive love of destruction—to assuage. As a preliminary, they assaulted the elegantly-attired waiters, and sent them flying for their lives.

Then they went for the good things upon the table.

Elegant dishes—pies, joints, *entrées*, all cold—bottles of wine, and the fittings and ornaments of the table, were caught up as in a whirlwind.

Huge grimy fists broke into the crowns of pies and tore out their toothsome contents; unwashed faces were buried in jellies; and joints were clawed asunder after the manner of wild beasts.

It was a pandemonium of revelry, and in the thick of it some malicious spirits cut the stays of the tent, and down it came upon the revellers within.

Of course, it was not likely to hurt them much, but when a man finds himself with a mob of people under heavily-pressing canvas, everybody struggling, kicking, and using the most explosive language, his sensations are inevitably the reverse of agreeable.

Outside, hundreds of lookers-on capered and screamed with delight. The guests on the terrace fled terrified into the house, and the doors were made fast.

"Well," said Bob, breathlessly, "if this isn't coming of age with a vengeance!"

"It is the result of trying to graft old customs upon modern times," said Jack; "but as a sample of manners, I must confess that it takes the cake."

At that moment several gentlemen on horseback came riding into the grounds before the house by a side and hitherto, as far as that day was concerned, unused bridle-path.

They reined up in the rear of the seething crowd, and gazed for a few moments with impassive faces upon the hideous spectacle.

Then one, who was foremost, motioned his desire to ride on, and the whole party rode forward, passing the boat-house, and disappearing by a path leading into a wood.

"I wonder who they were?" remarked Don.

"The foremost man was the Prince," replied Jack Ford, "and the others are noblemen, you can see by their bearing. You can see it was their intention to come along quietly, avoiding the crowd on the road."

"They little expected to find such a lively party here," said Tom Drummond.

"Disgusted with the row," said Bob, "they have ridden on, and unless the son and heir, for whom these festivities were arranged, has glimpsed him from the window, he will see nothing of royalty to-day."

And it may here be said that the royal party *was* seen from the house, and loud were the unavailing lamentations therein. Mr. Gimpson-Smith openly tore his hair, and young Gimpson-Smith swore almost as terribly as the "army did in Flanders," as we have been told on the authority of the immortal author of "Tristram Shandy."

CHAPTER CLXXXV.

THE USE MADE OF THE PUNT.

"IN course," said Botch, who had joined the boys with Bunn, "it is a very bad way to treat a man; but then, he brought it on himself. He wasn't satisfied to give a feed to his friends and neighbours, but must go in for getting the whole country here. They told me in Malmesbury that he had even advertised it in the papers, which ain't the way people of good breeding does things."

"It occurs to me," said Bunn, "that this is a festival that will be long remembered by the people hereabouts."

"You may bet on that," said Botch; "and look at the people now, still coming in. Blowed if I don't think they will go for the house next!"

There were some rough men indeed clamouring at the door, but, as no notice was taken of them, they soon desisted, and playfully broke a few windows with stones.

But now the more orderly element came awhile to the front, and there was a cry of "Shame!"

It was resented by some of the guilty ones, who struck inoffensive people standing near, and who had been taking no part in the proceedings beyond looking on.

Free fights soon became the order of the day, and defeated ones fled in every direction. The flower-beds were remorselessly trampled on for the next hour, and the proceedings were of a most riotous description.

Then half a dozen mounted police suddenly appeared, and the mob, with the usual courage of such assemblies, bolted away through every available opening.

In twenty minutes the lawn was clear of everything but the police and the wreckage.

"Justice prevails," said Bunn, as he lighted a cigar —one of his favourites, sometimes called by the scurrilous "cheap knock-outs."

"A few police on 'oss-back," said Botch, "can work wonders; but it's the 'osses as people thinks the most on."

"That matters not," rejoined Bunn, "so long as justice, as in the present case, is satisfied."

"Nobody seems to have been locked up," remarked Don.

"But somebody probably *will* be," drawled Bob.

They all looked at him. He was seated upon the towel-chest, swinging his legs to and fro.

"Come away from the window, all of you," he advised.

"Why?" asked Tom.

"Because," said Bob, "the police, if they find us here, will satisfy justice by locking us up as the least of all the offenders of to-day."

A general expression of dismay assented to this view. Now that Bob mentioned it they all saw it.

"Of course," said Bunn, "in a strictly legal sense, we are trespassers; but taking our social position——"

"We should get it hotter from the magistrates," said Botch, "who will tell us that we ought to have known better."

"It will be assumed," said Bob, who was well on the job of playing Job's comforter, "that, having assisted in working the ruin to be seen outside, we hid away here to escape the consequences."

"Suppose we go out at once in a casual way?" suggested Bunn.

"We ought to have done it before," said Jack.

He peered out of the window, keeping a distance from it.

"The police," he added, "are looking about among the shrubberies, and routing out all hiding there. By jingo! the boys are scuttling out like rabbits. There's a man—well-dressed, too. He can run. They are after him. Down he goes—they've got him!"

"If we kept quiet," said Bob, easily, "they may try the door of this caboose, but, on finding it fast, they will be satisfied. They will naturally think the family left it so."

"And how long are we to remain here?" asked Bunn.

"Until it is dark or the police go away."

"A lively look-out, truly!" said Bunn. "But I am a child of destiny, and with all my heart I yield myself to my fate. Everything in my life is wrong, and nothing matters. Mr. Botch, if you do not mind, I will step down and take a slight dose of refreshment."

They all went down, as the back room certainly seemed the safest place under the circumstances.

As the cottage was built over the terrace, the windows of this apartment were safe from spies without. Perhaps, if they kept quiet, they would not be discovered.

They kept very still for a time, merely exchanging an occasional word in whispers. Luckily, they had been careful in this respect, for presently the hoofs of a horse sounded outside, and the door was tried.

"Where is the key of this place?" demanded an authoritative voice.

"Master keeps it," answered a gruff speaker. Probably it was a keeper.

"What is it used for?"

"Bathin' and boatin'; nuthin' else."

The speakers passed on. Our friends breathed freely again. During the short colloquy they had held their breath.

"Once out of this," said Botch, "no more on it. All the chaps in creation may come o' age, and they will have to come it alone, for me."

He referred to his watch, and found that it was half-past four o'clock. There was yet a considerable time to the hour of darkness.

But there was no help for it. There they thought it would be wise to stay.

If discovered now, their guilty participation in the days' proceedings would be taken for granted. The hour to risk showing themselves was gone by. And, as Bob suggested, no doubt Mr. Gimpson-Smith would be glad to avail himself of the opportunity of avenging his social fall by taking a rise out of them.

They whiled away the time as well as they were able. Every now and then one of the boys crept upstairs and cautiously peeped outside. It was not until twilight had come that they were free of the police, who, in recognition of their services, were being hospitably entertained upon the lawn.

But at last they rode away, presuming that the neighbourhood was free of all dangerous characters.

"Now is our time," said Bunn. "If we leave this hut now, and assume the air of tourists——"

"Better ware until it's quite dark now," said Botch. "Another half-hour will do it."

They all assented to the proposition, and slowly the darkness came down. They waited in silence for it, and when they could only barely distinguish their outlines in the gloom, Botch was about to make the signal to start, when Jack said: "Hush!"

"What is it?" inquired Bunn.

"Be quiet, please," said Jack; "there is somebody on the lake in a boat. It is coming this way."

Thoughts of cunning police coming from the rear to arrest them flashed through the brains of all, for long waiting had in a measure unstrung their nerves. They were all as still as mice until Bob was heard to whisper:

"It's the punt. Can't you hear the pole bumping against the side as they draw it out?"

"Bob's got punt on the brain!" muttered Tom.

Jack asked all to keep quiet, and creeping up to the door, he opened it an inch or so. At the same moment the punt, with two men in it, glided under the boat-house.

One of the men had a dark-lantern with him, which he turned on and flashed about, but not upwards in the direction of the door; the punt came to the steps, where there were two posts; he made it fast. Jack was about to close the door and bolt it as a preliminary to escaping the other way, when a word from the man with the light checked him.

"Good!" he said; "we've done the trick so far."

Jack had been taking note of the appearance of the two men. One was a liveried servant, and the other wore the dress of a keeper. In his voice Jack recognised the gruff tones of the man who had been outside the other door with the police officer earlier in the day.

"How are we to get it away, do you think?" demanded the other.

"What's to stop us?"

"The perlice will be about all night lookin' arter suspicious characters. The country swarms with 'em, as I knew it would."

"And that is why you told me to shove all the plate into the punt by the willows as soon as old Plummer had cleaned it?"

"In course. It will soon be missed, and who will be suspected, do us think? Us? No. It will be laid at the door of one or more of that lot as has been here to-day. Well, we knows the boat-house won't be used, because the water is a bit too cold for 'em. So all we have to do is to sink the stuff here, under the steps, and fetch it when we can get it safe off."

"That's a good idea," assented the other. "You are a *cute* 'un, Barnes."

"I am as cute as most as is going," said Barnes, with a grin, "so you make a note on it, Pinks."

Jack carefully recorded the names of these two worthies in his mind, and watched them as they removed a sack, evidently filled with plate, and carefully tucked it under the steps out of sight, and, as he judged, in about three feet of water.

In the gloom of the covered waterway, even by day, it was not likely its presence would be suspected or detected.

"There!" said Barnes, with a grin, "there it is, carefully tucked in, just as if it wor a bed. Now, what does we do? Why, jest go out with the punt agin—shove it back among the willers, and use it agin when we wants to move the stuff. Coming of age! I reckon that old Gimpson-Smith will remember it as long as he lives. He's had a toughish time of it."

"Missus have been a-crying," said Pinks, "ever since the Prince cut off without coming in to see her."

"Serve her right!" said Barnes, disgusted; "wot's she got to do with princes? Now, I douses the light, and if you will ketch hold of that boat we'll work our way out and be off."

A minute later the precious pair were gone, and Jack, closing the door, said, softly:

"You hear what was said?"

"Every word," replied Botch. "The thieves!"

"There will doubtless be a reward for the stolen plate," said Bunn, "and as a source of revenue, or I may say income, a reward honestly earned is not objectionable."

"We ought to let them know about it at the house," said Botch.

"I don't agree with either of you," said Jack. "If you will take my advice——"

"It's took afore you utters it!" interposed Botch.

"If we go to the house," said Bunn, "I should certainly stipulate that we receive a reward before revealing the secret of the hidden treasure."

"We must have nothing to do with it," said Jack; "as far as we are concerned, myself and chums, we really have no time to waste hanging about here awaiting the trial of these rascals. I have a better plan in my mind."

"What is it?" asked Bunn, coldly.

"I will explain it when we get to Malmesbury," replied Jack. "Now I think we may start and take everything with us save the empty bottles."

Bunn still demurred. It was not in the course of common-sense or sound practice to throw away the chance of obtaining a well-earned reward. But Jack's views were acceptable to all the rest, and he had to bow to his decree.

They packed the hamper with the remnants, and as it was considerably lightened, it could be carried with ease.

Cautiously sallying forth, they found a bright, starlight night, and, unobserved, gained the highroad in safety.

"It was just as well we brought something with us," said Botch with a laugh, as he lighted a cigar, "otherwise we should have had to fight for it or starve."

"A coming of age in the olden times," said Bob, thoughtfully, "may have been a joyful thing, but in these modern times it has its drawbacks."

"It's all on account of them railways," said Botch: "they ruins everything."

The roan mare and the waggonette had found refuge at one of the Malmesbury inns, and while they were being got ready Jack wrote a letter to Mr. Gimpson-Smith, which he read to his companions.

"I regret to say that I am obliged to make it anonymous—a class of thing I object to," he said, "but in this case it is not malicious, and therefore pardonable."

The letter was as follows:

"A visitor to your place this day was a witness to the stowing away of certain property of yours in the water under the steps of the boat-house. The thieves are two of your servants, Barnes and Pinks. You will do well to set a watch and catch them in the act of removing it—which may not be attempted for a day or two—so that justice may be done to them. Business of a pressing nature is the reason for the writer not coming forward as a witness."

This letter was approved of by all except Bunn, who was still of opinion that it was a wicked, wanton waste of a good opportunity not to go for a reward.

The letter was, however, posted by Jack at the office in the town, and the party started gaily for home.

On the whole, now that it had ended happily, they thought the outing rather enjoyable than otherwise.

"I reckon," said Bob Stockton, "that it is about our last adventure hereabouts."

He was right. What else was to occur to them was of comparatively minor importance.

It was a jolly ride home, for the fragments of the feast and the remains of the wine and so on sufficed to satisfy their requirements.

About ten o'clock they arrived home, where they found Mrs. Botch looking out some old crape for mourning.

Wild stories of the riots at Bolsover Court had come to Smudgem Bender. Fifty people were reported slain, and the good woman had numbered her husband among them.

But, on the whole, she did not appear to very deeply lament his being still in the land of the living. She insisted on the boys having something hot for supper, and afterwards allowed Bunn and Botch to make merry until the small hours of the morning.

We may here state that Jack's letter secured the capture and conviction of the two thieves, who spent much of their time in prison in endeavouring to solve the problem of how they were found out.

And they never did it.

CHAPTER CLXXXVI.

A LETTER FROM LINGO.—AN INVITATION FROM SIR CHARLES BARSTOW.

BUNN went off next morning early to work another district. The two lovely black eyes which garnished his face, he hoped would be of considerable service to him, as he accounted for them by saying that a falling beam, as he was rescuing the pupils of his academy from their beds, had fallen on him. He had the gift of making some sort of capital of everything.

In the afternoon Lingo unexpectedly arrived. He found the boys in the village mooning about, having nothing to do. He came in a cab, in state.

"I am doing the toff," he said, as he shook hands with them, "because that noble old fellow, Sir Charles Starchback, has given me fifteen hundred pounds. Each of you boys are to have the same amount. In fact, it is lying at his banker's ready for you. You can tip your friends the story of the find now, if you like. Oh, and I almost forgot: Sir Charles is back at his house up Swindon way, and his wife having gone to Paris with some of her relatives for a week or so, he will be glad if we will all go to him for a change. He's got the lot of the armour home. Went down in the same train as it, and kept his eyes upon it until it was safely landed. He's got armour on the brain, bless him!"

The message was backed up with a short note from Sir Charles to Jack. The boys were to go on to Steepdene, his abode, in a day or two.

"And after that we make for home," said Jack. "What will you fellows do? We ought to have a long holiday together, especially as we can afford it."

"I shall not write home about my share of the lucre," said Don; "but just tell mother that I am going to spend a few days with a baronet. That will make her happy. I can save the chief joy until I get home."

"We had all better do the same," said Tom Drummond. "Fifteen hundred pounds! What a pile! But I suppose it will be invested, and all that sort of thing, for us, and we shall not be allowed to play highjinks with it."

"Quite right, too," said Lingo; "you will be glad of it when you are men. But you can stand out for a holiday. No reasonable parent would refuse you a few pounds for that."

Having written more letters home, and sent an acceptance of the invitation, with their thanks, to Sir Charles, the boys were about to go out for a stroll, when they saw Bunn coming down the village street.

He was not so buoyant as on the day before. His second attempt to collect funds for burnt-out pupils had not been entirely successful. He had met mostly with refusals, and at one house he had been detained as an impostor while a constable was being fetched.

It was only on his most fervent assurance that he was the real master of the Abbey that he was allowed to depart, and he was comforted with the promise that inquiries would promptly be made concerning him.

This was not exactly what he wanted. Inquiries could only lead to unpleasantness, and he was mentally arranging his future when he came upon the boys.

"Not gone!" he exclaimed. "I understood that this day I was to lose you all."

"We are going to-morrow," replied Jack. "Sir Charles Barstow has invited us to stay with him."

"Sir Charles Barstow!" Bunn's eyes loomed out of darkness around them.

"Yes," said Jack; "for a week or so."

"I suppose," murmured Bunn, "that he has not extended the invitation to *me?*"

"Not in the letter we received."

"Strange. But, of course, it was an oversight. Where is he staying?"

"At Steepdene—up Swindon way."

"Ah! just so," said Bunn. "And you go to-morrow; by an early train. I presume?"

"By the 11.40," said Jack.

Penny Bunn nodded pleasantly and strolled on to the "Cowley Arms." There was a cab at the door, and Susan was standing with a young man of the agricultural persuasion near it. The young man held in his arms a huge bundle, and there was a box at his feet. These were Susan's effects.

"Going away?" said Bunn, with his most gracious air.

"Yes, sir," answered Susan; "but this cab is for missus. She says she *won't* pay me my wages, and I'm going to see about that. She isn't going to have all her own way with me."

"Not a bit on it," said the young man, breathing hard, "and if you was a man *you* would pay up. It ain't much. Two-pun-ten."

"It is not much to the affluent, my friend," said Bunn, "but to a man just burnt out of house and home it is a small fortune. But Susan shall not depart without a drop of comfort. I will give her an I O U for the——"

"Blow your higher you!" said the young man, suddenly depositing the bundle on a seat near the door of the inn; "she is agoin' to have her money,

onless you wants your head knocked orf. I didn't quite favour the notion of her pitching inter missus, but seeing as you wasn't home, there warn't nought else to be done. Here, you pay up!"

"My friend," pleaded Bunn, "this violence——"

"I ain't begun yet," said the young man; "pay up or I'll have the werry clothes off your back!"

"Susan," urged Bunn, "I have been a kind master, and I ask if I am to be subjected to this sort of thing?"

Susan said nothing, and her young man began to show that he was on the warpath indeed, by putting up two huge fists, each about the size of an ordinary football.

Bunn hastily bade him follow him into the coffee-room, and he would see if he "had any change" in his pocket.

They retired together, and Susan waited quietly outside. She was a calm sort of girl, but she knew her rights, and could at a pinch stand up for them.

It was fully ten minutes ere her young man returned, and then there was a grin on his face.

"I've got it all but fourpence," he said. "Fust o' all, he wanted me to take a suvrin and a higher you for the rest. But I holds my fist close to his nose, and he brings out ten shillings more. He took a fearful hoath that he hadn't another penny about him, but I waggles this hand o' mine again, and he outs with some more. So I drawed him until I'd got all but fourpence, and he asked me to leave him that to carry him on to Chippenham, where he has friends who will help him to make a respectable living."

"Did he say that?" asked Susan.

"He did," answered her young man, "and then he kind o' snivelled, and said he was a horphan and everybody gave him knocks. So I comed away."

"We've got more than I ever expected," said Susan, "and I'm sure I wish nobody any harm, but if master don't come down to be a regular tramp and beggar, I shall be astonished."

As the pair vanished round a bend in the road Miriam and her aunt appeared outside the inn, dressed ready to depart. The man was not on the box, he having dropped into the tap-room for a drink while he waited.

Miriam glanced round, and not seeing anyone, exclaimed, "The girl is gone!"

"She was only bouncing," said Miss Astracan. "What an impudent lot they are!"

Bunn came gliding out of the inn. He had seen his wife come downstairs, and was inspired by another happy thought.

"Yes," he said, "Susan is gone. She asked me for her wages, saying that you would pay them when you came down. I borrowed the money from the landlord in your name——"

" You *liar !*" hissed Miriam ; and then she laughed harshly. " It was only right that you should part from me with a falsehood upon your lips. The landlord is *not at home !* I saw him go out with a friend an hour ago. Where is that driver ?"

" Here, mum," responded the man, as he came hurrying out of the inn.

" To Chippenham station," said Miriam, as she helped her aunt into the cab, " as quickly as you can."

Bunn put his hands into his pockets and smiled bitterly. Not another word, not even a look, came from his wife, and so they parted not to meet again for many a day.

Somehow Penny Bunn felt sorry that they had parted in this way, but he jingled his money and sought comfort from the music thus created.

" It will soon be time for me to go," he muttered, " but I must wait till night and steal away. I will leave an I O U for the landlord to meet my bill. I wish to part on good terms with the man."

When night came, and it was as dark as it would be, Penny Bunn ordered some drink to be brought to him in the cool of the evening, outside. He wished, he said, to enjoy the night air.

The time was come for him to depart. The letter to the landlord, with the I O U enclosed, was written and left upon the dressing-table upstairs. There was in it a promise to meet the I O U " at no distant date "—a vague time of payment which most people would demur to.

Bunn sat alone. The village was quiet, and nobody was abroad. The only sounds he heard came from the frequenters of the coffee-room and tap. Overhead there was a clear sky. It was a chilly night.

Suddenly Penny Bunn was roused from rather dismal reflections by something cold touching his hand.

He glanced downward and saw, by the light coming from the door of the inn, a small dog—*Dolphus !*

There was no other dog built on the same lines in Smudgem Bender, and probably not in the world, as Miriam's pet. *But was the dog alive ?*

Bunn could hardly credit the evidence of his senses, but, as the nose of Dolphus touched his hands again, he was convinced. By some miracle the animal had escaped from death ; probably it fell upon a tree and rolled from branch to branch, and so fell to the ground without breaking its neck.

And more, it was a changed dog. The spirit of hatred and defiance it had always shown towards Bunn was gone. He had by one act completely cowed it, and its eyes were raised to his pleadingly.

As he shifted, Dolphus retreated a step, and by his movements showed that he was lame. Penny Bunn felt his heart moved to the one thing left to him of all that he had known in the Abbey.

It is true that Dolphus was the last creature he would have originally thought of as deserving his care, but all things were changed.

" I am alone, old man," he said, tearfully ; " and you have lost your missus. Both are friendless and forlorn. If you like to go with me I'll do the best I can for you. I'm glad I haven't got your murder on my spirit. Come, Dolphus—come !"

He rose up, and softly stole away, with the dog limping behind him. That which he had most hated and despised was the only thing left to comfort him. What a strange world it is, and how things work round, to be sure !

Penny Bunn and Dolphus roaming the world together ! Marvellous !

CHAPTER CLXXXVII

WITH SIR CHARLES.—HARRY BARSTOW.

THE morning came, and the boys were packing up to start for Steepdene, when Gubbles unexpectedly arrived, and had an interview with Lingo.

The ex-tutor had been furnished with all the particulars of recent events, and he reproached himself for having gone away.

" I might have thought of the fellow hiding in the Abbey," he said.

" In Chunder Loo," replied Lingo, " you have no common rascal to deal with. When I think of the way he worked, exhibiting himself—but there ! what is the use of talking about it ? He did us all round."

" Do you think it possible he has gone to London now ?"

" I do. The very place for him. There is nothing to detain him here."

" Will you come back with me ? I suppose you know London well ?"

" Fairly well," said Lingo. " The shady parts of it, anyway."

" Perhaps we might unearth him," suggested Gubbles.

" We might, and we might not," returned Lingo. " If we don't, the police won't, because they can't. The boys are going to stay with Sir Charles Barstow."

Then he told Gubbles all about the confession Jack Ford had felt it necessary to make, and it gave Gubbles unqualified delight.

" Who would have thought that so much good would have come out of such a tangle of evil ?" he said.

When the boys assembled, an hour later, they were delighted to find their old friend had arrived. They all had a chop together, and as time was valuable to the men, they decided to go on to London in the train that was to take the boys to Swindon.

Botch dropped into the inn for a final good-bye, and the parting with him was quite affecting.

"I didn't understand you youngsters at the first," he said; "but then, you see, I never had any sons of my own, which I wish I had. I hope I shall see or hear from you some day. The place will be mighty dull now that the Abbey school is busted up. When I come to think of it, I see that it was the only bit of life in this dull hole. We are a slow lot hereabouts!"

As this was a fact that nobody could deny, they did not attempt to do so. The boys said they would certainly write and let him know how they were getting on, and if they ever again came within a moderate distance of Smudgem Bender, they'd assuredly pay him a visit.

Thus, with mutual good will, they parted, the waggonette of Botch being lent by him to convey them to the station. He could not drive them to the station himself, as he had an appointment with a man who wanted to buy some calves; and business was a thing Botch would not neglect for friend or foe.

As Sir Charles had been apprised by telegraph of the hour of their coming, he sent a carriage for the boys. It was accompanied by the fattest of coachmen and the most genteel of footmen, both of whom were condescendingly deferential to the four friends.

Lingo and Gubbles went on as arranged, and the carriage whirled away in a northward direction from the town.

A drive of three miles brought them to Steepdene. It was as the boys expected it would be, a mansion ripe with age.

Sir Charles would have pined and faded away in the most gorgeous modern structure.

The building was of the time of the Tudors, and stood back from the road in the heart of a park, rich with trees planted by men long since dust.

"It makes one feel quite old to look at it," said Bob Stockton, as the carriage rolled along the drive. "So far from the madding crowd's ignoble strife."

"Bob," said Tom, warningly, "don't fall away into poetry, for your head will not stand it."

"It really is a delightful old place," said Jack Ford. "I can hardly wonder if the owner of such a home does get what Lingo would call starch-backed. But in the pride of the true gentleman there is no arrogance, which cannot be said of some of the upstarts who get rich and live in big houses, nowadays."

The carriage drove up, and the footman leaped nimbly down to ring the bell, as if royalty had arrived. At least so it seemed to Don.

The oaken door swung open wide, and a hall porter was seen in all his majesty. Then another servant came out to take the luggage, and the boys entered the hall, rich with many trophies of war and the chase.

Yet another attendant ushered them into a room, whither Sir Charles presently came and gave them greeting.

"I am expecting my son to-day," he said; "until this morning I had no idea he was near home. He is passionately fond of the sea, and, although not yet two-and-twenty, has been twice round the world in his yacht.'"

"What a happy life he must have!" said Don.

"Up to the present," said Sir Charles, "I think he has walked in pleasant places; but I fear, from his telegram that something is wrong. He went away the last time with his friend Norton Truscott—they have been inseparables from boyhood, and he does not mention him. I have, however, ordered both their rooms to be prepared."

As they had lunched at the "Cowley Arms" they declined the baronet's offer of refreshment, and he bade them go out and look around the place.

"I have some letters to write," he said, "and an old man is no company for you. Pray consider yourselves entirely at home. The stables may interest you, and there is a boat on the lake."

They thanked him, and departed by way of a French window in the room, which opened on the terrace fronting the hall.

They went first to the stables, where they were taken in hand by the chief groom, a white-haired old man, almost as aristocratic in appearance as Sir Charles himself. He showed the boys horses that were fed and taken care of as if they had been human beings—better, indeed, than many human beings ever were or could hope to be.

Everything was wonderfully clean and in perfect order. A place for everything and everything in its place.

From there they went down to the lake, about two furlongs from the hall, where they discovered the boat-house without much trouble. It was big enough to contain half a dozen varieties of boats, small and big, and several canoes.

Jack said he could handle one of the latter, but they agreed to go together in a skiff built for double sculling.

Jack took stroke and Tom Drummond bow; Don and Bob sat in the stern, the latter handling the tiller-ropes.

"I call this real enjoyment," said Bob. "It would take very little more to make me feel like a sultan being rowed up the Bosphorus by galley-slaves."

"Bless your cheek!" growled Tom Drummond, who, not having handled an oar for a year or more, was really labouring at the work.

"For my part," said Jack, who was pulling easy,

"I feel as if I were giving two helpless duffers a treat. Trim the boat, Bob. If you can't do anything else you might sit straight."

It was good-humoured chaff, of course, and there was a lot of it as the boat glided here and there about the lake. It was so enjoyable that they had more than an hour of the quiet fun, and then were far from tired.

Once they thought they heard wheels in the avenue, but from where they were they could see neither the drive nor the chief entrance of the hall.

"It may be the son of Sir Charles," suggested Don.

And so it proved, for by-and-bye, as they were gliding along on the southern shore of the lake, where there was a belt of willow and larch trees, a young fellow suddenly appeared.

He was attired in a quiet tweed suit, but there was something in his bearing that proclaimed the sailor, and Don thought he was the handsomest fellow he had ever seen.

"How do you do?" he said, in a voice as clear and as musical as a bell. "Sir Charles has told me of your coming, and deputed to me the task, a pleasant one, of playing host. Shall I come into the boat, or are you tired of it?"

Jack said he supposed they had had enough of it, and proposed to row back to the boat-house.

"No; pull in here," said Harry Barstow—they soon learnt his name was Harry—"one of the men will see her, and put her up."

They got out, and fastened the painter to the roots of a tree upon the water's edge. Then he asked their names, and they were all on the best of terms right away.

Harry Barstow was, as we have said, a very handsome fellow, and he had all the amiability of his father, made still more delightful by the natural affability of youth. He was cheerful, too, but under his light way of speaking Don thought he saw a tinge of sadness. It was not long ere he enlightened them as to the cause of it.

"If at times you find me a little dull," he said, as they strolled through the belt of trees, "you must forgive me. I am not here on an ordinary visit home. I have lost a friend under very painful circumstances."

"Drowned?" said Jack, thinking of the sea.

"No," said Harry Barstow, thoughtfully, "and I do not believe he is dead, for reasons I can hardly explain to you now. You are almost too young to understand the depth of a strong friendship."

"We four are the closest friends," said Jack.

"No doubt," replied Harry Barstow, with a faint smile; "and your friendship is true. But the bud is not the ripened fruit. True friendship is not of mushroom growth. It must blossom, form into fruit, and ripen, as it only does with manhood, to be really known."

"And the blossom often gets nipped with the frost," said Don, softly.

"It does," said Harry Barstow. "Not one boyish friendship out of ten lasts through the time of probation, the years between fifteen and twenty. But Norton Truscott and myself grew up as one, with the same hopes, aspirations, and an undying love for and faith in each other. He has been taken from me, and I must endeavour to find him. That I cannot do unless I can go with a few brave men who can fight and a ship that shall at least be armed with sufficient guns to get on even terms with the proas of the traders of the Eastern Archipelago."

"I thought you were going to say pirates," said Jack.

"No," answered Harry Barstow, "the men-monsters who have spirited my friend away are something worse than the ordinary loafer and thief of the sea. It is not plunder they seek. But I will not say more to you now than that I am here to endeavour to induce Sir Charles to fit me out a smart little craft that will carry about thirty or forty men and a half-dozen small guns that can be used for shot or shell. The moment I can get on the kind side of him I shall be off to obtain the ship I want; and I think I know where it can be obtained."

"You have your crew, I suppose?" said Jack.

"No; I must look for the men as soon as I am ready to get afloat."

"I suppose that I am not old enough?"

Harry Barstow turned upon Jack with a look of surprise. He did not answer for the moment, and the boy hastened to add:

"I am as strong as many men, and I not a coward. As for going to school again I do not mean to do it. If you do not take me I shall try elsewhere."

"I should like to go, too," said Bob Stockton.

Don and Tom eagerly said the same thing, and Harry Barstow surveyed them each in turn with a growing appreciation.

"You are four likely-looking youngsters," he said, "and a year or two at sea would do you good; but I am going—if I can get my ship—upon a very perilous expedition."

"That is what we want," said Jack. "We are not softies. I am sure that if you will consent it can be arranged. We need not tell them at home that we are going to run any great risk, because I feel certain that with you we shall not come to any harm."

"You express great faith in me on a very short acquaintance," said Harry Barstow.

"I feel what I say," said Jack.

"Well, we shall see," said Harry Barstow. "When

I have had my answer from Sir Charles I shall be able to say more about it."

"I hope you do not mean that as a polite rejection," said Jack.

"By no means," was the smiling reply. "I know what some of the middies have done in the way of plucky fighting, and I am certain that what they have done you will, after a little training, be able to do. I like the notion of taking you; but I must think it over a bit. Five o'clock," he said, as an old timepiece in a tower of the hall solemnly boomed out the hour. "We do not dine until seven, so you had better come in and have a cup of tea."

CHAPTER CLXXXVIII.

A STIRRING TIME.—HEY! FOR A LIFE ON THE BRINY DEEP.

NEVER had four boys a happier time than those four or five days spent by the young visitors at Steepdene when Sir Charles was debating with himself the advisability of granting his son's request.

Fitting out a vessel such as he required was a very different affair from keeping the yacht in which Harry Barstow had hitherto enjoyed a life at sea; and there was also the nature of the expedition to be considered.

Harry was the sole heir, in direct descent from Sir Charles, to the estates, and if he lost his life there would practically be an end to the Barstows.

Per contra, there was the fact that he was bent on seeking his lost friend, who had been taken from him under startling circumstances, about which Harry was reticent to the boys, and to an extent, probably, to his father also.

Added to that there was the regard for Norton Truscott, which the baronet had always entertained, and he knew that unless he was restored to his son, thenceforth a shadow would rest on the life of Harry.

But Sir Charles was a man of method, and he would not give an answer until he had fully meditated on the subject.

Lady Barstow need not be consulted, as Harry, being the son of the baronet by a former wife, would not be likely to put up a barrier to the expedition, as his real mother might have done.

While the baronet considered, Harry took the visitors about here and there, so that they grew to know each other with an ever-increasing regard.

They told him, modestly enough, the story of the barring-out and all the subsequent events which attended their life at Littlecote Abbey, which entertained him vastly, and really created in his mind a fixed determination to take the boys with him, should the means for the expedition be supplied.

The upshot of the meditations of Sir Charles was that he decided to assent.

He had some idea of asking the Government to help with a gunboat, but, on naming it to Harry, he was speedily induced to change his mind.

"I shall be there and back," said Harry, "while the red-tapemongers of the Admiralty are corresponding with each other about what ought to be done."

"Then you must have your way, Harry," said Sir Charles, with a sigh. "Of course, after your return"— there was a slight huskiness in his voice as he spoke— "the vessel can be sold for something, and the expense will not be so great."

"I hope to make it pay for itself," said Harry, with a meaning smile.

"When will you be leaving?" asked the baronet.

"Moments are golden," replied Harry. "I ought to go at once to the Clyde. There is a craft building there and nearly complete, which ought to be the very thing I require. It was ordered by the Chilian Government, but I understand there is a hitch about the payment. I can, if I am smart, step in and secure it. Then I must look up the men, and fix on somebody to see to the stores. Finally, I can have a few more days at home, and then away."

"Very well, my son, so be it."

Harry lost no time in seeking the boys and telling them of his good fortune, as he termed it. Then came the question of their own.

"I will take you," he said, "if your friends consent. Leave it until you go home. There is time enough and to spare. Your outfit can be got together in a few hours. Give me your addresses, in case I wish to write to you."

They did so, and shortly after he left them in a state of bubbling excitement. One and all immediately fell into a flutter of fear as to the view their friends would take of the proposition.

"We can only stand out and vow we will run away and turn tramps if they at first refuse," said Bob.

"You would make a good sort of tramp," remarked Tom, sarcastically. "How would you get on when you had to bully women living in lonely houses? What would you do when you found children going on errands with money in their hands? Would you take it from them politely?"

"I shouldn't take it at all," replied Bob, "nor bully lonely women!"

"Then you would be a failure as a tramp," said Tom, emphatically; "they get their chief living from these sources."

Their stay at Steepdene soon came to an end, and when Sir Charles politely asked them to extend it to a few days longer, they told him of the arrangements they had made with his son.

He was astounded, but at the same time pleased.

"It is such boys as you," he said, "who make our nation what it is."

When the time came for parting, he presented each with a cheque for fifteen hundred pounds, their respective shares of the value of the old Abbey treasure.

"I have crossed them," he said, "and therefore they are not negotiable to a stranger. If you should lose one of them—boys are careless now and then—wire to me and I will stop it at the bank and send you another."

He was kind and thoughtful to them to the last, and they went away with a feeling that they had been in a better human atmosphere at the old hall than is to be found anywhere in the cold, hard world.

Jack and Don parted with Tom and Bob, who were going on to London. Tom lived north of the metropolis and Bob down Kensington way.

Jack Ford also might be considered a Londoner, but as his home lay on the south side, he elected to travel by the South-Eastern Railway from Reading, so as to accompany Don, who otherwise would travel alone. All but Don had wired to their respective friends to announce their coming home, Don wishing to give his mother a pleasant surprise.

"She will hardly know you," said Jack, as they journeyed on their way. "I never met with a fellow who grew so fast or changed—shall I, without being suspected of buttering you, say—for the better, as you have done."

"I feel years older," said Don, musingly, "and I think I know to whom I owe that change in me. You have an inspiring power about you, Jack, such as I never met with before."

"Well, I am glad to hear it," said Jack.

"I can hardly realise that we are going abroad," said Don, later on.

"You have quite made up your mind that you *are* going?" said Jack.

"Rather. Haven't you?"

"Of course. But there is somebody at home, you know."

"I always had my way, and I mean to have it now!"

"Don, you take a tip from me. Don't go on the old bouncing system. Be firm, if you like, but don't make a disturbance. I have no doubt that if you go the right way to work your father and mother will consent."

Jack was going on the further of the two, and they parted at Smallwell Station, with the usual promises to write as soon as possible.

Don left his luggage to be brought on by an outside porter, and sauntered in the direction of home.

He had not been away a year, and yet it seemed to him that the place was strangely altered. The streets did not not look so wide as they used to do, and the shops had a meaner appearance.

It was market day, and there was a lot of bustle in the thoroughfares, traps rushing here and there, and cattle and sheep on the way to the butchers' slaughter-houses, there to be turned into prime beef and mutton—a fact they seemed to have some inkling of by the way they objected to enter "their last home."

Don met two or three people he used to know in a casual way, but, instead of addressing him, they only stared in a doubting way and passed on.

"I must have grown and changed a lot," he murmured.

"Ah, there is the old shop," he said, a moment later, as he pulled up short and gazed at his unpretentious home.

That, too, seemed changed. There was certainly not so much ironware in the window, and what there was had a neglected, dusty appearance.

But perhaps it was nothing but his fancy, and putting on the air of casually dropping in, he entered the shop.

CHAPTER CLXXXIX.

IN THE NICK OF TIME.—GOOD LUCK ALL ROUND.

THERE were no customers in the shop, but Mrs. Peebles was behind the counter engaged in sorting out some small packages of screws and nails.

As his father was generally in the shop, Don was beginning to wonder if something was wrong. His mother, hearing his footsteps, looked up.

"What can I get for you, sir?" she said, in the old, wan, quiet, hopeless way.

"Nothing, thank you. None of your larks, mother. You *must* know me."

She grasped the counter, and for a moment it seemed as if she would faint; but as he nimbly leaped over the counter, she uttered a cry of joy and folded him in her arms.

"I didn't know you," she said—"so grown, and altered so much for the better. I thought it was one of the young gentlemen from the Manse. You are something like their eldest boy."

"I am like your boy, mother, and none other," said Don. "How's father?"

A sudden pallor came over her face, and the heart of Don stood still.

"Mother," he cried, "don't tell me he is *dead!*"

"No, no," she answered, "but he is poorly, worried, and is in bed. Don, my boy, it's a terrible thing, but you must know it. We have a bailiff in the house."

"Oh, indeed!" said Don, positively laughing, "and how much is he in for?"

"Fifty pounds, and we have hardly as many shillings to bless ourselves with. Trade has been so bad, and we can't get our money in. If we could, we might pay everybody and look for a place where there is a chance of a better trade."

"Look at that, mother!" said Don, hauling out his cheque and laying it on the counter. "Fifteen hundred pounds, payable to Donovan Peebles, Esquire—that's me—and signed by Sir Charles Barstow, who is good for half a million. Here, I'll pop this into the bank in father's name and they will let him draw out enough to settle half a dozen bailiffs. Who is the creditor?"

"A loan society," replied Mrs. Peebles, feebly; "we got twenty pounds to meet a bill, and they've run it up to fifty. But, Don, dear, you are sure that this cheque is real—it isn't a joke of yours? I don't mind it for myself, but it would kill your father."

"Mother," said Don, "I was a thoughtless, selfish cub when I left home, but I have had a lot of nonsense knocked out of me now, and I could not play a cruel joke on you to save my life. The money is all right, and it is all for you except a few pounds I shall want for my outfit. I will tell you about that by-and-bye. I'll run up and see father, and make him happy. You are sure there is nothing really bad the matter with him?"

"Nothing but low spirits, which don't kill people, or I should have died long ago. But I am not going to be low-spirited any more. Oh, my dear boy! I always said you would one day be a blessing to us, and that is what you are to us this day. I have been uncommonly cool to the bailiff, but the poor man can't help his being such a miserable sort of creature, and before he goes away he shall have a chop for tea."

Don knew his way upstairs, as a matter of course, and as he approached the staircase he had to pass through the parlour, where the bailiff—a dejected, mouldy specimen of his calling—was sitting mournfully by the window.

Don gave him good-day in a cheery voice, and he was too much surprised to respond. The boy bounded upstairs to his father's room, and knocked at the door.

"Come in!" responded a melancholy voice.

Don entered, and saw his father lying half-dressed upon the bed, weary of life, as most men are when things go hopelessly wrong with them in their affairs.

Over the interview between father and son we draw a veil. A quarter of an hour later they came down together. Peebles, senior, clothed and in his right mind, Don radiant with joy.

After embracing Mrs. Peebles, who had also become buoyant even to the borders of playfulness, they went out to interview the manager of the local bank, with such a satisfactory result that in half an hour the bailiff had departed from the house of Peebles.

In another hour a local printer had a bill ready to put into the window, informing the inhabitants that for the next three days there would be, in consequence of removal, a sale of the stock of the shop. No reasonable offer refused.

"It will pay all round, my dear," said Mr. Peebles, to his wife; "we shall get rid of a lot of useless rubbish, and the rest of the stock will go for more than it is worth. We can then take a rest, and look round for a more promising place of business."

That night Don told the full story of how he became possessed of the money, and the amazement of his parents was unbounded. Mrs. Peebles thought it "very wicked" of Lingo to go about as a parson when he wasn't one; but her husband assured her that he had just as much right, and perhaps a little more, to be considered a good Christian as many others who not only wore the clothes of the class, but preached every Sunday.

Then came the subject of Don's going abroad, and he led up to it with the skill of a diplomat.

First of all he dilated on the merits of Harry Barstow, and how well they had got on together. Then he went into the matter of the lost friend, and robbed the proposed expedition of its terrors by merely stating that they were "going to look for him."

"I suppose," said Mrs. Peebles, "that he is on some lonely island, like poor Robinson Crusoe, with only a parrot and a poor ignorant savage to talk to. I am afraid, Don, that you will be sea-sick. Your father is a very bad sailor. Do you remember, my dear, going out at Brighton in the 'Skylark' with sixty other poor creatures, and how bad you all were?"

Mr. Peebles, with a shudder, remembered.

"We started each other off," he said, "and there was no stopping us until we got to shore again. It was a lot of misery for a shilling."

Don said he was going in a bigger vessel, and the chances of sea-sickness were thereby much reduced. He could not, he said, if he suffered "ever so," go against such a good friend as Sir Charles. Besides, they were not going away for ever, but only for a few months—a year at the outside.

"It will do the boy good," said Mr. Peebles, "although we shall be sorry to part with him. A boy always tied to his mother's apron-strings rarely makes a man in the world."

"And he will be a hero in Smallwell, too," said Mrs. Peebles, after thinking the subject over. "That stuck-up Mrs. Roper, the butcher, had to send her boy on a common merchantman, and our Don is going in a pleasure-yacht with the son of a baronet. But suppose he gets wrecked in some lonely part of the sea, and have to live on an island? Mr. Crusoe was there more than twenty years."

"Ships were scarcer in these days," suggested Don. "In these days he would not be there two months."

He had won the day, and ere he went to bed he wrote a long letter to Jack, and a shorter one to each of his other friends, informing them that he "done the trick."

It seemed that they had also written to him that night, and on the following morning three letters arrived for him.

Jack Ford and Tom Drummond had made matters right, and Bob hoped to do so. His father, it seemed, was a bit of a fad in some things, and he was anxious to have Bob's chest sounded ere he allowed him to go to sea.

"And I have lungs like a blacksmith's bellows," Bob wrote; "but it seems that about the time of George the First, a member of our family died of consumption, and it is supposed to crop up sooner or later among us. If the doctor who supplies the pills and potions at home thinks he is going to find anything wrong with me, he will find himself up a tree."

With things in this happy state, Don went about the town, showing himself, as Bob would have said; and he was a bit of a hero there, for his mother had told of his coming home with a "small fortune" given to him by a baronet "for his good behaviour" in rescuing and taking care of a lot of treasure found in the Abbey. The public mind having giving itself up to speculating on the amount, magnified the sum into tens of thousands.

The reporter of a local paper interviewed Don, without results; then he fell upon the father, and failed there; but he got copy out of the mother, mostly irrelevant to the subject.

Smallwell was fairly in a ferment, and the rush to buy the stock in the shop of Peebles, senior, was prodigious.

A man in his position could afford to sell cheap, and no reasonable offer being refused, the stock of his shop went at highly remunerative prices.

CHAPTER CXC.

IS IT CHUNDER LOO?—THE "ALBATROSS."

WHILE things were thus moving on well with the boys, Lingo and Gubbles were at work in London, hoping to get some clue to the whereabouts of Chunder Loo.

Lingo was well up in the intricacies of the East-end, but all his inquiries there ended in nothing. He also sent flying messages among the showmen attending the various fairs, bidding them to keep a lookout for the Hindoo, and offering a reward of a hundred pounds for such information as should lead to his capture.

All this was done, and for a week there was no result.

Gubbles was staying at a quiet family hotel, where he was visited almost daily by Lingo, who was not staying anywhere in particular, but, like a bird on the wing, roamed here and there, searching for his lawful prey.

On the evening of the seventh day they were together, talking over their prospects of success, when one of the attendants brought in the evening paper and laid it on the table.

Gubbles took it up and glanced over the short leaderettes.

"On my word," he exclaimed, "these newspaper fellows find out everything!"

"What have they discovered now, sir?" asked Lingo—"nothing of interest to us?"

"Of interest, certainly, but not helpful. Listen.

"'The small cruiser built on the Clyde for the Chilian Government, and refused nominally by that Government, the real cause of non-delivery being the want of punctuality in payment, has been purchased by Sir Charles Barstow for his son, who is about to start on a third voyage round the world. As on a previous occasion Mr. Harry Barstow was attacked by savages and very nearly lost his life, he will now take with him means to protect his life and property. The gallant little craft has been named the 'Albatross,' and she will start in a day or two on a trial run to the Thames, where she will take in stores and a fitting crew, and proceed to sea.'

"Pretty accurate for a newspaper," muttered Gubbles. "Hallo! here is something else."

The paragraph that now caught his eye he read through two or three times ere he gave the nature of it to the wondering Lingo. Here it is:

"On board the P. and O. steamer the 'Rainbow,' which sailed two days ago, there was an Eastern magnate, who had been unostentatiously residing in this country for some time past. It is not exactly known who he is, for he travels strictly *incog.*, but it is known that he is connected with the Avishnus, or serpent worshippers, and is probably a high dignitary among them. The singular thing in connection with him is, that he is not going to India, but will be dropped at Malta. We are inclined to think that he is about to visit some of the islands of the Archipelago, where an offshoot of that race of worshippers has been settled for a century or more. The probability is that he is about to pay them a pastoral visit."

"What do you think of that?" asked Gubbles, breathlessly.

"It reads like Chunder Loo," replied Lingo, staring at the paper as if it had been an oracle and suddenly made some portentous announcement.

"Personally, I have no doubt it is the brute," said Gubbles: "if so, what a bold scoundrel he must be!"

"Can't we stop him with a wire to Malta?"

"We might stop this fellow if we could interest the

authorities, and make them believe as we do. But they will want strong evidence ere they move, and we have none to give. But we can follow on his track. Still, I must wait and know that Berry Mawston is safe."

"He's safe enough," said Lingo; "there isn't a feather-chance for him."

But Gubbles knew that in this life there are many slips between the cup and the lip, and nothing would have induced him to leave the country until the fate of one of the murderers of his friend had paid the penalty of his crime.

The time was not far distant, for Berry Mawston had been committed to take his trial at Devizes, and the assizes opened in a few days.

Gubbles and Lingo would be there, and if the case of the merchant failed to convict, he would be tried for the murder of Hone.

The chief thing against him was the confession of his son Mulberry, who had been placed under the care of a police-officer, who had instructions to keep him under close surveillance, or under lock and key.

The official thought that locking him up in an attic would suffice; but, a few days prior to the evening when Gubbles read out the two paragraphs as described above, it was discovered that Mulberry had got away.

He was locked up in the morning, after an hour's exercise, and at noon the officer took up his dinner.

He found the door of the attic open and the lock lying upon the floor. Mulberry, with the aid of a pocket-knife, had taken out the screws, and in the simplest manner possible set himself free.

The dismay of the force was almost ludicrous, and they kept the matter a secret as long as they could, quietly scouring the country in search of the missing boy.

But they never found him, and what became of him is a matter of the future.

Suffice it to say that he did not remain in England, and that the friend he flew to for help to get away was Chunder Loo.

When thieves are suddenly scattered by extra attention to their movements, they invariably have some place where they can find each other, just as people visiting a crowded resort arrange with their friends, if they should get separated, to meet here or there, as they may appoint.

That this was the case with Chunder Loo and Mulberry there was no doubt, and the pair succeeded in showing a clean pair of heels to those on the lookout for them.

Wherever they went to, we must leave them for the present, and turn our attention to the London Docks, where the "Albatross" in due time put in an appearance, with Harry Barstow, her builders, and a temporary crew on board.

She had been built as a steamer and sailing vessel combined, the latter being her most prominent feature, as it was expected she would mainly have to trust in canvas, and used steam only on special occasions.

Her burden was about eight hundred tons, but owing to her build, which was light in appearance, she would not have been credited with it by a casual observer.

On the way from the Clyde she had been tested as a steamer and a sailer, in both of which respects she gave the greatest satisfaction.

For her size she was undoubtedly one of the fastest vessels afloat.

Harry Barstow was, of course, commander; but he had secured through the firm of shipbuilders from whom he bought the "Albatross" two officers—first and second—respectively named Richard Darnley and Benjamin Walton, the former about twenty-eight years of age, and the other just on the wrong side of thirty.

There was also a very important assistant secured in the person of one Bill Oakley, to act as boatswain, as tough an old seaman as ever trod the deck of a ship.

He was empowered to get a crew together, as he was justly considered to be a good judge of the material that makes the right sort of men for an expedition which had the element of danger rather prominent in it.

"As there is to be good pay, good grub, and fust-rate officers, sir," he said to Harry Barstow, "I'll get the men. I suppose, sir, I'm also to engage sich persons as the fo'castle cook and a swab to help him?"

"Certainly," said Harry Barstow; "get what you think is requisite."

This arrangement was likely to affect the lives of more than one person already familiar objects in our story.

It was estimated that it would take a fortnight to put the finishing touches to the "Albatross" and get in her stores; and at the end of that period of time it was settled that she was to spread her wings over the sea.

————

CHAPTER CXCI.

PENNY BUNN IN LONDON.—HE MEETS WITH AN AGREE-
ABLE STRANGER.—THEY GET APPOINTED TO THE
"ALBATROSS."

THE exigencies of our story compel us to follow for a short space of time the fortunes of Penny Bunn, who, on leaving Snudgem Bender, made his way to London.

He took Dolphus with him, for the dog was a companion to him, almost miserably abject in its servility.

The arrogant spirit of the dog had been cowed on the night when Bunn hurled it into space. For the time, anyway, Dolphus had not the pluck to bark at a kitten.

So they came to town together, and the ex-schoolmaster, with nearly twenty pounds still left in his pocket—he carried it in a leathern purse—proceeded to enjoy himself a bit, prior to settling on a new line of business.

Dolphus had to be left at home and content himself with a morning and evening run. The broken creature did not demur to the arrangement by so much as a single bark or howl during the absence of his master.

Penny Bunn, parading the Strand one morning, with the air of a man who had come up to favour the metropolis by spending a few thousands of loose cash, stopped by the window of a filter-seller, to admire the glass swans going round a dish, and the cork balls bob up and down on the summit of a little fountain of pellucid water.

"Most ingenious arrangement that," said a voice in his ear.

He turned and saw at his elbow a young man in clerical attire, and of remarkably benevolent aspect.

"I suppose there is no trickery in it?" responded Bunn.

"None at all," was the cheerful rejoinder; "it is simply a matter of force and gravitation. Not but what there is a great deal of trickery in the world, especially in this mighty city. They call it the modern Babylon, but the original Babylon was a village to it. You have visited the ruins of that ancient place, I presume?"

"Well," said Bunn, immensely flattered at his being taken for an Eastern traveller, "I have not been quite so far. My duties as principal of a college compelled me to return home sooner than I wished."

"I have a sympathy for you, having once filled a similar post," said the stranger, "but I have been fortunate in being appointed to a rectorship of yonder church"—he pointed to St. Clement Danes with a smile—"the duties are light and the emoluments good. Would you like to look over the sacred building?"

"I think I should enjoy it immensely," answered Penny Bunn.

"The church is closed, but I have a private key," feeling in his pockets. "Dear me, how vexing! I have left it at home—most annoying, as I reside at Kensington. This weather is conducive to thirst. May I offer you, as a compensation for the disappointment I have caused by making you an offer I am unable to fulfil—may I offer you some refreshment?"

Bunn refusing refreshment would have been a phe-

nomenal thing, and he, as a matter of course, assented readily.

Then came the question of where they should go.

The clerical stranger could not, as he declared, be seen going into one of the public places in the Strand, and suggested they should walk as far as "a retired hostelry" he knew of, where privacy with the best whisky combined to amend for a somewhat dingy interior.

He led Bunn down through the Temple, across Blackfriars Bridge, and finally landed him in a doubtful-looking public-house in a back street.

It was, in all conscience, about as uninviting to a sensitive man as a public-house could possibly be.

The bar was divided into boxes with high partitions, and into one at the far end the clerical gentleman escorted Bunn.

"Here," he said, "we can have our refreshment in peace."

A flashy-looking girl served them with some liquor, and they got into conversation. Bunn naturally talked about himself, confining his statements entirely to the realms of fiction. In the midst of a glowing account of an entirely imaginary college which brought him in two thousand a year, a man entered the retired box.

He was attired in the apparel of a moderately well-to-do farmer or dealer, and his face was beaming with a satisfied but rather vacant expression.

"Marnin'," he said.

"I beg your pardon," said the clerical gentleman, "but this box is private."

"Beg pardon, zur," said the countryman, "but I be entirely abroad in this ere Lunnon. Blame it, I waddent ha' coom up if it ha'n't been to take a fortin as my brother left me in Australey."

"We have nothing to do with that," said the clerical gentleman, coldly.

"But I think you may ha' summat to do wi' it," said the countryman. "This 'ere brother o' mine leaves ten thousand, but two on it ha' got to be given to the desarvin' poor o' Lunnun; for Jim had rough times 'ere afore he went to Australey. But I doan't know the desarvin' poor, and I want to find someone as does, and can be trusted. I seed you coom in here, and thowt as you was two likely gentlemen to take a thousand apiece and do the wark for me, as I'm sick of this noise and bustle, and want to get back to the farm."

The clerical gentleman looked covertly at Bunn, and winked. Bunn felt a glow all over him. What if this flat consented to entrust him with a thousand pounds? He knew one deserving poor man who would make good use of it, and that was himself.

But he said nothing, as the clerical gentleman was leading up to the desired result.

A SPLENDID SCHOOL STORY.

NEVER BEFORE PUBLISHED.

By E. HARCOURT BURRAGE,

Author of "Ching Ching," "Monkey Mat and Roving Dick," "The Brave Boy of the Basilisk," &c.

THE LAMBS OF LITTLECOTE

E. COUCHENSPIDT

BUY AND READ

24 PAGES

THE CARFIELD BOYS JOURNAL

BLIND FROM BIRTH

SCREECHEMS PILLS 1ᴰ WEEKLY

A terribly sarcastic voice rang in his ear "What's your game, you hypocrite?" Opening his eyes Penny saw a stout, red-faced man in seedy nautical attire.

"If we consented to dispense this money in our names," he said, "when will it be ready?"

"I ha' got 'em here," answered the countryman, drawing out a roll of notes—"twenty on 'em for a hundred each. But I must fust know if *you* are honest enough to trust me. Let me walk out with that 'ere watch o' yourn for a minute."

The clerical gentleman not only trusted him with his watch, but his purse also.

The countryman went out, and returned in five minutes. During the interval, Bunn and his friend had another drink.

"You be honest as the sunlight," said the countryman, as he handed back the watch and purse, "and there be your thousand pounds."

He counted off ten of the notes in a careless way, rolled them up, and handed them to the clerical party, who favoured Bunn with a very sly wink as he put them into his pocket.

"Maybe you, sir, would take the rest?" said the countryman, to the perspiring Bunn.

"I shall be delighted, in the cause of charity, to accept your offer," replied Bunn, tremulously.

He had no watch, but there was the leathern purse, which the countryman was entrusted with, and he opened and counted the contents with the utmost *sang froid* before leaving—"just to make it clear that he handed every penny back." Then he went out, and the clerical party ordered another drink.

They waited ten, twenty, thirty minutes, and the countryman did not return. The clerical gentleman was certain he had lost his way or been taken ill, and suggested that he should go and look for him.

"I'll be back in a minute," he said, "and should he really have lost himself, I will share my thousand with you."

He vanished, and Bunn waited there alone, penniless and forlorn. Dark doubt began to hang over his head. But he could not at first believe that men could be so vile as to deceive and rob him.

Presently he asked the barmaid if she knew the clerical gentleman?

"Yes," she answered, curtly; "but I don't know any good of him. He ain't a clergyman at all. What's he been doing? Borrowing money of you?"

Penny Bunn, in a state of cold perspiration, told the story of the countryman and his fortune, and the girl laughed.

"You've been took in by confidence-trick men," she said, "and had better go to the police at once. Don't lose no time."

Bunn staggered out of the public-house, and having found a policeman, repeated his story. He was referred to the police-station, where he told it again, and the inspector made a note or two in a book, and told him to call in on the morrow.

He said he thought that Conky Smith and the Fibber had been working the oracle, but couldn't be sure. He would see into it.

Bunn went out blind, or nearly so, with misery.

On returning to the coffee-house he thought over his prospects, and hit upon a source of income.

The next day he was parading the Strand with Dolphus on a string, and a board attached to the lapel of his coat, on which was crudely inscribed the legend, "Blind from my birth."

The game paid.

In three hours he had quite a lump of coppers in his pocket, and having edged his way into a quiet street, he recovered his sight, put the board in his tail-coat pocket, and removed the string from the neck of Dolphus.

"I have found my vocation at last," he thought, as he counted the money in the secrecy of his meagre bedroom. "Eighteen-and-tenpence. I am a Rothschild from this hour."

Wisely he resolved to work in a new neighbourhood every day, and for a week he was in clover.

But one morning, as he was crawling down the Commercial Road—it was his first visit to the East-end—he was suddenly grasped by the arm, and a terribly familiar voice rang in his ear:

"What's your game, you hypocrite?"

Bunn nearly fainted away. But he was pushed up a court by his interlocutor, and then he opened his eyes. Before him stood a stout, red-faced man, in seedy nautical attire.

"Well," he said, in excellent spirits, "you are a nice young man. What put it into your head?"

"I am compelled temporarily to do this thing," replied Bunn, as he stowed his hoard away. "In a moment of folly I laid a wager with a friend that I would walk through London as a blind man."

"A big humbug you are, and I hate humbugs," said the other; "but let me tell you, young man, that you run the risk of getting six months as a himposter."

"Never!" exclaimed Bunn.

"It is true," said the other. "Now look here, my name's George Rammer, known in naval suckles as the 'Royal George,' owin' to my being none o' your common, low-born muck. I'm cook on a private cruiser, and I want a mate. What do you say to going to sea for a bit?"

"In what capacity?" asked Bunn.

"As my assistant," replied Rammer.

And then he told Bunn how he had seen an account of the arrival of the "Albatross" in the docks, and being on the lookout for a berth to hide a month or two, he went down to see her. There he tumbled over Oakley, the boatswain, who asked him if he could cook. He jumped at the idea, and engaged himself at once. He was left to choose his own assistant.

No. 26.

"I believe," said Rammer, "that the 'Albatross' is agoing out to seek for a lost treasure. If so, we shall get a bit. Will you come with me?"

It was tempting. Walking about the streets with his eyes shut, or nearly so, was getting monotonous, and then there was the risk of getting into prison. Finally, the prospect of sharing in a treasure was to be thought of, and in five minutes Bunn had consented to join the "Albatross."

No two men could be more opposite in character, but, strange to say, both were pleased at having met, to such sore straits does loneliness—and both were lonely, and there is no loneliness like being without a friend in a great city—drive a man.

There was one thing neither of them knew, and that was the arrangement made by Harry Barstow to take four boys with him.

Bunn did not for a moment fancy that though the captain of the "Albatross" was the son of his old landlord, he would so much as know his name.

Had he dreamt that he would again be thrown into the society of the four Littlecote Lambs, the "Albatross" would have had to look elsewhere for a cook's assistant.

But it was destined that he was to go abroad, and that night Bunn settled the matter with Oakley, to whom he was introduced by Rammer.

The canine recruit was to be smuggled in secretly, as Rammer had doubts if Oakley would allow him to come on board.

"But when we gets afloat," he said to Bunn, "and the dog is discovered, he must allow him to stop or chuck him overboard."

CHAPTER CXCII.

BERRY MAWSTON TRIED.

THE day of the trial of Berry Mawston fell within the fortnight that elapsed before the appointed time for the sailing of the "Albatross."

Although the trial for the original murder did not personally affect Jack Ford and his friends, they had to be in the court in case they should be wanted on a further charge.

No matter how base a man may be, there is something pitiable in his standing in the dock on a charge that is leading him to an ignominious death.

The thought that, vile as he had proved to be, he was once a babe in arms, nursed and caressed by a loving mother, who perchance had high hopes of his future, and now all her dreams, as his life, were to end on the scaffold, is extremely painful.

Only the vilest nature could find a pleasure in such a scene.

Berry Mawston, humanely speaking, did not deserve

mercy, and he got none. The evidence of his guilt was sufficiently clear to enable a jury to return a verdict of guilty.

"Prisoner at the bar," said the judge, "have you anything to say why the sentence of death should not be passed upon you?"

Then the despairing man denied his guilt.

"It was not I, but Chunder Loo, who killed him," he cried. "It was arranged that he should be drugged and robbed. I was always against the murder. But Chunder said that Mehala, his serpent, had declared that without murder there would be no success, and the man must die. It was Chunder who slew him."

The judge, in passing sentence, pointed out that the excuses of the prisoner condemned him as an accessory. He would therefore have to be taken back to the place from whence he came, and from thence taken to the scaffold, where he would be hanged by the neck until he was dead, and might Heaven have mercy on his soul!

No hope of mercy from earthly authority was held out to him. He was led from the dock, to expiate his sins ere long upon the scaffold.

His case was made memorable from the fact that nobody—not even the knock-kneed sentimentalists who take no interest in the better classes, but give all their tender sympathies to vice—moved to save him from his doom.

After the trial Lingo and Gubbles promptly returned to town.

"I have never been in such a scene before," said Jack Ford, as they left the court and got into a cab that was to convey them to the station, "and I hope I shall never be in it again."

"He is a clever man," said Don, "and might have been rich and prosperous if he had gone the right way."

"To go right—to do right, without cant or humbug," said Jack Ford, "is the way to live. The rest we must leave. Boys, I am sick of this part of the world. I long for the pure air of the sea."

"So do I," rejoined Bob Stockton. "Our family doctor, having found that I have the chest of a grampus, has kindly given a certificate to the effect that I may try the sea and see how I like it. Bless him for a learned booby, what a rigmarole he made of it!"

"I was afraid at one time," said Don, "that you would not have gone with us."

"I would have gone with you," fervently replied Bob, "if I had to be hooped up in a barrel and labelled 'Pickled Pork.'"

"'Preserved Gentility' would have been a more appropriate label," murmured Tom Drummond.

Bob aimed a playful blow at him, and then they adjourned to an adjacent hotel for a late dinner.

CHAPTER CXCIII.

THE SAILING OF THE " ALBATROSS."

HARRY BARSTOW, not being personally concerned in the trial of Mawston, was not in the court. He was engaged in town in seeing to the fitting up and taking in the stores of the "Albatross."

Nor was it to be expected that he would feel concerned in the disappearance of Mulberry Cork, which was, however, a matter of strong interest to the four boys who were going with him.

Jack Ford was of opinion that they had not seen the last of him, but how and when and where they were to meet him again he could not tell.

"I have read somewhere," he said, " that there are certain lives linked together until one comes to an end. There are links of hatred as well as friendship, and Mulberry is one with whom I could never be friends."

"He was a beastly vulgar fellow," remarked Bob, as he held out his plate for another chop. Tom, who was presiding, gave him one, as he remarked :

"Vulgar, but not a fool. I have a belief that there is a lot in Mulberry."

"Of the wrong sort of stuff," said Don.

"Just so : but there is talent of the wrong as well as of the right."

"Let us change the subject for a moment," said Jack. "I learn from our noble captain, as they would call him in the play, that the sooner we are on board the 'Albatross' the better, as we ought to be acquiring a technical knowledge of the rig of a ship. Then we have a lot to learn in the way of the use of arms. He makes no secret of the possibility of our being called on to fight. The 'Albatross' is, in short, a miniature man-of-war, and we are the middies."

"I can turn up in two days," said Don, "and I could have been there sooner, but I did not think we should be wanted, but I promised to have a short time with the mater. She is dead certain that I shall be wrecked on an island. I suggested that I should take a parrot with me, so as to have a companion like dear old Crusoe. Of course, it was a joke."

"A poor one," said Bob.

"Yes, but my own," returned Don. "It fell flat. My dear mother took it seriously, and she would see if one could be got in Smallwell. Luckily there were none for sale."

"Well," said Jack, "can you all be on board in two days' time ?"

They thought they could, and Jack wrote before he left the hotel to Harry Barstow to that effect. An hour afterwards they were all bound for their respective homes—light of heart enough, and little dreaming how long it would be when they went away ere they saw their friends again.

Meanwhile Bunn had, as stated, succeeded in getting appointed by Bill Oakley to the "Albatross." He had no idea of the nature of the duties he would be called on to perform, but it was part of his nature to do all that he undertook in a thoroughgoing fashion.

Having a little spare money, he bought himself a seaman's rig-out of the old school, more worn by the typical pirate than honest-going sailors.

It was, in fact, a rig-out that had been worn in some private theatricals and been sold cheap to a dealer, who assured Bunn that it was the latest fashion of the service.

It consisted of a striped stocking-cap, a short blue jacket with brass buttons as big as the old crown-pieces, a striped jersey, and trousers big enough to ramble about in.

Thus attired, he created a sensation as he wended his way with Rammer through the intricacies of the docks on the way to the "Albatross."

The latter carried Dolphus in a fish-basket, for it was necessary that the dear dog should be smuggled on board. He with Bunn was asked all sorts of pertinent and impertinent questions as they ambled along.

One man wanted to know "who let 'em loose," and why their keeper "didn't stick to 'em ?" Another asked Bunn why he wasn't hung for mutinying off the Nore? A third offered to fight him for a fool; and so they went on, Rammer contenting himself with scowling at the querists, and Penny Bunn charmed with the sensation he was undoubtedly creating.

They found the "Albatross" with her deck in all the confusion of preparation for sea. Boxes and bales lay about in apparent hopeless confusion ; a seaman, urged on by the stentorian tones of Bill Oakley, moved briskly about, evolving order out of disorder.

Harry Barstow was standing aft in conversation with Darnley, his first officer—a smart-looking fellow with a bright pair of eyes and a resolute mouth.

Neither of them espied the pair that had just come aboard, but the watchful Bill Oakley observed them instantly.

Rammer he knew, but Bunn at the outset he failed to recognise, having only seen him once before.

"Well," said the bo'sun, after a long stare at Bunn, who smiled sweetly upon him, " where the blankity did you come from ?"

"Come aboard, your honour, according to orders," replied Bunn, hitching up his trousers and affecting the free-and-easy air of a thorough old salt.

"Oh!" said Bill, " I see who you are now. Well, where did you get that blankity-blankity rig-out from ? Who's been making a rampageous fool of you ?"

Bunn explained that he had bought a suit so as to have apparel in harmony with his duties on board.

"You will know more about your duties by-and-bye," returned Bill. "Meanwhile, young man, you get below down the fore-companion, and I'll send something for you to wear."

"My dear sir——" began Bunn, but he was cut short by being twisted round and favoured with a kick of undoubted power and precision.

"No argument," said Bill, "is allowed to swabs here. What the blankity next? Perhaps you would like to order me about? As for that infarnal toggery, you keep it till you go a-courting some blind gal ashore. Down you go!"

Rammer had already vanished, and Bunn, with a sensation that a sea life was not all tobacco and jars of honey, limped down the companion.

"Scuttle my hold!" muttered Bill, as he returned to his duties, "if I don't think I've shipped a rum 'un. But if I can't shape him into something, my name isn't Oakley."

Rammer and Bunn were below for about ten minutes, discussing the probabilities of their life on board, when a sailor came down with a pair of canvas suits, which he tossed at their feet.

"Shove your carcases into them things." he said, "and come on deck to bear a hand with the stowing."

There was nothing fancy in the make of the apparel provided, each garment being distinguished by a simplicity of cut that would have made the hair of a masher fly off his head and leave him prematurely bald; but the two recipients had nothing else to do but to attire themselves therein and go upon deck.

There Bill set them to work "bearing a hand," and if we had time and space, we would gladly put on record all they went through with during the next four or five hours.

Rammer worked in a slow, sulky fashion; but Bunn, feeling that he ought to do something towards his being eventually promoted to the command of the "Albatross," threw any amount of enthusiasm into his labour, that caused him to collide with other men, to drop parcels and packages, and in a general way to richly earn the florid epithets and the occasional kicks, more demonstrative than really painful, which Bill Oakley bestowed upon him.

By the evening the deck was clear, and the cleaning of it up was carried on by the light of a full moon. Bunn wielded a mop, and upset buckets, and splashed himself all over, and daubed himself with tar, until he was in personal appearance qualified for an engagement as stoker at a gasworks.

At a late hour he and Rammer were allowed to retire for supper—wonderfully plentiful and good when compared with the food generally served on board. and having eaten their fill, they retired and slept as if they never intended to waken more.

Rammer had a cook's cuddy under the fore-deck, to the care of which he was appointed on the following morning. Having been a showman and a wanderer in his time, he knew something about plain-cooking and was so far at home.

Bunn was taken away by Oakley for some brass polishing on deck, and it was about noon when he staggered into the cuddy and sank upon a tub of fat pork, which his old master was about to open.

"Rammer," he said, "we are in for it!"

"That's news," sneered Rammer. "I should like to know how long it isn't since I was not in for something or t'other."

"You don't understand," said Penny Bunn, smearing his face with a polishing rag, until he had spread the dirt well over it, unintentionally making a mulatto of himself. "Who do you think has come on board?"

"The mayor of London, or a beadle, perhaps."

"Worse than all the beadles and mayors that ever lived. It is four boys—Ford, Peebles, Stockton, and Drummond, the biggest little imps in creation!"

"Good ivens!" exclaimed Rammer. "What are they doing here? Looking over the ship?"

"No," said Bunn, in accents of an overwhelming despair, "they have come to stay! They are going with us! At this moment their traps are being taken down to a fore cabin they are to occupy together, and the captain has invited them in the most friendly manner to partake of refreshments in his own cabin."

"Boys," said Rammer, "are rat-pison to me. We must get out of this."

"We must—but how?"

"As soon as it is dark we must sneak off and run for it."

"I am with you, Rammer. It will be impossible for us to remain here without being subjected to all sorts of things calculated to drive a sensitive man mad."

When the night was drawing nigh the tide was on the ebb, and served for outgoing ships. The "Albatross" was ready, and the tug engaged to take her down to the broader reaches of the Thames.

At half-past seven the dock gates swung open, the hawser of the tug lying just outside was taken on board and made fast. Then the gallant little craft was drawn out into mid-stream.

The idea of flight was hopeless now. In the cuddy two men sat upon empty boxes and exchanged glances of despair. For good or ill their lot was now cast in with the "Albatross."

An inkling that the vessel was bound on some secret mission had got abroad, and there was a considerable number of spectators on the shore and in boats, to see her depart. As she glided down stream they gave a hearty cheer.

The boys and the officers and all the crew were on deck, and they responded with a will. It stirred the blood of the youngsters, flushing their cheeks and brightening their eyes.

" This is really a beginning of life," said Jack Ford.

" A new life with a glorious outcome, let us hope," said Don.

As they passed Blackwall there was a loud shouting from the pier, and Don, gazing in that direction, saw his father and mother, who had, unknown to him, come so far to get a last glimpse of their darling boy.

He sprang into the ratlines and waved his cap as long as they were in sight. But the bend of the river speedily hid them from view.

Then he jumped down to the deck, and Bob Stockton saw that there were tears in his eyes.

" I'm not blubbering because I am leaving them for a time, but as I stood up there a sudden feeling came over me that I was taking a final leave of them."

" Which you are not doing, of course," replied Bob, cheerily.

But Don made no rejoinder. For the time there was a sadness on him that would not be driven away until they were passing Greenwich, and the moon was in the sky.

Then he rallied, and joined his friends in commenting on the delights of the trip down the river.

Presently the tug cast off, and, with a favouring wind almost astern, the "Albatross" went alone on her way.

All on board were very quiet—thinking of home, it might be. By the man at the wheel, Harry Barstow was pacing to and fro, with his gaze fixed ahead, as if he saw in the sombre horizon something of the end of the voyage.

On, on, down the noble river, past Tilbury Fort and other well-known places. Half an hour after midnight they glided by Southend and headed for the Nore, famous or infamous for the mutiny of Parker and his misguided followers.

Here the "Albatross" fell in with a pilot engaged to take her down the Channel. He was in a boat that drew up and received a rope cast from the "Albatross," and in a minute he was on board.

The rope was loosened and the boat headed for the shore.

The pilot took command, and his voice was heard for a time giving orders for an additional spread of canvas, until it was like a huge cloud overhead, and the vessel speeding on, dashing the spray from her bows.

The land was left behind, and the only indication of its presence was the line of lights twinkling like stars resting on the horizon.

All this time the boys had kept on deck, but now a voice was heard calling on them to go below.

It came from Harry Barstow, who said :

" There is nothing more to see, my lads, and it is time to turn in."

They bade him good-night, and descended the companion to the cabin in which their hammocks had been slung ready for their use.

" To-morrow," said Jack Ford, " when we awake we shall be upon the open sea."

" It is all so new and so very delightful," murmured Don.

They were tired, for the day had been a fatiguing one, and they were soon in their hammocks. For a while they continued to talk softly, and then one by one they were silent in sleep.

So through the night the "Albatross" bore them away towards scenes that were new, and to places in which they were to find peril and go through adventures that would tax the courage for which they had already so justly earned a name.

CHAPTER CXCIV.

AMONG THE HUNDRED ISLANDS.—THE MISSING YOUTHS.

" I DON'T know as ever I felt it so eternally hot!"

" Yes, indeed, the air may be considered to be overcharged with caloric."

The speakers were George Rammer, cook of the "Albatross," private cruiser, and Penny Bunn, his assistant, and, as he was sarcastically called on account of his comparative uselessness, "general utility man of the vessel."

Around them, viewed from the fore-deck on which they stood, shaded by an awning, was a glorious expanse of the bluest sea, dotted all over with islands of various sizes. Some were mere specks in the distance, others of fantastic form, that gave them the appearance of antediluvian monsters reposing on the waters, and a few assumed dimensions of considerable importance, notably one near which the "Albatross" lay at anchor.

To all outward appearance she was a peaceful pleasure craft, a yacht of extra size, such as many millionaires of the day travel in. She was fitted to steam or sail, but her two funnels were smokeless, and every stitch of canvas was furled.

It was high noon, and not a breath of wind was stirring. It was indeed as hot a day as they ever get in one of the warmest quarters of the earth or sea, for the "Albatross" was anchored in the almost untraversed portion of the Indian Ocean that lies four hundred miles south of Socotra.

"Overcharged with cholic," said Rammer; "then Heaven have mercy on us, for down here it's bound to dewelop into cholera morpus."

"I fear," said Penny Bunn, "that you do not understand me. There's a wide gulf between caloric and cholic."

"What's the differs?" curtly asked Rammer.

"Caloric," explained Bunn, "is heat. Cholic is pain."

"Well," said Rammer, "if ever you gets cholic you will find it warm enough, so there ain't any differs arter all. But it's like you cutting in with your would knows when they ain't wanted."

"Kick him overboard!" growled somebody hard by.

This recommendation came from a huge, thickset sailor, lying upon his back in the scuppers, with his head resting on his hands. He was a dark man, with a strong but close-cut beard, a nose like the beak of an eagle, and two close-set, dark eyes.

"Your one panacea for the ills of life," remarked Penny Bunn, with his nose in the air, "appears to me to be the violent and unjustifiable use of your pedal extremities. I am disgusted with you, Mr. Matthews!"

"My name is Dirk Matthews," said the sailor, "and I am Dirk to them as loves me. So don't mister me, if you please."

"Dirk to those who love you," said Penny Bunn, in a musing tone. "Ahem!"

The "ahem" was a cough of doubt implying that those who loved Dirk Matthews were few and far between, if they existed at all.

So it was taken by the seaman, who made as if he would rise, muttering:

"Blamed if I don't shoeleather you up to the stars, you *worm!*"

"Shut up, Dirk," advised a seaman, squatting on his haunches on the opposite side of the vessel. "Are you going to fire lead at a fly?"

"I'm sick of it," answered Dirk. "Look at him. Got up as if he was aboard a man-o'-war, and chief gunner there, and yet the warmint is only a cook's scab, and that cook none of the best. Got bust up in a cheap beef-shop, I reckon, and so was drove aboard for a livin'."

This reflection on the qualifications of Rammer for his post raised his ire. He walked up to Dirk Matthews, who had stretched himself out again. He exhibited a slight limp in his gait, and when he stopped there was a curious little jerky movement, as if he had put the break on somewhere.

"You talk to me in that way!" he said. "Me, as have been afloat from my birth, being born on one of the finest ships afloat——"

"Give her a name," growled Dirk Matthews.

"I decline to do so!" answered Rammer, standing very straight and stiff. "It's enough for me that, through my birth and my long service at sea, I've been knowed as the Royal George all my born days."

"You was born on the 'Royal George,' perhaps?" sneered Dirk Matthews.

"Maybe I was," replied Rammer, in a manner that implied an affirmative.

"Good heavens!" exclaimed Dirk Matthews. "Out of my way, or, I must git up a——"

He finished the sentence with the dumb motion of lifting his foot, and Rammer was about to ask him to carry out his threat, when, casting his eyes aft, he saw the young captain of the "Albatross," Harry Barstow, come up from below.

There was an awning aft, under which he stood. In the shade cast by the vertical sun, his slim, handsome figure and white clothing stood out like a being of light. Silence fell on the wranglers forward. Rammer, with a cautious gliding motion, shifted to the side of Penny Bunn, and the pair stood together with their eyes on their commander.

There were several of the seamen lying about, and it seemed as if they were instinctively aware of the coming of their captain on deck, for, one after the other, in quick succession, they got swiftly on their feet. All but Dirk Matthews, who, like a gun that hangs fire, did not rise until some moments after the rest.

And then he did it in a sullen, resentful way, as one who was inclined to dispute both influence and authority.

Harry Barstow just glanced at the men, and then turned his eyes to the shore of the island by which the "Albatross" lay.

It was a beautiful spot, a gem of the sea, rich with tropical foliage and swelling hills, with a belt of sand that glistened as gold in the sunlight. On the beach, in a line with the "Albatross," was a boat, and a few yards from the slowly-heaving sea, sat two men under the shade of a low-growing tree, with huge, down-hanging leaves.

After a while, the young captain of the "Albatross" turned round, and twice struck a small spring-bell fixed near the binnacle. It gave out a curiously-clear yet unaggressive sound.

In response, Bill Oakley came hurrying up from the fore-cabin, and presented himself before his captain, with an old-fashioned salute.

"Oakley," said Harry Barstow, "it is time the party of survey returned."

"Much the same thought was in my own 'ed, sir," answered Oakley, "seeing as your orders was to get back afore noon."

"Ask Mr. Darnley to step up to me," said Harry Barstow.

Oakley vanished down the aft companion, and in a minute, Dick Darnley, first officer of the "Albatross," aged twenty-eight, and as good a seaman and fellow as ever drew breath, came bounding to the deck.

"Darnley," said Harry Barstow, "the boat is still on the beach, waiting for Walton and the boys. Something must have gone wrong with them. My orders were explicit. Go as far as the first line of hills, take a survey of the island, and be back before noon."

"And it isn't like Walton to exceed orders," said Darnley; "he is comparatively such a steady old file. Quite a Methusaleh of thirty-three years."

A faint smile just stirred the upper lip of the captain. Bill Oakley, as an inferior, did not show any sign that he heard what was said.

"Dick," said Harry Barstow, "it's cruel work to send out the men at this hour—at least before they are seasoned to this climate—but I am uneasy. I don't understand why there should be any delay. Will you mind going ashore in the gig? Take half a dozen men with you and have a look round. But don't go too far inland."

"I will go with pleasure," replied Darnley.

A sign to Oakley sufficed, and the old boatswain walked forward, singing out, "Lower the gig there. Smart and lively, every mother's son of you! Half the morning watch going ashore with Mr. Darnley."

"What's that for?" growled Dirk Matthews. "Is it to see how we can lay in a stock of sunstroke?"

"You just obey orders, Matthews," said Oakley, "and don't turn your tongue at me, or I'll tan your hide for you. Into the boat with you!"

"All right, Mr. Oakley," said Dirk, with glinting eyes and a feigned humility, "I wasn't a-turning my tongue, but just axing a natral question."

"You'd no call to question," said Oakley, "and don't you do it again. There's too much jabber about you all round."

Dirk Matthews dropped in a haphazard, careless fashion into the boat which had been lowered. Five other men took their places, and then Dick Darnley, with a wonderful lightness, leaped down into the stern.

"Give way, men," he said. "I'll serve out arms as we go along."

He opened a locker behind the back seat and took out a sufficient number of revolvers and cutlasses for the party. There were enough in the locker for double the men, if they had been required.

"The revolvers are loaded, I presume?" he said.

"They ought to be, sir," answered one of the men.

"But they are not," said Darnley, throwing open one of the chambers. "Whose work was it to see to them?"

"Mine, sir," replied Dirk Matthews.

"Then why wasn't it done?" sternly demanded Dick.

"I'm sorry, sir," said Matthews, "but it went right out of my head. I cleaned them last night, and, seeing there was no cartridges in the locker, I intended to ask Mr. Oakley for some, but he got a-bullyragging me for something, and put it out of my head."

"What became of the usual supply of cartridges?" asked Darnley. "Every boat is supposed to be kept well supplied. Although we have had no occasion to use them as yet, there is no saying when they may be wanted."

The matter of the disappearance of the cartridges none of them admitted they were able to solve. Darnley replaced the revolvers in the locker and told the men to gird on their cutlasses.

"I will look into this when we return. Some serious neglect is apparent here."

The men rested on their oars, one at a time, as they girded on their weapons, and, when all were ready, pulled slowly towards the shore. The excessive heat checked anything like real exertion.

The boat stranded on the beach, near the one already lying there. The two seamen under the broad-leaved palm rose up and saluted Dick as he stepped ashore.

"Have you heard anything of Mr. Walton?" asked Dick.

"No, sir, nothing since he went away with the four young gentlemen. He said he wouldn't be more than an hour, and its nigh on three now, sir. We come ashore in the middle of the forenoon watch."

"And you have not heard anything at all of them since?"

"Nothing, sir. They went up by the wood through them two big cedars, and the young gentlemen was laughing and chatting as usual. Mr. Walton walked on in front, thinking like."

Dick Darnley glanced uneasily in the direction indicated.

It certainly was strange that the exploring party of five should be so long away.

They had not far to go, for the hill selected by the captain to get a view of the interior of the island was only a short distance from the belt of wood. The summit of it could easily be reached in half an hour, ten minutes would suffice for a look round, and then another twenty minutes would be ample allowance for the return journey. They ought to have been back fully an hour and a half prior to Dick's starting from the "Albatross."

"Something must be wrong," said Darnley. "Now men, follow me. We shall soon find out what it is."

CHAPTER CXOV.

CUT OFF FROM THE SHORE.—A STRANGE EXPE-
RIENCE.

DICK expected to find a clear trail of the missing party in the wood, and he was not doomed to disappointment.

The ground was literally carpeted with ferns and flowers, growing with amazing luxuriance under the tall trees that reared their feathery crowns proudly to the sky.

To all appearance the spot had until that morning been unvisited by man. The only indications of a path had been made by the five explorers from the "Albatross."

They had walked one in advance and four abreast behind. Occasionally there was a widening out to avoid a tree of unusual dimensions. Dick strode on quickly, his men keeping up with him, with Dirk Matthews in the rear.

There was a malevolent grin upon his face, which he strove to suppress; but if it had been seen by his fellow-seamen they would not have commented on it as anything unusual. Dirk's saturnine nature was well known. He enjoyed nothing so much as the misfortunes of others.

The belt of wood was soon crossed, and then they came to the base of the hill, where a surprise awaited them.

From the sea it presented the appearance of an ordinary slope, covered with green, and here and there bushes and trees, easy to ascend. But the base was all broken up with huge rents to the right and left, traversing each other, but, most marvellous of all, spanned by bridge-like strips of earth.

There was no sign of a living being in sight, and in a moment Dick Darnley divined what are happened.

The party of exploration had trusted to one of these presumably natural bridges, and it had given way with them.

It turned him sick with apprehension, as he thought of them lying dead in some unfathomable depth.

There was a perfect network of these rifts in the side of the hill. Had it been level it would have borne a strong resemblance to a floe of ice being broken up in spring. Dick stepped up to the edge of the first rift and peered over. It was too deep for his eye to fathom.

A short distance down, lying coiled up on a shelf of earth, was a serpent of some sort, and he judged it was at least twenty feet long.

As he looked down, it lazily raised its head, hissed, and then coiled itself up again.

To the left was one of the natural bridges, and

drawing back with a shudder, Dick walked up to it and cautiously tested its strength.

The men drew up behind him, looking on curiously and in silence.

Halfway across he observed the faint outline of a footstep. The missing party had no doubt crossed there, and he went boldly over to the solid ground upon the other side.

"Shall we come, sir?" asked one of the men.

"There is no need to risk your lives," was Dick's reply. "Stay where you are, all but one, who had better go back to the 'Albatross' for a spare topmast or two, a couple of pulleys, and a hundred feet of rope. We are not likely to find much use for more," he added, sadly.

"I'll go, sir," said Dirk Matthews, with unwonted alacrity.

It was very rarely he volunteered his services at any time, showing rather a tendency to shirk. As Oakley said, he talked too much, and big talkers are rarely big workers.

"Bring back two or three more hands with you," sang out Darnley, as Matthews turned away.

"Ay, ay, sir."

Seemingly forgetful of the heat, he broke into a run and vanished. Dick Darnley advised the remaining men to seek the shade, but not to lose sight of him.

"If I go down anywhere," he said, grimly, "it will be some sort of satisfaction for you to know exactly where I am."

He feared that his friends were lost, and in bitterness of heart, he moved on and upward.

Forgetting the burning sun and ignoring the stream of perspiration that ran down his face, he tested another bridge and crossed a second crevice.

Then he stopped, and putting his hands to his mouth, sent forth a shout both loud and clear.

Was it an echo, or did he hear a faint, answering cry?

He could not tell from whence it came, and all he could do was to repeat the cry and be more watchful for the answer or echo.

Once more he sent up a shout and stretched his ears to listen.

The reply was longer in coming this time, and it was therefore no echo. Furthermore, he could make out the word.

"*Here.*"

Here; but where?

He moved to the left and shouted a third time, standing near another crevice.

The reply came up almost from his very feet.

Then he saw hard by the remnants of one of the bridges that had broken down, portions sticking out jaggedly from the sides of the crevice, and knew that he had by good fortune lighted on the very spot.

Throwing himself down, he gazed into the depths, and, as luck would have it, it ran parallel with east and west, and the sunlight went directly to what appeared to be the bottom. He estimated that it was thirty-odd feet, narrowing to almost a point; but he could see no signs of living beings.

"It was an echo!" he cried, despairingly.

Lying down, his voice—he spoke loudly—travelled into the depths, and promptly the reply came back.

"It wasn't anything of the sort, Mr. Darnley. We're all here, shaken up a bit, but no bones broken."

"Who that is speaking?" he asked, in bewilderment.

"Jack Ford."

"All well, you say?"

"As can be expected."

"Yes, but where are you?"

"Down at the bottom of this crevice. It curves under, and we are out of sight. The slope is too much for us. *It is of polished stone, and we can't climb it.*"

"What do you mean by polished stone?"

"What I say. It is a regular well—a trap."

"It is quite true, Darnley," said a deep voice. "Get us out as soon as you can, and we will tell you all about it."

"I suppose I had better not talk. Matthews will soon be back. But you must make allowances for his having to go to the 'Albatross.' With your permission I will have a cigar."

"Smoke away," was the answer.

He drew back, immeasurably relieved, but with a mind puzzled about the polished stone. Nature smooths, but seldom polishes, especially in the bowels of the earth. And they were in a sort of well, too. Uncommonly strange thing, that.

But he could only wait for a fuller description of the mishap which had befallen his friends, and lighting a cigar, he smoked with as much serenity as he could command.

He could hear them talking below, but there was confusion in the sound to his ears, now that he was away from the chasm. Now and then a light musical laugh would come up from the mysterious depths below, and a responsive smile flit across his face.

"Light-hearted, always," he said. "I don't wonder at Barstow being fond of the boys. Boys, do I call them?—men in heart and courage."

It was a long wait, as all such waitings are. Time lags or flies according to circumstances; but Dirk Matthews, with three extra men and the required material, appeared at last, and Dirk showed a great anxiety to do his full share of the work of rescue.

"The cap'en, sir," he said to Dick Darnley, "is mighty put out, and would have come hisself if there had been a officer to leave aboard."

"We shall soon be able to reassure him," answered Dick, cheerily.

They laid a couple of topmasts across the chasm, and fixed a rope in the pulley. One end was taken by the men and the other dropped into the chasm.

"Coming up!" shouted a lively voice.

Then, in a few moments, the face of a handsome but somewhat sad-looking man in uniform of a first officer appeared above the ground.

He let go of the rope, grasped the topmasts, and deftly swung himself to firm ground.

"Jack Ford," he said, "will wait to the last. He wants to find out what it would feel like to be down there alone."

"Just like Jack," said Darnley, as he gave his brother officer a congratulatory shake of the hand; "goes the whole hog or none, right through."

The first of the younger officers of the "Albatross" was Tom Drummond. He came up looking as if he had had enough of underground habitation, but pretty cheerful.

Then arrived Bob Stockton, who politely thanked all who had been concerned in the rescue, individually and collectively.

The third to come to the surface was Don Peebles, and he intimated that, if convenient, Jack Ford would prefer being left below for ten minutes or so.

"What's the crank?" asked Dick Darnley.

"Jack wishes to get experience of underground solitude," replied Don, laughing. "He says that you never can tell what you may have to go through with one day."

As the rescue was now as good as complete, they could afford to wait a little while. One of the men was sent forward to signal to the ship that all was well. The rest stood about chatting, until Darnley, looking at his watch, discovered that they had given Jack a full twenty minutes.

An indication was given that they were ready for him, and as soon as they felt his weight upon it, the rope was hauled in. Jack, the boldest, strongest, and bravest of a quartet of handsome, brave, strong boys, was soon among them.

"How long did you leave me there?" he asked.

They told him.

"Quite long enough," he remarked, in his quiet way.

Four straight-limbed youngsters were the companions of Harry Barstow's quest.

He had come thither in search of his lost friend, Norton Truscott, spirited away from him under most mysterious circumstances, and he had given to each and all the position of middies on board the "Albatross."

Though so pacific-looking, the "Albatross" had her

teeth, which could be shown on very short notice, and it was understood among the crew that they were on no mere voyage of pleasure, but might be called upon to fight, if certain contingencies arose.

Yet none outside those in command knew what or whom they were seeking, and all sorts of stories were afloat among the men as to the real object for which they had signed articles.

It was not to be expected that ordinary seamen would have shipped on such mysterious conditions. Adventurers were wanted, and adventurers had been obtained.

There had been no prying into their past, and, truth to tell, it would have been better for the "Albatross" if some on board had never joined.

Among these was Dirk Matthews.

There was a dark record behind the man, and he had joined with the hope and belief that the "Albatross" was bound on a mission in which the getting of money was the first thing thought of, and the morality of the way it was got a matter of after-consideration.

But as by degrees he became convinced he had fallen into an error, so he became dissatisfied. The result of this we shall see anon.

Before leaving the spot Mr. Ben Walton explained the "mishap," which was afterwards considered to be no mishap at all.

On making the discovery of the real nature of the ground at the foot of the slope, he at first was inclined to go back. As an old Alpine climber he had had some experience of the treacherous nature of natural bridges, especially when formed of snow, but the youngsters had urged him to go on.

Jack Ford set an example by crossing the first bridge alone, then in company with Don, and after that they all crossed.

The same example was set with the second, which appeared to be much stronger than the former one.

They crossed it singly, in twos, in threes, and finally all together.

There was not the least sign of its yielding, until it suddenly gave way, and they were precipitated into the depths below.

Falling on comparatively soft ground, they were not hurt, but when they shot off at an angle they discovered it was a serious matter.

One and all were precipitated into a tank of moderate dimensions, but of sufficient depth to debar them from getting out of it without assistance.

And the sides were of marble.

"Polished," said Jack Ford, "as smooth as a mirror. You could see your face in it."

CHAPTER CXCVI.

A COUNCIL ON BOARD.—A CIRCLE OF BARRIERS.

HARRY BARSTOW was one of the first to welcome the party on their return. He, in common with most on board, had entertained serious apprehensions that something was wrong. To hear the story of the mishap he held a council under the awning aft, when refreshment had been duly provided for what Jack Ford merrily termed "the sufferers."

"It is all very well to make light of it," said Walton, "but there was but an off-chance of our being rescued."

"I do not quite understand those pits," said Harry Barstow. "From you I gather that there is one under each bridge."

"It is only a surmise," said Ben Walton.

"But the one you fell into was artificial?"

"Without a doubt."

"Ancient man made pitfalls," said Harry.

"So have modern ones, and they also use those made by men long since dust."

There was a short silence. The minds of all were busy with speculation.

"You have a theory," said Harry Barstow. "Like many others, you have read vastly. Tell us what you think of your experience to-day."

Ben Walton stood up, and with a motion of his hand towards the island, said:

"Take note of the shape of yonder land. Ere we dropped anchor we discovered that it was of a certain form. What was it?"

"Practically circular," replied Barstow.

"And the hills—what are they?"

"To me hills, and nothing more."

"They follow the shape of the island, like the lip of a cup. Now, I believe the fissures to be natural, the result of some great upheaval of the earth. The bridges are the work of men, designedly crude to deceive strangers. The centre of the island between the hills is a huge basin, an extinct volcanic crater, levelled and partly filled in by time. What a place for those whose lives are tainted by unholy rites!"

The eye of Walton was lighted up with animation as he speculated on the probable. The listeners sat silent, almost breathless.

"Who is it we have come to seek?" he resumed. "The Avishnus, the worshippers of the serpent, a race as secret as the Thugs, and as cruel and vile. Driven from their native haunts in India, it is supposed by the thoughtless that they are extinct, but do we not know that, like the Mormons, they have simply sought out a home where they can pursue their ways of evil undisturbed? Have we not, strong in that belief, sought for twelve long months their skulking-ground?

Do you not know, Captain Barstow, that if your lost friend, Norton Truscott, be yet alive, he is among these heathens?"

"It is so," murmured Harry Barstow.

"Then there lies your goal," said Ben Walton, with another sweeping motion of his hand. "Beyond the rent and riven ground, where we nearly lost our lives to-day, is the haunt of Avishnu. Happily for us, help came speedily. They may not yet have heard of the coming of the 'Albatross,' for this is the month of September, when they gather together for one of their great festivals. But ere long they would have marked the broken bridge, and then the end would have come. If we could have stood the test of the serpent, not only would our lives have been spared, but we should have been worshipped and kept closely hidden away, as men hide their sacred things. It would have been a fate more terrible than death, perhaps. Solitary imprisonment for life is worse even than the scaffold."

"What is the test?" asked Jack Ford.

"The man to be sacrificed or worshipped, according to circumstances, is thrust into a pit, similar to that in which we were this morning. Then one of the huge serpents that are worshipped is thrown in with him. Care is taken that it is hungry. The man and reptile are then covered from the sight, and left *for three whole days!* At the end of that time the pit is opened, and if the man be yet alive, he has stood the test, and is saved."

"But would the brain of any man stand the test?" asked Dick Darnley, his thoughts reverting to the serpent he had seen.

"The mind of man varies," replied Walton. "Some can endure much ordinary trouble; others are impregnable to all attack."

"Walton," said Harry Barstow, rising, "I am inclined to think with you, that we have lighted on the haunt of the accursed race which robbed me of my friend. It now only remains to make sure it is so. The way is simple. We must make another circle of the island, land here and there, and explore a short way inland. If the Avishnus are there, they must have some outlet by which they secretly come and go. On the island itself there is not the means of subsistence for them. The wind has come to us for days with the first dog-watch. It will be here in an hour and a half. All night it blows from the south, and shifts to the west at dawn. Thus far it will favour us."

He left them somewhat abruptly, as was his wont after talking of his lost friend. How deep must have been the affection between them thus to disturb him!

Dick Darnley had some duty to perform, and Walton was left with the boys.

"Mr. Walton," said Don, softly, "you have often spoken to us of the Avishnus. How is it you know so much of them?"

"First by reading, and then by experience," he replied; "but you must not ask for too much. I can never recall a portion of my past without mental suffering for many hours. Sometimes I am sleepless for days when the memory of it comes back and haunts me."

That the mate of the "Albatross" had known sad and bitter experiences was understood by all on board, but of their nature little had been revealed.

He was a reticent man, but it was impossible not to like him. Under his half-hidden sorrow there was the geniality of a sterling man.

He left the boys, and they continued their talk of the past and speculations as to the future.

It may serve the purposes of our story well if we put on record the salient features of the conversation that ensued.

It was about eighteen months since they left school. All had grown, and much of the boy had departed from them for ever.

In Jack Ford this was more marked than in the rest, for he had ever given promise of an early manhood. Not that manhood had yet come to him, for the bloom of youth was on his cheek; but he was tall, well knit, and with a resolute, self-reliant bearing, which served him well in the place of the more mature strength of the time to come.

Don Peebles had grown fast during the year he had been at sea. His figure was tall and straight, with well-squared shoulders. Tom Drummond promised to make a man of medium height, thick-set and muscular—one of the class who plant their feet down, and are not to be moved by anything less than the arrival of a cannon-ball or an earthquake.

Bob Stockton, the Chesterfield of the old school-days at Littlecote Abbey, had naturally developed into a bit of a dandy.

He was slimmer than his chums, and looked somewhat delicate. This impression was heightened by his assumed languid air and the sleepy look in his deep blue eyes.

The men, according to the way of sailors, had a name for each. Bob was "The Dandy," Jack "Young Fireaway," Don "There When Wanted," and Tom "The Bull-Dog."

In a rough and ready way these nicknames were very appropriate. They, as it were, outlined the characters of the four friends.

CHAPTER CXCVII.
MORE OF THE ISLAND MYSTERIES.

"IT would be a marvellous thing," said Jack, with a dreamy glance towards the island, "if we should there find a common foe."

"Sure to be that, if a foe at all," said Tom Drummond.

"Harry Barstow," said Jack, "has told us the story of his lost friend on that never-to-be-forgotten night, when we lay off Malta. You remember it?"

"Can we ever forget it?" returned Don. "The sky so darkly, deeply, beautifully blue, as the poet hath it; no breath of air, a sea that rose and fell with a curious, sighing sound, the lights ashore, and the far-off sounds of music. Ourselves on board in the curious light that was more felt than seen—a light that seemed to gather like a faint halo around all things—and Harry Barstow with us lounging at ease. It was a dream."

"He told us," continued Jack, "of the time when he lay off an island apparently uninhabited, a patch of earth in the Archipelago between Greece and Turkey. Norton Truscott, moved by the spirit of a sportsman, landed with his gun. One shot was heard, and then no more. The day passed away, and he did not return. At eve our captain went ashore to seek his friend, sought him all night, and found no trace of him. In the morning a wand was discovered on the beach, sticking in the sand. The top was cleft, and in it was a paper, on which was written:

"'Under compulsion, and yet with a desire to ease your mind as to my fate, I write these words. Harry, old friend and more than brother, I am in the hands of a strange people, who are about to bear me hence. I may not name them, for if I do you will never receive a word from me. I go to my death, or to a life that is worse than death. But I will not despair. Perhaps in the time to come I may find some means of escape, but do not imperil your life by seeking me. Adieu. I leave my heart behind me, comforted with the knowledge that I take yours with me.'

"That letter," said Jack, "was in the handwriting of Norton Truscott. Of course, Harry Barstow disobeyed the injunction as to seeking his lost friend. He did all that he could under the circumstances—searching the island through and through, and finding nothing. There wasn't the faintest clue to the fate of Norton Truscott."

"Until he was enlightened when he stopped at Mitylene," said Don, "and there he learnt that a strange body of men from India, it was thought, had landed there. They had huge serpents with them, as seen by a scared fisherman who was hiding on the island. It was plain that they had come and gone, like thieves in the night."

"As we all know," resumed Jack, "our captain obtained a clue as to the route they had taken in their boats. At Suez they boarded a ship, evidently waiting for them, and journeyed down the Red Sea. From point to point they have been traced to here—the sea with a hundred islands—and here he believes they have made their home."

"I judge from Walton's manner he believes that home is on yonder island?" said Tom.

"Just so," said Jack; "and I am almost certain of it, too. And now I come to a matter that closely concerns ourselves. Take your minds back to the old school, with Chunder Loo and his fetish serpent, Mehala."

Little trouble was it for them to do so. All too vivid in their minds were some of the scenes in which that malevolent Hindoo played a part.

"Now recall again that night at Malta," continued Jack; "after we had heard the captain's story, what did we do?"

"Took a boat and had a quiet row together."

"Out beyond the forts and back to the harbour. We landed, and the hour being late, we had the place almost to ourselves. You remember how you three fellows went on a little way, leaving me sitting by the sea?"

"Yes," they replied, in chorus.

"And when you came back I appeared to be somewhat excited?"

"For you," said Don.

"Well, I was put out about something. Can you recall what that was?"

"You said you had fallen asleep, dozed off, and that Chunder Loo came to you in your dreams."

"It was no dream," said Jack. "I was in the condition that is between sleeping and waking. On the morrow I learnt by inquiry that such a man had been in the harbour town, and had left in a trader, bound through the Red Sea. Now, then, tell me what you think of that?"

"Nothing," replied Don, after a pause given to thought; "it might have been Chunder Loo, or not. Say that it was. He was fleeing from justice, and he was naturally making for his home in India, where he occasionally informed us he was born."

Tom and Bob laughed as they recalled a familiar phrase that had fallen so often from the lips of Chunder Loo, but Jack was very grave.

"Boys," he said, "I am not given to talking at all times, and I allowed that meeting to drop out of your sight, but I kept it in mine. The memory of it has come back to me again and again, and stronger than ever this day."

"Why to-day?" asked Bob.

"Who are the people that spirited away Norton Truscott?" asked Jack.

"The serpent worshippers," they chorussed.

"And what was Chunder Loo?" pursued Jack—"a serpent worshipper. He carried that horrible little fetish with him wherever he went, until Don killed it that day he lay insensible in the wood. You cannot have forgotten that?"

"Forgotten it?" said Don. "No! I wish I could.

Like you, Jack, I am not a talker about some things. I can keep them to myself. But I can tell you now that times and oft I have dreamt that scene over again, and more often than ever of late. Last night, as I lay in my hammock—I believe I was asleep, but will not be sure—I saw it all as vividly as I did on that terrible day. But with an addition I have not known before. I saw Chunder Loo rise up and curse me for what I had done, and threaten to have my life for that which I had taken. And then he suddenly changed to the figure of a fiend, and vanished."

"Had too heavy a supper," languidly suggested Bob.

"No," said Don, "I am not troubled that way. Nor am I going to worry over a dream. But as it came to me, I tell it to you. Think what you like of it."

"I think," said Jack, "that if the serpent worshippers are on yonder island, Chunder Loo is there too."

"Rather speculative, that," murmured Don.

"Don't quite see it," added Tom.

"Nor do I," admitted Jack, "but I *feel* it. In the old days"—he spoke as if the schooltime was a matter of fifty years before—"I used to experience the same thing. I divined this or that to come with an indefinable feeling, and, if you remember, I rarely was wrong."

"It is true," said Bob, "and all I hope is, that you may be right. Nothing would give me greater pleasure than being the custodian of Chunder Loo on his way back to the old country, there to be taken to the place from whence he came, and to be removed from thence and hanged by the neck until he is dead, dead, *dead!*"

"Boys," said Jack, "we have had a placid, happy time up to now, but more stirring times are at hand. The real work for which the 'Albatross' has been fitted out, is about to begin."

"The light farce is over," said Bob, "and the curtain rises on the scene of the tragedy. Here's Penny Bunn. Suppose we have a light drink. I am fearfully thirsty. Bunn!"

"Sir," said Bunn, who was engaged in coiling a rope, amidships.

"Come hither."

Bunn came over to them and stood in the attitude of an experienced waiter expecting an order.

"Claret and water," said Bob.

"Yessir."

Bunn vanished below, and was speedily back again with a bottle of wine, tray, glasses, and jug of water, complete.

"Well, Bunn," said Bob, "how goes it with you now?"

"As well as I can expect, sir," answered Bunn; "there is, however, a lack of personal freedom here which scarcely harmonises with my love of liberty."

He poured out some wine into each of the four glasses, added water until told to stop, and handed the drinks round.

"You have fallen naturally into your true position, Bunn," said Bob; "you are a born waiter."

"I am made of adaptable stuff, sir," answered Bunn, "otherwise I never could have endured my old employer, Snicker."

"Or accepted the joys of matrimony so readily as you did," remarked Don.

"The joys of matrimony, sir," said Bunn, "in my case were somewhat mixed. There was a little too much acid in their composition. But for all that the society of my dear departed and still, I trust, living wife was far preferable to the company of such ruffians as Dirk Matthews."

"He is rough," admitted Don.

"He is a dark-souled, desperate, designing, murderous villain, gentlemen," said Bunn, lowering his voice. "Rammer is ignorant, aggressive, and offensive, but he stops at words. Dirk Matthews is given to violence, and is dangerous. I have come to the conclusion that it would have been better for the 'Albatross' if——"

"The first puff of wind!" cried Tom, springing up, "and here is Mr. Darnley. Up comes the anchor, and off and away!"

The hour for leaving their anchorage ground had arrived.

In a few moments the deck was alive with men. Harry Barstow and his officers, Bill Oakley, and others, were there — some to obey orders, others to give them, and all glad to welcome the cooling breeze.

Even the men attached to the engine of the vessel, who invariably spent their leisure time in sleeping below, came up and sat forward, a grimy crew of five.

Down tumbled the canvas, the anchor came up from the deep, and with a gracefully slow lurch to starboard, the "Albatross" moved on before the wind.

From a soft breeze, as gentle in its action as the breathing of an infant, the wind rose to a steady blow. On sped the "Albatross," showing her sailing powers to be of the finest.

The sea swelled and broke into waves, and all on board rejoiced in the sense of motion.

Keeping well in towards the shore, with a man in the chains with a lead to give warning of possible shoaling, the swift vessel pursued her way, her captain and the two second and third in command busy with their powerful telescopes scanning the shore.

For miles they saw nothing but the belt of wood, and strip of golden sand with the distant crown of hill, but coming at length to a break, it was a mere gap in the wood, the word was given to shorten sail, and the "Albatross" was brought up into the eye of the wind.

A boat was lowered, and Harry Barstow in person decided to pay a brief visit to the shore.

Bill Oakley and half a dozen of picked men were ordered to accompany him.

Nothing as yet had been said about Dirk Matthews' neglect of the duty of seeing that the firearms kept in the locker of every boat were provided with ammunition, but the precaution was taken to examine those in the boat that was lowered.

As in the previous case, there was no ammunition.

Still nothing was said, and Harry Barstow quietly gave the order for the defect to be remedied.

"It seems a strange thing, sir," said Jack Ford, "that *all* the lockers should be empty as far as ammunition is concerned."

"It will be looked into anon," replied the second mate.

Harry Barstow was absent about an hour. When he returned night was at hand. The sun was already within touch of the horizon, and a full moon would soon appear in the eastern sky.

All were anxious to know if he had discovered anything of importance, but he said nothing immediately after his return. His first care was to see the "Albatross" put before the wind again.

That done, he left Dick Darnley in charge of the deck, and beckoned for Ben Walton, the second mate, to follow him below.

As he put his foot on the top stair of the companion, he espied the boys close by, in a group.

"You may as well come, too," he said; "after your experience to-day, it is only right that you should know everything."

So they all went down together to the captain's cabin, and he closed the door.

"All doubts any of us may have entertained," he said, "about the island being inhabited, may now be put aside. Nature has been aided by man in fortifying it, and the means adopted have been the work of a superlative cunning."

It seemed that he had discovered that the strange crevices in the earth were still in evidence on the hillside through the gap in the wood, and that gap had been made and kept up by man.

There was no doubt about it, for although traces of the removal of trees had to a great extent been hidden by the laying down of turf, or what was equivalent to it there, the keen eyes of Harry Barstow, born and bred to a country life at home, had seen signs of the artificial arrangement.

And beyond that there had been an extension of the sham bridge system in the complete covering of the lowest crevice for a space of a hundred yards or more.

"It has been so well done," he said, "that I was nearly deceived. But for your adventure to-day, which gave me a key to the doings of the people on the island, I should indubitably have lost my life. But suspecting the stability of a particular spot, I tested it by throwing a fair-sized stone upon it, and it broke through. The covering was a mere shell of light sticks and earth, on which the seeds of weeds had been sown. Growth of such things here is rapid, and judging by the imperfect development of the plants, I should say that the work was done not more than a week ago. We broke away a few feet of it, and saw that at a depth of twenty feet spiked pieces of wood had been fixed in the bottom of the crevice. A man falling on one must have been impaled."

"There must be some strong reason for all these precautions against invasion," said Ben Walton.

"Undoubtedly," replied Harry Barstow; "and there must also be some vulnerable joint in the armour. This we must find out. They could never travel to and from the sea by the hills."

"All sorts of possibilities arise in my mind," said Walton; "but it is useless to speculate. Our work now is to find out the joint in the armour of the island."

"With a full moon," said Harry Barstow, "we can sail on the night through. But every foot of the shore must be scanned closely lest we pass by that which we seek."

Then the boys, as with one voice, asked that they might share in this duty. Hitherto they had done little or nothing beyond learning the craft of seamanship from the two mates and Bill Oakley, and study navigation from books in their leisure.

Up to then they had done nothing to repay Harry Barstow for all his kindness to them.

He readily consented, and divided them into watches of two each, to be independent of the ordinary watches of the ship.

Don and Jack were to take the middle watch, and Tom and Bob the first watch.

By this arrangement the two latter would be on duty from eight o'clock until midnight, and Jack and his chum Don from midnight until four in the morning.

CHAPTER CXCVIII.

THE BUDDING OF A MUTINY.

"I WONDER how long we are going to sneak about in this way?" said Dirk Matthews; "that wasn't what *I* come afloat for."

He sat on a locker in the fore cabin, and around

him were about half of the crew of the "Albatross." Near the door Rammer and Penny Bunn stood in the hesitating, doubting way of those who had no great love for their company, and knew not whether to stay or go.

There was no light in the cabin, but the door was open, and a lamp in the passage without relieved the gloom. Still, neither Bunn nor Rammer, standing in the deep shadow, had been observed by Dirk Matthews, who had only just come below.

"Mates," he went on, "I look at you and see some as are of my way of thinking. What say you, Bates?"

"It is a sickening game," answered Bates.

"And you, Goffer?"

"I've given you my sentiments afore," was the reply. "Springtop?"

"Afore you open your heart too free and your mouth too wide," said Springtop, "let me just remark that neither old Rammer nor his slab, All Toplights, are likely to help us in our meditations."

"All Toplights" was the nickname for Penny Bunn, being a cheerful sarcasm on the fact of his having nothing outside his learning worth looking at. Dirk Matthews turned with an oath towards the pair.

"What yer mean by skulking here?" he demanded.

"Skulking!" repeated Bunn. "Really, I was under the impression that when off duty my quarters were here. If you have any complaint to make in that respect, Mr. Oakley or one of the chief officers is open to receive it."

"Mr. Oakley and the officers be——" growled Dirk Matthews. "Get out, the pair of you!"

"I was born afloat," said Rammer, "and I've lived afloat, respected and loved, I may say, by all aboard, and have allus had my company in the forecastle considered an honour rather than t'otherwise. Didn't I get this limp o' mine off Cape Wincent——"

"Off where?" snarled Dirk Matthews.

"Cape Wincent, where the sea fight was—not for the fust time."

"Good heavens!" exclaimed Dirk Matthews—"a born liar. Now, of course, having lived aboard, you could run a ship if she was left to your charge?"

"I rayther fancy," said Rammer, "that I *have* run a few in my time. Traders, also war vessels—likewise cruisers."

"Name 'em," said Dirk Matthews, with an oath.

"I don't see where you come in, ordering people about," replied Rammer.

"Well, tell me," said Dirk Matthews, "wot you would do with a ship as was waterlogged with a sou'-west wind on her beam, and making headway for starboard breakers?"

Suppressed chuckles were heard from the men lying about near Dirk Matthews, who in an undertone growled at them to be quiet.

"I should do wot every other man would in sich a case," replied Rammer; "but wot it would be, *you* ain't agoing to learn from *me*. I don't give lessons in seamanship except to them as is able and willin' to pay for the same."

Dirk Matthews sprang up, with an oath, exasperated by this undoubtedly evasive reply, which amused some of the listeners.

"Git out smart," he said. "I've put off my shoes, but if you drives me to putting them on again I shall make good use of 'em."

He gave Rammer a rough push, which sent him hopping towards the door, with his right leg sticking out straight behind him.

Dirk Matthews laid hold of it. Rammer gave vent to a fearful yell that could be heard all over the ship.

Dirk, yielding to the sudden alarm of the moment, let it go.

"What the deuce is the matter with you?" he growled.

Rammer, leaning against the side of the door, panting and groaning, replied brokenly:

"This yere leg o' mine, iver since it was wounded with a splinter fired from a forty-ton gun, have—— Oh, what hagony!—been all narves. I can't abear to touch it myself, and the hands of others is liquid fire on it. Oh, lor! oh, lor! not a wink of sleep shall I get to-night."

"What do you mean by having sich a leg?" demanded Dirk Matthews.

"I ain't responsible for it," answered Rammer. "Bunn, help me out of this hole."

Penny Bunn gave him his arm, and the pair went out, Dirk Matthews angrily banging the door behind them.

Rammer sat down upon a coil of rope and groaned.

"That leg of yours," said Penny Bunn, "seems to be a most remarkable piece of human anatomy."

"It's alive with a galwanic apparatus," replied Rammer; "the least touch sets it agoing like forty clocks all just wound up, and every tick is a stab. It's torters worse than the Holing Crimposition."

"I assume you mean the Holy Inquisition?" suggested Bunn.

"I mean wot I says, and I says no more than wot I mean," grunted Rammer. "You can't do t'otherwise. A nice sort of chap you are, standing by and seeing me handled in that way by a skunk!"

"It was a matter of your own self-defence," replied Bunn.

"I am bound, on account of my leg, not to fight," answered Rammer. "The least sudden movement, and I'm alive with pain."

"Passing from that subject," said Bunn, "what do you think is hatching among that lot, inside there?"

"Wot should be hatching?" asked Rammer.

"Though not born at sea," said Penny Bunn, with some emphasis, "nor blessed with an extensive circle of friends, mainly composed of the chief officers of vessels of war, I have read stories of the sea, and among others, those referring to mutinies. Did you ever have experience of one?"

"Been in several," was the curt reply. "Put an end to one single-handed."

"What, with that leg of yours?" exclaimed Bunn.

"It hadn't been conflicted with a splinter then," said Rammer.

"I beg your pardon," said Bunn. "Your life is, of course, divided into two portions—the ante and after splinter ages. Well, as you are so experienced in mutinies, let me ask, if you do not think one is brewing on board the 'Albatross'?"

"Who is to brew it?" asked Rammer.

Penny Bunn jerked his thumb in the direction of the forecastle cabin. The nose of Rammer, which was a good substantial protuberance upon his countenance, assumed an almost corkscrew form expressive of entire disapproval of the suggestion.

"Mutiny!" he exclaimed. "Who is to mutiny?"

"That lot," said Bunn.

"You are a fool," said Rammer, "and idiot. Mutiny! Wot for, and how? It takes born seamen to mutiny, them as is by nature and sperience fitted to command. Them chaps in there ain't got the brains. Don't make me hill with suggestives of that natur'."

"But I am sure——"

"Wot do you know about it? A landsman who never see the inside of a ship till he was growed up. Don't talk to me!"

"Very well," said Penny Bunn; "but allow me to remark that although I have not your nautical gifts, I am not an absolute fool. I am endowed with reason, and I have a comprehensive knowledge of the English language, embracing the more violent forms thereof."

Rammer got up, and, with a sniff of scorn, ascended to the deck.

Bunn, left alone, hesitated a moment, and then crept up to the door of the cabin. In it, near the bottom, was a small hole from which a knot in the wood had been removed. Penny Bunn lay down at full length, and placed his ear to it, with the air of a man who was not performing the feat for the first time.

It was not so good for listening purposes as the ordinary keyhole, but it served, and he was enabled to hear all that was being said.

Dirk Matthews was addressing the men in his company, expatiating on the fitting up and stores of the "Albatross."

"There's guns," he was saying, "and ammunition, and stores for a run among shipping for six months or more before they've got a scent of what is going on. It takes time for news of piracy to reach home, and then they have to locate the pirate and send out cruisers in search of him. Before that we could lay hands on enough to hide away, say in one of the southern republics, all rich men."

"But we've got to take the ship," urged a speaker, whom Bunn judged, by his voice, to be Bates.

"True," returned Dirk Matthews, "and we've got to pick the right moment for working. Given the captain and Mr. Darnley away, and it can be done. Say it is our watch on deck. We are all together, and we've talked it over. Them as is below has to be battened down. The stores and ammunition are aft. We've got them. We put to sea and no boat can follow us. Once there we let out the rest one by one. Those who are willing to join can be swore in, and the t'others will have to walk the plank. I know how it is done, for I've been in it!"

There was a silence of a few moments, and then some whispering, finishing with an assent to his scheme.

Bunn rose up with his hair on end. He had read many stories of mutinies at sea with their attendant horrors, and he knew that he would have but scant mercy from the ruffians who were scheming to get the "Albatross" into their own hands.

The question was, what was the course for him to take?

Holding an inferior position on board, he stood in awe of the captain, and was not on speaking terms with the first and second officers. His one time pupils, the four youths, were always disposed to chaff and ridicule him, and if he went to them with his story, they might ask for proof ere they acted, and he had none to give.

Say that he charged Dirk Matthews with being a conspirator, and the charge was denied, in what position would he be?

It was a hundred to one if the recreant seaman would not be believed before him.

But he had already spoken to Rammer, and to him he again resolved to go for advice.

They slept in the cuddy, where they performed their daily cooking duties, and when Bunn went thither he found that Rammer was already in his hammock in the full enjoyment of a final pipe ere he sought sleep.

He told him of the fresh evidence he had obtained, but Rammer only laughed him to scorn.

"They knowed you was a-listening," he said, "and plummed you up so that you might make a fool of yourself."

"You think so?" said Penny Bunn, miserably.

"I am sure on it," answered Rammer. "It's an old

A SPLENDID SCHOOL STORY.

NEVER BEFORE PUBLISHED.

By E. HARCOURT BURRAGE,

Author of "Ching Ching," "Monkey Mat and Roving Dick," "The Brave Boy of the Basilisk," &c.

ONE MOMENT THEY SAW THE CLIFF IMMEDIATELY OVERHEAD AND THEN THEY SHOT INTO DARKNESS.

☞ PRICE ONE PENNY. ☜

ALDINE PUBLISHING CO., 9, Red Lion Court, Fleet St., and 1, 2, & 3, Crown Court, Chancery Lane, London.

game at sea; they does it to all land lubbers. Bless you, they don't try it on *me*, knowing as I am up to every move afloat. You can go and tell the yarn to the captain, if you like, and he will just laugh or order a bucket of water to be throwed over you, jest to cool your imagination."

"But I'll swear they spoke in earnest," said Bunn.

"Well, if you think so, offer to jine 'em and make sure. Say that I am in it, too; and when we've got the lot in a corner we can do the blowing on 'em. Now, don't you worry me any more. This 'ere leg o' mine is uncommonly painful, and I want to get to sleep."

"I yield to your superior knowledge of sea matters," said Bunn, as he began to sling his hammock; "but as a commonplace man of the world I think you are wrong. However, as I think your advice is worth having, I will play up as one burning to join in the plot. It may lead to something."

He was on sure ground there. It might—and did.

CHAPTER CXCIX.

A DISCOVERY IN THE MIDDLE WATCH.

AT midnight Jack Ford and Don Peebles came on deck punctual to the moment to relieve Tom Drummond and Bob Stockton.

It was Dick Darnley's watch also, and he replaced the second mate.

There was nothing, it seemed, to report.

Under a steady breeze the "Albatross" had pursued her way favoured with deep water, so that she was able to keep close in shore.

She was now, however, on the north side of the island, opposite to her anchorage ground of the morning, and the wind not having shifted as it had done on previous days, she had to make short tacks to and fro to make any headway at all.

This of course impeded her progress, and there was little hope of getting many miles further ere the wind died away.

The moon shone brilliantly, more so than it ever does in our less favoured home clime; but it was not as bright as day. The moonlight never comes within measurable distance of sunlight; the talk about its being "as bright as day" is absolute fudge and nothing else. It is an exaggeration of the most glaring kind.

Nevertheless, the island stood out wonderfully clear as the "Albatross" approached it on the shoreward tack.

The curious monotony of bolt of sand, strip of wood, and crown of hill had been practically unbroken ere Jack and Don came on deck.

Shortly after the sands began to narrow and the wood to thin, and finally in both cases became merged in tall cliffs, against which the sea dashed with moderate force under the action of the breeze.

Night-glasses had been supplied to the boys, and by the side of Dick Darnley they scanned the cliff-bound shore.

Forward the men of the watch stood whispering together. Among them was Dirk Matthews.

The short tacks kept the men pretty busy, and the orders given by Darnley in an undertone were transmitted to them by old Bill Oakley, who stood amidships.

Presently he was heard rating somebody, and a few moments later he came aft to make his report.

"Matthews insolent, sir," he said. "Says he's tired of humbugging about doing nothing but run aloft and furl or loosen sail."

"Send Matthews to me," said Dick Darnley.

Matthews was longer in coming than he ought to have been, and he came along the deck to where Darnley and the boys were standing in a high-shouldered, dogged fashion.

"Matthews," said Darnley, sternly, "what is the meaning of your conduct? You are reported for insolence."

"I didn't mean to be insolent, sir," answered Dirk Matthews, slowly. "I only said that the work we are doing isn't what I shipped for."

"You shipped to do as you were told."

"Begging pardon, sir, but I understood it was to be *active* work. And it ain't me alone, neither. There's several of us as have been accustomed to taking sarvice wherever there was a bit of a fight and something hanging to the end of it in prospect."

"Well, there may be some fighting soon," said Darnley; "but the time for it is not to be of your choosing. This is not the first time there has been a complaint against you. Hitherto we have not reported it to the captain; but it will be done if occasion to do so is given again. Go back to your duty, and let me hear no more of you."

Dirk Matthews saluted in form respectful enough, but there was something in the action that conveyed covert insolence.

As he slouched forward, Dirk remarked to the boys that he was an ugly-looking fellow.

"I never liked him," said Jack Ford. "He doesn't look one straight in the face."

They thought no more about him just then, for the "Albatross" was on the land tack, and Don had espied with his night-glass a dark speck on the face of the cliff, close to the sea.

It was a mere blot when first seen, but on getting in nearer, which they did very slowly in the falling wind, it was seen to be the mouth of a cave.

There was not much in the discovery, apparently, and they might have passed it by without comment, but it was not to be. The breeze suddenly died away, and there was nothing to be done but to drop the anchor, which was done in eight fathoms of water and about two hundred yards from the cave.

There is always something fascinatingly alluring to the young in a cave. This one soon became an especial attraction to Jack and Don.

" I wonder if Mr. Darnley would allow us to take the gig and explore it ?" said Jack.

" Perhaps there isn't much to explore," hinted Don.

" Well, I should like to see. Notice the waves how they roll in, and *they don't beat back*. That cave goes right under the cliff."

" Shall I ask Darnley ?"

" Yes. He can only say no."

Dick Darnley had just given orders for some of the main canvas to be furled, and was about to lighten the monotony of the night-watch with a smoke. He looked up in the act of igniting a cigar, and listened to Don's request with an amused face.

" And what do you think you will find there ?" he asked—"a robber's store, or a peck of diamonds ?"

" It will be something to do, sir," replied Don, " and there isn't the least risk. Mr. Oakley will get us a ship's lantern."

" He had better go with you," said Darnley, " and if you find the cave penetrates to any depth, say over a hundred feet, you had better return."

Don thanked him and sought out Oakley, who was not in favour of the proposed expedition.

" You niver can tell what's in them holes, especially in parts like these. Mayhap we will light on a devil-fish."

" Did you ever see one ?" asked Don.

" Once," was the dry reply, " and I don't want to see another."

" Then we had better go alone," said Don, gravely. "Your curiosity about devil-fishes appears to have been fully satisfied. Ours is not, and therein lies the difference."

Bill Oakley turned to the man, and ordered the gig to be lowered. Then he went off for a lantern, with which he soon returned.

Don and Jack were already in the boat, and he dropped down beside them.

" Oh, you are coming, after all ?" said Don.

" Young fools sometimes want an old fool to look arter 'em," answered Oakley, sententiously.

Dick Darnley peered over the side to give them a parting word of advice.

" You remember what I told you boys. Don't run any risk. If the cave is very deep, don't go too far."

" I hardly know, sir," said Oakley, " why you let 'em go at all."

" No more do I," replied Darnley, " but they would have been groaning with disappointment if I had said no."

It was evident he had no fears, and the boys, having tossed their oars in merry salute, pulled for the cave. Bill Oakley, with a wooden countenance as far as expression went, did the steering.

" The tide is a-coming in," he said, " and it's kind o' spurting through the mouth of that cave. I reckon it goes in a tidyish way."

" All the better," said Jack ; " there will be more to see."

" But once in," rejoined the boatswain, " you won't get back till the tide gives you leave."

" What do you mean by that ?"

" You will have to remain till it turns. Young gentlemen, if I was you I wouldn't bother to go in there."

" We will just peep in at the mouth," said Jack.

" And go no furder," urged Oakley.

They did not answer him, but pulled on to the mouth of the cave, standing off a bit at first, and turning round in their seats so as to get a look at it.

" I do not think there is any great rush of water in there," said Don.

" It is being sucked in," replied Oakley ; " look how quiet it goes. There's no obstacle, and that shows how deep it is. Steady—no furder."

But Jack had given two pulls, and the boat shot on to the front of the cave. In a moment it was making towards it, carried by the tide.

" Back water !" cried the old boatswain.

But it was already too late.

The current had a force in it not visible to the ordinary eye, and it caught the boat in its grip and bore it to the cave. One moment they saw the cliff immediately overhead, and then they shot into darkness.

" Heaven have mercy on us !" ejaculated Oakley.

For an instant the boys repented of having come, and then the old love of adventure warmed their hearts.

" It is all right, Oakley," said Jack ; " the water that takes us in will bring us out again."

" In six hours, if at all," was the dolorous response.

The water made little noise, save a swishing sound against the sides of the cave, which was about thirty feet high and as many wide, with sides smooth as if chiselled by a mason.

The oars were shipped as useless, and Jack went forward with a lantern. Bill Oakley steered.

" No monster yet," Jack reported, a minute later.

" Better be ready for one sir, anyhow," replied the boatswain. " Mr. Peebles, will you pass me a cutlass and a revolver ? Also take one each yourself."

There was no harm in acting upon this advice, and

from the store in the locker aft they armed themselves.

On glided the boat, Jack holding the lantern aloft, and saw nothing until they suddenly swung round a bend in the cave, and shot out into the moonlight again.

It was all so sudden and unexpected that they could not for a brief spell realise what had taken place, but on recovering themselves they saw that they were in a huge basin, or bay, covering many acres, and surrounded on all sides by towering rocks.

Into this inner receptacle the tide was rushing, and spreading out in the process of filling it.

The rapid motion of the boat ceased, and as it was borne along, in a circular direction, their eyes became fully alive to things around. They espied on the far side a number of long boats, stranded in a line.

And close to them there was a flight of steps cut in the solid rock.

"Gentlemen," said Oakley, in a thrilling whisper, "we've got into dangerous quarters. Them's pirate proas."

"But there is nobody in them," said Jack.

"Where the proas is," said Oakley, "pirates ain't far away. If they should show up afore the tide turns, we are cooped up and caught."

The position was certainly a dangerous one, and Jack proposed to have just one try to see if they could pull through the cave again.

Bill Oakley, with a grim smile, said they might try.

They tried, but the boat was as powerless in their hands to penetrate the cave as a cork is to fight against the rush of a mill-stream.

They were in a trap, and would have to remain there at the very least until the moon overhead drew the waters in her wake and turned the tide.

CHAPTER CC.

DICK DARNLEY IN TROUBLE.—DIRK MATTHEWS PREPARES TO MOVE.

ONE of the chief points in the character of Dick Darnley was his good-humour. It is a feeling which is allied to generosity, and he invariably did the kind thing first, and thought of the consequences afterwards.

It was his good-nature that had prompted him to yield to the request of the boys to go ashore, or rather to explore the cave. But the moment the boat disappeared from view he felt that he had done an unwise thing.

As if to accentuate the position, Harry Barstow immediately afterwards came on deck.

Awakening from a light sleep, he had, with a sailor's knowledge, realised from the rocking of the "Albatross" that it had come to anchor. As he had not expected the wind would fall so soon, he dressed, and came on deck to see if anything outside the breeze had caused the anchor to be lowered.

The stillness of the air answered that question satisfactorily. The next thing that gave rise to a slight feeling of surprise in him was the absence of the youngsters who had volunteered to share the night watch.

He remarked upon it, and Dick Darnley explained. The brows of Harry Barstow were slightly knitted, as he said:

"It is so like you, Darnley. The request of the boys ought to have been refused. No good can possibly come of their prowling about alone."

"I admit I was wrong," answered Dick, "but I thought that it was to be a mere trip by boat in the moonlight. It never occurred to me that they would go further than the mouth of the cave."

"It seems to me," said Harry Barstow, "that the tide is racing into it. If so, it is certain that it is a mere tunnel through the cliff to some inland place."

"They will soon find that out."

"Yes, and what then?"

"Why, they will come back again."

"Not until the ebb. What power have they to pull against the certain rush of water through that hole?"

"I am a fool!" muttered Dick, tilting his cap over to the back of his head.

"You are a thorough good fellow," returned Harry, "an able officer in every way, but do a thing too often on impulse. Walton would never have made such a mistake."

"No," said Dick, "he thinks a bit, and looks before he leaps, but now and then he thinks and looks so long, that it is too late to leap."

A faint smile passed across the face of Harry Barstow.

"I am not reproaching you. I trust that no ill will come of the adventure. The boys have nerve, and Oakley is cool-headed."

"What if I went after them?"

"Of what would that avail? I cannot spare you many men, and whoever went now would have to await the turn of the tide. If they do not come back on the ebb, then something must be done."

A soft, shuffling sound immediately behind them caused them both to wheel round. Close up near them was Dirk Matthews, with naked feet.

"Axing your pardon, sir," he said, saluting, "but Mr. Oakley being away, there ain't nobody in charge of the watch, and I think as somebody ought to be appointed. It ain't the duty of any of us, without orders, to call the relief."

"Let it be your duty," said Harry, abruptly.

Dirk Matthews touched his forehead and skulked back to the forecastle.

"There is something about that man, Dick, I don't quite like."

"No more do I. And there are others on board, too, whose physiognomy might be improved."

"In selecting the crew I needed," said Harry, thoughtfully, "I left it to Oakley to choose men who would not be squeamish as to where they went, or, indeed, what they did so long as they were well-paid. Naturally we were bound to have a few rough ones."

"Naturally," assented Dick, "and it follows that we must keep an eye on the rough ones."

"Such men must be kept employed," said Harry: "to-morrow we will have the guns up and put the 'Albatross' into fighting trim. Perhaps it ought to have been done before."

Dirk Matthews meanwhile had rejoined the men of the watch. With two exceptions they were his chosen confederates in the scheme he had in his mind.

Drawing aside with Bates and Goffer, he told them that he had overheard the talk of the two officers, and at ebb tide on the following day there would be a weakening of the crew to go in search of the trio who had ventured into the cave.

"Perhaps the cap'n will go himself," he said; "if so, with old Bill Oakley away, I think we might venture to make a move. At the ebb we shall be off duty, and it won't be us that will have to go in the boats. Pass the word to the others."

"It's early to risk it," said Bates, uneasily.

"Take the first chance, or you may never get none at all," said Dirk Matthews. "All we have to do is to be prompt. Say the cap'n goes; then there will be Mr. Darnley and Mr. Walton left in command. One of 'em is bound to be below. See here, I've got weapons and ammunition in my chest. I takes a revolver tucked inside my shirt, and I goes up to the officer on deck and says a word or two ordinary. Then afore he answers me I shoots him down."

"Yes," assented Bates, "that's easy work."

"Then you and t'others as are in it, being ready, rushes on deck and battens down the fore-cabin. I stand aft and shoots the other officer as he comes up to know what is the matter. Then the ship is ours."

Still Bates appeared to be dubious.

"But the boats will return," he suggested, "and then we should be in trouble."

"Let 'em come," said Dirk Matthews; "afore they can reach us I'll undertake to have a gun fixed and the ammunition ready to sink 'em. There are ten of us in it."

"A small crew for a pirate craft."

"Just so. But the rest will join when it is to save their lives. And as for more crew, I know where to find 'em. But if you are turning soft, and want to go on fuddling about on ordinary pay like a merchantman swab, say so, and I'll drop the business. Which is it to be?"

"I'm with you," said Bates, who was one of those men who seldom originate an evil scheme, but are always ready to follow a determined leader.

"All right," said Dirk Matthews; "then pass the word and look out by-an'-bye for the signal."

CHAPTER CCI

THE TRIO IN THE LANDLOCKED BAY.—A TERRIBLE DAWN.

WHILE things were progressing thus on board the "Albatross," the three adventurers shut off from their friends had passed an anxious time.

The land-locked bay in which they were afforded them no place of concealment from a possible coming foe. As they viewed it the conviction that it was the work of man, and the cave also, gradually came upon them.

There was nothing in its appearance to show that it was the result of the ordinary action of nature.

The cave was a tunnel with smooth sides and arched roof, smooth as tools could make it. The bay was nearly circular, and the high banks round it presented the appearance of having been blasted or dug out like a railway cutting.

There were the steps, near the boats, too, which they decided to row up and inspect. They proved to be made of a stone, differing from the rocky material around, and well smoothed and polished.

The material seemed to be a sort of marble, unlike anything the boys had ever seen before. It was veined and spotted in a very beautiful fashion, with varying shades and colour.

The boats were tethered to posts of the same material sunk in the softer ground on the edge of the bay.

"This is no an island peopled by savages," said Jack. "Walton is right. We have dropped upon the haunt of the Avashnus."

"It isn't so very far to the top," murmured Don, glancing upwards.

"I must put my veto on your going there," said Bill Oakley, "uncommonly sorry I am, and it may be a bit of imperence on my part, but you are not to leave this 'ere boat."

"Nonsense, Billy," said Don, "it would not take long to climb up, and we may be able to make sure if there is any occasion to fear an enemy or not."

"Anyway, you don't go," said Oakley, obstinately, "not if I can hold you."

"Listen!" exclaimed Jack.

They all sat still, and from over the hill-top there floated towards them a medley of sounds, in which music and cries of pain seemed mingled. They ceased almost as suddenly as they had begun.

"What a beastly uncanny noise!" said Don, with an involuntary shiver.

"I have an idea," said Jack. "Here we are, and over there we have certainly some enemies. Here are their boats. Well! Anon they may come down and spot us. There isn't a shadow of a chance of our escaping observation. What will they do?"

"Come for us," replied Don.

"My idea is to keep them off as long as possible," said Jack, "and that can be done by unfastening those boats, tying them together, and taking the lot into the middle of the bay."

"It may stave off mischief," said Don.

"It's an idea to be acted on," said Bill Oakley, "but it will take time. I reckon that there are thirty of these proas. We can't pull out the lot."

Jack said they could take some at a time, leave Don in one to keep them in position, while he and the boatswain went to and fro until the whole were were secured in the middle of the bay.

There, owing to the action of the in-flowing water, was comparative stillness. The trouble of keeping the boats from the shore, having once got them here, would be very little.

The work was carried out without a hitch or a sign of the enemy. It was by that time close on five o'clock. In another hour the daylight would come upon them with a rush.

There is little dawn in that latitude. Darkness comes and goes as if from the rising or falling of a curtain. And when the day came they would still have an hour ere they could hope to be served with the ebb.

What might happen in that time it was impossible to say. But they resolved not to anticipate evil, but keep up a hopeful spirit.

The proas, once huddled together in the middle of the bay, gave no trouble worth mentioning. A touch here, a pull there, kept them in place.

Twice during the hour the medley of sounds they had heard was repeated. But there was no sign of life upon the hills around.

The moon shone in the heavens all the time, but they had lost it for an hour or more behind the hills, when the first flash of sunlight spread across the sky.

The herald of the sun, the "oosha," as the Persians call it, came and died quickly away. Then there was a moment's rest, and daylight was there.

A deep gloom that had rested on the bay vanished.

But never had daylight been less welcome than it was to the trio in the boat. If darkness could have remained a while longer, until the wished-for ebb arrived, they would have been thankful. But time, and light, and darkness take their regular courses without regard to the needs of particular individuals, and daylight was there.

Together, by instinct, the three pairs of eyes were turned towards the marble steps, and what all dreaded to see was there.

A man was coming down.

He was tall and thin, and dark of countenance. On his head he wore a turban of some material that shone like gold. His body was clad in a garment that shone resplendently with jewels.

So brilliant was his attire that at first they did not observe he held a serpent like a rod in his right hand.

But ere long they saw it slowly twisting in his grasp.

He held it from him at the outset, but as he descended he slowly raised it until it was over his head, and there it remained until he was almost to the bottom of the long flight of marble steps.

Then suddenly he stopped.

He was staring fixedly at the water, and missed the boats.

"Down, all of us," whispered Jack.

They were on the further side of the cluster of proas slowly turning on the water, and it flashed on Jack that if they were unseen for a time they might obtain a sort of respite. There was only an hour to wait, and if during that time they could bamboozle the enemy their escape was almost certain.

It was not the one man they feared. He was the indication of many being in the neighbourhood. His garments and the serpent in his grasp showed that they were indeed the mystic and justly dreaded Avishnu people.

And there was one thing more which gave rise to a natural fear, a knowledge that from the serpent-worshippers no mercy could be hoped for if they fell into their power.

Don had not only seen the man, but recognised him.

As they lay on the bottom of their boat he looked at Jack, whose face wore a puzzled expression.

"You recognise him?" whispered Don.

"I scarcely noticed the face," replied Jack, "but there was something in the figure——"

"Have you forgotten Mehala?"

"Merciful heavens! Chunder Loo!"

They paled a little in spite of their courage, for they knew that this man-monster was to be dreaded. If he got the boys—they were no more—into his power in this lone spot on the earth, where he possibly reigned supreme, what would be their fate?

There was no torture he would not devise for their punishment for having so successfully thwarted his villainous plans in the old schooldays.

"I am no coward," whispered Jack, "but I pray that he has not seen us."

"I wonder what he is doing," muttered Don. "Would it be too risky to take one peep?"

"I hear sounds as of someone swimming," said Bill Oakley, in a low, gruff voice.

They all listened.

Above the sounds of the lapping water and the boats slowly grinding together, they undoubtedly heard the short, sharp breathing of a swimmer.

"Only one," whispered Jack, "and that one Chunder Loo. Don, if he comes to us what shall we do?"

"Kill him," answered Don; "it will be no crime, or if it is I will share it with you."

Bill Oakley lay curled up in the after part of the boat. He had shifted round so as to have his eyes on the boys. They motioned to him to keep still, and with great care drew their cutlasses.

During the year they had spent on board the "Albatross" they had been taught the use of the weapon, but hitherto had not drawn one save in play.

Now they were about to stain the brightness of the steel with the life-blood of a *man*.

It is true that he was a villain of the deepest dye, a thief, a murderer, and their remorseless enemy; but the first taking of life, even though it be in fair fight, is a serious thing.

A man never does it without hesitation, and what could be expected of two youths like Jack and Don?

And yet it must be done, to save themselves.

They were conscious, in the slow eddying of the mid waters of the bay, that the proas and their own boat had swung round, and they were now on the shore side of the group.

The swimmer would, in all probability, have discovered the presence of the strange craft.

But he was still coming on.

Nearer drew the sounds of his panting breath.

And the boys lay still.

Bill Oakley had also drawn his weapon, and was ready for action.

He understood something of what was in the minds of the boys, but not all. He had no knowledge of the swimmer being an old enemy, but he understood that they looked upon his death as, in self-preservation, a most desirable thing.

Chunder Loo, that arch-villain, was now so near that they could have risen up and shot him.

But the noise of firearms might bring about the disaster they dreaded.

The echoing report would be heard by those beyond the hills, and in a brief space of time the enemy would be swarming down to avenge him.

Nearer came the swimmer, until, as Jack judged he could not be more than a few feet from the boat.

That he was heading for it was certain, unconscious perhaps of its being occupied.

Jack gave the signal, and in an instant he and Don were on their feet.

As one takes in a whole picture at a glance, so they saw that Chunder Loo had divested himself of his gorgeous raiment, and left it on the shore.

Beneath it was his mahogany skin, and his upturned face dispelled all possible doubts of his identity.

Aloft, above the water he held the writhing serpent, one of a brilliant-coated species, unknown, even in natural history, to the boys.

They saw its glittering, evil eyes, its gleaming coat, all things before them, indeed, in one moment, including the sardonic grin on the face of Chunder Loo which showed that he knew they were in the boat and recognised them.

That he should be so audacious as to venture alone to take them prisoners surprised them, but such proved not to be his purpose.

Ceasing swimming, he assumed an upright position in the water, and, with a fiendish laugh, hurled the serpent into the boat.

Then he turned over and struck out for the shore.

The scaly reptile struck Jack on the face, and fell upon the bottom of the boat.

Ere he had recovered from the shock, the twisting creature coiled itself up and sprang at Bill Oakley, round whose neck it twisted its sinuous body.

It was the work of a moment, and poor Bill's eyes under the enormous pressure suddenly put upon his throat, stood out of his head.

It was a fearful spectacle, and the boys for a moment were unable to stir. But the horrible fascination happily did not last.

They sprang forward, side by side, at the risk of upsetting the boat, and struck at the serpent together.

Jack's blow severed its head, and Don cut off a foot or so off the tail.

The hold of the rest on Bill's throat relaxed and fell upon the bottom of the boat.

The severed pieces writhed and twisted like three serpents, leaping and turning about in a horrible way.

In a frenzy of loathing, more than fear, the boys cut at it again and again, hacking the portions of the serpent until the floor of the boat was bespattered with blood and naught but quivering fragments of the reptile remained.

Meanwhile Bill Oakley lay perfectly still, as to body, opening and shutting his mouth in a gasping way, and staring ahead like a man in a dream.

When Jack and Don had completed their work of killing the serpent they went to his aid, and assisted him into a sitting position.

"Bill," said Jack, "pull yourself together. You are not dead yet."

"Wot a sensation!" gasped Bill; "it was like a circular wice, and cold as ice. Where is the warmint?"

"Here is all that is left of it," said Don, pointing to the pieces of the reptile.

Bill shivered.

"I'll swab this 'ere boat out," he said. "Ugh! I seed the finish of my airthly wanderings when it put the grip on."

He had not got over it by a long way, and as he wriggled his neck, with many distortions of countenance, Jack and Don could scarcely forbear laughing.

But their position was altogether too serious for mirth.

Chunder Loo, who proved to be a strong swimmer, was already out of revolver-shot, on his way to the shore, there to give the alarm and rouse the people at his command to action.

It wanted yet half an hour to the ebb. The tide, though it had slackened outside, still swiftly poured its waters through the cave, and any attempt to row against it would have been futile.

What could Chunder Loo do in that half-hour?

In the first place he would have to resume his attire, and then ascend the flight of steps. There surmise came to a dead stop. He might have help at hand, or he might be obliged to seek it inland.

Then came the question as to the nature of that help.

If it should prove to be men with firearms, then the end would speedily come, for half a dozen decent marksmen could riddle the boat and slay the inmates in five minutes, or less.

If it consisted of a people without the modern instruments of warfare, then they would be obliged to swim to the boat. Even in that case, numbers, with courage, must prevail, for the killing of two or three would not stop a host.

"We have eighteen shots and our cutlasses," said Jack: "after that we have nothing."

He looked up at the cliffs on the sea-side, and saw that there was no hope in that direction.

In an ordinary country they might have landed and made their way to the beach, and by signals attracted the attention of their friends; but things were against them in that respect.

They had no clear idea of how far they were from the sea, to begin with. The swift passage through the cave or tunnel had left them nothing to gauge the distance. It might be one, two, three, or more miles. And to land on any part of the surrounding rocks, save that of the sea, appeared to be throwing themselves into the arms of a remorseless foe.

No wonder, then, that they watched with anxious eyes the speeding of Chunder Loo to the shore.

He swam—adopting the modern side-stroke—strongly, shooting through the water straight as an arrow from a bow, but with less speed, of course.

They saw him land, climb upon the lower step, and proceed, with great coolness, to dress himself.

With his simple attire, it did not take long.

Not once did he look back upon the boat and its occupants. He seemed to be perfectly assured of their being in his power.

Proceeding deliberately up the marble steps, he gained the summit, and there he stood for a moment looking down.

At that height he was no more than a dot to the eyes of those below. It was not possible to discern the expression of his features, but Jack and Don, who had seen so much of him of old, pictured the look he cast towards them.

They affected to be occupied with assisting Bill Oakley in ridding the boat of all signs of their unwelcome visitor.

Still they had one eye for the heights above, and they saw Chunder Loo spread his arms, as if cursing them, and then face inland, and put his hands to the sides of his mouth.

He sent forth a shrill cry, that was only human in the sense that it came from a man.

It rang far and wide. It dived down to the bosom of the enclosed bay, and echoed there. It spread abroad over the island, and was heard even as far as the deck of the "Albatross," where it sounded like some far-off cry of pain.

The Australian "coo-ee," a sound that travels miles in still air, had not its penetrating power.

A few moments elapsed, and then the answer came back.

Not in one voice but in many.

The morning air rang with the responses of the unseen, and the trio who heard then guessed with some reason that a horde of enemies would soon be upon them.

By-and-bye they came upon the hill-top.

First one man, then two, and after that in small companies, a wild, dark-skinned people.

Some were clad in raiment that shone with many colours in the sunlight.

Others in more sober garb stood up darkly lined against the radiant sky, and a few had no raiment worthy of the name.

But in the hands of all weapons were revealed.

The greater part had naught but the sword or the

dagger, or perchance a long, gleaming knife. The remainder were armed with firearms, varying in form from the Arab's long musket to the latest rifle.

They formed round Chunder Loo, who leaped upon a clump of rock and addressed them briefly, but to a terrible purpose.

His sayings ended, they came pouring down with cries that were as the roaring of rushing waters, and with less promise of mercy in the resonant utterances that rent the air in twain.

"Don," said Jack, "we are in for it now."

"Let us make for the cave," advised Don, "and fight it out there."

They both looked at Bill Oakley, who shook his head mournfully.

"No chance of getting through yet," he said; "the tide is still strong. The force of it is still felt by that narrow hole."

"We can but try," said Don. "It will give them further to swim to us, anyway."

"But we must leave the proas to drift in their direction," said Jack.

"Let it be so," said Don. "The cave is our only chance. What matters it if we take a dozen lives and lose our own?"

There was a force in this argument that could not be ignored, so they loosened the painter of their own boat, and the two youngsters took the oars. Bill Oakley resumed the helm.

The old boatswain's face was rigid.

It was not the first time he had been in peril of losing his life, and he had little thought of that. It was the young and hopeful companions of his danger that he thought of. To him they were what children are to some fathers, and he would gladly have laid down his life to save theirs.

"Pull steadily," he said; "you may want your strength by-and-bye."

As they rowed they faced the swarm of foes now dashing down towards the inland bay. With watchful eyes they noticed that Chunder Loo was not among the foremost, but followed in the midst, speaking to those around him as he came.

They could not hear his words, but they instinctively judged that he was bidding his followers take the captives alive.

A death by the sword or rifle would not satisfy him now. He wanted them in his power, at his mercy, to be tortured, so that he might have full vent for his malevolence.

They knew it by that intuitive feeling by which the keen intellect judges the actions of men, and with set teeth they resolved not to be taken alive.

Down they came, a howling horde of fanatics, and, reckless of themselves, plunged into the water and swam towards the boat.

The mouth of the cave was reached and the frail barque headed for it. The rowers threw all their strength into the oars, but beyond a certain point they could not go.

The strong tide still drove them back.

CHAPTER CCII.

THE FIRST FIGHT WITH THE AVISHNUS.

AS the time passed on and day drew near Harry Barstow became more and more uneasy about the missing trio.

Apart from the love he had for Don and Jack, which had grown by association at sea, he valued Bill Oakley as one of those rare birds, a faithful man, at once a servant and a friend.

He had a hope that nothing would happen to them, and he recognised the fact that they were unable to return by the way they went until the change of tide permitted it. But that they must be undergoing some strange experiences he had not the least doubt.

At length, as the dawn approached, he decided to wait no longer, and, in case of there being a tangible foe to deal with, to take with him eight or ten good men.

"I wish," said Dick Darnley, "that you would let me go in your place. I am responsible for the whole thing, and ought to see the boys out of it."

"I will go myself," said Harry.

The boat was got ready, and eight men volunteered for the service. Dirk Matthews was not among them, nor, indeed, any of the disaffected ones who had been misled by him.

They all kept well out of the way until the boat was gone.

At the last moment Tom and Bob came on deck to take another turn at watching. On hearing that their chums were missing they asked to be allowed to go in the boat. Harry Barstow hesitated a moment, and then said "Come."

Thus were thirteen on board taken away, making sixteen in all.

Dirk Matthews exultingly looked upon the "Albatross" as already in his possession.

For the present we must leave him to carry out his scheme to the best of his bad ability, and accompany the party of rescue.

The precaution was taken to arm the men, and strong in numbers and in weapons, they headed for the cave.

At sea the tide was already weakened, but the run of water through the narrow way was still brisk. It had, however, lost much of its power.

The men, in obedience to orders, backed water by

the mouth of the cave, while their captain endeavoured to fathom its depths. But all was darkness there.

A lighted lantern was ready, and Tom was sent into the bows with it to give warning of any peril ahead. Then came the word, "Give way, men," and the boat shot out of the open air into the inner darkness just as the "oosha" flashed athwart the sky.

The rowers did not ship oars, but they pulled gently, Harry Barstow steering, guided by the light of the lantern in the bow, which sufficed to reveal the proportions of the place. The velocity with which the first boat shot through may be guessed at from the fact that the party of rescue were half an hour in darkness ere they came to the bend around which was the opening into the bay.

In silence they had travelled, none being in a humour for conversation. The seamen had a natural repugnance for the cave, and the boys were thinking of the absent ones.

The sight of daylight ahead roused them all from their semi-apathy, and a shout was on their lips, when the rattle of firearms was heard from without.

"Bend to your oars, men!" cried Harry.

The men had been pulling somewhat leisurely, but, roused by the command, they gave half a dozen smart tugs at the oars, and then they were in the light of day.

Shooting out at a great speed, they nearly collided with a boat hard by.

Their eyes being half-blinded for the moment by the glare, they did not perceive anything clearly. But they had ears to hear, and the shout of welcome that burst from the occupants in that boat showed them that they had fallen upon the lost ones.

A few moments later, their eyes being no longer holden, they could see clearly. But there was no time for more than a word of greeting, for the enemy was at hand.

On the shore were the men with the rifles, firing in a desultory manner. The bosom of the water swarmed with human heads. A host of swimmers, with knives between their teeth, were making for the boats.

On the base of the flight of steps, a conspicuous figure, even among so many that were striking, was Chunder Loo, urging on the Avishnus with piercing voice and wild gesture.

The enemy were not practised riflemen, for their aim was wild, and the boats were fully two hundred yards away; but the leaden pellets fell dangerously near to the boats, and that in which Jack and Don were had a hole in it not far from the water-mark.

Harry Barstow took in the advantages and disadvantages of the position at a glance. Standing erect in the stern of his boat, he gave his orders calmly but rapidly.

"Hook on to the rocks there. Forward oars keep going to steady her. Oakley, pass on your painter and tie to our stern. Cool and steady, all of you. The tide will be near the ebb in a few minutes. Don't waste a revolver-shot, but when one of those fellows gets near enough, drop him!"

The boats tethered together swung out in a line with the approaching swimmers, whose vulture-like countenances and small, dark, gleaming eyes curiously suggested water-rats.

There was no fear or hesitation in their advance. Like all fanatic people they were set to do something, and they were there to do it or die.

While they were yet some thirty yards away, that being about the distance of the foremost, one of their number was seen to leap up suddenly in the water, throw out his arms, and, with a wild yell, disappear.

He had been struck by one of the bullets despatched by his friends ashore.

It was marked by Chunder Loo, who was observed to motion for the firing to cease.

It was afterwards judged that it had been exercised only as a means of distracting the attention of those they sought to capture, Don, Jack, and Oakley. The assumption was not without foundation.

A desultory fire from the shore could not fail to attract their attention, to a degree, from the swimmers.

They came on through the water as wild birds fly in the air, in the form of a wedge.

The foremost was a man with the shaven head of a dervish, grizzly and ferocious in expression of face, a leader of the Avishnus.

He had his eyes on the revolvers held in the hands of those in the boats.

The coming of the second one must have been an unpleasant surprise to them, but they showed no signs of it. Not one man halted or turned back.

"Shoot low!" cried Harry Barstow, "and aim steadily!"

He set the example by aiming at the foremost at the distance of twenty-five yards. The grizzly old man immediately dived, and reappeared ten yards nearer to the left.

The young captain was watching for him, and ere his eyes were clear of water, had taken aim and fired.

On the bald part of his crown a small round hole appeared, proving how well the shot had told. The Avishnu heeled over, lay for a moment on the surface of the bay, and then disappeared.

As in the beginning of a great battle so it was now. The sight of one man shot roused the warlike spirit of all who looked on. The banner of the god of war metaphorically floated on the breeze.

A thrill went through the younger portion of the occupants of the boats.

It was their first taste of actual warfare, and the momentary qualm, that comes to the bravest at such a time, having passed away, they were ready for anything.

Each and all singled out a swimmer as a mark, and coolly waited for him. Harry Barstow cast a quick glance at them, and seeing their eager eyes fixed on the foe and the cocked weapons ready, knew that he could leave them to take care of themselves.

And the men, all but those engaged in keeping the boats close up to the cave, were prepared likewise.

They uttered no sound or cry, but stood as cool as if on some ordinary deck duty, erect in the boat, each man in his place.

Ping! Ping!

Don and Jack, being the nearest to the foe, had fired, One man clapped his hands to his face, screaming and plunging about in the water. The other vanished as if he had been drawn under by some powerful monster.

"Well done, boys!" cried Harry Barstow.

The defenders were inspirited, and the attacking party maddened, by the success of the first three shots.

On came the latter, cleaving through the water with strong, practised arms—on to within a few yards of the boats, and then to go under in turn from the unerring aim of the seamen. But these only composed the thin end of the wedge; the thick end was to come. Each successive line of the Avishnus was broader than the one preceding.

Anon they would swarm around in a semicircle, and, with the blindness of their race, come on to death or victory.

Not a sound escaped them.

When one of their number went under, the nearest to him just turned their eyes for a moment towards where he had been, and then came on and on.

Still, it was death for them to come within reach of the boats. The water was tinged with the blood of the slain. Some wounded did not sink, but kept afloat, grim and ferocious. One laid hold of the smaller boat, and was climbing in, when Bill Oakley, with a chopping action, cut off one of his hands.

The fanatic still held on, and the other had, perforce, to be removed. It was done, and, with bleeding stumps raised in the air, as if appealing for vengeance from his fellows, he joined those already under the surface.

Then another gained a hold upon the larger boat, only to loosen it as his skull was cloven; then another gained almost a hand-hold, receiving a cutlass-thrust that made a wide gap in his breast, and let out the life-blood in a stream.

There was strife and death in every movement.

And through all the young captain was coolly watching for the time when the boats could beat a retreat.

Wisely, he understood that in point of numbers and in arms he was no match for the horde of foes in such a place.

The boats offered but a poor means of defence. There was no stability in them, and only a sailor could have kept erect in the rocking created by the unavoidable movement.

Three of the foe had fallen to Harry Barstow's share, when he observed that there was a sudden lull in the movement of the water from the cave. The ebb was at hand.

"Stand by for the oars!" he cried. "Ready—let go! Pull, men!"

The orders were given in rapid succession, and in three moments the men were in their places.

With the oars they seized they beat off two or three who had gained the boats, and then they pulled for their lives.

Slowly at first, and then more quickly, they glided into the dark shadow, with the smaller boat attached in the rear.

Down dropped Don and Jack, overboard went the blades of their oars, and they bent to them with all the strength at their command.

Then, and not till then, did a shout burst from the lips of the men.

It could not be one of absolute victory, but it was of triumph to an extent, and also of derision.

As the hindmost boat glided into the cave, Don and Jack became conscious of a sudden drag upon it.

Then over the stern appeared a dark brown face, with eyes that shone like those of some wild beast in the night.

"Look out, Bill!" shouted Jack.

The old boatswain, who was steering, faced about. Over him stood a lithe form, and a glittering knife was descending upon him.

He dodged aside, and seizing the invader by the legs, threw him heavily, partly in the stern of the boat, and head and shoulders over it.

In a moment the active Avishnu had wriggled in again, and they closed.

Again Bill thought of the serpent that had nearly made an end of him in the open bay. There was a curious resemblance between the grip of the reptile and the hold of the man—there was also the same sense of writhing and twisting.

So, the pair struggling, they were borne into the darkness, for both lanterns had, in the struggle outside, been extinguished, and nobody had thought of relighting them.

CHAPTER CCIII.

PLOT AND COUNTER-PLOT—PENNY BUNN EARNS A REWARD HE IS NOT LIKELY TO GET.

AS soon as the boat with the captain and others had left the "Albatross," Dirk Matthews went up to the deck to take stock of the situation.

Mr. Walton, the second mate, was on deck talking to Dick Darnley. Forward there was the watch, reduced to four men, owing to the draft made upon the crew to man the captain's boat.

The two officers being on deck rather checked the plans of the would-be mutineers.

He could have shot one easily, but with two the chances were that he would get shot in return.

If he fell, even though he was only slightly wounded, but crippled for the time, he knew that his brother-conspirators would give in.

Apart from himself, they had not one who could take place as leader.

But there was still plenty of time, and he could wait awhile. Sullenly he went below to the cabin where the men who intended to act with him were in waiting.

"We must hold off a bit, boys," he said. "Both of the mates are on deck."

"Can't we do the thing with a bold rush?" asked Goffer.

"Bold rushes cost lives," replied Matthews, "and we have none to spare. Close that door."

It was done, and the only light now in the cabin came in from the porthole windows.

In the semi-gloom they sat about, and presently began to smoke.

"You don't seem in no hurry to begin," remarked Springtop.

"I'm giving them time to get away from each other," replied Dirk Matthews. "If I go pottering upstairs every few minutes they will smell a rat. Anyways, they will want to know what the deuce I want."

There was another silence, and then Dirk Matthews arose and went to his trunk, which stood at the far end of the cabin. It was locked, and with a key he opened it.

"Now here," he said, "are a brace of barkers for each of you. I've been careful to see that they was loaded, and I was careful to see that them in the boat's lockers was *not* !"

"What was the need of your interfering there?" said Bates.

"I'll tell you why one day, perhaps," answered Matthews; "there's wheels within wheels everywheres, and I'm in a wheel as you haven't set eyes on yet. Now you have all got shooters, and for the rest you must trust to your knives. Who is that snorting?"

"Didn't hear anyone snorting," answered one of the men.

"Snuffling, then. Up in the corner. There, by the door?"

Dirk Matthews looked in that direction and having assured himself of the fact, put two revolvers inside his shirt and locked the chest.

"Two minutes more," he said, "and I'll go on deck. You foller close at my heels and wait till you hear me fire. Then rush up, and some of you cover the watch with your poppers. The t'others can give me a hand if I should want it. Order the watch down below, and put on the hatches."

They nodded in assent, breathing hard. Now that the great moment had come, the majority were rather inclined to hang back. They were not so sure of entire success as their leader was.

He waited two or three minutes, ostentatiously smoking in a fashion expressive of the utmost coolness. Then he knocked the ashes out of his pipe, trod upon the few sparks that fell, and walked to the door.

"Cool and steady," he said, "and we are masters of one of the finest little crafts afloat. Six months hence we shall all be rich men and blowing our 'bacca under the vine-trees of our plantations in the south of Amerikey. There we shall have ease and drink, and as many wives for the axing as a Turk. Remember my orders."

He stepped up to the door and turned the handle. A jerk inward failed to open it.

"What the deuce is the matter with it?" he growled.

There was no lock that required a key. The handle being turned, the door ought to have opened. But it only yielded the fraction of an inch.

"Some fool has been playing a trick on us," he growled; "this yere door is tied up somehow."

"Then we are caged," said Bates.

"Seems so."

"But who should do it?"

"How am I to tell?"

"But there is a reason for it," urged Goffer. "Whoever did it means to keep us here till the cap comes back, I reckon."

"Here," said Bates, pulling out his two revolvers, "shove these things into your chest ag'in. I don't want to be convicted on circumstantial evidence afore I've done anything."

"Here, take mine!"

"And mine!"

The men all wanted to get rid of the weapons, and they thrust them on the furious and disappointed Matthews in a very peremptory manner.

"We ought to stand or fall together," he said, with an attempt to work up a friendly smile.

"I'm not going to fall if I can help it," said Goffer, and so said they all.

"But why not put 'em in your own chests?" urged Dirk Matthews; "it will be sharing with me in a way."

But they all refused to do so, and called on him, not in the politest tones, to do as he was told.

He raved and threatened in no stinted fashion, but they were firm, and finally he had to resume possession of the weapons. But he would not retain them as evidence against himself. There was the open port window, and he could dispose of the revolvers by dropping them into the sea.

"It comes hard," he said, "as I paid for every one of 'em."

"Don't they belong to the 'Albatross'?" demanded Bates.

"No, they don't," returned Matthews. "I dursn't take the ship's tools at the start. They would be sure to be missed. I bought these 'ere things at Malta."

"Stole 'em, you mean," said Springtop; "you hadn't any money when you signed articles."

"I *got* 'em at Malta," insisted Dirk Matthews, "and they was paid for honest. Now will that content you?"

As he was speaking he quietly, one by one, pushed out the weapons and dropped them into the sea. After the fall of each he stood and listened for any sign that he was attracting attention. But there was none.

No movement or voice above showed that his action was observed.

In turn he disposed of all the weapons, and finished by despatching others he had in his chest to the bottom of the deep sea.

He had not the slightest doubt that he was a suspected man, and with all evidence of his premeditated guilt destroyed, he thought that he could face his accusers.

"It's a blooming sell," he muttered; "but if you all stick out that we was up to nothin', then we shall be all right; but if you go snivelling and a-blowing what you know, every man Jack of you will swing, if I knows the cap'en. He can be uncommon kind when he likes, but if you puts his back up he won't stick at trifles."

"There's somebody outside with a broom," said Goffer.

"Bunn, on his morning sweeping job," said Dirk. "Ask him what is the matter with the door."

Goffer went across the cabin and shouted out:

"Bunn!"

"What is it?" asked the cheery voice of that gentleman.

"What is the matter with our door?"

"How should I know?"

"It's fastened up, ain't it?"

"Not that I can see."

Goffer turned the handle and the door opened. Penny Bunn, with a broom in his hand, stared in with an expression of wonder on his face.

"What could have induced you to think that the door was fastened? It hasn't a lock."

"We tried it a few minutes ago," replied Goffer; "leastways, Matthews did, and it wouldn't open."

"Matthews could not have tried very hard," said Bunn, resuming his sweeping.

"Look here," growled Dirk, "I strongly suspect you have been up to some fool's game. Now, if you have, out with it!"

Penny Bunn went on with his sweeping as he made answer.

"The fool's game I have been guilty of," he said, "is to oversleep myself. As I am behind with my duties of the morning, I will thank you not to impede me."

"Let him alone," muttered Goffer; "the door was all right, only you were shaky and bungled with the opening of it."

Dirk Matthews turned the handle to and fro, and found it did not always act. The mystery of its presumably being fast was, to an extent, explained.

"Anybody on deck?" he asked Bunn.

"Only Mr. Walton," answered Bunn, "who, for the want of something to do, is dozing in an easy-chair. Mr. Darnley is below."

Dozing in an easy-chair. How easy it would have been to shoot him! But the idea of a mutiny must for the time be abandoned.

It was a chance thrown away, but yet it was some relief to learn that they were not suspected after all.

Bunn finished his sweeping with a flourish, gave the broom two or three scientific knocks against the wall, and stepped lightly away to the cuddy, where Rammer was heating the water for the cocoa.

"Friend George of the royal name," he said, "I have this morning put the break on a mutiny."

"How?" asked Rammer, tasting the contents of the packet, to make sure it was cocoa he was about to put in the pot.

The action was noticed by Bunn, who asked him if he could not trust to the labels.

"I trusts to nothing but my senses," replied Rammer.

"But it is so plainly printed thereon—'Cocoa, absolutely pure, with all the insoluble parts removed.' Read it."

Rammer held the packet at arm's-length, and gazed at it, as if reading the instructions thereon.

"You have it upside down," said Penny Bunn.

"I know that," snarled Rammer. "I was a just taking in the shape of the packet. It is as good a thing as you can go by."

"Indeed?"

"Yes, indeed. But what have you been doing to save the ship?"

Bunn's face brightened, and he told what would seem to some people to be a very strange story indeed.

Going down below a little before his accustomed hour to do some sweeping, he heard voices in the fore-cabin, and, impelled by curiosity, he lay down near the small hole created by the absence of a knot in the wood of the door, and listened.

Practically, but with some inevitable circumlocution, he told the story of the recent failure.

"It was I who tied up the door temporarily." he said, "my intention being to keep the villains there until the captain returned, and then hand them over to justice. But when that nefarious scoundrel Matthews dropped the revolvers into the sea, I saw there was no reason for keeping them fastened in. so I removed the rope."

"And what do you intend to do?" asked Rammer, stirring the cocoa, with his nose in the air.

"On the return of Captain Harry Barstow." replied Bunn, "I shall report the whole thing to him."

"And you expect him to believe you?"

"Certainly."

"Then you must be unkimmonly green."

"Don't you believe me?"

"I do *not*," was the emphatic reply. "It comes to this, young man. If you was an old salt like myself, you wouldn't try on sich palpitating lies. It won't do at sea. You was a schoolmaster once, I believe?"

"I was," replied Bunn, stiffly.

"Then that accounts for it," said Rammer. "I never knowed a schoolmaster as was worth feeding on horse-beans. They are a naterally bad lot—impostors, humbugs."

"You must have gone to a very poor school," remarked Penny Bunn.

"I went to one of the best to be got for love or money," returned Rammer, "so don't you insinivate to the contrary."

"You think that I should not be believed?" said Bunn, meditatively.

"I am sure on it. There isn't anything in your favour. The yarn is too childish. It is the sort of thing that might have gone down with a infant school, sich as I reckon you kept, but not here among old seamen."

"Well," said Bunn, "the next time a mutiny is on the *tapis*, I shall allow it to come to a head."

"On or off a tarpee," said Rammer, "keep your mouth shut until you can open it with bits of truth. There is nothing that riles me like a liar."

"How is your leg this morning?" abruptly asked Bunn.

"Well, it's better," replied Rammer; "the nerves seem to be a bit quieter."

Bunn sniffed.

"Wot! You don't believe as I suffers with my leg?"

"I do *not*."

"Well, of all the——"

"Stop a moment," interposed Bunn. "What proof have you that you suffer? Show us the nerves of your leg in action. Until you do that you have no *proof*. Besides, *I know that you can't suffer from it.* Now, then!"

"Bunn," said Rammer, with a face that paled, save at the tip of the nose, "it ain't manly to drop on me."

"Do you believe my yarn?"

"In course I does."

"All right: then I will let that leg of yours alone."

He nodded meaningly, and Rammer, with the sleeve of his shirt, wiped his heated brow.

Humming an air, his assistant disappeared.

"Good Heaven!" ejaculated Rammer, "to think that he's got hold of it. And nobody else in it. I shall have to cut it small when talking to him in future. Blow him, how did he get at it?"

Whatever might be the secret of that leg, the fact that Bunn had fathomed it troubled him sorely, and the cocoa that morning was not so good as usual.

As for Bunn, he saw on reflection that Rammer was a fair index of the general man. He would have some difficulty in getting anyone to believe his story. The evidence that would have helped him was at the bottom of the sea, ten fathoms down.

So for a while he would be dumb.

CHAPTER CCIV.

JACK FORD'S SCHEME.

THERE is always something peculiarly terrible about a struggle in the dark. In the case of Bill Oakley it was especially so, as it threatened to upset the boat and involve others besides the combatants in the issue.

The leading boat was obliged to go slowly, owing to the inability of those in charge of it to be fully certain of the course.

Twice there was a check, owing to a collision with the sides of the cave occurring while one of the men, by command of Harry Barstow, was groping about for the lantern.

It was eventually found and lighted. Meanwhile, the leading party only imperfectly understood that something was wrong with the boat in tow.

Jack and Don had ceased rowing and drawn their cutlasses, but were unable to use them. When the light of the lantern illumined the cave, they saw Bill Oakley kneeling on the body of his foe, who was writhing like a serpent, with one hand grasping a glittering knife, ready to strike.

Bill had hold of the wrist, and the only sounds emitted by either was a slight hissing from the Avishnu, and sundry grunts and gasps from the boatswain.

"What is the matter there?" asked Harry Barstow.

"Avishnu on board, sir," replied Jack. "Oakley has hold of him."

"Shoot the fellow and pitch him overboard!"

"Steady!" gasped Bill, "I've got him."

As he spoke, he gave the arm of his enemy a twist that compelled him to let go of the knife. Then rising, he quickly laid hold of his heels and tossed him over the stern.

The Avishnu went under with a splash, but was instantly on the surface again, and once more grasped the stern of the boat, but, instead of climbing in, endeavoured to overturn it.

He was so far successful that he upset Bill into the water, and there would have been another struggle in that dangerous position but for Jack, who, with his revolver, shot the Avishnu through the head.

He let go then, and sank to rise no more.

Bill, in falling, had spread-eagled himself upon the water, and Don promptly laying hold of the waistband of his trousers, prevented his going under.

"Take it easy, Mr. Oakley," said Don.

Bill spluttered something in reply, his mouth being filled with water, and laid hold of the side of the boat. He would have overturned it in good earnest if both the youngsters had not thrown their weight upon the opposite gunwale.

Notwithstanding the serious position of Bill Oakley, who, as it afterwards turned out, was no swimmer, the seamen in the other boat roared with laughter.

This exasperated the boatswain, who had a strong objection to being grinned at by those whom he usually commanded and occasionally rope's-ended.

"Stow that, you sons of sea-cows!" he growled, "or I'll put you dancing to a tune of my own when I get you on board."

All immediate peril was over, and he was got into the boat, soaked to the skin and filled with justifiable wrath.

The tide had now fairly turned, and the men settling to their oars, the boats glided along.

A man in the bow of the first boat signalled when it was necessary to steer to the right or left to avoid grazing the sides of the cave, and without any further mishap they eventually reached the welcome sunlight and the open waters again.

A cheer burst from their lips, and it was answered back from the "Albatross."

All hands there seemed to be on deck, and the sailors climbed into the ratlines, enthusiastically waving their caps.

And none were more exuberant in their demonstration of joy than Dirk Matthews.

The boats glided up to the side of the "Albatross," and were speedily empty. For the boys there was a more than hearty welcome from Dick Darnley and Ben Walton, which was supplemented with congratulations when the story of the recent adventures was told.

"I was right, then," said Walton; "the Avishnus are there."

"Our goal is reached," replied Harry Barstow. "There lies the highway to and from the island. It must be blocked for a beginning, and after that we must devise some means of exterminating the band."

It was a surprise to the second mate to learn that Chunder Loo, of whom the boys had often spoken, was apparently the chief, the high-priest, of the uncanny worshippers of the serpent.

Judging by the record of the man they had to deal with—a man of unsurpassable cunning, ferocity, and brute courage—the road to successfully carrying out the object of Harry Barstow, bristled with danger. But there was the comforting assurance that Norton Truscott was either dead or perfectly safe.

"If," said Walton, "he came alive out of the ordeal of the serpent, a dozen Chunder Loos dare not lay a hand upon him, for he, in the eyes of the people, is a sacred thing."

The time had come for the "Albatross" to be put into fighting trim.

During the day the enemy, if he ventured to attack, would not appear. Low tide was about half-past one, and after the turn the proas would be unable to come out until the ebb, which took place about seven p.m.

The moon rose about the same hour.

Tired and hungry, the trio of adventurers, who had passed a night they would remember for many a day, the inner man had first to be thought of, and a late breakfast was laid out for them on the aft deck.

Penny Bunn and Rammer attended to this matter, while the rest of the crew, under the captain's orders, proceeded to put the "Albatross" in "fighting trim."

There was a lot to be done. The heavy guns had to be got up from the hold, fixed on the carriages, and put into position.

Small-arms had to be looked to, and each man appointed to his especial spot in time of action.

But the work, though in a sense heavy, was not of a very trying nature. Everything was ready, like the portions of a machine fresh from the workshop, down to the smallest rope.

The portholes for the guns hitherto had been concealed from ordinary eyes by close-fitting shutters, which a few minutes sufficed to remove.

The men went to work with a will. The long inactivity was at an end. Fighting was the business of the majority, and they rejoiced in what they called "the prospect of a brush."

Bill Oakley, having refreshed himself with a heavy meal, and a bottle of wine as an extra thing after his late experiences, gave a hand; and to show that he had a good memory, he singled out the men who had had the audacity to laugh at him in the cave for a full amount of harrying, and on the least provocation for a taste of the bit of rope he carried at other times in the depths of his capacious trousers-pocket.

They accepted it all as a *quid pro quo*, knowing that they had been guilty of a breach of discipline in daring to laugh at an officer.

Meanwhile Jack and his three friends, lolling at their ease in camp-chairs, looked on, chatting together.

As we all enjoy summer after the chill blasts of winter, so did they revel in the ease that followed a night of bodily and mental strain.

"To think," said Tom Drummond, "that here, on the other side of the world almost, we have lighted on that beast Chunder Loo, fairly takes my breath away."

"Some fellow said somewhere," remarked Bob Stockton, dreamily, "that the world is a very little place, after all."

"You ought not to quote unless you do it more explicitly," said Don.

"Well, it has been said," drawled Bob.

"And the fact remains that we have seen Chunder Loo," said Jack. "Now it is clear that those fellows with him are not afraid of a fight. They will naturally want to have a go at us for more reasons than one. In the first place they will resent our having dropped upon their haunt."

"That is a certainty," said Don.

"Then Chunder Loo will not rest until he has settled with us."

"That is equally certain."

"Therefore, on their discovering, as they surely will, and may have already done, that we do not mean to budge, they will come out and have a go at us."

"There are lots of them," mused Don, "and it will be a big fight."

"My opinion is that they will come for us on the night ebb," pursued Jack; "they will come in their proas, with which they can move about, as we cannot in the 'Albatross,' without wind. Now, having once come out, I think they ought to be stopped from going back again."

"Can we do that?" asked Don. "Have we boats and men enough?"

"It need not be a task for the men and the boats," said Jack. "I've been thinking out a scheme which I propose to lay before our captain. It can be carried out by half a dozen of us, or less. There is a risk in it, of course, but I am willing to take my share of it."

"What is your scheme?" asked Tom.

"I will propound it to the captain first. If he accepts it, then I will proudly acknowledge it. If he says it cannot be carried out, then I will dry up and say no more about it."

"Believing, at the same time," said Bob, "that the captain is an ass for not seeing things as you do?"

"Naturally," said Jack; "but I'll bet you anything that he *does* accept it."

By this time the appearance of the "Albatross" had been totally changed. All the peacefulness of it, the air of being afloat for pleasure, had vanished. She bristled with the armaments of war.

To Penny Bunn the change was a ghastly one. It sent a thrill through him as he looked upon the big guns, and noted the smaller weapons carried by the men.

But he was not going to show what he felt to the outside world.

Having a short time of leisure, he walked about the mid and forward decks, critically examining the arrangements, smiling approvingly on some and frowning on others.

Aft, he saw Captain Harry—as the commander was affectionately called by his friends—and Jack Ford in close conference, the youth apparently pressing some point which his leader deprecated.

At length it appeared that Jack had carried the day, for he went below and soon returned with the second mate, and together they ordered a boat to be lowered—a light gig which would only carry a few persons, and was fit for smooth weather only.

In this they put some instruments which the mate had brought up with them, and a small box which they handled with exceeding care.

Their movements were watched with considerable interest by the majority of those on deck. It was evident that their nature puzzled the seamen, and Dirk Matthews was heard to mutter to those near him: "There is something on that we ain't to take part in."

When the boat was apparently ready, Don, Tom, and Bob were seen to be drawing lots with three pieces of string of different lengths, held by the mate. On comparing them Bob Stockton cut a caper, thereby showing that he had won whatever he had drawn for.

The others turned aside with an air of good-natured disgust. Jack and Bob dropped into the boat.

Penny Bunn advanced to the side and peered over it. The mate, at that moment, was saying something to Captain Harry in a low tone, and did not finish his remarks for a minute or more.

That minute was destined to lead Penny Bunn into some extraordinary adventures.

"Mr. Ford," he said to Jack, "if not intrusive, might I ask a favour?"

"Certainly," answered Jack.

"It is to accompany you on shore," said Bunn. "For many weeks I have not set foot on *terra firma*."

Jack was about to refuse, when Bob, moved by the spirit of mischief, said, with a drawl:

"Oh! let him come, Jack. His knowledge of chemicals may be useful."

"Yes, I remember how far that went at Littlecote," remarked Jack, with a smile.

"Anyway, he could be left in the boat to look after it. Let him come. The poor old chap has a general rough time of it."

"Very well."

Bob signalled to Penny Bunn to descend, and with a face lighted up with joy, the assistant cook of the "Albatross" glided down into the boat and took a seat forward.

Immediately afterwards Ben Walton joined them, and stared as he saw the addition to the party.

"It is Bob's whim," explained Jack. "He thinks that Bunn may be made useful in looking after the boat."

Ben Walton, knowing the old relation between Bunn and the boys, said nothing more, but took up the rudder-lines, and Jack and Don settled to the oars.

The boat was steered for the base of the cliff at the point where it sloped down to the wood.

On the deck of the "Albatross" Harry Barstow was closely scanning the shore to see if any of the foe were visible. Had he detected any signs of them, a signal would have been given for the boat to return by firing a revolver into the air.

But, without any warning, the boat gained the shore and they all got out. Bob Stockton took charge of the box which had hitherto been handled so carefully, and carried it a short way from the sea.

Then he gave Penny Bunn a bag containing some tools.

"Put that with the box," he said, "and mind you don't drop it, unless you wish to go up in pieces to the stars."

"Explosive, I presume?" said Bunn, affecting to be at his ease.

"A new one," answered Bob, "to which all others are but feebleness itself. If you hear any sounds of a jingling nature, get rid of the bag with all speed. Steady, now."

Penny Bunn was remarkably steady in his movements.

With every hair of his head bristling, and a sensation of having an ice-plaster on his back, he went gingerly forward in the direction of the box.

When within a few feet of it, he heard a slight jingling sound within the bag. Quickly, as if it had become suddenly red-hot, he dropped it, and wheeling about, fled back towards the boat.

It was being hauled up by the mate and the two boys, to be hidden among some mimosa bushes in the wood. Bob was facing him, and despite his command of countenance, he could not look serenely upon the face of the terrified Bunn, but burst into a roar of laughter.

"Be quiet, for goodness' sake," said Jack.

"I beg pardon," said Jack; "but it is too ridiculous. I gave Bunn the tool-bag to carry carefully to avoid an explosion. He has dropped it."

But Bunn had guessed from the experience of former years what that laughter meant. He had been, in the old school parlance, "sold again."

In an instant his fright vanished and he became comparatively calm.

Stopping short, he put a hand upon his hip and affected to be softly whistling.

"You have been saved by a miracle," said Bob.

"Really, sir," answered Bunn, "while anxious not to imply or suggest that you have imposed upon me, I venture to suggest that the explosive power of the contents of that bag are practically *nil*."

The boat was placed in a position that hid it from ordinary inspection, well under the bushes, and the ascent of the cliff begun. Penny Bunn, being under the impression that he was to remain with the boat, did not stir until Bob beckoned him to follow.

"You may as well come with us, Bunn," he said; "we are going to do a bit of blasting that may interest you."

Penny Bunn was powerfully interested already.

He began to think that, after all, he had better have remained on board, for it was now evident that they were bound on an expedition with the element of peril very prominent in it.

Ere they had gone far Ben Walton said they must now proceed in silence and with the utmost precaution.

"I must point out to you that we are out of sight of the ship, and a warning signal to return would be lost on us. We shall not see the 'Albatross' again until we are working along the face of the cliff."

Working along the face of the cliff!

Bunn heard those portentous words, and turned icy all over. On what mad errand were they bound?

The scheme which Jack had conceived and propounded to the captain was this.

Over the cave, on the face of the cliff, there was a considerable ruggedness, and at one place projected a

A SPLENDID SCHOOL STORY. NEVER BEFORE PUBLISHED.

By E. HARCOURT BURRAGE,

Author of "Ching Ching," "Monkey Mat and Roving Dick," "The Brave Boy of the Basilisk," &c.

No. 28. *A Handsome Coloured Plate Presented with Every Number.*

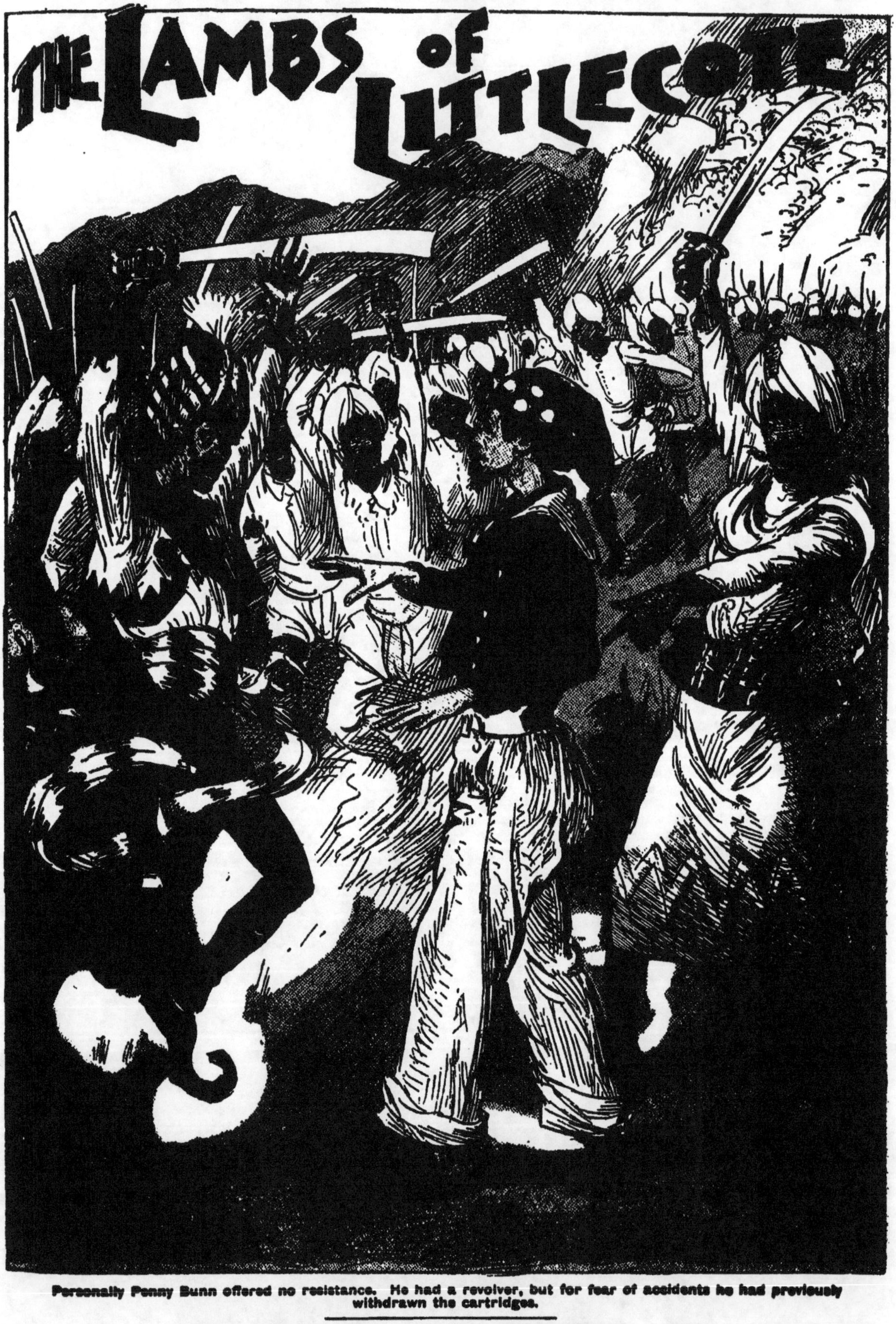
THE LAMBS OF LITTLECOTE.

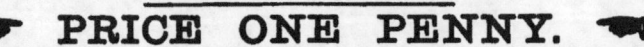

Personally Penny Bunn offered no resistance. He had a revolver, but for fear of accidents he had previously withdrawn the cartridges.

PRICE ONE PENNY.

Red Lion Court, Fleet St., and 1, 2, & 3, Crown Court, Chancery Lane, London.

rock of considerable dimensions which appeared from below to have a table surface.

This, Jack believed, could be reached by what looked like a natural path along the face of the cliff, beginning about a hundred yards nearer to the wood.

Having reached it, the rock could be prepared for blasting in an hour or so, and a fuse being attached, those who had done the work were to await the coming of the proas when evening fell.

It was considered a certainty that the enemy would endeavour to cut out the "Albatross," for the very existence of their faith, and the possession of their haunt as a place of security, depended on her not being allowed to depart.

After sunset the wind would come and the "Albatross" be free to move, if it was thought necessary for her to do so.

Say that the proas were out, they could not overhaul her with the aid of rowers only.

She could, therefore, tack to and fro and destroy them with her guns at leisure.

That is, unless they retreated through the cave.

Probably a time would be chosen when the tide would just serve to bring them out and carry them back within the hour.

It was to prevent their retreat that Jack's scheme had been conceived and accepted.

Immediately the proas were all out it was the intention to light a fuse attached to the blasting preparation and beat a retreat.

Then, if all had been well prepared, a huge mass of the cliff would be sent down and the mouth of the cave blocked.

There would be no means of retreat for the proas, save by flying to the right and left, and no road to return to the inner part of the island save by the dangerous route they had prepared for strangers.

This was the scheme, which promised to thwart the enemy's designs and compass their entire destruction.

We have now to record how far it was successful.

CHAPTER CCV.

PREPARING FOR THE FOE.

"DICK," said Captain Harry, as he closed his telescope, "they are out of sight, and I see no signs of the worshippers of the serpent. So far all goes well. Walton has had some engineering experience, and there won't be any mistake with the blasting of the rock."

Dick Darnley did not immediately reply. He was staring with thoughtful eyes at the summit of the cliff.

"See any impediment there, Dick?"

"No-o-o-o," answered Dick, slowly, "but I was thinking—well, it is nothing, perhaps, but it might have been thought of ere the expedition was finally decided on."

"What have you on your mind?"

"You believe that there is only one way into the interior of the island?"

"I have that belief."

"Well, Harry, as there is only one, are we not running a risk by blocking it up?"

"What risk?"

"The risk of never being able to get to the interior where Norton Truscott, if alive, is to be found."

This remark set the captain of the "Albatross" thinking also. It opened up a wide field of unpleasant speculation.

"I am not usually a croaker," pursued Dick Darnley, "but I think that a hasty decision has been come to. It is not likely that Truscott will be with the proas."

"No," said Harry.

"Nor that he would be left alone. A strong guard will inevitably be left with him."

"I see what you are driving at, Dick. You think that when those who are left behind find that they have lost many of their number, they may avenge themselves on Norton?"

"That is my view of the affair, certainly."

"Dick," said Harry, "we must take our chance of that. Walton says that Truscott is safe from injury if he survived the awful ordeal of the Avashnus. As for getting to the interior of the island, where there is a will there is a way. If we are to be attacked, it will be by a powerful body, comprising three-fourths of the Avashnus. If we succeed in destroying them surely we are men enough to settle the rest."

"I am glad you take a hopeful view of it," said Dick, "as I only mentioned the matter at all so that you might, if necessary, take some step to prevent a fiasco."

"Quite right," said Harry; "but I do not fear a fiasco. I believe that we shall be successful."

As the time wore on and night drew near, preparations for meeting an attack were carried through.

It might have been half an hour before sunset when Don, who was on the lookout for his chums with a glass, reported that there were three figures moving along the face of the cliff.

Immediately this was known all work was suspended for the time and attention concentrated on the three fly-like specks high up near the summit of the rugged rocks.

They were moving cautiously when first observed, with their backs to the cliff, and shifting with a side action, thus showing that the route they were taking was at that point very narrow.

Ben Walton, Jack, and Bob could be distinguished, but nothing was seen of Penny Bunn.

"They have had to leave him behind," said Don. "What head has he for such a job as that?"

"None at all," replied Tom.

The trio were watched as they progressed, and the dangerous nature of the path was indicated by the fact that they occasionally halted and consulted as to the way to go.

Here and there they had to drop, or climb up, a few feet, and now and then to jump. It sent a shiver through the breasts of the watchers as they realised the peril of the task Jack had taken upon himself.

"And the return is by moonlight," muttered Don. "What is the time-fuse they have with them?"

"I believe it allows them a quarter of an hour to get away," returned Tom.

"A quarter of an hour, and by that road? Great Heaven!"

The table rock was reached, and the adventurers stood and moved about there at their ease.

Ere long they were observed to be busy with the preparations for blasting.

Ben Walton directed the movements of his companions, while he seemed to be getting ready the cartridge for blasting.

While they were thus engaged the night came down.

There was an interval of darkness, covering half an hour, ere the moon rose up to give her borrowed light to the scene.

It was a time of anxiety on board the "Albatross." Every man was on deck ready for action, the seamen divided into two parties, one under Bill Oakley's command, and the other looked after by Dick Darnley.

Harry Barstow, of course, was in general command, with Tom and Don by his side to act as bearers of orders to Oakley and Darnley.

Quietude was essential, for there was no wind as yet. It lagged behind, and not a breath of it was stirring when the moon rose out of the sea.

The hour for the coming of the enemy, if he came at all, was at hand. Nearly every eye was turned to the mouth of the cave.

Only one pair may be excepted, and those were in the head of Rammer.

That gallant old seaman was in the cuddy with the door closed.

Though born and reared at sea, nurtured, as one may say, on the deck of fighting vessels, accustomed to war in all its terrors, he was at times in the bluest of blue funks, and endeavouring to rake up from the depths of his turbid memory some long-forgotten prayer for the safety of those at sea.

"Blamed if I'd have j'ined if I'd known that it would ever come to real fighting," he muttered; "all the pluck is taken out of me by this 'ere leg. Cuss it! why couldn't I say at the start that I'd got it? Then old Bill Oakley would have seen me jiggered ten time over afore he'd have allowed me to sign articles. I've been livin' a lie aboard here from the beginning, and now I've got to pay for it. Heaven ha' marcy on me! I'm a miserable sinner."

He knelt down by the door and put his ear to the hole of the lock. There was a rattling sound as of drawing arms. Then came a softly-uttered command:

"Stand steady and keep cool, men. Guns all loaded with grape?"

"Ay, ay, sir."

"Wait for the word to fire. Aim forward of the boats. Here they come."

"A procession," Bill Oakley's voice was heard to declare. "Why, they ain't left one behind 'em, I reckon. Goodness save us! there's four hundred warmints in them proas, if a man."

"Four hundred," groaned Rammer, "and we not more'n thirty odd. It's all up. Why in the name of all that's idjiotic *did I run away from home?*"

CHAPTER CCVI.

THE FIGHT IN THE MOONLIGHT.—BLOCKED.

NO wind, and the proas, as it was conceived would be the case, were stealing out from the dark hollow of the cave.

They came on in single file, with no sound that reached the deck of the "Albatross," the foremost making straight for the vessel first, but, when half the distance had been accomplished, swerving out to seaward.

The occupants all sat with their faces to the "Albatross."

Paddles were used in place of oars, and they were in the hands of dexterous men.

One would have thought that it was a peaceful procession at some moonlight festivity, a panorama of boats that would have gone down at "Olympia": but nothing could be more dreadfully and murderously in earnest than the occupants of the proas.

Fanatical, by nature ferocious, steeped to the lips with the wild, unholy lore of their hideous faith, they had come forth to kill, capture, and torture.

The sacred precincts of their faith had been invaded, and those who had the temerity to enter there must die or be disposed of according to the Avishnu law.

The bow of the "Albatross" was turned towards the foe.

It had a gun ready, so constructed that it could be depressed and play havoc with anything within a hundred yards of the "Albatross." If the foe were nearer than that it would be of no avail.

Harry Barstow took in the position, and guessed at the plans of the foe aright.

Their purpose was to form a circle round the "Albatross" and then at a given signal close in from all points.

"This plan must be thwarted at the outset, if at all," he thought. "What a host of them there is compared to us! Oakley!"

"Here, sir."

"Give them the contents of the bow gun."

"Ay, ay, sir."

Bill Oakley went forward with a quiet step, and all else was wonderfully still.

In the boats there was silence, on the deck of the "Albatross" silence, too.

No wind as yet, and the sea lazily resting for the turn of the tide.

"Boom!"

The stillness was broken.

One of the proas was ripped to pieces, and forty men in that and the two adjacent ones killed and wounded.

At that short distance the shot could not, if well aimed, be otherwise than terribly effectual.

The Avishnus woke out of their silence: a general cry, so wild and fierce that all who heard it involuntarily shuddered, rent the air.

"Horrible!" exclaimed Don, who was standing with Tom Drummond by the man who in case of wind had been placed at the wheel.

"It gives one the creeps," said Tom. "Here they come!"

The proas had broken order and were coming on anyhow and nohow, as one of the men remarked.

The ripping and rending of their foremost boat had roused them. All were bent on avenging it, but as it often is with semi-savage people, they took individual action instead of combining their forces.

A loud voice was heard from one of the rearmost boats calling on them to stop. It was Chunder Loo, who was standing up in the stern of a proa in all the glory of his gorgeous raiment.

Bill Oakley saw and recognised him, and as the bow gun was reloaded he aimed it in the direction of the arch-villain.

Without waiting for the word of command he fired, and the spreading, old-fashioned shot which had wisely been used played terrible havoc among the proas in the rear.

Being at an increased distance, the shot spread out among them, and the proa in which Chunder Loo was standing, was seen to heel over and sink.

Immediately afterwards there was a sharp cracking—it was no more—from the region of the summit of the cliff, followed by a thunderous roar that checked the movements of the Avishnu paddlers.

Down from aloft came the table rock, rent into a hundred pieces, with a tail of a million fragments of stone, and a cloud of dust rose up in the moonlight.

The rending of the table rock was, so far, a great success. It was, without doubt, a complete surprise to the Avishnus, and they did not know what to make of it.

True to the design of Jack Ford, the *débris* piled itself up before the mouth of the cave and closed it up, so that no boat or aught else could find entrance there.

A loud cheer burst from the deck of the "Albatross."

It was answered, so Don thought, by a faint cry from above.

But he could not make sure of that, for now a third assistant towards the confusion of the Avishnus came to hand.

The wind arose, sweeping over the sea with more force than it had shown for days on its coming, as if in a hurry to make amends for its lagging.

As a sufficient portion of the canvas of the "Albatross" was already set to catch the breeze, all that was needed was to weigh the anchor.

The command was given. Round the capstan trotted the men, and the moment the anchor was free of the bottom of the sea the "Albatross" was moving.

On she went before the wind like a thing of life, making straight for the proas.

The object of the captain was now to run down as many as possible, and destroy others with the aid of his guns.

Darnley received orders to keep them going, and as the "Albatross" sped on her way the starboard guns, three in number, opened fire.

The deep boom of their report reverberated back from the face of the cliff, and a hundred echoes added to the uproar. The crashing of the proas, the yells of the wounded men, the fierce cries of those who were cast into the sea and were swimming for their lives, made up a chaos of sound that was deafening.

The bow of the "Albatross" struck a proa, crashing in its stern.

The sound was scarcely heard above the general din.

And now an unexpected foe had to be reckoned with.

From the proa on the point of sinking the Avishnus hurled a number of snakes of various sizes on the deck of the "Albatross."

Don and Bill Oakley, having already had some slight experience of the venomous reptiles, called out for the men to be wary of them.

"Kill the brutes!" yelled Bill.

Then the cutlasses, which had been sharpened for

an encounter with men, had to be employed in the destruction of snakes.

The reptiles glided about, coiled themselves up, and sprang at their assailants, hissed a bit at them, behaving, indeed, as if they had been trained to fight against their masters' foes.

It was a fantastic, horrible fight while it lasted, and had the "Albatross" been at anchor the diversion created by the serpents would have enabled the Avishnus to swarm on deck and destroy the crew.

But she was going swiftly before the wind, and ploughed her way clear of the enemy, who were scattering in every direction.

Harry Barstow kept cool, directing the man at the wheel when the time came to bring the "Albatross" round to the wind.

The sailors slashed and cut at the serpents, cursing them as they hissed and writhed. One could have laughed if it had not been so serious a matter.

One poor fellow who had been bitten badly was seen writhing on the deck and calling for mercy, as if he were suffering the most terrible tortures. Others had wounded themselves in their efforts to destroy their loathsome foes.

Cold steel prevailed in the end. One by one the serpents were cut in pieces and destroyed, until it was hoped and believed that all were dead.

Then Harry Barstow had the "Albatross" put about, and with her canvas spread she returned to the attack on the proas.

But they were all scattered far and wide now. Some were going seaward, others creeping along by the cliff, and the rest hastening in the direction of the open coast.

A shot or two was fired, but without effect. The fight for the time was over.

"I'm derned if this ain't been about as queer a fight as iver I was in," muttered Bill Oakley. "It don't seem natoral to me, sir." He addressed his captain, who was glancing round at the retreating proas with a dissatisfied face.

"It has been successful up to a point," he said, "and that is all. Oakley, we have let too many of them get away."

"How could we help it, sir? It took all our time to look after the snaky varmints."

"Set the men cleaning the deck, and we'll drop anchor in our old ground for an hour to pick up the boat with Mr. Walton and the young gentlemen."

"Yes, sir."

Aloft went the men to furl the canvas, and the anchor dropped rattling down to the bottom of the sea. With mop and bucket the seamen proceeded to wash the deck clean of the presence of the loathsome reptiles.

"There is one poor fellow who won't get over it, I fear," reported Dick Darnley. "I've got him below, and it seems to me that he is going raving mad."

"I'll go down to him," said Harry.

"You will find the boys with him."

Harry went forward and descended to the cabin where the young seaman was. He had been put into his hammock, where he lay very white, and occasionally shifting with an exclamation of pain.

Beside him stood Tom and Don.

"It's Startop," said Harry. "My good fellow, how are you?"

"Bad, sir," was the reply. "I takes it kind of you to come and see me; but it's all up."

"Don't say that."

"I'm p'izened through and through," said Startop. "While I was a-wrestling with a biggish warmint about four feet long, a little thing—it warn't bigger than a four-ounce eel—crept up my trousers and bit me on the calf."

"I've read somewhere, sir," said Don, addressing Captain Harry, "that in cases of bites whiskey is a good thing."

"There is a bottle in the top locker of my cabin," said Captain Harry. "Here is the key. Run for it. Also bring a corkscrew."

Don flew up the cabin-stairs, and while he was gone Harry inspected the injured limb. It was fearfully swollen, and must have been very painful.

"You bear it well, Startop," he said.

"Howlin', sir, won't mend matters," was the reply; "but it is bad, I'm bound to say."

Don was back pretty sharp with the bottle, and he uncorked it neatly. In the pocket of his jacket he had brought a tumbler ready, which he half-filled with the liquid.

"He has to take it neat," he said, "and lots of it."

"Anyhow," remarked Captain Harry, "it cannot do him any harm."

Startop drank the whiskey off at a draught.

"It will make me drunk," he said, "but that won't matter now."

"If it does," whispered Don, "it won't help him; but if he keeps sober he will get well again."

They stood silently watching him for a while as he lay back breathing in a quick, feverish way. Presently he opened his eyes and said:

"The pain is easier, captain. I believe the whiskey is doing me good."

"Has it got into your head?"

"Not a bit, sir."

"Give him some more, Peebles."

Don did so, and the sailor drank it, with a faint smile on his lips.

"This will make me wild. I go that way when on the drink.

"It won't," said Don; and it did not.

He kept silent for a time, lying with his eyes shut. Opening them suddenly, he almost shouted:

"Captain, the pain is quite gone. I'm a saved man!"

"I congratulate you," said Harry. "Now, keep quiet for a time, and I will come and see you again."

"This young gentleman," said Startop, rising on his elbow and looking at Don with grateful eyes, "is knowed to us as 'There When Wanted.' He have come up to his name to-day, and from this time, if he wants a man to lay down his life for him, here he is, by Heaven!"

"I hope you will never have occasion to put your promise to the test," said Harry, as he left the cabin.

"He thinks I am only speaking for the moment," said Startop, turning his eyes again on Don; "but I mean it. There When Wanted! By all that is good and true, you was so to-day, sir, and I shall not forget it."

"It was nothing but a thought that came into my head," replied Don—"a memory of something I had read."

"It was there when wanted, sir," laughed the glad seaman. "I'm a saved man!"

Don would have urged him to think no more about it, but at that moment the sound of firing was heard in the distance.

"What is that?" asked Tom Drummond.

"Revolvers from the coast," replied Startop; "there's fighting going on. It may be the party as went ashore is in trouble."

"Will you mind being left alone now?" asked Don.

"Me, sir—not a bit, and thanky for what you've done," answered Startop. "'There When Wanted.' Blowed if ever I come across so 'propriate a name. It wins all the prizes for prophecy I ever heard of."

Don did not wait to hear further commendatory remarks from the man saved by whiskey, but dashed out of the cabin, followed by Tom Drummond.

There was assuredly something wrong ashore, for the firing of revolvers was going briskly on, and shouts were heard from the direction of the wood near the beach.

CHAPTER CCVII

TWO MISSING.

THE proas had all vanished out of sight. The only sign of life apart from the ship was to be seen shoreward in the form of the flash of revolvers, and otherwise indicated by the shouting.

"Lower the long-boat!" sang out Captain Harry. "Man her. Take your small-arms. Darnley, will you take command of the boat? See what is the

matter, but don't run into unnecessary danger. I was afraid of this when I saw the direction taken by some of the Avishnus."

He was quite cool, but he was nevertheless keenly anxious about those who were of a surety being attacked by the enemy.

On the part of those deputed to go to the rescue there was no seeming haste, no flurry, and yet not a moment was lost.

The long-boat under two minutes was lowered, manned, and ready to start.

"Pull as you would for a big prize," said Darnley.

Tom and Don would fain have gone in her, but were too late.

With a feeling of disappointment, they saw the long-boat shoot away in the direction of the spot where the firing had been heard.

Ere it had travelled half-way, a black speck was seen approaching it, and a shout went up that the other boat was returning.

This was the case, and the two met.

Then it was seen that in the smaller boat only two persons instead of four were visible.

"Who are they, sir?" asked Don, tremulously.

"One is Mr. Walton," replied Captain Harry, "and the second is one of the boys. The other two may be lying wounded in the boat."

The long-boat shortly after came slowly back with the other in tow. When they were close to the "Albatross," it was seen that only two of the four who had so successfully carried out the blasting were there. One was Ben Walton and the other Bob Stockton.

What had become of Jack Ford and Penny Bunn?

The boats arrived, and one of the first on deck was Bob.

He was no longer the languid swell, but, with every nerve in his body quivering with excitement, he grasped the hands of Tom and Don.

"It's all over with poor Jack. The Avishuus have got him!"

"It *can't* be!" moaned Don.

"It is, worse luck," said Bob; "and it all came about through Penny Bunn, and they have got him, too!"

He sat down upon an inverted bucket and groaned aloud. A sympathetic audience gathered round. There was another higher up, listening to the narrative.

"When we got to the cliff," said Bob, "and it came to crawling along the face of it, Bunn shirked the job. It was hardly to be expected that he would be up to it. So we left him behind squatting on the level ground, under the promise not to stir until we returned.

"It was all my fault," continued Bob, looking up,

sadly; "one of my fool's tricks. I took Bunn with us more for fun than anything. Nobody else wanted him."

"He did not stop there as he was told?" hinted Don.

"Not he!" said Bob. "When we had done the trick—and I must say that it was well done—we went back slowly to the level where we expected to find Bunn, but he was gone. It was my suggestion that the explosion had scared him to run down to the boat, and we hastened down. When near the bottom we heard Bunn crying up aloft somewhere for help."

"And you went back to help him?" said Tom.

"No," answered Bob; "only Jack, who was quicker than we, went. When we were ready to start we found an enemy coming up from the opposite quarter. As the best thing to be done was to run the boat down to the sea, we started off with it, pushing it with one hand and holding a revolver in the other.

"It was not our intention to leave Jack behind," pleaded Bob. "The sea was only a few yards away, and our thought was to have the boat ready to get off. We shouted to Jack and he answered back, but he did not return, as a swarm of those fiends got between us."

"Poor old Jack!" groaned Don.

"They must have heard him shout back to us," resumed Bob, "for a score immediately went in the direction of his voice. We blazed away at the gang, who, fortunately for Walton and myself, had no firearms, and we could hear Jack doing the same. I counted twelve shots, as if I had been a machine, and then there was a screeching, which told us those beasts had got him. By that time we had nothing but empty barrels, and to save our own lives we were obliged to come away. You don't think it was cowardly, I hope?"

"Bless ye, sir," said one of the men, "what were you to do? It wasn't any use giving up your own lives for nothing."

"I suppose they killed him!" groaned Tom Drummond.

"It's odds on his having fought to the last," replied Bob, "and really, although I shall never get over his loss, I wish him dead rather than alive and in the power of those fiends. They will have a bitter revenge for what we did to-night."

There was no sound on shore. All was as still there as if the island had been uninhabited.

The inference was that both Jack Ford and Penny Bunn were dead, and the general feeling was one of intense grief.

It is true that Dirk Matthews rejoiced. He had only one sentiment in the matter, and that arose from the belief that it was better for him that one so bold as Jack Ford was away. He had not entirely given up all hopes of getting possession of the "Albatross."

Nor was Rammer very sorry when he heard of the fate of his assistant.

Immediately after the destruction of the reptiles—when all danger was over—Rammer appeared on deck and helped in the minor work of cleansing away the signs of that peculiar contest.

He had a deal to say about what he was *going* to do, if he had not been kept in the cuddy "by his door being jammed."

"I hollered and hollered until I was hoarse," he said, "and nobody took the trouble to let me out."

This statement was received with considerable doubt, even to the utterance of such words as "Gammon!" "What next?" and suggestions about the advisability of reserving that yarn for his grandmother, and other exasperating indications that he was not dealing with the truth.

Rammer, conscious of his moral strength and rectitude, bore up against it all, and on hearing of the loss of Penny Bunn he hoped to bear up against that, too.

"He knowed a bit too much," thought Rammer, "and was getting cheeky. He's best gone."

And that he was gone, and Jack Ford lost to all his friends for ever, few could doubt.

The grim silence on the shore was portentous of their untimely death.

CHAPTER CCVIII.

THE FATE OF THE MISSING ONES.

HAPPILY for the interest of our story and for their own welfare, neither Penny Bunn nor Jack Ford had lost their lives.

But they were, nevertheless, in a very unpleasant position.

Briefly, we must return to the time when Penny Bunn was left upon the high-level ground at the top of the cliff, with instructions not to stir until his friends returned. He was, in short, left till called for.

But a man of Bunn's temperament is eminently qualified for getting into trouble on the slightest provocation.

Having passed the remaining portion of daylight in obedience to orders, it occurred to him that he might take advantage of night to get up for a little while and go through the familiar process often spoken of as "stretching one's legs."

It was not absolutely dark, for there were the stars overhead, and the sea below was throwing off a faint phosphorescent light, which would save him, if he moved about, from mistaking his course and going over the cliff.

So he got up and began strolling up and down, endeavouring to impose upon himself, having nobody else to practise imposition on, that he was as cool and collected as a man need be.

And yet, in good sooth, he was horribly afraid.

The time, the place, the gloom—all helped to raise a fever of fear in his breast, and, with eyes that were wandering round at all the points of the compass every half-minute or so, he shuffled slowly up and down.

Presently the moon rose, and he felt a little better. But he could not resume his seat.

He felt like a man who momentarily expects to have to run for his life, and he naturally wished to be ready to get away on the first alarm.

Suddenly he heard the boom of a gun below, and started off. Then, remembering himself, he pulled up, and was about to return, when the blasting shot was fired, and the rush and roar of the *débris* followed.

Penny Bunn now fairly lost his head, and ran he knew not whither.

Three minutes of this unwonted activity cooled off the rush of fear, and he stopped again, finding himself in among the bush, out of sight of the sea.

Wearily he once more sought the trysting spot, which, if he had reached it, would have been of no service to him, for his companions had already missed him and gone down.

But he never attained it, for on emerging into the open he found himself promptly surrounded by a party of men, whom he at first did not think were mortals, but beings of another world.

Some were most fantastic in their attire, with twisted turbans round their heads, and feathers stuck therein. Their bodies were partly covered with raiment of the most gorgeous colours. Some were almost naked, having paint in lieu of clothing, and all had bright, gleaming swords in their hands, and eyes that were brighter than their swords.

On seeing Bunn they hissed at him like snakes, and pouncing on him, threw him down. It was then that he uttered the shout which brought Jack Ford to his rescue.

Personally Penny Bunn offered no resistance.

He had a revolver in his belt, but, for fear of accidents, he had previously withdrawn the cartridges.

If he had attempted to use it, he would as likely as not have shot him himself first as a preliminary to attempting to shoot other people.

Finding he was passive, the enemy did not treat him with undue violence. But they bound his legs and arms, and it was while this was being done that Jack Ford dashed up, with a revolver in his left hand and his cutlass in his right, and used both—an extra revolver in his belt—with such effect that he had laid out three of the Avishnus ere they could seize and disarm him.

He struggled gallantly, but what was he against the score or more of lithe, determined men?

They got him down, bound his legs and arms, and laid him beside Bunn upon the ground.

Then all but two hastened down in the direction of the boat, with the obvious intention of assisting at the capture of Ben Walton and Bob Stockton. In this, as we know, they were doomed to disappointment.

The mental faculties of Penny Bunn were never in a more active condition. They were strained to the utmost by the whirl of thought that passed through his brain.

"Mr. Ford," he said, "what do-o-o-o you think they will do to us?"

"Cannot say," briefly replied Jack, "but it is all owing to your disobedience to orders that we have got into this fix. On my return to the 'Albatross' I shall report you!"

"If we only could return," said Penny Bunn, "I would gladly assent to half a dozen reports with fitting punishment. All that could be done to me would be bliss compared to my present position."

"Well," said Jack, "pluck up a little heart, and whatever happens, don't let these vermin see the white feather in our tails."

"Stimulated by your noble example," replied Bunn, "I will endeavour to exhibit a spirit becoming a British born man. I have no data to go upon as to my precise nationality, but I rather think that I have Welsh blood in my veins. I remember that my father had an extraordinary partiality, almost a passion, for leeks."

"You are not to eat them here," said Jack, "remember that. I wonder if these two fellows understand what we are talking about?"

The men in charge of them were two half-naked men, with skins almost as black as ebony. But their features were not Nubian.

They had hooked noses, thin lips, and dark, restless, close-set eyes.

Neither had shown that they took an interest in the talk of the prisoners, but that a close watch was kept by them was evident.

They stood still as statues in front of the captives, with their ugly-looking swords, shining as bright as looking-glass in the moonlight, ready to cut them down if they should attempt to escape.

But the bonds about the pair were too well fastened. Jack had quietly tested them, and discovered that he could not shift a single knot the fraction of an inch.

"Perhaps, if you asked them," suggested Bunn, "they would let you know if they are acquainted with the English tongue. Or shall I do so?"

"If you will," said Jack.

Penny Bunn cleared his throat and proceeded to do so.

"Gentlemen," he said, "may I have a word with you?"

"You not to talk," replied one of the men, in very good English. "It is an accursed thing for one of the faithful to have speech with those who worship not the serpent."

"But we may speak to each other, my good, kind friend?" urged Bunn.

"Silence!" was the stern rejoinder.

The prisoners said no more. Bunn was frozen up, and Jack was thinking.

He knew that the position he was in was a terrible one. At the very best his life would only be spared by his going through the Avishnu ordeal of the serpent, of which Ben Walton had told him.

That Walton spoke of a matter of which he was personally acquainted was pretty certain, notwithstanding his reticence about his past.

And that the Avishnus were the people of the island there could be no shadow of doubt.

"Truly," thought Jack, "I have brought my pigs to a charming market this time."

He was very sorry for Penny Bunn, who was ill-fitted in nerve or anything else for the ordeal he might have to undergo. But Jack had no time to think pityingly of himself.

He gave up his thoughts to two problems. Would he be able, unaided, to escape from his enemies, or would his friends succeed in rescuing him?

Of the former he had little hope, for he would assuredly be closely guarded and kept confined in some place of security. The only chance for him, as far as he could see, was in the ability of his friends to rescue him from the clutches of the Avishnus.

The main party came back soon, walking in a disorderly fashion, and talking together in an excited manner, a proof that they were without a leader.

The language they used was incomprehensible to the prisoners. It was a curious mixture of the guttural and the hissing sound. The trail of the serpent appeared to be over all they said and did.

Even their motions had something serpentine about them.

The sweep of the arms, the turn of their lower limbs suggested the reptile they adored; and to Bunn every word and action bore a weird unearthliness suggestive of the whole thing being a dream.

The legs of the prisoners were set free, and a sign was made for them to stand erect.

Jack sprang to his feet, thus showing how little he cared for the temporary inconvenience he had sustained; but Penny Bunn was very slow about it.

A quiet prick with a sword, however, hastened his movements, and energetically rubbing the afflicted spot, he fell in by the side of Jack, and a forward movement to the summit of the cliff began.

But even in this their captors could not proceed like ordinary men, marching steadily on with their prisoners in their midst.

It is true that they kept them in the centre, but the men shifted constantly, twisting and turning round, now in front and now behind, in a most bewildering manner.

Possibly this was done with a purpose, a reflection of the fascinating twirling of the serpent when it is in the presence of its prey.

Jack suspected as much, and half-closed his eyes so as to diminish the effect; but Penny Bunn, with his eyes wider open than usual, went through all the stages of giddiness without exactly falling. He was spared that by an occasional lurch against his companion or one of the ever-moving guard.

The summit of the cliff was attained, and for a moment or two Jack had a view of the sea.

Down below he saw the "Albatross" at anchor, and how his heart went down to her may be guessed.

Penny Bunn being occupied in recovering his disordered wits, saw nothing.

One moment's pause, and then the descent on the other side began.

Down by an unmarked but known way the Avishnus led their prisoners. For a time they had to proceed without any gyrations, for the road was rugged with rock, and dotted with bushes that were covered with thorns.

From some of the latter, as they passed by, came a hiss; but at the sound the Avishnus uttered a peculiar cry, and the noise instantly ceased.

So they went on, all silent now, save when interrupted as described, taking a slightly circular direction, until the gleaming of water told Jack that they were approaching the inland bay where he had already gone through such strange adventures with Don and Bill Oakley. It was reached, and the Avishnus skirted it, going in the direction of the flight of steps.

Jack glanced over the placid waters, henceforth to lose the addition of the inflowing tide, a mere lake that, unless replenished by draining from the hills, would dry up and become a hollow.

The proas were gone—not one was left. All had been engaged in the attack on the "Albatross." The blasting had been entirely successful, and the mouth of the cavern was closed for ever.

What his captors thought of it he could not tell. They made no reference to it, or to anything else, but, their first excitement over, became silent and grim.

Up the steps swiftly, and silently as to speech.

The only sounds to be heard were, the rattling of swords, the soft swish of naked feet, the light stepping of Jack, and the panting of Penny Bunn.

Th last step was attained, and Jack found himself upon a level platform of stone, commanding a view of the interior of the island.

The Avishnus spread out their arms as they formed in a line, saluting the scene below as the Persian hails the sun at dawn.

And what a spectacle it was for the strangers!

The interior of the island was a huge basin, a smoothed crater where the fires of the volcano had been out for a thousand years, and the soil grown rich and fertile.

All that makes the beauty of a tropical country, in the way of wood and flowers, was there, and in the heart of it all, shining in the refulgent moonlight, were the domes of a great city, shining white as snow.

CHAPTER CCIX.

THE CITY OF THE AVISHNUS.—THE HIGH-PRIEST.

"WHAT a glorious scene !" was the involuntary exclamation that burst from Jack.

"It is the home of the faithful and the blessed," said one of the Avishnus near him ; "for you to visit it is to die, or to live as a god."

"You speak our language," said Jack, "how is that ?"

"It is taught us by our Great Ruler, who is above even our high-priest."

"Who is he ?" asked Jack.

"I may not tell," replied the Avishnu ; "to utter it to one not blessed by the ordeal is to be accursed."

"It has often been on my lips," said Jack. "I knew him well in another land, my own country."

The Avishnu looked at him curiously, but made no rejoinder.

"Shall I speak ?" asked Jack.

"If you dare," was the reply.

"I dare," returned Jack, "for I do not fear him. In my native land he was a hunted man, a criminal who had forfeited his life."

They were moving on now down the gentle slope that led to the city. The Avishnu, impelled by a powerful curiosity he could not wholly conceal, fell in by the side of Jack. He indulged in a gesture of supreme contempt.

"Our Great Ruler," he said, "was never in your land. He would not set foot among the accursed."

"I may be mistaken," replied Jack. "Is he always with you ?"

"He leaves us sometimes to go to the spirit-land to ask advice of the Maker of the Serpent."

"And whither does he go ? To what place ?"

The Avishnu swept his hands upwards, embracing the firmament. Jack smiled. He understood all now.

"The name of your Great Ruler," he said, "in my country was Chunder Loo."

The shaft went home, but although the Avashnu did not show it, he had received a great shock. It was clear that Chunder Loo was Chunder Loo at home as well as abroad.

"It was not our Great Ruler," he said, "but Epha, the Evil One, who goes about in his form to work him ill."

"Is your Great Ruler in yonder city ?" inquired Jack.

"No, he went with the proas to-night, but he will return."

"Perhaps."

"He will. What can keep him away ? He is not in fear of death, for no man could kill him. Neither mountains, nor seas, nor wind, nor rain, nor storm can stop him. He will come back to us."

"If he does," said Jack, "you will see that he will kill me at once, lest my tongue should speak of him. Among my people he was a murderer, a thief, and a liar !"

Jack expected to receive a rebuff for his daring to speak of one in the position of the Great Ruler. He also wondered, after the communication he had received from one of his guards when first captured, that his present companion should be so free of speech. But there was no offence taken.

The Avishnu, though simply clad, appeared to be better than his fellows. His face had less ferocity, and more of the real spirit of intelligence. He only shook his head.

"It was Epha, the Evil One," he said, "and you have rightly said he is vile. As for the Great Ruler, he will not kill you now."

"Why not ?"

"You are a captive. It is against our laws to kill those we hold in our hands, and not even Chunder Loo would dare break them. You will be food for the serpent or live with the blessed."

"Have you many strangers among you ?" asked Jack, hesitating.

He held his breath while waiting for an answer. He was thinking of Norton Truscott.

"Two," was the quiet away.

He would have asked more, but a murmuring arose among the other Avishnus, which increased in power until it became a monotonous chant.

Then, as a plain of moderate size was reached, they drew their swords, and broke away into a dance so wild and bewildering that even Jack could not resist its influence.

Of the grace of the motions there could be no two opinions. The men were as lithe of body as willow wands and as supple of limb as a Taglioni.

Hither and thither they went, gliding, turning,

leaping, chanting, and hissing like beings possessed, but through all they could not have lost sight of their prisoners, for Jack Ford and the dumbfounded Penny Bunn were ever in the midst of a circle.

"I can't stand it," murmured Bunn. "You will excuse me, sir, if I sit down upon the ground."

"I think you had better not," advised Jack.

But Penny Bunn could not retain his feet, and, with his eyes closed, he gently subsided to the ground.

In a moment the dancing came to an end, and with wild yells of triumph the Avashnus rushed upon Penny Bunn and hoisted him into the air.

"Mercy!" he gasped, but his voice was drowned in their shouts.

What it all meant neither the victim of these demonstrations nor Jack could make out. But they feared the worst.

On they went across the plain, through a pathless wood of huge trees, with trunks that rose like mighty columns in the air, and so on to more open ground.

And there, a hundred yards or so away, stood the walls and a gate of the Avishnu city, flanked by dome-capped towers.

Strong of nerve as Jack was the sight fairly took his breath away, for the massiveness of the stonework was beyond anything of the sort he had hitherto seen.

And though he had only the moonlight to aid his vision he could see that these walls and towers were not the work of recent times.

Penny Bunn gazed and said nothing.

He was not going to speculate at all upon it, for at last he had made up his mind that it was all a nightmare.

"I shall be roused directly," he mused, "by Miriam asking me if I am going to get up to-day. She will dig me in the ribs, and I shall open my eyes and gaze upon my chamber in dear old Littlecote Abbey School. How delightful that will be!"

So he yielded himself up to the belief that nothing around him was real, and went on cheerfully to the city.

Two massive gates of iron or bronze, it was not easy to discern which in the shadow, stood open to receive them.

But there was no guard, nobody to welcome them.

Through a passage—it was fairly a tunnel—under the walls they went, emerging by an open way into the city itself.

A narrow street with tall, massive houses, pierced with glassless windows of every conceivable shape, a pavement of coloured marble, quaint carvings of stone, but no living man or woman.

Down by the narrow way, with every footstep, soft or loud, giving out an echo as they journeyed.

The Avishnus were silent again, and they bore Penny Bunn aloft upon their shoulders as heroes of the football or cricket field are borne to the tent after some notable feat.

He was quite resigned, although he wished they would carry him with his head a little higher up and his legs a little lower down.

It would soon be all over, anyway. Miriam certainly would not allow him to lie in bed much longer.

A turning in the street was reached, and down yet a narrower way glided the captors and the captives.

At the lower end was a tower, with a gate and archway.

As Bunn, borne in front, approached it he saw the gate turn on its hinges without visible hands, and he smiled.

"Now," he murmured, "the moment for awakening has come. I fancy I hear the boys below in the playground. And surely that is Miriam's footstep on the stairs."

But there was no playground, no boys, no Miriam, in that uncanny spot.

Beyond the gateway was a square, covering an acre or so of ground, entirely surrounded by a mass of buildings that appeared to be practically one place.

The corners were ornamented, dome-crowned towers; in the centre was a group of statuary and a fountain. The entrance to the buildings was by flights of broad marble steps.

And there was the silence of death over all things.

CHAPTER CCX.

A DAY OF DOUBT.—DIRK MATTHEWS SEES HIS CHANCE AND EMBRACES IT.

IT is only the weakling who gives up all hope while there is a chance of escaping for those in trouble.

On the "Albatross" there was a feeling, practically a conviction, that Jack and Penny Bunn were lost, but none yielded to despair.

"Jack is not the fellow to be done by a lot like that," said Tom Drummond. "He'll circumvent them, somehow."

The three youngsters were dallying over a morning meal, for which they had little appetite. Bob Stockton stirred his coffee mechanically, with his eyes dreamily fixed upon the island.

"Walton knows a lot about those fellows," he said; "perhaps he may have some power over them, or be able to save their lives, if he would only go ashore and see some of them. I suppose they would respect a flag of truce?"

"You may divest yourself of any hope of my being

able to assist them in that way," said a voice behind them.

Ben Walton had come up unobserved, and was standing behind them with his arms gloomily folded on his breast.

"For me to fall into the hands of the Avishnus," the mate went on, "would be to meet with a punishment equal to the heavy death of the Chinese. I am an escaped priest of their caste."

There was a movement of surprise among the boys, but they said nothing. Ben Walton drew up a chair and sat down beside them.

"Never," he said, "have I told my story in full to living man, but I think that reticence upon it is no longer needed. The details are not called for. In short, I have been a prisoner among the Avishnus, have gone through the ordeal of the serpent, come out victorious, and was made one of their high-priests against my will. As soon as I could, I escaped. To be again in their power would entail penalties too horrible to describe."

"You did not tell me this, Walton."

It was Harry Barstow who this time had stolen up unobserved. Walton moved uneasily in his chair.

"Had I done so," he replied, "you would have refused to allow me to come."

"True, and why did you?"

"Because I wished to give what aid I could," answered Walton, with eyes that suddenly flashed fire, "towards the extermination of the accursed race!"

"That may be beyond our power. We are few and they are many."

"They are a dwindling people," said Walton; "at one time they were both numerous and wealthy. Some of the richest princes of India belonged to them, and in secret indulged in their rites. Furthermore, I believe that although the number of the Avishnus has decreased, the wealth remains."

"Who holds it?"

"A certain section of the priests. There is a great ruler, whom I do not doubt is this Chunder Loo, but he has not the handling of the treasury."

"How do you think he obtained his dignity?"

"By right of birth, probably."

"And why should he occasionally leave them, as he appears to do? Witness his adventures at Littlecote Abbey."

"He was in England for some object, no doubt. I believe it was to get some assistance to rob the Avishnus of their wealth. Such a man cannot be one of the true people at heart. He is simply a scoundrel. In England he appears to have fallen into bad company, become poor, and committed crimes that, but for his superlative cunning, would have got him into the hands of the hangman. If we could only get hold of him, we could make good use of the scoundrel."

"How?"

"With the Great Ruler in our power we should be able to make terms with regard to Ford and Bunn, provided they are yet alive."

"True," said Harry Barstow, pursing his under-lip, "but how is it to be done?"

"There are two things to look at in our favour," replied Walton. "I speak as one knowing the people. First of all, it is certain that Chunder Loo was with the proas, and that the particular one in which he was seen was sunk by one of the shots fired from the bow gun. If not killed, he was at least thrown into the sea. Query, then—did he drown?"

"He appears to have been a good swimmer."

"Yes, and that points to the probability of his being alive. In all likelihood he was picked up by one of the other proas. Well, then, he is yet alive, say, and is making for home. Now comes the second point in our favour. I am of opinion that all routes to the heart of the island, save that which we have closed, are either very devious or perilous. Even those acquainted with the place will have to proceed with caution. Now, if a few of us went ashore and scaled yonder cliff, I fancy we could see our way inland as far as the lake or bay. Chunder Loo is sure to make for the other side of the island rather than run the risk of another encounter with us here. We might either reach his stronghold, and with a little exercise of caution rescue our friends, or intercept and capture him."

"Walton," said Harry Barstow, "it is my duty to go to the aid of those we have lost."

"And mine to accompany you," replied Walton, "if only for my knowledge of the people we have to deal with. A half-dozen good men is all we shall require. Darnley could be left in charge of the 'Albatross.'"

"It must be done at once," said Harry. "You see to the men, while I talk over things with Darnley. There are certain things he must do in case anything happens to us. You bear in mind the great risk you run, Walton?"

"I remember it. I am prepared—nay, I insist on the privilege of running it."

"Then there is no more to be said on that score."

Unconscious of the secret hopes and aspirations of Dirk Matthews, Harry Barstow shortly after called the men together, told them of his intention to go to the rescue of Jack Ford and Penny Bunn, and asked for volunteers. One of the first to come forward was Startop. Others soon followed, and the required number was made up.

The proffered aid of Bill Oakley and the trio of youngsters was refused.

"You will be wanted on board to see to the men, Oakley," said Harry Barstow, drawing him aside. To the boys he explained that they would be left as assistant officers.

Finally Harry Barstow instructed Dick Daruley as follows:

"Keep a sharp lookout for us. When the wind serves, tack about as close in shore as convenient. Sink without palaver any proa you may come across, and if we are not back within a week, set sail for home, report the whole thing to the authorities there, and leave them to so deal with this nest of vermin as they please."

He also pointed out sundry things he should desire his people at home to receive, and wrote a short letter to Jack Ford's friends, asking them to forgive him for having indirectly deprived them of so noble a son.

By that time the boat and the men, with all they were likely to need during their short sojourn ashore, were ready, and Harry Barstow took leave of the boys.

"All or none," he said, "will return. Keep up a good heart while we are away."

"It is not easy work," replied Don, "but we have great faith in Jack. If there is half a loophole he will squeeze through it."

"And for Penny Bunn," remarked Bob Stockton, "although gifted with the power of falling into mischief on the slightest provocation, he is endowed with the instinct that leads him with impunity among red-hot ploughshares blindfolded. I think we shall see them both again."

The boat, with two extra men in her to bring her back to the "Albatross," departed, watched by all, but by none more keenly than Dirk Matthews.

It had not reached the shore, when he hurried below, being off duty. He found Bates and Goffer smoking in the cabin.

"If we had arranged the whole thing it couldn't have been better," he said. "Now, boys, if you will stand by me, the 'Albatross' in a few hours will be ours."

CHAPTER CCXI.

TWO VERY STRANGE PRIESTS.—JACK IS STAGGERED.

THE two prisoners of the Avishnus, Jack Ford and Penny Bunn, were taken up one of the flights of steps already described, into a vast hall for the most part wrapped in gloom.

In the centre of it, on a sort of altar, a dull fire of red-hot ashes was smouldering, and beside it stood two men in long robes with twisted rods, suggestive of the serpent, in their hands.

Hearing the footsteps, they came forward and exchanged some words in a low tone with the Avishnu who had been so free of speech with Jack.

From the demeanour of the two men it was plain that they now received the first intimation of the disaster that had befallen the proas, for they raised their rods aloft, and sent forth from their lips a most dolorous yet somewhat forced wail.

Then they waved them to and fro, wildly cursing the foe that had brought confusion upon their Great Ruler.

The informant appeared to offer them some comfort in the way of an assurance that the unassailable might of their head would in the end prevail.

The two prisoners were handed over to the two priests as a balm to their wounded feelings.

They advanced to them, and grasped both Jack and Penny Bunn by the arms, with a peculiar fervour that at the time was inexplicable.

The bonds that had hitherto confined their arms were removed, and the priests motioned to them to follow.

In the almost complete darkness—for the fire gave but little light—Jack could only see the priests in outline. Owing to their headdress, a sort of turban with long flaps that fell around their ears like the wig of a chief justice, he could see nothing clearly of their features, but he could make out that they were two men of different mould.

One was tall and well set-up, with something of the military man in his air.

The other was short, with an impatient, jerky way of moving, and not a particle of grace in his movements. He was certainly an oddity.

They conducted the prisoners to a door, which they opened, and the taller one motioned for the prisoners to enter.

"You will pass the night there," he said, gravely, in such good English that Jack was startled. "Food will be brought you. I counsel you not to talk loudly, for you are in the sacred precincts of the chief temple of the serpent. Enter. When the morrow comes you will be visited by myself or one of my brother priests."

He turned away as they passed through the dark doorway. Bunn was quite jaunty, for he had not the slightest faith even now that he was acting a part in the real drama. Jack walked in with a careless grace, and halted a few paces from the door.

The short-statured priest lingered, instead of shutting them in at once, as Jack expected. He was seen to move about as if looking round for a possible spy. Then he thrust his head in, and whispered:

"Keep your pecker up, my noble Romans. Nothing like it You are in a hole, but, like all holes, *the way in is also the way out!*"

Then the door closed and he was gone, leaving them in the most utter darkness Jack ever remembered being in. It was as the darkness over the land of Egypt, that might be felt.

The words, the manner of the little priest completely bewildered him. It was such a contrast to the presumed dignity and mystery of his office.

"It beats anything I ever came across," said Jack, aloud; "what do you think of it, Bunn?"

"It is quite useless to think of it at all," serenely answered Bunn. "I will give you my opinion of it when I wake up."

"If you think that you are asleep and dreaming," replied Jack, "I should advise you to divest your mind of the idea. It is all too bitterly real."

"We naturally argue in that way in our dreams," said Penny Bunn, with exasperating persistence. "I have dreamt a hundred times of finding bags of gold, and on each successive occasion, I have said to myself: 'All other dreams of finding gold have been swindles, but *this* is a reality.' For all that I have in due time awoke, and found myself as poor as ever."

"I only wish that I could endorse your belief, but it is real enough. Listen!"

There was a click and a sliding sound. Jack looking towards the door, from whence the sound proceeded, was able to make out the outline of a small square opening.

"Here is your tommy," whispered a voice, which Jack recognised as that of the little priest; "it is what they call bread here. Wholesome, but tough. Not a drop of yeast to be got for love or money. Some fruit, too. Also coffee, cold. Better than nothing. The water here is inclined to be brackish. Some of it tastes like medicine. Once more, keep a stiff upper-lip. Think of the girl you left behind you. Good-night!"

He was gone again, and Jack, groping his way to the door, found upon a small shelf fixed in it an earthenware bottle and a flat, heavy loaf, with some fruit wrapped in a huge leaf of some sort. He took possession of these things, and invited Penny Bunn to partake with him.

"Food," he said, "will enable us to keep up our strength. We may need it on the morrow."

"Although well aware of the futility of seeking nourishment from visionary food," replied Bunn, "I must confess that I feel a shadowy hunger, and will partake."

Jack shared the viands as well as he could in the dark, and they both made a fairly hearty meal.

Jack did so because he knew the need of it, and he was not going to give in. Bunn ate on the ground that it was not of the slightest consequence whether he did so or not.

The cell or room in which they were confined was very dry and warm. Inspecting it by groping about after food, Jack discovered some kind of rush matting in one corner. The dimensions of the place he judged were about twenty feet square.

"We may as well lie down and sleep," said Jack, "if we never get the chance again."

"Certainly, why not, Ford?" cheerfully responded Bunn. "You do not mind, I hope, my addressing you as in my waking hours?"

"Not at all," answered Jack, "but on our return to the 'Albatross' you will have to resume your ordinary position there. It is a matter of discipline."

"Ah! the 'Albatross,'" lightly said Bunn. "I have a faint remembrance of a ship which played a part in my earlier dreams. Yes, I will do anything you like, Ford—when we get there."

Jack was already stretched out with his hands clasped under his head in preparation for sleep. Penny Bunn lay down near him.

"I think," he said, half to himself, "that when Miss Astracan is mentally regaled with the story of my visionary experiences she will shake her sides with laughter."

"Good-night, Bunn," said Jack, abruptly.

"You have forgotten the Mister, Ford," hinted Bunn.

"Good-night, *Mr.* Bunn," said Jack.

"Good-night," answered Bunn; "and by the way, Ford, I shall be glad if you will give the boys a hint, when the bell rings in the morning, that they ought to go downstairs more quietly. Although no sluggard, I by choice lie in bed a while in the morning mentally arranging the work for the day, and the scampering of so many feet disturbs me. It also irritates my dear wife."

"I'll remember, sir," said Jack, to humour him.

Bunn curled himself up, and being really by this time pretty well worn out, was soon asleep.

Jack, although kept awake for a time by his thoughts, was not long in following him

---

CHAPTER CCXII.

THE FINDING OF NORTON TRUSCOTT.—POOR CHIPPY BUNYONS.

A CRASH and a clanging as of brass musical instruments played just anyhow and nohow.

Penny Bunn opened his eyes and stared about him. He was in complete darkness.

After the clashings, which lasted only a few seconds, there was silence, broken only by the steady breathing of Jack, who still slept on.

Penny Bunn thought over his recent adventures, clinging to the notion of its being all a dream.

"It is perfectly clear to me," he said, "that I am still asleep. For length and novelty this is the most remarkable night of dreams I have ever experienced."

Clash! Clang! Clang!

Bunn started into a sitting position and rubbed his eyes violently. Jack stirred and awoke.

The darkness was for a moment bewildering, but the clashing again ceased, and he recalled the terrible experience of the fight and capture of himself and companion before he asked if Bunn was awake.

"I am, in a sense," replied Bunn, "but I fear that something is going on wrong below. There appears to me to be a smashing of crockery going forward. The result will be ruinous."

Jack declined to argue the question. Bunn could think what he pleased, and on the whole he was not sorry he did take that view of it. If his old schoolmaster once fairly realised the true state of things he would morally go to pieces and become a lost man.

Better, therefore, that he should live in the faith that it was all unreal.

After the second burst of discord without, there was a short stillness and a chanting, weird and monotonous was heard. It lasted but a few minutes, and then ceased.

"Something like humming tops," murmured Penny Bunn.

Jack made no reply. It was quite useless talking to Penny Bunn in his condition of mind. As the old man in his second childhood returns mentally to the scenes of his boyhood, so had Bunn wandered back to the old days of Littlecote Abbey Academy.

It was but a short time afterwards, to be counted by seconds, when the door, that fitted so closely as to shut out all light, was opened, and the tall priest they had seen the night before beckoned to them to come forth.

Jack Ford knew him by his square-set figure and his upright bearing. He did not utter a word, but simply beckoned.

They rose up, Bunn with a juvenile alacrity born of that wild conviction he entertained, and went out.

Then, for the first time, Jack had a clear view of the hall in which they had been received.

It was of vast extent, squarely built, with two rows of fluted columns, that gave it something of the appearance of a cathedral nave.

These columns were of polished marble of many colours. The floor was of the same material, and the only thing in the way of fitting up was the altar on which the fire had been and was still smouldering.

No others of the Avishnus were in sight. The prisoners and the priest were alone.

With stately step the latter crossed the hall, passing between the columns on either side, to another door which stood open.

He paused at the entrance and motioned for Jack to enter.

In a chamber, rich with walls of many-coloured stone, carved and polished, and furnished with the luxuriousness of a Turk's harem, stood the little priest who had been so kind with his advice on the previous night.

He had a full face, a nose inclined to protuberance, and small eyes. His mouth was that of a man who was in trouble and had no hope of getting out of it, pursed and on the right side drawn slightly awry.

The tall priest, at whom Jack had scarcely looked until the door closed upon them all, was a handsome man, not more than three or four-and-twenty, fully fifteen years younger than his brother priest, and of unmistakable English origin.

As a completion of the assurance of his nationality, the moment the door was closed he grasped Jack by the hand, exclaiming:

"In the name of all that is unfortunate and pitiful, how came you here?"

The little priest had also seized the hand of Penny Bunn and asked the question, not in the same words, but with a similar air of pained inquiry.

"It is a long story," replied Jack. Bunn merely smiled, as if he thought the inquiry superfluous, considering how soon he was going to wake up. "May I first ask you another question?"

"Assuredly," was the rejoinder,

"Is your name Norton Truscott?"

The tall priest flushed to his eyebrows, and then turned as pale as death itself.

He stared at Jack as if he too doubted the evidence of his senses.

"It is my name," he answered, drawing a deep breath.

"Then it was seeking you that brought us here," said Jack.

"Sit down," replied the priest, whom we must henceforth call by his rightful name, "tell me all—at once—I will not once interrupt you."

As he threw himself down upon a pile of cushions that flanked one of the walls of the chamber, he put his hands to his brow for a moment and stood quietly with a set face, looking white under the tan of his skin.

Penny Bunn and his companion also subsided into a sitting position, and held their peace while Jack as briefly as possible told his story.

That it was a complete surprise to the two listeners was evidenced by their faces and the occasional suppressed exclamations that burst from their lips.

When all was told, Norton Truscott covered his face with his hands, and for a while remained still, save for a slight quivering of his tall figure.

At length he looked up.

"Your name, you tell me, is Jack Ford," he said "a name ever to be held in remembrance dear to me

But alas! you will be sacrificed in the vain effort to save me."

"Perhaps not," answered Jack, dreamily; "but whatever befalls me, I shall to the end rejoice that I have found you. Are there no means of escaping from here?"

Norton Truscott shook his head.

"Take things at their best," he said— "that is, from your point of view, and mine, too—there are still fifty of the accursed Avishnus remaining. Though I was apparently a free agent this morning, we were, in fact, all closely watched and guarded."

"But why are we allowed to communicate at all?" asked Jack.

"Because it will be my office to conduct you to the scene of your ordeal. It will not take place until Chunder Loo returns, but there will be no shirking it."

"Perhaps our friends meanwhile may come to our aid?"

"No, the way is too perilous and their numbers too few. You thought you passed along a safe way in coming hither?"

"I did. There was nothing to induce me to think otherwise."

"You were mistaken. The road is dotted over with a hundred pitfalls for those who are not initiated into the mysteries of the place."

"You know them?"

"I do."

"Could we not then escape unaided?" asked Jack.

"To attempt to leave the palace would be certain destruction to us all, unless——"

"Unless what?" asked Jack, as he paused.

"Something happened to Chunder Loo. They will do nothing until their Great Ruler, as they call the unmitigated scoundrel, returns. Should he be heard of or brought back as dead, we might have an opportunity, in the general confusion of despair arising from a faith falsified, to make our escape."

"I should like to know if you have really gone through the ordeal of the serpent?"

Norton Truscott, looking straight ahead, answered in a hushed voice, as one who speaks of a past horror:

"I have."

"And this gentleman?" said Jack, turning towards the little priest.

Ere Norton Truscott could reply, the individual referred to burst into a semi-savage speech upon the subject.

"Have I gone through the orjeal?" he cried. "Rather! Look here, my name is Chippy Bunyons—at home I was the proprietor of a steam roundabout and did well; but one day a party in black, with a smug kind of face, comes to me and says, 'Mr. Bunyons'—I oughter to have been wide—o when he tacked the Mister on my name—'Mister Bunyons,' he says, 'what a fortune there would be in this thing among the benighted inhabitants of the Gold Coast!'"

Chippy Bunyons stopped to groan, and then went on:

"He shoved a yarn into me of having a handful of gold popped down by savages as is burdened with it. He told me they dusted the floors of their rooms with gold, and he so jammed me up, that I'm blessed if I didn't take his tip and go afloat with the machine, including the steam band, in pieces, ready to land on the fust available island, put it together, and make my fortune."

"You must have had some faith in him," remarked Jack.

"I *had*," was the emphatic response, "the more so as he offered to go with me. Well, we started, and instead of tumbling on a island, as I expected, a few miles out, we come on and on right through the Red Sea down to here, where we was wrecked. I come ashore on one of my own wooden horses, getting the grab on it when I was a-floundering about the sea, and I was one of the four that was saved. The chap as plugged me was among 'em.

"You know what happened," he continued, addressing his brother priest, "seeing that we were thrown on this island——"

"Tell your own story," said Norton Truscott, with a kindly smile.

"Well," said Chippy Bunyons, "there we was, all dripping wet and confusicated by being knocked about in the sea, standing on the shore, and not one could have betted safely on the p'int of being on his head or his heels, when up comes some of these hero 'Vishnus and marches us right here. That was a year ago yesterday. Blessed if it don't seem ten."

He stopped short, wiped his heated brow, and stared at Penny Bunn, who nodded in a kindly way, implying that he was at liberty to proceed as a story more or less would not matter, the whole thing being but a night vision.

"We went through the orjeal," resumed Chippy Bunyons, "and if you have heard of it—as I suppose you have—I needn't go on with the description of it. We was four, and they put us in with four cyphons——"

"Pythons," corrected Norton Truscott.

"Yes, pythons, bless 'em, I never can remember that word. There we was in a sort of pit with the varmints gliding in a greasy way about us. Dear! what a sight it was, and the way Smivel —the man as got me to come—howled and roared makes me wild to think of now. Pussonally I didn't make the least noise, because I couldn't. I was reg'lar choked up. The other two men were sailors and didn't say much, 'cept cuss now and then.

Presently one of them cy—pythons goes for Smivel, and just wrops him round, and then I faints right away and knowed no more."

"It was the fainting that saved him," explained Norton Truscott; "the python will not touch food that seems as dead."

"When I come to," Chippy Bunyons went on, "there was the sound of drawing back the bolts of the place I'd been in. T'other three *had disappeared*, and three of the—pythons was swollen frightful about the necks. The fourth chap was curled up as if asleep to stave off hunger. The door opens, and in rushes a lot of them warmints—Avishnus—and they ketches me up and carries me away and make a priest of me, and here I am, and of all the queerest games as ever was, this beats the lot."

He stopped short, with the perspiration pouring down his face. The memory of his time of suffering was very trying. Norton Truscott sat thinking until roused by a question from Jack.

"How was it, Mr. Truscott, that you escaped?"

"I seized the python," was the quiet reply, "about five feet from his head, and beat out its brains against the wall. But it was a close shave. Before I could settle it, its folds were about me, and I had lost my breath when I finished it. It is uncanny talking. Let us end it."

"But as I must go through the same ordeal," urged Jack, "it will be well for me to know the *worst*."

"All depends on the possible return of Chunder Loo. I pray Heaven that he is at the bottom of the sea!"

"Amen to that!" responded Jack.

"To the sober man," said Penny Bunn, oracularly, "the snake has no terrors."

Norton Truscott gazed at him in surprise.

"He thinks it is all a dream," quietly explained Jack.

"Happily for him if he never awakes to the reality," said Norton Truscott; "and now, Chippy, I think we ought to have breakfast."

"I will procure it," replied Chippy, rising. "What a game it is, to be sure! They feed the serpents first and themselves afterwards. Did you hear that clashing and humming this morning?"

"I did, the whole of it," replied Bunn.

"That was for the reptiles. Them as was in turn to be victualled. Old and young, little and big, they comes out of their dens and take their tommy. Then back they go to snooze it off. But the pythons only stop in their dens; they are kept sharp all the year round for them as breaks the Avishnu laws, and for *visitors!* Good Heaven! how I'd like to put some of the men warmints down their 'lastic throats!"

CHAPTER CCXIII.

RETURN OF CHUNDER LOO.—JACK AND THE PRIEST.

THOUGH they partook of breakfast together, Jack could not remain long with the lost friend of Harry Barstow.

It was explained to him by his host that it would not be politic to remain together.

"By right of my position among the priests," he said, "I have received you here, ostensibly to question you as to your antecedents. Chunder Loo would, in case of complete strangers, have expected a report."

"For what purpose?" asked Jack.

"Well, I think he has made good use of information he obtained concerning some of his victims. But I hear little. They dare not kill me now, but they will not wholly trust me."

Jack would very much have liked to learn something about the office he held, but as Truscott offered no information on that head, he did not venture to ask any questions. He called to mind how little Ben Walton cared to talk about the matter.

Chippy Bunyons had taken very kindly to Bunn, who placidly returned his friendship. In a body they all went out, recrossed the hall, and the prisoners were once more confined in the dark cell.

Jack found it hard to bear up against the impenetrable gloom, and he almost envied the semi-idiotic satisfaction of his companion, who had no faith in the reality of his surroundings.

Penny Bunn, like a muddy stream swollen with rain, placidly followed on.

He talked a little to himself, crooned fragments of songs, and chuckled as he thought of the fun it would be on the morrow when he awoke and told the story of his dreaming adventures.

But Jack had had enough of it. The subject was now exasperating.

"Look here, Bunn——" he began, but he was immediately interrupted.

"I really must, even in my present impalpable state of life, insist, Ford, on the forms of school-life being observed."

"Go to Jericho," said Jack, as he lay back, and was still for the next ten minutes, save in a restless shifting of his legs.

But Bunn was in the mood to lecture him on the first laws of politeness, and he held forth for a time with great fervour on the subject. Presently an exclamation from Jack stopped his tongue.

"What is it?" asked Bunn.

"Something cold passed over my face."

"Possibly a draught of cold air."

A SPLENDID SCHOOL STORY.

NEVER BEFORE PUBLISHED.

By E. HARCOURT BURRAGE,

Author of "Ching Ching." "Monkey Mat and Roving Dick," "The Brave Boy of the Basilisk," &c.

THE LAMBS of LITTLECOTE

A Handsome Coloured Plate Presented with Every Number.

No. 29.

R. P. Rowse   Marshall Sc

"NOT A DREAM," MURMURED PENNY BUNN, VACANTLY, "A REALITY."

PRICE ONE PENNY.

ALDINE PUBLISHING CO., 9, Red Lion Court, Fleet St., and 1, 2, & 3, Crown Court, Chancery Lane, London.

"It was not only cold, but had a slimy feeling. There it is again!"

"Fancy—mere fancy," murmured Bunn.

Jack had risen, and confounding Bunn for an idiot, felt his way to the wall, where he stood quiet for while.

Bunn also, in a reclining position, hummed an air, portion of an old song.

"Ah," he said, stopping short, "there is nothing like the old ditties. They beat all of the present day—— Confound it!"

"What ails you?" asked Jack.

"Something passed over *my* face," said Bunn.

"Fancy," said Jack, curtly.

"With your accustomed smartness," said Bunn, "you have had me there. Hang it! There's another. I've got him! No, I haven't. Dear me, I had no idea that this place is haunted with eels!"

"Not eels," replied Jack, "but serpents. There are several crawling about the floor—let loose upon us, I suppose, by way of preparing us for the good things to come."

"We must bear them," said Bunn, gaily.

"Here is one crawling up my leg now," said Jack, hurriedly. "Ugh!"

The exclamation was wrung from him by the horror of the situation.

The darkness, absolutely impenetrable, was in itself hard to bear, but the presence of snakes or serpents as unsought companions was maddening.

Bunn heard him moving rapidly about and wondered what he was doing, until his voice was heard again.

"I've got the grip of it, Bunn. Stand aside. I am going to dash its brains against the wall!"

Bunn, his belief in its being a dream to the contrary notwithstanding, felt there was need of urgency of movement, and skipped out of the way.

Standing with a shivering sensation about his legs, he heard the sounds of something soft being struck against the wall.

Once, twice, thrice.

"If the brute survives *that*," said Jack, "it is welcome to live and work as much mischief as it pleases."

He cast it from him, and as he was not able to to judge of the exact position of Bunn, he unintentionally threw it in his face.

"Ford," exclaimed Bunn, "really I——There seems to be no limit to the acts of insubordination you are guilty of."

"But it is all a hallucination," urged Jack.

"Hem!" coughed Bunn, "there is some truth in that." "Dear me! I've trodden on another. Serpents," he added, "figure strongly in the history of man. By a serpent he fell——"

Here a stamping movement of his foot was heard, followed promptly by his falling seemingly upon the flat of his back.

"Dear me—this is very terrible," he said, after a pause, during which Jack was only kept from laughing by the serious nature of their position generally.

"Having more than once experienced a fall from the incautious way boys and men throw orange-peel about on the pavement, I ought to have been prepared on this occasion for a similar result when I stepped upon a slimy intruder. I will examine my bones to see if any are broken. But why waste my time? All's well."

How the serpents were introduced into the cell was a mystery.

They certainly were not there when first they returned to their place of confinement, and it was equally certain that there were many creeping over the stone floor.

The size of the one killed was not very great. It could not have been more than four feet long.

But others of more imposing proportions seemed to be there—one at least nine feet long—for just as Jack was beginning to congratulate himself on their having departed by the way they came, a more solid body touched his leg and slowly glided by.

He did not venture to touch it, for he could feel that it was as thick as his own leg at the start, and gradually diminished in size until it dwindled to a point and was gone.

The sensation produced by this strange experience almost overwhelmed him. The reptile must have deliberately rubbed against him as a dog might have done, and then passed on his way silently.

If Jack had been possessed of even more courage than he could boast of he could not have coolly endured this awful experience.

The perspiration burst from his forehead, and he backed until he came in contact with the wall, against which he leant for support.

"There is no end to their infernal ingenuity," he thought; "and what may be in store for me I dare not think. But I will be strong. Chunder Loo shall never say with truth that he made me flinch by means of his fiendish tricks. One can die but once."

After the passing of the big serpent he was troubled no more with his slimy, uncanny visitors.

Gathering heart, he slowly felt his way round by the wall, occasionally thrusting out his foot, cautiously seeking them. But there was naught but the floor, and by-and-by he crossed it, walking slowly.

Bunn asked him what he was doing, but he did not answer him.

Step by step he traversed the cell in every direction, and finding nothing of his late visitors, he came to the conclusion that they were gone.

No. 29.

And indeed they were.

By some secret way they had been sent into the cell, and by their own will, or as a result of training, had departed again. But where that means of exit and entrance was Jack was unable to discover.

Having recovered himself, he resumed a lounging place upon the floor, with no other companion than Bunn. Even the serpent he thought he had slain had vanished, and the method of its going was as deep a mystery as anything else he had met with in the strange home of the Avishnu people.

So the time passed, and it was about noon—Jack fancied the night must have come again—when the clashing of discordant music was heard again.

Wondering what it meant, Jack rose up, and, walking to the door, planted his ear against it.

He had little hopes of overhearing anything, but to his surprise he could distinctly hear voices in the hall, and among them the well-known tones of Chunder Loo.

The Great Ruler of the Avishnus had a voice which, once heard, would be likely to be remembered. It was not loud, but it had a penetrating shrillness that had the effect of chilling a sensitive listener.

"He has returned," said Jack, aloud; "now what mercy may we expect from him?"

"Who has returned?" asked Bunn.

"Chunder Loo."

"Dear old Chunder: though born in India, a free disposer of the drinks of Old England, I shall be glad to see him again."

"Bunn," said Jack, sharply, it is time you awoke—"

"So I have been thinking."

"To the reality of things."

"To the reality—of—things?"

"Yes," said Jack, "if you imagine you are dreaming——"

"Stop!" interposed Bunn, with a sort of a scream; "you do not mean to say that it is possible for our surroundings to be *real?*"

"They are, so I want you to face them like a man, and not like a child. Hark! there are footsteps approaching. They are come to put us through the ordeal. Here, give me your hand. We will go out together."

Bunn was close up behind him, and he put out his hand. Jack groped about until he grasped it.

"That is it," he said; "brace yourself together. Never let these brutes get the laugh of us, as they will if we show fear."

"*Not a dream,*" murmured Penny Bunn, vacantly— "*a reality!*"

The click of the fastening without was heard, and the door was thrown open.

For a moment Jack was blinded by the light, and then he prepared to go out.

Before him stood Chunder Loo, rich-robed, swarthy, and saturnine, of feature as heretofore.

"Stand!" he cried, "let me look at you. Ha! it is not he who slew my Mehala. I am so far disappointed, but you will serve."

Behind him was a line of men robed as priests, the foremost Norton Truscott and Chippy Bunyons. Further on was a loosely-arranged body of Avishnus, forty or fifty in number.

Some alterations had been made in the appearance of the hall. The altar had been removed, and in its place was a raised chair of carved stone, which would serve as a throne.

Chunder Loo motioned for the priests to advance and take charge of the prisoners. Then he retreated to the throne and took his seat thereon.

It was Truscott who took Jack by the arm.

"Be quiet," he whispered; "show no signs of a defiant spirit save in a placid, non-resistant way."

They stepped forward, and immediately after them came Penny Bunn, staring straight ahead, and helped along by Chippy Bunyons.

Chunder Loo glanced at the captives with a grim smile of satisfaction on his face.

"Your names?" he cried.

"You know them," answered Jack.

"Your names," was the question repeated.

"Answer him," Truscott advised, with a nudge.

"Jack Ford."

"You are English?"

"Yes."

"Your name?" to Penny Bunn.

"Really," answered Bunn, "considering the old and jolly times we have had together——"

"Silence!" cried Chunder Loo, fiercely. "Dog, how should I have old times with you when we have never met before?"

"All right," said Bunn, "if you wish it; but I should have thought, after the liberal way I treated you——"

"Gag him!" said Chunder Loo, fiercely; "for by the mouth of Epha, the Evil One, he speaks."

Chippy Bunyons, with every appearance of business-like alacrity, produced a short piece of wood attached to a cord, and thrusting it into the mouth of Penny Bunn, expertly gagged him. But at the same time he gave him no pain.

"Worshippers of the mighty serpent," said Chunder Loo, rising and addressing the priests *en masse*, although he studiously avoided the eye of Truscott, fixed somewhat contemptuously upon him, "once more we have children of the accursed with us. There is but one way in which they can be brought to us, and that is by the ordeal. Go, all of you but those who hold the prisoners, and prepare the chambers of trial. One to Luva and the other to Kala, as it is my will that those two should be tried apart."

The priests, all but Truscott and Chippy, fell into a line and marched away chanting a mournful dirge, which Jack afterwards learnt was their song for the doomed.

The members of the ordinary Avishnu tribe followed them, and only Chunder Loo and the four composed of prisoners and guard remained.

He surveyed them with a very ugly look in his close-set eyes, beginning with Jack and finishing with Norton Truscott.

"To you," he said, addressing the latter, "I have a word of warning. You are a priest of the Avishnu faith, and as such you must live or die."

No answer was given him. Passing over Chippy Bunyons he came to Penny Bunn, who was now fully alive to his position; very white, but assuming a firmness he did not feel.

He ordered Chippy to remove the gag and it was done.

"In your country," said Chunder Loo, "which has been visited by Epha, the Evil One, in a semblance of myself"—the cool impudence, mingled with sly enjoyment of the scoundrel, almost took away the breath of Bunn—"you have a proverb about fools rushing in where their betters fear to tread. What brought such a ninny as you *here?*"

"Sir," replied Bunn, after a preliminary cough, "you ask me a question I decline to answer, on the ground that it would entail going into my private affairs, with which you have no concern. But I am in a position to assure you that, if I could have kept away from this most undesirable place, I would gladly have done so. Also, if my society is offensive, as it appears to be, I am ready to depart forthwith."

A smile—half-snarl, as it used to be in the old school days—lifted the upper lip of Chunder Loo. He turned to Jack, who met his gaze unflinchingly.

"Your object," he said, "or, rather, the object of the man who brought you here, I know. I do not quarrel with him, because he has lost that which he hopes to recover, but can never regain." His eyes rested for an instant on Norton Truscott. "But what have you cubs to do with the matter? Need you have been so officious as you have been in blocking up the portal of the Avishnu home?"

"What I have done," answered Jack, "I would gladly do again."

"A reply that I might have expected of you," returned Chunder Loo. "You were a dangerous boy, are now a dangerous youth, and unless nipped in the bud, will become a dangerous man. Had I the power I would have you roasted alive to-day. That pleasure is, however, denied me."

He ceased speaking, and his eyes once more scanned them one by one.

"Fifty of my people," he presently resumed, "lie at the bottom of the sea, a few more are in the bosom of the sacred lake, and two score on their way home from the coast have fallen victims to the pitfalls designed for the stranger. But we are still nearly three hundred strong, and can defy the puny power that seeks to exterminate us."

"What is all this to me?" demanded Jack.

"It is not so much for you as for those who are of us," replied Chunder Loo. "To those whose duty it is now to put you through the ordeal of the serpent, I speak. Let them do their duty, for the eyes of the Avishnu are on them. The penalty of disobedience is to suffer a hundred deaths and *yet live!*"

"Is it to be my task to send this youth to certain death?" asked Norton Truscott.

"It is," answered Chunder Loo, "for is it not my office to appoint the priests for such work? To you," addressing Chippy, "falls the task of putting yonder booby in the den of Luva—Jack Ford is the food for Kala. Both pythons are hungry. Each has its own den. Away with them!"

"If I might be spared this office," said Norton Truscott, with the perspiration of pain on his brow, "I would gladly undergo--—"

"You will undergo all that you could desire in case of refusal," interposed Chunder Loo, "and yet he,"—pointing at Jack—"will not be spared. Bandy no words with me, but *obey!*"

He hissed out the last word, and his eyes flashed with venomous rage. There was a responsive fire in the eyes of Norton Truscott, but he answered, quietly, "So be it."

"In half an hour," said Chunder Loo, "all will be ready. Meanwhile, you are mercifully allowed to spend the time together. You dogs of Englishmen! destroyers of our race in India! tyrant masters of all our people! this is but a deed of justice. Could it be known over there in our sunny land, rich with the memories of a wonderful past, how many breasts would throb with secret joy! To put to torture, and compel your brethren to torture you, is surely a sweet revenge for all our wrongs. Go!"

He sprang up and put his hand to his side, where a sword was hanging, but he did not draw it. Not one flinched. A death by that means would not have had many terrors just then.

Norton Truscott took Jack by the arm and led him away to the chamber where they had breakfasted that morning, and Chippy Bunyons piloted Penny Bunn, who walked with a decided weakness about the knees, to another chamber lower down the hall.

"Why are we parted?" asked Jack. "At such a time as this poor Bunn has need of a friendly hand."

"You are parted from him," answered Norton Truscott, gravely, "probably in this world to meet no more. Any attempt to have taken leave of each other would have been checked. Anon we shall be summoned in turn, but whether he or you goes first, you will not know."

"But why the delay?" asked Jack.

"It is part of the system of torture," said Truscott. "The fiend-man who sits as ruler here knows that suspense is worse than actual pain; but there is another reason. The pythons are hungry—I can scarcely bring myself to speak on this matter to you—and they will be fiendishly angered by the display of food—a sheep or a goat, which will be taken away when the appetite of the reptiles is fully roused. Oh, Ford! little as I have seen of you, I have already learnt to love you as a younger brother. How shall I bear this thing? To think that it was my hand that thrust you into a den of the monstrous creatures will haunt me ever after. Hitherto I have held in my breast a hope of one day escaping from my captivity, but what will freedom be to me now? I shall live a haunted man."

"You cannot help me," said Jack, gently, "though you sacrifice your own life. Do not forget that there is a *chance* of my coming out victor. You strangled the python, and why should not I? Trust me in the struggle for my own life I shall not show the white feather."

"That I can well believe."

"Here, grip my arm. It is that of one who is little more than a boy, but I am strong. I have muscles of steel. When we were at Gibraltar, a Levantine ruffian in the street, mad with some coarse drink he had been partaking of, insulted me first and then assaulted me. I had my bare hands; in his was a knife. But I threw him, and left him lying as one dead, upon the ground. I do not speak of this in a boastful spirit, but to give you hope of my coming free from the ordeal."

"I could have throttled that worm!" said Truscott, "as he sat upon his mimic throne, but it would not have helped us. My boy, my brother in misfortune, you shall be led to your trial by me, and if you perish, I——"

He stopped suddenly, seeing a look of pained surprise in Jack's eyes.

"You must live," said the youth, "for Harry Barstow's sake. For me to die is to live in your memories both honoured and loved, and that for me will suffice. Should you ever get back to the old country and leave me *here*, you can tell my friends at home how I died. It will not be as a coward, but as one who despises the heathens at whose hands he met his death."

CHAPTER CCXIV.

PENNY BUNN ASTONISHES A PYTHON.

CHIPPY BUNYONS was quite overwhelmed with grief, but he hid it from outward observance until he and Penny Bunn were in the chamber to which he escorted his prisoner.

It was his own, and somewhat similar to that of Norton Truscott, but less luxuriously furnished.

"Old man," he said to Bunn, "I feel as if I had taken on a job of murder at a price. What can you think of me? Here we are, we two, made, as I may say, for pals, and yet I have to pop you into a den and see that you are either done for or get the better of the sinewy, slimy warmint."

"I suppose," said Bunn, miserably, "that there is no back-door out of this place?"

"There is no getting away at all," answered Chippy. "There isn't a shadow of a chance of it. I'd run any risk if I thought it would help you or me. I feel as if I'd had a heavy meal and took two hours right orf on one of my own roundabouts."

"Friend Chippy," said Bunn, shivering, "your sentiments do you honour. I feel that my life's gratitude—limited but fervent—ought to be yours, and it is. Say no more. I suppose you have not such a thing as a drop of good old brandy here? If you have, it might help me to—to—to bear my lot with something like fortitude."

The eyes of Chippy beamed with pleasure. He was in a position to gratify the last dying wish of his recently-acquired friend.

"Among our stores we have a lot of spirit 'in bond,'" he said "It is for the use of the priests only, and the quantity allowed to me and Truscott is rather limited. But now and then I have succeeded in boning a bottle of something strong. It has been necessary for me now and then to have a quiet, merry evening all to myself. Truscott never goes on the bust. I do so as orfen as I can."

He turned back some of the cushions, beneath which was the paved floor.

The blocks were small squares, one of which he prised up with a knife, disclosing a small hollow below. In it nestled a full bottle of French brandy.

"You are welcome to the lot, Bunn," said Chippy, "if you can carry it."

"In such an emergency as this," replied Bunn, "I can carry a cargo."

Chippy had no corkscrew, but he expertly knocked off the top of the bottle as clean as if it had been removed with a cutting-machine, and handed it to his companion.

"Drink, and take it steady," he advised; "you will find it strong—only ten under proof."

Bunn took a sip, and smacked his lips.

"Prime," he said; "ten years old, if a day."

Then he indulged in a pull, and Chippy did the same. After that they began to view matters more hopefully.

"You may come out of it as I did," he remarked, "if you take enough of this. Only you must hold your breath while the varmint kind o' sniffs you."

Bunn had another drink.

"It's an awful thing," he said, with a clicking in his throat; "but—but—excuse me if I take a little more."

He was in the act of doing so, when Chippy uttered a sharp exclamation of alarm.

"The priests are coming," he said.

Bunn instinctively popped the bottle inside his shirt, and held it tightly under his arm, to keep it upright, and prevent its precious contents from being spilled. Outside a chanting of about a dozen voices was heard.

The sound swelled as the priests approached, the doorway opened, and immediately there was one of the now familiar clashes of musical instruments.

A dozen swarthy men in long, flowing robes and turbans, each with a pair of cymbals or some other instrument in his hands, stood awaiting the coming forth of the man doomed to go through the ordeal.

"Steady," whispered Chippy, himself both white and shaky.

Penny Bunn, strong in brandy, put on the air of a haughty baron going to execution, stalked out, and stared defiantly at the priests.

No other of the Avishnus was in sight. Nor was Chunder Loo to be seen.

Bunn was motioned to take his place at the head of the party, which he did with Chippy, half blind with tears, by his side. There was another clash of music, and then they started marching to the sound of the chant of death.

It was but a monotonous melody, and yet it was very impressive. It had a tendency to depress, and Bunn, ere he had reached the bottom of the hall, would gladly have paid another visit to the bottle, but he dared not.

At the end of the hall was a passage, into which the solemn procession entered. It was of a considerable length, with two turnings in it, and it landed them eventually in a courtyard, in the centre of which were two stone erections without windows, and presenting the appearance of gigantic beehives, save that each had a door, heavily barred.

"The homes of Kala and Luva," softly groaned Chippy, by way of explanation. "Luva is the reptile for you."

Bunn made no answer.

The chanting now suddenly ceased, and two of the swarthy priests advanced to the door, ready to open it at the right moment.

Chippy half led, half pushed Penny Bunn up to the side of the priest.

"I must push you in," he whisperingly groaned, "as we have to be smart in case the python should get out."

Another of the priests climbed up to the top of the building, with naked feet that seemed to cling to the sloping stonework, and peered through a small opening in the crown of it.

He was watching the movements of the python inside for a few moments ere he made a sign, and then the action of his hand indicated that it was moving to and fro.

Suddenly he threw his arm up, and the two priests by the door whipped off the bars and opened it a foot or so.

The whole body joined in a simultaneous yell of execration, Chippy propelled Bunn through the opening, and the door closed.

Clang went the bars as they fell into their places; then again the priests yelled—this time with demoniacal satisfaction—and Chippy, with absolutely colourless cheeks, rocked to and fro upon his heels in his effort to maintain his composure.

The priest on the roof slid down, his object in giving up such a pleasant spectacle—to him—of an unbeliever being destroyed by a python being to avoid distracting the attention of the reptile.

The sudden forward movement shook up Penny Bunn a bit, and set the brandy within him at work. It leaped to his head, and the spirit of bravado took possession of him.

"Houp la!" he shrieked; "here we are again!"

He found himself in a circular room, with perfectly bare walls, and all the light in it admitted through a small hole in the roof.

On one side was a pile of blankets on which the python had been sleeping. But now it was awake, slowly winding about its sinuous thirty feet of head, body, and tail, a hideous, fearsome-looking reptile which might well have daunted a much stronger-nerved man than Penny Bunn.

As he caught sight of it, he whipped out his bottle and put it to his lips, pouring out the brandy with a free hand, so that it ran from his mouth and down his clothes. Finally it choked him.

"Poof! pah!" he gasped. "Ugh! ugh! Oh! my stars and garters——" Here he began to dance and cough and kick as few men have danced and kicked and coughed before.

The python, with its head reared, regarded him with all the unqualified amazement that it was capable of feeling.

For the time its hunger was forgotten, and when

Penny Bunn became calmer and from wild antics and loud coughing settled down to rubbing his chest and gasping, it subsided into a coil, with its head lying idly over the top of it, but with its eyes still fixed upon its involuntary visitor.

The additional brandy was soon felt by him who had imbibed it.

If not absolutely intoxicated he was not far off it, and fear was no longer in his breast.

The bravado that often accompanies Dutch-courage took possession of him.

Seeing the python curled up, apparently indisposed to stir, he ventured nearer to it.

Still it remained quiescent.

" Come, old chap," said Bunn, with a drunken smile, " wake up or you will lose your dinner. Have a nip beforehand—juss a pappytiser, you know."

He proffered the bottle to the python, whose eyes became fixed upon its shining exterior.

The glitter of it attracted the reptile.

"Have a drink," said Bunn, with heavy-eyed gravity. " Don't be bashful. It's all free—yah—help ! murder !"

The python had suddenly raised its head and sprung at the bottle, with so true an aim that it got it, top foremost, in the grip of its jaws.

Down poured the half-bottle of brandy still left into its throat, and as Bunn, sobered and scared out of his wits, fell upon his back, the reptile started gyrating with lightning-like rapidity, so that it looked like one of those chromotypes with which juvenile magic-lantern entertaiments are concluded.

Outside the priests had vanished.

Chippy Bunyons had gone too, for by the laws of the Avishnus some hours at least, or even days, would have to expire ere the door was opened again to see if man or reptile had conquered.

CHAPTER CCXV.

JACK GOES THROUGH HIS ORDEAL.

PENNY BUNN was the first of the pair to be called on to go through the ordeal. Jack Ford's turn was yet to come.

He was kept in suspense for fully an hour, then the clashing and chanting of the priests was heard, and Norton Truscott told him that the moment had come.

"Give me your hand, my brave lad," he said. " I may not be able to grasp it again."

They exchanged a fervent grasp, but there was no more time for words, as the door opened and the voice of a priest was heard summoning them to come forth.

Chippy Bunyons was with them in the rear, and his presence made Norton Truscott acquainted with the fact that Penny Bunn had gone to meet his fate.

The glance that he exchanged with his fellow-priest was not comforting. It conveyed an intimation that there was little hope of Bunn coming safely out of the trial with the python Luva.

But there was no attempt to convey so much to Jack.

Better that he should, for his own sake, remain in ignorance of his old associate's fate.

With a light step the youth left the cell, and took his place in the centre of the priestly group.

For some reason a change was made in the order of his going from that of Penny Bunn. Chippy and Norton Truscott both fell into the rear. The priests before and behind Jack were entire strangers to him

Both were dark, and one was almost black enough for a negro, and he was taller than any man there save Truscott.

He differed in garb somewhat from the rest, which, as he was in front of Jack, the youth observed.

In a girdle round his waist, close to the side under his left arm, was a knife in a leathern sheath. None of the other priests bore any visible weapons.

On this knife the eyes of Jack became fixed the moment the line was formed with him in the centre.

It was a long knife of the bowie description, only that its blade was quite straight. To have it in his possession would be something for Jack to defend himself. It would give him a chance for his life, if only for a few hours.

Perhaps the slaying of the python under any conditions would fulfil the law of the Avishnus. If so, what might not that weapon be worth to him ?

The bearer of the weapon walked with a swinging gait. He carried a pair of cymbals, which at intervals he clashed over his head, varying the movement with beating them together with extended arms.

What was the risk of attempting to steal that knife ?

Jack did not know, and he was not disposed to care. Risk could be hanged at such a time.

They were clear of the hall and in the passage leading to the courtyard when Jack made the attempt to secure the knife—and succeeded. The semi-gloom favoured him.

He was quick of hand and sure of eye, and in a moment it was done. The knife rose out of the sheath as if it had passed through air, and without any flurry Jack secured it in his breast, holding it under his arm as Penny Bunn had carried the brandy-bottle.

It was a double-edged knife, and undoubtedly keen of edge. It had that feeling as he pressed it close to his side.

Now he felt strong, and there was a bright light on his face as he emerged into the open air.

A halt was called, and one of the priests crept up to the door of Luva's home and listened. He could hear nothing.

"The unbeliever has perished," he said.

This was the first intimation Jack received of the fact that Penny Bunn had preceded him. There was a pang at his heart as he thought of the old days with the eccentric tutor and schoolmaster, whose vagaries had given him many a hearty laugh.

But if the unbeliever had perished it was against the law to verify it as yet.

To the den of Kala they turned, and a priest, as before, climbed to the summit and gazed through the orifice made for light and air.

Norton Truscott stepped up to Jack's side and stood there quite still until the signal was given to open the door. Then he whispered, "It is my duty to thrust you in."

"I will spare you that," was the reply, in the same tone.

Then the door opened, and Jack, to the astonishment of the main body of the priests, leaped into the den.

They closed the door and gazed at each other in astonishment.

"Of such material is my country made," said Norton Truscott, sternly. "His blood be on the heads of you dogs!"

"Ha!" cried an elderly, swarthy priest, "dare you speak thus to the Avishnus?"

"I dare, Guacha," replied Norton Truscott; "what matters? The life I lead is a torture, I do not fear the end of it. Would you snarl at me, you cur? Stand out of my path!"

"Seize him!" cried Guacha, "he is false to the Avishnus. Let him be taken before the Great Ruler!"

There was a movement on the part of the priest to seize him, but Norton Truscott rose as one of might in his fury and struck right and left with his fists, bowling over one after the other. Chippy Bunyons also became as one inspired.

"Chippy is my name!" he cried, "and here I must chip in or go mad!"

He dashed at the tall priest who had preceded Jack, and who was now wonderingly fumbling for his lost knife, and butting him in the stomach with his head, sent him to the ground.

The alarm was now general, and cries for help went up.

"Clear out," cried Norton Truscott, "through the Temple! It is our only chance."

Kicking a semi-prostrated priest out of his way as if he had been a football, he dashed into the passage, followed by Chippy, and disappeared.

The priests remaining continued to cry for help, but did not go in pursuit. Suddenly Chunder Loo sprang with a tigerish movement from the passage.

"Cease this bawling!" he cried. "What ails you? Speak, Guacha!"

"The English priests have sought to kill us, and failing, have disappeared!"

"And do you think your baby-cries will bring them back again?" demanded Chunder Loo. "Away—give the call about the city! Arm yourselves! If they get away we are *lost!* The Avishnus will die the death of dogs at the end of a rope!"

He was wild with rage and excitement, and seeing that Guacha, who had been half-stunned by a blow from Norton Truscott, did not stir himself briskly, he raised his hand and struck him.

A great cry went up from all who witnessed it, and they stared at Guacha, who had staggered back.

He was himself overcome with mortal terror, for it was part of the faith of the Avishnus that a blow from the Great Ruler would wither a man to ashes and doom him hereafter.

It was in haste and without thought that Chunder Loo had struck the priest, proving by his own act that his potency was a fraud.

But it was not in that light the priests took it.

To them it was not their Great Ruler who had struck the blow.

"It is Epha, the Evil One!" shouted Guacha. "He who turns himself into the image of our Ruler. Brethren, let us slay him!"

Chunder Loo cursed himself for the deed he had done in haste, but no explanation would avail him then. And to remain was to be torn to pieces by the fanatical body. So he turned and fled, and they, with the ardour of a pack of hounds, went in pursuit of the Evil One.

Meanwhile Jack was in the den of Kala the python, and we must see how he fared.

Kala was a reptile a foot longer than Luva, and reputed to be endowed with enormous strength. It was said of him that he could crush the bones of an ox within his folds.

When Jack leaped into the dark chamber Kala had taken a whim into its head to retire under the blanket, and only its head was protruding when Jack, with apprehensive eyes, looked round.

A minute before, or less, the reptile had been gliding about, restless with hunger.

It espied the youth, and raising its head, gave vent to a hiss.

It was an inspiration surely that came to the aid of Jack. The thought was not to wait for the attack of Kala, but to take the initiative and fall upon it while in the folds of the blanket.

Jack never hesitated at any time when prompt action could be of service.

He sprang forward, knife in hand, and threw himself down upon the reptile, striking at its head, that was moving to and fro.

Jack's hand seized it by the neck, but he felt that, with his still undeveloped strength, he could not emulate the deed of Norton Truscott. By the knife alone he must win or lose his life.

Up rose the sinewy body of the python enveloped in the blanket, and a struggle ensued between it and Jack, which might end in the death of both, but assuredly of one or the other.

Jack tried to keep cool, but he was pressed over by the advance of the reptile, and he struck blindly and furiously.

Blood spurted out from somewhere—he could not see where—covering his hands and face, but there was no apparent diminution of the powers of his foe.

He could hear its tail beating on the stone floor as its body writhed in the effort to shake off the blanket covering, and momentarily expected to feels its fatal folds about him.

But he kept on hacking with the knife and still holding on to the neck of the monster.

At last the time came for the fulfilment of his fears.

There was a quick movement on the part of the python, then a mass of it fell upon him; he was turned over, and the cable-like folds put about him.

At first they were loose, but soon tightened, as a cord is drawn round the wrist.

Jack felt his breath going, he could feel the bending of his ribs, and fancied he heard them being crushed together, and then darkness came over him and he knew no more.

CHAPTER CCXVI.

DIRK MATTHEWS TRIES ANOTHER MUTINY.

IT was afternoon on board the "Albatross," and the good ship lay sweltering in the heat of a cloudless sun.

The sky was as lurid as if it were a dome of molten metal; the sea shifted as liquid brass does in the furnace. It was hotter than it had ever been before since the vessel reached that latitude, and hotter than anything previously experienced by those on board.

Work was not to be thought of. It was not expected or demanded; and although the usual watch was kept, the men had practically leave to do what they pleased to keep themselves cool.

Under the awnings, fore and aft, there was shade, but the warmth was that of an oven. The cabins below were simply unendurable.

"This cannot last," remarked Dick Darnley to the boys; "it will end in some fearful storm. I trust it will hold off until the captain returns."

"The heat is simply frightful!" remarked Don, fanning himself with a book he had been trying to read.

They had nothing on but a thin silken shirt, trousers, socks, and shoes; but, as Bob Stockton said, "it was too much."

"Who was the fellow," he asked, drowsily, "who on a hot day in England expressed a desire to take off his flesh and sit in his bones?"

"Sydney Smith," replied Darnley.

"I feel as he must have done," said Bob. "If it is as bad on the island I do not believe they will have the strength to get along. Phew! it is a scorcher!"

Bill Oakley, with his face shining like a full moon, came slowly across the deck, mopping his forehead with a handkerchief that in case of emergency would have served for a banner.

"I was a-thinking, sir," he said, saluting Darnley, "that by about nightfall we shall get a change of weather. There is something brewing."

"A storm, Oakley?"

"Sure, sir, I should say. It will come from the south, and it won't do to be lying here, sir, longer than we can help."

"We must await the return of the captain."

"Well, sir, if he isn't back by sunset, and we can get a capful of wind, we ought to stand off the coast. Should it come on to blow, as I believe it will, we are bound to go ashore. The anchorage here is as light and rotten as it can be."

Bill was an authority on the weather, and his prognostication created a feeling of uneasiness. It was a sure thing that the more prudent course to take would be to stand off. But suppose it came on to blow, and Harry Barstow returned to the shore with or without those he went in search of, how could they help him?

"Well, Oakley," said Darnley, "we must hope for the best. It is no use meeting trouble half-way. If it threatens to blow by-and-by we must get further out."

"I'm afeard, sir," said Bill, "that it isn't a blow only that is coming. Some years ago I was off Otaheite in similar weather to this, but not so hot. The air warn't so muddy. In a few hours there was lightning, thunder, and such rain as you never dreamt of, and I reckon a sort of airthquake under the sea. The water b'iled up as if it had been in a big kettle. It was fearsome, and how the 'Euphrates'—the ship I was in—lived through it is more than I can tell. She got a fearful towzeling, anyway."

"We will do our best, Oakley, to be ready for an emergency."

"There is another matter as I wished to speak on,"

said Bill, hesitating, "and it's about the men—some on 'em—who seem to be kind of hatching and brooding over something."

"Brooding over what?"

"There's that Dirk Matthews, for instance. I'm sorry I shipped him for the captain, and in my opinion he is a bad lot."

"We can hardly expect all the men to be saints," said Darnley, laughing.

Bill shook his head, gravely.

"There ain't many of that spechies afloat," he said, "and nobody looks for 'em. But I do think an eye ought to be kept on that Matthews."

"Keep an eye on him, then," said Darnley, lightly, "and if he shows himself inclined to be disagreeable, bring him to me. I will talk to Mr. Matthews in a way that will make him sit up."

Bill Oakley scratched his head, sighed, and, after a moment's hesitation, walked away. Dick Darnley lit a cigarette, lay back in his lounging-chair, and composed himself for an afternoon nap.

The hints thrown out by Bill made an impression on the younger listeners, but they were too inexperienced to decide if the latter idea at least had any justification in it.

They could not tell Dirk Matthews was at that very moment arranging for the seizure of the "Albatross" at sunset, "between the lights," when the afternoon watch was to be changed.

He and his especial friends would then have charge of the deck and the other men probably go below.

The old idea was to be worked up.

Dick Darnley, as officer in command, was to be shot, and the men not in the secret of the affair to be battened down.

The three boys Dirk Matthews hardly counted.

They could be frightened into submission, just as he might take it into his head. There was really no occasion—in the opinion of Matthews—to think of them at all. Possibly he might toss them overboard as useless human lumber.

CHAPTER CCXVII.

TRUSCOTT AND CHIPPY IN HIDING.

THE rapidity of the movements of Norton Truscott and his companion, when they fled away, enabled the pair to speedily put a considerable gap between them and their pursuers. Indeed, it seemed as if their escape from the city would prove to be an easy matter.

They ran across the great hall of the temple, and at the entrance met two of the priests, Olga and Waff by name, who had been abroad that morning performing some rite of their unholy faith.

Seeing Truscott and Chippy dashing towards them, they pulled up short and stared hard at them, such an undignified thing as running being rare among the priesthood.

The spirit of an Englishman was still uppermost in the breast of Norton, who promptly gave directions in an undertone to his companion:

"Hit out, and hit hard! Take the left-hand fellow. I will land the other one."

Chippy promptly responded, and with good effect.

Both the priests were fixed with surprise, and, not anticipating an attack, were bowled over, and rolled down the steps, yelling their loudest.

The noise they made brought out some men from the houses below, and the retreat of Norton and Chippy was cut off.

But with his mind in full activity, and his wits at their keenest, Norton Truscott decided, in the tenth of a second, how to act.

"Back!" he cried.

Seizing Chippy by the arms, he dragged him back from the entrance, pushed him aside into the shadow, and in a twinkling had him through a doorway.

"Do you know where you are going?" gasped Chippy.

"Hush! It is our only chance," whispered Truscott. "Up you go—smartly!"

Inside the door was a winding staircase, up which they rapidly ascended. It was dimly lighted with small openings here and there in the wall.

All that has been described, from the first moment of flight up to this moment, covered a wonderfully small space of time, little more than a minute, in fact. Just for an instant the pair paused when they had ascended a dozen stairs. The rush of feet was heard below, then a sudden hush, broken by the voice of Chunder Loo.

He spoke in the language of the Avishnus, which both the listeners understood.

"How say you—worms—you met them here?"

"It was so, Great Ruler," replied a voice, which they recognised as that of Olga.

"And you did not stop them in their flight?" demanded Chunder Loo.

"How could we, Great Ruler," was the answer, "not knowing they were fleeing away from thee? And more—they struck us ere we were aware of their purpose."

A cold, chilling laugh escaped from Chunder Loo. But he suddenly changed his tone, and said:

"It is to be supposed you did your uttermost to stop them. Let it pass. Which way went they?"

"Great Ruler," commenced Waff, in a terrified tone of voice, "we do not know."

For a moment there was silence, and then the voice of Chunder Loo again was heard:

"It matters not; they cannot escape from the island; and, for the present, let all the gates be watched. Anon we will go forth and seek them. The temple must not be deserted; besides, I have a ceremony to perform. Await me here."

"Hasten," hurriedly whispered Norton Truscott, and Chippy went on ahead up the stairs, both treading lightly, and with a pardonable palpitation of the heart.

For the door below had opened, admitting, as they could easily guess, the Great Ruler—Chunder Loo.

He was coming up slowly, his movements betrayed only by the rustling of his garments.

So keen was their hearing under the excitement of the moment that they could hear this clearly.

Onward they went, up fully two-score stairs, and then they came to a chamber, the door of which fortunately stood open.

It was the sanctum of Chunder Loo, the one apartment in the temple they had never seen, for it was forbidden to all to enter on pain of the most torturous death.

Facing the door by which they entered was another, also open, and for this the fugitives made with all speed.

There was no time to examine the apartment, but Norton Truscott hastily took in its general features at a glance.

He was astonished to find very few signs of luxury there.

In one corner was a bed, and there were also a table and chair, but by far the greater portion of space was taken up by a bench, similar to that used by carpenters, on which there was a display of tools, some of them of a very minute size, but all beautifully made.

It was just such a display as one might look for in the private room of a rich amateur mechanic.

Of all things in the world Norton Truscott would not have expected such a sight as this, but at the same time it let a little light into certain things that had always been a mystery to him.

Having no time to dwell upon the matter now, he hastened through the second door, where another staircase was discovered, up which the pair fled.

Ere they had gone far they heard the door below close with a bang, and knew that for the time they were safe.

Their place of retreat was not suspected.

But how long would they be able to remain there in security?

Ascending the second flight of stairs, they found it led to another chamber above, but different from the other, for it was almost dark, as the only light it received came from a series of small holes in the stonework, so made that from one or the other the whole city was under survey.

Beyond this room, evidently a secret one, built long ago in the thick walls, there was no place to hide in.

The pair were fairly boxed in.

"Well, Chippy," said Norton, "we have caged ourselves to a certainty."

"So it seems, sir," answered Chippy, dolorously, "but it can't be helped. That warmint Chunder, I daresay, will soon be coming up here, and then——"

"He will never go down alive," coolly whispered Truscott, "unless he leaves me a dead man behind him."

"Same here," said Chippy; "he will have two of us to reckon with."

It was exceedingly exasperating to find themselves in such a place, but there was no helping it now.

For a short time they occupied themselves in peering out of the holes in the wall, but the moments lagged wearily, and they soon tired of it.

"Chippy," said Truscott, "I am going down below." He kicked off his slippers as he spoke, but only to listen at the door. "I wonder what that villain is up to."

"Can't I come, too?" asked Chippy, "in case of a row with him?"

"No," was the reply; "our best game is to avoid a disturbance, if possible. I shall be careful, you may depend."

"All right, sir," said Chippy, resignedly; "only, if you *do* get into a fix, just holler, will you, and I'm there."

Norton glided out of the chamber and slowly descended the stairs. He was astonished to find there were so many. In their hasty flight upstairs they had not thought of estimating their number.

There were fully seventy between the upper chamber and the door below.

Having reached it, he stood quietly listening. Inside there was a whirring sound such as accompanies a turner's lathe.

Remembering the bench and tools he had seen, Norton understood its nature, and marvelled.

Chunder Loo at work, after such thrilling scenes as he had recently gone through, bordered on the incredible.

But the whirring soon ceased, and was followed by a tapping sound of a small hammer. After that there was silence, until the closing of the other door proclaimed that Chunder Loo was gone.

Norton Truscott hastened back to his companion, and was about to suggest their descending and seeking some other way of escape, when a scene below riveted his attention.

————

CHAPTER CCXVIII.

CEREMONY OF THE AVISHNUS.—SOMETHING WRONG WITH THE ORACLE.

THE sound of brazen instruments was heard outside the temple, summoning the people to assemble in the square.

It had a most unearthly sound, the like of which has seldom fallen on mortal ears.

It was not so much that the music was loud and harsh, for there would have been nothing uncommon in that; it had a peculiar ring in it—a twang that was unlike any other sound extracted from instruments by mortal lips.

Ere long, the people—the common herd, if we may so term them—began to assemble, and by the gravity of their countenances the serious nature of a coming ceremony was foreshadowed.

They uttered no sound, exchanged not a word with each other, but gathered in a circle round the centre of the square and awaited the coming of their superiors with the stillness of so many statues.

A few minutes elapsed, and then the minor priests began to appear.

They stepped out of the temple in couples, making perhaps a score in all, and as they drew near the circle an opening was made to allow them to pass through. That opening remained, for others were expected, Olga, Waff, and Chunder Loo—Epha no longer to any there.

It was a part of the sardonic programme of the latter to make the other two his bodyguard, as if they were his best friends and most trusted confidants; but they were, on the contrary, deeply mistrusted by him, through having allowed Norton and Chippy to escape, and but for the Avishnu law he would long before have wreaked his hatred upon them.

For them, if he could have proved them traitors, would have been death by torture, and such torture as only the most cruel savages could devise—more cruel than the reader can guess at, although we know that there is such a thing as the "Heavy Death" in the Chinese code, supposed by many to be without parallel in the long list of punishments inflicted upon the helpless by savage persecutors.

And now, indeed, it was his hour for testing a new oracle at the expense of Olga and Waff.

With respect to the escaped men, he could not now aim at their bodies, but he knew he had struck them deep in their hearts by incarcerating Jack and his companion in the serpents' dens. So far, well, but much remained to be done.

He walked with a hand on each of the shoulders of the two priests, his face assuming a sadness he assuredly did not feel.

"A sorrowful occasion," he said, in a soft tone of voice, as they were descending the steps, "but the laws of our great people must be obeyed, and Kala and Luva must be fed."

No answer was given him. The faces of both were rigid.

"You are dumb," said Chunder Loo, with a snarl. "It is not right that I should speak and be favoured with no reply."

"What can we say?" asked Olga. "If we say it is a sorrowful day, you will declare we favour the prisoners and the escaped ones. If we rejoice in the fate of the captives, we contradict you, Great Ruler, and we die. Have mercy on us!"

Chunder Loo turned away and smiled in his cruel way. He knew of mercy only in name.

The chamber in which our friends were concealed was a veritable sounding board. They could hear every word, as well as see all that went on.

"May they have help in their trouble, varmints though they are!" murmured Chippy. "But that poor creetur' Bunn—who could hope for him to escape?"

Chunder Loo, assuming his loftiest bearing, now strode into the centre of the circle, where by this time the minor priests had fitted up piecemeal a sort of altar, on the top of which was an apparently solid carving of stone, representing a serpent coiled about the stump of a tree.

It was a strange thing to the Avishnu people, judging by the way they gazed at it, half in curiosity, half in terror.

A new ceremony, with a novel test, was about to be introduced to them.

Chunder Loo ascended the two steps that formed the base of the throne, and, with his hand upon the serpent, addressed his people.

His voice was low but peculiarly clear, and it had a thrilling effect upon his listeners.

"My people," he began, "a few days ago I was away from you for awhile conferring with the Great Spirit that gives wisdom to our serpents. From that mighty source I learnt that we should have two prisoners in our power—to put to the test."

He paused, and there was a stir among the people. Norton Truscott and Chippy from their elevated post looked at the serpent curiously.

Norton fancied he saw that the solidity was only apparent, and that the head and a portion of the body was made to move.

Glancing lower down, he noticed that the hand of Chunder Loo rested on what looked very much like a mechanical spring.

Remembering the sounds he had recently heard, and wondering what trickery was about to be performed, he glanced at Chippy, whose face might have been cut out of marble, so rigid was it.

"Do you know aught of this?" he asked.

"A few," enigmatically replied Chippy Bunyons.

"By our laws," pursued Chunder Loo, "those who are shut in with the serpents have a certain time of grace—that is a time of anxiety and doubt to us—therefore I besought the Great Spirit to give me something that would indicate to us *at once* whether the prisoners or captives will conquer."

He stopped again, and gazed round at the thrilled circle, every man implicitly believing every word he said.

"Are not Kala and Luva great?" he asked, "and if they kill their prey, shall they not be left in peace for the weeks that are required for them to digest their food? Answer me——"

There was a shout by way of reply, although it was clear that many had not as yet conceived what he was aiming at.

But Norton Truscott had grasped it.

Chunder Loo was going to *make sure* of his prisoners. There was no loophole for them to escape by.

If the figure signified that the serpents would conquer, then there was an end of the matter, and Kala and Luva, having partaken of their stupendous meal, would be left to themselves *for weeks*.

And even if, by anything approaching a miracle, Jack and his companion in misery overcame their reptile foes, they must in the end perish.

For by the laws of the Avishnus the sacred serpents must not be approached within a distance sufficient to cut off from outside hearing any cries that might escape the captives.

"Doubly and trebly cunning villain!" said Norton Truscott between his teeth, "he will leave no loophole for them in his malice."

And now the clear voice of Chunder Loo resumed:

"I will put our new oracle to the test."

Prostrating himself by the altar, so that his hand still rested on the spring, he proceeded to offer up a prayer, of a nature we cannot put on record here, finishing with an earnest adjuration of the idol-like thing to answer it.

"If these our captives will die," he said, "raise your head, oh! holy serpent. If they are to conquer, be still."

There was no doubt he pressed the spring, for the effect was visible to the two watchers in the hidden chamber; but the Avishnu people could not see it, for, like their "Great Ruler," they were prostrate.

But though he pressed the spring, the serpent did not stir; the head remained stationary.

Hearing no further word from their leader, the people raised their heads and saw that the head had not stirred.

Then a great cry burst from their lips.

"The unbelievers will be spared, and become as we are—true worshippers of the serpent."

There is much joy over converts everywhere, but among these people it was a matter for much rejoicing.

Diminishing fast in numbers, any addition to their body was hailed with the most extravagant delight.

Chunder Loo dared not show his feelings, but, on the contrary, had to feign sharing in them.

So he raised his hands over his head, and there was a general song of joy sung by the people.

Not that they cared a straw personally for either Jack or Bunn, but it was the fact that they would be stronger by two men of the white race.

The song ceased, and then one of their number came into the centre and burst into an impromptu chant, singing each line by himself, and then repeating it with the people joining in:

"Behold! at the dawn Kala and Luva arose, and cried: 'To-day shall we eat of the flesh of the unbelievers!'

"And so the unbelievers were cast into their dens and left to die.

"But as they entered, the light of Avishnu burst upon them, and they saw the true faith. So Kala and Luva passed them by unharmed.

"And now they live in harmony together, and at the setting of the sun the prison doors will be thrown open and they will be free."

The song ceased with a great clashing of instruments, and the ceremony was over.

CHAPTER CCXIX.

CHUNDER LOO'S RAGE.—THE SECOND ATTEMPT TO ESCAPE.—THE PRIESTS DENOUNCED.

CHUNDER LOO, while the people formed in a line to return to the temple, stood as a man stunned by some terrible misfortune.

Owing to some unforeseen hitch in his idol, made by his own hands, it had failed to work.

And now, at sunset, unless he could ward off their intentions, the doors of the cells would be thrown open, and then—— Ah! what then?

If either, or both, of the prisoners had conquered their sinuous adversary, he or they would step forth free.

And sacred in the eyes of the Avishnu people so long as he or they dwelt in peace among them.

But if the serpents had conquered, as seemed most likely, then Chunder Loo would stand discredited in the eyes of his people.

He would be branded as a liar who had boasted of communing with the Unseen, and his idol proclaimed to be a false one.

Convinced of that, Chunder Loo would be as naught their eyes—he would be a doomed man.

This was so apparent to the watchers above, that, Chunder Loo descended wearily from the altar, by chuckled aloud:

"It strikes me," said Chippy, "that he is in a bit a fix."

"Oh, he will find a way of wriggling out of it," plied Truscott. "What we have to worry over is: re we are boxed up, and no way of getting out ible."

"Wait till night and throttle the warmint as he eps," suggested Chippy; "or go down now and t behind the door, so that as he comes in we may ain him with some of the tools he works with."

"And then?"

"Well, then we shall have time to think over what e can do."

"There is something in the notion, Chippy," said orton Truscott, "but I do not care to kill a man nawares."

"Is he a man?"

"Well, perhaps not. Anyway, we can slip down and ee what can be done."

They went quietly down the stairs, but ere they cached the bottom they heard Chunder Loo moving about below.

Not in his quiet, stealthy way, but as one who walks n a rage. They could hear him muttering to himself, and presently he burst out:

"Curses! who has played me this trick? Some fool must have touched it, or thrust something into the springs as it stood in the hall this morning. May the curse of Mehala fall upon him!"

Chippy Bunyons nudged the arm of Norton, who looked at him, and was favoured with a wink of intense meaning.

It conveyed to him the fact that Chippy was responsible for the idol being "out of order."

"Shoved a bit of wood into the hole of the spring."

His mouth framed the words—to utter them would have been dangerous; but Norton Truscott understood him, and smiled grimly.

Thwarting Chunder Loo was, in any case, a highly satisfactory proceeding.

After communing angrily with himself for awhile, Chunder Loo, in a sudden paroxysm of passion, cast the idol on the floor and danced upon it.

Finally he was heard breaking it up with a hammer, and the listeners felt inclined to laugh aloud. But the serious nature of their position forbade it.

Having so far satisfied his embittered feelings, Chunder Loo left his room, and ten minutes afterwards the others entered it.

On the floor lay the broken idol and the shattered works whereby Chunder Loo intended to make it exhibit occult powers. The construction was very simple, being mainly on the lines of the Jack-in-the-box principle.

The release of a spring would have sent the neck of the serpent up with a jerk, and what at home serves as an amusing feature of a toy, would have been received by the Avishnus with awe and reverence, as practically a vision from the spirit-world.

"The simplest forms of humbug," said Norton Truscott, "are the most effectual."

Time being precious, they did not linger, but followed after Chunder Loo, who was by this time in the hall, where the Avishnus were assembled in tumultuous discussion.

The subject was, of course, the imprisonment of the two captives with the serpents, and the promise of their being everlastingly in safety, given by the new oracle.

But Chunder Loo was about to upset their theories and hopes, and a spirit of malevolence prompted him to assuage his wrath by punishing the two unfortunate priests, Waff and his companion.

There is no limit to the possibilities when ignorance and superstition are governed by a crafty intellect.

Chunder Loo, with an assumption of majesty, stalked into the thick of them and called for silence.

Immediately every tongue was still and the eyes of all turned upon him.

"The Great Spirit is angry," he said.

A dull, dumb look of terror was upon the gaze of all, including the priests. The arch-villain who had inspired this feeling stalked to the centre of the hall, where there was an altar, and ascending its three steps, looked around him.

"I am here," he said again, "to tell you that the Great Spirit is angry. You are accursed, for you have those in your midst who have favoured the escape of traitors!"

He pointed at the two unfortunate priests, Olga and Waff, who threw up their arms and shrieked out:

"We are not guilty!"

"To those who do this thing," pursued Chunder Loo, relentlessly, "there is but one fate—that which was due to those they have aided to flee away. But let me tell you that it was owing to their presence that the serpent refused this day to raise its head and foretell the doom of the two men thrown to Kala and Luva."

Norton and Chippy, standing at the foot of the stairs, could hear every word that was said, and from the latter involuntarily burst the exclamation:

"What a liar he is!"

It was spoken so loudly that some of the Avishnus on the outside of the circle, and therefore nearest to the two men in hiding, started and looked about them apprehensively.

Fortunately Chunder Loo again claimed their attention.

"Our oracle," he said, with feigned sadness, "has been taken from us. As I bore it to my chamber, where alone I commune with the Great Spirit, it was taken from me—it melted away in my grasp and vanished."

"Well, of all the——" muttered Chippy.

"Pray be quiet," said Norton Truscott. "Our one chance of escape lies in their taking away those two poor wretches to torture. Hush!"

"I cannot promise you that the serpent of stone, that speaks and moves, will be restored to you," resumed Chunder Loo; "but it may be so, if you will but hearken to the voice of wisdom. Shall the false ones live?"

There was a wild, general shriek of "No! they must die!"

"Wisely spoken," said Chunder Loo. "They know their fate, and you know in whose hands lies the execution of it. Let justice be done!"

CHAPTER CCXX.

A FIGHT FOR LIFE.—A CHASE THROUGH THE CITY.

BUT the two priests, Olga and Waff, though denounced, were neither ready nor willing to die. Like all human beings endowed with health, they were, like cornered rats, stimulated to fight.

Each drew a dirk, and backed against the wall, where they stood wildly hacking and hewing the throng that pressed upon them.

Desperate men are hard to beat, and five of their assailants were lying in the agonies of death upon the pavement ere the denounced men were secured.

But at last they went down, and, struggling to the last, were securely bound.

For the dead and wounded there might be wailing, but the triumph of having secured the "traitors" rose high above all else.

Shouting and sounding their brass instruments, they accompanied the captives to the altar, on which the two men were laid.

Though eager to sacrifice them, the Avishnus, as a body, were not fully prepared to inflict the "full torture" upon them.

There were things to be done at which even they might shrink, so Chunder Loo, to work them up to the requisite pitch, commanded a drink to be served out. It was of the nature of arrack, and highly intoxicating.

About the quantity that would fill a wine-glass was served in cups to each man, the bottle from which it was poured being made of leather.

As soon as swallowed its potency was attested by the shouting and laughing of the men, all of whom eventually formed in circles round the altar, and danced more like maniacs than men.

"Now is our time, if at all," said Truscott, who had softly opened the door, so that he could peep forth.

"Go on, sir," replied Chippy. "I am with you."

The whirling of the dancers would prevent their seeing anything, and Chunder Loo was standing erect, with his eyes closed to prevent his suffering from the giddy effect of the turning circles of men.

He stood on the steps, his head far above the rest, and, if his eyes were open, his seeing the fugitives when they came into the full glare of the light was a certainty.

"We must rush and take our chance," said Norton.

He was out in a moment, with Chippy close behind him, and the pair made for the entrance to the temple.

If they hoped to escape being discovered they were in error, for the eyes of Chunder Loo were not fully closed, after all.

He had merely shut them sufficiently to make everything misty before him, and he was gazing over the heads of the mad dancers into the daylight in the streets beyond.

As Chippy and Truscott darted out he saw them.

Then at once, as one inspired, he understood the secret of their temporary escape, and, in a black fury, he yelled at the dancers for them to stop.

But they had no ears for him, nor sight or thought for anything but their wild, frenzied movements, and by ordinary pushing he could not break his way through.

So he furiously threw himself upon them, and the circles were checked and broken.

Then came a scene of commotion, the people struggling with each other, not knowing what to make of the interruption.

Those nearest Chunder Loo, seeing who it was, fought in terror to get away from him. The peril of laying a hand upon his sacred person was too well known.

But do what they might, they were thrust against him, insomuch that he stumbled and fell.

But he was speedily on his feet again, and in bubbling tones of wrath a few denunciatory words fell from his lips.

Then he told them he had seen the two men—he called them "traitor priests"—and urged them on to pursue.

He was too wary of his own person to risk encountering them single-handed.

Norton Truscott was of the class that fights well and, when life is at stake, most desperately.

So he waited until his followers comprehended him, and then in a body, like a pack of hounds, they tumbled down the steps in a reckless way, but saw nothing of the fugitives. They could only estimate the way they had gone.

"To the great gate !" cried Chunder Loo.

It was the gate with which the reader is already familiar, and Chunder Loo thought of it as the most probable point the fugitives would make for, as it faced the side of the island where the "Albatross" lay at anchor.

There was one street through which they must pass to reach it, and there they found an Avishnu sentry pacing up and down.

From him they ascertained that nobody had passed that way.

"It is their only real road of escape," muttered Chunder Loo ; "but perhaps they have doubled again."

Aloud he said : "They are still within this city, my people, and may make no effort to escape until nightfall. For us there is a duty to perform on other traitors. Let us return to the temple."

So they returned, and there performed the cruel office on the supposed traitors set them by their faith.

It was barbaric, inhuman, and from our point of view incredible.

Inch by inch these poor wretches were slain, and the fiendish acts were not desisted from until the last muscle had ceased to quiver.

Then all that was left of the two hapless priests was taken out and cast into a well behind the temple.

So far Chunder Loo was satisfied, but he was eager to ascertain the fate of the two captives, particularly Jack, for whom he had ever entertained a burning hatred.

It was forbidden to approach the dens of the huge serpents until the testing time had expired ; but Chunder Loo, having bidden his people go and refresh themselves after their labours, crept by a roundabout way back to the dens.

First of all he lay down by the door of the den where Penny Bunn was incarcerated, and listened.

He fancied he heard a slight sound—a rustling, or a slight scraping, of which he could make nothing.

"It matters little what becomes of him," muttered Chunder Loo.

Next he passed to the den occupied by Jack and the serpent appointed to kill him.

There he fairly glued his ear to the door, but heard no sound.

All within was as silent as the desert at midnight.

"It is *over*," he muttered, exultingly. "At last he who foiled all our plans at Littlecote is dead !"

He stood up, and in his unearthly elation leaped three times in the air, striking his hands and heels together.

Then he went back to his people, and singling out a dozen of them, went forth to seek the lost Norton and Chippy.

Satisfied that they had not left by the main gate, he did not go thither again, but sought them in other directions.

What an uncanny place it was !

So weird its architecture, and so tortuous its narrow streets, to the uninitiated it must have been quite a maze.

But Chunder Loo knew it as well as if he had been born there, and lived among its shadows all the days of his life.

But only here and there did they come across some lone creatures of whom to ask the question :

"Have you seen the priests hurrying past ?"

The answer was always, " No, Great Ruler," and Chunder Loo went on unsatisfied.

Once upon a time there must have been many more inhabitants than the city could now boast of, as in the quarter which they passed there was accommodation for many thousand people.

But the majority of the houses had that lifeless, dreary look one sees in all places which had been long uninhabited.

The doors were gone, the windows were black and staring, and the stones, yielding to time, chipping slowly away.

Swiftly here and there went Chunder Loo, and found nothing.

So back he hied to the temple.

Meantime Norton Truscott and Chippy were hiding in a deserted house in the very street where the sentry was passing to and fro, of whom Chunder Loo had made inquires.

The question of slaying this man had been discussed, but Norton was averse to taking him unawares. He wished to get away from his accursed surroundings with as little blood upon his hands as possible.

By-and-by he would perhaps return and avenge Jack, or rescue him, in fair fight. Then indeed must none of the Avishnus look to him for mercy.

He was not a warrior, had never been one, but he felt an overpowering longing to grasp a sword and rush into the thick of the Avishnus.

Right nobly would he leave his mark upon them.

As for Chippy, as he lay quiet in the house, his thoughts turned also to war, but instead of sword, his mind reverted to a certain truncheon he had seen in his early days at home, a relic of the time when his father was called on to do duty as a special constable.

What a handy little thing it was, in every way suggestive of smart blows and broken pates !

To have that in his hand, and fifty Avishnu heads to crack with it, was desiring happiness he knew could never be fulfilled.

"Chippy," said Norton, suddenly, "I cannot linger here. He is one, and we are two. Let us make a bold bid for liberty."

As before, Chippy expressed his readiness, and they peered forth at the sentry, who, to their astonishment was advancing upon the house.

He must have heard their voices, for the place was full of acoustic surprises, and was coming to see what the noise meant.

He carried in his hand a long dirk or dagger, that gleamed like a mirror in the sunlight.

It was a formidable weapon in the hands of a powerful man, but Norton Truscott did not flinch.

He motioned to Chippy to stand on one side of the doorway, while he took up a position on the other side.

Both held their breath, and the Avishnu drew nearer.

He paused outside as if in doubt what to do. Then he moved a step backwards, as if satisfied that nobody was there.

But a sense of duty prevailed, and he again advanced towards the doorway and entered.

In a moment both men were upon him.

Norton Truscott seized the hand that bore the weapon, and Chippy Bunyons threw his arms about his neck, making an effort to throw him.

But the Avishnu was a sinewy man, well-practised in the arts that made the race of serpent worshippers so dangerous to their foes.

He had the elasticity of limb of a contortionist and the strength of an athlete, so that he was not conquered by merely being seized.

He writhed this way and that, throwing poor Chippy with so much violence against the wall that he saw innumerable stars, and rockets, and bluelights, all products of a disordered imagination.

But Chippy held on, and, if he did nothing else, he prevented the Avishnu from indulging in his wish to shriek for help.

Given the opportunity, he would have emitted sounds that would have been heard all over the city, for he had a throttle, and the streets were built for the conveyance of sound.

Down they all went together upon the stone floor, the Avishnu underneath. His head gave out a remarkably distinct sound as it struck the ground.

To all appearance he was dazed, and Norton Truscott, believing it to be the case, released his hold upon the fellow's wrist.

It was a terrible mistake, and might have had fatal results.

With a wrench he got free and leaped up, and seemingly had both his assailants at his mercy.

In a moment more he might have stabbed them both, but Chippy, seizing his ankles, jerked his legs from under him, and he fell upon the stone floor with a thwack that effectually scattered his wits.

"I think we have him this time," said Chippy.

"No doubt," answered Norton Truscott, as he breathlessly went to work removing a scarf from the man's waist.

They tore it in two, and having securely bound his legs and arms, went on their way.

CHAPTER CCXXI.
THE PARTY OF RESCUE.

FROM the summit of the cliff the party of rescue looked down upon the interior of the island.

Exercising due caution, they crouched behind the broken rocks and talked in an undertone, knowing how the still air might convey the sound of their voices to a distance.

The reader is acquainted with the nature of the spectacle that lay at their feet in all its quaintness and weird splendour.

Despite the deep anxiety in their hearts, they could not but feel its influence as they peered down upon it cautiously ; and even the ordinary seamen, not accustomed to give way to romantic feelings, opened their eyes and marvelled.

"A purty place," muttered one of the men, "but don't seem wholesome-like."

"Kind o' got a tinge o' summat evil," muttered another.

Harry Barstow was thoughtful and Ben Walton silent, until the latter remarked on the strange quietude of the air.

"It does seem peculiarly quiet," assented Harry Barstow. "Although we have had calms and calms, this seems to be something special."

"It is so ; but what it portends I shall not pretend to say. Shall we move on now ?"

"I think it will be as well. Steady, men ! do not show yourselves more than you can help."

Just as they were about to move, a strange sound, that was like music and not music, was borne to them on the air.

Ben Walton shuddered.

"What is that ?" asked Harry.

"I suppose it is what those fellows call music," replied Walton.

"It is very strange music."

"It is ; I have heard it before."

Harry turned an inquiring glance upon him. The face of Ben Walton was very pale.

"It is a summons to a sacrifice," he said, "with a triumphant burst proclaiming its completion."

"It must be for our friends—poor fellows !"

A SPLENDID SCHOOL STORY.
NEVER BEFORE PUBLISHED.
By E. HARCOURT BURRAGE,
Author of "Ching Ching," "Monkey Mat and Roving Dick," "The Brave Boy of the Basilisk," &c.

THE LAMBS OF LITTLECOTE.

"MERCIFUL HEAVENS!" CRIED HARRY. "CAN IT BE YOU, NORTON?"

PRICE ONE PENNY.

"It may be or not; we cannot tell. With the Avishnus sacrifices are sometimes of almost daily occurrence. There are so many of their laws so easy to break."

"And is there but one punishment for them all?"

"But one, unless the offence is very small. Death is the sentence, differing in the matter of the amount of torture, but nothing more."

"If it should be a summons to witness the end of Nor——"

"Then we are too late. Our hope, if he is alive, lies in getting into the city unseen. The summons, if summons it was, calls all the people, save such as are sentries, together."

"Let us go on," said Harry, hurriedly.

"I beg of you to use the utmost caution," urged Walton.

"There does not seem to be a single person about," remarked Harry Barstow.

"No," said Ben Walton, thoughtfully, "and probably there is not. Quite recently, however, some of the Avishnus have passed this way. Look a few feet down, to where there is a patch of soft soil between the stones. What do you see there?"

"A mark or scratch."

"Note its shape."

"I see. It is a crude resemblance of a serpent."

"And that dot at the lower end is meant for the head, and it signifies that they have gone down. But there is more than that to observe. There are footmarks—indefinite, it is true, because the Avishnus walk with slippered feet. But I think I can detect the mark of a heel such as Ford or Bunn might have on their boots."

"Let us see what we can make of it," said Harry Barstow.

He motioned to the men to keep as they were, and he and Walton went down to the spot they had been inspecting from a short distance.

There was no doubt about it. Heel-marks were to be seen, and one was particularly clear.

"We may hope," said Walton, "they are yet alive."

"We must follow this trail," said Harry Barstow; "it seems to be open."

"The path down here is not marked out in an ordinary way, but it is clear enough to the initiated," said Walton. "Like most of the roads of the Avishnus, it takes the form of the reptile they worship. Possibly on either side of it they have constructed pitfalls—their cunning in that direction surpassing that of man generally. We must, therefore, proceed with caution."

"You had better lead the way," suggested Harry.

"Assuredly."

The men were summoned with a motion of the hand and told to fall into Indian file, and to be sure to follow exactly in the footsteps of Mr. Walton.

The second mate then proceeded to guide them down the rugged slope.

He was exceedingly—and some of the men thought absurdly—wary. Harry Barstow was inclined to think so, too, and he gave away his thoughts with a slight movement of impatience when they were about halfway down.

Ben Walton turned to him with a smile.

"You think that I am wasting time?" he said.

"Well, I should like to get on quicker," answered Harry. "Every moment is precious."

"See here," said Walton.

He stepped cautiously off the route, put one foot forward, and gave a stone a touch with it. Though of considerable size and weight the stone immediately rolled away, revealing a hole about six feet across, dug out like a well, and penetrating to a depth of twenty feet.

"It is on account of these trifles," he said, calmly, "that I am so cautious."

"Forgive me," said Harry.

They went on again, and Walton guided them safely to the bottom by the borders of the sheet of water.

He glanced around and said that they could push on now, and they did so, round by the bank, to the flight of steps, which they ascended until the topmost was reached, and there the men were commanded to lie down.

The nature of the view we know.

It came upon Harry Barstow as a complete surprise, but Walton accepted it almost as a matter of course.

"Let us sit down and keep out of view," he said; "for the present we can go no further. In yonder city our friends are prisoners, alive or dead."

They sat down, and Startop was desired to crawl forward and place himself in position to see and give warning of the approach of the foe.

He crept over the summit and lay down by a bush, sufficiently well concealed from anyone in the distance below.

"How long must we wait here?" asked Harry Barstow. "I am guided by you in all things, of course. It is on your experience of these people we must rely to carry us through."

"Being a small party," replied Walton, "it would not be safe for us to move down the city before nightfall; we have to discover our friends and keep ourselves concealed."

"Who would have dreamt of such a people building a noble city like that before us?"

"They did not build it; but their priests have books relating to nations and peoples long since extinct.

They have records of hidden cities of vast proportions to be used as refuges when driven, as they knew they would be, from place to place. The Avishnus have always recognised that the hand of every man, outside themselves, was and ever will be against them."

They talked awhile of these things, Walton speaking freely of things on which he had hitherto been reticent. And so the time passed until the sunset hour was at hand.

Meanwhile, of course, the men had partaken of food. With exemplary patience they bore the infliction of inactivity, for nothing was seen or heard to interest them until the time named, when the warning voice of Startop was heard :

"Man coming out of the city."

Lying low, all fixed their eyes in that direction.

By the city, Startop meant the wood that skirted it. A solitary figure, little more than a speck, was seen hurrying as one runs for his life.

He was attired in a rich robe, which he had gathered to his knees to enable him to run freely. At the first it seemed as if he were coming straight on towards Harry Barstow's party, but he soon changed his mind, and bore away to the left.

"A refugee of some sort," said Harry Barstow.

"His skin appears to be dark," answered Walton ; "he is not one of our friends, I fear."

"See, he halts and throws himself down by that clump of bushes."

"Look there—another refugee !"

This time it was a smaller man, less richly attired, and although he pounded along, he travelled like a man who was in need of breath.

He bent his steps towards the men on the summit of the slope, but was stopped short by a cry from the other man in hiding.

Wheeling about he cut a caper, and, running up, joined him by the bushes.

"Now, who may they be ?" asked Harry Barstow.

"Not Avishnu, though in Avishnu attire," answered Ben Walton.

"Can they be refugees ?"

"Possibly."

"Would it be wise to signal to them ?"

"As they are refugees, plainly no harm could come of it, as far as they are concerned. But we might be seen by those who, in all likelihood, are pursuing them."

"Suppose I went down alone," said Harry. "I could keep out of sight until I was near enough to them without being seen."

Walton scanned the intervening ground quickly, and said :

"I think you might venture ; but do nothing further than is necessary to see what these men are. We can follow you cautiously one by one."

Harry Barstow felt his heart beat quicker than it had done of late. A hope he dared not fully define was in his breast. It seemed to be too wild and improbable, nay, impossible of realisation.

Rushing up, he swiftly passed over the brow of the hill, and, taking advantage of every prominence and bush, travelled swiftly down.

The two men lay under the bushes, evidently watching towards the city for a possible pursuer. They never once looked up towards the summit of the hill.

Harry Barstow hurried on until he came in sight of the two men again. They were then not more than a hundred yards apart.

He stopped and stared at them with eager eyes. The taller of the two had his face turned from him, but he could see a portion of his profile.

The eyes of Harry Barstow dimmed for moment with emotion, and then, with a gasping cry upon his lips, he ran forward.

The two men heard his advancing steps, and springing to their feet, stood upon the defensive. They had naught but stout sticks to defend themselves with.

But the taller of the two dropped his almost as soon as he raised it, and dashed forward to meet Harry Barstow.

They met without a word, fell upon each other necks and embraced with the strong clasp of true friendship.

Thus for some moments they stood, and then drew a little apart, but still holding on to each other by the arms.

"Merciful Heaven !" cried Harry, "can it be you, Norton ?"

"It is Norton," was the answer, "and you are Harry. Come in search of me, as I know. A friend, indeed—a brother."

"How did you know of my coming ?"

"I had forgotten for a moment," said Norton Truscott, regretfully, "I have seen your young friend, Ford."

"What of him ? Is he alive ?"

"I cannot tell. But see here ; one who has suffered with me—a faithful fellow."

"Chippy Bunyons by name," said Chippy, who had hitherto stood quietly in the rear ; "not at all a pot, but a man as will stand by a friend to the last drop in his pewter, to use a piece of poetical allegory."

Harry shook hands with him, and, Walton now coming up, he was introduced to Norton Truscott and Chippy with joyous ceremony.

The seamen also came gliding on one by one, and by the advice of Norton Truscott the whole party hid themselves among the bushes.

"We are sure to be pursued," he said, "unless the sun sets before they have ascertained the way we took. It was rather quick work evading them."

"A neat bit of doubling on your part," said Chippy, "making as if you were going t'other way, and then harking back through the empty part of that there city to the gate, where with one blow under the ear—a fair knock-out—you settled the sentry for half an hour or so."

"After dark," said Norton Truscott, "no Avishnu within the city will leave it."

―――――

CHAPTER CCXXII.

WHAT OF FORD AND PENNY BUNN?

"AND now," said Harry Barstow, "tell me about Ford and Bunn."

Briefly the story was told, and it brought little hope to the hearers. Norton Truscott was not aware that Jack had possessed himself of a knife, or there might have been a ray of it. As for Bunn, it seemed practically certain that he had become food for Luva the python.

"And not a bad sort of fellow," said Chippy Bunyons, tearfully; "just the sort of chum I like. No pride or nonsense about him, and yet up to snuff."

"The sun is about to dip," remarked Norton Truscott; "as soon as it is dark we can return and make sure that poor Ford is dead or alive."

"You ought not to run the risk," said Harry.

"You are going?"

"Yes."

"That is of course. Why, then, should I hold back? I know the place, too, so well, that I could walk through it blindfold. There is no need for more to go."

"We cannot leave you," said Walton, and the men murmured.

"Take our friend here," said Harry Barstow, "and return with him to the summit of the hill, and there await us till midnight. If we are not with you then, go back to the 'Albatross.'"

"Too many of us," said Norton Truscott, "would only be embarrassing—fatal to our project, perhaps. We are not going to carry the city by assault, but simply to ascertain if two poor fellows are dead or alive. The place of their confinement is free of the Avishnu presence, for it is against their faith to go near the home of their accursed serpents while feeding, or within some hours or days of their satisfying their hunger. If alive, we can bring away our friends. If dead, there will be naught to bring away."

As he said this the sun went down, and darkness fell upon the earth.

There was something ominous in this, in the thoughts of many there.

The close of day might be indicative of the shutting out of hope.

"Go now," said Norton Truscott, gently, "and fear nothing for us. Together we old friends are strong. If any of you can spare me a weapon I shall be glad. A sword and revolver—anything."

They proffered him more than he could possibly need, and he accepted a cutlass and a pair of revolvers.

"At the worst," he said, cheerily, "I shall not live for the tortures they inflict on a recreant priest. Chippy, if you see no more of me――"

"Oh! don't say that!" burst out Chippy; "it would break my heart if I didn't see you again. Here, let me go. I know the way as well as you."

"No, no, that would be parting two friends who have been apart too long," replied Truscott. "Don't think of it, Chippy. How hot the air is!"

"It reminds me of a London bakehouse," said Chippy, "one of them in a cellar, and without ventilation. Well, if you will go, you must."

"We must get through our work before the moon rises," said Norton. "Harry, I am ready."

A few more words of advice and hope were exchanged, and then they parted, Harry and his restored friend going towards the Avishnu city, and Norton leading the rest back to the top of the hill.

"Norton," said Harry, "I have a flask with me. I think that a little of its contents might do you good."

"I am not in need of Dutch courage," answered Norton, smiling; "but I must confess to a curious sensation a moment ago, as if the ground shifted slightly from under my feet, and I feel out of sorts."

"I experienced the same sensation," replied Harry, quietly.

"It was excitement, or the fruits of it, perhaps. There it is again. Did you feel it?"

"Yes."

They stopped short, and waited a moment side by side, but the sensation did not return.

Each took a pull from the flask and proceeded.

The sun was down, but the heat that had marked the latter part of the day was not lessened.

On the contrary, it appeared to increase, and there was a curious *thickness* in the air that made it oppressive breathing.

"I have never felt anything like this before," said Norton Truscott, "although the clime here is often very sultry."

"There is a storm brewing, perhaps," said Harry, looking up. "Norton, what has become of the stars?"

Norton Truscott raised his eyes and saw that the stars overhead had all assumed a blood-red colour, arising from some peculiar haze in the atmosphere.

"Harry," he said, "I don't care for the state of things. Let us hurry on."

"What does it portend?"

"Some serious atmospheric and possibly terrestrial disturbance, I should say."

They attained the wood, and passed through it slowly to avoid coming in contact with the trunks of trees, or bushes with thorns. Norton made no mistake, and they emerged from it almost opposite the great gate.

Voices from the inner side fell upon their ears—the voices of men talking in excited tones.

"What are they saying?" asked Harry. "I do not understand them."

"They are speaking in the Avishnu tongue," said Norton. "Listen!"

From the Babel of voices which each moment gathered in strength, Norton was able to catch, and mentally interpret, the following:

"It is Epha the Evil One—he is transformed into the Great Ruler—he hides in the city—the holy priests seek him with the sword—it must have been one of his demons who slew the sentry—see, he has no wound—he lies as one asleep."

"By George!" muttered Norton Truscott, "I *killed* that fellow when I hit him under the ear. Can't say I'm sorry, though. One Avishnu less is a betterment of the world."

Whoever was discussing the untimely death of the sentry did not linger to carry the matter to a definite conclusion.

There were dissentients to the suggestion that Epha, the Evil One, had sent a special messenger to put an end to him, but they were in a minority, and were told that they knew nothing about it.

Then the whole body went off wrangling into the town, and the gate was left free for anyone to enter by.

"Let us go on," said Harry Barstow, feverishly. "I feel as one who knows that a moment may be fatal to one he loves. Norton, you will not be jealous when I tell you that Jack Ford has wound himself about my heart. Indeed, all the youngsters have, for they are, as the Yankees say, 'true grit.'"

"I am more than jealous," answered Norton Truscott; "but I long, with an eagerness I cannot describe, to know the fate of the poor youth. What does it matter, in a jealous sense, whether he lives or dies? In either case he will be in your heart as he is in mine."

He finished with a wave of the hand, and they passed through the gate together into the passage, and so on to the quiet street.

It was deserted, as it had been on the previous night, when Jack and the dreamy Penny Bunn were led through it captives.

The Avishnu people had gone on in search of Epha, the Evil One, as schoolboys boldly go to a churchyard in hope of a ghost, and when there is the least intimation of one being about to rise, they make a rapid movement to the rear.

Norton Truscott had been more than a year in the strange city, record of an unknown people long since extinct.

He went boldly forward, and, by ways that savoured of the uncanny, through narrow windings and by underground roads which he declared were sacred to the priests, he arrived at the palace wherein Jack and Penny Bunn had gone through their awful ordeal.

To Harry Barstow it was all new, and Norton told him, as they descended a flight of steps, that led to the great hall, in which the altar had been, that if there was anything in the Avishnu faith an unbeliever could not tread foot there alive.

But Harry Barstow trod there, and did not die.

The great hall was deserted, and there was no light to guide them. Not a sound gave warning of a living being there. The stillness of the deserted catacombs rested on the place.

"I wonder what this silence portends," said Norton, in a low tone. "Be wary. The Avishnus may even now be on the watch for us."

"Can they know we are here?" asked Harry.

"I cannot tell, but they are cunning," was the reply.

Norton took his friend by the hand and led him on. In silence they crossed to the passage that led to the dens of Luva and Kala. In silence they emerged into the open courtyard beyond.

Both instinctively raised their eyes to the stars above.

They were still visible, but the red colour they showed a short time before had deepened.

It was now that of blood.

"There is mischief in the air," said Norton Truscott; "we must do our work and away."

He crossed the courtyard, and, with the air of one secure from interruption, walked up to the den of Kala, grasped the bars that held fast the door, and tore them from their sockets.

He cast them on the ground with a clanging sound, and opened the door.

With Harry Barstow close behind him he peered in.

"Jack!"

They called aloud together, and there was for a moment no answer. The worst was feared in their hearts, when they heard a faint response.

"Here!"

They rushed in, calling aloud to him again, for the den was very dark, and they could see nothing.

"Jack Ford!—where are you?"

"Here," was the reply. "I am hurt, and the body of the python holds me as a ship's cable."

By that time their eyes were used to the gloom, and they could faintly see the gallant youth lying on the ground with the flaccid body of the dead python wound about him.

Its head and throat were gashed and torn out of all shape by the thrusts the brave Jack had dealt it with the knife which he still held in his enfeebled hands.

They lifted him up and dragged him into the starlight, perforce also taking the body of the python with them.

Thrice had it wound its body about him, and but for the loss of blood and the subsequent fading away of its strength, it would have crushed his bones, as the giant of old used to smash those of his victims, to make its bread.

But it was dead, and Jack was yet alive—barely so.

In a few minutes more he must have died under the weight of those enormous coils.

But Norton Truscott tore away the yielding mass, and the youth was free.

He drew a deep breath and smiled.

"I felt that I was not doomed to die here," he said. "Who is it that has so nobly rescued me? I cannot see you."

"It is I. Harry Barstow and Norton Truscott."

"I am satisfied," answered Jack, "for you have not come hither in vain. You are together again."

"There is yet your poor simple friend to be looked up," said Truscott. "It would be too much to hope that he is alive."

"Where is he?" asked Harry.

"There, in the den of Luva."

"I fancy I hear a slight scratching at the door."

Norton Truscott rushed to it, whipped up the bars, and opened the door.

Penny Bunn walked out in a mechanical way.

"I think," he said, "that drink will be old Snicker's ruin. He is lying dead drunk inside. I was just taking a sip of brandy when he rushed at me and *swallowed the bottle.* But, of course, it is all a dream. I should like to be pinched, or kicked, or pounded. For goodness' sake, wake me up!"

They could not comprehend his meaning; but Norton Truscott, peering into the den, saw Luva the python feebly writhing about upon the ground. He closed the door and put up the bars again.

"It is no time for explanation," he said; "this poor fellow has been saved, as I judge, by a miracle. Our task now is to rejoin our friends. Will you kindly walk as quickly as you can?"

He addressed Penny Bunn, who smiled, in a self-satisfied way, as he replied:

"I see no need for any hurry in the matter. Did you ever hear of the intoxicated gentleman who, on finding the street whirling about him, sat down in the gutter and waited for his door to come past?"

"We have nothing to do with him," said Harry Barstow, who was assisting Jack to his feet.

"Granted," answered Bunn; "but his case and mine are in a degree synonymous. I am going to sit down and wait until I *wake up.*"

Thereupon he dropped to the ground in a sitting position, and burst into the refrain, "Wait till the clouds roll by, Jenny," in the most melancholy voice that ever came from the throat of a human being.

"What is to be done with him?" asked Truscott; "time is precious."

"Stick a pin into him," said Jack, with a smile; "it is what we should have done to him at school."

Norton Truscott had no pin available, but he had his cutlass, and spurred on by the necessities of the situation, he drew the weapon he carried, slid it along the ground, and gave the melodious Bunn a pointed application of it.

"Murder!" roared Bunn, as he leaped to his feet.

"Enough of this!" said Harry Barstow, sternly. "If you still think you are dreaming, remain where you are and perish. If convinced that you are awake, follow us."

"There is a reality about the pointed request of this gentleman," said Bunn, "that dispels all doubts as to the reality of things around me. But I must say that it is the most remarkable experience ever undergone by man. The antics of that python under the influence of liquor it involuntarily swallowed were edifying, or would have been so to a man not on the borders of what schoolboys call 'funk.'"

"This way," said Norton Truscott. "Ford, can I give you an arm?"

"I think I can get on," said Jack, with an effort. "I am coming round, but I feel a bit tight about the chest."

"No bones broken, I trust?"

"None, I hope."

"Hark!" cried Harry Barstow; "what is that?"

It was a slight humming sound that might have been near or afar off, for they could not locate it. It was very peculiar. Then there was a sensation, felt by all, as if the air affected their heads and made them giddy.

"Hasten!" said Norton Truscott, briefly.

He would not be denied by Jack, but taking one arm—Barstow had the other—he hurried him into the passage and down to the hall.

Penny Bunn kept close upon their track, not yet quite certain that things around him were real, but acting like a reasonable man on the off-chance that they might be so.

Across the great hall down to the main entrance, by which Jack had originally entered, they went. Norton Truscott, for a reason he afterwards explained, no longer trusted to devious underground ways.

They stepped outside, and found the square alive with the Avishnus.

"Back!" cried Truscott, hurriedly.

Too late! They had been seen, and a yell, as fierce as ever leapt from human throat, rent the air.

It was answered, not by those they threatened, but by a roaring sound, coming from nobody knew whither.

It was above, below, around them, it was everywhere.

It checked the rush of the Avishnus, and stopped the retreat of the escaping party.

For a moment or so all stood still, and then the earth shook and lightnings flashed from the sky.

The stars disappeared, and appalling thunder rent the air, as if chaos had come again.

CHAPTER CCXXIII.

THE FLIGHT THROUGH THE CITY OF THE AVISHNUS.

IT was impossible for the voice of a single human being to be heard.

But for the lightning, which played from one quarter or another unceasingly, it would also have been impossible to see a sign made by Norton Truscott to follow him for their lives.

That the peril was great of their being buried alive was apparent to all but Penny Bunn, on whom this fresh horror had the effect of restoring his bewilderment. Left to himself he would have remained rooted to the spot and perished.

But the kindly hand of Truscott grasped him by the arm, and they hastened towards the gate from which they could leave the square.

None of the Avishnus sought escape in that direction.

In a state of mad bewilderment and terror they burst into singing, and danced round in circles, or with the gliding, sweeping motion peculiar to their religious rites.

Once more the earth rocked, and the huge temple recently vacated parted in the centre. At the same moment Luva the python, released from prison, came forth with a stealthy glide, its head slightly raised and its glittering eye fixed on the whirling body of Avishnu people.

It was seen by the fugitives, and, notwithstanding their mortal peril, they stopped by the gate, impelled by an irresistible fascination to watch the movements of the reptile.

They stayed long enough to see it reach one of the outside dancers, and, with the action of a whip plied by a human hand, twist itself about the doomed man's body.

In the light of the electric fluid they marked the man's face as he realised his fate, and saw the eyes bulge out of his head with unspeakable terror. On they fled, unable to bear the sight of more horror there. Just in time, for, with a roar that haunted them for months afterwards, the earth heaved up, rocked to the right and left, and the whole square collapsed into ruins.

They had scarcely passed through the gate when it was blocked by the falling masonry, thus shutting out all hope of escape for the imprisoned Avishnus in the square.

It was a race from there to the outside of the city.

Spurred on by their natural fears, they ran. Jack Ford for the time had all his old activity renewed, and Penny Bunn instinctively put his best foot foremost.

On every side the buildings were collapsing. In the narrow street by the main outer gate the houses were leaning over towards each other as they raced through. There was an incessant and all-bewildering crash behind them, but none were struck, although huge stones fell from the housetops above, in front, and beside them.

They got clear of the city, but could not go far.

They could stand clear of the masonry, breaking up and raining in huge pieces to the ground, but they dared not attempt to pass through the wood.

The trees were swaying about as reeds swept by a hurricane. Branches were breaking and huge trunks were uprooted in every direction.

Between the shattered walls of the city and the wood they were comparatively safe.

But the fearful sensation that is experienced by those who taste the horrors of an awful earthquake chilled their blood and held the strongest nerved of the four in the bondage of fear.

There comes a time to every man when he feels how poor and frail a thing he is, and at no time more clearly is this conviction forced upon him than when he stands in the face of that mightiest phenomenon of our globe—an earthquake.

Penny Bunn sank to the earth, and they let him lie there. The other three stood with bowed heads, awaiting the issue of the terrible riot of the elements above and below.

The motion of the earth at such a time is peculiar. It is of a billowy nature, a tidal movement of the soil.

Sometimes the surface is unbroken, but now and then it cracks or opens, so that whole buildings, and even portions of forests, disappear.

Thus it was on that eventful night.

There was a swift shifting of the ground, and then it ripped up, and the city wall, a remnant of the towers abutting the gates, vanished into the bowels of the earth.

Beyond, the rest of the city lay a heaped-up mass of stones.

This was the final effort of the earthquake.

A slight thrill, an after-shudder, passed through the island, and then all was still save a gentle wind that was as the sighing of the sick after a long course of pain.

The haze above melted away, the stars came out bright and clear, the trees still standing slowly subsided into their usual quiescent state. Peace, the peace of exhaustion, was on all things.

It was some time ere the voice of Norton Truscott was heard, soft and low, as of one who stands in the presence of a reposing monster and fears to wake it.

"For our merciful escape," said he, "let us be devoutly thankful."

Then there was another silence, which was eventually broken by Jack.

"How many anticipating these things could live through them?" he asked.

"Nobody," answered Harry Barstow; "but the future in all cases is mercifully veiled from us."

"The accursed Avishnus," cried Norton Truscott, holding out his arms, "have perished to a man! They are extinct. Oh, Harry, old friend, if I could bring myself now to speak of the horrors of the rites of that vile body, you would scarcely credit me. You would think that the earthquake had unhinged my mind. I am not presumptuous enough to declare that there is a special punishment for them in this wreck of their late home, but I may be pardoned for thinking that it is a fitting end for them all."

"Let us get away from here," said Harry. "Bunn, my good fellow, you had better get up. It is time we were moving back to the coast."

"I am somewhat fatigued," answered Bunn, wearily, "and reflection under the light of the stars is pleasing to me. Perhaps, since you are bent on going forward to the town, you would not mind ordering a cab for me?"

"Come, Bunn," said Jack; "you were always a man great in an emergency. Brace yourself up and come—home, shall I say?"

"It is late," said Bunn, "and Miriam objects to sit up for me. If I ask her why she *does* sit up, I am rebuked as impertinent. But, as you say, there is no place like home, and I will endeavour to get there."

They started on the back journey, and entered the wood. It was blocked here and blocked there, but they eventually got through it.

Then there was another surprise in store for them. In the line of hill and cliff that fringed the sea there was a huge gap half a mile wide, and through it they could see the sparkling waters, still in agitation.

The portion that had yielded to the power of the earthquake was the very place where Ben Walton and the men with Chippy Bunyons were told to wait for them.

If indeed they had gone thither they were lost.

It was a terrible blow, coming as it did when the fulness of joy was arising from their wonderful escapes from peril; but viewing things in a hopeful light, they pursued their way to the coast.

Here and there they came across slight fissures in the ground, mere cracks, which they leaped over; but slight as they were, some appeared to be of great depth.

From others arose a sulphurous smell, but they did not linger to examine one or the other. They were too eager to get on and learn the fate of their friends.

CHAPTER CCXXIV.

THE MUTINY ON THE "ALBATROSS."

DIRK MATTHEWS had selected the time of change of the afternoon watch as the better hour for the carrying out of his mutinous work. Not a single soul on board, outside the conspirators, had the least idea of what was in store.

There was not even a Penny Bunn to get at the facts, and be afterwards laughed at and derided by a sapient George Rammer.

It is true that Bill Oakley had his suspicions, but they did not lead him to imagine that an immediate mutiny was impending. The boatswain was a man of slow thought, and he took his time in working out such mental problems as occasionally presented themselves to his understanding.

Therefore, when the time drew near for Dirk Matthews and his companions to make a move, all things pointed to the probable success of the nefarious project.

There being murder in the programme, it was, of course, necessary for the person to be murdered to be within available distance of the would-be murderer.

It was essential that Dick Darnley should be on deck at four o'clock when the watch would be changed.

But when the time arrived he was below, and the only occupants of the after deck were Don, Tom, and Bob. Bill Oakley was below with the first mate, the pair being probably in conference on some matter appertaining to their friends ashore or the future management of the "Albatross," in case none of them ever returned.

It was Bill Oakley's intention to see that the usual routine was carried out with punctuality and promptitude; but he was spared the task by the change men, who comprised the entire body of mutineers, coming on deck a few minutes before the time.

The men on duty were not loth to leave their posts and get below for a quiet pipe, chat, or nap, according to their desires, and Dirk Matthews was master of the situation.

He had his revolver ready, but the first mate was not there to be disposed of.

Here was a slight hitch in the arrangements, but Dirk was not deterred from proceeding.

"Batten down fore and aft," he said to his followers, who had already been told off to their respective portions of the work.

As they divided and proceeded to close and make secure the two companion-ways, Dirk Matthews, with a revolver in each hand, advanced to the trio of youngsters, who were naturally in a state of surprise bordering on bewilderment.

"Young gentlemen," said Dirk Matthews, "I'll trouble you to take off them toasting-forks you carry by your side and hand over them barkers in your belts."

The toasting-forks and barkers, being the cutlasses and revolvers of the boys, could not be left in their possession. The latter, unfortunately, were not loaded.

"It ain't necessary, if you behaves yourselves," continued Dirk, "to make cold meat of you; but it will be done if you give us the least bother."

The youngsters looked at each other, still in doubt as to the real purpose of the fellow. Bob Stockton, fortunately, as the most diplomatic of the three, undertook to put certain queries to the mutineer.

"Will you kindly explain what this means?" he asked.

"Suttinly," answered Dirk Matthews, with a grin; "it's a mutiny."

The face of Don flushed, and the brow of Tom grew dark; but Bob restrained them with one of his quiet looks.

"A mutiny!" he repeated. "And why is there one on board the 'Albatross'?"

"Becos," answered Dirk Matthews, roughly, "we've had enough of being sat on and bossed about."

"Indeed?" said Bob. "I was inclined to think that as seamen you have been remarkably well treated."

"As shipping goes," admitted Dirk, "there ain't no cause for grumbling; but we ain't men of or'nary build. We was led to believe when we signed articles that we was going in for active work."

"Then your great complaint," rejoined Bob, with a wonderful suavity when the circumstances are considered, "appears to be that you have not had enough to do?"

"Enough to do be blowed!" growled Dirk Mat-

thews; "we've had enough, and to spare. Wot we j'ined for was to get the *right* sort of work—cutting out and sinking vessels, and making a bit of money."

"Oh," said Bob; "you thought the 'Albatross' was a pirate craft?"

"Yes; mostly of the class knowed as privateers."

"You were mistaken," said Bob, as he unbuckled his cutlass, "and it is a pity that you have allowed your disappointment to prey upon your mind and lead you to do such a thing as this."

"Wot I've done," said Dirk Matthews, roughly, "I'm ready to answer for. I'm running no more risk in this than I thought I was going to when I j'ined."

The three friends gave up their weapons—they could do no less—and Dirk Matthews swaggered away with them to see how his men were getting on.

They were engaged in screwing up and making fast the two entrances to the cabins below.

"Merciful Heaven!" exclaimed Don, in an undertone, "what horrible misfortune is this that has come to us?"

"Don't give way," answered Bob, quietly; "and, above all, keep your head cool. Without falling in with these scoundrels, we can sham completely giving in to them. It is our one chance of recovering the ship."

"A poor one," said Tom.

"What power have we three to do it?" asked Don.

"I will adopt our dear friend Jack's old piece of advice," said Bob. "Wait and see."

It was at this moment that a knocking was heard at the aft cabin doors, and Dirk Matthews motioned for the men to cease their labours. The voice of Bill Oakley broke the stillness that followed. It sounded like the roar of a lion with his head muffled in a sack.

"Who's having games here with this yere door? Young gentlemen, I'm ashamed of you, larking at such a time!"

Dirk Matthews beckoned Bob to come to his side, and at the same time cocked a revolver as an intimation that prompt obedience was essential to his safety.

Bob prudently did as he was commanded.

"Tell him that there is a mutiny aboard," he hoarsely whispered; "but don't mention no names."

"In a grammatical sense," murmured Bob, "that is a permission to name all concerned. But I understand your meaning."

Advancing to the door of the cabin-way:

"Mr. Oakley," he called out.

"Here, and be durned to you!" Bill growled, in reply.

"You desire the door to be opened, but it cannot be done. I regret to say that there is a mutiny on board the 'Albatross,' and the deck is in possession of the men."

"Gammon!"

"It is true. We have given up our arms, and are practically prisoners."

This was evidently a staggering piece of information to the boatswain, for he did not immediately reply. Presently a question came from him.

"Are all the men in it?"

"Not all."

"Stow that!" growled Dirk Matthews.

"How many are on the job?" roared Bill Oakley.

"That is a thing I am not allowed to say," answered Bob. "Of course, I could tell you, but I should get my head blown off for my audacity, and you will not expect me to run the risk of that."

The voice of Dick Darnley was now heard.

"What is the matter there, Oakley?"

Bill Oakley was presumably explaining in reply, but although a series of growling sounds could be heard, nothing intelligible reached the ears of the listeners.

The next thing clear from below came from Dick Darnley.

"Stockton."

"Yes, sir."

"I presume you are speaking on behalf of the mutineers under compulsion?"

"I am, sir."

"Tell them from me that if they will give up their ringleader, and promise to behave better in the future, they will be forgiven. But if they do not promptly set me free, that by-and-by I will hang every man of them!"

There was no need to repeat the message, for Dirk Matthews, standing beside Bob, could hear every word of it. He grinned contemptuously.

"You needn't answer that," he whispered, and motioned for Bob to retire to his friends.

Declining further parley with the two officers incarcerated below, Dirk Matthews proceeded to coolly inspect the means that had been taken to securely keep those below as prisoners until it should please him to set them free.

Satisfied they were all that could be desired, he filled and lit his pipe, and proceeded to look about him as a monarch of all he surveyed.

The mutineers were nine in number, all told, and the chief spirits among them—the ruling element—were their leader, Dirk Matthews, Bates, Coffer, and Springtop. The rest were merely black sheep that followed the flock.

CHAPTER CCXXV.

GEORGE RAMMER AS RENEGADE.—THE "ALBATROSS" IN THE STORM.

WITH the coming of the afternoon wind Dirk Matthews proposed to put to sea. It could hardly be expected that a man of his caste would feel any compunction about leaving the adventurers to their fate on the island.

Indeed, he looked upon it as a lucky piece of assistance—almost providential—that the captain and the first mate, and the seamen with them, should be away on an errand that might cost them their lives.

Monarch of all he surveyed! Undoubtedly.

There was the deck in the hands of his own men—the boys, as we know, he did not think worth counting—and all who might have opposed him were securely battened down below.

They could be let out on conditions by-and-by, barring the two officers, who, as soon as they could be conveniently got at, would have to die.

Dirk Matthews reflected that it was necessary to dispose of them, feeling convinced that he would never be able to induce either of them to serve under his flag.

With the men it was different. They could easily be led to see that it was to their advantage to recognise in Dirk Matthews the fitting commander of the "Albatross." So reasoned the leader of the mutiny.

He glanced aft, where the trio of youngsters were leaning against the side of the vessel, staring at the island, and apparently silent. From them his eyes roamed forward, and they fell upon the cuddy where Rammer undoubtedly was.

"I forgot him," muttered Dirk Matthews; "he must be swore in."

He called to Bates and Goffer, and made them rout out the cook and bring him before his chief.

In two minutes that redoubtable son of the sea was to be seen coming along between the two men with a quick step, with his accustomed occasional half-hop, half-halt.

Saluting Dirk Matthews with his knuckles to his forehead, he said, with a briskness that bordered on cheerfulness:

"Fine evening, cap."

"Fine evening be hanged to you!" snarled Matthews. "Wot do you mean by your infarnal familiarity?"

"I beg pardon, cap," said Rammer, aghast, "not meanin' anything more than was iver respectful."

"Look here," said Matthews, "you are aweer that I've laid hands on the 'Albatross'?"

"I ham aweer on it, cap," answered Rammer, "and I was intendin' to bear a hand in the job if you'd only been gracious enough to ask me. But I didn't like to intrude myself by offering."

Dirk Matthews surveyed him for a moment or two, with suspicion in his eyes.

"Whether you were going to offer or not," he said, "you've got to take on now. Down on your knees, and take the oath!"

As Rammer sank down, the youngsters turned round, and seeing him in that humiliating position which is rarely adopted in matters mundane, drew up and heard the following oath administered to him, and also his acceptance of it:

"I, George Rammer, known to them as chaff me as R'yal George, swear on my bended knees to serve Dirk Matthews, cap of the 'Albatross,' as assistant pirate when called on, and as cook and gineral swab at all times. If I'm not true to him may " (here came in some strong allusion the internal arrangements of Rammer with much detail) "be cut up, and throwed to carrion-crows, all of which is to be done arter I've been hung up by the heels ontil I'm dead."

The final bit of affirmation being blasphemous we cannot give here, but the oath all round was strong enough to bind a hundred men.

Rammer arose a full-blown pirate, and saluting again, asked if the captain had any orders for him.

"Yes," said Dirk Matthews, haughtily, "you may serve out a noggin of grog to each man."

"Excuse me, captain," said Rammer, "but I ain't nothing to do with the grog. Mr. Oakley has the key of the sperrit-room, and that's below."

Dirk Matthews frowned. This was a matter of detail he had overlooked.

"What can you give us, then?" he demanded.

"Well, not much in a gineral way, captain," answered Rammer, humbly, "for the fact is I don't keep the main store. Mr. Oakley has that, and jest now I've run out of most things, being in the mind to renoo 'em to-night. Indeed, captain, I guv Mr. Oakley an hour ago a list of things as was wanted, and he would have give me the same if you hadn't——"

"*What* have you got, curse you?" roared Dirk Matthews.

"There's a matter of a quarter of pound of coker," replied the alarmed Rammer, "and two ship's biscuits, maybe, reckoning the crumbs, as good as three——"

Here was another and most important hitch in the arrangements. Not even the most ardent of mutineers can get along without eating and drinking, especially the latter. Dirk Matthews had overlooked the most important item of provisioning himself and his followers, and for the lack of something better to vent his wrath upon, he rose up and knocked Rammer down.

That somewhat doubtful naval hero fell upon his back and groaned out an appeal for mercy.

"Get up," hissed Dirk Matthews, "or I'll shoot you through that thick head of yours! What yer mean, yer skunk, by bein' out of *everything?*"

"It was hoversight," murmured Rammer. "Excuse me this once, it won't happen *the next time you mutiny.*"

There must have been something exasperating in this answer, for it induced Dirk Matthews to kick the prostrate Rammer on that leg of his. The howl he set up could be heard a mile off.

Scrambling to his feet, with the assaulted leg in a very stiff state, he hopped off to his cuddy with the agility of a goat with wooden limbs.

Dirk Matthews had to explain matters to his followers, which he did, assuring them at the same time of his being in a position to get at the provisions and drink below within an hour or two.

"As soon as the wind comes," he said, "and we have set the 'Albatross' in the seaward track, we'll let out the officers—they are only two to nine of us—and *quiet 'em.* Arter that we have all the ship's stores to make free with."

It was now between four and five in the afternoon, and as yet there was no wind.

The dreadful sultriness of the day in nowise abated, but seemed rather to increase as the hour of sunset drew nigh.

All on deck experienced the pangs of thirst, in its early stages, but there was nothing to drink. The mutineers smoked or chewed tobacco as relief, and the three youngsters bore their pangs with fortitude. Conversation all round flagged.

Rammer, having got under the sheltering roof of his cuddy, remained there, preferring solitude and gloom to the doubtful and dangerous society of Dirk Matthews and his fellows.

The minutes crawled away, and at its appointed time the sun went down, but there was no wind.

Dirk Matthews fancied that now and then he felt the slightest puff, and wetting his forefinger, held it up to get at the quarter from whence the breeze was coming. This an old sea-going expedient. A wet finger is more sensitive than a dry one. The slightest puff of air will cool the side that is nearest to the moving air. But he felt nothing.

Darkness and no wind.

Now was the time to set the two officers free of their place of confinement, and get at the stores below; but there was no movement in that direction on the part of the mutineers.

A sense of depression lay upon them all.

Overhead were the red stars, the like of which in colour none had ever seen before.

The men glanced up at them and shivered. There

was something horribly ominous in the blood-red sparks aloft, that did not give a tenth of their usual light.

Bates sidled up to Dirk Matthews, who sat upon an upturned empty barrel, smoking, and assuming a bravado he did not feel.

"Matthews," he said, "I don't like the look of things."

"Wot's the matter with 'em?" demanded Matthews.

"Look up—see them stars."

"Well, wot of them?"

"Can't you see they are *blood-tinted?*" said Bates, lowering his voice, "and I don't like this orful stillness. I tell you, Matthews, I'm sorry we started on this job."

"Havin' started," returned Matthews, "you've got to go on with it. There is no going back now."

"There niver was for you," grunted Bates, "but Mr. Darnley said as we should be let orf if we was only follerers."

"Yes—at the time he was speaking—but not *now*."

Bates felt the force of this rejoinder, and sighed heavily.

"It's the ticklishest game I iver was in," he said, "and I'm more'n sorry I wentured on it."

Here the voice of Goffer, who was hanging over the land side of the vessel, was heard.

"There summat rum going on at the bottom of the sea," he said. "Jest as if old Neptune was a-boiling of his kettle."

There was a general movement to the spot where he was standing, and all eyes were turned down to the water.

True enough, below the surface, and apparently at the bottom of the sea, there was a curious phosphorescent light.

And as they stared at it some bubbles, also illuminated, rose to the surface, and breaking, sent up a sulphurous smell.

"Durn me," cried Springtop, "if that is nateral!"

The phosphorescence increased, and later there was quite a burst of light from below.

The men fell back, uttering exclamations of terror.

From the direction of the shore came a humming sound, with a somewhat similar noise from the westerly horizon on the sea.

Dirk Matthews made an effort to pull himself together. Unless he did so, he was in danger of being seized by his confederates and handed over to Darnley by his fast collapsing followers.

"Here comes the wind, my lads!" he shouted. "Up with the anchor, brace the mainsail, haul in the slack of the jib—smart there—helm hard a-port!"

The men obeyed from sheer force of instinctive obedience to the stronger spirit.

They brought up the anchor smartly, and, with the exception of Jones, who took the helm, ran aloft as briskly as the darkness permitted.

A short, sharp, angry puff of wind bellied out the sails for an instant and died away again.

From the shore arose sounds of sharp cracking, as of nuts broken by giant hammers. The sea around the ship bubbled and hissed.

The three youths, who through all the time had quietly kept together, now moved away from the aft deck towards the lower deck. They separated as they came, each looking about him keenly in search of something that might, in case of emergency, be used as a weapon.

It was not easy to see even big objects upon the deck, for the light of the stars, though faint before, was growing each moment fainter still. Of all three Don was the only one who laid hands on anything that could be of real service. He succeeded in getting possession of a short iron bar.

Again the wind came, and with it the little light remaining from the stars went out, and a terrible darkness lay upon the ship.

It was not dispelled, but in a curious way intensified by a number of scarcely discernible patches of phosphoric light upon the water.

From the sea there also arose hissing sounds, and from the shore an increase of the cracking before alluded to. Rocks could be heard falling from above into the waters below.

Though the men were half-palsied with fear, the "Albatross," insensible to the influences of the terrible time, paid off before a steadily increasing force of intermitting wind.

She wheeled outward, and, with her prow seaward, slowly left the place so fraught with peril.

But barely was she well on her way, when a great gust of wind swept up and tore the mainsail from her lower stays. It spread out horizontally for a moment; though unseen, all on board could feel it was in that dangerous position.

The men were coming down from aloft, travelling as blind men do by the sense of touch. They completed the rest of the journey in a hurry, narrowly escaping in two instances going overboard.

Then crack!—the top gear of the mainmast went, and the huge sail was torn from the bolt-ropes and vanished for ever. No man on the "Albatross" ever saw it more.

It was a great loss, but the good ship was not yet a complete wreck.

Some of the canvas on the mizzen-mast and the jib held, and she sped along clear of the island, from where there now arose a chaos of awful sounds. The sea heaved, not in waves, but in huge hills that sank again almost as soon as formed.

The mutineers, all but Dirk Matthews, crouched upon the deck and gave themselves up for lost. He, the arch-villain of the lot, still retained some of his head.

Fearing from the motion of the vessel that the man had deserted or fainted away at the helm, he groped his way to it and found the seaman was not there.

"Curse him!" he muttered, as he grasped the wheel.

A fierce light flashed from above. It was a bar of lightning.

He was half-blinded by it, and would have cursed that, too, if he had not received a blow from behind that laid him as senseless as a log upon the deck.

———

CHAPTER CCXXVI.

A REUNION OF FRIENDS.—WHERE IS THE "ALBATROSS"?

HARRY BARSTOW, with his three companions, whom we left hurrying towards a tremendous gap made in the cliffs and other high lands by the earthquake, reached the spot where the flight of steps that ascended from the lake had been the night before.

Both the slope and the steps were gone, and the lake was now nothing more than a scattered series of insignificant pools and puddles divided by the enormous masses of earth and rock that had fallen in its midst.

The place where the two boys and Bill Oakley had gone through their adventures was a thing of the past.

Across the rough ground and around the small pools the quartet picked their way.

They were all silent, save that now and then an exclamation or a brief query and still briefer reply broke the stillness.

Penny Bunn said absolutely nothing. Reviewing matters as well as he was able in his troubled mental condition, he arrived at the conclusion that all the troubles he knew at home, and when experienced conceived by him to be the most terrible, sank into insignificance beside his recent sufferings.

For once in his life, at least, he admitted that he was a terrible fool to have ventured to sea.

They got over the ground at last, and went down to the beach. There, as elsewhere, all things were changed.

The portions of the cliffs on either side of the gap, though still remaining, had been shorn materially about their summits.

Masses of rock had fallen down, forming a rough beach that prevented the incoming sea reaching their base as it had done before.

It was now possible at high or low tide to walk along a shore that was but a few hours old.

This was so far helpful to the adventurers, but in other matters how desolate was their condition!

Their friends were not in sight, and the "Albatross" was nowhere visible on the sea.

To all appearances they were the sole survivors of all who but a day before had been alive.

"The Avishnus and our friends," said Harry Barstow, "alike have perished."

"Then we are alone upon the island," said Jack. "Life is very dear to us, but to me it is not worth so much as it has cost."

"I would not say that," gently remonstrated Norton Truscott. "Life is a valuable possession, and it is early days to be certain that we have lost them all."

"I should like to ask a question," said Bunn, passing a hand across his brow.

They turned their faces towards him and awaited the query. After a moment's thought, it came.

"Being cast, or left—practically the same thing, I imagine—on a lone island, what are we to do for a wrecked ship laden with the necessaries of existence? It seems to me," he added, rather vacantly, "that there is something faulty in the arrangements. I feel as if I were playing a part in an imperfectly-written story. The work of a crude hand, if I may so put it."

"There is hardly a royal right to a wrecked ship for every wrecked man," answered Norton Truscott; "but perhaps, if you are patient, all your requirements may be met."

He was very hopeful again. After his fearful experiences with the Avishnus, and his unexpected and almost miraculous escape from their clutches, it was natural he should be buoyant. And he became more so every moment.

"To me," he said, "there is a promising glitter on the sea. Feel the gentle breeze. How it fans the cheek! How unlike the recent sultry mornings—heavy, foreboding, and oppressive!"

"The end cannot be here," said Harry Barstow.

The question was, what should they do? Remain where they were, or explore along the coast?

They finally decided to go as far as the place where Jack Ford and Penny Bunn, in the company of Bob and Walton, had landed, and there remain until they saw something of their missing friends or gave up all hope of meeting them again.

They found the wood had suffered in the earthquake, but not to a serious extent. The greater part of the trees still remained, and some of them bore fruit, for the better part ripe and eatable.

And here, too, the beach being unchanged, some edible classes of shellfish were to be found.

Bunn was told off to gather some, while the others

did the best they could towards constructing a shelter that would shield them from the sun by day and from possible dews at night.

Picking up shellfish or trifles generally from the seashore is a light and not brain-taxing pursuit. It was just the sort of thing for Bunn, in his strained mental condition.

Using his black handkerchief as a receptacle, he began his task, and could have collected all he required from the spots within a few minutes' walk of the camping-ground.

But under such conditions man becomes an epicure.

With so many to take, only the finest would suit Penny Bunn, choice in his shellfish, strayed on and on, and ere long was out of sight.

He was a mile, or probably a little more, from his friends by the time he had filled his handkerchief, and then, feeling tired, sat down with his back against a tree and surveyed the rippling sea.

"If this was one of Albion's shores," he murmured, "I should at this moment be a happy man. But it isn't. It's a wild, lonely spot where the alluring photographer, with his samples in frames, which he doesn't tell you are extra until you've got your bob portrait in paper, would fail at the start. The old lady with shell pincushions and bits of coral would do no trade, and even the man with the overdate novelettes at three a penny, originally sold by the publisher as waste, would die in despair. If he sold any it would be to himself, and no bookseller or newsvendor ever reads anything except the contents bills as they come in."

Communing thus with himself on the unbusiness air of the island, he had ten minutes to himself ere an interruption came.

It was of the most startling nature.

Something—at first he could not tell what—came up to his eyes, from above or below or around, and pressed tightly against them.

The foreign substance was rather soft, and not unpleasantly warm.

There was something human in its grasp, and this was confirmed by a squeaky, feigned voice crying out:

"Guess who it is!"

Penny Bunn had never been a good guesser in his life, and in his startled condition of mind one could not look for him to be correct in a guess right away.

"Is—it—Miriam?" he asked.

"No," was the answer; "try again."

"Can't be Snicker, sure—ly."

"No, not Snicker, whoever he may be."

"Don't tell me," said Bunn, beginning to shake, "that it is my wife's aunt, Miss Astracan. If it is she may have to stop here for life, as no boat could carry her to a ship. A woman of her size would have to be floated off."

"Wrong again," was the answer; "it is not a Miss of any sort."

"Then I must give it up," said Bunn, desperately.

"All right, old man. Here you are!"

His eyes, released, were blind for a few moments, and then from out of a sort of fog there loomed the figure of Chippy Bunyons.

"Ha, ha!" he laughed; "fancy my playing that old game on you, and you not getting at me!"

"Chippy," said Penny Bunn, with emotion, as he grasped the hand extended to him, "friend and companion of—a day or two—sharer with me in Avishnu atrocities and—and—earthquakes—I am completely overcome. I never hoped for this hour. Of the rest —speak! Are they yet alive?"

"Rather," replied Chippy, "more by luck than wit. But come along. They are having dinner not far off. You are alone, of course?"

"Not a bit of it," said Bunn. "A short distance, in a retrograding direction, you will find young Ford and the two gentlemen, one lately a priest, and Truscott by name, the other, the benevolent and gentlemanly commander and owner of the 'Albatross.'"

Chippy Bunyons let go of Bunn's arm, in which he had affectionately linked his own, and turned a wheel as neatly as it was ever performed by a street Arab.

"Hurrah!" he cried; "but stop. Let us be mum for a bit. Together we will hark back and bring them forward together. A surprise, like a fortune, will be more effectual in a lump than it would be piecemeal."

Penny Bunn, with his parcel of shellfish, escorted his friend back to where the others had been left. The meeting between Chippy and Norton Truscott was marked by tears, that silently coursed down the cheeks of the former. Poor little Chippy! He might be rather rough, and in the eyes of some people a common specimen of humanity, but he was very tender-hearted.

The explanation of the manner of the escape of his party from destruction was given by him on the way back.

It appeared that, instead of going to the summit of the slope as arranged, Ben Walton decided to camp below in sight of it.

"I have a presentiment, or, rather, a conviction," he said, "that we shall have either a violent storm or some other natural disturbance this evening, and we shall be better if not exposed on yonder ridge. A hurricane would shave us off as so many straws."

Then, by-and-by, as the night fell, and the first intimations of the approaching earthquake were given, he showed his prudence again in moving the party still lower down to a perfectly open spot where there were neither rocks nor trees to injure them when falling.

Of the terrors of that night we have already said enough.

They went through the horrors of the time with as much courage as most men. There was, however, no sleep for them, and, drenched to the skin, they witnessed the destruction of the trysting-spot.

As soon as there was a ray of light in the morning Ben Walton crept up the way of the high land that had escaped destruction, and, without going to the top, he saw through a gap in the lower wood the piled-up ruins of the city, and, the towers by the gates having in addition vanished from sight, he returned and gave it as his sorrowful conviction that their friends had been buried beneath that wonderful work of the past.

He suggested that they should seek the shore and get further help from the "Albatross" to explore the island, or at least survey it sufficiently carefully to be certain that all hope of seeing the lost ones was dead.

A feeling of superstition prompted them to avoid the way they came, and instead of passing through the gap in the cliff, they worked their way round the western base of it to the shore.

Not seeing anything of the "Albatross" there, they wandered on with the hope that, in turning one of the points of land, they would sight her. In this way they reached the spot where Penny Bunn unconsciously followed them, and but for their seeking shade in the wood, he would have tumbled across the whole party.

Chippy Bunyons had left them just to run down to the beach to see if the "Albatross" was in sight. Seeing Penny Bunn seated against a tree, he was at first taken aback, but recovering, he played an old-time joke upon him, and the rest we know.

The reunion of the entire party led to much rejoicing, but there was an undercurrent of sadness in it owing to the absence of the "Albatross."

Where was the gallant little craft?

Had she succumbed to the power of the storm?

If so, what would be their fate?

For a time they might live upon the island on the fruit and herbs to be found there. They could have fish, also, of the lower sort of crustacea, and they might use such ammunition as they had for the shooting of birds and animals. But such means would soon be exhausted.

"And after that," said Ben Walton, grimly, "our clothes would go, and we must perforce sink down to the level of savages in appearance. The chances of a ship coming this way are very remote."

It was not a very exhilarating lookout, but Jack Ford was one of the first to rally.

"Looking at things squarely," he said, "I think we have much to be thankful for. For the present I say, 'Keep up a bold heart and *wait*.' A month hence will be time enough to despair."

"Well said, youngster," cried Norton Truscott. "I saw the moment we met the stuff *you* are made of. Wait we must, whether we will or no. Meanwhile let us talk over what we ought to do to make sure of attracting the attention of the 'Albatross' or any other vessel that may come near us."

In that and other matters they spent the next hours weighing the pros and cons of things, and thus engaged, we for the present leave them, to renew our acquaintance with the "Albatross."

CHAPTER CCXXVII.

A DISABLED VESSEL.—UNDER STEAM.—A SAIL.

TWENTY miles from the Avishnu island and on the open sea, out of sight of all land, lay the "Albatross."

She was in a crippled condition, and the wind was dead against her, thus hampered, beating back to the island. It blew as a matter of fact direct from the scene of their recent experiences.

On the deck the whole of the crew excepting one man were assembled. There were also, on the after-deck, Dick Darnley, Bill Oakley, and the three youths, who had recovered their arms and now wore them proudly, this time with the revolvers loaded.

With the exception of Bill Oakley, none of the seamen carried arms.

Owing to the impossibility of returning to their old quarters, and being undesirous of getting further away from them, the "Albatross" had been brought to, and lay idly rocking on the sea.

The officers had been holding a discussion, which terminated just at the moment we find them.

"I think, gentlemen," said Bill Oakley, "that you couldn't arrange things better if you talked for a month. I'll pipe all hands aft."

This he did, and the men promptly responded. Many of them were ready, but others came sneaking up from below in a shamefaced manner. The latter were the companions of Dirk Matthews's attempt to get possession of the "Albatross."

How it was in the end completely foiled we shall soon see.

Bill Oakley walked up the centre of the vessel, and as the men advanced, he divided them into two parties on either side, the faithful from the false.

While he was thus engaged, Don, Tom, and Bob disappeared below, and speedily returned with a bundle of cutlasses and some small-arms.

They laid them on the deck close to Bill Oakley,

who proceeded to distribute them among the loyal men.

"They was took away from you last night," he explained, "as a matter of form, pending the decision of Mr. Darnley as to things. Feeling that there isn't any call to doubt men so honest as you are, he wishes them to be returned to you with the 'surance that he is certain you will never disgrace 'em."

A cheer arose from the recipients. The humiliated rascals on the other side of the deck hung their heads with shame and secret rage.

One and all cursed the day and hour they had listened to the tempter Dirk Matthews.

He was not among them, but in safe keeping below.

His place of confinement was near the engine-room, where Jim, the stoker, and the other engineers were getting the furnace ready, and oiling the engine for early use.

It will be remembered that the "Albatross" was so constructed as to be used as a steamer, but only in case of great emergency. She had not the means of carrying any great quantity of fuel, and the fifty tons of coals in the bunkers would not last long.

Hitherto her engines had not been used, and, as is too often the result of long inactivity, when the time came to put them in motion, it was discovered that idleness had clogged the more delicate parts of the machinery.

Hence the delay and the inactive lying out at sea. But for that the "Albatross" would have before then steamed her way back to the island.

Trussed like fowl with rope and pieces of stout stick, Dirk Matthews squatted in a corner of a closed chamber, and with many inward but unavailing lamentations, cursed his fate.

But let us return to the deck, where Dick Darnley was about to impart to the other mutineers his opinion of them and their recent conduct.

"I am not going to act as your judge at present," he said, addressing the crestfallen ones; "that office, I hope, will be filled by-and-by in a more worthy manner by your captain. But pending his return to the 'Albatross,' I should like to gather from you the facts of the origin of this precious attempt to seize the 'Albatross.' Truth-telling will be found advantageous to you. Now, who speaks first?"

Bates stood forward a step and knuckled his forehead.

"May it please you, sir," he said, "to hear me. Since last night, when most of us was fetched a whack in the dark by one or all the young gentlemen, and took prisoners as it were while in an onsensible state, we have talked this yere matter over, and I'm appointed to make a clean breast on it, feeling as we've all been fools and desarve whatsomever we may get for it."

"You are, as a matter of fact," said Dick, "the spokesman of all, with the exception of Matthews, I presume?"

"Matthews," replied Bates, "must speak for hisself. Here we are, a lot of idjots. We don't want to make Matthews out worse than he is, and we ain't a-going to try to make him better than he's showed hisself to be. He started the idea and we took on with it, being as I may say truly and without ewasion, as they say in the law-courts, and we are all mighty sorry for it. If so be as you thinks we're to get the cat o' nine tails or be hanged, then we must try to bear it like men. But if you or the captain can see a way to overlook what we've done, we'll sarve him truly and well, or may we suffer as all varmints and skunks as is dead to all good feelin's ought to do!"

Having got through this—for him—very elaborate address, Bates made a bow and resumed his place in the ranks of the mutineers.

"I am not in a position to say what will be the final outcome of this affair," replied Dick Darnley, "but I may tell you that it is a very serious thing to mutiny. It cannot be lightly passed over. But what the nature of your punishment is to be remains to be seen. I hope on our return to the Avishnu island to find our lost friends awaiting us. Meanwhile, you will resume your duty with the understanding that on the least sign of a mutinous spirit you will be shot. The loyal men have been armed with the object of carrying out this decree should it be considered necessary."

Once more Bates stood forward, looking, if possible, more shamefaced than ever, and yet happier in his heart, as was shown by the tears in his eyes.

"We are thankful, sir," he said, "to find that there is sich a kindly, noble sperrit aboard, sir. We are thankful, and there ain't no fear of our making ourselves fools again. I'd like to say more, but the whack I got over the head larst night ain't any help to hellyquench"—he sympathetically touched the side of his head as he alluded to this painful experience—"but all I says is, for myself and t'others, bar Matthews, who can speak for hisself and be blowed to him!—that we are thankful."

"That will suffice for the present," said Dick Darnley. "Oakley, set them to work. Get the funnel fixed, and I will hurry up those fellows with the engines."

In an hour the "Albatross" was a changed vessel. Between the main and mizzen masts certain portions of the deck were taken out and the box and funnel of a steamer, both of which had been stored in sections below, were fixed.

Below there was activity with the engines, and the fire in the furnace was lit.

No great steaming power was to be expected, but

it was known that her engines were of the best, capable of exhibiting the maximum of speed with the minimum of fuel when compared to anything of the class up to date.

Bill Oakley recognised the use of machinery in the emergency, but he naturally looked upon it with contempt. He hated all things in opposition to the old sea-going style with a deep, undying hatred.

"It may take us back to the island," he said to Don, as the pair watched the first cloud of smoke coming from the funnel, "but evil will come of it. You mark my words, sir!"

"I always do mark them," answered Don, pleasantly, but vaguely, "for they are words of wisdom and experience. What do you think our chances are of finding our lost friends?"

"Well," said Bill, reflectively, "if so be as they are on the cliff or shore awaiting for us, we shall drop on 'em all right, but if as they ain't there, and they've got kind of buried somewhere by the earthquake, we shall have difficulties. There's what you gentlemen call the helement of doubt about it. Howsomever, it is our duty to be hopeful."

Having spoken thus oracularly, Bill departed to attend to his duties, and Don turned his attention to the signs of getting up steam below.

The portion of the story relating to the mutiny and the failure thereof is soon told.

It was Bob Stockton who, taking advantage of a flash of lightning, laid Dirk Matthews low upon the deck.

It was part of a plan he had arranged with Don and Bob, who were to have assisted him by honouring the other mutineers with similar attention, but, failing to secure a weapon, they took another task upon themselves.

They followed up Bob, and bound the man whom Bob had laid low upon the deck.

It was a cool piece of work, performed during the chaotic turbulence going on at sea and on land, and while the "Albatross" was driven before a perfect hurricane of wind.

How she lived through it all was a mystery even to those accustomed to the turbulent moods of the ocean.

The mutineers were terrified out of their wits by the riot of the elements, deeming it all to be the outcome of their crime.

Though not cowards under ordinary circumstances, conscience took all the courage out of them. Superstition did the rest.

From the fallen man the three youngsters obtained arms, and were masters of the deck when the worst was over, and the "Albatross" lay idly rocking on a still turbulent sea.

Under threats of shooting them without more ado,

they compelled two of the mutineers to open the companion-ways and set free the officers and the loyal men.

What they had gone through with during their hours of confinement boots us not to tell. Nor need we dwell on the very strong language used by Bill Oakley and the loyal men when they learned all that had transpired.

If it had not been for the coolness and forbearance of Dick Darnley, every offender would there and then have been tossed overboard.

He stood between them and the men's anger, asking them to forbear awhile and leave the punishment of the rascals to a more fitting time.

"Let it suffice for to-night," he said, "that we have escaped a double peril—mutiny and earthquake. For that let us be grateful."

Only one offender escaped mention in the matter, and that was Rammer. He kept carefully out of sight on seeing how things were going, after having passed a night of terror that amply punished him for his brief misconduct as a mutineer.

The reason for this escape lay in the clemency of the boys.

"He would have made a poor pirate, anyway," said Bob, "and he seemed to join under compulsion."

"And it will be a good thing to hold over his head," said Don. "I fancy he rubs it into Penny Bunn, and should our old friend of Littlecote be restored to us, the threat of exposure would not be a bad weapon to place in his hands."

"Rammer," remarked Tom, "is a rank old humbug. By the way, I wonder what *is* the matter with that precious leg of his?"

"The subject can be investigated," said Bob, "when we have the heart and opportunity for lighter things than looking for lost friends."

"Listen!" cried Don. "Is that not the first turn of the screw?"

It was.

They heard the peculiar swish of it for the first time.

There was nothing peculiarly melodious about it, yet it was sweet music in their ears, for it promised them a speedy return to the spot where they had been severed from their friends.

The "Albatross" trembled from stem to stern, as if struck and shrinking from the blow.

Then she moved slowly forward, and Dick Darnley ordered the man at the helm to bring her round a bit, and steer as due north as the needle could take him.

The wind was against her, but it was only a steady breeze, and as the steam got up the "Albatross" made better headway, cutting through the waves in a fashion that gladdened the hearts of those on deck.

A SPLENDID SCHOOL STORY. NEVER BEFORE PUBLISHED.

By E. HARCOURT BURRAGE,

Author of "Ching Ching," "Monkey Mat and Roving Dick," "The Brave Boy of the Basilisk," &c.

The LAMBS of LITTLECOTE

"You think I'm going to die here," snarled Matthews. "BUT I AIN'T!"

No. 31. **PRICE ONE PENNY.**

ALDINE PUBLISHING CO., 10, Red Lion Court, Fleet St., and 1, 2, & 3, Crown Court, Chancery Lane, London.

"We shall sight the island in a few hours, at the outside," said Dick.

But as he spoke, the voice of a man, who as a matter of discipline had been appointed as lookout, was heard.

"A sail!" he cried.

"Where away?" was the prompt query by Bill Oakley.

"Nor'-west-by-west, sir."

Every eye was turned in that direction, and through the clear air they saw the tapering masts of a vessel laden with canvas.

Her hull was still down below the horizon.

"She's a big craft and a swift one, I'll swear," uttered Bill Oakley, "and what is she doing in these waters? It ain't in the line of traffic. Blowed if I like the look of her."

———

CHAPTER CCXXVIII.

THE CAMP BY THE SEA.—A DISTANT BOOMING.

AFTER the wearying experiences of the previous night hard work was out the question for those detained upon the island.

Nor, indeed, could they do much in any case, as they had no tools to work with.

The seamen with their cutlasses chopped off a lot of boughs to form additional shelter for sleeping under, and erected in their handy way a long, low building that would have served for cattle, at home.

A store of food such as the island provided for them was collected, some empty shells gathered to serve as drinking-cups, and with pipes for some and cigars for two or three, the entire party lay upon the sandy shore.

Their eyes were fixed longingly seaward, and the theme of conversation was a general one. When would the "Albatross" appear?

"Dick prudently took her out to sea," said Harry Barstow, "and the wind is against her returning so promptly as he could wish. She has to beat up with dead in her eye."

Norton Truscott, who was still obliged to wear his priest's attire, in the full enjoyment of a cigar, long a forbidden luxury to him, put a pertinent question.

"Is she not built for steam as well as sailing?"

"As I live!" exclaimed Harry, "I had forgotten that."

And then there was a silence.

If still afloat, and capable of using her steam power, why had she not returned?

They went into the matter, allowing time for everything, and it was clear that she ought to have been back hours ago. Evening was at hand, and in a little while it would be night.

"It looks bad," said Harry, "but we will not despair."

Chippy Bunyons and Penny Bunn were wandering together closer down by the sea. Chippy had borrowed a pipe of a sailor and puffed vigorously at it. Bunn, not to be behindhand with anything, was also furnished with one, but he indulged in the luxury of smoking as if he were handling some tremendous explosive.

Suddenly the pair stopped and stared to seaward. Bunn pointed in a westerly direction; Chippy directed a finger further south.

"They can hear or see something," remarked Jack Ford, who had been watching the movements of the pair.

"See what it is," said Harry.

Jack jumped up and ran down to the spot where Chippy and Bunn were still discussing something.

"It was over there, I am sure," Bunn was saying.

"More to the right," insisted Chippy.

"What is it?" asked Jack, as he drew up beside them.

"A kind of booming sound, sir," replied Bunn.

"More like the bang of a drum than anything else," said Chippy; "just the sort of thing a show party gives as a signal for the company to wake up and go on the platform to parade."

"There it is again," said Bunn.

Jack heard it this time, and his heart leaped within him, for he recognised the sound.

It was that of a distant gun.

He lost no time in speeding back with a report. Harry Barstow immediately called on all around him to be still. The seamen ceased to laugh and chatter, and in breathless silence they listened.

Boom!

Soft and evidently afar off, but unmistakably the firing of a heavy gun.

"It is said," remarked Walton, "that as every shepherd knows his individual sheep, so does a sailor recognise the sound of the guns of his ship."

"It is a legend," said Truscott, shaking his head.

"Be still for one moment," said Harry.

Boom! Boom!

"Two this time, and nearer," said Jack.

"I cannot recognise the voices of my guns," said Harry Barstow, "having heard but little of them."

"Can it be a signal for us that they are coming?" suggested Jack.

"They would hardly waste powder for that purpose," replied Ben Walton; "besides, those guns are shotted."

"How can you tell that?" asked Truscott.

"In a way not to be explained," answered Walton, "but one gets used to the difference in the navy. We feel it."

Once more the solemn, portentous sound was heard as the whole party gathered together.

Now that the meaning of it was known to all, every boom sent a thrill through the hearts of the listeners.

The signalling theory would not hold water now, for it was beyond belief that the firing for that purpose should be continued on the "Albatross." It had to be abandoned, and cast into the regions of the incredible.

How they strained their eyes for some distant indication of the coming of the ship, whether it was the "Albatross" or not. But the sun sank low, and they could see nothing.

At last it dipped, and darkness hurried up to take possession of the earth.

For ten minutes or so nothing more had been heard seaward, but now again the booming of the distant gun awoke the stillness. Then there was another interval of silence.

It lasted a long time, more than half an hour, and then again it floated towards them.

Now it was undoubtedly nearer.

To add to the excitement of the time, half a dozen guns were fired in quick succession, and then once more there was that portentous stillness.

The wind was falling slowly, with the promise of a calm by midnight, thus reversing the order of things prior to the earthquake.

Fully an hour elapsed ere another gun was heard, and at last the flash of it was seen, not by one only, but by all.

To judge of its distance from the shore was to a man of Walton's experience a moderately easy task.

"The ship is about six miles out, and coming slowly in."

Boom!

A flash in another direction, a third of a mile east of the former one. All doubts were now dispelled.

"It is a fight," cried Harry Barstow, "and between the 'Albatross' and another craft."

"But who on earth is there to pitch into her?" asked Jack.

"Impossible to say," answered Walton.

Only two more flashes were seen, and then silence.

In vain they listened and watched. There was no more firing. The strain of anxiety was terrible.

All sorts of conjectures were afloat.

After all it might not have been the "Albatross" engaged in warfare, especially as she was hardly prepared for it. But if so, who was her foe, and which had conquered?

It was proposed, but negatived, to light a fire upon the beach as a signal, until they knew more about the encounter they had imperfectly witnessed; it might be perilous to do so.

If an enemy, unknown hitherto, had attacked and beaten the "Albatross," it would be madness to bring him to the island to complete his work.

One thing was clear. Such an enemy could not be a legitimately appointed war vessel of any civilised country.

And who it could otherwise possibly be, none of them could conjecture.

Penny Bunn's suggestion that the whole thing might be a novel form of natural phenomena did not meet with the reception it deserved. All but Chippy laughed at it as ridiculous.

The latter had a growing feeling of admiration for Bunn as a talented and learned man. He believed in him.

He asked the originator of the remarkable theory later on, in private, to explain to him what he meant.

"It was a theory," exclaimed Bunn, "and no more. But it is remarkable in the history of science that all the theories of its most able men have, at the outset, been treated with derision and scorn, sometimes with persecution. It is a thankless task enlightening the ignorant."

Having thus by a side-wind heaped scorn upon the heads of the deriders, Bunn entered into a learned exposition on explosive sounds in general.

It was not based on any known line of thought and experience, but it was very mystifying to Chippy, and he was charmed.

"You mark my words," said Bunn, in conclusion, "the supposed firing is but a forerunner of another earthquake. I should say, judging by the altitude of Aries and the declination of the Dog Star, the two being antagonistic, I reckon that the quake will start about four in the morning."

Chippy had had enough of earthquakes, and was proportionately so disturbed on hearing from so sound an authority another was expected, that when a general order was given to retire for rest, he crept under the shelter provided, but could not sleep.

Bunn, on the other hand, having no particular faith in his own predictions, yielded to fatigue, and slept soundly.

In time all were in a state of forgetfulness, save the sentry appointed from the men, who paced slowly up and down on the soft soil, watchful and ready to give the alarm if anything created occasion for it.

But the hours wore on, and the stillness remained unbroken.

The sentry in due time, using the stars as a guide to the time, awoke his relief and slept in his turn.

Thus the night passed and the dawn came.

It was but a minute after the coming of the welcome day that the prophet Bunn, who had slept throughout the night dreaming of the old country, was aroused from a vision of a banquet, at which he was the honoured guest, toasted by royalty. He started up with the cry of voices in his ears:

"The 'Albatross'! Hurrah, the 'Albatross'!"

CHAPTER CCXXIX.

A STARTLING STORY.—ARE THERE TWO CHUNDER LOOS?

LYING off the shore, about half a mile distant, was the ship that all knew so well.

She was changed, owing to the damage to her rigging and the putting up of the funnel, but in other respects she was unmistakable to those who had been so long acquainted with her.

There was not at the moment any sign of life on board, but as the shouts from the party on shore awoke the stillness of the morning air, several heads appeared above her side, and immediately afterwards a boat was lowered.

Of the dozen or so who hurriedly tumbled into her, Bob Stockton and Bill Oakley were easily recognised.

Jack knew the slim form of his old schoolfellow, and the ample proportions of the boatswain were not to be mistaken by anybody.

The rest of the occupants appeared to be members of the crew.

The boat started, and other faces appeared at the side. Two men ascended halfway up the rigging of the mizzen mast.

Suddenly there was a cheering and waving of caps, but those in the boat did not stop rowing.

They pulled like men who were endowed with treble their ordinary strength.

It was a short pull ashore to such men, and then as the boat grated on the beach there was more shouting and much grasping of hands.

Bob Stockton fairly hugged Jack, and danced about with him in a manner widely diverging from his usual placid, languid bearing.

"Never expected to see you again, old fellow," he gasped, "and what a pull I've got over Don and Tom! They are below—hurt, but nothing serious."

"What has happened?" asked Jack.

"Oh! lots," replied Bob. "I must take in a fresh stock of breath before I can tell you a quarter of it. I must shake hands with—why, who is this gorgeous nobleman? Not——"

"Yes," said Jack, delighted, "it is Truscott. And just look at Penny Bunn shaking hands with Bill Oakley, and embracing him as if they were long-severed brothers. You may have a story to tell, Bob, but we have one to match it, for anything you like up to the extent of my worldly possessions."

"And who is that little chap, in the stage get-up, Bunn is introducing to Bill?"

"Chippy Bunyons, another prisoner of the Avishnus. Looks like a priest, doesn't he? Ha, ha!"

Jack was almost hysterical in his glee.

It was a moment of joy that acted like laughing-gas upon them all.

Everybody had something to say, and there were more talkers than listeners.

Harry Barstow gave his hand to Bill Oakley, who grasped it affectionately.

"This is better than a fortin' to me," said Bill.

"Mr. Darnley," said Harry, "is he well?"

"As well as can be expected," replied Bill. "You see, he and two of the young gentlemen have been damaged by splinters, and old Rammer is laid up in his bunk. Got a knock on the leg, and won't let anybody look at it, but swears he is going to die. There ain't nobody else hurt, but I reckon we've stopped the perceedings of some of the others."

"You have had an encounter—whom with?"

"Well, sir, I should reckon he is a pirate or some secret trader, but we niver got at the facks. He come up and opened fire on us right away, without offering to inspect our papers, or telling who or what he was. He's a smart sailor, and he's heavily manned. Bar the steam, we might have got it worse, being short-handed, and it was a running fight. The men stood to their work, and, for the 'sperience they've had, handled the guns wonderfully well. We punched a few holes in the warmint, and last night, when we was off yonder, he sheered away."

"You must give me the particulars later on," said Harry Barstow; "I must get on board at once. The rest can follow, and the sooner we are out of this latitude the better."

"We shall be obliged to repair the 'Albatross' fust, sir," said Bill; "it ain't no use trusting to steam to get us through the Red Sea. We ain't got a quarter coals enough. What o' them 'ere 'Wishnus, sir?"

"You need not be troubled about them any more," replied Harry. "Now, Oakley, I will go on board. Mr. Truscott and Mr. Ford will accompany me."

Jack was anxious to see his two friends, who were in a wounded condition, and he gladly sprang into the boat. Bob, by way of a change, elected to stay ashore, and hear from the lips of Ben Walton the story of their experience on the island.

There was, indeed, so much to tell all round that it was difficult to tell where to begin. The mutiny, however, took a foremost place, and Bill Oakley briefly explained to his captain how it had begun and ended.

There was a frown upon the brow of Harry Barstow, but it presently cleared away, and he spoke of the matter quietly.

"The blackguards," he said; "must of necessity bo punished, and Dirk Matthews cannot be forgiven in any way. I never liked the look of the scoundrel. But that is a matter which can wait."

The "Albatross" was reached, and the arrival of the captain and his companions hailed with a burst of cheering. Even the mutineers, who were on deck in force, joined in heartily, although they had good reason to dread meeting him.

Dick Darnley was in the mate's cabin, the boys were in their own. Jack Ford dived down the companion, and found them lying in their hammocks, looking pale, but, on the whole, very happy.

"Jack, old man!" was all Don could say, and he held out his hand.

Tom also extended his, and Jack grasped both.

"Now, what is the damage to you two?" he asked.

"Tom has a splinter, or had one, near his ribs, and I have one in the small of my back," replied Don, with a smile; "neither are of much account, but Bill Oakley says we have to lie quiet for a day or two, and live decently, if we don't want the wounds to fester."

"Is Darnley seriously hurt?"

"He has an ugly gash on the chest, but he swears it is nothing. He will get over it."

"Now tell me about the fight," said Jack—"unless you think that talking isn't good for you."

"I don't jaw with the small of my back," answered Don, smiling. "We sighted the warmint, as Bill calls him, when we were making for the island, after having got the engines ready. You have heard how we were damaged and driven to sea?"

Jack nodded. "I have heard the story in outline," he said.

"Well, with the wind against us we could not sail in our crippled condition," resumed Don, "and that fellow *could*. He shoved himself between us and the shore, and opened fire upon us. Darnley was not caught napping, and our guns were ready. So we returned the compliment. Then we sheered off westerly, intending to get round him if possible, but he got between us and the land again, and we harked back. It was a sort of game of see-saw, and it lasted all day, until just before night came we sighted the island. It was about that time he did us any real damage; a shot dropped right along the deck from aft to fore, as we were showing him a clean pair of heels. It wounded us, and I believed damaged Rammer in some way. And that's all."

"How many hours were you fighting?" asked Jack.

"Taking the dodging in," replied Tom, "four hours or more."

"And that was the only time you were fairly hit?"

"No; we got a smack or two in the ribs, but nobody was hurt. The fellows were poor gunners, but there was a swarm of them, and if they could have boarded us we should have had to go under, for numbers will tell, and it's no use talking humbug about it."

"Chunder Loo," said Don, "was on board, but not in command."

"Chunder Loo!" exclaimed Jack—"impossible!"

"It was he," said Don; "I had a good look at him through the glass. He was standing on something that elevated him a foot or more above the rest, and I could not be mistaken."

"But I tell you it is impossible," insisted Jack; "he perished last night in the city of the Avishnus."

And then he told his story, but it did not convince Don.

"It was Chunder Loo or his ghost," he said; "there could not be another like him in the world."

One thing was clear: the strange vessel had had enough fighting for the present.

More than one shot from the "Albatross" ploughed through her crowded crew on the deck, and many must have lost their lives. Don was of opinion that at least forty were wounded.

Taking advantage of the tail end of the breeze, the stranger departed, but, like the lover in the song—in one respect, at least—it was expected "he would return."

CHAPTER CCXXX.

REPAIRING THE "ALBATROSS."—THE PUNISHMENT OF
DIRK MATTHEWS.

THE explanations were all made; the stories all told and commented on; congratulations had been exchanged all round, when Penny Bunn, urged by the spirit that governed the Good Samaritan, came on board to look after his old associate, Rammer.

Already preparations had begun for replacing the injured mast with the best material from their stores and on the island, and the ship had been brought in as near to the shore as the depth of water permitted. She was very close in, about two cables-lengths from it.

Bunn had reason to be proud of his recent adventures. In none of the records of the wonderful doings of man had he come across a parallel case of a hero overcoming a python by the simple means of a pint or so of brandy.

He was in a position to patronise Rammer, whose records of heroism were supported by his personal evidence alone, without anything or anyone to confirm them.

Bunn opened the door and entered the cuddy. A groan burst from Rammer, who was lying on his back in his hammock.

"Who's there?" he feebly demanded.

"I—Bunn," was the answer. "I have come to see what I can do for you."

"You can't do nuthin'," answered Rammer. "Go away, and leave me to die in peace."

"You are hurt in the leg, I believe?" said Bunn, calmly.

"I ham," replied Rammer.

"Seriously?"

"Mortifully."

"When I was one of the junior physicians and surgeons of a leading London hospital," said Bunn—"a position I occupied at the early age of eighteen, owing to my superior ability—wounded legs was my speciality."

"I don't care about that," said Rammer, gruffly; "you can't tackle mine."

"They brought me all sorts of legs," pursued Bunn, ignoring this assurance of the hopeless nature of the case—"legs bent, legs broken, legs ripped, and legs cut, legs with every form of injury that was appalling to the eye. Others, men of medical eminence, shrank from the task, but I cured them all. I will now look at your leg."

"Hands orf!" roared Rammer, as Bunn attempted to uncover the injured limb.

"Rammer," said Bunn, firmly, "am I to see that leg, or *tell the truth about it?*"

"What do you mean?" asked Rammer, with his eyes starting out of his head.

"Medicine cannot cure it," said Bunn. "The surgeon's scalpel is not needed. *It is a case of tacks or glue being required.* You are the possessor of a *cork leg*—a forbidden article of human wear on board ship."

Rammer lay back in his hammock, gasping. The truth was out at last, and he feared that it meant ruin to him.

"You need not fear that I shall betray you," continued Bunn, "especially if you behave yourself with the becoming humility of a low-born *humbug*, to a gentleman. What's the matter with the leg?"

"One of the springs is bu'st," groaned Rammer. "It got a bang from a bit of wood a canning-ball ripped up from the deck."

"Next to my skill as a surgeon," said Bunn, "comes in my inherited genius as a mechanic. Are you aware that I am the sole inventor of perpetual motion?"

"I think I remember reading of something about it."

"*Where?*"

"In the daily papers, or summit in that way."

"Your memory has done you a good turn," calmly returned Bunn. "Hand out that leg."

Rammer brought it out without delay. It had been previously detached from his body.

"As a cork leg, it is a very good piece of workmanship, and must have cost a good lump of money."

"Forty pounds."

"Where did you get the money from?"

"Let me alone, will you?" groaned Rammer. "Can you put it right?"

"I can," said Bunn, confidently. "But not now. Later on in the evening I will return. You will understand that if I put it right you are to give me credit for having almost miraculously healed your wound."

"I'll say anything you like—swear to it," said Rammer, readily.

"It is enough," said Bunn. "And now I must leave you to join a festive party which is about to meet on deck to celebrate the many victories over our foes, of which I may justly claim my share."

He could not help it. The old spirit had taken possession of him, and he was the original Littlecote Bunn again.

But it was not a festive party that he saw as he emerged from the cabin—far from it.

Once more a court-martial had assembled, this time with Harry Barstow presiding, and Dirk Matthews was the prisoner.

There was no need to receive evidence, for he made no attempt to deny his guilt. It only remained to decide what should be his punishment.

To keep such a man on board was impossible, and to hang him was distasteful to the captain, for in the hour of joy, it would have gone against the grain of all to have had such a ghastly ceremony carried through.

Something that would avoid this, and yet be an ample punishment, was needed, and it came to Harry Barstow, as he sat with his eyes sternly fixed on the hang-dog-looking ruffian, standing with bowed head before him.

"Matthews," he said, "I will not waste words on a man of your stamp. Rightfully I could order you to be hanged, but I will spare you that humiliation and myself the disgrace of the 'Albatross' being turned into a place of execution." There was a faint gleam of exultation in the eyes of the rascal. "But you will not remain here. On yonder island you will be left to make your home." A dreadful pallor spread over the face of the prisoner. "A few necessaries will be given you, no more."

"I shall starve, sir," muttered Matthews.

"You need not do that, as there is food and to spare for a hundred or more better creatures than you are. I am not concerned about your ultimate fate."

"If you will forgive me," said Matthews, hoarsely, "I will make a clean breast of everything, and serve you as true as a dog."

"There is nothing for you to tell. I know all."

"I was set on to this, and offered a big reward if I would spoil your chances of rescuing your friend. It was at Malta, and the party gave me something on account. He said he was an Indian prince, and could make me a rich man. I'm a poor one, sir, and I've longed all my life to be rich. If you had been in my place, you might have been tempted to do as I did."

There was something in this, but Harry Barstow was not to be moved.

"I give you a chance of your life," he said, "and that is more than you would have given anyone here, if you had got us in your clutches. As for the story of the Indian prince, I believe there is some truth in it, but it does not matter now. He is dead. Oakley, take Matthews ashore and turn him adrift at the spot I have told you of. If he should come near us during our short stay upon the island, hunt him down as you would a wild beast, and hang him!"

Matthews uttered a loud cry, and fell upon his knees.

"I can't abear the notion of living *alone!*" he cried; "it's too awful, and in that spot, where fires of brimstone seem to be smouldering under it. Captain, I'd rather hang!"

"Take him away," said Harry Barstow, rising, and the men appointed to convey him ashore laid violent hands upon him. They dragged him to the side of the vessel and dropped him into the boat, where he lay curled up, groaning for mercy.

One of the most assiduous of his escort was his late assistant conspirator, Bates.

It is the way of the world, and men who have risked their lives, and lost, in the effort to gratify ambition, from monarchs downwards, have had experience of the convenient way their one-time helpers have of turning their coats to save their skins.

CHAPTER CCXXXI.

THE LEAVING OF DIRK MATTHEWS.—THE RUINED CITY.

THE instructions given to the men who conveyed Dirk Matthews ashore, were to take him up to the summit of the cliff and there desire him to start for the interior of the island, and *see that he went.*

Bates, as became a repentant sinner, was very hard upon his late associate, just as bibulous men who sign the pledge are down upon all who still adhere to their drinking habits.

"Hurry up!" he said, as they began the ascent of the slope. "We ain't got any time to waste on you."

"I hope to have a bit to waste on you some day,"

growled Dirk Matthews, casting an evil eye on him. "If ever we meet again *in private*, I'll arrange for your being wiped out like the bit o' human *fungis* as you are!"

"A civil tongue, if you please!" snarled Bates, giving him a kick.

Dirk Matthews looked for a moment as if he would have resented it, but he restrained himself.

Startop, who was also of the party of escort, laid a forefinger on the shoulder of Bates.

"There isn't any call," he said, "for you to be so mighty hard on him. There ain't a bit of need for you to pile up on the captain's sentence."

Bates took the hint, and interfered no more with Matthews.

They conveyed him to the top of the hill, where he was given rations of biscuit for a week, a clasp-knife, a bundle of clothing belonging to him, needles and thread, some lines and hooks for fishing, and a few other small necessaries.

"Off you go," said Startop, "and you know the consequence of showing near us."

"I knows it," growled Matthews. "I don't feel as if I wanted any more of your company. A white-livered lot, all of you. Yah! you think I'm going to die here. *But I ain't.*"

Startop did not think much of this utterance at the time, although he afterwards remembered it. There was more of the spirit of prophecy in it than he suspected.

They returned to the "Albatross," after having watched Dirk Matthews, until he was a mere speck in the distance, bearing for the ruined city. The men were already busy putting the "Albatross" in repair, so as to fit her for the return voyage. The object of Harry Barstow in coming out had been accomplished, and the thoughts of all turned to home.

It was expected that the better part of a week would be occupied in this work. Meanwhile, it was advisable to keep a sharp lookout for the strange vessel that had already given such trouble. The fire of the engine was kept ready for getting up steam under short notice, and with the exception of the heavy guns being shotted, the "Albatross" was in all things prepared for action.

The wounded promised to progress favourably, including Rammer, who, according to Bunn, was getting along, and would resume his ordinary duties in a day or two.

For a brief space of time we must follow Dirk Matthews, who was destined to be the hero of a great discovery, outcast and scoundrel though he was.

That he felt his position was true, but it was a solace to him to find that his life had been spared. With it there is always hope to the meanest and most villainous.

He went on, as we have stated, straight to the Avishnu city. It was a mass of ruins, with scarcely a single building left standing.

Although no information on the subject had been imparted to him, he guessed that it was the recent earthquake that had laid it low, and the chaotic mass had a strong fascination for him as he climbed over the shattered masonry.

He was of that breed of man who instinctively feels that in the ruin of others his harvest was at hand.

In time of war he would have been a camp-follower and plunderer of the dead; in civic riots he would have been one of the first to join the army of thieves who rob shops and private houses. So now he at once began to look for plunder.

"There's bound to be something among these stones," he muttered.

But he could do nothing more than take stock of the surface as he climbed here and there, now and then coming upon a hand or an arm of some serpent-worshipper buried beneath the ruins, and anon arrived at the spot where the temple had been.

He had no idea what place he stood on, but he noted that there was a look of superiority about the tumbled-up masses, and he climbed about, peering into hollows and crannies, looking for anything that was valuable, or would be if he ever got clear of the island.

By-and-by he felt hungry and thirsty, and the latter compelled him to retrace his steps to find water.

There was any amount of it without the city lying in pools, and he went back to the open ground.

There he ate and drank and lounged about awhile. When the evening was coming on he returned to the ruins, and once more sought the vicinity of the temple.

But little of it remained standing.

The great hall and the adjoining chambers were all ruined, the passages beyond and the recent homes of the pythons down. That of Luva was rent in twain, revealing a dark hollow beneath.

Ignorant of the use to which it had been put, he stepped up to the spot and peered into the opening revealed. A flight of steps, terminating he knew not where, but beginning in the floor of the den, met his eye. Whither did those steps lead?

His curiosity was powerfully excited, and after a moment's hesitation he stepped in and descended the first half-dozen. Then he stopped and peered down once more.

He fancied that he could see a chamber below, and not of very great extent. There also appeared to be a number of boxes and cases roughly made.

But it was all very indefinite from where he was, and he went lower, walking slowly. His eyes grew accustomed to the gloom, and before he reached the bottom, he saw that the early view had not deceived him.

It was a small stone chamber, not more than fourteen feet square, and in it there were a number of square boxes, about the size of a seaman's chest.

They were of the crudest make—mere packing-boxes, in fact—and on trying the lid of the nearest, he found that it could be removed without trouble, not being fastened in any way.

He turned it aside, and then from the interior there flashed up a thousand little sparks of light.

He staggered back, not knowing at the moment what to make of it. It came upon him as such an overwhelming surprise.

He stepped forward again, and thrust in his hands. He felt the hard stones, saw the glitter as he dabbled his fingers among them, and knew that he had lighted upon the wealth of a monarch.

Among other of the needful gifts bestowed upon him, he had received from Startop some matches, so that he could light a fire. He drew out the box with a trembling hand and lighted one. By the glare of it, he saw the precious stones as thick as kernels of corn in a bin.

From once chest to another he went, pulling off the lids until he had got through all. Of the eleven cases, only one was empty—the rest were full or partly so, with this wonderful accumulation of treasure.

"I'm the richest man on airth!" he gasped, and sitting down upon the steps, held his head tightly between his hands, feeling for a moment as if it would burst.

He had no thought of time. The night was at hand, but he heeded it not. The one absorbing thought in his mind was this sudden acquisition of wealth.

The richest man on earth!

Undoubtedly, with the exception of two or three absolute potentates, who claim as a divine right the entirety of the nations they govern.

What should he do with it? How spend half of it?

He tried to think it out, but it was only chaotic thought that surged through his brain. Suddenly the sun went down and night was there.

As the darkness fell upon him he awoke from his day-dreams, with a start. In an instant his head was clear.

"How shall I spend it?" he shrieked. "I *can't* spend it. I'm boxed up in this accursed island for *life!*"

Then he fell to raving and cursing those who had set him there, oblivious of the fact that, but for the sentence of banishment from the "Albatross," he would never have known of the great treasure of the Avishnu people, or of its hiding-place, laid bare by the earthquake.

He crept up the steps and stood under the light of the stars, thinking. What if he went to his late captain and told him of the wonderful discovery he had made, would he not be content with half as payment for taking Dirk Matthews with the remainder away from that accursed island?

"No, he would not be satisfied," muttered Matthews. "He would want _all_, and he would take it. After what's happened he would not show me a pinch of mercy. I dursn't tell him, nor anyone else. But how am I to get away from here?"

He stopped short, for he fancied he heard a footstep hard by. His wild eyes roamed here and there, but he saw nothing.

"Maybe they think they will rob me of it," he muttered, drawing his knife; "but what a fool I am! Nobody but myself knows of it. It is _all_ mine—_mine_! But where am I to get the ship to take me home? To think that I'm worth _millions_, and yet can't spend one penny of it, but must drag out the life of a wild dog here! I can't stand it! It will drive me mad in a day or two. What's that?"

Once more he fancied he heard a sound, and coming from the direction of the ruined temple. He stepped upon a pile of fallen stones, and remained there for awhile watching for signs of an interloper. There was light enough from the stars for him to have seen a man, or even one of the smaller animals, moving, but there was nothing moving. The stillness was impressive —profound.

"It was fancy," he growled. "I'm a-worriting myself about nothing. It isn't likely any of them would follow me here, as the Avishnus are all dead and buried under the piles of stone. I've got the place and all that precious stuff to myself."

But he was not so certain that he could safely leave the spot.

He had no fancy for sleeping in the ruined city, much less in the dark chamber underground, but he could not tear himself away.

He was afraid of going lest during his absence some thief might come along and rob him of all.

Descending to the level ground, he lay down to rest. The stones were chilly, and he fancied there was a dew falling, so he sought a sheltered and warmer spot, from whence he could keep his eye on the entrance to his treasure-house.

It was his intention to keep awake and watch all night, but the day had been an exciting one, and he slept but little the night before. Gradually, as his mind became easier, sleep stole upon him like a cloud and shut out all things. And it was a sleep that was as sound as if he had been dead.

CHAPTER CCXXXII.

GONE!—WAS IT A DREAM?

FROM dreams of the old country and life on board ship Dirk Matthews awoke, and found that it was day.

It was early as yet. The sun may have been up an hour, but not more. He stretched his arms, extended his legs lazily, and then, with a mental bound, realised his position.

He scrambled to his feet and looked about him. Too true, he was a prisoner, and alone on that island, but was he not rich? There was the entrance to the chamber below. That was as real as all else, and he _was_ the richest man on earth.

"And hang you all!" he hissed, as he shook his fist in the direction of the "Albatross." "I'll get the better of you one day. _I'm_ worth _millions!_ D'ye hear?"

In his excitement he bawled out this startling piece of information, and then confounded himself for being a fool, "blabbing his business to everybody."

"Not as there is anybody to hear me," he muttered, "but it is jest as well to be keerful."

He was in no hurry to go below. What was there was perfectly safe—as safe, and safer, than it could be in any bank. He would have breakfast before he looked it over.

But he could not go far away in search of water, and after looking about him, he discovered a small pool of it among some portion of the ruins hard by.

There was enough for his present needs. By-and-by he would go and live without the walls, and bury his treasure somewhere handy, so that he could keep an eye upon it, and live at ease in mind and body.

He ate his biscuit, munching it slowly, with sweet contentment, dwelling on his acquired property, and laying out plans for future enjoyment "when he got off the island."

The morning meal disposed of, he had a look round in a perfunctory fashion, just as a matter of form, to make sure nobody was about.

Of course it was impossible, but it was only the right thing to be careful. It was better to err on that side than on that of carelessness.

Still he was in no hurry to go down.

It was so enjoyable dwelling on the time of discovery and the sensation it gave him.

What a musical rattle it was that accompanied the trickling of the precious stones through his fingers! It was worth living for.

But at last he began the descent of the flight of steps, and he felt his way down, keeping his eyes tightly shut. He did not want the sweet vision to return to him by degrees, but to come upon him with a rush.

When he got below he would open his eyes and take it in all *at once*.

So down to the bottom he went, and satisfied at last he was there, he opened his eyes.

All dark for a brief spell, and then——

He stared and stared as the state of the chamber forced itself upon him and refused to change.

It was empty!

As he was at the outset unable to realise the extent of his discovery, so now was he too much overcome to grasp the nature of his loss.

"*It can't be!*" he gasped at last, and rising to his feet—for he had sunk to the ground in the moment of his utter amazement—went about groping for the vanished chests as if they had been so many pins dropped in the dark.

It was a feeble, futile thing to do, and presently he crawled up to the outer air and lay down to think.

"Was it a dream?" he asked himself, with the sickening sensation of despair. "No, it wasn't. It was true enough. *But who is the thief that's robbed me?* Is it the man who sent me here?"

The thought of this was maddening in its intensity.

To be robbed at all was exasperating in the highest degree, but to think that he had been deprived of the wealth of a monarch by Harry Barstow, or, indeed, by anyone on board the "Albatross," was unendurable.

But how was he to learn the truth?

If he ventured down to the beach, where a party of men had again landed from the "Albatross" for a purpose we shall make clear anon, he would be shot right away. There would be no time given him to offer an explanation.

In his impotent fury Dirk Matthews lay at full length upon the ground and tore at the stony ground with his fingers, as if he was resolved to dig up the truth by that primitive means.

But it all ended in torn nails and bleeding fingers; and, in a state bordering on exhaustion, he at length arose, and shouldering the bag containing his necessaries, he wearily left the spot.

He had no definite idea of going anywhere in particular, beyond that it would be wise of him to avoid the southern beach of the island. In an opposite direction he turned his steps.

Over the huge piles of broken masonry, stone, and cement, and shattered marble columns, he pursued his way, getting clear of the ruined city after nearly an hour's toilsome journey.

He was now on the other side of it, with the sloping crater rising upwards several hundred feet, and there unbroken by the action of the earthquake.

There were clumps of trees of various sizes, some approaching the dignity of a wood, but many of them had suffered, for the trees had been thinned out, and lay upon the ground, their tops crushed and broken.

He passed on to one of them to gather some of the fruit, for now he felt that there was a fever growing in his blood.

He entered it, forcing his way through a fringe of undergrowth.

Barely had he passed through it when he received a blow from behind that stretched him senseless to the ground.

* * * * *

When Dirk Matthews woke to a knowledge of things again he found himself lying on the deck of a ship, the character of which a man of his experience could not mistake.

The craft was long, with a low deck and rigging that raked aft. She carried guns, and around a number of swarthy, loosely-attired half-castes were busy in various ways.

Some were cleaning their weapons, others occupied in the ordinary duties of a seaman, but the vast majority were smoking, and there was a free-and-easy air about the whole of them that is only to be found on a privateer, not averse to a bit of piracy when a prize comes into view.

The vessel lay at anchor close under the bluff of an island. Dirk Matthews had no doubt it was the same where he had recently found a vast fortune—and lost it.

He was not secured in any way, but apparently was free to get up and look about him. His captors had brought him on board, and thrown him down to recover without giving him any more thought or care.

He got up, and the movement attracted the attention of two ruffians close by, who turned their eyes upon him and grinned.

"Tell me, mates," said Dirk Matthews, "how came I here?"

"*We* brought you," was the cool reply.

"Wot for?"

"To make a good seaman of you, instead of a molly-coddle on board that toy boat, the 'Albatross.'"

The fellow was dark-skinned, but his English was good. Dirk Matthews realised that he was on board a ship after his own heart, and he ought have been content. But he was not exactly comfortable.

"Tell me, mate," he said, "if I ain't axing too much, what you was a-doing ashore?"

"Gathering fruit," was the grinning answer. "We saw you coming—prospecting, we supposed—and as we lost a score or more of men in the fight we had with the 'Albatross,' we thought one of you would help fill up the gap—which you have to do, or be chucked overboard."

"Of course I'm willing to jine," said Dirk Matthews. "It's a life that suits me. But may I ax another question?"

"Forty, if you like."

"Was you ashore larst night?"

"No, we went off at dawn."

"But you've been on the island other times?"

"Never been near it till the middle of last night, that I know of."

Dirk Matthews reflected for a moment. It was plain that the man knew nothing of the lost treasure. How would it do to mention the matter to their chief?

"I suppose," he said, insinuatingly, "that it would be too much to ax for the priwilege of speaking to the captain?"

"Not a bit," said the other. "He said, when you woke up out of your nap you were to be brought to him. Come along; he's below."

Dirk Matthews felt a little weak about the head, but he was a hardy ruffian, and a blow or so more or less was not of much moment to him. He recovered sufficiently on the way to the cabin of the pirate chief to walk straight and speak clearly.

The leader of the crew was a small, wiry man, nationality doubtful, but bearing a resemblance to the ordinary Portuguese adventurer.

His hair was grizzled, and he was apparently about fifty years of age.

He looked at Dirk Matthews as a keen judge of cattle surveys an ox for the first time, reading him as a book, and estimating his points of good and evil.

It was the evil he was most interested in.

"You belong to the 'Albatross'?" he said, curtly.

"I did," replied Dirk Matthews; "but now, of course, I am going to join *here*."

"Not so fast," said the pirate captain. "What were you doing on the island?"

"Looking about me in a general way, cap," replied Dirk Matthews, "and I come across some rum things."

The pirate captain gazed at him inquiringly.

"The airthquake," said Dirk, "had rumpussed up the city where them 'Wishnus was holding high jinks. You've heerd of them, maybe, sir?"

The pirate captain shook his head.

"No," he said. "What are they?"

"Sarpint worshippers," answered Matthews; "and they've got a city, or *had*, that would make you stare, sir. It's in ruins now, but in the thick of them ruins I come across a treasure that was enough to make the eyes of any man bulge out."

"What was it?"

"Bushels of jewels!"

The pirate captain smiled.

"Tell me all about it," he said.

Then Dirk Matthews warmed up to his theme, and told the whole story, as he viewed it. According to his notions, Harry Barstow, or some of those under him, had watched and robbed Dirk while he slept.

"And you expect me to believe this story?" said the pirate captain, calmly.

"Well, sir," pleaded Dirk Matthews, "it *is* the truth!"

"Is it?" was the rejoinder. "Say, then, what you expect me to do."

"Nothing, sir; only if the 'Albatross' have got the stuff aboard, look what a prize——"

He was interrupted with a gesture of contempt.

"With the 'Albatross,'" said the pirate captain, "I hope to have another brush, but not because you have chosen to tell me a yarn as old as the hills, Matthews —that, I believe, is your name?"

"It is, sir."

"The next time you spin that yarn in my presence I'll hang you as an incurable liar! Go about your work, and mind you do your duty!"

Dirk Matthews reeled out of the cabin like a drunken man. He had given away everything to a rascally pirate chief, and instead of being received with open arms as a benefactor and a friend, was stigmatised as a liar.

"There never was sich luck for a man," he muttered, "but I'll be even with the lot yet, if I die for it!"

CHAPTER CCXXXIII.

THE FOE THAT CAME IN THE NIGHT.

THE men who were busy on shore preparing materials for the repairs of the "Albatross," slept on board at night. For the time much of the accustomed routine of the vessel had to be abandoned. The watches, for instance, were broken up, and about half the number performed this duty.

This was absolutely unavoidable, for a man who has been cutting timber, hauling and trimming it all day, is not fit for the work of standing about deck looking after an enemy. And that one might appear at any moment was not to be ignored.

A steady breeze now blew continuously night and day, and if it only held in the same quarter, it would be very favourable to the "Albatross" on her way home, for it came from the south.

Therefore was the work on hand hurried forward, and it was hoped that within a week they would leave a spot fraught with many terrible associations.

It was believed that the Avishnus perished to a man. The only element of doubt arose in their thoughts of Chunder Loo. Don and Tom Drummond were both positive that they saw him aboard the pirate craft, but their companions were inclined to think they had been misled by a strong resemblance.

Five days elapsed, and nothing being seen of Dirk Matthews, it was conceived that he had accepted his banishment in a becoming spirit. They had no inkling of the fate that had fallen on the hapless head of the mutinous rascal.

The subject of the wealth of the Avishnus cropped up on the evening of the fifth day. Work for the day was over, and the toilers were on board. On the aft deck there was a merry party partaking of dinner. Penny Bunn was once more the attendant, and it must be confessed that he made a most admirable waiter.

The subject of hidden treasure has ever had an absorbing interest to mankind. Previous experience had accentuated it in the mind of the late schoolmaster of Littlecote.

The conversation, open enough, of the party, was quite fascinating to him.

"I know for a certainty," said Norton Truscott, "that the wealth of the Avishnus amounted to millions, and their treasury was formed of jewels, like most of the wealth of the old Indian princes."

"But where was it?" asked Harry Barstow.

"Somewhere in the temple," answered Truscott, "and, of course, now buried from mortal eye. perhaps for ever. It could only be got at by carrying out excavations on the line that has unearthed Pompeii."

"All idea of getting at it has to be given up," said Jack Ford, with a sigh.

"Yes," said Truscott, "it will be better so. Let the thing slide."

"We might have one day ashore on the off-chance of finding something," suggested Don.

"If you once begin the search," replied Norton, "you will not give it up. It would be like going into the Court of Chancery to recover unclaimed property. Your whole life would be sacrificed to the fever of hope. No, let the thing go."

Penny Bunn cleared the table, put on wine and cigars, and went off to his own quarters.

There Chippy Bunyons, by choice, had taken up his abode. Rammer, one time "boss" of the cuddy, had fallen from his high estate to that of Penny Bunn's servant.

But with regard to the rest of the ship, he was still in his old position of cook.

Chippy, as well as Norton Truscott, had cast off the Avishnu robes and assumed seaman's attire. It is a becoming dress to most people, but on the spare form of Chippy it had something of the burlesque in it. He looked like a comic edition of T. P. Cooke, the old famous delineator of the British tar.

"Hurry up, Rammer," said Bunn, as he bounced into the cuddy and sank into a chair. "I've seen other people eat their fill, and now feel as if I could do justice to my own dinner. Chippy!"

Chippy, who was engaged in endeavouring to tie some of the knots for which seamen are famous, looked up inquiringly.

"They've been talking about the jewels of the Avishnus," continued Bunn, "worth *millions*."

"They were worth a pile," said Chippy.

"Did you ever see any of them?"

"I saw the lot once. There is one day in the year—or rather there was—when they brought out the lot, and *spread them on the floor of the temple*. You niver see sich a sight in your life. There was a good cartload of them."

"And where did they keep them?"

Chippy shook his head.

"Ah! that was one of the things they did not trust us with. Both Truscott and myself was locked in when they fetched the pile out and put them away."

"I was wondering," mused Penny Bunn, "if they could be dropped on."

"Whoever does it," said Chippy, "won't want bread and cheese while he lives."

"If we had a look around——"

"Don't put me in the *we*, Bunn, for forty millions wouldn't tempt me to go prowling around for the stuff. The very thought of that infernal place makes me sick. I've got away, and I don't want to set eyes on it any more."

"Well," sighed Bunn, "it only occurred to me that it seemed a pity to let so much money lie idle. All my life I have walked hand in hand with impecuniosity. It would be such a delicious sensation to feel *rich*, if only for an hour. Rammer, if you don't hurry up with dinner I'll have that cork leg of yours off and sell it on the forecastle by auction!"

"Coming, sir—coming," replied Rammer, as he raised a flap table from the wall, and proceeded to lay a cloth upon it.

And the way he hopped about showed how completely he had been subjugated by his late assistant.

Bunn and Chippy ate their food together; Rammer, as became a dependant, partook of his afterwards, which he did with an outward humility strongly contrasting with his inward exasperation.

By the door of the cuddy Bunn and Chippy sat in lounging-chairs smoking cigars.

It was almost dark when things had got to this stage, and the cool breeze fanned their brows. It was the hour of contentment and peace.

"After all," said Bunn, "there is much that is enjoyable in a life at sea. How restful, how charming is the hour!"

At this moment Bill Oakley was seen to hurry aft

and descend to the captain's cabin. A minute later, and all the officers were on deck.

"It's yonder I saw it," they heard Bill say—"there by the point, stealing up; "but I'm afeard it is too dark to see it now."

The darkness was indeed rapidly descending. Objects half a mile away were lost in the coming gloom of night.

Some command was given to Bill, who came hurrying aft.

"Mr. Oakley," said Bunn, "may I ask what it is you have discovered?"

"A sail," gruffly answered Bill. "Some warmint is stealing up to us, and he's got an ugly look. We may have a bit of fighting afore another hour."

He passed on and said something quietly to Startop, who vanished below.

"Really," said Bunn, "the peace of a seaman's life is delusive. Chippy, old man, if ever we get safe home, we will, as the song says, 'never come back no more.' It is not grammatical, but it expresses my feelings to a hair."

Up from below came the men without the least noise or bustle.

They had received their orders, and each went to his post.

Every hand and all the officers were now on deck, so many shadows to the eye, for the night had fully come.

There was a slight creaking sound as the guns were gently run back and loaded ready for action. In a whisper every command was given.

"Chippy," said Bunn, softly, "how do you feel?"

"Creepy," was the answer.

"We can be of no service here."

"Not until there's somebody hurt as wants looking to."

"Hurt," said Bunn, with a sickly smile. "Cannon-balls are no respecters of persons. If an emperor stood in the line of progress of one of them he would *go down*. Humble as we are, we cannot hope to escape the result of being in the wrong place. Let us go inside, and it will be as well for both if we devote a short time to meditation. Chippy, I've been an awful sinner."

"Not wuss than most on us, perhaps," murmured Chippy.

"Worse than any of you, worse than anybody except Rammer. He is vile enough to bring the direst catastrophe upon us."

They glided into the cuddy, where Rammer sat smoking his pipe in gloomy meditation.

"Now," whispered Bunn, "out you go!"

"Wot for, sir?" asked Rammer.

"There's danger in the air," answered Bunn. "Yet a little while and we shall have shot and shell raining upon this devoted vessel! I do not want additional peril to be put upon the cuddy by the presence of so vile a man as you. Out you go! Let them see that you are not a liar, but one born to fight and bleed for his country. Sharp, now!"

Rammer shook all over from the crown of his head to the toes of his valiant body. But he did as he was told, and laying down his pipe, stole softly out.

CHAPTER CCXXXIV.

A RANDOM FIGHT.

"WHO has the best sight of you youngsters?" asked Harry Barstow.

It was difficult to say, but Don got the credit of being the happy possessor of eyes that could be compared to those of the eagle.

"Go with Oakley," said Harry; "he will tell you what is required of you."

Don joined Bill, who was standing forward with his eyes directed towards the point where he had seen the sail.

He could see neither the one nor the other now, nor indeed anything three hundred yards from the ship, for the stars were not shining so brightly as usual.

"Mr. Oakley," whispered Don, "the captain sent me to you."

"Stand well forrard," said Bill, "and let me know if you can see anything."

"Shall I get out on the bowsprit?"

"If you ain't afeard of falling into the sea."

Don smiled as he took off his cutlass and laid it upon the deck. The next moment he was over the bows and sprawling along the bowsprit. He went right on to the end and lay there, just discernible to those on deck.

The silence on board was now profound. On the first alarm of the approaching stranger there had been some thought of shifting their ground in the darkness; but it could not be done without making a noise which would be a practical guide to the other craft. So a hasty consultation was held between the captain and his mates, and it was resolved to sham being asleep—playing the weasel, in fact.

That it was a foe approaching was pretty certain, especially as he showed no lights. Deluded by the stillness on the "Albatross," and having no guide from lights on her deck, he would probably come on unsuspecting the preparations made to give him a warm reception until well within range.

Then he could be made the recipient of all the shot that could be thrown into him, and the advantages of a first blow reaped by the "Albatross."

That was the plan arranged, and in silence all were watching for a sign of the enemy's approach.

Don lay out upon the bowsprit for ten minutes or more, and then his voice was heard:

"Mr. Oakley!"

"Yes, sir."

"I can see her. She is creeping up by the shore, wonderfully close."

"There ain't water enough for her to get between us and the shore," muttered Bill; "besides, it would be *too* nigh. The fust fire would blow one on us clean into the hair. How far away, sir?"

"Half a mile."

"Come back, sir. We shall have to bring the bow-gun to bear upon her."

Don came gliding back, and he and Bill stood side by side. The youth pointed out where the vessel was.

"She is only a shadow," he said—"just a blurred outline."

"I can't see her yet," muttered Bill. "Jest slip aft and tell the captain."

Don disappeared, and Bill strained his eyes to catch a glimpse of the strange vessel. He fancied he saw her heading from the shore, but it was the faintest picture of her.

"All in good time," he muttered. "When we do fire a shot it oughtn't to be wasted."

There was a quiet, intense excitement around. Somehow, without being told verbally, all the men knew that the expected enemy was, as the Yankees say, "on hand." And they managed to locate him pretty accurately, too, for every face was turned to the forward part of the vessel.

Suddenly Bill Oakley stooped down and looked to the sight of the bow-gun. He shifted it, settled it to his satisfaction, and then there was a flash of light and a boom that shook the craft from stem to stern.

It was immediately followed by a crash of timber in the distance.

"Hit!" cried a dozen voices. "Bravo, Bill!"

A chorus of yells from voices a furlong away was heard, and then came the answering shot. It whistled overhead, somewhere among the rigging, but did not seem to do any damage.

"She's tacking out, sir!" cried Bill.

They could all see her now—a long, low-built craft, with enough canvas for a man-of-war—a ghost of a ship in the gloom.

She was wearing round, so as to get broadside on to the "Albatross."

And now Harry Barstow, Dick Darnley, and Ben Walton moved down among the men, inspiring them, with quiet bearing and calm utterance, to keep cool.

Walton sighted one of the broadside guns, and sent a second shot into the foe. It hit her somewhere in the hull, and she answered with a broadside of five guns.

A shot struck Goffer squarely, and dashed the life out of him. He fell in the scuppers on the shore side, a shapeless mass, and died without a groan. A second shot went right through the cuddy, hurt no one, but it left Bunn speechless on the floor, and Chippy feeling for his head. Rammer, who was crouching by the door, howled like a dog.

"Steady, men!" cried Harry Barstow.

Again the guns of the "Albatross" gave tongue, but without effect, judging by the derisive shouts of the foe.

As a cloud of mist sweeps over a moor, so could they see the stranger gliding by.

"She is going to get to windward of us, sir," said Bill Oakley, who had deserted his now useless bow gun.

"Up with the anchor," said Harry Barstow, "and shake out all the canvas she can bear. Cool and steady!"

It was the work of some minutes, and ere it was done a second broadside was fired by the foe. The crash of a shot in the hull, somewhere in dangerous proximity to the water-line, was heard.

Jim the stoker came up from below, three stairs at a time.

"Cap," he cried, hoarsely, "the engine's crippled, and my mate won't whistle or sing any more. There's a hole big enough to shove your head into, and the water's bubbling through it!"

"Go down and plug it," was the answer. "Darnley, will you see that it is done?"

Not another shot was fired from the "Albatross" until her anchor was up and she was moving under a fair spread of canvas.

She was not quite fit for sea, but she was no longer a complete cripple.

"Head her for that fellow!" was the command next given.

Jack Ford and Tom Drummond sprang to the wheel. They knew how to steer her, and their undertaking the work would leave a man free to serve at the guns.

As she swung round, with her bow pointed at the stranger, Bill once more took up with the bow gun.

There were four of the men in charge of her, and, under the boatswain's direction, she was rapidly reloaded.

The stranger grew clearer to the eye, and the buzz of voices on her deck could be plainly heard.

Bill lost no time in giving the enemy the contents of his gun, with an aim so true that the air was laden with the shrieks of wounded men.

Immediately afterwards she swung herself astern the "Albatross" to the sea.

She had had enough of it, and was making tracks to get away.

Any attempt to follow her would have been a waste of time. The "Albatross" was not in racing condition, but they sent a shot or two after her with no visible effect, and then she vanished in the darkness of the night.

It was still uncertain if she had really beaten a retreat or not, and the "Albatross" stood steadily out to sea until she was six or seven miles from the shore, and then, as nothing more was seen of the foe, she slowly beat back again, anchoring finally near her old ground.

Three of the men were found to be slightly wounded, and Goffer was dead. In the gloom they picked him up, and winding a piece of canvas about him, consigned him to the deep.

He was so terribly mangled that he could not be kept on board till the dawn.

Jim the stoker's chum was not killed, but the strength of his cranium had been severely tested by its being struck with a portion of the machinery. Happily it was made of strong material, and beyond a time of insensibility and some hours of confused thought, he was none the worse for it.

But the engine was ruined. Until they got to some port where it could be repaired, the "Albatross" would have to rely upon her canvas.

One thing was certain: she was in dangerous quarters, and the sooner she got away the better.

It was possible that the craft that had assailed them would have a consort somewhere, for the pirate seldom works without two strings to his bow. An encounter with the double force could only end in the sinking of the gallant little vessel. Right goes a long way in a fight, but it yields to overpowering might.

So, with one consent, she was got ready to depart with the return of daylight.

When the morning broke the sea was clear of the foe.

Those who had shared in the previous encounter were of opinion that the vessels in both cases were one and the same, but doubt there could not help being, owing to the lack of light during the last brief but telling fight.

"We could swear to her in daylight," said Bill Oakley.

So said others, but the opportunity to swear to —or, as Bob Stockton remarked, "at her"—was not to be theirs for many days.

And yet they were to fall in with her later on, and learn all about her and the man who commanded her, and other things concerning the craft.

The repairing of the "Albatross" was now so far advanced that the rest of it could be done at sea

Therefore, early on the following day, her anchor was again raised; and with few regrets, but many things to keenly remember, the gallant crew bade farewell to the Avishnu island for ever.

CHAPTER CCXXXV.

AT ALEXANDRIA.—A MYSTERIOUS RAJAH.

IT was about two months later when Jack Ford and Don Peebles, arm-in-arm, were strolling about Alexandria. The time was early in the night, and the occasion some public festivity, probably the birthday of the Khedive or the anniversary of an event prominent in the annals of the country.

But whatever it was, the two friends were ignorant of it, and not at all curious. It was enough for them that the streets were filled with strange men of many tribes and nations, wonderfully picturesque in the glittering light of the varied illuminations.

They sauntered on, apparently unheeded, save that now and then some dark-skinned son of the desert cast a sidelong angry glance at them, as representatives of the dominant nation.

By one of the score or so of *cafés* in a main thoroughfare Jack suddenly stopped.

"What do you say to a cup of coffee, Don?" he said.

"I am ready for it," replied Don; "it is the only drink to be got here to suit our taste."

"You forget the sherbet, famous in history and in song."

Don made a wry face.

"I made better stuff years ago with carbonate of soda, tartaric acid, and a little sugar," he said.

"Well, it *is* a fraud," remarked Jack, as they entered the *café*.

It was a big place glittering with light, a cosmopolitan house of refreshment, with a French proprietor, and attendants of half a dozen nationalities.

There was a good company, the place being pretty full, but they found a small table unoccupied in a corner, and sat down.

A sprite-like French waiter was in instantly in evidence.

"Coffee, gentlemen?"

"If you please."

He vanished, and Jack, casting a look around, drew Don's attention to a long, loose-limbed fellow, attired in a dress that reminded one of a Neapolitan fisherman. He sat at a table on the other side of the *café* with his back to them.

"Doesn't that strike you as a familiar figure, Don?" he said.

"Ye-e-es," answered Don, hesitating; "but when I have seen him before I can't tell!"

"Coffee, gentlemen."

The attendant was there with two pots, one with hot coffee, the other with milk.

"Black coffee," said Jack.

It was poured out, and he put an English sovereign down to pay for it.

"You must change him, sar, at ze bureau," said the attendant.

He pointed towards an office at the bottom of the *café*. Jack went off to exchange his sovereign for Egyptian money, which was promptly done.

On his return he paid the attendant, who had meanwhile looked to the wants of some new arrivals.

"That fellow in the fisherman's dress is gone," said Don, as he stirred his coffee.

"Did you glimpse his face?" asked Jack.

"Yes, and who do you think it was?"

"Can't say."

"Dirk Matthews."

"Oh, come, Don, none of your gammon!"

"It was Dirk Matthews or his twin brother," insisted Don; "he did not notice me, but I got a good look at him. He spoke to our waiter as he went out with the air of an old acquaintance."

"Suppose we ask a question or two about him?"

Jack beckoned to the attendant, and asked who the sailor was that had just gone. "He spoke to you as he left," he said, to assist the man's memory.

"I know him no more zan he is a servant of ze great Rajah," was the reply of the attendant.

"And who is the great Rajah?"

The attendant raised his eyebrows in surprise.

"You not know him? He vith more money zan ze Khedive. It is strange!"

"We have only been in Alexandria a few hours," explained Don.

"So," said the attendant, "I see him now. Ze Rajah make us what you Englees call *hum*. He spend money, he haf big house—he haf feast—much drink —he throw money to ze beggar like water."

"A Rajah, eh? What is his title—of what place is he Rajah?"

"He gif no name. He say he is Rajah. It is enough. He haf money, so all go to see him. Hi! Yes, sir, I am ready."

Responding to the beckoning finger of an Englishman with a military air, who had just come in, the attendant glided away. Jack tasted his coffee, put in more sugar, and said:

"I feel curious about this Rajah. You know my speculative way."

"I do," said Don, smiling; "building all sorts of theories on the slightest foundation."

"But some of them have stood firm. Dirk Matthews—the great Rajah—well, there isn't much there, perhaps."

"They can have nothing to do with each other, Jack."

"No-o-o. Perhaps not. But I've got it into my head that they have. Of course, it may not be Dirk, after all."

"I am certain of it, Jack."

"Well, so be it. Say he got taken off the island— he won't want to renew acquaintance with any of us. Do you remember how, as we came through the Red Sea, Alexandria cropped up persistently in our talk, until Barstow suggested that we should put in there for stores and repairs? Then how eagerly we jumped at the idea, although we are all in a hurry to get home."

"Natural curiosity, I suppose, Jack."

"It was more than that. I feel we *had* to come."

"For what purpose?"

"Can't say. But I think it is so, and that the Rajah has something to do with it."

"You *are* a strange fellow, Jack," said Don, as they left the *café*, "and if you were a stranger to me, I should feel inclined to laugh at your conceptions. But I've seen before how your mind intuitively grasps a lot of odd material, as the magnet does particles of steel, and proceeds to put it into shape. It is a wonderful instinct."

They strolled about the streets and into the bazaars for another hour.

The varied tongues were for the most part strange to them, but now and then they came across persons who spoke in French, or the more familiar English, and in four cases out of five the Rajah was the subject of conversation.

"We must find out more about him to-morrow," said Jack, "and now I think we may head for home. It is a strange word to use under the circumstances, but we Britishers are fond of it. It fits in with every hole where we may be staying for a time."

"Barstow has given us more than a hole to put our head in," said Don, in genial reproach.

"I wasn't thinking of our 'drum,' only generalising," said Jack.

Early that morning the "Albatross," after a slow voyage, during which she lay a fortnight becalmed off Aden, dropped her anchor outside the line of forts guarding the town. Harry Barstow, who had been there before, immediately landed, saw an agent, and secured as a temporary residence the house and grounds of some Eastern potentate who had "gone wrong."

Ruined by a change of policy of the Government, he had retired in disgust to some inland place with as many wives and servants as his means permitted of.

He was not averse to adding to his income by letting his town residence.

"It will be better than an hotel for the boys," said

Harry; "with Bunn, Rammer, Startop, and another man or two, and a sprinkling of native attendants, we shall rub along."

It was a fine residence, on a slope overlooking the forts and the sea. The house stood in a splendid but neglected garden, which was surrounded by a high wall. There were two entrances, one for the upper caste, the other for the servants, strong doors keeping out intruders in both cases.

It was about nine o'clock when Jack tapped lightly upon one of them, and it was promptly opened by a Nubian, who bowed low as they passed through.

The moon was shining brilliantly on the orange-trees that mingled with a score varieties of fruit-bearing trees, the almond and the olive predominating.

In the midst of the silvered foliage the house stood, a substantial structure of stone, with a low dome rising from the roof. There were windows of many quaint shapes, from mere slits to the solid square, but the majority were dark. Here and there one was lit up, and these were in the lower part of the building.

From a distant part of the garden arose the sound of some stringed instrument, accompanying a clear tenor voice in a song.

"I feel," said Jack, as they glided on with softened steps, "as I used to do when reading the stories of the Arabian nights."

"There has been some romance in our lives," remarked Don, sententiously, "and there may be more to come."

CHAPTER CCXXXVI.

THE FACE OF THE RAJAH.

IT was Norton Truscott who was singing. He lay in a hammock swung between two citron-trees, with a guitar resting lightly on his knee. Near him Harry Barstow and Dick Darnley lounged in camping chairs. Bob Stockton and Tom Drummond reclined upon some rugs on the ground. Penny Bunn and Chippy had the care of a table on which was spread the dessert that had followed dinner.

Jack and his companion stole up quietly, listening to the song, which soon came to an end with every sign of approval from the listeners.

"You have quite recovered your voice, Truscott," said Harry.

"Yes," was the thoughtful reply, "but I remember one night when alone in my 'drum' with the Avishnus, I tried to sing, and there was not a note in me—not one."

"That was not to be wondered at," said Chippy, in an undertone to Penny Bunn. "I used to be *oh fay* on the penny-whistle, but I couldn't have tootled 'Sally come up' in that infernal hole."

"There was a time," sighed Penny Bunn, "when my performance on the accordion excited a considerable amount of admiration, but I fear that I could do little on it now."

"Well, Jack," said Darnley, "what do you think of Alexandria?"

"We have enjoyed ourselves," answered Jack. "What do *you* think were the chances of Dirk Matthews getting off that island?"

"A curious question to pop into the thick of a conversation on Alexandria. Three million to one, I should imagine."

"We have seen him to-night. Don could swear to him."

There was a general exclamation of surprise. Jack repeated their experiences of the evening, including all they had heard about the Rajah.

"Some adventurer," said Norton Truscott, contemptuously, "who will vanish one morning in debt everywhere. A Lambri Pasha, I should say."

"If Dirk Matthews is in Alexandria," said Harry Barstow, "I shall make it my business to move him on. Have some claret, boys. Then some of you give us a song."

"We can oblige you with a chorus," said Jack, "one of our old school-day performances. You remember our singing, Bunn?"

"I do, indeed, sir," answered Bunn, with emotion, as he poured out some claret for Jack and Don. "You were younger then, and your voices had the sweetness of boyhood. I used to lie and listen and think of angels."

They laughed on hearing this tribute to their innocent past.

"You can't help it, Bunn, I suppose," said Bob Stockton. "It is your powerful imagination that glosses over the defects of our younger days."

They sang one of their old school songs, written by Herbert May. At the conclusion there was a round of applause.

"Stop a moment," said Bob. "I must take another rise out of Bunn."

Turning to that faithful servitor, he asked him if he thought they sang as sweetly as when they did at school.

"Precisely the same," answered Bunn, "if anything, sweeter."

"No change in the tone?"

"None in the least, sir."

"Strange," mused Bob, "at school we all sang treble or contralto, and now Ford is a baritone, Don and myself tenor, and Drummond a bass, and yet no change of tone, although in the course of nature there is a change of voice. Bunn, you have no ear for singing."

"I fear, sir," answered Bunn, readily, "that travel-

A SPLENDID SCHOOL STORY.

NEVER BEFORE PUBLISHED.

By E. HARCOURT BURRAGE,

Author of "Ching Ching," "Monkey Nat and Roving Dick," "The Brave Boy of the Basilisk," &c.

"Backsheesh!" demanded the Arab.   "That's nothing but cheek," observed Chippy.
"Hit him in the eye, Bunn!"   "I am not aggressive," said Bunn, mildly.

j g has somewhat impaired it. Years ago it was considered that my ear was unrivalled. As a boy, the
village choir in which I sang, having no organ, they
considered me their *tuning fork*."

"It's no use," said Jack Ford, with a gasp, "let
him go."

Bunn was dismissed, and he set to work carrying
some of the materials of the board into the house as
no longer required. He went away quietly, but returned at a hand-gallop.

His hair stood up, his eyes were out of his head; he
is the embodiment of fright.

"Save me!" he gasped. "I am stabbed in a vital
part. I am dying!"

He fell upon the sward, rolling his eyes as Chippy
rushed to his assistance. The entire company gathered
in haste round the prostrate Bunn.

"Stand back a moment," said Norton Truscott. "Let
us see what is the matter with him."

Kneeling down, he asked Penny Bunn to point out
where he was injured, and to explain who had hurt
him.

"Behind—in the small of my back," gasped Bunn.

He was turned over as gently as possible, and there,
sure enough, was a wide gash in his clothing from the
small of his back downwards.

"I don't think you are hurt," said Norton Truscott.
"There is no blood."

"I distinctly felt the point of the knife," asserted
Bunn, struggling into a sitting position. "As I
emerged from the house I saw the villain crouching
in the shrubbery, swarthy, and villainous of eye.
'What are you doing there?' I asked him, sternly.
Instead of answering me, he whipped out a knife, and
struck at my heart. I instinctively wheeled about,
and *moved away* with the intention of asking if he had
a right to do this thing. It was then that I was
wounded."

"The main injury is in your clothing," said Norton.

Turning to Harry Barstow, he said, in an undertone:

"He has been attacked in a vicious manner, and
escaped a serious wound by a hair's-breadth. It
could not be one of your native servants."

"The wall is high," returned Harry, "and an intruder would have some difficulty in getting away."

"The house and grounds ought to be searched."

"Yes; let us do it."

They were divided into two parties; Harry undertaking to search the house, and Norton the grounds.

The latter was accompanied by Bob and Jack.
Bunn was with them, and Chippy went with the captain and the other youngsters.

In a quarter of an hour they reassembled by the
door of the house.

No signs of an intruder had been found.

"He is not in the house," said Harry Barstow.

"Nor in the grounds," said Norton. "Nor could a
man without assistance get over the wall. There are
no ladders, and the top of the wall is built projecting. It is sound everywhere. Your Eastern potentates
know how to guard themselves from intrusion."

"Did you speak to the gatekeeper, Haska Waffa?"

"No. He was at his post, but I thought it as well
not to show that we had occasion for alarm."

"I will go down and speak to him. Come with me,
Norton. The rest of you remain here. There is no
need for a crowd."

———

CHAPTER CCXXXVII.

HASKA WAFFA, THE INGENIOUS.

HASKA WAFFA stood within the gate, erect,
and with his hands clasped before him, and
his eyes raised to the stars. So absorbed was he in
thought that he did not hear approaching footsteps
until Harry Barstow and his friend were close upon
him.

With a start he brought his eyes to their level, and
immediately became a bowing machine.

"Haska Waffa," said Harry, "who has passed
through the gate to-night?"

"Only my lord and his friends, whose countenances
are as the light of the sun."

"You have not seen a stranger in the garden?"

"Am I not my lord's servant, and if one intruded
here, shall I not slay him?"

He bowed before and after each answer, and while
waiting to be addressed again was the image of
humble simplicity.

They left him, and when they were out of earshot
Norton said:

"That fellow is a liar."

"All the Eastern scoundrels are liars."

"True. But I am referring to the fact that there
has been a stranger in the grounds to-night, and
Haska Waffa knows it. Probably let him in and out
again."

"That is a serious suggestion, Norton."

"I make it seriously, because I believe it to be
founded on fact."

"But why should he deceive me?"

"Why should he be true to you if it is to his
interest to be otherwise? These Orientals may have
souls, but they have no conscience. Where did you
pick him up?"

"I took him with the house. He was a servant to
the departed pasha."

"And why did not the pasha take Haska Waffa
with him?"

"That is more than I can tell."

"Thereby hangs a tale, perchance. But we will not get excited over the matter, Harry, although it is as well to keep an eye open. Perhaps it is nothing more than some relative of Haska's coming round for anything that may be picked up. It is difficult to make certain."

"But the attempt to stab Bunn?"

"Oh, an Oriental stealing a doormat, will, if detected, attempt to hide his crime by taking a life. The breed of rascals are very particular about their insects—they will not kill one for money—but they will let daylight into a man and the life out of him for twopence."

Norton Truscott understood what he was talking about. It was as true as ever anything that ever was said or written. Insect and animal life is precious to the Oriental, but human existence is as cheap as dirt.

Nothing more was seen or heard of the vanished visitor that night. Precautions, however, were taken to prevent intrusion into the sleeping-chambers by bolting the doors. The windows had been barred long before by the suspicious pasha.

As a further precaution, Haska Waffa was shifted from his post on the following day, and another native put in his place pending the arrival of a couple of Jack-tars from the "Albatross," who would take turn and turn at keeping the gate.

With plenty of "'bacca" Jack would think little of the task, but would rather enjoy it.

But as nothing was really known against Haska Waffa it would have been unjust to dismiss him altogether, and he was appointed as attendant on the younger portion of the party.

In this capacity he accompanied them on the morrow in their further explorations of the town.

He was the most abject of servants. To answer a question without bowing his nose to the dust seemed impossible. It rather disgusted Jack, who liked politeness, but detested servility.

"I should like to cure him of ultra-civility," he said.

"Suppose we test him," suggested Bob.

"How?"

"Keep on asking him questions. Ask him if he knows the great Rajah without a name, for a start."

They were in one of the bazaars at the time, crowded with men of all nations, some on foot, some on donkeys, and all united in creating a state of the atmosphere that was stifling.

Haska Waffa had to keep up close so as not to lose "his young lords."

Of course he was not listening.

"Haska Waffa," said Jack, stopping short.

"My lord, son of the stars," replied Haska Waffa, stopping and bowing with a suddenness that led to his violently colliding with a strolling magnate in a turban, of fearful weight and size.

"Pig!" said the turban-wearer, with a gasp.

"If my young lord speaks shall I not answer him?" demanded Haska Waffa, who, like a true servant, felt that he could be insolent to anyone but his employer.

"May wild asses kick you to death!" hissed the turban-wearer, "and vultures prey upon the corpse of your mother!"

"Perhaps he hasn't a mother, old cock," suggested Bob, suavely.

"A curse upon you all!" snarled the turban-wearer.

"Certainly—why not? Wherefore?" assented Bob. "May your garment be one day subjected to a washing, and that bulging turban on your turnip head be cut up into pocket-handkerchiefs for the poor!"

There was something so fearfully novel in this anathema that the turban-wearer suffered immediate defeat. He retreated, followed by the laughter of Bob's companions. Haska Waffa demurely waited with his eye upon the ground.

"Haska Waffa!" said Jack again.

Haska Waffa bowed once more, and this time he sent the protruding portion of his anatomy into the stomach of a negro with a basket of fruit balanced on his head.

By performing some wonderful antics, the negro succeeded in saving himself from a fall, and his fruit from coming to the ground.

"Yah!" he cried, "you cussed *black man!*"

This was cool, considering that he was fully two hundred shades darker than Haska Waffa, and it gave unqualified delight to the youngsters.

"Slave!" hissed Haska Waffa.

This was also cool, when one comes to think that Haska Waffa was part of the goods and chattels of the pasha, and was let with the house and grounds.

The negro popped his basket down upon a board protruding from one of the shops of a bazaar laden with beastly little bits of earthenware, sham manufactures of a bygone Egyptian age.

Then he drew a knife from his sash and slashed at Haska Waffa, who skipped out of reach like a goat, and bowled over a man with a tray of dirty sweetmeats.

A regular riot ensued, but it only lasted two minutes; for one in authority, an Egyptian armed with a stout cane, appeared on the scene and belaboured all three, Haska Waffa, the nigger, and the sweetmeat man, until they howled for mercy.

None of the ordinary passers-by took the least notice of the performance, but went their way as if nothing unusual was going on.

When the official, policeman or gendarme, or whatever he was, had tired himself out, he left off, and the row was over.

Haska Waffa fell into a position behind his young

lords, the nigger grabbed his basket and glided away, and the sweetmeat man picked up his stock-in-trade from the dirt, brushed some with the sleeve of his garment, licked others, put the lot on his tray, and went on howling the price of his peerless wares.

"If you question that beast in this busy place again, Jack," said Don, "we shall have a revolution in the city."

Jack thought it would be as well to say no more for the present, and waited until they were in a quieter and more open thoroughfare, and then he went at it again.

"Haska Waffa."

"My lord—balm to my eyes," was the response.

"Have you heard of such a person as the Rajah?"

"Am I not as others?" asked Haska Waffa. "Shall not the sun shine upon me, though I am as one born of the dirt upon the ground?"

"Which means," said Bob, "that he has heard of the Rajah."

"Why can't these fellows give a straight answer?" asked Tom Drummond.

"Because they are crooked by nature," replied Bob.

"We should like to see the house where the great Rajah lives," said Jack.

"If my lords will go on to where the street turns, and condescend to go on the side that is the left, and bless the street by walking a few yards, behold! he shall see the abode honoured by the Rajah."

"A true-born Britisher," said Bob, "would have said, 'Fust turnin' to the left, guv'nor, and if you've the price of a pint o' beer about you, I should be glad on it.'"

The others laughed as they walked on to the next turning and entered a thoroughfare that was very narrow, but not meagre in the matter of buildings.

One side was nearly filled by a tall palace-like erection with a wide gate in the centre, by which stood two Nubians armed with swords.

"Let my young lords' eyes rest on the abode of the Rajah," said Haska Waffa, "and behold! he cometh forth soon, for the warning guards are at the gate."

They asked him what the warning guards were, and he told them they were men appointed to come forth and bid all idlers stand aside and not block the way of their master.

Naturally the listeners immediately felt a strong desire to take up a position near the gate.

Haska Waffa clasped his hands, rolled his eyes, and told them it would be perilous to do so, especially as his young lords were not armed.

"You are mistaken," said Jack; "we have our poppers, although we do not intend to use them unless to defend our lives."

They went on and took up a position opposite the guards, who warned them with angry gestures to stand aside. Before they could do more the gates were opened, and a carriage, drawn by a pair of magnificent horses, came out.

It was an open carriage, and seated in it was a man in the apparel of an Indian prince.

His dress was white, save a sash of gorgeous colours and his turban, which was scarlet.

Around his neck was a collar covered with diamonds and other precious stones. His turban had a featherette of priceless gems. Resting on the cushion by his side was a sword with a hilt that was blinding in its glitter to look upon.

He was a dark man with a beard and moustache, and eyes that rivalled the jewels in their flashing of light.

In front of the horses ran two swarthy natives, armed with stout sticks. Their office was to strike at all comers who dared to stand in the way of the great man's equipage so as to retard his progress by the fraction of a second.

Haska Waffa laid himself out upon the dust. The four friends stood quietly regarding the turn-out as it whirled past, raising a cloud of grit from the stony ground.

As soon as it was round the corner the two guards vanished within the palace, and the gates clanged to. Haska Waffa rose from the dust.

"It is good to see the mighty in their glory," he murmured; "my young lords have looked upon the Rajah."

"Yes," said Jack; "and if I have not seen him before, I'm a native of the Cannibal Islands."

"I thought there was something familiar in his face," remarked Don; "but I was most taken with the jewels. He has a fortune round his neck."

"Haska Waffa," said Jack.

"My lord," gasped that humble servitor, with his nose bobbed down to his knees.

"Go on ahead a bit. To the corner of the street."

"My lord, I fly."

"I wish he would walk; it would suffice," muttered Jack.

"Cast an eye on the flying Waffa," said Don, derisively.

He flew at the rate of about three miles an hour, and took up a position at the corner with one of his leery eyes upon them.

"Boys," said Jack—and how much he reminded them of the old Littlecote days at that moment!—"the Rajah wears a wonderful dress, and he has grown a beard; but for all that he is *Chunder Loo!*"

———

CHAPTER CCXXXVIII.

HOW CAN WE SNARE HIM?

NOW that Jack named it, the light of recognition came down upon them all. Without a doubt that hooked nose and eyes were the same as Chunder Loo's; and as for the beard, he had had ample time to grow it to its present extent—fairly long, thick, and dark.

The addition or removal of a beard makes a wonderful change in a man, even though he be so peculiar in the matter of physiognomy as Chunder Loo.

"I have no doubt," said Jack, "it is the scoundrel, and he did not perish with the Avishnus. I kept my eyes fixed upon his face, and fairly looked through him."

"Did he turn his face to us?" asked Don.

"Apparently not," answered Jack; "but do not come to a conclusion on that account, that he did not see us. The fellow is a hawk."

"Suppose he saw and recognised us?"

Jack shrugged his shoulders.

"If he saw us, he recognised us."

"We are changed," urged Tom Drummond. "He hasn't set eyes on us since we were boys."

"'Since we were boys, merry, merry boys together,'" hummed Bob. "We are old men now."

"There are two things to look at," said Jack, "in the event of his having recognised us. He may not think that we know who he is, or, believing that we do, decides upon treating us with contempt."

"He has been guilty of murder, and could be extradited," said Don.

"Not by us, I fear," said Jack. "Gubbles is the man to move in that matter, and he isn't here."

"I wonder where he is?"

"Still looking for the other murderer of his friend. He sent Mawston to the scaffold, but he won't rest until Chunder Loo follows him there."

"I wonder," mused Bob, "how Chunder Loo got hold of the tin to flash it about in this style?"

"He may be a mere adventurer," said Jack, "or somehow secured of the wealth of the Avishnus Walton told us about."

"We must have a general confab about what is to be done at home," suggested Don. "Our position is this: we are not personally concerned in the crimes of Chunder Loo, and Harry Barstow is in the same boat. The object for which he came out is attained, and he may not be disposed to interfere."

"We can but tell him Chunder Loo and the Rajah are one, and let him do as he pleases," said Tom.

"Well, boys," said Jack, "let us move along."

They strolled on up the street to where Haska Waffa was standing with his back towards them, wrapt in meditation.

"Attention!" said Jack, sharply.

The Egyptian skipped round, and bowed as he murmured: "My young lord, I am here."

"We want you to show us the sights, as our country cousins say at home. What is there to see?" asked Jack.

"All things," answered Haska Waffa, with an indescribable, half-smothered leer upon his face. "It is what my young lords wish to see."

"Well, name something."

"There are places, my lord, where the sinful play for money, and win and lose."

"At this time of the day?"

"Oh, young light of the sun, they play all day and all night; there is no ceasing. But in the daytime it is grave, quiet men who throw the dice and toss the cards one to another. At night come the men who get hot and angry, and use the knife and pistol sometimes."

"I don't see why we should not see these places," said Bob Stockton. "For my part, I am not inclined to be a gambler."

"Only duffers cannot be tempted without falling headlong into the pit," said Tom Drummond.

"Haska Waffa," said Jack, "lead on, and remember this: if you get us into a row, you will have to take your share of the fighting."

"Oh, son of the glistening stars," said Haska Waffa, with tears in his eyes, "it is not given to me to fight. In my youth, I tended the flocks and herds of my father on the banks of the Nile. I am a peaceful man, and I know not how to handle the weapons of war."

"All the worse for you," replied Jack. "We don't mind a bit of a shindy, but we are not eager for it. Go along!"

"And I obey my young lord," said Haska Waffa, "for is not my life thine?"

"Isn't he a beautiful fraud?" whispered Don.

The object of this complimentary remark was now moving on ahead, and they followed him. Jack was thoughtful for a time, and his companions, knowing his disposition, let him have his think out, and waited for him to speak. Presently he said:

"I think that something might be done by strategy. If Barstow has no objection, we could possibly snare a certain wild beast and convey it to England."

"One of Jack's ideas in the ova state," said Bob.

"It will hatch into something with life in it," returned Jack; "but for the present be mum. Haska Waffa is a child of ancient Egypt, a babe in the form of a man, but I mistrust him."

They spoke low, and it was hardly possible that Haska Waffa could hear; but his ears, which he had the animal power of moving, were thrown back, and he was certainly listening.

But he kept steadily on through a number of streets until he came to a bazaar, the narrowest and dirtiest the four friends had hitherto seen.

The shops exhibited nothing but odds and ends for sale, and although men went in and out, no visible business was done.

The customary haggling of the busier places was not heard. An ordinary shopkeeper will ask of the stranger a sum for an article equivalent to two pounds English money and end by taking a shilling, and then make a hundred per cent. profit. Nowhere, however, do they solicit custom.

A shopkeeper squats by the door and makes no sign until a question is put, or somebody falls over him.

"See, oh, great and good children of the earth," said Haska Waffa, "the place where men play."

"Which shop is it?" asked Jack.

"All shop," asked Haska Waffa, with touching simplicity, "all play. If you ask to buy they are deaf, or swear much."

"Well, show us into a den."

Haska Waffa entered the bazaar, in which were few people, all men and no women. There were no riders on the usual donkeys or mules. All were on foot.

Haska Waffa stopped in front of a door where a greasy Turk sat upon a mat, smoking a chibouque.

"Father of mighty men," he said, "here are four strangers who would look upon the joys of your abode."

The old Turk made no reply. He did not even remove the pipe from his lips, but simply held out his hand.

"I am not going to shake a paw that hasn't been washed for a week," said Jack.

"He desires not to shake," said Haska Waffa, "to your greeting he would but answer by reviling the father of my young lord. It is money for entrance he asks."

As it was only a small amount that was demanded, they paid it, and squeezed past the old Turk, who refused in his scorn of the infidel to budge one hair's-breadth for their convenience.

"Confound the old hound!" muttered Bob, "I should like to apply a stout shawl-pin to his anatomy and make him skip."

"Do nothing of the sort," advised Jack.

"For the present," said Bob, "I spare the malodorous skunk."

CHAPTER CCXXXIX.

THE GAMBLING-DEN.—AN OLD ACQUAINTANCE AT PLAY.

THE inside of the shop was barren of goods, unless a few mangy mats could be considered stock-in-trade. At the top end was a passage which Haska Waffa entered with the confidence of one who knew his way about.

There were several curtained doors from behind which murmurings could be heard, but Haska Waffa paused not until he reached the end of the passage, where he drew a curtain of extra heaviness and revealed a chamber of considerable size, built of stone and lighted from the roof by a number of round holes glazed with horn.

In the centre was a roulette-table, and dotted about other tables for cards or dice. Men were scattered about playing, and there was a good attendance on the rolling ball, but all were very quiet.

Not a word was uttered save by the croupier at the roulette-table, and no other sound but his voice heard beyond the whirr of the wheel, the sharp clicking of the dice, and the faint swish of the shuffled cards.

It was a matter of surprise to the friends that very few natives were in attendance. The company consisted almost entirely of men who, from an Egyptian standpoint, were foreigners.

There were Frenchmen, Germans, Austrians, Russians, and an Englishman or two—men of rather a low intellectual type, but well dressed and with plenty of money, judging by the way they risked it.

The floor of the chamber was covered with a thick carpet that completely deadened the footsteps. The whole place was a striking contrast to the meagre shop without.

The entrance of the four youths with their attendant might have been expected to cause surprise; but not a face was raised, not an eye turned towards them—absolutely no notice whatever was taken of them.

This was a relief, as it enabled them to take the part of spectators without joining in the play. They went up to the roulette-table and quietly watched the play.

The croupier spoke in French, his words falling from his lips in low but clear tones. The translation of his chief utterances, repeated again and again, is as follows:

"Roulette—a game of absolute chance, with no advantage to the table—all fair and square—you can back your number while the ball is rolling—until it stops money can be put down—no limit—what you like in silver, gold, or notes—notes must be English—make your game while the ball is rolling—seventeen is the number this time and on seventeen I pay.

Messieurs, this is an absolutely honest game with even chances."

Dumb, and intent upon the game, the players staked their money, and won or lost. Not a word escaped their lips ; but occasionally, when some man lost rather heavily, the dew of agony would burst out upon his forehead, or he would bite his underlip.

But that was all.

They had wonderful command of themselves, and there was something horribly fascinating in the mere looking on.

Suddenly a new-comer joined the ranks of the players on the opposite side of the table.

He was rougher in his manners than the rest, and was the first among the players to break the stillness.

" I want to stand here, if you don't mind," he said ; " it is my lucky spot."

The men on either side of him shifted without a word, so as to give him room to stand, and he began to play. Jack, meanwhile, had hastily motioned for his friends to move back a little out of sight.

It was Dirk Matthews who appeared thus unexpectedly upon the scene.

He wore the dress that he had on in the café when first seen in Alexandria by Jack and his companion, and it was now observable that the materials of which his apparel was made were of the best. No ordinary seaman or fisherman would have had such an outfit for every-day wear, or, indeed, for any purpose whatever.

Moreover, Dirk Matthews had a bag of gold, with fully a hundred pounds in it, which he ostentatiously placed upon the table. He did not cast a glance towards the youthful visitors. As with the rest, his whole attention was taken up with the table.

When he spoke of his lucky spot it was not without justification, for as soon as he began to play the tide of fortune was in his favour.

He backed the ten and won, then the eight and won, on eleven he lost, but came to the fore again with the twelve. So he went on, the contents of his bag swelling fast.

Meanwhile, Jack had been thinking of this strange meeting, and pondering on what to do.

It was not necessary, and might not be expedient, to make themselves known to him.

The rascal had committed an offence which he had expiated by being confined on a lone island. As he had had the good luck to be taken off, he could not be punished again.

The better course appeared to be to let him go his own way, and take no notice of him whatever ; but Jack was imbued with a conviction that Dirk Matthews could be made useful.

How was it that he had escaped from the island, and was in such a flourishing pecuniary condition ?

Might it not have some connection with Chunder Loo and his playing the Rajah ?

Jack touched Don on the arm, and motioned towards the door. The signal was passed on to the others, and they moved away. Haska Waffa, who had been in abject attendance all the time, waiting for the commands of his lords, lifted the curtain for them, and they passed out.

" Lead the way," said Jack. " I like to have you in front of me."

" You relieve the monotony of the landscape," said Bob.

Haska Waffa bowed and glided to the front, and in this order they passed on to the shop.

The old Turk was at his post, still smoking, and to save his chibouque from being trodden on or tumbled over by passers by, he had placed it behind him.

Bob Stockton saw his opportunity for revenge for the cool insulting ways of the old villain, and embraced it.

Quietly removing a cartridge from his revolver, he hung behind the rest.

When it came to his turn to go out he paused a fraction of a second, and in that short period of time lifted the lid of the chibouque, and inserted the cartridge, bullet downwards, in the glowing tobacco.

By this arrangement he had a minute or more of grace to get away ere the explosion took place.

Nothing very serious would come of it, but at any rate the Turk might get a scare which would rouse him from his lethargic condition.

Whether Haska Waffa made some sign whereby the old Turk knew that the youngsters had not been playing, is uncertain. Nobody saw him do it. But the fact remains, the old rascal in his heavy way cursed them under his breath.

If curses went for anything, or were worth breathing for their productive power, not one of the four would have been alive another hour.

By sunset they would have been ashes.

When they reached the outside of the bazaar, Jack made a proposition to his friends to go home and leave him behind for awhile.

" In the name of the Prophet," cried Don, " why?"

" I am going to waylay Matthews and have a word with him," said Jack.

" And get shot or stabbed for your pains."

" Not in the streets and in daylight. Now be good boys, and do as you are told."

" Appealed to in that way," murmured Bob, " we cannot but obey your commands."

If Haska Waffa was astonished to find himself short of one to guide, he did not show it. On being told to lead the way home he complied, after the usual bow and address, and Jack remained to watch for the coming forth of Dirk Matthews.

It was more or less risky of Jack to stay in the neighbourhood alone.

But for the daylight, he was surrounded by men, skulking in the surrounding houses, who would gladly have cut his throat for a florin, and thought no more of it than of smoking a pipe.

But the tender-hearted ruffians, acting up to the precepts of their faith, would not destroy vermin.

Jack sauntered up and down without taking his eyes off the entrance to the gambling-den. About three minutes had elapsed, when he heard a sharp crack, and saw the Turk spread-eagle himself upon the pavement, or what passed for such, in front of his door.

He did not say anything, but soon got upon his feet, and holding up a yard and a half of pipe-tube detached from the chibouque, regarded it for a minute with stolid amazement.

Then he went into the shop, and presently reappeared with the shattered chibouque in his hand.

Several of his neighbours and a few idlers gathered about him, until there was quite a little crowd.

Jack, knowing nothing of the nefarious act of which the jovial Bob had been guilty, strolled up to ascertain what was the matter.

The old Turk was holding forth in a mixture of languages, to meet the needs of his varied audience, on the affair.

He had bought the tobacco he had been smoking of a pig, one Hassan, whose father drove asses in the desert around the Pyramids, and the old Turk suspected from the price that the said tobacco was either stolen or cursed by witches.

He asked Hassan if it were not so, and the vendor had sworn on the Koran that it was neither one nor the other, but tobacco sold cheap to get another ass for a birthday present for Hassan's father.

"But the pig lied," said the old Turk, "and for it I will poison the water from which the asses drink. I will choke the dog Hassan with the broken pieces of my chibouque, which I have smoked these many years. It was a gift from the Khedive to my father."

Then he howled and cursed the innocent Hassan again, and showed the portions of his chibouque around as if they had been curious specimens of fossils or something in that way.

Everybody seemed to be much interested, and in the thick of a discussion as to nature of a fitting punishment for Hassan having attempted to choke or blow up so worthy a man as the old Turk, Dirk Matthews emerged from the gambling-house.

He was no longer elated, but depressed. In his hand he carried an empty bag, which he swung viciously to and fro.

The action told its own story. Dirk Matthews had been cleaned out.

Jack Ford returned to the street and awaited his coming. It was not until they were close to each other that their eyes met.

Dirk Matthews pulled up and stared hard at Jack, who looked at him calmly.

"Matthews," he said, "I should hardly have expected to meet you here."

"Nor I to see you, sir," replied Matthews. "But I suppose I have as much right to stand in this street as you."

"Certainly."

"Whatever I did has been worked out, and paid for up to the last farthing."

"I must admit as much," said Jack; "and it is not my intention to talk to you about the great mistake you made when on board the 'Belvedere.'"

"It was a mistake," said Matthews, "and I admit it. I made that 'ere mistake because I was a idjot. I thought I was fit to be a pirate-leader, but I ain't. I ain't a quarter strong enough in the murdering line for it."

"Matthews," said Jack, "tell me honestly—would you like to lead an honest life again?"

"I wants to get a decent living," answered Matthews, after a pause, "and to have my rights."

"Your rights?"

"Yes. When a man drops on a pile of hidden stuff, I suppose he's got a right to some of it, especially when there ain't no living owner."

"I should say so; but I should like to have that matter put clearer to me. Shall we walk a little way together?"

"Mr. Ford," said Matthews, "I ought to feel honoured, and I do, but it's too risky unless you are here alone."

"I am not here alone. The 'Albatross' is in the harbour."

Jack could see no use in concealing this fact, as it could be ascertained by anyone who chose to take the trouble to look for himself.

"Oh, she is, is she?" said Matthews, licking his dry lips. "Then, in course, the captain will be down on me."

"What did he say to you when you were sent to the island?"

"He said as how I were to do the best I could for myself."

"Did he not state as clearly as was necessary that it was to be your complete punishment?"

"He said as much as that."

"And is he a man to go back on his word?"

"No. He's a gentleman, if he is nothing else."

"Now, Matthews," said Jack, "think a moment, and tell me if you were not let off lightly? Would not Captain Barstow have been justified in hanging you?"

"He would."

"Well, then, you having got away, he has no grievance against you."

"No, but I have ag'in' other people. It's a matter I can't talk of here."

"Here is a quiet *café*. Suppose we go in together."

The *café* in question was in a street into which Jack and Dirk Matthews had strolled. It was the quietest time of the day, and it was absolutely empty. Even the waiters were taking a rest on the lounges, and one of them was asleep.

The entrance of two customers aroused the attention of a swarthy attendant, who came forward for an order. Dirk Matthews said he wanted wine, and Jack ordered a bottle for him. He asked for coffee for himself.

Jack was in no hurry. He had hooked his fish, and could take his time in playing him.

He waited till the wine and coffee were served, and then he went on with the conversation.

"You did not see us in that gambling-den?" he said.

"Saw who?" asked Matthews, staring.

"Myself and three friends, with a servant."

"Not me, sir. I never set eyes on you. When I get into a crib of that sort I don't see anything but the board and the money."

"We left you in your lucky corner."

"Lucky corner be hanged!" said Matthews. "It was so yesterday, and it started fair with me to-day, but it put me in a hole at the finish. I ran right out on wrong numbers.

"But you have a means of obtaining money?" hinted Jack.

"I'm 'lowed twelve pound a month," said Matthews, "and I took it yesterday. Last night I made a hundred on it. To-day, at this moment, I haven't change for sixpence."

"Who allows you that money?" inquired Jack.

"That's tellings."

"Confide in me, and it shall go no further."

"I dursn't do it yet", said Matthews; "but I'll put a case to you. Say you stopped on a island to starve, or go to the deuce, just as might happen, and you found a pile of stuff as was worth millions, wouldn't you consider it your own—specially if you knowed there was no real owner to it?"

"I think I should stick to it if I could," said Jack.

"Naterally, sir. But supposing it was stole from you in the night, and you, when looking for it, was press-ganged on board a pirate and compelled to serve—you would think that hard?"

"I would not serve. I would die first!"

"Different people has different notions, accordin' to breed, sir," said Matthews. "I, being a ruffian, thinks I'll sarve fust and git away when I can. But,

supposing, when you was aboard, you got a inkling that the stuff you was robbed of was there—you would speak on it, maybe?"

"I should like to, but probably I should say nothing, and endeavour to get my own again in some way."

"Just my notion at the time, sir," said Matthews, as he drank his wine. Jack filled his glass again. "Well, I got the inkling, and proved it was so. Moreover, there was a party aboard, a great friend of the pirate, and *he'd* got the stuff that will run inter millions. I said nothing until I was pretty safe here ashore, and then I opens my mouth."

"With what result?"

"They cussed me at first, and would have had me throttled or summat, but I said as I'd made purwision for others to go in for my rights if I was put away, and then they says, 'Here's three pun a week, and if you like to take it, and lay close and quiet, it's yours.' I lay close and took it."

"But," said Jack, as he replenished the glass, which Matthews emptied at a gulp that expressed his feelings—"you are not satisfied?"

"I should think not, sir! Satisfied? No, I'll have a bit of my own if I dies for it!"

Jack had got the whole story in outline now. He understood who the friend of Matthews was, and the nature of the "stuff," the loss of which hung so heavily on his heart. The question now was, how far would it be advisable to trust Matthews? He decided not at all.

"Well, Matthews," he said, "as a man for whom I felt sorry for having done a foolish thing, I was not sorry to see you alive and well, and if I could help you to get your own I would. Perhaps I may be able to do so."

"You are a bold young gentleman," said Matthews, hoarsely, "and can do a lot when you put your shoulder to the wheel. I'll think over things a bit afore I tell you more, and then if I thinks we can work together and get at the stuff, then there is half for you and half for me, so help me——"

He finished with a blow upon the table with his fist, and Jack filled his glass, and so emptied the bottle.

"I must be going now," said Jack, rising, "and will leave you to think the matter over. You know the pasha's house down by the chief fort? It has a wall entirely round it."

"I can find it," answered Matthews, "for I've a notion where it is."

"Be outside there to-night at nine o'clock, and let me know what you will do."

"Very good, sir."

"If you decide not to confide in me the name of your friend, you will make a mistake, but that will be your look-out. If you will do as I wish you, then you may live to be thankful. Good-day."

"Good-day, sir."

Jack sauntered out of the café, and Dirk Matthews was left alone. He filled his pipe, and sat smoking and sipping his wine until the glass was empty. Then he would have renewed the bottle, but he had no money.

At length he arose.

"I'll give the Rajah a chance of doing me justice," he muttered, "and if he don't, I'm blowed if I don't let daylight into him."

CHAPTER CCXL.

THE RAJAH'S IDEA OF JUSTICE.

THE afternoon was pretty well on as Dirk Matthews turned into the street. The heat of the day was waning, and the society of the town coming forth to enjoy the air.

The beggars were much in evidence also, and every form of human distortion of limb and general malformation was about soliciting aid from the charitable.

Dirk Matthews was solicited as he walked along to assist the afflicted, and he gave all he had—a hearty curse, for which he received from the sufferers quite as good as he sent, with a trifle over.

Doggedly he pursued his way to the abode of the Rajah, and rang the great bell at the gate. It was responded to by a negro, who recognised him as an old acquaintance, and grinned him a welcome.

"Is the Rajah at home?" asked Matthews.

"He am, sar," answered the negro.

"Will you tell him I am here and wish to speak to him on a matter of great importance?"

The negro was doubtful if he could do so, but would see, and Dirk Matthews was left cooling at the gate for a full half-hour ere he appeared again.

"The Rajah see you, sar," he said.

"I thought so," said Dirk Matthews, as he swaggered through the gate opened to admit him.

There was a broad archway on the other side that led to a courtyard. The house was a square, with most of the windows on the inner side.

In the centre of the courtyard was a fountain, playing with a cooling effect upon the atmosphere. On the marble pavement a number of armed men, richly attired, lay about at their ease.

They were mostly of the Bedouin and dervish class, dark-skinned and ferocious in look, men ready to slay upon the slightest provocation or pecuniary inducement, unscrupulous fanatics, to whom all unbelievers were as dogs.

They scowled at Dirk Matthews, who returned their angry glances to the full value as he crossed the square to a door on the opposite side. A doorway admitted him to the Rajah's portion of the building.

Into a passage and up a broad staircase covered with carpet they pursued their way. Pictures on the walls, rich hangings, wondrous plants and flowers —signs of wealth everywhere. So on to a suite of rooms on the first floor, and in one of them sat the Rajah, smoking a hookah.

He was not alone.

Beside him sat the little pirate captain who had taken Dirk Matthews into his service when he was brought from the island.

On the right and left stood half a score of negroes, mutes, who had suffered all the barbarous mutilations sanctioned by the Turk for his attendants' security from doing evil.

Dirk Matthews entered with a swagger, but on encountering the eye of the Rajah, better known to us as Chunder Loo, his heart sank into his shoes.

"Pestro," said Chunder Loo, "he is here."

"I behold him," was the calm reply.

"Come nearer, most excellent Matthews," said Chunder Loo, in his oiliest tones, "and tell me what has brought you hither so soon again."

"I've blew all my tin," said Matthews, with affected ease, "and thought as you might dub up a little more."

"He has spent his allowance," remarked Chunder Loo to his companion. "You hear him, Pestro?"

"Perdition! yes," was the rejoinder.

"And how have you disposed of your monthly allowance?" asked Chunder Loo.

"I gambled it away," replied Matthews, sullenly. "It ain't much for a man to live on, and I thought as I would add to it."

"You have grasped at the shadow and lost the substance," smoothly remarked Chunder Loo, "and because you have done so you think I ought to find you with some more money."

"You wouldn't miss it, seeing all you've got which I found fust, and by every law of right ought to have it."

"Pestro," said Chunder Loo, "something must be done for our persistent friend."

"I think so," replied the pirate chief. "It would be a pity to wholly disappoint him. Say, what shall it be?"

Pestro added something in a low tone, and Chunder Loo motioned to the mutes standing near.

In a moment they had seized the astounded and alarmed Matthews, and were divesting him of the arms he carried—a brace of revolvers and a knife.

"What the deuce is the game?" he demanded.

Another sign from Chunder Loo and his arms were bound.

"If I don't——"

A third sign, and his legs were grasped and his feet turned soles upwards. In turn his shoes and stockings were whipped off.

Then Dirk Matthews began to realise what was in store for him, and he set up a howling for mercy that could have been heard half over the place, despite the thickness of the walls and the closely-covered doors.

One of the dumb slaves brought out a stout, pliable cane, and, on receiving the necessary sign, laid on with all his might, and gave Dirk Matthews a bastinadoing that would have lamed a rhinoceros.

He begged, he implored, he howled, he shrieked, but the arm of the dark wielder of the cane did not flag.

And Chunder Loo sat looking on with a quiet air of thorough enjoyment, while Pestro twirled his moustache and grinned delightedly.

It was a cruel, remorseless punishment, and when it was completed, Dirk Matthews lay gasping and groaning on the carpet, suffering indescribable tortures.

"Put on his shoes and stockings," signed Chunder Loo.

It was done, the stockings being drawn on, and the shoes squeezed over the swollen feet.

"You will be placed outside the gate of this—*my* palace," said Chunder Loo, with sudden ferocity, "and if you come howling here again for money I'll have your feet cut off!"

"Chopped," added Pestro, "with an axe, and dipped into boiling pitch to stop the bleeding. It was the good old way of amputation. A pity it has been superseded by the more namby-pamby art of surgery."

The miserable Dirk Matthews was picked up. He ceased to groan, and he fixed his eyes on the face of the mad fiend who had commanded him to be tortured with a look that it would have been wise to interpret.

But Chunder Loo, careless in the belief of his impregnable position, allowed Matthews to be carried forth.

What did it matter if he went and complained to the authorities? Would not the rich man prevail? Apart from his being poor, Dirk Matthews was an infidel dog, and would be laughed to scorn.

But it did dawn on Pestro that it would have been better to dispose of him in a more complete way.

"Chunder," he said, as the mutes disappeared with their burden, "why not have sent him to the Land of Eternal Silence?"

"It will do the dog good to live on in remembrance of to-day," answered Chunder Loo.

"You forget that your enemies are here."

"A straw for them—a breath of air! Who cares? How can Matthews go to them when he mutinied, and would have murdered them if he had got the chance? Hasn't the hound boasted of it?"

"Still," urged Pestro, "those who are silent for ever, cannot speak."

"Fear not," said Chunder Loo; "I have a plan—a net prepared, into which I will get *all*—the young, the old—of those who had a hand in destroying my people."

"Your people? Pshaw! Have you not got all that you longed for? Did not the fools play the game for you?"

"Not of their own free will," said Chunder Loo; "but is not any peg good enough to hang our revenge upon? *I hate them all!* Enough, good Pestro. Let us have the dancing-women in and have a good time. Merry to-day and dead to-morrow—that is the luck of man."

———

CHAPTER CCXLI.

BUNN AND CHIPPY MAKE A NIGHT OF IT.

"CHIPPY," said Penny Bunn, "I have solicited, like the ordinary domestic, for an evening out, and have obtained permission to take it to-night."

"I'll go with you just to see that you don't get into mischief," replied Chippy.

Bunn smiled serenely.

"I am a man of the world, and can take care of myself," he said; "nevertheless, your society will be welcome. Excuse me, old friend, but are you ever given to gallivanting?"

"What's that?" asked Chippy.

"Hovering round the girls," answered Bunn, with a smirk and wink of much meaning.

"Can't say ever I did much of it," said Chippy, after thinking a bit.

"Prior to my marriage with Miriam," said Bunn, "I was as gay a dog as you would meet; but union with a sweet but very decided woman, acted as a deterrent. Now I am to all intents and purposes a free man."

"If you are going a-galliwanting to-night," said Chippy, "I think you had better go alone."

"I have nothing definite in view," said Penny Bunn.

He spoke with the air of a roaming gallant—a gay young dog who might, or might not, go forth to conquer and deceive. Chippy believed in him with his whole heart.

"I see," he said, "I must go with you to keep you straight."

When the evening came, the sun had gone down, and the stars were in the sky, they started together, both really about as fit to roam about Alexandria by night as the two babes were to wander in the wood.

Even Chippy, with all his experience, retained much of his original simplicity.

When they got to the gayer part, with the *cafés* lighted up, and the hordes of cosmopolitan people passing to and fro, Bunn paused to contemplate the scene.

"It is a dream," he murmured, "or a realisation of the Arabian Nights. I feel like a modern Ali Baba."

"*You*, with all your learning, feel like a barber!" said Chippy; "a man busting, as I may say, with learning, taking on the feelings of a shaver."

"You misunderstand me," said Bunn; "the Baba I refer to is an historical personage—B, a, b, a, is the way it was spelt. By strategy he acquired the property of forty thieves, accumulated in the usual way. Now, here comes a fair maid, veiled and shrinking. See me fix her with my eye."

The fair maid in question was an old harridan veiled according to the custom of her people—she belonged to a desert tribe—on her way home after a rather unsuccessful day of begging.

Bunn put on a pensive air as she approached, and Chippy, in a gasping state, waited to see the result of his lover-like bearing.

"Ahem!" coughed Bunn. "Fine evening."

The woman stopped and regarded him curiously through her veil. Her knowledge of English was slight, but she guessed from the tone that Bunn was in a pleasant mood.

Thrusting out her hand, she softly said, "Backsheesh."

It was the native way of asking for relief, a sort of "Give me a penny, sir," but Bunn did not realise her meaning. He gently and reverently took the skinny hand and raised it to his lips.

It was such a staggerer for the old woman, that for the moment she was incapacitated from saying or doing anything but stare. Penny Bunn, glowing with the conviction that he had made a conquest, went a little further.

"May I ask you to partake of coffee," he said, "or of any other native drink to your taste?"

Limited as her knowledge of English was, the old woman had mastered some of its more offensive expressions.

"Fool!" she hissed; "you laugh. Pig!"

"Eh?" exclaimed the startled Bunn, "what did you say?"

"Worm! Dog!" spluttered the old woman; "you English! You much laugh at me——Abdul Hoolah!"

She called out the last two words, and in response a battered old ruffian, a true son of the desert in difficulties, glided up.

He was attired in dirty white garments, crowned with a turban in which he apparently slept; he had a sword by his side rusty but formidable, and in his sash two old-fashioned pistols about the size of blunderbusses.

"Lelah," he cried, "light of my eyes! What is it with these strangers?"

The old woman said something to him in Arabic, and he clapped one hand upon his sword, holding out the other, saying:

"Backsheesh!"

"That's blooming cheek," said Chippy. "Hit him in the eye, Bunn."

"I am not aggressive," said Bunn, mildly.

The veil of the old woman had blown aside for a moment, giving him a glimpse of her withered, hideous face. All his gallantry went down to the heels of his boots.

"If you won't, I will," said Chippy, who had a fair amount of pluck.

Abdul Hoolah was conveniently looking at Bunn at that moment, and was therefore not prepared to ward off the blow. Chippy hit him in the eye, and he hit him hard.

Moreover, he sent him flying so that he collided with the old woman, and the pair fell into the road together.

"Let us bolt!" said Chippy, hurriedly.

He laid hold of Bunn's arm and hurried him round a convenient corner. There was a *café* a few yards down, and into this place of refuge they hastened.

It was well filled with people, but there were vacant seats, one of which Chippy took possession of.

"Sit down, old man," he said, "and get your wind. Keep as quiet as you can, and turn your back to the door."

"Chippy," gasped Bunn, "you have saved my life. What a murderous old scoundrel!"

"The gal's father, perhaps."

"She was more likely his mother, Chippy. The woman was a hundred, if a day; but the sex were deceivers ever. Heigho!"

"I should turn up galliwanting here," advised Chippy; "it can't pay. That old man would have put his sword through you in a minute if I hadn't hit him, and he'll do it now if he comes across you."

"You think so?" murmured Bunn, faintly.

"Odds on it," said Chippy. "The amount of venom in that old man would fill a bucket. I knows the breed."

"Under the circumstances," said Bunn, "perhaps it would be politic to remain here until the old gentleman has retired for the night."

"Perhaps he don't go to bed at all," suggested Chippy, "not having one. We must keep our weather eye open for him."

"Coffee, shentlemon?" said a French waiter, gliding up.

"I think I should like something stronger. Brandy, for instance."

"One corfee," said Chippy, "and a ody wee."

"Pardon?" queried the waiter.

"Brandy," said Chippy, louder. "The thickhead,"

he added, as the waiter glided away, "not to know his native drink brandy, is called ody wee!"

"O. D. V.," murmured Bunn—"oh, yes, of course."

A dose of coarse strong brandy restored the troubled nerves of Bunn, and in a quarter of an hour or so he proposed to start afresh.

"No more galliwanting, though," warningly said Chippy.

"No more, certainly not, in this country, where every woman seems to be eighty years old on the day she is born."

They went out cautiously, peering up and down the street in search of Abdul Hoolah, who had vanished.

So they went back to the scene of their original adventure, which was now thronged with people.

There was music, too, of a sort, stringed instruments played in a fashion that entitled the performers to ten years' penal servitude—singers whose voices had all the rasping charms of the East.

The inevitable seller of sweetmeats was also much in evidence.

Whatever may have been the individual offensiveness of the gathering, as a whole the scene was pleasing to the eye. Still, it had its drawbacks.

"I should think," said Chippy, as they strolled along, "that this would be a lovely country for people not blessed with noses."

"There is certainly an aroma in the air," replied Bunn, "to which the British nasal organ has not been educated."

"Abdul Howler," said Chippy—"quick! Cut it!"

Yes, there was the old man not two yards from them, soliciting arms from a languid tourist who was groping in his pocket for a small coin.

The ferocious son of the desert was unconscious of the vicinity of the pair, and they got out of the neighbourhood undiscovered.

From there they went to a bazaar, which, being narrower than the street, was more inconveniently crowded.

"There is an accession of native odours here," said Bunn, "allied to additional safety. Chippy, I feel that in the old scoundrel who haunts us I have met my fate."

"I don't tumble," said Chippy. "What do you mean?"

"Simply, that the feud between us will only end in his life or mine being sacrificed."

"Then the old man's got to go, for he ain't of much account, and the life of a man of learning like you is of wally to the country. Here's a shop where they sell knives. We had better buy one each."

"Surely you would not slay him?" said Bunn.

"Not me, but you must," said Chippy. "Now come in. What's the price of these knives, mister?"

The "mister" was a greasy half-breed of some sort, probably half-Turk, half-Arab. He signified that any of his knives would be cheap at two-pounds-ten apiece, British money.

"We must find a cheaper place than this," said Chippy.

They were about to go away, but the owner of the shop detained them.

He would take half that sum—a quarter—for he loved all Englishmen, and looked on them as his brothers, and then with a rush he came down to seven shillings apiece for the knives, and there he stranded.

"They are really good stuff," said Chippy, testing the spring of the blade of one he held in his hand. "Not dear for out here. All right, mister."

He paid for them in Egyptian money, but, in reckoning up, the dealer succeeded in cheating them out of a sum equivalent to three farthings, and was happy. Chippy shut up his knife and put it into his pocket. But he advised Bunn to have his open, ready for action.

"Since it's got to be him or you," he said, "we can't allow of any hesitation. When you meet, stick him right away, and run."

"Certainly," murmured Bunn, dismally. "I suppose they hang here for murder?"

"They don't even arrest you—sticking is free," asserted Chippy; and in the simplicity of his heart he believed it.

Penny Bunn was not qualified to take part in warfare, general or private. With the open knife in his pocket, he sauntered along by the side of his friend, oppressed with a sense of being in peril of his life.

He could take no joy in anything. The varied scene, that at another time would have had a charm for him, was now a dreary blank. The evening he had hoped would be so bright with joy was as dark as the lifeless desert on a moonless night, with a sandstorm raging.

"Backsheesh!"

The voice came from the rear, but Bunn knew it. It was that wretched old woman again. He started forward, but was detained by Chippy grasping his arm.

"What is the matter, old man?" he asked.

"She—behind us—with her beastly backsheesh!" groaned Bunn. "The old man can't be far away."

Chippy looked round, and saw the old woman right enough, but her spouse was not near.

"Backsheesh!" she said again, in a manner that showed she did not recognise Chippy or his friend.

Before Chippy could reply with a gift or a few appropriate words of refusal, there was a sudden commotion among the crowd, a pressing to the right and left, and cries were heard of warning and alarm.

Everybody seemed to be anxious to get behind somebody else, and somehow Bunn and Chippy got hustled into the front rank of a lane formed in the roadway.

Then came two runners along, wielding pliant canes, and striking to the right and left, without hurting anyone unless they kept doggedly in the way.

Close behind them appeared the carriage of the Rajah, and Chunder Loo in all his glory burst upon their view.

Penny Bunn was endowed with a sort of shrewdness of observation that was near ability. He could see through a disguise fairly well, and he recognised in the richly-attired potentate his old assistant.

Their eyes met, and two persons of such strong individuality in the front of the ranks of the motley crew could not escape the watchful eyes of Chunder Loo.

A malevolent smile wreathed itself about his lips. A word from him, and the carriage was pulled up short.

The wielders of the cane hastened to the door of the carriage to receive orders.

"Back!" said Chunder Loo.

The carriage wheeled round and dashed back again, the crowd closing in behind it, commending the richness of the turn-out—for wealth in the East commands almost as much respect as it does in the West, and people will endure its overbearing power with resignation or sycophantic gratitude, just as they do here.

"Chippy," said Bunn, "did you recognise him?"

"Who?" asked Chippy.

"The fellow in the carriage."

"No."

"It was your Great Ruler and my Chunder Loo."

"Bunn," said Chippy, hurriedly, "let us get home, and never come out again while he is about. I can't understand how he came here such a flowery swell, but in any state he is dangerous."

"But how can he harm us?" urged Bunn.

"Any way and every way," replied Chippy. "Now, Bunn, do not be a fool. Home, I say!"

"All in good time," said Bunn, suddenly developing one of his peculiar gifts of doing the wrong thing; "we are perfectly safe. The town is open to all. Let us have something else to drink."

"Better go without it."

"One more, Chippy."

"Well, one, and then we will clear out."

They looked about them for a *café*, and one being near, they entered it. Scores of people were there, drinking, smoking, chatting, and playing dominoes.

"Brandy for two," said Chippy to an attendant.

It was served them, and they partook of it. Chippy was in a state of nervous terror, and again he urged Bunn to hasten.

"You don't know that warmint," he said; "if he spotted us he will be up to mischief."

"He certainly stared at *me*," replied Bunn, jauntily, "and I fancied he quailed under my eye. Probably he fears exposure——"

"Oh, dear!" gasped Chippy, "I can't help saying it, Bunn, but you are a fool! That Chunder Loo is a demon, I know. He fears nothing."

He took Bunn by the arm, and led him out of the *café*. They paused for a moment, uncertain of their way home.

"To the right," said Chippy.

"To the left," said Bunn. "I am not likely to make a mistake. The bump of locality is abnormally developed on my head."

"Something is fully developed there," muttered Chippy; "but as I ain't certain, I'll be guided by you."

So to the left they went, passing through the crowd as quickly as possible, and unconsciously exciting some attention by their haste.

Bunn affected to be at his ease, but Chippy made no secret of his apprehension, and his eyes were wandering here and there as they hastened along.

"Yes," said Bunn, as they came to a turning; "I am right. This is the way we came."

"I don't remember this street," said Chippy.

"A good bump of locality," said Penny Bunn, "never deceives its owner. But if you like, we can ask our way."

"No; if you know the road, let us go along. Who are these fellows?"

Half a dozen men lounged up and passed them. They were all armed, and had the appearance of being members of an Arab tribe.

"They are simply loafers," answered Bunn. "Chippy, old man, you see a foe in every post."

"Well, I know what Chunder Loo can be guilty of."

It was a quiet street they were in, and Chippy hurried his companion on. Penny Bunn was in a very humorous frame of mind.

"It is absolutely funny," he said.

"What is?" asked Chippy, shortly.

"This dreadful anxiety of yours. Why——"

The men who had passed them now suddenly wheeled about, and faced the two friends. As one man, they whipped out their swords, and there was a hissing command for them to stand.

"I feared it!" cried Chippy. "Bunn, you are a most exasperating ass!"

Bunn had no power to reply, nor would Chippy have heard him if he had spoken, for some person, creeping up behind, enveloped each in a heavy cloth. Ropes were cast about them, drawn tight, and knotted, and then the staggered pair were lifted up and borne away.

CHAPTER CCXLII.

DIRK MATTHEWS KEEPS HIS APPOINTMENT.

PRECISELY at nine o'clock, Jack Ford emerged from the gate of the grounds around the Pasha's mansion, and looked about for Dirk Matthews.

But he was not there, nor anyone in view.

Ahead lay the fort in outline, silhouetted against the glittering sea. To the right, minor forts, and to the left the shimmer of the lights of the town.

"He will not come—the blackguard has deceived me," Jack muttered; "but something is coming here What is it—a dog?"

Creeping along by the wall, slowly and painfully, was a dark object that would have scared a more nervous spectator.

It bore no resemblance to any man or beast that Jack had ever seen, so clumsy and uncouth, and of no particular shape.

Jack felt for a weapon to defend himself, if need be, and kept his eyes upon it.

Slowly it came near, and gradually took the shape of a man crawling on his hands and knees.

"One of the begging monstrosities of this place," thought Jack; "but what is the horrible creature doing here?"

He shuddered, in spite of his courage, for he had a natural loathing of all things hideous, especially distortion of the human form divine.

Still he would not retire. If a beggar, he would bestow a few petty coins upon the creature, and receive the customary blessing.

Then the shape by degrees took a more recognisable form, and he was able to distinguish that it was Dirk Matthews.

He hurried up to him, and the wretched man pulled up, and lay huddled against the wall.

"You have met with an accident, Matthews?"

"Accident! No, sir. It isn't an accident. It is one of the Rajah's bits of amusement."

"What has he done to you?"

"I went to him for a bit of my own—it is that, and nothing less—and he set his mutes on to bastinado me. Look at my feet, sir! I've had to cut off my boots that they forced on me, and wrap 'em up in rags. They are red-hot now. They ache horrible —they smart, they shoot, and I suffer in a way that would send a dog howling mad."

"Tell me all about it," said Jack.

Dirk Matthews told his story, interlarded with a few oaths that came naturally from the lips of such a man. Jack listened to it with a certain amount of sympathy, but on the whole he was not sorry, for he saw that now he could rely on Matthews to aid him in bringing Chunder Loo to grief.

"After this," he said, as Dirk Matthews finished, with a bitter invective on the head of Chunder Loo, "you will never again be lured into his service?"

The answer was a look and clenched hands raised. Jack was satisfied.

"Something must be done for you," he said. "To-night, as it happens, Captain Barstow is not at home, which favours a plan I have thought of. The house in which we reside has dozens of empty rooms in it —whole suites, in fact—and if I can get you in there quietly, you can lay up at your ease until you have recovered from your injuries."

"Bless you, sir!" said Matthews, fervently.

"I do it for a purpose of my own," said Jack, candidly, "although I must in any case have felt sorry for you. In return, you will have to do something for me."

"I'll do anything for you."

"Do you know much of the Rajah's palace? I call him the Rajah, as by that name he seems to be known here. But he is no more of a Rajah than one of the lowest of Indian caste."

"I've been about the place a good deal," replied Matthews, "all over it, I may say."

"Could you draw me a plan of it?"

"I could chalk it out on a board, or pencil it on paper, sir."

"What I want is a rough sketch of the various rooms, who occupies them, and the way to get to any of them quietly."

"I can help you to that, sir," said Matthews, brightening, "and I can guess who you want. What's he done?"

"If he can be got to England he will be hanged for murder."

"Get him there," said Matthews, in thrilling tones, "and if I can only stand in the street and have the joy of seeing the black flag go up for him, you may hang me the next minute! I don't want to live for more than that."

"It will be a tough bit of work," said Jack, "but I think it may be done. Stay here a moment. I have something to say to the sentry at the gate."

He went up to the door and knocked. The gate was opened by Startop, who was one of the men that replaced Haska Waffa, deposed.

"Startop," said Jack, "you know me, I believe?"

"Lord love you, sir," answered Startop, "yes, and your friend Mr. Peebles, and the other gentlemen. I knows you all as some of the best going."

"Well, I am going to do something extraordinary."

"There wouldn't be much that is extraordinary in that, sir."

"Thank you for the compliment, Startop. I want to smuggle a cripple into the house, and not a word to be said about it."

Startop stared, his eyes gradually emerging from his head, until they threatened to leave it altogether.

"And that cripple is Dirk Matthews."

Startop passed his hand across his brow. There was an unreal element about Jack's statement.

"I have a great object and a good one in view," continued Jack; "what it is you will know one day. Meanwhile you must take my word that everything is right."

"I am not to report to the captain, sir?" asked Startop, recovering himself a little.

"No."

"Not to Mr. Darnley?"

"To no one, not even to my special friends of my own age. I have a scheme I want to mature alone, although I shall want help to carry it out, and I am sure I shall want you."

"But Dirk Matthews, sir? Wasn't he—he left on that 'ere island?"

"Yes, undoubtedly. But he got away and is here, and I want to make use—good use—of him. Come, Startop, time presses. I want you to say if you will do as I wish, absolutely?"

"All right, sir," said Startop, resolutely; "if it's your job, it can't be anything wrong. I'm in it."

"And you will keep my secret."

"Faithfully, sir."

"Then come and help me to get him in, I may tell tell you the secret of his injuries. He has been crippled by a brutal bastinadoing."

"That's a whacking on the feet with sticks, ain't it, sir?"

"Yes."

"It's a warmint Turkish trick. I've heerd on it. I'd like to bastinader some of 'em somewhere else. I'll back that when I'd done with 'em they wouldn't ax for a hard seat for six months."

Startop was not very warm in his greeting of Matthews; that could hardly be expected; but he assisted him into the grounds, and Jack Ford went on to see if the way was clear to the house.

The seniors of the party were gone to the "Albatross" to see into certain matters, but the other youngsters were about somewhere, and Jack did not mean to take them into his confidence just at present.

His motive for this reticence was a very unselfish one. If bringing Matthews into the place resulted in any form of fiasco, Jack would take all the blame.

By-and-by, when there was a prospect of success in carrying out his plans, his friends should have a share in the profit of it.

The abode of the pasha was, as we have pointed out, of a very roomy nature. There were several entrances to it for the inmates and servants, and in the security of being in an enclosure, these were generally left open.

Selecting one rarely used, Jack went into the house and up to a suite of rooms wherein none of the house rarely, if ever, now set foot.

This was a fact testified to by the neglected, dusty condition of the furniture.

What with the seclusion of it and the curtained recesses, of which there were at least a dozen, ample hiding-place was afforded for Dirk Matthews, if he could be got there unseen.

The suite was, indeed, one that had been, when occupied, set apart by its owner for guests.

It lacked nothing, and Dirk Matthews would have a regal lodging, the like of which he had never known before.

And into this place Jack and Startop succeeded in smuggling him.

The only light came from the moon through the windows as he lay down in one of the recesses on a pile of cushions.

"I'm more than thankful," he said. "I shall soon get well here."

"I will bring you some food before I go to bed," said Jack.

He went back with Startop to the gate, well pleased with being so far successful in his undertaking.

Jack meant to capture Chunder Loo, and when he had him secure, to make an appeal to Harry Barstow to permit of his being taken to England in the "Albatross."

Once there, the authorities would take charge of him pending his trial for murder.

"I should hesitate to hang a man, as a rule," thought Jack, "but not Chunder Loo.

"Startop," he said, aloud, "you have done me a service. But if you have any doubts——"

"Doubts, sir? Not a bit of it!" interposed the sailor. "I'm with you, sir, whatever may be the game, if I lose my life on the job!"

"I will not threaten you as to what may happen if you are not faithful," said Jack, "but I will say this, that it is your only chance of living henceforth in safety. Behave honestly, and you will do much to retrieve the past."

Then Jack left him to his reflections, which were, on the whole, more pleasant than they had been for many a day.

CHAPTER CCXLIII.

PENNY BUNN AND HIS OLD ENEMY.—FIENDISH FUN.

THERE are certain things one ought to hesitate ere attempting to describe, and one of them is the feelings of Penny Bunn when he found himself captive in unknown hands.

And it was all his own fault, too. That was what troubled him bitterly. He was so very sure there was no danger that he had lingered while his enemy got ready the trap and caught him.

He had suffered much during his varied career, but only when with the python in the home of the Avishnus had he experienced anything like what he endured now.

His captors hurried him along, and must presently have come to some building, for there were challenges —presumably from sentries—and a clanging of opening and shutting of gates.

Then more hurrying on, and finally a stoppage, when he was put upon his feet and the muffling garments about him removed.

He was conscious at first only of a blinding light, which presently sank down to the glare of a lamp suspended from the ceiling of a magnificent chamber, fitted up in the Oriental style.

On either side were ranged a number of negroes, in white apparel, and armed with drawn swords. They stood motionless, the only sign of life they showed being an occasional shifting of their dark eyes.

The men who had brought in the captive were of a different nation. They were Bedouins—the wild, fierce, ungovernable tribe of the desert. Penny Bunn mechanically counted six of them standing in close attendance upon him.

He looked for his companion in misfortune, Chippy Bunyons, but he was not there.

Bunn would have speculated on his fate if he had not been so miserably apprehensive about his own.

The grim silence of the room was oppressive.

Not a word was said, not even so much as a whisper exchanged. Like the deaf and dumb warriors spoken of in an ancient story, the swarthy negroes and Bedouins stood awaiting the coming of one who was to arrange the punishment for the prisoner.

Presently he came, with a dozen armed men as an advance guard, and a companion by his side.

Penny Bunn knew Chunder Loo too well. Pestro up to that moment had been a stranger to him.

Chunder Loo was clad in a rich silken garment that about the collar and wrists blazed with jewels. By his side hung a sword that was worth a fortune. Pestro was more simply attired, but in his scarf and on his fingers rich and rare diamonds gleamed in the eyes of the looker-on.

"Bring the fellow forward," said Chunder Loo, as he subsided into an easy position upon the pile of cushions at the upper end of the room. Pestro remained standing, by choice, as his air betrayed.

The prisoner was pushed forward several feet until he was within a few paces of Chunder Loo.

"Well, P.Y.," he said, in a mocking tone of greeting, "how's Miriam and dear old auntie, Miss Astracan?"

"I am unable to inform you," answered Bunn, endeavouring to maintain his composure and dignity, "not having had the pleasure of seeing them lately."

Chunder Loo grinned and snarled at him like a wild cat.

"You have not seen them lately," he said; "when do you expect to see them again?"

Penny Bunn made no reply.

He knew too well how much it depended on the will of the sarcastic man-fiend who had him in his power.

"Do you hear me? Answer my question!" cried Chunder Loo, ferociously. "Don't sham being dumb with me, or, by the light of the sun!"—his eyes were blazing now—"I'll make a dumb man of you in reality!"

"I would answer you," replied Bunn, with an effort, "if I had any idea when I am likely to meet my dear wife again."

"Your *dear* wife! Well, she wasn't cheap," sneered Chunder Loo, "but you got her at a price—the old screw!—and you had auntie thrown in. Pestro, what think you of him?"

"A rare bird," replied the pirate captain, "who hath left his feathers at home."

"Well answered," drily responded Chunder Loo; "be it our task to refit him. P.Y., my good old friend, attention!"

Bunn was all attention, with his eyes well out of his head.

"Now that I have you once again in my grasp, tell me how it was that you escaped the python—Luva, was it not?"

"It was named something like that," answered Penny Bunn. "As for the way I escaped, it was by the road so many go wrong by—by the help of the bottle."

"Is this dog a humourist?" asked Pestro.

"By nature," answered Chunder Loo, "as other born fools are. Explain yourself, you pedagogue."

"I had a bottle of brandy with me," recklessly answered Penny Bunn, "and myself and the python got drunk together. We made a night of it."

"None of your ill-timed jests with me!"

"It is a fact, and it was no jest to me."

Bunn then explained how he had got the better of the python, and Chunder Loo listened with every sign of appreciation.

"Truly," he said, "you have a fool's luck. Now, I, like the monarchs of old, am dull at times, and need a fool to make me merry. You shall be my fool."

"Kill me," murmured Penny Bunn, driven to make the plea by fear of torture; "it will be more merciful."

"Kill you?" exclaimed Chunder Loo; "not I. A dead man offers nothing in the way of sport or satis-

A SPLENDID SCHOOL STORY.

NEVER BEFORE PUBLISHED.

By E. HARCOURT BURRAGE,

Author of "Ching Ching," "Monkey Mat and Roving Dick," "The Brave Boy of the Basilisk," &c.

THE LAMP OF LITTLECOTE

"I WILL DO MY BEST TO DANCE," SAID PENNY BUNN—AND HE DID!

PRICE ONE PENNY.

faction to the revengeful. He is gone. There is an end of him, and he gives us nothing. I am not the man to kill the goose that lays the golden eggs of mirth. I must have sport out of you. Strip him," he added, in the Arabic tongue.

The guard, hitherto in ignorance of what was being said, understood now. They denuded the hapless Bunn of everything by the simple process of cutting and rending off his clothes to rags.

"By the stars," said Chunder Loo, "a rare figure of a man. What a chest! It would serve for a cannibal soup-ladle. What legs! Walking-sticks for the aged. Bring me here the paint that fades not in the scorching heat of the sun nor will be washed away by water or by spirit. Quick, you dogs! for I long to see my fool in the gay garments of his office."

One of the Arabs ran from the room and speedily returned with three pots of paint, blue, red, and yellow.

Chunder Loo proceeded to give directions for the embellishment of the quivering Bunn.

"Put a cloth about his waist," he cried. "There, that will do. Now paint him half and half—red and blue, and dot him with yellow, like the wild beast he is."

Bunn made no resistance.

It was policy to submit, although he judged that they were making him hideous for ever.

The grave old Bedouins, who may possibly have seen a joke in the proceedings, but did not show it in their faces, went to work and made a parti-coloured man of him. One cheek, one side, and one leg were painted blue, the other red. The paint dried quickly.

Penny Bunn could feel it soaking into his skin with the chillness of ether.

Then they put on the spots with care, with two that were as staring eyes upon his chest.

"Pestro," said Chunder Loo, "how does that strike you?"

"He should have a crown of feathers," answered Pestro.

"Good!"

Chunder Loo said something to the artists engaged in the work, and one of them vanished as before.

He speedily returned with a pot of some gummy substance and a small linen bag.

The former he emptied in part over the head of Bunn, and rubbed it in with his hands.

From the latter he took out a handful of small white feathers, which he sprinkled over the sticky crown of the victim.

Then more of the gummy matter was sprinkled over, then an addition made to the feathers.

This was done three or four times, until the head of Penny Bunn was like a monstrous feather dusting-broom.

No doubt the general effect was exceedingly comical, but there was no laughter.

The Bedouins and the negro guard looked on with immovable faces. Chunder Loo and Pestro merely grinned sardonically.

"Done, and neatly done," said the former. "Now, as I feel sad, we will have a dance."

With a wave of his hand he dismissed the guard, and with the Bedouins and the negroes they silently glided from the room.

Penny Bunn and Chunder Loo and Pestro were left together.

"Now, P.Y.," said the mock Rajah, "if I remember rightly, there is no accomplishment you were not a master of at one period of your life. Therefore you dance. Give us something worthy of Taglioni or Fanny Ellsler."

"I regret to say," replied Bunn, frozen with dismay, "that dancing was not one of my accomplishments."

"In the natural course of your overwhelming modesty," said Chunder Loo, "you make that statement. Probably you miss the music?"

"Music," moaned Bunn, "would not help me."

"You need a stimulant of some sort to awaken your dormant memory. Pestro, old friend, prick him with your knife."

"Pray don't," cried Bunn, hastily. "I will do my best to dance."

And he did.

To describe how they worried, badgered, cursed, and ridiculed him as he went through a multitude of curious contortions of the body would fill several pages. We have not the time or space for it.

In the end he fell upon the floor in a state of exhaustion.

Then Chunder Loo, rising from his seat, came and stood over him, looking down at the unfortunate man with a fierce, implacable malevolence.

"This is but a beginning," he said, "of what I will do to repay your hospitality at Littlecote. I would not forgive if I could, I cannot forget if I would: I never forget or forgive."

"I was never cruel to you," gasped Bunn.

"You were as kind to me," said Chunder Loo, "as you were compelled to be—no more. Remember now, that if you escape from here you will have to go through life *as you are!* There is no removing the paint that adorns your accursed body. The feathers that crown your booby head can only be removed in part unless the scalp goes with them. Both paint and feathers are part of your physique for the rest of your days."

Bunn groaned, but said nothing.

"As for your friends outside," resumed Chunder Loo, "the net is spread for them, and I will haul them in one by one, and no man will know whither they are gone. Those of my servants who are not really dumb are silent for their own interest. And could they speak it would be in vain."

Bunn groaned again. Chunder Loo laughed with the sound of a rattling steel chain.

"Behold my friend Pestro," he said, pointing at the pirate captain, "a faithful friend and true, who was ever ready to help me, who watched and waited for the time when he could help me to be what I am—*the richest man on earth!*"

He drew his spare form up in exultation, and his eyes seemed to positively blaze with triumph.

"Here," he said, "money does everything. Your Government might demand me as a murderer, or what they will, and the authorities would open a hundred channels of escape for me. I can bribe the highest native in the land. They would swear I was not here now, or I never set foot in the land, hide me in inaccessible places—laugh at your people, in short."

He meant what he said, and Bunn believed him. He gave up himself as a lost man.

"I thi-i-ink," he said, feebly, "that you go a little too far."

"Do I not tell you that I have only just begun?"

"You say so, but you cannot go on for ever. Human nature can't stand it. What have you done with Chippy? At least, let me have him as a companion."

The face of Chunder Loo assumed a most awful expression of malevolence.

"Chippy," he said, "is a foresworn priest of the Avishnus. Did you ever hear of the heavy death of the Chinese?"

"Only as something very terrible," moaned Bunn.

"It is torture that goes on for days," hissed Chunder Loo, "and changes its character every day—so terrible that one would think that no human being could suffer it and live for an hour, and yet so discreetly balanced that one torture acts as a saving medium to another until the final course—when all are rolled into one—and death comes at last."

"Horrible! Awful!"

"Yet all that is nothing to what is in store for your friend as a false priest of the serpent worshippers. Think of that, and rejoice over my clemency that gives you your life. Pestro!"

"I am here, most merciful of foes and kindest of friends," answered the pirate captain.

"It is time that we went forth to finish the evening. As for this worm, he may lie here until we return. We may need him as a jesting balm to the losses of the gaming-table. You hear?"

He spurned Bunn with his foot, and the recipient of that unwelcome attention admitted in hushed accents that he heard.

"Leave here at your peril until we return!" said Chunder Loo, as he glided from the room with Pestro swaggering behind him.

Penny Bunn remained as he was, prone on the floor, for some minutes. Then he slowly got upon his feet and stared about him.

"I suppose it is all real," he muttered; "anyway, it is very horrible. So I'm painted, enamelled for life! Once I had fondly hoped to meet my Miriam again, but now—*never!*"

———

CHAPTER CCXLIV.

THE MISSING MEN.—APPLICATION TO THE AUTHORITIES. —JACK AND DIRK MATTHEWS.

HARRY BARSTOW came back in the morning, leaving Ben Walton on board the "Albatross." The necessary repairs were proceeding slowly, for in the East the workmen are a leisurely class.

But for all that, it was expected the yacht would be ready to start for home in a fortnight.

"For my part," said Harry Barstow, "I shall not be sorry to get out of the place. It looks very well in a picture, but the reality is a beastly swindle."

"Artists omit to fully illustrate the dirt," remarked Dick Darnley; "they also varnish up the figures and put a gloss upon them."

They were at the gate of the house now, and tapped lightly. Startop opened it. His face was very grave.

"Asking your pardon, captain," he said, as he saluted, "but there is something wrong. Mr. Bunn and his friend have been away all night."

Norton Truscott, who was with Harry Barstow and Dick Darnley, looked up quickly.

"Do you mean Mr. Chippy Bunyons?" he inquired.

"That is the gentleman, sir," replied Startop. "I've just heerd of it from one of the young gentlemen. They are with Rammer, who's been going on dreadful, threatening to strike becos he ain't got anyone to help him with the cooking. The native beggars ain't up to nothin', he says."

Voices on ahead drew the men to the more open part of the garden, where the four youngsters were with Rammer.

He had a soup-ladle in his hand, and seemed to be in a very excited frame of mind.

"I ain't overbearing," he was saying, "and I ain't, as you young gentlemen puts it, onreasoning. If I went on the loose all night, I should be brought up short in the morning."

"If you came back, certainly," said Bob Stockton, "but if you did not turn up, what could be done to you? With all courtesy, I beg to say that I cannot help thinking you are a very unreasonable old fool."

"I don't ax for no more than to have Bunn dropped on," pleaded Rammer.

"Well, here's the captain," said Don; "speak to him."

Rammer immediately came down from his pedestal, and, taking off his hat, bowed to the verge of grovelling.

Harry Barstow got at the simple facts. Bunn and Chippy went out the night before for an hour or two, and had not returned.

"What do you think of it?" asked Harry of Norton Truscott.

"Bad. I don't like the look of it at all," was the reply.

"You think they have got into bad company?"

"Certainly. I have no doubt of it."

"And have been robbed and murdered?"

"Robbed to a certainty, but not necessarily murdered. Probably drugged and carried away to some of the outside ruins of the town. An experienced native could tell us where to look for them."

"Haska Waffa," suggested Jack.

He was troubled about the disappearance of Bunn and Chippy, and had been thinking over the advisability of revealing to Harry Barstow and Norton Truscott the fact that the supposed Rajah was Chunder Loo, but it would have spoiled his plot.

And furthermore, he feared that the steps Harry Barstow might be disposed to take would end in nothing but the showing Chunder Loo what cards to play. Jack had already learnt enough about Egypt to feel certain that so powerful a criminal, in a pecuniary sense, could not be got at through the ordinary channels.

"Bring Haska Waffa here," said Harry Barstow to Rammer, who limped away to seek the wily one.

As a rule, when wanted he could rarely be found without a lot of trouble. On this occasion Rammer tumbled over him hovering about the garden not far away.

"Haska Waffa," he said, "you are wanted. Cut along sharp."

"Sharp yourself," said Haska Waffa, who could, in common with all grovellers, be rude when dealing with persons of no importance. "Go bother. Blow your head off."

"Yah! you black spider," growled Rammer, raising his arm. "I'll land you one if you give me any tongue."

Haska Waffa showed his teeth, and put a hand on a knife in his sash. Rammer aimed a back-handed blow at him, which he dodged.

"As you ain't goin' to obey orders," said Rammer, "I'll report as sich to the captain. Alser that you drawed a knife on me."

"I not draw him; I put my hand so, for pain of stomach," said Haska Waffa.

"What a owdacious liar you are!" said Rammer. "But I've given my message, and I shall take your answer."

He made as if he would have returned to his captain, but Haska Waffa shot past him, and quickly subsiding into his ordinary humility, vanished round a cluster of bushes.

"The warmint," muttered Rammer, "oily as a sardine-tin arter it is opened. What he don't know about hevil places it ain't no use guessing at. As for them as is missing, why, let 'em stay where they've put their heads inter. I don't see no call to be sorry for 'em."

And away he stumped back to his cooking domicile, growling all the way, and long after he got there.

Haska Waffa, on being questioned by Harry Barstow, first declared there were no wicked places where a stranger could be robbed and murdered in Alexandria.

Then he vowed, by all sorts of things, that if there were he knew nothing about them.

Finally he admitted that it would be possible for him to get at such information from people he knew, as would enable a search-party to visit the most likely places where the missing ones would be found.

Harry Barstow and Norton Truscott started with him on the journey of search.

Haska Waffa led them here and there, and was so far *bonâ fide* that some information was obtained about the missing men. They were traced to one of the *cafés* where they had partaken of refreshment, and the man and wife in search of backsheesh, with whom Bunn had a slight disagreement, were unearthed.

According to their statement, Bunn was going on anyhow—they did not put it exactly that way, but more floridly—with all the women he met.

"Mere childish folly," said Harry Barstow, as they walked on.

"But it may get him into trouble," said Norton Truscott.

Beyond a certain point they could obtain no information of the two friends, and Harry suggested seeing the British consul. Haska Waffa knew him very well, but seemed shy of visiting his abode.

"Me show you, lord duke," he said, bursting into a higher range of titles, "but me stop outside."

"Why?" asked Harry Barstow.

"Consul a wild, angry man. Curse Haska Waffa for nothing."

"Well, stop in the street," said Harry, curtly. "Only hurry up and get there as quickly as you can."

The consul's quarters were not far away, and Harry Barstow, having sent in his card, was soon admitted.

The consul, a genial, quiet-spoken man, listened to the story of the disappearance, and shrugged his shoulders.

"I am afraid," he said, "that I can help you very little. Disappearances are too common here. It is the gambling-houses that are at the root of it all. If a man loses and grumbles, they kill him. If he wins, the chances are that he will be followed and murdered for his money."

"I do not think this is a case of the gambling-rooms," said Harry.

"Whatever it is I can do little," said the consul. "There is law and order here of a sort, but it is very loose in its working. Have you done anything?"

They told him they had been round with Haska Waffa, and, hearing he was in the street, the consul went to the window and peered out through the blinds.

Haska Waffa stood meekly at the corner, lower down.

"Is that your man?" he asked.

"Yes," was Harry's answer. "He was not anxious to come in with us."

"If he had," coolly returned the consul, "I would certainly have kicked him out again—notwithstanding the unwritten law that forbids a man to interfere with the servants of another."

"You know him?" said Harry Barstow.

"As the biggest thief and scoundrel in Alexandria," was the answer. "He was too bad for the pasha, whose home you occupy, to keep in his employ; and when it comes to being rejected by a pasha, it means something extra in the way of villainy."

"I took him with the house," said Harry, "and I must keep or pay him."

"Keep your eye on him, that is all," said the consul. "With regard to your missing friends, I venture to state that they will turn up again without your help, if they are to turn up at all. I wish I could have given you more assistance."

He shook hands with them, and they departed, neither satisfied nor made hopeful by the interview.

Haska Waffa gazed at them out of the corners of his eyes as they approached, probably thinking he would hear of something to his disadvantage, but not a word was said to him.

"We had better just keep an eye on the fellow," was Norton's advice, as they left the consul's office, "and the moment he is caught tripping, kick him out of the place."

While they were away from home, Jack had managed to slip away from his friends and pay a visit to Dirk Matthews in his hiding-place.

It was in Jack's mind to put a few questions to Dirk Matthews on the subject of the disappearance. He found him still suffering from the bastinadoing, being as yet unable to rise.

"The smart's gone out of 'em a bit, sir," he said, "but they are still as tender as you please. If I looks at the soles of my feet very 'ard, they aches."

Jack told him of the absence of Penny Bunn, and asked him if he thought Chunder Loo had got hold of them.

"Not unlikely, sir," he answered, "for he's a keen-eyed 'un, and have spies all over the place; but if he has, it is no use looking for 'em now. He's put 'em clear out of the way, and to go to the palace and kick up a bobbery would be to spoil your chance of landing him by-and-by."

As this coincided with his own views, Jack accepted it as good advice.

Dismissing Bunn for the time from his mind, he produced some sheets of paper and a pencil, and asked Matthews if he thought he could make a rough map of the palace where Chunder Loo resided, and mark the places where admission, without leave, could possibly be obtained.

"Ah, sir," said Matthews, shaking his head, "there is only one spot as I knows on that could be called wulnerable, and all the maps I could make would not enable you to find it unless I take you to it myself."

"And will you faithfully do it?" asked Jack.

"Bet your life I will," answered Dirk Matthews. "I'll risk anything to circumwent that warmint. After all I've done for him, too, to go a-bashing my feet about so that I can't stand! I'm with you, sir. Why, I could take you right to 'is own rooms, his sant santorium, as I thinks he calls it."

"You shall do it by-and-by," said Jack. "Now let me know exactly what you are likely to want to-day, as I can only pay you one more visit."

The list was a small one. Food and drink, a screw of tobacco and a pipe, for the one he usually smoked had been broken when he was maltreated in the palace.

For the rest of the day Jack was thinking over and maturing plans for the capture of Chunder Loo. It was a daring scheme, which will be fully revealed when we come to describe the way it was carried out.

Furthermore, he thought of getting hold of some of the hoard of wealth with which the mock Rajah was making a sensation.

It was not his; it belonged to no man except to him in whose hands it might fall.

In many respects it was different from the old treasure found at Littlecote. There at least a legal owner had some right to it. In the case of Chunder Loo's holding there was none.

Even those who may have had a shadowy claim to it—the Avishnus—were dead. Jack, if he could get possession of it, had as much right to it as any living being.

"Especially after Chunder Loo has paid for his

crimes upon the scaffold," he said, grimly. "If I cannot get help to take him to the old country, I——"

Jack stopped short. He had not yet quite made up his mind what he would do in that case.

CHAPTER CCXLV.

PENNY BUNN MEETS WITH AN OLD ACQUAINTANCE IN THE PALACE OF THE RAJAH.—HE HEARS SOMETHING STRANGE BUT TRUE.

THE palace occupied by Chunder Loo was a vast, rambling place, with ample accommodation for the host of followers and servants of various grades.

They were split up into various bodies, the power of caste being felt throughout. Each race lived, or rather herded, by itself.

The general style of living was wild and Bohemian to a degree.

The Bedouins camped in the open courtyard or square, and the negroes occupied a secluded portion of the palace.

The mutes also had a nook for their use, and each and all helped themselves to such food as they needed from ever-open store-rooms.

Penny Bunn found himself isolated from the rest.

Being released from the confinement of the room in which he had involuntarily shown his gifts as a dancer, he was told by Chunder Loo to look out for himself, report himself at headquarters in the morning and evening in case his entertaining services should be required, and to make no attempt to escape.

"Try it," said Chunder Loo, with one of his catlike grins, "and you will be stopped and brought before me. Your punishment will be, slowly boiled to death in oil. It was a remedy not unknown among you Christians a few centuries ago."

Bunn, not being desirous of restoring in person a fiendish custom of the past, decided to settle down to his new life and make the best of it until he got a chance of getting away.

"But what am I, in this rig-out," he thought, "to do in the world?"

It was a problem, certainly, but, pending his return to the world, he left the solution unsolved.

It was his nature to be sociable.

If he could not have one sort of company, he could try another. He was not proud, and for the lack of white men, he tried to ingratiate himself with the dark-skinned races.

But they would have none of him.

The mutes were out of the question, and the negroes still blessed with tongues, when spoken to only stared at him sullenly in silence.

The Bedouins, on being addressed, significantly placed a hand upon their swords, and so cut short what might have possibly have developed into an interesting conversation.

Travel had sharpened the wits of the ex-schoolmaster.

He speedily noted the way of living adopted, and selected an apartment for himself half up one of the towers of the palace.

It was a big room hung with faded tapestry, and the floor covered with a thick carpet, in which a vast variety of moths had found a home.

As some sort of bedding was necessary, Penny Bunn prowled about, and when an opportunity offered itself, he "borrowed" a cushion from one room and a second one from another, then a third, until he had got a goodly pile from various apartments.

By this discreet conduct he minimised the chances of the purloining being discovered.

Then he got a Turkish hookah from a disused room, that with a little furbishing up was quite pretty. The store-room furnished him with tobacco and matches, and the only thing wanted to make him tolerably happy, as far as comforts were concerned, was " a drop of the usual."

But there was no strong drink in the store-room. That was prudently kept from the fiery followers of Chunder Loo.

But of course the greatest miss of all was the companionship of his friend Chippy.

During the first two days of his captivity Penny Bunn was haunted by thoughts of the unfortunate man, who, according to Chunder Loo, was to die in a manner to which the Chinese heavy death was as nothing.

Where was he?

Had the fiend, the head of the place, carried out his threat?

Was Chippy dead, or, if alive, enduring torture?

These were momentous questions that at the outset worried Bunn, and led him to be indifferent to the million or so of moths that came out in the evening and fluttered about the room.

Some were as big as butterflies, others the size of an English house-fly, but they were all fond of Penny Bunn.

They settled upon his hands and face in little clouds, and if they did not bite or sting, their crawling about him was excessively aggravating.

After dark a species of rat or mouse also came out—Bunn, having no light, could not say which for certain—and careered about the room, squeaking.

They ran over him, too, and got under the cushions of the bed, and they nibbled at the feathers that garnished his head.

He did his best to drive them away, banging about

blindly with a cushion, but the vermin seemed to enjoy it as a joke, for they only ran over him the more and squeaked the louder.

Four times did Bunn present himself at the chamber of his master, twice in the morning and twice at eve, and each time was told with a curse to go away. He was not sorry he was not wanted.

It was on the morning of the third day that he found a companion, the last he would have expected to meet with in such a place.

He was ascending the stone staircase that led to his room with some rice, biscuits, and fruit he had furnished himself with from the store-room, when most unexpectedly he met a negro boy.

At least he thought he was a negro, for his skin was as black as jet, and he wore the usual white turban and tunic of the race.

Penny Bunn was satisfied he had not seen this boy before.

Had he been a man not a word would have passed, for Bunn had given up all hope of finding a companion among the men; but it occurred to him that the lad might be made of more genial stuff, and stopping short, he smiled.

"It is a nice morning for the time of year," he said.

This remark, in a country where the climate goes regularly through its stated changes of fine months and a wet season, partook of the ridiculous.

The boy pulled up and stared at him.

"Who are you?" he asked, in good cockney English, "and who do you think you are getting at?"

"Gracious powers!" exclaimed Bunn, "you are a countryman of mine—or, to be absolutely correct, a country boy—and I seem to know your voice."

"And I know yours," replied the boy, "but I'm blowed if I can twig your phiz. Were you ever shown as a curiosity down Whitechapel way?"

"No," replied Bunn, "but I hope to have the chance of being so one day. What is your name, my little friend?"

"Look here," said the boy, savagely, "don't come the weekly visitor with me! I never could stand it, and I ain't going to begin now. In a place like this a cove has to be pertickler about who he lays hisself out afore. Tell me your name?"

"It is Bunn," was the soft reply.

"What?"

"P. Y. Bunn, Esq., known to my Littlecote boys as Penny Bunn. Ah me! they were a merry lot. A strong love existed between us."

"Of a sort—yes," was the semi-scornful reply. "Who got you up in this rig?"

"Chunder Loo."

A grin spread over the boy's face.

"Permanent paint, I suppose?" he queried.

"I believe so," sighed Bunn. "I am informed it is, by the man who arranged for it to be put upon me."

"How you came here," said the boy, with a meditative air, "is a licker to me. But you can tell me about it by-and-by. Can't you guess who I am?"

"Who you are?" mused Bunn, falling into his old habit. "Hem! I ought to, for in my earlier days I had no rival in penetrating disguises. It was quite a gift. That eye—the almost classical nose—the—the—well-poised head—where did we meet?"

"I was at Littlecote Abbey School," said the boy. "Now, then, roll it out. You must know me."

"Surely it cannot be Ford—no, the tongue is different——"

"Cut it short. You don't know me. I'm the cove you knew as Mulberry Cork."

Penny Bunn nearly fell down the staircase in his astonishment. Of all the boys this was the last he would have thought of.

"Of course you will turn up your nose at me," said Mulberry, bitterly, "because my father was hanged for murder, and I did my best for him when he was alive. But I ain't committed no murder, and if you had been brought up as I was, you wouldn't have been much nearer an angel than I am, perhaps."

"My boy," said Bunn, gently, "I am one of the last of men to blame the child for the errors of the parent. It is true that he played me a trick that was a facer at the time, and led to all sorts of complications; but that is past and forgiven."

"I'm glad to hear it," said Mulberry Cork, and he spoke as if he meant what he said.

"I must confess," continued Bunn, "that meeting with you here is a facer—a knock-down blow—a staggerer; but I am truly glad to see you, especially if it is possible for us to associate and be friends."

"I'll be glad if you will," eagerly exclaimed Mulberry Cork. "I live a horrible life here. Not speaking to anyone for days together, and then only to Pestro, who curses and kicks me as if I were a dog."

"My poor boy," said Bunn, "where do you abide?"

"I'm hanging out nigh the top of the tower. I've done it a-purpose, and I'll tell you what it is by-and-by, if you won't peach."

"We ought to trust one another," said Bunn, warmly. "Come, Cork, let us adjourn to my room, and you shall tell me your story, and I will tell you mine."

"You are sure you are Bunn?"

"Quite sure."

The boy seemed doubtful, but after a keen look at the face of the transformed man, he smiled quietly and followed him to his chamber.

CHAPTER CCXLVI.

MULBERRY CORK REVEALS SOME STARTLING THINGS.— NEWS OF CHIPPY.

"BE seated," said Bunn. "Owing to the furniture, you must do it in the Oriental style. For my own part I have acquired Eastern tastes, and while we talk, I will, with your permission, smoke my hookah. The tobacco is exceedingly mild."

"It ain't more powerful than hay," said Mulberry, contemptuously.

They sat down, and Bunn, having filled the hookah and lighted it, bade the boy start off with his yarn.

"You know my father was hanged for murder," Mulberry Cork began, "which he didn't do, but he was in the robbery that led up to it. Chunder was the man as killed the merchant; but there is no use in talking about that. I looked on him as the only friend I had in the world, and when I got the chance I hooked it out of the room where I was put by a chuckle-headed officer, who didn't notice that the lock could be taken off with a powerful knife. I went orf straight to where I hoped to find him."

"And where was that?" asked Bunn, blowing off a cloud of smoke with the air of the Grand Turk.

"At an East-end opium-den," replied Mulberry; "there I *did* find him, and together we got out of the country, crossed the Continent, and went to Malta. There Chunder stopped for a short time in a house with Pestro, a pirate, who was waiting for him. I didn't exactly know their game, but from what I picked up now and then, it was to get hold of a lot of jewels from some savage sort of coveys that Chunder was to be mixed up with, and had knowed afore. Pestro was to lie off and on an island until the time came to shift the stuff, and I was to go on board with him."

"Yes," murmured Bunn, "I see. Pestro is not an entire stranger to me. He is a little man."

"He is a fiend," said Mulberry, "a beast and a brute. I was sent with him, and he made me wait on him. The ship he commanded had two fights with a swell's yacht, and didn't get the best of it. One was afore we shipped the stuff, t'other afterwards. Chunder was aboard the second fight, and he made Pestro sheer off, though he was so savage at losing his men. Then we come on here."

The boy stopped, and a frown passed over his face. Bunn blew a big cloud of smoke aloft.

"You were not—*coloured* then?" he said.

"No," replied Mulberry Cork; "but I was treated as bad as the darkest nigger. Pestro kicked me, Chunder ignored me, and at last I told him one day I wouldn't stand it. I was a fool, but I was goaded to it, and I up and at him. 'Don't forget,' I says, 'that

when you wanted bread and a bed, my father gave you both; and that he was hanged for a crime *you* committed. Anyways,' I says, 'you ought to have been hanged with him.' Pestro was there at the time, and he looked at Chunder in a way that showed he knew nothing about affairs in England. Chunder, in his cool way, said I was a liar, and had the chaps in to turn me into a nigger, and here I am."

"How long was that ago?" asked Bunn.

"About a month," replied Mulberry.

"And there is no sensible diminishing of the *tone* of your face?"

"Not a bit of it. I'm black all over, and it seems to get darker every day."

Penny Bunn blew off more smoke, and groaned.

"My boy," he said, "I am sorry for you, even as I am sorry for myself. By the way, before I tell you my story, let me ask you a question: Do you know Chippy Bunyons?"

Mulberry shook his head.

"He is an unfortunate friend of mine who has mortally offended Chunder Loo. He is threatened with a torturous death."

"Who threatened him?" asked Mulberry.

"Chunder Loo."

"And where is he?"

"A prisoner here."

"Then it is all up with him. Chunder will keep his word."

"I only want to know where he is to, make sure," said Bunn. "I could bear it, perhaps, if I knew for certain that he was dead and out of his misery, but picturing him, as I do day by day, and hour after hour, suffering all sorts of agonies, is more than I can bear."

"I think I could find out what has become of him," said Mulberry. "You, of course, can't prowl about everywhere?"

"Not without bringing myself under suspicion."

"They don't mind me as I am only a kid, and I've been in the habit of running here and there jest as I please."

"If they should learn that we are friends, they might be suspicious."

"I don't see how they can. Nobody knows or cares where I hang out. Chunder is satisfied that nobody can come in or go out without his knowledge, and Pestro is always off for a gamble. If we lay dark, nobody will bowl us out. I'll find where your friend is. What was he afore they nabbed him?"

"In the old days he was a sort of priest—against his will—among a lot of savages, of which Chunder Loo was the head. The whole of the tribe were swallowed up by an earthquake."

"I've heard 'em talking," said Mulberry, as light broke in upon him. "Chippy cut and run?"

"He did."

"Then," said Mulberry, emphatically, "I wouldn't stand in his shoes for a million."

"Poor fellow!" moaned Penny Bunn. "Cork, if we could only find him, and all get away, what a joyous hour it would be. You have no desire to stay, I suppose?"

"Not unless I see a chance of roasting them two wermin as they lay asleep."

There was an intensity in the way this was said that showed the old dogged spirit was not dead within him. Cruelty had not even scotched it.

"There's one way out of here," he said, after a silence, "and no more, as far as my optics can see, and that is by dropping down from the top of the tower. By a rope, in course."

"And what is the height?" asked Bunn.

"A hundred feet, at least; but if we had rope enough it could be done."

"Very little rope would suffice for me," murmured Bunn, shutting his eyes tightly. "I should make a start, perhaps, and then let go. My descent would be distinguished by a fatal rapidity."

"Not if you make up your mind not to think of the height," said Mulberry, "but I ain't got more'n forty feet of rope in odd bits yet. It's awful scarce here, 'cept when there's anybody to be turned off"—he illustrated the act of throttling somebody with a rope.

Bunn shivered.

"Have you seen it done?" he asked.

"Twice," replied Mulberry, as he rose to go. "Now you keep here for an hour or so, and I may bring you back something."

He left Bunn with his hookah, which he smoked with more contentment than he had done hitherto. Hope was once more with him. His nature was very elastic.

Not more than half an hour had elapsed, when Mulberry came gliding back.

"I've found our pal," he said.

"Good boy!" exclaimed Bunn. "Well done!"

"Leastways I know where he is. They've got him in one of the underground places, a cell worse than any coal-hole in England."

"Could I see him?"

"Yes," replied Mulberry, drily, "arter you'd settled four of them beddings—I think they call theirselves. They're on duty outside."

"Then he hasn't been tortured yet?" said Bunn, eagerly.

"Can't say," answered Mulberry, "but I should say not. They are making preparations for something in one of the small courts near Chunder's rooms. You can see it from the tower."

"Preparations?"

"Yes, there's a sort of frame, with chains and pulleys. It is to stritch a chap out on, I guess, and pincers, and

long, thin knives, and a copper with a jar of ile standing near it, and the niggers as was getting ready was a-jabbering together as if they was going to have a fair."

"Is it possible," exclaimed Penny Bunn, "that these things can be done in the heart of a populous place like Alexandria?"

"That's jest it," said Mulberry. "Like having a thing in your own 'art, it's there, but them as is outside knows nothing about it. *If you don't talk yourself,* not a blessed covey in here will open his mouth—no, not if you was to flay 'em."

"*It's* a fearful place," sighed Bunn. "Poor Chippy! I'd die with you if it would do you any good, and was made a bit easier for a fellow. But it is a fact, Mulberry, that I am not a good hand at bearing pain. Still, if anything *can* be done for a true friend, ungrammatical in speech, but with a heart of gold, I'll do it."

———

CHAPTER CCXLVII.

HASKA WAFFA PLAYS THE SPY.

WHILE Bunn was spending his time in captivity, efforts to find out his whereabouts were not lacking. But they were all in vain.

In the opinion of the Egyptian police there was no hope of ever hearing of him again.

Haska Waffa guided Harry Barstow and Norton Truscott to every place where it was likely some clue to the mystery of the disappearance of the two friends might be obtained, but beyond that he made no suggestions.

One night—it was the third after the vanishing of the pair—he suggested that they could go to a distant part of the city, where, he said, there were some places often used for the temporary concealment of murdered men and women.

It was so well known—so Haska Waffa declared—that the authorities paid periodical visits to it in search of missing people, but if they lagged a few hours too long, they rarely found anything but bones.

"It is the dogs, my lords," said Haska Waffa; "they're hungry, and they eat anything."

"I see no good in going," said Norton Truscott. "We have done all in our power. The poor fellows are gone for ever."

Harry Barstow was of the same opinion, but Haska Waffa ventured to urge them again, using all the flowery language at his command. He was too earnest, in short.

"He has some motive in inducing us to go," said Norton, in an undertone. "Suppose we test the rascal?"

"Very well, do," assented Harry.

"You are sure there is no peril in going?" said Norton, addressing Haska Waffa.

"Not to my lords," he answered.

"Well, then, if you will give us full directions of the road to take, we can go alone. You will remain here in charge of Startop and the other men, who, failing our return by midnight, will hang you as a traitor and a liar!"

"My lord," said Haska Waffa, cringing to the very ground, "am I so unfaithful a servant that you would do this to me?"

"We will trust you as far as we can see you, but no further," replied Norton.

"There are those within these walls," said Haska Waffa, raising his eyes to the two men, "who profess to love my lord and owe him much, but still work to bring him ruin and death."

"What do you mean?" demanded Harry Barstow, sternly.

"I will answer my lord when I have full proof," said Haska Waffa, "but for to-night I will be bound hand and foot, and my lords shall go forth to the place I will tell them of, and they will return in peace. If they do not, let me die by the sword or fire, or how my lords may command."

He gave them a description of the route to take, and when the night came Haska Waffa was bound and handed over to the care of Startop.

"At midnight," said Harry, "if we are not back, hang him, and risk the rest."

About an hour prior to this Haska Waffa had thrown over the wall a small ball of paper, and after waiting a minute, heard a cry, to indicate that it was found by one watching for it.

Harry and Norton went forth, and were back, unharmed, by eleven o'clock. They had, of course, discovered nothing.

Haska Waffa was released in their presence, and he ventured humbly to call attention to his not having deceived them.

"I said to my lords, 'Behold, the road is safe,' and they would not believe me. But they have gone thither, and returned in safety."

"Yes, so far you spoke the truth," said Harry Barstow; "but you spoke of one who is a traitor to me. Who is it?"

"My lord, the time is not yet ripe to speak. To-morrow, it may be, I will reveal him to you."

"Do it," said Harry, quietly, "or I will make you eat your words. My friends are not to be lightly charged with being false to me."

"My lord, I will suffer the bastinado if I prove nothing."

Obeying a contemptuous signal to be gone, he crept away into the house, and after lingering for a time in the entrance hall, stole upstairs with a silent step.

First into one room, then into another he went, until he came to the unoccupied chambers adjoining that in which Dirk Matthews was in hiding.

Now the stealthiness of the man became a thing to see.

No tiger in the jungle scenting its prey ever approached with more caution. There was absolutely no sound as he glided on over the rotting, dingy carpet, once so pleasing to the eye.

At last he reached the curtain that shut off the room in which Dirk Matthews was. Or, to be more correct, the room in which the alcoves were, one of which was occupied by the man in hiding.

Haska Waffa lifted the curtain an inch, and crouching on the ground, peered under it.

There was no light in the room itself, but he could see that there was one in an alcove, also protected by the ubiquitous curtain of the East.

Now was the moment for the rascal to show what he was worth as a spy.

He was born for that much-despised calling.

There was no ear attached to the head of man that could have heard him as he approached and placed one of his dark, snake-like eyes to the slight opening left by the imperfectly closed curtain.

Inside were two persons—Jack Ford and Dirk Matthews.

They were kneeling on the floor, looking intently at a sheet of paper, on which a map or plan had been rudely drawn.

Jack Ford, in an undertone, was addressing his companion.

"It is a rough bit of work," he said, "but it is very clear. I see no reason why we should not attempt it, if you are bold enough."

"Try me," said Dirk Matthews. "I am not afraid. I have been in and out this way a score of times for the fun of it."

"Then as to the rest, that will be a matter of boldness and swift execution," returned Jack.

"One blow, and he will be mum enough for a good half-hour," said Matthews, "and I know where to hit him. I had a go at the ring in my young time."

"You are sufficiently recovered to walk, you say?"

"My feet have got over the licking they had, as if by a miracle."

"That being so we will start in an hour. Startop goes with us. He is faithful and true."

Haska Waffa strained his eyes to get a good look at the paper, but one side of it was turned up sufficiently to hide the drawing on it from being clearly viewed.

Whatever notions may have got into his head with regard to the secret consultation of the two apparent conspirators, they were on the wrong tack.

This was the second time he had played the spy upon them.

He had heard all he desired to know, and it now only remained for him to wait awhile and watch them go on whatever errand they may have been upon.

He had, among other items of information, picked up the knowledge that Matthews was looked on by Harry Barstow as a villain, and he also knew that he was a follower of Chunder Loo, cast out of the fold of the mock Rajah for some delinquency.

Coupling these things together, he formed an idea of his own which was destined to bear fruit.

Of the nature of that fruit, and who had to eat it, we say nothing at present. In due time the particulars of the feast will be laid before the reader.

Haska Waffa stole from the room and out of the house into the garden.

Sneaking down to the vicinity of the gate, he hid away among a cluster of shrubs, and with Eastern patience awaited the development of events.

Startop was on duty, but he was to be relieved at midnight, and at that hour another of the crew of the "Albatross" took his place.

He hastened to the house, but was soon back again.

"I am going out, mate," he said, "with Mr. Ford and a party you don't know, on a job that will please everybody if it comes off right. If it doesn't, then it will be a waste of breath to grumble at us, and in the morning you can report us to the captain as missing."

"Does he know you are going?" asked the relief sentinel.

"Ask Mr. Ford," answered Startop.

"Not me," was the rejoinder; "if he is in it, I am sure all is right."

Shortly after Jack and Dirk Matthews—the latter muffled up so as to hide his identity—came quietly down to the gate.

It was opened for them, and with Startop they went out.

Haska Waffa felt his heart beat wonderfully fast —for one of Eastern blood—and wriggling out of his hiding-place, he glided back to the house where he hoped to find Harry Barstow still stirring.

In this he was not disappointed, for the captain of the "Albatross" was in one of the lower chambers, smoking a final cigar with his friend Norton Truscott.

He was no favourite with either, and as he sidled into the room with his back bent and his head down, they regarded him with the strongest disfavour.

"What now?" asked Harry Barstow.

"My lord, it was but an hour ago when I spoke of a false friend of thine," replied Haska Waffa, "but behold, there are two!"

"Go on," said Norton Truscott, as Haska Waffa stopped, apparently for breath.

"Behold, my lords," continued Haska Waffa, rolling his eyes, "they have had concealed in this house one known as Dirk Matthews——"

An exclamation escaped both hearers, but they checked the words of surprise that rose to their lips.

"One Dirk Matthews," repeated Haska Waffa, "a man of evil well known in Alexandria, and to-night they have gone, as they have done before, forth in his company."

"For what purpose?" demanded Harry Barstow.

"My lord, I know not," answered Haska Waffa, with the meekness of a good man who knew no evil, "save that men do not go forth at night for good. There are places for gambling, and robbery and murder are known when the lights of the town are put out. Or perchance some are stealing about to hide the plunder they take from the houses where they are trusted?"

"Who are the men that have gone out with this Matthews?"

"One is but a youth. My lord speaks to him as Ford."

"And the other?"

"He is a seaman, and called Startop. They all went out as friends."

"You say that one Matthews has been hiding here," said Harry Barstow. "Describe him."

Haska Waffa did so, and there could be no doubt that so far he spoke the truth.

The rest remained to be proved.

"Well," said Harry Barstow, with assumed indifference, "I do not see much in the information you have given us. You may go to your quarters for to-night. I daresay they will all be back in the morning."

Haska Waffa was disappointed. He expected something more than this, although he hardly knew what it would be. As the two friends turned to their cigars again, he glided out of the room, but not to go to his quarters.

He slipped into a recess in the hall and waited.

By-and-by the two young men came out of the room and went upstairs. Waffa sneaked after them.

Their object was to visit the sleeping-chambers of the four youngsters, and they discovered, of course, that Jack was not there.

Their next move was down to the gate, where the relief sentry was passing to and fro.

"Mr. Ford returned yet?" carelessly asked Harry Barstow.

"Not yet, sir," answered the man.

"It is late, but he has Startop with him, and one of his friends."

"Yes, sir."

"Let me see, which of the young gentlemen was t?"

"None of 'em, sir. It was a man, a biggish fellow. I couldn't see who it was, as he was muffled up like a party with a cold in his head."

"Oh, yes, I remember," said Harry. "It was"—he murmured something indefinite, supposed to be the name of the third member of the party—"of course. Good-night."

They left the man at the gate, without saying anything more until they were out of earshot.

Pulling up short, Harry Barstow asked Norton in a low tone what he thought of it.

"It is a mystery to me," was the answer. "Don't see anything but mist in ——. Ford is young, with a lot of go in him, and he may have taken a fancy to a bit of gambling——"

"But *Dirk Matthews here?* What do you make of that?"

"Nothing—absolutely nothing. We knew the fellow was here, but why Jack should take up with him beats me. But when they come back, perhaps an explanation may be forthcoming."

"I shall demand it, for his sake and my own," said Harry Barstow, "but I fear that there is some secret agency at work. Bunn is gone, so is Chippy, and now Ford. We are being whittled down or weeded out by somebody. But it is useless to speculate. We must wait until the morning."

With heavy hearts, burdened with doubt, they sauntered into the house.

A few minutes afterwards, Haska Waffa, who in hiding had heard every word, followed them with an evil smile upon his face.

CHAPTER CCXLVIII.

MORNING AND NOT RETURNED.—NO HELP FROM ANYWHERE.

THE four youngsters slept in two rooms. Don was Jack's companion, and Tom Drummond with Bob Stockton occupied the other chamber.

The two latter were awake early on the following morning, but had not risen when Don entered the room, interrupting a discussion about a way of spending the day.

"I say, you fellows," he said, "what has become of Jack?"

"That question," replied Bob, "partakes of the nature of the ordinary conundrum. He who puts it is the only person able to supply the answer."

"He hasn't been to bed all night," said Don; "the last thing, as I was going upstairs, played out by the heat, he told me that he was going out for a bit, but

would not be long. I supposed he meant into the garden for a cooler."

"I thought yesterday that Jack was up to some game," said Tom Drummond. "He was off and on in one of his thoughtful moods. You know the style of them—a ' can't see you' look in his eyes—set lips, and a general appearance of his mind being out on the opposite side of the earth."

"I don't like the look of it," said Bob, "because if Jack is making a move, it is against Chunder Loo."

"But what can he do alone?" exclaimed Don.

"He can do as much as anybody of his age, and more," replied Bob. "But it is possible he may try too much."

"He might have confided in us."

"So he might, Don, but you may reckon that he has kept his game quiet for the love of us. He is up to something awfully risky, in which he did not wish us to share."

"Kind of him," said Tom, as he began to dress, "but he ought to give us the option of risking our lives with his if we wish to do it, after all we've gone through together."

"Yes; but it isn't selfishness," insisted Bob. "Jack doesn't want all the honour and glory, and if there is profit in it he will make it a point of honour to share with us."

"Hang the profit!" muttered Don. "All I want is Jack."

Don felt rather sore over it. He was convinced that Jack's absence meant real business of some sort, and he would eagerly have gone into it with him.

Before Bob and Tom had completed their toilet—and they were pretty smart about it—Norton Truscott came into the room.

"I see," he said, "that you know Ford has vanished. Tell me, do you know anything about the reason of his going?"

They were silent for a moment. Then Bob returned an evasive answer.

"He said nothing to us about it," he said.

"Were you aware that Dirk Matthews was in hiding here?"

The look of unqualified surprise that sprang into their faces was a satisfactory answer without the denial in words they gave him.

"Well, it seems that Ford had him here, and last night they went out together with Startop. The whole thing is so mystifying to Barstow and myself that we should be glad of the slightest thing to lead us to a solution."

The minds of the youngsters were busy. They all guessed that something had happened quite outside their ken, but what it was they had no idea, save that it led up on an unknown path to Chunder Loo.

As they could not apparently help him in any way

Norton Truscott left them, and when he was gone they eagerly discussed what was to be done.

"Suppose we let out all that we know about Chunder Loo, what would happen?" said Bob.

"Barstow and Truscott would go to the authorities and tell them that the Rajah is a murderer wanted in England."

"How would he prove it? He has no papers, no authority, no anything. But it is this Dirk Matthews business that licks me. Jack's got him in tow, making use of him."

It was an aggravating, torturous mystery to them, but, recalling the past, they made up their minds not to worry.

As soon as the *cafés* and shops were open, Harry Barstow and Norton Truscott went about making inquiries, with the result that no news was obtained of the missing ones.

Then they called upon the British Consul, who appeared to be getting worried with applications of that nature.

"Every day I hear of something wrong or somebody missing," he said. "Why can't people stay at home? You appear, Mr. Barstow, to have a very troublesome or foolish lot of followers and friends."

"We have some enemy here," said Harry; "of that I am convinced."

"Go to Mustapha Pasha," said the consul; "he has the command of the gendarmes here. I will give you a letter of introduction. His residence is not five minutes' walk from here."

They went on with their letter of introduction, and presented it at the house of the pasha, and were informed that he was very busy. But they were at liberty to wait, if they thought it advisable to do so.

They waited, as a matter of course, and at the end of two weary hours obtained five minutes with the pasha.

He was awfully polite, and promised to help them. Inquiries should be made, and any information obtained should be promptly conveyed to them.

With this they were obliged to be content, and walked wearily homeward,

"That old rascal won't budge an inch to help us," said Norton Truscott.

"I wish we had crawled home with a crippled yacht," sighed Harry Barstow. "All was well with us when we put in here. Now I fear we shall depart with our flags half-mast high."

"I would not loose heart dear fellow. Remember all we have gone through and the series of miracles that have helped us."

"Miracles cannot go on for ever."

"Let us hope they have not yet come to an end.,'

CHAPTER CCXLIX.

JACK FORD GETS INTO THE RAJAH'S PALACE.—CHUNDER
LOO MAKES A NIGHT OF IT.

IN the darkness, for the lights of most of the streets were extinguished, Jack Ford and his companions stole towards the palace of the Rajah.

There was need of caution, for, as Dirk Matthews truly told them, any dark corner or gateway might be the hiding-place of some needy native, wolf-like on the look-out for prey.

They walked in the middle of the road, with a revolver in their right hands, ready for use.

"If you see a man making for you, sir," said Matthews, "shoot first, and afterwards ask him what he wants."

He must have been blessed with the bump of locality, for he led them through a maze of streets that twisted and turned, and apparently harked back, until he came to a high wall in a miserable lane, devoted, it seemed, to the depositing of domestic rubbish, such as old rags, broken pottery, and kitchen refuse.

They had escaped molestation on the way, which was probably owing to there being three in company.

"It ain't a nice place to bring a gentleman to," said Dirk Matthews; "but we can't be particular if there's only one road to travel."

Jack looked about him, and, judging by things as he could see them in the faint light, there was an end to the journey.

The end of the alley was a blank, and each side was flanked by a high wall.

Dirk Matthews stopped short about half-way down, and after a close examination of a lot of loose rubbish, kicked some of it aside.

Then he thrust his hands into it, and pulled up a small grating about two feet square.

"I covered it up," he said. "Not that there was much fear of anyone troubling to open it, but a thing can't be kept too close. You've only a drop of a few feet, sir. I'll come last, and shut up."

The possibility of the whole thing being a trick flashed on Jack, but he decided to risk everything, and lead the way down. The drop was nothing—at the outside, not more than seven feet.

He stood aside, and Startop followed. Then came Matthews, who held the grating over his head, as he slipped down, and dexterously restored it to its place.

"Now, sir," he said, "I'll go first. I've a light on ahead."

By that he meant he had a lamp lying in wait for him, and presently it shone with a mild radiance, showing that they were in a narrow passage formed of stone. The roof was arched and plain.

"There's a lot of these passages," said Matthews, "running outwards, all round the building, like the spokes of a wheel, and they all meet in a big underground chamber, propped up with columns, just as the big churches are at home. It's the rummiest crib for a cellar I ever see."

A short journey brought them to the place he spoke of, and the lamp, burning more brightly, revealed a portion of an underground chamber, with massive columns about fifteen feet apart.

There was something very impressive in their stateliness, and the stillness of the place was complete.

"This is not a cellar," said Jack, after a pause, "but one of those wonderful underground water-tanks to be found about the East in great cities."

"A water-tank, sir?" exclaimed Startop.

"Yes," said Jack; "a siege of many months, or even years, was a common thing, comparatively, in ancient times, and, for the defenders to hold out, water was absolutely necessary. They had no knowledge of pump-making, so they brought the water in the rainy season to such places as these, and stored it for the dry day that might come. The passages, which Matthews says remind him of the spokes of a wheel, are for the purpose of ventilation. But for them these tanks would have become foul—unbearable—and the water undrinkable."

"And the water is all gone," said Startop.

"These reservoirs underground have not been needed for a century, and the heat has drawn off the water to the outer air by evaporation."

"We live and learn, sir," remarked Matthews. "Blessed if I didn't put the whole thing down to be a wine-cellar."

"How do we gain access to the palace?" asked Jack.

"There's a flight of steps at the end of an opening over yonder, and it leads right up to a sort of cupboard in one of the end chambers occupied by that fraud of a Rajah. I diskivered it one day when waiting a couple of hours for him. The room ain't got a bit of furniture—nothing but odds and ends—and nobody ever sets foot in it, to my thinking, let alone the cupboard. It's got a stone door."

"A stone door?"

"Yes, sir, as I live; and I shouldn't have found it out if it hadn't been ajar. The wind blows it, I reckon, for it turns easy on a swivel, unless you pulled it tight; but, in any case, you've only got to shove in a certain place to open it."

As he was speaking he led the way across the underground reservoir to an opening, similar to that they had recently passed through, save that a short way in there were the steps he spoke of.

"Better not talk much now, sir," he said, "till we make sure that the warmint isn't at home. He's bound to be late, anyway, for he is going the pace and will soon burn the candle out at both ends."

There were forty steps and the way was straight. At the top there was a landing with a narrow doorway, just about wide enough to let a stout man pass through. Beyond it was the cupboard.

"The door is closed," whispered Matthews; "now I'll put out the light and open the door. Keep quite still."

He blew out the lamp, and handed it to Startop with the wick aglow. This the seaman snuffed with his fingers.

A moment later and Jack could see the door, as Matthews called it, turn on its hinges, thanks to a faint light, a reflection from an adjoining room on the other side.

The sound of a voice, laughing in a mocking glee, reached their ears. Jack recognised it as that of Chunder Loo.

"Ha, ha! my friend made beautiful for ever!" he cried. "You must dance to-night, while Pestro will touch the light guitar. Dance, trip it lightly, and beware of faulty steps. For every one I'll have a toe cut off to-morrow! It will be a rare day for us all. You shall see how gaily we tickle our foes. Are you ready?"

There was a reply given in a low tone, the nature of which they could not catch. Then the twang of the guitar followed, playing a lively air.

Dirk Matthews slipped outside, and disappeared. The music continued, accompanied by the thud of feet on a thick carpet.

Matthews was soon back.

"If you want to see how that fiend amuses himself," he said, "go on through the next room. Take a peep from behind a red curtain you will see there. It is in the opening between the two rooms. The warmint won't see you, as you will be behind him."

Jack picked his way through the lumber-chamber to the next room, evidently by its luxurious fittings a sleeping-chamber.

It was from the next apartment that the sounds of music and dancing came.

There was a light burning in the bed-chamber, and Jack slipped quietly up to the curtain. Pushing it a little aside he peeped into the next room.

What he looked upon was this.

Lying back upon the pile of cushions, with a cigar in his mouth, was Chunder Loo. By his side sat Pestro the pirate, and at their feet several wine-bottles with glasses.

The only other occupant of the room was the unfortunate Penny Bunn, whom, of course, Jack failed to recognise, in all the glory and misery of his paint and feathers, dancing to the best of his ability, for the edification of his tormentors.

It was a most ludicrous spectacle without a doubt, and, not knowing the sufferer, Jack was fairly tickled, and narrowly escaped giving way to a burst of laughter.

But he stifled it, and stayed awhile watching the fun and the movements of the instigators of it.

To his great satisfaction he observed that both Chunder Loo and Pestro were drinking deeply. Every few moments one or the other went to the bottles.

"You dog! you scorpion! you reptile!" yelled Chunder Loo, "do you call that dancing?"

He picked up an empty bottle and hurled it at the head of the tortured dancer, who ducked his head. The bottle struck a mirror on the opposite side of the chamber, breaking it, and at the same time smashing the bottle.

This result seemed to rouse Chunder Loo to a pitch of mirth bordering on frenzy. He roared and shrieked, kicking up his slippered heels. Pestro stopped playing.

"Curses!" he said. "You are going mad!"

"Look at him!" shrieked Chunder Loo. "The dog that had the impudence to try his low wit on me in the days gone by! There's a worm got up as a viper, for you! But you are right, Pestro. There should be an end to foolery. I'm on the blood-trail to-night, and I'll chop him down as a butcher does the carcase of a sheep!"

He sprang to his feet and drew a gleaming dagger from his belt. Pestro, who may not have been in the humour to see the richly-furnished chamber turned into a slaughter-house, sprang up, too, and caught him round the waist.

"Peste!" he hissed, "have done with mad folly. Out of the room, you dog! To your quarters!"

Penny Bunn vanished like a ghost at cockcrow, and Chunder Loo, after wrestling awhile with Pestro, without getting himself free, gave in.

"The fit is over!" he said, in an exhausted voice. "It doesn't often come upon me, but it is very strong while it lasts. Give me something to drink."

He dropped down upon the cushions, and Pestro opened another bottle of wine.

"Faith, friend," he said, "but you are going on ahead. You burn too much oil. The lamp will soon be going out."

"Better a brilliant flash for a moment than a spark for a year!" answered Chunder Loo. "Give me the wine."

A cupful was handed to him, and he quickly drained it to the bottom.

"I am myself again," he said, as he threw the goblet aside. "Now sing to me, Pestro, one of your soft, sentimental songs about the girl you loved in your boyhood, or if you like, about your mother."

"My mother—no," replied Pestro; "she is no theme for to-night. This is not the place to sing of holy things. Could you sing of yours?"

"Mine?" said Chunder Loo, with a hard laugh. "She *was* a woman. She was quiet, but a woman to be feared. Those who offended her died—if not to-day, to-morrow. Some went suddenly—others slowly. It was the last she hated most. She was a gifted poisoner. Now, sing!"

Pestro glanced at him with something akin to aversion in his face, but he picked up the guitar, tested the strings, strung them tighter, and began.

He had a sweet tenor voice, and he was well trained in the art of making the most of a melody.

"The title of my song," he said, "is:

"DESPAIR.

"'Far from its source the streamlet flows
In wanton mazes through the plain;
Each blooming flower reflecting glows
Beneath the waves without a stain.

But when it leaves the city walls,
The brightness, pureness are no more
And darkly, deeply, downward falls
The poisoned torrent to our door.

Oh! thus in fairy hours of youth
The heart is bright without a care;
Awake alone to love and truth,
Knows no deceit and dreads no snare.

But soon, alas! in scenes of strife,
Where all is falsehood, guile, and gloom;
Corrupted is the stream of life,
And falls despairing to the tomb.'"

He ceased, and there was a moment's silence. Then Chunder Loo suddenly burst out with an imprecation.

"In the name of the fiend," he asked, "what led you to sing that song?"

"I was in the humour to sing it," answered Pestro.

"To eternal perdition with your humour!" cried Chunder Loo; "what have we to do with despair? If it dogs your heels, drink and drown it."

As he spoke he filled up his goblet again, and drained it as before. Then he filled for the pirate captain.

"Drink!" he said.

Pestro, with a melancholy air, did as he was told, saying: "What matters? There is no going back. We had better die drunk than sober."

"Die?" laughed Chunder Loo; "you and I, men in our prime! Ha, ha! Is there anything that we cannot command? Since you will not sing gay songs——"

"I cannot, for my heart is heavy."

"Then lighten it with wine. This is rare old stuff, fermented for the gods of fabled history. Drink, drink!"

And he drank, as the demoniac given over to the

power of alcohol drinks in the hour of his weakness.

Another bottle was opened, and he divided it between them, insisting on "the melancholy Pestro," as he jeeringly called his companion, imbibing his full share.

Then another bottle, and another, until the pirate captain tumbled back upon the cushion as senseless as a log.

Chunder Loo was going the same way, but he managed to get upon his feet, with a goblet of wine in his hand, and in muttering accents he drank a toast to the confusion of all his enemies.

"Though born in India," he said, heavily, staring about him, "I—pick—up English customs—drink toast—any of you——"

He emptied the goblet, cast it with a wild aim at the prostrate Pestro, and reeled in the direction of his bed-chamber.

Jack, who had watched the scene throughout, thought it was time to go, and glided back to Startop and Dirk Matthews, who were impatiently awaiting him.

———

CHAPTER CCL.

THE MORNING FOR THE TORTURE.—MULBERRY CORK'S LADDER.—DESPAIR OF PENNY BUNN.

"I THINK," said Mulberry Cork, "that there is enough of the ladder now. Anyways, if it comes to a drop, it can't be more than ten feet."

It was early in the morning in the day that he had learnt that Chippy Bunyons was to undergo the torture.

All efforts to get at him had been in vain, but Mulberry had not given up all hope of rescuing him.

The boy had a species of courage that was not to be despised, and his life in the palace had strengthened it by the daily bitterness of his existence.

"Yes," murmured Bunn; "the ladder I think will do—for anyone who can hold on to it. But is it not a figure of speech to call a single rope a ladder?"

"It's got knots which will do for steps," said Mulberry. "You can hold on it tightly if you've a mind to."

Bunn shivered, as he had done many times when contemplating the descent.

"It just comes to this," said Mulberry; "you've got to do it or stay here. Perhaps we sha'n't get the chance, though. You may make a mess of the bomb."

"I may, it is true," murmured Bunn. "It is a parlous thing."

Mulberry, who had been engaged in testing a long rope made up of pieces knotted together, got up and walked across the room.

From under a long cushion he brought out a six-inch shell of modern make, such as is fired from modern ship-guns.

"It's bound to go off, if you drop it on the hard stones," he said; "for you see these bits sticking out. They was made to run in the grooves of the gun—I learnt that on board the pirate—and there's free play for the top, until the shell gets away and strikes something outside. Then as it's made so that it is sure to hit one or other of the pieces, it's bound to bu'st."

"Go over the plan again," said Penny Bunn.

"I found this 'ere thing," said Mulberry, "among the military stores, and I knowed what it was, so I smuggles it up here, and I says to you, 'Now, look here, Mr. Bunn, if you've pluck enough, I see a chance of rescuing your friend.'"

"The very words, I believe," said Bunn.

"Then," continued Mulberry Cork, "I proceeds to point out to you how it can be done. This 'ere tower looks four ways, don't it?"

"It does."

"And one of 'em looks into a street—a back one, by which we hope to get away?"

"That is also the case."

"And another side gives you a look down into the yard where they proposes to worry your friend?"

"It does."

"Then what we have to do is this: *You* stand on the top of the tower with this in your hand; I goes below and stands by a door, back out of sight, that leads to the yard. I has a knife in my hand ready for action."

"A knife!—yes."

"When the soldiers bring in Mr. Chippy, they will first pop him on a sort of stritcher, made like a gridiron. He will be bound with ropes, as I knows it is their habit so to do. Well, the moment they pop him down, you drop the bombshell down a bang!"

Bunn started as if it had exploded, and he cautioned Mulberry not to illustrate by raising and lowering the heavy shell he held in his hands. The boy put it down, with a smile.

"There'll be a few of them niggers tumbling about, and a general confusion, alser a lot of smoke. In the thick of it out I goes, cuts the ropes, say a few words to Chippy, get him along up the stairs to the top, and then down we go, one after the other—*free!*"

"It sounds well," said Penny Bunn, "and it *may* go off all right. I'll do my best."

But although his words were hopeful his tone was somewhat hopeless. Mulberry gave an impatient shrug of the shoulders as a rejoinder, and picking up the shell, said:

"I'll place it at the top of the tower ready. In another half-hour we shall get our chance. The time app'inted to begin is an hour after sunrise, becos," he added, grimly, "they want to have a long and happy day of it."

Left alone, Penny Bunn got up and walked to and fro in a state of extreme agitation. There could be no two opinions that the rescue about to be attempted required nerve and dash. He never wanted it more than he did at that moment.

"If I could only summon up courage—such as distinguished my youth. No," he muttered, "I can't play that game on myself. I was always a duffer when it came to a fight, and invariably gave in or ran away. Still, I must not forget what Chippy has done for me. But for him, I must have been made a meal of by that python. P. Y., think of your *one* real friend in the world, and *be a man*."

He struck himself upon the chest thrice, which seemed to do him good, for his eyes lighted up and his nostrils dilated. For a moment he felt as brave as a lion.

But the feeling was transient. He was soon again the old Penny Bunn.

Mulberry Cork, having carried up the shell, came back for the rope, which he proposed to make fast and leave it ready to throw over when the time to attempt the descent arrived.

He invited Bunn to come up and see the arrangements.

They went up, and Mulberry showed him the shell placed ready to be lifted and dropped over, also the coil of rope, with one end lashed to a portion of the projecting stonework.

"I point out these 'ere things," he said, quietly, "in case me or Chippy, or both, get settled by the shell. We have to run that risk, you know."

"I never thought of that," said Bunn. "It will be terrible!"

"If we are killed, it will be better than livin' on here," said Mulberry.

"And I shall be left alone," murmured Bunn, pathetically.

"I can't stand no more of it," said Mulberry, with sudden asperity. "If you ain't game to go on, say so, and I'll give it up. It is your friend, not mine, I'm thinking of rescuing of."

"Forgive me," pleaded Bunn; "it is my over-sensitive nature that leads me to display so much emotion. We will go on to the end, if it leads to our being picked up in pieces!"

Mulberry peered over the parapet and quickly drew his head back.

"There's some of them nigger sodgers there. They are laying a bit of fire under that grate. Blowed if I don't think they mean to roast him!"

"Horrible!" groaned Bunn.

"Now," said Mulberry, "I'm orf. You know what you have to do. Don't fail. Drop the shell egzactly over where I've placed it. It will fall to the right of the doorway where I shall be, and so give me a chance of not being knocked on the head. That will be something. It will alser give me the smoke on my side. Now, steady; if you never was a man before, be one now."

"I will be true, though I die," said Bunn, laying a hand upon his heart.

Mulberry slipped away, and was speedily down at the base of the tower, where a small open doorway without a door admitted him to the yard.

But he did not go beyond the entrance, and was then careful enough to keep in the shadow.

About a score of the Nubian mutes were busy laying a fire under a huge grating, standing on four stout iron legs in the middle of the yard.

They did not light it, however, but, the preliminary work being done, one of them ignited a torch and stood ready.

On one side a chair of rude structure was placed on a raised platform. Behind this a number of Bedouin guards, shortly after the fire was prepared, came in and ranged themselves as a bodyguard to whoever sat upon that extemporised throne.

That it was intended for Chunder Loo, Mulberry could but believe, and a feeling akin to regret that it was away from the spot where the shell ought to drop came over the boy.

"I'd like nothing better," he muttered, "than to see *him* blowed sky-high in *strips*."

All the arrangements were carried out in grim silence. Soon after the guard formed behind the throne, another body appeared with the prisoner Chippy, who was very pale.

His arms alone were bound, somewhat in the style of pinioning in our home prisons, but as the reporters would put it, he walked with a firm step.

He cast a quick look around, and seeing the place he was in, his head drooped. He did what a vast majority would do in a similar case—he gave up all hope.

They did not put him on the "grill," but stood him beside it, near to Mulberry, but with his back to the boy.

"Hang it," thought Mulberry, "I didn't reckon on that. He's bound to be blown to smithereens!"

And with a quailing spirit he waited for the shell to fall.

But it did not come.

And furthermore, there appeared to be something wrong with the arrangements, for the guard cast inquiring and even anxious glances towards the door by which Chunder Loo ought to appear.

But he did not arrive.

There was an officer in command of the guard, and after some minutes' delay, he said something to his men and went off to make inquiries.

A SPLENDID SCHOOL STORY.

NEVER BEFORE PUBLISHED.

By E. HARCOURT BURRAGE,

Author of "Ching Ching," "Monkey Mat and Roving Dick," "The Brave Boy of the Basilisk," &c.

THE LAMBS OF LITTLECOTE

"You know 'em both," said Chippy.   "Hanged if I do," returned Don.   "But you are wrong, sir.
One you knowed at school and haven't seen for years, t'other is—guess now."

No. 34.   PRICE ONE PENNY.

ALDINE PUBLISHING CO., 10, Red Lion Court, Fleet St., and 1, 2, & 3, Crown Court, Chancery Lane, London.

Then there was a shuffling about, and anxiety expressed in various ways by those he left behind him.

Suddenly there was a breaking-up and a buzzing as of bees among the men. Even the mutes partook of the excitement. Though deprived of speech, they could hear.

The officer was back again, and he was giving them some information in a wild-eyed, gesticulating way.

Those near Chippy moved forward to hear better.

He was left standing by himself.

Mulberry Cork saw that he had a chance of doing something.

It might be now or never.

He had his knife ready, and slipping out, he glided up to Chippy and began slashing at his bonds.

"Not a word, mister," he whispered. "I am a friend. Come with me."

The bonds were cut, and seizing the astounded and half-bewildered Chippy by the arm, he dragged him a pace or two away.

"Turn and follow me!" he said, hurriedly.

Chippy turned, saw the swarthy figure of the boy, and coupling it with his Cockney tongue, was more staggered than ever.

But he was too much awake to his own interests to waste time by asking any questions. He followed Mulberry into the tower, and at his bidding did his best to race up the stairs.

Half-way up they heard a shouting and yelling below.

"They have 'discovered you've hooked it," cried Mulberry. "Slip along!"

There was a crash below that shook the tower to its foundations.

Chippy stopped short.

"That's the shell!" cried the excited Mulberry Cork. "Never mind that. Hurry up, old man!"

They could hear fragments of masonry tumbling about below, mingled with cries of rage and dismay.

"On—quick!" said Mulberry.

On they went up to the top of the tower, where they saw Penny Bunn, who ran and folded Chippy in his arms.

"Stash it!" cried Chippy. "What now? Cut it short!"

He had no idea that the strange figure was Bunn; and when that worthy spoke in tearful accents he recognised the voice, but was more staggered than he had been right through.

"Don't waste time," said Mulberry. "If they guess where we've come to, they will be here in a minute."

"It can't be Bunn," said Chippy.

"It is," said the owner of that name. "What a game they've been having with me! I can't tell you about it now."

Mulberry again called on them to hurry up, and

explained in a word or two to Chippy the method he had arranged for escape, at the same time throwing over the coil of rope.

Chippy peered over the tower and shivered.

"It's a long way down," he said; "but anything will beat stopping on here. I'm off after you."

"No, you first," said Mulberry. "I'll be the next."

Chippy did not argue the matter further. It was his only apparent chance of escape, and swinging himself over, he shut his eyes and slid down the rope.

He swayed to and fro at the start, but as he got lower the motion ceased. At length he reached the ground in safety.

Looking up, he saw that Mulberry had made a start in his turn, and with monkeyish activity the boy accomplished the descent without making a mistake.

Then came the turn of Penny Bunn.

They saw him peer over the edge of the tower and draw his head back with a jerk.

The action was easily interpreted.

"He will never do it," said Chippy, in accents of despair. "We ought to have made him come first."

But the most timorous of men will sometimes do the most daring things. Strung up to a certain pitch, there is nothing they will not at least attempt at the moment.

Bunn suddenly popped over the top of the tower, clinging to the rope, and with his legs widely extended.

"Good heavens!" exclaimed Chippy. "He can't come down in that style!"

"He is getting the grip on with his legs," remarked Mulberry Cork, who was watching the antics of the suspended Bunn with the interest of one who looks on a daring performance.

"He's coming!" gasped Chippy. "Hold on, Bunn. Come easy, or you will flay your hands."

Bunn did not hear him.

The intense excitement he was labouring under made him deaf to all sounds, and blind to everything but the wall before his eyes.

He started slowly, and every time he came to a knot he gave a gasp as if he had been pulled up short by an enemy.

But he held on, and all went well with him until he was about forty feet from the ground.

Then his courage gave way, and relaxing his hold, without exactly letting go, he slipped down at the rate of a mile a minute.

"Steady!" cried Chippy, as he rushed close up to ease the fall of his friend.

He forgot for the moment how heavy a man is in such a case, and the force with which Penny Bunn fell upon him laid him out flat upon the ground, with a thousand lights dancing before his eyes.

But he had played the part of safety-buffer to Bunn,

who, although he, too, came to the ground, was practically unhurt.

"Saved!—*free*!" he gasped.

Mulberry helped Chippy to his feet, and as he slowly recovered his wits he clasped the hand of Bunn.

"We have gone through a lot together," he said, "and we've each done the other a good turn. Friends for life we are."

"Bosom friends," murmured Bunn.

They were in the blind street in which the grating was, and a portion of it was visible among the rubbish. But it was not an object of interest to any of them.

There were no people in the street. Their descent had not been marked by any human eye.

It was daylight, and they could pass through the streets unobserved, unless the extraordinary feather headgear of Penny Bunn attracted attention.

It was more than likely it would do so, and Mulberry Cork again came to his aid.

He slipped off his upper white tunic, and twisted it about Bunn's head so that it made a very fair turban. The feathers were all hidden.

"Now," he said, "you can go home."

"And what are you going to do, my lad?" asked Chippy.

"Oh, I shall hang about and get a job aboard ship and work my passage home. As a nigger I can get a living in London sweeping a crossing. Old women at home are always more generous to niggers than they are to white boys."

"That's true enough," said Chippy, as they walked up the street; "but you are not going to sweep a crossing if I know it. You've saved my life, my boy, and I'll help you along better than that."

"But I can't go back with you," said Mulberry, shrinkingly. "I know who are there, and they will be down on me."

"If it comes to that," said Bunn, "they will not know you—any more," he added, with a wail, "than they will *me*."

"You are certainly a derned pair of curiosities," said Chippy, looking at them with twinkling eyes, "but, lor! what matters, so long as the 'art is in the right place? The colour of the skin is nothing."

"The moment I spoke, Ford or one of them would bowl me out," said Mulberry Cork; "they are as sharp as anything!"

"Now, if I know them young gentlemen," said Chippy, "they will give you a welcome when they learn what you've done. Whatsomever there may have been in the past, which I don't know nothing about, they will no more think of throwing it into you teeth than *I* should. Anyway, you've got to come home with me, and if they turns their backs on you I will turn mine on them. Hallo! here's a row. Hadn't we better sheer off?"

They were at the top of the street, from whence a view of the chief entrance to the palace could be obtained.

Around the gates there was a seething mob of people, pushing and struggling, apparently with the idea of forcing their way in.

Others, mainly the off-scourings of the mixed populace, were coming up, loosening the knives they carried in leathern sheaths, or brandishing sticks in the air.

"Down this way," said Chippy, hurriedly, "and take our chance of finding a road home. There's danger for us here. Cut it!"

———

CHAPTER CCLI.

THE MURDERED MAN.—WHERE IS THE RAJAH?

BUT Chippy was mistaken in thinking that the excitement had anything to do with him or his companions. It arose from another source, and they could have passed through the crowd unheeded.

A terrible discovery had been made in the palace.

Pestro, the pirate, had been assassinated.

He was found lying on the cushions upon which he had sunk in a drunken sleep, with a dagger buried in his heart.

And the dagger was known to be one worn by the Rajah, as he was called—Chunder Loo.

The Rajah, to add to the mystery, was nowhere to be found.

The empty broken bottles lying about the room told a tale of dissipation, followed, as the discoverers believed, by a quarrel and assassination.

It was this discovery that caused the excitement in the small courtyard in which the arrangements for the torture of Chippy had been made.

By means of it he had been able, with the aid of Mulberry, to escape, and the timidity of Penny Bunn fortunately delayed the dropping of the shell until he was out of danger from it.

The murder of Pestro, the vanishing of the Rajah, and the subsequent slaughter of some of the Nubian soldiers by means of the shell, all served to set the inmates of the palace in a ferment.

They had no idea of the nature of the terrific explosion, beyond that it had taken place. No eye had seen the shell fall from the tower.

Maddened by terror, some of the men hurried out of the place into the street, and there, in the declamatory way of the East, cried out the tidings of crime and disaster.

Hence the rush of the idle, vicious, and curious to get within the gates.

But the mob was not permitted to enter.

Some officer in command of the Nubian attendants rallied them, closed the gates, and ordered the howling throng outside to stand back.

As the horde failed to obey, the command was given to fire upon them, and the rattling of rifles was followed by the fall of a few to rise no more and the groaning of many wounded.

The report of firearms being heard by the officers of the town, a number of the gendarmes speedily arrived.

They were admitted to the palace, and in the name of the Khedive took charge of it.

The dead and wounded in the street were left to look after themselves for the time.

Most of the latter crawled away to get what help they could from their friends. Half of those remaining were dead when at last men came to carry their bodies away.

Pestro, the companion of the Rajah, slaughtered, and the Rajah missing!

The wonderful intelligence—wonderful in the unlooked-for horror of it—flashed all over the town.

Mustapha Pasha came in person, with some soldiers, took possession of everything, and gave orders for no person to leave without a permit from him.

He came with the hope of securing some of the wealth of the Rajah.

Whatever was the nature of it, it was not banked in the ordinary way. That the pasha knew. Therefore it must be in the palace.

When found, he (the pasha) would, pending the claims of relatives or the reappearance of the Rajah, take care of it.

The latter he did not fear.

There could be no doubt whatever, in the official mind, that Chunder Loo had murdered his friend.

If he showed up again he could be speedily disposed of, and Mustapha, having got hold of his money, would need some very strong persuasive force, to say the least, to be induced to part with it.

In person he proposed to superintend the ransacking of the palace.

As for Pestro, little was known of him save that he was a kind of major-domo to the Rajah, and the sooner he was buried the better.

It would be folly to keep his corpse above-ground for an hour in that climate.

So orders were given, and the pirate was hurried away to the cemetery, where he was unceremoniously laid in a portion of it devoted "to those dogs—the Christians."

Not a single follower accompanied his remains to the grave.

Alive and strong the night before, by noon he was in the ground and of no more account to the natives than the lowest creature on earth.

Meanwhile the search was going on.

In turn all the apartments occupied by the Rajah were searched, and the curtains torn down, the carpets taken up, every cushion ripped open, and they found nothing.

Then to other parts of the palace the pasha and his assistants turned, searching and searching until the day was almost spent, and found nothing.

Then a suspicion began to lay hold on the mind of the Eastern potentate.

Might not this Rajah have been, after all, nothing more than a gigantic swindler?

He inquired into his ways, and learning that he had been in the habit of attending with Pestro nightly the gaming-tables of certain haunts, the Pasha ordered the proprietors of these dens to be brought before him.

They had one and all won large sums from the missing Chunder Loo, but they swore by the graves of their mothers and the beards of their fathers that it was he who had fleeced them.

"He was a cheat and a liar," they said, feeling strong in the knowledge that the "Rajah" was guilty of murder.

Last of all came Harry Barstow and Norton Truscott to the palace to demand audience of the pasha, as people who had important information to give concerning the missing scoundrel.

Don and his two friends, hearing of the break-up at the palace, had at last told all they knew concerning Chunder Loo.

"It was Jack's wish," they said, "we kept it secret. We always trusted and believed in him, and we thought that he had some scheme in hand which would have been spoilt by our saying anything."

"And now," said Harry Barstow, bitterly, "it has ended in your losing him."

It was past noon then, and nothing had been seen of Jack or Startop, nor, of course, of Dirk Matthews. They had been twelve hours away, and hope of seeing them again alive was waning fast.

But to return to Harry Barstow, who was admitted to the presence of the pasha.

In a few words he told his story, as far as was necessary.

His young friends had known for days that the supposed rajah was no rajah at all, but one Chunder Loo, a notorious villain, wanted in England for complicity in a murder.

Of his supposed wealth Harry would say nothing. He left the pasha to believe exactly what he believed about that, and the belief the pasha entertained after he heard the story was that Chunder Loo was simply a daring adventurer.

"He had not a shekel!" he hissed, "he lived by fraud—the mangy dog!"

Harry Barstow in his story simply confined himself to Chunder Loo in England and Chunder Loo in Alexandria. He said nothing about the Avishnu business at all, for various reasons.

He did not consider it was helpful in any way.

As soon as the pasha came to the conclusion that Chunder Loo was nothing more than a gambling adventurer, he called the mock Rajah's followers together and told them that they must quit the palace forthwith.

When they asked the pasha about the pay due to them, he drily informed them that they must await the return of their master.

On some of them showing a disposition to be troublesome he ordered the soldiers he had prudently brought with him to clear the lot out at the point of the bayonet, which they did with a promptitude that left nothing to be desired on the score of dutiful obedience.

Finally he himself retired, closing the gates and taking the keys with him. He also set his seal upon the lock, to make sure that nobody could break in and steal without his knowledge.

"One day," he thought, "I may return and renew the search. But there is no treasure. The reptile was a fraud and a liar!"

Certain of this, yet far from satisfied in another sense, he returned to his own abode and gave directions for a strict search to be made for Chunder Loo.

"Let me get hold of the dog!" he said, "and I will make him sorely repent of having deceived me."

CHAPTER CCLII.

PENNY BUNN'S RETURN.—MULBERRY CORK'S RECEPTION.—MORE STARTLING NEWS.

IT was about the time when Harry Barstow was closeted with the pasha, when Don, mooning disconsolately near the gate of his temporary abode, saw three persons hurrying towards him.

In one, to his amazement and delight, he soon recognised the lost Chippy.

He ran to meet him and fairly hugged him.

"Why, Chippy!" he cried, as he pushed him gently off, holding him by the shoulders, "this is a sight to make me glad. Where have you been, and what have you done with Bunn—the great, the glorious, the refulgent Bunn?"

"I ain't done nothing to him," replied Chippy, "but t'other have been up to a game or two with that unfortunate man. Lor, what a lot I've gone through with! See these parties here?"

Don glanced at the strange couple, but not with any keen interest. He had grown accustomed to all sorts of human curiosities during his stay in Alexandria.

"Where did you pick them up?" he asked, thinking that Chippy had gone in for two attendants.

"You know 'em both," said Chippy.

"Hanged if I do!"

"But you are wrong, sir. One you knowed at school, and haven't seen for years. T'other is—guess, now."

"I'm afraid if I guessed for years I should still be wide of the mark."

Then Chippy, helped along by Bunn, told everything, and Don was obliged to take a seat upon a big stone before the story was concluded.

"I have heard and read of people being limp with astonishment," he said, "but not till now did I understand what it was to feel so."

"The narrative of my sufferings and transmogrification," said Bunn, sadly, "would naturally touch even the hardest heart."

Don got up a sigh, but he was obliged to put a hand before his mouth to conceal a smile. Turning to Mulberry, he said:

"In the old days I used to think that there was some true grit in you, but it was swamped by—as I suppose I may, without hurting your feelings, put it—your evil associations. I regret to find you as you are, but I am sure that now all that is black in your nature is to be seen outside."

"Nicely put—neat," murmured Chippy. "I knowed it. You will be all right with us."

Don shook hands with Mulberry, and, bidding Penny Bunn take comfort from the fact that he was yet alive, said:

"I will go in and prepare the others to see you so changed. My friends are in the garden, reading, I believe. You may come along in, say, two minutes."

Don hurried back, and being admitted by the sailor at the gate, told him that Chippy and "two strangers" were shortly coming in. Then he dashed down to a favourite haunt of his friends, whom he found lounging upon a seat, talking of Jack Ford's disappearance, which they now placed to the charge of Chunder Loo.

"Dirk Matthews was the decoy," Tom was saying. "Somehow he persuaded Jack to go to some place where Chunder was in ambush. But it is all up with the villain now."

"Hallo, Don," exclaimed Bob, "you seem to be merry, considering the state of things."

"I can't help it," said Don, as he dropped down

beside him. "If I were walking to the scaffold this moment I must laugh. Chippy's back."

"Never?"

"Fact, and so is Bunn. Such a yarn! Chunder Loo got hold of them—he's made a permanent nigger with a cockatoo's head of poor Bunn. You will hear all about it. But who do you think is with them? But there, you would never guess—Mulberry Cork."

"Stash it, Don."

"It is true, and how he came with them I've yet to learn; but it is he who saved Chippy and Bunn. There's good in the fellow, after all. He's rather shy of coming in, but if you meet him kindly it will put him at his ease. He deserves it, too."

"We have no quarrel with the poor beggar," said Bob. "He hadn't the ordering of his father or perhaps he would have secured a better article. Of course, it's all right."

"Here they come. Just look at Bunn! He's taken off his turban, so that you may realise the full extent of the iniquity he suffers from, and sympathise with him accordingly. Don't laugh if you can help it."

And they did not.

Bunn was received with due gravity, congratulated upon his escape, and the trio were sent into the house to refresh themselves, prior to relating in full their recent experiences.

On the effect created by Penny Bunn's get-up on Rammer we need not dwell. The cork-legged mariner was fairly dumbfounded, and he was proceeding to sympathise with him, but Bunn would have none of it from him.

"Let me have something to eat, and cease your prattle," he said. "I decline to receive pity from *subordinates!*"

Penny Bunn was himself again.

Haska Waffa was prowling around, and came upon the trio as they sat at table eating with the appetites of the hungry.

He stared at Bunn as if he had been some low-class loafer on his domain. He evidently considered him to be a member of some hitherto unknown tribe.

"I see," he said, "my lord hath engaged others to serve him."

Bunn got up from the table and advanced upon Haska Waffa, breathing scorn and shooting small fire-works from his eyes.

"Swarthy *hound*," he said, "get out—*door*."

Haska Waffa was too much astonished to stir. The language, the air, were so different from what he expected.

Penny Bunn, with an angry hiss, seized him by the shoulders and twisted him round.

"Door!" he said, as he propelled Haska Waffa forward with his foot—"*door—door!*"

Haska Waffa shot into the passage and fell upon his hands and knees. In that attitude he remained for a moment in a state of bewildered reflection.

He would have remained longer if Penny Bunn had not given him a final application that caused him to spring up like a fly.

"The wo-o-o-rm!" hissed Bunn, as he resumed his seat. "Though painted like the figure-head of a ship, the old indomitable spirit remains intact within me."

"There is no doubt," said Chippy, "that you've got a lot of go—of a sort," and Mulberry Cork had a quiet little laugh on his own account.

When the narrative of their adventures was told to Bob and the youngsters, they not only derived some amusement from it, but gathered hope of seeing Jack again.

It was difficult to say why they did so. It was more of a shadowy feeling of hope than a conviction with some ground to it. All round they were more light-hearted than they had been since Jack went away.

By-and-by Harry Barstow and Truscott came back with further information about the startling events of the previous night and that day. But they had not the slightest information concerning Jack.

At seven they dined, and the two elders went away to the "Albatross" to see how the repairs were getting on.

Night was at hand, and shortly after, as the trio lounged about in the short twilight, Startop suddenly appeared before them.

They could see that he was pale, considering the deep tan of his skin, and his manner was nervous and agitated.

"I've come back, gentlemen," he began; but they interrupted him in a chorus of inquiry after Jack.

"He's all right," answered Startop, " 'cept, like me, he ain't had anything to eat and drink since last night. I've come for something for us all, and for help to get our prisoner home."

"Your prisoner?"

"Yes, gentlemen, him as you know as Chunder Loo. We've got him," he added, lowering his voice and looking cautiously round, "in a big water-tank under the place where he lived. He's gagged and he's bound, and we want a vehicle o' some sort to bring him on here."

For a moment the listeners were silent, and then with one voice they cried, "Hurrah for Jack Ford!"

"We ought never to have doubted he would come out right," said Don. "Hadn't we better come back with you, Startop?"

"No, gentlemen," said the seaman, "I'll get back alone, and you must wait till ten o'clock or so. Then if you could hire a sort of truck or barrer, and bring it along to a narrow street, the first past the big gates of that warmint's place, we will be ready for you. Mr. Ford says as you'd better bring along some wraps, too, so as to cover him up, and Dirk Matthews says he can get us here without going into any of the main thoroughfares. What's to be done with this 'ere Chunder Loo all depends on the captain. If he won't have him on the 'Albatross,' Mr. Ford says he'll string the warmint on a tree and chance it."

"If Ford said that," Don emphatically rejoined, "it will be done. You have heard of all that's happened at the palace?"

"I've heerd nuthin', sir. I just come along straight as I was told without saying a word to living mortal."

"Stay there," said Tom Drummond, "and I'll pack you a basket in a twinkling. I am an old hand at catering."

He referred to the 'old days when he filled the office of caterer at Littlecote Abbey, and he smiled in memory of the time as he ran off to prepare the much needed refreshment.

Startop, during his brief absence, explained to the others that on the previous night they had secured Chunder Loo when in a drunken, helpless condition. They seized and bound him, and carried him below; but, owing to the impossibility of carrying him through the streets without attracting attention, they remained with him right through the next day.

"More'n once," he continued, "I had a go at getting out of the crib, but ginerally there was somebody in the street. All round there have been a mob through the day until now, when at last the people cleared away. It was all on account of the Rajah, I reckon."

"And Pestro?"

"What's come of him?"

"He was found with a dagger in his heart."

"Oh!" exclaimed Startop, opening his eyes; "that is the job Dirk said he had to do arter we got Chunder Loo inter the tank. Well, I don't think that he ought to be hung for it. Anyways, Pestro earned all he's got."

"A tank," said Bob, "must be a very small hiding-place for you all."

"Bless you, sir! it's half as big as this 'ere garden, I reckon. I shouldn't have knowed it for a tank at all, if Mr. Ford hadn't said it was one. It's under the palace, and it's got a lot of pillars in it. It ain't been filled for a century or more."

"I think I know what he means," said Don. "There's an account of the underground reservoirs for water in the 'Guide to the East.' In Constantinople there are several of them. But here is Tom with prog for a decent-sized picnic party."

Tom handed a bulky basket to Startop, who took his departure. Then the three friends proceeded to discuss the ways and means of getting hold of the class of vehicle required.

"Stop a minute," said Don, in the midst of the discussion; "I've seen a long barrow kicking about the grounds somewhere. It seemed to me to have been used for clearing away the rubbish. It is rather short to carry a man, but we can double the beggar up. Let us have a look round for it."

CHAPTER CCLIII.

THE BRINGING HOME OF CHUNDER LOO.—HARRY BARSTOW'S DECISION.

TEN o'clock in Alexandria, and the streets lively as usual with the teeming mob of natives and strangers.

The cafés are lighted up—there is a sound of tinkling music and screechy voices, with the cries of the vendors of different wares.

Everything is cried in a manner peculiar to the country.

"In the name of the Prophet, figs!" screeches a woman, with a basketful of the soft, green fruit upon her head.

"By the beard of our Ruler, behold the best of sweets."

"Slay me, if here are not the juiciest of pines."

Now and then there is a brawl, more or less serious, but through it all, Tom and Don and Bob proceed with a long barrow on four small wheels.

They have discarded their uniforms, and put on rough, well-worn clothing. In addition, they have smudged their faces, and Tom has mounted a short pipe, filled with mild tobacco.

It occasionally happens that a curious pair of eyes are cast on them, but nothing comes of it. Without hindrance they go on direct to the palace where Chunder Loo so recently lived in all his glory. They pass the gates, and turn down the narrow blind-way, and find themselves alone.

"Not here yet," said Tom, as he stopped about half-way down. "A nice place for an assignation. Dust contractors' yard, I should say."

"They have no dust contractors here," said Don. "The wind does all the sweeping there is, and the dogs are the scavengers."

"Hist!"

They stared about them, hearing the sound, but saw nothing, because they did not look low enough down.

It was Startop who hailed them thus, and his head was just thrust above the grating.

"Hist! this way. Bring the barrer higher up."

They saw him now, and muttering, "Well, I'm jiggered!" Tom propelled the barrow on until the grating was reached. Then Startop came quickly out.

"Smart's the word," he said; "no wasting of time."

He stooped down and hoisted up what at first appeared to be a big bundle, assisted by somebody below.

It proved to be the lithe form of Chunder Loo, bound, gagged, and partly enveloped in a shawl. Jack and Dirk Matthews quickly followed, and Chunder Loo was bundled into the barrow.

"Jack, old man!"

"Your hands a moment. No talking till we get him safely locked up. Villain that he is, we cannot get him through the streets if they guess what we are carrying away."

Wraps had been thought of, and they covered him up. Don caught a sight, for a moment, of his eyes, glistening with fury, and laughed softly to himself.

They packed in Chunder Loo, close and warm.

"Scatter a bit," whispered Jack; "but act as a guard. I'll walk alongside, for if I see a chance of his being taken away from us, I'll shoot him through the head."

His resolute air showed that this was no idle threat. Startop took the shafts of the barrow, Dirk Matthews walked on a few paces ahead as a guide to the way, the others walked on either side a short distance away, and in irregular order.

Thus ignominiously was Chunder Loo borne away from the scene of his temporary splendour, bound like a tricky beast, and in a vehicle usually devoted to the removal of rubbish and offal.

It was a fall from a great height down to the lowest depths of degradation.

And no doubt he thought it so, for although he was too tightly secured to move, the violence of his emotions made the barrow quiver and tremble as Startop, with a seaman's phlegm, pushed it through the streets.

Through by-ways so narrow and foul that even in the night the sight of them sent a shudder of loathing through the youngsters, Dirk Matthews guided them. There the inhabitants were asleep, or prowling round in more populous thoroughfares in search of crude employment, or the chance of robbing somebody.

On in silence they went, unchallenged, to their home.

The sentinel at the gate, already prepared for their coming, as soon as he heard the grinding sound of wheels upon the shingle, opened the gate and let them in.

"Safe so far," said Ford, breaking the silence. "Has the captain returned?"

"Came in, sir, half an hour ago."

"Bring him down to the house," said Jack. "I will see if he can be taken charge of here. If not, there is only one thing to be done. It is not safe for this monster to be abroad."

They took the wraps off Chunder Loo and looked down upon him, curled up in a manner curiously suggestive of a wounded snake.

Being gagged he could not speak, but the expression of his eyes dispensed with the need of speech.

Not a word was said to him.

They contented themselves with looking quietly at the captive until Norton Truscott came hurrying out of the house.

"At last," he exclaimed; "and *the* last of a cruel race. There never was a deed better done. Matthews, you have retrieved your past."

"I am thankful to hear you think so, sir," answered Matthews, saluting. "Now, if I might be so bold as to advise you, I would say—settle him at once."

"I fear we can scarcely do that," returned Truscott, "but Captain Barstow will decide."

Jack Ford and the captain now appeared. Behind them were Bunn and Mulberry Cork.

"I have decided to take this villain home a prisoner in the 'Albatross,'" said Harry Barstow; "it goes against me to play the part of executioner. He will be kept here for a few hours, while a strong-room is being prepared for him aboard. How long has he been thus?"

"Since we captured him," replied Jack. "It was impossible to release him in any way. The risk was too great."

"He has paid a part of his debt," said Harry Barstow, grimly. "Take out the gag. But if he makes the least noise, replace it."

It was done, and they also sat him up. He worked his mouth like one getting free of a stiffness, for a time, and then attempted to speak. But the effort was useless, and Harry Barstow bade Penny Bunn get him a little wine.

"I have no desire," he said, "that he should cheat the hangman."

Chunder Loo closed his mouth with a snap. It was a feeble way of gnashing his teeth. Bunn got the wine and placed it to his lips. He drank with the fevered haste of a drunkard partaking of a "morning reviver."

Then he found tongue, and turning his face towards Harry Barstow, said, in a broken way:

"You will repent of this. Do not forget where you are. My friend will see the pasha, and he will hang the lot of you."

"What friend?" contemptuously asked Jack Ford.

"Pestro, the all-powerful," answered Chunder Loo.

"Do not rely upon him. He is dead."

"Dead?"

"He was found with *your* dagger in his heart," said Harry Barstow. "There is a reward offered for your apprehension as his murderer. Your palace is in the hands of Mustapha Pasha. Whether you stay here or are taken to England, you will die the death of an assassin."

"All this is lies," said Chunder Loo, wildly.

"It is true," replied Harry Barstow. "Truscott, will you go on board and make arrangements for his safe keeping? Bring him in, Matthews; you and Startop can carry him."

"Permit me to have a hand in the joyful task," said Penny Bunn. "Little did I dream of this pleasure in store. Chunder Loo, shall I dance to you to-night? I feel as if I could come out strong in a few new figures."

"Anyhow," said Chunder Loo, maliciously, "I have made something of you for the rest of your life."

"And I will make the best of it," replied Penny Bunn, cheerfully, "especially after you have had a short but effective interview with the hangman."

A shudder ran through the form of Chunder Loo. Cool villain as he was, it was indicated by his face that he dreaded the punishment in question.

"I'll take his head," said Bunn. "Ha! would you bite, you *snake*—you human tiger? Hoist him up. Never mind his heels being higher than his head. A little inconvenience will do him good."

They carried him in, and the rest followed. By the advice of Jack he was conveyed upstairs and placed in the alcove, where Dirk Matthews had recently been in hiding.

"We can keep watch over him here," said Jack; "he must not be left alone for a moment. Startop, just run over his bonds and see that none of them have been loosened."

They laid him down, and the bonds having been examined and found secure, Don and Tom Drummond offered to take the first watch. It was accepted, for all concerned in his capture were in need of rest.

Jack, however, though scarcely able to stand for lack of sleep, would not go further than the entrance to the alcove.

Stretching himself out upon the floor with his arm for a pillow, he was gone in a moment to the land of dreams.

And the rest, all but the two watchers, retired to rest pending the return of Norton Truscott.

CHAPTER CCLIV.

A DISSATISFIED PASHA.—TRUSCOTT UNDER ARREST.

THERE are some people who are never satisfied, and the pasha, who had been hungering for Chunder Loo's wealth, was one of them.

He was not satisfied with his failures, but still hoped on. Therefore did he summon to his presence one Alum Kay, renowned for his wisdom and cunning.

Alum Kay had been a sort of medicine-man in the desert, where he went about with uncombed hair and an unwashed face. When an Arab chief lost a horse he visited this sage, who forthwith drew some backsheesh on account and shut himself up in his tent.

There he went into a trance, which lasted just as long as the fee received demanded, and in coming round he again sent for the disconsolate chief.

More backsheesh was, of course, required, and if the owner of the horse could not or would not pay it, there was an end to the matter.

As a rule the helpless chief, who had more power than riches, put up with the robbery; but sometimes he kicked, and then Alum Kay got up another trance for the money, and fixed the theft on some person so described as to answer to the appearance of thousands of the children of the desert.

Where variety in clothing was little known this was no difficult matter.

Perhaps the thief would be caught, and then the medicine-man had a good time of it. But his failures were many.

The desert children had had almost enough of their sage, when he one morning levanted and wandered to Alexandria, where he proclaimed his calling, boasted of his wondrous powers, and did a good business with the ignorant in the many ways of the charmer and deceiver.

The pasha had him attached to his house at the cheap rate of finding him board and lodging, with a little cast-off clothing, with the idea that he might one day be made useful.

The hour of Alum Kay had now come.

As a last resource the pasha sent for him to say what the wealth of Chunder Loo consisted of, and what had become of it.

Naturally, he declared that the wealth consisted of jewels and gold. There is no other recognised form of wealth in the fiction of the East.

But where it was, he found a very hard nut to crack.

What he lacked in wisdom he, however, made up in cunning, and by the merest chance hit upon "the nest of Englishmen" as the present possessors of it.

He did this, knowing that the pasha would think twice ere he interfered with them, the English race having a way of resenting interference that was very often highly inconvenient to potentates in the East.

But Alum Kay reckoned without his host.

The pasha thought twice, and then resolved to try his luck with the Englishmen, recognising the fact that he must proceed warily.

Indeed, he decided to appear in it personally as little as possible, and he deputed Alum Kay to carry out his plans.

"Go," he said, "take ten mutes and secure the head Englishman. Bring him here in secrecy."

Alum Kay rather demurred to the commission.

"I am not, oh! ruler of the moon," he said, "a man

of war, but one who finds out the path for others to take.”

“Go,” said the pasha, “ or I will shave your head and bastinado your feet until you will not be able to crawl !”

All pashas when they threaten to punish keep their word, so Alum Kay demurred no more, but chose his ten mutes, and departed with them on his errand.

He knew where the Englishmen were to be found —all Alexandria knew it—but he had not the least idea who the head one was.

It was possible also that the pasha was equally ignorant. That was the hope in his heart as he set forth.

It so chanced that his coming, it was at night, timed almost to the minute with the departure of Norton Truscott to see that a fitting place was prepared on board the “ Albatross” for Chunder Loo.

Alum Kay had just arrived and posted his men on either side of the house, when Norton approached it, calling to the seaman on guard to unlock the gate.

As the gifts of the medicine-man did not extend to seeing through stone walls or strong wooden doors, he adopted the tactics of an ordinary mortal, and peeped through the key-hole.

He could by that means just see Norton Truscott approaching, and, judging by his air and authoritative voice, he concluded that the man he sought was approaching.

He ejaculated a thanksgiving, and drawing back, motioned for the mutes to stand flat against the wall and be prepared to obey his signal.

Then he began to hobble to and fro, doubling himself up, as if in pain, after the manner of Eastern beggars when they desire to attract the notice of sympathetic persons.

Norton Truscott came out, and the gate closed behind him. Attracted by the antics of Alum Kay, he saw nothing of the mutes.

“My lord, backsheesh !” gasped Alum Kay.

“At all hours of the day and night,” replied Truscott, “the streets are impeded by men of your stamp. Get out of my way !”

“ Backsheesh,” persisted Alum Kay.

Norton gave him a push, being weary of the beggars of Alexandria, and then Alum Kay threw up his arms. That was the sign.

Swiftly and silently the mutes pounced upon Norton Truscott, each man doing his set share of the work.

One threw a shawl over his head, a second pinioned his arms, two each grasped a leg, and the rest rapidly and skilfully bound a rope about him.

Had he been twice as strong as he was, he would have been helpless. The mutes were brawny, muscular men, and not at all dainty in handling a victim.

As soon as Norton Truscott was secured they raised him up, and by deserted byways carried him to the pasha’s palace, entering it by a back way.

As it was the time when the man in authority was indulging in sleep, he was not disturbed. The prisoner was convey to a chamber, and the shawl removed.

That Norton Truscott was staggered and troubled by thus being forcibly carried away goes without saying. Any man would have felt so, but he had been mixed up in too many dangerous adventures to entirely lose his nerve.

He knew he was not in the power of Chunder Loo. That was impossible. But he feared he had fallen into the clutches of one of his agents or emissaries.

The place in which he found himself was strange, of course, but he recognised it as a portion of a residence inhabited by a man of means.

Alum Kay and the mutes he had not, to his knowledge, seen before.

“Why am I brought here ?” he demanded.

Alum Kay made a sign signifying that he did not understand.

This was a bit of subterfuge. During his varied life he had picked up sufficient English to converse fairly well.

Norton Truscott looked closely at him; and saw the lie written in his face. He repeated his question. Then Alum Kay spoke.

“I know not,” he said. “I but obey the orders of my lord.”

“And who is your lord?” demanded Truscott.

“He will reveal himself anon,” was the answer.

“Can I not have some of my bonds severed ?” asked Norton.

“Yea; but beware of violence. It will cost you your life.”

“Give me some freedom, so that I may rest,” said Norton. “I am tired.”

He would not lie to the man, for it was his intention to seize his opportunity and make a bid for liberty. Still those ten muscular, armed men set him thinking on the nature of the task.

His bonds were taken off, and he threw himself down upon one of the piles of cushions that were scattered about the room.

Alum Kay regarded him with the complacency of a privateer captain who has secured a valuable prize.

Half an hour passed by, and Norton found no opportunity to attempt to escape. Alum Kay walked up and down with his eye upon him. The mutes stood motionless but watchful.

Norton Truscott’s arms—those that had been visible —had been taken from him but in a pocket at the back of his trousers, near the belt, he had an extra revolver which had not been touched.

He had kept it there for a long time to be used in

a case of great emergency. He had almost forgotten it, and the remembrance of it came to him with a rush of joyous feeling.

It was something, but not all he required.

There were six cartridges in it, but if every shot took effect there would still be five men to cope with.

Too many by three, at least. Therefore must he wait a little while.

CHAPTER CCLV.

THE PASHA REJOICETH.—ALUM KAY WEEPS.

HIS mightiness the pasha was awake in an hour, and his first thought was of Alum Kay and his mission. He inquired of a slave in attendance if that puissant person had returned.

The slave was not sure, and on being threatened with the loss of his head, and having listened to the cursing of his parents in good round Eastern fashion, sped away to make inquiries.

His absence was short, for slaves are not laggards if they can help themselves. He speedily returned with Alum Kay in his train.

The medicine-man was subduedly jubilant.

He assumed the air of one who had done a great thing, but was used to it, and was thereupon not unduly elated.

It was a little something he had knocked off in the way of business; no more.

"Well?" said the pasha, who was always out of temper, just a trifle crusty, after sleep.

"My lord, he is here," answered Alum Kay.

"Did he come willingly?"

"Nay, my lord; I was instructed to bring him by force."

"Pig! Liar! An Englishman to be brought here by force! Woe to you if you have hurt a hair of his head!"

Alum Kay was dumbfounded. This was scarcely the return he expected for a meritorious service—rapidly and skilfully performed—let alone the luck of it.

"My lord," he gasped, "he has not suffered. We brought him hither quietly."

"Help me to change my robe," grumbled the pasha.

Washing is not and never has been very popular in the East. Even pashas occasionally neglect their morning ablutions.

Having slept in his robe, a change was advisable, and there being a variety of garments hung upon the walls, Alum Kay selected one, and assisted the pasha to cover his portly frame with it.

"What manner of man is this Englishman?" he asked.

"He is young," answered Alum Kay, "and wears the garb of a sailor."

"Humph!" muttered the pasha, with a frown, "how looked he?—pleased?"

"He has not complained," said Alum Kay, "and regards the palace with a look of awe."

"Humph!" muttered the pasha again, "lead the way."

They had the length of a passage to go, and about half-way down it both were startled by several shots being fired in rapid succession. Both stopped short and exchanged a stare of mingled astonishment and alarm.

"You left him armed?" cried the pasha.

"No, by the beard of the Prophet—no!" cried Alum Kay.

Two or three more shots were fired, and all the time there was a distant sound of feet beating upon a soft carpet. There were no cries, because one of the combatants was mute by choice, and the others because, poor wretches, they could not help it.

"See to it!" cried the pasha, as he turned tail and hastened towards his sleeping-chamber.

Alum Kay stood stock still and moved not, until a solitary figure emerged from the chamber ahead, and rushing towards him, smote the medicine-man upon the nose with the butt end of a revolver.

In the desert, where the air is clear, Alum Kay had often looked at many stars, but never so many at one time as now, and all of them shooting ones.

Then the pasha, with his back to the oncoming peril, received a blow on the side of the head, and rolled over like a felled bullock.

He was not insensible, but he prudently lay quiet for a time—until, indeed, Alum Kay came to his assistance.

Bewailing his misfortunes, the medicine-man picked up the pasha, who faintly inquired:

"The infidel Englishman—where is he?"

"My lord, he is gone, and four mutes lie dead in yonder room."

The pasha rubbed his eyes, gasped and cursed for a while, then he bade Alum Kay strike the gong and summon the household.

The gong hung by a cord suspended from the ceiling. On a bracket fixed to the wall was a species of drumstick.

Alum Kay seized the latter, and made the whole palace resound with the booming of the gong.

Its reverberations speedily brought a number of men, slaves and retainers, armed and unarmed, to the spot.

The pasha bade them follow him to the room where the mutes had been left with the prisoner.

Five dead and five living they found, the air reeking with the smoke of powder, all the cushions kicked here and there, the surviving mutes bleeding and panting, and too bewildered to know what to do.

"Remove those men," said the pasha, pointing to the dead.

It was done with celerity by some of the servants; others put the room in order.

When it was done the pasha squatted down and called for Alum Kay to be brought before him.

Now that command meant that Alum Kay, erstwhile so potent, was a prisoner, and ready hands hauled him into the presence of his master.

"Dog!—traitor!" hissed the pasha, "how is it that you dare betray me?"

"Nay, my lord," pleaded Alum Kay, "I did my duty, as I believed, faithfully and well."

"What duty?"

"My lord, you bade me seize the Englishman——"

"A lie! You are no medicine-man, but a mangy dog—impostor! Off with the lying locks of hair from his head—shave him close!"

The men to do this work were not lacking. As if by magic the necessary implements and materials were forthcoming.

Alum Kay, when his head was shaved, looked more like an idiot than a wise man of the desert.

But there was no laughter; save when the pasha indulged in it, it was rarely heard within those walls.

"You seized an Englishman," he said, "to bring me to dishonour and disgrace! For you the bastinado! Selim!"

A man, answering to the name, stood forth.

"Let it be known throughout the city how I have punished the transgressor. Bastinado him!"

It was done, but less cruelly than when Chunder Loo directed the operation.

But or all that it left Alum Kay in a parlous condition.

When he tried to walk, it was with the gait of a pilgrim with unboiled peas in his shoes.

"Now turn the dog into the street!" said the pasha.

This was done, and, shorn of all his glory, Alum Kay was turned loose among a populace who would now look upon him as a fox shorn of his tail.

The pasha, with the air of a judge who has administered the law under trying circumstances, ordered a light morning meal to be prepared and his carriage got ready for a visit he proposed to pay to the British consul, with the object of clearing his noble self from all implication in the outrage upon Norton Truscott.

———

CHAPTER CCLVI.

THE PASHA IN TROUBLE.—HARRY BARSTOW ON THE WRONG TACK.

IN the bazaars the story of the just pasha's dealing with the impostor, Alum Kay, was rife within the hour. Notwithstanding their affectation of indifference to all things around them, all Eastern men are the veriest gossips in existence. The difference between them and Western chatterers lies in the fact that intolerate laziness leads them to tell their story in as few words as possible.

When the pasha rode away from his palace he was the object of much admiring criticism, and when he condescended to salute the people, they returned the greeting with much humiliation of body and many worded blessings.

In the East, by the way, it is the great people who offer the first salutation; in our country it is expected to come from the poor man. Why the customs should be the very opposite is a matter we must leave the learned to explain.

But it is a fact.

Now the pasha fully expected to hear from the consul that a complaint had been lodged against him by Norton Truscott, whom, it may be stated, he did not know by name.

He only knew him as the chief of the English party—rather indefinite, but all-sufficient, as he conceived, for his purpose.

The consul was at home, and received the pasha with that lofty affability which distinguishes many of our representatives abroad when dealing with foreigners holding minor offices.

He did not appear to understand why he was honoured with the visit, and the expected complaints were not forthcoming.

The pasha, therefore, instead of being called upon to find excuses—at which all his race are adepts—found it fell upon him to accept the more onerous duty of explaining.

He began with a tirade levelled at the disgraced Alum Kay, on whose head, and the heads of all his people, both present and to come, he invoked a perfect blizzard of diseases.

Then he deplored his own weakness in having allowed his charitable heart to get the better of his judgment so as to make that impostor a humble member of his household.

Finally he told the story "of the most unaccountable outrage," and the punishment he had meted out to the offender.

The consul was not so interested as he might have been. To him it appeared that the only serious sufferer was Alum Kay, who was no more to him than one of the semi-wild dogs that infested the streets of Alexandria, doing the duty of scavengers, but living as well as they could on the offal and refuse thrown from the houses.

"I am not in a position to say anything one way or the other," said the consul. "Had you not better call on the gentleman—who has not honoured me with a call—and explain?"

The pasha was doubtful. He feared the Englishman would be violent.

"If he lodges a complaint with me," said the consul, casually, "I shall be compelled to send it on to the Home Government. In that case, it may lead to some diplomatic inquiries."

This was exactly what the pasha did not want, and he declared that he would call at once upon the aggrieved party.

"Perhaps if you were to accompany me," he hinted, "it might smooth the road to peace."

But this the consul would not do. If trumpery Eastern potentates got themselves into trouble, they must get out of it as best they could. He pleaded despatches to write, and sent the pasha on his way.

One incident only happened on the road.

It arose from his meeting with Alum Kay, just outside the busier part of the town, to which the hapless outcast had been driven by a derisive mob of people.

He saw the pasha approaching, recognising the carriage first and the occupant afterwards.

Fury burned within his heart, the passion of revenge sent sparks of fire from his eyes.

He gathered up an armful of street refuse, and crouching down, awaited the passing of the great man.

At the right moment he sprang up and hurled the rubbish at the pasha, covering him with dirt and confusion.

When the potentate had recovered from the shock, he found the carriage had stopped, and one of his attendants was engaged in rubbing him down.

Alum Kay had fled right away into the desert, and was never more heard of.

Probably he skulked about alone until his hair had grown again, and then fastened himself on to a strange tribe in his old *rôle* of medicine-man.

A born humbug, like an inveterate drunkard, rarely abandons his evil ways for good and all. He may reform for a time, but, as a rule, he returns to the mire.

The pasha having been rubbed fairly clean, and eased his tortured soul with sundry additional curses of great potency and originality on the offender, proceeded on to Harry Barstow's residence.

Now, nobody there had the least idea of the events that had recently transpired. No sound of the attack on Norton Truscott, so stealthily carried out, reached the ears of the man at the gate.

And since then nothing had been heard of the victim of the pasha's reprehensible conduct.

He had gone forth to make arrangements for the safe keeping of Chunder Loo on board the "Albatross," and it was naturally assumed that he was engaged in preparing a fitting place of confinement for that slippery scoundrel.

Therefore, when the arrival of the pasha was announced to Harry Barstow, it flashed upon him that the potentate had obtained some inkling of the capture of Chunder Loo, and had come thither to demand his release.

"Sooner than do that," he muttered, "I will make the pasha a prisoner, get Chunder Loo aboard, sail away, and leave the settlement of the whole matter to the future."

CHAPTER CCLVII.

THE PASHA IS ENTERTAINED TO HIS OWN SATISFACTION AND THAT OF OTHER PEOPLE.

FIRST sending word to the pasha that he would join him immediately, Harry hastened up to the room where Chunder Loo was confined.

There he found that Tom Drummond and Don Peebles had gone off watch for the day, intending to resume it at night.

Jack, however, was as resolute as ever not to go far from the prisoner until he was safe on board the "Albatross."

Drawing him aside, Harry Barstow briefly explained the position, as he viewed it. Jack thought it was very grave.

"Come what may," said Harry Barstow, "the pasha must be detained."

"But suppose he declines to stay?" said Jack.

"We must keep him by force."

"Can you ask him to dinner with a prospect of his accepting? If he has really come for Chunder Loo, you must, once in a way, tell a fib, and say he is not here."

"I won't do that," replied Harry Barstow, resolutely; "but I can send the pasha's carriage away unknown to him, and inform his servants that he will return home in mine."

"A first-rate idea. But suppose we shut the man up, won't there be a row?"

"Yes, but when it comes off I hope to be far away at sea."

"Suppose the pasha won't stop, and insists upon taking Chunder Loo?"

"I will give you a timely warning. When there is

nothing else to be done I will shoot him with my own hand."

"Why should you get into trouble over *our* affairs?" urged Jack.

"Have you not endured much for me?" was the answer. "Now I will go and see this arrogant potentate."

The arrogant potentate was expecting him with his heart in his slippers. When Harry Barstow entered the room he bowed low. Up to that moment he had not ventured to seat himself.

Now it will be remembered that he had not fairly seen Norton Truscott when a prisoner, and therefore may be pardoned for thinking that he saw his late captive before him.

"As a duty, noble sir," he began, "I have called to see you concerning the outrage perpetrated last night."

"Be seated, I beg of you," returned Harry Barstow.

The pasha was astonished by his amiable reception. But knowing something of the craft of wicked man' he was still uneasy.

He seated himself on the cushions that formed a portion of the furniture, and Harry Barstow, not to be behind with anything conciliatory, squatted down beside him.

"The hookah," he said, "is a great assistance to thought, and helps in a consultation. Will you smoke, pasha?"

Would a duck swim? The pasha did not exactly use the words, but he said something synonymous, and Harry Barstow summoned an attendant by striking a bell.

Penny Bunn responded, his appearance overwhelming the pasha with astonishment.

"Of what tribe is your slave?" he asked.

"He comes of a tribe beyond the sea," replied Harry, gravely.

Bunn received his orders, and fetched two hookahs, which he duly filled and lighted. He certainly had the requisite aptitude to make a good servant.

With the tobacco going there came a long silence. Neither of the smokers seemed to care to renew the matter that was in his mind.

The pasha felt that, so far, he had got along pretty well, but the natural suspicions in his mind refused to be entirely lulled.

Harry Barstow wanted to feel his way to a knowledge of what the pasha required of him, and not being a born diplomatist, did not see exactly how it was to be done.

But he eventually broke the silence.

"Perhaps," he said, with a faint attempt to smile, "you are wondering what I intend to do?"

"No," replied the pasha, "I never wonder. It is a waste of time."

"What do you think I ought to do?"

"I never think at all, if I can help it."

It was to the pasha as if he had been a prisoner convicted of a crime, and called upon to pass sentence on himself.

Now it is known, and has been referred to by many travellers, that the Turks have the gift of sitting still thinking of absolutely *nothing*. By what arrangement of the brain this gift is created has often puzzled learned men; but it is a fact.

Many Turks and other Eastern men have the gift of sitting still, wide awake, and yet with their mental faculties entirely at rest.

Harry Barstow remembered having read of this some time before in a work written by a physician, who was in Turkey at the same time with the Lady Mary Wortley Montagu of undying fame, some eighty years ago.

Therefore he was not so much astonished as he might otherwise have been by the Pasha's reply.

"Well, it comes to this," said he, resolutely. "I mean to have my way in the matter. "I have truth and justice entirely on my side."

"Yes," said the pasha, in that tone in which assent and dissent are so evenly proportioned. So there is no more to be said, and therefore I propose to take my leave of you."

"Not yet; the hookah is but half-smoked."

"It can remain until I come again."

"Pardon me; but this is your first visit, and it must be the last."

The pasha was alarmed, but he strove to hide it by vigorously smoking. Harry Barstow kept him company, and presently spoke again.

"I was thinking," he said, "of detaining you for the rest of the day. You must not think of leaving me."

It was merely a polite way of offering hospitality, but the intended guest was more and more alarmed.

To him it was a covert way of informing him that he was a prisoner.

"You are an Englishman," he said, "and, true to the bent of your race, carrying things with a high hand."

"If circumstances compel me to," was the answer.

"Do not forget who I am," hissed the pasha. "I am high in authority here."

"But yours is an authority," replied Harry Barstow, "I am not disposed to recognise."

The pasha dropped the mouthpiece of his hookah and endeavoured to rise to his feet.

"Let my attendants be called," he said, "to escort me to my carriage."

"They are not here." No; I have despatched them home, with an intimation that when you return it will be in a carriage of mine. When the time comes, I will hire one for you."

Every vestige of colour outside the natural brown fled from the cheeks of the pasha.

Visions of a violent death and his body cast into the sea, floated before his eyes.

In a moment or two he went through the whole scene, following it up with all the lies the murderous Englishman would tell of his having been sent back to the palace and probably murdered on the way.

He turned to Harry Barstow, with his hands clasped and tears running down his cheeks.

"I am an old man," he said, "and not worth the killing. I am poor, or I would bribe you to spare me."

"I do not want a bribe," replied Harry Barstow; "nor is it my intention to slay. All I ask of you is to stay here until the evening—my guest."

"Until the evening?"

"Yes; and sacrifice the prejudices of your race and dine with me."

"Poison!" thought the pasha, and the dew of fear stood out upon his brow.

"I never dine with strangers," he faltered.

"Forego your rule for once," said Harry Barstow. "Indeed, you must!"

"My lord—noble sir—I beg of you not to press me in this matter! I am a poor, forlorn old man, put into an office in which there is little to be got from a contumacious people; but if——"

"I have told you," said Harry Barstow, "that I want nothing and will take nothing. But here you must remain—willingly, I hope. If not, you will be detained."

He rose up, and walking to one of the windows, threw it open. Outside, the gardens were illuminated with all the glory of a perfect day.

"You know these grounds," he said, "having probably visited them in days gone by. They are surrounded by a high wall, which you cannot scale. My servants will be about the grounds, armed and instructed to prevent you from making your escape. I advise you not to attempt it; and as you will not eat or drink with me, I must leave you. Your wants will be attended to."

And without waiting for further remonstrance from the terrified pasha, he left the room.

CHAPTER CCLVIII.

NORTON TRUSCOTT'S RETURN.—A COMPLICATED POSITION.

"I'VE done it now," thought Harry Barstow, as he walked down the passage. "The old gentleman seems to be rather astonished; but, really, I do not see what else could be done."

He had no fear that the pasha would attempt to escape. He was such a bulky old man, and evidently unaccustomed to exercise, and the bare idea of his trying to scale the walls gave rise to ludicrous visions of failure.

He could get into the gardens and shout, of course, but there was nobody to hear him; and if by any chance a stray native passed that way, he would not consider it his business to interfere.

But Harry Barstow was not entirely satisfied with his position.

He would much rather have had the pasha stay as his guest, and he looked upon his refusal as the outcome of the arrogant pride of Ottoman caste.

Anyway, now that he had gone so far he could not retreat. He considered that setting him free now would result in very serious complications with the authorities.

His first care was to look up Bunn and instruct him to take in food and wine to the guest, his second to instruct the victim of Chunder Loo's brutality to lock the door on the outside, and, thirdly, he appointed himself as sentry in the grounds to check the involuntary guest should he attempt to get out of the window.

"If the pasha speaks to you," he said to Bunn, "affect not to understand. He may attempt to bribe you to help him to escape. It is my desire that he remains here to-day."

Bunn entered upon the task of ministering to the wants of the pasha with a natural zest, and he placed before that functionary the best the house afforded, including two bottles of Moët's champagne.

As Harry Barstow premised, the pasha made an offer to Bunn of a vast amount of wealth if he would help him to escape, but without making any effect upon him.

Penny Bunn pretended he did not understand, throwing up his hands, as he said:

"Non comprenny, mossoo."

The pasha did not understand French, especially when uttered in a petrified form, and he made signs which he hoped would be understood.

Bunn shook his head, and looking outwardly indignant, left the room.

Meanwhile Harry Barstow had taken up a position near the window, out of sight of the unwilling guest.

He could hear him groaning and puffing, and calling down all sorts of pains and penalties on those within the house, but nothing escaped the lips of the pasha to give him a clue to the actual facts.

As the time passed, he began to wonder why Norton Truscott did not return, but as at the outset, he thought that he was merely detained by the necessities arising out of the putting up of a strong cell for Chunder Loo.

By-and-by Tom Drummond came strolling along, and finding him there—the window was at the back of the house—expressed his surprise.

Harry Barstow explained the state of things, and bade Tom get him some food.

Tom was exhilarated beyond measure by the thought of having a real live pasha a prisoner in the house, and he went off exultingly to do Harry Barstow's bidding.

As he came round by the front of the house, he saw no less a personage than Norton Truscott coming down the path from the front gate.

To him Tom must needs impart the good tidings.

"A pasha a prisoner!" exclaimed Norton. "What brought him here?"

"He came to demand the release of Chunder Loo, I believe," replied Tom.

"How did he know the brute was here?"

"That I can't tell," said Tom. "You will find Barstow at the back of the house; he will explain everything."

Off went Tom to get some food as desired, and Norton Truscott, in a complete fog, wended his way to the back of the house.

"Good heavens, Harry!" he exclaimed, "what is the matter now?"

"I will tell you in a minute," replied Harry. "What has made you so long?"

"I have had an adventure," replied Truscott, "and deuce a bit can I make out what it all means. I was seized as I went out last night and carried away."

He then, as briefly as he could, related his adventures. Up to the time when he floored the pasha the reader is acquainted with them. There is little more to tell, and we give it in his own words:—

"As soon as I bowled the old fellow over, I shot along down the passage and got into a perfect maze of rooms. Shortly after a gong sounded, and I hopped into an alcove that was curtained in front. Then came a lot of fellows rushing by, in response to the gong, I suppose, and the instant they were past I came out again and took the way they had come.

"By great good luck," he added, laughing, "I came to a passage that led to a small door, secured only by a bolt. I opened the door, and found myself in a narrow street. I cleared off as quickly as I could, going on, as it were, blindfold—and so eventually got wrong, of course. I went right away to the opposite side of the town."

"I begin to see a little light," said Harry.

"It was not my desire to fall in with these blackguards again," resumed Norton Truscott, "so I worked my way, in a roundabout fashion, to the quay, and went off to the 'Albatross.' Everything there will be ready in a few hours, but not, I fancy, much before the morning."

"Why did you not come back and tell me what had happened to you?" asked Harry.

"Well, I thought my story would keep," replied Truscott.

"Now, I have something to tell you," said Harry, and he gave him an account of the coming of the pasha, and what he had done with him.

Norton Truscott listened with an amused face.

"And you think that he has come to demand the release of Chunder Loo?"

"What else can he have come for?"

"He certainly would have done it in a different way. Has he positively stated that is his errand?"

"No; but I took it for granted that that was his object."

"There is more in this than is clear at present," said Norton. "Suppose we go and ask him direct what brought him here?"

"I shall be only too pleased, but I think it is needless. He can have no other object."

So they went together, in by the open window, and found the pasha sitting gloomily before the viands he had not ventured to taste.

He received them with a quivering lip and a tear rolling from either eye, believing that his doom had come, and Norton Truscott was to be his executioner.

But there was not murder in the air of that gentleman as he sat down beside the pasha and asked him plainly what had brought him hither.

Then came the explanation, to which Harry Barstow listened with dumb amazement.

Norton Truscott grasped the old man by the hand, and revealed himself as the person outraged.

"I knew," he said, "that no man of position was responsible for the affair. What could be the object of this Alum Kay?"

"He got it into his accursed head," replied the pasha, "that you knew where the wealth of the sham rajah was hidden."

"And what has become of the sham rajah?" asked Norton, suavely.

"A murrain seize him!" hissed the pasha. "What care I? He is a murderer—he has fled—may his bones rot in the desert!"

The whole thing was out now, and it was as much as Norton Truscott could do to keep from laughing aloud; especially when he saw the grave face of Harry Barstow, who was wondering how he was to explain his conduct to the pasha.

But Norton Truscott put everything right.

He informed the pasha that his long absence had made his friend anxious, and that *he* was the person outraged; but with the explanation given he was perfectly satisfied.

"I fear," he said, by way of conclusion, "that my

friend thought you were guilty—he will, of course, apologise."

Harry did so in a most handsome manner, and the pasha, glad to find that he had nothing to fear, shook hands with him.

Nay, more, he consented to stay and dine, and Tom Drummond, having been informed through the window, when he appeared with the tray for Harry Barstow, that he could take it back again, the trio had a little preliminary feast, the pasha showing that he was not entirely innocent of the merits of champagne.

The dinner was a glorious success, and the pasha swore eternal friendship for his hosts.

Just about the time when Don and Tom Drummond resumed the night-watch—Jack had again taken to sleep after a wakeful day—the pasha was sent home in a hired carriage, most ingloriously drunk.

"It was the old beggar's own scheme that was foiled," said Norton Truscott, "but I think we may consider that the blue funk you put him in, Harry, squared the whole business."

CHAPTER CCLIX.

THE NIGHT-WATCH.—HASKA WAFFA GETS INTO TROUBLE.

HELPLESS, save in the matter of speech, Chunder Loo lay almost at full length upon the floor. At his back was a cushion on which his head rested.

Tom Drummond and Don Peebles stood facing him, resolved to make their watch a thorough one.

The glittering eyes of the rascal were fixed in turns upon them.

For awhile there was silence, and then he spoke, addressing himself to Don.

"It was you," he said, "who, in the old days in Littlecote Abbey, killed my friend."

"I killed nothing in Littlecote Abbey," replied Don. "And if by your friend you mean that little reptile snake—I admit I killed it in the wood."

"Ah-h-h-h-h!" exclaimed Chunder Loo, with a curious drawing in of his breath. "You thought it was a great thing to do, perhaps?"

"I considered it was a good thing," calmly answered Don, "for it put a stop to your unholy worship of the reptile. But why recall that? It was long ago, or it seems so to me. Surely you have got over your great loss?"

"You sneer because you do not understand," said Chunder Loo. "Mehala, my little snake, was more than a friend. It was a wise and sure counsellor. But vast as was the loss to me, I forgive you."

His eyes belied this assertion. Don smiled.

"It matters nothing to me," he said, "whether you forgive or not."

"You are wriggling about," said Tom. "Do that again and I shoot! We know you of old."

He went up to Chunder Loo, turned him half over, and carefully examined his bonds. Assured that they were still fast, he resumed his position by the side of Don.

"Better not talk to the fellow," he said, in an undertone.

Don nodded assent, and although Chunder Loo persistently addressed them again and again, they gave him no answer.

He seemed to have some object in continually speaking, for at last Don got a bit out of patience with him.

"If you are not quiet," he said, "you will be gagged again. We are provided with the necessary article."

Chunder Loo answered with a snarl, but he was quiet for a time. Anon—it may have been half an hour afterwards — his face gradually assumed a listening expression. Don observed it, and his suspicions were aroused.

But he made no sign, and lounging carelessly against the wall, yawned as if tired of his task.

The silence became profound in the alcove, and the only sound without that he at first could hear was the light, regular breathing of Jack Ford.

But as he listened with all his ears, he fancied he heard a slight, shuffling noise, as of one stealthily crossing the carpet.

A sidelong glance at the face of Chunder Loo showed that he heard it also.

The inference to be drawn from it was that there was danger in the air.

Don yawned again, put his hand before his mouth, and looked in the direction of his companion watcher.

Their eyes met, and Tom received at a glance the information that there was something wrong, and also a request to keep still.

Tom obeyed him, remaining so still that he might have been taken for a waxwork figure. He kept his eyes on Don, who, with head a little on one side, put his hand to his mouth and yawned.

Chunder Loo closed his eyes and drew a long breath as if sinking into sleep.

But it was a little overdone, for his breast heaved as if he were agitated. There were indications of suppressed excitement in the quivering of his hands. That something of a startling nature was impending was evident.

Again Don turned his attention to the sound in the room, and with a slow movement he got his hand upon one of his revolvers.

The moment he had succeeded in doing this he

A SPLENDID SCHOOL STORY. NEVER BEFORE PUBLISHED.

By E. HARCOURT BURRAGE,

Author of "Ching Ching," "Monkev Mat and Roving Dick," "The Brave Bo*v* of the Basilisk," &c.

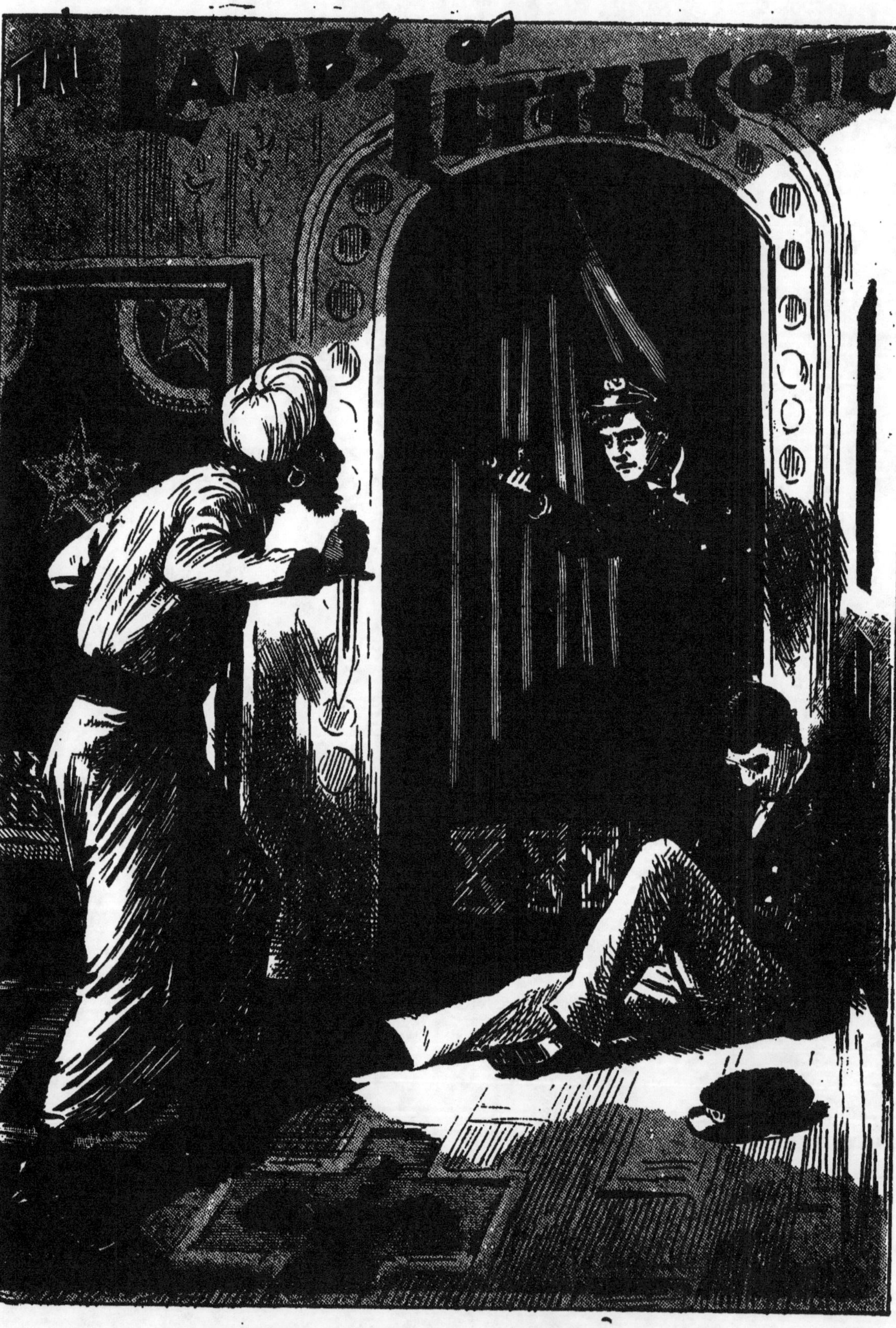

"STAND!" ORIED TOM. "DROP THAT KNIFE, HASKA WAFFA!"

No. 35. PRICE ONE PENNY.

ALDINE PUBLISHING CO., 40 Red Lion Court, Fleet St., and 1, 2 & 3 Crown Court, Chancery Lane, Lond.

suddenly whisked aside the curtain and saw Haska Waffa, with a long, thin knife in his hand, creeping up upon his hands and knees.

He was within a few feet of Jack, who was doubtless the object of his coming. It was his intention to assassinate him.

As the light flashed upon him, he leaped upon his feet.

"Stand!" cried Don. "Tom, don't lose sight of Chunder Loo! Drop that knife, Haska Waffa!"

"Stab them!" shrieked Chunder Loo, and then he cried out something in a strange tongue that inspired Haska Waffa with the fury of a fanatic.

Uttering a wild yell, he leapt towards Don, shaking the knife in the air, its blade glittering with a dazzling effect. There was a species of fascination in the movement that might have been fatal to Don if he had not kept cool.

He saw that it would be madness to hesitate, and taking steady aim, he fired.

Haska Waffa pulled up short, stood upright for a moment with a fixed and ghastly expression in his eyes, and then fell, as a tower comes to the ground, straight and stiff, upon his face.

He was shot through the heart.

The report of the weapon awoke Jack, and he sprang up awake and alert on the instant. From distant rooms there came the sound of voices, as the inmates called to each other.

"What is the row, Don?" asked Jack.

"The skunk was creeping up to assassinate you, Jack," replied Don, as he tossed aside the empty cartridge-case from the revolver and replaced it with another, "and I brought him down."

Jack patted him on the shoulder and turned his eyes down the room, where Harry and Bob Stockton appeared, heading the rest of the occupants of the house.

A hurried explanation was given of the event, and angry exclamations were heard from all around.

The attempt at assassination, coupled with previous things, established the fact that Haska Waffa had been the tool, or in the pay, of Chunder Loo.

"It appears," said Harry Barstow, addressing him, "that you have a very extensive connection among the knaves and murderous scoundrels in every part of the world."

Chunder Loo made no reply, but a curious smile curled his lip.

"After this," said Norton Truscott, in an undertone, "it will be better to get our prisoner on board the 'Albatross.' The original idea of keeping him until a place is prepared for him must be modified. There is no knowing how many ruffians he may have in his pay."

"They will go short of their wages now," said Harry, with a dry smile; "but I agree with you. Send Startop with a lantern to signal for a boat."

Truscott departed, and Harry dismissed all but the youngsters and Dirk Matthews to their beds again. Dirk especially pleaded to be allowed to remain to assist in getting Chunder Loo on board.

"And there I'll stop, with your leave, sir, and if he gets away from me, I'll cheerfully pay for it with my life."

"There is one thing I would like to say before you take me away," said Chunder Loo, "but it is not for the ears of boys, and if Captain Barstow will give me a minute, I will look upon it as a favour."

"'Ware treachery," said Jack.

Harry Barstow smiled and bade them leave him, but to keep within call.

So they went out, and turning to the prisoner, he said:

"Now say what you have to say, and get over it speedily."

"Drop the curtain," said Chunder Loo.

Harry hesitated, and a jeering laugh burst from the prisoner.

"Armed to the teeth," he cried, "and afraid of an unarmed man bound hand and foot! Truly, you English are a brave race!"

"You mistake my hesitation altogether," calmly answered Harry Barstow. "I was merely wondering if it were not a degradation to hold private conference with such a wretch as you."

Having said this he dropped the curtain.

CHAPTER CCLX.

CHUNDER LOO'S OFFER.—JACK WORKS OUT ANOTHER PROBABILITY.

"IT would be folly for me to pretend that I am about to make you an offer, save for my own benefit," said Chunder Loo. "I am about, to put it shortly, to make an effort to buy back my life."

"You have no hope of its being spared in England?" returned Harry Barstow.

"Not an atom. They will, if they get me, hang me as high as the law allows, and once in an accursed British prison, the chances of escape are reduced to a minimum. Neither your judges nor your gaolers can be bribed. Even your executioners are incorruptible."

"They are helpless," said Harry.

"Yes—perhaps," replied Chunder Loo; "but to come to the point I have to speak of: How much money or money's worth will you take for my life?"

"The offer is ridiculous—childish."

"It may be. But that time would prove, if you are

willing to make a bargain. What say you to a hundred thousand pounds?"

"Your life is not mine to sell. It has been forfeited to the laws of my country."

"Two hundred thousand?"

"I tell you——"

"Three hundred thousand—four—I can tell you where to find it. Think of it. *A half-million then?* Come, there was never so big a price offered for so worthless a life as mine."

"I have enough for my needs," said Harry Barstow. "No sum would tempt me to shield a murderer from justice. Besides, you are not my prisoner. It was Ford who was the chief instrument of your capture."

"From the time I met him and his friends," hissed Chunder Loo, "they have been my curse. If you will not listen to reason, call him hither."

"You will waste your breath," replied Harry Barstow; "but I will ask him to come here."

He called to Jack, and he responded quickly.

"Chunder Loo has an offer to make you," said Harry.

Jack, with a sarcastic smile, turned his eyes upon the prisoner, who struggled to keep cool, but was evidently in a burning fever of rage.

"I want to buy my life," he said, "at a price that will give you a princely fortune."

"Well," said Jack; "name the sum you think you are worth."

"Half a million."

"Of course," said Jack, drily, "you have the money about you?"

"I can tell you where it is to be found," said Chunder Loo, knitting his brows, "and I will trust to your honour to release me on obtaining possession of it."

"All right," said Jack, easily, "I will think it over."

"If I tell you now——"

"Pray keep your secret for the present. The offer requires a little reflection."

Harry Barstow was much surprised to hear Jack speak in this fashion. He expected him to indignantly refuse the offer. His face betrayed his thoughts, and Jack looked at him with a smile.

"If you will come outside with me," he said, "I will tell you why I gave him that answer."

They drew aside, and Jack, dropping his voice, said:

"I was but giving him back some of his own physic. Let him have a ray of hope for the present. It will be extinguished by-and-by. As for his half-million and the rest, if it exists I mean to have it, and keep him too. There is no bribe that could induce me to set him free. He has forfeited his life a hundred times."

"Spoken well, as I expected you would," said Harry Barstow. "Now you and the other boys get to bed. I will watch here."

"And what of *that?*" asked Jack, pointing to the body of Haska Waffa.

"Oh, that will be left here for the pasha who palmed the scoundrel on me. To-morrow, or the next day at the least, we shall all be on board the 'Albatross.' The repairs will be hastened by our presence, and there will be more assurance of the safekeeping of——"

And he pointed to Chunder Loo.

Jack left with his friends, and on the way to his chamber he signified that he would be glad of a chat with them.

"I don't know how it is with you," he said, "but as soon as I am awake, no matter how short the sleep I have had, I feel as if I shall never sleep again. In other words, I am as fresh as paint."

They all declared they were ready for anything he wanted them for, and they adjourned to his room—he shared it with Don—and throwing himself in an easy attitude upon his couch, he prepared to say what was on his mind.

The trio sat side by side on Don's bed.

"Now open confession is good," began Jack, "and you may as well admit being a bit sore over my not calling you in to help in the capturing of Chunder Loo."

"We thought you *might* have given us the tip, anyway," said Bob.

"Just so," laughed Jack. "Well, the reason I did not was that it was a job for few to help in, and the fewer the better. If we had all been of the party, we'd have been too numerous. Now, to make amends, I have another task to carry out, in which I shall want the help of you all."

"Hear, hear!" cried Don.

"Dirk Matthews," said Jack, "discovered the wealth of the Avishus just in time to be robbed of it. Full particulars can wait a bit. As time presses, I will condense facts. Chunder Loo got possession of it, and it is hidden away somewhere under his palace."

"You think there *is* a real treasure?" said Don.

"I am sure of it, and whoever gets hold of it has a right to keep it."

"If he can," said Bob.

"Of course. If he can. Now the difficulty is to locate that treasure; but, thinking the matter over, I fancy I have an inkling of the spot where it lies hidden. You have all heard about the water reservoir, and that Dirk Matthews discovered it through the curious pivot-door in the lumber-room being partly open?"

"Yes, yes," they said

"Well, then comes the question, Why was that door

open?" said Jack. "It must have been closed for a long time prior to Chunder's occupancy, as none of the servants of the palace appear to have any knowledge of it. The answer is, that Chunder Loo, who is as keen on the scent of hidden places and secret ways as a pig is after truffles in a French forest, discovered the reservoir and hid his money there."

"Got it again," said Don. "You are a marvel, Jack."

"Oh, blow your compliments," replied Jack, "especially for hitting upon such a simple matter. Chunder Loo must have come up one day, and omitted to properly secure the door. Dirk Matthews found it, but had no idea that there was below all that he had lost, or, as he puts it, was robbed of."

"I see more light," said Bob.

"But the reservoir is a big place," continued Jack, "and will take a lot of looking over. So I propose that we have a day and a night of it there. We can take some prog and lighting material, and rummage the place from end to end. If we can't find it—it isn't there, that's all."

"We are with you, Jack," said Don. "When do we start?"

"As soon as Chunder Loo is on board," answered Jack. "I sha'n't feel easy till he is there, but when he is stowed away, I *know* he will be secure. Truscott will see that he is kept tight, and there is no chance of his being rescued by any of his villainous connections. Of course I must get leave of Barstow, for we can never tell what is going to happen, and if we risked our lives and lost them, it might not be agreeable to him to have Chunder Loo left as a legacy."

"It is all, or nearly all, we have to leave him," said Bob, pathetically.

"There is Bunn—and Mulberry Cork," said Don.

"Yes, there are two prize curiosities. One must laugh," said Tom Drummond, "but at the same time it is impossible not to feel sorry. The malevolent invention of Chunder Loo is unapproachable."

"Having settled that matter," said Jack, "I advise you all to lie down and rest, if you don't want to sleep. I shall give the next hour or so to think over my plans."

He began to think right away, and thought so hard that in five minutes sleep came back to him again.

And it came to the others, so that when they awoke broad daylight had come once more to brighten the party and make glad the hearts of all honest men.

———

CHAPTER CCLXI.

IN THE RESERVOIR.—THE PASHA THINKS HE WILL HAVE ANOTHER HUNT FOR THE POSSIBLE HIDDEN WEALTH.

"HAVE you not had enough of adventure in this hole of a place?" asked Harry Barstow, with a smile, when Jack Ford spoke to him concerning the expedition in search of the treasure of Chunder Loo.

"There is little or no risk," answered Jack; "the palace is deserted—nobody is on the same quest."

"It appears to me," said the captain of the "Albatross," thoughtfully, "that there is always a risk in prying about these Eastern dens; but I suppose you are bent on going?"

"I think it is too good a thing, sir, to leave untouched."

"Very well—go; but you had better have a man with you—Startop, or someone you can trust in an emergency."

"We would rather, if you do not mind, sir, work this thing without any help. It isn't greediness, but we have so often done things in company with unvarying success, that we feel we are strong enough to carry it through unaided."

After that there was no more to be said, and leave was granted them, on condition that should a night's work bring forth no fruit, they were to give up the search and report themselves on board the "Albatross."

Jack readily assented to this, and went off to his friends, delighted beyond measure.

He told them that so far they were on the road to success, and preparations for the search were at once begun.

They had the whole day to themselves, and the first thing to be done was to see to their arms and a proper supply of ammunition.

The latter they placed in sportsmen's belts, to be worn round the waist.

Next they looked up lanterns, with a fitting supply of candles. Oil was voted to be messy and uncertain in giving light. With composite candles there was no trimming of wicks required.

Last of all they made due provision for the inner man, in the shape of a packet of sandwiches, and a flask of wine for each.

With impatience they awaited the coming of night, and to kill some of the time, in the afternoon they took a trip to the "Albatross," lying off the shore, and had a peep at Chunder Loo in confinement.

He was placed in an empty store-room, with a stout door, not only secured with lock and key, but with strong bolts also. Two men were on guard outside, and Truscott or Bill Oakley were always within the hail of a "whisper" from the sentries.

Night came at last, and as soon as the sun vanished the four friends started in pairs, with a score or so paces between them, so as to lessen the chances of attracting unwelcome attention.

Jack and Don led the way through the town, and barring the inevitable applications for backsheesh, for the really or falsely afflicted, met with no obstruction on the way.

Backsheesh having been refused some of the earlier applicants, they were eventually left at peace to pursue their way. Had they weakly yielded to the first demands, they would have had a train of cripples in their wake, importunate to a degree, and not to be easily shaken off.

They found the region round the palace of the departed "Rajah" quite deserted.

To the populace Chunder Loo had come and gone as a meteor of the night. He was but as one of the passing file of figures in a show.

The gates, however, were fast, and the seal of Mustapha Pasha intact.

"He is not likely to come this way again," said Jack. "We shall have the whole show to ourselves."

But Jack, for once in a way, was in error.

The pasha was at that very moment meditating another visit to the palace to look round, on the off chance of finding something to account for the recent display of Chunder Loo.

The old thirst was upon him.

It is astonishing how it clings to a man. Having got the notion that there ought to be a treasure hidden away somewhere behind those stone walls, he reasoned in vain against it.

In his heart he could not believe he would get anything to reward his labours, but the feeling that he must have another hunt, was too strong for him.

Therefore did he say to one Ali Bey, a faithful follower of his, and almost as big a rogue as Alum Kay:

"Ali, son of Meshach, we will go forth, and, unaided by others, search the palace alone."

"My lord hath well spoken," answered Ali Bey.

"And therefore, oh, Ali, son of Meshach, do thou prepare for the going thither. Get wine and oil, and also some tobacco, in the form of the infidel cigar. See, likewise, that the lamp thou takest is in good order, on pain of dismissal from thine office. For, governor as thou art of a province, I am mightier than thou."

"And for that which he seeketh," said the bey, "if it should so befall that we find it, what shall be my share thereof?"

"We will apportion it afterwards—or what say you to an honest fourth?"

"It is not enough," replied the bey, shaking his head. "Let it be a third, or you go alone."

"A third it shall be," said Mustapha Pasha, solemnly, "I swear it by the beard of the Sultan!

"And, furthermore, do thou get two disguises for us, lest peradventure the people discern us and ask themselves why we walk abroad without an escort."

Ali Bey went about the business he was commanded to do, and with a rare wit hit upon two disguises that not only hid their personality but their sex.

In short, he assisted the pasha to disguise himself as a woman.

The clothing and the veil hid all that indicated his being a man, and when Ali had got himself up they made two elephantine women to the eye.

Meanwhile Jack and his friends had gained admission to the passage leading to the reservoir without attracting attention, and after a careful creeping through the entrance, dark as pitch, gained the vast underground hall where they could consider themselves safe.

The lamps were all lighted, as they had an abundant supply of candles in bags swung upon their backs.

"Now the first thing to do," said Jack, "is to arrange a system to work upon."

"You mean," said Don, "to go to work so that we do not travel over the same ground more than once?"

"Just so."

"This doesn't look a likely place for the hiding of valuables," remarked Tom.

It did not. To all appearance the floor was smooth and bare, and the stately columns concealed nothing. Jack walked straight across until he came to the wall. There he halted, and taking out his knife, scraped away some of the small fungi that clustered thickly upon it.

"We shall know this place when we come to it again," he said, "now forward." A dozen steps brought them to one of the spoke-like passages that led to the ventilating holes. Jack held up his light above his head and peered down it. "All black here," he said. "Perhaps the way is blocked."

Leaving his lantern upon the ground, and bidding the others hold theirs up so as to give him as much light as possible, he walked in slowly for a dozen feet, and then found the way blocked by fallen masonry.

"No thoroughfare here," he said; "the way is blocked."

They all turned back, and in a few moments came to another, down which they penetrated, and found that it led to a ventilator in the heart of a double wall.

By this arrangement it was concealed from prying eyes, for the outlet was somewhere on the summit, and doubtless where it would not be found and seen by ordinary observers.

So they went on inspecting some half-dozen, all of

which, save the one with the fallen masonry and that by which they had entered, were built so as to terminate in a double wall.

At last they came to that which led up to the palace rooms where Chunder Loo recently held his weird, hideous revels.

Jack, of course, was, in a sense, familiar with the chambers, but the others had not seen them, and were naturally anxious to do so.

"We have lots of time," said Don; "it can't be more than ten o'clock now."

"I'll give you half an hour up there," said Jack, "then we must come back here. I feel certain we shall land something before the morning."

He led them up to the door, that turned upon a swivel, and showed them how it worked.

"Now see," he said, "a push here does the trick."

And putting his shoulder to one side of the door, he turned it.

He showed them the lumber-room and the chamber in which Chunder Loo had fallen into a sudden sleep from which he awoke to find himself a prisoner.

Then on to the room where Pestro the pirate had met his death at the hand of Dirk Matthews.

So little account did the authorities take of the deed that the room was as it had been left on that eventful morning. There was the cushion on which the pirate had slept his last sleep. It was of crimson velvet, and there was the dark stain made by his life's blood as it flowed from his breast.

They were commenting on the weird interest of the place, when Jack called on them to be still for a moment.

"I fancy I hear voices," he said. "Listen!"

They listened, and all could hear the muffled tones of speakers, apparently in the passage without.

"Back to your burrow!" hastily whispered Jack.

They slipped away, like scared rabbits, through the intervening rooms, and took refuge behind the pivot door.

Jack lingered till the last—lingered until he saw the curtains that covered the entrance to the rooms agitated by a human hand, which was thrust through to draw them back.

Then he joined his companions with all speed and bade them get down below.

He closed the door, and they vanished down the steps, wondering who it was that had come and so unexpectedly disturbed them.

"It is the Pasha, I reckon," muttered Jack. "He has got scent of there being something worth prowling round after, and if he is a true Oriental he will nose it out like a dog. Come, boys, we must not idle now."

They went rapidly through the rest of the ventilating passages, and then began to examine the flooring, walking in a line across the reservoir, and taking it in sections.

But there was nothing to give them encouragement in the close-fitting, grimy flags. Not a sign of anything that could possibly lead to a hidden receptacle for jewellery was to be found.

"You are on the wrong tack for once, Jack," said Bob Stockton. "For my part, I think the beggar has shipped the lot off to somewhere, say London, or Paris. It was not his game to live on here."

"Not to London," said Jack; "too risky. Stay, boys, I feel sure the stuff is here, and"—he paused, as a light suffused his face, for breath—"by Jehosaphat! I've got it! Or, failing it this time, we shall not get it at all."

He cast a quick glance round, as if getting at his precise locality, and then, as the carrier-pigeon goes for home, made for the place that had flashed across his mind.

CHAPTER CCLXII.

MUSTAPHA PASHA AND ALI BEY MAKE MERRY.—THE PASHA RECOGNISES AN ARRANGEMENT FOR SECRECY.

ALI BEY, of some province which we have no record of, did not forget the inner man in the preparations he had made for searching the house.

Unlike his leader, he was not very keen upon it. He did not believe that there was anything to find, although he had, with Oriental caution, stipulated for his share if a prize should turn up.

Under the petticoats in which he had arrayed his portly person, he had hung about his waist sundry bottles of wine and a box of cigars.

Food he intended to bring, but somehow omitted to do so.

"What says my lord to a little refreshment ere we proceed further?" he said.

"In truth, bey, I am prepared for it," sighed the pasha. "Wine is a mocker, however. It will not do to put too much into the blood."

Ali Bey produced a bottle with the modern invention of a corkscrew that acted as a lever and gave no trouble. Among other things he had brought two silver cups, which he now proceeded to fill up.

"Drink, my lord," he said.

"Though wine be forbidden to the true believer," sighed the pasha, "it is needed for my blood. I will drink it for the sake of my health."

And he drained the cup.

Ali did the same, and filled up again.

"Solitude," he said, "is not good for anything. Therefore shall a lone cup make us sad, wherefore if we swallow another to keep it company, our hearts shall be merry."

And they both drank again. Ali Bey produced the cigars, handed them to his principal, and lit one himself.

"If we had a sportive dancing girl to cheer us," he said, meditatively, "my lord, we should be truly merry."

But the sportive girl not being available, they took refuge in the bottle, and then Mustapha Pasha bethought himself of the work he had to do.

"Come, Ali," he said, "we will now search the rooms of the Rajah murderer. There, methinks, the mystery of the lost wealth will be revealed."

"We shall find it in the air," said Ali Bey, merrily, "but as you will. As the boys in the street yell when a comrade picks up anything, I now cry, 'Halves.' Ha, ha!"

"I have no mind for unseemly mirth," said the pasha, as he threw back his veil and waddled from the room. "Of what avail is it to play the fool if thou art high in office?"

Ali followed with a light, and the pair penetrated to the lumber-room. There an exclamation burst from the pasha.

"Behold," he said, pointing to the pivot door, which was partly open. "There is the hiding-place of the Rajah's wealth."

There must have been some fault in the catch, which had played Jack the scurvy trick it had played on Chunder Loo, and revealed the secret of its working to one who had no recognised right to it.

"It is a cupboard," said the pasha.

"It is more than that," said Ali Bey, as he drew near, "behold, there are steps—and are—my lord, *there are men moving about below!*"

The pasha listened closely for a moment, and a frown passed over his face. He put his hand to his side in search of a sword, but it was not there.

"A curse upon the folly that led you to clothe me thus!" he said to Ali; "but lead the way, and drop thy veil so that the men when they see and believe it is a woman may not harm thee."

Ali dropped his veil, and the pair having squeezed their fat figures through the doorway, they began the descent of the stairs.

Ali, as the inferior, led the way, it being his duty to run the first risk of peril should there arise anything of the sort.

He held the lamp above his head, and endeavoured with indifferent success to pierce the gloom below.

When near the bottom his foot slipped, and down he went with the lamp to the bottom, performing the usual feat on such occasions of scraping his spine against the edges of the steps.

The lamp was put out, and they were in darkness.

"Now a murrain seize upon thee for a fool!" cried the pasha. "Of what use are such feet as thine?"

At the bottom of the steps the bey lay groaning. Exasperated by the smarting of his back, he retorted tartly:

"And a plague upon thy carcase for bringing me here on such a fool's errand!"

The pasha was about to make a fitting rejoinder to this piece of insolence, when he received a blow in the pit of the stomach that laid him gasping upon the steps.

Naturally he attributed it to Ali Bey, and he cursed him as only an angry pasha can.

He anathematised his parents, long since made mummies of or turned to dust, he reviled the day of his birth, and expressed a strong desire to shortly attend upon him as a mourner at his funeral.

The bey heard him, and replying in kind, got up, and succeeded with the aid of a modern match in relighting the lamp.

He was seemingly astonished to find the pasha also upon his back.

"And hast thou fallen likewise?" he asked.

"Ask me that, darest thou," howled the Pasha, "even while thy hand tingles with the blow thou gavest me?"

"I struck thee not," said the bey; "the wine of the infidel hath got into thy stomach, and giveth thee much pain."

He held up the lamp to get a better view of the prostrate pasha, and immediately it was dashed from his hand with a crash that echoed weirdly and horribly about the reservoir.

This astounding event was followed by wild shrieks of demoniac laughter that made bristly the beards of the listeners.

Without seeking the lamp, or so much as lighting a match to guide them on their way, they scrambled up the steps upon their hands and knees, and having gained the lumber-room, tumbled down upon a heap of rubbish.

"Perchance, oh, Ali Bey," groaned Mustapha Pasha, "there is a lamp hereabouts. Strike another match, and give me light."

Ali did so as much on his own account as that of the pasha, for it was not pleasant remaining in the dark, and he speedily found one of the original lamps used in the time of Chunder Loo's occupation of the palace.

By its light they felt more at ease, but were not disposed to remain where they were.

"Ali," said the pasha, "what makest thou of what has happened?"

"The halls of this place," replied Ali, "are stained deeply with blood. I have heard that the spirits of the dead arise at times to confound timorous man. Perchance it may be so now."

"It seemeth so to me," said the pasha, "therefore

we will abandon the search, and come with a guard on the morrow in the daylight. Then we will depute certain of our followers to search—below."

Convinced that this was the better course, and certainly the more agreeable one to take, they left the scene of the recent tragic death of Pestro, and retreated towards the palace gates, intending to retire and hasten homewards.

But they were suddenly checked by a murmuring of voices and the glare of a torch.

"What new terror is this?" demanded the pasha, aghast.

And they both stood still, listening with palpitating hearts to the gathering murmur of voices.

CHAPTER CCLXIII.

THE RESULT OF THE BROKEN SEAL.—A GRAND HAUL.

THE fact was, the breaking of the pasha's seal had been discovered, and the report of it having spread, there had been a quick gathering of loafers and rascals, bent on looting the palace.

Like their class all over the world, they were prepared to carry away with them anything and everything not too hot or too heavy.

The nature of these unexpected and unwelcome visitors was soon made clear to the two dignitaries.

Had they been in their ordinary attire they could speedily have checked the tide of loafing rascality, but the misfortune was that they were fully and properly attired as women, the double apparel having been voted inconvenient owing to the heat.

What a position for them to be in, if they should be discovered!

A pasha and a bey in petticoats!

What a commotion it would make among Mahomedan circles, and how the men would despise the pasha and his companion! For women are of little account to your true Mahomedan, who does not grant them the possession of a soul.

They are, in short, the mere slaves of the Oriental lords of creation.

And there was no real place of hiding for the ponderous officials, who were in a state of profuse perspiration as they retreated from room to room, followed by the plunderers, who increased in numbers every moment.

The palace was filled with a howling mass of the scum of Alexandria.

At last the precious pair were brought to bay in a room from which there was no escape.

They were discovered, and the appearance of two such ponderous females delighted the crowd beyond measure.

"The Rajah when he fled," they cried, "found these two much too heavy for him to carry away."

Then, in a spirit of mockery, they tore off the veil of the bey, and howled with delight when they saw his beard.

There is no knowing what they might have done in the exuberance of their joy, if the pasha, feeling impelled to take the bull by the horns, had not unveiled himself, and, with a dignity that was natural to him when in the presence of his inferiors, called upon them to be still.

There were men there who knew him, and they were terrified at their temerity, as it would be considered, in laughing at a pasha to his face.

"Fools!" he cried, "is it because the Prophet commands me once a year to humble myself in this garb that thou darest make a jest of *me?* Stand back!"

They stood back in a hurry, and the pasha led the way out.

As a telegram precedes the advance of royalty, so did the word fly acquainting the roughs of the discovery made.

There was practically a free passage to the gates, and a man there was commanded to fetch a couple of palanquins, which being brought, the two adventurers sought refuge therein, and were conveyed home.

But in the East as in the West, the tongues of the people were not to be stilled by word or threat from the highest in the land, and the story of the pasha and the bey in petticoats was destined to make much laughter at their expense for many a day.

Moreover, it anon reached the ears of the Sultan, whose influence was brought to bear on the removal of officials who could so far forget the true dignity of Oriental manhood as to wear the apparel of soulless women.

This by the way.

Let us see how it fared with the other adventurers of the night.

The idea that Jack had got into his head was that the fallen rubbish was a matter of recent date, and it flashed upon him that it was artificially brought about; in short, it was under this rubbish, if at all, that the treasure of the Avishnus would be found.

And it *was* there, packed in wooden boxes of small sizes for removal by hand.

Moreover, each box was corded round so as to be carried easily, or slung upon the shoulders.

There was no need to open the boxes to test their contents.

The newness of them, the past history of the treasure, and the peculiarity of the hiding-place, all pointed to Jack's having once more hit the right nail upon the head.

It was the work of an hour to shift all the rubbish.

and set free the dozen or so of boxes, each about a foot square.

The treasure being precious stones, the boxes were not particularly heavy. The youngsters could carry three apiece without being marvellously overburdened.

All but Jack had assumed their portion of the burden, when Ali Bey came a cropper upon the staircase.

He promptly hid the lights, extinguishing all but one which he put behind a pile of rubbish.

With a piece of rock in each hand he went out to see what was the matter.

He guessed that somebody was prowling round, and hearing the voice of the pasha, he took aim in the direction of it with so true a result that, as we know, the ponderous official was put *hors de combat.*

Jack having done this, waited to see what would happen next.

He was anxious, if possible, to avoid the shedding of blood.

The bey, it will be remembered, lighted his lamp, which Jack, with another well-aimed stone, promptly extinguished. All that followed in the movements of the pair of officials has been recorded.

Jack, as soon as he was sure they had retreated, returned to his friends, and having assumed his portion of the burden, they hastened to the place of exit in the blind thoroughfare. It was clear, and they got away, Jack calling to mind the route taken by Dirk Matthews on a previous occasion.

He acted as guide the whole way, and made no mistake. It was scarcely past midnight when he and his friends arrived at an appointed spot by the sea, where a boat was waiting on the chance of their returning.

With high-beating hearts they were taken to the "Albatross," where they met with an enthusiastic reception.

In fact, a night of merriment followed, and dawn found them still rejoicing over the complete success of their final adventure in Alexandria.

For it was to be so.

Their work was done there. Chunder Loo a prisoner on board, and the treasure of the Avishnus securely stowed away in secret in Harry Barstow's cabin, pending overhauling at a more convenient time.

All that now remained to be done was to hasten the completion of the repairs of the "Albatross," and then away for the old country and for home.

By bribes, hard words, and an occasional blow, the native workmen were induced to hurry on with their labours, and in three more days the repairs were completed.

The account was settled, papers asked for, and with the aid of "tips" to the Government officials, promptly obtained. Coals having been taken on board, it was decided to steam until they were well out in the Mediterranean.

There were no hosts of friends to bid them farewell, for they had sought none and made none.

Therefore the usual adieux were not looked for or missed.

They parted with all they had known there and the place itself without one pang of regret.

CHAPTER CCLXIV.

THE WILD BEAST IN HIS CAGE.—A BID FOR LIBERTY.

THE place of confinement for Chunder Loo was small but strong.

It was no bigger than a cabin for one on the lesser ocean liners, and light was admitted through a small porthole scarcely bigger than the fist of a man.

The door, originally a stout one, was strengthened with planks of oak, and a small hole was drilled through it, so that the movements of the prisoner could be watched from without.

When the door was opened to give food, or otherwise minister to his wants, there was always a guard of four men, armed, and ready to shoot him down if he made the slightest attempt to give trouble.

When the "Albatross" had been two days at sea, and steam had been abandoned for the sail, a certain amount of freedom was allowed him. His legs were set free, and his arms were simply strapped from behind.

He could raise his hands to his face, and the tips of his fingers just met, but he was powerless to do mischief with them.

Bill Oakley was responsible for the condition of his bonds, and every time the cell was entered he made a personal examination of the strong straps that held the prisoner fast.

Once a day at least Harry Barstow or Dick Darnley visited Chunder Loo, and silently inspected him and his cell. If he addressed them, they gave him no answer. Very rarely did any of his guards speak to him.

Chunder Loo was not going to risk being shot down. Cunning, cruel, and, in a coarse, animal way, courageous, he yet feared to die. Strange to say, he trembled at the thought of it.

Above all did he dread the death of the criminal by the hands of the hangman.

The evening of the third day arrived, and Bill Oakley, walking the deck, with an eye aloft and around the horizon, on the lookout for one of those sudden changes often experienced in some parts of the Mediterranean Sea, was startled by the sudden appearance of Startop, who came bounding up from below.

The young sailor, at the time, was one of the sentries outside the cell of Chunder Loo.

The officers and most of the men were on deck also, talking, smoking, or lounging at ease, in the full enjoyment of a glorious sunset.

"What's the matter, my lad?" asked Bill.

"Prisoner lying on the floor as if dead," answered Startop.

His answer was heard by all, and there was a general stir of excitement, especially among those more nearly concerned in the prisoner's fate.

Jack Ford came over to the old boatswain's side to get further particulars.

"Perhaps he is only lying down asleep," he said.

"No, sir," replied Startop; "he's all in a heap, just as he fell off the seat, and the expression of his face is awful."

Jack immediately started off down the companion, followed by Oakley, the young seaman, and several others, among them Bob, Tom, and Don.

The door was opened, and there, sure enough, lay Chunder Loo, apparently "as dead as Phary," as one of the men remarked.

They picked him up, and listened for the sounds of breathing. None came from him.

The half-closed eyelids revealed eyes that were fixed and glassy, and it seemed as if he were growing cold.

"He's gone," said Bill Oakley.

They rubbed his hands, pulled off his shoes, and chafed his feet, but no indication of returning life rewarded their efforts.

From the cell he was carried up to the deck, and two of the men, with an effort, straightened his limbs. All the signs of his being gone for good and all were there.

"He has cheated the gallows," remarked Norton Truscott. "It seems to me that he has somehow managed to conceal poison and swallow it."

"What is to be done with him?" asked Harry Barstow.

"We ought not to consign him to the sea with Malta in sight," replied Truscott, pointing to a speck on the sea ahead. "Our better course will be to keep him until we get there, and then make a statement of facts to the authorities. They may deem it advisable to have a post-mortem examination. Anyhow, let us have everything open and above-board."

"Assuredly. Let him be taken below again, Oakley."

"Axing your parding, sir, but a dead man won't be very pleasant keeping in that close place. It is as much as he will keep right on deck for twenty-four hours."

"Shall we get to Malta to-night with this wind?"

"It's shifting a bit for'ard, but I think the 'Albatross' will be off the island by midnight."

"Well, carry him forward, cover him up, and get on as fast as you can. I think the 'Albatross' would bear a little more canvas."

"Don't put it on her, sir," said Bill Oakley, earnestly. "The wind's shifty, and if we get a white squall, as we may do, with little notice, we may not be able to shorten in time to stop mischief."

Harry Barstow always yielded to Bill's advice. He was such a thoroughly experienced old seaman that his opinion was invaluable. So the "Albatross" went on as before, under a fair amount of sail, beating up against the wind, for the island of Malta.

Of all on board there was only one at that time who did not believe that Chunder Loo was dead.

It seemed incredible that he could be alive and not breathe. The fixed features and the growing coldness of his body all pointed to the end of a turbid, bad life having arrived.

But the solitary exception was Jack Ford.

He was afraid that a trick was being played by the man who had shown himself to be a past-master in the art of dissimulation.

He had no fear that—provided it was a piece of shamming—Chunder Loo would make any attempt to escape while there was nothing but deep water around the ship. The possibility was that he had cunningly timed feigning death so that he would have a chance of escaping at Malta.

There it was certain he had friends or confederates, who would find means of hiding him away.

Jack, however, did not openly confide his opinion to all. He contented himself with drawing Don Peebles aside and asking him what he thought of it.

"I don't see how he could sham the thing so completely," said Don, doubtfully.

"Have you ever read any of the stories of the fakirs?" asked Jack.

"Yes, now that you name the subject."

"You remember that they have the art of suspending animation so as to deceive even a doctor?"

"I have read it, but could scarcely believe it."

"A fakir," said Jack, "has voluntarily allowed himself to be buried in a vault, the earth put over it, corn grown, gathered in when ripened, and then, when that was done, he has been brought forth again and restored to animation."

"Yes, but hasn't he had what may be called professional assistance to carry the thing through?"

"I believe it generally is so; but this man, Don, is a marvel of cunning and experience in the uncanny arts. You remember when we first became acquainted with his fetish, the little snake he called Mehala?"

"Yes, it was at the 'Cowley Arms.'"

"I picked it up, and it appeared to be dead. We even thought it was stuffed."

"The little beast was feigning to be dead."

"Just so, as the spider and the beetle do in an emergency. Now, does it not seem to be reasonable that what Mehala did Chunder Loo can do?"

"It may be so."

"In my opinion," said Jack, "Chunder Loo is making a bold bid for liberty, and, dead or alive, a close watch ought to be kept on him. If he is shamming, he is entertaining the idea that he will be taken ashore and placed in a mortuary, if there is one at Malta, or that on arriving there he will have a chance of getting away. I shall make it my business to stop that little game."

"You are a wonderful fellow, Jack," said Don, "but this time I think you are extra cautious. However, I will help you to keep an eye upon him."

"Turn and turn about," said Jack. "Of course, I am not certain, and I don't want to be laughed at. Here's Mulberry Cork. Let us see what he is after."

CHAPTER CCLXV.

OFF MALTA.—FOILED AGAIN.—A STRUGGLE BY MOONLIGHT.

MULBERRY CORK had been below, sleeping, he afterwards said, during the commotion attending the discovery of the state of the prisoner.

He arrived on deck yawning and rubbing his eyes.

"Have you heard the news?" asked Jack.

"What news?" asked Mulberry, who, clad in seaman attire, presented the appearance of a half-caste sailor youth.

The deep staining of his skin had not changed in the slightest.

"Chunder Loo was found dead in his cell."

The eyes of Mulberry Cork opened wide. He gave vent to an incredulous grunt.

"Did he die of fright?" he inquired.

"No. He was simply found in a heap, still and breathless. There he is, forward, lying under that bit of canvas."

Mulberry Cork walked to the forecastle, and the other two followed him. Uncovering the face, he stared at it steadily, and then covered the unsightly object again.

"Oh, he is dead," he said. "There isn't much chance of his troubling you again."

Then he looked steadily at them, winked, and covertly pointed aft, as if he wished to adjourn there.

"Dead?" he said, as he sauntered back. "I should think so. It's a pity, for he ought to have suffered as my father did. He was the worst of the two."

It was not until he got right away to the aft-deck that his manner changed. His face expanded in a grin, and he winked again.

"You think he is shamming?" whispered Jack.

"Bet a million on it and win," replied Mulberry. "I never see him do it but once, and then he didn't know I was looking at him. It was in a room he was staying in with my father. I was under the table, which was covered with a cloth too big for it, so that it came close to the ground. I was spying on them, for I wanted to know what game they were up to."

"Was this before the murder?" asked Don.

"Yes, a week before, perhaps more. They were smoking and drinking together and talking over all sorts of things. Chunder asked my dad if he had ever seen a live man look like a dead man? Dad said, 'No.' 'Then I'll show you,' said Chunder, and he lays hisself down close to the wall of the room and goes orf. It wasn't nice to see him, and dad was scared. He thought Chunder was really dead, and I could have laughed to see him trying to bring him round if I hadn't been scared, too. But all he did 'mounted to nothin'. He couldn't bring him to life again; but presently he comes round hisself, and laughs fit to split. I never saw such a game in my life."

"Thank you, Cork," said Jack; "you have fully confirmed my suspicions. But say nothing. I'll see Chunder Loo gets a startler when he comes round."

"Yes," grinned Mulberry; "let him have all you can."

"I'll bring him to," said Jack. "Don, get Tom and Bob, also Startop and old Bill. I want them here. Chunder Loo, in a very few minutes, will be restored to life."

From that moment Jack was busy in making his preparations for once more confounding Chunder Loo. First of all he had a quiet talk with Bill Oakley, that set the old boatswain grinning. Then he, in turn, confided his plan to his three chums and Startop, and they all gathered round the covered form of the assumed dead man.

"It is a pity he is gone," said Jack, in a casual sort of way, "as so great a scoundrel deserved a harder fate."

"Hear, hear!" murmured the listeners.

"Still," continued Jack, "he was no common man to have done such things as we have seen and heard of. Mr. Truscott says that there must be something peculiar about his physical organisation. He is a bit of a surgeon, you know."

Expressions of surprise were heard. Jack assured them it was a fact.

"He was diffident about turning any portion of the 'Albatross' into a dissecting-room," pursued Jack, "but the captain told him he was welcome to do as he pleased."

"And what is he going to do?" asked Bob Stockton.

"Why, make a post-mortem examination of Chunder Loo," replied Jack.

"But if we put in at Malta——"

"We are not going to put in at Malta after all. Not unless he finds there is something peculiar in the physical arrangements of Chunder. Then he intends to call the attention of certain doctors residing there to it. But if he has simply died in a fit, he will be heaved into the sea, and the report of his death reserved for the authorities at home."

Jack spoke slowly; with his eyes upon the piece of canvas that covered the form of Chunder Loo. He was almost certain it stirred a little.

He motioned to his friends to be on the alert for any movement he might make.

And the movement was made just in time.

There was a sharp, snapping sound, as Chunder Loo burst the straps that held his arms, and with a bound he was upon his feet.

Much as they had seen of him, they were not fully prepared for the extraordinary agility and ferocity he displayed.

Tossing aside the canvas covering that clung to him for the fraction of a second, he leaped upon Jack Ford, making an effort to grasp him by the throat.

It would have fared ill with Jack if he had been successful in the effort.

But Jack, with a quick movement, dodged under his extended arm, and the long bony fingers of the Indian only succeeded in grasping the cap he was wearing.

It came off, naturally, as soon as touched, and Chunder Loo pitched forward right into the arms of Bill Oakley.

The moment of surprise past, they all fell upon him.

It was a brief struggle, but terrible in its way, mainly because the movements of Chunder Loo were like nothing ever seen or felt by those who struggled with him.

It was not a human being they were struggling with, but with a huge reptile. That was how they felt as his sinewy form writhed and twisted from one grasp to another.

The cries, the heavy treading of feet, brought upon the deck all who were not asleep in their hammocks. Among them were the three chief officers.

They were surprised to find the supposed dead man spread out upon his back on the deck, his arms and legs extended, and each limb grasped by one or more assailant.

The desperate effort, the outcome of a fit of mad fury, was past. Chunder Loo had shot his bolt, and he lay helpless as a child gasping for breath.

"I thought he was not dead," said Jack, looking at Barstow and Truscott, "and we got up a sham preliminary to a post-mortem examination. That woke him up."

A wild cry burst from the lips of Chunder Loo. It was so unnatural that all who heard it shuddered.

Then he began to talk rapidly and fiercely in an unknown tongue. It was a delirious gabbling that was horrible to hear. For a time the man of many crimes was insane.

They carried him below, bawling and screeching in the unknown tongue. Norton Truscott declared that he was uttering some sort of curse upon the head of somebody.

"My head," said Jack, "but:

"Notwithstanding that horrible curse,
I do not feel an atom the worse.'

It is a great comfort to me to think that I have spoiled his little scheme, that might have ended in his getting clear away."

"He won't get another chance of imposing on us without paying the penalty," said Harry Barstow. "The next time he shams death, a shot shall be put about his feet, and he will be dropped into the sea."

All night long, with rare intervals of silence, Chunder Loo cursed and raved.

About his hands were put steel handcuffs, and for further security against his violence, his legs were put in irons.

When the morning came he had exhausted his venom, and was broken down.

The old Chunder Loo was dead and gone, and a broken-spirited, defeated man in his place.

He asked to see Jack Ford and the other youngsters, and after consulting with Harry Barstow, they consented to visit him.

Jack led the way into his cell and found him seated, his back to the wall and his head upon his breast.

His eyes were cast down, and for a few moments he remained in that attitude. They waited for him to speak.

————

CHAPTER CCLXVI.

THE BREAKING OF CHUNDER LOO.—THE WHITE SQUALL.

WHEN Chunder Loo looked up, it was seen that the old spirit—the evil, sarcastic, mocking spirit—was gone.

His eyes, up to then notable for the fires smouldering in their depths, were the eyes of a cowed and beaten man.

"I have sent for you," he said; "shall I say what for?"

"As you please," replied Jack; "we ask for nothing and will promise nothing."

"I desire to yield wholly and completely to you," said Chunder Loo.

They did not answer him, and a silence followed. He presently terminated it with a deep-drawn sigh.

"When I first set foot in Littlecote Abbey," he said, "or, to be correct, within the district, I ought to have known that I was on the turning point of my fate. Once before I had been in trouble, but Mehalah never failed to rally me. You do not believe in Mehala, perhaps?"

"Go on," was all Jack said.

"In Mehala," resumed Chunder Loo, with knitted brows, "I had a guide, a counsellor. One ever strong in the hour of misfortune, a helper in the time of need. When I was within the influence of your sphere at Littlecote, Mehala suddenly showed symptoms of giving way. You smile."

"Mehala," remarked Don, "was a miserable reptile."

"Mehala was something you will never know of," replied Chunder Loo, "and be thankful for it. Mehala was the minute monster I had raised by arts unknown to your people. But to go on. Mehala felt his influence on the wane and sank into a state unknown to me, that was like unto death. I lost Mehala in one of your drinking-holes, called the 'Cowley Arms.' One of you found him."

"I did," said Jack, curtly.

"It matters not who. He was found," continued Chunder Loo, "and you carried my fetish to the wood, where he recovered his life—I ought to say called it back. Meanwhile, I was dying, and it was while I was in a state of extremity that Mehala with his intelligence, beyond that of this world, found me and restored me."

The listeners all recalled the scene of Chunder Loo lying stretched out at the base of the cliff, and shuddered.

"No man stained with the sins of man could have slain Mehala," resumed Chunder Loo, "but he eventually perished at the hand of unstained youth. A thing of evil, he was not proof against the blow dealt him by Peebles. It was enough. I had lost him, and although I might flourish for awhile, it was set down in the book of fate that my career would be brief, and that you four, my curse, would bring me—to what I am.

"There were times," he went on, after a catching of the breath, "when I tried to think it was all a lie —a superstition, and I strove hard against the inevitable. Strive as I might, the end was to be, and I am here."

He spoke with the intensity of hopeless despair, born of a conviction that he was a doomed man.

They could see the perspiration on his tattooed forehead, and had it been possible to feel pity for one so vile, punished and brought down, they would have entertained it.

But the memory of his crimes was not to be obliterated by his present condition, and in silence they awaited to hear the rest he had to say.

"It is not only death I fear," he said, "but the knowledge that it was owing to my shortcomings that my race has been exterminated weighs me down. If there is a paradise for the Avishnu in the Great Beyond the grave, it is not for me. I am now of no race and no creed. I am a lone outcast—a pariah among the countless hordes created since the world began. It may be some satisfaction for you to know that I feel it is so."

"You would hardly look to us for sympathy," Jack said.

"No, I have no hope," was the wailing reply, "broken, crushed—I have sent for you, as my conquerors, to tell you that the spoils of the fight are yours by right of conquest, and when I, positively the last of the Avishnus, am gone, all the accumulated wealth of my people is *yours*."

"We have it in our possession," said Tom Drummond. "Why do you take the trouble to say this?"

"Because I know you," returned Chunder Loo; "you have a high sense of honour that I cannot understand, while I admit and know it exists. By-and-by you will get talking among yourselves, or you would have done, and come to a conclusion that the vast treasure you hold is by rights the property of your Government, or as it is technically put, the Queen. It is nothing of the sort, for it was taken out of India prior even to the occupation of the East India Company, and there is no living heir to it now that the serpent worshippers have become, save for myself, of brief existence, extinct."

"You must have some motive in telling us this," said Jack.

"I have none," was the answer, "outside the desire to say that I am completely beaten. The fight is over —the victory and the spoils are yours. The Government of your country has done nothing to earn it. Hold fast to that which you have so righteously earned."

He ceased, and his head sank once more upon his chest. Jack spoke to him after awhile, but he only spread out his hands without looking up, and murmured:

"I have no more to say. My last word to you is spoken."

He motioned for them to go, and they left him.

The door was closed and made fast, and they adjourned to their own cabin.

"What do you think of that?" asked Jack.

"He has spoken the truth—for once in his life," replied Bob Stockton.

The others assented.

"Then the treasure, you consider, is all our own?" Jack said.

"Every fraction of it," they replied.

"To do as we please with?"

"Yes."

"Then we will stick to it," said Jack—"subject, of course, to the approval of Barstow and Truscott."

"Suppose we go to them at once?" suggested Don.

They assented, and were on the way to the chief cabin, when the "Albatross" suddenly heeled over and lay almost on her beam ends.

There was a rush of feet, a tumbling about, and a clambering up a gangway that was a long way out of the perpendicular, and they were on the deck.

To keep their feet was impossible, and they slid into the lee scuppers.

A fierce wind was blowing, the like of which they had only known once before, and that was at the time of the great earthquake.

In the light of the moon they could see a film overspreading the sky. The men on deck had tumbled about in every direction. Some of the sails were gone, torn from the bolt-ropes, to be carried away like a puff of smoke and lost for ever more.

The nature of the disaster was apparent to them.

The "Albatross" had been struck by a white squall.

It transpired afterwards that Bill Oakley had gone down for a few moments for a glass of grog, anticipating no evil. The sky was clear when he left the deck. Ten minutes later the squall, coming up with prodigious speed from nobody knew where, was upon them.

Harry Barstow was on deck with all speed, and, the first big blast over, the "Albatross" righted and lay almost on an even keel.

But the weather was not to be trusted, and the word was given to shorten sail.

Aloft sprang the men to furl the canvas that was left, the job being much lighter than it would have been half an hour before.

Then storm-sails were set, as the breeze blew steadily from the north.

But the weather could no longer be relied upon for a minute.

Presently another squall struck the "Albatross." But she was prepared, and, beyond heeling over for a few moments, no disturbance took place.

Across the sky there spread a huge sheet of cloud that almost obliterated the light of the moon. Then rain began to fall, first in big drops, then in a shower, and finally in sheets.

The "Albatross" was in for a night of it; being rapidly driven out of her course, she had to go round the south side of Malta, instead of putting into the eastern harbour.

"We must make for Tunis, sir," said Bill Oakley to Harry Barstow, in response to a question put to him; "it is our best chance of safety. Though the wind is shifting to the south-east, it won't go south far enough for days after the squall to allow us to weather Cape Bon. It never does."

"How long will it take us to get there?" asked Harry Barstow.

"About three days, sir."

"Then head for Tunis," replied the captain of the "Albatross" "although, crippled as we are, I would rather go on to Gibraltar, before we come to anchor, for rest and repairs."

"If the wind softens, sir," said Bill Oakley, "we can bend fresh sails as soon as daylight comes."

CHAPTER CCLXVII.

AT TUNIS.—A COMMAND FROM THE BEY.

THE city of Tunis lies on the west side of a lagoon, shallow and, beyond a limited area, unnavigable. The lagoon extends thirty miles inland, where it gets lost in the sandy country.

As there is a considerable trade done with silks, oil, gold-dust, coral, and other things there is generally a fair sprinkling of vessels in the anchorage-ground.

The "Albatross" arrived on the afternoon of the third day succeeding the squall, and dropped her anchor.

Within half an hour, an official of Arab breed, accompanied by two men of the Berber race, arrived in a boat, and requested to be taken on board.

His business was to inquire into the nature of the vessel, look at her papers, inquire into the prospect of trading with her commander—in short, learn all about her.

He was very courteous, gave his name as Sadyk, chief officer of Customs, and seemed disposed to make the inquiries merely of a formal nature.

He could speak the English tongue fluently, also French, and at a pinch, so he declared, could make himself intelligible in German.

"It is my business," he said, agreeably, "to know all tongues."

Although not apparently persistent or unduly curious, he managed to get at the fact that there was a prisoner on board.

"You have arrested him?" he said.

"It is so," answered Harry Barstow.

"May I ask where?"

"In Alexandria."

"You have papers, of course, authorising his arrest?"

This was spoken in the most careless way imaginable.

"No; but if I can have an interview with the English consul, I could explain matters to his satisfaction."

"Your consul," said Sadyk, "is ill with fever. But it is of no matter. I can see the prisoner, I suppose?"

He could hardly be refused, and Bill Oakley was desired to prepare Chunder Loo for the visit.

To the astonishment of the old boatswain, Chunder Loo objected to it.

"It is making a show of me," he said, hotly. "Tell this jack-in-office to go hang himself!"

A message of this description could not obviously be delivered, but Bill did say that the prisoner objected to being disturbed.

"He's in a bad humour, sir," said Bill.

But Sadyk said he was not accustomed to consulting the feelings of a prisoner, and as a matter of duty he must look at him.

So he was taken down to the cell, where Chunder Loo sat with his head down, and on being commanded to raise it, refused to do so.

"It is of no consequence," remarked Sadyk, easily, as he rolled a cigarette and lighted it; "the dog may have his will in so small a matter."

He left the cell, and having partaken of a cup of coffee with the officers of the "Albatross," was taken back in his boat.

"I am glad he is gone," said Harry Barstow, with a sigh of relief, "for at first I feared there would be some trouble with our having Chunder Loo. All these dark-skinned people have a knack of fighting against us of a whiter breed."

"They cling to each other," returned Norton Truscott, "whether right or wrong."

All who were interested in the fate of Chunder Loo were anxious to avoid any trouble with the Bey respecting his detention. Jack Ford had quietly observed the coming and going of Sadyk, and the fear that their captive might be taken away took possession of him.

He and others wondered why they had not thought of it prior to anchoring off Tunis.

The feeling of relief was speedily damped about an hour before sunset, by the return of Sadyk.

He was amiable and suave as ever, but he had a portentous message to deliver.

It was from the Bey, or some person high in authority, to the effect that the "Albatross" would find it convenient to remain where she was for the time.

Meanwhile the Bey would be glad to receive a visit of courtesy from all her chief officers.

They expressed willingness, of course, for the Bey's invite amounted to a command.

Now, every appearance of having been a fighting-craft had long since been removed, and to all appearance the "Albatross" was only a private yacht. Sadyk did not on either occasion look into her hold where the guns and other armaments had been stowed away, but after his little experience he evidently suspected something was wrong; it was just possible he had smelt a rat.

Harry Barstow expressed great pleasure at the honour conferred on him by the Bey, and Sadyk was about to depart, when Penny Bunn, still in his involuntary disguise, appeared on deck.

The men and officers had ceased to smile at his appearance, and he was getting used to it. Sadyk eyed him curiously.

"Of what nation or race?" he asked Harry Barstow.

As there was nothing like telling the truth, the facts of Penny Bunn's get-up were stated.

Sadyk, in a quiet way, was intensely amused.

"When you honour the Bey with a visit, bring him with you. It will amuse his Highness. Perhaps he will purchase him of you."

Harry explained that it was impossible. It would be against the laws of his country to sell Penny Bunn or any other man.

"Ah! Just so," murmured Sadyk. "I had forgotten. At all events, bring him as one of your train."

There could be no objection to this, unless it portended the detention of the entire party. But Harry Barstow perforce said that Bunn should be one of the party.

Then Sadyk, with many polite expressions, took his departure.

Among other notable buildings observable from the deck of the "Albatross" was the Citadel, an erection of historical interest and imposing appearance.

Mounted on the summit of it were some modern guns of rather heavy calibre.

A movement was apparent among the guns at sunset, and Harry Barstow inspected it with his glass.

"What is going on up there?" asked Dick Darnley, who was with him at the moment.

"They are training their guns upon us," answered Harry Barstow. "If we attempted to raise anchor they could sink us. I don't like that. It has an ugly twang about it."

"It has," assented Dick, "but it may not mean anything serious after all. These African potentates are fond of making displays of their power. I do not see one of our war vessels here."

"No, but one is sure to put in soon, I should say. Anyhow, there are French and Italian craft here, and if anything happens to us, tidings of it are sure to be conveyed home."

"It will be a comfort to us after the Bey has bowstrung the lot of us," said Harry Barstow, grimly, "for our Home Government to demand compensation of the Bey. But it is no use anticipating evil. We shall know all about it on the morrow."

CHAPTER CCLXVIII.

WITH THE BEY.—EMBARRASSING ACTION OF THAT POTENTATE.—THE "ALBATROSS" WITHOUT AN OFFICER.

THE palace of the Bey is the finest building in Tunis.

It is not so very striking outside, although it is built of marble, for the outline is almost a plain square. It is when one gets a glimpse of the interior that its magnificence is revealed to the spectator.

In the centre of it is a court-yard and garden, and all the rooms open into it.

There, embowered among beautiful flowers and rare tropical plants, a number of fountains are ever at play, cooling the air.

The servants in white robes, and the fierce desert retainers in their gorgeous apparel, flit to and fro or lounge at ease in the shade.

Outside the upper windows there are carved marble balconies which, uniting, form a shady verandah below.

It was under the southern side of the verandah that the Bey sat in state.

It was his custom on certain days to hear complaints, to receive homage from the chiefs of dependent tribes, and perform other offices belonging to the ruling of one who has absolute power.

The smile of the Bey is prosperity, his frown, death. And there is no Court of Appeal from his judgments, whether they be good or ill.

Achmet Bey, the potentate ruling Tunis at the time of our story, was a white-bearded old man, with eyes as black as a coal. They were seemingly the only part of his face that ever moved in public.

When he spoke his voice came through his beard, that hid the movement of his lips, in terse sentences.

He never argued nor explained why so and so was to be done. He simply ordered, and expected immediate obedience.

There were about a dozen criminals, arrested for offences of different degrees of criminality, ranged before him.

They were all men of the lower classes of various tribes, and their accusers men of a higher position.

Achmet Bey heard the accusation, and was not troubled with more than two attempts at defence.

The criminals, truly or falsely charged, as a body, knew that Achmet Bey was not favourable to a defence, and were silent. Innocent or guilty, the dumb ones got off with comparatively light sentences, whereas those who had the temerity to assert their innocence and attempt to prove it, received full measure.

One man was sentenced to be beheaded before sunset, so he relieved his feelings by cursing his aged judge in good strong Arabic.

He had better have died without demur, for the Bey, objecting to being compared to the lower form of swine, and a jackass without a tail, commanded that he be soundly whipped an hour before being beheaded.

The criminals disposed of, one of the officials of the court announced that "the English officers, with an attendant, were awaiting the gracious pleasure of the Bey." A wave of the hand expressed a command to admit them.

Fearing that any omission of the "officers" of the "Albatross" would give offence, Bill Oakley had been left in command, and all above him were there. Penny Bunn, in the garb of an ordinary seaman, presented a striking appearance as he brought up the rear.

In almost any European country he would have excited the spectators to laughter, but there he was received with marked gravity.

As Harry Barstow, Dick Darnley, Ben Walton, Norton Truscott, and the four youngsters formed in line and bowed, the Bey scarcely noticed them, but turned his dark eyes on Penny Bunn, for whose coming he had evidently been prepared.

Sadyk stood on the right of the Bey to act as interpreter, the mighty potentate being too great a man to learn any language but that of his native country.

The following colloquy, which took time, owing to the necessary intepretations, then ensued.

"Which is your chief?"

Harry Barstow signified that he was in command.

"You are owner of the vessel that has cast anchor in our waters?"

"Yes."

"Are you on a voyage of pleasure, and are you outward or homeward bound?"

"I have been on a voyage of business of a private nature, and am homeward bound."

"You have a prisoner on board your vessel. Of what tribe and nation is he?"

Harry Barstow thought it better to be perfectly candid on the personality of Chunder Loo, and he made as brief a statement of it as he could.

The Bey listened with an owlish expression of face, as though it was of no interest to him at all.

But he was listening closely for all that, as they afterwards had reason to know.

When Harry Barstow finished, the Bey gravely nodded his head and turned to Penny Bunn, who, in imitation of some of the Berber attendants, had put on an air of grave ferocity, standing with one hand upon his hip, his left knee bent, as he glared haughtily round him.

"Who is that slave?"

The Bey put that question with more animation than he had hitherto shown. Harry Barstow explained that he was not a slave, but one of the men of the "Albatross."

He would have stopped there, but the Bey was persistent, and the story of the dyeing and feathering of Penny Bunn by order of Chunder Loo had to be told.

It was received with all the gravity due to a funeral oration.

"And is he thus stained for life?" was the next question.

"It is to be feared so," answered Harry Barstow.

"How will he fare at home? Your people are given to mocking those who have a dark skin from their birth. Will they not persecute *him*?"

Harry Barstow was not sure. People in England, friends of Penny Bunn, would get used to him, he hoped. The Bey dissented with a shake of the head.

"He will have no honour in his own country," he said; "leave him here with me. What is his price?"

It was imperative to explain very clearly that Penny Bunn was not for sale. The Bey seemed to be astounded.

"What is to be done?" he asked "I want him. If he remains here he will be given a post of honour. He will stand on my right, and have slaves of his own. Tell him so."

Penny Bunn listened to the offer with some amazement. He could hardly understand the meaning of it.

But he was rather pleased than otherwise, and he bowed graciously to the Bey.

"I am grateful to your royal highness for your offer," he said, "and with your leave will take time to think it over."

"The Bey gives no time," said Sadyk, before interpreting this reply. "He must have a yea or nay at this moment."

"Then," said Penny Bunn, with his original impulsiveness, "inform his royal highness that I accept his offer."

It was done.

There was no going back.

In a few words, quickly spoken, Sadyk informed the Bey that Penny Bunn was willing to enter his service.

It is needless to say that the party from the "Albatross" stared at the reckless Bunn.

"I suppose," said Harry Barstow, with some sternness, "that you know what you have done?"

"The life of the African and the Oriental," replied Penny Bunn, "has always had a charm for me, from my youth up. To ride upon an ostrich, to battle with the lion of the desert, were ambitions of my youth. To reside in the palace of a Bey has been the chief ambition of my riper years."

"Well," said Jack Ford, "I suppose you cannot help it, but you *are* a caution."

"It is the command of the Bey that you take your stand on his right hand," said Sadyk.

With a swinging step and a proud air, Bunn stepped forward, bowed low, and took up the position named

"What a dear old ass he is!" murmured Don.

"There is yet one matter more," said Sadyk: "the Bey commands that your prisoner be brought ashore to undergo examination before him. Our mighty lord is just. He hears both accuser and accused, and judges the right and the wrong. It is his desire that you remain here, while I take a written message from you for the delivering up of Chunder Loo."

CHAPTER CCLXIX.

PRISONERS ALL.—CHUNDER LOO GIVEN UP TO SADYK.

THE command of the Bey came like a thunderclap upon them all.

It was so full of evil portent that the boldest—and all were bold—quailed.

Not that they thought so much of themselves on the score of their liberty, so far as the Bey was concerned. It was the galling idea that Chunder Loo would get his freedom that troubled them.

And having gained it, might he not use it to avenge his own capture? Would he not claim the treasure of which he had been deprived, and, charging them with theft, place the whole party in a very awkward position?

Achmet Bey was absolute ruler in his own country, but in dealing with Englishmen, he would not go to the length he did with his own people.

At the very worst, he would only imprison them for awhile. But to lose Chunder Loo and that vast treasure would be hard to bear.

Sadyk, having received the written message from Harry Barstow, scribbled with a pencil on a slip of paper, beckoned to an officer of the Berber guard, and said something to him in an undertone. The officer wheeled about and signed to the Englishmen to follow him.

They were unarmed and helpless. As occupants of an assumed pleasure-yacht, they could not well have come ashore with sword and revolver. In the bitterness of their weakness they could only obey the sign.

Bowing in turn to the Bey, with outward calm they filed out of the courtyard behind the swarthy Berber chief.

A SPLENDID SCHOOL STORY.

NEVER BEFORE PUBLISHED.

By E. HARCOURT BURRAGE,

Author of "Ching Ching," "Monkey Mat and Roving Dick," "The Brave Boy of the Basilisk," &c.

THE LAMBS of LITTLECOTE

"Well," said Bill, staring at the unmoved bearer of the message, "this beats cock-fighting."

No. 36. ☞ PRICE ONE PENNY. ☜

ALDINE PUBLISHING CO., 10, Red Lion Court, Fleet St., and 1, 2, & 3, Crown Court, Chancery Lane, London.

He led them into the main building by a door under the verandah. Inside they found themselves in an apartment with a polished marble floor, and lounges of the same material, on which shawls and skins were laid, round the room.

"It is the command of the all-powerful Achmet," he said, in French, "that you remain here, giving your word not to stir hence until he summons you."

In the name of all Harry Barstow gave that word.

There was something hopeful in the condition by which they escaped being under lock and key.

Leaving them to discuss their position as to the possible outcome of Chunder Loo being released from captivity on the "Albatross," we will follow Sadyk, who, with a guard of a dozen men, took a boat and were conveyed to the vessel's side.

Bill Oakley and Chippy were walking the deck together, and espying them approaching, guessed something was wrong.

But, as with those on shore, so with those on board—fighting was not to be thought of. There were no preparations made to resist, and Sadyk came on deck, followed by his guard, without hindrance.

"Who is in command here?" asked Sadyk.

"I am," answered Bill, gruffly, eyeing Sadyk with no great favour.

"I bear a message from your commander to you."

As Sadyk said this he handed out the slip of paper, and Bill, with the assistance of Chippy, deciphered it. The message was very brief:

"The bearer of this will take charge of Chunder Loo to convey him on shore. Place no obstacles in his way.

"H. BARSTOW."

"Well," said Bill, staring at the unmoved bearer of the message, "this beats cock-fighting."

"Possibly," answered Sadyk; "although I know nothing of that form of warfare. My master, the Bey, is of impatient blood. If he is kept waiting he may make me suffer. Be considerate to his servant by being prompt."

"You are sure of the handwriting?" whispered Chippy.

"That's right enough," answered Bill, softly; "but what do it mean? Anyways, good riddance to the warmint, says I, if they are going to hang him right orf."

"I think," he said, "that you know the sort of party you have come for. He's slippery."

Sadyk bowed.

"Then come this way," continued the old boatswain, still in a bit of a fog, not being able to grasp the bearings of the case.

It was such an unexpected command from his captain, after the trouble taken to keep Chunder Loo in security, for the purpose of having him tried for murder at home.

Chunder Loo was crouching in his cell when the door opened, and Bill commanded him to come forth.

"What am I wanted for?" asked Chunder Loo, distending his eyes with a look of sudden alarm.

"Going ashore," briefly answered Bill.

"I will not go," cried Chunder Loo, as he threw himself upon the floor.

This unexpected conduct was as much of a staggerer to Bill as anything that had preceded it.

"Come," he said, "no more of your tricks. Up you get and ashore you go. There's a party come to escort you like a nobleman."

"I'll not go," yelled Chunder Loo. "If you are a man, with a spark of pity for one down in the very depths of misery, keep me here. Kill me, but do not send me ashore."

Bill Oakley, wondering more than ever, drew aside, and Sadyk with three of his followers pushed their way into the cell.

Chunder Loo screamed as they laid hands upon him, and writhed about in the fear of a child who expects a whipping.

But he was unceremoniously picked up, carried to the deck, and there securely bound hand and foot.

All the time he cried out for those belonging to the "Albatross" not to allow him to be taken away.

"Where is your captain?" he cried, "or Ford, or any of them? Surely they are not responsible for the giving up of one in my position. I am wanted in England for murder. Take me there. The gallows is nothing to the torture-house of the Bey!"

No response was made to his cries.

Sadyk calmly superintended his being bound and transferred to the boat. That done, he bowed to Bill, thanked him for ready obedience to the message, and descended to the side of the still pleading prisoner.

It was about half a mile to the shore, and as the boat glided away, the cries of Chunder Loo became fainter and fainter. Bill, leaning on the side of the yacht, scratched his head and rubbed his hair in a puzzled way.

"Chippy," he said, "you are a man of wisdom. What do you make on it?"

"Blessed if I see the game, but I'm afeard that trouble will come out of it. I don't like the captain not coming hisself to deliver up that warmint."

"And I don't see why they've claimed him."

"No, but he ain't certain of their being friendly, or he wouldn't have hollered so."

This seemed the strangest part of the whole affair. But neither Bill nor Chippy could make head or tail of the business, save that they feared the Bey would give trouble.

"All we can do, Chippy," said Bill, "is to quietly get out a few weppins, and have 'em handy if there's need to use 'em. I sartainly don't like the appearance of the captain and all of 'em being kept ashore."

So Bill went to work, and prepared for a possible position of emergency.

———

CHAPTER CCLXX.

THE BEY AND THE PRISONER.—ANOTHER RECORD OF CHUNDER LOO.

WHILE Sadyk was gone for Chunder Loo, the Bey retired from his seat of justice in the court.

During his absence the various members of his guard lay about like dogs in the sun or shade, according to their fancy. There was a narrow window in the chamber where our friends were confined, through which Harry Barstow surveyed the strange scene of quietude.

The others sharing his captivity lay about in twos and threes, feeling even in that shady chamber the effect of the full heat of the day.

On board the "Albatross" they would have had the benefit of the sea-breeze—there the air was still naturally stifling.

"I wish I understood what is in store for us," said Harry Barstow. "It was a mistake our coming ashore."

"We could not help ourselves," said Ben Walton. "If we had refused, they would have fetched us. As for getting away, two turns of the capstan to raise the anchor would have brought the fire of the fort upon us."

"Coming here at all was the mistake," remarked Jack Ford, who was lying upon his elbow, fanning his face with his cap; "but I suppose, sir, it could not be avoided?"

"No," replied Harry Barstow, "it was almost impossible to weather the Cape. The conduct of the Bey is inexplicable. He is on the most friendly terms with our Government, I believe."

"Chunder Loo is at the bottom of it all," said Jack.

"The fiend had connections all over the world," said Don, "but I am not so sure that he is among friends here. I think we are all right."

There was a curtain at the lower end of the chamber, shutting off other apartments. It was now raised, and the Berber chief appeared with a half-score negro slaves, bearing food and wine, behind him.

"It is the command of my mighty and resistless lord, the Bey," he said, "that you are refreshed."

A slave spread out a white cloth upon the floor, and the viands were placed in order thereon.

Then cushions were laid upon the floor, and the prisoners invited to sit.

"If you need more," said the Berber chief, "a clap of the hands will bring a slave into your presence for commands."

He bowed low and retired. The slaves also vanished, and the captives, as they considered themselves to be, squatted round, feeling both hungry and thirsty.

"I presume," said Bob Stockton, as he helped himself to some sweet biscuits and a bunch of grapes, "that this is *not* ordinary Tunis prison-fare."

"We are detained for something," replied Ben Walton. "Make up our minds to that. Claret, and good, too"—he sipped some from a glass—"I can recommend it."

They ate and drank merrily enough, and the jest passed round. At the noise of their laughter, some of the loungers and sleepers in the courtyard were aroused, and lifting their heads, stared about them, surprised at the unwonted sound.

Perhaps they were a little disgusted, too, with the noise, for they were men reared and bred to be silent and grave. If not reared to it, they would have become so by the nature of their daily lives.

In that grim palace—grim in spite of its architectural beauty—the sounds of merriment were rarely if ever heard.

From the Bey downwards, solemnity of bearing was cultivated.

Presently one of the Bey's runners appeared in the open.

One word he uttered, and every man was on his feet, and reassuming the positions they occupied at an earlier hour.

Then appeared Sadyk and his men, bearing the bound form of Chunder Loo on a sort of trestle or stretcher. He had ceased to cry out, and lay still, with eyes fixed as one who sees a coming horror, or the shadow of a dreadful end sinking down upon him.

The party within the chamber had lunched and fared well, and from the openings in their temporary prison-house beheld the bringing in of Chunder Loo.

"It is three to one against this being a friendly visit," said Bob Stockton. "There's a warm time in store for Chunder."

"Don't make too sure of that," muttered Ben Walton. "Here is the Bey again."

The great man had come in and resumed his seat. Calm as his ordinary demeanour was, it was now made manifest that he could, on occasions, be excited, for his eyes flashed, and there was a quickness in the movement of his hands not usual with him, as he motioned for the captive to be brought nearer.

They brought up Chunder Loo until there was but

a foot or two between them, and then the Bey, bending over him, hissed out the one word "*Dog!*" with a fierce intensity that was absolutely startling.

On the right of the Bey stood Penny Bunn, now armed with a species of wand of authority—a bamboo stick with a bunch of ostrich-feathers upon it. Round his neck was a heavy chain of gold, and he bore himself with an assumption of dignity that the Emperor of Russia would in vain have endeavoured to copy.

For all that, Don, who took particular notice of him, was sure that Bunn was not exactly happy.

Already the canker of greatness was getting at him, as the worm gets at the bud.

As the Bey hissed out the epithet, Chunder Loo was seen to curl himself up closer, as if stung. A shiver passed through him, but he made no reply.

"Let the Englishmen be summoned," said the Bey, in his accustomed tone of voice.

Sadyk glided up to the door of the chamber, and beckoned them to draw near.

"One word with you," he said, in a whisper. "Be wise, and yield to the will of the Bey. If so, all will be well; but it is not good to cross my mighty lord and master."

He backed out of the chamber ere they could offer him any reply, motioning for them to follow him.

"Be guided by me in all things. Do as I do," said Harry Barstow.

"This is a precious go," whispered Don to Bob, who shrugged his shoulders, and put on an air of languid indifference.

"Whatever happens," he said, "it will be all the same a century hence."

Harry Barstow came of a good old stock. He belonged to the class of men who are cool when looking down the mouth of a cannon, with an enemy at the other end prepared to fire.

Bearing himself gallantly, he walked into the court-yard, and presented himself before the Bey.

His followers ranged themselves alongside, and there was a short silence, broken only by a faint moan from Chunder Loo. Sadyk took up his original position on the left of the Bey to act as interpreter.

The powerful potentate—powerful in his own district, anyway—opened the conference that ensued with the air of a man who meant to have his own way in everything.

"You see this dog, Chunder Loo? On what grounds have you held him prisoner?"

"He is a murderer," answered Harry Barstow, "and his life is forfeited to the laws of my country."

"Were you empowered to arrest and carry him thither?"

"No."

"Was it a friend or a relative of yours he murdered?"

"I do not at the moment even remember the name of the man."

The Bey looked as much surprised as one so mighty as he could do under the circumstances, and asked the next question in a petulant manner.

"Why should you interfere?"

"Because," replied Harry Barstow, "I know him to be guilty of a hundred infamous crimes. He was the head of a tribe, now happily extinct, of unholy worshippers of the serpent—the Avishnus. At their hands my friend Truscott," he motioned towards him, "has suffered much. It was only by a miracle that he escaped an awful death at their hands."

The Bey slightly shrugged his shoulders.

"My demands," he said, "are that you voluntarily give up this Chunder Loo to me, and undertake never to reveal what you have done."

"I cannot do that," was Harry's rejoinder.

"Why not?"

"Because, according to the laws of my country, every man must be tried and found guilty by twelve men ere he can be punished. I take him back at my own risk, but I have no right to give him up to you."

"He is here," was all the Bey said to this, "and I cannot let him go. Let all of you swear on your own Holy Book that you will be dumb concerning him, and you are free."

"And if we refuse?" inquired Harry Barstow.

"Then you will be detained here as long as it is my will."

The eyes of the listeners flashed. They were not disposed to quietly submit to this petty yet arbitrary potentate without demur.

"You will at least inform us," said Harry, "what you intend doing with this man?"

The Bey intimated that he intended to do nothing of the sort.

"Is he to be set free?"

A shrug was the only answer.

"Do you charge him with any crime, and will he be punished for it?"

"He is to be left here as *mine!*" returned the Bey, "to do as I please with."

A murmur of dissent arose from the listeners.

The fact was they mistrusted the whole proceeding and looked upon it as a farce, a scene in which the Bey and Chunder Loo were the chief actors.

In the minds of all was a conviction that Chunder Loo, on being left with the Bey, would immediately be set free. And what devilish schemes he might conceive as a free man, and carry them out, perhaps, they all knew.

Was this to be the end of the successful capture effected mainly through the boldness of Jack Ford?

They rebelled against the notion, and Jack was particularly bitter about it. But what could they do?

"Get time if you can, sir," he softly whispered.

Already he was conceiving a plan for the recapture of Chunder Loo and conveying him once more on board the "Albatross."

Then an effort might be made to get away in the night-time, and carry the scoundrel across the sea to his just doom.

There was Penny Bunn, of course. But he was personally responsible for his position, and they could not help him. Among the youngsters there was also the conviction that their old acquaintance would come out of the trouble somehow.

Bob Stockton once said of him that "he was in and out of mischief, like a dog in the fair," and there was a strong element of truth in that observation.

Harry Barstow asked for a few hours to think over the proposition, also that meanwhile a message might be sent to his friends on board the "Albatross" of a reassuring nature as to their prospective early return.

The Bey granted the few hours—until the morrow, in fact—and promised to send word to the yacht that it was his pleasure to detain the party for a time as his honoured guests.

Then the proceedings having terminated, Sadyk descended from his place by the Bey and ushered the captives, for such they were, back to the chamber.

As they were bowing to the Bey before departing, a short, gasping cry escaped the lips of Chunder Loo.

"Do not in mercy leave me here!"

But they paid but little heed to it, knowing how excellent an actor he was and past-master in deceit and chicanery.

CHAPTER CCLXXI.

PENNY BUNN TO THE RESCUE.—THE BEY'S PALACE AT NIGHT.

SADYK, having ushered them into the chamber, stood by the door, regarding them with wistful eyes.

"You have not done well," he said; "my master is angry."

"He has asked us to do an unreasonable thing," replied Harry Barstow. "Granted that he has power to detain Chunder Loo, he has not the right to bind us to silence."

"He does it," rejoined Sadyk, "because he fears that your Government will demand the extradition of Chunder Loo, although we have no treaty. And what your people demand is generally enforced."

"Why will he not give up Chunder Loo?"

"When the demand comes it will be impossible."

"Suppose we refuse to be silent," asked Harry Barstow, "what will be our fate?"

"You will remain here," answered Sadyk "within these walls as long as you live."

"But does your master in his madness think that he will go unpunished?"

"He will be asked about you, perchance, but he will know nothing, save that you sailed away in the night."

"But there is my yacht, with my men——"

Sadyk interrupted him, with a hard laugh.

"That," he said, "will never more be heard of. I can say no more. Be wise. When the morrow comes yield to him. He knows your race, and will believe your promise will be kept. But your parole is now at an end. You are prisoners, and any attempt to leave this or the adjoining chamber will result in your being shot. Our guards are numerous, and their eyes keen."

He bowed low and departed. In anger, mingled with dismay, the captives sat down or lounged upon the floor.

A long discussion ensued, ending with the resolve to do nothing until the morning. Whether it would be wise to yield at the last moment was a question none would answer in the affirmative.

"This old potentate," said Dick Darnley, "would never dare to take our lives."

"I would not be sure of that," said Ben Walton. "Indeed, I think he is resolute on the subject. Sadyk, knowing more of the world's affairs, is anxious to avoid that extremity. He understands the risk the old fool will run. How on earth is it that this scoundrel, Chunder Loo, has friends wherever he goes?"

They could not answer the question.

An agreeable change from discussing the position was afforded them by the return of the negro slaves with the evening meal—meat, bread, a variety of biscuits, sweets, and wine.

Whatever might be the ulterior designs of the Bey, he was as hospitable as ever.

The feast was supplemented with cigars, pipes, and good tobacco. They had eaten and drunken well, and were enjoying their smoke, when Penny Bunn suddenly appeared in the doorway.

"Hush!" he whispered, "a friend approaches." Penny Bunn was nothing if not dramatic. They knew that, but they could see that his visit was really burdened with portentous matter.

"In another hour," he said, as he glided in, "the sun will set and the night come on. May I, without being considered intrusive, sit down?"

Jack made room for him by his side, and Penny Bunn squatted on the floor.

"I am sorry to see you gentlemen in this position,"

e said, "and I am here to see if I cannot, in my present capacity of major domo of this establishment, elp you in some way."

"Can you do so without getting yourself into rouble?" asked Jack. The others all quietly listened.

"I can," replied Bunn, firmly. "Whatever happens, need fear no harm. The base trick played upon me, which I looked upon as one of the greatest misfortunes of my life, has developed into a blessing. I am boss of this show."

They did not exactly believe it, but they all expressed pleasure on hearing that his post was so important.

"Boss—absolutely *boss*," repeated Penny Bunn. "My word is law, my frown annihilation. I am virtually the Bey. The original article is as clay in my hands."

"I am not surprised to hear that," said Don. "In the old days at Littlecote I always felt you were a man born to command."

A complacent smile spread itself across the painted face of Bunn. He helped himself to a cigar and lit it.

"The berth will suit me," he said. "Now as to yourselves. What are your plans?"

They did not immediately answer. Bunn, especially in his position, was hardly the man they would trust with their present designs.

"You hesitate—naturally," he said. "Let me make a guess. You wish to get away from here?"

"You must be a thought-reader," said Bob Stockton, and the rest had to struggle with a tendency to laugh.

"I possess the gift," answered Penny Bunn, in his aggravating, complacent way, "to a degree. Now for my second guess. You desire to get Chunder Loo on board the 'Albatross,' and carry him to England?"

They did not answer him, nor was there any indication of merriment now. Bunn, like the boy playing hide-and-seek, was "getting warm."

"Be guided by me," he said, "and you shall be successful in both."

"If," said Harry Barstow, "you can help us to get away and to take Chunder Loo with us, you will earn our lasting gratitude. But it must not be done at the cost of your own life."

"My life is safe here," asserted Bunn. "I have, as I may say, the whole place—house, garden, native savages, servants, and the Bey under my thumb."—he pressed it in the table-cloth as he spoke thus boldly—"and if you will listen to me all will be well. First of all, the Bey is an old humbug."

They were surprised to hear it, or professed to be. Bunn continued:

"He intends this night to give a feast in your honour, *but you won't be there.*"

Real surprise was now felt by all. The light of day was getting dim. There were long shadows in the courtyard. The clank of arms carried by the man on guard was heard on the quiet air.

"Already," continued Bunn, lowering his voice, "I can read the old rascal like a book. The feast will be a sham. It will consist of an illumination of his palace for the outside world to see, but inside there will be nothing unusual to eat or drink—no song, no dance, no guests—and why?"

He paused, as if expecting an answer to a conundrum; but getting none—for what could they say?—he went on:

"Why all this humbug? Simply to say, in the future, *if you should never be heard of again*, that he gave a feast in your honour, and you left him to return home. Already the report has been spread abroad in the town. Sadyk, who confides in me as a man on whose judgment in intricate matters he can rely, tells me that this is a sign that the Bey will never permit you to leave here *alive*.'"

"But we have until to-morrow to decide," said Harry Barstow.

"To-morrow is nothing. It never comes. The Bey is offended by your hesitation. It is now too late!"

There was a convincing air about Penny Bunn that made them all serious and thoughtful. He was, no doubt, dreadfully in earnest, and, for once, had abandoned dealing in fiction.

"Too late," he resumed, "and in the stillness of the night, I know for certain that an attempt will be made to seize the 'Albatross,' kill all on board, and scuttle her. Thus all record of its existence will be swept away. A story will be set afloat that she went down in a squall. Who is to prove anything to the contrary?"

He was wonderfully logical, more so than he had ever before been known to be. There was something peculiar about the way he delivered himself that struck Jack Ford, but he did not divine its nature until afterwards, when it was too late.

"You think, therefore," said Ben Walton, "that we ought to do our best to get away."

"Assuredly," answered Bunn, "and you need not go without Chunder Loo. He is lying in a small place near the main gate. Now I can do two things for you. I can give him a drug—I found a bottle of it in my own room—and make him insensible. Then I can wrap him up so that he will look like a bundle of clothes. If you are seen bearing a man to the shore, you may be stopped and questioned; but a parcel of what looks like clothes is nothing."

"And when we get to the shore?" queried Jack Ford.

"I will have a boat ready for you," said Bunn.

"The risk I run is nothing, and if you get clear off I shall be happier than I can ever be if anything happens to you. Should you arrive safe in England and meet my wife, you will conceal the ornamental way I have been got up, and merely tell her that I have been appointed ruler of a province in the wilds of Africa, and any attempt to reach me would result in her being made a meal of by some lion."

They promised, and, as it was now dark, he left them, after enjoining them not to have a light. Should a slave come and offer them one they were to declare they would rather be left to sleep.

No slave came near them to make the offer, and they remained quietly chatting and smoking for two hours or more.

Then the courtyard was lit up with a glare, and they conceived that Achmet Bey was illuminating in honour of supposed guests who were in reality his prisoners.

It made them very exasperated against the aged potentate, and the longing to thwart his plans in respect to Chunder Loo grew strong within them.

It was well supplemented, of course, by a desire to get out of his clutches.

Brighter and brighter grew the glare outside, and anon the sounds of weird Moorish music were heard.

It originated in some part of the palace on the opposite side of the courtyard.

Dick Darnley went over to one of the narrow windows and looked out. He expected to see the accustomed number of swarthy figures lying about or moving to and fro, but the place was deserted.

He reported this to his chief, who judged that the men were at their evening meal, or had been taken away to assist somehow in the mock festivities.

Brighter and brighter became the glare, and, oh! how slowly the minutes passed away!

The question of whether Penny Bunn would be able to keep his word or not burned within them. But they talked little.

By-and-by Dick softly reported that Bunn had crossed the courtyard with a flagon, presumably containing wine, in his hand. He was moving in the direction of the principal gate.

"He is on the way to drug Chunder Loo," said Don.

Then the light of hope burned brightly in their hearts, and with ill-restrained impatience they waited the coming of their rescuer.

It was a long time—hours, it seemed—ere he appeared—not, as they expected, from the direction of the courtyard, but by the door at the back of the chamber.

"Hush!" he said, dramatically, "the hour has come. Art thou prepared?"

"All ready," answered Harry Barstow.

"Then go forth in Indian file and keep well against the wall where the deeper shadows lie. The moon will be up in half an hour. You must be away ere it shows its silver crown above the horizon. Ahem!"

"Fearfully and wonderfully poetic," muttered Don, as he filed out close behind his friend Jack.

Bunn went first, holding up a warning finger for the utmost caution to be used.

At any other time he would have excited uproarious laughter, but all were very much in earnest, and remained dumb.

Along by the wall until they came to the corner of the square yard nearest them. Twenty feet on ahead was their only means of exit—the chief entrance from the outer gate.

"Excuse me," whispered Bunn, "while I go forward to reconnoitre."

He went forward on tiptoe, a weird figure in the gloom. Then back again he came to report all clear, and once more the entire body moved on.

They gained the passage and entered it. Bunn stealthily called a halt. Then the click of a lock was heard, and he asked for four of their body to follow him into a pitchy dark room.

As the men were the stronger, and more fitted for the work of carrying a burden, they followed him.

Inside he bade them wait a moment and listen.

The sound of heavy breathing was heard.

"Hear him?" muttered Penny Bunn. "He sleeps. The potion has done its work. Ha, ha!"

It must not be assumed that he laughed aloud. It was a soft yet demoniac chuckle that burst from his lips.

He guided them to a trestle in the centre of the room on which the sleeper was lying. The man was muffled from head to foot in a thin cloth.

"Chunder Loo," remarked Bunn, "used to be a light sleeper. To-night he is clean gone. You might jump upon him, and he would not wake."

They got into position, and each taking hold of a limb, lifted the tall spare form from the trestle.

The doorway was visible, being a little less dark in the passage without.

They carried their burden out, and Bunn again assumed the lead.

Down, right to the big iron gates that guarded the entrance to the palace, they went. No sentry was there, and Bunn with a giant key turned the lock.

One of the gates swung silently back, and they filed out. Bunn instantly closed the gate again and stood with his face against the bars.

"Good-bye, and Heaven bless you, gentlemen," he said, in a voice of deep emotion. "Perhaps in the distant future we may meet again on earth. If not—aloft."

"Why not come with us?" suggested Harry Barstow.

"No," hurriedly replied Bunn, "I must soon be missed, and then there would be an alarm. That would be fatal to us all. I sacrifice myself for you to-night. In the hour of prosperity and happiness remember me."

He vanished for a moment, and as they were about to proceed with their burden, he was back again.

"Should you ever set eyes on that arrant rascal, Snicker," he said, "ask him to come here and I will find a place for him. In the matter of warmth it will lack nothing. Remember me to my wife, also, and likewise Miss Astracan. Tell them that they little dream of the sort of man they have lost."

"You had better leave with us," urged Jack Ford.

"No, the sacrifice would be imperfect if I did that," murmured Bunn. "Adieu—*au revoir*—good-bye—farewell!"

And then he vanished again, this time for good.

They waited a minute or so, and, as he did not re-appear, they felt that it would be only prudent to get away with all speed.

Accordingly the burden of the motionless drugged man was resumed, and through silent deserted ways they proceeded to the sea.

It struck them all that there was something truly remarkable in this absence of the population, wont to be abroad at night in the cool; but it was by the poorer thoroughfares they travelled, and they deemed it possible that the inhabitants had gone to more popular places.

But as they proceeded on their way, they did not know that the occupiers of the queer houses came stealing out to squat by their doors, smoking and talking in whispers.

It was like rising water dogging the heels of travellers, but the tide of humanity never overtook them so as to reveal itself, and they safely reached a landing-stage lapped by the waters of the lagoon.

There a boat was in waiting, but no man was in her.

The oars were ready, and the little craft was simply tethered by a rope.

Jack Ford, glancing round, observed that the same strange absence of human beings that had marked their route was still observable.

He did not attempt to account for it, but lightly sprang into the boat, and assumed the position of stroke oar.

His chums took up the other three oars, and the insensible burden was laid in the stern.

Dick Darnley loosened the painter and pushed off.

"Give way, and pull quietly," said Harry Barstow, "for the peril of being seen is not yet over."

CHAPTER CCLXXII.

THE WARNING ROCKET.—THE "ALBATROSS" READY.— UNDER FIRE.

THE boat glided on evenly over the bosom of the lagoon. On the other side, close to the horizon, was a faint light, heralding the coming of the moon.

Behind lay the town, a blaze of light in honour of the guests who were escaping from the tender mercies of their host.

It was not so perilous as some adventures they had passed through, but it was the strangest they had ever known.

The foremost emotion in their breasts was thankfulness at their escape from the clutches of the Bey. The second feeling was one of exultation at having thwarted the plan to rob them of Chunder Loo.

Not a word was said, for they knew that water carried sound to a great distance. The oars were dipped and pulled with scarce a response to the movement. There was a little grating in the rowlocks, but that was all.

Half the distance to the "Albatross" was covered, when suddenly a rocket shot into the sky.

It so happened that no one in the boat was looking shoreward at the moment. The rowers had their heads down, and the men their backs to the shore.

But they all saw it, high in the air, rising to a great height, poising itself an instant as a bird does on the wing, and then bursting with the report of a gun.

A stream of bluish light followed, illuminating both land and sea, and Jack Ford saw some men hurrying to the landing-stage.

"We are missed, sir," he said, quietly.

"So it appears," replied Harry Barstow. "Pull with all your hearts. We cannot tell what may be done to stop us."

There was a soft breeze blowing from the south. It favoured the boat, and it would favour the "Albatross" if she got under way.

There was the question of her being ready, of course, but Bill Oakley, it was hoped, would be on the alert.

Meanwhile, would the forts take any steps to stop them?

Whirr!

Another rocket spurted upwards and burst, showing a red light this time. The glare of it made the lagoon of a blood-red colour.

And now a responsive rocket was seen from the chief fort.

Jack bent to his oars and pulled as if he aimed at cracking his heart-strings.

His companion rowers followed his example. The boat ploughed through the water at a great rate.

"Steady! The 'Albatross'!"

It was the captain who gave the warning. Then a voice came from the deck.

"Who's there?"

"The captain and the rest of us," replied Dick Darnley.

"Lower a rope there. We have something helpless in the boat."

It was Ben Walton who spoke now. The bow of the boat just touched the side of the vessel, was steered round, and brought alongside.

The rope fell, and a running noose being made, it was fixed under the armpits of their inanimate prize.

"Haul away and run him down below," cried Harry Barstow. "Up with the anchor. Every man must work for his life!"

He gave these commands as he climbed on board. The others followed, and the borrowed boat was cast adrift to float where it willed.

Boom!

A gun spoke from the fort, and a shell—they knew it from a shot by its shrill screaming—passed along to the right, struck the water, and burst, sending up a fountain forty feet high.

"All ready, sir," cried Bill Oakley. "I've expected there was mischief in the air."

"Well done, Oakley," said Harry Barstow. "Aloft there—set every stitch of canvas. We shall want it in this bit of wind."

The men at the capstan fairly ran round as they weighed the anchor.

All that could be spared climbed like cats aloft, and the canvas spread out before the feeble breeze.

"Is that man safe below?" asked Dick Darnley.

"All safe, sir," replied Startop, "and locked in."

A second gun awoke the stillness of the night, and rocket after rocket rose up from the palace of the Bey.

The second shell struck the water fully a hundred yards short, but it was in the right direction, and with feverish haste Harry Barstow urged the men to get every sail out before the wind.

The anchor was up and made fast. The "Albatross" paid before the breeze lazily, as if loth to leave the region.

"Keep her away," sang out Harry Barstow. "Show her stern to the fort, or they will hit us."

"And then who will pick up the pieces?" muttered one of the men.

To add to the peril of their position, the moon, broad and brilliant now, rose above the horizon.

The "Albatross" was between it and the fort in a direct line. If the gunners were worthy of their name they could not fail to hit her now.

But there seemed to be something wrong with them or their guns, for several minutes elapsed ere another shot was fired. The shell flew wide of the mark.

"Blowed if they won't hit some of the other shipping," muttered Bill Oakley.

There were many vessels at anchor around, and from their decks arose the voices of men cursing either the object aimed at or those who fired at the "Albatross."

Startop, at the helm, was the only man on deck who did not turn his eyes towards the shore.

His simple duty was to keep the head of the yacht for the open sea. Pending his getting there, he conceived that it would be a very good thing to put one of the vessels at anchor between the "Albatross" and the fort.

A lumbering Dutchman was the nearest craft, and he headed to get outside it. On her deck were a number of sturdy figures watching the scene.

One as stout as a prize pig put his hands to his mouth, and called on the "Albatross" to sheer off.

But as he spoke in Dutch it could not be expected that Startop should understand what was said, and he steered a little closer.

"Keep her away," sang out Harry Barstow.

"Going round the Dutchman, sir," answered Startop, respectfully.

Boom!

A shot, better aimed than any of the former, ploughed between the two vessels, and the fat skipper of the Dutchman raved in half a dozen languages.

He fished out a speaking-trumpet from the deck, and sent out a blast of expostulation.

"Sthand offs!" he bellowed, "keep more *out*. Ach, vhat you vill come more near—*pig—jackass!*"

In impotent fury he hurled his speaking-trumpet at the "Albatross," and, as she was forty yards away, it fell into the sea.

The Dutchman capered about the deck, and as another shot was fired he fell upon his stomach.

"They've killed him," said Jack, regretfully.

"Nothing of the sort," said Ben Walton; "that last gun fired blank cartridge. There he is, up again and as lively as ever."

It was true. The Dutchman was again upon his feet, bounding about like a cricket-ball, and cursing until the "Albatross" was out of hearing.

The fort was silent then.

"They have given up the notion of sinking us," said Harry Barstow. "We are well away, my lads."

A cheer, partly in derision of the gunners, and partly in the joy of having escaped the peril of being sunk, responded to the young captain's congratulatory words. As if to help them, the breeze freshened.

On the shore the lights of the Bey's palace were extinguished. Only the faint glimmering of the town lamps remained.

"All right now," said Bob Stockton, rubbing his hands gleefully.

"What's come of Bunn, sir?" asked Chippy Bunyons, coming up. "I've been looking for him everywhere."

"He stayed behind with the Bey," was the reply.

In vain was it explained to Chippy that his friend had of his own free will remained. He was not to be comforted or consoled.

"If he's there I ought to be there too," he said. "Blow me, if I don't try and swim ashore, may I be shot!"

In any case it seemed probable that he would come to an early end, for there was only one way he would go, if he attempted to swim, and that was to the bottom.

Ben Walton came up from below at a speed that excited general attention. His movements were usually rather deliberate than otherwise.

Harry Barstow turned an inquiring glance upon him.

"That man below!" he gasped.

"What of him," was the next question.

"It is not Chunder Loo!"

CHAPTER CCLXXIII.

SOLD BEYOND RECALL.—ON TO OLD ENGLAND.

THERE was a general exclamation of anger and dismay, then a rush down below. There they saw Startop shaking up a man, who had the appearance of having been heavily drinking.

It was not Chunder Loo indeed, but a wretched Arab of an inferior caste. He was about the same height as Chunder Loo, and of a like build. But that was all the resemblance between them.

He gazed about him heavily with lack-lustre eyes. There was no sign that he had the least comprehension of his surroundings.

"*Sold!*" said Jack Ford, bitterly.

He stood just behind his captain, feeling as if he would like to do something to somebody, without exactly knowing what.

"To think that we should have been taken in so neatly," said Ben Walton. "The whole thing from our arrest to the firing upon us was a farce. The Bey wanted Chunder Loo, and to get him without complicating himself with the British authorities. He has succeeded to admiration."

"It was Sadyk that pulled the strings and made us dance to his own tune," said Jack Ford.

For once he felt himself completely outwitted.

There was nothing to be done but to restore the Arab to his wits, and take him with them until he could be landed at some convenient spot, then make for home.

Leaving the navigation of the "Albatross" to Dick Darnley, there was a consultation in the chief cabin, at which the first mate, Ben Walton, and the youngsters assisted.

There was a suggestion of stating the facts at home, and asking the authorities to demand the extradition of Chunder Loo; but Ben Walton and Norton Truscott both declared that it would fail.

"Say that the authorities moved in it," said the latter. "The Bey, or those who act for him, would put so many obstacles in the way that we should be defeated. They would stick at nothing, and probably swear that they returned precisely the same man they took away, and the change must have been effected at some earlier period. It would all come to nothing, and we should get no thanks for having interfered without due authority."

"I am sorry I helped to bring such a ridiculous fiasco upon us," said Jack.

"No blame can be attached to you," replied Harry Barstow; "on the contrary, I think you have acted most commendably. You have one consolation in still holding the treasure you wrested from the scoundrel."

There was considerable consolation in that, the more so because it was clearly seen that the Bey could make no claim upon it unless he declared he had possession of Chunder Loo, and that he was a subject of his realm.

So far the triumph was theirs, but no farther. The consultation ended as it began, in the knowledge that nothing could be done, and Jack retired with his friends to their cabin.

There they confounded Sadyk and all his works for two hours before getting into their hammocks, and even there continued to rail at him until they fell asleep.

Meanwhile, Bill Oakley headed for Gibraltar, and Chippy Bunyons, abandoning the idea of swimming ashore, gave himself up to unavailing grief.

Mulberry Cork endeavoured to console him with the suggestion that it was the best thing that could have happened to Penny Bunn, for in his present rig-out he would gain little or no honour in his own country. But Chippy mourned and refused to be comforted.

"He will be all right," he said, "so long as that blackguard the Bey holds him in favour; but he will boil poor Bunny in oil, or skin him alive, if he does anything to offend him."

It was not proposed to put into port again until they arrived at Gibraltar, where Harry Barstow would have the opportunity of consulting someone in authority and obtaining a little advice as to the better thing to do. To reach there they had to sail close upon a thousand miles, passing the wild countries of Algiers and Morocco.

The next day the Arab victim of Sadyk's scheming was sufficiently recovered to be questioned by Ben Walton, who was the only person on board able to talk to him in his native tongue.

He said his name was Ab Hulli Hassan, which seemed rather a long and important one for such an insignificant being.

He had no desire to be sent back to Tunis or to be landed anywhere until he got to England.

Of that country he had a hazy idea of the authorities being always glad of foreigners, whom they fed and clothed without calling upon them to do any form of work.

On being asked where he got that notion from, he said it was generally supposed to be so by all the poor in Tunis. That was all he knew.

He was no more anxious to work than to be put ashore, and on being informed that he would be expected to do something for his board and lodging, he suddenly became very dignified, and declined to soil his hands in the company of unbelievers.

Finally he was handed over to Bill Oakley, who prepared a special rope's-end to stimulate him, and he was told to burnish some of the brass-work of the binnacle to show what he could do.

He refused even to touch the rags as being "defiled" until the rope's end was applied with so good an effect that he commenced his labours with all the vigour of a promising young man just entering upon a new situation.

But he soon flagged, and from there to the harbour of Gibraltar his waking hours became a turn and turn about of miraculous energy and reprehensible laziness.

Ab Hulli Hassan and Bill Oakley during that time were the light comedy in the life on board.

Owing to occasional contrary winds, it was seven days ere the "Albatross" dropped her anchor before the historic rock with the quaint little town on the spur of land at its foot.

It was noon at the time, and soon after the heat of the day Harry Barstow went ashore, taking the boys with him. He was going to see some man in authority, to ask him permission to see as much of the galleries and guns which so well assist in the holding of the place against all comers.

Bill asked Chippy if he would like to go ashore and have a bit of a fling, "jist to cheer him up."

"Nothing will ever cheer me again," replied Chippy, glimly, "each day sees me farther from Bunny. I shall never smile again."

CHAPTER CCLXXIV.

ASHORE AT GIBRALTAR.—PROPOSED EXCURSION, AND A MEETING WITH A NEW FRIEND.

THE town of Gibraltar is of more considerable extent than is generally supposed by those who have not interested themselves in its history.

It is inhabited by nearly twenty thousand people of mixed nationality—English, Spanish, Jews, and Moors. The main features of it are that it consists of three long, parallel streets, and the mixed nature of its architecture, which is partly British, such as we see at home, and partly Spanish. Harry Barstow ascertained the position of the residence of the governor, and walked thither. His dress and bearing obtained him ready admittance.

Having sent in his card by an equerry, he was shown into the presence of the great man, the boys awaiting his return in an ante-room, where they were entertained by a young subaltern—he could not have been more than nineteen—who put on the airs of a man, and in a pleasant way patronised them.

"Come ashore to see our drum, I suppose?" he said. They admitted that was their idea.

"It will interest you," he said, with a yawn, "as it did me at first, but a week of it is enough. You will have to get a pass and some fellow as a guide."

"Captain Barstow," said Jack Ford, "is going to ask the governor for a pass."

"I could have got you one," replied the subaltern. "Men in my position have only to ask for such things."

"Will it be rude if I ask what your position is?" inquired Don. They were all amused by the youngster, who was boyish in his appearance to a degree.

"I am a portion of his excellency's household. But I do nothing but lounge about. Here, suppose I offer to be your guide? It will be a change for me to do something."

"Do you think you could be spared?" suavely asked Bob Stockton.

"If I put it as a favour to you," was the grave rejoinder. "What do you say to that suggestion?"

They said they would be delighted, and he promised to make it all right.

"By the way," he added, "my name is Heathcote. What is yours."

They told him.

"You are trotting about the sea for pleasure, I presume?"

"We have had something to do, but it is of private nature. We are homeward bound."

"I would I were going with you," sighed Heathcote. "Hallo, here's your chief."

Harry Barstow entered the room, accompanied by

an equerry. He brought with him the required pass, which he handed to Jack.

"His excellency says you must be accompanied by somebody—a private soldier or a non-commissioned officer," he said.

"I will go with them," said Heathcote, briskly. "I suppose I may?"

He looked wistfully at the equerry, who calmly replied:

"Certainly, and go to the deuce for a young imp!"

"What leave of absence can I have, sir?" asked Heathcote, drawing himself up.

"As long as you choose to stay away, provided you don't leave the rock."

Heathcote saluted by way of thanks, and the equerry, after a few whispered words with Harry Barstow, left the room.

Heathcote was then, by his own desire, introduced.

"You can leave these boys safely with me," he said. "I suppose, Captain Barstow, that you would not mind their being ashore for the night?"

"I would rather they did not remain in the town."

"They will not be in the town. I propose to camp up the rock. All we shall want will be a blanket a piece, which I can supply, and sufficient grub for supper and breakfast. It is impossible to see the rock properly in an hour or two."

"As you please," said Harry Barstow. "I shall not sail for a week at least."

The arrangement was voted to be A 1 by the four friends, and Harry Barstow having cautioned them, and told Jack in private that the governor was going to see what he could do in the matter of Chunder Loo, took his departure.

"A good fellow, I should say," remarked Heathcote, carelessly.

They admitted he was right, and then the details of the provisioning for a night upon the rock were discussed.

Heathcote frankly admitted that he could not entertain them in a fitting manner, having anticipated his pay for three months, and "blown" the half-yearly allowance he had from home. Jack told him it was of no consequence, as they had plenty of money—more, in fact, than they knew what to do with.

"By George!" he exclaimed. "I should like to see more than I could do with. It would have to be a precious pile.

"Now, I daresay," he said, "that you think the rock is barren?"

"It certainly appears so from the sea," replied Tom Drummond.

"You were never more preciously mistaken in your life," returned Heathcote. "High up there are hollows big enough for wooded glens, some lovely enough for fairies to dwell in; and there's lots of game, pigeons, rabbits, partridges, woodcocks, and curious fawn-coloured apes. No shooting, however, is allowed, for military reasons."

"What is the use of the game, then?" asked Jack.

"I'll show you," replied Heathcote, confidently. "There are ways of getting at them. The birds we can nobble after dark. There are thousands of them, and they are pretty tame, not being shot at. We shall want nothing but bread and wine, and a pot for cooking. I'll give you a taste of the native wild asparagus for a vegetable, and if you don't say it's prime, call me what you like."

He then suggested getting ready and going at once. Jack handed him a couple of sovereigns, and desiring them to await his return, he sauntered from the room.

CHAPTER CCLXXV.

IN THE GLENS OF GIBRALTAR ROCK.—HEATHCOTE SHINES AS A CATERER.—THE SPANISH FOES.

THOUGH apparently remarkably leisurely in his movements, Heathcote was soon back with all the needful material. But he was not himself the bearer. He was accompanied by a young Spaniard, whom he casually introduced in the ordinary way as Don Alguazil.

"He is a nobleman in difficulties," he said to Jack, in a lower key than he usually spoke; "poor, but not ashamed to earn his bread. For five shillings he will be our porter."

It was very convenient having someone to bear the burden of the blankets and a basket filled with bread and wine. Don Alguazil was therefore a welcome addition to the party.

He was good-looking, with a somewhat sombre face. In years he was not more than five-and-twenty.

With the basket in his hand and blankets strapped to his back, he led the way.

"He knows a path up the rock that will enable us to avoid the galleries. We shall have to pass through one of the outside forts, but that won't matter. Your pass will carry us along; besides, I am with you."

Being off duty, he had thrown off the shell jacket and regimental trousers he was wearing when they arrived, and was dressed in mufti—that is, in ordinary walking-attire.

He asked, in an undertone, if they had any arms, and being shown their revolvers, expressed his approval.

"There is not much probability of our requiring them," he said, as he exhibited one of his own, "but you never can tell. This place swarms with Spanish smugglers who come ashore and run their goods over the rock into the interior. Sometimes they are troublesome."

The idea of there being a spice of danger in the trip seemed to give it the requisite zest in the eyes of the listeners, and with light hearts they left the governor's house.

On the way through the streets to the west of the town they excited some attention, but nothing more than curiosity on the part of the mixed population was shown.

Heathcote nodded to some officers he met, but being in private attire none of the rank and file they encountered took any notice of him.

That is true etiquette in the army, or was at the time of our story.

We need not occupy the time of the reader with a description of the town. On reaching the end of it, the ascent was begun over the broken and rapidly-rising surface of the rock.

It was then about four in the afternoon, and Don Alguazil, as Heathcote called him, said their camping-ground would be reached an hour before sundown.

"Provided, of course," he added, "that the young senors are not too tired to complete the journey."

The "young senors" smiled at the supposition.

The fort they had to pass through was five hundred feet from the sea, built on a projecting rock, and jealously guarded by sentries without and within.

The pass was shown, and they were allowed to go on after a brief glance at the guns and the bomb-proof casemates which made the fort practically impregnable to a foe.

Then on again, up—up over rocks and along ledges invisible from below, from whence they had a magnificent view of the panoramas of land and sea.

But it was not the view they had come for, and after briefly admiring it, they proceeded on their way. Occasionally the road—if it can be called by that name—was perilous, but within the time named—that is, an hour before sunset—they arrived at a hollow of considerable extent on the side of the rock, where they were to pass the night.

Don Alguazil had borne his burden bravely, but he had had enough of it, and was glad of a rest. So were they all.

Throwing themselves down upon the greensward, the visitors looked around them, and beheld a scene of exquisite beauty.

They were on the verge of a miniature wood, where the trees were richly foliaged and flowers abounded. When they began to talk, the whirr of partridges on the wing immediately followed, and a number of fawn-coloured apes appeared on the tree-tops, and peered downward with that preternatural gravity with which the monkey generally is credited.

Then some pigeons of a common tribe, but prettily marked, came fluttering down, almost as tame as those by the Guildhall, St. Paul's, and other well-known buildings in London.

"You see what the birds are where the gun is not in use," said Heathcote; "tame as white mice. By-and-by we shall have some for supper."

"Doesn't it seem a pity to kill things so tame?" suggested Tom Drummond.

"We eat fowls," returned Heathcote, with a shrug. "Don Alguazil, light a fire."

"Is that his real name?" whispered Jack.

Heathcote laughed softly.

"What his real name is nobody knows. At least, I don't," he said. "He puts up for being a swell, and I named him Don Alguazil. It is about equivalent to Mr. Magistrate or Mr. Bobby at home."

"You meant it to be sarcastic?"

"Originally. But he took it seriously, and appeared to be highly complimented. So I let it stand. Now I will get you some asparagus for supper."

"Asparagus?"

"It grows wild here. Did I not hint at it before?"

The fire was lighted, and some water having been found, the pot was filled and slung over the blazing sticks, gipsy fashion. Heathcote disappeared for awhile, but soon returned with an armful of asparagus and half a dozen pigeons.

"As the farmer spares the feelings of a town visitor by killing the fowls in the barn, so have I in secret wrung the necks of these toothsome creatures for supper. I hope you are not too sensitive to help to pluck them."

They were not—far from it; and while the work was going on, Heathcote explained that he had merely gone up quietly to a spot where scores of pigeons were settling on the lower branches of a tree for the night, and selected some of the younger ones.

The pigeons were prepared, and the asparagus trimmed of all superfluous matter. Then the whole was put into the pot.

"In twenty minutes," said Heathcote, "supper will be ready. Meanwhile, what do you say to a cigarette?"

He had brought several boxes of the popular but injurious smoke, and they lighted up.

Don Alguazil made his own from tobacco and a sort of paper leaf he carried. The dexterity with which he rolled them was surprising.

"It is an art," explained Heathcote, "that the true Spaniard cultivates from his childhood."

The sun dipped below the western horizon, and night came on. There was no moon, but they had the light of the fire by which to eat their supper.

The stew was served in small bowls made from the cocoanut, and they ate it with wooden spoons, which

Heathcote explained cost but a trifle, and could be thrown away after use.

Altogether it was very delightful, and after the meal the fire was made up, and they gathered about it while Don Alguazil cleared away the remnants of the feast, and prepared a place for sleeping on by tearing off light branches and strewing them on the grassy ground.

But though their sleeping had been arranged for, they were not yet in the humour for rest.

Heathcote had led a leisurely life that had not sapped his energies in any way, and our friends were inured to hardship.

Strange to say that they were, notwithstanding their many adventures and strange experiences, as much charmed with their outing as if they had been fresh from school.

Possibly this arose from their healthy organisation, which enabled them to enjoy everything in life calculated to give pleasure.

"My idea of Gibraltar," said Tom, as he blew away the smoke of a mild cigar he had been tempted to try, "was a big rock sticking out of the sea, honeycombed with places for guns, and soldiers living in the holes, like—like——"

"Like wildfowl," suggested Heathcote.

"Yes, like wildfowl, seagulls—anything; but here I find a sort of miniature Paradise stowed away in the hollows of quite a country."

"Hardly that," said Heathcote; "but still, the rock is very different from what most people, who have not seen or read about it, believe. It is a wonderful place, reeking with legend and story."

"And not without romance still," suggested Jack,

"No, indeed," replied Heathcote. "Ask Alguazil, there—but he is dozing. The beggar has a hundred good yarns to tell, but they are all matter-of-fact to him."

"How is that?"

"Well, they have been part of his daily life— things that have happened in the struggle to live. When a man hasn't fields to cultivate, what does he do?"

"Work in the towns," suggested Don.

"But suppose there is nothing to do in the towns," said Heathcote, "or no towns in which to look for work? Then the bread-seeker must look for something. In some countries he takes to robbery— around here the most legitimate business is smuggling, and in viler regions the lowest form of man becomes a cannibal. We all of us feel the dire necessity of living, although it is not everybody else who agrees with us."

"You are quite a philosopher," remarked Jack.

"In a retail way—yes," replied Heathcote, calmly. "It is cultivated in the army and navy, and in all Government places abroad. We are taught by precept and example to feel nothing, or, if we must, not to observe it, and we end in not caring for anything or anybody—not even ourselves."

"A pleasant way of living, truly," said Don; "but surely all do not drift into this state of stagnation?"

"Most of our fellows do," sighed Heathcote. "By the way, I will tell you a short yarn illustrative of it."

"Make it a long one, if you like," said Jack; "I am just in the humour to listen."

CHAPTER CCLXXVI.

ON THE CAST OF THE DIE.

"IT happened about a year ago," began Heathcote, "just before the time for the relief of the Fourty-fourth fellows. They were all tired of being here, and had been for a long time, and as the day for the arrival of the exchange troops drew near, the time crawled with them. I heard the officers growling about it—and the two who said the least were those who felt the most. Among them were two fellows, Williamson and Corbett. They were subalterns—'subs' we call them for short—of the regiment.

"They had been fast friends, once upon a time, but for a year or more there had been a coolness between them. Some girl had to do with it, I believe. According to *my* experience, there always is a girl in anything especially disagreeable."

There was a general smile as Heathcote made this portentous announcement, but nothing was said, as he was looking into the fire with a face expressive of his being perfectly serious.

Evidently, he looked upon himself as quite a man of the world.

"Now, as far as I could make out at the time," continued Heathcote, "Corbett and Williamson, who had not exchanged a word, off parade, for ever so long, were drawn together by their mutual impatience to be gone. It was not so much for the sake of getting away from the Rock, although that was strong enough for anything, but from a desire to know what luck awaited them at home. You will understand that I had to piece this story together with such odd bits of information as I could get."

"Yes; we take that for granted," said Jack,

"But I think I have got the thing pretty correct," resumed Heathcote, "even to the conversation that took place between them at a café—that came from the waiter. Williamson was seated there when Corbett strolled in. A nod was exchanged.

"'Only another week,' said Corbett.

"'Seven days that will be seven ages,' replied Williamson.

"Then there was a short silence.

"'Corbett,' said Williamson, suddenly, 'you remember the conversation that made us ill friends?'

"'Yes,' replied Corbett.

"'We both had the portrait of *her*. I needn't mention her name.'

"'Not at all necessary. She had encouraged us both.'

"'To an extent,' said Williamson, 'and each thought the other was the favoured one, so we wrangled and rowed.'

"'Like two fools,' muttered Corbett.

"'Just so,' continued Williamson. 'Now I've got an idea.'

"'That is something novel,' said Corbett, in the good-humoured, chaffing way of the mess-room.

"'Well, I have it,' said Williamson, 'and it is this: *She* cares as much for one as the other. Our chances are about even.'

"'I have often thought so,' assented Corbett.

"'Now, instead of wrangling and rowing when we get home, why not put a stop to it here?'

"'How?'

"'Corbett, we can't both have her, that's plain. With even chances, it will be a tug-of-war, unless we come to some arrangement. They can let us have a box and dice.'

"'You propose to throw for her?'

"'Certainly. It won't affect *her*, you know. She seems to like one as well as the other.'

"The dice were brought," said Heathcote, as he pushed some of the burning sticks forward with his foot, "and then the strangest thing that ever happened with dice took place. They both threw sixes."

"Nothing very wonderful in that, is there?" asked Jack.

"Wait a minute," returned Heathcote. "They threw again, and both got *threes*. They stared at each other, as you may reckon.

"'This something strange,' said Williamson.

"'Unnatural,' muttered Corbett.

"Once more they threw, and, for a third time, tied with the lowest cast of all.

"'Six—three—one,' said Williamson. 'That is coming down a peg or two.'

"'But we are still level,' said Corbett. 'Shall we go on?'

"'No,' replied Williamson; 'it will be useless. Things will have to remain as they are. We must be rivals still, but let us put it off till we get back. If it is for the last time, let us be friends.'

"And they were," said Heathcote, "for the last time. There is no doubt they drank more than was good for them, and while they were making merry the mail-boat came in."

"An important arrival," suggested Don.

"Yes, although it is fairly frequent now," said Heathcote; "but those two fellows knew nothing about it. They were busy toasting the fair one and wishing each other good luck, as men will do when they have imbibed the red, red wine. At a late hour they returned to their quarters, and have never been seen since."

The sudden and startling termination to an apparently prosaic story caused the listeners, with quick movement, to raise their heads and stare at the narrator.

Heathcote was lying back, resting on an elbow, his face perfectly serious, dispelling the thought that came into Jack's mind of the story being nothing but a jest.

"Not seen since?" he echoed.

"No," rejoined Heathcote. "They vanished as completely as if they had been taken away to the heart of Africa by a tornado."

"And was there no clue to their disappearance?" asked Don.

"None to—most people; but I got at something."

"You?"

"Yes, I, which is more than even the governor did. When they could not be found there was a hubbub, you may guess, and all the queer houses in the town searched. But that was a needless trouble."

"Why?"

"Because neither Williamson nor Corbett had taken anything with him. Their watches were both found in their rooms, so it was certain they went back there when they left the café."

"What a terribly strange thing!" said Bob.

"It was. The investigation—it was practically an inquest without the bodies—took place, and the café waiter was called. He told us just what I have given to you."

"He must have listened pretty closely," remarked Don.

"He did," said Heathcote, "and he was very candid about it. He said there were few customers in the café, and he listened because he had nothing else to do. With a child-like air, he said that he always listened to what customers were saying when he had the chance of doing so."

"What breed was he?" asked Bob.

"Something in Alguazil's line, only more of a fool. Well, what do you make of it?"

"It is a fact, and not a conundrum, of course?" hinted Drummond.

"It is the solid truth."

"Perhaps they quarrelled again," suggested Don, "and kind of destroyed each other."

"How?"

"I can't tell."

"No, that won't do," said Heathcote, "because they went home, and Corbett evidently threw himself down upon his bed to read the letters and papers that had come in by the mail. They both had a copy of the London *Times* sent to them. I saw them both, because during the inquiry we had everything at our kennel."

"Was there anything special in their getting newspapers?" asked Jack.

"No, but there was a special paragraph marked by some kind friend, who was, to my thinking, responsible for their death. It related to the marriage of a lady with a nobleman. I have called it a paragraph, but it was almost a column in length."

"I begin to see," exclaimed Jack; "it was the girl they both loved."

Heathcote nodded.

"Without a doubt," he said.

"Might I ask her name?" inquired Bob, politely.

"I think it had better remain a secret within my breast," said Heathcote. "I can't blame her. I daresay she did no more than hundreds of pretty women, I may say thousands, do yearly. She had a mild flirtation with them and they took her seriously. I have been had myself that way once. But," he added, firmly, "never again. They won't hit this old bird in the wing never no more, as the song says."

His listeners smiled, but they were too keenly interested in the story to extract any mirth from it, or anything relating to it, just then.

"Perhaps you have solved the mystery," suggested Jack Ford.

"I have, to my own satisfaction," replied Heathcote. "Now follow me: there were two spoony fellows, excited by an evening out; they drank a lot, for I saw the book of the waiter. They were unstrung by long service in the Rock, and weakened by impatience to get home to see the girl they thought loved them. You have the matter so far."

"Yes," said Jack.

"Now you come to the throwing of the dice with a ten-million-to-one chance of a tie three times in succession. A kind of superstitious fear gets hold of them, they feel that they have to remain rivals to the end, but they drink and try to forget it. After they get home—or on the way—they remember it, perhaps; and if the latter, I daresay they got boastful. Lots of fellows do it in their cups."

"Assuredly," said Don, as Heathcote paused for breath.

"Say that without actually quarrelling," pursued Heathcote, "they taunted each other with prospective failure. Nothing more likely. Then they parted. Each went to his rooms, and there found their letters

and papers. Every fellow runs over the headings of the papers before he reads his letters. They did so. The marked column catches their eyes. They read it, and it maddens them. Take their condition of mind and body they were in, and you will see that they were ripe for anything."

"You think they committed suicide?" said Jack.

"Yes, I do; and they did it because one should not be laughed at by the other. Their minds were morbid, and they were bent on disappearing. Each went out, and each did it his own way."

"But their bodies would have been found?"

"Not if they went up to one of the higher galleries and threw themselves into the sea. It was an idea that would naturally come to them, for they were often there on duty. Their bodies would be sucked away by some eddy or current sweeping past the straits. They would be borne down far away into the bosom of the Atlantic, and, as happened, they would never be seen or heard of again."

CHAPTER CCLXXVII.

THE TWO LIGHTS IN THE SEA BELOW.

"YOU have come to a conclusion," said Tom Drummond, "that would do credit to the most expert detective."

"I flatter myself I got at something nearer the mark than anybody here," replied Heathcote, "and I have kept it to myself until now, because I find that my ideas are not appreciated. Take the governor, now. What do you think his view was?"

They made several guesses, but Heathcote said they were all wrong.

"The governor," he declared, "went for their being smuggled away in a state of intoxication and sold as slaves in Algiers. He had a long correspondence with the French authorities about it, and all sorts of doubtful characters were hauled in to give an account of their doings for the past week or two. Some were able to do so, but others seemed to be in a difficulty in the matter. Still there was nothing got out of them to account for the disappearance of the two men. Hallo! what's that?—a gun?"

The boom of a gun from the sea below, brought them all to their feet, save Don Alguazil, who merely looked up.

"That's one of our small craft," said Heathcote, "firing blank cartridge."

"What is the sense of that?" asked Don.

"It's a notice for some suspicious boat to heave to and allow itself to be overhauled. It's a hundred to one on a smuggler being about."

"Then he will lose his run?"

"He will run for it—into the bay, perhaps. Let us go up and see. We can follow the dodging about by the lights of our own craft."

They climbed up to the point of an adjacent rock, from whence they could command a view of the sea.

It was only faintly to be seen, but there were many lights attached to the ships below lying at anchor, and in a westerly direction two were moving onward, one following the other.

"The smuggler and one boat," chuckled Heathcote. "Same old game, which our people will never see through."

He did not say what the game was, and they did not ask him. All were keenly interested in the two lights, and, in imagination, they saw the boats, one crowded with alarmed smugglers, and the other manned by cool, determined men.

The foremost light went on ahead in a westerly direction for a time, then bore to the north, and shortly afterwards disappeared.

The second light went on the same tack, passing almost immediately under where the youngsters were standing.

Then it turned back, closer in-shore.

"The old style—the old style," said Heathcote; "and they will cruise about all night and catch nothing."

"I suppose the smuggler has been too smart for them?" said Don.

"He has," returned Heathcote, drily. "Now, see this. *That* light—the one which has vanished—was *not* on the smugglers' boat, but on a decoy."

"I don't see the use of that," said Tom.

"No, perhaps not," said Heathcote. "But I, knowing the beggars, do. There are two boats, one with the goods for the run, the other to draw off our people. The first carries no light, the second one does. While our people were dancing after the second, the first has run in, and the goods are either landed or well on the way."

"That's a cunning move."

"It is the simplicity of it that does the trick. I am sure it has been practised a dozen times since I first honoured the Rock with my august person. I saw through it long ago, but I didn't mention it. I have nothing to do with the Spanish revenue, and never hesitate to buy a thing smuggled when I get the chance and have the money. I never often have the chance, though, to possess the money."

This dolorous confession of chronic impecuniosity made them laugh, and Heathcote joined in. It amused him as much as anybody.

"I first got an idea of how it was done," he went on, "one night when I was prowling about, amusing myself with looking round, because I had nothing else to do. I found a seat on the east side of the town, close to the sea. Luckily it was in a hole, which I selected, because it kept off the night dew. If I had been lying in the open I should not be here yarning the truth to you now.

"Suddenly I heard a gritting sound upon the rocks, and heard whispering voices. Poking my head out, I saw the outlines of a dozen or more men, who were very busy landing a lot of packages from a boat. They were hard at work, and having a diffidence about interfering with them, I drew my head in again, scarcely breathing. When one is resolved upon not interfering with what does not concern us, one cannot be too cautious."

"Hear, hear!" said Bob, politely.

"They had quite a cartload of stuff," said Heathcote, "and having got it ashore, the boat sloped off, and they proceeded to make up packages, by binding parcels together, for each man to carry—the usual thing is lace or silk, as the case might be. Sometimes they run brandy, but it is neither so light to carry, nor so profitable, as the other things.

"When they had made up everything, it was discovered that there was one odd package, and as each man had as much as he cared to be worried with, there was a wrangle as to who should take it. Finally, one of their number proposed to leave it hidden and come back for it. He said, truthfully enough, that it could be disposed of in the town."

Heathcote paused, and drew a deep breath, as if the memory of that night excited him. But he soon resumed his story.

"I was, as I told you, in a hole. It was deep—almost a cave running under the rocks. The man who proposed leaving the package took it up and came towards where I was lying. I rolled quietly back, and waited to be found out.

"You may imagine my feelings when he threw that package in, carelessly, as if it had been a bundle of old clothing, and hit me fairly in the ribs with it. I pledge you my word that it knocked all the breath out of my body. It was fully half a minute before I could gasp, and that short space of time saved me. The men were in a hurry, and they were off in a twinkling, like successful burglars with a bobby coming up the street."

"Suppose they had found you out?" asked Tom.

Heathcote passed his hand across his throat.

"Without the least compunction or the slightest hesitation," he said, "they would have done it, and then one of the chief of our luminous lights would have been extinguished. I gave them lots of time to get away, and then came out. Thinking it would be a pity to leave the package exposed to the night air, I took it home with me."

"And what did it contain?" asked Jack.

"Lace—newly manufactured—but of the best. I

A SPLENDID SCHOOL STORY.

NEVER BEFORE PUBLISHED.

By E. HARCOURT BURRAGE,

Author of "Ching Ching," "Monkey Mat and Roving Dick," "The Brave Boy of the Basilisk," &c.

THE LAMBS of LITTLECOTE

On seeing the youngsters round the fire, the smuggler pulled up short. "I salute you, senors," he said, with profound respect.

No. 37. ☞ PRICE ONE PENNY. ☜

ALDINE PUBLISHING CO., 10, Red Lion Court, Fleet St., and 1, 2, & 3, Crown Court, Chancery Lane, London.

orget how many yards there was of it, but I know hat I was able to send home a lot to my mother and isters, and there was a tidy bit left for a maiden aunt who has money, and whose kindly interest on my behalf in her will I hoped to stimulate."

"Let us hope you have done so," suggested Don.

"I can't say," was the doubtful reply. "From some I received letters thanking me—they evidently believed the story that accompanied the gift. My aunt is a hard-hearted woman of the world, and she merely acknowledged it, hoping I had come by it *honestly.*"

"What was the yarn you pitched?" asked Don.

"It was something about a lost child I picked up after a shipwreck. The father was a French lace manufacturer, who in gratitude piled up his stock-in-trade upon me—part of it, anyhow. My sister Alma —she's a jocular little beggar—asked me when I was going to start novel writing. If there was a tinge of doubt it was in her gentle breast."

"Life has not been altogether dull for you here," remarked Jack, as they stepped down the road on their way back to the fire.

"Not entirely," replied Heathcote; "it is the sense of being confined in a small area that is so aggravating. If you want adventure, you can get it here. Half a dozen words with some of the semi-savages will lead up to a fight, if you are inclined that way."

"Perhaps you are?"

"No; I have no desire to cultivate the pugnacious art. I am satisfied with playing spectator to the street rows. You should see a Moor and a half-caste nigger go for each other. It is a real treat. The Moor stands on his dignity, erect as a marble monument. The nigger goes for him ram-fashion, head down and bent on butting him. If he gets in first the Moor goes down upon his back, and while he is counting the stars, real and imaginary, the nigger jumps on him until his internal anatomy isn't worth a cent for a month to come. But if the Moor gets his knife home in time, the nigger has nothing to do but to think of his native land, say good-bye to his mother, and close his eyes in peace."

All this was very amusing to the listeners. It was an insight into a life that was new to them. But they were to have their own adventures in the Rock ere they left it, as we shall see anon.

During their absence the fire had burned low, but the Don, waking up, hastened to replenish it in a silent, listening way, as if he expected something or somebody to come along that way.

Sleep was a stranger to the eyes of the friends; indeed, they felt more wakeful than before. Stretching themselves upon the ground, they were silent for awhile. Don broke the quietude by asking if anybody had anything more to talk about.

Heathcote was, of course, curious to learn what his new friends had seen during their travels. They told him a lot about the Avishnus, and their adventures with that strange, but now happily extinct body, which interested him immensely.

Don Alguazil still lay a little apart, listening with the inherent gravity of a true-blooded Spaniard. Suddenly he arose to his feet and disappeared.

"What is the matter?" asked Jack, who had noted the movement.

"He has heard something," answered Heathcote, carelessly. "The smugglers use this road, I believe. Our Don, I strongly suspect, is in the line, or was in it. A very brisk business he carried on."

"But why is it allowed?"

"It is a matter for the Spanish Government to look to on the other side of the low neck of neutral ground between the rock and Spain proper."

Don Alguazil came back, and from his manner it was seen that something was wrong.

"Senors," he said, "I regret to inform you that the band of Luigi is approaching."

"What of that?" asked Heathcote, raising his eyebrows. "We have done nothing to Luigi, and if we had we should not be afraid of him. He knows very well what would happen if he interfered with us."

"It is not with you, senor, he will interfere with," said Don Alguazil, "but myself. We were friends once, but now——"

"If you want to have a row," replied Heathcote, "you must go away and have it out. We can't be bothered with you."

"Luigi," said Don Alguazil, "is here."

Not only was Luigi there, but he had half a dozen followers with him, all laden with packages of contraband goods.

The leader of this band, Luigi, appeared to be a cross between the Spaniard and the Italian. Coming from a mixture of two such races he could not be less than fiery, and on occasion ferocious.

On seeing the youngsters around the fire he pulled up short, and bowed low.

"I salute you, senors," he said, with profound respect; "it was not given to me to know it was you who were here. I see a fire, and I say, we shall find comrades there. But it was a mistake. Pardon."

"Oh, it is of no consequence," replied Heathcote, coolly. "There is room for us all. What are you running through to-night?"

"Lace and silks, senor," replied Luigi; "but if we rest here we will not intrude. Our fire shall be lighted at a respectful distance."

Up to this time Don Alguazil had been standing in the shadow, and Luigi was not aware of his presence, but in turning slightly to give instruction to his men he saw him.

Fire seemed to positively flash from his eyes, and his right hand clutched the handle of a knife he had in his sash.

" *You* here, dog !" he hissed.

" Yes, *pig !*" replied Don Alguazil, coolly.

"Look here," said Heathcote, "if you two want to row, go and have it out yonder. What right have you to disturb us ?"

"Pardon, senor," said Luigi, with an effort; "but I was not aware this jackass was with you."

"Nor did I think," said Don Alguazil, "that this spavined mule would intrude upon you."

"Well," said Heathcote, carelessly, "you seem to have some ill-blood between you. Go and have it out."

The two men exchanged a sign and withdrew to a portion of the glade higher up.

The carriers of the bales followed, and having deposited their burdens on the ground, proceeded to light a fire.

While this was being done the two enemies stood apart with their arms folded.

"What is the cause of the row ?" asked Don.

"A woman, I should say," answered Heathcote; "they seldom fight about anything else."

"Are they serious, do you think?" inquired Bob Stockton.

"The woman will have but one lover left when it is over," said Heathcote. "I can tell by their manner that they mean business."

"Can't something be done to stop it?" suggested Jack. "I have no fancy for seeing a man laid out in death to-night."

"You may try what you can do, of course," said Heathcote, "but I fear a failure."

"I'll have a shot at it," said Jack, as he rose to his feet.

He walked over to the place where the fire was just beginning to burn, and was followed by the rest. Heathcote casually remarked that he would bet ten to one on a failure.

The bearing of the two enemies pointed in the direction that if he got a taker he would win.

CHAPTER CCLXXVIII.

THE DUEL BY FIRELIGHT.

" I HAVE no right to interfere with you," said Jack, addressing Luigi, "but I should like to put matters square if I can. Is your quarrel a very serious one ?"

Luigi took off his hat and bowed low.

"Senor," he said, "it's most serious."

"Can't I adjust things for you ?" inquired Jack.

"Impossible," said Don Alguazil.

"Spare your breath, Ford," said Heathcote. "I knew how it would be. You have a lady in the case, Senor Luigi ?"

"It is so," answered the smuggler. "While both are alive she will have neither."

"Then both should give her up," said Heathcote; "the woman is unreasonable."

"Love does not reason," said Luigi, sententiously.

"Let them fight it out," whispered Heathcote; "it will be just as well, as they are bound to have a go in sooner or later."

Jack said no more, and with his friends drew a little aside to watch the issue of the coming fight.

It was a scene that would fix itself on the memory of any living being endowed with ordinary powers.

The blazing fire cast dancing shadows around, and the foliage and flowers gleamed in the glare. The smugglers in their coarse yet picturesque attire also aided in giving a romantic charm to the picture. Then there was the position on the historic rock, high above the sea, and the shining stars overhead. Altogether a thing to be remembered.

When it was considered there was light enough the combatants pulled off their jackets, twisted them round their left arms, and drawing their knives, advanced upon each other.

Stooping slightly, with their eyes fixed intently on the face of their foe, they drew up step by step.

All the spectators were still. They scarcely breathed.

The glade, also, was quiet, for the wind, blowing from the other side of the rock, was not felt. There seemed to be a feeling of expectancy on all things around.

The feelings of Jack may be taken as an illustration of those of his friends.

He was deeply moved, as he might have been if he had seen two tigers advancing upon each other to fight to the death. There was, indeed, something of the action of wild beasts in the movements of the men.

Having got within three paces of each other they paused and stood as still as figures of stone. Each waited for his foe to make the first spring.

It was a pause of but a few moments only, and then Luigi leaped upon the Don.

There was a flashing of steel in the firelight, and then they had each other by the wrist.

Both had struck and been foiled by the jacket around the left arm, and then hold was taken.

It was now a question of strength.

If one could wrest away the other's weapon the end was certain. The grip on the wrist was a matter of life and death.

Although there was no wild movement, no quick

stepping here and there, or staggering to and fro, the sight was most thrilling.

Wonderfully evenly matched in the matter of muscle, they held to each other, scarcely stirring, but straining quietly ever; sinew to get the better of the fight.

Don Alguazil's arm was forced back a little, only to be thrust forward again with an effort. Then the same thing was done with Luigi.

But after awhile, it could not have been more than a minute or two, a change came over the scene.

Luigi suddenly endeavoured to throw his foe, but failing, was in his turn thrown with tremendous violence on his back.

There was a hoarse cry from the watching band of smugglers, expressive of dismay. Jack spoke again :

"Can't this thing be stopped?" he asked. "It is too brutal and horrible !"

" You can do nothing," asserted Heathcote.

Nor could he.

All the ferocity of the Spanish and Italian natures was to the front. It was a fight to the bitter end, and the end soon came.

It was impossible for any of the spectators to turn away from the weirdly impressive finale to the fray.

Inch by inch Don Alguazil forced down the knife he held until it pierced the clothing of his foe.

Then Luigi gave in, and with a bitter cry, that rang out horribly on the night-air—yielded himself up.

There was a sharp down-thrust with the knife, another cry less piercing, but as painful to hear, and all was over.

The smuggler chief would never more go a-wooing.

As Heathcote remarked, the woman who had caused the affair would on the morrow have no choice of lovers. Only one was left.

Don Alguazil arose and wiped the stained blade upon the grass prior to restoring it to its sheath. His anger was over now, and as he looked down upon his dead enemy Jack observed that there was a tear in his eye.

"We were friends once," he murmured, loud enough for those nearest to him to hear, "and now thou art dead, and I have killed you. And all for a woman—*curse her !*"

"Come away," said Heathcote. "It is even money the woman has lost both her lovers. I suppose she set them on to fight. There is nothing a Spanish woman is so proud of as having a man killed for her sake."

They sat down by their own fire again and were silent for a time.

The smugglers carried away their dead chief to another part of the wood, probably, and returning for their bales, bore them off also, and were seen no more.

The Don came up and asked permission to go away also. He was anxious to confess to the priest and obtain absolution without delay.

Permission was readily given him, for all felt that he would be less acceptable as a guide after the incident of the night.

Not that they were disposed to judge him harshly, knowing nothing of the way the duel was brought about.

But his hands were red with recently spilled life-blood, and they could not have borne with him as a companion on a pleasure-excursion.

"It is rather awkward," said Heathcote, "as I wanted him to guide us through the lower galleries, which are rarely visited. But I think I may be able to carry you through without him. I think it is time to turn in. One cigarette in the blankets, and then to sleep. We must be up with the dawn. The cooing of the pigeons will wake us."

They were all ready to lie down and be quiet, if not to sleep, and having made up the fire for the last time, they lay down and talked no more.

CHAPTER CCLXXIX.

HEATHCOTE AS A GUIDE.—DODGING THE SENTRIES.

THE party of five all slept soundly until they were awakened by the cooing of pigeons and the chattering of apes.

The latter joined in with the former much as a beating of a light tattoo would do with the droning of a low-toned chant.

"Up, boys !" cried Heathcote, rolling out of his blanket. "One of you get a fire going ; I'll see to breakfast. Put the pot on, too, as we are going to have stewed rabbit."

He performed a rapid toilet and vanished. Tom Drummond, once the Littlecote caterer, now became cook.

"You fellows can take your ease," he said. "I am the man for the making of rabbit-stew."

The embers of the previous night's fire being still aglow underneath, all that had to be done was to put on fresh fuel and fan it into a blaze. That done, the pot was put on and the water was on the boil when Heathcote returned with a pair of rabbits.

"I put down a couple of snares in their run," he said. "My proper avocation is that of a poacher. My governor at home has big preserves, and I've done a bit of it to mystify the keepers."

"Now there is the programme for the day," said Heathcote later on, when a delightfully gipsy breakfast was in full swing. "It may be expressed in a few words as a visit to the galleries. You have heard of them, perhaps?"

They had all read about them, but had forgotten half their reading.

They believed that the galleries were passages of considerable extent tunnelled through and about the rock. Some were comparatively modern, say a couple of centuries old, but others had an origin lost in the mists of a forgotten past.

"Now when we started," said Heathcote, "it was supposed by our misguided friends that we were going the usual tourist round, but seeing the sort of fellows you were, I made up my mind to try at something more worthy of us. Shall I open my mind?"

"By all means," said Jack.

"Well, then, my idea was to explore the *under* galleries that lie below the four-hundred-feet level. That is the point where the prohibition comes in."

"Why prohibition?" asked Jack.

"Because it is supposed to be dangerous to go lower. Anyway, there are no perforations for guns to the outer air. But, then, why go lower at all?"

"For magazine purposes, perhaps," suggested Don.

"No. The galleries were made long before gunpowder was thought of, and therefore could not be wanted. I have been lower than I ought to have gone, disobeying orders, and heard the murmuring of the sea below. I went with a midshipman of the 'Ariadne.' Such a plucky little devil. He was killed the other day fighting with the blacks, somewhere on the African coast. Got let in for an ambush, and having given a dozen niggers beans, died covered with glory."

"What you want us to do," said Jack, "is to accompany you in an effort to get to the bottom?"

Heathcote admitted as much.

"I invested a portion of your tin in candles," he said, "for which I hope you will forgive me."

"Shall we pardon him?" asked Bob Stockton, with mock dubiousness. "For my part, I think he ought to have tested our nerves ere he brought us here."

"You have no nerves to test," returned Heathcote.

"Oh, forgive him," said Don. "Now, how do we get to the galleries?"

"There are two ways known to me," said Heathcote, "one the authorities are aware of, and another they know nothing about. It is one of the smugglers' secrets, but I wormed it out of Alguazil the last time we were here."

"What are the advantages of the secret way?" asked Jack.

"The ability to go alone is all I know of, and it is

everything," replied Heathcote. "If we go by the ordinary route a private or a non-commissioned officer will be told off to accompany us, and it will be his duty to see that we go so far and no lower."

"But if we tip him?"

"If you tip him all your pockets, and throw your head in, you would not induce him to swerve from his duty. You may subsidise a bobby, but never a soldier. Which is the result of the severer discipline, and not on account of the morality of the man."

They had three bottles of wine, which Heathcote proposed to take with the remains of the cooked rabbit and the bread that was left.

The blankets, he said, had better be left behind.

"We shall not sleep there," he remarked, adding, casually, "unless it will be the longest sleep of all."

"What time shall we be back?" asked Tom.

"Before night, if nothing intervenes," was the answer; "but don't let me take you unless you wish."

They were all for going, and the preparations for the start at once began.

The candles, matches, and provisions were divided into equal portions, not so much for the proper sharing of the burden, as on the off chance of their becoming separated. In that case it would be very hard for some to have all the candles and provisions, and others none at all.

When they were ready to start, Heathcote led the way to what may be termed the back of the hollow, the upper side of the rock in which it was situated.

There the stone was upright in cliff form, and up the face of it a variety of creeper had climbed.

Some of it, of the virginia-creeper tribe, hung down in festoons, and, parting it, Heathcote disclosed an opening in the rock about the width and height of an ordinary man.

"Enter," he said, "and don't leave hope behind. Mind how you go, as there is a flight of steps just inside."

They entered, and he dropped "the curtain," as he expressed it. A light, he told them, was not immediately necessary, as at the bottom of the flight of steps to which they groped their way they would be in a gallery lighted from without.

"It has long been deserted," he said, "and there is nothing to look at but some old guns that would be as much use in a fight in these days as so many peashooters."

The steps were many, fully a hundred, and they had come almost to the bottom ere a ray of light came to their relief.

It was very feeble at first, but speedily growing stronger, they were eventually guided into a gallery which, in comparison with the place they had left, was fairly bright.

The opening through which the daylight penetrated was covered with foliage, which accounted, as Heathcote explained, for their being unknown. The light filtered through the foliage.

Lying by the openings were portions of old guns, some dismounted from their wooden carriages by suddenly-applied force, while others had rotted and fallen in a slower way, covering a term of years perhaps.

Rusty pike-heads and portions of armour were also scattered about.

"Who held this gallery, and came to grief in it, nobody knows," said Heathcote; "it isn't mentioned in any of the guide-books."

"But it is known to the smugglers?" said Bob.

"To a few of them, and the beggars have no romance in their characters. They simply use it in case of emergency for storing some of their contraband goods. But that isn't very often, as they generally have a clear run."

The gallery was semicircular in shape, and they passed round it to the far end, where they came to what appeared to be a rugged blank wall.

"Beyond this," said Heathcote, lowering his voice, "there is a gallery, where a sentry may generally be found. I don't think there is one so early in the day, but I'll make sure before we attempt to get through."

He pulled out a piece of rock, and applied his eye to a small hole. In a few moments he withdrew it with a sigh of satisfaction.

"All clear," he said. "Now then. Open Sesame!"

He thrust his hand into the hole, and dragged out the end of a small but strong steel chain.

Pulling hard, he removed a stone of sufficient size to enable them in turn to pass through.

At his bidding they did so, and he came last, and dragged the stone back into its place with the chain. Then he closed up the hole he had looked through with a smaller stone.

"Safe, so far," he said. "Now we have to run the gauntlet of at least three inquisitive sergeants ere we get to what is known as the lowest gallery, which it isn't by a long way."

The galleries of Gibraltar have all been cut out of the solid rock.

No shot or shell, even of the present day, could break through the natural wall, and wherever possible, bomb-proof casemates have been placed for defending soldiery.

Passing many signs of modern defence, Heathcote, turning a corner, came upon a sentry. The man's rifle, ready bayoneted, was brought to the level, and barred the way.

"The word?" he cried.

"Here is our pass," replied Heathcote. "I am one of the staff of the governor."

"Can't let you pass without the sergeant's permission. Here he comes, sir."

The sergeant came up, looking very fierce, until he saw and recognised Heathcote. Then he saluted him. So it appeared to Jack that what was military etiquette in the streets was the reverse in the galleries.

"We are going to the lower galleries," said Heathcote; "here is the pass. It was signed yesterday."

"You've got here early," said the sergeant. "I don't remember seeing you pass, sir."

"We are here, anyway," coolly replied Heathcote. "Of course, you do not expect us to provide you with eyes to see with?"

"No, sir."

"Very well, then, lead us to the next gallery, and explain that we don't want to be bothered any more about our pass."

The sergeant, still puzzled, passed them on to the next gallery. He was far from satisfied.

"They came here unseen," he said, "and they are up to some game. I'll keep an eye on them."

Unconscious of having excited especial attention, the five visitors were passed on through a series of galleries and passages, where the bristling guns and watchful sentries conveyed the impression of a warlike time being at hand. But it is always so there, for Gibraltar is ever prepared for an enemy.

It has once been taken by surprise. It is our duty now that it never be so again.

At last they reached the lower gallery, where they were supposed to stop. There the last embrasure had been cut through and the last gun hoisted. Below that all was darkness.

There was a way out to an open-air fort, and by that they were supposed to go; but Heathcote, while pretending to make his way thither, watched until the sentry, pacing to and fro, had his back turned to them, and then bore abruptly to the right, striking into a narrow passage as dark as the shades of night.

"Hurry up!" he whispered. "Keep a hand on the wall, and move as quietly as you can."

There was no pursuit, however, and they were soon able to stop and rest. Heathcote lit one of the candles, and taking the lead when they started again, presently came to an opening in the wall about four feet wide and feet high.

"This leads down to the forbidden ground below, and now our real work as explorers begins," said Heathcote. "There is a legend that the air is so foul that we shall not be able to breathe, but so long as the candles burn we are all right."

Jack said it was so, but they had better proceed with caution; and they passed on.

CHAPTER CCLXXX.

DOWN TO THE LOWER DEPTHS.—A DISCOVERY.

INSIDE the crude doorway there was a flight of steps travelling in a zig-zag fashion. They were like the galleries above, wonderfully dry.

About a hundred of these steps had been traversed ere they came to a landing in the form of a small chamber cut out of the solid rock.

The only ventilation came from a similar opening to that above; but there appeared to be plenty of it.

"I have been as far as this before," said Heathcote, "and it strikes me that the air seems to be fresher than it was when last I was here. There is quite a rush up from below."

It was so, insomuch that when they renewed their downward journey, it became imperative to shield the candles with their caps.

Another chamber was soon reached, and there they paused and looked around them with amazement.

All round the sides of it, save at a third opening, were ranged a quantity of rifles and small-arms. It was, in fact, an armoury of no inconsiderable proportions.

This discovery excited more amazement in Heathcote than in the rest. It also troubled him, for reasons that will be presently explained.

Holding a candle aloft, he walked through the chamber until he had completed the circle.

"All of the latest make and invention," he said. " I say, you fellows, we have dropped on something, I can tell you."

"Why should our people hide arms here?" asked Jack.

"It is not our people who have placed them there," answered Heathcote, "and that is where the mischief comes in. Who has done it, is what we have to find out. Now we must proceed with the utmost caution. If you talk, let it be done in a whisper."

Forward and downward again they went by many steps, arriving anon at another storehouse of war ammunition, in the form of cases and boxes, which Heathcote declared were filled with powder and cartridges.

"Of Spanish make," he said, thoughtfully.

As there was some probability of an accident of considerable magnitude taking place if they lingered there with the naked candles, they proceeded onward by a passage that had a slight downward slope.

Like all the places they had been in, it was hewn out of the solid rock, but here and there they came upon recesses varying from a few feet to many yards deep.

Some were empty, while others had packages placed there in a loose fashion, and evidently left for future removal above.

"It occurs to me," said Heathcote, halting, "that we are now getting into very dangerous ground. Of course I have no hope of scaring you fellows when I tell you that our being found here would result in our being unceremoniously murdered."

"By whom?" asked Don, wonderingly.

"Again, I cannot say," replied Heathcote; "but by somebody who has no love for us as a people, you may take your davy. To come to the point: I propose going on with one of you, and the rest are to go back to where we dodged the sentry. There they must remain, say for two hours."

"Why?" asked Bob.

"Here," said Heathcote, speaking very low indeed, "I see arrangements made to wrest Gibraltar from us. It cannot be done from the outside, so the attempt is to be made from within."

"Traitors in the camp?" suggested Tom Drummond.

"No," answered Heathcote, "I judge that there is some means of communicating with some place below, of which our people have not the slightest suspicion. If we can find out what it is, we shall be doing a great service to the country and gain us a lot of credit, if nothing else. I wish Ford to accompany me."

"Why me?" asked Jack.

"Oh, you seem to be sort of leader among your set."

"I never said so, or hinted at it."

"Perhaps not; but you can always tell who is the man in command before he opens his mouth."

The others were not jealous. Jack was their acknowledged leader, their hero, and they readily fell in with the proposition that they should return, await the coming of Jack and Heathcote for two hours, and if they did not reappear, the rest were to hasten with all speed to the Governor's house, and report on the discovery which had been made.

So the party divided, and Don, Tom, and Bob went back, with special instructions not to linger in the powder-magazine.

Jack and Heathcote proceeded on their way.

The passage suddenly terminated in a door which, to their great satisfaction, opened without trouble.

On the other side of it was a cellar, with coal and wood strewn about the floor.

"This place belongs to a house," said Heathcote, softly. "We have found our way right down into the town."

The question that now arose was, what ought they to do? It was soon answered by both declaring for going on.

They discovered that there were three cellars in all, communicating with each other, and terminating in a flight of brick steps, with a trap-door overhead. In one of the cellars there was a considerable store of

SERGEANT FARREL IS BUMPTIOUS.   583

wine in cask and bottle. Heathcote, surveying them, again became thoughtful.

"There is only one man in Gibraltar," he said, in a whisper, "who could have such a lot of good stuff, and that is the Spanish trader, Maragua. I have heard that he is a big swell with another name, and that he was exiled from Spain for being mixed up with Don Carlos. He is a big pot in his way, but gloomy. He doesn't keep much company, but those who have been invited to his feasts say they are something to remember."

"Being exiled from his native country," said Jack, "why should he interest himself in Gibraltar?"

"Well, suppose he wrested it from us, which *could* be done from the inside, what a present it would be to make to the Spanish people! He would be the biggest man in the country, and able to bowl over the present king and place Don Carlos on the throne, if he had a mind to."

"Perhaps Don Carlos——" Jack began, but was checked by Heathcote, who laid a hand upon his arm.

"Out with your candle," he whispered. "Somebody is moving overhead."

They blew out their candles and pressed down the wicks, so that no tell-tale odour might arise therefrom.

Steps and voices overhead could be heard, and the trap-door above was opened.

The youngsters slipped behind a cask, and crouching down, felt for their revolvers, so as to be ready to defend themselves in case of emergency.

It is needless to say that they held their breath as far as possible, and listened with all their ears.

There were two men. One elderly, with a grave face of Spanish mould. The other a Frenchman, of middle life. They were talking in the language of the latter. We give a translation of their conversation, carried on with the freedom of persons assured of being alone.

"Maragua, my friend," said the Frenchman, "there is nothing like prompt action."

"Many a good cause, Lantenant," answered the Spaniard, "has been ruined by too much confidence, and the resulting hasty action. Still, I think that too long a delay is not good."

"It is weakness," said Lantenant. "Now, on Monday next there is one of the festivals of the Church, and that it should attract many from other places is not to be marvelled at. There are a thousand already in the town willing to assist us. Another three or four hundred will suffice to seize the upper galleries and forts, which can play the very deuce with the lower ones. To possess them is to have Gibraltar. Shall it be on Monday?"

"As you will," answered the Spaniard. "But they must enter my house warily."

"It will be an open one that day, you being a good giver at festive times."

"In any case it would be so. They must begin to arrive early, because there is but one way up. That closed, our plans would fail."

"Such provisions as they may need they will bring with them. But for wine—is it here?"

"It is at the service of the cause, but it must not be left for every fool to help himself. You are here for the purpose of looking at the cellar, and making arrangements for the removal of the wine to my rooms above, and there place it under lock and key. If possible, let it be done in the night."

"To-night it shall be done. My men are already ashore. I know where to find them. Maragua, you may rely upon my doing this work with the silence and discretion that have marked all my movements in the cause of——"

"In *my* cause," said Maragua. "Gibraltar mine, Spain will rise as one man to welcome me. Then will be the hour of triumph. Mine enemies will feel the grinding power of my heel."

"It was to me a wild dream at first," said Lantenant "but now I see it is possible. Still, if aught should go wrong——"

"If there were no risks to run, where the honour and glory? Of what good would it be to me?"

The Spaniard moved away, with a gesture of disdain for the expressed fears of the other, and in turn they passed up the stairs.

"I was right," said Heathcote, as the trap fell. "That is the old man's idea. If he could carry it out, he would have not only the sympathy of his own people, but the veiled approval of the rest of the world. We should be the laughing-stock of nations. Outwitted and ousted from our stronghold by a Spanish outcast and a French adventurer!—what a glorious thing it would be for France. Then they could cry out, with something in it, 'Waterloo is avenged!'"

He quietly lit a match, and set the candles going again.

There was nothing more to be done but to hasten back and report the affair to the governor, who would see that steps were promptly taken to secure the arms and defeat the plotters.

CHAPTER CCLXXXI.

SERGEANT FARREL IS BUMPTIOUS.—WITH THE GOVERNOR.

"I SHALL take you all to the governor. Where are the other two?"

It was the sergeant who had been suspicious of the movements of our friends who spoke thus, and he spoke as one having authority. The persons he addressed were the trio who had been sent from below to await the return of Jack Ford and Heathcote.

"I should advise you not to be in too great a hurry," said Bob Stockton. "We are doing no harm."

"I knew you were going to break through the regulations," said the sergeant, whose name was Farrel. "And it's my duty to report you to the governor. Mr. Heathcote is on his staff, and he ought to have known better."

"You will wait for him, of course?" suggested Don.

"I'll do as I like about that," wrathfully replied the sergeant. "Where are they?"

"Coming on directly," said Tom.

"The idea of risking your lives against orders!" growled the sergeant. "Come out into the daylight!"

He had come upon our friends on their return to the upper chamber. As he was accompanied by a file of soldiers they could only obey him, and they all went up to the gallery above. There they had not so very long to wait, for Jack and Heathcote hastened back with all speed and presented themselves before the sergeant in rather a breathless condition.

"Well," said he, sternly, "and what have you to say for yourselves?"

"Nothing, thank you," replied Heathcote, "and don't you say too much, sergeant, for it will not end in either pleasure or profit to you!"

But the sergeant was bent on reporting the breach of discipline to his officer in command, and he did so.

This personage was in one of the outer forts, and he happened to be a fiery old major, who hated subalterns and all "cubs" of the army, forgetting of course, that he had himself been one in the long ago.

"Take them down to the governor," he said. "Heathcote is the chief offender," growling to himself, "the little beggar. Laughed at me as I was walking with the Scotch widow the other day. I hope the villain will be sent home!"

Descending from the galleries by the ordinary route, our friends were conducted to the house of the governor; the manner of the sergeant in the street conveying to the public mind that they were all his prisoners.

They made very light of it, and, as a reporter would say, "smoked their cigarettes with an air of defiance."

By the door of the house they were met by an equerry, who asked what was the matter.

"Mr. Heathcote, sir," said the sergeant, "been prowling down in the lower galleries, against orders."

"What was the sentry doing?" asked the equerry.

"They dodged him, sir."

"Heathcote," said the equerry, "you ought not to have done this. It is true it is at your own risk, but it can't be permitted. You have done this before."

"I am afraid I have," said Heathcote, coolly, "and I wish to report myself to the governor. He can cashier me if he likes."

"Don't be rude. Go and report yourself, and be hanged to you for an impudent cub!"

"May I take my friend Ford with me?"

"Take the lot, if you like."

"I have something very serious to report," said Heathcote, lowering his voice, "it would make your hair stand up like quills upon a fretful porcupine!"

"Get along," said the equerry, wheeling round; "the idea of your dealing in anything serious is too ridiculous."

Beckoning to Jack, Heathcote ascended to a room on the first floor, and, having knocked, it was opened by an orderly. The governor was seated in an inner chamber, into which Heathcote led Jack.

Stopping in the doorway the subaltern respectfully saluted an elderly man in uniform, seated at the table.

"Something to report, sir."

"What is it?"

"An attempt is about to be made to wrest the Rock from us, sir!"

The governor stared angrily at Heathcote, who preserved an immovable countenance.

"Heathcote," said the governor, impressively, "you are doing a weak and silly thing to jest with me. You presume on there being ties of blood between us."

"No, sir. It is a fact, I assure you. Here is a witness to prove it. Attack to be made from the inside!"

"Come and tell me what you mean," said the governor, with sudden interest.

They went up to the table, and Heathcote told the story, which Jack confirmed. The amazement and perturbation of the governor were complete.

"This is more serious than I deemed possible," he said. "It cannot fail to be serious for me in any case. To think that such a plot should be conceived, and be possible to carry out, and I know nothing about it! What will they say at home?"

"Needn't know anything about it, sir," said Heathcote. "Two trusty men could close up the passage near the cellar, and Maragua might get a hint to move. Then, sir, you could take possession of his house and stop all chances of his ever coming that game again —I mean ever renewing his nefarious operations."

"Your friend will say nothing?" asked the governor.

"Not a word."

"We can all keep a secret, sir," said Jack. "If you do not wish it, the world will never hear the story from our lips."

"You will have earned my everlasting gratitude if you do not talk of this discovery," said the governor. "Though I can hardly be blamed, it will be conceived by the Home authorities that there has been neglect on my part that the matter should have gone so far without my knowing it. Heathcote, you have done well. Send Sergeant Farrel in here."

"Won't he get a wigging!" said Heathcote. "We might casually wait and see him after the interview is over."

This they did. The interview was a short one, but it sufficed to bring the countenance of the sergeant to the colour of boiled beef.

He saluted Heathcote hurriedly as he passed by.

"Got a wigging for interfering with his superiors," said Heathcote. "Now, boys, suppose we celebrate our safe return from peril by having a dinner at one of the cafés. I would stand Sam but for my impecunious condition, but as I cannot, I will cheerfully dine at your expense."

They were all ready for dinner, and on their way to the café Jack asked what would be done.

"I'll let you know. Now that the governor has got the office from us he will bottle up that lot. Here we are. My word, I am thirsty! Let us have a big light drink all round as a preliminary."

They had a sherry-cobbler apiece and then ordered dinner to be got with all speed.

Those who had had no share in the main discovery were let into the secret of the full nature of it, and enjoined to secrecy.

It is needless to say that they promised to be dumb, and superfluous to state that they kept their word.

In the afternoon they returned to the "Albatross," where they related their adventures to a certain point. They were able to speak of the duel and the pleasant night in the hollow, also of their visit to the galleries, but of the discovery of arms they said not a word.

Late at night a boat brought a man to the "Albatross" with a letter and parcel for Jack Ford.

It was from Heathcote.

The letter ran :

"DEAR FORD,—All has been done. *Blocked for ever !* If you spun your yarn now the B. P. could say you were a liar, and you would not be able to prove you weren't. *Everything shut in*, to be found a few thousand years hence by explorers slicing up the rock, with the latest machinery, like a cucumber. Parcel contains a ring for each of you boys. Memento from the G., who is in a state of high-blown relief. Has tipped me some tin. You don't want it—therefore rings. Love to the lot of you.—Yours serenely,

"JIM HEATHCOTE."

"Not a bad little affair all round," said Jack, as he distributed the rings. "Diamond, and plain setting of the general make ; but Heathcote doesn't say a word about the Frenchman or the Spaniard. Perhaps we may hear more of them."

He was destined to become a prophet. On the morrow they heard of them for the last time.

CHAPTER CCLXXXII.

A FIGHT IN THE STREETS OF GIBRALTAR.—OFF AND AWAY.

SO quietly had everything been done, that in the town of Gibraltar there was not the slightest suspicion of anything unusual having taken place.

But in the house of Maragua the merchant, and in the apartments Lantenant the Frenchman had taken on shore, there were dismay and fury.

Late on the evening of the discovery made by Heathcote and Jack Ford, one of the equerries of the governor, who acted as his private and confidential secretary, called upon the merchant with a portentous verbal message for him.

"I am instructed by his excellency," he said, "to inform you that your plot has been revealed to him, and you will be well advised to leave Gibraltar at your earliest convenience."

The merchant tried to put a bold face upon the matter, but on the equerry entering into details, and informing him that the secret way was already blocked, Maragua caved in, and humbly promised to depart from Gibraltar on the morrow.

Left alone, he gave way to unavailing wrath, and charged his fellow-conspirator with being a traitor.

"When I meet the dog," he hissed, "old as I am, he shall be made to answer for his falsity !"

The equerry went direct from the merchant's house to the temporary residence of Lantenant. He was fortunate in finding him at home.

The bare fact of his being honoured with such a visitor showed the Frenchman that something was wrong. He received him, however, politely, and begged to know why he was thus favoured.

"You are directed, on pain of being arrested, to leave Gibraltar and not return again," said the equerry ; adding, in words identical with those used to the merchant, "Your plot has been revealed, and the stores collected by you seized. The secret passage is blocked. Need I say more ?"

"His excellency," said Lantenant, "must have some motive in permitting me to depart ?"

"He simply does so to avoid public discussion, which would not redound to your credit. Few of your countrymen would look with favour on your conspiring with an untrustworthy Spaniard."

"Perhaps, if I sail to-morrow," said Lantenant, "his excellency would be satisfied ?"

"To-morrow will do," said the equerry ; "but there must be no longer delay."

Lantenant was certain that the "untrustworthy Spaniard, Maragua," had betrayed him—with the notion, of course, of saving his own skin, and getting one of the time-honoured enemies of his country into trouble.

Each nation cordially hates some other nation, but the hatred existing between the ordinary Spaniard and the Frenchman passes all others.

It was early on the following morning when Lantenant left his abode for the purpose of making arrangements to depart in a craft he used for trading or smuggling, as the times served.

A goodly proportion of the population was abroad to enjoy the cool of the early day. A short way from home he espied Maragua, also abroad making arrangements for his departure.

The moment they espied each other, all the passion of their respective races blazed up within them.

Not a word was uttered. Neither was in the humour to waste time in making accusations.

The Spaniard drew his knife, and the Frenchman whipped out a revolver. The handier weapon was first brought into play. Two shots were fired, and Maragua was seen to stagger.

But he did not fall.

Uttering a scream, such as might have emanated from a wounded eagle, he sprang upon Lantenant, and struck at him with terrible ferocity. It was at this moment that a boat landed Jack and his friends from the "Albatross." They were going to look up Heathcote, with the idea of getting full particulars of the seizure of the secret stores from him.

Jack alone was able to recognise the two men, and he hastily told his friends who they were.

But, at the same time, he was unable to account for the scene.

But yesterday they were close friends, conspiring to do a deed that would have astounded the world To-day they were fighting like remorseless foes.

Lantenant received the knife in his chest, and fell. The blood poured from the wound with horrible rapidity, dyeing the ground near him.

But, cat-like, he had great tenacity of life. He could fight to the last.

Maragua, having struck his assailant down, would have fled, and turned to do so.

But he had already two bullets in his body—a fact afterwards ascertained by the doctors—and as he wheeled round, he staggered like a drunken man.

Lantenant, raising himself upon his elbow, fired again, hitting him in the back, and, with a hoarse cry, the Spaniard threw up his arms and fell back dead.

Ere the many witnesses of the tragedy could fully ascertain its full import, Lantenant sank down, and spreading out his arms, expired with a deep groan.

Both were well-known men, and supposed to be friends. That they should meet thus and slay each other was inexplicable.

The officers, who arrived on the scene too late to save either, took possession of the bodies and bore them away to the police-station, followed by a mixed crowd of people.

Jack and his friends went on to the governor's house, where they found Heathcote. On his hearing what had happened, he said that it was "a queer ending to a queer business."

"The governor won't be sorry," he added, "for it is pretty certain that the secret of the way up to the galleries was known only to themselves. They would never trust the common ruck until the moment of action came."

Thus ended the whole affair, which was so closely kept at the time that none knew of it beyond those who had played a part in the strange drama.

Whispers of it were afterwards heard, and a paragraph got into one of the papers at home, hinting at a narrow escape of our "important rocky possession," but it was looked upon as a *canard* got up during the "silly season."

We have given it as one of the memoirs of the adventurous lives of our friends, and it now passes out of our story, for Jack Ford and the trio with him faithfully kept the secret and never hinted at it afterwards.

The "Albatross" stayed at Gibraltar three more days, the time mainly occupied in being entertained ashore and entertaining on board.

Then the time of parting came.

Heathcote spent the last evening on board the "Albatross," and he bade adieu to those whom he made friends of with unwonted emotion.

"I feel," he said to Jack Ford, "that I am about to lose the dearest friend of my life."

"But we may meet again," suggested Jack.

"We may," replied Heathcote, "but life is an awfully uncertain thing. I expect to be sent to India shortly. I have an uncle there who is boss of a big district, and he feels he can't do without me, I suppose; or it may be that my friends at home feel that I shall do better with him. They arrange my life between them. Anyway, I'll write to you, and you can write to me."

With many expressions of good will they parted, and at sunrise on the morrow the "Albatross" once more spread her white wings, this time for home, without a prospect of a halt by the way.

The end of the adventures of our friends was drawing nigh—the time of rest approaching. But there are a few more threads of their story still to be gathered together.

CHAPTER CCLXXXIII.

IN THE OLD COUNTRY.—A FAMILIAR NAME ON A BILL.—THE MAN FISH.

ON the voyage back, for the most part uneventful, Harry Barstow had more than one consultation with the four youngsters concerning the treasure of the Avishnus of which they had become possessed.

He had no doubt that by every moral right it was theirs and theirs alone, but still he was of opinion that they ought to talk little about it, in case Chunder Loo might, through the Bey of Tunis, lay claim to it.

"If that scoundrel was dead," he said, "it would be quite another matter. Living, he might be a dangerous claimant."

"But how would he fare with our authorities?" said Jack; "he is wanted here for murder."

"I forgot that for the moment," said Harry Barstow, "but the danger still exists of his making a claim through the Bey, who would make it a desideratum, perhaps, that the treasure be first passed on to him before he could entertain the idea of extraditing Chunder Loo. Anyway, I should say nothing about it, but, pending further intelligence of the scoundrel, have your prize stored away, say in one of our most trustworthy banks."

They agreed with him, and for the purpose of storage, the cases were battened and strongly hooped with iron.

On arriving in England it was proposed that Harry Barstow should proceed with them to London with the treasure, and arrange for its safe depositing. Messrs. Coutts was the firm finally selected for the purpose.

"They are as safe as anything on earth," said Harry, "and never ask a lot of needless questions of their clients. My father banks with them."

One morning Jack Ford, always an early riser, went on deck and saw the long white line of cliffs of Old England before him. Two hours later they passed the Needles, and before noon had dropped anchor in the Solent.

Then came the time of usual excitement. Everybody was eager to get ashore, but all could not be spared.

As soon as possible the "Albatross" was to be laid up for cleaning and further repairs. Then all would be free.

There was one aboard who was not so eager as the rest to land, and that was Mulberry Cork.

The dye with which his face had been stained was as deep as ever. It really seemed to be permanent, and as one of the white races he could never appear again.

But Norton Truscott suggested that he should be dressed in ordinary attire, as many negroes are in this country, and he was taken ashore for the purpose of obtaining clothing for him. Having been rigged out at a ready-made store, he became quite presentable, and pending arrangements for his future, he was to accompany Jack Ford to London.

Dirk Matthews had to be thought of as the original discoverer of the treasure. But what had to be done for him must be done quietly. If he knew the whole story, there was no knowing what extravagant and unjustifiable claims he might make.

As the great ambition of his life now appeared to be to settle down in a public-house, he was promised the money for the purpose. He looked upon it as a reward for his services generally, and professed to be very grateful.

George Rammer, who had for a long time been living in the obscurity of the cuddy, was another not so eager for the shore, and he confessed to Chippy that Portsmouth was his original home. He had, indeed, left a wife there prior to his coming to sea.

"But what are you afeard of?" asked Chippy.

"That she will claim me again," replied Rammer.

"No fear of that," said Chippy, contemptuously.

There was something in this remark that seemed to hit Rammer home. He thought it over, and after a while asked Bill Oakley, who had been left in charge of the "Albatross," if he might go ashore.

"Yes," was the answer: "to-morrow you will be paid off. There's a lump due to you. Make good use of it."

Rammer, more thoughtful than ever, hailed a boat, and was taken ashore. Then, with considerable doubt and hesitation in his gait, he wandered off to one of the by-streets of the town.

It was a poor street and it swarmed with children playing at such games as the place and materials available permitted.

Rammer cast his eyes over the lot, and presently espied a boy about ten years of age.

"Jim," he said, hoarsely.

The boy was hopping about on one leg as a lively and cheap amusement. He stopped short and stared at Rammer. Then a light broke in upon him.

"It's dad!" he exclaimed. "My eye! Won't mother warm yer!"

"Will she?" said Rammer, dolorously.

"That she will," said the boy; "having all of us to keep, and nothin' but washing to do it on."

"Go and tell her," whispered Rammer, "that I'm sorry I ever runned away, and that I'm waiting round the corner to know if she will welcome me home. You might mention cashewilly that I've a stiff bit of pay to take to-morrow."

The boy grinned and vanished up the street.

Rammer retired to the corner, ready for flight in case of his wife appearing on the warpath.

Presently he saw her coming along with "all sail spread," wiping her hands upon her apron. He cast a critical eye over her, and decided that she was only "fairly vicious."

So he stayed, and she came up to him, a wiry, hard-working woman, with an eye like a corkscrew.

"So you've come back?" she said.

"Yes, Polly," he replied, meekly.

"Been to sea, I hear?"

"Yes, Polly."

"Had enough on it?"

"Yes, Polly."

"Got some pay to take?"

"I has, Polly. To-morrer."

"Will you run away any more?"

"No, Polly."

"Then come home and help me with the mangle."

So Rammer, the sailor who had been born at sea and gone through half the naval battles of the world, according to his own account, went meekly back to the washing business, and was seen no more by those with whom he had shared the perils of the deep. Polly on the morrow went to the "Albatross" for his pay and received it.

Meanwhile many of our friends had taken up their quarters at the "Blue Posts," pending the paying-off and getting the "Albatross" into dock.

The hotel has been famous for many years as the resort of midshipmen and naval officers of the lieutenant class.

Marryat made much of the "Blue Posts" in his novels, and it was there that Peter Simple and other kindred characters took up their quarters.

Now the navy is a service of which we are all very proud, and the majority of the young officers in it are thorough good fellows; but there are exceptions, as in every other walk in life.

When the "traps" of our four friends had been taken to the "Blue Posts" by some men of the "Albatross," and deposited in the hall, pending the arrival of their owners, the travel-stained portmanteaus attracted considerable attention.

Lounging about in the doorway and in the hall were half a dozen middies and two sub-lieutenants—the latter recently promoted.

The names of the pair just elevated from the midshipman's level were respectively Jobson and Farlowe.

Not being "born swells," they might very well have been modest in their bearing, but the reverse was the case.

What they lacked in breeding they made up in hauteur, and were very much down upon anyone who had no birthright entry into society.

The arrival of the luggage engaged their attention, and Jobson, screwing an eyeglass into its recognised position, surveyed it curiously for a time.

Farlowe did likewise, and hard by half a dozen or so of middies sauntered about or leaned against the doorposts, for the lack of something better to do.

"Who the deuce sent this stuff here?" exclaimed Jobson.

"Nobody in the se-e-ervice," stuttered Farlowe. He occasionally had an impediment in his speech.

"Service? No; more likely a bagman."

"More than one ba-a-agman; two at least——"

"Cases of samples, I suppose?"

"So-o-o I should sa-a-ay."

Jobson, seeing that the back of the hall-porter was turned towards him, heaved up one end of the portmanteau, and allowed it to drop again.

Something rattled inside.

"Travels in tin ware," he said.

"No-o-o," said Farlowe, "looks more like drapery, or bu-u-uttons."

"Have you got all *your* buttons?" inquired a middy who was leaning against the doorpost.

This inquiry, in a tone of tender solicitation, raised a laugh from the other middies.

Farlowe turned haughtily upon the querist, who met his gaze with sleepy indifference.

"What did you say, Gunner?" he demanded.

"I merely wished to know if you had *all* your buttons," answered Gunner. "No offence, I hope. If you are one or two short, you cannot help it."

"Do you forget whom you are speaking to?"

"For the moment I had forgotten," replied Gunner, rousing himself and feigning a terror that seemed to amuse his brother middies even more than the button question, "you were promoted two hours ago. Pray forgive me. *Don't* have me hung at the yardarm for mutiny."

"Cub!" sneered Farlowe.

"Insufferable idiot!" chorused Jobson.

Gunner calmly surveyed the pair in turn. He was probably two years their junior, but he was quite as tall, and there was a fighting look in his build.

"If either of you repeat your insults," he said, "I'll kick you, and risk being cashiered for striking my superior officer."

"You say the owner of this baggage trades in tin?" said Farlowe, presenting his back to the pugnacious Gunner.

"Bet you a sov. on it," replied Jobson.

"Done!"

"And you say drapery?"

"Ya-a-as. Bet you a sov. on that."

"How are we to tell what's his line?"

"Ask him."

There was a sound of light footsteps behind them, of which neither took heed.

"There's another thing to be-e-et on," said Farlowe.

"What's that?" asked Jobson.

"One or two bagmen. I say two."

"And I say one. Another sov. on that?"

"You are both wrong," said somebody behind them. "There are four of us."

The precious pair wheeled about and faced Jack and his friends, whom they regarded with unqualified surprise.

That they were not of the navy was certain—nor were they of the merchant service.

What then were they?

"You gentlemen seem to be interested in our baggage," said Jack Ford, with quiet scorn.

"Been shaking it to make the tin-ware rattle," put in Gunner.

Jack turned upon him and saw that he was smiling pleasantly enough.

"The tin-ware is Jobson's idea," said Gunner. "He bets on it. Farlowe bets on drapery—on buttons."

"Their own drapery, perhaps," said Bob Stockton, with his accustomed suavity. "They look like a pair of old women masquerading as penny-steamboat captains. But I would not advise them to bet on a full allowance of buttons."

"Just my idea," remarked Gunner, approvingly. "I tackled Farlowe on the button question myself."

"It appears to me," said Jack Ford, addressing the two subs, now presenting the appearance of two defeated roosters, "that you have been guilty of a grave and unwarrantable impertinence. But as you appear to be interested in our baggage——"

"No, hang the stuff!" said Jobson, insolently.

"Deuced natural to take it for a bagman's lot," said Farlowe.

"You think so?"

"Strange," said Jack, "that I should take you for a bagman. Your name is Farlowe, I believe?"

"It is, and be hanged to you!"

"Any relation to Farlowe, cheap draper, High Street, Islington?"

Farlowe turned deadly pale.

"Son, I believe?" said Jack. "Why, you miserable cub, I knew you when you were seven years old, running about the streets in an old woollen comforter and crying with cold. Your father stood by his door then selling off the job lots on Saturday nights."

"The deuce!" exclaimed Jobson. "You going to stand that, Farlowe?"

"Would you have me fight a *cad?*" asked Farlowe, recovering himself a bit.

The next moment he received a blow that sent him sprawling upon the baggage. The hall-porter moved forward.

"No fighting allowed, gentlemen, please!" he urged.

"There won't be any," said Bob Stockton. "The gentleman who bet on buttons stops short at crowing. He doesn't fight."

And so it seemed.

Farlowe got up scowling, and turning to Jobson, loftily inquired:

"Will you act for me in this matter?"

"Certainly," replied Jobson.

"Then I leave you to arrange the details of a meeting," said Farlowe. "Meet me on the esplanade in half an hour."

With a scowl on his face, that was all the more ludicrous owing to a rising bump under his left eye, he stalked out of the hotel.

"Whew!" whistled Gunner, "this affair is likely to end very seriously."

CHAPTER CCLXXXIV.

THE DANGER OF PLAYING THE GAME OF BLUFF.

FARLOWE having departed, Jack was about to see to their rooms, when Jobson interposed.

"My time is precious," he said, "will you please name your friend?"

Jack stared at him.

"What do you mean?" he inquired.

"You have insulted Lieutenant Farlowe."

"No, he insulted me at the onset, and it ended in my knocking him down."

"A blow cannot be passed over."

"Why did he not return it?"

"Gentlemen do not settle their differences that way."

"Oh!"

Jack as yet did not quite understand. He looked up at his friends for inspiration.

"You must be summoned before a magistrate," said Tom Drummond.

"Or have an action brought against you," said Don Peebles.

"Probably in the county court," suggested Bob Stockton.

"Good," exclaimed Gunner, who, with the other middies, had drawn up closer to watch the fun.

"Really," said Jobson, haughtily, "you are either very obtuse or you will not understand."

"Well, explain yourself," said Jack.

"With this crowd around us?"

"I think I see what it is this gentleman is aiming at," said Bob Stockton. "Suppose you leave him to me?"

"Very good," replied Jack, as he walked away to the clerk's office; "don't forget—luncheon at one."

"Now, sir," said Bob to Jobson, "I am entirely at your service."

"Excuse me one moment," interposed Gunner. "Before you have an interview with this bloodthirsty person, may I have one word with you?"

"Just one," said Bob, lazily.

"I will await you outside," growled Jobson.

He left the hall, and Bob drew aside with Gunner, who waved his companion middies away.

"I don't know who you are," began Gunner, "nor is it any business of mine, but you seem to be a very decent fellow."

"Thank you," replied Bob, with much humble gratefulness; "the smallest commendations thankfully received."

"No chaff—I mean it," said Gunner. "You know what the game is, I suppose?"

"I guess it—a duel is meant."

"Yes."

"A duel here in these days would be ridiculous."

"So they know, but they are coming the scaring dodge."

"Playing the game of bluff?"

"Just so."

"Then they have got hold of the wrong fellow," said Bob. "If that sub has the cheek to challenge Jack Ford, he will have to fight him."

"He won't do it," said Gunner, shaking his head, "he dare not."

"I do not suppose it will come to that," rejoined Bob, "but he will have to fight or eat the leek."

"He will eat it," said Gunner, cheerfully. "Why, if it got wind that he had challenged your friend, it would get him into trouble."

"How?"

"Our commander does not encourage bullying, and that is Farlowe's game. He wants to frighten your friend."

"He can't do that."

"I wish you would do me a favour," said Gunner, wistfully.

"If it is not out of my power or too expensive," said Bob, "I will do it. But we common folks have to be careful of our money."

"It will cost you nothing," said Gunner. "All I want is to know how this affair goes off. Keep me posted in it."

"H'm! I don't quite grasp your meaning."

"Jobson, acting for Farlowe, will talk a lot of stuff about the honour of an officer and a gentleman, and at the outset just hint at a duel."

"Yes—and then?"

"He will expect you to object—to funk it, in short."

"Oh, indeed?"

"Now, if you or that——"

"My dear fellow, if you knew Jack Ford, you would not dream of talking such stuff."

"You have been travelling, I think?"

"Yes."

"Private yacht?"

"Yes, belonging to a friend."

"Had any fun?"

"Lots. But to the point about these fellows. If they are asses enough to go right through with a duel we shall not draw back."

"I thought you wouldn't," said Gunner, gleefully, "and that is why I want to be there. You will let me know the place of meeting, will you?"

"But you mustn't talk about it."

"I will only mention it to two or three fellows, who will keep it as close as wax. They would not be such asses as to spoil their own fun."

"Very well," said Bob, "I will leave you a note in the office. What name?"

"Gunner—*Mister* Gunner. If you put esquire they will think it is for some other fellow. You know the law of duelling, I suppose?"

"No, I know nothing about it."

"As the challenged, you will have the choice of weapons."

"That is worth knowing. Jack Ford is a dead shot. He will select pistols—revolvers."

"Farlowe could not hit an elephant at twenty paces," said the delighted Gunner. "My eye! what a lark!"

Bob went his way and found Jobson outside, impatient for his coming.

"I thought you had changed your mind," he said. "Where shall we go? This is a matter that must be kept quiet, as it is an affair of life and death."

His tone was very solemn, but Bob was not troubled.

"You don't say so," he carelessly returned. "Here's a coffee-shop, shall we turn in here?"

It was a coffee-shop of the lowest class, and Bob had purposely selected it because he knew that it would be objectionable to Jobson.

It was quite deserted at that hour of the day, as they could see through the open doorway.

"We shall not be interrupted here," urged Bob.

"Beastly hole!" muttered Jobson, as he followed Bob in.

Jobson would have sat down just inside in a corner by the window, where they could not be seen from the street, but Bob, with apparent unconsciousness of his desire, walked halfway down the shop, and take a seat in a most conspicuous place.

With a suppressed groan Jobson dropped into a seat facing him.

A slatternly girl, astounded by the advent of such customers, came up for orders. Bob coolly ordered two cups of coffee, and giving the girl a shilling, told her to keep the change.

"Now," he said to Jobson, "let us get to business."

"My friend," began Jobson, "has been insulted."

"Waiving that question," said Bob, "what does he want?"

"As a gentleman and a man of honour he must have satisfaction."

"Provided he can get it, of course."

"But he must have it—he will insist. Nothing but a meeting will satisfy him."

"A duel, you mean?"

"I do," blustered Jobson.

"All right," easily responded Bob, "we are willing."

"Sh—did you say you are willing?"

"More than willing—eager for it. Ford will fight your friend Barlow——"

"Farlowe."

"Farlowe, then ; and I will fight you, if you like."

"I am acting for my friend at present," said Jobson, hastily.

"Very good," said Bob. "When Ford has settled with your friend I can tackle you."

"We will first arrange the duel between Farlowe and your friend," said Jobson, "that is, unless you apologise——"

"Nonsense!" said Bob, sharply. "What are you thinking of?"

"Apologies are often offered in these days, and nobody thinks the worse of a man for them."

"You won't get one from us," said Bob, "and your man has to fight, or Ford will lead him by the nose for an hour up and down Southsea Common. We have the choice of weapons, and I select pistols—revolvers."

"Are not revolvers unusual?"

"We have the choice, and I select revolvers because they give a fellow an extra shot or two without the bother of reloading. The time—to-morrow morning, as early as possible. The place——"

Bob stopped short, and taking down a railway time-table, looked it over, while the other man wondered.

"Yes," said Bob, "that will do. There is an early train that will land us at Hayling Island by seven o'clock. We couldn't have a better place. Not the slightest chance of being interrupted, as there is only one man living there, I believe, and he is generally in bed. Anyway, he only gets up in the afternoon to see what o'clock it is. Don't forget, this is the train. We can travel by it in separate carriages, and be strangers until we arrive on the ground. Good morning."

Before the semi-bewildered Jobson could muster any form of reply of assent or dissent he found himself alone, with two untasted cups of coffee before him.

He stared at them for awhile, and slowly returned to himself.

"Hang it !" he muttered, "the fellow will fight—a duel here—with a fellow unknown, and supposed to be a bagman. Blow it ! the whole thing is deuced ridiculous. We can't go to the police to stop it. It will surely get into the papers. We can't shirk it without Farlowe getting his nose pulled. We can't do anything but fight, and do what we will, if Farlowe isn't killed we shall be the laughing-stock of everybody. The game of bluff doesn't pay."

CHAPTER CCLXXXV.

THE STOPPING OF A DUEL.

"IT seems our luck," said Don Peebles, "always in for something."

"But this is a mere farce," observed Bob. "Will you pass the pepper, please?"

They were at dinner in a room overlooking the street, and the subject of the impending duel was being discussed.

"It may not be all farce," remarked Jack Ford, "although a duel, as a duel, according to modern English notions is ridiculous."

"He will fight, I suppose?" said Tom Drummond.

"And fall upon his back at the first shot," asserted Bob. "We ought to have blank cartridges."

"Which would make us ridiculous," said Jack, quietly. "It is a pity, for the whole thing arose from a very trivial cause. But, as Don says, it was our luck."

"Would it not be as well to suggest to Farlowe that we drop it?" said Tom.

"And get branded as a coward," replied Jack, with a smile. "No, I fancy that will not do. We had better let things slide. What time does the train leave in the morning?"

"Six thirty," returned Bob.

"That does not leave us much time for breakfast.'

"I'll see to it. In fact, I have mentioned it. The' waiter has promised to have something on the table at five forty-five."

"Doesn't he want to know where we are going?"

"Yes, Jack, he was curious, and I mysteriously informed him that it was a matter which could not be spoken of until we returned. Then, of course I should be happy to tell him everything if he could keep the business a secret. He swore upon two rows of tumblers that he would."

"Don't be absurd."

"I am not. The tumblers were there—so were three forks and a gravy-spoon. I did not mention the latter, for fear you should think I was exaggerating.

He laid his hand upon the tumblers when he swore not to breathe a word."

Jack Ford did not like the affair, and in this respect he shared the feeling with Farlowe, who about the same hour sat at dinner in another room with Jobson.

They were both disgusted with the result of playing the game of bluff, and each was disposed to throw the blame on the other.

"If you had let the baggage alone," said Farlowe, "we should not have had any trouble with these fellows."

"And if you had not been so bitter about being remembered when a boy," said Jobson, "there would have been no fight."

"I don't remember him, anyway," muttered Farlowe. His stutter left him when in earnest.

"Well, don't let us row over it. Neither of us is in the peerage. Here's luck to you—a shot or two and no wounds, in the morning."

Farlowe made no reply, but gloomily tossed off his wine, and presently said that he wanted to be alone, as he had letters to write home.

"Surely you do not anticipate being killed?" exclaimed Jobson.

"I don't know, and I don't care," was the sullen reply. "Bother it! there never was anything more exasperating."

"You can withdraw your challenge," said Jobson.

Farlowe looked at him with a very bitter expression upon his face.

"And apologise to that young fellow—what is his name?"

"Ford."

"In one sense I should be right in doing so," said Farlowe, quietly, "for we began it. He did not interfere with us. It was we who interfered with him. But, having gone so far, an apology is *quite* out of the question."

"Still, you need not take so gloomy a view of it," urged Jobson. "Say you are winged——"

An impatient gesture from the other stopped him.

"I have had enough talking about the matter," said Farlowe, "and shall be glad to be left alone for an hour."

"Can't you come on to the pier by-and-bye?"

"Perhaps I may."

"Nine o'clock?"

"Yes, at nine, if I come at all."

Jobson rose and left the room. He could not understand the mood of his friend a bit. He was naturally inclined to attribute it to cowardice.

"And after all it may be a case of bluff on both sides," thought Jobson. "Well, I can always say that I carried it through for a joke."

Farlowe, left alone, wrote several letters. They were all short, and the tone of them all was that of a dying man bidding adieu to all he loved on earth.

He wrote rapidly, sealed and addressed the letters, laid them on the table, and went out.

It was night, but the shops were not yet closed, and he went on up the main street until he came to a gunsmith's.

There he paused, and took stock of the contents of the window.

There were guns, rifles, and revolvers on view, apparently of every known revolver maker. Some of the latter could be carried in the waistcoat-pocket, others were almost too heavy for anyone but a strong man to use with ease.

Farlowe's eyes roamed from one weapon to another as if seeking a particular pattern. Whatever he wanted, he could not decide upon any on view, and he entered the shop.

As he did so, Jack Ford, who was also in the mood of being alone, came sauntering by.

He caught sight of his antagonist in the shop, and stopping short, peered at him between the rows of rifles.

The obliging shopman recognised in Farlowe a naval man at a glance. He would have guessed his profession if he had been clothed in sackcloth.

"I want a revolver," said Farlowe.

"I know, sir," replied the shopman, producing one of heavy calibre. "Here is a thing that is very popular in the service."

"Too heavy," said Farlowe. "I want something lighter. For shooting at a short distance, I may say."

"For practice, sir?"

"Well—yes—for practice."

Several revolvers were laid upon the counter, and after testing the triggers of two or three, he selected a light one. Then he asked for cartridges.

A box of fifty satisfied his wants, and he loaded one of the barrels of the revolver as if testing the fit of the cartridges.

"Better load the lot, sir, or none, sir," advised the shopman. "A gentleman puts a cartridge in and forgets it. Another party picks up the weapon, and seeing the other chambers empty, snaps the trigger at somebody, just for fun. It's a foolish practice, but they will do it, and it more often causes the loss of a life than not. And a life is very valuable."

"Certainly—very," said Farlowe, drily.

He finished loading the revolver, and left the shop. Outside, he stood thinking for a moment, and then walked rapidly in the direction of Southsea.

On reaching the common he strode across it, at an angle, in a bee-line for the old fort on the parade.

It is very lonely there at night, and just then Farlowe very much wanted to be alone.

The Island School

Ready on APRIL 5th.

A NEW, ORIGINAL AND THRILLING SCHOOL TALE.
By the Author of "The Lambs of Littlecote."

Ready on APRIL 5th.

No. 2 GIVEN AWAY WITH No. 1.   Coloured Pictures and Presentation Plate Gratis.

THE LAMBS OF LITTLECOTE

"Gracious goodness!" exclaimed Professor Lingo. "To think of seeing you again after all this time."

No. 38.   **PRICE ONE PENNY.**

In front of the fort there was an old cannon captured in one of the battles against the French. It has a concrete platform all to itself, and the muzzle was half-full of small stones, which the mischievous boys were fond of placing there.

Farlowe mounted the platform, and leaning on the gun, looked out at the sea. In the far distance were the lights of Ryde; overhead, the everlasting stars.

"It is rough," he muttered, "but I have been a fool, and there is no other way out it."

He drew the revolver from his pocket and cocked it. In the act of raising it to his forehead his wrist was grasped by a strong hand.

"Don't be a fool! What are you thinking of?"

He did not at first know the voice, but in turning his head he saw that it was Jack Ford, although he could only see his outline.

"Why are you here?" asked Farlowe, hoarsely. "Let me alone!"

"I saw you in the gunsmith's shop," replied Jack, "and thinking that you looked very strange, I watched and followed you here."

"To make a jest of me?" said Farlowe, bitterly.

"No," answered Jack. "But, pardon me, I don't see why you are going to do this dreadful thing. It does not show that you were afraid of fighting."

"I was not afraid of it, but to fight would have been my ruin. It must have got wind, and I should have been dismissed the service."

"That would have been a serious thing."

"Not to fight you after having challenged you would have been worse. I should be laughed at—derided by everybody."

"That I can see."

"So I thought I would dash a line home, explaining what an ass I had made of myself, and then blow out my brains."

Jack took the revolver from his now unresisting hand, and put it into his pocket.

"We are both to blame," he said. "Let us shake hands and go back to the hotel together."

"I think you are a good fellow, and meeting with you will do me good," said Farlowe. "Foolishly I have encouraged false notions of what a man ought to be. I have made a puppy of myself, and there is too much of it in the service. I thought it the correct thing to screw a bit of glass in my eye, and feign a contempt for anything and everything out of the service. We create false standards for a gentleman, and I was idiot enough first to insult you and then to play a game of bluff. You beat me at that, you beat me all round, but I am not sorry for it."

Now about this time Bob left a letter for Gunner, informing him where the place of meeting was, and Gunner, shortly after arriving with quite a little host of chums, received it.

He had just read it aloud for their edification, and they were expressing their delight, when Jack and Farlowe entered arm in arm.

This was too much for Gunner, who, leaning back against the wall, gasped with surprise.

"This *is* a facer," he said, as the pair disappeared upstairs.

"What does it mean?" cried the others.

"Blessed if I know," replied Gunner. "It is a mystery. I don't think either of them is exactly afraid to fight, but it *is* a blessed mystery. I must go out for a breath of fresh air. Who will have an hour with me at the music-hall?"

They said they would all go, and trooped out. In the qualified delights of the music-hall Gunner forgot the whole business.

But he afterwards recalled it and pondered deeply on the affair, and it is a mystery to him to this day.

CHAPTER CCLXXXVI.

AN OLD FRIEND.

THE next morning Farlowe went on board his ship and remained there on duty. He simply told Jobson that he had met Jack Ford and they had come to an understanding which would satisfy any honourable man.

Jobson on his part was satisfied. He considered that both himself and his friend were well out of a hole into which their folly had tumbled them, and that was an end to the matter.

Meanwhile Jack remained at the hotel, going in and out in a casual way, but spending most of the time in the hotel.

The four youngsters were there, and in the evening Jack Ford and Don Peebles wandered out in search of recreation.

In one of the streets near the station they came upon a variety-hall with a big glaring star of gas flaring over the doorway.

They stopped to look at the bill of attraction, and found the greater part of it absorbed by a familiar name.

This portion of the announcement ran as follows:

"PROFESSOR LINGO, THE MAN FISH.

EATS UNDER WATER.
DRINKS UNDER WATER.
SMOKES UNDER WATER.
LIVES UNDER WATER.

"This extraordinary man, who possessed from his birth marvellous diving powers, has so cultivated them that he is practically amphibious. He has even gone so far at times as to SLEEP under water.

"It was not until recently that he decided to exhibit his great gift, having up to now contented himself with indulging in it for the amusement of himself and his numerous family. The opportunity to see him may never occur again, as he is about to show himself to Royalty at home and upon the Continent. After which he will retire into private life.

"Therefore, do not let the precious opportunity slip by. Come and see him

TO-NIGHT.

ENGAGEMENT CONCLUDES ON SATURDAY NEXT."

"Can there be two Lingos?" asked Jack.

"I should say not," replied Don; "at least, not two such Lingos as ours. Shall we go in?"

"Certainly. If it is our man I should dearly like to see him again."

They paid sixpence apiece at the door, ascertaining from the money-taker that the professor would be "on" in about twenty minutes' time.

It was not a first-class hall, but the people were very orderly, if somewhat demonstrative, in their applause. A comic singer was doing a turn when they went in.

Having listened to him, and wondered what there was in his song to laugh at, they ordered some bitter beer and sat down at a table. Jack produced his cigarette-case, and they lighted up.

As they had their sea toggery on, not having had time yet to get shore clothing, they were just the pair of youngsters to attract attention.

Many admiring eyes were cast upon them, among others several pairs in the possession of women, fair and otherwise.

But, indifferent to the attention he received, they impatiently awaited the exhibition of the marvellous man fish, for whose appearance considerable preparations, it seemed, were needed.

A curtain was lowered in front of the stage, and while the orchestra played some lively music a vast amount of heavy shifting and banging about went on behind.

By-and-bye the lively music changed to something slow and solemn. The curtain rose, revealing the front of a huge tank of water. It was of glass, and the dark background of slate on the other side was seen through the transparent medium.

A man in evening dress stood upon a raised platform and pointed out first that there was something lying at the bottom of the tank.

"It is Professor Lingo," he said, "and when I have concluded my address he will go through his marvellous performance."

"See here," he said, dabbling his hand in the water and setting it in motion, eddying about, "some people say there is no water here. Judge for yourselves. See, again and again I stir it."

There could not be the least doubt about the matter. It was water he moved about, and he exhibited it dripping from his fingers.

The audience applauded loudly.

Then he proceeded to recapitulate the various things the professor would do, speaking leisurely, as if time were no matter to the man lying at the bottom of the huge tank.

His address concluded, the lecturer tapped upon the glass front, explaining that the human voice would not penetrate under water. The figure immediately assumed a sitting position, and the well-known features of the original Professor Lingo, friend of their days at Littlecote Abbey, were revealed to the two friends.

They sat quietly watching him while he ate and drank, the latter from a bottle, under water. As a final feat, the exhibitor carefully passed down the stem of a pipe, apparently leaving the bowl just above the surface of the water.

A match was applied to it, and the professor, with great deliberation, puffed out smoke that rose slowly up and disappeared.

Great applause followed the dropping of the curtain, and a man near our friends drew out his watch, remarking, as he looked at it, "Six minutes and a quarter. Really a marvellous performance."

So it seemed, and how it was done fogged Jack completely.

"I know what a minute under water is," he said, "and I never yet met a diver who could keep down three. Lingo is a marvel."

In response to a call, only the exhibitor appeared.

He explained that the professor was in such a damp condition that he was at present unable to appear before the public. Moreover, he was exhausted with his efforts, and he ought not, according to his medical attendant, who was always near him behind the scenes, to be subjected to excitement, such as demonstrative public approval would create.

More applause followed this statement, as if it were a clever thing for a man to be in such an exhausted condition, and another performer of the vocalising order came upon the stage.

"Suppose we go round to the stage-door," suggested Jack, "and ask to see the dear old fellow?"

They left the hall, and having found the stage-door, knocked thereat. It was opened by a man of resolute appearance and a doubting eye.

"Well, young gentlemen," he said, "what do you want?"

"Can we see Professor Lingo?" inquired Don.

"No, you can't."

The door was about to close, when Jack hurriedly said, "If you take in our names, he will be glad to see us."

"Let's have 'em," said the man, as doubtful as ever.

They gave them, and he closed the door, locking it with a demonstrative sound.

A delay of a minute or two ensued, and then it was reopened with a flourish.

"Ontray," he said. "I had no idea you were old pals."

They entered, and he guided them down a particularly small passage to a particularly small room, where they found Lingo smoking a pipe, but not in a tank this time. He sprang up, holding out both his hands.

"Lord love us all!" he exclaimed, "to think of seeing you again after all this time! I never expected it. My eye! what a change there is in you! And yet there is the same old look that carries my mind back to Snicker and Co. Where have you been, and what have you been doing?"

"Too long a story to tell now," replied Jack, "but tell us of yourself. What on earth ever made a fish man or a man fish of you?"

CHAPTER CCLXXXVII.

LINGO'S EXPERIENCES.—NEWS OF GUBBLES, AND GOOD TIDINGS FOR MULBERRY CORK.

PROFESSOR LINGO sighed.

"I went abroad a bit with Gubbles," he said, "in search of that 'ere warmint of warmints, Chunder Loo. But we couldn't find the least trace of him, and came back again. Gubbles went to a post at the Fenley Institute to keep his hand in work as a chemist. He didn't want the pay, of course. I put my money in a circus, got hold of a drunken partner, and lost it all. After that I had many ups and downs, until I hit upon the man-fish idea."

"And does *that* pay?" asked Don.

"Middling," answered Lingo; "but there are so many who must be paid to keep it dark that there is not more than fifteen bob a night left for me."

"But why pay them?" inquired Jack, "why keep it dark?"

Lingo looked at him and laughed.

"Are these the clothes I wore in the tank?" he asked.

"I think so."

"Feel 'em, both of you."

They did so.

"The clothes are perfectly dry," said Jack.

"Just so. What should they be? Do you think any living man could keep under water six minutes without kicking the bucket?"

"It doesn't seem credible. But we saw you do it."

"Did you?"

There was a world of dryness in his voice as he made this rejoinder. They began to think that there was more in the man-fish business than met the eye.

"But we saw the fellow who exhibited you dabble in the water," urged Don.

"Granted. And what else?"

"We had a clear view of the slate back of the tank."

"Certainly. But you didn't twig the sheet of plate-glass that divided the tank, did you?"

They were too much staggered to do more than shake their heads.

"It is a neat trick," said Lingo, "if you can only keep the public off the stage. *We* have no end of trouble in stopping the Paul Prys who want to see me in the tank, over the side of it. But it won't do. The man fish has got to be seen from the front, or he wont work."

"Then excuse me," said Jack, "the man fish isn't a fish at all?"

"Not he!" contemptuously replied Lingo, "he is a fraud, just as other things are. Nothing is what it seems nowadays. Lots don't believe in me. They write offensive letters, and want me to go to their houses and experiment in their own tanks. I'd like to see me a-doing it."

"How do you stall them off?" asked Jack.

"Some one way, some the other," said Lingo, "we accept the offer of one now and then at a price, say fifty pounds, playing up the exhaustion theory. Others are surprised when they come to the hall and see for themselves all is fair and square. Not one, however, seems to get at how it is done. At the outside they say it's a fraud of some description."

"And yet it is so simple—now that we know it," said Jack.

"That's it. The thing is so simple. Now, did you guess it when you were in front?"

"I must confess that I did not."

"Just so, and you are no fool, whereas most people we have to deal with *are* fools. Are you in a hurry?"

"No. We are staying at the 'Blue Posts Hotel.'"

"Swell, of course. I am obliged to lie close in obscure lodgings, or some of the eager ones would be getting at me. However, it will be all over on Saturday next. I was thinking that we might have a bit of a quiet supper somewhere. It would be nice for me to hear what you have been doing."

"I think we shall astonish you," said Jack.

"I'll be ready in five minutes," said Lingo, as he rose and put on a close red wig and beard that fitted him to perfection, and changed him so completely that they would not have known him.

"Obliged to do it," he said. "Some men stopped me the other night, and wanted to see how long I could keep at the bottom of a pond. They were larky young swells, and they offered me a pound a minute."

He smiled grimly, as he added : "If I had won a ten-pound note of them I should have been a loser."

Having disguised himself to his satisfaction, and ascertained from the stage-doorkeeper that the street was clear of the curious, he went out with Jack and Don, and acting on his advice, or rather expressed wish, they adjourned to a quiet restaurant close to the station.

There a supper was ordered, and Jack gave Lingo an outline of their adventures, which fairly staggered him.

"Of course," said Jack, "we know we can trust you about that Avishnu wealth."

"I should think so," replied Lingo. "And fancy Bunn being with the Bey of Tunis! Turned into a nigger, too! What a useful man he would be to his missus just now!"

"How?" asked Jack, with a puzzled look on his face.

"Oh, of course I haven't told you. Mrs. Penny Bunn has been exhibiting her fat aunt—what's her name—as the fattest woman on earth, and she ain't far out of it. They've done pretty well, as the fat is real. Let me see—the last time I come across them was at Barnet Fair. Mrs. Bunn was got up as a Greek gal—long loose dress, with golden girdle, and a cap of liberty on her head. She was painted up to her eyes, but she didn't look bad."

They asked after Fontenoy Snicker, and Lingo shook his head.

"Gone utterly to the bad," he said. "Got mixed up with the teetotals, and been exhibiting himself as a specimen of what drink will do for a man."

"He was reformed, of course?"

"He pretended to be, but one night—let me see, it was a year ago—I came across a bill announcing that Fontenoy Snicker, Esq., late Headmaster of Littlecote Abbey School, would lecture on the evils of drink. I knew he was on that lay, and, having nothing to do, went in to hear him. The place was crowded, for admission was free.

"On the platform there was a lot of respectable men, all clothed in black, as ever I set eyes on. They looked as if butter wouldn't melt in their mouths, and they were waiting for Snicker, as I could make out by the way they kept on looking at their watches. Presently he came on—with a rush."

Lingo stopped to laugh, and his listeners laughed, too.

They pictured that old humbug as a temperance lecturer.

"He was drunk, and had been down in the mud," continued Lingo, "and somebody had torn the crown of his hat almost off so that it hung over the side in a weak way; the brim of it was round his neck. His tie was gone, and his coat was split clean up his back."

Lingo had another laugh at the recollection of it, and went on with his story.

"I can see him now, a-standing glaring at the amazed nobs, as I supposed they were, on the platform. He wanted to know why they should think they were better than any other people, and whether he wasn't at liberty to get drunk without their making an exhibition of him. Then he hit the smallest of the party on the nose, and sent him flying like a rocket off the platform. After that he went for the rest, and there being no police handy for a few minutes, he made skittles of them, until the meekest of the lot pulled off his coat, and, with as much science as you would want to see, went to work.

"It was a sight to do your heart good the way he polished off Snicker, who being strong in liquor fought while he could. But he had to go down at the finish. Everybody said it was a rare treat, the more so as it was unexpected. For my part, I think it was the only temperance meeting that ever edified me. Not that I don't believe in temperance, but I don't want to be forced by Act of Parliament to be better than I am."

After this he asked many questions about the Bey of Tunis, and they answered them as far as their judgment would allow.

Shortly after they parted.

"We must come and see you again, Lingo," said Jack, "and if you don't mind, I should like to help you to the doing of something better."

"We can talk of that another time," said Lingo. "Of course I know that you are all as good as gold, but I am self-reliant. If I can do anything whereby I can get a bit of money, I'm on. Another time I may be glad to listen to you. Where are you going to stay in London?"

"At Morley's, I believe," replied Jack.

"Well, I'll write to you there, and let you know exactly what I am going to do. For the present good-bye, my young nobles."

They shook hands with him, and went home, laughing and chatting on the way about the things they had heard. The exhibition of Miss Astracan, the aunt of Mrs. Bunn, as the fattest woman on earth was especially edifying.

CHAPTER CCLXXXVIII.

DIRK MATTHEWS ON THE WRONG TACK AGAIN. — A PROPOSED ROBBERY.

THERE are some men who after a bad career may lead a good life for a time, but are sure in the end to fall back again.

Dirk Matthews was one of this class of delinquents.

He had done a good thing in Alexandria, and been rewarded in more ways than one, and now on his return home he had the chance of settling down into a quiet life. To all appearance he was ready to do so.

But inwardly he was far from satisfied.

He had got hold of the notion that the wealth of the Avishnus was in the possession of our friends. How it came into his head he could not have described, but it was there, and the old false sense of being wronged laid hold of him.

If they had it, it was on board the "Albatross," and being there, would it not be possible to get it away, if he could procure a little assistance?

He was a man of crude ideas, yet cunning withal, and his wits being put to work, he laid his plans.

He had marked the hooping and strengthening of the boxes containing the jewels, and knew, as others knew, that they were stored in the cabin of the captain.

The captain had gone ashore and taken the key of his cabin with him. But a lock and key did not count much with Dirk Matthews.

He would get at the boxes easily enough, provided he had the opportunity of smuggling them ashore.

Why should he not pretend to somebody that he was only smuggling ordinary goods? There were scores of men who would help him on that tack. Yes, that was the way to put it.

Conversing with Bill Oakley, he ascertained that the captain would not return that night. So far well.

Then he learnt that he would be put in the middle watch, the old discipline being kept up as a matter of form. But he knew it would be a matter of form only.

Lying at anchor in the Solent, with lamps alight, there would be little danger.

But he thought he had better make quite sure of the non-interference of the men, and made his arrangements accordingly.

Having obtained leave for an evening ashore, he went into the town, and in the lowest part of it paid a visit to a chemist's shop, a very dingy specimen of its class, and there obtained a small quantity of a certain drug—which, for obvious reasons, we cannot here specify—which he said he wanted to "still the toothache."

The intrinsic value of the quantity he purchased was about threepence. Nevertheless, the chemist, a very bibulous-looking personage, demanded half-a-sovereign for it, which Dirk Matthews paid without the slightest demur.

The drug was done up in a piece of perfectly plain paper. There was nothing to show where it had been purchased.

"A grain or two is quite enough," said the chemist, warningly; "don't take an overdose of it, or you may go to sleep for a month, or longer."

Dirk Matthews replied that "he knew how to use it, having taken it afore," and left the shop.

From thence he went on to a public-house in a back street, one of the very lowest in the town. Entering the bar, he found a half-dozen loafers hanging around, talking in undertones, except in the case of two, who were on the verge of a quarrel over some transaction vaguely named as "on the joint."

Being "on the joint," we may explain for the edification of the reader, is going out in company on a thieving or swindling expedition, the proceeds of which have afterwards to be shared by all who take part in it.

There is no forgiveness for the thief who does not act "on the square" with another thief, and one of the rascals was now inveighing against the other on the ground of his "dishonesty."

Dirk Matthews, after a quick glance round, glided up to the two men and cut into the quarrel by bidding them "Good evening."

They stopped and stared at him with no particular favour, and the denunciatory party asked him what he wanted.

"Nothing but good fellowship," answered Dirk Matthews. "Have a drink with me. What's the use of quarrelling?"

"Wot use it may be," was the answer, "is our business, not yours."

"All right," said Matthews, airily, "do you drink or not? Am I to go further afield? If you drink give it a name."

To refuse drink would have been utterly at variance with the tenets of the loafers, so they named their respective liquors, and Matthews ordered a liberal supply.

It was so liberal, indeed, that both scented business, and became more deferential.

"I want to talk with you two," said Matthews, after they had pledged each other with some fervency. "Not here, I suppose?"

"The bar-parlour is free," was the reply.

The bar-parlour was a horrible little den at the back, very often in request for private consultations. Thither they adjourned, taking their drink with them.

"First of all," said Dirk Matthews, as they settled down, "can you two put aside your little differences for a few hours?"

They thought they could, and promised to do so, provided they were paid separate.

"What's your names?" asked Matthews.

"Call me Waller," answered one, "and him's Buckles."

"That will do for me," said Matthews. "It's so

okkard talking to people who hasn't a name of some sort."

"It are," they admitted.

"Well, then, to the p'int," said Matthews. "I've just come home from a voyage in a private yacht, and I've brought a few things back with me as I want to get ashore without troubling the excise to help me."

"Only a bit o' smuggling!" said Buckles, in disgust. "I thought it was a job that could be well paid for, some henemy shoved into the water or bashed about."

"There's five pounds apiece hanging to it," said Matthews.

"Add another to it, and we says yes," said Waller.

"Well, I don't mind six," said Matthews; "but I can't go a penny more if I am to get anything for myself."

"In course not," they drily said.

"Did you see the yacht come in to-day—the big 'un?" asked Matthews.

They nodded.

"And you know where she lays?"

They knew it very well. Could find her "blindfolded in a thunderstorm," Buckles declared.

"Can you be under her stern with a boat about one in the morning?"

Of course they could, and they knew where a boat was kept for people who wanted a late row. He might depend on them.

Dirk Matthews, having other business to attend to, gave each of the rascals half-a-sovereign as earnest-money, and left them.

From the public-house he went into a better part of the town, where the houses were of the respectable if poor class, and there he engaged apartments for himself under the simple but useful name of Smith.

He was first mate of a steamer that had been just been paid off, he said, and in place of reference paid a week's money on account.

Now the greater part of his arrangements were completed. The final thing was the getting of a bottle of rum, uncorking it, putting in a portion of the drug he had purchased, and recorking it. All of which he carried out with a master-hand.

It was then nearly ten o'clock, and he returned by a hired boat to the "Albatross."

CHAPTER CCLXXXIX.

DRUGGING THE WATCH.—THE ROBBERY.

UNSUSPECTING evil, Bill Oakley took things easily on the yacht.

He felt that he might even relax in the presence of the men, and when the watches of the night were changed, he ordered all of the middle watch a noggin of grog, and saw that they had it—full measure.

Then he went below to have a nightcap in his own cabin, in the form of a stiff glass of rum, prior to his turning in.

Dirk Matthews was this far favoured, for Bill had been previously "softening his clay" with libations as a celebration of his safe return to his native land, and was asleep before he got into his hammock.

As a matter of fact, he went off sitting on his chest, and snored so that the rasping nasal sounds he emitted could be plainly heard on deck.

"Old Bill is agoing of it," said one of the watch.

"Had his dose to-night," remarked another; "but it is a poor heart that never rejoices, and if a sailor can't go on the bust arter a voyage, who ought to?"

"Hear, hear!" said Dirk Matthews, "and that was my feelings to-night when I went ashore. So I says to myself, says I, 'To-night, Matthews, you are in the middle watch, which ain't no watch under the sarcumstances to speak of, and therefore you just take back with you a bottle of rum inside your jacket to cheer the 'arts of your shipmates.' That was what I says, and here is the bottle I alluded to."

He drew out the bottle, and holding it up so that they could see it, gave vent to a chuckle, which was followed by a pleasant laugh from the rest.

"It was thoughtful of you, Matthews," said one.

"We'll drink to each other all together," said Matthews. "One of you slip down and bring up a few tin mugs. We'll toast our safe return arter a voyage of trouble and triberlation."

The tin mugs were fetched, and Matthews, making some ado over the drawing of the cork, which he said was the tightest in he had known for many a day, filled them halfway up, except in the case of his own, where he only shammed doing it.

"Now all together," he said. "Luck to us ashore, and luck when we are going afloat agen."

The men tossed off the spirit, and Dirk Matthews put his empty cup to his lips.

"Hallo!" said one of the men, "that is queer-tasting stuff."

"It's the cork," replied Matthews, hurriedly. "I knowed it was a rum 'un by the way it stuck in the bottle."

"You're a liar!" answered the man. "I've been took in afore, I knows the taste. Mates, he's drugged us!"

As he spoke, the man lunged forward with the idea of striking Matthews, but the poison was already at work, and he simply staggered and fell.

The other men, too astounded at the outset to do anything but stare, now began to cry out they were poisoned and all dead men. One shouted for help, but only once, his voice dying quickly away as he subsided senseless to the deck.

Then another and another fell, the last with a shout that rang far away over the sea.

Dirk Matthews stood aghast.

"I've overdone it," he muttered. "What in the name of goodness is the strength of the stuff?"

He stood still, listening for sounds of movement below, but nobody was disturbed there. Sailors in time of rest sleep soundly. But from the sea there came the sound of oars and an approaching boat.

It speedily hove in sight, and proved to be a boat with some Revenue men in her.

"What's up there?" demanded the officer in the stern.

"Skylarking and on the drink," replied Dirk Matthews.

"Well, make a little less row, all of you. I thought somebody was being murdered. Give way there!"

The men bent to their oars, and the boat glided away.

Dirk Matthews wiped the perspiration from his forehead.

"I'm jiggered if I didn't think the whole thing was spoilt. Blow the howling lot of worms! What do they mean by it?"

He spurned the nearest of them with his foot, and stole below. It was the aft cabins he was going to visit. Bill was in one of the furthest from the captain's.

Guided by the prodigious snoring of the boatswain, Dirk Matthews went to the door, and finding it was not fast, softly opened it.

By the light of a swinging lamp he saw Bill sitting with his chin on his breast and his hands in his pockets, safe and sound.

He could go to work, and producing a small steel jemmy from his pocket, he speedily broke open the door of the chief cabin, making no more sound than that created by the cracking of an ordinary nut.

Inside all was dark, but he had matches and candle ready in his pocket, and lighting up, he took a look round.

The precious boxes, which he rightly suspected contained the treasure, stood in a far corner. There were six in all, strongly bound and hooped with iron.

His heart beat fast with exultation, but it suddenly stopped as a thought flashed on him.

"Suppose they hunts me up for robbery?" was the idea that came to his mind.

If they did, and brought it home to him, his project would simply end in his being sent to prison. That would not do.

"I mustn't be caught," he muttered; "there ain't much difficulty in lying close. Besides, there ain't many as would believe the yarn. Anyway, I can't leave these boxes, and I've got to risk the taking of 'em."

One by one he carried them on deck, placing them well aft ready for the boat he was expecting. It was late in coming, for the clocks of the town had struck one half an hour when he placed the last box upon the deck and sat down.

He had another quarter of an hour for thinking, and he utilised it by conceiving a plan of evading pursuit. It was to get up a sham suicide.

Or perhaps he might so manage matters that some innocent persons would be looked upon as murderers. There was the trifling difficulty of the finding of the body, but he thought he could get over that.

How, he could hardly conceive, but the main idea remained. He would have to sham being dead.

There was a light dipping of oars over the stern, and he rose, peering upon the feebly gleaming water.

"That you, mates," he whispered.

"It are," was the answer. "Blow that ere Revenuer. We've had to lie off for nigh an hour a-dodging it."

"Look out!" said Matthews. "I'm going to sling over the boxes. They contains good French brandy, and are fairly heavy."

They were not so heavy that he could not lower them with perfect ease, and that done, he dropped over the side.

"Better make for the fort and land there," he said. "It's quiet."

He had taken apartments on the Southsea side of the town, and his plan was get the boxes across the common and home one by one.

He had no doubt that his assistants, after being paid, would sheer off, leaving him to complete the rest of the work alone. They on their part had a plan of their own to carry into execution.

"We had better go to the east end of it," said Buckles.

"Why?" asked Matthews.

"It's quieter there."

"The tide's a-running out. Don't bear away too much."

"We knows how to manage," said Waller, sulkily.

"If you do, it's my opinion you are making too much down east."

"If you let us alone," growled Buckles, "we'll land you right enough."

"Not in this heavy boat," insisted Matthews, "she's three times as big as she need have been."

"We hadn't the chance of picking and choosing," muttered Waller. "It seems to me you are mighty particular."

"Where's her rudder-lines?" suddenly demanded Matthews.

"She ain't got none," said Buckles; "we rows and steers as one."

"Then pull your starboard oar, will you? It won't be possible to fetch the fort if you go much further out."

"Let's see where we are," said Buckles, resting on the oar he grasped.

Waller did the same, and they were a minute or more resting ere Matthews uttered an impatient exclamation.

"I suppose," he said, "that you know how far you've drifted?"

"We does," said Buckles, as he jerked the oar into the boat; "we shall do here, Waller."

Then in a moment he had thrown himself upon the startled Matthews, and dragged him from his seat to the bottom of the boat.

Waller at the same time plunged aft, and rubbed a handful of some powder over the face of the doomed man.

It stifled, it choked him. He could not cry out for help, nor could he do more than feebly struggle.

Moreover, he knew the nature of that powder, and that in a few minutes it would overpower him.

The whole of the awful truth flashed upon him.

The rascals he had hired to assist him in a crime intended to cap it by murdering him and taking possession of the whole of the proceeds.

As soon as he was in a helpless condition they would merely have to drop him over the side of the boat, and he would go down to the bottom.

The outgoing tide would carry his body far out to sea, and it would be many days, if ever, ere his fate was known.

The sham death was to become a real one.

And, again, the scoundrels would be perfectly safe.

There was nothing to connect them with the murder or robbery.

They would be the possessors of enormous wealth that he had sinned to become possessed of. It was galling—maddening.

These many thoughts tumbled over each other in his brain, even while Waller was engaged in rubbing the powder into his nostrils. It was only a matter of moments, but a long time to the doomed man.

The agony he endured was awful, but it was soon over.

Insensibility came upon him, and he lay like a log at the bottom of the boat with the two brutes kneeling beside him, and grinning over the success of their nefarious scheme.

"He'll do now," said Buckles, coolly. "Help me to heave him over."

"Wait till I've emptied his pockets," muttered Waller; "the less there is for identification the better.

They took everything from him without compunction, and then, after a look round, heaved him over into the sea.

CHAPTER CCXC.

DICK DARNLEY GOES OUT TO DINE.—THE RESULT OF KEEPING LATE HOURS.

YET one more of our friends must we accompany on this eventful evening and night we have been dwelling on.

It was Dick Darnley, who happening to meet some old friends, bachelors, almost as soon as he was ashore, had accepted an invitation to dine with one of them.

It was one Sam Briscoe who was to give the dinner, and half-a-dozen or so of choice spirits were invited to meet Dick and partake of it in his company.

They were mostly young, and being well endowed with health and this world's goods, were all in the highest spirits. The result was that the dinner and the subsequent proceedings led to very late hours.

It was half-past one when the first to go, an officer who had to be on duty at seven in the morning, took his leave of his host. After that they departed one by one until only Dick was left. It was getting on for three o'clock.

"I don't like late hours," said Briscoe, "so I shall walk to your hotel with you."

"But that will make you later than ever," urged Dick.

"Oh, no," replied Briscoe; "if I go there with you I shall not go to bed at all, and I can therefore conscientiously and truly say that I was up very early."

"No, old fellow, I won't trouble you."

"It is no trouble. We can have a quiet stroll along the shore to see the sun rise. It is a treat, I can assure you, one of the coolest and most refreshing sights imaginable."

"Very well," said Dick. "Like you, I think I will make an early riser of myself by not going to bed at all."

"Have another cigar, and then we will start."

"Thanks, I'm ready. No more wine, unless you wish me to become intoxicated."

"Which you never have been, of course?"

"Well, hardly ever."

"Don't play that old joke on me, but light up and come along."

They turned out, and walked down to the sea, striking the shore about half-a-mile eastward of the fort. Then, in an easy fashion, they lounged along over the shingle, taking things quietly, and talking of the days when they were boys together at school.

Everything was so still that the least sound outside the lazy lapping of the retreating sea was heard with great distinctness.

Briscoe suddenly stopped, and pressed Dick's arm.

"Listen!" he whispered. "Somebody's rowing ashore."

"Much in that?" asked Dick.

"Well, it is an unusual thing. Somebody doing a quiet line in smuggling, I reckon. Let's have a bit of fun with them."

"What can we do?"

"You leave it to me. Steady. Keep quite still."

They stood for a short time listening. From the seaward came the sounds of oars, and men breathing quickly.

"Pulling against tide and close in," whispered Briscoe.

There were only the stars overhead, and they were outside the lights of the town. With a dark background they became invisible from the sea.

But to add to their security from early discovery, Briscoe quietly drew his companion behind an old boat that had been lying on its side slowly rotting for years.

Then the voices of men were heard.

"Blowed if I iver had such a job a-pulling ag'in' the tide."

"It is a bit stiffish."

"Better have made for Hayling Island."

"Hayling Island be blowed! How was we to get orf there without being nobbled? You ain't got no head, Buckles."

"As good a head as yours any day. Didn't I work out the notion of playing the right game orf on that feller from the 'Albatross'?"

"You did, and it was a good notion, coming from you. I wonder what is in these 'ere boxes?"

"*Not* brandy, you may bet, although that covey said so. They don't iron-bind brandy as these 'ere things are."

"Briscoe," hurriedly whispered Dick.

"Well, old man?"

"You heard about the 'Albatross'?"

"Of course, and—why, it is your ship."

"Yes, and those boxes contain something that we must get hold of. A big robbery has been perpetrated."

"We have nothing but our fists," said Briscoe, complacently. "I can see the men pretty well. There doesn't seem to be more than two of those fellows."

"What I want to do is to get hold of those boxes without any fuss," whispered Dick. "There is a strong reason why it should be done."

"No arrest?"

"None. It is not my affair. But I can vouch that it is all right."

"Leave it to me," said Briscoe, softly.

"They are pretty close in, now."

"I'm ready for them."

"I don't think we shall do better than here," said the voice of Buckles, about a dozen yards from the shore.

"Better go higher up. We sha'n't have so fur to carry 'em."

"I can't pull no furder. My blessed hands are blistered. Blow me, if I'd a known it we'd had old Walster's boat. It's lighter."

The grating of the keel of the boat upon the shingle followed. Briscoe nudged the elbow of Dick Darnley as a sign for him to keep still.

Then he stole down towards the boat with the step of a wildcat bearing on its prey.

"Pull her up a bit," said Buckles, who had stepped out with his companion. "She'll have to lie here till next tide."

"Now, men," shouted Briscoe, "seize them!"

His voice rang out like a trumpet-blast upon the ears of the startled villains.

Always at war with society, and ever in terror of arrest with imprisonment, "without beer and 'bacca," Buckles and Waller dashed away into the darkness, vanishing from sight and soon after from hearing.

Briscoe continued to call upon his men to follow until he was satisfied that the pair had cleared off, and then he stopped for a quiet chuckle.

"These fellows, these law-breakers," he said, "have no heart in them. About a year ago I scared a boat-load of rascals who had come ashore with quite a cargo of brandy and tobacco. They were part of the crew of one of the royal yachts. They left all their stuff behind them as soon as I called on my imaginary men to arrest them."

"And what became of the cargo?" asked Dick.

"I took care of it in case they ever returned," replied Briscoe, "but I have not seen them since. The cargo has dwindled somewhat. You know, Dick, if I had handed it over to the police, or any of that lot, *they* would have enjoyed it quite as much as I have done, and they had no real right to it. Like Norval, I had scared away the enemy, and felt I had a right to the spoils."

"I should say so," said Dick, who was leaning over the side of the boat and examining the boxes by touch. "I hope you will not claim the run this time?"

"Not if it belongs to you."

"It is the property of my friends, and how it came here is a mystery of no common order."

"Well, what shall we do with it?"

"Will you mind staying here while I run up to the 'Blue Posts'? Barstow and one or two more must be got out of bed to help back with the cargo."

"All serene," said Briscoe. "I'll have a smoke while you are gone. Only hurry up, as it is lonely."

CHAPTER CCXCI.

BILL OAKLEY'S DESPAIR.—RESTORED.

BILL OAKLEY awoke from the sleep that was heavy while it lasted, if not especially refreshing. He was astonished to find himself sitting on his chest, and meditated thereon.

"Seems to me, Bill," he said, "that you've been a-indulgin' of yourself in too much licker. That won't do. When them in command goes wrong the rest can't go right."

Feeling it was a matter of duty to see that others had not been backsliding, he unhitched the lantern and left the cabin, a bit dry about the throat and decidedly acid in his temper.

It was still night, and on his way up the companion he had to pass the door of the captain's cabin. It was standing wide open, and the sight of it brought him to a standstill.

"What the tarnation now?" he groaned. "Surely the cap didn't come back."

He peered in cautiously, and saw the cabin was empty.

Then his eyes fell on the shattered lock, and he fairly leapt with a sudden terror.

Bill knew of the boxes in the cabin, and he mentally booked them as something uncommonly particular. Entering, he looked round for them, and discovered they were gone.

"A robbery!" he gasped.

Wild with alarm, he bounded upstairs with an unwonted agility.

On the deck the members of the watch lay about like fallen leaves.

His suspicions were aroused that something very wrong had happened. Fearing the men were dead, he examined them one by one, and found they were alive, but in a state that his experienced eyes saw was no commom state of intoxication.

"Drugged," he muttered, "and that warmint Matthews not among 'em. I thought the captain was wrong in having him aboard arter what had happened. He was repentant, he was! Oh, yes! The skunk!"

His only resource was to arouse the men who were in their hammocks, and this being done, half a dozen growling sailors came on deck, wondering why there was no more peace at anchor than there had been in mid-ocean.

"Mates," said Bill, "the watch have been drugged, Dirk Matthews is gone, and the captain's cabin robbed."

It roused them thoroughly, and as they assisted Bill in his efforts to restore the drugged men, they vowed vengeance on the offender.

But the men could not be brought round. The more they were shaken up the more like logs they were. Bill became alarmed. There was the appearance in more than one case of a probable fatal end to the victim.

"I dunno what to do," exclaimed Bill, in despair. "We ought to have a doctor, and the police, but I don't like to act without orders. Mason, you go ashore to the 'Blue Posts,' and get the captain up. You can explain matters all right. Good Lord—I must have been drugged, too."

Bill shirked seeing Harry Barstow, feeling all the shame of a guilty spirit on him. Mason was a sober, cool-headed seaman, quite capable of bearing a message and delivering it in a fitting manner.

"You may tell him," said Bill, "that Matthews p'isoned myself and the watch, and then bu'st open the cabin-door. He took with him some boxes when he runned away. What boat did he take?"

"None, sir," replied Mason, "all in their davits."

Bill was more puzzled than ever, but delay was dangerous, and Mason, with a companion rower, was sent ashore in the gig.

They pulled for the pier and grounded on the beach near it. As they stepped out they heard the voice of their captain, and saw him coming from the direction of the town, in company with Dick Darnley, Jack Ford, and Don Peebles.

The first faint light of the morning was beginning to dispel the darkness. Mason stepped forward and saluted.

"Come ashore, sir," he said. "Mr. Oakley sent me to report summat wrong. He's been drugged with the watch, your cabin broken open, and Dirk Matthews gone."

"Pull round below the fort," said Harry Barstow. "You have come in the nick of time."

"Mr. Oakley thinks, sir, a doctor ought to be fetched."

"Is he so bad?"

"No, sir. But the men are insensible. Mr. Oakley have come round."

"Drugged men seldom die," said Dick Darnley. "Time presses in the other matter. If seen taking boxes on board by the Revenue people, you may be asked questions you would not care to answer."

The boat was taken round to where Briscoe was waiting. The party from the hotel walked along the beach.

"The whole story is now clear," said Dick Darnley. "Dirk Matthews suspected what was in those cases—got some friends to help him in the attempted robbery and they have, like many other and better friends, turned against him for their own ends."

"It seems next door to a miracle," said Jack Ford, "that you should come along at the very moment. But, then, I suppose it was to be."

"I wouldn't give much for Matthews's chance of being alive," said Don. "I wonder who his friends were?"

"That we needn't trouble ourselves about," said Harry Barstow; "by ridding the world of him, they have done good service to the State."

"And have met with no reward," said Jack, grimly.

Briscoe asked no question about the boxes. When the boat came round he helped to put them in, and accompanied the party on board.

"A bit of a blow and a breakfast at sea will wake me up," he said.

Daylight was well on hand when the boat drew up to the side of the yacht, and Bill Oakley, peering over the side, saw the missing cases in the stern.

He could hardly believe his own eyes.

"Bad business, sir," he said to Harry Barstow, when he reached the deck, "and how he got *me* to take the drug I can't tell."

"I suppose not, Oakley," was the quiet reply; "but the most miraculous thing is the way you have recovered from it. These are the drugged men, I see."

They had been laid out on the fore-deck, just like so many slain warriors awaiting interment. Dick Darnley carefully examined them, and declared that all they could do was to allow the men to sleep off the effects of the potion.

"It will leave them shaky for a day or two," he said, "but nothing more."

"Ford," said Harry Barstow, later on, when they were alone, "there will be no rest for us until we have deposited the treasure in the bank. If we run up by the twelve train, we can be back again in the evening. Or you can remain in town, just as you please."

"I think I had better let my people know I have returned."

"Quite right. And the others might do the same."

"I will take Mulberry Cork with me," said Jack. "There is a possibility of his being put right by an old friend of mine. You remember my speaking of him —Gubbles, who played the part of private detective?"

Harry Barstow nodded.

"Of course I do. Well, at twelve o'clock we start."

With the fortunate restoration of the money Bill Oakley became comparatively happy again. The only reproaches he suffered from came from himself, and in a spirit of repentance he went ashore to sign the pledge.

But on arriving there he thought better of it, and decided, liké a wise man, to keep to a moderate allowance of good things in the future.

He set a seal upon this resolve by treating himself and sundry seamen he met in the bar of an inn to a stiff glass of grog.

Then he returned to the "Albatross," and that morning she was towed into dock for repairs.

Meanwhile the men had partly recovered from the ill effects of the drug, and loud and deep were the curses they hurled at the head of Matthews.

But he could not hear them, nor did he ever hear human voice again.

The tide that carried him out to sea did not bring him back again, and he was never heard of more.

CHAPTER CCXCII.

MULBERRY CORK.

DON, Tom, and Bob resolved to run home and visit their friends and rejoin Jack at Morley's Hotel at the end of the week. Jack's friends living in London were relieved from all anxiety about him by his calmly walking in on the morning after his arrival, as his father and family were sitting down to breakfast.

There was a mighty hubbub over him and a lot of embracing, especially on the part of his mother; but we need not dwell upon the scene, agreeable as it was, because this is not a story of domestic life.

Jack explained that he would be at the hotel for a time on business, but would see them every day until he could come home for a long stay.

He said nothing concerning the possession of a fortune. All round the four friends had decided to be reticent on that matter.

Harry Barstow arranged everything at the bank, and at last the vast treasure of the Avishnus, after being carried here and there for years and years, was safely housed. Until the time came for the realising of it into current coin no further anxiety need be entertained.

On the second day after putting up at Morley's Jack was honoured by a visit from Sir Charles and Lady Barstow, both of whom expressed themselves as delighted to see him.

"You left us two years—or was it more?—ago a boy, and you return a man. I suppose you will write a book about your travels?"

"I have not done travelling yet, I hope," replied Jack, with a smile, "and if ever I take to writing, it will be when I have done travelling."

They stayed to luncheon with him, and Jack did the honours in a style that delighted Lady Barstow. She told Sir Charles, in confidence, as they were driving away:

"Jack Ford is the handsomest fellow in the world. And if I run away with him, do not be surprised," she added, archly.

Sir Charles looked as if he had no fear of that coming to pass.

"He is a manly, sensible fellow," he said.

In the evening Jack had another visitor in the person of Professor Lingo, no longer a man fish, but clothed in ordinary attire, in which he looked like a well-to-do theatrical manager.

Jack gave him cordial greeting, and inquired the finish of the man-fish business.

"It stopped on Friday night, instead of Saturday," said Lingo, laughingly. "Somehow a suspicion of the truth had got abroad, and a lot of naval cadets were coming on Saturday night to investigate the genuineness of the man fish in a very simple manner."

"Indeed. And what was that?" asked Jack.

"They were going to shy a big stone at the front of the tank, which would of course shatter the glass and let the water out. But I got scent of it through one of them talking about it at the bar of an inn. I happened to be in the next compartment."

"That was lucky."

"It was; but I had a fear that something was known. I think I must have been blown upon by somebody connected with the hall. Anyway, I was prepared for them, and the man fish was taken ill on Saturday morning."

Lingo stopped to laugh again.

"I was to be paid as usual," he resumed after awhile. "I made the arrangement with the proprietor. The hall, we knew, would be fuller than ever with the friends of the imps who were coming to spoil the show. As soon as the doors were open the whole of the front seats were taken by cadets, and by eight o'clock the body of the hall was crammed by the general public. At nine the manager came forward and announced the sudden indisposition of the man fish, who, in a swell coat and blue spectacles, was at the back of the hall. You never heard such a howling row. It was a case of five hundred cubs being deprived of their mothers. They howled with rage, and one of them got upon a table and said the whole thing was a fraud. 'Somebody has blown the gaff!' he roared. Then he was pulled down by a policeman and led out. Others wanted their money returned, but as they had stayed during a portion of the entertainment, that request could not be entertained. Finally they all got outside, and making things lively in the street, were eventually dispersed by the police and a patrol of soldiers. It was the first swindle of the sort I have ever played principal in, and it shall be the last."

Then he came to the main object of his visit. He had called on Gubbles, and told him about Jack's return and the staining of the countenance of Mulberry Cork.

"He thinks he can remove it," said Lingo; "but, anyway, he will be glad to see you to-morrow at luncheon. His address is in Berners Street. Here is his card."

He had further information for Jack concerning old friends. If he wished to see the gentle Miriam (Mrs. Penny Bunn), he would find her at a shop on the other side of Blackfriars Bridge, where she was exhibiting Miss Astracan.

"I will certainly call and see her," said Jack. "She does not know you and I are friends, I suppose?"

"Well, I think she guesses it. On my way here I dropped in and had a chat with her. I fancy she has had enough of show life, poor thing. It gets tiring after a time to those who are born in it. To those who only drop into it because they can do nothing else it must be *poison*."

On the morrow Jack took Mulberry Cork to a house in Berners Street, where he was received by Gubbles, over whose head time had passed lightly. He was quite emotional in his reception of Jack.

"I've recalled a hundred—nay, a thousand times the days I spent with you at Littlecote Abbey. I have wished that I could claim you or one of our friends as a son. How are they?"

"Well," replied Jack, "they have run home to see their friends."

"Ah!" sighed Gubbles, "it is a great thing to be young. I suppose you think of adopting some profession?"

"I mean to see the world from end to end," said Jack.

"Are you not yet tired of wandering?"

"I have only begun to taste the joys of it."

Gubbles turned to Mulberry, who was standing near, and looked at him steadily.

"I cannot recall your face as it is," he said; "but you are grown, and that helps further to disguise you. Come nearer to the window and let me have a good look at you."

Mulberry drew up to the window, and Gubbles carefully examined his stained features. Then he opened a drawer in the table and brought out a bottle of light-coloured liquid and a camel's-hair brush.

With great care he uncorked the bottle, quickly dipped in the brush, and corked it up again.

Then he lightly painted a small circle on the forehead of the youth, and stood for a minute or more watching the result.

Jack and Mulberry awaited his announcement of good or ill result with breathless interest.

"I can remove it," he said, "but it will take time. Cork had better stay with me. He can make himself useful, instead of paying me my professional fee."

"I will do anything for you, sir," said Mulberry, gratefully.

"How long will he have to stay with you?" asked Jack.

"A month at least," was the reply. "Meanwhile I shall be glad to see you whenever you have a spare hour."

Jack promised to look in after luncheon, and then went his way.

"The clouds are clearing up for us all," he thought, "and Chunder Loo, with all his cunning and knowledge, is an all-round failure."

That was all very well, but Jack, nevertheless, felt galled as he thought of his old enemy safe at Tunis, and, in all probability, plotting further mischief. Never could he rest until he knew that the earth lay over him, or that he was many fathoms under the sea.

It was about four o'clock as he wandered down the Strand, and the thought of Mrs. Bunn and her show in the Blackfriars Road flashed upon him.

It would be as good a time as any other to visit her, for he knew that her class of show was best patronised in the evening.

"I hope she will take my call as a kindly one, as I mean it to be," he thought, as he climbed up a Road-car to have a pennyworth to Ludgate Hill. "I wonder what has been the fate of Bunn. Anyhow, I don't think he will come back to do any harm. He has the knack of falling *soft*, no matter how hard the ground may be."

CHAPTER CCXCIII.

GUBBLES'S EXPERIMENT.

LEFT alone with Mulberry Cork, the learned Gubbles beckoned the boy over to him.

"Stand there," he said, "by the window and let the light fall upon you."

All his life Mulberry had been shy of being inspected. It was a thing inherited, born in him, for he came of a long line of law-breakers.

Anything like being looked at in the way desired by Gubbles savoured so much of the police-court and inquiring detectives.

The boy held back instinctively, and Gubbles smiled.

"All I want," he said, "is to get a good look at the colour laid upon you. I am in the position of a picture-cleaner, who is called in to clean a work of art."

Mulberry shuffled up to the window and stood there, still in a shamefaced manner.

"I never did like being stared at," he said.

"No," replied Gubbles, coolly. "There are a great many things none of us like, but we have to put up with them. You have had teeth drawn occasionally, I suppose?"

"Several, years ago, sir," replied Mulberry.

"And you did not like the operation?"

"No, sir. The chap I went to nearly screwed my head off."

"But you were glad when the teeth were out," said Gubbles; "and if I can bring back your natural complexion you will not be sorry. Humph! there are some new ingredients here."

He turned the boy to the right and left, so as to allow the light to fall upon different parts of his face. Finally, he examined the skin with a powerful magnifying glass.

"Permanent dyes," he said, "are, to my thinking, unknown. Everything fades in time, but the people of India, or rather the master-minds of those people, have got at the nearest thing to permanency."

"You will be able to get it off, sir?" inquired Mulberry, anxiously.

"I will try," replied Gubbles. "Until I saw you I had only the dye Chunder Loo used upon himself in my eye. But there have been improvements—developments in his art. He is a wonderful man."

"He is, sir," assented Mulberry, "but a bad 'un."

"Never a worse," said Gubbles. "Had he applied his talents to a proper use, he might have become a ruler in the world. But he has allowed the blacker side of him to rule, and with the usual result."

"He isn't beaten yet," hinted Mulberry.

"He will be—he must be!" said Gubbles. "It is a law that never fails. Evil may flourish for a time, but it has a root in shifting ground, and in the end it must fall."

He opened a drawer and took out a small bottle and a short stick with a small piece of sponge fixed to one end of it.

Mulberry eyed the bottle apprehensively.

In common with most people not well up in chemistry, he mistrusted everything related to it.

"Will it burn, sir?" he asked.

"No," replied Gubbles. "Stand still. I will try the lobe of the ear as the most impressionable part."

He opened the bottle, and poured out a few drops of the liquid upon the sponge. Then he applied it to the ear of Mulberry.

The moment it touched the boy he shrank back.

"Come; you must not say it burns," said Gubbles, good-humouredly.

"Burn, sir—no," replied the boy; "it's the coldest thing I ever felt."

"I think it is inclined to be chilly," murmured Gubbles. "Yes; it will act, I think, but not so well as I should like it to do."

"Am I to be rubbed all over with that stuff?" asked Mulberry, with a shiver.

"Not in its present form," replied Gubbles; "you could never endure it. Besides, it would cost a fortune; I could not afford it. And last of all there is another reason. If I painted you with this, as it is, in an hour you would be dead."

"Perhaps I had better remain as I am," said Mulberry, faintly.

" What ! a boy of your pluck talk like that ?"

" I'll go through with it," said Mulberry, between his teeth.

" It is a matter of baths for a time," said Gubbles. " I will prepare you one at once. Come upstairs and see me do it."

They left the room, and on the way to the bath-room Mulberry saw many things which pointed to the pursuits and tasks of the chemist.

To some people it would have been a veritable nightmare of a house, with its mysterious cases filled with chemicals, its stuffed specimens of birds and lizards, and strange, creeping things.

To Mulberry it was something calculated to inspire awe, and he dumbly followed Gubbles, who paused here and there upon the staircase to survey with rapt admiration some hideous specimens of the taxidermist's art.

They were to him what a fine picture is to others, things of beauty and a joy for ever.

The bathroom was no less awe-inspiring to Mulberry ; for out of that usually prosaic place Gubbles had made much mysterious capital.

There were batteries and bells and wires, shelves with coloured bottles, and curious brushes, sponges, and other necessaries.

There was even a towel made of fine wire, so deftly woven that it was almost as pliable as the ordinary huckaback.

Gubbles bade Mulberry undress, and while he was removing his attire, turned on the hot and cold water taps until the bath was half full.

The next thing was to test the temperature, which he did to a nicety, and finally brought out the bottle containing the icy fluid and counted twenty drops into the water.

" Lie in that for twenty minutes," he said, " then get out and first give yourself a rub with the wire towel. After that use the huckaback ones. There's a clock in the corner to test the time by."

He left Mulberry to himself, and the boy got into the water, not without some misgivings ; but there was nothing unusual in the feeling it inspired at the outset.

But after the lapse of a few minutes Mulberry felt a pricking sensation, that slowly increased until it became a bit of a nuisance.

He glanced at the clock.

Five minutes had barely expired.

" Blessed if I think I can stand this," he muttered.

But then he remembered what a disadvantage it would be for him to have to go through life with a dark skin.

For a real nigger it was perhaps bad enough, but for a sham one it would be unendurable.

Then the boys in the street—how well he knew them and understood their little ways—how soon they would find him out ! His very tongue would betray him.

What would they not say and do under the circumstances ?

Beyond that, there was the long life before him.

He had seen black men about the streets whose lives were a burden to them. White-faced young villains reviled them, as if to have a dark skin was a deadly sin ; and the black man, as a rule, is patient under insult.

But Mulberry felt that he could not be so.

He could never stand the "chaff" and the pushing and the pelting with refuse whereby the young Britisher expresses his contempt of the swarthy foreigner.

He would strike them, and perhaps kill one in the end.

Then there would be the usual trial, judge, jury, executioner—ugh ! It was too terrible to think of.

Mulberry Cork, you see, was endowed with a fervid imagination, and it did him good service that day.

It scared him into enduring the irritating tingling of that confounded bath.

Was there ever such a blessed clock as that in the bath-room ?

It travelled so slowly that it hardly seemed to move at all.

But it indicated at last that ten minutes had expired, and Mulberry shut his eyes as he muttered :

" Half time."

A man sentenced to ten years' penal servitude might have uttered the words in the same tone when five years were up.

Mulberry resolved to keep his eyes shut until the whole term of the twenty minutes had expired.

So he screwed them up as tight as he could, and tried to think of other things. It was just about as easy as to go to sleep with a legion of mosquitos at work upon one.

When he thought that the time was up, and more than up, he opened his eyes.

Twelve minutes were recorded by that remorseless clock.

A groan burst from the lips of the boy, and he was half inclined to get out of the bath and have no more of it.

But the thought that he had got over the worst of it restrained him.

So he closed his eyes again, and this time he was determined to have no more disappointments as regards the time, and closed his eyes tighter than before.

" I *won't* be licked," he muttered.

He was a very resolute boy when thoroughly screwed up, and he had kept his eyes shut for some time, but not long enough, in his opinion, when he heard the voice of Gubbles.

"Here, are you not going to get out of that bath to-day?"

He opened his eyes and stared at the clock.

Three-quarters of an hour it recorded.

From the clock he glanced at Gubbles, who was referring to his watch with the gravity of a physician when feeling the pulse of a patient.

"Have I been in so long as that?" he said, in a breathless way.

"You have," replied Gubbles. "Get out and give yourself a good rubbing, and then come down to me."

Mulberry was not eager to remain in the bath, and he was out in a moment.

Even the rasping of the wire-towel was quite pleasant after his recent experience.

In ten minutes he was with Gubbles in the room below. The latter seemed to be in a laughing humour.

"What induced you to remain in the bath so long?" he asked.

"It was all the clock, sir," replied Mulberry. "First of all, it seemed hardly to go at all, and then it regularly jumped—at least I thought it did."

"It was no fancy," said Gubbles, "and as you will not have to endure another bath of that description, I can let you into a secret. It *is* a jumping-clock."

Mulberry stared. The idea of a jumping-clock was new to him.

"It is my own invention," said Gubbles. "I got it up for myself, for I have had in my time to take baths that covered a comparatively long time. Three-quarters of an hour was necessary for you, but if I had told you so, would you have endured it? No. So when you were getting ready I quietly set the 'jumper' at work, which includes a piece of machinery which compels the clock to do a preliminary crawl."

"It is all wonderful, sir," said Mulberry, "and as you say, sir, if I had known I was to be kept in the bath for three-quarters of an hour, I never could have stood it. Thank you very much, sir."

"The rest of the process," said Gubbles, "will not worry you."

CHAPTER CCXCIV.

MRS. BUNN'S SHOW.—A MARVELLOUS MEETING.

THERE are in certain districts places known as "unlucky shops," where all efforts to carry on ordinary commerce indubitably fail.

You may find them in all of the poor parts of London, and in not a few of the more prosperous districts, standing out in bold but dismal relief, ghastly failures in the heart of success.

After a time they become neglected. The landlord doesn't see the fun of painting and garnishing them for tenants who come in at the beginning of a quarter and vanish just before the rent becomes due. Nor will he go to the expense of repairing windows that boys of the neighbourhood will break again almost before the putty is dry. So, paintless and with broken windows, these unlucky shops remain, until a tenant is found in some wandering showman, who takes them by the day, and pays up his rent smartly every night as long as his exhibition is a success.

It was on the right-hand side going south of the Blackfriars Road that Mrs. Bunn had secured an "unlucky shop" for her show. Over the doorway, and of sufficient size to hide the broken window on the first floor, was a big canvas with the form of a lady of impossible proportions, attired in regal robes, painted thereon.

At the bottom of it those who could read might learn that the above depicted lady "could be seen inside *alive*," the "alive" being written in letters four inches deeper than the rest.

The windows of the shop were whitewashed, so as to defeat the efforts of those who endeavoured to get unpaid-for peeps at the vast lady within.

These would-be "deadheads" of the penny exhibition are mostly boys, and Jack found them swarming against the window like flies upon a patch of treacle plastered on the wall.

"I can see her!" shouted one with his eye against a hole about the third of the size of a pin's-head. "Oh, ain't she a big 'un!"

"Bigger than the picter?" asked a boy behind him.

"Five times as big," was the answer.

"*Let's* have a peep."

"You be blowed!"

Then there was a scrambling struggle, and the discoverer of the one oasis of view in the desert of whitewash was jerked away, and his place taken by another, who, before he could make certain of the coveted spot, was likewise pulled back.

Jack stopped to watch the youngsters for a few minutes, immensely edified by the struggle to get a brief glimpse of Miss Astracan. Then he turned his gaze to the picture over the door, but could find no likeness to her in it.

Showmen artists do not, as a rule, descend to minute matters in their sketches, but rather trust to a vivid imagination to make the best of a subject.

He peered in at the door, which was screened from the room by a bit of green baize nailed upon a rough wooden frame. There was another screen on the opposite side standing further back, the space between forming an entrance-passage to the room.

In this space there was a portion of a lady's dress visible. It seemed to belong to someone sitting down, and Jack, screwing up his courage to enter, found that it was indeed the Miriam of old.

And not much changed, unless it was for the better.

Her face no longer wore the hard, grinding look of old. Time and tribulation must have softened her.

She was seated at a table to take money, and it must have been a very quiet time, for she was actually dozing when Jack appeared.

Her attire, by the way, was eminently classical, consisting of the simple Grecian dress with a gilt girdle round the waist.

On her head was the Phrygian cap of liberty Lingo spoke of.

"One penny, please," she exclaimed, smartly, as she opened her eyes.

"Have you change for that?" asked Jack, as he laid down a sovereign.

She stared at the coin, and then at him, wonderingly.

"No, I haven't," she answered.

"Then I will call for it to-morrow," said Jack.

"To-morrow I may not be here."

"But if I leave my address, you can send it on to me."

She was still staring at him as one who doubts the evidence of her senses. Suddenly she burst out with, "Oh, I know you now. Why do you come here to pain me?"

And then as she covered her face with her hands, he saw a tear trickle between her fingers.

"It is such a shame of you! So mean."

She sobbed now convulsively.

"Excuse me," said Jack, softly, "but I hadn't the least notion of annoying you. I came with another object entirely."

"What else could you come for?" she asked, still bitterly, but in a quieter tone.

"Well, I thought I might help you for the sake of old times."

She brushed aside her tears, and looked him full in the face.

"I believe you were always generous, Ford," she said, "but I have no desire of taking advantage of it. A few pounds would not help me much."

"Granted," said Jack. "One moment—is there any-one inside to hear us?"

"There is no company. It is the quietest part of the day."

"And Miss Astracan?"

"She is kept behind a curtain until wanted, and as she has a nice easy-chair, you may reckon she is fast asleep. She sleeps a great deal now. More than ever."

"I want to have a long talk with you," said Jack. "Could you shut up this place?"

"I do sometimes in the afternoon," said Miriam. "Here is a board I hang upon the door."

She brought out a board about a foot deep and eighteen inches wide. On it was painted the following notice: "Closed until six o'clock."

"That will do for the present," said Jack. "Here, I'll hang it up."

"You must nail through the cord," said Miriam, "or the dreadful boys will pull it down and run away with it. I used to think the Littlecote Lambs very bad, but they were angels to the London boys."

She gave Jack a hammer and a nail, and, having secured the notice to the door, he closed it and slipped the bolt.

There was a yell of derision from the outside, and a boyish voice asked through the keyhole "what they meant by shutting him out just as he had got his penny ready?" following up the query by giving two vicious kicks at the door.

"He hasn't a penny," said Miriam; "but that is the way they go on. They are simply dreadful."

They retired behind the screen to the place the public was supposed to fill. It would have held forty people at a pinch. At the back was a small platform, with a screen closely drawn.

"Auntie," said Miriam, pointing to the latter, "is behind there. Perhaps you have something to say to me before you see her?"

"I have," replied Jack, "provided you would care to hear it. It is about your husband."

"Poor P. Y.!" said Miriam, with emotion, "he was a great fool in some things, but he had some excellent qualities."

"Would you care ever to see him again?"

"I would, indeed. I was very hard upon him. Auntie says so, too, and so she was. She admits it."

"Under any circumstances?"

"I would gladly see him anyhow and anywhere."

"I must confess," said Jack, as he seated himself on the edge of the platform, "that the chances of your doing so appear to me to be very remote. But so many wonderful things have happened that one need never despair. He is with the Bey of Tunis."

Miriam stared at Jack, aghast.

"He is in high favour with the Bey. At least, he was when we left him."

"Oh, dear!" exclaimed Miriam, clasping her brow, "do not play any of your old jokes upon me. I deserve all I get, but I am not strong enough to endure it."

"I am telling you the truth," said Jack. "Penny Bunn, as we used to call him, has been abroad with Mr. Harry Barstow and a lot of us, and he has gone through some of the most startling adventures you ever heard of. I ought to tell you that he went with us by the merest accident. If you wish, I can soon run through his whole story."

The Lambs of Littlecote.

R. Prowse

No less a person than Penny Bunn himself stalked majestically in, strangely attired, with a noisy crowd at his heels

No. 39.   ☞ PRICE ONE PENNY. ☜

ALDINE PUBLISHING CO., 10, Red Lion Court, Fleet St., and 1, 2, & 3, Crown Court, Chancery Lane. W.

"Do," urged Miriam, "and I won't interrupt you with a word."

So Jack told the story in his telling, terse way, and she listened in a state of utter amazement that assisted materially in keeping her dumb.

When she heard of his being coloured a sweet mahogany brown, she first faintly smiled, and then looked very angry.

"Oh, that Chunder Loo!" she cried, breaking a long silence on her part, "I wish I had him here!"

"I wish you had," said Jack; "and now we come to the point. Something must be done to get your husband home. He is sure not to long retain the favour of the Bey. Those Eastern potentates are very fickle in regard to their favourites."

"What can be done?" asked Miriam.

"Ah, there I am at present at a loss. But I am never so long. I will think it over," said Jack. "And now, if you think it advisable to wake up Miss Astracan, I should like to have a little talk with her."

"Assuredly you shall, and a cup of coffee with us," said Miriam; "this is about our time. She will be surprised and charmed."

She arose, having been seated, as Jack had been during the narration of the story, on the edge of the platform, and was about to ascend it, when a shouting was heard outside, and it was immediately followed by a loud knocking at the door.

———

CHAPTER CCXCV.

YET ANOTHER SURPRISE.—CAN THIS BE HE?

"NOW, who can that be?" exclaimed Miriam, wonderingly. "It can't be the man for the rent, as he, by arrangement, doesn't come until ten o'clock. He is a jobbing cabinetmaker, and lives in Stamford Street."

"Shall I see who it is?" inquired Jack.

"Listen before you open the door," replied Miriam; "it may only be some man the worse for drink. We had one here last night, and he wanted to kiss aunt before he went away. He said she was the sort of woman he had been looking for for years. He liked a lot for his money, and he reckoned that if he married her, she would be as good as any two ordinary wives. I verily believe auntie would have allowed him to kiss her, for she is a bit vain still. But I called for a policeman, and he went away."

The knocking was now renewed, and again there was shouting of boys. Jack plainly heard one crying, "Hooray! here's another of 'em. To be seen alive and nothing to pay!"

Motioning to Miriam to keep still, Jack walked to the door and listened.

He could now clearly hear what was going on.

"Go away, boys," said a mild, expostulating voice that was familiar to his ear. "In this age of cheap education you ought to have better manners. A distinguished traveller, like myself, is entitled to be received by the lower orders with courtesy."

"Where's your banjo?" yelled a boy. "Play up. Give us a breakdown."

"I am not a vulgar street-performer," replied the previous speaker. "Really, I shall be obliged to chastise you if you don't go away."

Then he knocked at the door again, and Jack opened it.

Attired in Moorish garments and wearing a huge, close-fitting turban, drawn down over his ears, no less a person than Penny Bunn stalked majestically in.

Coming from the stronger light he did not immediately recognise Jack.

"I have just met an old friend, Professor Lingo, down near London Bridge, who informs me that I shall find Mrs. Bunn here."

"She is here," said Jack, with a gasp. He was fairly overcome with surprise.

"What is this?" exclaimed Bunn—"my fellow-traveller Ford?"

"Yes, I too have just paid Mrs. Bunn a visit. But had I not better prepare her to meet you?"

"I know his voice," said Miriam, faintly; from within; "let him come to me."

"'Tis she!" cried Bunn, as he vanished round the screen.

A scream burst from the lips of Miriam.

"Bunn, it isn't you! It can't be!"

"But it is, my own. Changed somewhat, but your own true Bunny all the same. To my arms, my Miriam!"

Jack allowed them to have a pretty long embrace, and then joined them. They were sitting side by side on the platform, as strange a pair as ever were seen by mortal eyes.

Bunn had his arm around the waist of his wife, and beamed and even perspired with contentment and happiness.

"To think that we should meet again," he said. "Had I been in ordinary attire it might never have been, but, wandering from the docks to London Bridge, I brought with me a train of boys, admiring or otherwise. They showed that innate ignorance of all English boys by looking upon my dark skin as that of a nigger. All black men are niggers to the youth of our nation. They will not cultivate a knowledge of nations and castes."

"So it was through the boys that you came here?" said Miriam, looking him all over still in a wondering way.

"It was," said Bunn; "they kept me close company.

Not to put too fine a point upon it, they chivied me into the doorway of a big merchant's office, where a beadle was on duty. He sought to eject me, forgetting that travel has given me a wondrous accumulation of muscle, such as I was famous for in my youth. In a short but telling struggle that ensued between us I threw him heavily. His hat fell off and was stolen with remarkable promptitude by a boy devoid of principle, who succeeded in getting safely away with it. The beadle called a constable, and he wisely refused to take me into custody, on the just grounds that *I* had not stolen the hat. But he expressed his willingness to take my name and address with a view to the beadle issuing a summons. For the lack of the real thing I gave him a visionary address, viz., the Moorish Embassy."

"Is there such an embassy in England?" asked Miriam.

"My love" said Bunn, "I don't know. There may be. If there is they will not there find Chief Halli Pastor Bey, which was the name I allowed the police officer to put on record."

"You will hear no more about it," said Jack.

"I trust not," answered Bunn. "Such indeed is the opinion of our friend Lingo, who, attracted by the commotion which stopped the entire traffic of one side of London Bridge for nearly five minutes, joined the eager crowd of sightseers. When I was free to go he came up and made himself known to me. How he knew me, as he certainly did, is a mystery I have not yet attempted to solve."

"He knows your story," said Jack; "I told it to him."

"That explains it."

"But I could not tell him everything. How is it that you have left the Bey?"

"I left him under circumstances that will take time to relate. Prior to laying it before you, I would like a cup of refreshing tea. By the way, I heard that Miss Astracan is with you, Miriam?"

"She is here," said Miriam, drawing back the curtain, revealing Miss Astracan, not asleep, but very wide awake, and staring in the old far-away style, transfixed, in short, with astonishment.

"Auntie," exclaimed Miriam, "you have heard all?"

"I have heard something," replied Miss Astracan, in sepulchral tones.

"Look at poor P. Y."

"I'm a-looking at him. And he says *he* is P. Y. ?"

"Yes, it's my own husband."

"I don't believe it," said Miss Astracan, firmly. "If you tried to hammer it into me with a sledge-hammer you couldn't do it. He's an impostor."

She was fatter than of yore, and she spoke slowly because it required an effort to get her words out. She also put in a wheeze at intervals, that was like letting the wind out of a big india-rubber bag.

"Auntie," said Miriam, "it was being woke up suddenly that gave you a shock. You will see that it is P. Y. by-and-by."

"Never," said Miss Astracan; "he may deceive you, but never me. Keep him off, Miriam. Hit him or scratch him if he comes near you. And get me a cup of tea, as I am famishing with thirst."

"Miss Astracan," said Penny Bunn, in a tone of lofty toleration, "in the past I made many allowances for you. I need not say why. Adipose matter is often cultivated at the expense of the brain. I pass that by. But when you state that a weary traveller, who has gone through things that would have reduced *you* to a skeleton, and comes back to the arms of a devoted wife, is an impostor, you exceed the bounds of decency."

"I didn't make you one," said Miss Astracan, curtly. "If you are P. Y. go, and wash your face, and don't come bamboozling and masquerading here."

"Aunt is always a little difficult to deal with immediately after sleep. Take no notice of her. I have the materials for tea in the back room. It will soon be ready."

CHAPTER CCXCVI.

PENNY BUNN RELATES A STORY OF STRONG INTEREST.

THE back room was sparely furnished with a table and two forms, which were the property of the landlord.

They sufficed for the use of his periodical tenants, but Miss Astracan required something more comfortable than a form, and, while the others had tea in the back room, partook of hers in solitary state in her exhibition chair.

"P. Y. dear," said Miriam, "after the night exhibition we had all better have a quiet supper together and hear your adventures."

"I cannot permit my wife," said Bunn, firmly, "to go on with the exhibition."

"It isn't very elevating, certainly," said Miriam, "but we have to live, dear, and you must not be foolish."

"I am not foolish," said Bunn; "at the present moment I am possessed of means of money value that will make us independent in a quiet style."

"I hope, P. Y., that you are not romancing. You used to have quite a gift that way."

It was a delicate way of putting it, and he smiled gently.

"No," he said "I am not romancing. I used to conceive wonderful things—it was a gift that made me famous in my earlier days—but all that I ever thought of falls into insignificance compared with the recent experiences of my life."

"I was about to suggest the same thing," said Jack, "but feared I might be deemed impertinent."

"There is auntie to deal with," said Miriam, thoughtfully; "she is quite proud of her popularity. But, of course, she could not take money at the doors and exhibit herself. Personally, I must confess it is distasteful to me."

"You shall do no more of it," resolutely replied Penny Bunn. "Miriam, there are bright days in store for both of us."

There were materials for writing notices in the house, in the form of a board or two, and a pot of paint and a brush. As soon as tea was over, Bunn and Jack put their heads together and concocted the following startling announcement for the benefit of the public:

"SUMMONED TO THE PALACE"

"Will Re-open Shortly with Additional Attractions."

What palace they were summoned to they did not know, but it would be naturally inferred that it was one inhabited by royalty.

Prior to its being put up, Jack slipped out and bought sundry refreshments and smoking material for the evening. He foresaw that there was a treat in store for him in the narrative to be told by Penny Bunn. Miss Astracan, after tea, went to sleep again, but shortly after woke up, and as her chair was a wheel one, they got her into the back room without much trouble.

"What is the meaning of this?" she demanded. "I thought the show reopened at six."

"It will not open to-night, auntie," said Miriam, gently.

"It must reopen," said Miss Astracan. "I cannot allow my admirers to be disappointed."

"I have to tell the story of my adventures," said Bunn.

"You may tell what you like," answered Miss Astracan, "and I shall not believe you. The truth was never in the real Bunn, and how it is to be in an impostor I can't see."

Jack uncorked a bottle he had brought in and mixed a little almost colourless liquid with water in a glass.

Handing it politely to Miss Astracan, he suggested she should "try it,"

She tried it, and, finding it to her taste, became more composed.

"Let him go on and say what he likes," she said, resignedly.

Then Bunn, also supplied with something to moisten his throat, began his story.

The first part of his wonderful adventures we know,

and Jack being able to confirm him, he found credence with his wife, who otherwise might reasonably have doubted him.

Miss Astracan went off to sleep, and woke up at intervals to declare "she did not believe a word of it."

Having thus entered her protest, she went off again.

Evening had deepened into night, and a lamp had been lighted, when Penny Bunn arrived at the stage of his adventures when he was left behind with the Bey of Tangier.

It is there we take up the thread of his story for the benefit of the reader.

"You remember," he said to Jack, "when I assisted you to carry away a person you believed to be Chunder Loo?"

"I do, very well," said Jack.

"Possibly you may have conceived that I was a party to the deception."

"It certainly struck me that you might have been obeying orders."

"No orders from the mightiest of potentates would have induced me to deceive my friends," said Bunn, firmly. "I would have been faithful on the rack to those with whom I had suffered."

"We know that, dear," said Miriam. "Go on."

"It was Sadyk who did the whole trick," resumed Bunn, "and he was obeying orders without a doubt. The Bey very much wanted Chunder Loo."

"As an old friend of his?"

"They were old acquaintances, certainly, Ford, as you will perceive ere I have finished my story. Shortly after you were gone, Sadyk came to me, and, in his oily way, summoned me into the presence of the Bey. I went, and found the old man in a state of extraordinary hilarity. I was inclined to think he had been drinking.

"He began with praising me for my faithful services, which he would remember for ever, if he lived long enough, and he gave me a sword, four feet or more long, to wear. It had a fearfully sharp blade, and a handle covered with jewels."

"P. Y.!" exclaimed Miriam, warningly.

"My love," said Bunn, "you shall see that sword. I confided it with some other things to the care of a trusty person—no other than the captain of the vessel in which I came home—and he will deliver the same as soon as I have a settled address."

"I beg your pardon."

"All right, my dear, I admit that my story seemingly wants something to help it down. Not only did he give me a sword, but he made me keeper of his jewels, and the stock he has is amazing. He could never wear a tenth of them if he covered himself from head to foot. Nor did he design to turn any into money. They simply lay there in his private room—rusting, as I may say."

"Chunder Loo was not with the Bey?" suggested Jack, to assist Bunn back to the more interesting part of his story.

"He was not," replied Bunn, with considerable emphasis, "for reasons I will now proceed to make clear to you."

———

CHAPTER CCXCVII.

THE FATE OF CHUNDER LOO.

"THE reason why Chunder Loo was not with the Bey," said Bunn, looking round the room as if he saw some terrible panorama passing by, "was that he was a prisoner and a doomed man."

"A doomed man!" exclaimed Jack.

"Hopelessly doomed," returned Bunn. "What he had done to the Bey I know not, beyond that it was a matter of years before, and must have been something very serious. I fancy that religion might have had something to do with it, but there it was, a deep and undying hatred in the old man's breast. First of all they made merry—he and Sadyk—over the way they had got hold of Chunder without getting into complications with the British authorities. Then, as a final portion of the entertainment, they had Chunder Loo brought in before them."

Bunn paused a moment, and when he resumed his narrative, spoke very slowly, as one who recalls every little detail, and sees the incidents vividly reproduced before his eyes.

"Four big, brawny black fellows, with muscles like those of a dray-horse, brought him in. He was loaded with chains, and could scarcely crawl under the weight of them. Never shall I forget the look on his face as he came before us.

"I stood on the right of the Bey with my gleaming sword in my right hand, ready, if necessary, to protect my chief, and Sadyk on his left. Chunder Loo looked from one to the other with eyes that seemed to belong to the dead, and were for a time unnaturally endowed with a semblance of life."

Bunn's listeners shuddered as they mentally pictured the once fierce, bright eyes of Chunder Loo in that condition. The simplicity of the description lent power to it.

"The old Bey," continued Bunn, "looked straight at him, and I could see every hair of his beard in a bristling condition.

"'Dog!' he hissed, '*At last I have thee!*'

"Then Chunder Loo uttered a cry of terror, and asked for mercy.

"'Mercy,' said the Bey, 'and for thee? Nay; by the sun and the moon, and the far-off stars, whose light burns for ever, there is none for thee. To-morrow I will reward thee for the past. Take him away,' he said, 'and let him lie on the bed of the condemned!'

"He was taken away howling—literally howling—and again I say I could not have believed, if I had not seen and heard, that Chunder Loo, cool fiend as he used to be, could be reduced to such a pass.

"Having seen and gloated over his prisoner, the Bey retired for the night, and Sadyk invited me to his particular chamber, declaring that he was a friend, and liked me, and I have no reason to suppose otherwise to this hour. Quite the contrary.

"In his chamber Sadyk had refreshments of the class not usually found among his people. They were of a strong-water nature, and we got very jolly, without, I may say, exceeding the bounds of discretion. In the course of conversation I asked him what the bed of the doomed was like. He said that it was hardly a bed at all in the true sense, being an arrangement of closely-laid iron spikes, which, so long as a man kept quite still, did not cause him any very great inconvenience, but the moment he stirred became irritating and painful to a degree.

"I passed the night in the chamber of Sadyk, and he also slept in some portion of it. I have reason to believe that, while I had the cushions, he had the bare floor, which he may have chosen in courtesy to a guest. But I won't be sure on that head."

"I should think not!" said Miriam, with something of her old dryness.

"On the morrow we were awakened early by the beating of a gong, and Sadyk got up in a hurry. As it was a warm morning, he suggested a bottle of qualified soda-water, which we partook of, and were refreshed. Then we felt fit for breakfast, and partook of it with relish. For the time I had forgotten Chunder Loo. But he was speedily recalled to my memory by Sadyk, who said it was time for him to go and see to the preparations for the execution of the man who seems to me to have been a general enemy to all mankind, and a friend to none.

"I went with him to see those preparations, and I sicken as I think of them. One can't expect that objection to torture shown by the civilised world to be in force everywhere. What the Inquisition did a few centuries ago in Europe may be reasonable punishment in Africa in the present day. I am not going to be hard on the Bey. He lives and acts according to the light within him. But, Ford, if you had wished the worst for your old enemy, you would have fallen short in your wishes to that which was prepared for him."

"There were instruments for giving pain of which you have no knowledge. I cannot and will not describe them, nor can I dwell upon the scene that I witnessed that morning ere the sun was high at noon.

I was obliged to be there in my high position as chief favourite of the Bey, and the death of Chunder Loo took place after the torture was inflicted in the square court in which you interviewed his mightiness.

"It may have been two o'clock when the officers of justice, as I suppose they are called, assembled there, with the Bey sitting in his composed way upon his throne.

"They brought in Chunder Loo, and they tortured him for two long hours, and as I am a living man, I believe that each moment was a minute to him!

"I shut my eyes half the time, another quarter of it I looked away—for how could I, as an Englishman, take pleasure in the torturing of a man, however vile? But I cannot say that I really pitied Chunder Loo. He was a scoundrel of scoundrels!

"Late in the evening, Sadyk, who had been quite at his ease through all, came to me and said that Chunder Loo was dead. I thought he was dead long before, and said so.

"'Oh, no,' replied Sadyk. 'He lingered, and talked a lot'—he did not use these exact words—'of those he had wronged in England.' Among other things I learnt from Sadyk was that Chunder Loo spoke of having set the old Abbey on fire, with the intention of roasting all in it to death, and that he had that day endured all the tortures he had designed for others.

"I went to look at him for the last time as he lay dead. I thought I might do that; but as I went into the prison-cell where he was lying, the black men on guard had just stripped him of his clothing, which were their perquisites. I can't describe to you the awful state he was in. Whatever he did to others, he paid for it in part in the end.

"I should be a hypocrite if I shed a tear over him," said Jack. "He was a man-monster, and he died an awful death. I am glad he is gone."

"For the rest of my story," said Bunn, "you may have little interest. It is so tame."

"Go on to the end," said Jack.

"After what I had seen," continued Bunn, "I felt a strong desire to abandon the service of the Bey and return to my native land. That desire was a natural one, especially as it was coupled with a longing to see my dear wife."

"Don't look at me like that," said Miriam, laughing. "Sentiment and a black face don't go well together. Poor old P. Y.! Never mind, I won't mind the colour of your face."

"I confided in Sadyk my desire," said Bunn, after a pause, "and he agreed with me that the sooner I could get away the better. Then came the question of how and when I should go. He said he would arrange it.

"I asked him what the Bey would think of it. He said he would make it all right with the Bey, but I was to be sure not to say a word to him. I am inclined to think now," said Bunn, meditatively, "that he had a personal motive in helping me to get away."

"Jealous of your influence with the Bey?" suggested Jack.

"Just so. But that is of no moment. I am grateful to him, anyway.

"You had been gone about a week, when one evening Sadyk suddenly announced that the arrangements for my departure were complete. I was to go aboard a British trader as a stowaway, and lie close until the ship was clear of the harbour. A boat would be on the shore, ready for me, at nine o'clock. 'It is the wish of the Bey,' said Sadyk, 'that you do not take leave of him. It is more than likely emotion might overcome him. He sends you your pay.'

"It was a parcel he gave me, which, when I afterwards examined it, I found to be filled with jewels of considerable value. The pay was very good indeed."

Bunn paused, and looked about him for a moment in a peculiar way ere he concluded his story.

"I was stowed away only a few hours, and on revealing my presence to the captain of the trader he said it was all right, and gave me some light duties to perform in payment for my food. I said nothing about the contents of my parcel, but sealed it up and asked the captain to take care of it for me. He is an honest man."

"I hope he is," said Miriam, uneasily.

"I am sure of it," said Bunn, complacently; "but if he fails us, I still have sufficient jewels sewn up in my clothing to meet our modest future requirements. The fact is, I was not sure the Bey would pay me my dues, and having access to a lot of loose material lying about, of which his mightiness has deprived some of the traders of his town, I helped myself. The parcel given me by Sadyk may be looked upon as supplementary pay."

"My dear P. Y.," said Miriam, "I hope you have not exceeded the bounds of honesty?"

"A Bey," replied Bunn, "is a thief on a large scale, and it is lawful to spoil him. He was my Egyptian. I merely borrowed from him without intending to pay back again, like the Jews of old."

At that moment Miss Astracan woke up for the thirtieth time, and said, with more emphasis than ever:

"There is not a syllable of truth in the whole story!"

"Allow me to mix you a little more, madam," said Jack, and she allowed it.

CHAPTER CCXCVIII.

THE COMING OF QUIET DAYS.

BEFORE leaving his friends that night, Jack Ford imparted to the Bunns the glad tidings that Gubbles had taken Mulberry Cork in hand, and should he be successful in removing the deep stain from his skin he would gladly perform the like office for Penny Bunn.

"But there still remain the feathers," urged Bunn.

"Get your wife to cut them off, then have your head shaved, and the hair will come again as of yore."

"Bless me! what a simple expedient!" murmured Bunn. "I should never have thought of it, though. But you always had a good clear head, Ford."

Arrangements were made for Penny Bunn and his wife to get quiet lodgings. Miss Astracan sternly declined to give up a public life.

"I have been exhibited with great success," she said, "and I will not go back to the old dreary existence."

This was embarrassing, but it occurred to Jack that Lingo might be of service here. Though not at all likely to personally undertake the management of the public life of Miss Astracan, he would be sure to know of someone who would gladly do so.

He mentioned the professor, promising to communicate with him at once, and Miss Astracan was pacified.

"All I want," she said, "is a public life, such as I have enjoyed for some months."

Miriam was not loth to let her go, and Penny Bunn said that, valuable as a domestic treasure to his future home as Miss Astracan might be, he was willing to do without her for her own sake.

The last thing Jack did that night was to write sundry letters to his friends, stating the particulars of the death of Chunder Loo, and one to Chippy, asking him to come up to town with all speed, and welcome back his old friend.

"You see, my dear," said Bunn to Miriam, "that we must make sacrifices for others; it is our duty."

"Yes, love," she replied.

"Aunt Astracan will be missed by us," mused Bunn. "A woman of her—of her—well, substance, could not be anything less than a loss. She will leave a vacuum."

"Dear old P. Y.," said Miriam, "you will never change."

"Not change, my dear? Who, looking at me at this moment, would recognise the old tutor, the instructor and leader, the moulder of the youthful mind?"

"I am not alluding to your feathers and paint, but to you—internally—to the spirit that governs you," she explained.

"By the way," said Bunn, "referring to these feathers, they must, of course, be removed; but while my skin retains its present hue——"

Miriam took him by the elbows and pressed him into a chair.

"Do not stir for a moment," she said. "Mr. Ford, please keep an eye upon him."

"I'll fix mine on him, too," said Miss Astracan, in her most sepulchral tone.

"Oh, blow *your* eye!" muttered Bunn. "I wonder, Ford," he added, with a seraphic smile, "what my darling intends to do?"

His "darling" was not long away. She came back with a huge pair of shears, which she had borrowed from a jobbing tailor who lived closed by.

"Keep still," she said.

Bunn obeyed her, looking at Ford with the air of one who dumbly says, "You see this child, I must yield to her little pleasant jests."

In a minute, or thereabouts, the feathery crown of Bunn was shorn off his head, and nothing but a curious collection of bristles remained.

This gave him a more extraordinary appearance than ever. But he was not conscious of it.

"I begin to feel a little more like myself," he said.

"You don't look it," grunted Miss Astracan. "Who tarred and feathered you, and what for? I know they do these things in America, but I wasn't aware they practised them in England."

"It was not done in England," said Bunn, firmly.

"I don't believe you," replied Miss Astracan.

"I assure you," Jack here remarked, "that he has been abroad, and was very badly treated there."

"You boys always made a fool of him," rejoined Miss Astracan, "and you will go on doing it to the end. Not that he wants any help in that direction, as we all know."

Bunn resumed his head-dress with a sigh.

"I shall not attempt to persuade you further to believe me," he said; "but let me assure you, aunt, that you have lost much by not travelling."

"What have I lost?"

"Many things. The love of the rich and powerful. There are some countries where you would have been raised to a throne."

Miss Astracan appeared gratified.

She was peculiarly open to flattery.

"I allude to those countries," pursued Bunn, dreamily, "which you may probably have heard of, where kings purchase their wives by *weight*. The woman who can turn the scale against all comers wins his love, and she wears the crown until some heavier lady comes along and deposes her. The fate of the rejected wife I will not dwell upon."

"You may as well finish," said Miss Astracan, eyeing him with that fixed expression which denoted a rising wrath.

"Well," said Bunn, "I have it on the highest authority that the deposed wife is immediately slain and salted or potted down."

"*What!*" cried Miss Astracan.

"P. Y.," whispered Miriam, "do not agitate her."

"I merely wish to state facts," replied Bunn, "which I have gathered from authentic sources. You need not be agitated, aunt, as you are not going abroad."

"I should like to catch the biggest king on earth salting down or potting *me!*" said Miss Astracan; "he wouldn't do it a second time."

This was an assertion that admitted of no argument, and was practically indisputable.

Jack Ford now thought it time for him to be gone, and he promised Miss Astracan to do his best to make her future life in harmony with her tastes and wishes.

Bunn went to the door with him, and excused himself for not accompanying his old pupil at least part of the way home.

"Even at this hour," he said, "I might be subject to a public ovation. One tires of popularity after a time. I really begin to sympathise with the Royal Family. Once upon a time I envied the great."

Jack said it was of no consequence, he did not expect Bunn to leave his wife for a moment even, so soon after his return, and shaking hands, on Bunn's side with much emotion, they parted for the night.

It is more than probable that Jack was not averse to Bunn's remaining at home.

Even at that hour the London boy was abroad, and there might have been, what Bunn was pleased to call, "a demonstration."

CHAPTER CCXCIX.

LINGO UNDERTAKES A TRULY HEAVY RESPONSIBILITY.

JACK wrote to Lingo before going to bed, and to Chippy Bunyons also, telling them the news of Bunn's return to the society of his wife.

He also, to the latter, stated the case of Miss Astracan, and asked the great professor if he could do anything for her.

"It has occurred to me," wrote Jack, "that you might know of somebody who would be glad to show her. She is bent on a public life, and will have no other."

In response, Lingo turned up by a late train that evening, and left word of his coming at the hotel.

He also appointed a meeting with Jack at the temporary residence of Bunn at the hour of noon.

Chippy Bunyons wired to say that he would be up that evening.

At the hour agreed on Jack was at the appointed place, where he found Lingo outside, with one of the unmistakable show fraternity in his company.

"Shifty Snorker—Mr. Ford," he said, by way of introduction.

"How do you do?" said Jack.

Shifty Snorker touched his hat.

"We have been busy here," said Lingo, "driving off the boys. They want the show open again, and have been shouting through the keyhole."

"There's no stoppin' of a eager public," said Snorker, in a gruff voice.

"Suppose we go in?" suggested Jack.

He knocked at the door with a cane he was carrying, but there was no response; nor was a second application more successful.

"They can't have gone away," said Jack.

"Or been turned away?" hinted Lingo.

"No; they have the money to pay the rent."

"Try again, sir."

Ford knocked the third time, and also called out through the keyhole. This time a soft footstep was heard in the shop.

"Come, Bunn," said Ford, "open the door."

"Is it really you, sir?"

"It is."

Then the door was opened, and Bunn was seen there in all his glory. Lingo and Shifty Snorker eyed him with the professional eye.

"Worth three quid a week," whispered Snorker.

"More," was the reply.

"I really must apologise for keeping you gentlemen waiting," said Bunn. "My wife is out, and Miss Astracan is not sufficiently active, even if she were so disposed, to get out of her seat and open the door."

"But you must have heard me knock?" said Jack.

"I did," replied Bunn; "but as we had not arranged a code of signals, I feared to respond. Miriam went out at nine this morning, and at half-past somebody knocked at the door."

"Wanted to come in?" suggested Lingo.

"Incautiously I opened it," said Bunn, "and there was quite a mob outside."

"That looks like money," said Shifty Snorker. "You didn't let them in, I hope?"

"I had a desperate fight with the ringleaders," replied Bunn. "One boy, I am sure, is now the possessor of a bump as big as a hen's egg. After an exciting struggle, I succeeded in closing the door."

"This looks as if the public was worked up to the right pitch," said Snorker.

"I beg pardon?" replied Bunn, as if not understanding him.

"The lady must be a tremenjous draw," said Snorker.

"Oh, yes—certainly," replied Bunn. "You would like to see her, perhaps?"

Shifty Snorker assented. "That was what he had come for," he said.

"You will find her behind the curtain," said Bunn.

The two showmen disappeared, and Penny Bunn sat down upon an empty packing-case.

"Mr. Ford," he said, "with you I am disposed, as I have ever been, to be honest. I cannot, and never could, deceive you."

"You never did," said Jack, knowing that it was a fact, arising from Bunn's failing to really deceive anybody, let him try as he would.

"That man with Lingo is a showman, of course?" said Bunn.

"He is."

"And he thinks that the crowd came to see her?"

"Undoubtedly."

"The crowd had no such idea in their heads—they were here to see *me*. There could be no doubt about it, although I could have wished them to be more complimentary. They called me Cannibal Joe, and a low-class man threw a dead rat into the shop and offered me twopence if I would eat it.

"The world is apt to misjudge us all," sighed Bunn. "Well, here are the worthy caterers for the public."

"It's as good as settled, gentlemen," said Shifty Snorker; "the lady rates herself rather high, but they all do that, even if they are nothing but skin and bone."

"You have gained a prize!" said Bunn, heartily. "Permit me to congratulate you."

Thereupon he shook hands with the showman.

"Now, if you would jine the lady," said Snorker, with a touch of pathos in his voice, "there would be a run that would astonish some people. We might have twopenny arternoons, and *might* be sent for by Royalty. There is no knowing."

"I am infinitely obliged to you, of course," replied Bunn, graciously, "and you mean well assuredly, but I am not accustomed to being shown for money. At present I am wearing—the—ahem! *court uniform* of an Eastern potentate, whose right hand I have been during a crisis, now happily past, that rocked his kingdom to its foundation."

"Well," said Snorker, "as you say, sir, I mean well, and I think you are running against your own interests to refuse to jine. If I was like you, I should consider it a public dooty to show myself."

He shook hands with Bunn again, touched his hat to Jack, and moved towards the door.

"One moment, professor," said Bunn. "You are not engaged this evening, I hope?"

"I am not," replied Lingo.

"Then perhaps you will look in about seven o'clock and spend an hour with us and a friend."

"I shall be most happy."

"I will not ask you," said Bunn to Jack; "the pressing attentions of higher society——"

"Can wait," said Jack. "I will come and bring my friends with me. We will have a jolly night of it. When does Miss Astracan leave?"

"I never allows things to wait," said Snorker, looking back, "and as soon as it is dusk the wan for the lady will be here."

"Then to-night we shall merry be," said Bunn, gaily.

And for a time they all parted company.

CHAPTER CCC.

POPULAR AS WELL AS PECULIAR.

MIRIAM returned shortly afterwards, with the look of a woman who has had a very fatiguing experience.

"I had no idea," she said, "that there would be any difficulty about getting apartments."

"I can conceive none," murmured Penny Bunn. "Surely, as we are in position pay the rent in advance——"

"It wasn't that, P. Y. Of course I had to tell them that my husband was a coloured gentleman, and that made everybody look at me askew."

"How strange!"

"Well, my dear, I thought it advisable not to say that you were of English extraction. It appeared to me to be better to let them assume that you are a foreigner."

"And what nationality did you bestow upon me, my love?"

"I said you were a Moorish Bey; but lots of people wouldn't have you. One woman told me she could not stand black men, as they were mostly cannibals."

"Did she look toothsome, my dear?"

"Far from it. She was a miracle of slovenly dressing, to begin with. But I have secured you apartments at the house of a very good man. He has something to do with missions, and he fervently declares that the blacker the man the more he loves him as a brother."

"He must be good."

"Yes, but he asked an exorbitant rent, and I had to pay it. He wishes, on our entering the house, to look into our boxes."

"What an extraordinary request!"

"He fears tomahawks being imported into his house. One of his brothers was killed and eaten somewhere abroad."

The apartments secured were in Smugger's Terrace, Clapham, and they were to be ready on the morrow.

Miss Astracan was in a patronising humour, having got it into her head that the Snorker engagement was something equivalent to being appointed to the post of Mistress of the Robes at Windsor Castle. Bunn encouraged the idea, his great object being to get rid of the ponderous lady.

"Snorker and fortune are synonymous terms," he said. "You will yet be a millionaire."

About dusk there was a knock at the door, and Snorker with four strong men, who looked like market porters, appeared.

"The wan," he said, "will be here in a minute, and then we must get her in with a rush."

As a preliminary step they carried her, seated in her accustomed chair, to the door.

A moment later and the van drove up, the driver backing it against the pavement.

"Now, then, all together!" cried Snorker.

The four porters laid hold of the legs of the chair and hoisted it up.

"Murder!" screamed Miss Astracan.

"Don't holler, miss," said Snorker; "it wobbles the chair and doubles the weight."

"Oh! this is dreadful," groaned Miss Astracan, as the men staggered across the pathway with their burden.

"If you drop me I am a dead woman! Bunn, you villain, this is all of your arranging. Oh-h-h-h!"

"In she goes," said one of the men, as the chair was shoved into the van.

"You scoundrels!" gasped Miss Astracan. "I——"

"Close the door!" grunted Snorker. "We can't afford to show a woman of her weight for nothing."

The door was closed, two little boys hurrahed, and Snorker jumping on the step, like an omnibus conductor, the van was rapidly driven away south.

He had previously paid the men, who disappeared in a northern direction.

"Poor auntie," sobbed Miriam. "It comes hard parting after having been so long together."

"It does," sighed Bunn; "but we must struggle to bear it. She leaves a big gap behind her."

He was more candid and truthful later on when talking the matter over with Jack Ford and his friends. Miriam was in another room laying the supper-table, entirely furnished from an adjacent restaurant.

"When Miss Astracan vanished," he said, "it was like removing a mountain from my breast. At last I inhale the air of true freedom—but with a wife it is necessary to dissemble. Hush! she comes."

She came in to announce the supper, and a very jolly evening followed. Miss Astracan was not referred to again.

CHAPTER CCCI.

MR. WISPER RECEIVES A MAN AND A BROTHER.

SMUGGER'S TERRACE, Clapham, if not exactly aristocratic, is eminently respectable. The rents are fifty pounds a year, which the occupants for the most part manage to meet by letting apartments.

There the landlady ghoul draws the life-blood in the form of cash from her victims, and the landlord spider spins the advertising web for prey.

There is no place in the wide world where a tenant of lodgings learns so well how he can be shaven and shorn, robbed, bled, and blistered.

Smugger's Terrace has been anathematised a thousand times, but it lives and thrives to this day.

Penny Bunn and his wife arrived in the afternoon in a four-wheeled cab. The eagle-eyed boy of the street had espied them on the way, and there was a goodly following of the impudent fry to see Bunn alight.

Mr. Wisper was the landlord's name, and he stood upon the doorstep to receive them.

He was a flabby, florid man, with a moist eye, and toes that turned out excessively.

He wore black clothes, a small ribbon necktie, and slippers, gingerbread brown in colour.

"Welcome!" he said to Bunn, holding out both his hands.

"Boora ba galloo," replied Bunn.

He could not help it. It was born in the man, and would die with him. Give him half a chance, and he must needs assume to be something he was not.

"Our dear friend," said Wisper to Miriam, "does not apparently understand English?"

Once upon a time she would have exposed her husband in the most merciless manner, but she was now more tender to his faults, and merely smiled in reply. The cabman, on being paid his fare, gruffly remarked that he *did* expect "a hextry tanner for carrying niggers," to which Miriam responded, "I saw by the look of you that it was your intention to be insolent, and so paid you your bare fare."

Wisper ushered Bunn into the front-parlour, a meagrely-furnished, stuffy little room, with the odour of last week's boiled greens lingering in the corners, and pressed him into the easy-chair as if he had been an invalid or a little child.

"Oh, my brother!" he exclaimed, clasping his hands and rolling up his eyes, "this is indeed a joyful day for me."

Miriam ordered some tea and dismissed him.

Left alone with her husband, she ventured to remonstrate with him.

"My dear," she said, "why will you be so ridiculous?"

"Ridiculous?" he exclaimed, as if the bare notion of his having been so astounded him.

"Shamming that you did not understand English," explained Miriam.

"Think for a moment, my dear," urged Penny Bunn; "how *could* I reconcile perfect English with this get-up? It is an impossibility."

"Something in that, dear."

"Then fancy having the curiosity of this vulgar man aroused. He would want to know everything, and there are episodes in my life which, I think you will agree with me, ought to be confined to our family circle."

Miriam could not deny it. Bunn's reasoning was sound.

"Well," she said, "I hope that having started you will keep it up all through."

"You may trust me, my dear," he said; "I shall, as I have ever done, exhibit all necessary reserve."

"If your friend Bunyons comes here he must be warned."

"He is sure to come here, and I will advise him as to the *rôle* I am playing."

Miriam sent their address to Gubbles that evening, and quietly intimated that she would like to have her husband restored to his natural condition as soon as possible, "or goodness only knows what would happen."

"I daresay you understand him," she wrote. "Though of excellent disposition, he is inclined to be eccentric, and is so easily led away."

Chippy Bunyons was also communicated with, and he turned up the next day.

Wisper happened to be in the room inquiring what he could "do for his dear friend and brother," and Chippy very nearly exposed the whole thing by crying out:

"What cheer, Bunn, my boy?"

Luckily Bunn, being a man of extraordinary resource, as we have seen throughout his varied career, turned, so as to have his back to Wisper, winked, and replied:

"Anarraka lu bella stun."

Chippy was taken aback, but he too was no common man, and, after a moment's pause, said:

"Gossma toolip."

"You understand our friend here?" said Wisper.

"What do *you* think?" replied Chippy.

"You knew him in his native land?"

"I did."

"Ah—yes—it was in——"

Wisper paused, but as Chippy was not enlightened in the matter of Bunn's latest native land, he did not supply the required information.

As the worthy Wisper had originally failed in endeavouring to pump Miriam, and could not hope to get the information from Bunn, he was left stranded and helpless on the barren shores of curiosity.

It was very trying, but he was a good man who had learned to suffer and be strong, especially in the petty ills of life—overdue rent, rates and taxes, and a laggard spirit exhibited by tradesmen when asked to leave their goods prior to payment thereof—and he bore up.

One thing was certain: he had a rare jewel in his house, a black pearl of great price, and he thought he saw a way of making something out of him.

CHAPTER CCCII.

RESTORATION.—ACT THE FIRST.

BY return of post there arrived a letter from Gubbles, asking Bunn to pay him a visit as soon as he could. Accordingly, he went at once, accompanied by Miriam.

Gubbles seemed to find in Bunn a perfect mine of matter for experiment. Astonished he was, of course—for who would not have been so?—but it was in the nature of the dyes used upon that hapless man that he found so much interest.

"Young Cork," he said, "was pretty well fixed, but your case is much more striking. What a clever brute the fellow must have been!"

"I trust," said Bunn, "that he has not succeeded in permanently fixing me up in this style?"

"I can't say for certain," replied Gubbles, "but let us hope not."

As with Cork, so with Bunn—various things were applied to the skin, some hot and some cold, and all intensely disagreeable.

At last Gubbles had got at what he wanted.

"I see now what it is," he said. "Mrs. Bunn, will you kindly wait here while I take your husband away for a time—I shall not be long."

He took Bunn away upstairs to the bath-room, but not for a bath. Bidding him strip to the waist, he brought out a bottle filled with a colourless liquid, which, however, belied its innocent appearance, for, when applied to the skin with a sponge, it fairly set Bunn dancing.

"Disagreeable, isn't it?" remarked Gubbles.

"The-e-e strangest sensation I ever experienced," replied Bunn; "not that it is painful—but do what I may I cannot keep still."

"Good," said Gubbles; "that is the right action. We shall do now. If repeated every morning for a month——"

"What!" exclaimed Bunn, staring aghast. "Shall I have to da-a-ance in this fashion every morning for a month?"

"No: the muscular sensation will slowly subside. I think that, after your other experiences, you will be able to bear it."

When Bunn returned to his Miriam there was a smile upon his face, as if he had been thoroughly enjoying himself; indeed, he did tell her that the process was peculiar, but agreeable.

So far, however, there was no change in his appearance. That was to appear by-and-by.

Reference was made to the necessity of getting his head shaved, and here Gubbles helped them again.

As Bunn remarked, "it would never do to walk into a hairdresser's shop like an ordinary customer, and ask for this to be done." The effect upon the mind of a common barber might be very serious.

Gubbles had a man whom he occasionally employed at all sorts of strange matters, and as he could shave, he was sent for.

He was a short, thick-set man, with a stolid face, who seemed incapable of exhibiting surprise. Nor was he inwardly astonished.

Having taken stock of Bunn's wretched cranium, he remarked: "This will take some lathering," and went to work.

The amount of lather it did take was prodigious, and the process of slowly shaving off the hair, mixed with feather-stumps, was a long and arduous task.

But it was done at last, and the effect created by the dark face crowned with a lily-white cranium was inexpressibly ludicrous.

They all laughed, even the shaver, although not a muscle of his face moved; and Bunn, when he surveyed himself in the glass, said:

"Never until this hour was I aware of the Shakespeare-like contour of my head. But then, I was always inclined to the dramatic element. When quite a boy, I——"

"P. Y.," said Miriam, holding up a warning forefinger.

"Certainly, my dear," he murmured. "If the reminiscences of my early days are distasteful to you, you shall not be troubled with them. Still, it cannot be denied, my head is Shakespearian."

He replaced his turban, and having thanked Gubbles for his kindness, departed with his wife.

CHAPTER CCCIII.

MORE MEN AND BROTHERS.

MR. WISPER was a member of one of the numerous Clapham sects who cultivate brotherly love as shown to the swarthy stranger, and whenever a specimen of any shade of colour except white could be landed—like a fish—by one of the brethren, it made him a shining light among them.

But too often the light, after flaring awhile, went out, leaving the brethren in gloom, as was the case when Brother Jobbs brought to the conventicle an escaped slave who had never been outside London in his life before—he had, indeed, been born in Whitechapel.

The discovery of this fraud, arising out of the escaped slave being wanted for robbery with violence, extinguished Brother Jobbs, and shook the conventicle to its foundation.

Something was wanted to strengthen it, to shore it up, and Brother Wisper rejoiced to think that he had found in Penny Bunn the very article required.

Wisper lost not a moment in letting his discovery be known, and on the evening of the second day there was a meeting of the brethren, and Wisper addressed them on the subject of "a brother who wanted their guiding hand to help him out of the darkness."

He was obliged to confess that he knew nothing of the nationality of Bunn, and that the trifling difficulty of his being unable to speak English stood in the way of free conversation; but he had a friend—a most worthy gentleman—named Bunyons, who would no doubt be pleased to act as interpreter.

As a preliminary canter, as it were, Wisper proposed that some of the brethren should drop in casually on the off-chance of being able to interview the interesting subject.

Accordingly, three or four of the brethren turned up the next day, and were favoured by fortune to the extent of Miriam being out, and Bunn at home with Chippy.

Wisper ventured to intrude himself upon them, and asked Chippy if he might bring his friends in for a few moments.

"What for?" Chippy naturally wanted to know.

"They are interested in all aliens and our heathen brethren," replied Wisper.

"Bring 'em in," said Chippy.

Wisper vanished, and a short, hurried consultation took place between the friends.

"Wot's their game, Bunny?" asked Chippy.

"Converting the heathen," replied Bunn. "You will be the interpreter, no doubt. Exercise your intellectual gifts, and give them some staggering replies."

"All right. I hear 'em coming."

The brethren, led by Wisper, entered the room on tiptoe, as if there were some sick person to care for; and Bunn, rising, favoured them with a low salaam and the salutation:

"Arraka clentnee!"

"Which means 'Greet you well,'" explained Chippy.

"The language is familiar to me," remarked one of the brethren. "Your friend is a native of——"

"He would rather not say," interposed Chippy, "as he is here on an important diplomatic business."

"How interesting!" was the general exclamation.

"The fact is," pursued the reckless Chippy, "that in his native land there ain't no cold-water associations, no wegetarians, no New Women, no nothing sich as we has in a civilised country, and he wants help to get them."

"Possibly," said Wisper, "there is an opening for an energetic missionary?"

"For a dozen," replied Chippy.

"And the climate?"

"It is 'eavenly."

"And rich in articles of diet, perhaps?"

"Nothing is wanted. Everything is ready to hand," said the veracious Chippy. "Fowls run wild and lay eggs by the hundred. Cows and all sorts of cattle browse on the hills and look after themselves. The choicest fruits grow in abundance."

His hearers gasped. Their mouths watered.

"And further than that," pursued Chippy, "it's a land o' gold, although that isn't generally known yet; and I feel sure that I can trust you not to talk about it."

Of course he could. They pledged their faith, and honour, and what not, upon it.

"There ain't no digging for it, neither," pursued Chippy, "nor no 'quartz-smashing, or any blooming hard work in getting it. No. You just pick up a handful, blow the sand away, and there you are— nothing but gold left. We could have brought tons away with us if we liked."

"Then you have been with our friend in his native land?" said one of the brethren.

"Rather," replied Chippy; "got wrecked there, and niver did I come across such charming people. They quite coddles you up with kindness."

The listeners were entranced.

Here was a life that would just suit them.

They were, for the most part, impecunious men, living from hand to mouth in various ways, and a life of ease under a tropical sun would suit them to a hair.

By degrees they led up to what was in their minds. Was their brother going back to his native land, and would he be pleased to take a stranger with him?

Chippy Bunyons addressed Bunn in Avishnu, which, of course, he could not understand, and Bunn replied in his own improvised tongue, which nobody could comprehend.

And the outcome of it was that in the end Bunn undertook to take back with him as many there as chose to go, pay all expenses of passage, bestow upon them delightful homes, and see that they were honoured by his countrymen.

No wonder, then, that all the little band of brothers declared it to be their intention to accompany him, and that day month was the time appointed for sailing.

There was much fervent hand-shaking at parting, and the two friends were left together at last.

"Well, Chippy," said Bunn, "I think you have done it. You've just been going it a bit."

"I did my best, old man, to come up to your standard," replied Chippy, modestly. "I knew that if you had the chance you would go it, so I went it."

"This day month," mused Bunn; "by that time Gubbles ought to restore me. Possibly I may not be called upon to return to my native land—ha, ha!"

CHAPTER CCCIV.

EUREKA!

A WEEK passed away, during which period Bunn daily went under treatment for his discoloration. The results were not so visible as either Bunn or Gubbles wished them to be.

"After all," said the latter, "I haven't got quite the right thing."

This was, in a measure, disturbing, but Gubbles bade Bunn cheer up. The thing would surely come out right in the end.

Meanwhile Wisper and his friends were making a noise abroad about their prospects of returning with an Eastern potentate who had promised to make them rulers, and the envy and hatred of the rest of their especial brethren, without mentioning other bodies, was very bitter.

It increased to such an extent that the brother who took the next Sunday duty—they did this in turn— preached on the sin of grasping greediness, which surely would bring its own punishment.

The parties thus assailed bore the blows administered with great philosophy. For them the lookout ahead was all that could be wished for.

It was their intention to see what could be done with the gold-lands Chippy had spoken of, and their general opinion was that they would become millionaires.

"We seem to have got the blind side of our brother the potentate," said Wisper, "and we must get a grant of land from him—a few square miles of the best."

"The cut-up must be fair and square," remarked one of the other brethren.

"Oh, of course. Honour among — ahem! — brethren."

What precious plans they furthermore got into their heads it bodes us not to tell, but there is no doubt they swallowed Chippy's yarn head and tail.

And he was punished for it.

He could neither come nor go when visiting Bunn without being waylaid by one or more of the brethren, bursting to hear more of the land which they termed "a country flowing with milk and honey," the milk being doubtless the softness of Bunn's nature, and the honey the gold they trusted to scoop up by the shovelful.

They waited, watched for him. When in the house they would remain outside until he left. Sometimes it would be as late as twelve o'clock ere he bade Bunn good-night, but the faithful were ever there.

"It is getting too stiff," said Chippy one evening; "the lies I have to tell would fill a bushel. If they weren't regular cormorants they couldn't swallow them."

But the hour of release was at hand.

One morning Bunn went off to see Gubbles as usual, and found him in one of his best humours.

"I've got it at last," he said, holding up a big bottle containing about a quart of liquid. "Go up to the bathroom and sponge yourself with it. Let me know the result."

Bunn hastened upstairs, stripped himself, and began his labour. Every wipe with the sponge brought off broad lines of colour. Gubbles could now indeed cry "Eureka!" for he had found it.

Barring a pallor of the face, natural enough under the circumstances, and the absence of hair on his head, Bunn was himself again.

He summoned Gubbles to behold his handiwork, and to receive thanks for the same. Mutual congratulations were uttered.

Now Bunn was never the man to do anything by halves. What had been a surprise to him must be one for Miriam also.

And the surprise must be complete.

She did not accompany him that morning—indeed, she had done so but once after the first visit—and Bunn suggested to Gubbles that she should receive a staggerer.

"With a becoming wig and a suit of fashionable clothes," he said, "I shall be in a condition to give her a shock."

There was also the idea of bewildering Wisper in his mind. Likewise the brethren would be the better for a lesson on "avarice and its fruits."

Bunn was in a very complacent and highly moral state.

Gubbles accompanied him to an outfitter's, and assisted him in the selection of a suit of clothes, including a tall hat of the newest shape, and an attenuated umbrella.

He dressed himself upon the premises, and went forth a new man. A convenient barber supplied him with a wig, and, feeling as light as a feather, he started for his temporary home.

His knock and ring brought Wisper to the door, and the man had not the least idea of his identity.

"You have a foreign potentate here, I believe?" he said.

"In a manner I have," replied Wisper, suspiciously. He scented a rival scouting for goldfields.

"In a manner you have; what do you mean by that?" demanded Bunn.

"He is staying here, but he isn't in," replied Wisper, haughtily.

"Then I'll come in and wait," said Bunn. "Ground-floor front, I believe?"

Before Wisper could stop him, Bunn had passed by and gained the sitting-room. Wisper followed, and looked about him as if counting the articles of furniture and ornaments, in case anything was missing after the stranger was gone.

"Well," said Bunn, "anything wrong?"

"In course I have to be careful who I admit into my lodger's rooms," replied Wisper; "we don't know who's who nowadays."

"Very good," said Bunn; "I will deal with you presently."

He dismissed him with a wave of the hand, and Wisper, not knowing what else to do, departed in a perturbed mood.

The more he saw of this gorgeously-attired stranger, the less he liked him.

Miriam, who had been out shopping, shortly afterwards returned. She let herself in with a latchkey and entered the room.

Bunn sat with his back towards her, reading a book, and as he had purchased a curly wig—it was *so* like him to do it—his identity was not clear to her.

"I beg your pardon, sir," she said, "but you must have mistaken the room."

"No, indeed, Miriam, my love," he replied, as he faced about; "behold your P. Y., restored like an old picture, by a master-hand."

She was more than delighted to see him, and Wisper, with ears listening at the door, was much scandalised on hearing sundry terms of endearment, such as "My own Bunny," and "the same P. Y.," with a kiss between.

"That foreign potentate wants a friend to give him the tip," muttered Wisper. "Hallo! there's the bell."

He waited a few moments before answering it, as if he had come up from the kitchen. He had done that sort of thing before, and could time himself to a second. Bunn required him, so that he might learn how to receive him in future, if "he should call."

"Now, my fine fellow," he said, "ask this lady if I am a friend of her husband."

"Of course, you are," said Miriam.

"Has he a better friend in the world?"

"Assuredly not!"

This reply was given emphatically; there was a tinge of the old Miriam in its tone.

"Now you understand—eh?" said Bunn.

"I do," replied Wisper; "but I am not supposed to know people's friends by sight."

"Insolent hind," said Bunn, dramatically; "begone!"

Wisper could but go, and he left the room more and more troubled. Shortly afterwards Chippy Bunyons knocked at the front door and Wisper opened it.

He ventured to tell Chippy of the arrival of this stranger, and completely fogged him.

"It must be the lady's brother, if she has one," he said.

"Whoever he is, he wants looking after," said Wisper, meaningly.

Chippy said he would look after him, and wondering what on earth it could be, he entered the room with the scant ceremony of a favoured guest.

One glance at Bunn sufficed, and a stentorian roar of "Bunn ahoy!" startled the listening Wisper, who stole away to the kitchen, fearing that he was mixed up with some very strange people.

CHAPTER CCCV.

WHERE IS THE POTENTATE?

"MIRIAM, my dear," said Bunn, "we must vanish this evening, or the whole thing may be blown, and I do desire to leave Wisper in a maze."

"It is conventicle night," said Chippy; "he goes at eight o'clock. The rent, of course, is paid?"

"In advance," said Miriam; "we lose a little in that."

"But gain much, disappointing that greasy lot," said Bunn.

"Leave the whole thing to me," advised Chippy. "Mrs. Wisper never comes out of the kitchen, or the coalhole, or wherever she may pass the time. At 8.15 I will have a cab at the door and see you off. You can put up at one of the hotels to-night."

"And to-morrow," said Bunn, "we will go on a little pleasure-trip together, my Miriam."

He promised to take her to see the "Albatross," "whose deck he had trod in sunshine and darkness, storm, and fine weather," and with that they would visit the Isle of Wight, which Miriam had never seen, and, in short, have their first real pleasure-trip together.

Wisper was bound to visit the brethren that night, as he had some unpleasant tidings to impart to them. That stranger hung about his neck like a millstone.

It was dolorous news he imparted to the brethren, and the "chosen few," as the elected body called themselves, felt that the bull must be taken by the horns.

The potentate must be forthwith secured, an never lost sight of again until he had conducted hi *protégés* across the sea.

Wisper escorted his friends back, and personally, a a preliminary step, dropped into the parlour.

There he discovered Chippy Bunyons with a glas of grog and a cigar, but that was all.

"Alone?" he said. "What's come of your frienc sir?"

"That is what I should like to know," replie Chippy. "He's gone."

"Gone!" echoed Wisper, in a whisper—"not left !

"Anyways," said Chippy, "he's took his traps. H doesn't owe you any rent, I know for certain. It's tha party as was here to-day as took him away."

Wisper sat down without an apology, for he did no know what he was doing. Here was a blow for th brethren, and after all the talk they had indulged in

"He may come back," he said, after a silence.

"No," replied Chippy, sadly, "the wrong man ha got hold of him. You saw that swell party here to day?"

"I did—the villain!" hissed Wisper.

"Well, he's got hold of the gold business, and i going to run it on his own account," said Chippy rising. "It's a pity, but you've one and all lost million apiece."

He put on his hat, and nodding, by way of adieu went out. Wisper was too much overcome to detai him, or to make an attempt in that direction.

Chippy lingered long enough to hear the wail agony that burst from the other brethren whe Wisper told them of their loss, and went his way smiling.

"It was worth while giving them a lesson," he saic "They are mighty fond of laying it on to others Jehoshaphat! never while they live will they forge the gold-mine they have lost."

Chippy went back to the "Albatross" for a day where he entertained the old bo'sun with the story o Bunn's being a potentate with large tracts of gol country to be given away, and within a day or tw Bunn brought his wife to see the wonderful littl vessel in which he had passed so many happy days.

While Chippy and the bo'sun were preparing a tea table "fit for a lady," with a bottle of rum as a side dish to the teapot, Bunn took advantage of thei absence to show Miriam round the vessel, namin; each bit of gear in his own fashion for her edification

She may have suspected something was wrong, bu it was an immaterial matter, and she questionec nothing, not even a reference to the capstan as "th anchor turnstile."

Bill did the honours of the table with unaffectec gravity, being persistent in the matter of "a spoonfu of rum to take the raw edge off the tea."

"If I drinks hot tea neat," he explained, "it lies like a ship's anchor on my chest."

They spent a very happy evening together, and at a late hour a boat conveyed Bunn and his wife to Ryde.

*   *   *   *   *   *

And now our story is practically at an end. The broadsheet is woven, and it only remains to put the last few threads in order.

After a year or so of peaceful show-life, during which Miss Astracan proved to be a little copper mine to her showman, she passed peacefully away.

Her last words were, "I don't believe his story. The man is an impostor." Which showed that she had Bunn on her mind to the end.

But could she have seen that gentleman, restored as to countenance, and happy in his home, to which the additional joy of a remarkably small baby had just been added, she might have been induced to change her opinion.

Now, as to the rest; and first of all the minor character, Ab Hulli Hassan Bey.

He was brought home in the "Albatross," and speedily found favour with a body of good men to whose tenets he professed to be converted.

As a show savage brought from darkness to light, he proved to be a very profitable commodity. His share of ten per cent of the profits of the meeting. held to show him to a delighted assemblage, and to listen to his experiences, kept him well in clover.

The vast wealth of the Avishnus was disposed of in a way that prevented any great amount of comment, even from the dealing fraternity.

There was a passage in one of the smartest of evening papers about "a glut of diamonds," but it was not taken up by the rest.

The proceeds of the sale were divided, by the desire of Jack and his three friends, in such a way as to give the more needy portion of the crew of the "Albatross" a part thereof.

Every man got something.

There was a fairish fortune for Ben Walton and Dick Darnley, and a big one for each of the four friends, the latter being invested for them until they came of age. They enjoyed the interest meanwhile.

Lingo had a good amount of proper pride, but he saw no reason for his refusing a loan to start a circus, and it speedily turning out a success, he was soon able to pay back the money, and is now at the present time, the proprietor of one of the best of our travelling circuses, to which he has given a grandiloquent name that we leave the reader to discover. Lingo has a great aversion to gifts, and above all things objects to a gratuitous advertisement coming form a friend, on the score that it must be biassed.

Mulberry Cork is with him as an assistant manager, and a very good one too he is.

Bill Oakley has had enough of the sea, and is now retired to a fashionable resort on the south coast, where he is a man of mark among those who go down to the sea in boats at sixpence a trip.

Startop is sailing-master of the yacht of a noble lord.

Harry Barstow and Norton Truscott are living down in the old spot, pursuing the even tenour of a country gentleman's life.

Tom Drummond, Don Peebles, and Bob Stockton are at college, where they are picking up some of the necessary knowledge to enable them to carry out the position of men of means, as soon as they are old enough to be considered men.

And Jack Ford, what of him?

Well, Jack bought the "Albatross" on tick, till he came of age, and the chief pleasure of his life is to cruise about in her around the islands of Great Britain. He is astonished to find how much there is that is interesting in the less frequented places.

He invariably has some of his family or a friend or two on board, and among those who share his pleasure-trips the old chums of Littlecote and the strange, thrilling adventures in the East.

It is true and often painful to reflect upon, that the friends of one's boyhood must be lost in after days. A widening out is inevitable, but such friendship as is felt still by the daring quartet for each other rarely dies wholly away, and there is a good prospect of it remaining in all its strength and beauty for many years to come.

www.ingramcontent.com/pod-product-compliance
Lightning Source LLC
Chambersburg PA
CBHW081353050726
47504CB00015B/1900

9 781535 813075